The Annotated Tales of

EDGAR ALLAN POE

Edited with an Introduction, Notes, and a Bibliography

by

STEPHEN PEITHMAN

AVENEL BOOKS • NEW YORK

DEDICATION

This book is dedicated to my parents,
to Larry Fanning, and especially to Ruth Eversole,
who showed me the love of learning.

ACKNOWLEDGMENTS

The research facilities and helpful assistance of the libraries
at the University of California, Davis, and Humboldt State
University, Arcata, California; Linda Shaffer; and Roscoe and
Laura Peithman, for their assistance and advice.

Copyright © MCMLXXXI by Stephen Peithman

All rights reserved.

This 1986 edition is published by Avenel Books, distributed
by Crown Publishers, Inc., 225 Park Avenue South,
New York, New York 10003, by arrangement with Doubleday
and Company

Printed and Bound in the United States of America

Library of Congress Cataloging in Publication Data

Poe, Edgar Allan, 1809-1849.
The annotated tales of Edgar Allan Poe.

Bibliography: p.
Includes index.
I. Peithman, Stephen.   II. Title.
PS2612.Al   1986   813'.3   86-3500
ISBN 0-517-61531-2

h g f e d c b a

Contents

HUMOR AND SATIRE

FLIGHTS AND FANTASIES

Introduction

I

The raven. The black cat. The house of Usher. The tell-tale heart. The pit and the pendulum. The Red Death.

More than 135 years after his death, Edgar Allan Poe continues to haunt our imaginations. In fact, he is practically inescapable. Children read him under blankets by flashlight, savoring each hair-raising moment of his tales of mystery and imagination. Adults rediscover him, discovering whole new levels of meaning that escaped them before. Film versions of his stories have been box office successes for decades and continue to draw large audiences on television and in revival houses. Each year, new books are added to an already impressive list dealing with Poe's life, his work and his legend. And through it all, literary critics and scholars continue to argue over whether Poe is, or is not, a great writer—or even a good one.

Just what is there about this man that has granted him such long-lasting notoriety? After all, there are other writers who have made careers (and a good deal more money) from writing fright stories.

The reason is simple: Poe wasn't merely out to scare. Oh, he knew well the trappings of Gothic fiction, all right, and used them to the hilt at times, but his chief interest lay in that complex mystery called the human mind. It makes little difference whether the tale is comic or dramatic, or whether we consider the events in the tale or their effect on the reader—in practically everything Poe wrote, there is an analytical streak, and this makes all the difference.

As early as 1845, James Russell Lowell observed that Poe "is a spectator *ab extra*. He analyzes, he dissects, he watches. . . ." His power of analysis, Lowell pointed out, "enables him to throw a wonderful reality into his most unreal fancies. A monomania he paints with great power. He loves to dissect one of the cancers of the mind, and to trace all the subtle ramifications of its roots" (*Works*, I, p. 378).

The Annotated Poe is for the reader who is attracted to, curious about, delighted with, or mystified by the tales of Edgar Allan Poe. Like most books of this kind, it is somewhat informal; while the Poe scholar will find much of interest here, I have always kept the general reader firmly in mind. The versions of the tales used are those with which most readers are familiar, but if there are significant departures from other versions or if literary scholarship has uncovered textual errors, these are mentioned. The real purpose of this book, however, is to bring together in convenient form explanations, definitions, interpretations, sources, and biographical information, adding to them information on works based on or inspired by Poe's work—in other words, to increase one's understanding, appreciation, and enjoyment of Poe.

The tales have been grouped in four categories: "Terror of the Soul," "Mysteries," "Humor and Satire," and "Flights and Fantasies." The second and third categories are self-explanatory; the first deals with Poe's tales of horror, and the last with his tales of fantasy and science fiction. In some cases, a tale might fit into several categories, but I have tried to place each one where I think it fits best: "The Angel of the Odd," for example, is a comic tale, but I have categorized it as fantasy to distinguish it from the otherwise similar "Bon-Bon" and "Duc De L'Omelette."

Most of the illustrations used here have at one time or another graced various published versions of Poe's tales. However, some of them were originally drawn for other stories and then appropriated for use later in magazines by publishers who found this cheaper than hiring new artists. Artists have been identified whenever possible.

Now, an introduction ought to give a reader a firm grasp of an author's intentions—and his prejudices. Here are mine:

1) What makes Poe so fascinating is that the more one reads the tales, the more one finds there. Poe's fiction is an embarrassment of riches: puns and other wordplay, mysterious allusions, obscure quotations, foreign languages, archaic phrasing, burlesque, parody, satire, political and historical commentary, mysticism, and hard science jostle for the reader's attention. The problem with Poe is not that there is no substance, but that there is sometimes too much, so that a mere quick reading can leave a person baffled, bored, or disturbed. Not all works of literature need to be annotated; Poe's tales cry out for this kind of help.

2) While one can argue over the exact meaning of the word "tale," excluded here are certain sketches, essays, and essay-like pieces, as well as those written in dialogue form (e.g., "The Colloquy of Monos and Una"). To be sure, some of the tales included come very close to these forms, but they also display a very obvious narrative approach. Also outside the scope of this book of tales are Poe's only novel, *The Narrative of Arthur Gordon Pym;* the fragment of his other attempt at long fiction, *The Journal of Julius Rodman;* and of course his poetry.

3) Annotations are restricted to definitions of unusual, foreign, and archaic terms; explanations of names, places, dates, and facts; translations of passages in other languages; interpretations representing various points of view; and historical and, where necessary, biographical commentary.

4) The lack of numerous biographical references is symptomatic of my firm belief that while one may legitimately compare events in an author's life with those in his writing, it is a mistake to constantly equate the two. We have gotten along just fine for four hundred years knowing very little of Shakespeare's life; simply because we know a good deal more about Poe is no reason to assume that his biography is the key to his tales.

5) We can easily fall into the trap of drawing parallels between Poe and his narrators, because most of the tales are written in the first person. But we should always remember that these narrators are *characters* created by Poe and each has a unique point of view. Poe often places them in extreme circumstances, and they are often unstable—occasionally mad—but his reasons are almost always the same: to portray the workings of the mind or to illuminate in some way his cosmological theories, which reach their climax in his enigmatic prose poem *Eureka* (1848). See the Introduction to "MS. Found in a Bottle" for a brief overview of this important work of Poe.

Poe's narrators are the real key to the tales, for it is through their eyes that we see the events and characters. "The weird events," notes G. R. Thompson, "are psychological delusions on the part of the narrators, delusions so subtly insinuated that the reader tends to see only from the narrator's point of view, even though he announces his madness, or nervousness, or terror, or some oddity or other that should cause the reader to pause for a moment to consider his distorted or eccentric view of the events he narrates. In their intricacy of design, Poe's Gothic tales contain telltale evidences for rational psychological explanation, yet rarely so obtrusive as to destroy their weird supernatural effect. . . ." (*Poe's Fiction,* Wisconsin, 1973; p. 36).

It would be foolish to claim that this or any other book has the final answer to the meaning of Poe's tales, for there really is no such thing. But there are *answers*. Poe carefully allows for multiple levels of meaning in his work, so that we often find remarkably opposing viewpoints on the interpretation of a particular tale. Included here are some of the more representative interpretations—and some of the more offbeat as well. In many cases, however, the reader is just as well off coming to his or her own conclusions.

6) The number of entries does not in any way relate to the quality of the tale; the more complex or difficult the tale the more annotations provided.

7) Finally, if you have not read some of these tales before, try reading them through once without the annotations (except to clarify certain points). Then go back and read them again, taking time to pause and browse through the notes as you please.

A friend once looked at me strangely when I told him that I hoped readers would find fun in this book. "Fun" is apparently not a word most people associate with Poe. But the truth is that there is a great deal of humor in Poe, for here is a man who sees both the tragedy and the absurdity of life and who can write of either—or both at the same time. Poe is a man who loves puns, hoaxes, swindles, satire, and parody. If this book helps readers discover the comic side of Poe, it will have done a great deal.

II

Edgar Allan Poe is a mass of paradoxes. He wanted to be remembered as a great poet, but most critics today agree that his tales are his great contribution to literature.

He is an American, and yet his stories are seldom set in this country and often seem alien to the American spirit. While he has always been popular here, he is even more so in Europe: in France, he has long been considered a major literary figure by critics, scholars, and other authors. In America, scholarly debate still goes on: is Poe a great writer, they argue, or merely a competent hack?

His tales are superficially simple and yet seem to provide numerous possibilities for interpretation. There are those who see his tales as reflections of his own, tortured psyche, as psychological case histories, as emblematic of numberless themes and symbols. His tales are complex; they are simple. They are Freudian; they are Jungian. They are biographical; they are pure fiction. They are obscure; they are straightforward. They are Christian; they are existential. They are romantic; they are classic.

And then there is the man himself. Always strapped for funds, Poe nevertheless played the part of the Southern Gentleman. He also had a drinking problem, was enormously defensive about his background and talent, and rewrote his life history to suit the moment and the mood.

He married his thirteen-year-old cousin (whom he called "Sis"), lived with her and her mother (whom he called "Muddie"), carried on "romances" with several other women while still married, and, after a period of prostrate grief, asked three women to marry him within months of his wife's death from tuberculosis. And yet there is no assurance that his marriage was ever consummated, or that there were even any sexual feelings in his other romances.

He gives the appearance of great learning in his tales, but his schooling was not as extensive as he would have us believe. Always he wrote for money, aiming his work toward the general reading public, but at the same time including other levels of meaning to impress the more erudite readers and critics of his day.

His last five days are a blank, and despite the work of more than 135 years, we still do not know for sure what happened to Poe before he was found delirious in Baltimore.

By his own request, the executor and final editor of his works was a man he disliked, and who repaid the feeling by distorting and fabricating Poe's biography to such an extent that even today we still think of that Poe, rather than the Poe that really was. Some say Poe knew this would happen, and that even when death came, he had his final joke. By allowing his name to be besmirched, he created a controversy that has kept his name and works alive to this day.

Even after death, Poe continues to puzzle and perplex.

III

Here, in brief outline, are the facts of Poe's life. [For those who wish to know more, I recommend Arthur H. Quinn's biography (Appleton-Century, 1941), or Julian Symons' *The Tell-Tale Heart* (Harper & Row, 1978).]

He was born in Boston, on January 19, 1809, the son of a talented actress, Elizabeth Arnold, and her second husband, David Poe, Jr., also an actor. David Poe deserted his wife, and she died on December 8, 1811, in Richmond, and the young Edgar was taken into the home of wealthy merchant John Allan, who became his godfather but did not adopt him.

In 1815, Allan, in an attempt to set up a European branch of his business, took his family to England. While there, Edgar attended Doctor John Bransby's academy at Stoke Newington (the basis for the early part of "William Wilson"), but, in 1820, business reverses forced Allan to return to Richmond, where Poe was sent to several good schools.

When Poe went to the University of Virginia, in February 1826, he was secretly engaged to Elmira Royster, but her family managed to intercept one of his letters and put an end to the romance by marrying her off to another man. Although he was a good student in languages, he stayed only one term at the university. His godfather refused to give him any spending money and Poe had taken to gambling as a way of getting more income. He wasn't successful, however, and merely piled up more debts, until Allan took him out of school.

It was at this point that stories began to circulate about Poe's drinking problem. While some of these accounts are exaggerated, it seems clear that Poe did have an abnormal reaction to even small amounts of liquor (especially wine).

Things continued to go badly between Poe and Allan, and when Poe returned to Richmond, he quarreled with his godfather and ran away to Boston. He managed to have a small volume of poems privately printed (*Tamerlane*, 1827), but he was unable to find work, and out of desperation joined the Army under the name of Edgar A. Perry. He was sent to Charleston's Fort Moultrie, on Sullivan's Island (the setting for "The Gold-Bug"), but soon found military life not to his liking—at least as a common soldier. He begged Allan to get him out of the service, but his godfather refused until his wife on her deathbed pleaded with him to reconcile with Edgar. Allan sent for Poe and the two made up their differences—on the condition that Poe enter West Point.

In 1829, Poe published another collection of poetry, and entered West Point the following year (after yet another quarrel with Allan). After Allan's remarriage, in October 1830, Poe realized that his fortune no longer lay in that direction, and apparently made a caustic comment to that effect to a friend in a letter—which came to Allan's attention. Poe was disowned, and now, without any financial support whatsoever, set about getting himself expelled from West Point. He succeeded.

New York was his next stop, where he published a third volume of poems, in 1831, and moved to Baltimore, where he began writing tales as well. He submitted several in a contest sponsored by the Philadelphia *Saturday Courier* in 1832, and although he did not win, they were published anonymously. The following year, the Baltimore *Saturday Visiter* awarded Poe $50 for his story "MS. Found in a Bottle." More tales followed, and through the auspices of a friend, novelist John P. Kennedy, he began to write for the *Southern Literary Messenger*, becoming its editor in 1835. During his tenure, readership increased from five hundred to thirty-five hundred, but he also began a series of attacks on other literary figures of the day, which immersed him in petty quarrels that would hurt his reputation and plague him for the remainder of his life.

Poe was now living with his aunt, Marie Poe Clemm, and she arranged a marriage between him and her daughter, Virginia, who was only thirteen. Because of the age difference and the close blood relationship between the two, Edgar and Virginia pretended to be brother and sister for the first two years of their marriage, living with Mrs. Clemm. The marriage was an odd one by any standard. Virginia read little of Poe's work, and he never wrote a poem to her while she was still living. There is no proof that the marriage was ever consummated. In fact, Poe seemed equally attached to Mrs. Clemm, who kept the family together through financial problems and Virginia's illnesses.

Now came a series of tales, poems, and his only complete novel, *The Narrative of Arthur Gordon Pym*. In January 1837, Poe resigned from the *Messenger*, where *Pym* was serialized in part, and moved to New York. In 1838 he went to Philadelphia to help Professor Thomas Wyatt with two books on natural history and in 1839 became an editor for *Burton's Gentleman's Magazine*, on whose staff he remained until June of 1840, when he and Burton had a falling out.

In the meantime, Poe brought out several prospectuses for a magazine of his own, to be called *The Penn* or *The Stylus*, but nothing came of it. When George R. Graham bought out Burton and began *Graham's Gentleman's Magazine*, in December 1840, Poe moved in as reviewer and stayed until May 1842. Once gain, circulation increased markedly during his time with the publication. His drinking problem was kept in bounds, and as in most of his editorial work, Poe seldom lost a day's work on account of alcohol.

He published his first volume of tales in 1840, but it did not sell well. He kept on writing, however, despite this failure. Then, in early 1842, disaster struck: Virginia broke a blood vessel while singing, and her health, which had never been good, declined rapidly, and she contracted tuberculosis. Poe, Virginia, and Mrs. Clemm moved back to New York, where he wrote for several publications. Fame finally came when his poem *The Raven* was published, in January 1845, and he became editor of the *Broadway Journal*.

Poe began to give lectures on poetry, and at this point met and fell in love with Mrs. Frances Sargent Osgood, apparently with Virginia's knowledge and acceptance. His drinking once again became a problem, perhaps from the strain caused by Virginia's decline, the continuing literary quarrels, and the financial pressures that continued to plague him. At a lecture in Boston, he read his poem *Al Aaraaf* while intoxicated, first baffling, and then outraging, his audience.

Poe took what money he had and bought out the *Broadway Journal*, but in January 1846 the paper folded. Once again he moved, this time to a cottage at Fordham (now in the Bronx). From here, a series of articles called The Literati of New York sealed his downfall. These were profiles of thirty-eight authors in New York City; one, on Thomas Dunn English, was so harsh that English

A watercolor painting of Virginia Clemm Poe *Artist unknown*

Sarah Helen Whitman *Artist unknown*

Rufus Griswold *Artist unknown*

replied scurrilously in print (the two had already come to blows over Poe's affairs with two women). Poe then sued for libel and won, but the publicity from the trial, which included stories of his purported drunkenness, ruined his reputation and firmly established him in the public mind as unstable and irresponsible.

Virginia died in early 1847, and Poe, seriously ill for much of the year, was nursed back to health by Mrs. Clemm and Marie Louise Shew. It was Mrs. Shew who sought out the famous Dr. Valentine Mott and from him learned that Poe suffered from a "brain lesion" and had not long to live. The lesion was perhaps responsible for Poe's manic-depressive behavior and possibly for his inability to tolerate liquor.

The crowning achievement to his career, Poe believed, was *Eureka* (1848), which he meant as a cosmological testament to the meaning of the universe. The public, however, was bewildered, and the prose poem was not well received. In September 1848, Poe moved to Providence and was engaged briefly to Sarah Helen Whitman, but the romance soon cooled, apparently after another one of his drunken lectures (one wonders if his odd behavior was actually caused by the brain tumor). That same year, he fell in love with Mrs. Annie Richmond, but again nothing came of it.

Once more in bad financial straits, Poe took to writing for a cheap newspaper, the Boston *Flag of Our Union*. In June 1849, he went to Philadelphia, where he reportedly went on a spree and was rescued by two friends and sent back to Richmond; he seemed to revive briefly in his old boyhood home, and became engaged to his childhood sweetheart, the now widowed Elmira Royster Shelton. Once again, however, he went on a drunk, and in August joined the Sons of Temperence.

In late-September 1849, Poe left Richmond for Baltimore, where, one story has it, he attended a birthday party, was offered a glass of wine in a toast, and once again went on a spree. The next five days are a blank, but on October 3, 1849, he was found wandering the streets of the city. While a widely circulated story has it that he was taken in a drunken stupor from poll to poll by unscrupulous political hacks, this is only a possibility. He was placed in the Washington Hospital, where he died without ever fully regaining consciousness. He was buried in what is now Westminster Churchyard on October 8; Mrs. Clemm and Virginia are now buried beside him.

Poe had named editor-writer Rufus Griswold as his executor, and Griswold, whose relationship with Poe was always tenuous, set about to destroy Poe's reputation once and for all. In his obituary of Poe, Griswold charged that the writer had no friends and no faith in humanity, that he had been expelled from the University of Virginia, that he had deserted the Army, that he had had an affair with the second Mrs. Allan, that he had been guilty of plagiarisms "scarcely paralleled for their audacity in all literary history," that he had had no redeeming virtues, and that he had been a slave to alcohol and possibly opium.

The Poe legend was born.

IV

Poe's theory of the short story is simple: an author should work toward a preconceived effect, structuring the tale and everything within it to produce that effect. Unity in the short story was an important development and one that has been followed by most writers since.

Poe was not always an original thinker, but he was a master of combination. He was a great reader, and he constantly made notes and clipped articles for use in his work. Newspaper and magazine accounts of the day, descriptions of historical events, snippets from poems and novels—all made their way into his stories. What is important is not that Poe borrowed so frequently but that he was selective in his borrowings and used the material only as a jumping-off point. In most cases, his creation is superior to the original from which it derives.

Poe's originality lies in his viewpoint, in his treatment of the human condition. Yet, as William Carlos Williams pointed out, Poe suffered by his originality:

"Invent that which is new, even if it be made of pine from your own yard, and there's none to know what you have done. It is because there's no *name*. This is the cause of Poe's lack of recognition. He was American. He was the astounding, inconceivable growth of his locality. Gape at him [Americans] did, and he at them in amazement. Afterward with mutual hatred; he in disgust, they in mistrust. It is only that which is under your nose which seems inexplicable.

"Here Poe emerges—in no sense the bizarre, isolate writer, the curious literary figure. On the contrary, in him American literature is anchored, in him alone, on solid ground. In all he says there is a sense of him *surrounded* by his time, tearing at it, ever with more rancor, but always at battle, taking hold" (*The Recognition of Edgar Allan Poe*, Michigan, 1966; p. 136).

Kenneth Allot adds that "an understanding of Edgar Allan Poe is a short cut to an understanding of the nineteenth century. His singularity is unmistakable, but it lies in the degree of intensity with which he held certain beliefs. He was strongly opposed to progress . . . but he could not help being interested in the scientific discoveries of his time. It is true that he was only interested in these things for the fantastic purposes they might subserve, but . . . the cultivation of individual fantasy was a fairly common reaction to a mechanical civilization. Poe represents an emphasis on the Gothic romantic side of the nineteenth century, but he was forced to use scientific and technical ideas to embody his fantasies. However peculiar and morbid he may seem, there was health in a reaction toward feeling and [away] from the overrationalistic mechanical universe with its standardization of response" (*Jules Verne*, Cresset Press, c. 1930).

Not all critics have been kind to Poe. For Yvor Winters, "the underlying defect in all of Poe's work" is "the absence of theme." W. C. Brownell suggests that "it is idle to endeavor to make a great writer of Poe because whatever his merits as a literary artist, his writings lack the elements not only of great, but of sound, literature. They lack substance" (*American Prose Masters*, Scribners, 1909; p. 193).

Yet Brownell bases his charge on the fact that Poe's stories "have no human interest because humanity did not in the least interest him"—the very point on which others have based their praise. Say Robert Scholes and Robert Kellogg, "Poe is rarely interested in expressing his own emotions, as such. The tales are noteworthy for their attitude of dramatic objectivity, a fact that should have discouraged autobiographical interpretation, although it has not done so. Poe is detached. . . . He was not out to exploit his own emotions. He was scarcely interested in them. He was out to exercise the power of the artist over the reader's attention, and thereby to master and to manipulate the reader's response. The naive reader always assumes that he is in control of the words before him. The experienced reader of Poe knows better. Poe is in control." (*The Nature of Narrative*, Oxford 1966; p. 101).

While critics argue over Poe's claim to greatness, none have defined just why Poe has survived both popularity and controversy. In another context, Joseph Campbell at least provides a clue, in his classic *Hero with a Thousand Faces* (World, 1971):

"The problem of mankind today . . . is precisely the opposite to that of man in the comparatively stable periods of those great coordinating mythologies which now are known as lies. Then all meaning was in the group, in the great anonymous forms, none in the individual. But [now] the meaning is absolutely unconscious. One does not know toward what one moves. One does not know by what one is propelled. The lines of communication between the conscious and unconscious zones of the human psyche have all been cut, and we have been split in two" (p. 388).

It is this idea that seems to permeate almost everything Poe wrote. If he is vague or obscure, it may be because he is groping for those lines of communication, all the while knowing that, like the narrator of "The Man of the Crowd," there are some secrets that do not allow themselves to be told.

V

"Mr. Poe has that indescribable something which men have agreed to call *genius*." James Russell Lowell, 1845

"Poe was always great not only in his noble conceptions but also as a prankster."—Charles Baudelaire, 1857

". . . there exists one characteristic that is singularly peculiar to Poe and which distinguishes him from every other writer, and that is the vigor of his imagination."—Fëdor Dostoevski, 1861

"With all due respect to the very original genius of the author of the 'Tales of Mystery,' it seems to us that to take him with more than a certain degree of seriousness is to lack seriousness one's self. An enthusiasm for Poe is the mark of a decidedly primitive stage of reflection."—Henry James, 1876

"Poe's genius has yet conquer'd a special recognition for itself, and I too have come to fully admit it, and appreciate it and him."—Walt Whitman, 1875

"His fame always puzzles me."—William Butler Yeats, 1899

"Above all, Poe is great because he is independent of cheap attractions, independent of sex, of patriotism, of fighting, of sentimentality, snobbery, gluttony, and all the rest of the vulgar stock-in-trade of his profession. This is what gives him his superb distinction."—George Bernard Shaw, 1909

"Poe had a pretty bitter doom. Doomed to seethe down his soul in a great continuous convulsion of distintegration, and doomed to register the process. And then doomed to be abused for it, when he had performed some of the bitterest tasks of human experience, that can be asked of a man. Necessary tasks, too. For the human soul must suffer its own disintegration, *consciously*, if ever it is to survive."—D. H. Lawrence, 1923

"Of his method in the Tales, the significance and the secret is: authentic particles, a thousand of which spring to the mind for quotation, taken apart and reknit with a view to emphasize, enforce, and make evident, the *method*. Their quality of skill in observation, their heat, local verity, being *overshadowed* only by the detached, the abstract, the cold philosophy of their joining together; a method springing so freshly from the local conditions which determine it, by their emphasis of firm crudity and lack of coordinated structure, as to be worthy of most painstaking study—The whole period, America 1840, could be rebuilt, psychologically (phrenologically) from Poe's 'method.' "—William Carlos Williams, 1925

"Poe has long passed casually with me and most of my friends as a bad writer accidentally and temporarily popular; the fact of the matter is, of course, that he has been pretty effectually established as a great writer while we have been sleeping."—Yvor Winters, 1937

"That Poe had a powerful intellect is undeniable: but it seems to me the intellect of a highly gifted young person before puberty."—T. S. Eliot, 1948

"His portraits of abnormal or self-destructive states contributed much to Dostoevski, his ratiocinating hero is the ancestor of Sherlock Holmes and his many successors, his tales of the future lead to H. G. Wells, his adventure stories to Jules Verne and Stevenson. It is not without interest that the development of such fiction in which the historical individual is missing should have coincided with the development of history as a science, with its own laws, and the appearance of the great nineteenth-century historians; further, that both these developments should accompany the industrialization and urbanization of social life in which the individual seems more and more the creation of historical forces while he himself feels less and less capable of affecting his life by any historical choice of his own. . . . As D. H. Lawrence says, . . . 'Poe had a pretty bitter doom.' . . . Doomed to be used in school textbooks as a bait to interest the young in literature, to be a respectable rival to the pulps."—W. H. Auden, 1950

*   *   *

"I doubt very much whether tales of the wild, improbable and terrible class can ever be permanently popular in this country. Charles Dickens, it appears to me, has given the final death blow to writing of that description."—J. E. Heath, explaining the rejection of "The Fall of the House of Usher" for publication in the *Southern Literary Messenger*, 1839

The Annotated Tales of Edgar Allan Poe

Terror of the Soul

METZENGERSTEIN

First published in the Philadelphia *Saturday Courier*, January 14, 1832, this was Poe's first short story to appear in print. In the tale's second edition, it was subtitled "A tale in imitation of the German," which indeed it is.

The Gothic tale was a German invention, but by Poe's time it had become widely popular in England and America as well. *Frankenstein, The Castle of Otranto*, and *Vathek* were all within this tradition, even though they were very different in content. In America, the Gothic tradition showed itself in Washington Irving, Charles Brockden Brown, and Nathaniel Hawthorne—and again, each author used the tradition according to his own bent.

"Metzengerstein" is closer to that tradition than it is to Poe's later tales, in which Gothic for its own sake is soft-pedaled in favor of psychological insight.

While the tale may be called "German" (Hungary was then part of the Germanic Holy Roman Empire), it derives in part from a poetic ghost story by Richard Henry Dana the elder, *The Buccaneer* (1827). In that poem, the main character is a pirate who poses as a captain of a merchant ship, murders most of the passengers, tries to rape a young widow, and after she flings herself into the sea, throws her horse in after her and burns the ship. The horse then reappears three times—the last time carrying the pirate into the sea to his death.

Another source seems to be Horace Walpole's *The Castle of Otranto* (1764), where we find a prophecy of doom, a picture that comes to life, and a gigantic ghost. One of Walpole's hero characters incidentally, is named Frederic. In the 1811 edition, edited by Walter Scott, there is an introduction which contains other ideas that found their way into "Metzengerstein."

Still another source seems to be Benjamin Disraeli's *Vivian Grey* (1826), which Poe reviewed favorably. In the third chapter we read of a portrait of one of Vivian's ancestors seated on a horse: "The horse seems quite living, and its fierce rider actually frowns upon us." Several other points in the story resemble Poe's tale, although as in all else, Poe took only ideas and developed them according to his own concepts.

"Metzengerstein" was one of the tales that made up the French-Italian film *Tales of Mystery and Imagination* (1968). The segment was directed by Roger Vadim and starred Jane and Peter Fonda in a much-altered version of the tale.

Pestis eram vivus—moriens tua mors ero.
          —*Martin Luther*   **1**

Horror and fatality have been stalking abroad in all ages. Why then give a date to the story I have to tell? Let it suffice to say, that at the period of which I speak, there existed, in the interior of Hungary, a settled although hidden belief in the doctrines of the Metempsychosis. Of the doctrines them- **2** selves—that is, of their falsity, or of their probability—I say nothing. I assert, however, that much of our incredulity (as La Bruyère says of all our unhappiness) "*vient de ne pouvoir être seuls.*"   **3**

1 "Living I have been your plague, dying I shall be your death" is part of a hexameter by Martin Luther (1483–1546) directed to the Pope.

2 Transmigration of souls, reincarnation. Poe makes use of the idea in several other tales, including "Morella," "Ligeia," and "A Tale of the Ragged Mountains." From the Greek word meaning "change of soul," metempsychosis describes the passage of the soul from one body to another, either human, animal, or inanimate. It is a fundamental doctrine of several religions originating in India, including Hinduism and Buddhism. The Druids of Gaul supposedly taught that the soul left the body after death to enter another, but the second body was not necessarily an earthly one.

Other famous believers in metempsychosis were Pythagoras, Plato, and Plotinus. In the Jewish Cabala, man has absolute free will, but his soul is tied and sullied by contact with matter. Demon souls interfere with the progress of the soul to its fulfillment in the divine plan, and punishment and atonement for sins is achieved by another incarnation. Transmigration was tolerated but not approved by official Judaism and was rejected entirely by the Christian Church.

3 "Mercier, in '*L'an deux mille quatre cents quarante*,' seriously maintains the doctrines of the metempsychosis, and J. D'Israeli says that 'no system is so simple and so little repugnant to the understanding.' Colonel Ethan Allen, the 'Green Mountain Boy,' is also said to have been a serious metempsychosist." [Poe's note]

The French in the text translates as "comes of being unable to be alone" and is from *Les Caractères*, by Jean de La Bruyère (1645–96), Section 99.

Louis Sébastien Mercier's book *L'An 2440* (1770), Chapter XIX, involves metempsychosis, but there is no record of any interest in that notion by Ethan Allen (1738–89), who is best known as a Revolutionary War hero and founder of the state of Vermont. He did, however, have a great white horse, in whose body, folklore said, he lived on.

4 Hindu believers

5 The soul "lives but one time in the material body: for the rest, a horse, a dog, even a man, there is only the intangible resemblance of those creatures." The Parisian mentioned here is still a mystery, and Poe may have merely made up the quote—as he did in other tales when he couldn't find one to suit his purpose.

6 Both names are Poe's creation. Berlifitzing may mean "little son of a bear," while Metzengerstein seems to be a combination of *Metzger* (butcher) and *Stein* (stone).

7 No real person is intended. The device is common in eighteenth- and nineteenth-century fiction in order to give an air of reality to the proceedings. ("You would know the name if I spelled it out.")

8 While "vibrate" means something different to most modern readers, in the sense of a pendulum swinging, the usage dates back to 1667.

In the original version of the tale, this paragraph followed:

"The beautiful Lady Mary!—how could she die?—and of consumption! But it is a path I have prayed to follow. I would wish all I love to perish of that gentle disease. How glorious! to depart in the hey-day of the young blood—the heart of all passion—the imagination all fire—amid the remembrances of happier days—in the fall of the year, and so be buried up forever in the gorgeous, autumnal leaves. Thus died the Lady Mary. The young Baron Frederick stood, without a living relative, by the coffin of his dead mother. He laid his hands upon her placid forehead. No shudder came over his delicate frame—no sigh from his gentle bosom—no curl upon his kingly lip. Heartless, self-willed, and impetuous from his childhood, he had arrived at the age of which I speak, through a career of unfeeling, wanton, and reckless dissipation; and a barrier had long since arisen in the channel of all holy thoughts, and gentle recollections."

But there were some points in the Hungarian superstition which were fast verging to absurdity. They—the Hungarians— 4 differed very essentially from their Eastern authorities. For example. "*The soul,*" said the former—I give the words of an acute and intelligent Parisian—"*ne demeure qu'une seule fois dans un corps sensible: au reste—un cheval, un chien, un homme même, n'est que la ressemblance peu tangible de ces* 5 *animaux.*"

6 The families of Berlifitzing and Metzengerstein had been at variance for centuries. Never before were two houses so illustrious, mutually embittered by hostility so deadly. The origin of this enmity seems to be found in the words of an ancient prophecy—"A lofty name shall have a fearful fall when, as the rider over his horse, the mortality of Metzengerstein shall triumph over the immortality of Berlifitzing."

To be sure the words themselves had little or no meaning. But more trivial causes have given rise—and that no long while ago—to consequences equally eventful. Besides, the estates, which were contiguous, had long exercised a rival influence in the affairs of a busy government. Moreover, near neighbors are seldom friends; and the inhabitants of the Castle Berlifitzing might look, from their lofty buttresses, into the very windows of the Palace Metzengerstein. Least of all had the more than feudal magnificence, thus discovered, a tendency to allay the irritable feelings of the less ancient and less wealthy Berlifitzings. What wonder, then, that the words, however silly, of that prediction, should have succeeded in setting and keeping at variance two families already predisposed to quarrel by every instigation of hereditary jealousy? The prophecy seemed to imply—if it implied anything—a final triumph on the part of the already more powerful house; and was of course remembered with the more bitter animosity by the weaker and less influential.

Wilhelm, Count Berlifitzing, although loftily descended, was, at the epoch of this narrative, an infirm and doting old man, remarkable for nothing but an inordinate and inveterate personal antipathy to the family of his rival, and so passionate a love of horses, and of hunting, that neither bodily infirmity, great age, nor mental incapacity, prevented his daily participation in the dangers of the chase.

Frederick, Baron Metzengerstein, was, on the other hand, 7 not yet of age. His father, the Minister G——, died young. His mother, the Lady Mary, followed him quickly. Frederick was, at that time, in his eighteenth year. In a city, eighteen years are no long period; but in a wilderness—in so magnificent 8 a wilderness as that old principality, the pendulum vibrates with a deeper meaning.

From some peculiar circumstances attending the administration of his father, the young Baron, at the decease of the former, entered immediately upon his vast possessions. Such estates were seldom held before by a nobleman of Hungary. His castles were without number. The chief in point of splendor and extent was the "Palace Metzengerstein." The

boundary line of his dominions waas never clearly defined;
but his principal park embraced a circuit of fifty miles.

Upon the succession of a proprietor so young, with a
character so well known, to a fortune so unparalleled, little
speculation was afloat in regard to his probable course of
conduct. And, indeed, for the space of three days, the behavior
of the heir out-Heroded Herod, and fairly surpassed the **9**
expectations of his most enthusiastic admirers. Shameful
debaucheries—flagrant treacheries—unheard-of atrocities—
gave his trembling vassals quickly to understand that no servile
submission on their part—no punctilios of conscience on his **10**
own—were thenceforward to prove any security against the
remorseless fangs of a petty Caligula. On the night of the **11**
fourth day, the stables of the Castle Berlifitzing were discovered to be on fire; and the unanimous opinion of the neighborhood added the crime of the incendiary to the already
hideous list of the Baron's misdemeanors and enormities.

But during the tumult occasioned by this occurrence, the
young nobleman himself sat apparently buried in meditation,
in a vast and desolate upper apartment of the family palace of
Metzengerstein. The rich although faded tapestry hangings
which swung gloomily upon the walls, represented the shad- **12**
owy and majestic forms of a thousand illustrious ancestors.
Here, rich-ermined priests, and pontifical dignitaries, familiarly seated with the autocrat and the sovereign, put a veto
on the wishes of a temporal king, or restrained with the fiat
of papal supremacy the rebellious sceptre of the Arch-enemy.
There, the dark, tall statures of the Princes Metzengerstein—
their muscular war-coursers plunging over the carcasses of
fallen foes—startled the steadiest nerves with their vigorous
expression; and *here*, again, the voluptuous and swan-like
figures of the dames of days gone by, floated away in the
mazes of an unreal dance to the strains of imaginary melody.

But as the Baron listened, or affected to listen, to the
gradually increasing uproar in the stables of Berlifitzing—or
perhaps pondered upon some more novel, some more decided
act of audacity—his eyes were turned unwittingly to the figure
of an enormous, and unnaturally colored horse, represented
in the tapestry as belonging to a Saracen ancestor òf the family **13**
of his rival. The horse itself, in the foreground of the design,
stood motionless and statue-like—while, farther back, its
discomfited rider perished by the dagger of a Metzengerstein.

On Frederick's lips arose a fiendish expression, as he
became aware of the direction which his glance had, without
his consciousness, assumed. Yet he did not remove it. On the
contrary, he could by no means account for the overwhelming
anxiety which appeared falling like a pall upon his senses. It
was with difficulty that he reconciled his dreamy and incoherent feelings with the certainty of being awake. The longer
he gazed the more absorbing became the spell—the more
impossible did it appear that he could ever withdraw his
glance from the fascination of that tapestry. But the tumult
without becoming suddenly more violent, with a compulsory

9 This line from *Hamlet*, III, ii, is a favorite of Poe's—
he uses it again in "The Masque of the Red Death" and
"William Wilson." It comes from Hamlet's instructions
to the players on how to portray characters, particularly
his warnings about those who overact in deference to
the lowest common denominator of theatergoers: "I
would have such a fellow whipped for o'erdoing Termagant, it out-herods Herod." Termagant was the name
of a supposed Mohammedan diety whom medieval
Christians pictured as violent and powerful.

The Herod here is the Herod who ruled at Jesus' birth
and ordered the massacre of the Innocents, not the one
who ruled when he was crucified. The earlier Herod,
who died in 4 B.C., married ten times, spent lavishly on
his cities, gradually went insane, and became more
bloodthirsty than ever.

10 Minute details or trifling points. Poe seems to have
done some research into Hungarian history, for some of
the country's nobility were indeed notorious. One of
these, Countess Elizabeth Báthori (d. 1614) was supposed
to have forced young peasant women to dance barefoot
in the dead of winter for her entertainment. And there
is also the famous Vlad the Impaler, the historical Count
Dracula.

11 Caligula (A.D. 12–41) was emperor of Rome (37–41).
His real name was Gaius Caesar Germanicus (he was
the son of Germanicus Caesar), but he was called Caligula
(Little Boots) because he wore military boots when a
child. After a serious illness he apparently went insane,
soon becoming well known for his ruthlessness and
cruelty. Legend has it that he made his horse a consul
and a member of a college of priests. He was finally
assassinated by a member of the Praetorian Guard.

12 Tapestries were more than decorations; they served
to keep room air from the cold stone walls. The draftiness
of these castles is well documented, and naturally the
tapestries would swing. Poe uses moving tapestries again
in "Ligeia."

13 "Saracen" was commonly used in the Middle Ages
to mean an Arab or Moslem. The Saracens invaded
France in the eighth century but were defeated by
Charles Martel in a decisive battle. Their cultural influence lingers on in Sicily, where they ruled from the
ninth to the eleventh centuries (see "Ligeia," n. 42).

The fact that the Berlifitzings have a Saracen ancestor
merely serves the "Arabesque" nature of the tale,
providing atmosphere and the possibility of supernatural
influence.

14 The words "sepulchral and disgusting" used with the normally mundane "teeth" is Metzengerstein's own interpretation and surely says something about him. It recalls Poe's "Berenice" and also the jaws of death (*Twelfth Night*, III, iv).

15 Men in charge of the stables; an archaic word by Poe's time, but it fits in with the medieval atmosphere of the tale.

16 The symbolism of the horse is complex and not easily defined. In Germany and England, to dream of a white horse was thought to be an omen of death (A. H. Krappe, *La Genése des mythes*, 1952). In legend and fable, horses are often said to be clairvoyant, and in ancient times they were thought to be endowed with powers of divination. Some cultures associate horses with burial rites.

17 "Any beast not wild, found within any Lordship, and not owned by any man [O.E.D.]."

18 Metzengerstein knows the horse is the reincarnated Wilhelm von Berlifitzing. He will not name it, but the initials on the forehead are proof enough.

exertion he diverted his attention to the glare of ruddy light thrown full by the flaming stables upon the windows of the apartment.

The action, however, was but momentary; his gaze returned mechanically to the wall. To his extreme horror and astonishment, the head of the gigantic steed had, in the meantime, altered its position. The neck of the animal, before arched, as if in compassion, over the prostrate body of its lord, was now extended, at full length, in the direction of the Baron. The eyes, before invisible, now wore an energetic and human expression, while they gleamed with a fiery and unusual red; and the distended lips of the apparently enraged horse left in **14** full view his sepulchral and disgusting teeth.

Stupefied with terror, the young nobleman tottered to the door. As he threw it open, a flash of red light, streaming far into the chamber, flung his shadow with a clear outline against the quivering tapestry; and he shuddered to perceive that shadow—as he staggered awhile upon the threshold—assuming the exact position, and precisely filling up the contour, of the relentless and triumphant murderer of the Saracen Berlifitzing.

To lighten the depression of his spirits, the Baron hurried into the open air. At the principal gate of the palace he **15** encountered three equerries. With much difficulty, and at the imminent peril of their lives, they were restraining the convulsive plunges of a gigantic and fiery-colored horse.

"Whose horse? Where did you get him?" demanded the youth, in a querulous and husky tone, as he became instantly aware that the mysterious steed in the tapestried chamber **16** was the very counterpart of the furious animal before his eyes.

"He is your own property, sire," replied one of the equerries, "at least he is claimed by no other owner. We caught him flying, all smoking and foaming with rage, from the burning stables of the Castle Berlifitzing. Supposing him to have belonged to the old Count's stud of foreign horses, we led **17** him back as an estray. But the grooms there disclaim any title to the creature; which is strange, since he bears evident marks of having made a narrow escape from the flames.

"The letters W. V. B. are also branded very distinctly on his forehead," interrupted a second equerry: "I supposed them, of course, to be the initials of William Von Berlifitzing— but all at the castle are positive in denying any knowledge of the horse."

"Extremely singular!" said the young Baron, with a musing air, and apparently unconscious of the meaning of his words. "He is, as you say, a remarkable horse—a prodigious horse! although, as you very justly observe, of a suspicious and untractable character; let him be mine, however," he added, after a pause, "perhaps a rider like Frederick of Metzengerstein **18** may tame even the devil from the stables of Berlifitzing."

"You are mistaken, my lord; the horse, as I think we mentioned, is *not* from the stables of the Count. If such had been the case, we know our duty better than to bring him into the presence of a noble of your family."

"True!" observed the Baron, drily; and at that instant a page of the bedchanber came from the palace with a heightened color, and a precipitate step. He whispered into his master's ear an account of the sudden disappearance of a small portion of the tapestry, in an apartment which he designated; entering, at the same time, into particulars of a minute and circumstantial character; but from the low tone of voice in which these latter were communicated, nothing escaped to gratify the excited curiosity of the equerries. **19**

The young Frederick, during the conference, seemed agitated by a variety of emotions. He soon, however, recovered his composure, and an expression of determined malignancy settled upon his countenance, as he gave peremptory orders that the apartment in question should be immediately locked up, and the key placed in his own possession.

"Have you heard of the unhappy death of the old hunter Berlifitzing?" said one of his vassals to the Baron, as, after the departure of the page, the huge steed which that nobleman had adopted as his own, plunged and curveted, with redoubled fury, down the long avenue which extended from the palace to the stables of Metzengerstein.

"No!" said the Baron, turning abruptly toward the speaker, "dead! say you?"

"It is indeed true, my lord; and, to the noble of your name, will be, I imagine, no unwelcome intelligence."

A rapid smile shot over the countenance of the listener. "How died he?"

"In his rash exertions to rescue a favorite portion of the hunting stud, he has himself perished miserably in the flames."

"I–n–d–e–e–d–!" ejaculated the Baron, as if slowly and deliberately impressed with the truth of some exciting idea. **20**

"Indeed," repeated the vassal.

"Shocking!" said the youth, calmly, and turned quietly into the palace.

From this date a marked alteration took place in the outward demeanor of the dissolute young Baron Frederick Von Metzengerstein. Indeed, his behavior disappointed every expectation, and proved little in accordance with the views of many a manœuvring mamma; while his habits and manner, still less **21** than formerly, offered any thing congenial with those of the neighboring aristocracy. He was never to be seen beyond the limits of his own domain, and, in his wide and social world, was utterly companionless—unless, indeed, that unnatural, impetuous, and fiery-colored horse, which he henceforward continually bestrode, had any mysterious right to the title of his friend.

Numerous invitations on the part of the neighborhood for a long time, however, periodically came in. "Will the Baron honor our festivals with his presence?" "Will the Baron join us in a hunting of the boar?"—"Metzengerstein does not hunt"; "Metzengerstein will not attend," were the haughty and laconic answers.

These repeated insults were not to be endured by an imperious nobility. Such invitations became less cordial—less

19 Unlike most of Poe's tales of the uncanny, "Metzengerstein" seems to have but one interpretation: it *is* a story of the supernatural (although some have thought it a parody of that form). Since someone else has seen the missing portion of the tapestry, we know the phantom horse is real and not merely the figment of a disordered mind. In all of Poe's later Gothic tales, he is careful to provide several possibilities for the bizarre events that occur.

20 I.e., metempsychosis

21 "Mamma" seems inappropriate at this point; why not "mother"?

frequent—in time they ceased altogether. The widow of the unfortunate Count Berlifitzing was even heard to express a hope "that the Baron might be at home when he did not wish to be at home, since he disdained the company of his equals; and ride when he did not wish to ride, since he preferred the society of a horse." This to be sure was a very silly explosion of hereditary pique; and merely proved how singularly unmeaning our sayings are apt to become, when we desire to be unusually energetic.

The charitable, nevetheless, attributed the alteration in the conduct of the young nobleman to the natural sorrow of a son for the untimely loss of his parents;—forgetting, however, his atrocious and reckless behavior during the short period immediately succeeding that bereavement. Some there were, indeed, who suggested a too haughty idea of self-consequence and dignity. Others again (among whom may be mentioned the family physician) did not hesitate in speaking of morbid melancholy, and hereditary ill-health; while dark hints, of a more equivocal nature, were current among the multitude.

Indeed, the Baron's perverse attachment to his lately-acquired charger—an attachment which seemed to attain new strength from every fresh example of the animal's ferocious and demon-like propensities—at length became, in the eyes of all reasonable men, a hideous and unnatural fervor. In the glare of noon—at the dead hour of night—in sickness or in health—in calm or in tempest—the young Metzengertein seemed riveted to the saddle of that colossal horse, whose intractable audacities so well accorded with his own spirit.

There were circumstances, moreover, which, coupled with late events, gave an unearthly and portentous character to the mania of the rider, and to the capabilities of the steed. The space passed over in a single leap had been accurately measured, and was found to exceed, by an astounding difference, the wildest expectations of the most imaginative. The Baron, besides, had no particular *name* for the animal, although all the rest in his collection were distinguished by characterstic appellations. His stable, too, was appointed at a distance from the rest; and with regard to grooming and other necessary offices, none but the owner in person had ventured to officiate, or even to enter the enclosure of that horse's particular stall. It was also to be observed, that although the three grooms, who had caught the steed as he fled from the conflagration at Berlifitzing, had succeeded in arresting his course, by means of a chain-bridle and noose—yet not one of the three could with any certainty affirm that he had, during that dangerous struggle, or at any period thereafter, actually placed his hand upon the body of the beast. Instances of peculiar intelligence in the demeanor of a noble and high-spirited horse are not to be supposed capable of exciting unreasonable attention, but there were certain circumstances which intruded themselves by force upon the most skeptical and phlegmatic; and it is said there were times when the animal caused the gaping crowd who stood around to recoil in horror from the deep and impressive meaning of his terrible stamp—times when the young Metzengerstein turned pale and shrunk away from the rapid and searching expression of his human-looking eye.   **22**

Among all the retinue of the Baron, however, none were found to doubt the ardor of that exraordinary affection which existed on the part of the young nobleman for the fiery qualities of his horse; at least, none but an insignificant and misshapen little page, whose deformities were in everybody's way, and whose opinions were of the least possible importance. He (if his ideas are worth mentioning at all) had the effrontery to assert that his master never vaulted into the saddle without an unaccountable and almost imperceptible shudder; and that, upon his return from every long-continued and habitual ride, an expression of triumphant malignity distorted every muscle in his countenance.

One tempestuous night, Metzengerstein, awaking from a heavy slumber, descended like a maniac from his chamber, and, mounting in hot haste, bounded away to the mazes of the forest. An occurrence so common attracted no particular attention, but his return was looked for with intense anxiety on the part of his domestics, when, after some hours' absence, the stupendous and magnificent battlements of the Palace Metzengerstein, were discovered crackling and rocking to their very foundation, under the influence of a dense and livid mass of ungovernable fire.   **23**

22 The horse's eye seems human, and the fact that everyone notices this is another indication that this is a true tale of the supernatural.

23 Has Metzengerstein set fire to his room before leaving, or does the fire start of its own accord—or through supernatural intervention?

"... a steed, bearing an unbonneted and disordered rider, was seen leaping with an impetuosity which outstripped the very Demon of the Tempest." *Illustration by Johann Friedrich Vogel, nineteenth century*

24 In the first version of the tale, this is followed by "and called forth from every beholder an ejaculation of 'Azrael!'" Azrael, the Muslim angel of death, is mentioned again in "Ligeia" and "Mesmeric Revelation." He separates the soul from the body with a sword.

"Demon of the Tempest" could refer to Arridu, the mountain genie of Aptolcater's *The Book of Power* (1724), or to Furfur, the commander of twenty-six infernal legions, who in the shape of a deer, winged and breathing fire, brings on storms. Other storm gods include the Sumerian Enlil; Adad, from Babylonia; and the Teutonic Fylgjur.

25 This is the first of many appearances of a whirlwind in Poe's tales. Whirlwinds always represent destruction, for they suck in everything they touch.

Note that fire is a purifier, traditionally sure death to infernal beings, such as witches. Burning at the stake was a means of purifying the soul, and thus fire is also an agent of regeneration (see "The Pit and The Pendulum," note 8).

26 Smoke rising heavenward is a traditional symbol of the *axis mundi*, the path of escape from time and space into the eternal and unconfined, again underscoring the supernatural origin of the horse. Smoke can also signify a soul ascending to heaven, purified by fire, so that the horse might represent the Baron himself.

In Christianity, smoke is often used to suggest the shortness of life and the vanity of fame or anger.

As the flames, when first seen, had already made so terrible a progress that all efforts to save any portion of the building were evidently futile, the astonished neighborhood stood idly around in silent if not pathetic wonder. But a new and fearful object soon riveted the attention of the multitude, and proved how much more intense is the excitement wrought in the feelings of a crowd by the contemplation of human agony, than that brought about by the most appalling spectacles of inanimate matter.

Up the long avenue of aged oaks which led from the forest to the main entrance of the Palace Metzengerstein, a steed, bearing an unbonneted and disordered rider, was seen leaping with an impetuosity which outstripped the very Demon of the **24** Tempest.

The career of the horseman was indisputably, on his own part, uncontrollable. The agony of his countenance, the convulsive struggle of his frame, gave evidence of superhuman exertion: but no sound, save a solitary shriek, escaped from his lacerated lips, which were bitten through and through in the intensity of terror. One instant, and the clattering of hoofs resounded sharply and shrilly above the roaring of the flames and the shrieking of the winds—another, and, clearing at a single plunge the gate-way and the moat, the steed bounded far up the tottering staircases of the palace, and, with its rider, **25** disappeared amid the whirlwind of chaotic fire.

The fury of the tempest immediately died away, and a dead calm sullenly succeeded. A white flame still enveloped the building like a shroud, and, streaming far away into the quiet atmosphere, shot forth a glare of preternatural light; while a cloud of smoke settled heavily over the battlements in the **26** distinct colossal figure of—*a horse*.

MS. FOUND IN A BOTTLE

First published in the Baltimore *Saturday Visiter*, October 19, 1833, this tale was entered in a contest with other material by Poe and won him the top fifty-dollar prize. It also marked his first major step into the limelight, since the story was well received and one of the judges was John Pendleton Kennedy, who became Poe's lifelong friend and supporter.

"MS. Found in a Bottle" is a remarkable tale in many ways. It is a fine mood piece, building to a shattering climax, and foreshadows both "A Descent into the Maelström" and Poe's only novel, *The Narrative of Arthur Gordon Pym*. It is also the first clear example of Poe's cosmological preoccupations.

What Poe was attempting, it seems, was to work out a satisfactory explanation of the workings of the universe, and to a great extent, he worked out his theories in his tales. This is not to say that each and every tale is merely a cosmological exercise, but that in many of them we can detect indications—sometimes fairly obvious—of his theory of unity.

Although not expressed fully until *Eureka* (1848), Poe's theory of unity was beginning to develop as early as "Metzengerstein." Briefly, Poe believed that originally all matter coincided with the Godhead but that an explosion or diffusion took place, in which all matter was hurled outward from its starting point, the Primordial Particle. Since that time, matter has been moving away from its source, but it still shares an identity with its Creator, still longs to be reunified with the Godhead.

When the momentum of that original diffusion slows sufficiently, the gravitational attraction of the source (and the individual particles of matter) will take charge, and from that moment all matter will rush back to the Godhead to be reunited (and annihilated) in one giant collision.

In Poe's concept, which predates yet anticipates the modern big-bang theory, there is a paradoxical yearning for unity (the merging with the Godhead) and a terror of the inevitable annihilation (the destruction of individual matter—and personality). It is this conflict which gives a certain underlying tension to many of Poe's tales and which represents itself in images of whirlpools and whirlwinds and other symbols of uniting force.

Despite the fact that *Eureka* was a financial failure, the book contains "some staggering, almost incredible insights," according to Colin Wilson (*Starseekers*, Doubleday, 1981). Wilson points out that Poe's concept of the origin of the universe predates Willem de Sitter's theory of the expanding universe (1917) by seventy years, and that his collapsing universe that ends in annihilation is almost identical to the black-hole theory, which we owe to modern radio astronomy. "Poe also throws off the casual suggestion that space and time are the same thing," Wilson says, "an insight that seemed obvious nonsense at the time, and that did not begin to make sense until Einstein's appearance." Poe also recognized that the Milky Way is a galaxy and not just a cluster of stars—something that would, again, be proved in this century. "And when Poe states that the universe ends in annihilation, and then begins all over again, he anticipates one of the most recent theories of cosmology: that a black hole does not continue to collapse indefinitely, but that it finally reaches a limit, and then explodes again." (pp. 10–11)

How did Poe, who was in no way a scientist, come to these remarkable conclusions? We do not know, for Poe left no record of how he came to write *Eureka*. For those who care to wade through his often pretentiously written and verbose essay, it is included in most complete editions of Poe's works.

Sources for "MS. Found in a Bottle" include the writings of Captain John Cleves Symmes (1780–1829), who proposed a theory that the world had openings at both poles, through which ships could navigate, and an internal world he called Symzonia. Symmes's book, *Symzonia* (1826), written under the pen name of Captain Adam Seaborn, struck Poe's imagination, as did the works of a

Symmes disciple, Jeremiah Reynolds, who actually proposed making an expedition to the polar cataract. [On his deathbed, Poe murmured, "Reynolds, Reynolds," leading some biographers to speculate that this polar theory continued to be vital to him.]

Although Poe suggests the polar openings are perilous, Symmes navigates them with ease in *Symzonia*. We might expect this if Poe were seeing them as symbolic of his destruction-in-unity principle.

Jack Scherting, in *Poe Studies* (Vol. I, p. 22), cites many similarities between Poe's tales and Melville's *Moby Dick* (comparisons have also been made between Melville's novel and Poe's *Narrative of Arthur Gordon Pym*). Ishmael and Poe's narrator have similar motives for going to sea. There is an enigmatic captain in both, an older, gray-haired man who suggests some higher authority. Both tales indicate a hostile, or at least uncaring, universe. And both end in a whirlpool.

Martin Donegan reads the story on disc (CMS 655).

---

1 "He who has but a moment to live, has no longer anything to dissemble," from *Atys*, by Philippe Quinault (1635–88), I, vi, 15–16.

2 Absolute skepticism. Pyrrho of Elis (c. 365–275 B.C.) founded the school of philosophy called "skeptics," after returning as a member of Alexander's expedition to India. Pyrrho left no written record of his work, but his ideas have come down to us through his pupil Timon of Phlius, who flourished around 280 B.C. Pyrrho held that it is impossible to understand the nature of reality or attain absolute knowledge, that man would be better off not trying to solve ethical problems, but instead to accept the world as it is.

"Pyrro" is the name of the narrator in the first draft of Poe's "Eleonora."

3 *Ignis fatuus* means a "fatuous fire"—that is, a will-o'-the-wisp. It has come to mean a Utopian scheme, or something wholly impractical.

"When thou runnest up Gadshill in the night to catch my horse, if I did not think thou hadst been an *ignis fatuus* or ball of wildfire, there's no purchase in money" (*I Henry IV*, III, iii).

4 Batavia was the former name for Jakarta, Indonesia. It was completely destroyed by an earthquake and flood in 1699. The name comes from the ancient Celtic tribe (the Batavi) who gave the Netherlands its original name.

5 Islands of the Malay archipelago, comprising the Greater Sunda (Sumatra, Java, Borneo, Celebes, and adjacent islands), and the Lesser Sunda, extending east from Bali to Timor.

6 Malabar is the coastal region of southwestern India on the Arabian Sea (the states of Mysore and Kerala). Teak (*Tectona grandis*) is the East Indian tree with a hard, yellowish-brown wood so valuable to shipbuilders.

7 The Laccadive Islands are Indian territory in the Arabian Sea, north of the Maldive Islands.

8 Coir is a stiff, coarse fiber prepared from the outer husks of coconuts, used to make mats and rope. Jaggery is an unrefined sugar made from palm sap or coconuts. Ghee is a semifluid clarified butter from India, usually made from buffalo milk.

9 The ship is carrying mostly staples, but the inclusion of opium may mean that Poe wants us to be aware of the

---

Qui n'a plus qu'un moment à vivre
N'a plus rien à dissimuler.
　　　　　　—Quinault—Atys.

1

Of my country and of my family I have little to say. Ill usage and length of years have driven me from the one, and estranged me from the other. Hereditary wealth afforded me an education of no common order, and a comtemplative turn of mind enabled me to methodize the stores which early study very diligently garnered up.—Beyond all things, the study of the German moralists gave me great delight; not from any ill-advised admiration of their eloquent madness, but from the ease with which my habits of rigid thought enabled me to detect their falsities. I have often been reproached with the aridity of my genius; a deficiency of imagination has been **2** imputed to me as a crime; and the Pyrrhonism of my opinions has at all times rendered me notorious. Indeed, a strong relish for physical philosophy has, I fear, tinctured my mind with a very common error of this age—I mean the habit of referring occurrences, even the least susceptible of such reference, to the principles of that science. Upon the whole, no person could be less liable than myself to be led away from the severe **3** precincts of truth by the *ignes fatui* of superstition. I have thought proper to premise thus much, lest the incredible tale I have to tell should be considered rather the raving of a crude imagination, than the positive experience of a mind to which the reveries of fancy have been a dead letter and a nullity.

After many years spent in foreign travel, I sailed in the year **4** 18—, from the port of Batavia, in the rich and populous island **5** of Java, on an voyage to the Archipelago of the Sunda islands. I went as passenger—having no other inducement than a kind of nervous restlessness which haunted me as a fiend.

Our vessel was a beautiful ship of about four hundred tons, **6** copper-fastened, and built at Bombay of Malabar teak. She was freighted with cotton-wool and oil, from the Lachadive **7,8** islands. We had also on board coir, jaggeree, ghee, cocoa- **9** nuts, and a few cases of opium. The stowage was clumsily **10** done, and the vessel consequently crank.

We got under way with a mere breath of wind, and for many days stood along the eastern coast of Java, without any other incident to beguile the monotony of our course than the occasional meeting with some of the small grabs of the [11] Archipelago to which we were bound.

One evening, leaning over the taffrail, I observed a very [12] singular, isolated cloud, to the N.W. It was remarkable, as well for its color, as from its being the first we had seen since our departure from Batavia. I watched it attentively until sunset, when it spread all at once to the eastward and westward, girting in the horizon with a narrow strip of vapor, and looking like a long line of low beach. My notice was soon [13] afterwards attracted by the dusky-red appearance of the moon, [14] and the peculiar character of the sea. The latter was undergoing a rapid change, and the water seemed more then usually transparent. Although I could distinctly see the bottom, yet, [15] heaving the lead, I found the ship in fifteen fathoms. The air [16,17] now became intolerably hot, and was loaded with spiral exhalations similar to those arising from heated iron. As night came on, every breath of wind died away, and a more entire calm it is impossible to conceive. The flame of a candle burned upon the poop without the least perceptible motion, and a long hair, held between the finger and thumb, hung without the possibility of detecting a vibration. However, as the captain said he could perceive no indication of danger, and as we were drifting in bodily to shore, he ordered the sails to be furled, and the anchor let go. No watch was set, and the crew, consisting principally of Malays, stretched themselves deliberately upon the deck. I went below—not without a full presentiment of evil. Indeed, every appearance warranted me in apprehending a Simoom. I told the captain my fears; but [18] he paid no attention to what I said, and left me without deigning to give a reply. My uneasiness, however, prevented me from sleeping, and about midnight I went up on deck.— As I placed my foot upon the upper step of the companion-ladder, I was startled my a loud, humming noise, like that occasioned by the rapid revolution of a mill-wheel, and before I could ascertain its meaning, I found the ship quivering to its centre. In the next instant, a wilderness of foam hurled us upon our beam-ends, and rushing over us fore and aft, swept the entire decks from stem to stern. [19]

The extreme fury of the blast proved, in a great measure, the salvation of the ship. Although completely water-logged, yet, as her masts had gone by the board, she rose, after a minute, heavily from the sea, and staggering awhile beneath the immense pressure of the tempest, finally righted.

By what miracle I escaped destruction, it is impossible to say. Stunned by the shock of the water, I found myself, upon recovery, jammed in between the stern-post and rudder. With great difficulty I gained my feet, and looking dizzily around, was, at first, struck with the idea of our being among breakers; so terrific, beyond the wildest imagination, was the whirlpool of mountainous and foaming ocean within which we were engulfed. After a while, I heard the voice of an old Swede,

dreamlike state that the drug produces, since this tale has that same quality.

10 The boat is unstable.

11 Grabs are East Indian boats of light draft and broad beam, and with two or three masts with triangular (lateen) sails extended by a long spar slung to the low mast.

12 The upper part of the stern.

13 This seems to describe the formation of cloud clusters, which tend to lie along bands running across the oceans parallel to the equator. From the sea, warmed by the sun and fanned by the trade winds, the air sucks up moisture and hot air, which then turns into rain at the surface plus a huge weight of hot air high above. When the air drops, it is compressed and becomes hotter; energy is given off and the air rises again. Says Nigel Calder in *the Weather Machine*, "This machinery that injects energy from the tropical oceans into the world's air pulsates like a great piston engine" (Viking Press, 1974; p. 22). It is from these cloud clusters that tropical storms develop.

14 A warning, as we see in "The Fall of the House of Usher," note 73.

15 The ship, in the transparent water, suggests an object floating in air. But the fact that the ship is in fairly deep water means that the transparency is abnormal, and therefore ominous.

16 A lead weight at the end of a rope or string, let down to mark the depth of the water, usually marked off in fathoms (a fathom is six feet).

17 Typical of the atmosphere in the tropical cloud-cluster formation. The hot, dry air that rises above the rain clouds over the ocean cools and returns to the surface, becoming a sort of sponge to soak up more moisture.

18 The Simoon (or Simoom) is a hot, dry violent wind laden with dust from Asian and African deserts. Poe uses it here in a more general sense as a storm wind.

19 A similar occurrence, but with less disastrous results, can be found in *Symzonia*, Chapter 19.

20 A hulk was originally a round-sterned, square-tucked sixteenth-century cargo carrier. A heavy, clumsy ship, by Poe's time its name had been transformed into the term for the body of an abandoned wreck.

21 Australia.

22 It was thought that the sun, at such low angle, would be weaker than when high in the sky, but although the sun does change in intensity when viewed on the horizon (because we view it through heavier atmosphere), *dim* light is often the result of either dust or other pollutants. When Krakatoa exploded in 1883, the volcanic dust spread throughout the world, creating spectacular sunsets for months.

23 Meaning both polarization (light waves filtered in such a way that the waves move in one plane instead of scattering) and the Pole itself

24 The image of the sun being swallowed by the sea is an ancient one (see *The Golden Bough*, V, Section 3) and, as always, represents a threat to existence itself.

25 The phosphorescence is mentioned in *Symzonia* but is also a common occurrence in certain latitudes.

who had shipped with us at the moment of our leaving port. I hallooed to him with all my strength, and presently he came reeling aft. We soon discovered that we were the sole survivors of the accident. All on deck, with the exception of ourselves, had been swept overboard;—the captain and mates must have perished as they slept, for the cabins were deluged with water. Without assistance, we could expect to do little for the security of the ship, and our exertions were at first paralyzed by the momentary expectation of going down. Our cable had, of course, parted like pack-thread, at the first breath of the hurricane, or we should have been instantaneously overwhelmed. We scudded with frightful velocity before the sea, and the water made clear breaches over us. The frame-work of our stern was shattered excessively, and, in almost every respect, we had received considerable injury; but to our extreme joy we found the pumps unchoked, and that we had made no great shifting of our ballast. The main fury of the blast had already blown over, and we apprehended little danger from the violence of the wind; but we looked forward to its total cessation with dismay; well believing, that, in our shattered condition, we should inevitably perish in the tremendous swell which would ensue. But this very just apprehension seemed by no means likely to be soon verified. For five entire days and nights—during which our only subsistence was a small quantity of jaggeree, procured with great difficulty **20** from the forecastle—the hulk flew at a rate defying computation, before rapidly succeeding flaws of wind, which, without equalling the first violence of the Simoom, were still more terrific than any tempest I had before encountered. Our course for the first four days was, with trifling variations, S.E. and by S.; and we must have run down the coast of New **21** Holland.—On the fifth day the cold became extreme, although the wind had hauled round a point more to the northward.— The sun arose with a sickly yellow lustre, and clambered a very few degrees above the horizon—emitting no decisive **22** light.—There were no clouds apparent, yet the wind was upon the increase, and blew with a fitful and unsteady fury. About noon, as nearly as we could guess, our attention was again arrested by the appearance of the sun. It gave out no light, properly so called, but a dull and sullen glow without reflection, **23** as if all its rays were polarized. Just before sinking within the turgid sea, its central fires suddenly went out, as if hurriedly extinguished by some unaccountable power. It was a dim, silver-like rim, alone, as it rushed down the unfathomable **24** ocean.

We waited in vain for the arrival of the sixth day—that day to me has not arrived—to the Swede, never did arrive. Thenceforward we were enshrouded in pitchy darkness, so that we could not have seen an object at twenty paces from the ship. Eternal night continued to envelop us, all unrelieved by the phosphoric sea-brilliancy to which we had been **25** accustomed in the tropics. We observed too, that, although the tempest continued to rage with unabated violence, there was no longer to be discovered the usual appearance of surf,

"In the next instant, a wilderness of foam hurled us upon our beam-ends, and rushing over us fore and aft, swept the entire decks from stem to stern." *Artist unknown*

or foam, which has hitherto attended us. All around were horror, and thick gloom, and a black sweltering desert of ebony.—Superstitious terror crept by degrees into the spirit of the old Swede, and my own soul was wrapped up in silent wonder. We neglected all care of the ship, as worse than useless, and securing ourselves, as well as possible, to the stump of the mizzen-mast, looked out bitterly into the world of ocean. We had no means of calculating time, nor could we form any guess of our situation. We were, however, well **26** aware of having made farther to the southward than any previous navigators, and felt great amazement at not meeting with the usual impediments of ice. In the meantime every moment threatened to be our last—every mountainous billow hurried to overwhelm us. The swell surpassed anything I had imagined possible, and that we were not instantly buried is a miracle. My companion spoke of the lightness of our cargo, and reminded me of the excellent qualities of our ship; but I could not help feeling the utter hopelessness of hope itself, and prepared myself gloomily for that death which I thought nothing could defer beyond an hour, as, with every knot of way the ship made, the swelling of the black stupendous seas became more dismally appalling. At times we gasped for

26 Navigation and the reckoning of time at sea depend on the visibility of the sun and stars.

27 The wandering albatross has a wingspread often to twelve feet and was called by sailors the Cape Sheep because large flocks of the white birds frequented the Cape of Good Hope. It gorges itself and then sits motionless on the waves; sailors believed it slept in the air, because in flight it glides without any apparent motion of its long wings. According to maritime tradition, it is bad luck to shoot an albatross, a superstition that is the basis for Coleridge's *Rime of the Ancient Mariner*.

The kraken is a beast from Norwegian folklore said to haunt the coast of Norway, destroying ships and eating sailors. Norwegian Bishop Pontoppidan in 1752 described the kraken as being of vast size, darkening the water around it by some excretion—suggesting that it was most likely a giant cuttlefish.

Krakens were also said to have been seen off the North American coast, and Pliny speaks of a sea monster in the Straits of Gibraltar that blocked the entrance of ships.

28 A ship of the Dutch East India Company, which was founded in 1602 to oversee trade with the Indian Ocean; it was put out of business by government decree in 1832. Its ships were bigger and faster than anyone else's, with twelve hundred tons typical in 1800. However, the ships were not as fast as some have suggested, because of their bluff bows. Time wasn't really of the essence until much later.

29 Some interpreters see this as a symbolic transition from one mental state (skepticism) to another (sensation), or from a waking state to a dream state.

Such a mid-ocean transfer is not impossible. In 1957 a passenger was hurled from his room on the ill-fated *Andrea Doria* to the Swedish ship *Stockholm*.

30 Partitions put up to prevent cargo from shifting.

"Almighty God! see! see!" *Artist unknown*

breath at an elevation beyond the albatross—at times became dizzy with the velocity of our descent into some watery hell, where the air grew stagnant, and no sound disturbed the **27** slumbers of the kraken.

We were at the bottom of one of these abysses, when a quick scream from my companion broke fearfully upon the night. "See! see!" cried he, shrieking in my ears, "Almighty God! see! see!" As he spoke, I became aware of a dull, sullen glare of red light which streamed down the sides of the vast chasm where we lay, and threw a fitful brilliancy upon our deck. Casting my eyes upwards, I beheld a spectacle which froze the current of my blood. At a terrific height directly above us, and upon the very verge of the precipitous descent, hovered a gigantic ship, of perhaps four thousand tons. Although upreared upon the summit of a wave more than a hundred times her own altitude, her apparent size still **28** exceeded that of any ship of the line or East Indiaman in existence. Her huge hull was of a deep dingy black, unrelieved by any of the customary carvings of a ship. A single row of brass cannon protruded from her open ports, and dashed from their polished surfaces the fires of innumerable battle-lanterns, which swung to and fro about her rigging. But what mainly inspired us with horror and astonishment, was that she bore up under a press of sail in the very teeth of that supernatural sea, and of that ungovernable hurricane. When we first discovered her, her bows were alone to be seen, as she rose slowly from the dim and horrible gulf beyond her. For a moment of intense terror she paused upon the giddy pinnacle, as if in contemplation of her own sublimity, then trembled and tottered, and—came down.

At this instant, I know not what sudden self-possession came over my spirit. Staggering as far aft as I could, I awaited fearlessly the ruin that was to overwhelm. Our own vessel was at length ceasing from her struggles, and sinking with her head to the sea. The shock of the descending mass struck her, consequently, in that portion of her frame which was already under water, and the inevitable result was to hurl me, with **29** irresistible violence, upon the rigging of the stranger.

As I fell, the ship hove in stays, and went about; and to the confusion ensuing I attributed my escape from the notice of the crew. With little difficulty I made my way unperceived to the main hatchway, which was partially open, and soon found an opportunity of secreting myself in the hold. Why I did so I can hardly tell. An indefinite sense of awe, which at first sight of the navigators of the ship had taken hold of my mind, was perhaps the principle of my concealment. I was unwilling to trust myself with a race of people who had offered, to the cursory glance I had taken, so many points of vague novelty, doubt, and apprehension. I therefore thought proper **30** to contrive a hiding-place in the hold. This I did by removing a small portion of the shifting-boards, in such a manner as to afford me a convenient retreat between the huge timbers of the ship.

I had scarcely completed my work, when a footstep in the

hold forced me to make use of it. A man passed by my place of concealment with a feeble and unsteady gait. I could not see his face, but had an opportunity of observing his general appearance. There was about it an evidence of great age and infirmity. His knees tottered beneath a load of years, and his entire frame quivered under the burthen. He muttered to himself, in a low broken tone, some words of a language which I could not understand, and groped in a corner among a pile of singular-looking instruments, and decayed charts of navigation. His manner was a wild mixture of the peevishness of second childhood, and the solemn dignity of a God. He at length went on deck, and I saw him no more.   **31**

*   *   *

A feeling, for which I have no name, has taken possession of my soul—a sensation which will admit of no analysis, to which the lessons of by-gone times are inadequate, and for which I fear futurity itself will offer me no key. To a mind constituted like my own, the latter consideration is an evil. I shall never—I know that I shall never—be satisfied with regard to the nature of my conceptions. Yet it is not wonderful that these conceptions are indefinite, since they have their origin in sources so utterly novel. A new sense—a new entity is added to my soul.   **32**

*   *   *

It is long since I first trod the deck of this terrible ship, and the rays of my destiny are, I think, gathering to a focus. Incomprehensible men! Wrapped up in meditations of a kind which I cannot divine, they pass me by unnoticed. Concealment is utter folly on my part, for the people *will not* see. It **33** was but just now that I passed directly before the eyes of the mate—it was no long while ago that I ventured into the captain's own private cabin, and took thence the materials with which I write, and have written. I shall from time to time continue this journal. It is true that I may not find an opportunity of transmitting it to the world, but I will not fail to make the endeavour. At the last moment I will enclose the MS. in a bottle, and cast it within the sea.

*   *   *

An incident has occurred which has given me new room for meditation. Are such things the operation of ungoverned Chance? I had ventured upon deck and thrown myself down, without attracting any notice, among a pile of ratlin-stuff and old sails, in the bottom of the yawl. While musing upon the singularity of fate, I unwittingly daubed with a tar-brush the edges of a neatly-folded studding-sail which lay near me on a barrel. The studding-sail is now bent upon the ship, and the thoughtless touches of the brush are spread out into the word DISCOVERY. *   *   *   **34**

I have made many observations lately upon the structure of the vessel. Although well armed, she is not, I think, a ship of war. Her rigging, build, and general equipment, all negative

31 That this is a ghost ship, with a dead crew, is suggested by the seamen's blend of childishness and godlike qualities. Ghost ships are part of the folklore of the sea, including the legend of the *Flying Dutchman*. Captain *Frederick* Marryat (1792–1848) wrote a novel called *The Phantom Ship*, which Poe probably knew.

32 The narrator begins as a man whose world is circumscribed, a man who is confident that all questions about the world can and will be answered. Now he sees that reality is infinite, that he can never fully understand his universe—yet he continues to try. The awesome nature of existence does not frighten him so much as it seems to inspire him on his quest, hopeless as it may be, in the true romantic spirit.

33 Another possibility is that the narrator and the ship are in different dimensions—parallel worlds, which overlap but do not allow complete integration.

34 "Discovery" may allude to the name of an explorer's ship, or to the narrator's realization about the nature of existence. *Symzonia* is subtitled "A Voyage of Discovery."

35 A more definite allusion to the legend of the *Flying Dutchman*. According to tradition, a captain had blasphemed and been condemned to sail forever (usually in the area near the Cape of Good Hope) or until a woman agreed to give up her life for him out of love. In one version, the captain, called Von Falkenberg, was condemned to sail forever around the North Sea in a ship without a helm or steersman, playing at dice for his soul with the Devil.

In Sir Walter Scott's poem *Rokeby* (1813), a note gives another version: the ship was a vessel loaded with great wealth, and after some horrible event on board, plague broke out and the wicked crew was condemned to sail forever looking for a port. Sailors consider the sighting of the *Flying Dutchman* the worst possible of all omens, Scott says.

Poe may also have read a story by William Gilmore Simms (1806–70), "A Picture of the Sea," which appeared in the Charleston *Southern Literary Gazette* in December 1828. Simms describes a passenger who, like Poe's narrator, is a rational, unsuperstitious man. A sudden storm hits the ship, but the narrator and several other passengers pass the time in playing cards—an act the captain fears will provoke the *Dutchman* to appear. Sure enough, a huge ship under full sail (ships usually take *in* their sails during a storm) rams the passenger ship, which sinks. The narrator and another passenger manage to grab hold of a piece of debris and are saved. The rest of the tale moves farther into the bizarre, and turns out to be a dream (in church, yet).

The *Flying Dutchman* legend is, of course, the basis for Wagner's opera of the same name (1843), probably through Marryat's novel. There is also the forgotten but haunting film *Pandora and the Flying Dutchman* (1951), which starred James Mason and Ava Gardner.

36 Wood used in shipbuilding must be hard and relatively nonporous, such as teak or oak. The narrator likens this ship's wood to Spanish oak—cork oak—which is hardly sturdy material for a sound vessel.

37 Whitman uses the same image in *Aboard, at a Ship's Helm:* "But O the ship, the immortal ship! O ship aboard the ship!/Ship of the body, ship of the soul, voyaging, voyaging, voyaging."

38 One of Poe's devices for signaling the limits of reason. Just as Roderick Usher's study is filled with similar useless instruments of music and science, so this crew finds that none of these navigational instruments work in this strange, new universe.

39 A truck is a small wooden cap at the top of a masthead, with holes for passing ropes through.

40 The studding sail is a light sail set at the side of a principal square sail.

41 The topgallant sail lies above the topmast and below the royal mast of a ship. The vessel must be rolling and pitching indeed to get these wet.

42 Even though it means certain death, the narrator would rather know the answer to the puzzle before him than live on in ignorance. In Poe's cosmology, our ultimate knowledge of the Godhead and the meaning of existence could only come at that moment when all is united—and annihilated. This knowledge, then, is both powerfully attractive and lethal.

a supposition of this kind. What she *is not*, I can easily perceive—what she *is* I fear it is impossible to say. I know not how it is, but in scrutinizing her strange model and singular cast of spars, her huge size and overgrown suits of canvas, her severely simple bow and antiquated stern, there will occasionally flash across my mind a sensation of familiar things, and there is always mixed up with such indistinct shadows of recollection, an unaccountable memory of old foreign chron-
35 icles and ages long ago. *   *   *

I have been looking at the timbers of the ship. She is built of a material to which I am a stranger. There is a peculiar character about the wood which strikes me as rendering it unfit for the purpose to which it has been applied. I mean its extreme *porousness*, considered independently of the worm-eaten condition which is a consequence of navigation in these seas, and apart from the rottenness attendant upon age. It will appear perhaps an observation somewhat over-curious, but this wood would have every characteristic of Spanish oak, if
36 Spanish oak were distended by any unnatural means.

In reading the above sentence a curious apothegm of an old weather-beaten Dutch navigator comes full upon my recollection. "It is as sure," he was wont to say, when any doubt was entertained of his veracity, "as sure as there is a sea where the ship itself will grow in bulk like the living body of the
37 seaman." *   *   *

About an hour ago, I made bold to thrust myself among a group of the crew. They paid me no manner of attention, and, although I stood in the very midst of them all, seemed utterly unconscious of my presence. Like the one I had at first seen in the hold, they all bore about them the marks of a hoary old age. Their knees trembled with infirmity; their shoulders were bent double with decrepitude; their shrivelled skins rattled in the wind; their voices were low, tremulous and broken; their eyes glistened with the rheum of years; and their gray hairs streamed terribly in the tempest. Around them, on every part of the deck, lay scattered mathematical instruments of
38 the most quaint and obsolete construction. *   *   *

I mentioned some time ago the bending of a studding-sail. From that period the ship, being thrown dead off the wind, has continued her terrific course due south, with every rag of
39 canvas packed upon her, from her trucks to her lower studding-
40,41 sail booms, and rolling every moment her top-gallant yardarms into the most appalling hell of water which it can enter into the mind of man to imagine. I have just left the deck, where I find it impossible to maintain a footing, although the crew seem to experience little inconvenience. It appears to me a miracle of miracles that our enormous bulk is not swallowed up at once and forever. We are surely doomed to hover continually upon the brink of Eternity, without taking a final
42 plunge into the abyss. From billows a thousand times more stupendous than any I have ever seen, we glide away with the facility of the arrowy sea-gull; and the colossal waters rear their heads above us like demons of the deep, but like demons confined to simple threats and forbidden to destroy. I am led

to attribute these frequent escapes to the only natural cause which can account for such effect.—I must suppose the ship to be within the influence of some strong current, or impetuous under-tow. *   *   * **43**

I have seen the captain face to face, and in his own cabin—but, as I expected, he paid me no attention. Although in his appearance there is, to a casual observer, nothing which might bespeak him more or less than man—still a feeling of irrepressible reverence and awe mingled with the sensation of wonder with which I regarded him. In stature he is nearly my **44** own height; that is, about five feet eight inches. He is of a well-knit and compact frame of body, neither robust nor remarkably otherwise. But it is the singularity of the expression which reigns upon the face—it is the intense, the wonderful, the thrilling evidence of old age, so utter, so extreme, which excites within my spirit a sense—a sentiment ineffable. His forehead, although little wrinkled, seems to bear upon it the stamp of a myriad of years.—His gray hairs are records of the past, and his grayer eyes are Sybils of the future. The cabin **45** floor was thickly strewn with strange, iron-clasped folios, and mouldering instruments of science, and obsolete long-forgotten charts. His head was bowed down upon his hands, and he pored, with a fiery unquiet eye, over a paper which I took to

43 The ship is now held by the current rushing toward the Polar opening. Although Poe stops short of entering the earth's interior, Jules Verne describes a vast underground ocean in *Journey to the Center of the Earth* (1864), and Edgar Rice Burrough's short novel *The Inner World* (1913) began a series of stories about life inside the hollow earth.

44 The captain resembles the captain of the *Flying Dutchman*. He also resembles in some ways Captain Ahab, in Melville's *Moby-Dick* (1851). Both this captain and Ahab are older, gray-haired, and seem to be agents of some higher authority. Poe's captain has a "well-knit and compact frame of body, neither robust nor remarkably otherwise." Ishmael describes Ahab's limbs as those of a man rescued from the stake before the fire had taken "one particle from their compacted aged robustness."

"I am Fate's lieutenant," Ahab tells Starbuck.

45 Plato speaks of only one sibyl, or prophetess, the Erythraean; Martianus Capella says there were two, the Eyrthraean and the Phrygian (the former being Amalthaea, the famous Cumean Sibyl of the *Aeneid*, Book VI); Solinus maintains that there were four, the Erythraean, the Samian, the Egyptian, and the Sardian; Varro tells us there were ten, the Cumaean, the Delphic, the Egyptian, the Erythraean, the Hellespontine, the Libyan, the Persian, the Phrygian, the Samian, and the Tiburtine; the medieval monks (in a form of sibling rivalry) reckoned twelve, adding the Cuman, the European, and the Agrippine, and dropping the Egyptian.

"His forehead, although little wrinkled, seems to bear upon it the stamp of a myriad of years." *Illustration by Johann Friedrich Vogel, nineteenth century*

46 A land of the ancients, from the old English word *eald,* "old." In Patricia A. McKillip's *The Forgotten Beasts of Eld* (1974), it is a fantasy world.

47 Three ancient cities: Balbec was in Mesopotamia; Tadmor (Tamar) is Palmyra, on the northern edge of the Syrian desert, northeast of Damascus; Persepolis is the former capital of Persia. Poe mentions them again in *Al Aaraaf,* II, 36–37.

48 Compare this first tale of Poe's in which a narrator finds himself in a baffling new world operating under different laws from those he has known before with "A Descent into the Maelström" and "The Pit and the Pendulum."

49 Compare "We are hurrying onwards to some never-to-be imparted secret" with Ishmael's "Uppermost was the impression, that whatever swift, rushing thing I stood on was not so much bound to any haven as rushing from all havens astern," and his comments on the "ungraspable phantom of life."

Note that here, as in "A Descent into the Maelström" and "The Pit and the Pendulum" (as well as *Pym*), the narrator has a moment of calm before the onslaught of catastrophe. One could compare this with the point in Poe's cosmology where expansion ceases and the universe pauses before contracting into ultimate union.

50 "Note: The 'MS. Found in a Bottle' was originally published in 1831, and it was not until many years afterwards that I became acquainted with the maps of Mercator, in which the ocean is represented as rushing, by four mouths, into the (northern) Polar Gulf, to be absorbed into the bowels of the earth; the Pole itself being represented by a black rock, towering to a prodigious height. (The Author)"—Poe's note

Gerardus Mercator (Gerhard Kremer, 1512–94) was the greatest cartographer of his day, famous for his Mercator Projection, which allowed the round globe to be pictured on a two-dimensional map (despite the loss of accuracy toward the poles). Mercator shows the north pole as a towering black rock.

Poe, no great shakes at accuracy when it comes to citations, gives the wrong publication date; 1833 is correct.

One of the paradoxes of Poe is that he often used similar themes or situations in drastically different tales, as in the openings of "The Fall of the House of Usher" and "The System of Dr. Tarr and Professor Fether"— and the climax here, which is echoed in the comic ending of "Mellonta Tauta." In both "Ms." and "Mellonta" a final catastrophe ends the narrator's life, and a message (that is, the tale) is left in a bottle to keep the narrator's experiences alive. In all Poe's other tales, the narrator manages to escape, to return and tell us his story. This, of course, calls for a great deal of imaginative writing in order to make his miraculous reprieve believable.

be a commission, and which, at all events, bore the signature of a monarch. He muttered to himself, as did the first seaman whom I saw in the hold, some low peevish syllables of a foreign tongue, and although the speaker was close at my elbow, his voice seemed to reach my ears from the distance of a mile. *   *   *

46 The ship and all in it are imbued with the spirit of Eld. The crew glide to and fro like the ghosts of buried centuries; their eyes have an eager and uneasy meaning; and when their figures fall athwart my path in the wild glare of the battle-lanterns, I feel as I have never felt before, although I have been all my life a dealer in antiquities, and have imbibed the shadows of fallen columns at Balbec, and Tadmor, and Per-
47 sepolis, until my very soul has become a ruin. *   *   *

When I look around me I feel ashamed of my former apprehensions. If I trembled at the blast which has hitherto attended us, shall I not stand aghast at a warring of wind and ocean, to convey any idea of which the words tornado and simoom are trivial and ineffective? All in the immediate vicinity of the ship is the blackness of eternal night, and a chaos of foamless water; but, about a league on either side of us, may be seen, indistinctly and at intervals, stupendous ramparts of ice, towering away into the desolate sky, and looking like the walls of the universe. *   *   *

As I imagined, the ship proves to be in a current; if that appellation can properly be given to a tide which, howling and shrieking by the white ice, thunders on to the southward
48 with a velocity like the headlong dashing of a cataract. *   *   *

To conceive the horror of my sensations is, I presume, utterly impossible; yet a curiosity to penetrate the mysteries of these awful regions, predominates even over my despair, and will reconcile me to the most hideous aspect of death. It is evident that we are hurrying onwards to some exciting knowledge—some never-to-be imparted secret, whose attain-
49 ment is destruction. Perhaps this current leads us to the southern pole itself. It must be confessed that a supposition apparently so wild has every probability in its favor. *   *   *

The crew pace the deck with unquiet and tremulous step; but there is upon their countenances an expression more of the eagerness of hope than of the apathy of despair.

In the meantime the wind is still in our poop, and, as we carry a crowd of canvas, the ship is at times lifted bodily from out the sea—Oh, horror upon horror! the ice opens suddenly to the right, and to the left, and we are whirling dizzily, in immense concentric circles, round and round the borders of a gigantic amphitheatre, the summit of whose walls is lost in the darkness and the distance. But little time will be left me to ponder upon my destiny—the circles rapidly grow small— we are plunging madly within the grasp of the whirlpool—and amid a roaring, and bellowing, and thundering of ocean and
50 of tempest, the ship is quivering, oh God! and—going down.

THE ASSIGNATION

First published as "The Visionary," in *The Lady's Book*, January 1834.

This and "Eleonora" are Poe's most romantic tales; here is spelled out a clandestine love affair and its consequences—a story of passion overshadowed ultimately by unrelenting fate. Here, too, the pathos of the two main characters is not disturbed by madness or grotesquerie.

Poe took as his models Lord Byron, after whom he modeled his protagonist, and two women whom Byron loved: Mary Chaworth and the Contessa Guiccioli, the latter the wife of a Venetian nobleman.

Poe also borrowed from Chapter 23 of Oliver Goldsmith's *The Vicar of Wakefield* (1776): "Matilda was married . . . to a Neopolitan nobleman . . . and found herself a widow and a mother at the age of fifteen. As she stood one day caressing her infant son in the open window of an apartment which hung over the river Volturna, the child with a sudden spring leaped from her arms into the flood below and disappeared in a moment."

Another possible source could be E. T. A. Hoffman's tale "Doge and Dogaressa," which involves a young man in love with a lady, and his rescue of her husband from drowning.

As "The Visionary," the tale has a different beginning, one that is far less effective than the present one. For the original, see Volume II of Thomas Ollive Mabbot's *Collected Works of Edgar Allan Poe* (Harvard, 1978), p. 150. It is interesting to note that in that original version Poe began with a quote from Goethe: "And if I die, at least I die/*With* her—*with* her." He must have removed it when he realized it telegraphed the ending of the tale.

So far no film has been made of "The Assignation," probably because it doesn't have the eerie or horror-ridden atmosphere of many of Poe's tales. Too bad—it would make a good film, something on the lines of *Don't Look Now* (1973), a top-notch horror film with both intelligence and sophistication, also set in Venice.

Stay for me there! I will not fail
To meet thee in that hollow vale.
[*"Exequy on the death of his wife,"
by Henry King, Bishop of Chichester*.]   **1**

Ill-fated and mysterious man!—bewildered in the brilliancy of thine own imagination, and fallen in the flames of thine own youth! Again in fancy I behold thee! Once more thy form **2,3** hath risen before me!—not—oh not as thou art—in the cold valley and shadow—but as thou *shouldst be*—squandering **4** away a life of magnificent meditation in that city of dim visions, thine own Venice—which is a star-beloved Elysium **5** of the sea, and the wide windows of whose Palladian palaces **6** look down with a deep and bitter meaning upon the secrets of her silent waters. Yes! I repeat it—as thou *shouldst be*. There are surely other worlds than this—other thoughts than the thoughts of the multitude—other speculations than the speculations of the sophist. Who then shall call thy conduct into question? who blame thee for thy visionary hours, or

1 "The Exequy" of Henry King (1592–1669) is an elegiac poem written to King's dead wife (an exequy is a funeral procession or ceremony). King was Bishop of Chichester; he wrote several poems that in some respects resemble those of Donne.

> Sleep on, my Love, in thy cold bed,
> Never to be disquieted!
> My last good-night! Thou wilt not wake,
> Till I thy fate shall overtake;
> Till age, or grief, or sickness, must
> Marry my body to that dust
> It so much loves, and fill the room
> My heart keeps empty in thy tomb,
> Stay for me there; I will not fail
> To meet thee in that hollow vale.

2 "Who, falling in the flaws of her own youth, . . ." *Measure for Measure*, II, iii. Also, Byron's *Childe Harold*, III, lxxviii: "His love was passion's essence, as a tree/On fire by lightning; with ethereal flame/Kindled he was, and blasted."

3 We should remember Poe's (and Coleridge's) distinction between Fancy and the Imagination. When one

21

imagines, one penetrates to the truth, but when one fancies, one is merely deceived by appearance. The former, then, is the realm of the true poet, while the latter is the refuge of the mundane intellect—and the lunatic.

". . . just as Poe in his critical reviews used the degree of imaginativeness present in the writings of others to best judge the success of that work, so in many of his own tales he allows the narrator's use of fancy or imagination to determine the ultimate failure or success of his . . . quest. If the narrator is described as fanciful in seeking the ultimate resolution to his problem the result seems to be inevitable failure. However, if the narrator had used instead more imagination, then one must assume that like Dupin he would have met with better results." (Marvin and Frances Mengeling, *University Review*, Vol. 33, p. 287)

4 "The valley of the shadow of death" is from Psalm 23; Poe uses the image many times in his work, most notably in one of his finest poems, *El Dorado*, and in "Shadow—a Parable."

5 Elysium, or the Elysian Fields, was the home of the blessed after death in Greek mythology. Ruled by Cronos, or Rhadamanthus, it was situated at the end of the world.

6 Andrea Palladio (1518–80) was the most influential of the great Italian architects. He designed palaces, villas, and churches, all in a surprisingly unpompous and unpedantic style, drawing heavily upon his study of the ancients. Palladianism is the name given to the style derived from his buildings and publications, which spread in the eighteenth century and arrived in America in the 1760s. Here it had a great influence; Thomas Jefferson, for example, was a classic example of the Palladian spirit in America.

7 The Ponte dei Sospiri is the bridge that leads from the Doge's Palace to the former prisons. It is wreathed in romantic legend because of the injustices perpetrated there long before the Baroque stone bridge was built in 1600. Byron mentions it in *Childe Harold's Pilgrimage*, iv, 1.

8 St. Mark's Square

9 5 A.M.

10 A bell tower over 320 feet high, which was rebuilt in this century after it collapsed.

11 The Palace of the Doge ("Doge" is a varient of the word for duke) was the seat of power under whom the communities around the area first organized themselves, in 697. The palace is in Gothic style.

12 The broad way that leads from St. Mark's Square along Canal San Marco.

13 Shaped like a reversed S, this is the main traffic artery of Venice.

14 Canal San Marco lies on the southern side of the main island; it is not really a canal, but a natural waterway that stretches from St. Mark's eastward to the tip of the island.

She stood alone. Illustration by F. S. Coburn, 1902

denounce those occupations as a wasting away of life; which were but the overflowings of thine everlasting energies?

7 It was at Venice, beneath the covered archway there called the *Ponte di Sospiri*, that I met for the third or fourth time the person of whom I speak. It is with a confused recollection that I bring to mind the circumstances of that meeting. Yet I remember—ah! how should I forget?—the deep midnight, the Bridge of Sighs, the beauty of woman, and the Genius of Romance that stalked up and down the narrow canal.

It was a night of unusual gloom. The great clock of the
8,9 Piazza had sounded the fifth hour of the Italian evening. The
10 square of the Campanile lay silent and deserted, and the lights
11 in the old Ducal Palace were dying fast away. I was returning
12,13 home from the Piazzetta, by way of the Grand Canal. But as my gondola arrived opposite the mouth of the canal San
14 Marco, a female voice from its recesses broke suddenly upon the night, in one wild, hysterical, and long continued shriek. Startled at the sound, I sprang upon my feet: while the gondolier, letting slip his single oar, lost it in the pitchy darkness beyond a chance of recovery, and we were consequently left to the guidance of the current which here sets from the greater into the smaller channel. Like some huge

and sable-feathered condor, we were slowly drifting down **15** towards the Bridge of Sighs, when a thousand flambeaux **16** flashing from the windows, and down the staircases of the Ducal Palace, turned all at once that deep gloom into a livid and preternatural day. **17**

A child, slipping from the arms of its own mother, had fallen from an upper window of the lofty structure into the deep and dim canal. The quiet waters had closed placidly over their **18** victim; and, although my own gondola was the only one in sight, many a stout swimmer, already in the stream, was seeking in vain upon the surface, the treasure which was to be found, alas! only within the abyss. Upon the broad black marble flagstones at the entrance of the palace, and a few steps above the water, stood a figure which none who then saw can have ever since forgotten. It was the Marchesa Aphrodite—the adoration of all Venice—the gayest of the **19** gay—the most lovely where all were beautiful—but still the young wife of the old and intriguing Mentoni, and the mother **20** of that fair child, her first and only one, who now deep beneath the murky water, was thinking in bitterness of heart upon her sweet caresses, and exhausting its little life in struggles to call upon her name.

She stood alone. Her small, bare, and silvery feet gleamed in the black mirror of marble beneath her. Her hair, not as yet more than half loosened for the night from its ball-room array, clustered, amid a shower of diamonds, round and round her classical head, in curls like those of the young hyacinth. **21** A snowy-white and gauze-like drapery seemed to be nearly the sole covering to her delicate form; but the mid-summer and midnight air was hot, sullen, and still, and no motion in the statue-like form itself, stirred even the folds of that raiment of very vapor which hung around it as the heavy marble hangs around the Niobe. Yet—strange to say!—her large lustrous **22** eyes were not turned downwards upon that grave wherein her brightest hope lay buried—but riveted in a widely different direction! The prison of the Old Republic is, I think, the **23** stateliest building in all Venice—but how could that lady gaze so fixedly upon it, when beneath her lay stifling her only child? Yon dark, gloomy niche, too, yawns right opposite her chamber window—what, then, *could* there be in its shadows— in its architecture—in its ivy-wreathed and solemn cornices— that the Marchesa di Mentoni had not wondered at a thousand times before? Nonsense!—Who does not remember that, at such a time as this, the eye, like shattered mirror, multiplies the images of its sorrow, and sees in innumerable far off places, the wo which is close at hand? **24**

Many steps above the Marchesa, and within the arch of the water-gate, stood, in full dress, the Satyr-like figure of Mentoni himself. He was occasionally occupied in thrumming a guitar, **25** and seemed *ennuyé* to the very death, as at intervals he gave directions for the recovery of his child. Stupefied and aghast, **26** I had myself no power to move from the upright position I had assumed upon first hearing the shriek, and must have presented to the eyes of the agitated group a spectral and

15 The condor is the largest bird of prey, predominantly black, and a native of the Andes and parts of California (where it is now rare). Poe seems taken with it as a symbol of overwhelming and depressing size, as well as by its soaring power. In *The Conqueror Worm*, we find "Flapping from out their Condor wings/Invisible Wo!" and in *Romance*, "eternal Condor years."

16 torches, although a French word seems out of place here.

17 "Livid" and preternatural light is typical of many of Poe's tales of horror, from "The Masque of the Red Death" to "The Fall of the House of Usher."

18 An exaggeration; the average depth of the canals is only nine feet. However, it's certainly deep enough to drown in.

19 Poe originally called her Bianca ("white") but chose the name of the Greek goddess of love instead. Considering her clandestine romance, the latter name makes more sense than one suggesting innocence.

20 "Intriguing" here means "scheming." As for the family name of Mentoni, it may come from the root word meaning "to lie, to tell a falsehood," although there is a town of Mentone on the French-Italian frontier.

21 Compare the description of the Marchesa Aphrodite to that of the subject of the poem, *To Helen:*

> Lo! in yon brilliant window-niche
> How statue-like I see thee stand,
> The agate lamp within thy hand!
> Ah, Psyche, from the regions which
> Are Holy-Land!

Helen also has "hyacinth hair," as does Ligeia (see "Ligeia," note 12).

22 There is a sculpture of this name in Florence, thought to be a copy of a work by Praxiteles or Scopas. Niobe was queen of Thebes in Greek myth; because she boasted of her fruitfulness, the gods killed all her children. She fled to Mt. Sipylus, where Zeus turned her into a stone that wept perpetually.

23 Still standing, although no longer in use, the prisons stand across the Bridge of Sighs from the Ducal Palace.

24 Even as a broken mirror, which the glass
    In every fragment multiplies; and makes
    A thousand images of one that was.
        (*Childe Harold*, III, xxxiii)

25 The satyrs were minor Greek gods, half man and half goat, followers of Dionysus (Bacchus) and represented in Greek literature as wild and licentious.

26 One wonders what goes on behind the scenes in this household. Mentoni seems an unsavory character at best, with little regard for his wife other than as a handsome piece of property (compare with Browning's *My Last Duchess*) and apprently no concern for the fate of his child. Or *is* it his child? (And does he *know* it isn't?)

"Thou hast conquered—. . . ." *Illustration by Byam Shaw, 1909*

27 While Pliny the Younger does mention acanthus in this way, the quote is more likely from Horace Smith's *Zillah* (1828) III, 220: "what Pliny calls the soft and almost liquid Acanthus." *Zillah* is the main source for Poe's "A Tale of Jerusalem."

28 The narrator is a poor detective, although admittedly he doesn't have all the facts. Otherwise he would have realized immediately that the young man had been standing near the window, waiting for the Marchesa in secret, and that the accident with the baby has now confirmed that fact to the already suspicious husband. Poe's original title, "The Visionary," appropriately refers to fanciful and unpractical ideas, speculative and dreamy.

ominous appearance, as with pale countenance and rigid limbs, I floated down among them in that funereal gondola.

All efforts proved in vain. Many of the most energetic in the search were relaxing their exertions, and yielding to a gloomy sorrow. There seemed but little hope for the child; (how much less than for the mother!) but now, from the interior of that dark niche which has been already mentioned as forming a part of the Old Republican prison, and as fronting the lattice of the Marchesa, a figure, muffled in a cloak, stepped out within reach of the light, and, pausing a moment upon the verge of the giddy descent, plunged headlong into the canal. As, in an instant afterwards, he stood with the still living and breathing child within his grasp, upon the marble flagstones by the side of the Marchesa, his cloak, heavy with the drenching water, became unfastened, and, falling in folds about his feet, discovered to the wonder-stricken spectators the graceful person of a very young man, with the sound of whose name the greater part of Europe was then ringing.

No word spoke the deliverer. But the Marchesa! She will now receive her child—she will press it to her heart—she will cling to its little form, and smother it with her caresses. Alas! *another's* arms have taken it from the stranger—*another's* arms have taken it away, and borne it afar off, unnoticed, into the palace! And the Marchesa! Her lip—her beautiful lip trembles: tears are gathering in her eyes—those eyes which, **27** like Pliny's acanthus, are "soft and almost liquid." Yes! tears are gathering in those eyes—and see! the entire woman thrills throughout the soul, and the statue has started into life! The pallor of the marble countenance, the swelling of the marble bosom, the very purity of the marble feet, we behold suddenly flushed over with a tide of ungovernable crimson; and a slight shudder quivers about her delicate frame, as a gentle air at Napoli about the rich silver lilies in the grass.

Why *should* that lady blush! To this demand there is no answer—except that, having left, in the eager haste and terror of a mother's heart, the privacy of her own *boudoir*, she has neglected to enthrall her tiny feet in their slippers, and utterly forgotten to throw over her Venetian shoulders that drapery which is their due. What other possible reason could there have been for her so blushing?—for the glance of those wild appealing eyes? for the unusual tumult of that throbbing bosom?—for the convulsive pressure of that trembling hand?—that hand which fell, as Mentoni turned into the palace, accidentally, upon the hand of the stranger. What reason could there have been for the low—the singularly low tone of those unmeaning words which the lady uttered hurriedly in bidding him adieu? "Thou hast conquered—" she said, or the murmurs of the water deceived me—"thou hast conquered— **28** one hour after sunrise—we shall meet—so let it be!"

*   *   *

The tumult had subsided, the lights had died away within the palace, and the stranger, whom I now recognised, stood alone upon the flags. He shook with inconceivable agitation, and his eye glanced around in search of a gondola. I could not do less than offer him the service of my own; and he accepted the civility. Having obtained an oar at the water-gate, we proceeded together to his residence, while he rapidly recovered his self-possession, and spoke of our former slight acquaintance in terms of great apparent cordiality.

There are some subjects upon which I take pleasure in being minute. The person of the stranger—let me call him by this title, who to all the world was still a stranger—the person of the stranger is one of these subjects. In height he might have been below rather than above the medium size: although there were moments of intense passion when his frame actually *expanded* and belied the assertion. The light, almost slender symmetry of his figure, promised more of that ready activity which he evinced at the Bridge of Sighs, than of that Herculean strength which he has been known to wield without an effort, upon occasions of more dangerous emergency. With the mouth **29** and chin of a diety—singular, wild, full, liquid eyes, whose shadows varied from pure hazel to intense and brilliant jet— and a profusion of curling, black hair, from which a forehead of unusual breadth gleamed forth at intervals all light and ivory—his were features than which I have seen none more classically regular, except, perhaps, the marble ones of the Emperor Commodus. Yet his countenance was, nevertheless, **30** one of those which all men have seen at some period of their lives, and have never afterwards seen again. It had no peculiar—it had no settled predominant expression to be fastened upon the memory; a countenance seen and instantly forgotten—but forgotten with a vague and never-ceasing desire of recalling it to mind. Not that the spirit of each rapid passion failed, at any time, to throw its own distinct image upon the mirror of that face—but that the mirror, mirror-like, retained no vestige of the passion, when the passion had departed.

Upon leaving him on the night of our adventure, he solicited me, in what I thought an urgent manner, to call upon him *very* early the next morning. Shortly after sunrise, I found myself accordingly at his Palazzo, one of those huge structures of gloomy, yet fantastic pomp, which tower above the waters of the Grand Canal in the vicinity of the Rialto. I was shown **31** up a broad winding staircase of mosaics, into an apartment whose unparalleled splendor burst through the opening door with an actual glare, making me blind and dizzy with luxuriousness.

I knew my acquaintance to be wealthy. Report had spoken of his possessions in terms which I had even ventured to call terms of ridiculous exaggeration. But as I gazed about me, I could not bring myself to believe that the wealth of any subject in Europe could have supplied the princely magnificence which burned and blazed around.

Although, as I say, the sun had risen, yet the room was still brilliantly lighted up. I judge from this circumstance, as well as from an air of exhaustion in the countenance of my friend, that he had not retired to bed during the whole of the preceding night. In the architecture and embellishments of

29 George Gordon, Lord Byron (1788–1824), was born with a clubfoot, which was made worse by incompetent doctors; it was always an embarrassment to him. He compensated by taking up sports, playing cricket, and becoming an expert boxer, fencer, horseman, and a powerful swimmer. He settled in Venice in 1817, where, he estimated, he had affairs with more than two hundred women, mostly from the lower classes.

30 Lucius Aelius Aurelius Commodus (A.D. 161–92) was the son and successor of Marcus Aurelius. His beauty was widely celebrated, and he was also known for his sexual escapades. He took part in gladiatorial combats, showing off his strength, and actually decreed that he should be worshipped as Hercules Romanus. He was finally strangled by a wrestler, on the orders of his advisers.

31 The Rialto is the largest of the bridges that cross the Venetian canals. Built in 1590, it was the only bridge over the Grand Canal until the nineteenth century.

32 "Grotesque" in the arts means a mixture of disparate elements, confusion, the fantastic, and an alienation from the world. For a thorough study of the grotesque, see Wolfgang Kayser's *The Grotesque in Art and Literature* (McGraw-Hill, 1966).

33 Since this is before Muzak, one wonders just what the narrator hears. A string quartet hidden behind an arras? Gondoliers? An Aeolian harp?

34 Compare this to the palace in "The Masque of the Red Death."

35 The decor here also echoes that of the study in "The Fall of the House of Usher."

36 A reference, perhaps, to gold from the Chinese province of Chihli, later called Hopeh or Ho-pei, now Hebei, in the northeastern part of the country near the Yellow Sea. Or Poe may have been alluding to Chile, which is better known for its copper deposits than its gold.

37 Propriety, seemliness. It's a pity that Poe didn't know enough Italian to salt this story with.

38 Referring to Chapter II of Jean Tixtier, Seigneur de Ravisy's *Theatrum Poetarum* (1520), entitled "De gaudio et risu mortuis"—"of rejoicing and laughing at death."

39 Sir Thomas More (1478–1535), beheaded for treason by Henry VIII, was known for his great personal charm, piercing wit, and unfailing good humor, which enabled him to jest even on the scaffold. Near the end, he told his executioner, "My neck is very short, take heed, therefore, thou strikest not awry, for saving thyne honesty" (from William Roper, *The Mirrour of Vertue in Worldly Greatnes*, Paris, 1626). More was canonized for his martyrdom.

40 The title of the book, first mentioned in note 38, is not *Absurdities*. Perhaps Poe read a commentary on Ravisy's book that characterized it as "absurdities" and mistook the critique for the title.

41 Sparta, situated on the Peloponnesus, was the strongest city in Greece in the seventh century B.C., and because it cultivated only the martial arts was virtually an armed camp.

In Plutarch's *Parallel Lives*, we find that one Sosibius had dedicated a statue to Laughter at Sparta. Chateaubriand (1768–1848) visited Greece in 1806, where he claimed to have found the remains of the statue's pedestal (socle).

The Greek letters as shown in the text here are found in most Poe editions, but they are actually a printer's error, corrected by Poe himself in the tale's 1840 edition. They should be ΓΕΛΑΣΜΑ (GELASMA), which Poe apparently found somewhere as being the Greek equivalent of "laughter." Dictionaries of ancient Greek do not show this variant but do give ΓΕΛΑΣΤΟΣ (GELASTOS), ΓΕΛΟΤΟΣ (GELOTOS), and ΓΕΛΟΣ (GELOS). Although rarely used today, the English word "gelasin," meaning a dimple caused by a smile, comes from the same Greek root.

the chamber, the evident design had been to dazzle and astound. Little attention had been paid to the *decora* of what is technically called *keeping*, or to the proprieties of nationality. The eye wandered from object to object, and rested upon none—neither the *grotesques* of the Greek painters, nor the sculptures of the best Italian days, nor the huge carvings of untutored Egypt. Rich draperies in every part of the room trembled to the vibration of low, melancholy music, whose origin was not to be discovered. The senses were oppressed by mingled and conflicting perfumes, reeking up from strange convolute censers, together with multitudinous flaring and flickering tongues of emerald and violet fire. The rays of the newly risen sun poured in upon the whole, through windows formed each of a single pane of crimson-tinted glass. Glancing to and fro, in a thousand reflections, from curtains which rolled from their cornices like cataracts of molten silver, the beams of natural glory mingled at length fitfully with the artificial light, and lay weltering in subdued masses upon a carpet of rich, liquid-looking cloth of Chili gold.

"Ha! ha! ha!—ha! ha! ha!"—laughed the proprietor, motioning me to a seat as I entered the room, and throwing himself back at full length upon an ottoman. "I see," said he, perceiving that I could not immediately reconcile myself to the *bienséance* of so singular a welcome—"I see you are astonished at my apartment—at my statues—my pictures— my originality of conception in architecture and upholstery— absolutely drunk, eh, with my magnificence? But pardon me, me dear sir, (here his tone of voice dropped to the very spirit of cordiality,) pardon me for my uncharitable laughter. You appeared so *utterly* astonished. Besides, some things are so completely ludicrous that a man *must* laugh or die. To die laughing must be the most glorious of all glorious deaths! Sir Thomas More—a very fine man was Sir Thomas More—Sir Thomas More died laughing, you remember. Also in the *Absurdities* of Ravisius Textor, there is a long list of characters who came to the same magnificent end. Do you know, however," continued he musingly, "that at Sparta (which is now Palaeochori), at Sparta, I say, to the west of the citadel, among a chaos of scarcely visible ruins, is a kind of *socle*, upon which are still legible the letters ΛΑΣΜ. They are undoubtedly part of ΓΕΛΑΣΜΑ. Now at Sparta were a thousand temples and shrines to a thousand different divinities. How exceedingly strange that the altar of Laughter should have survived all the others. But in the present instance," he resume, with a singular alteration of voice and manner, "I have no right to be merry at your expense. You might well have been amazed. Europe cannot produce anything so fine as this, my little regal cabinet. My other apartments are by no means of the same order; mere *ultras* of fashionable insipidity. This is better than fashion—is it not? Yet this has but to be seen to become the rage—that is, with those who could afford it at the cost of their entire patrimony. I have guarded, however, against any such profanation. With one exception you are the only human being besides myself and my *valet*, who has been admitted within the mysteries of these imperial precincts, since they have been bedizened as you see!"   **42**

I bowed in acknowledgement; for the overpowering sense of splendor and perfume, and music, together with the unexpected eccentricity of his address and manner, prevented me from expressing, in words, my appreciation of what I might have construed into a compliment.

"Here," he resumed, arising and leaning on my arm as he sauntered around the apartment, "here are paintings from the   **43** Greeks to Cimabue, and from Cimabue to the present hour. Many are chosen, as you see, with little deference to the opinions of Virtû. They are all, however, fitting tapestry for a chamber such as this. Here too, are some *chefs d'œuvre* of the unknown great—and here unfinished designs by men, celebrated in their day, whose very names the perspicacity of the academies has left to silence and to me. What think you," said he, turning abruptly as he spoke—"What think you of this Madonna della Pietà?"   **44**

"It is Guido's own!" I said with all the enthusiasm of my   **45** nature, for I had been poring intently over its surpassing loveliness. "It is Guido's own!—how *could* you have obtained it?—she is undoubtedly in painting what the Venus is in sculpture."

"Ha!" said he thoughtfully, "the Venus—the beautiful Venus—the Venus of the Medici?—she of the diminutive head   **46** and the gilded hair? Part of the left arm (here his voice dropped so as to be heard with difficulty), and all the right are restorations, and in the coquetry of that right arm lies, I think, the quintessence of all affectation. Give *me* the Canova! The   **47** Apollo, too!—is a copy—there can be no doubt of it—blind fool that I am, who cannot behold the boasted inspiration of the Apollo! I cannot help—pity me!—I cannot help preferring   **48** the Antinous. Was it not Socrates who said that the statuary   **49** found his statue in the block of marble? Then Michael Angelo   **50** was by no means original in his couplet—

> *'Non ha l'ottimo artista alcun concetto*
> *Che un marmo solo in se non circonscriva.'* "   **51**

It has been, or should be remarked, that, in the manner of the true gentleman, we are always aware of a difference from the bearing of the vulgar, without being at once precisely able to determine in what such difference consists. Allowing the remark to have applied in its full force to the outward demeanor of my acquaintance, I felt it, on that eventful morning, still more fully applicable to his moral temperament and character. Nor can I better define that peculiarity of spirit which seemed to place him so essentially apart from all other human beings, than by calling it a *habit* of intense and continual thought, pervading even his most trivial actions—   **52** intruding upon his moments of dalliance—and interweaving itself with his very flashes of merriment—like adders which writhe from out the eyes of the grinning masks in the cornices around the temples of Persepolis.   **53**

I could not help, however, repeatedly observing, through

42 Dressed in a vulgar or gaudy way. The origin of the word is unknown.

43 Cimabue (c. 1240–1302?) is generally placed at the beginning of modern art as the supposed teacher of Giotto (which he may, in fact, have been). The basis for his fame is Dante's use of his name to represent the transitory nature of earthly glory: "Cimabue thought that he held the field in painting, but now Giotto is acclaimed and his fame obscured" (Purgatory, XI, 94–96).

44 The speaker's point is only that paintings can be exhibited together regardless of their era or school.

45 There were two Guidos. Guido Reni (1575–1642) was a Bolognese painter who enjoyed the highest reputation in the seventeenth and eighteenth centuries but was downgraded by influential Victorian critic John Ruskin. Today, in spite of his sentimental religiosity, his pictures seem to be returning to favor.
    Guido da Siena was the all but mythical founder of the Sienese school, who signed only one picture and dated it 1221. There are other paintings, also in Siena, associated with him and dated 1262 and the 1270s, which may mean that the 1221 date is the result of tampering and should have been 1261.

46 The Venus of the Medici, or Medicean Aphrodite (named after its most famous owners), belongs to the third century B.C. and is probably derived from Praxiteles' Aphrodite of Cnidus, which was destroyed. It now stands in the Uffizi Gallery, Florence (see "Ligeia," note 15).

47 Antonio Canova (1757–1822) was a famous neoclassic sculptor whose most famous work, a portrait of Napoleon's sister (1808), hangs in Rome's Borghese Gallery.

48 The most celebrated status of Apollo is the Apollo Belvedere, which is in the Vatican. A Roman copy, dating from the early empire, of a Greek original in bronze, it had the right forearm and left hand restored by a pupil of Michelangelo. The statue represents the god as a vigorous and triumphant young man, naked except for the chlamys (mantle) draped over his extended left arm. Byron was said to be its twin.

49 Antinoüs (c. 110–130) was the favorite of the emperor Hadrian. His beauty was legendary, and Hadrian mourned him greatly when he drowned in the Nile (some say in saving Hadrian's life), elevated him to deity, and founded the city of Antinoöpolis, in Egypt, in his honor. Canova used him as the subject for one of his works.

50 Socrates "often said that he wondered at those who made stone statues, when he saw how careful they were that the stone should be like the man it was intended to represent, but how careless they were of themselves, as to guarding against being like the stone" (Diogenes Laërtius, *Lives*, Book II, "Socrates," Section XVI).

51 "The best of artists does not have a concept, that the marble block does not circumscribe" (Michelangelo, Sonnet XV in J. A. Symonds' translation).

52 He sounds suspiciously like Roderick Usher from "The Fall of the House of Usher."

53 An ancient city of Persia and ceremonial capital of the Achaemenid empire under Darius I and his successors. Alexander looted the treasury in its citadel.

54 Exaggerated or pretended earnestness of manner

55 Again, compare with Usher after his sister's entombment.

56 Angelo Poliziano, or Politian (1454–94), the Italian poet and humanist, wrote *Orfeo* (1480), one of the earliest plays in Italian. Although not written in acts, it had been reworked in the modern fashion by Poe's time. Poe also wrote an unfinished play called *Politian* (1835).

57 This poem, composed by Poe, is also known as "To One in Paradise," but when it was printed separately, Poe dropped the fifth stanza. The poem resembles some lines that Byron wrote for Mary Chaworth, an early love who did not return his affection in the same, passionate way. She married another, and Byron was devastated. Poe's poem also echoes Byron's *Hills of Annesley* (1805) and *The Dream* (1816). James Thurber lampoons "a green isle in the sea" in "Casuals of the Keys," a sketch in the 1960 Broadway revue *A Thurber Carnival*.

the mingled tone of levity and solemnity with which he rapidly descanted upon matters of little importance, a certain air of **54** trepidation—a degree of nervous *unction* in action and in speech—an unquiet excitability of manner which appeared to me at all times unaccountable, and upon some occasions even filled me with alarm. Frequently, too, pausing in the middle of a sentence whose commencement he had apparently forgotten, he seemed to be listening in the deepest attention, as if either in momentary expectation of a visiter, or to sounds **55** which must have had existence in his imagination alone.

It was during one of these reveries or pauses of apparent abstraction, that, in turning over a page of the poet and scholar Politian's beautiful tragedy "The Orfeo," (the first native **56** Italian tragedy,) which lay near me upon an ottoman, I discovered a passage underlined in pencil. It was a passage towards the end of the third act—a passage of the most heart-stirring excitement—a passage which, although tainted with impurity, no man shall read without a thrill of novel emotion—no woman without a sigh. The whole page was blotted with fresh tears, and, upon the opposite interleaf, were the following English lines, written in a hand so very different from the peculiar characters of my acquaintance, that I had some difficulty in recognising it as his own.

> Thou wast that all to me, love,
>   For which my soul did pine—
> A green isle in the sea, love,
>   A fountain and a shrine,
> All wreathed with fairy fruits and flowers;
>   And all the flowers were mine.
>
> Ah, dream too bright to last;
>   Ah, starry Hope that didst arise
> But to be overcast!
>   A voice from out the Future cries
> "Onward!"—but o'er the Past
>   (Dim gulf!) my spirit hovering lies,
> Mute, motionless, aghast!
>
> For alas! alas! with me
>   The light of life is o'er.
> "No more—no more—no more,"
> (Such language holds the solemn sea
>   To the sands upon the shore,)
> Shall bloom the thunder-blasted tree,
>   Or the stricken eagle soar!
>
> Now all my hours are trances;
>   And all my nightly dreams
> Are where the dark eye glances,
>   And where thy footstep gleams,
> In what ethereal dances,
>   By what Italian streams.
>
> Alas! for that accursed time
>   They bore thee o'er the billow,
> From Love to titled age and crime,
>   And an unholy pillow—
> From me, and from our misty clime,
>   Where weeps the silver willow!

That these lines were written in English—a language with which I had not believed their author acquainted—afforded me little matter for surprise. I was too well aware of the extent of his acquirements, and of the singular pleasure he took in concealing them from observation, to be astonished at any similar discovery; but the place of date, I must confess, occasioned me no little amazement. It had been originally written *London*, and afterwards carefully overscored—not, however, so effectually as to conceal the word from a scrutinizing eye. I say this occasioned me no little amazement; for I well remember that, in a former conversation with my friend, I particularly inquired if he had at any time met in London the Marchesa di Mentoni, (who for some years previous to her marriage had resided in that city,) when his answer, if I mistake not, gave me to understand that he had never visited the metropolis of Great Britain. I might as well here mention, that I have more than once heard, (without of course giving credit to a report involving so many improbabilities,) that the person of whom I speak was not only by birth, but in education, an *Englishman*.   **58**

*   *   *

"There is one painting," said he, without being aware of my notice of the tragedy—"there is still one painting which you have not seen." And throwing aside a drapery, he discovered a full length portrait of the Marchesa Aphrodite.

Human art could have done no more in the delineation of her superhuman beauty. The same ethereal figure which stood before me the preceding night upon the steps of the Ducal Palace, stood before me once again. But in the expression of the countenance, which was beaming all over with smiles, there still lurked (incomprehensible anomaly!) that fitful stain of melancholy which will ever be found inseparable from the perfection of the beautiful. Her right arm lay folded over her bosom. With her left she pointed downward to a curiously fashioned vase. One small, fairy foot, alone visible, barely touched the earth—and, scarcely discernible in the brilliant atmosphere which seemed to encircle and enshrine her loveliness, floated a pair of the most delicately imagined wings.   **59** My glance fell from the painting to the figure of my friend, and the vigorous words of Chapman's *Bussy D'Ambois* quivered instinctively upon my lips:

> He is up
> There like a Roman statue! He will stand
> Till Death hath made him marble!   **60**

"Come!" he said at length, turning towards a table of richly enamelled and massive silver, upon which were a few goblets fantastically stained, together with two large Etruscan vases,   **61** fashioned in the same extraordinary model as that in the foreground of the portrait, and filled with what I supposed to be Johannisberger. "Come!" he said abruptly, "let us drink!   **62** It is early—but let us drink. It is *indeed* early," he continued, musingly, as a cherub with a heavy golden hammer, made the apartment ring with the first hour after sunrise—"It is *indeed*

58 Considering the clues that have been practically served up to him, the narrator seems doubly dense for still not figuring out what has happened.

59 In Poe's first version, her foot rests on a scroll that says, "I am waiting but for thee."

60 George Chapman (1559?–1634), English dramatist, translator, and poet, wrote *Bussy d'Ambois*, one of his best-known tragedies, in 1607. Oddly enough, he also wrote a play entitled *The Conspiracy and Tragedy of Byron* (1608). As is sometimes the case, Poe quotes inaccurately: ". . . I am up,/Here, like a Roman statue I will stand/Till death hath made me marble" (*Bussy d'Ambois*, V, iv, 96–98).

61 The Etruscans reached their peak of power and wealth during the sixth century B.C. Their art, including their pottery, is similar to the Greek but with an underlying barbaric energy quite unlike the quiet classicism of the Hellenic spirit.

62 Johannisberg, in Hesse near the Rhine, is celebrated for its white wines.

63 A large cup or glass of wine, filled to the brim and used for toasts. The name probably came from the custom of bumping the cups together.

64 A thing of beauty is a joy forever:
Its loveliness increases; it will never
Pass into nothingness; but will keep
A bower quiet for us, and a sleep
Full of sweet dreams, and health, and quiet breathing
(Byron's *Endymion* [1818], Book I)

65 Ionia is the coastal region of Asia Minor, plus the two islands of Chios and Samos. Its principal city was Lydia, and in its favorable position between the civilizations to the west and to the east, it made an immense contribution to Greek art by supplying much of the oriental influence we find there.

66 The speaker apparently feels that the classical, pure style of Greece is compromised by the primitive works of art.

67 See note 1.

68 The page must have brought messages from the Marchesa many times before. He obviously knows his way around.

69 Venetian glass was of such high quality that it was believed that it would crack if it touched poison.

70 Marie Bonaparte, in her Freudian review of Poe's life and work, sees "The Assignation" as a retelling in veiled words of the "archaic drama, which to-day, in civilized peoples, only survives deep in the unconscious but which, in prehistoric times, must often have taken place in dark primeval forests—the murder, by the avenging father, of the son who has possessed himself of one of the father's women; mother or sister. A clue to the crime for which punishment is inflicted, may be seen in the manner of the chosen death: that by poison. For the convulsions that result from poison, often, in the unconscious, stand for the sex orgasm. Thus the Marchesa and the stranger, as perfect Lovers, at the same moment and together, experience the ultimate, supreme orgasm." (*Edgar Allan Poe, a Psychoanalytic Study*, Imago, 1949; p. 272)

63 early, but what matters it? let us drink! Let us pour out an offering to yon solemn sun which these gaudy lamps and censers are so eager to subdue!" And, having made me pledge him in a bumper, he swallowed in rapid succession several goblets of the wine.

64 "To dream," he continued, resuming the tone of his desultory conversation, as he held up to the rich light of a censer one of the magnificent vases—"to dream has been the business of my life. I have therefore framed for myself, as you see, a bower of dreams. In the heart of Venice could I have erected **65** a better? You behold around you, it is true, a medley of **66** architectural embellishments. The chastity of Ionia is offended by antediluvian devices, and the sphynxes of Egypt are outstretched upon carpets of gold. Yet the effect is incongruous to the timid alone. Proprieties of place, and especially of time, are the bugbears which terrify mankind from the contemplation of the magnificent. Once I was myself a decorist; but that sublimation of folly has palled upon my soul. All this is now the fitter for my purpose. Like these arabesque censers, my spirit is writhing in fire, and the delirium of this scene is fashioning me for the wilder visions of that land of real dreams whither I am now rapidly departing." He here paused abruptly, bent his head to his bosom, and seemed to listen to a sound which I could not hear. At length, erecting his frame, he looked upwards and ejaculated the lines of the Bishop of Chichester:—

67
*Stay for me there! I will not fail
To meet thee in that hollow vale.*

In the next instant, confessing the power of the wine, he threw himself at full length upon an ottoman.

A quick step was now heard upon the staircase, and a loud knock at the door rapidly succeeded. I was hastening to anticipate a second disturbance, when a page of Mentoni's **68** household burst into the room, and faltered out, in a voice choking with emotion, the incoherent words, "My mistress!—my mistress!—poisoned!—poisoned! Oh beautiful—oh beautiful Aphrodite!"

Bewildered, I flew to the ottoman, and endeavored to arouse the sleeper to a sense of the startling intelligence. But his limbs were rigid—his lips were livid—his lately beaming eyes were riveted in *death*. I staggered back towards the **69** table—my hand fell upon a cracked and blackened goblet—and a consciousness of the entire and terrible truth flashed **70** suddenly over my soul.

BERENICE

First published in the *Southern Literary Messenger*, March 1835, "Berenice" is a strange, morbid, and gruesome tale. Apparently even Poe felt it was a bit too much, for he took out four rather graphic paragraphs. Even so, after its publication, the *Southern Literary Messenger* received complaints about the subject matter, and in a letter to the editor, T. W. White, Poe admitted that the "subject is far too horrible. . . . The Tale originated in a bet that I could produce nothing effective on a subject so singular, provided I treated it seriously. . . . I allow that it approaches the very verge of bad taste—but I will not sin quite so egregiously again" (April 30, 1835).

Poe then goes on to explain his method and to further defend "Berenice" on the grounds that it is similar in nature to tales in the fiction magazines of the day.

"The history of all Magazines shows plainly that those which have attained celebrity were indebted for it to articles *similar in nature—to Berenice* . . . in what does this nature consist? In the ludicrous heightened into the grotesque: the fearful coloured into the horrible: the witty exaggerated into the burlesque: the singular wrought out into the strange and mystical. . . . But whether the articles of which I speak are, or are not, in bad taste is little to the purpose. To be appreciated you must be *read,* and these things are invariably sought after with avidity. They are, if you will take notice, the articles which find their way into other periodicals, and into the papers, and in this manner, taking hold upon the public mind they augment the reputation of the source where they originated. . . . To be sure originality is an essential in these things—great attention must be paid to style, and much labour spent in their composition, or they will degenerate into the turgid or the absurd."

The bet in question apparently derived from a story in the Baltimore *Saturday Visiter* (February 23, 1833) that told of graves being robbed to obtain teeth for dentists.

The historical Berenice was the sister-in-law of Ptolemy III (d. 221 B.C.), who vowed to sacrifice her hair to the gods if her husband returned home the vanquisher of Asia. She suspended her hair in the temple of the war god, but it was stolen the first night, and Conon of Samos told the king that the winds had wafted it to heaven, where it still forms the seven stars, near the tail of Leo, called Coma Berenices.

Pope, in his *Rape of the Lock*, converted the stolen locks into a star or meteor, "which drew behind a radiant trail of hair" [Canto V].

Elements of Poe's tale were added to the plot of Roger Corman's film *The Premature Burial* (1962). A recorded version of the tale is available (CMS 626) with actor Martin Donegan, and another with Vincent Price (Caedmon 1450).

Dicebant mihi sodales, si sepulchrum amicae
visitarem, curas meas aliquantulum fore levatas.
      —Ebn Zaiat.   **1**

1 My companions told me I might find some little alleviation of my misery, in visiting the grave of my beloved," from the French book *Bibliothèque Orientale* (1697), which in turn quotes the *Kitab al-Aghani* (*Book of Songs*). Ebn (Ben) Zaiat was a grammarian and poet who died about A.D. 218; he wrote an elegy on the loss of a slave girl he loved.

Misery is manifold. The wretchedness of earth is multiform. Overreaching the wide horizon as the rainbow, its hues are as various as the hues of that arch—as distinct, too, yet as intimately blended. Overreaching the wide horizon as the rainbow! How is it that from beauty I have derived a type of

2 Several biblical allusions are tucked into this paragraph. The rainbow, of course, was God's covenant with Noah ("I do set my bow in the cloud, and it shall be for a token of a covenant between me and the earth," Genesis 9:13).

3 ". . . in sorrow thou shalt bring forth children" is God's sentence upon Eve (Genesis 3:16).

4 Egeus is the name of Hermia's father in *A Midsummer-Night's Dream*, a man who does not understand the meaning of love.

5 "Visionary" means fanciful and impractical, dreamy, as in the original title for Poe's "The Assignation."

6 It is interesting that his mother gave birth to him in a library, and apparently died in doing so. Egeus is thus born in an "unreal" surrounding, spends all his time there as he grows, and gains little knowledge of the world outside.

In a tale called "The Visionary," which appeared in *The Casket*, November 1832, we read of a woman named Beatrice who from childhood spends her time in the family library, preferring to "wander alone and live in the imaginings of her own wild fancy." Her mother had rejected the daughter, because she was born on the day the father died, and Beatrice turns to her nurse, who fills her full of "tales of superstition and dread." Eventually Beatrice dies, "the victim to a deluded and overwrought imagination," after her lover is killed by her brother.

7 Reincarnation, or metempsychosis (transmigration of souls), is prominent in some of Poe's other tales, including "Ligeia," "Metzengerstein," and "Morella."

8 Plato held that the soul is immortal and exists independently of the body both before and after death. Wordsworth's *Ode on the Intimations of Immortality* (1807) proposes that the soul only gradually loses "the vision splendid" after birth, contrary to Plato's idea that the knowledge of Eternal Ideas, which the soul has acquired by direct acquaintance, is totally lost at the moment of birth and must be "recollected" through one's lifetime. Wordsworth—and Poe's narrator here—more closely echo the Neoplatonists, who held that the glory of the unborn soul is gradually dimmed as it descends into the darkness of matter:

> Our birth is but a sleep and a forgetting:
> The Soul that rises with us, our life's Star,
>   Hath had elsewhere its setting,
>   And cometh from afar:
>   Not in entire forgetfulness,
>   And not in utter nakedness,
> But trailing clouds of glory do we come
>   From God, who is our home:
> Heaven lies about us in our infancy!
> Shades of the prison-house begin to close
>   Upon the growing boy, . . .
>   (*Ode*, V, 59–70)

9 Poe sets the stage for events to come: the narrator is prey to delusions and seems to be tottering on the brink of madness.

10 Pronounced either "Bear-uh-nye-see" (as it was in Poe's day) or "Bear-uh-nee-chay" (in the Italian manner)

11 "Berenice" provides us with the first in a series of odd love relationships in Poe's tales. Here, as in "Ligeia," the narrator is obsessed with a beautiful, superior

2 unloveliness?—from the covenant of peace a simile of sorrow? But as, in ethics, evil is a consequence of good, so, in fact, out **3** of joy is sorrow born. Either the memory of past bliss is the anguish of to-day, or the agonies which *are* have their origin in the ecstasies which *might have been*.

4   My baptismal name is Egæus; that of my family I will not mention. Yet there are no towers in the land more time-honored than my gloomy, gray, hereditary halls. Our line has **5** been called a race of visionaries; and in many striking particulars—in the character of the family mansion—in the frescos of the chief saloon—in the tapestries of the dormitories—in the chiselling of some buttresses in the armory—but more especially in the gallery of antique paintings—in the fashion of the library chamber—and, lastly, in the very peculiar nature of the library's contents, there is more than sufficient evidence to warrant the belief.

The recollections of my earliest years are connected with that chamber, and with its volumes—of which latter I will say **6** no more. Here died my mother. Herein was I born. But it is mere idleness to say that I had not lived before—that the soul **7** has no previous existence. You deny it?—let us not argue the matter. Convinced myself, I seek not to convince. There is, however, a remembrance of aerial forms—of spiritual and meaning eyes—of sounds, musical yet sad—a remembrance which will not be excluded; a memory like a shadow, vague, variable, indefinite, unsteady; and like a shadow, too, in the impossibility of my getting rid of it while the sunlight of my **8** reason shall exist.

In that chamber was I born. Thus awaking from the long night of what seemed, but was not, nonentity, at once into the very regions of fairy-land—into a palace of imagination— into the wild dominions of monastic thought and erudition— it is not singular that I gazed around me with a startled and ardent eye—that I loitered away my boyhood in books, and dissipated my youth in reverie; but it *is* singular that as years rolled away, and the noon of manhood found me still in the mansion of my fathers—it *is* wonderful what stagnation there fell upon the springs of my life—wonderful how total an inversion took place in the character of my commonest thought. The realities of the world affected me as visions, and as visions only, while the wild ideas of the land of dreams became, in turn—not the material of my every-day existence but in very **9** deed that existence utterly and solely in itself.

*   *   *

10   Berenice and I were cousins, and we grew up together in **11** my paternal halls. Yet differently we grew—I ill of health, and buried in gloom—she agile, graceful, and overflowing with energy; hers, the ramble on the hill-side—mine the studies of the cloister—I living within my own heart, and addicted body and soul to the most intense and painful meditation— she roaming carelessly through life with no thought of the shadows in her path, or the silent flight of the raven-winged **12** hours. Berenice!—I call upon her name—Berenice!—and from the gray ruins of memory a thousand tumultuous recollections are startled at the sound! Ah! vividly is her image before me now, as in the early days of her light-heartedness and joy! Oh! gorgeous yet fantastic beauty! Oh! sylph amid the shrubberies **13** of Arnheim!—Oh! Naiad among its fountains!—and then— **14,15** then all is mystery and terror, and a tale which should not be told. Disease—a fatal disease—fell like the simoom upon her **16** frame, and, even while I gazed upon her, the spirit of change swept over her, pervading her mind, her habits, and her character, and, in a manner the most subtle and terrible, disturbing even the identity of her person! Alas! the destroyer came and went, and the victim—where was she? I knew her not—or knew her no longer as Berenice.

Among the numerous train of maladies superinduced by that fatal and primary one which effected a revolution of so horrible a kind in the moral and physical being of my cousin, may be mentioned as the most distressing and obstinate in its nature, a species of epilepsy not unfrequently terminating in *trance* itself—trance very nearly resembling positive dissolution, and from which her manner of recovery was, in most instances, startlingly abrupt. In the mean time my own **17** disease—for I have been told that I should call it by no other appellation—my own disease, then, grew rapidly upon me, and assumed finally a monomaniac character of a novel and **18** extraordinary form—hourly and momently gaining vigor—and at length obtaining over me the most incomprehensible ascendancy. This monomania, if I must so term it, consisted in a morbid irritability of those properties of the mind in metaphysical science termed the *attentive*. It is more than probable that I am not understood; but I fear, indeed, that it is in no manner possible to convey to the mind of the merely general reader, an adequate idea of that nervous *intensity of interest* with which, in my case, the powers of meditation (not to speak technically) busied and buried themselves, in the contemplation of even the most ordinary objects of the universe.

To muse for long unwearied hours with my attention riveted to some frivolous device on the margin, or in the typography **19** of a book; to become absorbed for the better part of a summer's day, in a quaint shadow falling aslant upon the tapestry, or upon the door; to lose myself for an entire night in watching the steady flame of a lamp, or the embers of a fire; to dream away whole days over the perfume of a flower; to repeat monotonously some common word, until the sound, by dint of frequent repetition, ceased to convey any idea whatever to the mind; to lose all sense of motion or physical existence, by **20** means of absolute bodily quiescence long and obstinately persevered in;—such were a few of the most common and least pernicious vagaries induced by a condition of the mental faculties, not, indeed, altogether unparalleled, but certainly bidding defiance to anything like analysis or explanation.

Yet let me not be misapprehended.—The undue, earnest, and morbid attention thus excited by objects in their own nature frivolous, must not be confounded in character with that ruminating propensity common to all mankind, and more especially indulged in by persons of ardent imagination. It

women. He also admits that his fantasies have taken over his life—yet he expects us to believe every word he says. Note that Poe and his wife were also cousins.

12 Certainly, to my mind, a more successful image than that in Tennyson's *Maud* (1855), I, xxii, 1: "Come into the garden, Maud,/For the black bat, night, has flown." Night was often personified as a winged woman who folds her wings around the world as night falls. Michelangelo set the image for all time in his statue of *Night*, in Florence.

13 A slender, graceful woman; from the name of the elemental being that inhabited the air according to Paracelsus.

14 The name of Arnheim comes from Sir Walter Scott's novel *Anne of Geierstein* (1829), whose heroine, the Baroness of Arnheim, inhabits a castle with a reputation for magic. In the tenth chapter of the novel, we hear of mysterious appearances by the lady in the forest at night. Poe uses the name again in "The Domain of Arnheim."

15 One of the nymphs who, in ancient mythology, inhabited rivers, lakes, and streams. "Fountain" here means a spring, or the source of a stream or river.

16 See "MS. Found in a Bottle," note 18.

17 Catalepsy, epilepsy, and catatonic states are also important in "The Fall of the House of Usher" and "The Premature Burial." Catalepsy is a trancelike state in which the muscles are rigid for long periods. One form of catalepsy is characteristic of catatonic schizophenia and of some forms of hysteria. Without sophisticated medical equipment, catalepsy was often mistaken for death, and the victim was sometimes buried while still alive.

18 An old term for paranoia, a disorder characterized by fixed ideas and delusions of persecution.

19 A printer's ornament. Baudelaire mistranslates the word as "motto," which is not what Poe has in mind.

20 This phenomenon is well known, and most people have probably observed it themselves at one time or another, although not to the extreme of the narrator. Gertrude Stein also noted it, basing much of her poetry on the use of words for their sound or suggestiveness, rather than their literal meaning. Her "A rose is a rose is a rose" is an example of this repetitive device, which strips the word of its normal connotation and demonstrates that a word is *not* the object it names, but a separate entity.

21 Incitement, incentive

22 This suggests that he has perhaps recovered from his insanity after the traumatic events of the tale.

23 Curio (1503–69) was an Italian Protestant who argued that Hell had fewer souls than Heaven—a remarkably optimistic idea for the era. His book was published about 1554.

24 St. Augustine wrote *De Civitate Dei (The City of God)* about A.D. 412 His argument was that God had created two mystical cities, one of God and one of the Devil—and to one or the other all mankind will ultimately belong. This was in part an argument that the Eternal City was not Rome, but Heaven. "The City of God" soon came to mean the Church, the whole body of believers, and later the kingdom of Christ (as opposed to the city of the World, which John Bunyan calls the City of Destruction).
"Austin" for "Augustine" dates back at least as far as 1384, according to the O.E.D., although it was archaic by Poe's time.

25 Tertullian (Quintus Septimus Florens Tertullianus (A.D. c.160–c.230) was the Roman theologian and apologist who was converted to Christianity about A.D. 197, and became the most formidable defender of the faith in his era. His writing is persuasive and still quoted today: "The blood of martyrs is the seed of the Church." *De Carne Christi (On the Flesh of Christ)* dates from A.D. 202–8.

26 "The Son of God has died, it is to be believed because it is incredible; and buried. He is risen, it is sure because it is impossible" (*De Carne Christi*, Section V).
The investigation is fruitless because a paradox such as this is impossible to make logical. It is a matter of faith, not reason.

27 Also known as Ptolemaeus Chennos. The quote here is apparently from Photius (c.820–92?), the Greek churchman and theologian, patriarch of Constantinople, whose works contain many citations from lost Greek writings. The reference is to a story mentioned in Jacob Bryant's *Antient Mythology* (1807) in which a rock is swayed by a blade of grass.
Asphodel is a symbol of death and appears again in "Eleonora" and "The Island of the Fay." It is a member of the lily family, in Greek mythology sacred to Persephone and associated with the Elysian Fields.

28 The narrator's mental state is thrown into a turmoil by the alteration in Berenice's appearance—no wonder, considering his obsession with immortality.
On another level, the narrator is involved in a love/hate relationship, as are the narrators of "Ligeia" and "Morella," and in her illness he may see a chance to turn the tables on this "superior" woman who has dominated his life.

was not even, as might be at first supposed, an extreme condition, or exaggeration of such propensity, but primarily and essentially distinct and different. In the one instance, the dreamer, or enthusiast, being interested by an object usually *not* frivolous, imperceptibly loses sight of this object in a wilderness of deductions and suggestions issuing therefrom, until, at the conclusion of a day dream *often replete with luxury,* he finds the *incitamentum* or first cause of his musings entirely vanished and forgotten. In my case the primary object was *invariably frivolous,* although assuming, through the medium of my distempered vision, a refracted and unreal importance. Few deductions, if any, were made; and those few pertinaciously returning in upon the original object as a centre. The meditations were *never* pleasurable; and, at the termination of the reverie, the first cause, so far from being out of sight, had attained that supernaturally exaggerated interest which was the prevailing feature of the disease. In a word, the powers of mind more particularly exercised were, with me, as I have said before, the *attentive,* and are, with the day-dreamer, the *speculative*.

My books, at this epoch, if they did not actually serve to irritate the disorder, partook, it will be perceived, largely, in their imaginative and inconsequential nature, of the characteristic qualities of the disorder itself. I well remember, among others, the treatise of the noble Italian Cælius Secondus Curio "De Amplitudine Beati Regni Dei," St. Austin's great work, the "City of God;" and Tertullian "De Carne Christi," in which the paradoxical sentence "Mortuus est Dei filius; credible est quia ineptum est: et sepultus resurrexit; certum est quia impossible est" occupied my undivided time, for many weeks of laborious and fruitless investigation.

Thus it will appear that, shaken from its balance only by trivial things, my reason bore resemblance to the ocean-crag spoken of by Ptolemy Hephestion, which, steadily resisting the attacks of human violence, and the fiercer fury of the waters and the winds, trembled only to the touch of the flower called Asphodel. And although, to a careless thinker, it might appear a matter beyond doubt, that the alteration produced by her unhappy malady, in the *moral* condition of Berenice, would afford me many objects for the exercise of that intense and abnormal meditation whose nature I have been at some trouble in explaining, yet such was not in any degree the case. In the lucid intervals of my infirmity, her calamity, indeed, gave me pain, and, taking deeply to heart that total wreck of her fair and gentle life, I did not fail to ponder frequently and bitterly upon the wonder-working means by which so strange a revolution had been so suddenly bought to pass. But these reflections partook not of the idiosyncrasy of my disease, and were such as would have occurred, under similar circumstances, to the ordinary mass of mankind. True to its own character, my disorder revelled in the less important but more startling changes wrought in the *physical* frame of Berenice—in the singular and most appalling distortion of her personal identity.

During the brightest days of her unparalleled beauty, most surely I had never loved her. In the strange anomaly of my existence, feelings, with me, *had never been* of the heart, and my passions *always were* of the mind. Through the gray of the early morning—among the trellised shadows of the forest at noonday—and in the silence of my library at night, she had flitted by my eyes, and I had seen her—not as the living and breathing Berenice, but as the Berenice of a dream—not as a being of the earth, earthy, but as the abstraction of such being—not as a thing to admire, but to analyze—not as an object of love, but as the theme of the most abstruse although desultory speculation. And *now*—now I shuddered in her presence, and grew pale at her approach; yet bitterly lamenting her fallen and desolate condition, I called to mind that she had loved me long, and, in an evil moment, I spoke to her of marriage.

And at length the period of our nuptials was approaching, when, upon an afternoon in the winter of the year,—one of those unseasonably warm, calm, and misty days which are the nurse of the beautiful Halcyon,—I sat, (and sat, as I thought, alone,) in the inner apartment of the library. But uplifting my eyes I saw that Berenice stood before me.

Was it my own excited imagination—or the misty influence of the atmosphere—or the uncertain twilight of the chamber— or the gray draperies which fell around her figure—that caused in it so vacillating and indistinct an outline? I could not tell. She spoke no word, and I—not for worlds could I have uttered a syllable. An icy chill ran through my frame; a sense of insufferable anxiety oppressed me; a consuming curiosity pervaded my soul; and sinking back upon the chair, I remained for some time breathless and motionless, with my eyes riveted upon her person. Alas! its emaciation was excessive, and not one vestige of the former being, lurked in any single line of the contour. My burning glances at length fell upon the face.

The forehead was high, and very pale, and singularly placid; and the once jetty hair fell partially over it, and overshadowed the hollow temples with innumerable ringlets now of a vivid yellow, and jarring discordantly, in their fantastic character, with the reigning melancholy of the countenance. The eyes were lifeless, and lustreless, and seemingly pupil-less, and I shrank involuntarily from their glassy stare to the contemplation of the thin and shrunken lips. They parted; and in a smile of peculiar meaning, *the teeth* of the changed Berenice disclosed themselves slowly to my view. Would to God that I had never beheld them, or that, having done so, I had died!

*   *   *

The shutting of a door disturbed me, and, looking up, I found that my cousin had departed from the chamber. But from the disordered chamber of my brain, had not, alas! departed, and would not be driven away, the white and ghastly *spectrum* of the teeth. Not a speck on their surface— not a shade on their enamel—not an indenture in their edges— but what that period of her smile had sufficed to brand in

29 As in "Ligeia," the narrator is almost totally intellectual, seemingly without the capacity for real love.

30 Some critics have made Poe out to be his narrator, worshipping the Shrine of Womanhood in the same obsessive, sexless manner, and it is true that nineteenth-century American society did idealize woman into something approaching the unearthly. For more on this subject, see Ann Douglas' eminently readable *The Feminization of American Culture* (Alfred A. Knopf, 1977), a fascinating exploration of the alliance of middle-class women and the liberal Protestant clergy, which preached a reverence for female timidity, piety, childish naïveté, and purity.

31 "For as Jove, during the winter season, gives twice seven days of warmth, men have called this clement and temperate time the nurse of the beautiful Halcyon.— *Simonides*." (Poe's note)
   This fragment of Simonides (c.556–468? B.C.) also appeared in an early version of "Morella." Halcyone, or Alcyone, in Greek mythology was daughter of Aeolus and wife of Ceyx. When her husband drowned, Halcyone in despair threw herself into the sea. Out of pity, the gods changed the pair into kingfishers (*halcyon* is Greek for kingfisher), and Zeus forbade the winds from blowing seven days before and after the winter solstice—the breeding season of the kingfisher.

32 In "Ligeia," the narrator in his drapery-clad bedchamber also thinks he senses the footfall of a shadow.
   There are two basic types of Gothic tales: the supernatural, and the "explained." In the latter, the author leaves clues that offer a logical explanation for all events. In Poe's tales, as in Hawthorne's, the clue lies in the reliability of the narrator. Can we trust his memory, his judgment, even his sanity? Since everything we know about events and characters comes from the narrator, we have to consider his particular viewpoint before we can decide what has occurred.

33 The forehead is still high, which in phrenological terms is an expression of ideality—but the dark hair and vivid eyes (symbolic, as always, of the soul) are stripped of mystery and life. See "Ligeia," note 11.

34 Plotinus (c.205–70), the great Neoplatonist, states that the human eye would not be able to see the sun if, in a way, it were not itself like the sun. Since the sun is the source of light, and light is symbolic of intelligence and spirit, sight can represent a spiritual act and symbolize understanding. The eye becomes a mirror of the soul, or the pathway to it, depending on the point of view (see "Ligeia"). Carl Jung considers the eye as symbolic of the maternal bosom, and the pupil as its child (J. E. Cirlot, *A Dictionary of Symbols*, 1962).

35 If her smile has a "peculiar meaning", it is only in the mind of the narrator, who seems to be hanging on to the last vestige of Berenice's beauty. Her teeth, being non-flesh, are unchanged, while the rest of her once-perfect body has altered greatly.

36 A specter or apparition, a somewhat uncommon usage by Poe's time.

37 Since white is a symbol of purity, one may see teeth here as an indication of the narrator's elusive dream of life everlasting, or suggesting pure reason, or as symbolic of Berenice's virginity, which the narrator "defiles."

38 "That all her steps were ideas." Marie Sallé (1714–56) was a dancer and close friend of Voltaire.

39 "That all her teeth were ideas."

40 One always wonders why, if victims of epilepsy or catalepsy were known to be susceptible to deathlike trances, they are in Poe's tales so invariably mistaken for dead.

In the early versions of the tale, Poe follows this paragraph with four more, which he removed after objections, from readers and editors, that they were in excessively bad taste:

"With a heart full of grief, yet reluctantly, and oppressed with awe, I made my way to the bed-chamber of the departed. The room was large, and very dark, and at every step within its gloomy precincts I encountered the paraphernalia of the grave. The coffin, so a menial told me, lay surrounded by the curtains of yonder bed, and in that coffin, he whisperingly assured me, was all that remained of Berenice. Who was it asked me would I not look upon the corpse? I had seen the lips of no one move, yet the question had been demanded, and the echo of the syllables still lingered in the room. It was impossible to refuse; and with a sense of suffocation I dragged myself to the side of the bed. Gently I uplifted the draperies of the curtains.

"As I let them fall they descended upon my shoulders, and, shutting me thus out from the living, enclosed me in the strictest communion with the deceased.

"The very atmosphere was redolent of death. The peculiar smell of the coffin sickened me; and I fancied a deleterious odor was already exhaling from the body. I would have given worlds to escape—to fly from the pernicious influence of mortality—to breathe once again the pure air of the eternal heavens. But I had no longer the power to move—my knees tottered beneath me—and I remained rooted to the spot, and gazing upon the frightful length of the rigid body as it lay outstretched in the dark coffin without a lid.

"God of heaven!—was it possible? Was it my brain that reeled—or was it indeed the fingers of the enshrouded dead that stirred in the white cerement that bound it? Frozen with unutterable awe I slowly raised my eyes to the countenance of the corpse. There had been a band around the jaws, but, I know not how, it was broken asunder. The livid lips were wreathed into a species of smile, and, through the enveloping gloom, once again there glared upon me in too palpable reality, the white and glistening, and ghastly teeth of Berenice. I sprang convulsively from the bed, and, uttering no word, rushed forth a maniac from that apartment of triple horror, and mystery, and death."

upon my memory. I saw them *now* even more unequivocally than I beheld them *then*. The teeth!—the teeth!—they were here, and there, and every where, and visibly and palpably before me; long, narrow, and excessively white, with the pale lips writhing about them, as in the very moment of their first terrible development. Then came the full fury of my *monomania*, and I struggled in vain against its strange and irresistible influence. In the multiplied objects of the external world I had no thoughts but for the teeth. For these I longed with a phrenzied desire. All other matters and all different interests became absorbed in their single contemplation. They—they alone were present to the mental eye, and they, in their sole individuality, became the essence of my mental life. I held them in every light. I turned them in every attitude. I surveyed their characteristics. I dwelt upon their peculiarities. I pondered upon their conformation. I mused upon the alteration in their nature. I shuddered as I assigned to them in imagination a sensitive and sentient power, and even when unassisted by the lips, a capability of moral expression. Of Mad'selle Sallé it has been well said, *"que tous ses pas étaient des sentiments,"* and of Berenice I more seriously believed *que toutes ses dents étaient des idées. Des idées!*—ah here was the idiotic thought that destroyed me! *Des idées!*—ah *therefore* it was that I coveted them so madly! I felt that their possession could alone ever restore me to peace, in giving me back to reason.

And the evening closed in upon me thus—and then the darkness came, and tarried, and went—and the day again dawned—and the mists of a second night were now gathering around—and still I sat motionless in that solitary room; and still I sat buried in meditation, and still the *phantasma* of the teeth maintained its terrible ascendancy as, with the most vivid and hideous distinctness, it floated about amid the changing lights and shadows of the chamber. At length there broke in upon my dreams a cry as of horror and dismay; and thereunto, after a pause, succeeded the sound of troubled voices, intermingled with many low moanings of sorrow, or of pain. I arose from my seat, and, throwing open one of the doors of the library, saw standing out in the ante-chamber a servant maiden, all in tears, who told me that Berenice was— no more. She had been seized with epilepsy in the early morning, and now, at the closing in of the night, the grave was ready for its tenant, and all the preparations for the burial were completed.

*   *   *

I found myself sitting in the library, and again sitting there alone. It seemed that I had newly awakened from a confused and exciting dream. I knew that it was now midnight, and I was well aware that since the setting of the sun Berenice had been interred. But of that dreary period which intervened I had no positive—at least no definite comprehension. Yet its memory was replete with horror—horror more horrible from being vague, and terror more terrible from ambiguity. It was a fearful page in the record of my existence, written all over with dim, and hideous, and unintelligible recollections. I strived to decipher them, but in vain; while ever and anon, like the spirit of a departed sound, the shrill and piercing shriek of a female voice seemed to be ringing in my ears. I had done a deed—what was it? I asked myself the question aloud, and the whispering echoes of the chamber answered me, *"What was it?"*

On the table beside me burned a lamp, and near it lay a little box. It was of no remarkable character, and I had seen it frequently before, for it was the property of the family physician; but how came it *there*, upon my table, and why did I shudder in regarding it? These things were in no manner to be accounted for, and my eyes at length dropped to the open pages of a book, and to a sentence underscored therein. The words were the singular but simple ones of the poet Ebn Zaiat, *"Dicebant mihi sodales si sepulchrum amicae visitarem, curas meas aliquantulum fore levatas."* Why then, as I perused **41** them, did the hairs of my head erect themselves on end, and the blood of my body become congealed within my veins?

There came a light tap at the library door, and pale as the tenant of a tomb, a menial entered upon tiptoe. His looks were wild with terror, and he spoke to me in a voice tremulous,

41 See note 1. The narrator has broken into Berenice's tomb.

"... si sepulchrum amicæ visitarem, curas meas aliquantulum fore levatas." *Illustration by F. S. Coburn,* *1903*

42 One assumes Berenice has survived, although the forced extraction of her teeth must have been a rather traumatic experience.

43 "Substances" seems the wrong word here; "objects" would be more appropriate. Poe, however, is probably alluding to another meaning of "substance"—that of essential nature, or essence.

44 While the narrator's fixation on teeth may mean nothing more than proof of Poe's winning the bet mentioned in the introductory note, we have already seen some possible symbolic intrepretations of his act, and there are others.

According to René Allendry (*Le Symbolisme des nombres*, Paris, 1948), teeth are the primeval weapons of attack, and an expression of life. Loss of one's teeth, then, signifies inhibition or failure in life. Ania Teillard (*Il Simbolismo dei Sogni*, Milan, 1951) says the loss of teeth represents an attitude that is the inversion of that of the Primitive, who commonly adorned himself with the teeth and claws of conquered animals.

Some interpretations underline the sexual significance of teeth. Marie Bonaparte sees Berenice's teeth in typical Freudian fashion: ". . . in psycho-analysis, many cases of male-impotence reveal, though more or less buried in the unconscious—strange as it may seem to many a reader—the notion that the female vagina is furnished with teeth, and is thus a source of danger in being able to bite and castrate. . . . Mouth and vagina are equated in the unconscious and, when Egaeus yields to the morbid impulse to draw Berenice's teeth, he yields to the yearning for the mother's organ and to be revenged upon it, since the dangers that hedge it about make him sexually avoid all women as too menacing. His act is therefore a sort of retributive castration inflicted on the mother whom he loves, and yet hates, because [of] his sex-love for her in infancy." (P. 218)

Also of interest is the Gnostic concept that the teeth constitute battlements, the wall and fortifications of the inner person, just as the eyes and the glance are the defense of the spirit. This suggests the negative symbolism of the loss of teeth, at least from this early Christian viewpoint.

husky, and very low. What said he?—some broken sentences I heard.

He told of a wild cry disturbing the silence of the night—of the gathering together of the household—of a search in the direction of the sound;—and then his tones grew thrillingly distinct as he whispered me of a violated grave—of a disfigured body enshrouded, yet still breathing, still palpitating, still **42** *alive!*

He pointed to my garments;—they were muddy and clotted with gore. I spoke not, and he took me gently by the hand;—it was indented with the impress of human nails. He directed my attention to some object against the wall;—I looked at it for some minutes;—it was a spade. With a shriek I bounded to the table, and grasped the box that lay upon it. But I could not force it open; and in my tremor it slipped from my hands, and fell heavily, and burst into pieces; and from it, with a rattling sound, there rolled out some instruments of dental surgery, intermingled with thirty-two small, white and ivory- **43** looking substances that were scattered to and fro about the **44** floor.

MORELLA

First published in the *Southern Literary Messenger*, April 1835, "Morella" is one of Poe's best tales of metempsychosis—the passage of the soul from one body to another—which he touched upon in "Metzengerstein" and would deal with again in "Ligeia," "A Tale of the Ragged Mountains," and "The Black Cat." (For more on metempsychosis, see "Metzengerstein," note 2).

"Morella" also involves two important superstitions of which Poe was obviously aware: that spirits must answer when their right names are spoken, and that the child who takes its first breath after its mother takes her last is a supernatural being.

The chief source for the tale is Henry Glassford Bell's "The Dead Daughter," which appeared in the *Edinburgh Literary Journal*, January 1, 1831. It is the tale of two sisters: after the elder one dies, her name (Paulina) goes to the second. The story line is similar to Poe's in some ways but suffers from the lack of a definite motive for Paulina's desire to return to haunt her father. In Poe, the mother's intellectual background and the change of the sister/sister relationship to mother/daughter make it easier to accept the transfer of Morella's soul at the moment she dies to her daughter (if we wish to accept the supernatural interpretation of the tale).

Whether we accept the tale literally or not probably makes little difference. Poe, in his tales of the uncanny, almost always gives us a choice. For, above all, he writes, one should in such tales avoid "*directness* of expression" and instead leave as much to the imagination as possible, "writing as if the author were firmly impressed with the truth, yet astonished at the immensity of the wonders he relates, and for which, professedly, he neither claims nor anticipates credence—in minuteness of detail, especially upon points which have no immediate bearing upon the general story . . . in short, by making use of the infinity of arts which give verisimilitude to a narration—and by leaving the result as a wonder not to be accounted for. . . . The reader . . . perceives and falls in with the writer's humor, and suffers himself to be borne on thereby. On the other hand, what difficulty, or inconvenience, or danger can there be in leaving us uninformed of the important facts that a certain hero *did not* actually discover the elixir vitae, *could not* really make himself invisible, and *was not* either a ghost in good earnest, or a bona fide Wandering Jew?" ("Sheppard Lee," *Southern Literary Messenger*, September 1836).

Since Poe is here criticizing tales of the supernatural that endeavor to explain events as a dream or similar hallucination, one might think that Poe's tales must therefore be taken literally. But Poe is not discussing whether or not events actually *occurred;* this should be left for the reader to decide. The tale itself must have its own reality, whether or not that coincides with what we know of reality outside the tale.

The 1962 film *Tales of Terror* uses "Morella" for the basis of one of its three parts, also drawing upon "The Black Cat." Recorded versions include one read by Vincent Price (Caedmon 1450) and one by Ugo Toppo (CMS 567).

1 From Plato's *Symposium*, which Poe found in Henry Nelson Coleridge's *Introduction to the Study of the Greek Classic Poets* (1831). Poe wrote the story in 1834 or early in 1835 but left the manuscript unfinished, and there quotes Coleridge correctly: "Itself—alone by itself—eternally one and single," but here has rephrased it in his own words. The original lines from Plato read thus: "He who has been instructed thus far in the things of love, and who has learned to see the beautiful in due order and succession, when he comes toward the end will suddenly perceive a nature of wondrous beauty (and this, Socrates, is the final cause of all our former toils)—a nature which in the first place is everlasting, not growing or decaying, or waxing and waning . . . but beauty absolute, separate, simple, and everlasting. . . ." (*Symposium*, translated by B. Jowett, Random House, 1937; pp. 334–35)

2 The name may have come from an article in *The Lady's Book*, September 1834, entitled "Women Celebrated in Spain for Their Extraordinary Powers of Mind." Among others, the article details the life of Juliana Morella of Barcelona, whose father, skipping the country after murdering a man, taught his daughter so well that by age twelve she was a renowned student of philosophy, and by her teens was said to have held a public disputation in the Jesuit college at Lyons. She was apparently skilled in philosophy, divinity, music, law, and philology, and could speak or read fourteen languages. Today she is known as Venerable Mother Juliana Morell (1595–1653).

Another reference could be to the morel, a poisonous weed sometimes called deadly nightshade (*Solanum nigrum*, but more properly *Atropa belladonna*).

3 Another in the series of narrators who worship the beauty and learning of an ideal woman but seem to have no sexual interest in them. Typically, the narrator seems to resent the woman for her superiority (despite his yearning for the understanding she might share with him), and the woman begins to fade away for lack of attention to her sensual side. As usual, however, the narrator is unaware of his distorted sense of love.

4 In other words, he finds her devotion for him a bit too good to be true, sowing the seeds of doubt which will blossom into fear and hatred later on.

5 Compare with the description of Ligeia.

6 Pressburg, besides being the site where the kings of Hungary were crowned until 1835, was the home of a great university—and considered by folklore to be the center for the Black Arts as well. The Czechoslovakian city is now Bratislava.

Poe mentions the city in "Von Kempelen," again for its association with magic and alchemy.

7 Johannes Eckhart (c. 1260–1328) believed in a divine differentiation into personality and self-expression, in a world of unity and ideas and a world of physical phenomena. God's purpose was to effect a return of everything to himself, and since all creation desires unity, everything craves a return to the Source.

Meister Eckhart's belief here is almost identical to Poe's, as expressed in his last great work, *Eureka* (see "Ms. Found in a Bottle," introduction).

Elsewhere in his writings, Eckhart states that the mortal soul has a spark of divinity, which is the link

"*And thus, joy suddenly faded into horror, and the most beautiful became the most hideous. . . ." Illustration by F. S. Coburn, 1902*

Αυτο καθ᾽ αυτο μεθ᾽ αυτου, μονο ειδες αιει ου.
Itself—alone by itself—eternally one and single.
—PLATO—*Symp*.

1

2 With a feeling of deep yet most singular affection I regarded my friend Morella. Thrown by accident into her society many years ago, my soul, from our first meeting, burned with fires it had never before known; but the fires were not of Eros, and bitter and tormenting to my spirit was the gradual conviction that I could in no manner define their unusual meaning, or

3 regulate their vague intensity. Yet we met; and fate bound us together at the altar; and I never spoke of passion, nor thought of love. She, however, shunned society, and, attaching herself to me alone, rendered me happy. It is a happiness to wonder;

4 it is a happiness to dream.

Morella's erudition was profound. As I hope to live, her talents were of no common order—her powers of mind were

5 gigantic. I felt this, and, in many matters, became her pupil.

I soon, however, found that, perhaps on account of her Pressburg education, she placed before me a number of those **6** mystical writings which are usually considered the mere dross of the early German literature. These, for what reason I could **7** not imagine, were her favorite and constant study—and that, in process of time they became my own, should be attributed to the simple but effectual influence of habit and example.

In all this, if I err not, my reason had little to do. My convictions, or I forget myself, were in no manner acted upon by the ideal, nor was any tincture of the mysticism which I read, to be discovered, unless I am greatly mistaken, either in my deeds or in my thoughts. Persuaded of this, I abandoned myself implicitly to the guidance of my wife, and entered with an unflinching heart into the intricacies of her studies. And then—then, when, poring over forbidden pages, I felt a forbidden spirit enkindling within me—would Morella place her cold hand upon my own, and rake up from the ashes of a dead philosophy some low, singular words, whose strange meaning burned themselves in upon my memory. And then, **8** hour after hour would I linger by her side, and dwell upon the music of her voice—until, at length, its melody was tainted **9** with terror,—and there fell a shadow upon my soul—and I grew pale, and shuddered inwardly at those too unearthly tones. And thus, joy suddenly faded into horror, and the most beautiful became the most hideous, as Hinnom became Ge–Henna. **10**

It is unnecessary to state the exact character of those disquisitions which, growing out of the volumes I have **11** mentioned, formed, for so long a time, almost the sole conversation of Morella and myself. By the learned in what might be termed theological morality they will be readily conceived, and by the unlearned they would, at all events, be little understood. The wild Pantheism of Fichte; the modified **12** Παλιγγενεσια of the Pythagoreans; and, above all, the doctrines of *Identity* as urged by Schelling, were generally the points of discussion presenting the most of beauty to the imaginative Morella. That identity which is termed personal, Mr. Locke, I think, truly defines to consist in the saneness of a rational being. And since by person we understand an **13** intelligent essence having reason, and since there is a consciousness which always accompanies thinking, it is this which makes us all to be that which we call *ourselves*—thereby distinguishing us from other beings that think, and giving us our personal identity. But the *principium individuationis*—the notion of that identity *which at death is or is not lost for ever*—was to me, at all times, a consideration of intense interest; not more from the perplexing and exciting nature of its consequences, than from the marked and agitated manner in which Morella mentioned them. **14**

But, indeed, the time had now arrived when the mystery of my wife's manner oppressed me as a spell. I could no longer bear the touch of her wan fingers, nor the low tone of her musical language, nor the lustre of her melancholy eyes. And she knew all this, but did not upbraid; she seemed conscious of my weakness or my folly, and, smiling, called it Fate. She

between man and god. Knowledge is derived from the senses and thus concerned only with the world of physical phenomena. One has to transcend the sensible and rational and renounce the world of images. The soul must withdraw from memory and understanding.

Poe also believed in the divine link, and wrote of the human inability to catch more than "brief, indeterminate glimpses" of the real world beyond our own.

Other early German mystics include Rielman Merswin and Jan van Ruysbroeck. For more on these and Eckhart, see Thomas Katsaros and Nathaniel Kaplan, *The Western Mystical Tradition*, College and University Press (1969), Vol. I, pp. 246–67.

Since the narrator does not define "early," he could also be referring to eighteenth century German literature, which set up the principles for the romantic movement.

8 Morella's Pressburg education (rare for a woman) indicates the possibility that she has studied the arts of magic, so that the "forbidden spirit" enkindled within the narrator could be his interest in the Black Arts. (Note the similarity between this passage and one in "The Murders in the Rue Morgue": "The vast extent of his reading. . . . I felt my soul enkindled by the wild fervor of his imagination.")

If we choose to take a psychological interpretation of "Morella," we might read this passage as a reference to the narrator's obsession with ultimate knowledge. The "forbidden spirit" may be his desire to control Morella, to absorb her learning, even her very being. He would be, in D. H. Lawrence's words, a "spiritual vampire" *Studies in Classic American Literature*, Viking Press, 1964, p. 70).

Still another possibility is that the "forbidden spirit" refers to ultimate knowledge itself, which in Poe's cosmology means destruction.

9 Many of Poe's women have musical voices. Aside from the poetic description, this echoes Poe's belief that music is the art closest to the Sublime. Music has no basis in reality—or at least in no earthly reality, as painting and writing do. It is totally subjective.

10 Thomas Hobbes, in *Leviathan* (1651), III, 38, explains that the ancient Jews named a valley near Jerusalem "The Valley of the Children of Hinnon," until some of their people committed the sin of idolatry there and sacrificed children to the god Moloch. The valley was then burned and used to store refuse and filth. From time to time, new fires were set to burn the refuse and kill the stench, and so the Jews took to calling their version of Hell *Gehenna*, or the Valley of Hinnon The usual spelling is "Hinnom," but both Hobbes and Poe use the same spelling.

"Moreover he burnt incense in the valley of the son of Hinnom, and burnt his children in the fire, after the abominations of the heathen whom the Lord had cast out before the children of Israel" (II Chronicles 28:3).

"And he [Josiah] defiled Topheth, which is in the valley of the children of Hinnom, that no man might make his son or his daughter to pass through the fire to Molech" (II Kings 23:10).

"And he [Manasseh] caused his children to pass through the fire in the valley of the son of Hinnom: also he observed times, and used enchantments, and used witchcraft, and dealt with a familiar spirit, and with wizards" (II Chronicles 33:6).

"Down to Gehenna, or up to the Throne,/He travels the fastest who travels alone" (Rudyard Kipling, "The Winners," in *The Story of the Gadsbys* [1888]).

11 Diligent or systematic search; research

12 Johann Fichte (1762–1814), a follower of Immanuel Kant, took his master's belief that knowledge is limited and developed from it the concept of the limitless potential of the imagination. For Fichte, ego is the only being, shaking the fundamental premise that there is both a subjective world and an objective one, so that objectivity as an ideal lost ground, and subjectivity became the rule for the romantics who followed.

The Greek word here is *palingenesia*, "birth again," another word for metempsychosis, of which Pythagoras was an ardent believer.

Friedrich Wilhelm Joseph von Schelling (1775–1854) helped develop the romantic idea of a harmonious partnership between nature and man. If there is to be knowledge of nature and understanding of the origin of intellect, he reasoned, then the principle of mind must be already manifest in nature. In *Of Human Freedom* (1809) he maintained that history is a series of stages progressing toward harmony from a previous fall and that God is also part of this development process.

"Freedom and necessity, which appear separated, must be united in an absolute identity, 'the eternal consciousness,' which like the eternal sun in the realm of spiritual beings, is hidden by its own unshadowed light. This absolute identity can never be an object of knowledge, but rather of faith, which Schelling calls a belief in Providence. All else is fatalism or aetheism." (Paul Tillich, *Mysticism and Guilt-Consciousness in Schelling's Philosophical Development,* Bucknell University Press, 1974).

13 Locke defines this in his *Essay Concerning Human Understanding* (1690), II, xxvii. Locke (1632–1704) and his rather commonsense theories seem somehow out of place in the more mystical company above, but we should remember that Locke did propose that the world of sensation—those things that we distinguish through our senses—is only a faithful representation of the real world beyond our reach.

14 Since there is no direct evidence that Morella practices magic, we are free to believe either that she does or that everything we are told is merely the product of the narrator's troubled mind.

15 Does Morella understand that her husband's hostility stems from his jealousy of her intellectual prowess? It seems so , although she is also helpless to fight it.

"Yet was she woman" refers to her nonintellectual nature, the human being who craves, but cannot have, the narrator's love.

16 In Dryden's *Absolom and Achitophel* (1680), Pt. 1, Achitophel is termed "A fiery soul, which working out its way,/Fretted the pygmy-body to decay:/And o'er-informed the tenement of clay."

The image originates in the story of creation in which God fashions Adam from the dust of the ground, although Aristophanes (450–385 B.C.) calls man "weak creatures of clay" (*The Birds,* l. 685).

17 This is certainly one of the most beautifully written passages in all of Poe, and if anyone doubts the skill with which Poe uses his sources, "The Dead Daughter" (see preface) reads "Pauline . . . died upon an autumn evening. . . . It was an autumn evening—sunny, but not beautiful—silent but not serene. . . ."

In his first draft, Poe writes, "It was the season when the beautiful Halcyon is nursed" and places an asterisk immediately after with an explanation. Apparently, when he looked up the source of the quote, he discovered "Halcyon" refers to the spring, not the fall (see "Berenice," note 31).

seemed, also, conscious of a cause, to me unknown, for the gradual alienation of my regard; but she gave me no hint or 15 token of its nature. Yet was she woman, and pined away daily. In time, the crimson spot settled steadily upon the cheek, and the blue veins upon the pale forehead became prominent; and, one instant, my nature melted into pity, but, in the next, I met the glance of her meaning eyes, and then my soul sickened and became giddy with the giddiness of one who gazes downward into some dreary and unfathomable abyss.

Shall I then say that I longed with an earnest and consuming desire for the moment of Morella's decease? I did; but the 16 fragile spirit clung to its tenement of clay for many days—for many weeks and irksome months—until my tortured nerves obtained the mastery over my mind, and I grew furious through delay, and, with the heart of a fiend, cursed the days, and the hours, and the bitter moments, which seemed to lengthen and lengthen as her gentle life declined—like shadows in the dying of the day.

But one autumnal evening, when the winds lay still in heaven, Morella called me to her bedside. There was a dim mist over all the earth, and a warm glow upon the waters; and, amid the rich October leaves of the forest, a rainbow 17 from the firmament had surely fallen.

"It is a day of days," she said, as I approached; "a day of all days either to live or die. It is a fair day for the sons of earth 18 and life—ah, more fair for the daughters of heaven and death!"

I kissed her forehead, and she continued:

"I am dying, yet shall I live."

"Morella!"

"The days have never been when thou couldst love me—but her whom in life thous didst abhor, in death thou shalt 19 adore."

"Morella!"

"I repeat that I am dying. But within me is a pledge of that affection—ah, how little!—which thou didst feel for me, Morella. And when my spirit departs shall the child live—thy child and mine, Morella's. But thy days shall be days of sorrow—that sorrow which is the most lasting of impressions, as the cypress is the most enduring of trees. For the hours of thy happiness are over; and joy is not gathered twice in a life, 20 as the roses of Pæstum twice in a year. Thou shalt no longer, 21 then, play the Teian with time, but, being ignorant of the 22 myrtle and the vine, thou shalt about with thee thy shroud on 23 the earth, as do the Moslemin at Mecca."

"Morella!" I cried, "Morella! how knowest thou this?"—but she turned away her face upon the pillow, and, a slight tremor coming over her limbs, she thus died, and I heard her voice no more.

Yet, as she had foretold, her child—to which in dying she had given birth, which breathed not until the mother breathed no more—her child, a daughter, lived. And she grew strangely in stature and intellect, and was the perfect resemblance of her who had departed, and I loved her with a love more 24 fervent than I had believed it possible to feel for any denizen of earth.

But, ere long, the heaven of this pure affection became darkened, and gloom, and horror, and grief, swept over it in clouds. I said the child grew strangely in stature and intelligence. Strange, indeed, was her rapid increase in bodily size—but terrible, oh! terrible were the tumultuous thoughts which crowded upon me while watching the development of her mental being! Could it be otherwise, when I daily discovered in the conceptions of the child the adult powers and faculties of the woman?—when the lessons of experience fell from the lips of infancy? and when the wisdom or the passions of maturity I found hourly gleaming from its full and speculative eye? When, I say, all this became evident to my appalled senses—when I could no longer hide it from my soul, nor throw it off from those perceptions which trembled to receive it—is it to be wondered at that suspicions, of a nature fearful and exciting, crept in upon my spirit, or that my thoughts fell back aghast upon the wild tales and thrilling theories of the entombed Morella? I snatched from the scrutiny of the world a being whom destiny compelled me to adore, and in the rigorous seclusion of my home, watched with an agonizing anxiety over all which concerned the beloved.

And, as years rolled away, and I gazed, day after day, upon her holy, and mild, and eloquent face, and pored over her maturing form, day after day did I discover new points of resemblance in the child to her mother, the melancholy and the dead. And, hourly, grew darker these shadows of similitude, and more full, and more definite, and more perplexing, and more hideously terrible in their aspect. For that her smile was like her mother's I could bear; but then I shuddered at its too perfect *identity*—that her eyes were like Morella's I could endure; but then they too often looked down into the depths of my soul with Morella's own intense and bewildering meaning. And in the contour of the high forehead, and in the ringlets of the silken hair, and in the wan fingers which buried themselves therein, and in the sad musical tones of her speech, and above all—oh! above all—in the phrases and expressions of the dead on the lips of the loved and the living, I found food for consuming thought and horror—for a worm that *would* not die.   **25**

Thus passed away two lustra of her life, and, as yet, my **26** daughter remained nameless upon the earth. "My child," and "my love," were the designations usualy prompted by a father's affection, and the rigid seclusion of her days precluded all other intercourse. Morella's name died with her at her death. Of the mother I had never spoken to the daughter;—it was impossible to speak. Indeed, during the brief period of her existence, the latter had received no impressions from the outer world, save such as might have been afforded by the narrow limits of her privacy. But at length the ceremony of baptism presented to my mind, in its unnerved and agitated condition, a present deliverance from the terrors of my destiny. And at the baptismal font I hesitated for a name. And **27** many titles of the wise and beautiful, of old and modern times, of my own and foreign lands, came thronging to my lips, with many, many fair titles of the gentle, and the happy, and the

In that first draft, he also has Morella murmur "in a low under-tone" a "Catholic hymn":

> Sancta Maria! turn thine eyes
> Upon the sinner's sacrifice
> Of fervent prayer and humble love
> From thy holy throne above.
>
> At morn, at noon, at twilight dim
> Maria! thou hast heard my hymn;
> In joy and Woe—in Good and Ill
> Mother of God! be with me still.
>
> When my hours flew gently by,
> And no storms were in the sky,
> My soul—lest it should truant be—
> Thy love did guide to thine and thee.
>
> Now—when clouds of Fate o'ercast
> All my Present, and my Past
> Let my Future radiant shine
> With sweet hopes of thee and thine.

The "hymn" is actually Poe's, and it appears in 1845 in briefer form independent of the tale.

While it might seem strange that a practitioner of black magic would pray to the Virgin, tradition has it that making a compact with the Devil does not mean one must renounce the Mother of God. Medieval belief also had it that Mary saved repentent witches who could not pray to God Himself.

On the other hand, if Morella is not a magician, this may simply be a prayer to save her soul, because she knows her husband is slowly starving the life out of her.

18 ". . . the sons of God saw the daughters of men that they were fair; and they took them wives of all which they chose"(Genesis 6:2).

19 The rhymed meter of the sentence indicates, perhaps, an incantation or spell, but, once again, placing it within a prose context gives some room for different interpretation.

20 From Virgil's *Georgics*, IV, 119: ". . . the rose gardens of Paestum, blooming twice" each year.

21 Anacreon of Teos (fl. c. 521 B.C.), who wrote of love and wine (see "Shadow," note 12).
Byron, in *Childe Harold*, II, lxiii: "Love conquers age . . . /So sings the Teian, and he sings in sooth."

22 "The days of our youth are the days of our glory;/And the myrtle and ivy of sweet two-and-twenty/Are worth all your laurels, though ever so plenty"(Byron, "Stanzas Written on the Road Between Florence and Pisa" [1821]).

23 It is a custom to bury one who has made the pilgrimage to Mecca in the robe he wore there.

24 An inhabitant, but also a foreigner admitted to residence

25 The "worm" could easily refer to the narrator's feelings of guilt, which are gnawing away at his vitals. The worm that destroys the dead body is a familiar image in Poe, but here it may indicate that the narrator is, in the spiritual sense, already dead. He is living out the same dreadful fixation with the daughter that he did with the mother.
He has created his own living Hell, reminiscent of the words of Isaiah 66:24: "And they shall go forth, and look upon the carcases of the men that have transgressed against me: for their worm shall not die, neither shall their fire be quenched; and they shall be an abhorring unto all flesh."

26 A lustrum is five years.

27 The fact that the daughter is being baptized in the family vault is evidence of the narrator's total obsession with the dead Morella. The dramatic moment comes as he utters Morella's name "by mistake." This is important, for in magic, the name of a being is the key to its power (see "Shadow," note 19), Speaking the name of the deceased is dangerous, according to folklore, because it may raise the dead.

"Oh, breathe not his name! let it sleep in the shade,/ Where cold and unhonor'd his relics are laid" (Thomas Moore [1779–1852], "Oh, Breathe Not His Name).

28 The obsession with her name parallels that of the lost Lenore in *The Raven*. In "Ligeia," the grieving narrator calls out to his dead wife constantly, and she, too, seems to return in the body of another.

29 Both trees have sorrowful connotations: the hemlock because of its association with the death of Socrates, and the cypress because of its use as coffin-building material.

"Come away, come away, death,/And in sad cypress let me be laid" (*Twelfth Night*, II, iv, 51).

"My heart aches, and a drowsy numbness pains/My sense, as though of hemlock I had drunk" (Keats, *Ode to a Nightingale*).

Actually, the hemlock that poisoned Socrates is not the tree, but a tall weed or herb (*Conium maculatum*).

30 In "The Dead Daughter," the protagonist, Walstein, dreams that after his daughter's death his first wife comes to him in a dream. "The vision became double. . . . Walstein trembled and awoke. A strange light glanced under his chamber door . . . an incredible impulse urged him to rush towards the room in which the body of his daughter lay. . . . The door of the chamber was open; the Hungarian dog lay dead at the threshold; *the corpse was gone.*"

In Poe's tale, however, we are free to conjecture whether Morella has indeed returned in the body of her daughter. If she has, however, why does the daughter die? If her will to live is so powerful, why would she allow her new body to pass away?

One possibility is that the narrator is unreliable as a witness. Certainly his guilt feelings over Morella's physical decline and death have colored his perception. Morella's curse remains imbedded in his consciousness. Consider what he tells us: He says that his daughter looks exactly like her mother. But it could be the narrator's own guilt feelings that make him see Morella's face in her daughter's. This guilt leads to aversion, and he shuts the girl away "in rigid seclusion." She is certainly not safer there from the spirit of Morella, if that is what he is afraid of. What he really fears, according to this interpretation, is this visible reminder of his trespasses against Morella.

There is also the possibility that the narrator murders his daughter, explaining why he sets the baptism ceremony in the family vault—because he can no longer face his actions. He tries to exorcise the spirit of Morella (or, rather, the spirit of his own guilt) by removing the last vestige of her presence, but it doesn't work. A Jungian would say that Morella is the narrator's *anima* figure (the female portion of the male unconscious), which cannot be destroyed without taking the ego (or self) with it (see "Ligeia," note 28).

One can always choose the supernatural interpretation, for Poe does leaves that option. But this does not answer the question of why Morella returns in the body of her daughter only to die again.

In such possibilities of interpretation, I think, lies the enjoyment of reading Poe.

good. What prompted me, then, to disturb the memory of the buried dead? What demon urged me to breathe that sound, which, in its very recollection, was wont to make ebb the purple blood in torrents from the temples to the heart? What fiend spoke from the recesses of my soul, when, amid those dim aisles, and in the silence of the night, I whispered within **28** the ears of the holy man the syllables—Morella? What more than fiend convulsed the features of my child, and overspread them with hues of death, as, starting at that scarcely audible sound, she turned her glassy eyes from the earth to heaven, and, falling prostrate on the black slabs of our ancestral vault, responded—"I am here!"

Distinct, coldly, calmly distinct, fell those few simple sounds within my ear, and thence like molten lead, rolled hissingly into my brain. Years—years may pass away, but the memory of that epoch—never! Nor was I indeed ignorant of the flowers **29** and the vine—but the hemlock and the cypress overshadowed me night and day. And I kept no reckoning of time or place, and the stars of my fate faded from heaven, and therefore the earth grew dark, and its figures passed by me, like flitting shadows, and among them all I beheld only—Morella. The winds of the firmament breathed but one sound within my ears, and the ripples upon the sea murmured evermore— Morella. But she died; and with my own hands I bore her to the tomb; and I laughed with a long and bitter laugh as I found no traces of the first, in the charnel where I laid the **30** second, Morella.

LIGEIA

First published in the Baltimore *American Museum*, September 1838, "Ligeia" is Poe's first undisputed masterpiece and his own personal favorite among his tales. It is also one of his most complex stories, and along with "The Fall of the House of Usher," and "The Masque of the Red Death" has stirred up the most critical controversy over just what it is all about. More on that later.

Sources include Sir Walter Scott's *Ivanhoe* (1820); specifically, the story of Rebecca and Rowena. In Scott's novel, Rebecca is wrongly accused of witchcraft. After her death, Ivanhoe marries Rowena and, we assume, broods over his first wife's death, a possibility that must also have occurred to Poe.

Another source is "A Madman's Manuscript," in Chapter 11 of *The Pickwick Papers*, which Poe reprinted in the *Southern Literary Messenger* in November 1836. The story contains several familiar elements, including a beautiful home, the hero's mental instability, his lack of love for his wife, his contempt for the wife's family for pushing her into a mercenary marriage, and also his inability to remember dates, facts, and incidents.

"I don't remember forms or faces now, but I know the girl was beautiful," Dickens' tale begins. "I *know* she was; for in the bright moonlight nights, when I start up from my sleep, and all is quiet about me, I see, standing still and motionless in one corner of this cell, a slight and wasted figure, with long black hair, which, streaming down her back, stirs with no earthly wind, and eyes that fix their gaze on me, and never wink or close."

The resemblance to "Ligeia" is unmistakable.

"Ligeia" has almost always been one of Poe's most critically acclaimed tales. "The story of the Lady Ligeia," writes George Bernard Shaw, "is not merely one of the wonders of literature: it is unparalleled and unapproached. There is really nothing to be said about it: we others simply take off our hats and let Mr. Poe go first." (*The Recognition of Edgar Allan Poe*, University of Michigan Press, 1966; p. 99)

But while critics agree that "Ligeia" is a masterpiece, few agree on what *happens* in the tale. The most common interpretations include:

1) The entire story takes place just as the narrator tells it; a tale of the supernatural.
2) Ligeia is real, but the narrator has given her qualities no human could possibly possess. His obsession with ultimate knowledge kills Ligeia and Rowena in turn, and causes his hallucination of Ligeia's return.
3) Rowena is real, but Ligeia is merely a figment of the narrator's wishful imagination. He is obsessed with his Ideal to the point where it takes on a life of its own, quite apart from his ability to control it.

The story, as the narrator tells it, is this: Ligeia is a woman possessed not only of genius but of a powerful will. She dies and the narrator remarries, this time to a woman who is the opposite in every respect of Ligeia. His second wife then sickens and dies, and on her bier the spirit of Ligeia momentarily takes over her body. End of tale.

If we take the narrator's word for all this, the tale is clearly supernatural. But *can* we believe him? For, along with his version of events appear some important clues that seem to cast doubt on his reliability. Ligeia is hardly human at all. He knows nothing of her past. He cannot describe her adequately, with the exception of her face, eyes, and hair. He is obsessed with the idea of the immortality of the soul, even though the supposedly willful Ligeia despairs of it on her deathbed. He takes opium. He perversely marries a woman who represents the opposite of everything he has worshiped in Ligeia. He brings his second wife to a room purposely designed to frighten her. He wishes her dead, and she does die, apparently from poison. At the sight of the resurrected Ligeia, horror overcomes him and he shrieks aloud.

So whom—and what—do we believe? If you prefer the supernatural interpretation, Poe has certainly given you enough support. But the nagging question remains: If Ligeia were real, and did in fact return from the dead in Rowena's body, why would Poe set out to make the narrator so totally unreliable? Wouldn't the story be more powerful if we knew for certain that every word was true?

Part of the answer lies in Poe's statement about "directness of expression," quoted in the introductory note to "Berenice." However, that answers only why Poe is not more direct in the tale; it does not answer the question of Ligeia's existence outside the mind of the narrator. Poe, as usual, is not satisfied allowing a good story to get along with only one possible interpretation. "Ligeia" has several levels of meaning, and its ambiguity is part of its appeal.

However, such ambiguity leads to critical interpretations that seem a bit farfetched. For example, Kenneth T. Reed, in *Poe Newsletter*, Vol. IV, p. 20, suggests "Ligeia" is structured on the nineteenth-century pattern of the sermon: 1) the exordium, or metaphysical pronouncement on the human will; 2) the exposition, here the recollection of Ligeia, enlarging the tale as the exemplum of Glanvill's text; 3) the division, here the poetry that classifies the particulars of the central argument; 4) the discussion, which argues, disputes, and proves; and 5) the conclusion, which recapitulates the central theme.

As Julian Symons says in his biography of Poe, *The Tell-Tale Heart* (Harper & Row, 1978) "Poe has become in these twenty years a fine academic property, whose works can be expounded and argued about endlessly in American Studies courses" (p. 231). The theories that result, he points out, do not so much explain the tales as explain them away. "This is partly because vagueness of meaning combined with particularity of detail mark Poe's finest work, and any attempt to clarify that vagueness runs the risk of damaging a story. It is also, however, because Poe knew only partly what he was doing" (p. 239).

Very well: the notes that follow may run the risk of damaging the story, but in the end it is still the reader who must make up his mind.

Roger Corman produced and directed a 1964 version of the tale called *The Tomb of Ligeia* (also known as *The House at the End of the World*, *Ligeia*, and *Last Tomb of Ligeia*), starring Vincent Price, Elizabeth Shepherd, John Westbrook, and Derek Francis. The film is closer to the spirit, if not the letter, of Poe than are most other adaptations of his work.

A recorded version, read by Martin Donegan, is available (CMS 653).

---

1 Joseph Glanvill (1636–80) was famous for his treatises in favor of the new science, as well as for religious works. This passage, however, has puzzled scholars for years. There is no trace of it in Glanvill's known writings, and so Poe may have simply made it up, ascribing it to a man who believed in the notion of spiritual manifestations and the eternity of the soul. He uses an actual Glanvill quote for "A Descent into the Maelström."

2 The facts that the events related took place a long time ago and that the narrator has undergone much mental suffering since, again strains our reliance on his accuracy. One way to approach "Ligeia" (and most of Poe's other tales) is as a dramatic monologue in which the speaker begins with an established viewpoint and is not really interested in self-analysis or in the truth, but in trying to impress his view upon the outside world. Thus meaning lies in what is implied, rather than in what is stated. Robert Browning is the great master of the dramatic monologue, in such poems as *My Last Duchess* and *The Bishop Orders His Tomb*.

3 The setting is in the German Gothic tradition, from which Poe (and other romantics) borrowed freely. The

And the will therein lieth, which dieth not. Who knoweth the mysteries of the will, with its vigor? For God is but a great will pervading all things by nature of its intentness. Man doth not yield himself to the angels, nor unto death utterly, save only through the weakness of his feeble will.

1

—*Joseph Glanvill.*

I cannot, for my soul, remember how, when or even precisely where, I first became acquainted with the lady Ligeia. Long years have since elapsed, and my memory is feeble through **2** much suffering. Or, perhaps, I cannot *now* bring these points to mind, because, in truth, the character of my beloved, her rare learning, her singular yet placid cast of beauty, and the thrilling and enthralling eloquence of her low musical language, made their way into my heart by paces so steadily and stealthily progressive that they have been unnoticed and unknown. Yet I believe that I met her first and most frequently **3** in some large, old, decaying city near the Rhine. Of her family—I have surely heard her speak. That it is of a remotely ancient date cannot be doubted. Ligeia! Ligeia! Buried in studies of a nature more than all else adapted to deaden impressions of the outward world, it is by that sweet word alone—by Ligeia—that I bring before mine eyes in fancy the image of her who is no more. And now, while I write, a recollection flashes upon me that I have *never known* the paternal name of her who was my friend and my betrothed, and who became the partner of my studies, and finally the wife of my bosom. Was it a playful charge on the part of my **4** Ligeia? or was it a test of my strength of affection, that I should institute no inquiries upon this point? or was it rather a caprice of my own—a wildly romantic offering on the shrine of the most passionate devotion? I but indistinctly recall the fact itself—what wonder that I have utterly forgotten the circumstances which originated or attended it? And, indeed, if ever that spirit which is entitled *Romance*—if ever she, the wan and the misty-winged *Ashtophet* of idolatrous Egypt, **5** presided, as they tell, over marriages ill-omened, then most surely she presided over mine.

There is one dear topic, however, on which my memory fails me not. It is the *person* of Ligeia. In stature she was tall, somewhat slender, and, in her latter days, even emaciated. I would in vain attempt to portray the majesty, the quiet ease, of her demeanor, or the incomprehensible lightness and elasticity of her footfall. She came and departed as a shadow. I was never made aware of her entrance into my closed study save by the dear music of her low sweet voice, as she placed her marble hand upon my shoulder. In beauty of face no **6** maiden ever equalled her. It was the radiance of an opium dream—an airy and spirit-lifting vision more wildy divine than **7** the phantasies which hovered about the slumbering souls of the daughters of Delos. Yet her features were not of that **8** regular mould which we have been falsely taught to worship in the classical labors of the heathen. "There is no exquisite beauty," says Bacon, Lord Verulam, speaking truly of all the forms and *genera* of beauty, "without some *strangeness* in the proportion." Yet, although I saw that the features of Ligeia **9** were not of a classic regularity—although I perceived that her loveliness was indeed "exquisite," and felt that there was much of "strangeness" pervading it, yet I have tried in vain to detect the irregularity and to trace home my own perception of "the strange." I examined the contour of the lofty and pale forehead—it was faultless—how cold indeed that word when **10** applied to a majesty so divine!—the skin rivalling the purest ivory, the commanding extent and repose, the gentle prominence of the regions above the temples; and then the raven- **11** black, the glossy, the luxuriant and naturally-curling tresses, setting forth the full force of the Homeric epithet, "hyacin- thine!" I looked at the delicate outlines of the nose—and **12** nowhere but in the graceful medallions of the Hebrews had **13** I beheld a similar perfection. There were the same luxurious smoothness of surface, the same scarcely perceptible tendency to the aquiline, the same harmoniously curved nostrils speak-

tales of E. T. A. Hoffmann and the early Gothic novels such as *The Castle of Otranto* (1765) provided its stock-in-trade: haunted castles and gloomy abbeys; thunderstorms; maidens in distress; shadowy corridors; oriental decor; ghostly apparitions; the Black Arts; and trappings of decay, darkness, and isolation. To mention Germany was almost enough to set the mood of a tale.

Poe was quick to disassociate himself from these Germanic props, and in reply to critics who charged him with shallowness, replied that the terror in his work was "not of Germany, but of the soul." In other words, he was more interested in the *psychology* of terror, the workings of the human mind under stress.

4 The vagueness of his recollection could be a clue that Ligeia is a product of his distorted consciousness. On the other hand, she may have refused to tell him her name because, as a sorceress, she knew that to divulge her name would grant him power over her.

Ligeia is a dryad in Virgil's *Georgics*, IV, 336, and one of the Sirens in Milton's *Comus*, line 880. The name probably comes from the Greek *ligys*, meaning highsounding, clear-toned, or shrill.

5 A goddess of the Sidonians, she was also known as Ashtoreth, Astarte, or Ishtar, the goddess of love to the civilizations of the ancient Mediterranean. The Egyptians honored the Phoenician Ashtoreth as a fertility goddess.

She has also been identified with Isis (the Greek rendering of the Egyptian Aset), who in turn was confused with Athyr, or Hathor, the Egyptian deity whom the Greeks identified with Aphrodite.

6 She sounds like a statue—or a corpse.

7 The early romantics were fascinated by opium, which they thought would gain them inspiration and insight, as well as open up new and often inexplicable vistas into the Unknown. It was this which drove Thomas De Quincey (1785–1859), author of *Confessions of an English Opium Eater* (1822). While in withdrawal from the drug (taken as laudanum, opium mixed with alcohol), he had the grotesque and terrifying dreams that he wove into his literary fantasies.

Coleridge tells us that *Kubla Khan* came to him in a dream after taking an "anodyne"—that is, a painkiller, which at the time could only have been opium.

There is no hard evidence that Poe used drugs, let alone used them frequently, although he was obviously aware of the effects of opium.

8 Delos is a Greek island in the Cyclades, the mythological birthplace of the twins Apollo and Artemis. Artemis was waited upon by maidens sworn to chastity, the "daughters of Delos."

". . . her face was an angel's. Oh! lovelier far than the visions of the Carian, or the shapes that floated before the eyes of the daughters of Delos" is from Bulwer-Lytton's "A Manuscript Found in a Madhouse," in *Conversations with an Ambitious Student*.

9 A reference to the *Essayes* (1625) of Francis Bacon (1561–1626). However, in "Of Beauty," Bacon uses the word "excellent," not "exquisite."

10 The description of Ligeia owes much to phrenology, a theory that maintained that the various mental faculties are situated in different parts of the head and that the development of each can be judged by the shape of the skull overlying its particular position. The theory was first proposed about 1800 by Franz Joseph Gall and popularized in the United States by Orson and Lorenzo Fowler.

11 In phrenology, the frontal region, behind the forehead, indicates intellect and Perception, the latter meaning the ability to observe both outward and inward. A "gentle prominence" indicates an area of strength; thus Ligeia shows a well-developed intellect and perception, as well as a love of life.

To one side of the forehead is the region of Ideality (appreciation of the beautiful and refined) and Sublimity (appreciation of the grand and awe-inspiring). See "Berenice," note 33.

12 A word that has much appeal to Poe (he uses it in _To Helen,_ among other works), the meaning doesn't refer to the color or scent of the hyacinth but to the convoluted texture and shape of the petals. The Homeric reference is to the _Odyssey,_ VI, 231, "locks like the hyacinthine flower." Milton uses the word, as does Pope, to mean curling hair. (See "The Assignation," note 21)

13 Perhaps referring to Hebrew coins, since Poe seems to favor the lines of the Hebraic nose to those of the Roman (which is straight from the bridge down). He must not have known that Jewish shekels had no human outlines on them.

14 The obsessive dwelling on Ligeia's features is another indication of the narrator's instability.

Novelist Richard Wright, who read Poe eagerly as a child and into adulthood, echoes this passage in his first story, "Superstition," when he describes Lillian, a beautiful yet somehow disembodied consumptive: "Her narrow face, pale and emaciated, attracted me. Her hair was brushed backward and revealed a broad, bulging forehead, below which, shining in contrast to her pallid features, were a pair of dark, sunken eyes. The most unusual thing about her was a timid and perpetual smile, a smile that seemed melancholy and slightly cynical. A peculiar air of resignation pervaded her whole being." (_Abbot's Monthly,_ April 1931, p. 46). See also "The Black Cat," note 25.

15 The Venus de' Medici bears the signature of Cleomenes, but it is generally assumed to be a late forgery (see "The Assignation," note 46). Apollo, the patron of the arts, is suggested here as the sculptor's inspiration, and Poe may have heard a story that the statue was created in a vision.

16 Eyes are traditionally the mirror of the soul, and the window to the workings of the mind. The eye sees outwardly and inwardly. When we look at anything, the object is reflected on the retina as on a mirror; but, in deep contemplation, the inward thought provides the image "in the mind's eye."

17 _The History of Nourjahad,_ by Sidney Bidulph, was an oriental romance actually written by Frances Sheridan (1724–66), published in 1767 and still popular in Poe's day. "All parts of the earth shall be explored for women of the most exquisite beauty" is from the 1767 Dublin edition, p. 34.

18 Poe followed Coleridge in making a distinction between Fancy and Imagination, although he carried the idea much farther. Imagination was the true artist's province, while Fancy could not lead to real art. Thus when the word "fancy" appears in one of Poe's tales, we may interpret it as indicating a confused perception. (See "The Assignation," note 3).

ing the free spirit. I regarded the sweet mouth. Here was indeed the triumph of all things, heavenly—the magnificent turn of the short upper lip—the soft, voluptuous slumber of the under—the dimples which sported, and the color which spoke—the teeth glancing back, with a brilliancy almost startling, every ray of the holy light which fell upon them in her serene and placid, yet most exultingly radiant of all smiles.

14 I scrutinized the formation of the chin—and here, too, I found the gentleness of breadth, the softness and the majesty, the fullness and the spirituality, of the Greek—the contour which **15** the god Apollo revealed but in a dream, to Cleomenes, the son of the Athenian. And then I peered into the large eyes of **16** Ligeia.

For eyes we have no models in the remotely antique. It might have been, too, that in these eyes of my beloved lay the secret to which Lord Verulam alludes. They were, I must believe, far larger than the ordinary eyes of our own race. They were even fuller than the fullest of the gazelle eyes of **17** the tribe of the valley of Nourjahad. Yet it was only at intervals—in moments of intense excitement—that this peculiarity became more than slightly noticeable in Ligeia. And **18** at such moments was her beauty—in my heated fancy thus it appeared perhaps—the beauty of beings either above or apart **19** from the earth—the beauty of the fabulous Houri of the Turk. The hue of the orbs was the most brilliant of black, and, far over them, hung jetty lashes of great length. The brows, slightly irregular in outline, had the same tint. The "strangeness," however, which I found in the eyes, was of a nature distinct from the formation, or the color, or the brilliancy of the features, and must, after all, be referred to the _expression_. Ah, word of no meaning! behind whose vast latitude of mere sound we intrench our ignorance of so much of the spiritual. The expression of the eyes of Ligeia! How for long hours have I pondered upon it! How have I, through the whole of a midsummer night, struggled to fathom it! What was it—that **20** something more profound than the well of Democritus—which lay far within the pupils of my beloved? What _was_ it? I was possessed with a passion to discover. Those eyes! those large, those shining, those divine orbs! they became to me twin stars **21** of Leda, and I to them devoutest of astrologers.

There is no point, among the many incomprehensible anomalies of the science of mind, more thrillingly exciting than the fact—never, I believe, noticed in the schools—that, in our endeavors to recall to memory something long forgotten, we often find ourselves _upon the very verge_ of remembrance, **22** without being able, in the end, to remember. And thus how frequently, in my intense scrutiny of Ligeia's eyes, have I felt approaching the full knowledge of their expression—felt it approaching—yet not quite be mine—and so at length entirely depart! And (strange, oh strangest mystery of all!) I found, in the commonest objects of the universe, a circle of analogies to that expression. I mean to say that, subsequently to the period when Ligeia's beauty passed into my spirit, there dwelling as in a shrine, I derived, from many existences in the material world, a sentiment such as I felt always aroused within me by her large and luminous orbs. Yet not the more could I define that sentiment, or analyze, or even steadily view it. I recognized it, let me repeat, sometimes in the survey of a rapidly-growing vine—in the contemplation of a moth, a butterfly, a chrysalis, a stream of running water. I have felt it in the ocean; in the falling of a meteor. I have felt it in the glances of unusually aged people. And there are one **23** or two stars in heaven—(one especially, a star of the sixth magnitude, double and changeable, to be found near the large star in Lyra) in a telescopic scrutiny of which I have been **24** made aware of the feeling. I have been filled with it by certain sounds from stringed instruments, and not unfrequently by passages from books. Among innumerable other instances, I well remember something in a volume of Joseph Glanvill, which (perhaps merely from its quaintness—who shall say?) never failed to inspire me with the sentiment;—"And the will therein lieth, which dieth not. Who knoweth the mysteries of the will, with its vigor? For God is but a great will pervading all things by nature of its intentness. Man doth not yield him to the angels, nor unto death utterly, save only through the weakness of his feeble will." **25**

Length of years, and subsequent reflection, have enabled me to trace, indeed, some remote connection between this passage in the English moralist and a portion of the character of Ligeia. An *intensity* in thought, action, or speech, was possibly, in her, a result, or at least an index, of that gigantic volition which, during our long intercourse, failed to give other and more immediate evidence of its existence. Of all the women whom I have ever known, she, the outwardly calm, the ever-placid Ligeia, was the most violently a prey to the tumultuous vultures of stern passion. And of such passion **26** I could form no estimate, save by the miraculous expansion of those eyes which at once so delighted and appalled me—by the almost magical melody, modulation, distinctness and placidity of her very low voice—and by the fierce energy (rendered doubly effective by contrast with her manner of utterance) of the wild words which she habitually uttered.

I have spoken of the learning of Ligeia; it was immense—such as I have never known in woman. In the classical tongues **27** was she deeply proficient, and as far as my own acquaintance extended in regard to the modern dialects of Europe, I have never known her at fault. Indeed upon any theme of the most admired, because simply the most abstruse of the boasted erudition of the academy, have I *ever* found Ligeia at fault? How singularly—how thrillingly, this one point in the nature of my wife has forced itself, at this late period only, upon my attention! I said her knowledge was such as I have never known in woman—but where breathes the man who has traversed, and successfully, *all* the wide areas of moral, physical, and mathematical science? I saw not then what I now clearly perceive, that the acquisitions of Ligeia were gigantic, were astounding; yet I was sufficiently aware of her infinite supremacy to resign myself, with a child-like confidence, to her guidance through the chaotic world of meta-physical investigation at which I was most busily occupied

19 A nymph of the Mohammedan paradise, the word comes from the Arabic word meaning black-eyed. The passages in the Koran that detail the delights of heaven have been called merely allegorical by many Moslem scholars.

20 Democritus (460–370 B.C.) said that "truth lies at the bottom of a well." A materialist, he believed that the soul was made of matter and that "in reality there is nothing but atoms and space."

21 The two bright stars of the constellation Gemini are Castor and Pollux, named for the twin sons of the mortal Leda and the god Zeus, who impregnated her while she had the shape of a swan (they did things the hard way in those days).
"... the Ledean stars, so famed for love" is quoted from Cowley in Isaac D'Israeli's *Curiosities of Literature*, in the section "Literary Friendships."

22 "Upon the very verge of remembrance" is reminiscent of Jung's collective unconscious, which all mankind shares, or of the knowledge that our soul has before we are born but that is lost after birth, according to Wordsworth's *Ode on the Intimations of Immortality*. (See "Berenice," note 8.)

23 The list here reflects the mysteries of birth, life, and death, and in particular the life force itself.

24 Lyra contains two double stars. The brightest is Vega, or Alpha Lyrae. The second, lower and to the left, is Epsilon Lyrae, which changes intensity, and as the narrator points out, can be seen only through a telescope. (See "Mellonta Tauta," note 48.)

25 Note that it is the narrator, and not Ligeia, who first expresses an obsession with the Glanvill quotation.

26 The narrator *says* that Ligeia is prey to violent passion, yet she never shows it outwardly. One wonders how much he is reading into her demeanor, or, for that matter, whether this is another sign that this unreal woman lives only in his fancies.

27 Although the narrator believes in Ligeia's all-encompassing knowledge, we know from Poe's view of existence that this is impossible. Ultimate knowledge in Poe leads only to destruction. If she *does* exist, then it must be as a real human being, of perhaps above-normal intelligence, but with the same needs as any human. The narrator's refusal to acknowledge this may be either a sign of his willful use of her to gain knowledge for himself, or a projection onto Ligeia of his obsessive demands of perfection.
Her one flaw—as far as the narrator is concerned—is her mortality, a theme that Hawthorne also pursued, in such tales as "The Birthmark" and "Rappaccini's Daughter."

28 Ligeia recalls the Jungian *anima*, that personification of all female psychological tendencies in a man's psyche—more specifically, one who (like the Virgin Mary) raises love (*eros*) to the heights of spiritual devotion, or the wisdom anima, whose knowledge transcends even the most holy and the most pure.

She also resembles the sibyls of ancient mythology (see "MS. Found in a Bottle," note 45), who fathomed divine will and acted as intermediaries with the gods.

29 Saturn is a poetic name for Italy (Virgil, *Georgics*, II, 173) as well as for lead in ancient alchemy and chemistry. Italian lead is graphite, which is very dull. "Lambent" means softly bright or radiant.

30 In Muslim and Hebrew mythology, the Angel of Death. The Hebrew word means "help of God." In the Koran, the angel severs the soul from the body. He will be the last to die, but will do so at the second trumpet call of the archangel.

31 Dependency is the enemy of love. He feels inferior to her and at the same time sees in her a means to the knowledge he craves. "What does she see in me?" he asks—and so might the reader.

32 "It is easy to see why each man kills the thing he loves. To *know* a living thing is to kill it. You have to kill a thing to know it satisfactorily. For this reason, the desirous consciousness, the SPIRIT, is a vampire."

"One should be sufficiently intelligent and interested to know a good deal *about* any person one comes into close contact with. *About* her. Or *about* him."

"But to try to *know* any living being is to try to suck the life out of that being." (D. H. Lawrence, "Edgar Allan Poe," in *Studies in Classic American Literature*, 1964; p. 70)

(See also "William Wilson," note 16.)

28 during the earlier years of our marriage. With how vast a triumph—with how vivid a delight—with how much of all that is ethereal in hope—did I *feel*, as she bent over me in studies but little sought—but less known—that delicious vista by slow degrees expanding before me, down whose long, gorgeous, and all untrodden path, I might at length pass onward to the goal of a wisdom too divinely precious not to be forbidden!

How poignant, then, must have been the grief with which, after some years, I beheld my well-grounded expectations take wings to themselves and fly away! Without Ligeia I was but as a child groping benighted. Her presence, her readings alone, rendered vividly luminous the many mysteries of the transcendentalism in which we were immersed, Wanting the radiant lustre of her eyes, letters, lambent and golden, grew **29** duller than Saturnian lead. And now those eyes shone less and less frequently upon the pages over which I pored. Ligeia grew ill. The wild eyes blazed with a too—too glorious effulgence; the pale fingers became of the transparent waxen hue of the grave, and the blue veins upon the lofty forehead swelled and sank impetuously with the tides of the most gentle emotion. I saw that she must die—and I struggled desperately **30** in spirit with the grim Azrael. And the struggles of the passionate wife were, to my astonishment, even more energetic than my own. There had been much in her stern nature to impress me with the belief that, to her, death would have come without its terrors;—but not so. Words are impotent to convey any just idea of the fierceness of resistance with which she wrestled with the Shadow. I groaned in anguish at the pitiable spectacle. I would have soothed—I would have reasoned; but, in the intensity of her wild desire for life—for life—*but* for life—solace and reason were alike the uttermost of folly. Yet not until the last instance, amid the most convulsive writhings of her fierce spirit, was shaken the external placidity of her demeanor. Her voice grew more gentle—grew more low—yet I would not wish to dwell upon the wild meaning of the quietly uttered words. My brain reeled as I hearkened entranced, to a melody more than mortal—to assumptions and aspirations which mortality had never before known.

31 That she loved me I should not have doubted; and I might have been easily aware that, in a bosom such as hers, love would have reigned no ordinary passion. But in death only, **32** was I fully impressed with the strength of her affection. For long hours, detaining my hand, would she pour out before me the overflowing of a heart whose more than passionate devotion amounted to idolatry. How had I deserved to be so blessed by such confessions?—how had I deserved to be so cursed with the removal of my beloved in the hour of her making them? But upon this subject I cannot bear to dilate. Let me say only, that in Ligeia's more than womanly abandonment to a love, alas! all unmerited, all unworthily bestowed, I at length recognized the principle of her longing with so wildly earnest a desire for the life which was now fleeing so rapidly away. It is this wild longing—it is this eager vehemence of desire for life—*but* for life—that I have no power to portray—no utterance capable of expressing.

At high noon of the night in which she departed, beckoning me, peremptorily, to her side, she bade me repeat certain verses composed by herself not many days before. I obeyed her.—They were these: **33**

> Lo! 't is a gala night
>   Within the lonesome latter years!
> An angel throng, bewinged, bedight
>   In veils, and drowned in tears,
> Sit in a theatre, to see
>   A play of hopes and fears,
> While the orchestra breathes fitfully
>   The music of the spheres.   **34**
>
> Mimes, in the form of God on high,
>   Mutter and mumble low,
> And hither and thither fly—
>   Mere puppets they, who come and go   **35**
> At bidding of vast formless things
>   That shift the scenery to and fro,
> Flapping from out their Condor wings
>   Invisible Wo!

I struggled desperately in spirit with the grim Azrael.
Illustration by F. S. Coburn for Century Magazine, *1903*

33 *The Conqueror Worm* was not part of the tale when it was first published. The poem appeared separately in *Graham's Magazine* in January 1843 and was first incorporated into the tale in 1845, in the *Broadway Journal*, September 27. It seems to have been inserted after Poe found that Ligeia's return suggested too strongly her success at escaping death, for the poem suggests otherwise.

The Russian composer Mikhail Fabianovich Gniessin (1883–1957) wrote a work for symphony orchestra and chorus based on the poem.

34 "Music from [of] the spheres" appears in *Twelfth Night*, III, i, and *Pericles*, V, i, as well as in the *Religio Medici* (Part II, 9) of Sir Thomas Browne (1605–82).

35 The metaphor of life as a play with the actors controlled by the script of fate was a popular Renaissance motif.

> The World's a theatre, the earth a stage
> Which God and Nature do with actors fill.
> (Thomas Heywood, *Apology for Actors* [1612])

> All the world's a stage,
> And all the men and women merely players:
> They have their exits and their entrances;
> And one man in his time plays many parts. . . .
>
>   (*As You Like It*, II, vii, 139)

> Life's but a walking shadow, a poor player
> That struts and frets his hour upon the stage
> Ans then is heard no more.
>
>   (*Macbeth*, V, v, 17)

That motley drama!—oh, be sure
  It shall not be forgot!
With its Phantom chased forevermore,
  By a crowd that seize it not,
Through a circle that ever returneth in
  To the self-same spot,
And much of Madness and more of Sin,
  And Horror the soul of the plot.

But see, amid the mimic rout,
  A crawling shape intrude!
A blood-red thing that writhes from out
  The scenic solitude!
It writhes!—it writhes!—with mortal pangs
  The mimes become its food,
And the seraphs sob at vermin fangs
  In human gore imbued.

Out—out are the lights—out all!
  And over each quivering form,
The curtain, a funeral pall,
  Comes down with the rush of a storm,
And the angels, all pallid and wan,
  Uprising, unveiling, affirm
That the play is the tragedy, "Man,"
  And its hero the Conqueror Worm.

36 "And though after my skin worms destroy this body, yet in my flesh shall I see God" (Job 19:26).

> No longer mourn for me when I am dead
> Than you shall hear the surly bell
> Give warning to the world that I am fled
> From this vile world, with vilest worms to dwell.
> [Shakespeare, Sonnet 71]

36

"Man doth not yield him to the angels, nor unto death utterly, save only through the weakness of his feeble will." *Illustration by F. S. Coburn for* Century Magazine, *1903*

"O God!" half shrieked Ligeia, leaping to her feet and extending her arms aloft with a spasmodic movement, as I made an end of these lines—"O God! O Divine Father!—shall these things be undeviatingly so?—shall this Conqueror be not one conquered? Are we not part and parcel in Thee? **37** Who—who knoweth the mysteries of the will with its vigor? Man doth not yield him to the angels *not unto death utterly,* save only through the weakness of his feeble will."

And now, as if exhausted with emotion, she suffered her white arms to fall, and returned solemnly to her bed of Death. And as she breathed her last sighs, there came mingled with them a low murmur from her lips. I bent to them my ear and distinguished, again, the concluding words of the passage in Glanvill—"*Man doth not yield him to the angels, nor unto death utterly, save only through the weakness of his feeble will.*"

She died;—and I, crushed into the very dust with sorrow, could no longer endure the lonely desolation of my dwelling in the dim and decaying city by the Rhine. I had no lack of what the world calls wealth. Ligeia had brought me far more, very far more than ordinarily falls to the lot of mortals. After a few months, therefore, of weary and aimless wandering, I purchased, and put in some repair, an abbey, which I shall not name, in one of the wildest and least frequented portions of fair England. The gloomy and dreary grandeur of the **38** building, the almost savage aspect of the domain, the many melancholy and time-honored memories connected with both, had much in unison with the feelings of utter abandonment which had driven me into that remote and unsocial region of the country. Yet although the external abbey, with its verdant decay hanging about it, suffered but little alteration, I gave way, with a child-like perversity, and perchance with a faint hope of alleviating my sorrows, to a display of more than regal magnificence within.—For such follies, even in childhood, I had imbibed a taste and now they came back to me as if in the dotage of grief. Alas, I feel how much even of incipient madness might have been discovered in the gorgeous and fantastic draperies, in the solemn carvings of Egypt, in the wild cornices and furniture, in the Bedlam-patterns of the **39** carpets of tufted gold! I had become a bounden slave in the trammels of opium, and my labors and my orders had taken a coloring from my dreams. But these absurdities I must not pause to detail. Let me speak only of that one chamber, every accursed, whither in a moment of mental alienation, I led from the altar as my bride—as the successor of the unforgotten Ligeia—the fair-haired and blue-eyed Lady Rowena Trevanion, of Tremaine.

There is no individual portion of the architecture and decoration of that bridal chamber which is not now visibly before me. Where were the souls of the haughty family of the bride, when, through thirst of gold, they permitted to pass the threshold of an apartment *so* bedecked, a maiden and a daughter so beloved? I have said that I minutely remember **40** the details of the chamber—yet I am sadly forgetful on topics

37 Ligeia has her doubts about immortality, even if the narrator fails to get the message.

38 Gothic literature also moved from Germany to England, where it had a warm reception.

39 See "Hans Pfaall," note 1.

40 That the narrator has already planned Rowena's death is suggested by his statement that her family would not have allowed the wedding to take place if they had known his intent.

41 An understatement, to be sure. It is typical of a great many of Poe's narrators that they are obsessed with details of their surroundings but cannot come to grips with the larger and more personal human elements.

42 Five-sided figures have traditionally been considered to have magical properties, and appear in many old spells, although not as pentagons, but as pentacles—five-pointed stars. Poe may also have wanted to stress the bizarre shape of the room, which is already a mass of strange decor.

According to J. C. Cooper, "The pentagon, being endless, shares the symbolism of the perfection and power of the circle," reminding us of the narrator's obsession with perfection. "Five is the marriage number . . . as the combination of the feminine, even, number two and the masculine, odd, three." Since this is the marriage-bed room, this interpretation is also worth considering.

The number five is also, variously, a symbol of the alchemic quintessence, Venus, the five qualities of Apollo (omnipotence, omniscience, omnipresence, eternity, unity), light, and the microcosm (in five-petaled flowers and five-pointed stars) (An Illustrated Encyclopaedia of Traditional Symbols, Thames & Hudson, 1978).

J. E. Cirlot says that the pentagon, or rather the number five, "traditionally . . . symbolizes man after the fall" and is "symbolic of the whole of the material world" and "the order of the cosmos" (A Dictionary of Symbols, Routledge, 1962).

43 Murano, a town on several small islands in the lagoon of Venice, was the center of the Venetian glass industry as early as the thirteenth century. The art was revived again in Poe's time.

44 "Saracen" was a medieval term for Arab, and by extension, Moslems in general. Strictly speaking, the terms applied only to the people of northwestern Arabia, who held Sicily and parts of southern Italy in the ninth to eleventh centuries. Palermo and Monreale have some excellent examples of the fused architectural styles of the Saracens, Byzantines, and Normans.

The word also recalls Poe's word "Arabesque," which he used to define his horor tales, after the bizarre twisting and turning patterns of Moslem decoration (see "Metzengerstein," note 13).

45 Occupying part of the site of Thebes, the temple of Luxor is the greatest monument of antiquity in the city. Built in the reign of Amenhotep III, it was much altered by later pharaohs, especially Ramses II.

Poe's fascination with Egypt (see "Some Words with a Mummy," and "Shadow") reflects the widespread interest of the period, spurred on by the deciphering of the Rosetta Stone by Jean François Champollion (1790–1832).

46 Arabesque figures, in the strict sense of the word, must be abstract, since Islamic law bans representational images. However, Poe here indicates they *are* representational—"ghastly forms"—meaning that the word is used only for its associational sense, or that Poe is as ignorant of one Semitic religion as he is of the other (see note 13).

47 The Normans (or Norsemen) invaded England and Normandy in the tenth and eleventh centuries, and struck terror in the hearts of the inhabitants of those areas, spurred on by what seemed to the defenders to be bloodthirsty gods.

"I told her that I was more hideous than the demons

41 of deep moment—and here there was no system, no keeping, in the fantastic display, to take hold upon the memory. The room lay in a high turret of the castellated abbey, was **42** pentagonal in shape, and of capacious size. Occupying the whole southern face of the pentagon was the sole window—an **43** immense sheet of unbroken glass from Venice—a single pane, and tinted of a leaden hue, so that the rays of either the sun or moon, passing through it, fell with a ghastly lustre on the objects within. Over the upper portion of this huge window, extended the trellice-work of an aged vine, which clambered up the massy walls of the turret. The ceiling, of gloomy-looking oak, was excessively lofty, vaulted, and elaborately fretted with the wildest and most grotesque specimens of a semi-Gothic, semi-Druidical device. From out the most central recess of this melancholy vaulting, depended, by a single chain of gold with long links, a huge censer of the same metal, **44** Saracenic in pattern, and with many perforations so contrived that there writhed in and out of them, as if endued with a serpent vitality, a continual succession of parti-colored fires.

Some few ottomans and golden candelabra, of Eastern figure, were in various stations about—and there was the couch, too—the bridal couch—of an Indian model, and low, and sculptured of solid ebony, with a pall-like canopy above. In each of the angles of the chamber stood on end a gigantic sarcophagus of black granite, from the tombs of the kings over **45** against Luxor, with their aged lids full of immemorial sculpture. But in the draping of the apartment lay, alas! the chief phantasy of all. The lofty walls, gigantic in height—even unproportionably so—were hung from summit to foot, in vast folds, with a heavy and massive-looking tapestry—tapestry of a material which was found alike as a carpet on the floor, as a covering for the ottomans and the ebony bed, as a canopy for the bed, and as the gorgeous volutes of the curtains which partially shaded the window. The material was the richest cloth of gold. It was spotted all over, at irregular intervals, **46** with arabesque figures, about a foot in diameter, and wrought upon the cloth in patterns of the most jetty black. But these figures partook of the true character of the arabesque only when regarded from a single point of view. By a contrivance now common, and indeed traceable to a very remote period of antiquity, they were made changeable in aspect. To one entering the room, they bore the appearance of simple monstrosities; but upon a farther advance, this appearance gradually departed; and step by step, as the visiter moved his station in the chamber, he saw himself surrounded by an endless succession of the ghastly forms which belong to the **47** superstition of the Norman, or arise in the guilty slumbers of **48** the monk. The phantasmagoric effect was vastly heightened by the artificial introduction of a strong continual current of wind behind the draperies—giving a hideous and uneasy animation to the whole.

In halls such as these—in a bridal chamber such as this—I passed, with the Lady of Tremaine, the unhallowed hours of the first month of our marriage—passed them with but little disquietude. That my wife dreaded the fierce moodiness of my temper—that she shunned me and loved me but little—I could not help perceiving; but it gave me rather pleasure than otherwise. I loathed her with a hatred belonging more to demon than to man. My memory flew back, (oh, with what **49** intensity of regret!) to Ligeia, the beloved, the august, the beautiful, the entombed. I revelled in recollections of her purity, of her wisdom, of her lofty, her ethereal nature, of her passionate, her idolatrous love. Now, then, did my spirit fully and freely burn with more than all the fires of her own. In the excitement of my opium dreams (for I was habitually fettered in the shackles of the drug) I would call aloud upon her name, during the silence of the night, or among the sheltered recesses of the glens by day, as if, through the wild eagerness, the solemn passion, the consuming ardor of my longing for the departed, I could restore her to the pathway she had abandoned—ah, *could* it be forever?—upon the earth.

About the commencement of the second month of the marriage, the Lady Rowena was attacked with sudden illness, from which her recovery was slow. The fever which consumed her rendered her nights uneasy; and in her perturbed state of half-slumber, she spoke of sounds, and of motions, in and about the chamber of the turret, which I concluded had no origin save in the distemper of her fancy, or perhaps in the phantasmagoric influences of the chamber itself. She became **50** at length convalescent—finally well. Yet but a brief period elapsed, ere a second more violent disorder again threw her upon a bed of suffering; and from this attack her frame, at all times feeble, never altogether recovered. Her illnesses were, after this epoch, of alarming character, and of more alarming recurrence, defying alike the knowledge and the great exertions of her physicians. With the increase of the chronic disease which had thus, apparently, taken too sure hold upon her constitution to be eradicated by human means, I could not fail to observe a similar increase in the nervous irritation of her temperament, and in her excitability by trivial causes of fear. She spoke again, and now more frequently and pertinaciously of the sounds—of the slight sounds—and of the unusual motions among the tapestries, to which she had formerly alluded.

One night, near the closing in of September, she pressed this distressing subject with more than usual emphasis upon my attention. She had just awakened from an unquiet slumber, and I had been watching, with feelings half of anxiety, half of vague terror, the workings of her emaciated countenance. I sat by the side of her ebony bed, upon one of the ottomans of India. She partly arose, and spoke, in an earnest low whisper, of sounds which she *then* heard, but which I could not hear—of motions which she *then* saw, but which I could not perceive. The wind was rushing hurriedly behind the tapestries, and I wished to show her (what, let me confess it, I could not *all* believe) that those almost inarticulate breathings, and those very gentle variations of the figures upon the wall, were but the natural effects of that customary rushing

which the image of a Northern savage ever bodied forth" (Bulwer-Lytton's "Manuscript Found in a Madhouse").

As for the monk's guilty slumber, it might be a case of overindulgence, a break with the vows of celebacy, or merely reference to the Gothic literary fixture of the mad monk.

48 This lovely Poesque word has a fascinating history all its own. It comes from two Greek words meaning "illusion" and "place of assembly," coined for an exhibition of optical illusions produced for the most part by slide projection and first shown by a man named Philipstal in London in 1802.

In the Phantasmagoria, the projected figures on the screen increased and decreased in size, advanced and retreated, dissolved, vanished, and passed into one another in a way that most spectators thought marvelous and mystifying.

The word soon came to mean any bizarre and dreamlike apparition.

49 His loathing for Rowena stems from her earthliness. She contradicts his ideal by her very existence, and cannot provide him with the same fantastic hope of ultimate knowledge that Ligeia did. What woman could?

50 Rowena may be hallucinating, under the influence of some drug or the victim of slowly increasing doses of poison.

of the wind. But a deadly pallor, overspreading her face, had proved to me that my exertion to reassure her would be fruitless. She appeared to be fainting, and no attendants were within call. I remembered where was deposited a decanter of light wine which had been ordered by her physicians, and hastened across the chamber to procure it. But, as I stepped beneath the light of the censer, two circumstances of a startling nature attracted my attention. I had felt that some palpable although invisible object had passed lightly by my person; and I saw that there lay upon the golden carpet, in the very middle of the rich lustre thrown from the censer, a shadow—a faint, indefinite shadow of angelic aspect—such as might be fancied for the shadow of a shade. But I was wild with the excitement of an immoderate dose of opium, and heeded these things but little, nor spoke of them to Rowena. Having found the wine, I recrossed the chamber, and poured out a goblet-ful, which I held to the lips of the fainting lady. She had now partially recovered, however, and took the vessel herself, while I sank upon an ottoman near me, with my eyes fastened upon her person. It was then that I became distinctly aware of a gentle foot-fall upon the carpet, and near the couch; and in a second thereafter, as Rowena was in the act of raising the wine to her lips, I saw, or may have dreamed that I saw, fall within the goblet, as if from some invisible spring in the atmosphere of the room, three or four large drops of a brilliant and ruby colored fluid. If this I saw—not so Rowena. She swallowed the wine unhesitatingly, and I forbore to speak to her of a circumstance which must, after all, I considered, have been but the suggestion of a vivid imagination, rendered morbidly active by the terror of the lady, by the opium, and **51** by the hour.

Yet I cannot conceal it from my own perception that, immediately subsequent to the fall of the ruby-drops, a rapid change for the worse took place in the disorder of my wife; so that, on the third subsequent night, the hands of her menials prepared her for the tomb, and on the fourth, I sat alone, with her shrouded body, in that fantastic chamber which had received her as my bride. Wild visions, opium-engendered, flitted, shadow-like, before me. I gazed with unquiet eye upon the sarcophagi in the angles of the room, upon the varying figures of the drapery, and upon the writhing of the part-colored fires in the censer overhead. My eyes then fell, as I called to mind the circumstances of a former night, to the spot beneath the glare of the censer where I had seen the faint traces of the shadow. It was there, however, no longer; and breathing with greater freedom, I turned my glances to the pallid and rigid figure upon the bed. Then rushed upon me a thousand memories of Ligeia—and then came back upon my heart, with the turbulent violence of a flood, the whole of that unutterable wo with which I had regarded *her* thus enshrouded. The night waned; and still, with a bosom full of bitter thoughts of the one only and supremely beloved, I remained gazing upon the body of Rowena.

It might have been midnight, or perhaps earlier, or later,

51 Since the narrator is in a drugged state, we must tread carefully here. One school of thought holds that Ligeia has returned and poisoned Rowena so that she may take over the second wife's body. Another has it that the narrator has done the poisoning but shut out the thought through both repression and opium. Another interpretation is that the ruby-colored liquid is the Elixir Vitae (Elixir of Life), which was also ruby-colored, according to alchemical tradition, representing the material form of Ligeia, which will eventually take over Rowena's body.

Rowena's symptoms strongly suggest arsenic poisoning. According to experts Alexander and Meredith Blyth, in *Poisons: Their Effect and Detection* (London, 1906), arsenic sulphide, or "realgar," is found in its natural state "in ruby-red crystals" (p. 55). The symptoms of arsenic poisoning commence within one hour, and besides vomiting and diarrhea, include coldness in the extremities, feebleness, faint pulse, and a pale face which later takes on a bluish, deathlike tint. The body temperature falls lower and the patient sinks into a collapse, with death occurring from five to twenty hours after ingestion. "A remarkable preservation of the body is commonly, but not constantly, observed" (p. 573).

Strychnine in its iodide form is a violet color and its effects include convulsions at intervals, which resembles Rowena's symptoms.

As for the Elixir of Life, another name for the Philosopher's Stone, in some cases it was dissolved in the "spirit of wine," which could account for its red color. But also, the "stone or powder of projection" was called "Red Lion," and Salomon Trismosin, in the sixth century, claimed to have restored to youthfulness a ninety-year-old woman with a medicine made from the Red Lion.

In Ben Jonson's *The Alchemist* (II,1) we find:

"He that has once the flower of the sun,
The perfect ruby, which he calls elixir,
Not only can do that, but, by its virtue,
Can confer honour, love, respect, long life. . . ."

But why should Ligeia want to give the Elixir of Life to Rowena? To keep her alive until Ligeia can take over the body? The true Elixir should have cured Rowena, instead of killing her—and yet it is a dead body in which the narrator says he sees the returned Ligeia.

for I had taken no note of time, when a sob, low, gentle, but very distinct, startled me from my revery.—I *felt* that it came from the bed of ebony—the bed of death. I listened in an agony of superstitious terror—but there was no repetition of the sound. I strained my vision to detect any motion in the corpse—but there was not the slightest perceptible. Yet I could not have been deceived. I *had* heard the noise, however faint, and my soul was awakened within me. I resolutely and perseveringly kept my attention riveted upon the body. Many minutes elapsed before any circumstance occurred tending to throw light upon the mystery. At length it became evident that a slight, a very feeble, and barely noticeable tinge of color had flushed up within the cheeks, and along the sunken small veins of the eyelids. Through a species of unutterable **52** horror and awe, for which the language of mortality has no sufficiently energetic expression, I felt my heart cease to beat, my limbs grow rigid where I sat. Yet a sense of duty finally operated to restore my self-possession. I could no longer doubt that we had been precipitate in our preparations—that Rowena still lived. It was necessary that some immediate exertion be made; yet the turret was altogether apart from the portion of the abbey tenanted by the servants—there were none within call—I had no means of summoning them to my aid without leaving the room for many minutes—and this I could not venture to do. I therefore struggled alone in my endeavors to call back the spirit still hovering. In a short period it was certain, however, that a relapse had taken place; the color disappeared from both eyelid and cheek, leaving a wanness even more than that of marble; the lips became doubly shrivelled and pinched up in the ghastly expression of death; a repulsive clamminess and coldness overspread rapidly the surface of the body; and all the usual rigorous stiffness immediately supervened. I fell back with a shudder upon the couch from which I had been so startingly aroused, and again gave myself up to passionate waking visions of Ligeia. **53**

An hour thus elapsed when (could it be possible?) I was a second time aware of some vague sound issuing from the region of the bed. I listened—in extremity of horror. The sound came again—it was a sigh. Rushing to the corpse, I saw—distinctly saw—a tremor upon the lips. In a minute afterward they relaxed, disclosing a bright line of the pearly teeth. Amazement now struggled in my bosom with the profound awe which had hitherto reigned there alone. I felt that my vision grew dim, that my reason wandered; and it was only by a violent effort that I at length succeeded in nerving myself to the task which duty thus once more had pointed out. There was now a partial glow upon the forehead and upon the cheek and throat; a perceptible warmth pervaded the whole frame; there was even a slight pulsation at the heart. The lady *lived*; and with redoubled ardor I betook myself to the task of restoration. I chafed and bathed the temples and the hands, and used every exertion which experience, and no little medical reading, could suggest. But in vain. Suddenly, the color fled, and pulsation ceased, the lips resumed the

52 An interesting possibility is that Rowena (like Madeline Usher) is a cataleptic and may not be really dead at all, which would account for her occasional stirring and her final resurrection—with Ligeia's face and hair supplied by the overactive and opium-bound mind of the narrator.

53 Conveniently, there are no witnesses to the truth of what follows.

Marvin and Frances Mengeling, in "From Fancy to Failure: A Study of the Narrators in the Tales of E. A. Poe" (*University Review,* vol. 34), make what seems to be a valid comment:

". . . when a narrator is described as fanciful or unimaginative the following conditions always seem to be present: first, the hero's mind is victimized by an 'immoderate' dose of opium. The important word is always 'immoderate' and not 'opium.' It is the excessive use of the drug which seems to contribute to failure, not simply the dope-taking per se. The second characteristic which seems to dog these narrators is a hyper-acuity of one or more of the senses. Finally, there is the almost inevitable 'shriek' occurring at the tale's climax, marking the narrator's complete descent into one of failure's darkest pits—insanity.

"These tales contain one other peculiar characteristic worth mentioning; the narrator is always brought into contact with old metaphysical books of one kind or another. The reading of such volumes seems neither casual nor symptomatic in terms of the narrator's fancifulness, for Poe strongly hints that true knowledge and understanding might well lead to attainment of the sought Ideal. It is one of Poe's better ironies that when such study is undertaken the narrator is denied the necessary mental equipment to grasp the true meaning. Poe's women are often much more deep-sighted when it comes to these books than are their relatively obtuse spouses. Ligeia, largely due to her studies, almost 'perfects' her will to return from the dead. Lack of understanding of these dusty tomes by the men clearly demonstrates a lack of imaginative and reasoned analysis on their part. They will 'perfect' nothing." (*University Review,* Vol. 34, p. 31)

... I might have dreamed that Rowena had indeed shaken off, utterly, the fetters of Death. *Illustrated by Johann Friedrich Vogel, 1856*

expression of the dead, and, in an instant afterward, the whole body took upon itself the icy chilliness, the livid hue, the intense rigidity, the sunken outline, and all the loathsome peculiarities of that which has been, for many days, a tenant of the tomb.

And again I sunk into visions of Ligeia—and again, (what marvel that I shudder while I write?) *again* there reached my ears a low sob from the region of the ebony bed. But why shall I minutely detail the unspeakable horrors of that night? Why shall I pause to relate how, time after time, until near the period of the gray dawn, this hideous drama of revification was repeated; how each terrific relapse was only into a sterner and apparently more irredeemable death; how each agony wore the aspect of a struggle with some invisible foe; and how each struggle was succeeded by I know not what of wild change in the personal appearance of the corpse? Let me hurry to a conclusion.

The greater part of the fearful night had worn away, and she who had been dead, once again stirred—and now more vigorously than hitherto, although arousing from a dissolution more appalling in its utter hopelessness than any. I had long ceased to struggle or to move, and remained sitting rigidly upon the ottoman, a helpless prey to a whirl of violent emotions, of which extreme awe was perhaps the least terrible, the least consuming. The corpse, I repeat, stirred, and now more vigorously than before. The hues of life flushed up with unwonted energy into the countenance—the limbs relaxed—and, save that the eyelids were yet pressed heavily together, and that the bandages and draperies of the grave still imparted their charnel character to the figure, I might have dreamed that Rowena had indeed shaken off, utterly, the fetters of Death. But if this idea was not, even then, altogether adopted, I could at least doubt no longer, when, arising from the bed, tottering, with feeble steps, with closed eyes, and with the manner of one bewildered in a dream, the thing that was enshrouded advanced boldly and palpably into the middle of the apartment.

I trembled not—I stirred not—for a crowd of unutterable fancies connected with the air, the stature, the demeanor of the figure, rushing hurriedly through my brain, had paralyzed—had chilled me into stone. I stirred not—but gazed upon the apparition. There was a mad disorder in my thoughts—a tumult unappeasable. Could it, indeed, be the *living* Rowena who confronted me? Could it indeed be Rowena *at all*—the fair-haired, the blue-eyed Lady Rowena Trevanion of Tremaine? Why, *why* should I doubt it? The bandage lay heavily about the mouth—but then might it not be the mouth of the breathing Lady of Tremaine? And the cheeks—there were the roses as in her noon of life—yes, these might indeed be the fair cheeks of the living Lady of Tremaine. And the chin, with its dimples, as in health, might it not be hers?—but *had she then grown taller since her malady?* What inexpressible madness seized me with that thought? One bound, and I had reached her feet! Shrinking from my touch, she let fall from her head, unloosened, the ghastly cerements which had confined it, and there streamed forth, into the rushing atmosphere of the chamber, huge masses of long and dishevelled hair; *it was blacker than the raven wings of midnight!* And now slowly opened *the eyes* of the figure which stood before me. "Here then, at least," I shrieked aloud, "can **54** I never—can I never be mistaken—these are the full, and the black, and the wild eyes—of my lost love—of the lady—of the LADY LIGEIA."

55

54 Note the Mengelings' comment in the previous note about shrieking.

55 The very thing he has desired for so long—Ligeia's return—seems to fill him with horror. Jay L. Halio writes, "Abetted by her husband's own infected will, or longing after her, Ligeia has brought about her resurrection through the sheer force of her will not to yield unto death utterly. But the effect, astonishing and powerful as it is, is also one of great horror. Far from making Ligeia God-like, her reincarnation . . . makes her demonic. Furthermore, her distraught husband, as we are told at the beginning, is finally left with redoubled loss, with "much suffering"—not joy." (*Poe Newsletter*, Vol. 1, p. 23) Halio sees "Ligeia" as a Faustian tale, with her death the result—paradoxically—of her intense will, her superhuman desire for life itself.

After the tale was published, Philip Pendleton Cooke wrote Poe that he "was shocked by a violation of the ghostly properties . . . and wondered how the Lady Ligeia—a wandering essence—could, in quickening *the body of the Lady Rowena . . . become suddenly the visible, bodily, Ligeia.*" Rather, he said, the transformation should have taken place gradually in the mind of the narrator.

Poe replied (September 21, 1839) that since he had dealt with the idea in "Morella," he had to be satisfied with a "sudden half-consciousness" on the part of the narrator that Ligeia stood before him. "I should have intimated that the *will* did not perfect its intention—there should have been a relapse . . . and Ligeia . . . should be at length entombed as Rowena." This he accomplished in part by the insertion of the poem *The Conqueror Worm*, which suggests the impossibility of Ligeia's cheating death totally.

The above correspondence seems to indicate that Poe wanted the tale to be taken literally as a tale of the supernatural, but some critics have said that other parts of the letter to Cooke indicate that Poe was pulling his leg. Perhaps.

Meanwhile, Marie Bonaparte suggests that the ending of the tale is Poe's unwitting declaration "that every later love from Frances Allan [the wife of his guardian] to Virginia and her successors, would never be other than a reincarnation of his first undying love for his mother—still living in his unconscious—and ever to be reactivated by each new passion. Here too, he also formulates one of the prime conditions of these passions: that the women with whom he is to make the effort to prove unfaithful to the mother he knew as a child must, like here, bear the marks of sickness and death. For it is only when death has taken her from him, that the husband can at last love Rowena, since only then can he superimpose Ligeia's corpse upon hers and so, once more in this gruesome fashion, re-experience his first erotic delights." (p. 236)

Since we note that in his description of Ligeia the narrator speaks as a child to and of its mother, Bonaparte's comments seem to have weight. On the other hand, as D. H. Lawrence so aptly phrases it, art is "a sort of subterfuge." The artist's goal, he says, is "to point a moral and adorn a tale. The tale, however, points the other way, as a rule. Two blankly opposing morals, the artist's and the tale's. Never trust the artist. Trust the tale. The proper function of a critic is to save the tale from the artist who created it." (*Studies in Classic American Literature*, p. 2)

THE FALL OF THE HOUSE OF USHER

First published in *Burton's Gentleman's Magazine*, September 1839, "The Fall of the House of Usher" is possibly Poe's finest short story, as well as his most popular.

Like "Ligeia," "Usher" is complex, and again scholars have debated over its exact meaning. In summary, the most prominent interpretations are these:

1) We are to take the tale literally as a tale of the supernatural, and thus everything takes place exactly as the narrator describes it.

2) The narrator, although rational enough at the start, by slow degrees comes under the influence of the mad Roderick Usher, so that by the end of the tale he is hallucinating. The tale thus represents the fall of reason, the inability of the rational mind to make sense of a chaotic universe.

3) Events and characters are symbolic of the workings of the human mind on the brink of insanity. In this theory, Madeline and Roderick (who are twins) represent the unconscious and the conscious, and when Roderick denies the other's existence, he seals his doom. The fall of the house represents his ultimate breakdown—suggested by his strong identification with the building and underscored by the poem *The Haunted Palace*. Some see Roderick as the Ego, Madeline as the Id, and the narrator as the Superego, or mediating force, concluding that the war between the first two is simply too strong for the latter to overcome.

4) The tale symbolizes what Poe termed the "hypnogogic" state—that condition of semiconsciousness in which the closed eye beholds a continuous pattern of vivid and constantly changing forms. The tottering condition of Usher's mind, say the proponents of this theory, and the equally shaky condition of the house, are symbolic of the drop into unconsciousness and the escape from the material world in sleep.

5) Events represent the dilemma of the romantic artist, who in his ever-continuing search for the Sublime may eventually come to a point where he leaves the·real world behind and plunges into madness. The romantic search is thus at once enticing and laden with hazards.

6) The tale is a working out, in their early stages, of Poe's theories of the creation and destruction of the universe—his concept of Unity, which is first made clear in "MS. Found in a Bottle." Since final union with the Godhead provides us with both ultimate knowledge and the means for our annihilation, the "incestuous" reuniting of Roderick and Madeline at the climax of the tale symbolizes the catastrophic event that Poe sees as inevitable (See "MS. Found in a Bottle," introductory note)

The problem with coming to a consensus once again lies in Poe's multiple layers of meaning. As with "Ligeia," he wrote for a mass audience, one steeped in the Gothic tales that were the mainstay of most magazines of the day. The trappings, then, are pure Gothic, but the content seems to hint at far more.

Sources for the tale include "Thunder Struck," in *Passages from the Diary of a Late Physician* (1835), by Dr. Samuel Warren, in which a young woman falls into a cataleptic trance and "dies"; a storm rages, the characters think they hear a sound coming from her burial place, and she returns covered with blood.

In E. T. A. Hoffmann's story "Das Majorat," we find a house not unlike Usher's, which also is a symbol for a family jeopardized by a death. However, there is no conclusive evidence that Poe ever read any of Hoffmann (1776–1822), even though the two share certain interests.

The tale's strong visual sense has prompted a number of film versions. The first, *Le Chute de la Maison Usher* (1929), was filmed in France by Jean Epstein and brought him his first acclaim.

Notable for its use of flying drapery, low-flying mists, gusts of wind, and guttering candle flames, the film is unfortunately hampered by poor model shots, which ultimately mar the poetic atmosphere of the whole.

A British semiprofessional group made a quickly forgotten version in 1950, and NBC-TV's *Matinee Theater* in 1958 did a version with Tom Tryon and Marshall Thompson. Roger Corman's 1960 production for American International is a good effort to transcribe the tale onto film, although it takes many liberties with the original (the narrator becomes Madeline's fiancé; the house burns, then sinks). Too, the film has little of the subtlety of the tale, since it takes only one point of view—the most literal, at that. [Apparently, the spectacular fire that consumes the house before it sinks into the tarn was expensive to film, for it pops up again and again in later Corman films.]

From 1890 to his death, in 1918, Claude Debussy was obsessed with turning "The Fall of the House of Usher" into an opera. He worked fairly steadily on the project from 1908 to 1910, and again in 1912. In 1916 he sent a completed libretto to his publisher and then abandoned his musical sketches. Unfortunately, Debussy had a habit of abandoning a current project when something new and intriguing came his way, and so, few of his most ambitious works were ever completed, says William W. Austin in *Music in the 20th Century* (Norton, 1966; pp. 1–4).

Other writers have borrowed consciously from Poe (Lovecraft does, as does Bierce on occasion, and Wilkie Collins), and at least one has done so without diminishing either his own reputation or that of Poe:—Ray Bradbury. In Bradbury's delightful "Usher II," in *The Martian Chronicles* (1950), we meet Mr. William Standahl, an earthly expatriate who has had a replica of Usher's house built for him on Mars. The opening gives a good idea of the story's flavor:

> "The House of Usher," said Mr. Stendahl with pleasure. "Planned, built, bought, paid for. Wouldn't Mr. Poe be *delighted?*"
>
> Mr. Bigelow squinted. "Is it everything you wanted, sir?"
>
> "Yes!"
>
> "Is the color right: Is it desolate and terrible?"
>
> "*Very* desolate, *very* terrible!"

The House of Usher. *Illustration by C. A. Stoddard*

"The walls are—*bleak?*"

"Amazingly so!"

"The tarn, is it 'black and lurid' enough?"

"Most incredibly black and lurid."

"And the sedge—we've dyed it, you know—is it the proper gray and ebon?"

"Hideous!"

Mr. Bigelow consulted his architectural plans. From these he quoted in part: "Does the whole structure cause an "iciness, a sickening of the heart, a dreariness of thought'? The House, the lake, the land, Mr. Stendahl?"

"Mr. Bigelow, it's worth every penny! My God, it's beautiful!"

With borrowings from other tales by Poe (and from Girardoux's *The Madwoman of Chaillot*), Bradbury brings the tale to a proper and fitting conclusion, as Stendahl battles—and defeats—the enemies of the imagination.

Recorded versions of the tale include a definitive reading by the great Basil Rathbone (Caedmon 1195), one by Martin Donegan (CMS 557), and another by Hurd Hatfield (SKN 992).

---

1 "His heart is a suspended lute;/Whenever one touches it, it resounds." The lines come from "Le Refus" (II, 41–42), a poem by Pierre Jean Béranger (1780–1857), but the original reads "my," not "his," heart. Poe uses the same image in *Israfel*.

A lute, by the way, is shaped somewhat like a heart.

2 Poe is a master of choosing the right word for sound, sense, and suggestiveness, as well as characterizing the mind of his narrator. Consider the words here: dull, dark, soundless, oppressively, alone, drearly, melancholy, insufferable, gloom, sternest, desolate, bleak, vacant, rank, decayed, depression, bitter, hideous, iciness, sinking, sickening, dreariness, torture, unnerved, mystery, shadowy, black, lurid, shudder, ghastly—and all this in the first paragraph!

There is an interesting parallel in Washington Irving's "Westminster Abbey" (in his *Sketch Book*): "One of those sober and rather melancholy days in the latter part of autumn, when the shadows of morning and evening almost mingle together, and throw a gloom over the decline of the year, I passed several hours in rambling about Westminster Abbey."

Note also the similarity between the opening of "Usher" and that of "The System of Dr. Tarr and Professor Fether," which has made some suggest that the latter is meant to be a burlesque of the former.

Ambrose Bierce pays tribute to one of his chief influences in his tale "The Haunted Valley." While the setting is the Old West, there is no doubt about the allusion:

"An indefinable dread came upon me. I rose to shake it off, and began threading the narrow dell by an old grass-grown cow-path that seemed to flow along the bottom, as a substitute for the brook that Nature had neglected to provide.

"The trees among which the path straggled were ordinary, well-behaved plants, a trifle perverted as to trunk and eccentric as to bough, but with nothing unearthly in their general aspect. A few loose boulders, which had detached themselves from the sides of the depression to set up an independent existence at the bottom, had dammed up the pathway, here and there, but their stony repose had nothing in it of the stillness of death. There was a kind of death-chamber hush in the valley, it is true, and a mysterious whisper above; the wind was just fingering the tops of the trees—that was

Son coeur est un luth suspendu;
Sitôt qu'on le touche il résonne.
—*De Béranger*.

During the whole of a dull, dark, and soundless day in the autumn of the year, when the clouds hung oppressively low in the heavens, I had been passing alone, on horseback, through a singularly dreary tract of country; and at length found myself, as the shades of the evening drew on, within view of the melancholy House of Usher. I know not how it was—but, with the first glimpse of the building, a sense of insufferable gloom pervaded my spirit. I say insufferable; for the feeling was unrelieved by any of that half-pleasurable, because poetic, sentiment, with which the mind usually receives even the sternest natural images of the desolate or terrible. I looked upon the scene before me—upon the mere house, and the simple landscape features of the domain— upon the bleak walls—upon the vacant eye-like windows— upon a few rank sedges—and upon a few white trunks of decayed trees—with an utter depression of soul which I can compare to no earthly sensation more properly than to the after-dream of the reveller upon opium—the bitter lapse into everyday life—the hideous dropping off of the veil. There was an iciness, a sinking, a sickening of the heart—an unredeemed dreariness of thought which no goading of the imagination could torture into aught of the sublime. What was it—I paused to think—what was it that so unnerved me in the contemplation of the House of Usher? It was a mystery all insoluble; nor could I grapple with the shadowy fancies that crowded upon me as I pondered. I was forced to fall back upon the unsatisfactory conclusion, that while, beyond doubt, there *are* combinations of very simple natural objects which have the power of thus affecting us, still the analysis of this power lies among considerations beyond our depth. It was possible, I reflected, that a mere different arrangement of the particulars of the scene, of the details of the picture, would be sufficient to modify, or perhaps to annihilate its capacity for sorrowful impression; and, acting upon this idea, I reined my horse to the precipitous brink of a black and lurid tarn that lay in unruffled lustre by the dwelling, and gazed down—but with a shudder even more thrilling than before—upon the re-modelled and inverted images of the gray sedge, and the ghastly tree-stems, and the vacant and eye-like windows. **7**

Nevertheless, in this mansion of gloom I now proposed to myself a sojourn of some weeks. Its proprietor, Roderick Usher, had been one of my boon companions in boyhood; but **8** many years had elapsed since our last meeting. A letter, however, had lately reached me in a distant part of the country—a latter from him—which, in its wildly importunate nature, had admitted of no other than a personal reply. The MS. gave evidence of nervous agitation. The writer spoke of acute bodily illness—of a mental disorder which oppressed him—and of an earnest desire to see me, as his best, and indeed his only personal friend, with a view of attempting, by the cheerfulness of my society, some alleviation of his malady. It was the manner in which all this, and much more, was said—it was the apparent *heart* that went with his request— which allowed me no room for hesitation; and I accordingly obeyed forthwith what I still considered a very singular summons. **9**

Although, as boys, we had been even intimate associates, yet I really knew little of my friend. His reserve had been always excessive and habitual. I was aware, however, that his very ancient family had been noted, time out of mind, for a peculiar sensibility of temperament, displaying itself, through long ages, in many works of exalted art, and manifested, of late, in repeated deeds of munificent yet unobtrusive charity, as well as in a passionate devotion to the intricacies, perhaps even more than to the orthodox and easily recognisable beauties, of musical science. I had learned, too, the very remarkable fact, that the stem of the Usher race, all time-honoured as it was, had put forth, at no period, any enduring branch; in other words, that the entire family lay in the direct line of descent, and had always, with very trifling and very temporary variation, so lain. It was this deficiency, I consid-ered, while running over in thought the perfect keeping of the character of the premises with the accredited character of the people, and while speculating upon the possible influence which the one, in the long lapse of centuries, might have exercised upon the other—it was this deficiency, perhaps, of collateral issue, and the consequent undeviating transmission, from sire to son, of the patrimony with the name, which had, at length, so identified the two as to merge the original title of the estate in the quaint and equivocal appellation of the "House of Usher"—an appellation which seemed to include, in the minds of the peasantry who used it, both the family and the family mansion. **10**

I have said that the sole effect of my somewhat childish experiment—that of looking down within the tarn—had been to deepen the first singular impression. There can be no doubt that the consciousness of the rapid increase of my supersti-

all."—*The Collected Writings of Ambrose Bierce* (Citadel Press, 1946), pp. 454–55).

The time of day in Poe's opening is wholly appropriate, for twilight is a symbol of uncertainty and ambivalence. As a threshold symbol, it represents the region between one state and another, and of the end of one cycle and the beginning of another.

3 Our first hint that the house and its occupants are somehow bound together.

4 See "Ligeia," note 7.

5 "The beauty of the horrid" was one of the strains of nineteenth-century romanticism. Reacting against the ordered world of the Enlightenment, romantic writers found inspiration in the bizarre, the grotesque, the mysterious, and the absurd. Many believed—and Poe seems to agree—that the truly poetic mind could trans-form these otherwise disturbing and possibly harmful fancies into the Sublime; that is, true poetry. Coleridge discusses this process in *Biographica Literaria*, Chapter XIII, and Poe takes it up in his essay *Fancy and the Imagination*.

6 The narrator's impressions at this point are totally intuitive and sensory, and seem at odds with his self-image of rationalist. He thus sets up his gradual evolution from reason to collapse, while providing us with a vivid portrait of his physical surroundings.

7 A tarn (from the Old Norse *tjörn*) is a small mountain lake with no major outlet, whose waters are dark from lack of circulation or by the action of peat.

Tarns are not always forboding. Wordsworth describes one in his *Scenery Lakes* (1823) without a hint of mystery. However, Sir Walter Scott, in *The Bridal of Triermain* (1813) echoes Poe: "Though never sunbeam could dis-cern/The surface of that sable tarn/In whose black mirror you may spy/The stars, while noon-tide lights the sky."

French phenomenologist Gaston Bachelard, author of a fascinating series of studies on the psychology of the imagination (*The Poetics of Reverie, The Poetics of Space, The Psychoanalysis of Fire*), sees Poe as a poet of water. He returns again and again to that element—and more specifically, to dark water, Bachelard says. It is this water, stagnant, heavy, and dead, that absorbs life or drains it away. In Poe, water is no longer something that is drunk, but something that drinks (*L'eau et les rêves*, Librairie José Corti, 1947).

8 Literally, a "good fellow," from the French *bon*.

9 Roderick's stubborn persistence in encouraging his old friend to come is never really explained, although one plausible interpretation is that he knows his own mind is slipping and needs a more rational viewpoint. This makes sense whether one accepts the tale as supernatural or as psychological. Speaking more prac-tically, however, if Usher's tale is to be told, somebody must observe *and* escape with his life.

10 The use of "house" for both a family and its home is of long standing, so that the local peasantry are not unusual. Poe merely wants to emphasize the link—when one falls, so will the other.

11 The narrator's rational façade has slipped a bit, and as it does he seems to become aware of deeper basic fears he would rather not face.

12 The mansion has already been described as isolated, and the notion that it has an atmosphere of its own removes it even farther from the real world.

13 In his attempt to make sense out of absurdity, the narrator sometimes makes unrealistic assumptions. Because he assumes that his observations and reactions are the result of fancies, he dismisses most of what he sees as mere "superstition," and the work of an overactive imagination—thus ignoring the existence of something basically wrong in this house.

14 The house even looks like a cadaverous head; compare with the description of Roderick Usher later on.

15 For those who prefer a logical explanation for the climax of the tale, Poe has made the house almost eaten away and ready to fall at any moment.

16 The causeway is still another barrier between the house and the real world. Critics who have interpreted the house as the narrator's unconscious mind, with Madeline and Roderick as buried portions of his personality, see his crossing the causeway as his delving into his own subconscious—a perilous process.

17 "Dark and intricate passages" are often symbolic of the hidden recesses of the human mind.

18 See "Ligeia," note 48.

19 An "usher" is one who has charge of the door and admits people to a hall or chamber, or one who goes ahead and announces the arrival of someone. Usher does, of course, "usher" in the narrator—to his mind, to his universe, to the narrator's own unconscious, or into a world of the supernatural, depending on the interpretation.

20 Since Usher and his house are one, this room represents his isolation, both mental and physical. In one view, the narrator has reached the main but not the deepest level of the unconscious. In another, the room shows Usher bringing on his own doom by shutting himself off from the outside world; his self-created universe is too fragile to last.

21 Rooms in Poe often represent states of mind, since they reflect the person who lives there. The costliness of the decor may suggest that Roderick is richly imaginative, as it may with other narrators (since imagination is a gift, it isn't surprising that wealth in Poe's tales is either found or inherited, never earned). Here, however, Usher's possessions "fail to give any vitality" to the room or his life. His mental furnishings are "tattered" and "comfortless," and his spirit is worn out. The scene also resembles an alchemist's laboratory pictured in Heinrich Khunrath's *Amphitheatrum sapientiae acternae* (1609), and reprinted in Allison Coudert's *Alchemy* (Shambala, 1980), p. 57.

22 "Bored," although it also can mean "troubled, bothered, worried."

23 How does the narrator know this if he hasn't seen Roderick since they were children?

24 Some say this is a description of Poe himself, while others suggest that it is a caricature of James Gates

tion—for why should I not so term it?—served mainly to accelerate the increase itself. Such, I have long known, is the paradoxical law of all sentiments having terror as a basis. And it might have been for this reason only, that, when I again uplifted my eyes to the house itself, from its image in the pool, there grew in my mind a strange fancy—a fancy so ridiculous, indeed, that I but mention it to show the vivid

11 force of the sensations which oppressed me. I had so worked upon my imagination as really to believe that about the whole mansion and domain there hung an atmosphere peculiar to themselves and their immediate vicinity—an atmosphere which had no affinity with the air of heaven, but which had reeked up from the decayed trees, and the gray wall, and the silent tarn—a pestilent and mystic vapour, dull, sluggish,

12 faintly discernible, and leaden-hued.

13   Shaking off from my spirit what *must* have been a dream, I scanned more narrowly the real aspect of the building. Its principal feature seemed to be that of an excessive antiquity. The discoloration of ages had been great. Minute fungi overspread the whole exterior, hanging in a fine tangled

14 webwork from the eaves. Yet all this was apart from any extraordinary dilapidation. No portion of the masonry had fallen; and there appeared to be a wild inconsistency between its still perfect adaptation of parts, and the crumbling condition of the individual stones. In this there was much that reminded me of the specious totality of old wood-work which has rotted for long years in some neglected vault, with no disturbance from the breath of the external air. Beyond this indication of extensive decay, however, the fabric gave little token of instability. Perhaps the eye of a scrutinising observer might have discovered a barely perceptible fissure, which, extending from the roof of the building in front, made its way down the wall in a zigzag direction, until it became lost in the sullen

15 waters of the tarn.
    Noticing these things, I rode over a short causeway to the

16 house. A servant in waiting took my horse, and I entered the Gothic archway of the hall. A valet, of stealthy step, thence conducted me, in silence, through many dark and intricate

17 passages in my progress to the *studio* of his master. Much that I encountered on the way contributed, I know not how, to heighten the vague sentiments of which I have already spoken. While the objects around me—while the carvings of the ceilings, the sombre tapestries of the walls, the ebon blackness

18 of the floors, and the phantasmagoric armorial trophies which rattled as I strode, were but matters to which, or to such as which, I had been accustomed from my infancy—while I hesitated not to acknowledge how familiar was all this—I still wondered to find how unfamiliar were the fancies which ordinary images were stirring up. On one of the staircases, I met the physician of the family. His countenance, I thought, wore a mingled expression of low cunning and perplexity. He accosted me with trepidation and passed on. The valet now threw open a door and ushered me into the presence of his

19 master.

20   The room in which I found myself was very large and lofty.

The windows were long, narrow, and pointed, and at so vast a distance from the black oaken floor as to be altogether inaccessible from within. Feeble gleams of encrimsoned light made their way through the trellised panes, and served to render sufficiently distinct the more prominent objects around; the eye, however, struggled in vain to reach the remoter angles of the chamber, or the recesses of the vaulted and fretted ceiling. Dark draperies hung upon the walls. The general furniture was profuse, comfortless, antique, and tattered. Many books and musical instruments lay scattered about, but failed to give any vitality to the scene. I felt that I breathed an atmosphere of sorrow. An air of stern, deep, and irredeemable gloom hung over and pervaded all. **21**

Upon my entrance, Usher arose from a sofa on which he had been lying at full length, and greeted me with a vivacious warmth which had much in it, I at first thought, of an overdone cordiality—of the constrained effort of the *ennuyé* man of the **22** world. A glance, however, at his countenance, convinced me of his perfect sincerity. We sat down; and for some moments, while he spoke not, I gazed upon him with a feeling half of pity, half of awe. Surely, man had never before so terribly altered, in so brief a period, as had Roderick Usher! It was **23** with difficulty that I could bring myself to admit the identity of the wan being before me with the companion of my early boyhood. Yet the character of his face had been at all times remarkable. A cadaverousness of complexion; an eye large, **24** liquid, and luminous beyond comparison; lips somewhat thin and very pallid, but of a surpassingly beautiful curve; a nose of a delicate Hebrew model, but with a breadth of nostril unusual in similar formations; a finely moulded chin, speaking, in its want of prominence, of a want of moral energy; hair of a more than web-like softness and tenuity; these features, with an inordinate expansion above the regions of the temple, **25** made up altogether a countenance not easily to be forgotten. And now in the mere exaggeration of the prevailing character of these features, and of the expression they were wont to convey, lay so much of change that I doubted to whom I spoke. The now ghastly pallor of the skin, and the now miraculous lustre of the eye, above all things startled and even awed me. The silken hair, too, had been suffered to grow all unheeded, and as, in its wild gossamer texture, it floated rather than fell about the face, I could not, even with effort, **26** connect its Arabesque expression with any idea of simple **27** humanity.

In the manner of my friend I was at once struck with an incoherence—an inconsistency; and I soon found this to arise from a series of feeble and futile struggles to overcome an habitual trepidancy—an execessive nervous agitation. For something of this nature I had indeed been prepared, no less by his letter, than by reminiscences of certain boyish traits, and by conclusions deduced from his peculiar physical conformation and temperament. His action was alternately vivacious and sullen. His voice varied rapidly from a tremulous indecision (when the animal spirits seemed utterly in abeyance) to that species of energetic concision—that abrupt, weighty,

Percival (1795–1856), poetaster, lexicographer, geologist, and full-time neurotic. A colleague of Percival's said, "His classical features, his blonde complexion, his large humid eyes with dilated pupils, the tear starting and then settling back into its well in the socket, his whole expression as of one who had no communion with those around him, attracted my notice and led me to inquire his name and character" (quoted in Henry E. Legler's *James Gates Percival* [1901], p. 30). Another observer: "His countenance was indicative of his extreme sensitiveness and timidity; pale and almost bloodless; the eyes blue, with an iris unusually large, and when kindled with animation, worthy of a poet; the nose rather prominent, slightly Roman in outline, and finely chiseled; while the forehead, high, broad and swelling out grandly at the temples, marked him as of the nobility of the intellect" (Legler, pp. 32–33).

Percival, besides being a poet of sorts, also sang and played the accordion. He designed and built a retirement cottage that Nathaniel Park Willis (see "The Duc De L'Omelette," introductory note) described as a "sarcophagus in a cathedral aisle. Three blind windows on the front of a square structure are the only signs of anything ever going in or coming out of it." (Legler, pp. 44–45). Percival attempted suicide by an overdose of opium, and his dilated pupils and dreamy behavior might mean he was an addict.

Poe mentions a Dr. Percival in a note later on (see note 48); he may have recalled a poem by Percival called *The Suicide* (1821), which seems to tie all this together:

> An outcast, self-condemn'd, he takes his way,
> He knows and cares not whither—he can weep
> No more, his only wish his head to lay
> In endless death and everlasting sleep.
>
> Ah! who can bear the self-absorbing thought
> Of time, chance, talent wasted—who can think
> Of friendship, love, fame, science, gone to nought
> And not in hopeless separation sink.
>
> Behind are summits, lofty, pure and bright
> Where blow the life-reviving gales of heav'n
> Below expand the jaws of deepest night,
> And there he falls, by pow'r resistless driven.

25 In phrenological terms, Roderick is possessed of great intellect and artistic sensibility. The system of phrenology (see "Ligeia," note 10) places above the temples the faculties of Ideality (taste, love of beauty, poetry), Sublimity (love of grandeur, vastness) and Spirituality (intuition, prescience).

Poe showed little or no interest in phrenology before 1836, when he reviewed Mrs. L. Miles's *Phrenology, and the Moral Influence of Phrenology*. Although he was initially impressed with the new theory, he was aware of its deficiencies as well, for he pokes fun at the pseudoscience in "Lionizing," "Some Words with a Mummy," "The System of Dr. Tarr and Professor Fether," and the essay, "Diddling."

In his tales of terror, however, Poe found phrenology suitably mysterious to add atmosphere to the proceedings. He also used phrenological descriptions as a kind of shorthand, to telegraph character traits to the reader, who was probably more or less familiar with the methodology.

Phrenology is effectively outlined in *The Practical Phrenologist* (1869), by O. S. Fowler.

26 According to phrenology, a "nervous" disposition was indicated by fine, thin hair, thin skin, a pale complexion, and unusually bright eyes. Note also the resemblance between Roderick's appearance and that of the house, given earlier.

27 Moslem law forbids images, so mosques have traditionally been decorated with intricate designs, usually flowing and often plantlike, bizarre in their beauty. The word came to mean "strangely mixed, fantastic," and the O.E.D. gives the first citation of this usage to Dickens in 1848, even though Poe had already used it in this sense much earlier.

28 Nineteenth-century readers would expect an artist to have more acute senses than the average person, but Roderick seems to have cornered the market in hypersensitive ailments.

Excessive sensitivity to touch, pain, or other sensory stimuli is termed *hyperesthesia;* it includes hyperesthesia optica (sensitivity to light), tactile hyperesthesia (sensitivity of touch), olfactory hyperesthesia (sensitivity to odors), and gustatory hyperesthesia (sensitivity to taste).

Usher also seems to suffer from either auditory hyperalgesia (a painful reaction to sounds not ordinarily unpleasant) or hyperacusia (overacute hearing due to an increased irritability of the sensory neural mechanism).

All of these may be the result of psychological, as well as physiological, factors.

29 Usher is a true hypochondriac—not in the popular sense, but in the medical sense of suffering from a melancholic disorder. Melancholia, or severe depression, may lead to isolation, and then to monomaniacal obsession with a single fear, and then to self-destruction as a result of that obsession. Roderick is obviously aware of his problem but is unable to do anything about it.

At the same time, it should be noted that it was generally believed in Poe's time that poets and artists were more prone to madness than most people. It was also thought by some that insanity could increase artistic ability—to a point; complete madness was regarded as "erroneous perception." The romantic ideal in many ways parallels the development of hypochondria: beginning in reclusion and the cultivation of the mind's power, moving on to the imaginative struggle to idealize the real, and ending in the absolute dissolution of reality in order to achieve complete union with ideality.

Excessive and habitual reserve is symptomatic of both states, as is the lack of active employment, the cultivation of the mind over the body, hypersensitivity of feeling, and an active imagination.

Thus we can see Roderick as a romantic artist breaking through to ideality, or as a man suffering from schizophrenia or manic-depressive psychosis. Poe gives both physical and moral causes for Usher's behavior, and the reader must ultimately decide whether Usher is a positive or a negative portrait of a tortured spirit.

30 The two French words here mean "matter" and "spirit." In Usher's world, these two opposites are combined. The house, the grounds, Madeline—all are in some way parts of Roderick's being.

On another level, Usher apparently cannot exist away from his mansion—or so he believes. This reflects either his insanity or the fact that the house represents his mind, and he cannot, of course, leave that, except through death.

unhurried, and hollow-sounding enunciation—that leaden, self-balanced and perfectly modulated guttural utterance, which may be observed in the lost drunkard, or the irreclaimable eater of opium, during the periods of his most intense excitement.

It was thus that he spoke of the object of my visit, of his earnest desire to see me, and of the solace he expected me to afford him. He entered, at some length, into what he conceived to be the nature of his malady. It was, he said, a constitutional and a family evil, and one for which he despaired to find a remedy—a mere nervous affection, he immediately added, which would undoubtedly soon pass off. It displayed itself in a host of unnatural sensations. Some of these, as he detailed them, interested and bewildered me; although, perhaps, the terms, and the general manner of the narration had their weight. He suffered much from a morbid acuteness of

28 the senses; the most insipid food was alone endurable; he could wear only garments of certain texture; the odours of all flowers were oppressive; his eyes were tortured by even a faint light; and there were but peculiar sounds, and these from stringed instruments, which did not inspire him with horror.

To an anomalous species of terror I found him a bounden slave. "I shall perish," said he, "I *must* perish in this deplorable folly. Thus, thus, and not otherwise, shall I be lost. I dread the events of the future, not in themselves, but in their results. I shudder at the thought of any, even the most trivial, incident, which may operate upon this intolerable agitation of soul. I have, indeed, no abhorrence of danger, except in its absolute effect—in terror. In this unnerved—in this pitiable condition—I feel that the period will sooner or later arrive when I must abandon life and reason together, in some

29 struggle with the grim phantasm, FEAR."

I learned, moreover, at intervals, and through broken and equivocal hints, another singular feature of his mental condition. He was enchained by certain superstitious impressions in regard to the dwelling which he tenanted, and whence, for many years, he had never ventured forth—in regard to an influence whose supposititious force was conveyed in terms too shadowy here to be re-stated—an influence which some peculiarities in the mere form and substance of his family mansion, had, by dint of long sufferance, he said, obtained over his spirit—an effect which the *physique* of the gray walls and turrets, and of the dim tarn into which they all looked down, had, at length, brought about upon the *morale* of his

30 existence.

He admitted, however, although with hesitation, that much of the peculiar gloom which thus afflicted him could be traced to a more natural and far more palpable origin—to the severe and long-continued illness—indeed to the evidently approaching dissolution—of a tenderly beloved sister—his sole companion for long years—his last and only relative on earth. "Her decease," he said, with a bitterness which I can never forget, "would leave him (him the hopeless and the frail) the last of the ancient race of the Ushers." While he spoke, the lady

Madeline (for so was she called) passed slowly through a remote portion of the apartment, and, without having noticed my presence, disappeared. I regarded her with an utter astonishment not unmingled with dread—and yet I found it impossible to account for such feelings. A sensation of stupor oppressed me, as my eyes followed her retreating steps. When a door, at length, closed upon her, my glance sought instinctively and eagerly the countenance of the brother—but he had buried his face in his hands, and I could only perceive that a far more than ordinary wanness had overspread the emaciated fingers through which trickled many passionate tears. **31**

The disease of the lady Madeline had long baffled the skill of her physicians. A settled apathy, a gradual wasting away of the person, and frequent although transient affections of a partially cataleptical character, were the unusual diagnosis. **32** Hitherto she had steadily borne up against the pressure of her malady, and had not betaken herself finally to bed; but, on the closing in of the evening of my arrival at the house, she succumbed (as her brother told me at night with inexpressbile agitation) to the prostrating power of the destroyer; and I learned that the glimpse I had obtained of her person would thus probably be the last I should obtain—that the lady, at least while living, would be seen by me no more.

For several days ensuing, her name was unmentioned by either Usher or myself: and during this period I was busied in earnest endeavours to alleviate the melancholy of my friend. We painted and read together; or I listened, as if in a dream,

31 Madeline is a mysterious and shadowy figure, and we never really get a good look at her. She is a ghost even before her death. Some see her as Usher's alter ego, while others hint at an incestuous relationship between brother and sister, one that brings on Usher's guilt, his nervous agitation, and eventually his breakdown. Still others see Madeline and her brother as the embodiments of Poe's cosmology: that all matter began as one particle (Roderick and Madeline are twins) and still yearns for union, even though it means annihilation.

32 Catalepsy is related to hysteria. The victim suffers an immediate suspension of feeling and will, followed by rigidity of either the entire body or only certain muscles. The cause is often emotional, the result of fright or long depression.

Other symptoms include insensibility accompanied by a statuelike appearance, so that the body retains any position it is made to assume. Organic and vital functions diminish to the lowest level this side of death, and the condition may continue for minutes, hours, or even days. Sometimes epilepsy can bring on the symptoms.

From the amount of mileage Poe gets from cataleptic states, one would assume that they were a common occurrence in the nineteenth century. Actually, Poe preys more on the fear of premature burial than its probability. It is true that medical science lacked sophisticated medical equipment for monitoring vital life signs and that people were sometimes entombed alive (see "The Premature Burial"), but it was not an everyday occurrence.

As Jessica Mitford points out in *The American Way of Death* (1963), if there is anything to be said about modern embalming practice it is that it makes recovery after burial highly unlikely.

While he spoke, the lady Madeline . . . passed slowly through a remote portion of the apartment, and, without having noticed my presence, disappeared. *Artist unknown*

33 That the narrator cannot recall the "studies" and "occupations" is good indication of the increasing influence of Roderick. He's beginning to sound like the narrator of "Ligeia," who also has a bad memory.

34 Karl Maria von Weber (1786–1826) was a pioneer of the German romantic school of music, but "The Last Waltz of Weber" was actually composed by Karl Gottlieb Reissiger (1798–1859) as one of his *Danses Brillantes* (1822). Weber had copied down the music for his friend and it was found in his effects after his death, and so attributed mistakenly to him.

35 While the narrator calls Usher's paintings "abstract," they seem, in the description that follows, to share more of the style of the twentieth-century surrealists, who often painted an idea—that is, attempted to portray the subconscious. At any rate, Roderick does seem to be ahead of his time, for André Malraux points out that modern art is ". . . the annexation of forms by means of an inner pattern or schema, which may or may not take the shape of objects, but of which, in any case, figures and objects are no more than the expression. The modern artist's supreme aim is to subdue all things to his style. . . ." (*The Voices of Silence*, Doubleday, 1953; p. 119)

A complicated but intriguing possibility is that the painting, and the crypt in which Madeline is buried, refer to alchemical symbols. The explanation of all this is much too detailed to give here, but interested readers may see "Usher Unveiled," by Barton Lévi St. Armand, in *Poe Studies*, Vol. 5, p. 1.

36 Henry Fuseli (Johann Heinrich Füssli, 1742–1825) was a painter who illustrated Shakespeare and Milton. Artistic memoirs of the period are full of anecdotes of his eccentricities and sarcasm. His art, with its extravagance of movement and gesture, its distortion and stylization of form, its exploitation of horror and fear, is not unlike that of Blake, although clearly of less visionary quality.

37 Cellars and catacombs often symbolize the irrational part of the mind in dream analysis. "When it comes to excavated ground," writes Gaston Bachelard, "dreams have no limit. When we dream there, we are in harmony with the irrationality of the depths." (*The Poetics of Space*, Beacon Press, 1969; p. 18)

On a more literal level, Usher's painting represents Madeline's tomb, although some scholars have also suggested that the description sounds like a view through the West Lawn Arcade at the University of Virginia, which Poe attended.

to the wild improvisations of his speaking guitar. And thus, as a closer and still closer intimacy admitted me more unreservedly into the recesses of his spirit, the more bitterly did I perceive the futility of all attempt at cheering a mind from which darkness, as if an inherent positive quality, poured forth upon all objects of the moral and physical universe, in one unceasing radiation of gloom.

I shall ever bear about me a memory of the many solemn hours I thus spent alone with the master of the House of Usher. Yet I should fail in any attempt to convey an idea of the exact character of the studies, or of the occupations, in which he involved me, or led me the way. An excited and highly distempered ideality threw a sulphureous lustre over **33** all. His long improvised dirges will ring forever in my ears. Among other things, I hold painfully in mind a certain singular perversion and amplification of the wild air of the last waltz **34** of Von Weber. From the paintings over which his elaborate fancy brooded, and which grew, tough by touch, into vaguenesses at which I shuddered the more thrillingly, because I shuddered knowing not why;—from these paintings (vivid as their images now are before me) I would in vain endeavour to educe more than a small portion which should lie within the compass of merely written words. By the utter simplicity, by the nakedness of his designs, he arrested and overawed attention. If ever mortal painted an idea, that mortal was Roderick Usher. For me at least—in the circumstances then **35** surrounding me—there arose out of the pure abstractions which the hypochondriac contrived to throw upon his canvas, an intensity of intolerable awe, no shadow of which felt I ever yet in the contemplation of the certainly glowing yet too **36** concrete reveries of Fuseli.

One of the phantasmagoric conceptions of my friend, partaking not so rigidly of the spirit of abstraction, may be shadowed forth, although feebly, in words. A small picture presented the interior of an immensely long and rectangular vault or tunnel, with low walls, smooth, white, and without interruption or device. Certain accessory points of the design served well to convey the idea that this excavation lay at an exceeding depth below the surface of the earth. No outlet was observed in any portion of its vast extent, and no torch, or other artificial source of light was discernible; yet a flood of intense rays rolled throughout, and bathed the whole in a **37** ghastly and inappropriate splendour.

I have just spoken of that morbid condition of the auditory nerve which rendered all music intolerable to the sufferer, with the exception of certain effects of stringed instruments. It was, perhaps, the narrow limits to which he thus confined himself upon the guitar, which gave birth, in great measure, to the fantastic character of his performances. But the fervid *facility* of his *impromptus* could not be so accounted for. They must have been, and were, in the notes, as well as in the words of his wild fantasias (for he not unfrequently accompanied himself with rhymed verbal improvisations), the result of that intense mental collectedness and concentration to which I have previously alluded as observable only in particular moments of the highest artificial excitement. The words of one of these rhapsodies I have easily remembered. I was, perhaps, the more forcibly impressed with it, as he gave it, because, in the under or mystic current of its meaning, I fancied that I perceived, and for the first time, a full consciousness on the part of Usher, of the tottering of his lofty reason upon her throne. The verses, which were entitled "The Haunted Palace," ran very nearly, if not accurately, thus: **38**

I

In the greenest of our valleys,   **39,40**
  By good angels tenanted,
Once a fair and stately palace—
  Radiant palace—reared its head.
In the monarch Thought's dominion—
  It stood there!
Never seraph spread a pinion
  Over fabric half so fair.

II

Banners yellow, glorious, golden,
  On its roof did float and flow;
(This—all this—was in the olden
  Time long ago)
And every gentle air that dallied,
  In that sweet day,
Along the ramparts plumed and pallid,
  A winged odour went away.   **41**

III

Wanderers in that happy valley
  Through two luminous windows saw
Spirit moving musically
  To a lute's well-tunèd law,   **42**
Round about a throne, where sitting
  (Porphyrogene!)   **43**
In state his glory well befitting,
  The ruler of the realm was seen.   **44**

IV

And all with pearl and ruby glowing
  Was the fair palace door,   **45**
Through which came flowing, flowing, flowing
  And sparkling evermore,
A troop of Echoes whose sweet duty
  Was but to sing,
In voices of surpassing beauty,
  The wit and wisdom of their king.   **46**

V

But evil things, in robes of sorrow,
  Assailed the monarch's high estate;
(Ah, let us mourn, for never morrow
  Shall dawn upon him, desolate!)
And, round about his home, the glory
  That blushed and bloomed
Is but a dim-remembered story
  Of the oldtime entombed.

38 *The Haunted Palace*, like *The Conqueror Worm*, was first published by itself, in this case in the Baltimore *American Museum*, April 1839—five months before it appeared in "The Fall of the House of Usher." The poem very possibly suggested the tale.

The palace is an allegorical representation of the human head and mind, and the poem suggests the development of madness in a poet—thus paralleling Usher's own state of mind. Poe very clearly points this out when he says, ". . . by the Haunted Palace I mean to imply a mind haunted by phantoms—a disordered brain" (John W. Ostrom, *The Letters of Edgar Allan Poe*, Harvard, 1948; I, 160.

The use of a palace to represent the mind was not new. Edmund Waller (1606–87) refers to the "palace of the mind," as does Byron in *Childe Harold*, Canto II (1812).

The film entitled *The Haunted Palace* (1963) is actually based on H. P. Lovecraft's "The Shadow over Innsmouth" and "The Case of Charles Dexter Ward."

39 Green is an ambivalent color, symbolizing both life and the lividness of death, as well as youth, hope, change, inexperience, and immortality. Here it underscores the vitality of the scene.

40 Valleys are the most verdant and fertile of lands.

41 The man is a poet and the "winged odour" is a poem.

42 The lute's "well-tunèd law" is a reference to the Pythagorean view of music as a microcosm, "a system of sound and rhythm ruled by the same mathematical laws that operate in the whole of the visible and invisible creation" (Donald Jay Grout, *A History of Western Music*, Norton, 1973, p. 7).

The Pythagoreans discovered that musical notes could be expressed in numerical ratios demonstrated by divisions of a stretched string. Thus the music by which the spirits move in the palace represent the ordered thoughts of the poet (the lute).

43 A word of Greek origin, meaning "born to the purple," i.e., of royal blood. Porphyry was a purple dye prepared from mollusks and reserved only for the royal family. The O.E.D. cites Poe for the first use of this form of the word.

44 The poet's soul

45 The mouth

46 His poetic utterances

47 A pseudo-archaic past participle of "to light," which the O.E.D., again, gives as a Poe coinage

48 "Watson, Dr. Percival, Spallanzani, and especially the Bishop of Landaff—See "Chemical Essays," vol. v." [Poe's note] Actually the only source is *An Essay on the Subjects of Chemistry* (1771), by Richard Watson, Bishop of Llandaff. Watson mentions Abbé Lazzaro Spallanzani's *Dissertations Relative to the Natural History of Animals and Vegetables* (1784) and Dr. Thomas Percival's article on the perceptive powers of vegetables in *Memoir of the Literary and Philosophical Society of Manchester* (1785), II, 114.

49 Consciousness. "Sentient" means having the power of feeling or sensory perception, and the O.E.D., once again, gives Poe the first use of this form (1839), although "sentient" was used as early as 1632.

Usher clearly believes that the house and its immediate surroundings have a life of their own, a tangible vitality with which he himself is inexorably bound. This is reinforced by the narrator's perception at the beginning of the tale, and by the theme of *The Haunted Palace*. The house of Usher can be seen as the physical body of Roderick Usher, and its dim interior as Usher's visionary mind.

50 Note the number of mirror elements in the tale. The house is reflected in the tarn. Roderick and Madeline are twins. Roderick's painting suggests Madeline's vault. The poem *The Haunted Palace*, suggests the relationship between the palace and the mind of its tenant.

51 Usher's library is a bizarre mixture of the occult and the esoteric. The titles foreshadow the burial and apparent resurrection of Madeline, and shed more light on Roderick's own state of mind.

Vert Vert and *Chartreuse*, by Jean Baptiste Gresset (1709–77) are anticlerical satires, full of lusty humor.

Machiavelli's *Belfagor* (c. 1515) tells how an infernal demon visits the earth to prove that women are the curse of mankind.

Swedenborg's *Heaven and Hell* (1758) proposes the continuity of spiritual identity through life and death. The Swedish religious teacher and mystic (1688–1772) gave himself to the work of making clear to mankind the true inner doctrines of the divine Word as, he claimed, they were revealed to him by direct insight into the spiritual world through visions and appearances of spirits and angels.

The Subterranean Voyage (*Iter Subterraneum*), by Ludvig Holberg (1684–1754) is another description of a return from death.

Occult divination through palmistry is the subject of the next three works: Robert Flud (1574–1637) was a British Rosicrucian; D'Indagine (*Chiromantia*, 1522) and Marin Dureau de la Chambre (*Principes de la Chiromancie*, 1653) were French pseudoscientists.

The Journey into the Blue Distance of Tieck" is actually the subtitle of *Das Alte Buch* (1834), by Ludwig Tieck (1773–1853).

The City of the Sun (1623) was written by Tommaso Campanella (1568–1639); it describes an ideal other world, situated in the sun.

The Inquisition Directorium was an account of the procedures and tortures of the Inquisition prepared by Nicolás Eymeric of Gironne (c. 1320–99), who acted as inquisitor-general for Aragon.

Pomponius Mela was a Roman geographer of the first century A.D., whose *Geography* was published in 1471, giving rise to the belief in the goatmen ("Aegipans") of Africa.

VI

And travellers now within that valley,
    Through the red-litten windows, see
Vast forms that move fantastically
    To a discordant melody;
While, like a rapid ghastly river,
    Through the pale door,
A hideous throng rush out forever,
    And laugh—but smile no more.

I well remember that suggestions arising from this ballad led us into a train of thought wherein there became manifest an opinion of Usher's which I mention not so much on account of its novelty, (for other men have thought thus,) as on account of the pertinacity with which he maintained it. This opinion, in its general form, was that of the sentience of all vegetable things. But, in his disordered fancy, the idea had assumed a more daring character, and trespassed, under certain conditions, upon the kingdom of inorganization. I lack words to express the full extent, of the earnest *abandon* of his persuasion. The belief, however, was connected (as I have previously hinted) with the gray stones of the home of his forefathers. The conditions of the sentience had been here here, he imagined, fulfilled in the method of collocation of these stones—in the order of their arrangement, as well as in that of the many *fungi* which overspread them, and of the decayed trees which stood around—above all, in the long undisturbed endurance of this arrangement, and in its reduplication in the still waters of the tarn. Its evidence—the evidence of the sentience—as to be seen, he said, (and I here started as he spoke,) in the gradual yet certain condensation of an atmosphere of their own about the water and the walls. The result was discoverable, he added, in that silent, yet importunate and terrible influence which for centuries had moulded the destinies of his family, and which made *him* what I now saw him—what he was. Such opinions need no comment, and I will make none.

Our books—the books which, for years, had formed no small portion of the mental existence of the invalid—were, as might be supposed, in strict keeping with this character of phantasm. We pored together over such works as the Ververt et Chartreuse of Gresset; the Belphegor of Machiavelli; the Heaven and Hell of Swedenborg; the Subterranean Voyage of Nicholas Klimm by Holberg; the Chiromancy of Robert Flud, of Jean D'Indaginé, and of De la Chambre; the Journey into the Blue Distance of Tieck; and the City of the Sun of Campanella. One favourite volume was a small octavo edition of the *Directorium Inquisitorum*, by the Dominican Eymeric de Gironne; and there were passages in Pomponius Mela, about the old African Satyrs and Ægipans, over which Usher would sit dreaming for hours. His chief delight, however, was found in the perusal of an exceedingly rare and curious book in quarto Gothic—the manual of a forgotten church—the *Vigiliæ Mortuorum secundum Chorum Ecclesiæ Maguntinæ*.

I could not help thinking of the wild ritual of this work, and of its probable influence upon the hypochondriac, when, one evening, having informed me abruptly that the lady Madeline was no more, he stated his intention of preserving her corpse for a fortnight, (previously to its final interment,) in one of the numerous vaults within the main walls of the building. The **52** worldly reason, however, assigned for this singular proceeding, was one which I did not feel at liberty to dispute. The brother had been led to his resolution (so he told me) by consideration of the unusual character of the malady of the deceased, of certain obtrusive and eager inquiries on the part of her medical men, and of the remote and exposed situation of the burial-ground of the family. I will not deny that when I called to mind the sinister countenance of the person whom I met upon the staircase, on the day of my arrival at the house, I had no desire to oppose what I regarded as at best but a harmless, and by no means an unnatural, precaution.   **53**

At the request of Usher, I personally aided him in the arrangements for the temporary entombment. The body having been encoffined, we two alone bore it to its rest. The **54** vault in which we placed it (and which had been so long unopened that our torches, half smothered in its oppressive atmosphere, gave us little opportunity for investigation) was small, damp, and entirely without means of admission for

The Vigil of the Dead was a common title in the Middle Ages, including two rare quarto editions bound in Mainz in 1500.

52 Does Roderick feel she might be mistaken for alive—or that she *is* still alive and he doesn't want her reviving where she might be found?

53 The stealing of bodies for use by medical students and in scientific experiments was a thriving business at one time. The idea of allowing a body to be "mutilated" was horrifying (as it still is to many people), possibly because of the early-Christian belief that the whole body must be buried to assure its later resurrection—one of the grounds against cremation.

Grave-robbing is stock-in-trade in Gothic fiction and is a major plot element in *Frankenstein* (1818).

54 The narrator's description of the tomb is important, for Poe goes to great lengths to make it clear that no one could escape from such a crypt once placed there and sealed in.

If one takes the view that Roderick is attempting to bury (repress) some vital part of his unconscious, then the tomb's great depth and isolation are clearly symbolic.

We . . . made our way, with toil, into the scarcely less gloomy apartments of the upper portion of the house.
Illustration by F. S. Coburn, 1903

. . . I beheld him gazing upon vacancy for long hours,
. . . as if listening to some imaginary sound. *Illustration by Aubrey Beardsley*

55 This is the first time that the narrator has had a good look at Madeline, and the first time that her twinship has been acknowledged. Some readers see here a hint of an incestuous relationship between Roderick and Madeline.

56 Since catalepsy was known to masquerade as death, and Madeline is a cataleptic, one wonders why the narrator doesn't suspect that Madeline may still be alive. Apparently, he is already too much under the influence of Roderick to think clearly.

57 Recalling the image of the windows in *The Haunted Palace*. Roderick has slipped over the edge.

58 Poe seems to be suggesting we read between the lines, that the narrator's judgment and perceptions should no longer be taken at face value.

59 Note how long Madeline has lain in her sealed crypt.

60 He is still attempting to impose rationality on events transpiring around him, but it won't work. He must deal with a world where the old rules simply don't work anymore.

light; lying, at great depth, immediately beaneath that portion of the building in which was my own sleeping apartment. It had been used, apparently, in remote feudal times, for the worst purposes of a donjon-keep, and, in later days, as a place of deposit for powder, or some other highly combustible substance, as a portion of its floor, and the whole interior of a long archway through which we reached it, were carefully sheathed with copper. The door, of massive iron, had been, also, similarly protected. Its immense weight caused an unusually sharp grating sound, as it moved upon its hinges.

Having deposited our mournful burden upon tressels within this region of horror, we partially turned aside the yet unscrewed lid of the coffin, and looked upon the face of the tenant. A striking similitude between the brother and sister now first arrested my attention; and Usher, divining, perhaps, my thoughts, murmured out some few words from which I learned that the deceased and himself had been twins, and that sympathies of a scarcely intelligible nature had always

55 existed between them. Our glances, however, rested not long upon the dead—for we could not regard her unawed. The disease which had thus entombed the lady in the maturity of youth, had left, as usual in all maladies of a strictly cataleptical character, the mockery of a faint blush upon the bosom and the face, and that suspiciously lingering smile upon the lip

56 which is so terrible in death. We replaced and screwed down the lid, and, having secured the door of iron, made our way, with toil, into the scarcely less gloomy apartments of the upper portion of the house.

And now, some days of bitter grief having elasped, an observable change came over the features of the mental disorder of my friend. His ordinary manner had vanished. His ordinary occupations were neglected or forgotten. He roamed from chamber to chamber with hurried, unequal, and object-less step. The pallor of his countenance had assumed, if possible, a more ghastly hue—but the luminousness of his

57 eye had utterly gone out. The once occasional huskiness of his tone was heard no more; and a tremulous quaver, as if of extreme terror, habitually characterized his utterance. There were times, indeed, when I thought his unceasingly agitated mind was labouring with some oppressive secret, to divulge which he struggled for the necessary courage. At times, again, I was obliged to resolve all into the mere inexplicable vagaries of madness, for I beheld him gazing upon vacancy for long hours, in an attitude of the profoundest attention, as if listening to some imaginary sound. It was no wonder that his condition terrified—that it infected me. I felt creeping upon me, by slow yet certain degrees, the wild influences of his own

58 fantastic yet impressive superstitions.

It was, especially, upon retiring to bed late in the night of the seventh or eighth day after the placing of the lady Madeline within the donjon, that I experienced the full power of such

59 feelings. Sleep came not near my couch—while the hours waned and waned away. I struggled to reason off the nerv-

60 ousness which had dominion over me. I endeavoured to

believe that much, if not all of what I felt, was due to the bewildering influence of the gloomy furniture of the room—of the dark and tattered draperies, which, tortured into motion by the breath of a rising tempest, swayed fitfully to and fro upon the walls, and rustled uneasily about the decorations of the bed. But my efforts were fruitless. An irrepressible tremour gradually pervaded by frame; and, at length, there sat upon my very heart an incubus of utterly causeless alarm. **61** Shaking this off with a gasp and a struggle, I uplifted myself upon the pillows, and, peering earnestly within the intense darkness of the chamber, hearkened—I know not why, except that an instinctive spirit prompted me—to certain low and indefinite sounds which came, through the pauses of the storm, at long intervals, I knew not whence. Overpowered by an intense sentiment of horror, unaccountable yet unendurable, I threw on my clothes with haste (for I felt that I should sleep no more during the night), and endeavoured to arouse myself from the pitiable condition into which I had fallen, by pacing rapidly to and fro through the apartment.

I had taken but few turns in this manner, when a light step on an adjoining staircase arrested my attention. I presently recognized it as that of Usher. In an instant afterward he rapped, with a gentle touch, at my door, and entered, bearing a lamp. His countenance was, as usual, cadaverously wan—but, moreover, there was a species of mad hilarity in his eyes—an evidently restrained *hysteria* in his whole demeanour. His air appalled me—but anything was preferable to the solitude which I had so long endured, and I even welcomed his presence as a relief.

"And you have not seen it?" he said abruptly, after having stared about him for some moments in silence—"you have not then seen it?—but, stay! you shall." Thus speaking, and having carefully shaded his lamp, he hurried to one of the casements, and threw it freely open to the storm. **62**

The impetuous fury of the entering gust nearly lifted us from our feet. It was, indeed, a tempestuous yet sternly beautiful night, and one wildly singular in its terror and its beauty. A whirlwind had apparently collected its force in our **63** vicinity; for these were frequent and violent alterations in the direction of the wind; and the exceeding density of the clouds (which hung so low as to press upon the turrets of the house) did not prevent our perceiving the lifelike velocity with which they flew careering from all points against each other, without passing away into the distance. I say that even their exceeding density did not prevent our perceiving this—yet we had no glimpse of the moon or stars—nor was there any flashing forth of the lightning. But the under surfaces of the huge masses of agitated vapour, as well as all terrestrial objects immediately around us, were glowing in the unnatural light of a faintly luminous and distinctly visible gaseous exhalation which hung about and enshrouded the mansion. **64**

"You must not—you shall not behold this!" said I, shudderingly, to Usher, as I led him, with a gentle violence, from the window to a seat. "These appearances, which bewilder

61 Nightmare

62 Storms are another device of the Gothic tale. They bring to the fore man's fear of elemental forces, particularly thunder and lightning. The thunderbolt is traditionally a symbol of celestial fire, terrible and dynamic. Storms also isolate people from one another, underscoring our basic helplessness in the face of nature's power.

63 Whirlwinds and whirlpools are important in Poe's work because they seem to represent his notion of the rush to unity and its resulting destruction. Whirlwinds draw everything to their center, just as, in Poe's cosmology, all matter must one day return to its source.

64 Probably methane, or marsh gas. It usually forms underwater in swamps and marshes through the decomposition of plant and animal matter. The "terrestrial objects" that glow could be the result of certain luminous fungi, perhaps the previously described "web-like" growths covering the house.

65 The electrical phenomenon is probably Saint Elmo's fire, a luminous discharge of electricity observed as brushlike fiery jets extending from some projecting object. It occurs when the atmosphere becomes charged and an electrical potential strong enough to cause a discharge is created between an object and the air around it.

66 Poe made up the title and extended quotations from this fictional work, although it bears a resemblance to some of Sir Walter Scott's prose.

Lancelot, of course, comes from Arthurian legend, while "Canning" probably derives from William Canynges, mayor of Bristol in the 1400s and hero of a poem by Thomas Chatterton (1752–70).

67 Poe carefully sets up the narrator's final fall from reason. During the storm, alone in his room, "an irrepressible tremour" overcomes him and "utterly causeless alarm" fills him, even before Roderick comes to his room. But his terror is hardly "causeless," and his careless dismissal of it as such suggests he is still blind to the extent to which Roderick has affected him.

The final blow, say some, occurs as he reads to Roderick. By this time, the suggestive force of Usher, the house, and the storm are working full tilt on his imagination, forcing him into his own "mad tryst" with Roderick. Both men become completely absorbed in their fantasies as the narrator surrenders himself completely to his friend.

68 The sound of the door shattering comes from somewhere within the house. It might be the storm, or it might be Madeline in the crypt. Poe allows for both possibilities.

65 you, are merely electrical phenomena not uncommon—or it may be that they have their ghastly origin in the rank miasma of the tarn. Let us close this casement;—the air is chilling and dangerous to your frame. Here is one of your favourite romances. I will read, and you shall listen;—and so we will pass away this terrible night together."

The antique volume which I had taken up was the "Mad **66** Trist" of Sir Launcelot Canning; but I had called it a favourite of Usher's more in sad jest than in earnest; for, in truth, there is little in its uncouth and unimaginative prolixity which could have had interest for the lofty and spiritual ideality of my friend. It was, however, the only book immediately at hand; and I indulged a vague hope that the excitement which now agitated the hypochondriac, might find relief (for the history of mental disorder is full of similar anomalies) even in the extremeness of the folly which I should read. Could I have judged, indeed, by the wild overstrained air of vivacity with which he hearkened, or apparently hearkened, to the words of the tale, I might well have congratulated myself upon the **67** success of my design.

I had arrived at that well-known portion of the story where Ethelred, the hero of the Trist, having sought in vain for peaceable admission into the dwelling of the hermit, proceeds to make good an entrance by force. Here, it will be remembered, the words of the narrative run thus:

"And Ethelred, who was by nature of a doughty heart, and who was now mighty withal, on account of the powerfulness of the wine which he had drunken, waited no longer to hold parley with the hermit, who, in sooth, was of an obstinate and maliceful turn, but, feeling the rain upon his shoulders, and fearing the rising of the tempest, uplifted his mace outright, and, with blows, made quickly room in the plankings of the door for his gauntleted hand; and now pulling therewith sturdily, he so cracked, and ripped, and tore all asunder, that the noise of the dry and hollow-sounding wood alarumed and reverberated throughout the forest."

At the termination of this sentence I started, and for a moment, paused; for it appeared to me (although I at once concluded that my excited fancy had deceived me)—it appeared to me that, from some very remote portion of the mansion, there came, indistinctly, to my ears, what might have been, in its exact similarity of character, the echo (but a stifled and dull one certainly) of the very cracking and ripping sound which Sir Launcelot had so particularly de- **68** scribed. It was, beyond doubt, the coincidence alone which had arrested my attention; for, amid the rattling of the sashes of the casements, and the ordinary commingled noises of the still increasing storm, the sound, in itself, had nothing, surely which should have interested or disturbed me. I continued the story:

"But the good champion Ethelred, now entering within the door, was sore enraged and amazed to perceive no signal of the maliceful hermit; but, in the stead thereof, a dragon of a scaly and prodigious demeanour, and of a fiery tongue, which sate in guard before a palace of gold, with a floor of silver; and upon the wall there hung a shield of shining brass with this legend enwritten—

> Who entereth herein, a conqueror hath bin;
> Who slayeth the dragon, the shield he shall win;

And Ethelred uplifted his mace, and struck upon the head of the dragon, which fell before him, and gave up his pesty breath, with a shriek so horrid and harsh, and withal so piercing, that Ethelred had fain to close his ears with his hands against the dreadful noise of it, the like whereof was never before heard."

Here again I paused abruptly, and now with a feeling of wild amazement—for there could be no doubt whatever that, in this instance, I did actually hear (although from what direction it proceeded I found it impossible to say) a low and apparently distant, but harsh, protracted, and most unusual screaming or grating sound—the exact counterpart of what my fancy had already conjured up for the dragon's unnatural shriek as described by the romancer.

Oppressed, as I certainly was, upon the occurrence of the second and most extraordinary coincidence, by a thousand conflicting sensations, in which wonder and extreme terror were predominant, I still retained sufficient presence of mind to avoid exciting, by any observation, the sensitive nervousness of my companion. I was by no means certain that he had noticed the sounds in question; although, assuredly, a strange alteration had, during the last few minutes, taken place in his demeanour. From a position fronting my own, he had gradually brought round his chair, so as to sit with his face to the door of the chamber; and thus I would but partially perceive his features, although I saw that his lips trembled as if he were murmuring inaudibly. His head had dropped upon his breast—yet I knew that he was not asleep, from the wide and rigid opening of the eye as I caught a glance of it in profile. The motion of his body, too, was at variance with this idea—for he rocked from side to side with a gentle yet constant and uniform sway. Having rapidly taken notice of all this, I resumed the narrative of Sir Launcelot, which thus proceeded:

"And now, the champion, having escaped from the terrible fury of the dragon, bethinking himself of the brazen shield, and of the breaking up of the enchantment which was upon it, removed the carcass from out of the way before him, and approached valorously over the silver pavement of the castle to where the shield was upon the wall; which in sooth tarried not for his full coming, but fell down at his feet upon the silver floor, with a mighty great and terrible ringing sound."

No sooner had these syllables passed my lips, than—as if a shield of brass had indeed, at the moment, fallen heavily upon a floor of silver—I became aware of a distinct, hollow, metallic, and clangorous, yet apparently muffled reverberation. Completely unnerved, I leaped to my feet; but the measured rocking movement of Usher was undisturbed. I rushed to the chair in which he sat. His eyes were bent fixedly before him, and throughout his whole countenance there reigned a stony rigidity. But, as I placed my hand upon his

"Madman! I tell you that she now stands without the door!" *Illustration by Johann Friedrich Vogel, 1856*

69 Roderick is talking to himself, and his speech is an interior dialogue between the rational side of his personality (by now sadly disintegrated) and the irrational. Note his rocking movement, which is characteristic of certain mental states, including schizophrenia—whose symptoms parallel those of Roderick at this point.

70 Roderick refers to himself, but also to the narrator, who by now is sharing completely his fantastic vision. Usher is mad, but he clings to no illusions of rationality. The narrator, however, still believes he is in control of his thoughts, even though it is Roderick who holds sway.

71 The entrance of Madeline Usher is dramatic and caps the development of the supernatural element of the tale.

The narrator and Roderick have borne her coffin to a vault that contains so little air that their torches are "half smothered in its oppressive atmosphere." The tomb lies at a "great depth" and is sheathed in thick copper, while the door is heavy iron, also sheathed with copper. Once the coffin is in place, the two men screw down the lid and secure the iron door—which takes both of their efforts to accomplish.

Having undergone a wasting disease for some time before her "death," it seems unlikely that a living Madeline could break out of her sealed coffin, open the iron door, climb the long stairs, and knock down the huge wooden door to the study. Indeed, with the little amount of air in the tightly sealed coffin, and in the crypt, it would be difficult for her to survive a few hours, much less a week.

The elaborate detail of Madeline's burial serves only one purpose: to underscore the improbability of the climax. Thus it seems we must either accept a return by a ghost (who can move through solid matter) with immense powers, or assume that the narrator's final vision is an hallucination.

"The American development of the Gothic tale inclined toward explained Gothic in psychological terms," writes G. R. Thompson, "a mode that preserved some ambiguity as to the real nature of events" (*Emerson Society Quarterly*, Vol. 18, pp. 19–29). It is this ambiguity which leaves "The Fall of the House of Usher" so open to varying interpretations. In the end, it is up to the reader to decide what has happened.

shoulder, there came a strong shudder over his whole person; a sickly smile quivered about his lips; and I saw that he spoke in a low, hurried, and gibbering murmur, as if unconscious of my presence. Bending closely over him, I at length drank **69** in the hideous import of his words.

"Not hear it?—yes, I hear it, and *have* heard it. Long—long—long many minutes, many hours, many days, have I heard it—yet I dared not—oh, pity me, miserable wretch that I am!—I dared not—I *dared* not speak! We *have put her living in the tomb!* Said I not that my senses were acute? I *now* tell you that I heard her first feeble movements in the hollow coffin. I heard them—many, many days ago—yet I dared not—*I dared not speak!* And now—to-night—Ethelred—ha! ha!—the breaking of the hermit's door, and the death-cry of the dragon, and the clangor of the shield!—say, rather, the rending of her coffin, and the grating of the iron hinges of her prison, and her struggles within the coppered archway of the vault! Oh whither shall I fly? Will she not be here anon? Is she not hurrying to upbraid me for my haste? Have I not heard her footstep on the stair? Do I not distinguish that heavy **70** and horrible beating of her heart? *Madman!*" here he sprang furiously to his feet, and shrieked out his syllables, as if in the effort he were giving up his soul—"*Madman! I tell you that she now stands without the door!*"

As if in the superhuman energy of his utterance there had been found the potency of a spell—the huge antique panels to which the speaker pointed, threw slowly back, upon the instant, their ponderous and ebony jaws. It was the work of the rushing gust—but then without those doors there *did* stand the lofty and enshrouded figure of the lady Madeline of Usher. There was blood upon her white robes, and the evidence of some bitter struggle upon every portion of her emaciated frame. For a moment she remained trembling and reeling to and fro upon the threshold, then, with a low moaning cry, fell heavily inward upon the person of her brother, and in her violent and now final death-agonies, bore him to the floor a corpse, and a victim to the terrors he had anticipated. **72**

71

From that chamber, and from that mansion, I fled aghast. The storm was still abroad in all its wrath as I found myself crossing the old causeway. Suddenly there shot along the path a wild light, and I turned to see whence a gleam so unusual could have issued; for the vast house and its shadows were alone behind me. The radiance was that of the full, setting, and blood-red moon which now shone vividly through that once barely-discernible fissure of which I have before spoken as extending from the roof of the building, in a zigzag direction, to the base. While I gazed, this fissure rapidly widened—there came a fierce breath of the whirlwind—the entire orb of the satellite burst at once upon my sight—my brain reeled as I saw the mighty walls rushing asunder—there was a long tumultuous shouting sound like the voice of a thousand waters—and the deep and dank tarn at my feet closed sullenly and silently over the fragments of the *"House of Usher."* **73**

72 Roderick and Madeline are joined together in death. Take your pick: a) symbolizing reunification in the Primal Particle; b) the repressed part of the psyche forces its way out and madness results; c) melancholia leads to obsession and self-destruction; d) the romantic idealist severs all ties with the real world; e) the narrator has succumbed to Roderick's insanity and has fallen into temporary insanity himself; or f) Madeline has her revenge, returning from the grave to drag Roderick down to his death, destroying in the process the house both as a physical structure and as a symbol of the family.

73 The oppressive atmosphere that surrounds the Usher estate may be tinting the moon red. On the other hand, an earthquake and a blood-red moon are the Sixth Seal of Revelation 6:12, further underscoring the notion of final catastrophe, as does the allusion to "his voice as the sound of many waters," from Revelation 1:15.

Compare the ending here with Poe's description of the end of the world in "The Conversation of Eiros and Charmion" (1839):

"For a moment there was a wild lurid light alone, visiting and penetrating all things. Then—let us bow down, Charmion, before the excessive majesty of the great God!—then, there came a shouting and pervading sound, as if from the mouth itself of HIM; while the whole incumbent mass of ether in which we existed, burst at once into a species of intense flame, for whose surpassing brilliancy and all-fervid heat even the angels in the high Heaven of pure knowledge have no name. Thus ended all."

"Water and fire are the two conflicting elements which will ultimately penetrate each other and unite; they represent all contraries in the elemental world," writes J. C. Cooper in his Illustrated Encyclopaedia of Traditional Symbols (1978), p. 188.

Certainly "The Fall of the House of Usher" is a powerful tale, and one that invites interpretation. As for its "one and only" meaning, I must beg off. It is against Poe's nature to provide any "final" answer. Two other critics put it very well:

"The ghosts in the tale of Usher, then, are those of the mind. Such an analysis does not deny the supernaturalistic surface level of the tale, or other significant matters such as the incest motif, the eerie hint of vampirism, the use of abstract art to suggest sexuality, entombment, or nothingness, or the carefully balanced themes of order and sentience that other critics have noted. Rather, such a reading incorporates them into its overall pattern, while wrapping a layer of dramatic irony about the whole." (G. R. Thompson, *Poe's Fiction,* University of Wisconsin Press, 1973; p. 96)

". . . the tale is no less self-consistent when we read it as a record of mania than when we read it as a tale of simple horror. But we must add that it is no *more* self-consistent: the two 'Literal' interpretations co-exist; they impinge upon one another only when our analysis presses them. And if these two literal readings are equally defensible—a situation which we can account for only by reference to Poe's great plotting skill—there remain other levels of meaning, other readings which we cannot ignore. . . . We shall not grasp Poe's full accomplishment in fiction until we hear each of the several voices of a tale as at once discrete and part of a harmonious totality." (Robert Regan, *Poe: a Collection of Critical Essays,* Prentice-Hall, 1967; pp. 11–12)

. . . the huge antique panels . . . threw slowly back, upon the instant, their ponderous and ebony jaws. *Artist unknown*

WILLIAM WILSON

First published in *The Gift*, Christmas 1839, this is one of Poe's undisputed masterpieces, a compelling portrait of a man at war with his own conscience. Unlike "Ligeia," "The Fall of the House of Usher," and "The Masque of the Red Death," "William Wilson" is remarkably straightforward. There is no list of complex and conflicting critical interpretations here, for Poe makes it quite clear that this is the tale of a man who dooms himself because he refuses to accept a long-repressed side of his personality.

In this, Poe anticipates much of what concerned the psychological movement later in the century and has continued to our own day. He writes, of course, before Freud, Jung, or Adler, and thus his vocabulary is not the same. He uses age-old symbols and myths to frame the tale, but so emphatically that "William Wilson" remains one of the most forceful parables of the divided self.

Thomas Mann has called this the classic story of the *Doppelgänger*, or double, a theme that occurs again and again in folklore and literature through the centuries and in widely differing cultures around the world. "Among primitives," says psychologist Otto Rank, "the designations for shadow, reflected image, and the like, also serve for the notion 'soul,' and . . . the most primitive concept of the soul of the Greeks, Egyptians and other culturally prominent peoples coincides with a double which is essentially identical with the body." (*The Double*, University of North Carolina, 1971; p. 83)

The comparisons between "William Wilson" and this concept of the double, and between Poe's portrait and the writings of Freud and Jung are particularly fascinating (and will be taken up as they occur in the story).

Poe's immediate sources include an article by Washington Irving, "An Unwritten Drama of Lord Byron," which appeared in *The Gift* for 1836. In a letter to Irving (October 12, 1839), Poe gladly admits the borrowing.

Irving, in his article, discusses a projected drama of Byron (which he did not finish) based on an old Spanish play that Shelley had given to him: "The hero, . . . Alfonso, is a Spanish nobleman. . . . His passions, from early and unrestrained indulgence, have become impetuous and ungovernable, and he follows their impulses with a . . . disregard of consequences.

"Soon after his entrance into the world, he finds himself followed, occasionally, in public places, by a person masked and muffled up so as to conceal both countenance and figure. . . . It is carried, by degrees, to such lengths, that he becomes, as it were, Alfonso's shadow—his second self. . . . In the giddy mazes of the dance, in which Alfonso is addressing his fair partner with the honeyed words of seduction, he sees the stranger pass like a shadow before him; a voice, like the voice of his own soul, whispers in his ear; the words of seduction die from his lips; he no longer hears the music of the dance. . . .

"Alfonso now thirsts only for vengeance, but the mysterious stranger eludes his pursuit, and his emissaries in vain endeavour to discover his retreat. At length he succeeds in tracing him to the house of his mistress, and attacks him with the fury of frantic jealousy, taxes him with his wrongs, and demands *satisfaction*. They fight; his rival scarcely defends himself; at the first thrust he receives the sword of Alfonso in his bosom; and in falling, exclaims, 'Are you satisfied?'

"The mask and mantle of the unknown drop off, and Alfonso discovers his own image—the spectre of himself—he dies with horror!

"The spectre is an allegorical being, the personification of conscience, or of the passions. . . .

"The foregoing sketch of the plot may hereafter suggest a rich theme to a poet or dramatist of the Byron school."

Poe may also have read or heard of Musset's *December Night* (1835), a poem in which a man tells us that since his youth a shadowy double has followed him everywhere, appearing, clothed all in black, at all the decisive moments of his life. He is unable to understand its purpose until, in later life, he addresses it directly, first as his evil fate, then as his guardian angel, and finally as his own reflection:

> Who art thou, countenance so pale and drear,
>   Somber likeness of sable hue?
> Sad fleeting bird, why just to me appear:
> Is it an empty dream, *my* image here,
>   Which within this mirror comes to view?

Finally, the dark figure identifies itself as "Solitude."

E. T. A. Hoffman writes of the double in his tales "The Story of the Lost Reflection" and "The Doubles," but neither is related to Poe's tale other than incidentally.

Poe's tale may have inspired Oscar Wilde's "The Picture of Dorian Gray" (1891), in which the evil twin is embodied in the portrait, which takes on all the physical results of Gray's profligate living, leaving him (on the surface, at least) unblemished. In Robert Louis Stevenson's *The Strange Case of Dr. Jekyll and Mr. Hyde* (1886), the theme is man's dual life, with the moral façade often hiding the forbidding half-self inside. However, in Stevenson's tale, the warning seems to be the danger of loosing that interior self when the exterior self no longer has enough strength to protect itself. Poe's conclusion suggests that one cannot repress one's moral nature; Stevenson's seems to reinforce the idea that without a moral sense man's evil nature will take over and destroy him.

In his review of Nathaniel Hawthorne, Poe remarks that in the tale "Howe's Masquerade" he finds "a very flattering coincidence of thought" between one section of that story and the climax of "William Wilson." He quotes a passage, italicizing those elements which resemble his own tale:

"*With a dark flush of wrath* upon his brow they saw the general *draw his sword* and *advance to meet* the figure *in the cloak* before the latter had stepped one pace upon the floor. "*Villain, unmuffle yourself,*" cried he, "You pass no farther!" The figure, without blenching a hair's breadth from the sword which was pointed at his breast, made a solemn pause, and *lowered the cape of the cloak* from his face, yet not sufficiently for the spectators to catch a glimpse of it. But Sir William Howe had evidently seen enough. The sternness of his countenance gave place to a look of wild amazement, if not horror, while he recoiled several steps from the figure, and *let fall his sword upon the floor.*"

Poe makes very little of this coincidence other than to point it out, and the tales are so different otherwise that indeed he could say no more.

Three German films, all called *The Student of Prague*, seem to be based in part on "William Wilson." The first, directed by Stellan Rye, appeared in 1913 and dealt with a student who signs away his mirrored reflection to a mysterious man. The 1926 version, directed by Henrik Galeen, starred Conrad Veidt, and the 1935 version, directed by Arthur Robison, starred Anton Walbrook. In 1968, "William Wilson" was part of *Spirits of the Dead*, a French-Italian production, in which Louis Malle directed Alain Delon and Brigitte Bardot in a rather free adaptation.

Martin Donegon narrates the recorded version (CMS 663).

What say of it? what say [of] CONSCIENCE grim,
That spectre in my path?
          —*Chamberlayne's Pharonnida.*   **1**

Let me call myself, for the present, William Wilson. The fair **2** page now lying before me need not be sullied with my real appellation. This has been already too much an object for the scorn—for the horror—for the detestation of my race. To the uttermost regions of the globe have not the indignant winds bruited its unparalleled infamy? Oh, outcast of all outcasts most abandoned!—to the earth art thou not forever dead? to

1 The lines are not from William Chamberlayne's *Pharonnida*, but a garbled quote from his play *Love's Victory* (1658): "Conscience waits on me like the frightening shades/Of ghosts when gastly [sic] messengers of death. . . ." Chamberlayne (1619–89) is today considered a minor playwright; George Sampson says, "The spirit which at its fullest inspiration produces Spenser and Shakespeare produces at its lowest Chamberlayne . . ." (*Concise Cambridge History of English Literature*, 3rd ed., 1972; p. 295).

2 Poe knew two men by this last name, both of whom did business with his foster father, John Allan. One was a Quaker, the other an agent for Washington College.

However, Poe could have easily picked the name William Wilson simply for its alliteration, or because it joins two commonplace names.

3 It is highly dramatic, but not very probable, that the narrator has been able to do so much evil in his short life. More likely, he is expressing his own self-hatred.

4 Apparently Wilson has gone on to worse crimes than card-sharking, drinking, and lusting, which are the low points of his sinful career mentioned in the tale.

5 Although Wilson has convinced himself of all this, the tale itself proves otherwise. His "virtue," whatever there was of it, did not "suddenly" drop away, as we can see from the careful description of his childhood and the slow development of his profligate life. He is unable to see the internal development of his personality, particularly the split between his carefully constructed exterior and his repressed inner self.

Freud says that the double is an "insurance against destruction to the ego" (*On Creativity and the Unconscious*, Harper, 1958; p. 141), the result of repressing those things which might endanger a person's conception of himself.

In Jungian terms, what we see here is the building up of the "shadow," which Jung says symbolizes our "other side," our "dark brother," who is an invisible but inseparable part of our physical identity. "Without shadow," he says, we are only a "two-dimensional phantom" (*Collected Works*, Pantheon Books, 1957; VII, p. 236). Our "dark side" is that part of us we reject for ethical, esthetic, or other reasons, and repress because it contradicts our conscious way of life. A child has no shadow, but it becomes more pronounced as he grows older, as qualities that the ego (the conscious self) does not need or cannot use are set aside and repressed.

The parallel between Wilson's comments and the development of the shadow provides us with at least one viable interpretation of Poe's tale.

6 See "Four Beasts in One," note 1.

7 One wonders if this is a confession before death, as in "The Black Cat" and (perhaps) "The Cask of Amontillado."

James Cox notes that Wilson "sounds like a fugitive from an asylum devoted expressly to the maintenance of ineffectual heroes escaped from sentimental and gothic romance" (*Virginia Quarterly*, Vol. 44, 1968; p. 70).

8 This passage helps explain the rather fantastic events that follow. Wilson is obviously no ordinary character, and so we can expect extraordinary things to happen. But he is not insane, although clearly neurotic, and so through him we come to understand what he does not: the reality of his self-induced downfall.

9 This is a classic case of what would later be called projection: attributing one's faults to others. While it may be true that Wilson's parents erred in their judgment, the very fact that he realizes that this may be so is evidence that he sees something wrong in his own behavior. But he shows no sign of any attempt to correct the problem, choosing instead to blame others and to continue repressing his reproving self.

The Manor House School at Stoke Newington. *Artist unknown, 1850*

its honors, to its flowers, to its golden aspirations?—and a cloud, dense, dismal, and limitless, does it not hang eternally **3** between thy hopes and heaven?

I would not, if I could, here or to-day, embody a record of my later years of unspeakable misery, and unpardonable **4** crime. This epoch—these later years—took unto themselves a sudden elevation in turpitude, whose origin alone it is my present purpose to assign. Men usually grow base by degrees. **5** From me, in an instant, all virtue dropped bodily as a mantle. From comparatively trivial wickedness I passed, with the **6** stride of a giant, into more than the enormities of an Elah-Gabalus. What chance—what one event brought this evil thing to pass, bear with me while I relate. Death approaches; and the shadow which foreruns him has thrown a softening influence over my spirit. I long, in passing through the dim valley, for the sympathy—I had nearly said for the pity—of my fellow men. I would fain have them believe that I have been, in some measure, the slave of circumstances beyond human control. I would wish them to seek out for me, in the details I am about to give, some little oasis of *fatality* amid a wilderness of error. I would have them allow—what they cannot refrain from allowing—that, although temptation may have erewhile existed as great, man was never *thus*, at least, tempted before—certainly, never *thus* fell. And is it therefore that he has never thus suffered? Have I not indeed been living in a dream? And am I not now dying a victim to the horror **7** and the mystery of the wildest of all sublunary visions?

I am the descendant of a race whose imaginative and easily excitable temperament has at all times rendered them re-**8** markable; and, in my earliest infancy, I gave evidence of having fully inherited the family character. As I advanced in years it was more strongly developed; becoming, for many reasons, a cause of serious disquietude to my friends, and of positive injury to myself. I grew self-willed, addicted to the wildest caprices, and a prey to the most ungovernable passions. Weak-minded, and beset with constitutional infirmities akin to my own, my parents could do but little to check the evil **9** propensities which distinguished me. Some feeble and ill-

directed efforts resulted in complete failure on their part, and, of course, in total triumph on mine. Thenceforward my voice was a household law; and at an age when few children have abandoned their leading-strings, I was left to the guidance of my own will, and became, in all but name, the master of my own actions.

My earliest recollections of a school-life are connected with a large, rambling, Elizabethan house, in a misty-looking village of England, where were a vast number of gigantic and gnarled trees, and where all the houses were excessively ancient. In **10** truth, it was a dream-like and spirit-soothing place, that venerable old town. At this moment, in fancy, I feel the refreshing chilliness of its deeply-shadowed avenues, inhale the fragrance of its thousand shrubberies, and thrill anew with undefinable delight, at the deep hollow note of the churchbell, breaking, each hour, with sullen and sudden roar, upon the stillness of the dusky atmosphere in which the fretted Gothic steeple lay imbedded and asleep.

It gives me, perhaps, as much pleasure as I can now in any manner experience, to dwell upon minute recollections of the school and its concerns. Steeped in misery as I am—misery, alas! only too real—I shall be pardoned for seeking relief, however slight and temporary, in the weakness of a few rambling details. These, moreover, utterly trivial, and even ridiculous in themselves, assume, to my fancy, adventitious importance, as connected with a period and a locality when and where I recognize the first ambiguous monitions of the destiny which afterwards so fully overshadowed me. Let me then remember.

The house, I have said, was old and irregular. The grounds were extensive, and a high and solid brick wall, topped with a bed of mortar and broken glass, encompassed the whole. **11** This prison-like rampart formed the limit of our domain; beyond it we saw but thrice a week—once every Saturday afternoon, when, attended by two ushers, we were permitted to take brief walks in a body through some of the neighbouring fields—and twice during Sunday, when we were paraded in the same formal manner to the morning and evening service in the one church of the village. Of this church the principal of our school was pastor. With how deep a spirit of wonder and perplexity was I wont to regard him from our remote pew in the gallery, as, with step solemn and slow, he ascended the pulpit! This reverend man, with countenance so demurely benign, with robes so glossy and so clerically flowing, with wig so minutely powdered, so rigid and so vast,—could this be he who, of late, with sour visage, and in snuffy habiliments, administered, ferule in hand, the Draconian laws of the academy? Oh, gigantic paradox, too utterly monstrous for **12** solution! **13**

At an angle of the ponderous wall frowned a more ponderous gate. It was riveted and studded with iron bolts, and sur- **14** mounted with jagged iron spikes. What impression of deep awe did it inspire! It was never opened save for the three periodical egressions and ingressions already mentioned; then, in every creak of its mighty hinges, we found a plenitude of

10 Poe makes use of memories from his own childhood at the Manor House School at Stoke Newington (see Introduction) in his description. However, the Manor House was not Elizabethan in style, and Poe may have confused it with the neighboring Fleet House, a large mansion.

It is interesting to note that, as the story progresses, the locale becomes increasingly vague and impressionistic. Even here, the fairly specific details have an ambiguous feel to them, as if the school and its environs are not quite real.

Note, too, that Wilson mistakenly assumes that the details of his early life are insignificant.

11 Harold Bayley, in *The Lost Language of Symbolism* (London, 1912), sums up two essential features of walls as representing the feminine element and as symbolizing matter as opposed to spirit. Wilson feels secure within the walls, and yet also hemmed in by the mundane environment.

Walls also symbolize the boundary between the profane outer space and the sacred inner space—in this case, perhaps, between Wilson's inner self and his worldly exterior.

12 Corporal punishment was dealt out in British schools for even trivial offenses. A particularly disturbing example is in James Joyce's *A Portrait of the Artist as a Young Man* (1914). A ferrule is a ring or cap of metal on the end of a stick to keep it from wearing or splitting. Poe probably means a cane here.

Draco, or Dracon (fl. 621 B.C.) was an Athenian politician and law codifier. While we have little of his work to judge from, accounts by Aristotle and Plutarch indicate that the penalty of death was prescribed for even minor crimes, and so "Draconian law" has become a synonym for harsh legislation.

13 Wilson cannot understand how a man who utters words of Christian charity and forgiveness can also deal out corporal punishment to his students. This underscores his complete (and perhaps willful) misunderstanding of Christian love, which holds that to severely punish a child is justified if it sets him on the right road. But as with so many of Poe's narrators, Wilson's view of the world is simplistic, with everything reduced to black or white. One is either good or evil, he seems to be saying, and whatever you are, you can't change. Common sense tells us different, and Christian thought teaches that although men are capable of sin, they are also capable of redemption.

Psychologically, this stresses the split within Wilson's psyche as he continues to repress these complexities further into his unconscious.

14 Gates and doors are important symbols, for they often mark the threshold between one world and another. To Gaston Bachelard, doors represent "the temptation to open up the ultimate depths of being, and the desire to conquer all reticent beings." Sometimes, he says, the door is "closed, bolted, padlocked," but at other times "there is one that is just barely ajar. We have only to give it a very slight push. The hinges have been well oiled. And our fate becomes visible.

"If one were to give an account of all the doors one has opened and closed, of all the doors one would like to re-open, one would have to tell the story of one's life." (*The Poetics of Space*, Beacon Press, 1969; pp. 222–24)

The wall and gate circumscribe Wilson's world, and in Poe's tales circumscription usually means the exclusion from the consciousness of the so-called real world ("The Fall of the House of Usher," "Ligeia").

Reverend John Bransby, M.A.—Poe's English school-master, circa 1820 *Artist unknown*

15 An ornamental garden with paths between the beds

16 As in "The Fall of the House of Usher," one can read this extensive series of hidden, tortuous passageways, gloomy interiors, underground vaults, and mysterious rooms as symbolic of the labyrinth of the human mind. Was there ever a building so bizarrely constructed? Perhaps these are only the impressions of the young Wilson, for we have all experienced returning to some childhood locale only to discover that the reality does not match our memory of the place. Bachelard has some pertinent observations about this: "For the real houses of memory, the houses to which we return in dreams, the houses that are rich in unalterable [dreamlike qualities], do not readily lend themselves to description. To describe them would be like showing them to visitors. We can perhaps tell everything about the present, but about the past! The first, the [dreamlike] house, must retain its shadows. For it belongs to the literature of depth. . . ." (*The Poetics of Space*, p. 13)

The nature of the school house may also echo Poe's recurring theme of the limits of human knowledge. In "The Power of Words," Poe's Agathos says that the "infinity of matter" is there for the soul to quench its thirst to know, even though this thirst "is for ever unquenchable within it—since to quench it would be to extinguish the soul itself."

17 Corner

18 Poe's schoolmaster at Stoke Newington was the Reverend John Bransby, but the schoolmaster of "William Wilson" seems to be a composite of Bransby and the Reverend George Gaskin, rector of the nearby church and a secretary for the Society for Promoting Christian Knowledge.

19 A Scottish word meaning both pedagogue and clergyman

20 "Strong and lasting pain," referring to pressing, a medieval penalty for refusing to plead guilty or not guilty

mystery—a world of matter for solemn remark, or for more solemn meditation.

The extensive enclosure was irregular in form, having many capacious recesses. Of these, three or four of the largest constituted the play-ground. It was level, and covered with fine hard gravel. I well remember it had no trees, nor benches, nor anything similar within it. Of course it was in the rear of

15 the house. In front lay a small parterre, planted with box and other shrubs; but through this sacred division we passed only upon rare occasions indeed—such as a first advent to school or final departure thence, or perhaps, when a parent or friend having called for us, we joyfully took our way home for the Christmas or Midsummer holydays.

But the house!—how quaint an old building was this!—to me how veritably a palace of enchantment! There was really

16 no end to its windings—to its incomprehensible subdivisions. It was difficult, at any given time, to say with certainty upon which of its two stories one happened to be. From each room to every other there were sure to be found three or four steps either in ascent or descent. Then the lateral branches were innumerable—inconceivable—and so returning in upon themselves, that our most exact ideas in regard to the whole mansion were not very far different from those with which we pondered upon infinity. During the five years of my residence here, I was never able to ascertain with precision, in what remote locality lay the little sleeping apartment assigned to myself and some eighteen or twenty other scholars.

The school-room was the largest in the house—I could not help thinking, in the world. It was very long, narrow, and dismally low, with pointed Gothic windows and a ceiling of

17 oak. In a remote and terror-inspiring angle was a square enclosure of eight or ten feet, comprising the *sanctum*, "during

18 hours," of our principal, the Reverend Dr. Bransby. It was a solid structure, with massy door, sooner than open which in

19 the absence of the "Dominie," we would all have willingly

20 perished by the *peine forte et dure*. In other angles were two other similar boxes, far less reverenced, indeed, but still greatly matters of awe. One of these was the pulpit of the

21 "classical" usher, one of the "English and mathematical." Interspersed about the room, crossing and recrossing in endless irregularity, were innumerable benches and desks, black, ancient and timeworn, piled desperately with much-bethumbed books, and so beseamed with initial letters, names at full length, grotesque figures, and other multiplied efforts of the knife, as to have entirely lost what little of original form might have been their portion in days long departed. A huge bucket with water stood at one extremity of the room, and a

22 clock of stupendous dimensions at the other.

Encompassed by the massy walls of this venerable academy, I passed, yet not in tedium or disgust, the years of the third

23 lustrum of my life. The teeming brain of childhood requires no external world of incident to occupy or amuse it; and the apparently dismal monotony of a school was replete with more intense excitement than my riper youth has derived from luxury, or my full manhood from crime. Yet I must believe that my first mental development had in it much of the uncommon—even much of the *outré*. Upon mankind at large **24** the events of very early existence rarely leave in mature age any definite impression. All is gray shadow—a weak and irregular remembrance—an indistinct regathering of feeble pleasures and phantasmagoric pains. With me this is not so. In childhood I must have felt with the energy of a man what I now find stamped upon memory in lines as vivid, as deep, and as durable as the *exergues* of the Carthaginian medals. **25**

Yet in fact—in the fact of the world's view—how little was there to remember! The morning's awakening, the nightly summons to bed; the connings, the recitations; the periodical **26** half-holidays, and perambulations; the play-ground, with its broils, its pastimes, its intrigues;—these, by a mental sorcery long forgotten, were made to involve a wilderness of sensation, **27** a world of rich incident, an universe of varied emotion, of excitement the most passionate and spirit-stirring. *"Oh, le bon temps, que ce siècle de fer!"* **28**

In truth, the ardor, the enthusiasm, and the imperiousness of my disposition, soon rendered me a marked character among my schoolmates, and by slow, but natural gradations, gave me an ascendancy over all not greatly older than myself;— over all with a single exception. This exception was found in the person of a scholar, who, although no relation, bore the same Christian and surname as myself;—a circumstance, in fact, little remarkable; for, notwithstanding a noble descent, mine was one of those everyday appellations which seem, by prescriptive right, to have been, time out of mind, the common property of the mob. In this narrative, I have therefore designated myself as William Wilson,—a fictitious title not very dissimilar to the real. My namesake alone, of those who in school phraseology constituted "our set," presumed to compete with me in the studies of the class—in the sports and broils of the play-ground—to refuse implicit belief in my assertions, and submission to my will—indeed, to interfere with my arbitrary dictation in any respect whatsoever. If there is on earth a supreme and unqualified despotism, it is the despotism of a master mind in boyhood over the less energetic spirits of its companions.

Wilson's rebellion was to me a source of the greatest embarrassment;—the more so as, in spite of the bravado with which in public I made a point of treating him and his pretensions, I secretly felt that I feared him, and could not help thinking the equality which he maintained so easily with myself, a proof of his true superiority; since not to be overcome cost me a perpetual struggle. Yet this superiority—even this equality—was in truth acknowledged by no one but myself; our associates, by some unaccountable blindness, seemed not even to suspect it. Indeed, his competition his resistance, and **29** especially his impertinent and dogged interference with my purposes, were not more pointed than private. He appeared to be destitute alike of the ambition which urged, and of the passionate energy of mind which enabled me to excel. In his

to a capital charge. A wooden plank was placed on the chest of the condemned and stones were heaped upon it until the victim was crushed to death.

21 Ushers were assistant teachers.

22 The huge size of objects that Wilson describes is further evidence that his memories are from a child's point of view.

23 A lustrum is a period of five years; the third lustrum would be age ten to fifteen.

24 Excessive

25 The *exergue* is that portion of a coin or medal between the rim and the bottom of the picture or design. The suggestion here is that the exergue would be less worn through circulation than the rest of the coin. In *Graham's* (March 1842), Poe writes, "Fifty years hence it will be difficult . . . to make out the deepest indentations of the *exergue*."

The coins (*médaille* means old coins no longer in circulation) are those of the Vandal king of Carthage, Gelimer (ruled 530–34); the exergue takes up almost half of the design.

26 Close study, committing to memory (from Middle English *connen*, to know, learn)

27 "Wilderness" here means a mingled or confused collection.

28 "Oh, what fine times, this age of iron!" is from Voltaire's *Le Mondain* (1736), but the meaning here is ironic, since the Iron Age was the symbolic last step in the progressive degeneration of mankind (beginning with the Golden Age) and a period of misery and crime.

29 Our first hint that the second Wilson is an extension of the first.

30 Poe means for the second Wilson to represent the first's conscience, as the letter to Washington Irving indicates. According to Freud, the conscience is the superego, the moral or judicial branch of personality, which develops out of the ego as a consequence of the child's assimilation of his parents' standards of what is good and bad. Through this process, the child replaces their authority with his own, inner authority. Perhaps because Wilson's parents gave him little guidance, his own conscience is not integrated into his conscious personality.

The superego enforces its rules by rewards and punishments, and here, since it is denied access to Wilson's ego (consciousness), takes on a life of its own in order to confront him with its existence.

The second Wilson is what Carl Jung calls the "personal shadow," containing psychic features that have been unlived since birth, or at least scarcely lived. Such shadows may appear to us as a figure from our consciousness, as an elder brother or sister, a best friend, or a twin.

The shadow, Jung says, is the counterpart of our conscious ego, and it grows and develops at the same pace. We seldom or never admit this dark mass of experience to our conscious life, and this bars the way to the creative depths of our unconscious. If a person does not admit the shadow's presence, and continues to repress it, he builds his external personality on a very shaky foundation. Such a person finds it difficult to enter into a genuine relationship or to do any really vital work, and as more and more repressions accumulate in the shadow, the person becomes increasingly neurotic.

"Everyone carries a shadow," says Jung, "and the less it is embodied in the individual's conscious life, the blacker and denser it is. . . ." (*Collected Works*, II, p. 76)

To confront one's shadow means to take a mercilessly critical attitude toward one's self, but more often a person may simply project any blame onto external sources. In analysis, patients almost always resist the exposure of the shadow, for the conscious ego fears that its painstakingly maintained edifice will collapse under the weight of this insight. Still, Jung says, as bitter as this experience may be, we must learn to distinguish ourselves from our shadow, by recognizing its reality as a part of our nature, for only then can we begin to build an objective attitude towaard the self.

Note that here Wilson refuses with all his will to acknowledge the meaning of his double.

Still another theory is that the second Wilson represents "astral projection." In this scheme of things, man has a second body, a spiritual one, which he inhabits after death but which can spontaneously leave the body in sleep, trance, coma, or anesthesia. However, according to this notion, the second body is usually invisible, and the material body normally remains inert while the spiritual body is out.

31 In the previous versions of the tale, Poe gives the years 1811 and 1809. In real life he gave all three years as his birth dates on various occasions, but he was really born on January 19, 1809.

Twins appear in myth and folklore in most cultures, usually representing opposing traits or forces, such as mortal/immortal, good/evil, and light/dark. Examples include the Egyptian myth of Osiris and Set, the Persian story of Ahura Mazda and Angra Mainyu (or Ahriman), the Iroquois myth of Hawneyn and Hanegoasegeh, and the Slavic legend of Byelobog and Chernobog. More familiar myths include those of Romulus and Remus, Apollo and Artemis, and Castor and Pollux.

rivalry he might have been supposed actuated solely by a whimsical desire to thwart, astonish, or mortify myself; although there were times when I could not help observing, with a feeling made up of wonder, abasement, and pique, that he mingled with his injuries, his insults, or his contradictions, a certain most inappropriate, and assuredly most unwelcome *affectionateness* of manner. I could only conceive this singular behavior to arise from a consummate self-conceit assuming

30 the vulgar airs of patronage and protection.

Perhaps it was this latter trait in Wilson's conduct, conjoined with our identity of name, and the mere accident of our having entered the school upon the same day, which set afloat the notion that we were brothers, among the senior classes in the academy. These do not usually inquire with much strictness into the affairs of their juniors. I have before said, or should have said, that Wilson was not, in the most remote degree, connected with my family. But assuredly if we *had* been brothers we must have been twins; for, after leaving Dr. Bransby's, I casually learned that my namesake was born on the nineteenth of January, 1813—and this is a somewhat remarkable coincidence; for the day is precisely that of my

31 own nativity.

It may seem strange that in spite of the continual anxiety occasioned me by the rivalry of Wilson, and his intolerable spirit of contradiction, I could not bring myself to hate him altogether. We had, to be sure, nearly every day a quarrel in which, yielding me publicly the palm of victory, he, in some manner, contrived to make me feel that it was he who had deserved it; yet a sense of pride on my part, and a veritable dignity on his own, kept us always upon what are called "speaking terms," while there were many points of strong congeniality in our tempers, operating to awake in me a sentiment which our position alone, perhaps, prevented from ripening into friendship. It is difficult, indeed, to define, or even to describe, my real feelings towards him. They formed a motley and heterogeneous admixture;—some petulant animosity, which was not yet hatred, some esteem, more respect, much fear, with a world of uneasy curiosity. To the moralist it will be unnecessary to say, in addition, that Wilson and myself were the most inseparable of companions.

It was no doubt the anomalous state of affairs existing between us, which turned all my attacks upon him, (and they were many, either open or covert) into the channel of banter or practical joke (giving pain while assuming the aspect of mere fun) rather than into a more serious and determined hostility. But my endeavours on this head were by no means uniformly successful, even when my plans were the most wittily concocted; for my namesake had much about him, in character, of that unassuming and quiet austerity which, while

32 enjoying the poignancy of its own jokes, has no heel of Achilles in itself, and absolutely refuses to be laughed at. I could find, indeed, but one vulnerable point, and that, lying in a personal peculiarity, arising, perhaps, from constitutional disease, would have been spared by any antagonist less at his wit's end than myself;—my rival had a weakness in the faucial or gutteral **33** organs, which precluded him from raising his voice at any time *above a very low whisper*. Of this defect I did not fail to take what poor advantage lay in my power. **34**

Wilson's retaliations in kind were many; and there was one form of his practical wit that disturbed me beyond measure. How his sagacity first discovered at all that so petty a thing would vex me, is a question I never could solve; but, having discovered, he habitually practised the annoyance. I had always felt aversion to my uncourtly patronymic, and its very common, if not plebeian prænomen. The words were venom **35** in my ears; and when, upon the day of my arrival, a second William Wilson came also to the academy, I felt angry with him for bearing the name, and doubly disgusted with the name because a stranger bore it, who would be the cause of its twofold repetition, who would be constantly in my presence, and whose concerns, in the ordinary routine of the school business, must inevitably, on account of the detestable coincidence, be often confounded with my own.

The feeling of vexation thus engendered grew stronger with every circumstance tending to show resemblance, moral or physical, between my rival and myself. I had not then discovered the remarkable fact that we were of the same age; but I saw that we were of the same height, and I perceived that we were even singularly alike in general contour of person and outline of feature. I was galled, too, by the rumor touching a relationship, which had grown current in the upper forms. In a word, nothing could more seriously disturb me, (although I scrupulously concealed such disturbance,) than any allusion to a similarity of mind, person, or condition existing between us. But, in truth, I had no reason to believe that (with the exception of the matter of relationship, and in the case of Wilson himself,) this similarity had ever been made a subject of comment, or even observed at all by our schoolfellows. That *he* observed it in all its bearings, and as fixedly as I, was apparent; but that he could discover in such circumstances so fruitful a field of annoyance, can only be attributed, as I said before, to his more than ordinary penetration.

His cue, which was to perfect an imitation of myself, lay both in words and in actions; and most admirably did he play his part. My dress it was an easy matter to copy; my gait and general manner were, without difficulty, appropriated; in spite of his constitutional defect, even my voice did not escape him. My louder tones were, of course, unattempted, but then the key, it was identical; *and his singular whisper, it grew the very echo of my own*.

How greatly this most exquisite portraiture harassed me, (for it could not justly be termed a caricature,) I will not now venture to describe. I had but one consolation—in the fact that the imitation, apparently, was noticed by myself alone, and that I had to endure only the knowing and strangely sarcastic smiles of my namesake himself. Satisfied with having **36** produced in my bosom the intended effect, he seemed to chuckle in secret over the sting he had inflicted, and was

32 Achilles, son of Peleus and Thetis, while still a baby was dipped by his mother in the river Styx to make him invulnerable to attack. But the heel she held him by was not immersed, and he was killed when Apollo guided Paris to shoot a poisoned arrow into his heel.

33 The O.E.D. traces the word back to 1807 and gives Poe's tale as the second of three citations. It comes from the word "fauces," the throat of a flower.

34 That no one else can hear him, again underscores that the second Wilson is the first's alter ego.

35 Poe should have authored a thesaurus. "Patronymic" means a family's name, which in Wilson's case he apparently feels is less than aristocratic, and "praenomen" means the first name. Poe, too, was sensitive about his station in life and often lied in saying his father was of upper-class stock, of a "family one of the oldest and most respectable in Baltimore" (in a note to Rufus Griswold in 1841).

36 "Sometimes, though not often, an individual feels impelled to live out the worse side of his nature and to repress his better side. In such cases the shadow appears as a positive figure in his dreams," writes M.-L. von Franz (*Man and His Symbols*, Dell, 1964; p. 182). This shadow makes him "aware of (and sometimes ashamed of) those qualities and impulses he denies in himself but can plainly see in other people" (p. 174).

37 David Halliburton suggests the second Wilson is symbolic of the first's own guilt feelings, a man who magnifies events "out of a sense of inferiority, which is privately felt, and which merges eventually with a sense of guilt. Guilt, too, is privately felt, although it is an emotion brought on by [his] relations to others. Guilt is a failure to meet their standards or expectations. . . . As it happens, they do not see [his] inadequacy or guilt any more than they see the likeness between [him] and the other." (*Edgar Allan Poe: a Phenomenological View*, Princetom, 1973; p. 303)

characteristically disregardful of the public applause which the success of his witty endeavours might have so easily elicited. That the school, indeed, did not feel his design, perceive its accomplishment, and participate in his sneer, was, for many anxious months, a riddle I could not resolve. Perhaps the *gradation* of his copy rendered it not so readily perceptible; or, more possibly, I owed my security to the masterly air of the copyist, who, disdaining the letter, (which in a painting is all the obtuse can see,) gave but the full spirit of his original **37** for my individual contemplation and chagrin.

I have already more than once spoken of the disgusting air of patronage which he assumed toward me, and of his frequent officious interference with my will. This interference often took the ungracious character of advice; advice not openly given, but hinted or insinuated. I received it with a repugnance which gained strength as I grew in years. Yet, at this distant day, let me do him the simple justice to acknowledge that I can recall no occasion when the suggestions of my rival were on the side of those errors or follies so usual to his immature age and seeming inexperience; that his moral sense, at least, if not his general talents and worldly wisdom, was far keener than my own; and that I might, to-day, have been a better, and thus a happier man, had I less frequently rejected the counsels embodied in those meaning whispers which I then but too cordially hated and too bitterly despised.

As it was, I at length grew restive in the extreme under his distasteful supervision, and daily resented more and more openly what I considered his intolerable arrogance. I have said that, in the first years of our connexion as schoolmates, my feelings in regard to him might have been easily ripened into friendship: but, in the latter months of my residence at the academy, although the intrusion of his ordinary manner had, beyond doubt, in some measure, abated, my sentiments, in nearly similar proportion, partook very much of positive hatred. Upon one occasion he saw this, I think, and afterwards avoided, or made a show of avoiding me.

It was about the same period, if I remember aright, in an altercation of violence with him, in which he was more than usually thrown off his guard, and spoke and acted with an openness of demeanor rather foreign to his nature, I discovered, or fancied I discovered, in his accent, his air, and general appearance, a something which first startled, and then deeply interested me, by bringing to mind dim visions of my earliest infancy—wild, confused and thronging memories of a time when memory herself was yet unborn. I cannot better describe the sensation which oppressed me than by saying that I could with difficulty shake off the belief of my having been acquainted with the being who stood before me, at some epoch very long ago—some point of the past even infinitely remote. The delusion, however, faded rapidly as it came; and I mention it at all but to define the day of the last conversation I there held with my singular namesake.

The huge old house, with its countless subdivisions, had several large chambers communicating with each other, where slept the greater number of the students. There were, how-ever, (as must necessarily happen in a building so awkwardly planned,) many little nooks or recesses, the odds and ends of the structure; and these the economic ingenuity of Dr. Bransby had also fitted up as dormitories; although, being the merest closets, they were capable of accommodating but a single individual. One of these small apartments was occupied by Wilson.   **38**

One night, about the close of my fifth year at the school, and immediately after the altercation just mentioned, finding every one wrapped in sleep, I arose from bed, and, lamp in hand, stole through a wilderness of narrow passages from my own bedroom to that of my rival. I had long been plotting one of those ill-natured pieces of practical wit at his expense in which I had hitherto been so uniformly unsuccessful. It was my intention, now, to put my scheme in operation, and I resolved to make him feel the whole extent of the malice with which I was imbued. Having reached his closet, I noiselessly entered, leaving the lamp, with a shade over it, on the outside. I advanced a step, and listened to the sound of his tranquil breathing. Assured of his being asleep, I returned, took the light, and with it again approached the bed. Close curtains were around it, which, in the prosecution of my plan, I slowly and quietly withdrew, when the bright rays fell vividly upon the sleeper, and my eyes, at the same moment, upon his countenance. I looked;—and a numbness, an iciness of feeling instantly pervaded my frame. My breast heaved, my knees tottered, my whole spirit became possessed with an objectless yet intolerable horror. Gasping for breath, I lowered the lamp in still nearer proximity to the face. Were these—*these* the lineaments of William Wilson? I saw, indeed, that they were his, but I shook as if with a fit of the ague in fancying they were not. What *was* there about them to confound me in this manner? I gazed;—while my brain reeled with a multitude of incoherent thoughts. Not thus he appeared—assuredly not *thus*—in the vivacity of his waking hours. The same name! the same contour of person! the same day of arrival at the academy! And then his dogged and meaningless imitation of my gait, my voice, my habits, and my manner? Was it, in truth, within the bounds of human possibility, that *what I now saw* was the result, merely, of the habitual practice of this sarcastic imi-tation? Awe-stricken, and with a creeping shudder, I extin-guished the lamp, passed silently from the chamber, and left, at once, the halls of that old academy, never to enter them again.

After a lapse of some months, spent at home in mere idleness, I found myself a student at Eton. The brief interval **39** had been sufficient to enfeeble my remembrance of the events at Dr. Bransby's, or at least to effect a material change in the nature of the feelings with which I remembered them. The truth—the tragedy—of the drama was no more. I could now find room to doubt the evidence of my senses; and seldom called up the subject at all but with wonder at the extent of human credulity, and a smile at the vivid force of the

38 "The maze of strange passages, chambers, and un-locked exits . . . is a symbol of the unconscious with its unknown possibilities" (Von Franz, *Man and His Symbols*, p. 175–176). The "closet" mentioned below is another word for small room, and not a place to hang clothes.

39 Eton College, the largest and most famous of the English public schools, was founded in 1440 by Henry VI. Unlike other public (actually private) schools, Eton is controlled by elected student representatives who enforce regulations and administer discipline.

Were these—*these* the lineaments of William Wilson? *Illustration by F. S. Coburn, 1902*

40 Poe uses the same "may have" that so tantalizes readers of Hawthorne's tales. Just as we question whether or not Hawthorne's Young Goodman Brown really met the Devil and saw his wife at a witches' sabbath, so here we question the memory and point of view of William Wilson.

41 Opium, perhaps, and orgies; the imagination runs wild at the possibilities.

Madly flushed with cards and intoxication, I was in the act of insisting upon a toast of more than wonted profanity. *Illustration by Johann Friedrich Vogel, 1856*

imagination which I hereditarily possessed. Neither was this species of scepticism likely to be diminished by the character of the life I led at Eton. The vortex of thoughtless folly into which I there so immediately and recklessly plunged, washed away all but the froth of my past hours, ingulfed at once every solid or serious impression, and left to memory only the **40** veriest levities of a former existence.

I do not wish, however, to trace the course of my miserable profligacy here—a profligacy which set at defiance the laws, while it eluded the vigilance of the institution. Three years of folly, passed without profit, had but given me rooted habits of vice, and added, in a somewhat unusual degree, to my bodily stature, when, after a week of soulless dissipation, I invited a small party of the most dissolute students to a secret carousal in my chambers. We met at a late hour of the night; for our debaucheries were to be faithfully protracted until morning. The wine flowed freely, and there were not wanting **41** other and perhaps more dangerous seductions; so that the grey dawn had already faintly appeared in the east, while our delirious extravagance was at its height. Madly flushed with cards and intoxication, I was in the act of insisting upon a toast of more than wonted profanity, when my attention was suddenly diverted by the violent, although partial unclosing of the door of the apartment, and by the eager voice of a servant from without. He said that some person, apparently in great haste, demanded to speak with me in the hall.

Wildly excited with wine, the unexpected interruption rather delighted than surprised me, I staggered forward at once, and a few steps brought me to the vestibule of the building. In this low and small room there hung no lamp; and now no light at all was admitted, save that of the exceedingly feeble dawn which made its way through the semi-circular window. As I put my foot over the threshold, I became aware of the figure of a youth about my own height, and habited in a white kerseymere morning frock, cut in the novel fashion of the one I myself wore at the moment. This the faint light enabled me to perceive; but the features of his face I could not distinguish. Upon my entering he strode hurriedly up to me, and seizing me by the arm with a gesture of petulant impatience, whispered the words "William Wilson!" in my ear.

I grew perfectly sober in an instant.

There was that in the manner of the stranger, and in the tremulous shake of his uplifted finger, as he held it between my eyes and the light, which filled me with unqualified amazement; but it was not this which had so violently moved me. It was the pregnancy of solemn admonition in the singular, low, hissing utterance; and, above all, it was the character, the tone, *the key,* of those few, simple, and familiar, yet *whispered* syllables, which came with a thousand thronging memories of by-gone days, and struck upon my soul with the shock of a galvanic battery. Ere I could recover the use of my senses he was gone.

Although this event failed not of a vivid effect upon my

disordered imagination, yet was it evanescent as vivid. For some weeks, indeed, I busied myself in earnest inquiry, or was wrapped in a cloud of morbid speculation. I did not pretend to disguise from my perception the identity of the singular individual who thus perseveringly interfered with my affairs, and harassed me with his insinuated counsel. But who and what was this Wilson?—and whence came he?—and what were his purposes? Upon neither of these points could I be satisfied; merely ascertaining, in regard to him, that a sudden accident in his family had caused his removal from Dr. Barnsby's academy on the afternoon of the day in which I myself had eloped. But in a brief period I ceased to think upon the subject; my attention being all absorbed in a contemplated departure for Oxford. Thither I soon went; the uncalculating vanity of my parents furnishing me with an outfit and annual establishment, which would enable me to indulge at will in the luxury already so dear to my heart,—to vie in profuseness of expenditure with the haughtiest heirs of the wealthiest earldoms in Great Britain.

Excited by such appliances to vice, my constitutional temperament broke forth with redoubled ardor, and I spurned even the common restraints of decency in the mad infatuation of my revels. But it were absurd to pause in the detail of my extravagance. Let it suffice, that among spendthrifts I out-Heroded Herod, and that, giving name to a multitude of novel [42] follies, I added no brief appendix to the long catalogue of vices then usual in the most dissolute university of Europe.

It could hardly be credited, however, that I had, even here, so utterly fallen from the gentlemanly estate, as to seek acquaintance with the vilest arts of the gambler by profession, and, having become an adept in his despicable science, to practise it habitually as a means of increasing my already enormous income at the expense of the weak-minded among my fellow-collegians. Such, nevertheless, was the fact. And the very enormity of this offence against all manly and honourable sentiment proved, beyond doubt, the main if not the sole reason of the impunity with which it was committed. Who, indeed, among my most abandoned associates, would not rather have disputed the clearest evidence of his senses, then have suspected of such courses, the gay, the frank, the generous William Wilson—the noblest and most liberal commoner at Oxford—him whose follies (said his parasites) were but the follies of youth and unbridled fancy—whose errors but inimitable whim—whose darkest vice but a careless and dashing extravagance?

I had been now two years successfully busied in this way, when there came to the university a young *parvenu* nobleman, [43] Glendinning—rich, said report, as Herodes Atticus—his [44,45] riches, too, as easily acquired. I soon found him of weak intellect, and, of course, marked him as a fitting subject for my skill. I frequently engaged him in play, and contrived, with the gambler's usual art, to let him win considerable sums, the more effectually to entangle him in my snares. At length, my schemes being ripe, I met him (with the full intention that

[42] See "Metzengerstein," note 9.

[43] Nouveau riche

[44] The name of the man who succeeded Poe as sergeant major of the 1st Artillery

[45] Tiberius Claudius Herodes Atticus (c. 101–c. 177), Greek Sophist, rhetorician, and patron of learning, who spend all his fortune to adorn Athens and other Greek cities.

46 T. L. Preston was a schoolmate of Poe's in Richmond, and a lifelong friend.

47 A game for two people in which the cards from two to six are excluded. A player may discard, or throw out certain cards from his hand, and replace them with fresh ones from the pack (*écarté* means to discard).

Poe may have borrowed the setting from David Watson's "The Gamesters," a chapter published anonymously from William Wirt's "Old Bachelor" series of 1810–13. Watson's story tells about a pair of twins, one a scoundrel and the other good, and how the good one is ejected from a card game when the other players mistake him for his brother, a notorious card cheat.

46 this meeing should be final and decisive) at the chambers of a fellow-commoner, (Mr. Preston,) equally intimate with both, but who, to do him justice, entertained not even a remote suspicion of my design. To give to this a better colouring, I had contrived to have assembled a party of some eight or ten, and was solicitously careful that the introduction of cards should appear accidental, and originate in the proposal of my contemplated dupe himself. To be brief upon a vile topic, none of the low finesse was omitted, so customary upon similar occasions that it is a just matter for wonder how any are still found so besotted as to fall its victims.

47 We had protracted our sitting far into the night, and I had at length effected the manœuvre of getting Glendinning as my sole antagonist. The game, too, was my favorite *écarté*. The rest of the company, interested in the extent of our play, had abandoned their own cards, and were standing around us as spectators. The *parvenu*, who had been induced by my artifices in the early part of the evening, to drink deeply, now shuffled, dealt, or played, with a wild nervousness of manner for which his intoxication, I thought, might partially, but could not altogether account. In a very short period he had become my debtor to a large amount, when, having taken a long draught of port, he did precisely what I had been coolly anticipating—he proposed to double our already extravagant stakes. With a well-feigned show of reluctance, and not until after my repeated refusal had seduced him into some angry words which gave a color of *pique* to my compliance, did I finally comply. The result, of course, did but prove how entirely the prey was in my toils; in less than an hour he had quadrupled his debt. For some time his countenance had been losing the florid tinge lent it by the wine; but now, to my astonishment, I perceived that it had grown to a pallor truly fearful. I say to my astonishment. Glendinning had been represented to my eager inquiries as immeasurably wealthy; and the sums which he had as yet lost, although in themselves vast, could not, I supposed, very seriously annoy, much less so violently affect him. That he was overcome by the wine just swallowed, was the idea which most readily presented itself; and, rather with a view to the preservation of my own character in the eyes of my associates, than from any less interested motive, I was about to insist, peremptorily, upon a discontinuance of the play, when some expressions at my elbow from among the company, and an ejaculation evincing utter despair on the part of Glendinning, gave me to understand that I had effected his total ruin under circumstances which, rendering him an object for the pity of all, should have protected him from the ill offices even of a fiend.

What now might have been my conduct it is difficult to say. The pitiable condition of my dupe had thrown an air of embarrassed gloom over all; and, for some moments, a profound silence was maintained, during which I could not help feeling my cheeks tingle with the many burning glances of scorn or reproach cast upon me by the less abandoned of the party. I will even own that an intolerable weight of anxiety was for a brief instant lifted from my bosom by the sudden

and extraordinary interruption which ensued. The wide, heavy **48**
folding doors of the apartment were all at once thrown open,
to their full extent, with a vigorous and rushing impetuosity
that extinguished, as if by magic, every candle in the room.
Their light, in dying, enabled us just to perceive that a
stranger had entered, about my own height, and closely
muffled in a cloak. The darkness, however, was now total; and
we could only *feel* that he was standing in our midst. Before
any one of us could recover from the extreme astonishment
into which this rudeness had thrown all, we heard the voice
of the intruder. **49**

"Gentlemen," he said, in a low, distinct, and never-to-be-
forgotten *whisper* which thrilled to the very marrow of my
bones, "Gentlemen, I make no apology for this behaviour,
because in thus behaving, I am but fulfilling a duty. You are,
beyond doubt, uninformed of the true character of the person
who has to-night won at *écarté* a large sum of money from
Lord Glendinning. I will therefore put you upon an expeditious
and decisive plan of obtaining this very necessary information.
Please to examine, at your leisure, the inner linings of the cuff
of his left sleeve, and the several little packages which may
be found in the somewhat capacious pockets of his embroidered
morning wrapper."

While he spoke, so profound was the stillness that one
might have heard a pin drop upon the floor. In ceasing, he
departed at once, and as abruptly as he had entered. Can I—
shall I describe my sensations?—must I say that I felt all the
horrors of the damned? Most assuredly I had little time for
reflection. Many hands roughly seized me upon the spot, and
lights were immediately reprocured. A search ensued. In the
lining of my sleeve were found all the court cards essential in
écarté, and, in the pockets of my wrapper, a number of packs,
fac-similes of those used at our sittings, with the single
exception that mine were of the species called, technically,
arrondées; the honours being slightly convex at the ends, the **50**
lower cards slightly convex at the sides. In this disposition,
the dupe who cuts, as customary, at the length of the pack,
will invariably find that he cuts his antagonist an honour; while
the gambler, cutting at the breadth, will, as certainly cut
nothing for his victim which may count in the records of the
game.

Any burst of indignation upon this discovery would have
affected me less than the silent contempt, or the sarcastic
composure, with which it was received.

"Mr. Wilson," said our host, stooping to remove from
beneath his feet an exceedingly luxurious cloak of rare furs,
"Mr. Wilson, this is your property." (The weather was cold;
and, upon quitting my own room, I had thrown a cloak over
my dressing wrapper, putting it off upon reaching the scene
of play.) "I presume it is supererogatory to seek here (eyeing
the folds of the garment with a bitter smile) for any farther
evidence of your skill. Indeed, we have had enough. You will
see the necessity, I hope, of quitting Oxford—at all events,
of quitting instantly my chambers."

Abased, humbled to the dust as I then was, it is probable

48 This third major encounter with the second Wilson comes at a point when the first Wilson admits that his conscience is bothering him.

49 Compare with Madeline's entrance in "The Fall of the House of Usher." With the candles out, it would be impossible to see the stranger clearly, yet Wilson has no trouble.

50 From *aronder*, meaning to dovetail

that I should have resented this galling language by immediate personal violence, had not my whole attention been at the moment arrested by a fact of the most startling character. The cloak which I had worn was of a rare description of fur; how rare, how extravagantly costly, I shall not venture to say. Its fashion, too, was of my own fantastic invention; for I was fastidious to an absurd degree of coxcombry, in matters of this frivolous nature. When, therefore, Mr. Preston reached me that which he had picked up upon the floor, and near the folding doors of the apartment, it was with an astonishment nearly bordering upon terror, that I perceived my own already hanging on my arm, (where I had no doubt unwittingly placed it,) and that the one presented me was but its exact counterpart in every, in even the minutest possible particular. The singular being who had so disastrously exposed me, had been muffled, I remembered, in a cloak; and none had been worn at all by any of the members of our party with the exception of myself. Retaining some presence of mind, I took the one offered me by Preston; placed it, unnoticed, over my own; left the apartment with a resolute scowl of defiance; and, next morning ere dawn of day, commenced a hurried journey from Oxford to the continent, in a perfect agony of horror and of shame.

I fled in vain. My evil destiny pursued me as if in exultation, and proved, indeed, that the exercise of its mysterious dominion had as yet only begun. Scarcely had I set foot in Paris ere I had fresh evidence of the detestable interest taken by this Wilson in my concerns. Years flew, while I experienced no relief. Villain!—at Rome, with how untimely, yet with how spectral an officiousness, stepped he in between me and my ambition! At Vienna, too—at Berlin—and at Moscow! Where, in truth, had I *not* bitter cause to curse him within my heart? From his inscrutable tyranny did I at length flee, panic-stricken, as from a pestilence; and to the very ends of the earth *I fled in vain*.

And again, and again, in secret communion with my own spirit, would I demand the questions "Who is he?—whence came he?—and what are his objects?" But no answer was there found. And then I scrutinized, with a minute scrutiny, the forms, and the methods, and the leading traits of his impertinent supervision. But even here there was very little upon which to base a conjecture. It was noticeable, indeed, that, in no one of the multiplied instances in which he had of late crossed my path, had he so crossed it except to frustrate those schemes, or to disturb those actions, which, if fully carried out, might have resulted in bitter mischief. Poor justification this, in truth, for an authority so imperiously assumed! Poor indemnity for natural rights of self-agency so pertinaciously, so insultingly denied!

I had also been forced to notice that my tormentor, for a very long period of time, (while scrupulously and with miraculous dexterity maintaining his whim of an identity of apparel with myself,) had so contrived it, in the execution of his varied interference with my will, that I saw not, at any moment, the features of his face. Be Wilson what he might, *this*, at least, was but the veriest of affectation, or of folly. Could he, for an instant, have supposed that, in my admonisher at Eton—in the destroyer of my honor at Oxford,—in him who thwarted my ambition at Rome, my revenge at Paris, my passionate love at Naples, or what he falsely termed by avarice in Egypt,—that in this, my arch-enemy and evil genius, I could fail to recognise the William Wilson of my school-boy days,—the namesake, the companion, the rival,—the hated and dreaded rival at Dr. Bransby's? Impossible!—But let me hasten to the last eventful scene of the drama.

Thus far I had succumbed supinely to this imperious domination. The sentiment of deep awe with which I habitually regarded the elevated character, the majestic wisdom, the apparent omnipresence and omnipotence of Wilson, added to a feeling of even terror, with which certain other traits in his nature and assumptions inspired me, had operated, hitherto, to impress me with an idea of my own utter weakness and helplessness, and to suggest an implicit, although bitterly reluctant submission to his arbitrary will. But, of late days, I had given myself up entirely to wine; and its maddening influence upon my hereditary temper rendered me more and more impatient of control. I began to murmur,—to hesitate,—to resist. And was it only fancy which induced me to believe that, with the increase of my own firmness, that of my tormentor underwent a proportional diminution? Be this as it may, I now began to feel the inspiration of a burning hope, and at length nurtured in my secret thoughts a stern and desperate resolution that I would submit no longer to be enslaved.

It was at Rome, during the Carnival of 18—, that I attended **51** a masquerade in the palazzo of the Neapolitan Duke Di Broglio. I had indulged more freely than usual in the excesses **52** of the wine-table; and now the suffocating atmosphere of the crowded rooms irritated me beyond endurance. The difficulty, too, of forcing my way through the mazes of the company contributed not a little to the ruffling of my temper; for I was anxiously seeking, (let me not say with what unworthy motive) the young, the gay, the beautiful wife of the aged and doting Di Broglio. With a too unscrupulous confidence she had previously communciated to me the secret of the costume in which she would be habited, and now, having caught a glimpse of her person, I was hurring to make my way into her presence.—At this moment I felt a light hand placed upon my shoulder, and that ever-remembered, low, damnable *whisper* within my ear.

In an absolute phrenzy of wrath, I turned at once upon him who had thus interrupted me, and seized him violently by the collar. He was attired, as I had expected, in a costume altogether similar to my own; wearing a Spanish cloak of blue velvet, begirt about the waist with a crimson belt sustaining a rapier. A mask of black silk entirely covered his face.

"Scoundrel!" I said, in a voice husky with rage, while every syllable I uttered seemed as new fuel to my fury, "scoundrel! impostor! accursed villain! you shall not—you *shall not* dog

51 Mardi Gras, the period just before Lent

52 Washington Irving mentions the Broglio, the piazzetta in front of the Doge's Palace, in Venice in "The Mysterious Stranger," whose title character is a nobleman from Naples. In Musset's *La Nuit de Décembre* (1835) [see introductory note] the climax is set at a masked ball in the palace of Di Broglio.

Thus it appeared, I say, but was not. *Illustration by Albert Edward Sterner for* Century Magazine, *1903*

53 Stuart Levine observes, "Hawthorne would have thoroughly understood what Poe was about when he wrote those lines. Was there another man in the room? Did Goodman Brown really see the figures in the forest? Wilson thinks his double was there; the reader does not care, for he now fully understands Wilson. It was not a mirror, says Wilson, but 'my antagonist—it was Wilson, who then stood before me in the agonies of dissolution.'

"Precisely so, Poe has reached the point at which he can speak of either of the two Wilsons without distinguishing between them. The check represented by the second Wilson, all that the narrator has heretofore repressed, is now to be wiped completely from the narrator's personality.

" 'William Wilson' has been called a study in schizophrenia; actually, if one must use psychological terms, Wilson exhibits symptoms more nearly akin to a more specific form of insanity, paranoia. Schizophrenia is a very big and very loose term, which includes a number of very different forms of maniacal behavior. One of these, paranoia, can be characterized by the illusion of a figure persecuting the sufferer."

Levine also feels that the story's moral is similar to one of Hawthorne's. "Wilson has cut himself off from humanity by his pride, he has committed the Unpardonable Sin. The psychological interpretation is of a man sinking into paranoia. A supernatural interpretation would not work." (*Edgar Poe: Seer and Craftsman*, Everett Edwards, 1972; p. 190)

If we interpret "William Wilson" in terms of a man at war with his own conscience, then the Hawthorne comparison is an apt one, for in destroying the possibility of that conscience ever governing his life, Wilson cuts himself off from God's grace.

Marie Bonaparte, in a Freudian analysis of the tale, sees it as a battle between the id and the superego for control of the ego. "Whether, however, the double be essentially *id* or *super-ego*, it always represents self against self. And though it is always the persecutor of the original whose reflection or shadow it is, this happens . . . by virtue doubtless of the mechanism which, in paranoia, converts the first love-object into the imaginary persecutor as a result of attaching to it the feelings, transformed into their opposites, which that object formerly inspired. Love, turned to hate, is projected from within ourselves upon it.

"Whom do we ever love better than ourselves, and who, in this manner, more than ourselves, may become our relentless persecutor?

"It is here that the motif of 'the double' impinges on the important and universal problem of homosexuality. For the double can only be of the same sex as the being from whom it sprang, and the same narcissistic roots underlie both the creation of the double and latent or manifest homosexual trends. . . . For . . . if Wilson-Poe's double, in essence, is part of Poe-Wilson himself, externally re-projected, it is just that part which was constituted, so to speak, by Poe's assimilating his educator and up-bringer, the 'father' John Allan, to whom, despite his rebellion, his attitude always remained passive. It was the moral bans, the inhibitions inculcated in Poe by his education, which saved him from the fate of a William Wilson, while his moral passivity—in spite of his hate—also contributed to that end. This attitude, in Poe, in fact, amounted to passive homosexuality. . . ." (P. 555)

Confused enough? Another interpretation, this time based on the Jungian "shadow" concept, notes that

me unto death! Follow me, or I stab you where you stand!"— and I broke my way from the ball-room into a small antechamber adjoining—dragging him unresistingly with me as I went.

Upon entering, I thrust him furiously from me. He staggered against the wall, while I closed the door with an oath, and commanded him to draw. He hesitated but for an instant; then, with a slight sigh, drew in silence, and put himself upon his defence.

The contest was brief indeed. I was frantic with every species of wild excitement, and felt within my single arm the energy and power of a multitude. In a few seconds I forced him by sheer strength against the wainscoting, and thus, getting him at mercy, plunged my sword, with brute ferocity, repeatedly through and through his bosom.

At that instant some person tried the latch of the door. I hastened to prevent an intrusion, and then immediately returned to my dying antagonist. But what human language can adequately portray *that* astonishment, *that* horror which possessed me at the spectacle then presented to view? The brief moment in which I averted my eyes had been sufficient to produce, apparently, a material change in the arrangements at the upper or farther end of the room. A large mirror,—so at first it seemed to me in my confusion—now stood where none had been perceptible before; and, as I stepped up to it in extremity of terror, mine own image, but with features all pale and dabbled in blood, advanced to meet me with a feeble and tottering gait.

Thus it appeared, I say, but was not. It was my antagonist—it was Wilson, who then stood before me in the agonies of his dissolution. His mask and cloak lay, where he had thrown them, upon the floor. Not a thread in all his raiment—not a line in all the marked and singular lineaments of his face which was not, even in the most absolute identity, *mine own!*

It was Wilson; but he spoke no longer in a whisper, and I could have fancied that I myself was speaking while he said:

"You have conquered, and I yield. Yet, henceforward art thou also dead—dead to the World, to Heaven and to Hope! In me didst thou exist—and, in my death, see by this image, which is thine own, how utterly thou has murdered thyself." **53**

sometimes a patient in analysis breaks off when confronted with his shadow and crawls back into the shelter of his illusions or neurosis, thus shutting himself off from the beneficial possibilities hidden in the unconscious and dooming himself to further mental problems.

One should also not overlook the Irish joke that is the basis for the ending of Poe's comic tale "Mystification" (note 17), in which a man shoots his mirrored reflection, or Lao's mirror in Goldsmith's *The Citizen of the World* (1762), xlv, which reflects the mind and its thoughts, or finally, James Boaden's *The Man of Two Lives* (1828), written under the pseudonym off Edward Sydenham, where we read:

". . . most men are permitted *two lives* even here; *one* of *action*, with its usual attendant *error*,—the other of *Reflection* as it ought to prove, of *Atonement*. To carry on the parallel, neither are *they* without a mysterious friend and guide, to whom the *Magnetic Mesmer* was but a shade, who comes upon them unannounced and knows them through all disguises. He is plain too and generally alarming in his addresses and urges them to take the only course that conducts to their real interest, their peace, their honor, and their final happiness. The reader *feels* that I can only here mean the power of *Conscience*."

A DESCENT INTO THE MAELSTRÖM

First published in *Graham's Magazine*, May 1841.

This is an impressive achievement, a fantastic yet believable tale that displays Poe's skill in combining source materials into a coherent whole. The chief source is a story in *Fraser's Magazine*, September 1834, entitled "The Maelstrom: a Fragment," by Edward Wilson Landor [not to be confused with William Landor, the pseudonym of Horace Binney Wallace]. Although Landor's tale is too long and lacks unity, one can easily detect those portions which sparked Poe's fertile imagination: a ship is destroyed in a whirlpool off the Norwegian coast while people watch from Mount Helseggen; the hero describes his sensations as he hurtles into the depths of the Maelstrom, and he escapes alive. But, in Landor's tale, the hero faints and comes to only after he has escaped, so that he and the reader—and perhaps the author—haven't a clue to how he managed it.

Poe must have seen both the possibilities and the unsatisfactory execution of such a tale, and apparently went immediately to the *Encyclopaedia Britannica* (3rd–6th editions, 1797–1836) and the *Mariner's Chronicle* (1834). Interestingly enough, the latter reprints without acknowledgment the *Britannica* piece, adding to it the experiences of an American captain who supposedly went into the Maelstrom and lived. The *Britannica* article on the Maelstrom was in turn lifted from *The Natural History of Norway* (1755), by Erik Pontoppidan, Bishop of Bergen.

A minor point: the O.E.D. cites Poe's use of the umlaut over the "o" in "Maelström" as the only such use.

"A Descent into the Maelström" demonstrates that Poe and his narrators should not be confused with each other. The often-heard criticism that Poe's language is "obscure," "vague," and "convoluted" is best answered by pointing out that this is so only when such language suits a narrator's state of mind. Since in most of his well-known tales the narrator is on the brink (or over) of catastrophe (mental or physical), we should expect such exaggerated expression. Here, however, the language is lucid and rational, and the narrator's descriptions of the whirlpool have a terrible clarity, which makes them all the more frightening.

Elements from the tale appear in the 1912 silent film *The Raven* and in *Wargods of the Deep* (aka *Warriors of the Deep* and *City Under the Sea*), a 1965 film directed by Jacques Tourneur, starring Vincent Price, Tab Hunter, Susan Hart, and David Tomlinson. Very little remains of Poe's tale in this story of an aquatic creature who kidnaps a woman and takes her to his underwater city.

Martin Donegan reads the story on the disc version (CMS 588).

---

1 From *Essays on Several Important Subjects* (1676), "Against Confidence in Philosophy and Matters of Speculation." The quote should read, "The *ways* of God in *Nature* (as in *Providence*) are not as *ours* are: Nor are the models we frame any way commensurate to the vastness and profundity of his Works; which have a *Depth* in them greater than the *Well of Democritus*."

Democritus (b. c.460 B.C.) said that truth lies at the bottom of a well.

The ways of God in Nature, as in Providence, are not as our ways; nor are the models that we frame any way commensurate to the vastness, profundity, and unsearchableness of His works, *which have a depth in them greater than the well of Democritus*.

—*Joseph Glanville*.

1

We had now reached the summit of the loftiest crag. For some minutes the old man seemed too much exhausted to speak.

"Not long ago," said he at length, "and I could have guided

96

you on this route as well as the youngest of my sons; but, about three years past, there happened to me an event such as never happened before to mortal man—or at least such as no man ever survived to tell of—and the six hours of deadly terror which I then endured have broken me up body and soul. You suppose me a *very* old man—but I am not. It took less than a single day to change these hairs from a jetty black to white, to weaken my limbs, and to unstring my nerves, so that I tremble at the least exertion, and am frightened at a shadow. Do you know I can scarcely look over this little cliff **2** without getting giddy?"

The "little cliff," upon whose edge he had so carelessly thrown himself down to rest that the weightier portion of his body hung over it, while he was only kept from falling by the tenure of his elbow on its extreme and slippery edge—this "little cliff" arose, a sheer unobstructed precipice of black shining rock, some fifteen or sixteen hundred feet from the world of crags beneath us. Nothing would have tempted me to within half a dozen yards of its brink. In truth so deeply was I excited by the perilous position of my companion, that I fell at full length upon the ground, clung to the shrubs around me, and dared not even glance upward at the sky— while I struggled in vain to divest myself of the idea that the very foundations of the mountain were in danger from the fury of the winds. It was long before I could reason myself into sufficient courage to sit up and look out into the distance. **3**

"You must get over these fancies," said the guide, "for I have brought you here that you might have the best possible view of the scene of that event I mentioned—and to tell you the whole story with the spot just under your eye."

2 The similarities between Poe's tale and Coleridge's *Rime of the Ancient Mariner* (1798) are striking. Both use the storytelling device, both narrators go through horrendous experiences at the mercy of the forces of nature, both are saved when they acknowledge the beauty and grandeur around them, and both are "reborn," pulled from the sea unrecognized by their companions.

Both tales parallel the age-old archetypal hero, described by Joseph Campbell in *The Hero with a Thousand Faces* (World Publishing Co., 1949): "A hero ventures forth from the world of common day into a region of supernatural wonder; fabulous forces are there encountered and a decisive victory is won; the hero comes back from this mysterious venture with the power to bestow boons on his fellow man" (p. 30).

It seems appropriate at this point to quote the Latin epigraph that opens Coleridge's poem, adapted by him from Thomas Burnet's *Archaeologiae Philosophicae* (1692): "I readily believe that there are more invisible than visible Natures in the universe. But who will explain for us the family of all these beings, and the ranks and relations and distinguishing features and functions of each? What do they do? What places do they inhabit? The human mind has always sought the knowledge of these things, but never attained it. Meanwhile I do not deny that it is helpful sometimes to contemplate in the mind, as on a tablet, the image of a greater and better world, lest the intellect, habituated to the petty things of daily life, narrow itself and sink wholly into trivial thoughts. But at the same time we must be watchful for the truth and keep a sense of proportion, so that we may distinguish the certain from the uncertain, day from night."

Poe must have read this with great interest.

3 The narrator at first seems the reasonable one, and the old man the one not to be trusted. But what seems madness on the part of the fisherman is really the result of his initiation into the mysteries of life and death.

High cliffs also appear in "The Imp of the Perverse" and *The Narrative of Arthur Gordon Pym*, in both cases emphasizing the perverse desire to jump or fall, which is at the heart of fears of height: "For one moment my fingers clutched convulsively upon their hold, while, with the movement, the faintest idea of ultimate escape wandered, like a shadow, through my mind—in the next my whole soul was pervaded with a *longing to fall;* a desire, a yearning, a passion utterly uncontrollable" (*Pym,* in *Selected Writings of Edgar Allan Poe,* Houghton Mifflin, 1956, p. 397).

It is probably this longing the old fisherman means when he mentions the narrator's "fancies."

"Now raise yourself up a little higher—hold on to the grass if you feel giddy—so—and look out, beyond the belt of vapor beneath us, into the sea." *Illustration by F. S. Coburn, 1902*

4 Lofoten and Vesteralen are two neighboring island groups inside the Arctic Circle, stretching from one to fifty miles offshore. The North Atlantic Drift gives these northern islands a relatively temperate climate. The chief islands of the Lofoten group are Rost, Vaeroy, Moskenesoy, Vestvagoy, and Austvagoy. The Vesteralen group, separated from the Lofoten by the narrow Raftsund, include the islands of Hinnoy (the largest in Norway, Langoy, and Andoy. Despite the treacherous tidal currents, which make operations dangerous and difficult, fishermen regularly ply the waters in search of the rich supplies of cod and herring found there.

5 Al-Idrisi, whose *Nuzhat Al-Mushtak* was a compilation by this twelfth-century Arabian scientist, poet, and traveler, written for Roger II of Sicily. Reprinted as *Geographica Nubiensis* (1619), it was mistakenly catalogued by the British Museum under "Nubian Geography."

In Jacob Bryant's *Antient Mythology* (1807), IV, 79, we read, "They were come into the sea of shades." "Mare Tenebrarum" (sea of shadows) is the name of the "Nubian" gives to the Atlantic Ocean.

6 Projecting, jutting; from "beetle-browed."

7 "Vurrgh" is actually "Vaeroy," and Poe originally had "Stockholm" instead of "Skärholm." The Encyclopaedia Britannica is at fault here, at least for "Stockholm." The other misspellings ("Iflesen" originally was "Islesen," "Hoeyholm" was "Hotholm," and "Kieldholm" was printed "Keildhelm") could easily have been misprints caused by a typesetter trying to read Poe's sometimes crabbed handwriting.

Errors aside, the philosophical message here is important. The fisherman is in an ironic mood when he says that these are the "true" names, for with his next statement he makes it clear that names of any kind are in no way definitions or explanations of a place or thing. This he has learned from his experience in the Maelstrom: that words, like time, laws, and society, are man-made conveniences, with little relation to the actual universe. The tale then becomes in a sense a metaphysical adventure, combining as it does the branches of metaphysics called ontology (the study of the ultimate nature of being) and cosmology (the study of the ultimate nature of the universe).

8 "Chopping" means veering with the wind; Poe may mean "choppy," referring to changeable or variable winds or seas.

"We are now," he continued, in that particularizing manner which distinguished him—"we are now close upon the Norwegian coast—in the sixty-eighth degree of latitude—in the great province of Nordland—and in the dreary district of **4** Lofoden. The mountain upon whose top we sit is Helseggen, the Cloudy. Now raise yourself up a little higher—hold on to the grass if you feel giddy—so—and look out, beyond the belt of vapor beneath us, into the sea."

I looked dizzily, and beheld a wide expanse of ocean, whose waters wore so inky a hue as to bring at once to my mind the **5** Nubian geographer's account of the *Mare Tenebrarum*. A panorama more deplorably desolate no human imagination can conceive. To the right and left, as far as the eye could reach, there lay outstretched, like ramparts of the world, lines **6** of horridly black and beetling cliff, whose character of gloom was but the more forcibly illustrated by the surf which reared high up against it, its white and ghastly crest, howling and shrieking for ever. Just opposite the promontory upon whose apex we were placed, and at a distance of some five or six miles out at sea, there was visible a small, bleak-looking island; or, more properly, its position was discernible through the wilderness of surge in which it was enveloped. About two miles nearer the land, arose another of smaller size, hideously craggy and barren, and encompassed at various intervals by a cluster of dark rocks.

The appearance of the ocean, in the space between the more distant island and the shore, had something very unusual about it. Although, at the time, so strong a gale was blowing landward that a brig in the remote offing lay to under a double-reefed trysail, and constantly plunged her whole hull out of sight, still there was here nothing like a regular swell, but only a short, quick, angry cross dashing of water in every direction—as well in the teeth of the wind as otherwise. Of foam there was little except in the immediate vicinity of the rocks.

"The island in the distance," resumed the old man, "is called by the Norwegians Vurrgh. The one midway is Moskoe. That a mile to the northward is Ambaaren. Yonder are Iflesen, Hoeyholm, Kieldholm, Suarven, and Buckholm. Farther off—between Moskoe and Vurrgh—are Otterholm, Flimen, Sandflesen, and Skarholm. These are the true names of the places—but why it has been thought necessary to name them at all, **7** is more than either you or I can understand. Do you hear any thing? Do you see any change in the water?"

We had now been about ten minutes upon the top of Helseggen, to which we had ascended from the interior of Lofoden, so that we had caught no glimpse of the sea until it had burst upon us from the summit. As the old man spoke, I became aware of a loud and gradually increasing sound, like the moaning of a vast herd of buffaloes upon an American prairie; and at the same moment I perceived that what seamen **8** term the *chopping* character of the ocean beneath us was rapidly changing into a current which set to the eastward. Even while I gazed, this current acquired a monstrous velocity.

Each moment added to its speed—to its headlong impetuosity. In five minutes the whole sea, as far as Vurrgh, was lashed into ungovernable fury; but it was between Moskoe and the coast that the main uproar held its sway. Here the vast bed of the waters, seamed and scarred into a thousand conflicting channels, burst suddenly into phrensied convulsion—heaving, boiling, hissing—gyrating in gigantic and innumerable vortices, and all whirling and plunging on to the eastward with a rapidity which water never elsewhere assumes except in precipitous descents.   **9**

In a few minutes more, there came over the scene another radical alteration. The general surface grew somewhat more smooth, and the whirlpools, one by one, disappeared, while prodigious streaks of foam became apparent where none had been seen before. These streaks, at length, spreading out to a great distance, and entering into combination, took unto themselves the gyratory motion of the subsided vortices, and seemed to form the germ of another more vast. Suddenly—very suddenly—this assumed a distinct and definite existence, in a circle of more than half a mile in diameter. The edge of the whirl was represented by a broad belt of gleaming spray; but no particle of this slipped into the mouth of the terrific funnel, whose interior, as far as the eye could fathom it, was a smooth, shining, and jet-black wall of water, inclined to the horizon at an angle of some forty-five degrees, speeding dizzily round and round with a swaying and sweltering motion, and sending forth to the winds an appalling voice, half shriek, half roar, such as not even the mighty cataract of Niagara ever lifts up in its agony to Heaven.

The mountain trembled to its very base, and the rock rocked. I threw myself upon my face, and clung to the scant herbage in an excess of nervous agitation.

"Thus," said I at length, to the old man—"this *can* be nothing else than the great whirlpool of the Maelström."

"So it is sometimes termed," said he. "We Norwegians call it the Moskoe-ström, from the island of Moskoe in the **10** midway."

The ordinary accounts of this vortex had by no means prepared me for what I saw. That of Jonas Ramus, which is **11** perhaps the most circumstantial of any, cannot impart the faintest conception either of the magnificence, or of the horror of the scene—or of the wild bewildering sense of *the novel* which confounds the beholder. I am not sure from what point of view the writer in question surveyed it, nor at what time; but it could neither have been from the summit of Helseggen, nor during a storm. There are some passages of his description, nevertheless, which may be quoted for their details, although their effect is exceedingly feeble in conveying an impression of the spectacle.

"Between Lofoden and Moskoe," he says, "the depth of the water is between thirty-six and forty fathoms; but on the other side, toward Ver (Vurrgh) this depth decreases so as not to afford a convenient passage for a vessel, without the risk of splitting on the rocks, which happens even in the calmest

9 From the *Mariner's Chronicle*: ". . . foaming, tumbling, rushing to its vortex, very much concave, . . . the noise too, hissing, roaring, dashing, all pressing on the mind at once, presented the most awful, grand and solemn sight I have ever experienced" (p. 441).

10 The true Norwegian word is *Moskenstraumen*, and the island's name is Moskenes. The origin of the word "maelstrom" lies in the Norwegian word meaning "to mill or grind," and in Scandinavian folktales the whirlpool is called "the mill of the sea."

According to legend, Frodhi, a Danish king, owned two magic millstones that ground out gold, peace, and good luck for him. But soon he became greedy, and the giantesses who turned the stones for him changed the spell so that they ground out warriors and bad luck. Mysinger, a Viking, murdered Frodhi, and took the stones (*grotti*) on his ship and bade them grind out salt— a valuable commodity in those days. But Mysinger was as greedy as Frodhi had been, and the stones ground out so much salt that his ship soon sank under the weight of it all, and the heavy millstones made a gigantic hole in the ocean floor. Thanks to Mysinger's greed, the seas are salty, and from the hole in the ocean floor the Maelstrom was born.

11 Jonas Ramus (1649–1718) was a pastor in the diocese of Aggershus, whose descriptions of Norway are quoted extensively by Bishop Pontoppidan, who is quoted by the Britannica, paraphrased in turn by Poe.

The Maelström. *Artist unknown*

12 A Norway mile is equal to about four and one half of our miles.

13 See Chapter 22 of Jules Verne's *Twenty Thousand Leagues Under the Sea:* "From every point of the horizon enormous waves were meeting, forming a gulf justly called the 'Navel of the Ocean,' whose power of attraction extends to a distance of twelve miles. There not only vessels, but whales are sacrificed, as well as white bears from the northern regions."

weather. When it is flood, the stream runs up the country between Lofoden and Moskoe with a boisterous rapidity; but the roar of its impetuous ebb to the sea is scarce equalled by the loudest and most dreadful cataracts; the noise being heard several leagues off, and the vortices or pits are of such an extent and depth, that if a ship comes within its attraction, it is inevitably absorbed and carried down to the bottom, and there beat to pieces against the rocks; and when the water relaxes, the fragments thereof are thrown up again. But these intervals of tranquility are only at the turn of the ebb and flood, and in calm weather, and last but a quarter of an hour, its violence gradually returning. When the stream is most boisterous, and its fury heightened by a storm, it is dangerous **12** to come within a Norway mile of it. Boats, yachts, and ships have been carried away by not guarding against it before they were within its reach. It likewise happens frequently, that whales come too near the stream, and are overpowered by its violence; and then it is impossible to describe their howlings and bellowings in their fruitless struggles to disengage themselves. A bear once, attempting to swim from Lofoden to Moskoe, was caught by the stream and borne down, while he **13** roared terribly, so as to be heard on shore. Large stocks of firs and pine trees, after being absorbed by the current, rise again broken and torn to such a degree as if bristles grew upon them. This plainly shows the bottom to consist of craggy rocks, among which they are whirled to and fro. This stream is regulated by the flux and reflux of the sea—it being constantly high and low water every six hours. In the year 1645, early in the morning of Sexagesima Sunday, it raged with such noise **14** and impetuosity that the very stones of the houses on the coast fell to the ground."

In regard to the depth of the water, I could not see how this could have been ascertained at all in the immediate vicinity of the vortex. The "forty fathoms" must have reference only to portions of the channel close upon the shore either of Moskoe or Lofoden. The depth in the centre of the Moskoe-ström must be immeasurably greater; and no better proof of this fact is necessary than can be obtained from even the side-long glance into the abyss of the whirl which may be had from the highest crag of Helseggen. Looking down from this pinnacle upon the howling Phlegethon below, I could not help **15** smiling at the simplicity with which the honest Jonas Ramus records, as a matter difficult of belief, the anecdotes of the whales and the bears; for it appeared to me, in fact, a self-evident thing, that the largest ships of the line in existence, coming within the influence of that deadly attraction, could resist it as little as a feather the hurricane, and must disappear bodily and at once.

The attempts to account for the phenomenon—some of which, I remember, seemed to me sufficiently plausible in perusal—now wore a very different and unsatisfactory aspect. The idea generally received is that this, as well as three smaller vortices among the Feroe islands, "have no other cause than the collision of waves rising and falling, at flux and reflux, against a ridge of rocks and shelves, which confines the water so that it precipitates itself like a cataract; and thus the higher the flood rises, the deeper must the fall be, and the natural result of all is a whirlpool or vortex, the prodigious suction of which is sufficiently known by lesser experiments."—These are the words of the Encyclopaedia Britannica. Kircher and others imagine that in the centre of **16,17** the channel of the Maelström is an abyss penetrating the globe, and issuing in some very remote part—the Gulf of Bothnia being somewhat decidedly named in one instance. This opinion, idle in itself, was the one to which, as I gazed, my imagination most readily assented; and, mentioning it to the guide, I was rather surprised to hear him say that, although it was the view almost universally entertained of the subject by the Norwegians, it nevertheless was not his own. As to the former notion he confessed his inability to comprehend it; and here I agreed with him—for, however conclusive on paper, it becomes altogether unintelligible, and even absurd, amid the thunder of the abyss. **18**

"You have had a good look at the whirl now," said the old man, "and if you will creep round this crag, so as to get in its lee, and deaden the roar of the water, I will tell you a story that will convince you I ought to know something of the Moskoe-ström."

I placed myself as desired, and he proceeded.

"Myself and my two brothers once owned a schooner-rigged smack of about seventy tons burthen, with which we were in **19** the habit of fishing among the islands beyond Moskoe nearly

14 The second Sunday before Lent, the latin word for "sixtieth," because a period of sixty days begins then, ending with the Saturday of Easter week.

15 The fiery river of Hades

16 Poe for once names his chief source of information.

17 Athanasius Kircher (1601–80) was a German Jesuit archeologist, mathematician, biologist, and physicist who was particularly interested in subterranean forces, the deciphering of hieroglyphics, and linguistic relations—all of which were Poe's interests as well. (Kircher also perfected the Aeolian harp, or wind chime, so beloved of English and American romantics.)

Kircher, and later Ramus, connected the Maelstrom with Charybdis, a whirlpool near Sicily, which figures in the twelfth book of the *Odyssey*, after the escape from the Sirens. Bishop Pontoppidan, in *The Natural History of Norway* (1755), states that Kircher believed the Maelstrom was "a sea-vortex, attracting the flood under the shore of Norway, where, through another abyss, it is discharged into the gulph of Bothnia" (p. 81). Bothnia is the body of water between Sweden and Finland.

Note the similarity here between the ideas of Kircher and Ramus and the hollow-earth theories of Symmes, which figure in "MS. Found in a Bottle" [see introductory note] and *The Narrative of Arthur Gordon Pym*.

18 While "abyss" usually refers to the underworld, in Poe it represents annihilation, that ultimate destruction of self which is the most horrifying of all experiences (see "The Pit and the Pendulum" and "MS. Found in a Bottle").

The spiral movements of the whirlpool "may be regarded as figures intended to induce a state of ectasy and to enable man to escape from the material world and to enter the beyond, through the "hole" symbolized by the mystic Centre" says J. E. Cirlot in A Dictionary of Symbols (1962), p. 305.

19 Danish *smak*, a sailing ship such as a sloop or cutter, which is used for fishing or sailing along the coast to Vurrgh. In all violent eddies at sea there is good fishing, at proper opportunities, if one has only the courage to attempt it; but among the whole of the Lofoden coastmen, we three were the only ones who made a regular business of going out to the islands, as I tell you. The usual grounds are a great way lower down to the southward. There fish can be got at all hours, without much risk, and therefore these places are preferred. The choice spots over here among the rocks, however, not only yield the finest variety, but in far greater abundance; so that we often got in a single day, what the more timid of the craft could not scrape together in a week. In fact, we made it a matter of desperate speculation—the risk of life standing instead of labor, and courage answering for capital.

"We kept the smack in a cove about five miles higher up the coast than this; and it was our practice, in fine weather, to take advantage of the fifteen minutes' slack to push across the main channel of the Moskoe-ström, far above the pool, and then drop down upon anchorage somewhere near Otterholm, or Sandflesen, where the eddies are not so violent as elsewhere. Here we used to remain until nearly time for slack-water again, when we weighed and made for home. We never set out upon this expedition without a steady side wind for going and coming—one that we felt sure would not fail us before our return—and we seldom made a mis-calculation upon this point. Twice, during six years, we were forced to stay all night at anchor on account of a dead calm, which is a rare thing indeed just about here; and once we had to remain on the ground nearly a week, starving to death, owing to a gale which blew up shortly after our arrival, and made the channel too boisterous to be thought of. Upon this occasion we should have been driven out to sea in spite of everything, (for the whirlpools threw us round and round so violently, that, at length, we fouled our anchor and dragged it) if it had not been that we drifted into one of the innumerable cross currents—here to-day and gone to-morrow—which drove us under the lee of Flimen, where, by good luck, we brought up.

"I could not tell you the twentieth part of the difficulties we encountered 'on the ground'—it is a bad spot to be in, even in good weather—but we made shift always to run the gauntlet of the Moskoe-ström itself without accident; although at times my heart has been in my mouth when we happened to be a minute or so behind or before the slack. The wind sometimes was not as strong as we thought it at starting, and then we made rather less way than we could wish, while the current rendered the smack unmanageable. My eldest brother had a son eighteen years old, and I had two stout boys of my own. These would have been of great assistance at such times, in using the sweeps, as well as afterward in fishing—but, somehow, although we ran the risk ourselves, we had not the heart to let the young ones get into the danger—for, after all said and done, it *was* a horrible danger, and that is the truth.

"It is now within a few days of three years since what I am

"Such a hurricane as then blew it is folly to attempt describing." *Artist unknown*

going to tell you occurred. It was on the tenth of July, 18—, a day which the people of this part of the world will never forget—for it was one in which blew the most terrible hurricane **20** that ever came out of the heavens. And yet all the morning, and indeed until late in the afternoon, there was a gentle and steady breeze from the south-west, while the sun shone brightly, so that the oldest seaman among us could not have foreseen what was to follow.

"The three of us—my two brothers and myself—had crossed over to the islands about two o'clock P. M., and soon nearly loaded the smack with fine fish, which, we all remarked, were more plenty that day than we had ever known them. It was just seven, *by my watch*, when we weighed and started for home, so as to make the worst of the Ström at slack water, which we knew would be at eight.

"We set out with a fresh wind on our starboard quarter, and for some time spanked along at a great rate, never **21** dreaming of danger, for indeed we saw not the slightest reason to apprehend it. All at once we were taken aback by a breeze from over Helseggen. This was most unusual—something that had never happened to us before—and I began to feel a little uneasy, without exactly knowing why. We put the boat on the wind, but could make no headway at all for the eddies, and I was upon the point of proposing to return to the anchorage, when, looking astern, we saw the whole horizon covered with a singular copper-colored cloud that rose with the most **22** amazing velocity.

"In the meantime the breeze that had headed us off fell away, and we were dead becalmed, drifting about in every direction. This state of things, however, did not last long enough to give us time to think about it. In less than a minute the storm was upon us—in less than two the sky was entirely overcast—and what with this and the driving spray, it became suddenly so dark that we could not see each other in the smack.

"Such a hurricane as then blew it is folly to attempt describing. The oldest seaman in Norway never experienced any thing like it. We had let out sails go by the run before it cleverly took us; but, at the first puff, both out masts went by **23** the board as if they had been sawed off—the mainmast taking with it my youngest brother, who had lashed himself to it for safety.   **24**

"Out boat was the lightest feather of a thing that ever sat upon water. It had a complete flush deck, with only a small hatch near the bow, and this hatch it had always been our custom to batten down when about to cross the Ström, by way of precaution against the chopping seas. But for this circumstance we should have foundered at once—for we lay entirely buried for some moments. How my elder brother escaped destruction I cannot say, for I never had an opportunity of ascertaining. For my part, as soon as I had let the foresail run, I threw myself flat on deck, with my feet against the narrow gunwale of the bow, and with my hands grasping a ring-bolt near the foot of the foremast. It was mere instinct

20 "Hurricane" is the name for a tropical storm. "Cyclone" is the general term for a circular storm (which seems to be the case here). The wind blows counter-clockwise in the northern hemisphere and originates as a wave or eddy in the surface of separation (i.e., the polar front) between the cold polar easterly winds and the warmer prevailing westerlies of the south. This wave, once it begins, is accentuated by a northerly flow of warm, moist air in advance of the center of low pressure, and by a southerly flow of cold, dry air behind the center. As the circular motion begins, the pressure in the center begins to drop.

As for the date given, July is not the usual season for the Maelstrom. The codfish gather on the eastern coast of the islands from February to April, and the herring on the western coast from August to September, and fishermen would most likely be out on the seas at these times. However, the weather patterns may have altered between the time of Poe's sources and the 1840s, or between Poe's time and the present day.

21 Moved quickly

22 Copper has a reddish tint, and in Poe's tales, a red sky or moon usually spells disaster. In Coleridge's *Ancient Mariner* [II, 11–14] we read: "All in a hot and copper sky,/The bloody Sun, at noon,/Right up above the mast did stand,/No bigger than the moon."

There is also the old saying "Red sky at morning, sailor take warning."

23 Completely

24 The fisherman's two brothers rely on traditional methods to save themselves, but both make the fatal assumption that the ship is the safest spot to be.

25 Instinct, perhaps, but hardly "mere." The fisherman still does not comprehend the importance of what he has done. His ability to think and *imagine* has saved him, and yet he doesn't understand this. Perhaps this is why he feels compelled to tell his story—so that by verbalizing his experience, he may understand what it all means.

26 Pronounced "ay-gue," a fit of shivering as in severe fever

27 In the eye of a storm, the sky and seas are often calm and clear. As for the moon, Frank Jordan (*Natural History*, October 1935) points out that in July the moon would just barely rise above the southern horizon in this locale, and in the land of the Midnight Sun, moonlight would be superfluous.

25 that prompted me to do this—which was undoubtedly the very best thing I could have done—for I was too much flurried to think.

For some moments we were completely deluged, as I say, and all this time I held my breath, and clung to the bolt. When I could stand it no longer I raised myself upon my knees, still keeping hold with my hands, and thus got my head clear. Presently our little boat gave herself a shake, just as a dog does in coming out of the water, and thus rid herself, in some measure, of the seas. I was now trying to get the better of the stupor that had come over me, and to collect my senses so as to see what was to be done, when I felt somebody grasp my arm. It was my elder brother, and my heart leaped for joy, for I had made sure that he was overboard—but the next moment all this joy was turned into horror—for he put his mouth close to my ear, and screamed out the word 'Moskoe-ström,!'

26 "No one ever will know what my feelings were at that moment. I shook from head to foot as if I had had the most violent fit of the ague. I knew what he meant by that one word well enough—I knew what he wished to make me understand. With the wind that now drove us on, were were bound for the whirl of the Ström, and nothing could save us!

"You perceive that in crossing the Ström *channel*, we always went a long way up above the whirl, even in the calmest weather, and then we had to wait and watch carefully for the slack—but now we were driving right upon the pool itself, and in such a hurricane as this! 'To be sure,' I thought, 'we shall get there just about the slack—there is some little hope in that'—but in the next moment I cursed myself for being so great a fool as to dream of hope at all. I knew very well that we were doomed, had we been ten times a ninety-gun ship.

"By this time the first fury of the tempest had spent itself, or perhaps we did not feel it so much, as we scudded before it, but at all events the seas, which at first had been kept down by the wind, and lay flat and frothing, now got up into absolute mountains. A singular change, too, had come over the heavens. Around in every direction it was still as black as pitch, but nearly overhead there burst out, all at once, a circular rift of clear sky—as clear as I ever saw—and of a deep bright blue—and through it there blazed forth the full moon **27** with a lustre that I never before knew her to wear. She lit up everything about us with the greatest distinctness—but, oh God, what a scene it was to light up!

"I now made one or two attempts to speak to my brother—but in some manner which I could not understand, the din had so increased that I could not make him hear a single word, although I screamed at the top of my voice in his ear. Presently he shook his head, looking as pale as death, and held up one of his fingers, as if to say '*listen!*'

"At first I could not make out what he meant—but soon a hideous thought flashed upon me. I dragged my watch from its fob. It was not going. I glanced at its face by the moonlight, and then burst into tears as I flung it far away into the ocean.

It had run down at seven o'clock! We were behind the time of the slack, and the whirl of the Ström was in full fury!   **28**

"When a boat is well built, properly trimmed, and not deep laden, the waves in a strong gale, when she is going large, seem always to slip from beneath her—which appears very strange to a landsman—and this is what is called *riding*, in sea phrase.

"Well, so far we had ridden the swells very cleverly; but presently a gigantic sea happened to take us right under the counter, and bore us with it as it rose—up—up—as if into the   **29** sky. I would not have believed that any wave could rise so high. And then down we came with a sweep, a slide, and a plunge, that made me feel sick and dizzy, as if I was falling from some lofty mountain-top in a dream. But while we were   **30** up I had thrown a quick glance around—and that one glance was all sufficient. I saw our exact position in an instant. The Moskoe-ström whirlpool was about a quarter of a mile dead ahead—but no more like the every-day Moskoe-ström, than the whirl as you now see it, is like a mill-race. If I had not known where we were, and what we had to expect, I should not have recognized the place at all. As it was, I involuntarily closed my eyes in horror. The lids clenched themselves together as if in a spasm.

"It could not have been more than two minutes afterwards until we suddenly felt the waves subside, and were enveloped in foam. The boat made a sharp half turn to larboard, and   **31** then shot off in its new direction like a thunderbolt. At the same moment the roaring noise of the water was completely drowned in a kind of shrill shriek—such a sound as you might imagine given out by the water-pipes of many thousand steam-vessels, letting off their steam all together. We were now in the belt of surf that always surrounds the whirl; and I thought, of course, that another moment would plunge us into the abyss—down which we could only see indistinctly on account of the amazing velocity with which we were borne along. The boat did not seem to sink into the water at all, but to skim like an air-bubble upon the surface of the surge. He starboard side was next the whirl, and on the larboard arose the world of ocean we had left. It stood like a huge writhing wall between us and the horizon.

"It may appear strange, but now, when we were in the very jaws of the gulf, I felt more composed than when we were only approaching it. Having made up my mind to hope no more, I got rid of a great deal of that terror which unmanned me at first. I suppose it was despair that strung my nerves.   **32**

"It may look like boasting—but what I tell you is truth—I began to reflect how magnificent a thing it was to die in such a manner, and how foolish it was in me to think of so paltry a consideration as my own individual life, in view of so wonderful a manifestation of God's power. I do believe that   **33** I blushed with shame when this idea crossed my mind. After a little while I became possessed with the keenest curiosity about the whirl itself. I positively felt a *wish* to explore its depths, even at the sacrifice I was going to make; and my

28 Like the Ancient Mariner, who is guilty of pride (*hubris*) in his killing of the albatross, the fisherman is also guilty of pride in his assumption that he has control over his environment simply because he has a watch. He forgets how little separates him from annihilation when he takes it for granted that this little piece of ticking machinery will take care of him. In addition, his two brothers show pride too, in their willful separation from the other fishermen, and in their reliance on strength and familiar skills to get them through the Maelstrom.

29 The after portion of the boat, from the waterline to the extreme outward swell or stern overhang

30 Compare with the opening of the tale.

31 Port (left)

32 Compare the fisherman here with the narrator of "The Pit and the Pendulum," whose "nervous energy of despair" enables him to escape from his various predicaments.

33 The Ancient Mariner is saved when he sees for the first time the beauty in the world around him, and blesses the water snakes: "O happy living things! no tongue/Their beauty might declare/A spring of love gushed from my heart,/And I blessed them unaware" (IV, 282).

Because the fisherman is calm enough to reflect on his surroundings, he, too, sees the beauty and grandeur of nature. With new eyes he begins to understand the workings of this new world, and in this lies his salvation.

principal grief was that I should never be able to tell my old companions on shore about the mysteries I should see. These, no doubt, were singular fancies to occupy a man's mind in such extremity—and I have often thought since, that the revolutions of the boat around the pool might have rendered me a little light-headed.

"There was another circumstance which tended to restore my self-possession; and this was the cessation of the wind, which could not reach us in our present situation—for, as you saw yourself, the belt of surf is considerably lower than the general bed of the ocean, and this latter now towered above us, a high, black, mountainous ridge. If you have never been at sea in a heavy gale, you can form no idea of the confusion of mind occasioned by the wind and spray together. They blind, deafen and strangle you, and take away all power of action or reflection. But we were now, in a great measure, rid of these annoyances—just as death-condemned felons in prison are allowed petty indulgences, forbidden them while their doom is yet uncertain.

"How often we made the circuit of the belt it is impossible to say. We careered round and round for perhaps an hour, flying rather than floating, getting gradually more and more into the middle of the surge, and then nearer and nearer to its horrible inner edge. All this time I had never let go of the ring-bolt. My brother was at the stern, holding on to a large empty water-cask which had been securely lashed under the coop of the counter, and was the only thing on deck that had not been swept overboard when the gale first took us. As we approached the brink of the pit he let go his hold upon this, and made for the ring, from which, in the agony of his terror, he endeavored to force my hands, as it was not large enough to afford us both a secure grasp. I never felt deeper grief than when I saw him attempt this act—although I knew he was a madman when he did it—a raving maniac through sheer fright. I did not care, however, to contest the point with him. I thought it could make no difference whether either of us held on at all; so I let him have the bolt, and went astern to **34** the cask. This there was no great difficulty in doing; for the smack flew around steadily enough, and upon an even keel— only swaying to and fro, with the immense sweeps and swelters of the whirl. Scarcely had I secured myself in my new position, when we gave a wild lurch to starboard, and rushed headlong into the abyss. I muttered a hurried prayer to God, and thought all was over.

"As I felt the sickening sweep of the descent, I had instinctively tightened my hold upon the barrel, and closed my eyes. For some seconds I dared not open them—while I expected instant destruction, and wondered that I was not already in my death-struggles with the water. But moment after moment elapsed. I still lived. The sense of falling had ceased; and the motion of the vessel seemed much as it had been before while in the belt of foam, with the exception that she now lay more along. I took courage and looked once again upon the scene.

34 The second brother has taken hold of a ringbolt, which, since it is fastened to the ship, seems a sensible thing to do, just as was the first brother's dash for the mast. Unfortunately, "sensible" no longer means anything here (or at least what was sensible outside the Maelstrom), and so he seals his doom just when the narrator takes his second step toward salvation.

"Never shall I forget the sensations of awe, horror, and admiration with which I gazed about me. The boat appeared to be hanging, as if by magic, midway down, upon the interior surface of a funnel vast in circumference, prodigious in depth, and whose perfectly smooth sides might have been mistaken for ebony, but for the bewildering rapidity with which they spun around, and for the gleaming and ghastly radiance they shot forth, as the rays of the full moon, from that circular rift amid the clouds which I have already described, streamed in a flood of golden glory along the black walls, and far away down into the inmost recesses of the abyss.   **35**

"At first I was too much confused to observe anything accurately. The general burst of terrific grandeur was all that I beheld. When I recovered myself a little, however, my gaze fell instinctively downward. In this direction I was able to obtain an unobstructed view, from the manner in which the smack hung on the inclined surface of the pool. She was quite upon an even keel—that is to say, her deck lay in a plane parallel with that of the water—but this latter sloped at an angle of more than forty-five degrees, so that we seemed to be lying upon our beam-ends. I could not help observing, nevertheless, that I had scarcely more difficulty in maintaining my hold and footing in this situation, than if we had been upon a dead level; and this, I suppose, was owing to the speed at which we revolved.

"The rays of the moon seemed to search the very bottom of the profound gulf; but still I could make out nothing distinctly, on account of a thick mist in which everything there was enveloped, and over which there hung a magnificent rainbow, like that narrow and tottering bridge which Mussulmen say is the only pathway between Time and Eternity.   **36** This mist, or spray, was no doubt occasioned by the clashing of the great walls of the funnel, as they all met together at the bottom—but the yell that went up to the Heavens from out of that mist, I dare not attempt to describe.

"Our first slide into the abyss itself, from the belt of foam above, had carried us to a great distance down the slope; but our farther descent was by no means proportionate. Round and round we swept—not with any uniform movement—but in dizzying swings and jerks, that sent us sometimes only a few hundred feet—sometimes nearly the complete circuit of the whirl. Our progress downward, at each revolution, was slow, but very perceptible.

"Looking about me upon the wide waste of liquid ebony on which we were thus borne, I perceived that our boat was not the only object in the embrace of the whirl. Both above and below us were visible fragments of vessels, large masses of building timber and trunks of trees, with many smaller articles, such as pieces of house furniture, broken boxes, barrels and staves. I have already described the unnatural curiosity which had taken the place of my original terrors. It appeared to grow upon me as I drew nearer and nearer to my dreadful doom. I now began to watch, with a strange interest, the numerous things that floated in our company. I *must* have been deliri-

35 "Imagine to yourselves an immense circle running round, of a diameter one and a half miles, the velocity increasing . . . gradually changing its dark blue color to white," writes Jules Verne in *Twenty Thousand Leagues Under the Sea*. Actually, according to Frank Jordan (note 27) the Malestrom does not form a funnel of any kind.

Here is the rest of Verne's description:

"The Maelstrom! Could a more dreadful word in a more dreadful situation have sounded in our ears! We were then upon the dangerous coast of Norway. Was the *Nautilus* being drawn into this gulf at the moment our boat was going to leave its sides? We knew that at the tide the pent-up waters between the islands of Ferros and Loffoden rush with irresistible violence, forming a whirlpool from which no vessel ever escapes. From every point of the horizon enormous waves were meeting, forming a gulf justly called the "Navel of the Ocean," whose power of attraction extends to a distance of twelve miles. . . .

"It was thither that the *Nautilus*, voluntarily or involuntarily, had been run by the Captain.

"It was describing a spiral, the circumference of which was lessening by degrees, and the boat, which was still fastened to its side, was carried along with giddy speed. I felt that sickly giddiness which arises from long-continued whirling around.

"We were in dread. Our horror was at its height, circulation had stopped, all nervous influence was annihilated, and we were covered with cold sweat, like a sweat of agony! And what noise around our frail bark! What roaring repeated by the echo miles away! What an uproar was that of the waters broken on the sharp rocks at the bottom, where the hardest bodies are crushed.

. . .

". . . we heard a crashing noise, the bolts gave way, and the boat, torn from its groove, was hurled like a stone from a sling into the midst of the whirlpool." (Chapter 22)

Verne, who acknowledged Poe as his master, has obviously read "Descent into the Maelström" but has also added material from sources of his own. He uses the whirlpool again in *The Sphinx of the Ice Fields* (1897), which also happens to be a continuation of Poe's *Arthur Gordon Pym*.

36 "Mussulmen" is often used as the plural of "Mussulman" (Muslim), but the correct form (according to the O.E.D.) is "Mussulmans," since the "man" here is a Turkish word, unrelated to the English "man."

The bridge referred to here is Al-Siraat. The rainbow is a traditional symbol of a bridge between heaven and earth in many religions.

37 Like the narrator of "The Pit and the Pendulum," he chides himself for the "frivolity" of his observations of the "minutiae" of his surroundings, and yet there is nothing frivolous at all about it.

Note that this beauty is not one that can be explained in technological or scientific terms (as one would expect from a practical seaman), so that his curiosity is not so much scientific as it is aesthetic.

38 In the *Britannica* article on the whirlpool that Poe read, is this description of one in the Orkneys:

"Whenever it appears, it is very furious; and boats, etc. would inevitably be drawn in and perish with it; but the people who navigate them are prepared for it, and always carry an empty vessel, a log of wood, or some such thing, in the boat with them; as soon as they perceive the whirlpool, they toss this within its vortex, keeping themselves out. This substance, whatever it be, is immediately received into the centre, and carried underwater; and as soon as this is done, the surface of the place where the whirlpool was becomes smooth, and they row over it with safety."

The reference in *Britanica*, however is to a disturbance of the spiral motion by throwing an object into the whirlpool, while in this story, the wooden object does not stop the whirling motion, but instead merely rides it out.

39 "See Archimedes, *"De Incidentibus in Fluido."*—lib. 2. [Poe's note] No such quote exists in *De iis quae in humido vehuntur* (the actual title), and the fact that the fisherman has forgotten the explanation underscores that Poe simply made it up.

ous—for I even sought *amusement* in speculating upon the relative velocities of their several descents towards the foam **37** below. 'This fir tree,' I found myself at one time saying, 'will certainly be the next thing that takes the awful plunge and disappears,'—and then I was disappointed to find that the wreck of a Dutch merchant ship overtook it and went down before. At length, after making several guesses of this nature, and being deceived in all—this fact—the fact of my invariable miscalculation, set me upon a train of reflection that made my limbs again tremble, and my heart beat heavily once more.

"It was not a new terror that thus affected me, but the dawn of a more exciting *hope*. This hope arose partly from memory, and partly from present observation. I called to mind the great variety of buoyant matter that strewed the coast of Lofoden, having been absorbed and then thrown forth by the Moskoe-ström. By far the greater number of the articles were shattered in the most extraordinary way—so chafed and roughened as to have the appearance of being stuck full of splinters—but then I distinctly recollected that there were *some* of them which were not disfigured at all. Now I could not account for this difference except by supposing that the roughened fragments were the only ones which had been *completely absorbed*—that the others had entered the whirl at so late a period of the tide, or, from some reason, had descended so slowly after entering, that they did not reach the bottom before the turn of the flood came, or of the ebb, as the case might be. I conceived it possible, in either instance, that they might thus be whirled up again to the level of the ocean, without undergoing the fate of those which had been drawn in more early or absorbed more rapidly. I made, also, three important observations. The first was, that as a general rule, the larger the bodies, the more rapid their descent;— the second, that, between two masses of equal extent, the one sperical, and the other *of any other shape*, the superiority in speed of descent was with the sphere;—the third, that, between two masses of equal size, the one cylindrical, and the other of any other shape, the cylinder was absorbed the more **38** slowly.

"Since my escape, I have had several conversations on this subject with an old school-master of the district; and it was from him that I learned the use of the words 'cylinder' and 'sphere.' He explained to me—although I have forgotten the explanation—how what I observed was, in fact, the natural consequence of the forms of the floating fragments—and showed me how it happened that a cylinder, swimming in a vortex, offered more resistance to its suction, and was drawn in with greater difficulty than an equally bulky body, of any **39** form whatever.

"There was one startling circumstance which went a great way in enforcing these observations, and rendering me anxious to turn them to account, and this was that, at every revolution, we passed something like a barrel, or else the broken yard or the mast of a vessel, while many of these things, which had been on our level when I first opened my eyes upon the wonders of the whirlpool, were now high up above us, and seemed to have moved but little from their original station.

"I no longer hesitated what to do. I resolved to lash myself securely to the water-cask upon which I now held, to cut it loose from the counter, and to throw myself with it into the water. I attracted my brother's attention by signs, pointed to the floating barrels that came near us, and did everything in my power to make him understand what I was about to do. I thought at length that he comprehended my design—but, whether this was the case or not, he shook his head despairingly, and refused to move from his station by the ring-bolt. It was impossible to force him; the emergency admitted no delay; and so, with a bitter struggle, I resigned him to his fate, fastened myself to the cask by means of the lashings which secured it to the counter, and precipitated myself with it into the sea, without another moment's hesitation.   40

"The result was precisely what I had hoped it might be. As it is myself who now tell you this tale—as you see that I *did* escape—and as you are already in possession of the mode in which this escape was effected, and must therefore anticipate all that I have farther to say—I will bring my story quickly to conclusion. It might have been an hour, or thereabout, after my quitting the smack, when, having descended to a vast distance beneath me, it made three or four wild gyrations in rapid succession, and, bearing my loved brother with it, plunged headlong, at once and forever, into the chaos of foam below. The barrel to which I was attached sunk very little farther than half the distance between the bottom of the gulf and the spot at which I leaped overboard, before a great change took place in the character of the whirlpool. The slope of the sides of the vast funnel became momently less and less steep. The gyrations of the whirl grew, gradually, less and less violent. By degrees, the froth and the rainbow disappeared, and the bottom of the gulf seemed slowly to uprise. The sky was clear, the winds had gone down, and the full moon was setting radiantly in the west, when I found myself on the surface of the ocean, in full view of the shores of Lofoden, and above the spot where the pool of the Moskoeström *had been*. It was the hour of the slack—but the sea still heaved in mountainous waves from the effects of the hurricane. I was borne violently into the channel of the Ström, and in a few minutes, was hurried down the coast into the 'grounds' of the fishermen. A boat picked me up—exhausted from fatigue—and (now that the danger was removed) speechless   41 from the memory of its horror. Those who drew me on board were my old mates and daily companions—but they knew me no more than they would have known a traveller from the spirit-land. My hair, which had been raven-black the day   42 before, was as white as you see it now. They say too that the whole expression of my countenance had changed. I told them   43 my story—they did not believe it. I now tell it to *you*—and I can scarcely expect you to put more faith in it than did the merry fishermen of Lofoden."   44

40 It may be relevant that a sphere is often a symbol for intellectual life, pure thought, and abstraction, while a cylinder represents material thoughts and the mechanistic intellect.

Note the echo in *Moby-Dick*, when Ishmael saves himself by clinging to a sealed coffin.

41 He is only temporarily speechless, for once he begins to ponder his experience, he finds he must tell it again and again, like the Ancient Mariner:

"Forthwith this fame of mine was wrenched
With a woeful agony,
Which forced me to begin my tale;
And then it left me free.

"Since then, at an uncertain hour,
That agony returns:
And till my ghastly tale is told,
This heart within me burns [VII, 578–85]."

42 I.e., the land of the dead. The fact that his hair has turned white adds to his ghostly look, but contrary to popular belief, hair cannot turn white overnight; any change of color will show only as the hair grows out.

The Ancient Mariner also feels that he has "died in sleep,/And was a blessed ghost [V, 305–6]."

43 The fisherman is not the same man; he is, in fact, "reborn." What he has learned (if still unconsciously) is that nature resists man's understanding. The Maelstrom is not a parable, it is a riddle. It denies both our comprehension of the universe and the notion that the universe is somehow sympathetic to our plight. While it would be simplistic to say that Poe here looks ahead to the existentialist belief that man is alone in the universe, there is much in common between Poe's attitude as expressed in "Descent into the Maelström," "MS, Found in a Bottle," "The Pit and the Pendulum," and *Pym*, and the concepts of Sartre and Camus, as well as such American exponents of naturalism as Stephen Crane ("The Open Boat"). The chief difference between Poe and the existentialists is that Poe still believes in a God (although not a personal one), and unlike Crane, admits the possibility of coming to grips with his universe through imagination.

44 The Ancient Mariner also leaves the Wedding Guest a "sadder but a wiser man." The last sentence was added to the 1845 version, once again allowing literal-minded readers a logical out.

The truth of the events in the story, however, is of less importance than their symbolic meaning, Poe's insistence that if we do not insist upon forcing our viewpoint on the world—if we do not try to control our environment—but instead let it shape our thoughts and actions, we may at least come to terms with it.

Psychological interpretations include Maria Bonaparte's assertion that the whirlpool, "which for all its terror, fatally attracts" the narrator, "expresses a version of the return-to-the-womb phantasy" (p. 352). This is reinforced by the fact that the whirlpool is a spiral, symbolic of the source of life and natural energy or magic. Jungians see the spiral as leading to the unconscious, so that the narrator's experience could be seen as a symbol of his encounter with subconscious truths that he only partially understands.

THE OVAL PORTRAIT

First published as "Life in Death" in *Graham's Magazine*, April 1842, the story was shortened considerably for its second appearance, with a new title, in the *Broadway Journal*, April 26, 1845.

The central theme here is similar to Hawthorne's "The Birthmark" (1843), but the concept of a painting having an intimate connection with a person's being is an ancient one, part of the belief that a representation of a living being "captures the spirit" of the original. Another famous story of this type is Oscar Wilde's "The Picture of Dorian Gray" (1891).

Some critics have interpreted this tale as Poe's subconscious restaging of his own marriage, for Virginia understood little about her husband's literary talents. In Poe's story the wife seems jealous of her husband's painting.

There is evidence that Poe was inspired in part by a painting (in an oval frame), by his friend Robert M. Sully, of a girl who holds in her hand a locket that is hanging about her neck by a ribbon.

Between the story's first and second appearances, Poe removed several lengthy descriptions at the beginning of how the narrator prepared and smoked opium and how he decided to use the drug to alleviate his feverish symptoms in the isolated mountain château that is the scene of the story. Poe was wise to delete this, for it blunts the story as we now know it by emphasizing too strongly the hallucinatory effect of the drug.

Elements from the tale were used in the 1925 French film. *The Fall of the House of Usher*, directed by Jean Epstein.

Martin Donegan reads the tale on records (CMS 630).

1 The Apennines are a mountain system traversing the entire length of the Italian peninsula. The peaks are mostly bare and wild, and settlers have always preferred the valleys for settlement. Once heavily forested, the Apennines present a far different appearance today, after centuries as Italy's chief source of wood.

2 Ann Radcliffe (1764–1823) was the first writer to fully exploit the romance of the past, the distant, the unfamiliar, the picturesque, and the supernatural. Her three most important novels—*The Romance of the Forest* (1791), *The Mysteries of Udolpho* (1794), and *The Italian* (1797)—are variations on the theme of the heroine beset by forces of evil, usually in a gloomy and terror-ridden castle.

3 Cut from the original version: "Day by day we expected the return of the family who tenanted it, when the misadventure which had befallen me would, no doubt, be received as sufficient apology for the intrusion." In this version, the absence of the household and the narrator's presence take on a much more mysterious tone.

4 After reading the description of the room, one wonders what the *truly* sumptuous apartments are like.

5 The tale is set in Italy, and the narrator's manservant is Spanish (his name is Pedro in the first version), but we don't know the narrator's nationality.

The château into which my valet had ventured to make forcible entrance, rather than permit me, in my desperately wounded condition, to pass a night in the open air, was one of those piles of commingled gloom and grandeur which have so long **1** frowned among the Apennines, not less in fact than in the **2** fancy of Mrs. Radcliffe. To all appearance it had been tem- **3** porarily and very lately abandoned. We established ourselves in one of the smallest and least sumptuously furnished apart- **4** ments. It lay in a remote turret of the building. Its decorations were rich, yet tattered and antique. Its walls were hung with tapestry and bedecked with manifold and multiform armorial trophies, together with an unusually great number of very spirited modern paintings in frames of rich golden arabesque. In these paintings, which depended from the walls not only in their main surfaces, but in very many nooks which the bizarre architecture of the château rendered necessary—in these paintings my incipient delirium, perhaps, had caused **5** me to take deep interest; so that I bade Pedro to close the heavy shutters of the room—since it was already night,—to light the tongues of a tall candelabrum which stood by the head of my bed, and to throw open far and wide the fringed curtains of black velvet which enveloped the bed itself. I wished all this done that I might resign myself, if not to sleep, at least alternately to the contemplation of these pictures, and the perusal of a small volume which had been found upon the pillow, and which purported to criticise and describe them.

Long, long I read—and devoutly, devotedly, I gazed. **6** Rapidly and gloriously the hours flew by and the deep midnight came. The position of the candelabrum displeased me, and outreaching my hand with difficulty, rather than disturb my slumbering valet, I placed it so as to throw its rays more fully upon the book.

But the action produced an effect altogether unanticipated. The rays of the numerous candles (for there were many) now fell within a niche of the room which had hitherto been thrown into deep shade by one of the bedposts. I thus saw in vivid light a picture all unnoticed before. It was the portrait of a young girl just ripening into womanhood. I glanced at the painting hurriedly, and then closed my eyes. Why I did this was not at first apparent even to my own perception. But while my lids remained thus shut, I ran over in mind my reason for so shutting them. It was an impulsive movement to gain time for thought—to make sure that my vision had not deceived me—to calm and subdue my fancy for a more sober and more certain gaze. In a very few moments I again looked fixedly at the painting.

That I now saw aright I could not and would not doubt; for the first flashing of the candles upon that canvas had seemed to dissipate the dreamy stupor which was stealing over my senses, and to startle me at once into waking life.

The portrait, I have already said, was that of a young girl. It was a mere head and shoulders, done in what is technically termed a *vignette* manner; much in the style of the favorite heads of Sully. The arms, the bosom, and even the ends of the radiant hair melted imperceptibly into the vague yet deep shadow which formed the background of the whole. The frame was oval, richly gilded and filigreed in *Moresque*. As a thing **7** of art nothing could be more admirable than the painting itself. But it could have been neither the execution of the work, nor the immortal beauty of the countenance, which had so suddenly and so vehemently moved me. Least of all, could it have been that my fancy, shaken from its half slumber, had mistaken the head for that of a living person. I saw at once **8** that the peculiarities of the design, of the *vignetting*, and of the frame, must have instantly dispelled such idea—must have prevented even its momentary entertainment. Thinking earnestly upon these points, I remained, for an hour perhaps, half sitting, half reclining, with my vision riveted upon the portrait. At length, satisfied with the true secret of its effect, I fell back within the bed. I had found the spell of the picture in an absolute *life-likeliness* of expression, which, at first startling, finally confounded, subdued, and appalled me. With **9** deep and reverent awe I replaced the candelabrum in its former position. The cause of my deep agitation being thus shut from view, I sought eagerly the volume which discussed the paintings and their histories. Turning to the number which

6 Originally: ". . . I gazed. I felt meantime, the voluptuous narcotic stealing its way to my brain. I felt that in its magical influence lay much of the gorgeous richness and variety of the frames—much of the ethereal hue that gleamed from the canvas—and much of the wild interest of the book which I perused. Yet this consciousness rather strengthened than impaired the delight of the illusion, while it weakened the illusion itself."

7 The frame is "fantastically" gilded in the first version. Poe adds "*Moresque*" in the second version (as a variation on arabesque) For Sully, see introductory note.

8 G. R. Thompson suggests that the entire tale can be read as "the dream of a man delirious from pain and lack of sleep" (*Great Short Works of Edgar Allan Poe*, Houghton Mifflin, 1979; p. 39).

9 Poe added, in the original, "I could no longer support the sad meaning smile of the half-parted lips, nor the too-real lustre of the wild eye.

". . . he was a passionate, and wild, and moody man. . . ." *Illustration by Jean Paul Laurens, nineteenth century*

10 Compare with the ending of Hawthorne's "The Birthmark": "As the last crimson tint of the birthmark—that sole token of human imperfection—faded from her cheek, the parting breath of the now perfect woman passed into the atmosphere, and her soul, lingering a moment near her husband, took its heavenward flight."

Poe's original ending: "'This is indeed *Life* itself!' turned round to his beloved—*who was dead*. The painter then added—But is this indeed Death?'"

Poe's tale echoes another of Hawthorne's tales—"The Artist of the Beautiful"—in which a marvelous mechanical butterfly symbolizes the artist's attainment of an ideal beauty, which is destroyed at the tale's climax.

Most interpretations of "The Oval Portrait" have used the Hawthorne tales as parallels, suggesting that Poe means to warn of the danger of pride, of refusing to accept the responsibility of one's humanity. Like the narrators of "Ligeia" and "Berenice," the artist of "The Oval Portrait" is obsessed with the beauty of the woman he paints but has little or no concern for her emotional needs.

"What is it that Poe, in *The Oval Portrait*, confesses?" asks Marie Bonaparte. "It is that, to achieve those sombre masterpieces in which his Madelines, Ligeias, Berenices, smile ever more wanly to our eyes, he has had to 'draw' the colour and life 'from the cheeks' of a dying woman. In order that Poe might become the kind of artist he was, a woman had first to die. In this story, the note of remorse, as regards the man, mingles with that of triumph; as regards the artist, it is as though the man in him felt responsible for the woman's death, since he thus relentlessly used her both for his pleasure and profit, as was dictated by his deepest wishes.

"And, indeed, while *The Oval Portrait* was being written, a woman, in fact, was dying at Poe's side. . . ." (P. 260)

Bonaparte refers to Virginia's first hemorrhage, in January 1842, three months before the first publication of "The Oval Portrait." Her ideas, as always, are intriguing, but there are enough obvious autobiographical references in the tale without digging into Poe's psyche post-mortem, and surely Poe can write of a character's monomania without being monomaniacal himself.

One could also point to the tale as another study of the relationship between a person and his double. The artist has created a "perfect" representation of the woman in question, and not only does this perfect twin better represent what the artist worships in her, but once the painting is done, there is no reason for the human twin to exist: the "real" woman is now the painting, as far as he is concerned.

"Life is short, art is long," says Seneca. The woman dies, but the painting endures.

designated the oval portrait, I there read the vague and quaint words which follow:

"She was a maiden of rarest beauty, and not more lovely than full of glee. And evil was the hour when she saw, and loved, and wedded the painter. He, passionate, studious, austere, and having already a bride in his Art: she a maiden of rarest beauty, and not more lovely than full of glee; all light and smiles, and frolicsome as the young fawn; loving and cherishing all things; hating only the Art which was her rival; dreading only the pallet and brushes and other untoward instruments which deprived her of the countenance of her lover. It was thus a terrible thing for this lady to hear the painter speak of his desire to portray even his young bride. But she was humble and obedient, and sat meekly for many weeks in the dark high turret-chamber where the light dripped upon the pale canvas only from overhead. But he, the painter, took glory in his work, which went on from hour to hour, and from day to day. And he was a passionate, and wild, and moody man, who became lost in reveries; so that he *would* not see that the light which fell so ghastly in that lone turret withered the health and the spirits of his bride, who pined visibly to all but him. Yet she smiles on and still on, uncomplainingly, because she saw that the painter (who had high renown) took a fervid and burning pleasure in his task, and wrought day and night to depict her who so loved him, yet who grew daily more dispirited and weak. And in sooth some who beheld the portrait spoke of its resemblance in low words, as of a mighty marvel, and a proof not less of the power of the painter than of his deep love for her whom he depicted so surpassingly well. But at length, as the labor drew nearer to its conclusion, there were admitted none into the turret; for the painter had grown wild with the ardor of his work, and turned his eyes from the canvas rarely, even to regard the countenance of his wife. And he *would* not see that the tints which he spread upon the canvas were drawn from the cheeks of her who sat beside him. And when many weeks had passed, and but little remained to do, save one brush upon the mouth and one tint upon the eye, the spirit of the lady again flickered up as the flame within the socket of the lamp. And then the brush was given, and then the tint was placed; and, for one moment, the painter stood entranced before the work which he had wrought; but in the next, while he yet gazed, he grew tremulous and very pallid, and aghast, and crying with a loud voice, 'This is indeed *Life* itself!' turned suddenly to regard **10** his beloved:—*She was dead!*"

THE MASQUE OF THE RED DEATH

First published in *Graham's Magazine*, May 1842, "The Masque of the Red Death" is an undisputed masterpiece in the genre of short-story writing and one of Poe's most unusual efforts. Note the complete absence of that Poe trademark the first-person narrator, and the use of allegory, which Poe disliked in general and attacked in the work of others. The tale is more consistently dreamlike than even "Eleonora" and "The Oval Portrait," and its language is more opulent and purely descriptive than any of Poe's other stories, giving the whole the quality of a poem.

The "masque" of the title refers both to the masque as a private entertainment, which flourished in Renaissance Italy, and to the masque (mask) of the mysterious figure at the tale's climax. (The original title was "The Mask of the Red Death. A Fantasy.")

The chief source for the tale is an account, by N. P. Willis, of a "cholera ball" he attended in Paris, described in the notes that follow, as well as Shakespeare's *The Tempest* and a portion of Boccaccio's *Decameron*.

Elements from Poe's tale have found their way into Wilkie Collins' "The Yellow Mask" (1855) and H. P. Lovecraft's "The Outsider" (1921), although the opening of the latter sounds like "Berenice" and the ending resembles that of "William Wilson."

French composer André Caplet (1878–1925) wrote a symphonic study based on the tale, as did Englishman Joseph Holbrooke (1878–1958).

Only two film versions have been made. The first was *A Spectre Haunts Europe* (1921), a Russian film directed by Vladimir R. Gardin. The more recent *Masque of the Red Death* (1964), like so many other films based on Poe's works, adds dialogue and characters (including an entire subplot based on Poe's "Hop-Frog"). The acknowledged zenith of director Roger Corman's love affair with Poe, this ninety-minute film stars Vincent Price and Hazel Court (reputed to be "the best screamer in the business"), and abandons the tongue-in-cheek style of most of Price's films, concentrating instead on the stylish, symbolic, and literary aspects of the tale—with mixed results. The film's outstanding photography is the work of Nicholas Roeg, whose *Don't Look Now* (1974) is one of the most disturbing of all horror films.

Disc versions include readings by Hurd Hatfield (SKN 992) and Martin Donegan (CMS 630).

The "Red Death" had long devastated the country. No pestilence had ever been so fatal, or so hideous. Blood was its Avatar and its seal—the redness and the horror of blood. There were sharp pains, and sudden dizziness, and then profuse bleeding at the pores, with dissolution. The scarlet stains upon the body and especially upon the face of the victim, were the pest ban which shut him out from the aid and from the sympathy of his fellow-men. And the whole seizure, progress and termination of the disease, were the incidents of half an hour.

But the Prince Prospero was happy and dauntless and sagacious. When his dominions were half depopulated, he summoned to his presence a thousand hale and light-hearted friends from among the knights and dames of his court, and

1 A variation on the Black Death, or bubonic plague, which killed three quarters of the population of Europe and Asia in just twenty years during the fourteenth century

Bubonic plague is characterized by very high fever, chills, prostration, delirium, and enlarged, painful lymph nodes (buboes), which may open and discharge a combination of whole blood, dead white blood cells, and the bacteria responsible for the disease, *Pasteurella pestis*.

While the disease is most often spread through fleas (which circulate between man and rat), a more virulent form, called pneumonic plague, may also develop, and the infection can then pass directly from human to human when droplets bearing bacteria are discharged into the air by coughing.

More information on the effect of plague on history may be gathered from William H. McNeill's fascinating *Plagues and Peoples* (Anchor/Doubleday, 1976).

2 "Avatar" means the concrete manifestation of some principle; it comes from a Sanskrit word meaning "descent," referring to the incarnations or rebirths of the Hindu gods, especially Vishnu.

"Seal" here refers to an official mark, such as one placed on a document to verify its signature. That the seal is blood indicates that the life principle is being forced out of the victims' bodies, where it becomes a visible sign of the disease's victory.

Compare the devastation of the Red Death to that of the plague of blood brought on by God in Exodus 7:19–21 ("and there was blood throughout all the land of Egypt").

3 No disease works this fast, although pneumonic plague was known to strike and kill within a day's time. Many critics have suggested that Poe here means the Red Death as an emblem of man's mortality—a reminder that our stay on earth is all too short.

4 From the Latin *prosperare*, meaning to cause to succeed, to make happy or fortunate. The most famous Prospero is the exiled Duke of Milan in Shakespeare's *The Tempest*, who flees from the world and by means of potent magic controls the destiny of each character in the play. Poe's Prospero also believes he can control his own destiny, and that of his friends, but in his case it is only an illusion.

In Shakespeare's climactic scene, Prospero stops a masque, confronts utter reality, and admits, in effect, that man's creative art cannot change the life-threatening forces of hostile nature.

Caliban, the brutish, rebellious slave of the magician, tells the Duke, "The red plague rid you for learning me your language," another intriguing parallel, and perhaps the origin of Poe's title.

In addition, the seven rooms of Prince Prospero's castle suggest the Seven Ages of Man of Shakespeare.

Another Prospero, much less well known but certainly more delightful than the other two, is the magician-hero of John Bellairs' *The Face in the Frost* (Macmillan, 1969), a fantasy tale no one should miss.

5 While the word means "gifted with acuteness of mental discernment; having special aptitude for the discovery of truth," Poe's intent is clearly ironic: this is *Prospero's* opinion of himself.

6 In Boccaccio's *Decameron* (1353), a group of people take refuge in a remote castle to avoid the plague, there to tell the one hundred witty and occasionally licentious tales that make up the book. The tales reveal man as sensual, tender, cruel, weak, self-seeking, and ludicrous—effectively putting the end to the courtly themes of medieval literature.

Boccaccio (1313–75) describes the folly of attempting to escape the plague:

"Some were of a more barbarous, though, perhaps, a surer way of thinking, avouching that there was no remedy against pestilence better than—no, nor any so good as—to flee before them; wherefore, moved by this reasoning and recking of nought but themselves, very many, both men and women, abandoned their own city, their own houses and homes, their kinsfolk and possessions, and sought the country seats of others, or, at the least, their own, as if the wrath of God, being moved to punish the iniquity of mankind, would not proceed to do so wheresoever they might be, but would content itself with afflicting those only who were found within the walls of their city. . . ." (Translated by John Payne, in *The Black Death: A Turning Point in History*, Holt, 1971; p. 9)

with these retired to the deep seclusion of one of his castellated **6** abbeys. This was an extensive and magnificent structure, the creation of the prince's own eccentric yet august taste. A **7** strong and lofty wall girdled it in. This wall had gates of iron. **8** The courtiers, having entered, brought furnaces and massy hammers and welded the bolts. They resolved to leave means neither of ingress or egress to the sudden impulses of despair **9** or of frenzy from within. The abbey was amply provisioned. With such precautions the courtiers might bid defiance to contagion. The external world could take care of itself. In the **10** meantime it was folly to grieve, or to think. The prince had provided all the appliances of pleasure. There were buffoons, there were improvisatori, there were ballet-dancers, there were musicians, there was Beauty, there was wine. All these and security were within. Without was the "Red Death."

It was toward the close of the fifth or sixth month of his seclusion, and while the pestilence raged most furiously abroad, that the Prince Prospero entertained his thousand **11** friends at a masked ball of the most unusual magnificence.

It was a voluptuous scene, that masquerade. But first let **12** me tell of the rooms in which it was held. There were seven— an imperial suite. In many palaces, however, such suites form a long and straight vista, while the folding doors slide back nearly to the walls on either hand, so that the view of the whole extent is scarcely impeded. Here the case was very different; as might have been expected from the duke's love **13** of the *bizarre*. The apartments were so irregularly disposed that the vision embraced but little more than one at a time. There was a sharp turn at every twenty or thirty yards, and at each turn a novel effect. To the right and left, in the middle of each wall, a tall and narrow Gothic window looked out upon a closed corridor which pursued the windings of the suite. These windows were of stained glass whose color varied in accordance with the prevailing hue of the decorations of the chamber into which it opened. That at the eastern extremity was hung, for example, in blue—and vividly blue were its **14** windows. The second chamber was purple in its ornaments **15** and tapestries, and here the panes were purple. The third **16** was green throughout, and so were the casements. The fourth **17,18** was furnished and lighted with orange—the fifth with white— **19** the sixth with violet. The seventh apartment was closely shrouded in black velvet tapestries that hung all over the ceiling and down the walls, falling in heavy folds upon a carpet **20** of the same material and hue. But in this chamber only, the color of the windows failed to correspond with the decorations. **21** The panes here were scarlet—a deep blood color. Now in no one of the seven apartments was there any lamp or candelabrum, amid the profusion of golden ornaments that lay scattered to and fro or depended from the roof. There was no light of any kind emanating from lamp or candle within the suite of chambers. But in the corridors that followed the suite, there stood, opposite to each window, a heavy tripod, bearing a brazier of fire that projected its rays through the tinted glass **22** and so glaringly illumined the room. And thus were produced

There was much of the beautiful, much of the wanton, much of the *bizarre*, something of the terrible, and not a little of that which might have excited disgust. *Illustration by F. S. Coburn, 1903*

7 In Thomas Campbell's *Life of Petrarch* (1841), a man named Barnabo shuts himself up in a castle, with a sentinel to ring a warning bell whenever anyone comes near. When some people do manage to get inside, Barnabo flees, only to die in the forest. Poe reviewed the novel in *Graham's,* September 1841.

Because Prospero attempts to create a symbolic equivalent of nature's elements inside his abbey, he can be seen as representing the impossibility of the romantic ideal of transcending reality—a theme treated more fully in "The Fall of the House of Usher."

8 "Massy" is an archaic form of "massive"; it means of great size and weight.

9 Note that the gates have been welded shut not only to prevent outsiders from getting in but to keep those inside from getting out. The "sudden impulses of despair or of frenzy from within" may refer to claustrophobia or some morbid state brought on by fear, but also foreshadows the events to come.

10 Referring back to "sagacious," which hardly describes either Prospero or his guests.

11 The source for the tale seems to be this account by Nathaniel Willis, which first appeared in the New York *Mirror,* June 2, 1832, describing a masked ball in Paris during a cholera epidemic:
"I was at a masque ball at the *Théâtre des Variétés,* a night or two since, at the celebration of *Mi-Carême,* or half-Lent. There were some two thousand people, I should think, in fancy dresses, most of them grotesque and satirical, and the ball was kept up till seven in the morning, with all the extravagant gayety, noise, and fun, with which the French people manage such matters. There was a *cholera-waltz,* and a *cholera-galopade,* and one man, immensely tall, dressed as a personification of the Cholera itself, with skeleton armor, bloodshot eyes, and other horrible appurtenances of a walking pestilence. It was the burden of all the jokes, and all the cries of the hawkers, and all the conversation; and yet, probably, nineteen out of twenty of those present lived in the quarters most ravaged by the disease, and knew perfectly its deadly character."

Two other sources have been suggested: William Harrison Ainsworth's *Old St. Paul's* (1841) and chapter eleven of Joseph von Eichendorff's *Ahnung und Gegenwart* (1815). The first describes a dance of death in which some of the participants are dressed as skeletons, while the second tells of a ball at which a masked knight wears a black costume with the hands of a skeleton. Neither, however, seems as likely a candidate as the more fully developed idea in the Willis article.

All these do, however, have one thing in common: all hark back to the medieval symbol of the *danse macabre,* in which a skeleton or a corpse leads his victims to their death.

Says Barbara W. Tuchman, "The dance itself probably developed under the influence of recurring plague, as a street performance to illustrate sermons on the submission of all alike to Death the leveler. . . . 'Advance, see yourselves in us,' say the figures in murals illustrating the dance, 'dead, naked, rotting and stinking. So will you be. . . . To live without thinking of this risks damnation. . . . Power, honor, riches are naught; at the

a multitude of gaudy and fantastic appearances. But in the western or black chamber the effect of the fire-light that streamed upon the dark hangings through the blood-tinted panes, was ghastly in the extreme, and produced so wild a look upon the countenances of those who entered, that there were few of the company bold enough to set foot within its precincts at all.   **23**

It was in this apartment, also, that there stood against the western wall, a gigantic clock of ebony. Its pendulum swung **24** to and fro with a dull, heavy, monotonous clang, and when **25** the minute-hand made the circuit of the face, and the hour was to be stricken, there came from the brazen lungs of the **26,27** clock a sound which was clear and loud and deep and exceedingly musical, but of so peculiar a note and emphasis that, at each lapse of an hour, the musicians of the orchestra were constrained to pause, momentarily, in their performance, hour of death only good works count.' " (*A Distant Mirror*, Knopf, 1978; pp. 505–6)

In the dance of Poe's tale, the frenzy is not to demonstrate man's mortality but to deny it. "To live without thinking of this risks damnation," yet Poe's dancers do not think of it, and are indeed damned.

12 Seven is the number of the universe and represents a completeness or totality. In Christian thought there are seven sacraments, gifts of the spirit, virtues, deadly sins, deacons, major prophets, last words from the Cross, liberal arts, angels of the Presence, devils cast out by Christ, periods of fasting and penitence, and sorrows of Mary; and the seventh day is God's holy day of rest. Much of this comes from the idea that since three represents the heavens and the soul, and four symbolizes the earth and the body, together they equal God's creation.

The seven rooms of Prince Prospero also progress east to west and change from blue to black, paralleling the movement of the sun during the day, and thus the cycle of life. The rooms also recall the Seven Ages of Man in *As You Like It:* the infant, the schoolboy, the lover, the soldier, the judge, second childhood, and the dotard.

13 Poe's tale seems to be a richly vivid contrast between illusion and reality, life and death. The setting dominates everything, and the magnificence and voluptuousness of the decor heighten the sense of worldly pleasure. At the same time, the truly bizarre setting is part of Prospero's attempt to create a microcosmic world, full of the beautiful, the grotesque, and the terrible. These are the "delirious fancies such as the madman fashions," Poe mentions, for the prince is attempting to shut out the inevitable.

14 Color symbolism is a tricky business, but there are traditions from which one can draw some idea of what the various hues may represent in these rooms.

Blue, for example, symbolizes the dawning of human life, as well as truth, intellect, and the void. It is also the color of morning.

15 Purple is blue plus red, and thus represents the quickening of life, as well as power, justice, and temperance.

16 Green symbolizes growth, youth and aspiration, fertility, change, and hope. A blend of blue and yellow—heaven and earth combined—green is the mystic color, and combines the cold blue light of intellect with the emotional warmth of the sun.

17 Orange is representative of midday, the high noon of existence, also of the harvest, and of pride and ambition.

18 White is all colors in one, associated with both life and love, death and burial. It is also the color of winter and marks the approach of old age and death.

19 Violet is colder than purple, suggesting approaching death. It is also a symbol of memory, knowledge, religious devotion, sorrow, and mourning.

20 Black is the no-color of primordial darkness, of the void, of evil, and of death. It symbolizes nothingness, corruption, destruction, and despair.

"The Masque of the Red Death." *Illustration by Aubrey Beardsley*

to hearken to the sound; and thus the waltzers perforce ceased their evolutions; and there was a brief disconcert of the whole gay company; and, while the chimes of the clock yet rang, it was observed that the giddiest grew pale, and the more aged and sedate passed their hands over their brows as if in confused reverie or meditation. But when the echoes had fully ceased, a light laughter at once pervaded the assembly; the musicians looked at each other and smiled as if at their own nervousness and folly, and made whispering vows, each to the other, that the next chiming of the clock should produce in them no similar emotion; and then, after the lapse of sixty minutes, (which embrace three thousand and six hundred seconds of the Time that flies,) there came yet another chiming of the clock, and then were the same disconcert and tremulousness

28 and meditation as before.

But, in spite of these things, it was a gay and magnificent revel. The tastes of the duke were peculiar. He had a fine eye

29 for colors and effects. He disregarded the *decora* of mere fashion. His plans were bold and fiery, and his conceptions glowed with barbaric lustre. There are some who would have thought him mad. His followers felt that he was not. It was necessary to hear and see and touch him to be *sure* that he was not.

He had directed, in great part, the moveable embellishments of the seven chambers, upon occasion of this great *fête;* and it was his own guiding taste which had given character to

30 the masqueraders. Be sure they were grotesque. There were much glare and glitter and piquancy and phantasm—much of

what has been since seen in "Hernani." There were arabesque **31**
figures with unsuited limbs and appointments. There were
delirious fancies such as the madman fashions. The was much
of the beautiful, much of the wanton, much of the *bizarre*,
something of the terrible, and not a little of that which might
have excited disgust. To and fro in the seven chambers there
stalked, in fact, a multitude of dreams. And these—the
dreams—writhed in and about, taking hue from the rooms,
and causing the wild music of the orchestra to seem as the
echo of their steps. And, anon, there strikes the ebony clock
which stands in the hall of the velvet. And then, for a moment,
all is still, and all is silent save the voice of the clock. The
dreams are stiff-frozen as they stand. But the echoes of the
chime die away—they have endured but an instant—and a
light, half-subdued laughter floats after them as they depart.
And now again the music swells, and the dreams live, and
writhe to and fro more merrily than ever, taking hue from the
many-tinted windows through which stream the rays from the
tripods. But to the chamber which lies most westwardly of the
seven, there are now none of the maskers who venture; for
the night is waning away; and there flows a ruddier light
through the blood-colored panes; and the blackness of the
sable drapery appals; and to him whose foot falls upon the
sable carpet, there comes from the near clock of ebony a
muffled peal more solemnly emphatic than any which reaches
their ears who indulge in the more remote gaieties of the
other apartments.

But these other apartments were densely crowded, and in
them beat feverishly the heart of life. And the revel went
whirlingly on, until at length there commenced the sounding
of midnight upon the clock. And then the music ceased, as I
have told; and the evolutions of the waltzers were quieted;
and there was an uneasy cessation of all things as before. But
now there were twelve strokes to be sounded by the bell of
the clock; and thus it happened, perhaps, that more of thought
crept, with more of time, into the meditations of the thoughtful
among those who revelled. And thus, too, it happened,
perhaps, that before the last echoes of the last chime had
utterly sunk into silence, there were many individuals in the
crowd who had found leisure to become aware of the presence
of a masked figure which had arrested the attention of no
single individual before. And the rumor of this new presence **32**
having spread itself whisperingly around, there arose at length
from the whole company a buzz, or murmur, expressive of
disapprobation and surprise—then, finally, of terror, of horror,
and of disgust.

In an assembly of phantasms such as I have painted, it may
well be supposed that no ordinary appearance could have
excited such sensation. In truth the masquerade license of the
night was nearly unlimited; but the figure in question had
out-Heroded Herod, and gone beyond the bounds of even **33**
the prince's indefinite decorum. There are chords in the hearts
of the most reckless which cannot be touched without emotion.
Even with the utterly lost, to whom life and death are equally

21 Blood red is an appropriate hue to join with the black of the seventh, and last, room.

22 Through this lighting arrangement, the rooms are suffused with color and flickering shadows. In many of Poe's tales, it is the sun which shines (sometimes feebly) through tinted panes, perhaps portraying those half states of mind in which dream and reality are blended. But here, in Prospero's castle, the dream is far deeper, and visionary consciousness has blocked out all sense of the external world. The braziers on their tripods act as artificial suns, illuminating each room as an individual world.

23 "Men fear death as children fear to go in the dark; and as that natural fear in children is increased with tales, so is the other" (Sir Thomas Bacon, *Essays*, "Of Death").

24 The black clock mercilessly measures time, another reminder that Prospero cannot ignore mortality.

25 "Clang" seems inappropriate, for a pendulum normally gives out a pleasant "tick-tock." Since "clang" is a metallic sound, Poe may be likening the pendulum to the scythe of Time, an image he uses in "The Pit and the Pendulum."

26 Poe uses "stricken" for its archaic sound (and sense). The OED cites its usage for a sound or a musical note.

27 While this may seem another odd word choice, we should remember that the word meant "made of brass" long before it meant "shameless." On the other hand, Death *is* shameless in its refusal to stay hidden even though we wish it would.

28 Poe calls the revelers "dreams," and indeed, they almost wake each time the clock strikes and reminds them of the reality of their mortality. As soon as it stops, however, they return to their fantasies.

29 From the Latin, meaning beauty, elegance, ornament, charm

30 Distorted and exaggerated. The word comes from the French form of the Italian *grottesca*, a "painting appropriate to grottos." *Grotte* (grottos) was the popular name in Rome for the chambers of ancient buildings that had been revealed through excavation, and which contained murals that were typical examples of what we now call "grotesque."

31 A play by Victor Hugo (1830) that takes place in the Spain of Charles V. It is a lyric work, one that ends in the death of its hero. Poe may be alluding to the glitter of the Spanish court, for nothing in the play even remotely resembles the bizarre quality of "The Masque of the Red Death."

32 Poe may have heard of the Strasbourg Cathedral clock, which had a death figure sound the hour, while at half past, a Christ figure emerged to vanquish Death.

33 See "Metzengerstein," note 9.

jests, there are matters of which no jest can be made. The whole company, indeed, seemed now deeply to feel that in the costume and bearing of the stranger neither wit nor propriety existed. The figure was tall and gaunt, and shrouded from head to foot in the habiliments of the grave. The mask which concealed the visage was made so nearly to resemble the countenance of a stiffened corpse that the closest scrutiny must have had difficulty in detecting the cheat. And yet all this might have been endured, if not approved, by the mad revellers around. But the mummer had gone so far as to assume the type of the Red Death. His vesture was dabbled in *blood*—and his broad brow, with all the features of the face, was besprinkled with the scarlet horror.

When the eyes of Prince Prospero fell upon this spectral image (which with a slow and solemn movement, as if more fully to sustain its *role,* stalked to and fro among the waltzers) he was seen to be convulsed, in the first moment with a strong shudder either of terror or distaste; but, in the next, his brow reddened with rage.

34 The figure "blasphemes" in denying Prospero's dreamworld.

34   "Who dares?" he demanded hoarsely of the courtiers who stood near him—"who dares insult us with this blasphemous mockery? Seize him and unmask him—that we may know whom we have to hang at sunrise, from the battlements!"

It was in the eastern or blue chamber in which stood the Prince Prospero as he uttered these words. They rang throughout the seven rooms loudly and clearly—for the prince was a bold and robust man, and the music had become hushed at the waving of his hand.

It was in the blue room where stood the prince, with a group of pale courtiers by his side. At first, as he spoke, there was a slight rushing movement of this group in the direction of the intruder, who at the moment was also near at hand, and now, with deliberate and stately step, made closer approach to the speaker. But from a certain nameless awe with which the mad assumptions of the mummer had inspired the whole party, there were found none who put forth hand to seize him; so that, unimpeded, he passed within a yard of the prince's person; and, while the vast assembly, as if with one impulse, shrank from the centres of the rooms to the walls, he made his way uninterruptedly, but with the same solemn and measured step which had distinguished him from the first, through the blue chamber to the purple—through the purple to the green—through the green to the orange—through this again to the white—and even thence to the violet, ere a

35 Prospero first sees the figure in the blue, or easternmost room, and follows it in a progression that may well symbolize the movement from birth to death.

Jean-Paul Weber takes an off-beat approach, suggesting that the abbey is itself a clock symbol, with Prospero and the masked figure the minute and second hands, which meet at midnight (*Poe*, Prentice-Hall, 1967; p. 86).

35 decided movement had been made to arrest him. It was then, however, that the Prince Prospero, maddening with rage and the shame of his own momentary cowardice, rushed hurriedly through the six chambers, while none followed him on account of a deadly terror that had seized upon all. He bore aloft a drawn dagger, and had approached, in rapid impetuosity, to within three or four feet of the retreating figure, when the latter, having attained the extremity of the velvet apartment, turned suddenly and confronted his pursuer. There was a sharp cry—and the dagger dropped gleaming upon the sable carpet, upon which, instantly afterwards, fell prostrate in death the Prince Prospero. Then, summoning the wild courage of despair, a throng of the revellers at once threw themselves into the black apartment, and, seizing the mummer, whose tall figure stood erect and motionless within the shadow of the ebony clock, gasped in unutterable horror at finding the grave-cerements and corpse-like mask which they handled with so violent a rudeness, untenanted by any tangible form. **36**

And now was acknowledged the presence of the Red Death. He had come like a thief in the night. And one by one dropped **37** the revellers in the blood-bedewed halls of their revel, and died each in the despairing posture of his fall. And the life of the ebony clock went out with that of the last of the gay. And the flames of the tripods expired. And Darkness and Decay and the Red Death held illimitable dominion over all. **38**

36 In an important sense, it is man who invests death with elements of terror, since it is actually only a natural ordering of things. He garbs death in "the habiliments of the grave" and then runs to escape it—or, in an equally futile gesture, to destroy it.

"Prince Prospero's flight from the Red Death is the poetic imagination's flight from temporal and worldly consciousness into dream," suggests Richard Wilbur. "The thousand dancers of Prince Prospero's costume ball are just what Poe says they are—"dreams" or "phantasms," veiled and vivid creatures of Prince Prospero's rapt imagination. Whenever their is a feast, or carnival, or costume ball in Poe, we may be sure that a dream is in progress." ("The House of Poe," in *Poe*, Prentice-Hall, 1967; p. 119)

In Wilkie Collins' "The Yellow Mask" (1855), a man named Fabio attends a masked ball in Pisa, his first social appearance since the death of his wife:

"He turned round immediately, and saw a masked woman standing alone in the room, dressed entirely in yellow from head to foot. She had a yellow hood, a yellow half-mask with deep fringe hanging down over her mouth, and a yellow domino, cut at the sleeves and edges into long flame-shaped points, which waved backward and forward tremulously in the light air wafted through the doorway. The woman's black eyes seemed to gleam with an evil brightness through the sight-holes of the mask. . . . Without a word or gesture she stood before the table, and her gleaming black eyes fixed steadily on Fabio the instant he confronted her." (*Works*, Collier [no date]; Vol. 19, p. 487)

The masked woman makes the others at the ball uncomfortable, and her presence hovers over the merrymaking. Like Prospero's palace, there are a number of apartments here, and the woman in yellow follows Fabio from one to another.

Fabio finally unmasks the woman, and beholds the face of his dead wife. He goes into shock, and hangs near death in its aftermath, but is gradually brought back to health by his first love, Nanina. The masked woman turns out to be someone in the hire of a mad monk who, for reasons too complicated to discuss here, had fashioned a mask of the dead wife, and so all ends tidily.

37 ". . . the day of the Lord so cometh as a thief in the night" (I Thessalonians 5:2).

38 Poe's last line echoes that of Pope's *Dunciad:* "And universal darkness buries all." Darkness, besides symbolizing death, is a principle of Chaos, from which God made the world. Decay takes place as matter returns to its original state, and Prospero's world, created out of chaos, returns to chaos.

. . . the Red Death held illimitable dominion over all.
Illustration by Albert Edward Sterner, 1903

THE PIT AND THE PENDULUM

First published in *The Gift*, 1842, this has always been one of Poe's most-read tales, a skillful exercise in suspense with an undercurrent of something much more complex than most readers fully understand, although they may sense it.

Poe's source was probably a paragraph in Thomas Dick's *Philosophy of Religion* (1825): "On the entry of the French into Toledo during the late Peninsular War, General Lasalle visited the palace of the Inquisition. The great number of instruments of torture, especially the instruments to stretch the limbs, and the drop-baths, which cause a lingering death, excited horror, even in the minds of soldiers hardened in the fields of battle."

Other background, as well as some of the incidents found here, was probably drawn from *Anales de la Inquisición de España,* written by Juan Antonio Llorente (1756–1823) in 1812 and published in English in 1826.

The Spanish Inquisition was independent of the medieval Inquisition, which began in 1233, when Pope Gregory IX commissioned Dominicans to investigate heresy among the Albigenses, in southern France. Established by Ferdinand V and Isabella in 1478 with the reluctant approval of Pope Sixtus IV, the later Inquisition was entirely controlled by the Spanish kings, and the popes were never reconciled to the institution, which they regarded as usurping a church prerogative. Like the Communist hysteria in the American fifties, the original purpose of the Inquisition was soon overshadowed by political witch-hunting, so that even St. Ignatius of Loyola and St. Theresa of Ávila were investigated for heresy. The Spanish Inquisition was not abolished until 1820.

Films include *Le Puits et le Pendule* (1910), directed by Henri Desfontaines (1910), a 1913 English version directed by Alice Guy Blanche, and a Roger Corman production in 1961. The latter film, with Vincent Price, John Kerr, and Barbara Steele, stretches the story by adding a wholly new framework about an Englishman (Kerr) who arrives at a Spanish castle to investigate the mysterious death of his sister. The acting is atrocious, but the shocks are good, especially the final shot of Steele locked in the Iron Maiden as Price unknowingly seals her inside the Inquisitional torture chamber forever.

Plot elements from Poe's story also have made their way into *Avenging Conscience,* a 1914 D. W. Griffith film with Henry B. Walthall, Dorothy Gish, Donald Crisp, Blanche Sweet, and Mae Marsh; as well as *The Raven* (1912), *Dr. Goldfoot and the Bikini Machine* (1965) (the title speaks for itself), and *The Snake Pit (Blood Demon),* a 1967 West German film with Christopher Lee.

Basil Rathbone narrates a superb recorded version (Caedmon 1115); Martin Donegan also reads one (CMS 652).

Impia tortorum longos hic turba furores
Sanguinis innocui, non satiata, aluit.
Sospite nunc patriâ, fracto nunc funeris antro,
Mors ubi dira fuit vita salusque patent.
[*Quatrain composed for the gates of a market to be erected upon the site of the Jacobin Club House at Paris.*] **1**

I was sick—sick unto death with that long agony; and when they at length unbound me, and I was permitted to sit, I felt that my senses were leaving me. The sentence—the dread sentence of death—was the last of distinct accentuation which reached my ears. After that, the sound of the inquisitorial voices seemed merged in one dreamy indeterminate hum. It **2** conveyed to my soul the idea of *revolution*—perhaps from its association in fancy with the burr of a millwheel. This only for **3** a brief period; for presently I heard no more. Yet, for a while, I saw; but with how terrible an exaggeration! I saw the lips of the black-robed judges. They appeared to me white—whiter than the sheet upon which I trace these words—and thin even to grotesqueness; thin with the intensity of their expression of firmness—of immoveable resolution—of stern contempt of human torture. I saw that the decrees of what to me was Fate, were still issuing from those lips. I saw them writhe with a deadly locution. I saw them fasion the syllables of my name; and I shuddered because no sound succeeded. I saw, too, for a few moments of delirious horror, the soft and nearly imperceptible waving of the sable draperies which enwrapped the walls of the apartment. And then my vision fell upon the seven tall candles upon the table. At first they wore the aspect **4** of charity, and seemed white slender angels who would save me; but then, all at once, there came a most deadly nausea over my spirit, and I felt every fibre in my frame thrill as if I had touched the wire of a galvanic battery, while the angel **5** forms became meaninglesss spectres, with heads of flame, and I saw that from them there would be no help. And then there stole into my fancy, like a rich musical note, the thought of what sweet rest there must be in the grave. The thought came gently and stealthily, and it seemed long before it attained full appreciation; but just as my spirit came at length properly to feel and entertain it, the figures of the judges vanished, as if magically, from before me; the tall candles sank into nothingness; their flames went out utterly; the blackness of darkness supervened; all sensations appeared swallowed up in a mad rushing descent as of the soul into Hades. Then silence, and stillness, and night were the universe.

I had swooned; but still will not say that all of consciousness was lost. What of it there remained I will not attempt to define, or even to describe; yet all was not lost. In the deepest slumber—no! In delirium—no! In a swoon—no! In death—no! even in the grave all *is not* lost. Else there is no immortality for man. Arousing from the most profound of slumbers, we break the gossamer web of *some* dream. Yet in a second afterward, (so frail may that web have been) we remember

1 "Here the wicked mob, unappeased, long cherished a hatred of innocent blood. Now that the fatherland has been saved, and the cave of death demolished; where grim death has been, life and health appear."

According to Baudelaire, the great romantic French poet and author, the Marché St. Honoré, which was built on the site of the old Jacobin Club, had no gates, and certainly no inscription. The Jacobins were the political club of the French Revolution, responsible for the Reign of Terror (1793), but who fell with their leader, Robespierre, in July of 1794.

2 The Spanish Inquisition was begun to discover and punish converted Jews (and later, Muslims) who were not true believers. The notorious Inquisition of 1483 reputedly saw two thousand persons burned at the stake.

3 Compare with "MS. Found in a Bottle": "As I placed my foot upon the upper step of the companion-ladder I was startled with a loud humming noise, like that occasioned by the rapid revolution of a millwheel." There is also the suggestion of the sensation often experienced when a person loses consciousness—as if one were on a huge wheel, spinning down, down, and around, with a loud humming or vibrating sound.

4 Poe may have in mind the seven candlesticks in the midst of which sits God the Judge, in Revelation 1:13. In "Shadow" he also speaks of the "flames of the seven lamps." The number seven has many interpretations (see "The Masque of the Red Death," note 12), but, among others, it is a symbol for pain.

In *Blackwood's*, July 1826, Poe may have read: "This was a large apartment under ground, vaulted, hung round with black cloth, and dimly lighted by candles placed in candlesticks fastened to the wall. At one end, there was an enclosed place, like a closet, where the Inquisitor in attendance and the notary sat at a table; so that the place seemed . . . the very mansion of death, everything being calculated to inspire terror." (Compare with the rooms of "Ligeia" and "Masque of the Red Death.")

5 See "Loss of Breath," note 25.

not that we have dreamed. In the return to life from the swoon there are two stages; first, that of the sense of mental or spiritual; secondly, that of the sense of physical, existence. It seems probable that if, upon reaching the second stage, we could recall the impressions of the first, we should find these impressions eloquent in memories of the gulf beyond. And that gulf is—what? How at least shall we distinguish its shadows from those of the tomb? But if the impressions of what I have termed the first stage, are not, at will, recalled, yet, after long interval, do they not come unbidden, while we marvel whence they come? He who has never swooned, is not he who find strange palaces and wildly familiar faces in coals that glow; is not he who beholds floating in mid-air the sad visions that the many may not view; is not he who ponders over the perfume of some novel flower—is not he whose brain grows bewildered with the meaning of some musical cadence **6** which has never before arrested his attention.

Amid frequent and thoughtful endeavors to remember; amid earnest struggles to regather some token of the state of seeming nothingness into which my soul had lapsed, there have been moments when I have dreamed of success; there have been brief, very brief periods when I have conjured up remembrances which the lucid reason of a later epoch assures me could have had reference only to that condition of seeming unconsciousness. These shadows of memory tell, indistinctly, of tall figures that lifted and bore me in silence down—down— still down—till a hideous dizziness oppressed me at the mere idea of the interminableness of the descent. They tell also of a vague horror at my heart, on account of that heart's unnatural stillness. Then comes a sense of sudden motionlessness throughout all things; as if those who bore me (a ghastly train!) had outrun, in their descent, the limits of the limitless, and paused from the wearisomeness of their toil. After this I call to mind flatness and dampness; and then all is *madness*—the madness of a memory which busies itself among forbidden **7** things.

Very suddenly there came back to my soul motion and sound—the tumultuous motion of the heart, and, in my ears, the sound of its beating. Then a pause in which all is blank. Then again sound, and motion, and touch—a tingling sensation pervading my frame. Then the mere consciousness of exist- ence, without thought—a condition which lasted long. Then, very suddenly, *thought*, and shuddering terror, and earnest endeavor to conprehend my true state. Then a strong desire to lapse into insensibility. Then a rushing revival of soul and a successful effort to move. And now a full memory of the trial, of the judges, of the sable draperies, of the sentence, of the sickness, of the swoon. Then entire forgetfulness of all that followed; of all that a later day and much earnestness of endeavor have enabled me vaguely to recall.

So far, I had not opened my eyes. I felt that I lay upon my back, unbound. I reached out my hand, and it fell heavily upon something damp and hard. There I suffered it to remain for many minutes, while I strove to imagine where and *what*

---

6 ". . . to swoon and awake in utter consciousness of any lapse of time during the syncope would demonstrate the soul to have been in such condition that, had death occurred, annihilation would have followed. On the other hand, when the revival is attended with remem- brance of visions (as is now and then the case, in fact), then the soul is to be considered in such condition as would ensure its existence after the bodily death—the bliss or wretchedness of the existence to be indicated by the character of the visions." (Poe, "Marginalia," CCIX)

Thus, for Poe, a fall into utter unconsciousness would indicate that the soul itself was near death, a perilous state. But when some traces of consciousness are left, as the narrator here clings to, there is still sufficient strength for the person to recover.

Note the parallel with astral projection—the idea that the soul can leave the body during unconsciousness (see "William Wilson," note 30).

7 According to Jung, the language of dreams is archaic, symbolic, and prelogical— in other words, it is the key to the subconscious. "The dream cannot be explained with a psychology taken from consciousness. It is a definite functioning which is independent of willing and wishing, of the intentions and conscious aims of the ego. It is involuntary, like everything that happens in nature." (*Psychology of C. J. Jung*, Yale, 1943; p. 73)

Thus the narrator does not understand his dreams and wonders why he has them, because they stir up the "forbidden things" of the unconscious.

I could be. I longed, yet dared not to employ my vision. I dreaded the first glance at objects around me. It was not that I feared to look upon things horrible, but that I grew aghast lest there should be *nothing* to see. At length, with a wild desperation at heart, I quickly unclosed my eyes. My worst thoughts, then, were confirmed. The blackness of eternal night encompassed me. I struggled for breath. The intensity of the darkness seemed to oppress and stifle me. The atmosphere was intolerably close. I still lay quietly, and made effort to exercise my reason. I brought to mind the inquisitorial proceedings, and attempted from that point to deduce my real condition. The sentence had passed; and it appeared to me that a very long interval of time had since elapsed. Yet not for a moment did I suppose myself actually dead. Such a supposition, notwithstanding what we read in fiction, is altogether inconsistent with real existence;—but where and in what state was I? The condemned to death, I knew, perished usually at the *autos-da-fé,* and one of these had been **8** held on the very night of the day of my trial. Had I been remanded to my dungeon, to await the next sacrifice, which would not take place for many months? This I at once saw could not be. Victims had been in immediate demand. Moreover, my dungeon, as well as all the condemned cells at Toledo, had stone floors, and light was not altogether excluded. **9**

A fearful idea now suddenly drove the blood in torrents upon my heart, and for a brief period, I once more relapsed into insensibility. Upon recovering, I at once started to my feet, trembling convulsively in every fibre. I thrust my arms wildly above and around me in all directions. I felt nothing; yet dreaded to move a step, lest I should be impeded by the walls of a *tomb*. Perspiration burst from every pore, and stood in cold big beads upon my forehead. The agony of suspense grew at length intolerable, and I cautiously moved forward, with my arms extended, and my eyes straining from their sockets, in the hope of catching some faint ray of light. I proceeded for many paces; but still all was blackness and vacancy. I breathed more freely. It seemed evident that mine was not, at least, the most hideous of fates. **10**

And now, as I still continued to step cautiously onward, there came thronging upon my recollection a thousand vague rumors of the horrors of Toledo. Of the dungeons there had been strange things narrated—fables I had always deemed them—but yet strange, and too ghastly to repeat, save in a whisper. Was I left to perish of starvation in this subterranean world of darkness; or what fate, perhaps even more fearful, awaited me? That the result would be death, and a death of more than customary bitterness, I knew too well the character of my judges to doubt. The mode and the hour were all that occupied or distracted me. **11**

My outstretched hands at length encountered some solid obstruction. It was a wall, seemingly of stone masonry—very smooth, slimy, and cold. I followed it up; stepping with all the careful distrust with which certain antique narratives had inspired me. This process, however, afforded me no means

8 *Auto-da-fé* is often translated as "act of faith," perhaps referring to the age-old demonstration of faith or truthfulness in which one places a hand in a fire. But in Portuguese *auto* means a public ceremony, so that a better translation would be "A public ceremony of faith."

Although the word originated in Lisbon, it is most often applied to the ceremony of the Spanish Inquisition at which, after a procession, Mass, and a sermon, sentences were read and the convicted person executed. Heretics were dressed in the ceremonial *San Benito,* a yellow penitential garment with a red cross on the front and back (grotesquely embroidered for the unrepentant), and they wore a yellow miter. Those sentenced to death were handed over to the civil authorities for execution within five days, usually by burning. The Church itself did not execute anyone.

Most of the great *autos-da-fé* took place when Tomàs de Torquemada was head of the Inquisition, between 1483 and 1498. The last in Spain was at Seville in 1781, although there was one in Mexico as late as 1815.

9 Toledo is the capital of Toledo province, in central Spain, and stands on a granite hill surrounded on three sides by a gorge. An important commercial center for centuries, it declined in the sixteenth century but gained as the spiritual capital of Spanish Catholicism.

10 I.e., to be buried alive. Actually, the Inquisition was involved in only two major tasks: to force an admission of heresy or sin from the accused (by torture, if necessary) and to save his or her soul by the purification of death by fire.

11 In Chapter 16 of Charles Brockden Brown's *Edgar Huntly* (1799), the hero finds himself in a pitch-black cave, and details his sensations as he attempts to find his way out.

Brown (1771–1810) is one American writer who should be better known than he is, especially among the readers of Poe, Hawthorne, and Gothic fiction in general. His *Wieland* (1798) deals with hypnotism, spontaneous combustion, and a murdering religious fanatic. *Ormond* (1799) tells of a woman who murders the man who tried to rape her. *Arthur Mervyn* (1800) chronicles a case of mistaken identity wrapped around a yellow-fever epidemic. *Edgar Huntly* may be the best, involving a hero who walks in his sleep, marauding Indians, and some effective Gothic touches all Brown's own.

Shelley, Scott, Keats, Cooper, Hawthorne, and Poe all admired Brown's work, and Van Wyck Brooks calls him a precurser of both Melville and Henry James. His most immediate importance, however, is that he led the way away from "puerile superstitions, Gothic castles and chimeras," as he phrased it, translating the European Gothic tradition into American terms.

of ascertaining the dimensions of my dungeon; as I might make its circuit, and return to the point whence I set out, without being aware of the fact; so perfectly uniform seemed the wall. I therefore sought the knife which had been in my pocket, when led into the inquisitorial chamber; but it was gone; my clothes had ben exchanged for a wrapper of coarse serge. I had thought of forcing the blade in some minute crevice of the masonry, so as to identify my point of departure. The difficulty, nevertheless, was but trivial; although, in the disorder of my fancy, it seemed at first insuperable. I tore a part of the hem from the robe and placed the fragment at full length, and at right angles to the wall. In groping my way around the prison, I could not fail to encounter this rag upon completing the circuit. So, at least I thought: but I had not counted upon the extent of the dungeon, or upon my own weakness. The ground was moist and slippery. I staggered onward for some time, when I stumbled and fell. My excessive fatigue induced me to remain prostrate; and sleep soon overtook me as I lay.

Upon awaking, and stretching forth an arm, I found beside me a loaf and a pitcher with water. I was too much exhausted to reflect upon this circumstance, but ate and drank with avidity. Shortly afterward, I resumed my tour around the prison, and with much toil, came at last upon the fragment of the serge. Up to the period when I fell I had counted fifty-two paces, and upon resuming my walk, I had counted forty-eight more;—when I arrived at the rag. There were in all, then, a hundred paces; and, admitting two paces to the yard, I presumed the dungeon to be fifty yards in circuit. I had met, however, with many angles in the wall, and thus I could form no guess at the shape of the vault; for vault I could not help supposing it to be.

I had little object—certainly no hope—in these researches; but a vague curiosity prompted me to continue them. Quitting the wall, I resolved to cross the area of the enclosure. At first I proceeded with extreme caution, for the floor, although seemingly of solid material, was treacherous with slime. At length, however, I took courage, and did not hesitate to step firmly; endeavoring to cross in as direct a line as possible. I had advanced some ten or twelve paces in this manner, when the remnant of the torn hem of my robe became entangled between my legs. I stepped on it, and fell violently on my face.

In the confusion attending my fall, I did not immediately apprehend a somewhat startling circumstance, which yet, in a few seconds afterward, and while I still lay prostrate, arrested my attention. It was this—my chin rested upon the floor of the prison, but my lips and the upper portion of my head, although seemingly at a less elevation than the chin, touched nothing. At the same time my forehead seemed bathed in a clammy vapor, and the peculiar smell of decayed fungus arose to my nostrils. I put forward my arm, and shuddered to find that I had fallen at the very brink of a circular pit, whose extent, of course, I had no means of ascertaining at the

12 The narrator has literally circumscribed his world. This is important, for it shows he has both brains and imagination, and that he can combine "trivial" discoveries with creative thought and come up with solutions to his predicament, as does the narrator of "A Descent into the Maelström."

He is an example of Poe's "passive" narrators, whose survival in a hostile environment is based on their willingness to forgo old assumptions and meet a new world on its own terms.

13 The image of the pit has, for centuries, been connected with Hell and destruction, as in Psalms 73:18–19: "Surely thou didst set them in slippery places; thou castedst them down into destruction. How are they brought into desolation, as in a moment!"

These lines are also part of "Sinners in the Hands of an Angry God," that remarkable tract by Jonathan Edwards (1703–58), the last apostle of New England Puritanism. While Poe was an alien to the New England tradition, there is a strong parallel between "The Pit and the Pendulum" and "Sinners in the Hands of an Angry God."

According to Edwards, the quotation from Psalms implies that sinners "were always exposed to *sudden* unexpected destruction. As he that walks in slippery places is every moment liable to fall; he can't foresee one moment whether he shall stand or fall the next; and moment. Groping about the masonry just below the margin, I succeeded in dislodging a small fragment, and let it fall into the abyss. For many seconds I hearkened to its reverberations as it dashed against the sides of the chasm in its descent; at length there was a sullen plunge into water, succeeded by loud echoes. At the same moment there came a sound resembling the quick opening, and as rapid closing of a door overhead, while a faint gleam of light flashed suddenly through the gloom, and as suddenly faded away.

I saw clearly the doom which had been prepared for me, and congratulated myself upon the timely accident by which I had escaped. Another step before my fall, and the world had seen me no more. And the death just avoided, was of that **13** very character which I had regarded as fabulous and frivolous in the tales respecting the Inquisition. To the victims of its tyranny, there was the choice of death with its direst physical agonies, or death with its most hideous moral horrors. I had **14** been reserved for the latter. By long suffering my nerves had been unstrung, until I trembled at the sound of my own voice, and had become in every respect a fitting subject for the species of torture which awaited me.

Shaking in every limb, I groped my way back to the wall; resolving there to perish rather than risk the terrors of the wells, of which my imagination now pictured many in various positions about the dungeon. In other conditions of mind I might have had courage to end my misery at once by a plunge into one of the abysses; but now I was the veriest of cowards. **15** Neither could I forget what I had read of these pits—that the *sudden* extinction of life formed no part of their most horrible plan.

Agitation of spirit kept me awake for many long hours; but at length I again slumbered. Upon arousing, I found by my side, as before, a loaf and a pitcher of water. A burning thirst consumed me, and I emptied the vessel at a draught. It must have been drugged; for scarcely had I drunk, before I became irresistibly drowsy. A deep sleep fell upon me—a sleep like that of death. How long it lasted of course, I know not; but when, once again, I unclosed my eyes, the objects around me were visible. By a wild sulphurous lustre, the origin of which I could not at first determine, I was enabled to see the extent and aspect of the prison. **16**

In its size I had been greatly mistaken. The whole circuit of its walls did not exceed twenty-five yards. For some minutes this fact occasioned me a world of vain trouble; vain indeed! for what could be of less importance, under the terrible circumstances which environed me, than the mere dimensions of my dungeon? But my soul took a wild interest in trifles, **17** and I busied myself in endeavors to account for the error I had committed in my measurement. The truth at length flashed upon me. In my first attempt at exploration I had counted fifty-two paces, up to the period when I fell; I must then have been within a pace or two of the fragment of serge; in fact, I had nearly performed the circuit of the vault. I then slept, and upon awaking, I must have returned upon my

when he does fall, he falls at once, without warning. . . . Another thing implied is that they are liable to fall of *themselves*, without being thrown down by the hand of another. As he that stands or walks on slippery ground, needs nothing but his own weight to throw him down. . . . That the reason why they are not fallen already, and don't fall now, is only that God's appointed time is not come. For it is said, that when that due time, or appinted time comes, *their foot shall slide*. . . . God won't hold them up in these slippery places any longer, but will let them go; and then, at that very instant, they shall fall into destruction; as he that stands in such slippery declining ground on the edge of a pit that he can't stand alone, when he is let go he immediately falls and is lost. The observation from the words that I would not insist upon is this,

"There is nothing that keeps wicked men, at any one moment, out of Hell, but the mere pleasure of God."

Poe, of course, is no Puritan, but if we substitute "fate" for "God"—or even Poe's concept of the God-head—the similarities become clearer. Man, both writers say, is a passive element in the universe, kept from destruction only by the whim of God/Fate. The narrator escapes the pit—*this* time. But Poe, like Edwards, suggests that there *is* an appointed time, as there is for the narrator of "MS. Found in a Bottle."

Despite his Puritan theology, Edwards was a highly original thinker who moved "out from an intense and sometimes fatalistic subjectivity to construct a vast, metaphysically ambitious correlative of the soul," says Daniel B. Shea, Jr., in *Major Writers of Early American Literature* (Wisconsin, 1972; p. 200). His words could just as easily refer to Poe, who is "Calvinistic" in his belief that the universe was created by a "fall" from unity and that man is estranged from God's ideal world.

14 Mental, psychological

15 The abyss is associated with nothingness, chaos, and annihilation. Writers after Poe have continued to use it in this manner. "An immense river of oblivion is sweeping us away into a nameless abyss," writes Ernest Renan in a memorable passage from *Souvenirs d'enfance et de jeunesse* (1883), and President Kennedy in 1962 said, "However close we sometimes seem to that dark and final abyss, let no man of peace and freedom despair."

16 His sleep "like that of death" ends, and he awakens in something very much like Hell. By "wild, sulphurous lustre," the narrator alludes to the burning of sulfur (brimstone), although that flame is usually blue and yellow, not the red that one would expect of hellfire.

17 Like the narrator of "A Descent into the Maelström," it is this "wild interest in trifles" that saves him.

18 Compare with the bedchamber of "Ligeia." Poe may have also been inspired by a description in Chapter Six of *Melmoth the Wanderer* (1820), by Charles Robert Maturin: "I started up with horror . . . on perceiving myself surrounded by demons, who, clothed in fire were breathing forth clouds of it around me. . . . What I touched was cold . . . and I comprehended that these were hideous figures scrawled in phosphorous to terrify me." Poe mentions *Melmoth* in a letter of July 1836 and in a review in *Graham's* of January 1842.

19 A belt or girth around the body of a horse to keep a saddle or pack on the animal's back, but also the girdle, or cincture, for a priest's cassock.

20 The figure of Time, as we now know it, is actually that of Saturn, who, according to tradition, carries an hourglass and a scythe. The scythe is the instrument by which Time "cuts down" all things according to their allotted span. Time can also be seen as a sort of sword of Damocles, which hangs over our heads.

Here the scythe is a pendulum, so that two symbols of Time are combined, with the pendulum adding the idea of slow, steady marking off of one's lifetime.

Poe no doubt borrowed the idea from the preface to Llorente's *History of the Inquisition* (1826), reprinted in a review in the Philadelphia *Museum*, April 1827:

"One of these prisoners had been condemned, and was to have suffered on the following day. His punishment was to be death by the *Pendulum*. The method of thus destroying the victim is as follows:—the condemned is fastened in a groove, upon a table, on his back; suspended above him is a Pendulum, the edge of which is sharp, and it is so constructed as to become longer with every movement. The wretch sees this implement of destruction swing to and fro above him, and every moment the keen edge approaching nearer and nearer: at length it cuts the skin of his nose, and gradually cuts on, until life is extinct. It may be doubted if the holy office in its mercy ever invented a more humane and rapid method of exterminating heresy, or ensuring confiscation. This, let it be remembered, was a punishment of the Secret Tribunal, A.D. 1820!!!"

steps—thus supposing the circuit nearly double what it actually was. My confusion of mind prevented me from observing that I began my tour with the wall to the left, and ended it with the wall to the right.

I had been deceived, too, in respect to the shape of the enclosure. In feeling my way I had found many angles, and thus deduced an idea of great irregularity; so potent is the effect of total darkness upon one arousing from lethargy or sleep! The angles were simply those of a few slight depressions, or niches, at odd intervals. The general shape of the prison was square. What I had taken for masonry seemed now to be iron, or some other metal, in huge plates, whose sutures or joints occasioned the depression. The entire surface of this metallic enclosure was rudely daubed in all the hideous and repulsive devices to which the charnel superstition of the monks has given rise. The figures of fiends in aspects of menace, with skeleton forms, and other more really fearful **18** images, overspread and disfigured the walls. I observed that the outlines of these monstrosities were sufficiently distinct, but that the colors seemed faded and blurred, as if from the effects of a damp atmosphere. I now noticed the floor, too, which was of stone. In the centre yawned the circular pit from whose jaws I had escaped; but it was the only one in the dungeon.

All this I saw indistinctly and by much effort: for my personal condition had been greatly changed during slumber. I now lay upon my back, and at full length, on a species of low framework of wood. To this I was securely bound by a long **19** strap resembling a surcingle. It passed in many convolutions about my limbs and body, leaving at liberty only my head, and my left arm to such extent that I could, by dint of much exertion, supply myself with food from an earthen dish which lay by my side on the floor. I saw, to my horror, that the pitcher had been removed. I say to my horror; for I was consumed with intolerable thirst. This thirst it appeared to be the design of my persecutors to stimulate: for the food in the dish was meat pungently seasoned.

Looking upward, I surveyed the ceiling of my prison. It was some thirty or forty feet overhead, and constructed much as the side walls. In one of its panels a very singular figure riveted my whole attention. It was the painted picture of Time as he is commonly represented save that, in lieu of a scythe, he held what, at a casual glance, I supposed to be the pictured **20** image of a huge pendulum such as we see on antique clocks. There was something, however, in the appearance of this machine which caused me to regard it more attentively. While I gazed directly upward at it (for its position was immediately over my own) I fancied that I saw it in motion. In an instant afterward the fancy was confirmed. Its sweep was brief, and of course slow. I watched it for some minutes, somewhat in fear, but more in wonder. Wearied at length with observing its dull movement, I turned my eyes upon the other objects in the cell.

A slight noise attracted my notice, and, looking to the floor,

I saw several enormous rats traversing it. They had issued from the well, which lay just within view to my right. Even then, while I gazed, they came up in troops, hurriedly, with ravenous eyes, allured by the scent of the meat. From this it required much effort and attention to scare them away.

It might have been half an hour, perhaps even an hour, (for I could take but imperfect note of time) before I again cast my eyes upward. What I then saw confounded and amazed me. The sweep of the pendulum had increased in extent by nearly a yard. As a natural consequence, its velocity was also much greater. But what mainly disturbed me was the idea that it had perceptibly *descended*. I now observed—with what horror it is needless to say—that its nether extremity was formed of a crescent of glittering steel, about a foot in length from horn to horn; the horns upward, and the under edge evidently as keen as that of a razor. Like a razor also, it seemed massy and heavy, tapering from the edge into a solid and broad structure above. It was appended to a weighty rod of brass, and the whole *hissed* as it swung through the air.

I could no longer doubt the doom prepared for me by monkish ingenuity in torture. My cognizance of the pit had become known to the inquisitorial agents—*the pit* whose horrors had been destined for so bold a recusant as myself— *the pit*, typical of hell, and regarded by rumor as the Ultima Thule of all their punishments. The plunge into this pit I had **21** avoided by the merest of accidents, and I knew that surprise, or entrapment into torment, formed an important portion of all the grotesquerie of these dungeon deaths. Having failed to fall, it was no part of the demon plan to hurl me into the abyss; and thus (there being no alternative) a different and a milder destruction awaited me. Milder! I half smiled in my agony as I thought of such application of such a term.

What boots it to tell of the long, long hours of horror more **22** than mortal, during which I counted the rushing vibrations of the steel! Inch by inch—line by line—with a descent only appreciable at intervals that seemed ages—down and still down it came! Days passed—it might have been that many days passed—ere it swept so closely over me as to fan me with its acrid breath. The odor of the sharp steel forced itself into my nostrils. I prayed—I wearied heaven with my prayer for its more speedy descent. I grew frantically mad, and struggled to force myself upward against the sweep of the fearful scimitar. And then I fell suddenly calm, and lay smiling at the **23** glittering death, as a child at some rare bauble. **24**

There was another interval of utter insensibility; it was brief; for, upon again lapsing into life there had been no perceptible descent in the pendulum. But it might have been long; for I knew there were demons who took note of my swoon, and who could have arrested the vibration at pleasure. Upon my recovery, too, I felt very—oh, inexpressibly sick and weak, as if through long inanition. Even amid the agonies **25** of that period, the human nature craved food. With painful effort I outstretched my left arm as far as my bonds permitted, and took possession of the small remnant which had been

21 The end of the world, the last extremity. Thule was the most northern point known to the ancient Romans. Pliny, Solinus, and Mela take it for Iceland, while others, like Camden, consider it to be Shetland, Bochart says it is a Syrian word and that the Phoenician merchants who traded to the group called it Gezirat Thule, or Isles of Darkness. Its etymology is unclear, but it could be the Gothic *Tiule*, meaning "the most remote land," and connected with the Greek *telos*, "end."

Poe mentions it again in his poem *Dream-Land,* where it is to be pronounced "Thuly," not uncommon in previous centuries.

22 Avails or profits (obsolete usage)

23 Compare with Thomas Mann's (a pseudonym for William Maginn) "The Man in the Bell" (1821). In that tale, which Poe pokes fun at in "How to Write a Blackwood Article," the narrator tells how "Every moment I saw the bell sweep within an inch of my face." "To look at the object was bitter as death," but he cannot keep his eyes from it. "The bell pealing above and opening its jaws with a hideous clamor" seems to be "a ravening monster raging to devour" him. At the same time, the cavern in which he is trapped seems to be full of hideous faces, which glare down on him "with terrifying frowns, or with grinning mockery, still more appalling. At last the devil himself, accoutred, as in the common description of the evil spirit, with hoof, horn, and tail, and eyes of infernal lustre, made his appearance. . . ."

24 He seems to be mesmerized by the moving, glittering object.

25 Lethargy caused, no doubt, by lack of food and water

spared me by the rats. As I put a portion of it within my lips, there rushed to my mind a half formed thought of joy—of hope. Yet what business had *I* with hope? It was, as I say, a half formed thought—man has many such which are never completed. I felt that it was of joy—of hope; but I felt also that it had perished in its formation. In vain I struggled to perfect—to regain it. Long suffering had nearly annihilated all my ordinary powers of mind. I was an imbecile—an idiot.

The vibration of the pendulum was at right angles to my length. I saw that the crescent was designed to cross the region of the heart. It would fray the serge of my robe—it would return and repeat its operation—again—and again. Notwithstanding its terrifically wide sweep (some thirty feet or more) and the hissing vigor of its descent, sufficient to sunder these very walls of iron, still the fraying of my robe would be all that, for several minutes, it would accomplish. And at this thought I paused. I dared not go farther than this reflection. I dwelt upon it with a pertinacity of attention—as if, in so dwelling, I could arrest *here* the descent of the steel. I forced myself to ponder upon the sound of the crescent as it should pass across the garment—upon the peculiar thrilling sensation which the friction of cloth produces on the nerves. I pondered upon all this frivolity until my teeth were on edge.

Down—steadily down it crept. I took a frenzied pleasure in contrasting its downward with its lateral velocity. To the right—to the left—far and wide—with the shriek of a damned spirit; to my heart with the stealthy pace of the tiger! I alternately laughed and howled as the one or the other idea grew predominant.

Down—certainly, relentlessly down! It vibrated within three inches of my bosom! I struggled violently, furiously, to free my left arm. This was free only from the elbow to the hand. I could reach the latter, from the platter beside me, to my mouth, with great effort, but no farther. Could I have broken the fastenings above the elbow, I would have seized and attempted to arrest the pendulum. I might as well have attempted to arrest an avalanche!

Down—still unceasingly—still inevitably down! I gasped and struggled at each vibration. I shrunk convulsively at its every sweep. My eyes followed its outward or upward whirls with the eagerness of the most unmeaning despair; they closed themselves spasmodically at the descent, although death would have been a relief, oh! how unspeakable! Still I quivered in every nerve to think how slight a sinking of the machinery would precipitate that keen, glistening axe upon my bosom. It was *hope* that prompted the nerve to quiver—the frame to shrink. It was *hope*—the hope that triumphs on the rack—that whispers to the death-condemned even in the dungeon **26** of the Inquisition.

I saw that some ten or twelve vibrations would bring the steel in actual contact with my robe, and with this observation there suddenly came over my spirit all the keen, collected calmness of despair. For the first time during many hours—or perhaps days—I *thought*. It now occurred to me that the

26 "Because of the limitations imposed upon him by an inquisitionary force, every act of balance or sanity only leads to a worsening of his situation; this paradox suggests that while Poe ordinarily remained true to his conception of the torture of the disordered personality, he did not overlook the possibility that sanity can be more terrifying than madness" (James Lundquist, *Poe Newsletter*, Vol. 2, 1969; p. 25).

bandage, or surcingle, which enveloped me, was *unique*. I **27** was tied by no separate cord. The first stroke of the razor-like crescent athwart any portion of the band, would so detach it that it might be unwound from my person by means of my left hand. But how fearful, in that case, the proximity of the steel! The result of the slightest struggle how deadly! Was it likely, moreover, that the minions of the torturer had not foreseen and provided for this possibility? Was it probable that the bandage crossed my bosom in the track of the pendulum? Dreading to find my faint, and, as it seemed, my last hope frustrated, I so far elevated my head as to obtain a distinct view of my breast. The surcingle enveloped my limbs and body close in all directions—*save in the path of the destroying crescent*.

Scarcely had I dropped my head back into its original position, when there flashed upon my mind what I cannot better describe than as the unformed half of that idea of deliverance to which I have previously alluded, and of which a moiety only floated indeterminately through my brain when **28** I raised food to my burning lips. The whole thought was now

27 All in one piece (archaic)

28 A half

Still I quivered in every nerve to think how slight a sinking of the machinery would precipitate that keen, glistening axe upon my bosom. *Illustration by Jules Descartes Ferat, nineteenth century*

29 A poem published in *Knickerbocker Magazine* of November 1837 tells the legend of Archbishop Hatto II of Mainz, who was supposedly eaten by mice in the tower he had built as a refuge. Poe may have had this in mind, as well as Robert Southey's verses "God's Judgment on a Wicked Bishop."

30 Rats are traditional symbols of infirmity ad death, and so the rat's kiss is horrifying beyond mere sanitary reasons. The animal also represents plague, decay, and—appropriately here—the underworld.

31 The narrator does not escape unscythed.

present—feeble, scarcely sane, scarcely definite,—but still entire. I proceeded at once, with the nervous energy of despair, to attempt its execution.

For many hours the immediate vicinity of the low framework upon which I lay, had been literally swarming with rats. They were wild, bold, ravenous; their red eyes glaring upon me as if they waited but for motionlessness on my part to make me their prey. "To what food," I thought, "have they been **29** accustomed in the well?"

They had devoured, in spite of all my efforts to prevent them, all but a small remnant of the contents of the dish. I had fallen into an habitual see-saw, or wave of the hand about the platter: and, at length, the unconscious uniformity of the movement deprived it of effect. In their voracity the vermin frequently fastened their sharp fangs in my fingers. With the particles of the oily and spicy viand which now remained, I thoroughly rubbed the bandage wherever I could reach it; then, raising my hand from the floor, I lay breathlessly still.

At first the ravenous animals were startled and terrified at the change—at the cessation of movement. They shrank alarmedly back; many sought the well. But this was only for a moment. I had not counted in vain upon their voracity. Observing that I remained without motion, one or two of the boldest leaped upon the framework, and smelt at the surcingle. This seemed the signal for a general rush. Forth from the well they hurried in fresh troops. They clung to the wood—they overran it, and leaped in hundreds upon my person. The measured movement of the pendulum disturbed them not at all. Avoiding its strokes they busied themselves with the anointed bandage. They pressed—they swarmed upon me in ever accumulating heaps. They writhed upon my throat; their cold lips sought my own; I was half stifled by their thronging pressure; disgust, for which the world has no name, swelled **30** my bosom, and chilled, with a heavy clamminess, my heart. Yet one minute, and I felt that the struggle would be over. Plainly I perceived the loosening of the bandage. I knew that in more than one place it must be already severed. With a more than human resolution I lay *still*.

Nor had I erred in my calculations—nor had I endured in vain. I at length felt that I was *free*. The surcingle hung in ribands from my body. But the stroke of the pendulum already pressed upon my bosom. It had divided the serge of the robe. It had cut through the linen beneath. Twice again it swung, **31** and a sharp sense of pain shot through every nerve. But the moment of escape had arrived. At a wave of my hand my deliverers hurried tumultuously away. With a steady movement—cautious, sidelong, shrinking, and slow—I slid from the embrace of the bandage and beyond the reach of the scimitar. For the moment, at least, *I was free*.

Free!—and in the grasp of the Inquisition! I had scarcely stepped from my wooden bed of horror upon the stone floor of the prison, when the motion of the hellish machine ceased and I beheld it drawn up, by some invisible force, through the ceiling. This was a lesson which I took desperately to heart. My every motion was undoubtedly watched. Free!—I had but escaped death in one form of agony, to be delivered unto worse than death in some other. With that thought I rolled my eyes nervously around on the barriers of iron that hemmed me in. Something unusual—some change which, at first, I could not appreciate distinctly—it was obvious, had taken place in the apartment. For many minutes of a dreamy and trembling abstraction, I busied myself in vain, unconnected conjecture. During this period, I became aware, for the first time, of the origin of the sulphurous light which illumined the cell. It proceeded from a fissure, about half an inch in width, extending entirely around the prison at the base of the walls, which thus appeared, and were, completely separated from the floor. I endeavored, but of course in vain, to look through the aperture. **32**

As I arose from the attempt, the mystery of the alteration in the chamber broke at once upon my understanding. I had observed that, although the outlines of the figures upon the walls were sufficiently distinct, yet the colors seemed blurred and indefinite. These colors had now assumed, and were momentarily assuming, a startling and most intense brilliancy, that gave to the spectral and fiendish portraitures an aspect that might have thrilled even firmer nerves than my own. Demon eyes, of a wild and ghastly vivacity, glared upon me in a thousand directions, where none had been visible before, and gleamed with the lurid lustre of a fire that I could not force my imagination to regard as unreal. **33**

Unreal!—Even while I breathed there came to my nostrils the breath of the vapour of heated iron! A suffocating odour pervaded the prison! A deeper glow settled each moment in the eyes that glared at my agonies! A richer tint of crimson diffused itself over the pictured horrors of blood. I panted! I gasped for breath! There could be no doubt of the design of my tormentors—oh! most unrelenting! oh! most demoniac of men! I shrank from the glowing metal to the centre of the cell. Amid the thought of the fiery destruction that impended, the idea of the coolness of the well came over my soul like balm. I rushed to its deadly brink. I threw my straining vision below. The glare from the enkindled roof illumined its inmost recesses. Yet, for a wild moment, did my spirit refuse to comprehend the meaning of what I saw. At length it forced— **34** it wrestled its way into my soul—it burned itself in upon my shuddering reason.—Oh! for a voice to speak!—oh! horror!—oh! any horror but this! With a shriek, I rushed from the margin, and buried my face in my hands—weeping bitterly.

The heat rapidly increased, and once again I looked up, shuddering as with a fit of the ague. There had been a second change in the cell—and now the change was obviously in the *form*. As before, it was in vain that I, at first, endeavored to appreciate or understand what was taking place. But not long was I left in doubt. The Inquisitorial vengeance had been hurried by my two-fold escape, and there was to be no more dallying with the King of Terrors. The room had been square. I saw that two of its iron angles were now acute—two,

32 He apparently sees the light from the furnace that heats the iron. This torture device is not only elaborate but fantastic, since heat would have to be provided on all four sides and somehow not interfere with the movement of the walls.

"How to Write a Blackwood Article" mentions a tale entitled "The Involuntary Experimentalist," about a man working inside a boiler who is trapped when someone, not knowing of his presence, fires the thing up.

33 The room has truly taken on the aspect of Hell.

34 What he sees is, of course, only a pit, but what he comprehends is annihilation.

35 Griswold, in his memoir of Poe (1850), accuses Poe of plagiarism, charging that the moving walls are stolen from "The Iron Shroud," by William Mudford (*Blackwood's*, August 1830). There, however, the room is built of blocks that are removed a few at a time, quite unlike Poe's. It is typical of Griswold's obsessive degrading of Poe that he trumps up this criticism but says nothing about the countless other borrowings that can be found in Poe's works (all of which have been throughly reworked).

36 The narrator would rather die by the red-hot walls than be cast into oblivion, to lose once and for all his sole claim to existence.

"Feeling, intellect, and will function together, and the hero escapes the pendulum—but he escapes into a more restricted and horrible situation. 'I had but escaped death in one form of agony, to be delivered into worse than death in some other,' he says as he enters the third and most horrible crisis. Even though the three faculties are perfectly unified when the glowing walls begin to close in, sanity can no longer help the hero. Through his feeling, his intellect, and his will, he comprehends the predicament and wants to escape, but there is no alternative left. He is completely limited in time, for no adjustment of the faculties can help him. His previous escapes have worsened his condition to the point where he gives up hope and yields at last. . . ." (James Lundquist, *Poe Newsletter*, 2, 1969; pp. 25–26)

37 It is only when we think about it afterward that we realize that the sudden, swift retreat of the walls—just in time to save the narrator—is impossible. However, within the context of the tale, it works beautifully.

38 General Antoine Chevalier Louis Colbert, Comte de Lasalle, entered Toledo during the Peninsular War of 1808. His arrival parallels the announcement of the Second Coming in Browning's *Childe Harold*: "He that endureth to the end shall be saved." The man who wants to enter Heaven must first go through Hell (or at least Purgatory).

Harry Levin sees the tale as an existential parable: "The hero is not less heroic because he suffers rather than acts; nor is he less contemporary in an epoch which has so vastly multiplied the sentence of political imprisonment, and which has visualized the ordeal of life itself—through the apprehensive eyes of Franz Kafka—as an arbitrary trial, an unjust imprisonment, and an unjustified condemnation. For Poe the will is constrained to choose between evils which, upon confrontation, seem worse than their alternatives: the pit or the pendulum, the frying-pan versus the fire. . . . His climactic adventure, 'The Pit and the Pendulum,' abandons him to the existential dilemma: the agony of the prostrate individual, isolated and immobilized, surrounded by watchful rats, threatened by an encroaching mechanism, and impelled toward a gaping abyss." (*The Power of Blackness*, Vintage, 1958; pp. 153–54)

Marie Bonaparte sees Poe as being caught between the male force (the pendulum) and the female (the pit), and recoiling from both. This, she says, is indicative of Poe's suppressed homosexual nature. He cannot let the scimitar "enter and split his heart—the scimitar replacing the phallus," and he cannot enter the pit—the female sexual organ—either. His escape is "the supreme wish-phantasy of Poe, for, in effect, he was always to be tossed between these poles of his bisexuality with never a hope of escape." (P. 592)

In Jungian analysis, the pit or hole is seen as symbolic of the passage from temporal to nontemporal existence, and for Poe that is frightening merely because we do not

consequently, obtuse. The fearful difference quickly increased with a low rumbling or moaning sound. In an instant the **35** apartment had shifted its form into that of a lozenge. But the alteration stopped not here—I neither hoped nor desired it to stop. I could have clasped the red walls to my bosom as a garment of eternal peace. "Death," I said, "any death but that of the pit!" Fool! might I have not known that *into the pit* it was the object of the burning iron to urge me? Could I resist its glow? or, if even that, could I withstand its pressure? And now, flatter and flatter grew the lozenge, with a rapidity that left me no time for contemplation. Its centre, and of course, its greatest width, came just over the yawning gulf. I shrank **36** back—but the closing walls pressed me resistlessly onward. At length for my seared and writhing body there was no longer an inch of foothold on the firm floor of the prison. I struggled no more, but the agony of my soul found vent in one loud, long, and final scream of despair. I felt that I tottered upon the brink—I averted my eyes——

There was a discordant hum of human voices! There was a loud blast as of many trumpets! There was a harsh grating as **37** of a thousand thunders! The fiery walls rushed back! An outstretched arm caught my own as I fell, fainting, into the abyss. It was that of General Lasalle. The French army had entered Toledo. The Inquisition was in the hands of its **38** enemies.

know what lies beyond. While physical death by the pendulum is terrifying, the death of the self, as symbolized by the pit, is even more so. Yet the Jungian self does at least have a hope of saving itself: "Whenever a human being genuinely turns to the inner world, and tries to know himself—not by ruminating about his subjective thoughts and feelings, but by following the expressions of his own objective nature such as dreams and genuine fantasies—then sooner or later the Self emerges. The ego will then find an inner power that contains all the possibilities of renewal." (M.-L. von Franz, *Man and his Symbols*, p. 234)

Still another interpretation can be stated in purely Christian terms: only when the narrator admits that his predicament is beyond his power to escape, and surrenders himself completely to God, can he be saved.

Thus "The Pit and the Pendulum" can be read as a simple tale of terror, a parable of man's existence, a representation of the emergence of the self, an unconscious reworking of Poe's ambivalent sexuality, or as Christian allegory. Poe seems to offer something for everyone.

THE TELL-TALE HEART

First published in the Boston *Pioneer*, January 1843, this is one of Poe's best tales, a dramatic monologue that tells of the events leading up to and following the murder of an old man both as the narrator sees them and as they really occurred. Since we view everything through the narrator's eyes, it is testimony to Poe's narrative skill that we understand completely what the narrator does not.

Poe drew upon the age-old superstition of the evil eye, and also from a pamphlet by Daniel Webster, *Argument on the Trial of John Francis Knapp* (1830):

"An aged man, without an enemy in the world, in his own house, and in his own bed, is made the victim of a butcherly murder, for mere pay. Truly, here is a new lesson for painters and poets. Whoever shall hereafter draw the portrait of murder, if he will show it . . . where . . . last to be looked for . . . let him not give it the grim visage of Moloch. . . . Let him draw, rather, a decorous, smooth-faced, bloodless demon; a picture in repose, rather than in action; not so much an example of human nature in its depravity, and in its paroxysms of crime, as an infernal being, a fiend, in the ordinary display and development of his character.

"The deed was executed with a degree of self-possession and steadiness equal to the wickedness with which it was planned. The circumstances now clearly in evidence spread out the whole scene before us. Deep sleep had fallen on the destined victim. . . . A healthful old man. . . . The assassin enters. . . . With noiseless foot he paces the lonely hall . . . and reaches the door of the chamber. Of this, he moves the lock, by soft and continued pressure, till it turns on its hinges without noise; and he enters, and beholds his victim before him. . . . The face of the innocent sleeper . . . shows him where to strike. The fated blow is given! . . . It is the assassin's purpose to make sure work. . . . The deed is done. He retreats, retraces his steps to the window . . . and escapes. He has done the murder. No eye has seen him, no ear has heard him. The secret is his own, and it is safe!

"Ah! Gentlemen, that was a dreadful mistake. Such a secret can be safe nowhere. . . . True it is, generally speaking, that 'murder will out' . . . the guilty soul cannot keep its own secret. It is false to itself; or rather it feels an irresistible impulse to be true to itself. It labors under its guilty possession and knows not what to do with it. The human heart was not made for the residence of such an inhabitant. . . . The secret which the murderer possesses soon comes to possess him; and like the evil spirits of which we read, it overcomes him, and leads him whithersoever it will. He feels it beating at his heart, rising to his throat, and demanding disclosure. He thinks the whole world sees it in his face, reads it in his eyes, and almost hears its workings in the very silence of his thoughts. It has become his master. . . . It must be confessed, it will be confessed." (Compare also with the ending of "The Imp of the Perverse.")

Another source may be Charles Dickens' "A Confession Found in a Prison in the Time of Charles the Second" (1840). This tale includes the elements of narrator's inability to look his victim in the eye as well as his placing a chair over the place where the body is secreted. When he refuses to move, the authorities grow suspicious and the body is uncovered. The tale is a genuine potboiler, however, inserted quickly into a publication when a series of chapters of a novel failed to win reader interest, while Poe's tale is a masterpiece.

Filmed versions of the story include a 1928 European version directed by Charles Klein and starring Otto Matiesen and Darvas. Surprisingly, it is fairly true to the original. Brian Desmond Hurst directed a 1934 British production, also known as *A Bucket of Blood*, starring Norman Dryden and Yolande Terrell. The best thus far is definitely a 1954 UPA animated version narrated by James Mason—a visually stunning, and truly frightening, film.

Elements from the story also appear in *Avenging Conscience*, a 1914 D. W. Griffith production, *Histoires Extraordinaires* (1948), *Manfish* (1956), *Master of Horror* (1960), and *The Horror Man* (1960—also known as *Panic I* and *Hidden Room of 1000 Horrors*).

Basil Rathbone has recorded the tale (Caedmon 1195), as has Martin Donegan (CMS 630).

True!—nervous—very, very dreadfully nervous I had been and am; but why *will* you say that I am mad? The disease had sharpened my senses—not destroyed—not dulled them. Above all was the sense of hearing acute. I heard all things in the heaven and in the earth. I heard many things in hell. **1** How, then, am I mad? Hearken! and observe how healthily— how calmly I can tell you the whole story. **2**

It is impossible to say how first the idea entered my brain; but once conceived, it haunted me day and night. Object there was none. Passion there was none. I loved the old man. He had never wronged me. He had never given me insult. For his gold I had no desire. I think it was his eye! yes, it was this! One of his eyes resembled that of a vulture—a pale blue eye, with a film over it. Whenever it fell upon me, my blood ran cold; and so by degrees—very gradually—I made up my mind to take the life of the old man, and thus rid myself of the eye for ever. **3**

Now this is the point. You fancy me mad. Madmen know nothing. But you should have seen *me*. You should have seen how wisely I proceeded—with what caution—with what fore-sight—with what dissimulation I went to work! I was never kinder to the old man than during the whole week before I killed him. And every night, about midnight, I turned the **4** latch of his door and opened it—oh, so gently! And then, when I had made an opening sufficient for my head, I put in a dark lantern, all closed, closed, so that no light shone out, **5** and then I thrust in my head. Oh, you would have laughed to see how cunningly I thrust it in! I moved it slowly—very, very slowly, so that I might not disturb the old man's sleep. It took me an hour to place my whole head within the opening so far that I could see him as he lay upon his bed. Ha!—would a madman have been so wise as this? And then, when my head was well in the room, I undid the lantern cautiously— oh, so cautiously—cautiously (for the hinges creaked)—I undid it just so much that a single thin ray fell upon the vulture eye. And this I did for seven long nights—every night just at midnight—but I found the eye always closed; and so it was impossible to do the work; for it was not the old man who vexed me, but his Evil Eye. And every morning, when the **6** day broke, I went boldly into the chamber, and spoke courageously to him, calling him by name in a hearty tone, and inquiring how he had passed the night. So you see he **7** would have been a very profound old man, indeed, to suspect that every night, just at twelve, I looked in upon him while he slept.

1 ". . . things in heaven, and things in earth, and things under the earth" (Philippians 2:10)

Typically, Poe's narrator is mad yet lucid—and not merely in order to tell the tale. It is this *insistent* lucidity that tips off the reader to his insanity.

2 Consider this passage from "The System of Dr. Tarr and Professor Fether": "[A lunatic's] cunning . . . is proverbial, and great. If he has a project in view, he conceals his design with a marvellous wisdom; and the dexterity with which he counterfeits sanity, presents, to the metaphysician, one of the most singular problems in the study of the mind. When a madman appears *thoroughly* sane, indeed, it is high time to put him in a straight [sic] jacket."

3 Eyes are also important in "Metzengerstein," "Ligeia," and "The Black Cat."

The evil eye is a feature of popular superstition in many countries, from Italy to Africa to parts of the United States. The person with such an eye is thought to have the power of casting spells on another, inflicting bad luck or pain of some sort. The evil eye may be unwittingly acquired, or it may be the weapon of a person possessed by the Devil. (Al Capp's Evil Eye Fleegle is a comic example, a shady character who puts the "whammy" on others for a price.)

The eye in general has traditionally represented understanding and light, so that one could interpret the narrator's irrational hatred as his fear of knowing himself for what he is, or that, because the old man knows he is insane, the narrator must rid himself of this threat to his existence.

4 "It is the power of attention and concentration that gives the small intellect its force," writes John Rea. "The small mind conquers by making a victim of the superior mind that does not readily notice details. The victim in 'The Tell-Tale Heart' fails to notice the narrator's excess of kindness, but the narrator gives one whole hour to the detail of opening a door." (*Studies in Short Fiction*, Vol. 4; p. 65)

5 A lantern with metal doors that can be shut to conceal the light when necessary

6 The narrator is a bundle of classic symptoms of varying degrees of psychosis. He rationalizes his behavior in order to appear justified in both his own eyes and those of the reader.

Through displacement, he represses the real source of his anxiety and attributes his distress to another source: the old man's eye. His personality is manic in its elation, excitement, hyperactivity, and low irritability threshold. He seems also to be a paranoid schizophrenic, with delusions of persecution accompanied by hostility and aggressiveness.

7 Some readers have suggested that the old man is the narrator's father, but since the narrator addresses him by his first name this cannot be the case.

"Who's there?" *Artist unknown, late-nineteenth century*

8 A key word in Poe's tales, almost always used ironically

9 Job 38:8–9: "Who watched over the birth of the sea, when it burst in flood from the womb? When I wrapped it in a blanket of cloud and cradled it in fog. . . ." The words are God's.

10 The deathwatches in the wall are *Atropus pulsatorius* or *Liposcelis divinatorius*, beetles whose sounds were supposed to foretell the death of someone in the house. Here, however, the sound is most likely in the narrator's mind.

Thoreau, in an article in the *Dial* of July 1842, wrote: "In the autumn days, the creaking of crickets is heard at noon over all the land, and as in summer days they are heard chiefly at night-fall, so then by their incessant chirp they usher in the evening of the year. Nor can all vanities that vex the world alter one whit the measure that night has chosen. Every pulse-beat is in exact time with the cricket's chant and the tickings of the deathwatch in the wall. Alternate with these if you can."

Poe, like Thoreau, was fond of wordplay, and "death-watch" is also a vigil held over a dying person. The narrator of "The Tell-Tale Heart" holds his own death-watch as he sticks his head in the room and regards the old man. But it becomes his own as his pulse and breathing merge with the old man's, in an image paralleling Thoreau's final comment above.

11 Compare with Montresor in "The Cask of Amontillado," who tells us at one point that he is "sick at heart" and then answers his victim's screams by screaming himself.

12 "He discovereth deep things out of darkness, and bringeth out to light the shadow of death" (Job 12:22).

"Must not all things at the last be swallowed up in death?" (Plato, *Dialogues: Phaedo*, 72)

"The Angel of Death spread his wings. . . ." (Byron, *Hebrew Melodies*, "The Destruction of Sennacherib," st. 3)

13 "To give light to them that sit in darkness and in the shadow of death" (Luke 1:7–9)

Upon the eighth night I was more than usually cautious in opening the door. A watch's minute hand moves more quickly than did mine. Never before that night had I *felt* the extent **8** of my own powers—of my sagacity. I could scarcely contain my feelings of triumph. To think that there I was, opening the door, little by little, and he not even to dream of my secret deeds or thoughts. I fairly chuckled at the idea; and perhaps he heard me; for he moved on the bed suddenly, as if startled. Now you may think that I drew back—but no. His room was **9** as black as pitch with the thick darkness (for the shutters were close fastened, through fear of robbers), and so I knew that he could not see the opening of the door, and I kept pushing it on steadily, steadily.

I had my head in, and was about to open the lantern, when my thumb slipped upon the tin fastening, and the old man sprang up in the bed, crying out—"Who's there?"

I kept quite still and said nothing. For a whole hour I did not move a muscle, and in the meantime I did not hear him lie down. He was still sitting up in the bed listening;—just as I have done, night after night, hearkening to the death watches **10** in the wall.

Presently I heard a slight groan, and I knew it was the groan of mortal terror. It was not a groan of pain or of grief—oh, no!—it was the low stifled sound that arises from the bottom of the soul when overcharged with awe. I knew the sound well. Many a night, just at midnight, when all the world slept, it has welled up from my own bosom, deepening, with its dreadful echo, the terrors that distracted me. I say I knew it well. I knew what the old man felt, and pitied him, although **11** I chuckled at heart. I knew that he had been lying awake ever since the first slight noise, when he had turned in the bed. His fears had been ever since growing upon him. He had been trying to fancy them causeless, but could not. He had been saying to himself—"It is nothing but the wind in the chimney—it is only a mouse crossing the floor," or "it is merely a cricket which has made a single chirp." Yes, he has been trying to comfort himself with these suppositions; but he had found all in vain. *All in vain;* because Death, in approaching him, had stalked with his black shadow before him, and **12** enveloped the victim. And it was the mournful influence of the unperceived shadow that caused him to feel—although he neither saw nor heard—to *feel* the presence of my head within the room.

When I had waited a long time, very patiently, without hearing him lie down, I resolved to open a little—a very, very little crevice in the lantern. So I opened it—you cannot imagine how stealthily, stealthily—until, at length, a single dim ray, like the thread of the spider, shot from out the **13** crevice and full upon the vulture eye.

It was open—wide, wide open—and I grew furious as I gazed upon it. I saw it with perfect distinctness—all a dull blue, with a hideous veil over it that chilled the very marrow in my bones; but I could see nothing else of the old man's face or person: for I had directed the ray as if by instinct, precisely upon the damned spot.

And now have I not told you that what you mistake for madness is but over-acuteness of the senses?—now, I say, there came to my ears a low, dull, quick sound, such as a watch makes when enveloped in cotton. I knew *that* sound well too. It was the beating of the old man's heart. It increased **14** my fury, as the beating of a drum stimulates the soldier into courage.

But even yet I refrained and kept still. I scarcely breathed. I held the lantern motionless. I tried how steadily I could maintain the ray upon the eye. Meantime the hellish tattoo of the heart increased. It grew quicker and quicker, and louder and louder every instant. The old man's terror *must* have been extreme! It grew louder, I say, louder every moment!—do you mark me well? I am nervous: so I am. And now at the dead hour of the night, amid the dreadful silence of that old house, so strange a noise as this excited me to uncontrollable terror. Yet, for some minutes longer I refrained and stood still. But the beating grew louder, louder! I thought the heart must burst. And now a new anxiety seized me—the sound would be heard by a neighbor! The old man's hour had come! With a loud yell, I threw open the lantern and leaped into the room. He shrieked once—once only. In an instant I dragged him to the floor, and pulled the heavy bed over him. I then smiled gaily, to find the deed so far done. But, for many minutes, the heart beat on with a muffled sound. This, however, did not vex me; it would not be heard through the wall. At length it ceased. The old man was dead. I removed the bed and examined the corpse. Yes, he was stone, stone

14 Like Roderick Usher, he seems to have a "morbid acuteness of the senses," but here there is no doubt that what he hears is only in his own, twisted mind.

I then took up three planks from the flooring of the chamber, and deposited all between the scantlings.
Illustration by F. S. Coburn,
1903

dead. I placed my hand upon the heart and held it there many minutes. There was no pulsation. He was stone dead. His eye would trouble me no more.

If still you think me mad, you will think so no longer when I describe the wise precautions I took for the concealment of the body. The night waned, and I worked hastily, but in silence. First of all I dismembered the corpse. I cut off the head and the arms and the legs.

15 Wooden supports under the flooring   **15**

I then took up three planks from the flooring of the chamber, and deposited all between the scantlings. I then replaced the boards so cleverly, so cunningly, that no human eye—not even *his*—could have detected any thing wrong. There was nothing to wash out—no stain of any kind—no blood-spot whatever. I had been too wary for that. A tub had caught all—ha! ha!

When I had made an end of these labors, it was four o'clock—still dark as midnight. As the bell sounded the hour, there came a knocking at the street door. I went down to open it with a light heart,—for what had I *now* to fear? There entered three men, who introduced themselves, with perfect suavity, as officers of the police. A shriek had been heard by a neighbor during the night; suspicion of foul play had been aroused; information had been lodged at the police office, and they (the officers) had been deputed to search the premises.

I smiled,—for *what* had I to fear? I bade the gentlemen welcome. The shriek, I said, was my own in a dream. The old man, I mentioned, was absent in the country. I took my visitors all over the house. I bade them search—search *well*. I led them, at length, to *his* chamber. I showed them his treasures, secure, undisturbed. In the enthusiasm of my confidence, I brought chairs into the room, and desired them *here* to rest from their fatigues, while I myself, in the wild audacity of my perfect triumph, placed my own seat upon the very spot beneath which reposed the corpse of the victim.

The officers were satisfied. My *manner* had convinced them. I was singularly at ease. They sat, and while I answered cheerily, they chatted familiar things. But, ere long, I felt myself getting pale and wished them gone. My head ached, and I fancied a ringing in my ears: but still they sat and still chatted. The ringing became more distinct:—it continued and became more distinct: I talked more freely to get rid of the feeling: but it continued and gained definitiveness—until, at length, I found that the noise was *not* within my ears.

No doubt I now grew *very* pale;—but I talked more fluently, and with a heightened voice. Yet the sound increased—and what could I do? It was *a low, dull, quick sound—much such a sound as a watch makes when enveloped in cotton*. I gasped for breath—and yet the officers heard it not. I talked more quickly—more vehemently; but the noise steadily increased. I arose and argued about trifles, in a high key and with violent gesticulations, but the noise steadily increased. Why *would* they not be gone? I paced the floor to and fro with heavy strides, as if excited to fury by the observation of the men— but the noise steadily increased. Oh God! what *could* I do?

I foamed—I raved—I swore! I swung the chair upon which I had been sitting, and grated it upon the boards, but the noise arose over all and continually increased. It grew louder—louder—*louder!* And still the men chatted pleasantly, and smiled. Was it possible they heard not? Almighty God!—no, no! They heard!—they suspected!—they *knew!*—they were making a mockery of my horror!—this I thought, and this I think. But any thing was better than this agony! Any thing was more tolerable than this derision! I could bear those hypocritical smiles no longer! I felt that I must scream or die!—and now—again!—hark! louder! louder! louder! *louder!*—

"Villains!" I shrieked, "dissemble no more! I admit the deed!—tear up the planks!—here, here!—it is the beating of his hideous heart!"   **16**

16 Compare with the words of Daniel Webster's speech in the introductory note to this tale.

"Villains!" I shrieked, "dissemble no more! I admit the deed!" *Artist unknown*

THE BLACK CAT

First published in the *United States Saturday Post*, August 19, 1843.

Between 1841 and 1844, Poe turned out some of his finest work, including "The Black Cat," a tale that treats the subject of perversity as mental illness in a way unsurpassed by any other writer. Except for a brief passage in Sir Walter Scott's *Letters on Demonology* (note 23), there are no known sources for the story. However, we do know that Poe owned a black cat and that, when he was young he supposedly killed a pet fawn that belonged to his guardian's wife.

Poe may have drawn on two old superstitions. One, from the Egyptians, held the cat as sacred; whoever killed a cat, even by accident, was punished by death. In the Middle Ages, the black cat was considered to be Satan's favorite form when he was abroad in the world, and witches used such a cat as a "familiar." (See *Nine Lives: The Folklore of Cats*, by Katherine M. Briggs [Pantheon, 1980])

Poe's tale was an immediate success—so much so that the following year Thomas Dunn English wrote a parody called "The Ghost of the Grey Tadpole." The most notable use of the story, however, is in Richard Wright's *Native Son*, detailed in note 25.

The only film to use the tale's plot is D. W. Griffith's *Avenging Conscience* (1914). Universal's 1934 and 1941 films of *The Black Cat* have practically nothing in common with Poe other than their titles. A 1959 Indian production comes closer, with a crime thriller in the Jekyll-and-Hyde mold; and an English version in 1966 tells of a man who thinks his cat is the evil reincranation of his father. Possibly the most bizarre adaption is the 1968 Japanese version that tells of a mother and daughter who turn into monsters and seek revenge on barbarian soldiers who raped and killed them.

Elements of the tale also appear in *Five Tales of Horror*, a 1919 German film; *Maniac* (1934); and *Tales of Terror*, a 1962 film by Roger Corman.

Martin Donegan reads the tale on disc (CMS 555).

---

1 Unaffectedly natural

2 Unfortunately for the narrator, it is *not* a dream—and he *is* mad. Like others in Poe, his vision is distorted and he attempts to rationalize the consequences.

3 The narrator turns to drink, gouges out the eye of his favorite pet, a cat, and then hangs it, goes looking for another cat even though he hated the sight of the first one, comes to hate the new pet as well and tries to kill it but is stopped by his wife, whom he kills instead. He walls up her body in the cellar wall, along with the cat, which lives on to signal his crime. So much for the narrator's claims to sanity *and* his "series of mere household events."

4 Bizarre

5 Like Roderick Usher, he desperately wants someone to make some sense of his life. What he can't see is that the answers are all inside himself.

"Obviously, then," says James Gargano, "the narrator's version of the 'mere household events' cannot be accepted uncritically, nor, I believe, can his self-exculpa-

---

1 For the most wild, yet most homely narrative which I am about to pen, I neither expect nor solicit belief. Mad indeed would I be to expect it, in a case where my very senses reject their own evidence. Yet, mad am I not—and very surely do

2 I not dream. But to-morrow I die, and to-day I would unburthen my soul. My immediate purpose is to place before the world, plainly, succinctly, and without comment, a series

3 of mere household events. In their consequences, these events have terrified—have tortured—have destroyed me. Yet I will attempt to expound them. To me, they have presented little but Horror—to many they will seem less terrible than *ba-*

4 *roques*. Hereafter, perhaps, some intellect may be found which will reduce my phantasm to the common-place—some intellect more calm, more logical, and far less excitable than my own, which will perceive, in the circumstances I detail with awe, nothing more than an ordinary succession of very

5 natural causes and effects.

From my infancy I was noted for the docility and humanity

of my disposition. My tenderness of heart was even so conspicuous as to make me the jest of my companions. I was especially fond of animals, and was indulged by my parents with a great variety of pets. With these I spent most of my time, and never was so happy as when feeding and caressing them. This peculiarity of character grew with my growth, and, in my manhood, I derived from it one of my principal sources of pleasure. To those who have cherished an affection for a faithful and sagacious dog, I need hardly be at the trouble of explaining the nature or the intensity of the gratification thus derivable. There is something in the unselfish and self-sacrificing love of a brute, which goes directly to the heart of him who has had frequent occasion to test the paltry friendship and gossamer fidelity of mere *Man*. **7**

6

I married early, and was happy to find in my wife a disposition not uncongenial with my own. Observing my partiality for domestic pets, she lost no opportunity of procuring those of the most agreeable kind. We had birds, gold fish, a fine dog, rabbits, a small monkey, and *a cat*.

This latter was a remarkably large and beautiful animal, entirely black, and sagacious to an astonishing degree. In speaking of his intelligence, my wife, who at heart was not a little tinctured with superstition, made frequent allusion to the ancient popular notion, which regarded all black cats as witches in disguise. Not that she was ever *serious* upon this point—and I mention the matter at all for no better reason than that it happens, just now, to be remembered. **8**

9

ting theory of perverseness. He is, of course, eager to introduce into a world of psychological and moral order a concept that eliminates the onus of responsibility and guilt. Indeed, one of the most telling points of 'The Black Cat' is the narrator's fatuous denial of a moral order at the same time that the reader observes its unfaltering operation. This dramatic irony seems to me one of the compelling artistic effects that make 'The Black Cat' an undisputed masterpiece." (*Twentieth Century Interpretations of Poe's Tales*, Prentice-Hall, 1971; p. 91)

6 He fails to understand that his single-minded affection for his pets is in itself abnormal, for he seems to be repressing the other side of his nature—as if he could be either wholly good or wholly evil. His exaggerated devotion to his cat and his wife turns out to be an ineffective stopper for the hostility bottled up in his unconscious.

7 Because it does go directly to the "heart" (that is, the soul) of the narrator, he will soon find it impossible to let this love continue to live. For what lies buried in his subconscious must remain hidden.

8 "Sagacious," in Poe's tales, is almost always used ironically. Whether or not the cat has the almost human powers of perception the narrator says it does, *he* thinks so, and that is enough.

9 In an article entitled "Instinct vs. Reason," in *Alexander's Messenger*, January 29, 1840, Poe says, jokingly, "Black cats are all of them witches."

"The Black Cat." *Illustration by Aubrey Beardsley*

10 Pluto was the ruler of Hades, the dark underworld of Greek mythology.

11 While he blames alcohol for altering his personality, most psychologists believe the drug actually accentuates psychic disorders or repressed feelings already present. Zwerling and Rosenbaum in 1959 found that alcoholics are depressive, hostile, schizoid, dependent, and sexually immature—all of which aptly describe the narrator of "The Black Cat" (*Abnormal Psychology: Current Perspectives*. CRM/Random House, 1972; p. 211).

12 Like the murderer in "The Tell-Tale Heart," the narrator invests the eye with the power to see into his soul, his repressed self. "Given that the sun is the source of light and that light is symbolic of the intelligence and of the spirit, then the process of seeing represents a spiritual act and symbolizes understanding," notes J. E. Cirlot in his Dictionary of Symbols (Routledge & Kegan Paul, 1962; p. 99).

13 First gin, and now wine. . . .

14 There is perverseness not only in his actions but in his refusal to acknowledge his own flawed perspective of good and evil, and in his obsession with rationalizing his actions. It doesn't take much for the reader to see that what happens in the tale is the culmination of a lifetime of repressing an important, although unpleasant, side of his personality.

10   Pluto—this was the cat's name—was my favorite pet and playmate. I alone fed him, and he attended me wherever I went about the house. It was even with difficulty that I could prevent him from following me through the streets.

Our friendship lasted, in this manner, for several years, during which my general temperament and character—through the instrumentality of the Fiend Intemperance—had (I blush to confess it) experienced a radical alteration for the **11** worse. I grew, day by day, more moody, more irritable, more regardless of the feelings of others. I suffered myself to use intemperate language to my wife. At length, I even offered her personal violence. My pets, of course, were made to feel the change in my disposition. I not only neglected, but ill-used them. For Pluto, however, I still retained sufficient regard to restrain me from maltreating him, as I made no scruple of maltreating the rabbits, the monkey, or even the dog, when by accident, or through affection, they came in my way. But my disease grew upon me—for what disease is like Alcohol!—and at length even Pluto, who was now becoming old, and consequently somewhat peevish—even Pluto began to experience the effects of my ill temper.

One night, returning home, much intoxicated, from one of my haunts about town, I fancied that the cat avoided my presence. I seized him; when, in his fright at my violence, he inflicted a slight wound upon my hand with his teeth. The fury of a demon instantly possessed me. I knew myself no longer. My original soul seemed, at once, to take its flight from my body; and a more than fiendish malevolence, gin-nurtured, thrilled every fibre of my frame. I took from my waistcoat-pocket a pen-knife, opened it, grasped the poor beast by the throat, and deliberately cut one of its eyes from **12** the socket! I blush, I burn, I shudder, while I pen the damnable atrocity.

When reason returned with the morning—when I had slept off the fumes of the night's debauch—I experienced a sentiment half of horror, half of remorse, for the crime of which I had been guilty; but it was, at best, a feeble and equivocal feeling, and the soul remained untouched. I again plunged **13** into excess, and soon drowned in wine all memory of the deed.

In the meantime, the cat slowly recovered. The socket of the lost eye presented, it is true, a frightful appearance, but he no longer appeared to suffer any pain. He went about the house as usual, but, as might be expected, fled in extreme terror at my approach. I had so much of my old heart left, as to be at first grieved by this evident dislike on the part of a creature which had once so loved me. But this feeling soon gave place to irritation. And then came, as if to my final and **14** irrevocable overthrow, the spirit of PERVERSENESS. Of this spirit philosophy takes no account. Yet I am not more sure that my soul lives, than I am that perverseness is one of the primitive impulses of the human heart—one of the indivisible primary faculties, or sentiments, which give direction to the character of Man. Who has not, a hundred times, found himself committing a vile or a silly action, for no other reason than because he knows he should *not?* Have we not a perpetual inclination, in the teeth of our best judgment, to violate that which is *Law,* merely because we understand it to be such? This spirit of perverseness, I say, came to my final overthrow. It was this unfathomable longing of the soul to *vex* itself—to offer violence to its own nature—to do wrong for the wrong's sake only—that urged me to continue and finally to consummate the injury I had inflicted upon the unoffending brute. 15 One morning, in cool blood, I slipped a noose about its neck and hung it to the limb of a tree;—hung it with the tears 16 streaming from my eyes, and with the bitterest remorse at my heart;—hung it *because* I knew that it had loved me, and *because* I felt it had given me no reason of offence;—hung it *because* I knew that in so doing I was committing a sin—a deadly sin that would so jeopardize my immortal soul as to place it—if such a thing were possible—even beyond the reach of the infinite mercy of the Most Merciful and Most Terrible God. 17

On the night of the day on which this cruel deed was done, I was aroused from sleep by the cry of fire. The curtains of my bed were in flames. The whole house was blazing. It was with great difficulty that my wife, a servant, and myself, made our escape from the conflagration. The destruction was complete. My entire worldly wealth was swallowed up, and I resigned myself thenceforward to despair.

I am above the weakness of seeking to establish a sequence of cause and effect, between the disaster and the atrocity. But I am detailing a chain of facts—and wish not to leave even a possible link imperfect. On the day succeeding the fire, I visited the ruins. The walls, with one exception, had fallen in. This exception was found in a compartment wall, not very thick, which stood about the middle of the house, and against which had rested the head of my bed. The plastering had here, in great measure, resisted the action of the fire—a fact which I attributed to its having been recently spread. About this wall a dense crowd collected, and many persons seemed to be examining a particular portion of it with very minute and eager attention. The words "strange!" "singular!" and other similar expressions, excited my curiosity. I approached and saw, as if graven in *bas relief* upon the white surface, the 18 figure of a gigantic *cat.* The impression was given with an accuracy truly marvellous. There was a rope about the animal's neck. 19

When I first beheld this apparition—for I could scarcely regard it as less—my wonder and my terror were extreme. But at length reflection came to my aid. The cat, I remembered, had been hung in a garden adjacent to the house. Upon the alarm of fire, this garden had been immediately filled by the crowd—by some one of whom the animal must have been cut from the tree and thrown, through an open window, into my chamber. This had probably been done with the view of 20 arousing me from sleep. The falling of other walls had compressed the victim of my cruelty into the substance of the

15 He can't deal with the reproach he senses in the half-blind animal, but the only way he can free himself of the constant reminder of his mad act is to kill it. His solutions are no more rational than the incidents that produced the problem in the first place.

16 The repression of his violent nature, far from turning him into a model citizen, only creates a tension that leaves him uncomfortable, without any understanding of the reason, and that ultimately explodes in his black rages. As his repressed feelings surface, he is unable to deal with them and piles more defense mechanisms onto his already overburdened conscience.

In fact, the narrator is practically a case study in neurotic and psychotic behavior. His search for the causes of his behavior in the outside world, and his refusal to examine and analyze his own motives, is a sign of *projection.* When a person learns he can avoid punishment and self-blame by inventing a plausible excuse and alibis for his misdeeds, he is, in effect, rewarded for distorting the truth.

Another defense mechanism is *reaction formation,* in which a person not only represses his true feelings but develops beliefs and patterns of behavior that reflect the exact opposite—in the narrator's case, his self-professed love and affection for the cat and his mildness of disposition.

Through *denial,* a person reports that a source of distress no longer exists, which implies that he is somehow more competent even though there is no visible change in either his behavior or his situation. Note the narrator's thoughts after killing the cat, and later, his wife.

The narrator betrays his feelings of inadequacy in his inability to accept the love of both Pluto and his wife, and one senses that it is this, coupled with the repressed energy of his aggressive nature, that eventually cracks the dam of repression.

Repression of the desire to punish oneself eventually causes one's subconscious to resort to punishing in indirect ways, such as making foolish mistakes. That he somehow buries a live cat along with his wife is a sign that this unconscious moral guardian is at work. Simply because one chooses to ignore that moral sense (the superego) does not mean that it ceases to exist.

17 The unpardonable sin, an important part of much of Hawthorne's work, is "the sin against the Holy Spirit," usually defined as a denial of God's mercy. The narrator exaggerates here, for although killing an animal is sinful, there is always hope of forgiveness and salvation for anyone who accepts the love of God.

Unfortunately, the narrator sees everything in terms of black or white. There is no middle ground. If he cannot be good, then he must be evil. Any sin of his becomes unpardonable, and there is no hope of God's forgiveness.

Note that in "William Wilson," Poe creates a similar situation, with a man whose traits of good and evil become totally separated, but with the repressed side of the personality manifesting itself as a human figure.

18 Figures in bas-relief are usually shown in profile, since the sculptural relief is only barely raised from its background.

19 Observers in Hiroshima immediately after the bombing found silhouettes of victims whose shadows were cast on walls at the moment of the explosion.

20 Perhaps in protest; at any rate, it adds to the impression that the narrator has never been well liked.

freshly-spread plaster; the lime of which, with the flames, and the *ammonia* from the carcass, had then accomplished the portraiture as I saw it.

Although I thus readily accounted to my reason, if not altogether to my conscience, for the startling fact just detailed, it did not the less fail to make a deep impression upon my **21** fancy. For months I could not rid myself of the phantasm of the cat; and, during this period, there came back into my spirit a half-sentiment that seemed, but was not, remorse. I went so far as to regret the loss of the animal, and to look about me, among the vile haunts which I now habitually frequented, for another pet of the same species, and of somewhat similar appearance, with which to supply its place.

One night as I sat, half stupified, in a den for more than infamy, my attention was suddenly drawn to some black object, reposing upon the head of one of the immense hogsheads of Gin, or of Rum, which constituted the chief furniture of the apartment. I had been looking steadily at the top of this hogshead for some minutes, and what now caused me surprise was the fact that I had not sooner perceived the object thereupon. I approached it, and touched it with my hand. It was a black cat—a very large one—fully as large as Pluto, and closely resembling him in every respect but one. Pluto had not a white hair upon any portion of his body; but **22** this cat had a large, although indefinite splotch of white, covering nearly the whole region of the breast.

Upon my touching him, he immediately arose, purred loudly, rubbed against my hand, and appeared delighted with my notice. This, then, was the very creature of which I was in search. I at once offered to purchase it of the landlord; but this person made no claim to it—knew nothing of it—had never seen it before.

I continued my caresses, and, when I prepared to go home, the animal evinced a disposition to accompany me. I permitted it to do so; occasionally stooping and patting it as I proceeded. When it reached the house it domesticated. itself at once, and became immediately a great favorite with my wife.

For my own part, I soon found a dislike to it arising within me. This was just the reverse of what I had anticipated; but I know not how or why it was—its evident fondness for myself rather disgusted and annoyed. By slow degrees, these feelings of disgust and annoyance rose into the bitterness of hatred. I avoided the creature; a certain sense of shame, and the remembrance of my former deed of cruelty, preventing me from physically abusing it. I did not, for some weeks, strike, or otherwise violently ill use it; but gradually—very gradually—I came to look upon it with unutterable loathing, and to flee silently from its odious presence, as from the breath of a pestilence.

What added, no doubt, to my hatred of the beast, was the discovery, on the morning after I brought it home, that, like Pluto, it also had been deprived of one of its eyes. This circumstance, however, only endeared it to my wife, who, as I have already said, possessed, in a high degree, that humanity

22 "Fancy" is another catchword in Poe's tales, the sign of an unbalanced mind, emphasized here by the narrator's search for a replacement for the hated Pluto. See "Ligeia," note 53.

22 The shape of the blotch is undefined (as in a Rorshach test), and so the "change" recorded by the narrator later on may be only in his imagination.

The new cat is black and white, while Pluto was all black. This in itself would be cause enough for the narrator's disturbance, for it contradicts his either/or view of the world.

of feeling which had once been my distinguishing trait, and the source of many of my simplest and purest pleasures.

With my aversion to this cat, however, its partiality for myself seemed to increase. It followed my footsteps with a pertinacity which it would be difficult to make the reader comprehend. Whenever I sat, it would crouch beneath my chair, or spring upon my knees, covering me with its loathsome caresses. If I arose to walk it would get between my feet and thus nearly throw me down, or, fastening its long and sharp claws in my dress, clamber, in this manner, to my breast. At such times, although I longed to destroy it with a blow, I was yet withheld from so doing, partly by a memory of my former crime, but chiefly—let me confess it at once—by absolute *dread* of the beast.   **23**

This dread was not exactly a dread of physical evil—and yet I should be at a loss how otherwise to define it. I am almost ashamed to own—yes, even in this felon's cell, I am almost ashamed to own—that the terror and horror with which the animal inspired me, had been heightened by one of the merest chimæras it would be possible to conceive. My wife had called my attention, more than once, to the character of the mark of white hair, of which I have spoken, and which constituted the sole visible difference between the strange beast and the one I had destroyed. The reader will remember that this mark, although large, had been originally very indefinite; but, by slow degrees—degrees nearly imperceptible, and which for a long time my Reason struggled to reject as fanciful—it had, at length, assumed a rigorous distinctness of outline. It was now the representation of an object that I shudder to name—and for this, above all, I loathed, and dreaded, and would have rid myself of the monster *had I dared*—it was now, I say, the image of a hideous—of a ghastly thing—of the GALLOWS!—oh, mournful and terrible engine of Horror and of Crime—of Agony and of Death!

And now was I indeed wretched beyond the wretchedness of mere Humanity. And *a brute beast*—whose fellow I had contemptuously destroyed—*a brute beast* to work out for *me*—for me a man, fashioned in the image of the High God—so much of insufferable wo! Alas! neither by day nor by night   **24** knew I the blessing of Rest any more! During the former the creature left me no moment alone; and, in the latter, I started, hourly, from dreams of unutterable fear, to find the hot breath of *the thing* upon my face, and its vast weight—an incarnate Night-Mare that I had no power to shake off—incumbent eternally upon my *heart!*

Beneath the pressure of torments such as these, the feeble remnant of the good within me succumbed. Evil thoughts became my sole intimates—the darkest and most evil of thoughts. The moodiness of my usual temper increased to hatred of all things and of all mankind; while, from the sudden, frequent, and ungovernable outbursts of a fury to which I now blindly abandoned myself, my uncomplaining wife, alas! was the most usual and the most patient of sufferers.

One day she accompanied me, upon some household errand,

23 The cat hardly seems real, but, rather, a supernatural being. In *Letters on Demonology* (1830), Sir Walter Scott tells about a lawyer who explains to his doctor: "I found myself . . . embarrassed by the presence of a large cat, which came and disappeared I could not exactly tell how. . . . I was compelled to regard it . . . [as having] no existence save in my deranged visual organs, or depraved imagination."

The second cat is no doubt real, but the narrator's viewpoint gives it a supernatural quality.

24 Again he attempts to separate himself from the brute, reasoning that because he is a creation of God, he is thus Godlike. He dooms himself because he cannot comprehend his own brute nature, which is also a part of that God-created self.

into the cellar of the old building which our poverty compelled us to inhabit. The cat followed me down the steep stairs, and, nearly throwing me headlong, exasperated me to madness. Uplifting an axe, and forgetting, in my wrath, the childish dread which had hitherto stayed my hand, I aimed a blow at the animal which, of course, would have proved instantly fatal had it descended as I wished. But this blow was arrested by the hand of my wife. Goaded, by the interference, into a rage more than demoniacal, I withdrew my arm from her grasp and buried the axe in her brain. She fell dead upon the spot, without a groan.

This hideous murder accomplished, I set myself forthwith, and with entire deliberation, to the task of concealing the body. I knew that I could not remove it from the house, either by day or by night, without the risk of being observed by the neighbors. Many projects entered my mind. At one period I thought of cutting the corpse into minute fragments, and destroying them by fire. At another, I resolved to dig a grave for it in the floor of the cellar. Again, I deliberated about casting it in the well in the yard—about packing it in a box, as if merchandise, with the usual arrangements, and so getting a porter to take it from the house. Finally I hit upon what I considered a far better expedient than either of these. I determined to wall it up in the cellar—as the monks of the middle ages are recorded to have walled up their victims.

For a purpose such as this the cellar was well adapted. Its walls were loosely constructed, and had lately been plastered throughout with a rough plaster, which the dampness of the atmosphere had prevented from hardening. Moreover, in one of the walls was a projection, caused by a false chimney, or fireplace, that had been filled up, and made to resemble the rest of the cellar. I made no doubt that I could readily displace the bricks at this point, insert the corpse, and wall the whole up as before, so that no eye could detect anything suspicious.

And in this calculation I was not deceived. By means of a crow-bar I easily dislodged the bricks, and, having carefully deposited the body against the inner wall, I propped it in that position, while, with little trouble, I relaid the whole structure as it originally stood. Having procured mortar, sand, and hair, with every possible precaution, I prepared a plaster which could not be distinguished from the old, and with this I very carefully went over the new brick-work. When I had finished, I felt satisfied that all was right. The wall did not present the slightest appearance of having been disturbed. The rubbish on the floor was picked up with the minutest care. I looked around triumphantly, and said to myself—"Here at least, then, my labor has not been in vain."

My next step was to look for the beast which had been the cause of so much wretchedness; for I had, at length, firmly resolved to put it to death. Had I been able to meet with it, at the moment, there could have been no doubt of its fate; but it appeared that the crafty animal had been alarmed at the violence of my previous anger, and forebore to present iself in my present mood. It is impossible to describe, or to

25 "Is the narrator overcome with remorse, prostrate with grief? Does he weep, does he lament the terrible accident? Not at all. "This hideous murder accomplished, . . ." This hideous *murder!* As though he can now admit it has been his unacknowledged purpose all along. How more plainly, without violating the dynamics of his tale, could Poe have told us that from the first the cat had been but a displacement of the wife!" (Daniel Hoffman, *Poe Poe Poe Poe Poe Poe Poe,* Doubleday, 1972; pp. 232–33)

When he was young, Richard Wright set fire to his grandmother's house, starting with the white curtains, and later hanged a kitten with a string, apparently as a gesture of resentment against his father. No wonder he was so impressed by Poe when he read "The Black Cat." Poe's tale pops up in Wright's *Native Son* (1940), where a cat owned by a character named Bigger is said to have the eyes of justice. When they turn their gaze on Bigger, they seem to be "two green pools—pools of association and guilt—staring at him from a white blur that sat perched upon the edge of the trunk." (Harper & Bros., 1940; p. 78)

And later, after a particularly violent murder: "It was the white cat and its round green eyes gazed past him at the white face hanging limply from the fiery furnace door. God! He closed his mouth and swallowed. Should he catch the cat and put it into the furnace too? He made a move. The cat stood up; its white fur bristled; its back arched. He tried to grab it and it bounded past him with a long wail of fear." (P. 79)

When newspapermen are searching the premesis for clues, the animal jumps onto Bigger's shoulders, and he is certain that "the cat had given him away, had pointed him out as the murderer of Mary. He tried to lift the cat down, but the claws clutched the coat. The silver lightning flashed in his eyes and he knew that the men had taken pictures of him with the cat poised upon his shoulder."

26 Poe seems to have taken a strong interest in bricks (see "The Cask of Amontillado"). In *Scribner's Magazine,* November 1875, R. T. P. Allen, of the West Point class of 1834 and superintendent of the Military Institute at Farmdale, Kentucky, gives an account of seeing Poe working once in a Baltimore brickyard.

imagine, the deep, the blissful sense of relief which the absence of the detested creature occasioned in my bosom. It did not make its appearance during the night—and thus for one night at least, since its introduction into the house, I soundly and tranquilly slept; aye, *slept* even with the burden of murder upon my soul!

The second and the third day passed, and still my tormentor came not. Once again I breathed as a freeman. The monster, in terror, had fled the premises forever! I should behold it no more! My happiness was supreme! The guilt of my dark deed disturbed me but little. Some few inquiries had been made, but these had been readily answered. Even a search had been instituted—but of course nothing was to be discovered. I looked upon my future felicity as secured.

Upon the fourth day of the assassination, a party of the police came, very unexpectedly, into the house, and proceeded again to make rigorous investigation of the premises. Secure, **27** however, in the inscrutability of my place of concealment, I felt no embarrassment whatever. The officers bade me accompany them in their search. They left no nook or corner unexplored. At length, for the third or fourth time, they descended into the cellar. I quivered not in a muscle. My heart beat calmly as that of one who slumbers in innocence.

27 Where have the police come from, and why? Have others known the narrator is unbalanced and noticed the absence of his wife? Or did somebody hear her scream? Poe doesn't say, probably because it is not important to the story—and certainly not important to the narrator's view.

The corpse, already greatly decayed and clotted with gore, stood erect before the eyes of the spectators. *Illustration by Hans Meyer, early-twentieth century*

28 Compare his bravado with that of the narrator of "The Tell-Tale Heart."

29 "Wife of my bosom," which also appears in "Ligeia," is an allusion to Deuteronomy 13:6 and 28:54.

30 Pluto sank his fangs into the narrator earlier in the tale, so that there is a purposeful parallel between the narrator's concept of the Devil and his perception of the cat.

31 "Finally . . . the illumination or insight that his catastrophe should force upon the narrator never comes. Perversely convinced that what has happened to him lacks cause and effect, he betrays almost complete moral insensitivity even as he is about to be executed by the agents of the very law he has flouted and attempted to explain away," says James Gargano. (P. 93)

In "The Black Cat" the narrator is not interested in the truth of his situation, but only in attempting to convince the reader that the rationalizations he offers are true. When a Poe narrator tries to impress his point of view on the outside world, he succeeds only in making clear his real motivations. After all, it is one thing to do a perverse thing once, but to do perverse things continually is something else again.

Critics have made much of this tale. Some see the narrator's attack on the cat as an attack on his own soul, because in a larger sense the animal (basic instinct), coupled with the rational, equals the soul. Others see the ending as symbolic of the triumph of the amoral self—the brute beast in himself, which he hoped to escape, is there all the time.

"Since the instincts and their wild and savage components form the primitive subsoil of the human psyche," writes Marie Bonaparte, "Poe was right in asserting 'perverseness'—here meaning the compulsion to gratify the instincts—to be one of our prime, basic endowments, and to swear it by his similarly endowed soul" (pp. 462–63). She points out that "the genital function was too repressed in Poe for us to find it openly expressed in its perversity," but she nonetheless interprets the story in terms of castration fears, birth anxiety, fear of conscience, and finally death anxiety.

I walked the cellar from end to end. I folded my arms upon my bosom, and roamed easily to and fro. The police were thoroughly satisfied and prepared to depart. The glee at my heart was too strong to be restrained. I burned to say if but one word, by way of triumph, and to render doubly sure their assurance of my guiltlessness.

"Gentlemen," I said at last, as the party ascended the steps, "I delight to have allayed your suspicions. I wish you all **28** health, and a little more courtesy. By the bye, gentlemen, this—this is a very well constructed house." [In the rabid desire to say something easily, I scarcely knew what I uttered at all.]—"I may say an *excellently* well constructed house. These walls—are you going, gentlemen?—these walls are solidly put together," and here, through the mere phrenzy of bravado, I rapped heavily, with a cane which I held in my hand, upon that very portion of the brick-work behind which **29** stood the corpse of the wife of my bosom.

But may God shield and deliver me from the fangs of the **30** Arch-Fiend! No sooner had the reverberation of my blows sunk into silence, than I was answered by a voice from within the tomb!—by a cry, at first muffled and broken, like the sobbing of a child, and then quickly swelling into one long, loud, and continuous scream, utterly anomalous and inhuman—a howl—a wailing shriek, half of horror and half of triumph, such as might have arisen only out of hell, conjointly from the throats of the damned in their agony and of the demons that exult in the damnation.

Of my own thoughts it is folly to speak. Swooning, I staggered to the opposite wall. For one instant the party upon the stairs remained motionless, through extremity of terror and of awe. In the next, a dozen stout arms were toiling at the wall. It fell bodily. The corpse, already greatly decayed and clotted with gore, stood erect before the eyes of the spectators. Upon its head, with red extended mouth and solitary eye of fire, sat the hideous beast whose craft had seduced me into murder, and whose informing voice had consigned me to the **31** hangman. I had walled the monster up within the tomb!

THE PREMATURE BURIAL

First published in the Philadelphia *Dollar Newspaper*, July 31, 1844.

Anyone who has read "Loss of Breath," "Ligeia," "The Fall of the House of Usher," "Berenice," "Morella," and *The Narrative of Arthur Gordon Pym* is aware of the fascination that live burial had for Poe.

One reason may have been his apparent fear of the dark. Susan Archer Talley Weiss, who knew Poe in his later years, said that a friend of hers who had gone to school with Poe spoke of "his timidity in regard to being alone at night, and his belief in and fear of the supernatural. She had heard Poe say, when grown, that the most horrible thing he could imagine as a boy was to feel an ice-cold hand laid upon his face in a pitch-dark room when alone at night; or to awaken in semi-darkness and see an evil face gazing close into his own; and that these fancies had so haunted him that he would often keep his head under the bed-covering until nearly suffocated." (*Home Life of Poe*, 1907; p. 29)

While the story seems to jibe with the ending of "The Premature Burial," Poe's childhood fears seem no more unusual than most people's. Marie Bonaparte suggests that the fear comes from a womb fantasy, which instead of exhibiting "calm, gentleness and blissful well-being [becomes] the anxiety-phantasm *in excelsis*. This it is, too, which lies at the roots of various claustrophobias and which, again, is expressed in that most fearful of all instances of morbid anxiety, fear of premature burial." (p. 586)

While rather farfetched today, premature burial did occur occasionally in Poe's day, although not to the extent one would think after reading his tales on the subject. Some instances are recorded in George Alfred Walker's *Gatherings from Grave Yards* (1839) [reprinted by Arno Press, 1977], apparently due to a lack of sophisticated medical equipment. In order to avoid this problem, a "life-preserving coffin" was invented in 1843, mentioned by N. P. Willis in the *New Mirror* of November 18, so constructed as to give the victim air and a means to signal to those above ground that he was alive.

The story was filmed in 1962 by Roger Corman, with elements from "Berenice" added to the production, which starred Ray Milland, Hazel Court, Richard Ney, Heather Angel, and Alan Napier. One can discern Poesque plot elements and details in *The Crime of Dr. Crespi* (1935), with Erich von Stroheim, and *Horror* (also *The Blancheville Monster*), a 1963 Spanish-Italian production, which borrows heavily from other Poe stories.

There are certain themes of which the interest is all-absorbing, but which are too entirely horrible for the purposes of legitimate fiction. These the mere romanticist must eschew, **1** if he do not wish to offend, or to disgust. They are with propriety handled only when the severity and majesty of truth sanctify and sustain them. We thrill, for example, with the most intense of "pleasurable pain" over the accounts of the **2** Passage of the Beresina, of the Earthquake at Lisbon, of the Plague at London, of the Massacre of St. Bartholomew, or of the stifling of the hundred and twenty-three prisoners in the Black Hole at Calcutta. But, in these accounts, it is the fact— **3**

1 The underlying black humor of the tale is present from the start. The narrator tells us that there are certain ideas too horrible to be told, and that his story is one of them—and then proceeds to tell us every loving detail!

Friedrich Schlegel (1772–1829) first set down the words "grotesque" and "arabesque" in the sense in which Poe later used them. For Schlegel, the darker, more ominous aspects of the grotesque are the key to the innermost secrets of existence. For Poe, "grotesque" refers to those terrible, inexplicable, incomprehensible, bizarre, fantastic, and often nocturnal events that bring us face to face with both the mysteries of the universe and our own unconscious.

2 "And painful pleasure turns to pleasing pain" (*The Faerie Queen*, III, 10, 60).

Writer L. Sprague DeCamp answers the question of why people like to read "stories of horror, terror, disaster, doom and despair" by pointing out the words of Joseph Addison (1672–1719):

"The two leading Passions which the more serious Parts of Poetry endeavour to stir up in us, are Terror and Pity. And here, by the way, one would wonder how it comes to pass, that such Passions as are very unpleasant at all other times, are very agreeable when excited by proper Description. . . .

"If we consider, therefore, the Nature of this pleasure, we shall find that it does not arise so properly from the Description of what is Terrible, as from the Reflection we make on our selves at the time of reading it. When we look on such hideous Objects, we are not a little pleased to think we are in no Danger of them. We consider them at the same time, as Dreadful and Harmless; so that the more frightful Appearance they make, the greater is the pleasure we receive from the Sense of our own Safety. In short, we look upon the Terrors of a description, with the same Curiosity and Satisfaction that we survey a dead Monster." (*Lovecraft*, Ballantine, 1976; p. 153).

3 The Berezina River, near Minsk, flows into the Dnieper. Near Borisov in November of 1812 the remnants of Napoleon's Grand Army, under heavy Russian attack, lost twenty-thousand men and yet saved Napoleon and his remaining forces from capture.

The city of Lisbon was almost destroyed by an earthquake in 1755, which took more than thirty-thousand lives. Voltaire mentions it in *Candide* as an almost unimaginable catastrophe.

The Plague of London was actually the last (1665) of several plagues to hit the city over three centuries, but it is the best-remembered, probably due to Daniel Defoe's highly fictionalized account, *A Journal of the Plague Year* (1722). Defoe's book is chock-full of horror, death, and suffering.

The St. Bartholomew's Day Massacre took place in August 1572, when Charles IX ordered the murder of the French Huguenot Protestants, upon the advice of his mother, Catherine de Médicis, and the Duc d'Anjou (later Henri III). The massacre spread from Paris into other sections of France, and the result was the resumption of civil war.

The Black Hole of Calcutta refers to the small, stifling room in which the Nawab of Bengal imprisoned the British garrison of Calcutta, after he had captured the city. Most of the men suffocated, and the British reacted with more force, retaking the city in 1757.

4 The archaic (and poetic) spelling of "woe" indicates the narrator's rather overdramatic nature, as it does in other Poe tales.

5 The narrator is building his case hand over fist, and we may assent to his statements before we have a chance to realize there *might* be some more horrible fates.

it is the reality—it is the history which excites. As inventions, we should regard them with simple abhorrence.

I have mentioned some few of the more prominent and august calamities on record; but in these it is the extent, not less than the character of the calamity, which so vividly impresses the fancy. I need not remind the reader that, from the long and weird catalogue of human miseries, I might have selected many individual instances more replete with essential suffering than any of these vast generalities of disaster. The **4** true wretchedness, indeed,—the ultimate wo,—is particular, not diffuse. That the ghastly extremes of agony are endured by man the unit, and never by man the mass—for this let us thank a merciful God!

To be buried while alive is, beyond question, the most terrific of these extremes which has ever fallen to the lot of **5** mere mortality. That it has frequently, very frequently, so fallen will scarcely be denied by those who think. The boundaries which divide Life from Death are at best shadowy and vague. Who shall say where the one ends, and where the other begins? We know that there are diseases in which occur total cessations of all the apparent functions of vitality, and yet in which these cessations are merely suspensions, properly so called. They are only temporary pauses in the incomprehensible mechanism. A certain period elapses, and some unseen mysterious principle again sets in motion the magic pinions and the wizard wheels. The silver cord was not for ever loosed,

"The Premature Burial." *Illustration by Aubrey Beardsley*

nor the golden bowl irreparably broken. But where, meantime, **6** was the soul? **7**

Apart, however, from the inevitable conclusion, *a priori* that such causes must produce such effects,—that the well-known occurrence of such cases of suspended animation must naturally give rise, now and then, to premature interments,—apart from this consideration, we have the direct testimony of medical and ordinary experience to prove that a vast number of such interments have actually taken place. I might refer at once, if necessary, to a hundred well-authenticated instances. One of very remarkable character, and of which the circumstances may be fresh in the memory of some of my readers, occurred, not very long ago, in the neighboring city of Baltimore, where it occasioned a painful, intense, and widely-extended excitement. The wife of one of the most respectable **8** citizens—a lawyer of eminence and a member of Congress—was seized with a sudden and unaccountable illness, which completely baffled the skill of her physicians. After much suffering she died, or was supposed to die. No one suspected, indeed, or had reason to suspect, that she was not actually dead. She presented all the ordinary appearances of death. The face assumed the usual pinched and sunken outline. The lips were of the usual marble pallor. The eyes were lustreless. There was no warmth. Pulsation had ceased. For three days the body was preserved unburied, during which it had acquired a stony rigidity. The funeral, in short, was hastened, on account of the rapid advance of what was supposed to be decomposition.

The lady was deposited in her family vault, which, for three subsequent years, was undisturbed. At the expiration of this **9** term it was opened for the reception of a sarcophagus;—but, alas! how fearful a shock awaited the husband, who, personally, threw open the door! As its portals swung outwardly back, some white-apparelled object fell rattling within his arms. It was the skeleton of his wife in her yet unmoulded shroud.

A careful investigation rendered it evident that she had revived within two days after her entombment; that her **10** struggles within the coffin had caused it to fall from a ledge, or shelf, to the floor, where it was so broken as to permit her escape. A lamp which had been accidentally left, full of oil, within the tomb, was found empty; it might have been exhausted, however, by evaporation. On the uppermost of the steps which led down into the dread chamber was a large fragment of the coffin, with which, it seemed that she had endeavored to arrest attention by striking the iron door. While thus occupied, she probably swooned, or possibly died, through sheer terror; and, in falling, her shroud became **11** entangled in some iron-work which projected interiorly. Thus she remained, and thus she rotted, erect.

In the year 1810, a case of living inhumation happened in France, attended with circumstances which go far to warrant the assertion that truth is, indeed, stranger than fiction. The **12** heroine of the story was a Mademoiselle Victorine Lafourcade, a young girl of illustrious family, of wealth, and of great

6 "Or ever the silver cord be loosed, or the golden bowl be broken, or the pitcher be broken at the fountain, or the wheel broken at the cistern. Then shall the dust return to the earth as it was: and the spirit shall return unto God who gave it." (Ecclesiastes 12:6–7). See also Poe's poem *Lenore:* "Ah, broken is the golden bowl. . . ."

7 The idea that the soul could roam free when the body was in a coma or other unconscious state is an important part of "A Tale of the Ragged Mountains" and Poe's other tales of metempsychosis.

8 A similar story appears in the Lancaster (Pennsylvania) *Democrat* December 5, 1845.

9 Compare with the interment of Madeline Usher.

10 Obviously, the body had not been embalmed.
"The difference between the end of a weak life, and the commencement of death, is so small, and the uncertainty of the signs of the latter is so well established, that we can scarcely suppose undertakers capable of distinguishing an apparent from a real death" (*Gatherings from Grave Yards*, p. 192).

11 More likely by asphyxiation, since the lamp left burning could easily use up all the available oxygen if there was no ventilation.

12 Poe's source here may be a story in the Philadelphia *Casket*, September 1827, entitled "The Lady Buried Alive," which in turn admits to borrowing from two older stories, one from Domenico Maria Manni (1690–1788) and the other from Gayot de Pitavol's *Causes Célèbres et intéressantes*, vol. XII, (1737).
As for the names, they are all Poe's invention, as is the date.

13 Why she didn't suffocate is not explained; perhaps she has learned Madeline Usher's secret.

14 Smelling salts (ammonia). In *Gatherings from Grave Yards*, G. A. Walker writes: "Coldness, heaviness of the body, a leaden livid colour, with a yellowness in the visage, are all very uncertain signs. M. Zimmerman observed them all, upon the body of a criminal, who fainted through the dread of punishment, which he had merited. He was shaken, dragged about, and turned in the same manner as dead bodies are, without the least signs of resistance, and yet, at the end of twenty-four hours, he was recalled to life, by means of the volatile alkali." (Pp. 192–93)

15 No such journal has been traced to Leipzig, although there was a *Zeitschrift für Chirurgen* in Poland in 1841–46. No one, however, has traced Poe's story to any of its issues, and so it may stem from a newspaper article that mentioned a German source.

16 Trepanning is the making of an opening into the skull. It has been found in evidence back to ancient times, usually made in the course of an operation to reduce pressure on the brain because of a tumor or cerebral hemorrhage.

personal beauty. Among her numerous suitors was Julien Bossuet, a poor *litterateur*, or journalist, of Paris. His talents and general amiability had recommended him to the notice of the heiress, by whom he seems to have been truly beloved; but her pride of birth decided her, finally, to reject him, and to wed a Monsieur Renelle, a banker and a diplomatist of some eminence. After marriage, however, this gentleman neglected, and, perhaps, even more positively ill-treated her. Having passed with him some wretched years, she died—at least her condition so closely resembled death as to deceive every one who saw her. She was buried—not in a vault, but in an ordinary grave in the village of her nativity. Filled with despair, and still inflamed by the memory of a profound attachment, the lover journeys from the capital to the remote province in which the village lies, with the romantic purpose of disinterring the corpse, and possessing himself of its luxuriant tresses. He reaches the grave. At midnight he unearths the coffin, opens it, and is in the act of detaching the hair, when he is arrested by the unclosing of the beloved

13 eyes. In fact, the lady had been buried alive. Vitality had not altogether departed, and she was aroused by the caresses of her lover from the lethargy which had been mistaken for death. He bore her frantically to his lodgings in the village. He employed certain powerful restoratives suggested by no

14 little medical learning. In fine, she revived. She recognized her preserver. She remained with him until, by slow degrees, she fully recovered her original health. Her woman's heart was not adamant, and this last lesson of love sufficed to soften it. She bestowed it upon Bossuet. She returned no more to her husband, but, concealing from him her resurrection, fled with her lover to America. Twenty years afterward, the two returned to France, in the persuasion that time had so greatly altered the lady's appearance that her friends would be unable to recognize her. They were mistaken, however; for, at the first meeting, Monsieur Renelle did actually recognize and make claim to his wife. This claim she resisted, and a judicial tribunal sustained her in her resistance, deciding that the peculiar circumstances, with the long lapse of years, had extinguished, not only equitably, but legally, the authority of the husband.

15   The "Chirurgical Journal" of Leipsic, a periodical of high authority and merit, which some American bookseller would do well to translate and republish, records in a late number a very distressing event of the character in question.

    An officer of artillery, a man of gigantic stature and of robust health, being thrown from an unmanageable horse, received a very severe contusion upon the head, which rendered him insensible at once; the skull was slightly fractured, but no

16 immediate danger was apprehended. Trepanning was accomplished successfully. He was bled, and many other of the ordinary means of relief were adopted. Gradually, however, he fell into a more and more hopeless state of stupor, and, finally, it was thought that he died.

The weather was warm, and he was buried with indecent haste in one of the public cemeteries. His funeral took place on Thursday. On the Sunday following, the grounds of the cemetery were, as usual, much thronged with visitors, and about noon an intense excitement was created by the declaration of a peasant that, while sitting upon the grave of the officer, he had distinctly felt a commotion of the earth, as if occasioned by some one struggling beneath. At first little attention was paid to the man's asseveration; but his evident **17** terror, and the dogged obstinacy with which he persisted in his story, had at length their natural effect upon the crowd. Spades were hurriedly procured, and the grave, which was shamefully shallow, was in a few minutes so far thrown open that the head of its occupant appeared. He was then seemingly dead; but he sat nearly erect within his coffin, the lid of which, in his furious struggles, he had partially uplifted.

He was forthwith conveyed to the nearest hospital, and there pronounced to be still living, although in an asphytic condition. After some hours he revived, recognized individuals **18** of his acquaintance, and, in broken sentences spoke of his agonies in the grave.

From what he related, it was clear that he must have been conscious of life for more than an hour, while inhumed, before lapsing into insensibility. The grave was carelessly and loosely filled with an exceedingly porous soil; and thus some air was necessarily admitted. He heard the footsteps of the crowd overhead, and endeavored to make himself heard in turn. It was the tumult within the grounds of the cemetery, he said, which appeared to awaken him from a deep sleep, but no sooner was he awake than he became fully aware of the awful horrors of his position.

This patient, it is recorded, was doing well, and seemed to be in a fair way of ultimate recovery, but fell a victim to the quackeries of medical experiment. The galvanic battery was **19** applied, and he suddenly expired in one of those ecstatic paroxysms which, occasionally, it superinduces.

The mention of the galvanic battery, nevertheless, recalls to my memory a well-known and very extraordinary case in point, where its action proved the means of restoring to animation a young attorney of London, who had been interred for two days. This occurred in 1831, and created, at the time, a very profound sensation wherever it was made the subject of converse.   **20**

The patient, Mr. Edward Stapleton, had died, apparently, of typhus fever, accompanied with some anomalous symptoms which had excited the curiosity of his medical attendants. Upon his seeming decease, his friends were requested to sanction a *post-mortem* examination, but declined to permit it. As often happens, when such refusals are made, the practitioners resolved to disinter the body and dissect it at leisure, in private. Arrangements were easily effected with some of the numerous corps of bodysnatchers with which **21** London abounds; and, upon the third night after the funeral,

17 Emphatic declaration

18 A condition of suspended animation produced by a deficiency of oxygen in the blood. N. P. Willis, in the New York *Mirror*, November 18, 1843, says that "asphyxia, or a suspension of life, with all the appearances of death, is certified to in many instances, and carefully provided for in some countries."

G. A. Walker says from his vantage point in 1839: "On many occasions, in all places, too much precipitation attends this last office, or if not precipitation, a neglect of due precautions, in regard to the body in general; indeed, the most improper treatment that can be imagined, is adopted, and many a person made to descend into the grave before he has sighed his last breath" op. cit., (p. 191). In England, he adds, care is taken "to preclude all apprehensions of premature interment."

19 See "Loss of Breath," note 25.

20 "The Buried Alive," which appeared in *Blackwood's Magazine*, October 1821, is the source. As "The Dead Alive," Poe mentions it in "How to Write a Blackwood Article." There, he uses only the bare bones, adding to it a date, the hero's name, the exhumation results, and the ending.

21 Note Roderick Usher's same wariness of physicians, which prompts him (he says) to bury Madeline where no one can get at her. It was not until 1857 that Britain passed the Burial Act, which made it a misdemeanor to disinter any human remains from any place of burial without lawful authority.

"In December 1960 . . . a man aged 33 was charged with removing a corpse from a grave in a cemetery without lawful authority. He told the police that when his mother died, in October, he had tried to revive her with electric treatment. He failed and she was buried. After attending the funeral he decided to have another attempt to revive her. That afternoon he hired a car for the day and . . . returned to the cemetery, jumped over the wall and opened the grave. He then opened the coffin and removed his mother's body. . . . He then started electric treatment by connecting her foot to the household circuit, but it appears a short circuit occurred. He believed he was doing the best for her. The man was later found to be suffering from mental disorder." (Polson, *The Disposal of the Dead*, 1962; p. 253).

And some people think Poe is bizarre. . . . .

the supposed corpse was unearthed from a grave eight feet deep, and deposited in the operating chamber of one of the private hospitals.

An incision of some extent had been actually made in the abdomen, when the fresh and undecayed appearance of the subject suggested an application of the battery. One experiment succeeded another, and the customary effects supervened, with nothing to characterize them in any respect, except, upon one or two occasions, a more than ordinary degree of life-likeness in the convulsive action.

It grew late. The day was about to dawn; and it was thought expedient, at length, to proceed at once to the dissection. A student, however, was especially desirous of testing a theory of his own, and insisted upon applying the battery to one of the pectoral muscles. A rough gash was made, and a wire hastily brought in contact; when the patient, with a hurried but quite unconvulsive movement, arose from the table, stepped into the middle of the floor, gazed about him uneasily for a few seconds, and then—spoke. What he said was unintelligible; but words were uttered; the syllabification was distinct. Having spoken, he fell heavily to the floor.

For some moments all were paralyzed with awe—but the urgency of the case soon restored them their presence of mind. It was seen that Mr. Stapleton was alive, although in a swoon. Upon exhibition of ether he revived and was rapidly restored to health, and to the society of his friends—from whom, however, all knowledge of his resuscitation was withheld, until a relapse was no longer to be apprehended. Their **22** wonder—their rapturous astonishment—may be conceived.

The most thrilling peculiarity of this incident, nevertheless, is involved in what Mr. S. himself asserts. He declares that at no period was he altogether insensible—that, dully and confusedly, he was aware of everything which happened to him, from the moment in which he was pronounced *dead* by his physicians, to that in which he fell swooning to the floor of the hospital. "I am alive," were the uncomprehended words which, upon recognizing the locality of the dissecting-room, **23** he had endeavored, in his extremity, to utter.

It were an easy matter to multiply such histories as these—but I forbear—for, indeed, we have no need of such to establish the fact that premature interments occur. When we reflect, how very rarely, from the nature of the case, we have it in our power to detect them, we must admit that they may *frequently* occur without our cognizance. Scarcely, in truth, is a graveyard ever encroached upon, for any purpose, to any great extent, that skeletons are not found in postures which suggest the most fearful of suspicions.

Fearful indeed the suspicion—but more fearful the doom! It may be asserted, without hesitation, that *no* event is so terribly well adapted to inspire the supremeness of bodily and of mental distress, as in burial before death. The unendurable oppression of the lungs—the stifling fumes of the damp earth—the clinging to the death garments—the rigid embrace of the narrow house—the blackness of the absolute Night—the

22 In Mary Shelley's *Frankenstein* (1818) the scientist Frankenstein brings a body to life using electricity.

23 Compare with this account from G. A. Walker: "Mr. B, inhabitant of Poitiers, fell suddenly into a state resembling death; every means for bringing him back to life were used without interruption; from continued dragging, his two little fingers were dislocated, and the soles of his feet were burnt, but all these having produced no sensation in him, he was thought decidedly dead. As they were on the point of placing him in his coffin, some one recommended that he should be bled in both arms and feet, at the same time, which was immediately done, and with such success, that, to the astonishment of all, he recovered from his apparent state of death. When he had entirely recovered his senses, he declared that he had heard every word that had been said, and that his only fear was, that he would be buried alive." (P. 193, quoted from *Mémoire sur les inhumations précipitées*, 1839) silence like a sea that overwhelms—the unseen but palpable presence of the Conqueror Worm—these things, with the thoughts of the air and grass above, with memory of dear friends who would fly to save us if but informed of our fate, and with consciousness that of this fate they can *never* be informed—that out hopeless portion is that of the really dead—these considerations, I say, carry into the heart, which still palpitates, a degree of appalling and intolerable horror from which the most daring imagination must recoil. We know of nothing so agonizing upon Earth—we can dream of nothing half so hideous in the realms of the nethermost Hell. And thus all narratives upon this topic have an interest profound; an interest, nevertheless, which, through the sacred awe of the topic itself, very properly and very peculiarly depends upon our conviction of the *truth* of the matter narrated. What I have now to tell is of my own actual knowledge—of my own positive and personal experience.

For several years I had been subject to attacks of the singular disorder which physicians have agreed to term cata-lepsy, in default of a more definite title. Although both the immediate and the predisposing causes, and even the actual diagnosis, of this disease are still mysterious, its obvious and apparent character is sufficiently well understood. Its variations seem to be chiefly of degree. Sometimes the patient lies, for a day only, or even for a shorter period, in a species of exaggerated lethargy. He is senseless and externally motion-less; but the pulsation of the heart is still faintly perceptible; some traces of warmth remain; a slight color lingers within the centre of the cheek; and, upon application of a mirror to the lips, we can detect a torpid, unequal, and vacillating action of the lungs. Then again the duration of the trance is for weeks—even for months; while the closest scrutiny, and the most rigorous medical tests, fail to establish any material distinction between the state of the sufferer and what we conceive of absolute death. Very usually he is saved from premature interment solely by the knowledge of his friends that he has been previously subject to catalepsy, by the consequent suspicion excited, and, above all, by the non-appearance of decay. The advances of the malady are, luckily, gradual. The first manifestations, although marked, are une-quivocal. The fits grow successively more and more distinctive, and endure each for a longer term than the preceding. In this lies the principal security from inhumation. The unfortunate whose *first* attack should be of the extreme character which is occasionally seen, would almost inevitably be consigned alive to the tomb.

My own case differed in no important particular from those mentioned in medical books. Sometimes, without any apparent cause, I sank, little by little, into a condition of semi-syncope, or half swoon; and, in this condition, without pain, without ability to stir, or, strictly speaking, to think, but with a dull lethargic consciousness of life and of the presence of those who surrounded my bed, I remained, until the crisis of the disease restored me, suddenly, to perfect sensation. At other

24 "Conqueror Worm" appears also in "Ligeia."

25 The narrator overstates his case so that Poe can set up his obsession with the subject of premature burial in order to justify the ending of the tale.

26 See "The Fall of the House of Usher," note 32.

27 True catalepsy is not usually of long duration; this sounds more like coma.

28 A fainting spell, lapsing into unconsciousness

times I was quickly and impetuously smitten. I grew sick, and numb, and chilly, and dizzy, and so fell prostrate at once. Then, for weeks, all was void, and black, and silent, and Nothing became the universe. Total annihilation could be no more. From these latter attacks I awoke, however, with a gradation slow in proportion to the suddenness of the seizure. Just as the day dawns to the friendless and houseless beggar who roams the streets throughout the long desolate winter night—just so tardily—just so wearily—just so cheerily came back the light of the Soul to me.

Apart from the tendency to trance, however, my general health appeared to be good; nor could I perceive that it was at all affected by the one prevalent malady—unless, indeed, an idiosyncrasy in my ordinary *sleep* may be looked upon as superinduced. Upon awaking from slumber, I could never gain, at once, thorough possession of my senses, and always remained, for many minutes, in much bewilderment and perplexity—the mental faculties in general, but the memory in especial, being in a condition of absolute abeyance.

In all that I endured there was no physical suffering, but of moral distress an infinitude. My fancy grew charnel. I **29** talked "of worms, of tombs, and epitaphs." I was lost in reveries of death, and the idea of premature burial held continual possession of my brain. The ghastly Danger to which I was subjected haunted me day and night. In the former, the torture of meditation was excessive; in the latter, supreme. When the grim Darkness overspread the Earth, then, with every horror of thought, I shook—shook as the quivering plumes upon the hearse. When Nature could endure wakefulness no longer, it was with a struggle that I consented to sleep—for I shuddered to reflect that, upon awaking, I might find myself the tenant of a grave. And when, finally, I sank into slumber, it was only to rush at once into a world of phantasms, above which, with vast, sable, overshadowing wings, hovered, predominant, the one sepulchral Idea.

From the innumerable images of gloom which thus oppressed me in dreams, I select for record but a solitary vision. Methought I was immersed in a cataleptic trance of more than usual duration and profundity. Suddenly there came an icy hand upon my forehead, and an impatient, gibbering voice whispered the word "Arise!" within my ear.

I sat erect. The darkness was total. I could not see the figure of him who had aroused me. I could call to mind neither the period at which I had fallen into the trance, nor the locality in which I then lay. While I remained motionless, and busied in endeavors to collect my thoughts, the cold hand grasped me fiercely by the wrist, shaking it petulantly, while the gibbering voice said again:

"Arise! did I not bid thee arise?"

"And who," I demanded, "art thou?"

30   "I have no name in the regions which I inhabit," replied the voice, mournfully; "I was mortal, but am fiend. I was merciless, but am pitiful. Thou dost feel that I shudder. My teeth chatter as I speak, yet it is not with the chilliness of the

29 "Let's talk of graves, of worms and epitaphs" (*Richard II*, III, ii, 145).

30 Compare with the last lines of "Shadow."

night—of the night without end. But this hideousness is insufferable. How canst *thou* tranquilly sleep? I cannot rest for the cry of these great agonies. These sights are more than I can bear. Get thee up! Come with me into the outer Night, and let me unfold to thee the graves. Is not this a spectacle of wo?—Behold!"

I looked; and the unseen figure, which still grasped me by the wrist, had caused to be thrown open the graves of all mankind; and from each issued the faint phosphoric radiance of decay; so that I could see into the innermost recesses, and **31** there view the shrouded bodies in their sad and solemn slumbers with the worm. But alas! the real sleepers were fewer, by many millions, than those who slumbered not at all; and there was a feeble struggling; and there was a general and sad unrest; and from out the depths of the countless pits there came a melancholy rustling from the garments of the buried. And of those who seemed tranquilly to repose, I saw that a vast number had changed, in a greater or less degree, the rigid and uneasy position in which they had originally been entombed. And the voice again said to me as I gazed:

"Is it not—oh! is it *not* a pitiful sight?" But, before I could find words to reply, the figure had ceased to grasp my wrist, the phosphoric lights expired, and the graves were closed with a sudden violence, while from out them arose a tumult of despairing cries, saying again: "Is it not—O, God! is it *not* a very pitiful sight?"

Phantasies such as these, presenting themselves at night, extended their terrific influence far into my waking hours. My nerves became thoroughly unstrung, and I fell a prey to perpetual horror. I hesitated to ride, or to walk, or to indulge **32** in any exercise that would carry me from home. In fact, I no longer dared trust myself out of the immediate presence of those who were aware of my proneness to catalepsy, lest, falling into one of my usual fits, I should be buried before my real condition could be ascertained. I doubted the care, the fidelity of my dearest friends. I dreaded that, in some trance **33** of more than customary duration, they might be prevailed upon to regard me as irrecoverable. I even went so far as to fear that, as I occasioned much trouble, they might be glad to consider any very protracted attack as sufficient excuse for getting rid of me altogether. It was in vain they endeavored to reassure me by the most solemn promises. I exacted the most sacred oaths, that under no circumstances they would bury me until decomposition had so materially advanced as to render further preservation impossible. And, even then, **34** my mortal terrors would listen to no reason—would accept no consolation. I entered into a series of elaborate precautions. Among other things, I had the family vault so remodelled as to admit of being readily opened from within. The slightest pressure upon a long level that extended far into the tomb would case the iron portals to fly back. There were arrangements also for the free admission of air and light, and convenient receptacles for food and water, within immediate reach of the coffin intended for my reception. This coffin was

31 Luminous bacteria may appear on decomposing flesh, just as luminous fungi produce a phosphorescent glow on the surface of rotting wood.

32 This is a classic case of hysteria, a disorder of personality that involves a pattern of emotional instability and overreaction, egocentricity, dependence upon others, and suggestibility. Because hypnotized patients could reproduce hysterical phenomena such as paralysis, deafness, or skin anesthesia, the French physician Liébeault (1823–1904) concluded that the psychological disorder of hysteria might involve some form of self-hypnosis.

33 He seems to be slipping into paranoia.

34 Concern for premature interment prompted the city of Frankfurt in 1829 to require that mortuaries be under the control of a medically trained cemetery inspector, competent in the knowledge of reviving the "dead."

"The bodies were placed in separate rooms and provision was made for those apparently dead to summon assistance. Their resuscitation was to be undertaken in a special animating room, reserved solely for that purpose; it had to be kept in order, ready at all times for immediate use. Constant watch was kept over the bodies, and no porter might leave his room until relieved. If a corpse showed any sign of life, the inspector had to be summoned.

"No body might be interred until there were unequivocal signs of decomposition. Either three nights must elapse or, in the case of an earlier disposal, the fact that decomposiion had begun had to be certified by the inspector. Similar regulations had been made in Munich in 1821." (*The Disposal of the Dead, supra,* p. 102) Similar regulations were not enacted in England until 1843.

35 The American Institute in New York held exhibits each year of new products and inventions, and in 1843 displayed a "life-preserving coffin," which N. P. Willis mentions in the New York *Mirror* that November:

" 'The life-preserving coffin' lately exhibited at the fair of the institute is so constructed as to fly open with the least stir of the occupant, and made as comfortable within as if intended for a temporary lodging. The proprietor recommends . . . a corresponding facility of exit from the vault, and arrangements for privacy, light and fresh air—in short all that would be agreeable to the *revenant* on first waking."

The narrator's "elaborate precautions" parallel some of the points made in the following note, attached to a sixteen-stanza poem, by Mrs. Seba Smith, entitled *The Life-Preserving Coffin*, in the *Columbian Lady's and Gentleman's Magazine*, November 13, 1845:

"[The coffin] is luxuriously made, softly stuffed, with an elevation for the head, like a satin pillow, and the lining of delicate white silk. In order to guard against the occurrence of a burial before life is extinct, the inventor has arranged springs and levers on its inside, whereby its inmate, by the least motion of either head or hand, will instantly cause the coffin lid to fly open. The inventor also advises families who may feel disposed to make use of his life-preserving coffin, to have their tombs or vaults constructed with a lock upon the door, that will open either from the inside or outside, and to have a key to the lock left within the tomb. He would also have the tomb provided with a bell that would be rung by its inmates."

warmly and softly padded, and was provided with a lid, fashioned upon the principle of the vault-door, with the addition of springs so contrived that the feeblest movement of the body would be sufficient to set it at liberty. Besides all this, there was suspended from the roof of the tomb, a large bell, the rope of which, it was designed, should extend through a hole in the coffin, and so be fastened to one of the hands of **35** the corpse. But, alas! what avails the vigilance against the Destiny of man? Not even these well-contrived securities sufficed to save from the uttermost agonies of living inhumation, a wretch to these agonies foredoomed!

There arrived an epoch—as often before there had arrived—in which I found myself emerging from total unconsciousness into the first feeble and indefinite sense of existence. Slowly—with a tortoise gradation—approached the faint gray dawn of the psychal day. A torpid uneasiness. An apathetic endurance of dull pain. No care—no hope—no effort. Then, after a long interval, a ringing in the ears; then, after a lapse still longer, a pricking or tingling sensation in the extremities; then a seemingly eternal period of pleasurable quiescence, during which the awakening feelings are struggling into thought; then a brief re-sinking into nonentity; then a sudden recovery. At length the slight quivering of an eyelid; and immediately thereupon, an electric shock of a terror, deadly and indefinite, which sends the blood in torrents from the temples to the heart. And now the first positive effort to think. And now the first endeavor to remember. And now a partial and evanescent success. And now the memory has so far regained its dominion, that, in some measure, I am cognizant of my state. I feel that I am not awaking from ordinary sleep. I recollect that I have been subject to catalepsy. And now, at last, as if by the rush of an ocean, my shuddering spirit is overwhelmed by the one grim Danger—by the one spectral and ever-prevalent idea.

For some minutes after this fancy possessed me, I remained without motion. And why? I could not summon courage to move. I dared not make the effort which was to satisfy me of my fate—and yet there was something at my heart which whispered me *it was sure*. Despair—such as no other species of wretchedness ever calls into being—despair alone urged me, after long irresolution, to uplift the heavy lids of my eyes. I uplifted them. It was dark—all dark. I knew that the fit was over. I knew that the crisis of my disorder had long passed. I knew that I had now fully recovered the use of my visual faculties—and yet it was dark—all dark—the intense and utter raylessness of the Night that endureth for evermore.

I endeavored to shriek; and my lips and my parched tongue moved convulsively together in the attempt—but no voice issued from the cavernous lungs, which, oppressed as if by the weight of some incumbent mountain, gasped and palpitated, with the heart, at every elaborate and struggling inspiration.

The movement of the jaws, in this effort to cry aloud, showed me that they were bound up, as is usual with the dead. I felt, too, that I lay upon some hard substance; and by something similar my sides were, also closely compressed. So far, I had not ventured to stir any of my limbs—but now I violently threw up my arms, which had been lying at length, with the wrists crossed. They struck a solid wooden substance, which extended above my person at an elevation of not more than six inches from my face. I could no longer doubt that I reposed within a coffin at last.

And now, amid all my infinite miseries, came sweetly the cherub Hope—for I thought of my precautions. I writhed, and made spasmodic exertions to force open the lid: it would not move. I felt my wrists for the bell-rope: it was not to be found. And now the Comforter fled for ever, and a still sterner Despair reigned triumphant; for I could not help perceiving the absence of the paddings which I had so carefully prepared—and then, too, there came suddenly to my nostrils the strong peculiar odor of moist earth. The conclusion was irresistible. I was *not* within the vault. I had fallen into a trance while absent from home—while among strangers—when, or how, I could not remember—and it was they who had buried me as a dog—nailed up in some common coffin—and thrust, deep, deep, and for ever, into some ordinary and nameless *grave*.

As this awful conviction forced itself, thus, into the innermost chambers of my soul, I once again struggled to cry aloud. And in this second endeavor I succeeded. A long, wild, and continuous shriek, or yell, of agony, resounded through the realms of the subterranean Night.

"Hillo! hillo, there!" said a gruff voice, in reply.

"What the devil's the matter now!" said a second.

"Get out o'that!" said a third.

"What do you mean by yowling in that ere kind of style, like a cattymount?" said a fourth; and hereupon I was seized and shaken without ceremony, for several minutes, by a junto of very rough-looking individuals. They did not arouse me from my slumber—for I was wide-awake when I screamed—but they restored me to the full possession of my memory.

This adventure occurred near Richmond, in Virginia. Accompanied by a friend, I had proceeded, upon a gunning expedition, some miles down the banks of the James River. Night approached, and we were overtaken by a storm. The cabin of a small sloop lying at anchor in the stream, and laden with garden mould, afforded us the only available shelter. We made the best of it, and passed the night on board. I slept in one of the only two berths in the vessel—and the berths of a sloop of sixty or seventy tons need scarcely be described. That which I occupied had no bedding of any kind. Its extreme width was eighteen inches. The distance of its bottom from the deck overhead was precisely the same. I found it a matter of exceeding difficulty to squeeze myself in. Nevertheless, I slept soundly; and the whole of my vision—for it was no dream, and no nightmare—arose naturally from the circumstances of my position—from my ordinary bias of thought—and from the difficulty, to which I have alluded, of collecting my senses, and especially of regaining my memory, for a long time after awaking from slumber. The men who shook me

36 This is a more successful character transformation than the one in "The Spectacles."

37 William Buchan (1729–1805) was the author of *Domestic Medicine, or The Family Physician*, first published in 1769 and into its twenty-ninth American edition by 1854.

38 *The Complaint, or Night-Thoughts on Life, Death and Immortality* (1742) was written by Edward Young (1683–1765) and was extremely popular in Poe's day—a perfect example of what we now call the graveyard school of poetry.

"The immense and long-enduring popularity of *Night-Thoughts* will not return," says George Sampson. "It is hard reading, nowadays, even for the most energetic lover of poetry." (*Concise Cambridge History of English Literature*, 1972; p. 434) Thomas Gray's *Elegy Written in a Country Churchyard* (1751) is a far less gruesome example of the graveyard school.

39 An old Celtic name, related to the Old French name for a demon, Bugibus

40 This remark places the reader in the same position the narrator formerly occupied, and the ironic tone is now directed outward.

41 Poe appears to be ahead of his time. Freud did not publish *A Case of Hysteria* until 1905, and psychologists were not always certain of the causes of neurosis until the end of the nineteenth century.

42 This paragraph is drawn from Horace Binney Wallace's *Stanley* (1838): ". . with all the ardor of desperation, he sounded passion to its depths, and raked the bottom of the gulf of sin; he explored, with the indomitable spirit of Carathis, every chamber and cavern of the earthly hell of bad delights" (II, 83–84). Also: "The passions are like those demons with whom Afrasiab sailed down the river Oxus, our safety consists in keeping them asleep; if they ever wake we are lost" (I, 124).

Carathis is the name of a wicked witch in *Vathek* (1786), who enjoys for a day the treasure of Hell before being condemned to eternal damnation. The name comes from the Greek mother of Caliph Haroun Vathek Billah (842–47), the inspiration for William Beckford's Gothic romance.

43 The legendary wicked king of Turan (now western Turkistan), who betrayed the Persian hero Rustum by means of a hidden pit bristling with spears and swords. Before he died, however, Rustum had the satisfaction of killing the villain with an arrow.

44 The Oxus (today the Amu Darya) is a 1,580-mile-long river in central Asia that flows into the Aral Sea. It figured importantly in the history of Persia and in the campaigns of Alexander the Great.

45 The Persian myths of Rustum and Afrasiab do not mention sailing down the Oxus in the company of demons; where Wallace got this allusion is not known.

The literary flimflammery here tells us that while the narrator may have learned to be less hysterical, he is still a man prone to reverie and fancies, who could find himself in another uncomfortable situation because of his overemotional nature.

The ending is appropriately upbeat, because, as Jung would tell us, the tomb is a symbol of the unconscious, and when a person returns from that forbidding and terrifying place, with luck the knowledge he has gained

were the crew of the sloop, and some laborers engaged to unload it. From the load itself came the earthy smell. The bandage about the jaws was a silk handkerchief in which I had bound up my head, in default of my customary nightcap.

The tortures endured, however, were indubitably quite equal, for the time, to those of actual sepulture. They were fearfully—they were inconceivably hideous; but out of Evil proceeded Good; for their very excess wrought in my spirit **36** an inevitable revulsion. My soul acquired tone—acquired temper. I went abroad. I took vigorous exercise. I breathed the free air of Heaven. I thought upon other subjects than **37** Death. I discarded my medical books. "Buchan" I burned. I **38** read no "Night Thoughts"—no fustian about church-yards— **39,40** no bugaboo tales—*such as this*. In short I became a new man, and lived a man's life. From that memorable night, I dismissed forever my charnel apprehensions, and with them vanished the cataleptic disorder of which, perhaps, they had been less **41** the consequence than the cause.

There are moments when, even to the sober eye of Reason, the world of our sad Humanity may assume the semblance of a Hell—but the imagination of man is no Carathis, to exlore **42** with impunity its every cavern. Alas! the grim legion of sepulchral terrors cannot be regarded as altogether fanciful— **43** but, like the Demons in whose company Afrasiab made his **44** voyage down the Oxus, they must sleep, or they will devour **45** us—they must be suffered to slumber, or we perish.

may change his life in some way. The narrator's death experience has been a dream, and dreams are the conscious mind's only door to the subconscious. The beginning of the story has shown us a man obsessed with being buried alive, but by the end, as Geoffrey Rans pointed out, "his analytical awareness of the nature of morbid fancy is made quite apparent" (*Edgar Allan Poe*, Oliver and Boyd, 1965; p. 78).

It feels good to be alive, but it feels even better to be free of obsessive fear.

THE IMP OF THE PERVERSE

First published in *Graham's Magazine,* July 1845.

Poe seems to have taken his idea from a passage in Lady Georgiana Fullerton's *Ellen Middleton* (1844): " 'The organ of destructiveness must be strong in you,' observed Mr. Escourt. . . . Again an icy chill ran through me . . . I felt that I was making an odious speech, I saw in Edward's face an expression almost of disgust. I felt that I was sinking every moment in his opinion; perhaps losing ground in his affections. . . . A spirit of reckless defiance took possession of me, and I completely lost my head. A torrent of words burst from my lips, of which I hardly knew the meaning . . . like Samson . . . I was dragging down . . . the ruin which had so long hung over my head." (Chapter 22)

Poe reviewed the novel and gave it high marks, and in fact mentions this very paragraph in another context in "Marginalia," LII. The "organ of destructiveness" of Fullerton's novel is a phrenologically termed faculty, although as such it does not exist in the head charts of the nineteenth century. Perhaps because of his decreasing support of phrenology, or perhaps to add a more darkly mysterious aspect to it, Poe chooses to rephrase it as the Imp of the Perverse.

Critics have generally given the story two interpretations. The most common is the literal one of the narrator's battle with the perverse desire to destroy himself. The Imp is taken to be a self-destructive force present in all of us but with important differences in each person according to the power of will and morality.

Another approach is to view the narrator's blaming his actions on an Imp of the Perverse as his way of avoiding responsibility for what he does. If there is any perversity here, they argue, it is in the narrator's refusal to see where the moral burden lies. Compare this with the narrator's character in "The Black Cat."

---

1 prime movers. *Primum mobile*, from the Ptolemaic system of astronomy, is applied figuratively to that "machine" which communicates motion to others, and thus to persons or ideas suggestive of complicated systems. In Ptolemaic terms, the motion of the *primum mobile* produced the alternation of day and night. Its axis was that of the equator and its extremities the poles of the heavens.

"They pass the planets seven, and pass the 'fixed' [starry sphere],/And that crystallin sphere . . . and that 'First Moved' " (*Paradise Lost*, III, 482).

2 For more on phrenology, see "Ligeia," note 10.

3 See "Some Words with a Mummy," note 36. The word seems to be used here for its evocative effects alone.

4 Performing more than required by duty

5 "Metaphysics" is the more common term. The *O.E.D.* cites Poe as first usage of this word, meaning "metaphysical philosophizing." "Metaphysician" dates from 1597.

In the consideration of the faculties and impulses—of the *prima mobilia* of the human soul, the phrenologists have failed to make room for a propensity which, although obviously existing as a radical, primitive, irreducible sentiment, has been equally overlooked by all the moralists who have preceded them. In the pure arrogance of the reason, we have all overlooked it. We have suffered its existence to escape our senses, solely through want of belief—of faith;—whether it be faith in Revelation, or faith in the Kabbala. The idea of it has never occurred to us, simply because of its supererogation. We saw no *need* of the impulse—for the propensity. We could not perceive its necesssity. We could not understand, that is to say, we could not have understood, had the notion of this *primum mobile* ever obtruded itself;—we could not have understood in what manner it might be made to further the objects of humanity, either temporal or eternal. It cannot be denied that phrenology and, in great measure, all metaphysicianism have been concocted *a priori*. The intellectual or logical man, rather than the understanding or observant man, set himself to imagine designs—to dictate purposes to God. Having thus fathomed, to his satisfaction, the intentions of Jehovah, out of these intentions he built his innumerable system of mind. In the matter of phrenology, for example, we first determined, naturally enough, that it was the design of the Deity that man should eat. We then assigned to man an organ of alimentiveness, and this organ is the scourge with **6** which the Deity compels man, will-I nill-I, into eating. **7** Secondly, having settled it to be God's will that man should continue his species, we discovered an organ of amativeness, **8** forthwith. And so with combativeness, with ideality, with **9** causality, with constructiveness,—so, in short, with every organ, whether representing a propensity, a moral sentiment, or a faculty of the pure intellect. And in these arrangements of the *principia* of human action, the Spurzheimites, whether **10,11** right or wrong, in part, or upon the whole, have but followed, in principle, the footsteps of their predecessors; deducing and establishing every thing from the preconceived destiny of man, and upon the ground of the objects of his Creator.

It would have been wiser, it would have been safer, to classify (if classify we must) upon the basis of what man usually or occasionally did, and was always occasionally doing, rather than upon the basis of what we took it for granted the Deity intended him to do. If we cannot comprehend God in his visible works, how then in his inconceivable thoughts, that call the works into being? If we cannot understand him in his objective creatures, how then in his substantive moods and phases of creation?

Induction, *a posteriori*, would have brought phrenology to admit, as an innate and primitive principle of human action, a paradoxical something, which we may call *perverseness*, for want of a more characteristic term. In the sense I intend, it is, in fact, a *mobile* without motive, a motive not *motiviert*. **12** Through its promptings we act without comprehensible object; or, if this shall be understood as a contradiction in terms, we may so far modify the proposition as to say, that through its promptings we act, for the reason that we should *not*. In theory, no reason can be more unreasonable; but, in fact, there is none more strong. With certain minds, under certain conditions, it becomes absolutely irresistible. I am not more certain that I breathe, than that the assurance of the wrong or error of any action is often the one unconquerable *force* which impels us, and alone impels us to its prosecution. Nor will this overwhelming tendency to do wrong for the wrong's sake, admit of analysis, or resolution into ulterior elements. It is a radical, a primitive impulse—elementary. It will be said, I am aware, that when we persist in acts because we feel we should *not* persist in them, our conduct is but a modification of that which ordinarily springs from the *combativeness* of phrenology. But a glance will show the fallacy of this idea. The phrenological combativeness has for its essence, the necessity of self-defence. It is our safeguard against injury. Its principle regards our well-being; and thus the desire to be well is excited simultaneously with its development. It follows,

6 The organ of Alimentiveness, according to the phrenologists, was situated at the front of the upper part of the ear, and represented appetite, relish, and greediness. "Perverted, it produces gourmandizing and gluttony, and causes dyspepsia with all its evils," writes O. S. Fowler in *The Practical Phrenologist* (1869), adding that "this faculty is more liable to perversion than any other, and excessive and fast eating occasions more sickness, and depraves the animal passions more than all other causes combined." (Pp. 90–92)

7 Willy-nilly. The meaning has changed in the interim. Originally "will-I, nill-I," meant "whether one likes it or not"; the modern usage to mean "undecided and every which way" dates to the 1880s.

8 The organ of Amativeness was situated at the back of the head, on the level of the lower part of the ear, and represented sexual love, passion, fondness, and that which attracts the opposite sex, "for the perpetuity and multiplication of all forms of life," says Fowler. "It creates in each sex admiration and love of the other; renders woman winning, persuasive, urbane, affectionate, loving and lovely, and develops all the feminine charms and graces; makes man noble in feeling and bearing; elevated in aspiration; gallant, tender and bland in manner; affectionate toward woman; highly susceptible to female charms; and clothes him with that dignity, power and persuasiveness which accompanies the masculine. Perverted, it occasions grossness and vulgarity in expression and action. . . ." (Pp. 66–67)

9 The organ of Combativeness indicated defense, courage, force, while Ideality meant love of beauty, poetry, and the sublime (see "Ligeia"). Causality meant planning, thinking, reason, and sense, while Constructiveness accounted for ingenuity and invention. All could be perverted, producing an obsessive pursuit of any of these traits.

10 Principles

11 The follower of Dr. Johann Gaspar Spurzheim, who with Dr. Franz Joseph Gall formulated the principles of phrenology. Spurzheim died in Boston in 1832.

The tone here implies that Poe may well have given up on phrenology as the answer to man's sometimes inexplicable behavior—if indeed he ever really embraced it wholeheartedly in the first place.

12 *Mobile* here means something capable of movement. *Motiviert* is German for "a reason for." To translate Poe, the sentence reads: "In the sense I intend, it [perverseness] is, in fact, something that moves without motive, a motive without a reason."

that the desire to be well must be excited simultaneously with any principle which shall be merely a modification of combativeness, but in the case of that something which I turn *perverseness*, the desire to be well is not only not aroused, but a strongly antagonistical sentiment exists.

An appeal to one's own heart is, after all, the best reply to the sophistry just noticed. No one who trustingly consults and thoroughly questions his own soul, will be disposed to deny the entire radicalness of the propensity in question. It is not more incomprehensible than distinctive. There lives no man who at some period has not been tormented, for example, by an earnest desire to tantalize a listener by circumlocution. The speaker is aware that he displeases; he has every intention to please; he is usually curt, precise, and clear; the most laconic and luminous language is struggling for utterance upon his tongue; it is only with difficulty that he restrains himself from giving it flow; he dreads and deprecates the anger of him whom he addresses; yet, the thought strikes him, that by certain involutions and parentheses this anger may be engendered. That single thought is enough. The impulse increases to a wish, the wish to a desire, the desire to an uncontrollable longing, and the longing (to the deep regret and mortification

13 of the speaker, and in defiance of all consequences) is indulged.

We have a task before us which must be speedily performed. We know that it will be ruinous to make delay. The most important crisis of our life calls, trumpet-tongued, for immediate energy and action. We glow, we are consumed with eagerness to commence the work, with the anticipation of whose glorious result our whole souls are on fire. It must, it shall be undertaken to-day, and yet we put it off until to-morrow; and why? There is no answer, except that we feel *perverse*, using the word with no comprehension of the principle. To-morrow arrives, and with it a more impatient anxiety to do our duty, but with this very increase of anxiety arrives, also, a nameless, a positively fearful, because unfathomable, craving for delay. This craving gathers strength as the moments fly. The last hour for action is at hand. We tremble with the violence of the conflict within us,—of the definite with the indefinite—of the substance with the shadow. But, if the contest have proceeded thus far, it is the shadow which prevails,—we struggle in vain. The clock strikes, and is the knell of our welfare. At the same time, it is the

14 chanticleer-note to the ghost that has so long overawed us. It flies—it disappears—we are free. The old energy returns. We will labor *now*. Alas, it is *too late!*

We stand upon the brink of a precipice. We peer into the abyss—we grow sick and dizzy. Our first impulse is to shrink from the danger. Unaccountably we remain. By slow degrees our sickness and dizziness and horror become merged in a

15 cloud of unnamable feeling. By gradations, still more imperceptible, this cloud assumes shape, as did the vapor from the bottle out of which arose the genius in the Arabian Nights. But out of this *our* cloud upon the precipice's edge, there grows into palpability, a shape, far more terrible than any

13 Note how the narrator begins with a simple, fairly tame example, with which most of us can sympathize, and then proceeds to skillfully build his own case, extending our sympathies as the situations become more complex and less defensible.

14 Chanticleer is the rooster in the moralistic folk tale of Reynard the Fox. The name comes from the Old French meaning to sing loudly, referring to the rooster's early-morning crow. In more superstitious times, the populace believed that from the witching hour, of midnight, until the cock's crow, ghosts and demons roamed abroad to prey on the unwary. (See *Hamlet*, I, i).

The "ghost" here seems to be procrastination.

15 Poe details such a cliff-hanging nightmare in Chapter 24 of *The Narrative of Arthur Gordon Pym* (see "A Descent into the Maelström," note 3.)

genius or any demon of a tale, and yet it is but a thought, although a fearful one, and one which chills the very marrow of our bones with the fierceness of the delight of its horror. It is merely the idea of what would be our sensations during the sweeping precipitancy of a fall from such a height. And this fall—this rushing annihilation—for the very reason that it involves that one most ghastly and loathsome of all the most ghastly and loathsome images of death and suffering which have ever presented themselves to our imagination—for this very cause do we now the most vividly desire it. And because **16** our reason violently deters us from the brink, *therefore* do we the most impetuously approach it. There is no passion in nature so demoniacally impatient, as that of him who, shuddering upon the edge of a precipice, thus meditates a plunge. To indulge, for a moment, in any attempt at *thought*, is to be inevitably lost; for reflection but urges us to forbear, and *therefore* it is, I say, that we *cannot*. If there be no friendly arm to check us, or if we fail in a sudden effort to prostrate ourselves backward from the abyss, we plunge, and are destroyed.

Examine these and similar actions as we will, we shall find them resulting solely from the spirit of the *Perverse*. We perpetrate them merely because we feel that we should *not*. Beyond or behind this there is no intelligible principle; and we might, indeed, deem this perverseness a direct instigation of the arch-fiend, were it not occasionally known to operate in furtherance of good.

I have said thus much, that in some measure I may answer your question—that I may explain to you why I am here— that I may assign to you something that shall have at least the faint aspect of a cause for my wearing these fetters, and for my tenanting this cell of the condemned. Had I not been thus prolix, you might either have misunderstood me altogether, **17** or, with the rabble, have fancied me mad. As it is, you will easily perceive that I am one of the many uncounted victims of the Imp of the Perverse. **18**

It is impossible that any deed could have been wrought

16 The death instinct, according to psychoanalytical theories, is a drive toward self-destruction. Freud did not precisely describe it, because he considered it buried too deep in the unconscious. However, like the life instinct, or Eros, it originates in the libido, the source of all energy in an individual. Freud supposes something not unlike Poe's "Imp" in his concept, particularly in its manifestations of destructiveness and aggression.

"Genius" is a genie.

17 *Prolix* means unduly prolonged, drawn out. The narrator is indeed overly defensive, and it is this over-reaction to everything around him which marks him for what he is: unbalanced. The whole tale, then, can be viewed as nothing more than an elaborate, but flawed, defense of his irrational actions, for which he desperately wants to blame something outside himself, as does the narrator of "The Black Cat."

18 Compare this paragraph with the opening of "The Tell-Tale Heart."

There is no passion in nature so demoniacally impatient, as that of him who, shuddering upon the edge of a precipice, thus meditates a plunge. *Artist unknown*

The fatal taper. *Artist unknown*

19 Madame Pilau is a character in "An Oddity of the Seventeenth Century," by Catherine Gore, which appeared in the *New Monthly Magazine*, December 1839. She nearly dies from a poisoned candle, placed near her bedside by her enemies, but is saved when an observant physician administers the proper antidote. George Lyman Kittredge, in *Witchcraft in Old and New England* (1929), also tells of such a candle (p. 347).

20 As usual, "fancy" is an important clue to the narrator's mental state (see "The Assignation," note 3).

21 His use of "impertinent" suggests his mental state, particularly since he goes ahead and gives a fairly good idea of what he has done. "Vex" us? He vexes us far more by *not* telling us, or rather, by *telling* us that he's not going to tell us. His perverse streak runs deep.

22 If he were really safe from himself, he would not need constant reassurance.
"I am safe" may be a wordplay on "saved" in the Christian sense. One aspect of salvation is the confession of sin, which in turn implies a moral compulsion to make a clean breast of things. But confession here is also a form of perversity, since it means capture and execution.

23 Compare a similar phrase in the opening of "The Fall of the House of Usher."

24 Shrieking is a Poesque clue to one's insanity: see the end of "Ligeia," and "The Tell-Tale Heart."

with a more thorough deliberation. For weeks, for months, I pondered upon the means of the murder. I rejected a thousand schemes, because their accomplishment involved a *chance* of detection. At length, in reading some French memoirs, I found an account of a nearly fatal illness that occurred to Madame Pilau, through the agency of a candle **19,20** accidentally poisoned. The idea struck my fancy at once. I knew my victim's habit of reading in bed. I knew, too, that his apartment was narrow and ill-ventilated. But I need not **21** vex you with impertinent details. I need not describe the easy artifices by which I substituted, in his bed-room candle-stand, a wax-light of my own making for the one which I there found. The next morning he was discovered dead in his bed, and the coroner's verdict was—"Death by the visitation of God."

Having inherited his estate, all went well with me for years. The idea of detection never once entered my brain. Of the remains of the fatal taper I had myself carefully disposed. I had left no shadow of a clew by which it would be possible to convict, or even to suspect, me of the crime. It is inconceivable how rich a sentiment of satisfaction arose in my bosom as I reflected upon my absolute security. For a very long period of time I was accustomed to revel in this sentiment. It afforded me more real delight than all the mere worldly advantages accruing from my sin. But there arrived at length an epoch, from which the pleasurable feeling grew, by scarcely perceptible gradations, into a haunting and harassing thought. It harassed because it haunted. I could scarcely get rid of it for an instant. It is quite a common thing to be thus annoyed with the ringing in our ears, or rather in our memories, of the burthen of some ordinary song, or some unimpressive snatches from an opera. Nor will we be the less tormented if the song in itself be good, or the opera air meritorious. In this manner, at last, I would perpetually catch myself pondering upon my security, and repeating, in a low under-tone, the phrase, "I **22** am safe."

One day, whilst sauntering along the streets, I arrested myself in the act of murmuring, half aloud, these customary syllables. In a fit of petulance, I re-modelled them thus: "I am safe—I am safe—yes—if I be not fool enough to make open confession!"

No sooner had I spoken these words, than I felt an icy chill creep to my heart. I had had some experience in these fits of perversity (whose nature I have been at some trouble to explain), and I remembered well that in no instance I had successfully resisted their attacks. And now my own casual self-suggestion, that I might possibly be fool enough to confess the murder of which I had been guilty, confronted me, as if the very ghost of him whom I had murdered—and beckoned me on to death.

At first, I made an effort to shake off this nightmare of the **23** soul. I walked vigorously—faster—still faster—at length I ran. **24** I felt a maddening desire to shriek aloud. Every succeeding wave of thought overwhelmed me with new terror, or, alas! I well, too well, understood that to *think*, in my situation, was to be lost. I still quickened my pace. I bounded like a madman through the crowded thoroughfares. At length, the populace took the alarm, and pursued me. I felt *then* the consummation of my fate. Could I have torn out my tongue, I would have done it—but a rough voice resounded in my ears—a rougher grasp seized me by the shoulder. I turned—I gasped for breath. For a moment I experienced all the pangs of suffocation; I became blind, and deaf, and giddy; and then some invisible fiend, I thought, struck me with his broad palm upon the back. The long-imprisoned secret burst forth from my soul. **25**

They say that I spoke with a distinct enunciation, but with marked emphasis and passionate hurry, as if in dread of **26** interruption before concluding the brief but pregnant sentences that consigned me to the hangman and to hell.

Having related all that was necessary for the fullest judicial conviction, I fell prostrate in a swoon.

But why shall I say more? To-day I wear these chains, and am *here!* To-morrow I shall be fetterless!—*but where?*

25 In the first version of the tale the narrator says, "It was no mortal hand, I knew, that struck me violently with a broad and massive palm upon the back." This reference to the intervention of a higher power echoes the *Iliad*, XVI, 954, in Pope's translation: "For lo! the God in dusky clouds enshrined,/Approaching, dealt a staggering blow behind."

His deletion of the passage may indicate that Poe wanted the source of the confession to be the narrator himself—his unconscious, as we would read it.

26 All repressions are shoved aside in a cleansing act that parallels a situation in psychoanalysis in which a patient blurts forth his repressed feelings, which have drained his energies before.

"Repression of the desire to punish oneself may cause a person to punish himself in indirect ways, such as having accidents, losing things and making foolish mistakes," points out Calvin S. Hall in *A Primer of Freudian Psychology* (Mentor Books, 1954; p. 88). The "foolish mistakes" are amplified here but are nonetheless examples of the behavior Freud first analyzed.

Note also Daniel Webster's 1830 speech quoted in the introduction note to "The Tell-Tale Heart."

The final irony of "The Imp of the Perverse" is that the narrator's real perversity—morally speaking—is the murder, of which he says very little. By all normal standards, the only just thing he does is to confess, yet the narrator plainly regards the murder as fully justified and the *confession* as perverse. Many readers are sucked in by his argument, but there is every likelihood that, unconsciously, he wants to be caught, just as do the narrators of "The Tell-Tale Heart" and "The Black Cat." None of them know why, but something inside acknowledges their crime and demands punishment.

I bounded like a madman through the crowded thoroughfares. *Artist unknown*

THE CASK OF AMONTILLADO

First published in *Godey's Magazine and Lady's Book*, November 1846, this is one of Poe's masterpieces, one of the greatest short stories ever written. Its success lies in the almost perfect balance between the horror of the situation and the ironic humor with which Poe invests it.

Six years before the tale was written, Poe, in a review of *The Spitfire*, by Frederick Chamier (1796–1870), wrote: "Villains do not always, nor even generally meet with punishment and shame in reality, and we would have been pleased if Captain Chamier had courageously departed from this common-place fiction and uncommon reality, and exhibited the success of an impudent rogue . . ." (*Burton's*, February 1840). This idea apparently lay dormant for some time, until Poe found a way to turn it into a tale that gave him satisfaction.

What finally sparked "The Cask of Amontillado" appears to be the libelous attack on Poe by one of his literary enemies, Hiram Fuller, in the New York *Mirror* (May 1846), followed by a similar assault by Thomas Dunn English in the same publication a month later. The verbal sparring between Poe and the two men continued for months—and it was during this period that he wrote "The Cask of Amontillado." It isn't hard to read the tale as a fictional working out of Poe's highly charged emotions about the whole affair.

As for the sources, research has turned up several good possibilities. In Scott's *Marmion* (1808), the author tells of finding the bones of someone buried alive in the ruins of the Abbey of Coldingham, and in Bulwer-Lytton's *The Last Days of Pompeii* (1834), Arbaces conducts Dalenus through a subterranean passage, promising to reveal his treasure chamber, and then pushes him into a cell to rot, despite his pleas.

Many critics cite Joel Tyler Headley's *Letters from Italy* (1845), one of which (published in the *Columbian Magazine* in August 1844) tells of a niche in the Church of San Lorenzo in the town of Don Giovanni, where workmen had recently uncovered the skeleton of one who had apparently died of suffocation after being walled up. Headley re-creates the moment in his mind:

"By the dim light of lamps, whose rays scarcely reached the lofty ceiling, the stones were removed before the eyes of the doomed man, and measurement after measurement taken, to see if the aperture was sufficiently large. . . . At length the opening was declared large enough and he was lifted into it. The workman began at the feet, and with his mortar and trowel built up with the same carelessness as he would exhibit in filling any broken wall. The successful enemy stood leaning on his sword—a smile of scorn and revenge on his features—and watched the face of the man he hated, but no longer feared. . . . With care and precision the last stone was fitted in the narrow space—the trowel passed smoothly over it—a stifled groan, as if from the centre of a rock, broke the stillness—one strong shiver, and all was over. The agony had passed—revenge was satisfied, and a secret locked up for the great revelation day."

Another story with which Poe may have been familiar is Honoré de Balzac's "La Grande Bretêche," which appeared in an adapted form in the *Democratic Review*, November 1843. It tells how a jealous husband walls up a closet in which his wife's lover is hiding—while she watches hopelessly.

Still other possible sources are "Apropos of Bores," in the New York *Mirror*, December 1837, which involves a guest and a porter trapped in the wine cellars of Lincoln's Inn, and a tale by Benjamin Franklin (see note 29).

Probably the most famous borrowing of the material in "The Cask of Amontillado" is in Chapter 35 of Vladimir Nabokov's *Lolita* (1958), discussed in note 24.

The story has been part of three films: *Histoires Extraordinaires* ("Fünf Unheimliche Geschichten,"

"The Living Dead," "Extraordinary Tales"), a 1931 German film remade in French in 1948; *Master of Horror*, a 1961 Argentinian production; and Roger Corman's 1962 *Tales of Terror*, which makes good use of the story's black humor.

The best recorded version is the hair-raising rendition by Basil Rathbone (Caedmon TC 1115).

The thousand injuries of Fortunato I had borne as I best could; **1** but when he ventured upon insult, I vowed revenge. You, **2** who so well know the nature of my soul, will not suppose, however, that I gave utterance to a threat. *At length* I would be avenged; this was a point definitively settled—but the very definitiveness with which it was resolved, precluded the idea of risk. I must not only punish, but punish with impunity. A wrong is unredressed when retribution overtakes its redresser. It is equally unredressed when the avenger fails to make himself felt as such to him who has done the wrong.

It must be understood, that neither by word nor deed had I given Fortunato cause to doubt my good-will. I continued, as was my wont, to smile in his face, and he did not perceive that my smile *now* was at the thought of his immolation. **3**

He had a weak point—this Fortunato—although in other regards he was a man to be respected and even feared. He **4** prided himself on his connoisseurship in wine. Few Italians have the true virtuoso spirit. For the most part their enthusiasm is adopted to suit the time and opportunity—to practise imposture upon the British and Austrian *millionnaires*. In painting and gemmary Fortunato, like his countrymen, was a quack—but in the matter of old wines he was sincere. In **5** this respect I did not differ from him materially: I was skilful in the Italian vintages myself, and bought largely whenever **6** I could.

It was about dusk, one evening during the supreme madness of the carnival season, that I encountered my friend. He **7** accosted me with excessive warmth, for he had been drinking much. The man wore motley. He had on a tight-fitting parti- **8**

1 "The Fortunate One," or perhaps "Fated"

2 One of the fascinating aspects of the tale is that we never learn just what Fortunato did to anger Montresor (literally, "my treasure"). Compounding the puzzle is the fact that Montresor calls him "friend" and seems somehow in awe of him—as well as jealous of his happiness and number of friends. As for Fortunato, he doesn't appear to be afraid of Montresor, and goes into the catacombs willingly. Could it be that he isn't aware of his transgression? Or could it be that there never really *was* any transgression at all, other than something Montresor has magnified out of proportion?

Poe's vagueness on the point reminds one of Alfred Hitchcock's remark after someone asked him why James Mason's wife in *North by Northwest* (1958) comes in to ask her husband to receive guests, when we never see any. "I know nothing about it," responded Hitchcock. "I don't know the lady in question. I've never met her. I don't know why she came in then, or why she said that."

Like Hitchcock, Poe's purpose is not to explain the "why" but to tell the "what," and so his characters often seem vague in their motivations. When it comes to interpretation, we must tread carefully—taking to heart the warning in the family coat of arms of the archvillain Montresor.

3 Compare Montresor's comments with those of the narrator of "The Tell-Tale Heart." Their similarity may be a significant clue to the state of Montresor's mind, particularly in terms of his obsession with Fortunato's "injuries."

4 One wonders what sort of position Fortunato holds, since Montresor fears his power.

5 Montresor's comments on the production of bogus art in nineteenth-century Italy suggests that he is not himself Italian.

6 Actually, Montresor (or Poe) shows an imperfect knowledge of wines as the story progresses.

7 Carnival is the period (of which Mardi Gras is the last day) just before Lent.

8 The multicolored garment worn by jesters and fools, here apparently a costume for the carnival

A scene in the catacombs of Paris, from which Poe is supposed to have gotten his description of the underground passages in "The Cask of Amontillado." *Artist unknown*

9 A pipe is a large cask, containing about 130 gallons!
"Thanks to Poe, Amontillado has become famous throughout the word. But had Poe done his homework he would have learned that you can't promise a cask of amontillado to anyone [he doesn't—he promises a "pipe"]. The cask is the empty vessel being cured; when filled, however, it is a butt. In any case, amontillado is aged fino [a dry, light sherry], acquiring through age a darker color, more depth and a fuller aroma than fino. Almost all amontillado marketed nowadays is an amontillado style obtained by blending, rather than by long ageing. For the consumer, there is a useful rule of thumb to follow: if an amontillado is less expensive or about the same price as a fino, it is most likely not genuine. Genuine amontillado must reflect the cost of labor and the amortization of its ageing out of fino." (William Fifield, "In Vino Veritas," *Vintage*, October 1976; pp. 34–39)
"Amontillado" means a sherry of the Montilla type, and sherry itself takes its name from the coastal town of Jerez, in southwest Spain. It is made in a solera, a series of interconnected barrels lying one on top of another, four or five tiers high. The wine is not protected from the air, but instead exposed to it, as well as to the cool of night and the heat of day. Newer wine is added to the casks in the topmost tier of the solera as evaporation takes place, and fully aged sherry is drawn from the bottom. The bottom tier is of course replenished from the second row, and that in turn from above. It is a slow process, but as the wine passes down through the solera, it "marries" the old and assumes its character.

10 In the first draft of the tale, the name is "Luchresi," which might have been meant as a wordplay on "look crazy," and be a slap at Hiram Fuller. Poe names a dancing master named Luchesi in "Why the Little Frenchman Wears His Hand in a Sling" (note 9).

11 Amontillado *is* sherry; what Fortunato means is that Luchesi can't tell the difference between the ordinary and the expensive varieties.

12 Niter is potassium nitrate (saltpeter), a naturally occurring compound that is soluble in water and has been used in the manufacture of gunpowder since the fourteenth century in Europe. Here it describes the deposits left by the action of water seepage through the mortar of the brick walls.

13 An overcoat

14 The catacombs were the burial place of the early Christians, arranged in extensive underground vaults and chambers. Among the Greeks and Romans cremation was the rule, but contrary to popular belief today, there was no law forbidding burial for Christians, and the catacombs were not built in secret. Ordinances did forbid entombment within the city limits, however, so they were built outside the gates.
"The most awful idea connected with the catacombs is their interminable extent, and the possibility of going astray in the labyrinth of darkness," writes Hawthorne in *The Marble Faun*, Chapter III.

striped dress, and his head was surmounted by the conical cap and bells. I was so pleased to see him, that I thought I should never have done wringing his hand.

I said to him: "My dear Fortunato, you are luckily met. How remarkably well you are looking to-day! But I have received a pipe of what passes for Amontillado, and I have my doubts."

9

"How?" said he. "Amontillado? A pipe? Impossible! And in the middle of the carnival!"

"I have my doubts," I replied; "and I was silly enough to pay the full Amontillado price without consulting you in the matter. You were not to be found, and I was fearful of losing a bargain."

"Amontillado!"

"I have my doubts."

"Amontillado!"

"And I must satisfy them."

"Amontillado!"

10 "As you are engaged, I am on my way to Luchesi. If any one has a critical turn, it is he. He will tell me——"

11 "Luchesi cannot tell Amontillado from Sherry."

"And yet some fools will have it that his taste is a match for your own."

"Come, let us go."

"Whither?"

"To your vaults."

"My friend, no; I will not impose upon your good nature. I perceive you have an engagement. Luchesi——"

"I have no engagement;—come."

"My friend, no. It is not the engagement, but the severe cold with which I perceive you are afflicted. The vaults are

12 insufferably damp. They are encrusted with nitre."

"Let us go, nevertheless. The cold is merely nothing. Amontillado! You have been imposed upon. And as for Luchesi, he cannot distinguish Sherry from Amontillado."

Thus speaking, Fortunato possessed himself of my arm.

13 Putting on a mask of black silk, and drawing a *roquelaire* closely about my person, I suffered him to hurry me to my palazzo.

There were no attendants at home; they had absconded to make merry in honor of the time. I had told them that I should not return until the morning, and had given them explicit orders not to stir from the house. These orders were sufficient, I well knew, to insure their immediate disappearance, one and all, as soon as my back was turned.

I took from their sconces two flambeaux, and giving one to Fortunato, bowed him through several suites of rooms to the archway that led into the vaults. I passed down a long and winding staircase, requesting him to be cautious as he followed. We came at length to the foot of the descent and stood

14 together on the damp ground of the catacombs of the Montresors.

The gait of my friend was unsteady, and the bells upon his cap jingled as he strode.

"The pipe?" said he.

"It is farther on," said I; "but observe the white web-work which gleams from these cavern walls."

He turned toward me, and looked into my eyes with two filmy orbs that distilled the rheum of intoxication.

"Nitre?" he asked, at length.

"Nitre," I replied. "How long have you had that cough?"

"Ugh! ugh! ugh!—ugh! ugh! ugh!—ugh! ugh! ugh!—ugh! ugh! ugh!—ugh! ugh! ugh!"   **15**

My poor friend found it impossible to reply for many minutes.

"It is nothing," he said, at last.

"Come," I said, with decision, "we will go back; your health is precious. You are rich, respected, admired, beloved; you are happy, as once I was. You are a man to be missed. For me it is no matter. We will go back; you will be ill, and I cannot **16** be responsible. Besides, there is Luchesi——"

"Enough," he said; "the cough is a mere nothing; it will not kill me. I shall not die of a cough."   **17**

"True—true," I replied; "and, indeed, I had no intention of alarming you unnecessarily; but you should use all proper caution. A draught of this Medoc will defend us from the **18** damps."

Here I knocked off the neck a bottle which I drew from a long row of its fellows that lay upon the mould.

"Drink," I said, presenting him the wine.

He raised it to his lips with a leer. He paused and nodded to me familiarly, while his bells jingled.

"I drink," he said, "to the buried that repose around us."

"And I to your long life."

He again took my arm, and we proceeded.

"These vaults," he said, "are extensive."

"The Montresors," I replied, "were a great and numerous family."

"I forget your arms."

"A huge human foot d'or, in a field azure; the foot crushes a serpent rampant whose fangs are imbedded in the heel."   **19**

"And the motto?"

"*Nemo me impune lacessit.*"   **20**

"Good!" he said.

The wine sparkled in his eyes and the bells jingled. My own fancy grew warm with the Medoc. We had passed through walls of piled bones, with casks and puncheons intermingling, **21** into the inmost recesses of the catacombs. I paused again, and this time I made bold to seize Fortunato by an arm above the elbow.

"The nitre!" I said; "see, it increases. It hangs like moss upon the vaults. We are below the river's bed. The drops of moisture trickle among the bones. Come, we will go back ere it is too late. Your cough——"

"It is nothing," he said; "let us go on. But first, another draught of the Medoc."

I broke and reached him a flagon of De Grâve. He emptied **22** it at a breath. His eyes flashed with a fierce light. He laughed

15 Joseph H. Harkey, in *Poe Newsletter*, Vol. 3, p. 22, actually goes so far as to count the number of coughs here and elsewhere in Poe's tales, and come up with "double coughs (*ugh! ugh!*), compound coughs (*ugh!—ugh!*), and single coughs (*ugh!*)," finding in them a "pattern of neo-classical balance." Ugh.

16 A touch of self-pity surfaces in Montresor's otherwise controlled and icy manner.

17 Unfortunately, only Montresor gets the joke.

18 Médoc is the wine area just north of Bordeaux, producing extremely fine wines indeed. However, Montresor's breaking off the neck of the bottle is hardly the action of a connoisseur—but, then, Fortunato isn't in any condition to appreciate wine etiquette anyway.

19 Heraldry dates back to the Middle Ages, when the herald, often a tournament official, had to recognize men by their shields; thus he became an authority on personal and family insignia. The practice of embroidering family emblems on the surcoat, worn over chain mail in the thirteenth century, accounts for the term "coat of arms." As time went by, arms were taken up by families, corporations, guilds, religious houses, inns, colleges, boroughs, cities, and kingdoms.

This family's arms include a golden foot on a blue background crushing a snake whose fangs are sunk into the heel—certainly an apt emblem for the vindictive Montresor.

"And the Lord God said unto the serpent . . . I will put enmity between thee and the woman . . . and her seed . . . shall bruise thy head, and thou shalt bruise his heel" (Genesis 3:14–15).

20 "No one provokes me with impunity." This is also the motto of Scotland, as well as the Scottish Order of the Thistle. Poe uses a free translation of the motto again in "The Duc De L'Omelette" and "The Literary Life of Thingum Bob, Esq."

21 Large casks; from the Middle French *poinçon*, of unknown origin

22 Graves is the name of the region in the Bordeaux district known for its gravelly soil. The wines are mostly white, but the area does produce some reds. Poe no doubt means a pun on the word "grave."

23 Freemasonry is thought to have sprung from the English and Scottish fraternities of stonemasons and cathedral builders in the early Middle Ages. Traces of the society have been found as early as the fourteenth century (members trace their heritage back to Egypt and Babylonia). The formation of the grand lodge in London (1717) marked the beginning of the spread of Freemasonry, which demands of its members morality, charity, and obedience to the law of the land. The first lodge in the United States was founded in Philadelphia in 1730, and Benjamin Franklin was a member.

As for the secret hand signal, masonic experts have not been able to explain just what Poe had in mind. But, then, Poe was not a Mason himself.

24 Montresor is a practical mason, not a spiritual one. His motive for murder could be a Catholic's hatred of Freemasonry, which would date the tale to perhaps the eighteenth century, when some Masons of the French and Italian lodges were actively hostile to the Church, resulting in Pope Clement XII's issuing a papal bull (*In Eminenti*) in 1739, condemning Freemasonry and threatening Catholic Freemasons with excommunication because the society was a "secretive and pagan" religion, and a possible threat to the Church. He also condemned Masonic oaths and ritual. If Fortunato was an excommunicated Mason, reasons James R. Rocks, Montresor would regard him as outside the sanctions of the Church, and could indeed "punish with impunity" (*Poe Studies*, Vol. V, p. 50). It is only in recent years that the Church has relaxed its condemnation of Freemasonry.

In Chapter 35 of *Lolita* (1958), Humbert Humbert, "lucidly insane, crazily calm," arrives at Pavor Manor, on Grimm Road, in order to murder Clare Quilty, who has seduced Lolita. Finding his victim, Humbert jests with him, delighted "to have him trapped, after those years of repentance and rage." He insists that his victim "must understand why he was being destroyed" (as opposed to Montresor), but even so, Quilty either fails or refuses to see that the "little dark weapon" in Humbert's hand is the instrument of his death: "That's a swell gun you've got there. What d'you want for her?" he asks.

Quilty is also described as having an "absurd, clown's manner," and while a party is going on elsewhere in his house, playfully cries, "Ah, that hurts, sir, enough! Ah, that hurts atrociously, my dear fellow. I pray you desist. Ah—very painful, very painful, indeed . . . God!"

When the crime is committed, Humbert says, "Far from feeling any relief, a burden even weightier than the one I had hoped to get rid of was with me, upon me, over me," and he leaves the house "with a heavy heart."

25 The description here parallels that of the catacombs of Paris that appeared in an article by that name in the *Knickerbocker* of 1838. The Italian and the Parisian catacombs each has a river flowing through it, and so Poe may have used the one to describe the other.

and threw the bottle upward with a gesticulation I did not understand.

I looked at him in surprise. He repeated the movement— a grotesque one.

"You do not comprehend?" he said.

"Not I," I replied.

"Then you are not of the brotherhood."

"How?"

"You are not of the masons."

"Yes, yes," I said; "yes, yes."

23   "You? Impossible! A mason?"

"A mason," I replied.

"A sign," he said.

"It is this," I answered, producing a trowel from beneath

24 the folds of my *roquelaire*.

"You jest," he exclaimed, recoiling a few paces. "But let us proceed to the Amontillado."

"Be it so," I said, replacing the tool beneath the cloak, and again offering him my arm. He leaned upon it heavily. We continued our route in search of the Amontillado. We passed through a range of low arches, descended, passed on, and descending again, arrived at a deep crypt, in which the foulness of the air caused our flambeaux rather to glow than flame.

At the most remote end of the crypt there appeared another less spacious. Its walls had been lined with human remains, piled to the vault overhead, in the fashion of the great

25 catacombs of Paris. Three sides of this interior crypt were still ornamented in this manner. From the fourth the bones had been thrown down, and lay promiscuously upon the earth, forming at one point a mound of some size. Within the wall thus exposed by the displacing of the bones, we perceived a still interior recess, in depth about four feet, in width three, in height six or seven. It seemed to have been constructed for no especial use within itself, but formed merely the interval between two of the colossal supports of the roof of the catacombs, and was backed by one of their circumscribing walls of solid granite.

It was in vain that Fortunato, uplifting his dull torch, endeavored to pry into the depth of the recess. Its termination the feeble light did not enable us to see.

"Proceed," I said; "herein is the Amontillado. As for Luchesi——"

"He is an ignoramus," interrupted my friend, as he stepped unsteadily forward, while I followed immediately at his heels. In an instant he had reached the extremity of the niche, and finding his progress arrested by the rock, stood stupidly bewildered. A moment more and I had fettered him to the granite. In its surface were two iron staples, distant from each other about two feet, horizontally. From one of these depended a short chain, from the other a padlock. Throwing the links about his waist, it was but the work of a few seconds to secure it. He was too much astounded to resist. Withdrawing the key I stepped back from the recess.

"Pass your hand," I said, "over the wall; you cannot help feeling the nitre. Indeed it is *very* damp. Once more let me *implore* you to return. No? Then I must positively leave you. But I must first render you all the little attentions in my power."

"The Amontillado!" ejaculated my friend, not yet recovered from his astonishment.

"True," I replied; "the Amontillado."

As I said these words I busied myself among the pile of bones of which I have before spoken. Throwing them aside, I soon uncovered a quantity of building stone and mortar. With these materials and with the aid of my trowel, I began vigorously to wall up the entrance of the niche.

I had scarcely laid the first tier of the masonry when I discovered that the intoxication of Fortunato had in a great measure worn off. The earliest indication I had of this was a low moaning cry from the depth of the recess. It was *not* the cry of a drunken man. There was then a long and obstinate silence. I laid the second tier, and the third, and the fourth; **26** and then I heard the furious vibrations of the chain. The noise lasted for several minutes, during which, that I might hearken to it with the more satisfaction, I ceased my labors and sat down upon the bones. When at last the clanking subsided, I resumed the trowel, and finished without interruption the fifth, the sixth, and the seventh tier. The wall was now nearly upon a level with my breast. I again paused, and holding the flambeaux over the mason-work, threw a few feeble rays upon the figure within.

A succession of loud and shrill screams, bursting suddenly from the throat of the chained form, seemed to thrust me violently back. For a brief moment I hesitated—I trembled.

26 Fortunato's "obstinate" silence is probably Montresor's interpretation, for he seems to give his motley-clad "friend" more determination and strength than we see here. His monstrous delight at the cruel and inhuman punishment he has devised is appalling, especially when he sits down to listen and relish it all the more.

"As for Luchesi—"
"He is an ignoramus."
Illustration by F. S. Coburn

27 If there is any doubt that Montresor is mad, consider how he echoes Fortunato scream for scream, shrieking even louder than his victim.

"Montresor wants his friend Fortunato to know how he, Montresor, repays friendship as he walls him up. This is perversity, not revenge. It he had cared about revenge, instead of echoing Fortunato, his last words would have been something about the insult that he says Fortunato has given him." (John Rea, *Studies in Short Fiction*, Vol. 4; p. 61)

28 Fortunato's bells jingle out a sort of death knell, and for a brief moment, Montresor shows some signs of humanity. He shudders—but quickly asserts that it is merely the cold, damp air of the catacombs.

29 May he rest in peace.

Whether or not Montresor escapes punishment is arguable, but in light of Poe's comment on villains (see preface), he may very well have meant for Montresor to get away with his crime completely. On the other hand, if after fifty years he still remembers every detail, one wonders if the deed still haunts him. There are those who read the story as a deathbed confession, finding in the last words an ironic comment on Montresor's own wish for peace at least, free of the burden of his crime.

A case for Montresor's telling his tale to a priest is strengthened by the discovery of a translation of a French "bagatelle" by Benjamin Franklin, published in America several years before "The Cask of Amontillado":

"An officer named Montresor, a worthy man . . . was very ill. The curate of his parish, thinking him likely to die, advised him to make his peace with God, that he might be received into Paradise. 'I have not much uneasiness on the subject,' said Montresor, 'for I had a vision last night that has perfectly tranquillized my mind.' 'What vision have you had?' said the good priest. 'I was,' replied Montresor, 'at the gate of Paradise, with a crowd of people who wished to enter, and St. Peter inquired of every one what religion he was of. One answered, 'I am a Roman Catholic.' 'Well,' said St. Peter, 'enter and take your place there among the Catholics.' Another said he was of the Church of England. 'Well,' said the Saint, 'enter and place yourself there among the Anglicans.' A third said he was a Quaker. 'Enter,' said St. Peter, 'and take your place among the Quakers.' At length my turn came, and he asked me of what religion I was. 'Alas,' said I, 'Poor Jacques Montresor has none.' ''Tis pity,' said the Saint; 'I know not where to place you, but *enter nonetheless, and place yourself where you can*.' " (*Works of Benjamin Franklin*, Hilliard, Gray & Co., 1840; Vol. II, p. 164)

Marie Bonaparte suggests that the story may be the result of Poe's antagonism toward the brother of a woman he had fallen in love with. Frances Osgood, with whom Poe had spent a great deal of time during the winter of 1845–46, had a brother who disliked Poe intensely and supposedly challenged Poe to a duel. This, Bonaparte says, reactivated his father-hatred, so that "The Cask of Amontillado" represents the final disposal of the hated John Allen. (Pp. 505–10)

Unsheathing my rapier, I began to grope with it about the recess; but the thought of an instant reassured me. I placed my hand upon the solid fabric of the catacombs, and felt satisfied. I reapproached the wall. I replied to the yells of him who clamored. I re-echoed—I aided—I surpassed them in volume and in strength. I did this, and the clamorer grew **27** still.

It was now midnight, and my task was drawing to a close. I had completed the eighth, the ninth, and the tenth tier. I had finished a portion of the last and the eleventh; there remained but a single stone to be fitted and plastered in. I struggled with its weight; I placed it partially in its destined position. But now there came from out the niche a low laugh that erected the hairs upon my head. It was succeeded by a sad voice, which I had difficulty in recognizing as that of the noble Fortunato. The voice said—

"Ha! ha! ha!—he! he!—a very good joke indeed—an excellent jest. We will have many a rich laugh about it at the palazzo—he! he! he!—over our wine—he! he! he!"

"The Amontillado!" I said.

"He! he! he!—he! he! he!—yes, the Amontillado. But is it not getting late? Will not they be awaiting us at the palazzo, the Lady Fortunato and the rest? Let us be gone."

"Yes," I said, "let us be gone."

"For the love of God, Montresor!"

"Yes," I said, "for the love of God!"

But to these words I hearkened in vain for a reply. I grew impatient. I called aloud:

"Fortunato!"

No answer. I called again:

"Fortunato!"

No answer still. I thrust a torch through the remaining aperture and let it fall within. There came forth in return only **28** a jingling of the bells. My heart grew sick—on account of the dampness of the catacombs. I hastened to make an end of my labor. I forced the last stone into its position; I plastered it up. Against the new masonry I re-erected the old rampart of bones. For the half of a century no mortal has disturbed them.

29 *In pace requiescat!*

HOP-FROG

First published in *The Flag of Our Union*, March 17, 1849.

One of Poe's most unusual tales of horror, "Hop-Frog" differs from most of the others in its third-person narration, its intricate plot, and its unrelieved black humor. Some have criticized it for a lack of subtlety, but there is no doubt that the climax is still every bit as effective as Poe meant it to be.

The sources for "Hop-Frog" have been well documented. The fiery climax comes from a true incident in the *Chronicles* of Jean Froissart (c. 1337–1410?), although Poe most likely read the story in an article, "Barbarities of the Theater," in the *Broadway Journal* of February 1, 1845.

Another source is "Frogère and the Emperor Paul," in the London *New Monthly Magazine*, June 1830, which tells how Czar Paul I pretended to exile his jester, and how that same jester years later discovered his emperor had been murdered.

Film versions include a 1910 French film directed by Henri Desfontaines, and a good portion of *The Masque of the Red Death* (1964), directed by Roger Corman. The latter is not a successful rendering of either story, although it boasts some good, moody photography and the presence of Vincent Price and Hazel Court.

I never knew any one so keenly alive to a joke as the king was. **1** He seemed to live only for joking. To tell a good story of the joke kind, and to tell it well, was the surest road to his favor. Thus it happened that his seven ministers were all noted for their accomplishments as jokers. They all took after the king, too, in being large, corpulent, oily men, as well as inimitable jokers. Whether people grow fat by joking, or whether there **2** is something in fat itself which predisposes to a joke, I have never been quite able to determine; but certain it is that a lean joker is a *rara avis in terris*. **3**

About the refinements, or, as he called them, the "ghosts" of wit, the king troubled himself very little. He had an especial admiration for *breadth* in a jest, and would often put up with *length*, for the sake of it. Overniceties wearied him. He would have preferred Rabelais's "Gargantua" to the "Zadig" of Voltaire: and, upon the whole, practical jokes suited his taste **4** far better than verbal ones.

At the date of my narrative, professing jesters had not altogether gone out of fashion at court. Several of the great continental "powers" still retained their "fools," who wore motley, with caps and bells, and who were expected to be **5** always ready with sharp witticisms, at a moment's notice, in consideration of the crumbs that fell from the royal table. **6**

Our king, as a matter of course, retained his "fool." The

1 The irony is heavy and begins immediately, already looking ahead to the tale's climax. Poe often said that all good stories are written backward from the ending, so that every detail, every bit of dialogue, and every word look to the inevitable conclusion.

2 The king is modeled in part after George IV, who was a practical joker and, in Poe's mind, "the filthy compound of all that is bestial" (review of *Charles O'Malley*, in *Graham's*, March 1842). Poe satirizes the king again in "Four Beasts in One."

3 "Rare bird in the world" (Juvenal's *Satires*, VI, 165)

4 Poe preferred Voltaire's *Zadig* to the work of Rabelais (c. 1490–1553), as is evident from a passage in "The Facts in the Case of M. Valdemar" and by his modeling of Dupin, in part, after the title character of Voltaire's novel.

5 A multicolored or checkered fool's costume

6 ". . . desiring to be fed with the crumbs which fell from the rich man's table . . ." (Luke 16:21, referring to the beggar Lazarus and the rich man, Dives; the latter ends up in the torment of Hell).

7 Dwarfism results from a combination of both genetic factors and endocrine malfunctions involving pituitary and thyroid deficiencies. Dwarfs vary in height between two and four feet, and some, known medically as achondroplastic, have stunted limbs but normal trunks. Dwarfs' bodies are not in proportion, unlike midgets'.

Dwarfs were great court favorites from earliest times and reached the height of fashion in Europe between the fifteenth and seventeenth centuries. Although considered playthings, they were frequently noted for wit and intrigue. The career of Jeffrey Judson, for example—knighted in jest by Charles I—could be matched by few adventurers of any period.

8 There is more irony here in the cruelty of the king and his courtiers: they laugh at Hop-Frog because he is less than human in form; while they are less than human in spirit.

9 Compare the character of Quasimodo in Hugo's *Nôtre-Dame de Paris*, with which Poe was well acquainted.

10 Her proportions indicate she is a midget, rather than a true dwarf.

11 Perhaps derived from "to trip," meaning to dance or skip, or possibly from the French *tripette*, a scrap of morsel

12 Poe seems to be unaware of the physical differences between dwarves and midgets.

fact is, he *required* something in the way of folly—if only to counterbalance the heavy wisdom of the seven wise men who were his ministers—not to mention himself.

His fool, or professional jester, was not *only* a fool, however. His value was trebled in the eyes of the king, by the fact of

7 his being also a dwarf and a cripple. Dwarfs were as common at court, in those days, as fools; and many monarchs would have found it difficult to get through their days (days are rather longer at court than elsewhere) without both a jester to laugh

8 *with*, and a dwarf to laugh *at*. But, as I have already observed, your jesters, in ninety-nine cases out of a hundred, are fat, round, and unwieldly—so that it was no small source of self-gratulation with our king that, in Hop-Frog (this was the fool's name), he possessed a triplicate treasure in one person.

I believe the name "Hop-Frog" was *not* that given to the dwarf by his sponsors at baptism, but it was conferred upon him, by general consent of the seven ministers, on account of his inability to walk as other men do. In fact, Hop-Frog could only get along by a sort of interjectional gait—something between a leap and a wriggle,—a movement that afforded illimitable amusement, and of course consolation, to the king, for (notwithstanding the protuberance of his stomach and a constitutional swelling of the head) the king, by his whole court, was accounted a capital figure.

But although Hop-Frog, through the distortion of his legs, could move only with great pain and difficulty along a road or floor, the prodigious muscular power which nature seemed to have bestowed upon his arms, by way of compensation for deficiency in the lower limbs, enabled him to perform many feats of wonderful dexterity, where trees or ropes were in

9 question, or anything else to climb. At such exercises he certainly much more resembled a squirrel, or a small monkey, than a frog.

I am not able to say, with precision, from what country Hop-Frog originally came. It was from some barbarous region, however, that no person ever heard of—a vast distance from the court of our king. Hop-Frog, and a young girl very little

10 less dwarfish than himself (although of exquisite proportions, and a marvellous dancer), had been forcibly carried off from their respective homes in adjoining provinces, and sent as presents to the king, by one of his ever-victorious generals.

Under these circumstances, it is not to be wondered at that a close intimacy arose between the two little captives. Indeed, they soon became sworn friends. Hop-Frog, who, although he made a great deal of sport, was by no means popular, had

11 it not in his power to render Trippetta many services; but *she*, on account of her grace and exquisite beauty (although a

12 dwarf), was universally admired and petted; so she possessed much influence; and never failed to use it, whenever she could, for the benefit of Hop-Frog.

On some grand state occasion—I forget what—the king determined to have a masquerade; and whenever a masquerade, or any thing of that kind, occurred at our court, then the talents both of Hop-Frog and Trippetta were sure to be called into play. Hop-Frog, in especial, was so inventive in the way of getting up pageants, suggesting novel characters, and arranging costume, for masked balls, that nothing could be done, it seems, without his assistance.

The night appointed for the *fête* had arrived. A gorgeous hall had been fitted up, under Trippetta's eye, with every kind of device which could possibly give *éclat* to a masquerade. **13** The whole court was in a fever of expectation. As for costumes and characters, it might well be supposed that everybody had come to a decision on such points. Many had made up their minds (as to what *rôles* they should assume) a week, or even a month, in advance; and, in fact, there was not a particle of indecision anywhere—except in the case of the king and his seven ministers. Why *they* hesitated I never could tell, unless they did it by way of a joke. More probably, they found it difficult, on account of being so fat, to make up their minds. At all events, time flew; and, as a last resort, they sent for Trippetta and Hop-Frog.

When the two little friends obeyed the summons of the king, they found him sitting at his wine with the seven members of his cabinet council; but the monarch appeared to be in a very ill humor. He knew that Hop-Frog was not fond of wine; for it excited the poor cripple almost to madness; and madness is no comfortable feeling. But the king loved his practical jokes, and took pleasure in forcing Hop-Frog to drink and (as the king called it) "to be merry."   **14**

"Come here, Hop-Frog," said he, as the jester and his friend entered the room; "swallow this bumper to the health of your absent friends [here Hop-Frog sighed] and then let us have the benefit of your invention. We want characters—*characters,* man,—something novel—out of the way. We are wearied with this everlasting sameness. Come, drink! the wine will brighten your wits."

Hop-Frog endeavored, as usual, to get up a jest in reply to these advances from the king; but the effort was too much. It happened to be the poor dwarf's birthday, and the command to drink to his "absent friends" forced the tears to his eyes. Many large, bitter drops fell into the goblet as he took it, humbly, from the hand of the tyrant.   **15**

"Ah! ha! ha! ha!" roared the latter, as the dwarf reluctantly drained the beaker. "See what a glass of good wine can do! Why, your eyes are shining already!"

Poor fellow! his large eyes *gleamed,* rather than shone; for the effect of wine on his excitable brain was not more powerful than instantaneous. He placed the goblet nervously on the table, and looked round upon the company with a half-insane stare. They all seemed highly amused at the success of the king's "*joke.*"

"And now to business," said the prime minister, a *very* fat man.

"Yes," said the king. "Come, Hop-Frog, lend us your assistance. Characters, my fine fellow; we stand in need of characters—all of us—ha! ha! ha!" and as this was seriously meant for a joke, his laugh was chorused by the seven.

13 Sparkle; brightness

14 Perhaps Poe is reflecting his own well-known reaction to alcohol (see Introduction).
". . . take thine ease, eat, drink, and be merry" is from Luke 12:19.

15 Drinking to "absent friends" is an age-old toast, but here it suggests that Hop-Frog has been taken away from his home and family to serve the king—which may be yet another reason for his anger.

Hop-Frog also laughed, although feebly and somewhat vacantly.

"Come, come," said the king, impatiently, "have you nothing to suggest?"

"I am endeavoring to think of something *novel*," replied the dwarf, abstractedly, for he was quite bewildered by the wine.

"Endeavoring!" cried the tyrant, fiercely; "what do you mean by *that?* Ah, I perceive. You are sulky, and want more wine. Here, drink this!" and he poured out another goblet full and offered it to the cripple, who merely gazed at it, gasping for breath.

"Drink, I say!" shouted the monster, "or by the fiends—"

The dwarf hesitated. The king grew purple with rage. The courtiers smirked. Trippetta, pale as a corpse, advanced to the monarch's seat, and, falling on her knees before him, implored him to spare her friend.

The tyrant regarded her, for some moments, in evident wonder at her audacity. He seemed quite at a loss what to do or say—how most becomingly to express his indignation. At last, without uttering a syllable, he pushed her violently from him, and threw the contents of the brimming goblet in her face.

The poor girl got up as best she could, and, not daring even to sigh, resumed her position at the foot of the table.

There was a dead silence for about half a minute, during which the falling of a leaf, or of a feather, might have been heard. It was interrupted by a low, but harsh and protracted *grating* sound which seemed to come at once from every corner of the room.

"What—what—*what* are you making that noise for?" demanded the king, turning furiously to the dwarf.

The latter seemed to have recovered, in great measure, from his intoxication, and looking fixedly but quietly into the tyrant's face, merely ejaculated:

"I—I? How could it have been me?"

"The sound appeared to come from without," observed one of the courtiers. "I fancy it was the parrot at the window, whetting his bill upon his cage-wires."

"True," replied the monarch, as if much relieved by the suggestion; "but, on the honor of a knight, I could have sworn **16** that it was the gritting of this vagabond's teeth."

Hereupon the dwarf laughed (the king was too confirmed a joker to object to any one's laughing), and displayed a set of large, powerful, and very repulsive teeth. Moreover, he avowed his perfect willingness to swallow as much wine as desired. The monarch was pacified; and having drained another bumper with no very perceptible ill effect, Hop-Frog entered at once, and with spirit, into the plans for the masquerade.

"I cannot tell what was the association of idea," observed he, very tranquilly, and as if he had never tasted wine in his life, "but *just after* your majesty had struck the girl and thrown the wine in her face—*just after* your majesty had done this, and while the parrot was making that odd noise outside the

16 It seems hard to believe that the king actually hears Hop-Frog grating his teeth—the sound wouldn't be loud enough.

At last, without uttering a syllable, he pushed her violently from him, and threw the contents of the brimming goblet in her face. *Illustration by Johann Friedrich Vogel, 1856*

window, there came into my mind a capital diversion—one of my own country frolics—often enacted among us, at our masquerades: but here it will be new altogether. Unfortunately, however, it requires a company of eight persons, and——"

"Here we *are!*" cried the king, laughing at his acute discovery of the coincidence; "eight to a fraction—I and my seven ministers. Come! what is the diversion?"

"We call it," replied the cripple, "the Eight Chained Ourang-Outangs, and it really is excellent sport if well enacted."

"*We* will enact it," remarked the king, drawing himself up, and lowering his eyelids.

"The beauty of the game," continued Hop-Frog, "lies in the fright it occasions among the women."

"Capital!" roared in chorus the monarch and his ministry.

"I will equip you as ourang-outangs," proceeded the dwarf; "leave all that to me. The resemblance shall be so striking, that the company of masqueraders will take you for real beasts—and of course, they will be as much terrified as astonished."

"Oh, this is exquisite!" exclaimed the king. "Hop-Frog! I will make a man of you."

"The chains are for the purpose of increasing the confusion by their jangling. You are suppose to have escaped, *en masse*, from your keepers. Your majesty cannot conceive the *effect* produced, at a masquerade, by eight chained ourang-outangs, inagined to be real ones by most of the company; and rushing in with savage cries, among the crowd of delicately and gorgeously habited men and women. The *contrast* is inimitable."

"It *must* be," said the king: and the council arose hurriedly (as it was growing late), to put in execution the scheme of Hop-Frog.

His mode of equipping the party as ourang-outangs was very simple, but effective enough for his purposes. The animals in question had, at the epoch of my story, very rarely been seen in any part of the civilized world; and as the imitations made by the dwarf were sufficiently beast-like and more than sufficiently hideous, their truthfulness to nature was thus thought to be secured.

17 The king and his ministers were first encased in tight-fitting stockinet shirts and drawers. They were then saturated with tar. At this stage of the process, some one of the party

18 suggested feathers; but the suggestion was at once overruled by the dwarf, who soon convinced the eight, by ocular demonstration, that the hair of such a brute as the ourang-outang was much more efficiently represented by *flax*. A thick coating of the latter was accordingly plastered upon the coating of tar. A long chain was now procured. First, it was passed about the waist of the king, *and tied;* then about another of the party, and also tied; then about all successively, in the same manner. When this chaining arrangement was complete, and the party stood as far apart from each other as possible, they formed a circle; and to make all things appear natural, Hop-Frog passed the residue of the chain, in two diameters, at right angles, across the circle, after the fashion adopted, at the present day, by those who capture chimpanzees, or other

19 large apes, in Borneo.

20   The grand saloon in which the masquerade was to take place, was a circular room, very lofty, and receiving the light of the sun only through a single window at top. At night (the season for which the apartment was especially designed) it was illuminated principally by a large chandelier, depending by a chain from the centre of the sky-light, and lowered, or elevated, by means of a counterbalance as usual; but (in order not to look unsightly) this latter passed outside the cupola and over the roof.

The arrangements of the room had been left to Trippetta's superintendence; but, in some particulars, it seems, she had been guided by the calmer judgment of her friend the dwarf. At his suggestion it was that, on this occasion, the chandelier was removed. Its waxen drippings (which, in weather so warm, it was quite impossible to prevent) would have been seriously detrimental to the rich dresses of the guests, who,

17 A knitted elastic material used chiefly in underwear

18 While they may well deserve to be tarred and feathered, Hop-Frog has much more in mind. See "The System of Doctor Tarr and Professor Fether," note 45.

19 Chimpanzees are native only to Africa, but orangutangs do come from Borneo. (See "The Murders in the Rue Morgue," note 92).

20 A large assembly or public room. As a drinking bar, it was not a common term until the latter half of the nineteenth century.

on account of the crowded state of the saloon, could not *all* be expected to keep from out its centre—that is to say, from under the chandelier. Additional sconces were set in various parts of the hall, out of the way; and a flambeau, emitting sweet odor, was placed in the right hand of each of the Caryatides that stood against the wall—some fifty or sixty all together.

21

The eight ourang-outangs, taking Hop-Frog's advice, waited patiently until midnight (when the room was thoroughly filled with masqueraders) before making their appearance. No sooner had the clock ceased striking, however, than they rushed, or rather rolled in, all together—for the impediments of their chains caused most of the party to fall, and all to stumble as they entered.

The excitement among the masqueraders was prodigious, and filled the heart of the king with glee. As had been anticipated, there were not a few of the guests who supposed the ferocious-looking creatures to be beasts of *some* kind in reality, if not precisely ourang-outangs. Many of the women swooned with affright; and had not the king taken the precaution to exclude all weapons from the saloon, his party might soon have expiated their frolic in their blood. As it was, a general rush was made for the doors; but the king had ordered them to be locked immediately upon his entrance; and, at the dwarf's suggestion, the keys had been deposited with *him*.

While the tumult was at its height, and each masquerader attentive only to his own safety (for, in fact, there was much *real* danger from the pressure of the excited crowd), the chain by which the chandelier ordinarily hung, and which had been drawn up on its removal, might have been seen very gradually to descend, until its hooked extremity came within three feet of the floor.

Soon after this, the king and his seven friends having reeled about the hall in all directions, found themselves, at length, in its centre, and, of course, in immediate contact with the chain. While they were thus situated, the dwarf, who had followed noiselessly at their heels, inciting them to keep up the commotion, took hold of their own chain at the intersection of the two portions which crossed the circle diametrically and at right angles. Here, with the rapidity of thought, he inserted the hook from which the chandelier had been wont to depend; and, in an instant, by some unseen agency, the chandelier-chain was drawn so far upward as to take the hook out of reach, and, as an inevitable consequence, to drag the ourang-outangs together in close connection, and face to face.

The masqueraders, by this time, had recovered, in some measure, from their alarm; and, beginning to regard the whole matter as a well-contrived pleasantry, set up a loud shout of laughter at the predicament of the apes.

"Leave them to *me!*" now screamed Hop-Frog, his shrill voice making itself easily heard through all the din. "Leave them to *me*. I fancy *I* know them. If I can only get a good look at them, I can soon tell who they are."

Here, scrambling over the heads of the crowd, he managed

21 The *flambeaux* are torches, apparently soaked in an aromatic oil. The Caryatides refer to pillars (on the Erechtheum, on the Acropolis) depicting the women of Caryae, whom the Spartans conquered and sentenced to hard labor. Somehow their presence seems appropriate to the king's court.

to get to the wall; when, seizing a flambeau from one of the Caryatides, he returned, as he went, to the centre of the room—leaped, with the agility of a monkey, upon the king's head—and thence clambered a few feet up the chain—holding down the torch to examine the group of ourang-outangs, and still screaming: "*I* shall soon find out who they are!"

And now, while the whole assembly (the apes included) were convulsed with laughter, the jester suddenly uttered a shrill whistle; when the chain flew violently up for about thirty feet—dragging with it the dismayed and struggling ourang-outangs, and leaving them suspended in mid-air between the sky-light and the floor. Hop-Frog, clinging to the chain as it rose, still maintained his relative position in respect to the eight maskers, and still (as if nothing were the matter) continued to thrust his torch down toward them, as though endeavoring to discover who they were.

So thoroughly astonished was the whole company at this ascent, that a dead silence, of about a minute's duration, ensued. It was broken by just such a low, harsh, *grating* sound, as had before attracted the attention of the king and his councillors when the former threw the wine in the face of Trippetta. But, on the present occasion, there could be no question as to *whence* the sound issued. It came from the

In less than half a minute the whole eight ourang-outangs were blazing fiercely. . . . *Illustration by H. Church,* *1903*

fang-like teeth of the dwarf, who ground them and gnashed them as he foamed at the mouth, and glared, with an expression of maniacal rage, into the upturned countenances of the king and his seven companions.

"Ah, ha!" said at length the infuriated jester. "Ah, ha! I begin to see who these people *are*, now!" Here, pretending to scrutinize the king more closely, he held the flambeau to the flaxen coat which enveloped him, and which instantly burst into a sheet of vivid flame. In less than half a minute the whole eight ourang-outangs were blazing fiercely, amid the shrieks of the multitude who gazed at them from below, horror-stricken, and without the power to render them the slightest assistance. **22**

At length the flames, suddenly increasing in virulence, forced the jester to climb higher up the chain, to be out of their reach; and, as he made this movement, the crowd again sank, for a brief instant, into silence. The dwarf seized his opportunity, and once more spoke:

"I now see *distinctly*," he said, "what manner of people these maskers are. They are a great king and his seven privy-councillors,—a king who does not scruple to strike a defence-less girl, and his seven councillors who abet him in the outrage. As for myself, I am simply Hop-Frog, the jester—and *this is my last jest*."

Owing to the high combustibility of both the flax and the tar to which it adhered, the dwarf had scarcely made an end of his brief speech before the work of vengeance was complete. The eight corpses swung in their chains, a fetid, blackened, hideous, and indistinguishable mass. The cripple hurled his torch at them, clambered leisurely to the ceiling, and disappeared through the sky-light.

It is supposed that Trippetta, stationed on the roof of the saloon, had been the accomplice of her friend in his fiery revenge, and that, together, they effected their escape to their own country; for neither was seen again.

22 In Chaper LIII of Froissart's *Chronicles*, we read how, in 1393, a Norman squire devised costumes made of linen covered with flax the color of hair, and dressed Charles VI of France and several others, including himself, in them to masquerade as savages at a gala wedding party.

The Duke of Orléans "was very inquisitive in examining them, to find out who they were; and, as the five were dancing, he took one of the torches from his servants, and, holding it too near their dresses, set them on fire. Flax, you know, is instantly in a blaze; and the pitch, with which the cloth had been covered to fasten the flax, added to the impossibility of extinguishing it. They were likewise chained together, and their cries were dreadful; for the fire was so strong, scarcely any dared approach. Some knights indeed did their utmost to disengage them, but the pitch burnt their hands very severely; and they suffered a long time afterwards from it.

"One of the five, Nantouillet, recollected that the buttery was near, broke the chain, and flying thither, flung himself into a tub of water which was there for washing dishes and plates. This saved him, or he would have been burnt to death like the others: but he was withal some time very ill. When the queen heard the cause of the cries, she was alarmed lest the king should be hurt, for he had told her he would be one of the six, and in her fright fainted and fell down: her ladies and knights hastened to her assistance; and the confusion was so great, no one knew what to do. The duchess of Berry saved the king by throwing the train of her robe over him, and detaining him, for he wanted to quit her. 'Where are you going?' said she: 'do you not see your companions are in a blaze? who are you? for it is not now a time to keep it a secret.' He then mamed himself, saying, 'I am the king.' 'Ah, my lord,' replied the duchess, 'put on quickly another dress, and show yourself to the queen, for she is very much distressed about you.' "

When the confusion was over, the horror was fully evident: "Of the four that were on fire, two died on the spot: the other two, the bastard of Foix and the count de Joigny, were carried to their hotels, and died two days afterwards in great agonies. Thus unfortunately did the wedding-feast end. . . ." (*Chronicles of England, France, Spain, and the Adjoining Countries,* S. W. Green, 1882; pp. 557–58)

In *A Distant Mirror* (Knopf, 1978), Barbara Tuchman also describes the scene (pp. 503–5): "The fatal masquerade came to be called the *Bal des Ardents*—Dance of the Burning Ones—but it could as well have been called the *Danse Macabre*. . . ."

Mysteries

THE MAN OF THE CROWD

First published in December 1840, in both Burton's *Gentleman's Magazine* and *The Casket*.

"The Man of the Crowd" shares much of the style and thrust of Hawthorne's work in its attempt to fathom the recesses of the human soul. Unlike Hawthorne, however, Poe does not reveal the crime responsible for the aimless wanderings of the Man of the Crowd. He seems content, rather, to indicate the existence of certain dark secrets in the human soul that cannot be understood by anyone.

In Hawthorne's "Ethan Brand," the title character has become obsessed with the Unpardonable Sin, "lost hold of the magnetic chain of humanity," and is "no longer a brother-man, opening the chambers or the dungeons of our common nature by the key of holy sympathy, which gave him a right to share in all its secrets. . . ." His obsession leads to his searching the world for the Unpardonable Sin, and ironically, his cutting himself off from humanity has produced the very sin he has feared he would find—in himself.

The analytical style of "The Man of the Crowd" is most closely matched in Hawthorne's "Wakefield," which tells of a man who unaccountably leaves his wife, and then, just as unaccountably, returns much later. Hawthorne, again, provides a plausible explanation for Wakefield's behavior.

Poe is, as always, much more interested in the mystery *as* a mystery, inspired perhaps by a passage in "The Drunkard's Death," in Dickens' *Sketches by Boz* (reviewed by Poe in 1836): "Strange tales have been told in the wanderings of dying men; tales so full of guilt and crime, that those who stood by the sick person's couch have fled in horror and affright, lest they should be scared to madness by what they heard and saw; and many a wretch has died alone, raving of deeds the very name of which has driven the boldest man away."

Like Hawthorne, Dickens gives the background of his drunkard, and unlike Poe, moralizes on the social evils of the day.

"The Man of the Crowd" also shares something with the legend of the *Flying Dutchman* (see "MS. Found in a Bottle," note 35), particularly the notion of a man doomed to wander endlessly until his crime is expiated.

The tale is a kind of mystery story, with the narrator as a detective who takes up sleuthing in order to determine the motives for the stranger's strange behavior. Unlike Dupin, however, he fails.

Ce grand malheur, de ne pouvoir être seul.
　　　　　　　　　—*La Bruyère*.　　　　　　**1**

1 "That great misfortune, not to be able to be alone," from *Les Caractères* ("De l'homme"), by Jean de La Bruyère (1645–96), also quoted in "Metzengerstein."

It was well said of a certain German book that *"er lasst sich nicht lessen"*—it does not permit itself to be read. There are **2** some secrets which do not permit themselves to be told. Men die nightly in their beds, wringing the hands of ghostly confessors, and looking them piteously in the eyes—die with despair of heart and convulsion of throat, on account of the hideousness of mysteries which will not *suffer themselves* to be revealed. Now and then, alas, the conscience of man takes up a burden so heavy in horror that it can be thrown down only into the grave. And thus the essence of all crime is undivulged.

2 Compare this passage with the passage from Dickens quoted in the introductory note.

3 "The mist that previously was upon them" is from the *Iliad*, V. 127, where Athene lifts the haze from Diomede's eyes so that he may see the gods while he fights.

4 Gottfried Wilhelm, Baron von Leibnitz (1646–1716) was the German philosopher and mathematician whose scholarship embraced the physical sciences, history, law, diplomacy, and logic. He asserted that since the universe is the result of a divine plan, ours must be the best of all possible worlds—a statement roundly satirized by Voltaire in *Candide*. Leibnitz never said the world was perfect, however, but the best it could be under the circumstances.

In his original draft of the story, Poe uses the name of George Combe (1788–1858), who advocated studying the natural world as a guide to behavior.

5 Gorgias (c. 485—c. 380 B.C.) asserted that nothing exists, or if it does exist it cannot be known, or if it can be known the knowledge cannot be communicated. Objective truth, therefore, is impossible.

6 This isn't meant as masochistic pleasure, but as an expression of the joy of living, despite occasional pain.

7 Wholesalers

8 From the Greek, meaning of noble ancestry; one of the hereditary aristocracy of Athens, and hence a patrician

"The Man of the Crowd." Illustration by Albert Edward Sterner for Century Magazine, *1903*

Not long ago, about the closing in of an evening in autumn, I sat at the large bow-window of the D—— Coffee-House in London. For some months I had been ill in health, but was now convalescent, and, with returning strength, found myself in one of those happy moods which are so precisely the converse of *ennui*—moods of the keenest appetency, when the film from the mental vision departs—the αχλυς ος πριν

3 επηεν—and the intellect, electrified, surpasses as greatly its every-day condition, as does the vivid yet candid reason of

4,5 Leibnitz, the mad and flimsy rhetoric of Gorgias. Merely to breathe was enjoyment; and I derived positive pleasure even

6 from many of the legitimate sources of pain. I felt a calm but inquisitive interest in every thing. With a cigar in my mouth and a newspaper in my lap, I had been amusing myself for the greater part of the afternoon, now in poring over advertisements, now in observing the promiscuous company in the room, and now in peering through the smoky panes into the street.

This latter is one of the principal thoroughfares of the city, and had been very much crowded during the whole day. But, as the darkness came on, the throng momently increased; and, by the time the lamps were well lighted, two dense and continuous tides of population were rushing past the door. At this particular period of the evening I had never before been in a similar situation, and the tumultuous sea of human heads filled me, therefore, with a delicious novelty of emotion. I gave up, at length, all care of things within the hotel, and became absorbed in contemplation of the scene without.

At first my observations took an abstract and generalizing turn. I looked at the passengers in masses, and thought of them in their aggregate relations. Soon, however, I descended to details, and regarded with minute interest the innumerable varieties of figure, dress, air, gait, visage, and expression of countenance.

By far the greater number of those who went by had a satisfied, businesslike demeanor, and seemed to be thinking only of making their way through the press. Their brows were knit, and their eyes rolled quickly; when pushed against by fellow-wayfarers they evinced no symptom of impatience, but adjusted their clothes and hurried on. Others, still a numerous class, were restless in their movements, had flushed faces, and talked and gesticulated to themselves, as if feeling in solitude on account of the very denseness of the company around. When impeded in their progress, these people suddenly ceased muttering, but redoubled their gesticulations, and awaited, with an absent and overdone smile upon the lips, the course of the persons impeding them. If jostled, they bowed profusely to the jostlers, and appeared overwhelmed with confusion.—There was nothing very distinctive about these two large classes beyond what I have noted. Their habiliments belonged to that order which is pointedly termed the decent. They were undoubtedly noblemen, merchants,

7,8 attorneys, tradesmen, stock-jobbers—the Eupatrids and the common-places of society—men of leisure and men actively engaged in affairs of their own—conducting business upon its own responsibility. They did not greatly excite my attention.

The tribe of clerks was an obvious one; and here I discerned two remarkable divisions. There were the junior clerks of flash houses—young gentlemen with tight coats, bright boots, well-oiled hair, and supercilious lips. Setting aside a certain dapperness of carriage, which may be termed *deskism* for want of a better word, the manner of these persons seemed to be an exact fac-simile of what had been the perfection of *bon ton* about twelve or eighteen months before. They wore the cast-off graces of the gentry;—and this, I believe, involves the best definition of the class.

The division of the upper clerks of staunch firms, or of the "steady old fellows," it was not possible to mistake. These were known by their coats and pantaloons of black or brown, made to sit comfortably, with white cravats and waistcoats, broad solid-looking shoes, and thick hose or gaiters. They had all slightly bald heads, from which the right ears, long used to pen-holding, had an odd habit of standing off on end. I observed that they always removed or settled their hats with both hands, and wore watches, with short gold chains of a substantial and ancient pattern. Theirs was the affectation of respectability—if indeed there be an affectation so honorable.

There were many individuals of dashing appearance, whom I easily understood as belonging to the race of swell pick-pockets, with which all great cities are infested. I watched these gentry with much inquisitiveness, and found it difficult to imagine how they should ever be mistaken for gentlemen by gentlemen themselves. Their voluminousness of wristband, with an air of excessive frankness, should betray them at once.

The gamblers, of whom I descried not a few, were still more easily recognizable. They wore every variety of dress, from that of the desperate thimble-rig bully, with velvet waistcoat, fancy neckerchief, gilt chains, and filigreed buttons, to that of the scrupulously inornate clergyman, than which nothing could be less liable to suspicion. Still all were distinguished by a certain sodden swarthiness of complexion, a filmy dimness of eye, and pallor and compression of lip. There were two other traits, moreover, by which I could always detect them: a guarded lowness of tone in conversation, and a more than ordinary extension of the thumb in a direction at right angles with the fingers. Very often, in company with these sharpers, I observed an order of men somewhat different in habits, but still birds of a kindred feather. They may be defined as the gentlemen who live by their wits. They seem to prey upon the public in two battalions—that of the dandies and that of the military men. Of the first grade the leading features are long locks and smiles; of the second, frogged coats and frowns.

Descending in the scale of what is termed gentility, I found darker and deeper themes for speculation. I saw Jew peddlers, with hawk eyes flashing from countenances whose every other feature wore only an expression of abject humility; sturdy professional street beggars scowling upon mendicants of a

9 "Flash" has several meanings: "fashionable," "void of meaning," "counterfeit or sham."

Poe is having a bit of fun with the business mind, which he detested, since "flash house" means "a lodging or tavern frequented by thieves and illegally favourable to them," according to *A Dictionary of Slang and Unconventional English* (Macmillan, 1970).

10 A fine word. Too bad nobody else has picked it up.

11 High tone; good breeding

12 "Swell" originally meant a fashionably or smartly dressed person, usually someone of the upper classes. Poe's use of it in juxtaposition with pickpockets is no doubt a commentary on the society of the day, and also reinforces the meaning of "flash house" suggested in note 9; that is, that businessmen are thieves, while thieves dress like businessmen.

13 Cuff

14 A frog is an ornamental fastening consisting of a spindle-shaped button, covered with silk or other material, that passes through a loop on the opposite side of the garment.

15 "Lucian, in describing the statue 'with its surface of Parian marble and its interior filled with rags,' must have been looking with a prophetic eye at some of our 'moneyed institutions.' " (Poe, "Fifty Suggestions," XXI).

The work of Lucian of Samosata (c. 125–c. 180) referred to here is *Somnium* (*The Dream*). Parian marble is the name of the variety from Paros, an island in the Aegean.

16 This is as close as Poe comes to describing a prostitute. The passage echoes Dickens' "The Pawnbroker's Shop" (*Sketches by Boz*), in which a woman's clothes are called "miserably poor, but extremely gaudy. . . . The rich satin gown with its faded trimmings—the worn-out thin shoes, and pink silk stockings—the summer bonnet in winter, and the sunken face where a daub of rouge only serves as an index to the ravages of squandered health. . . ."

17 Jean-Louis Guez de Balzac (1594–1655) said this about Tertullian (160–230) in *Menagiana* (1694).

better stamp, whom despair alone had driven forth into the night for charity; feeble and ghastly invalids, upon whom death had placed a sure hand, and who sidled and tottered through the mob, looking every one beseechingly in the face, as if in search of some chance consolation, some lost hope; modest young girls returning from long and late labor to a cheerless home, and shrinking more tearfully than indignantly from the glances of ruffians, whose direct contact, even, could not be avoided; women of the town of all kinds and of all ages—the unequivocal beauty in the prime of her womanhood, putting one in mind of the statue in Lucian, with the surface **15** of Parian marble, and the interior filled with filth—the loathsome and utterly lost leper in rags—the wrinkled, bejewelled, and paint-begrimed beldame, making a last effort at youth—the mere child of immature form, yet, from long association, an adept in the dreadful coquetries of her trade, and burning with a rabid ambition to be ranked the equal of **16** her elders in vice; drunkards innumerable and indescribable—some in shreds and patches, reeling, inarticulate, with bruised visage and lack-lustre eyes—some in whole although filthy garments, with a slightly unsteady swagger, thick sensual lips, and hearty-looking rubicund faces—others clothed in materials which had once been good, and which even now were scrupulously well brushed—men who walked with a more than naturally firm and springy step, but whose countenances were fearfully pale, whose eyes were hideously wild and red, and who clutched with quivering fingers, as they strode through the crowd, at every object which came within their reach; beside these, piemen, porters, coal-heavers, sweeps; organ-grinders, monkey-exhibitors, and ballad-mongers, those who vended with those who sang; ragged artizans and exhausted laborers of every description, and all full of a noisy and inordinate vivacity which jarred discordantly upon the ear, and gave an aching sensation to the eye.

As the night deepened, so deepened to me the interest of the scene; for not only did the general character of the crowd materially alter (its gentler features retiring in the gradual withdrawal of the more orderly portion of the people, and its harsher ones coming out into bolder relief, as the late hour brought forth every species of infamy from its den), but the rays of the gas-lamps, feeble at first in their struggle with the dying day, had now at length gained ascendancy, and threw over every thing a fitful and garish lustre. All was dark yet splendid—as that ebony to which has been likened the style **17** of Tertullian.

The wild effects of the light enchained me to an examination of individual faces; and although the rapidity with which the world of light flitted before the window prevented me from casting more than a glance upon each visage, still it seemed that, in my then peculiar mental state, I could frequently read, even in that brief interval of a glance, the history of long years.

With my brow to the glass, I was thus occupied in scrutinizing the mob, when suddenly there came into view a countenance (that of a decrepit old man, some sixty-five or seventy years of age)—a countenance which at once arrested and absorbed my whole attention, on account of the absolute idiosyncrasy of its expression. Any thing even remotely resembling that expression I had never seen before. I well remember that my first thought, upon beholding it, was that Retzsch, had he viewed it, would have greatly preferred it to **18** his own pictural incarnations of the fiend. As I endeavored, during the brief minute of my original survey, to form some analysis of the meaning conveyed, there arose confusedly and paradoxically within my mind, the ideas of vast mental power, of caution, of penuriousness, of avarice, of coolness, of malice, of blood-thirstiness, of triumph, of merriment, of excessive terror, of intense—of supreme despair. I felt singularly aroused, startled, fascinated. "How wild a history," I said to myself, "is written within that bosom!" Then came a craving desire to keep the man in view—to know more of him. Hurriedly putting on an overcoat, and seizing my hat and cane, I made my way into the street, and pushed through the crowd in the direction which I had seen him take; for he had already disappeared. With some little difficulty I at length came within sight of him, approached, and followed him closely, yet cautiously, so as not to attract his attention.

I had now a good opportunity of examining his person. He was short in stature, very thin, and apparently very feeble. His clothes, generally, were filthy and ragged; but as he came, now and then, within the strong glare of a lamp, I perceived that his linen, although dirty, was of beautiful texture; and my vison deceived me, or, through a rent in a closely-buttoned and evidently second-handed *roquelaire* **19** which enveloped him, I caught a glimpse both of a diamond and of a dagger. These observations heightened my curiosity, and I resolved to follow the stranger whithersoever he should go. **20**

It was now fully night-fall, and a thick humid fog hung over the city, soon ending in a settled and heavy rain. This change of weather had an odd effect upon the crowd, the whole of which was at once put into new commotion, and overshadowed by a world of umbrellas. The waver, the jostle, and the hum increased in a tenfold degree. For my own part I did not much regard the rain—the lurking of an old fever in my system rendering the moisture somewhat too dangerously pleasant. Tying a handkerchief about my mouth, I kept on. For half an hour the old man held his way with difficulty along the great thoroughfare; and I here walked close at his elbow through fear of losing sight of him. Never once turning his head to look back, he did not observe me. By and by he passed into a cross street, which, although densely filled with people, was not quite so much thronged as the main one he had quitted. Here a change in his demeanor became evident. He walked more slowly and with less object than before— more hesitatingly. He crossed and re-crossed the way repeatedly, without apparent aim; and the press was still so thick, that, at every such movement, I was obliged to follow him

18 Friedrich August Moritz Retzsch (1779–1857) was a German painter and engraver best known for his illustrations for Goethe's *Faust*.

19 A knee-length coat (properly *roquelaure*), mentioned also in "The Cask of Amontillado."

20 "And it came to pass, that, as they went in the way, a certain man said unto him, Lord, I will follow thee withersoever thou goest" (Luke 9:57).

21 City Hall Park in New York City

22 In Dickens' "Thoughts About People," a passage about St. James's Park contains a description of a man who "walked up and down before the little patch of grass on which the chairs are placed for hire, not as if he were doing it for pleasure or recreation, but as if it were a matter of compulsion."

closely. The street was a narrow and long one, and his course lay within it for nearly an hour, during which the passengers had gradually diminished to about that number which is **21** ordinarily seen at noon on Broadway near the park—so vast a difference is there between a London populace and that of the most frequented American city. A second turn brought us into a square, brilliantly lighted, and overflowing with life. The old manner of the stranger re-appeared. His chin fell upon his breast, while his eyes rolled wildly from under his knit brows, in every direction, upon those who hemmed him in. He urged his way steadily and perseveringly. I was surprised, however, to find, upon his having made the circuit of the square, that he turned and retraced his steps. Still more was I astonished to see him repeat the same walk several times—once nearly detecting me as he came round with a **22** sudden movement.

In this exercise he spent another hour, at the end of which we met with far less interruption from passengers than at first. The rain fell fast; the air grew cool; and the people were retiring to their homes. With a gesture of impatience, the wanderer passed into a by-street comparatively deserted. Down this, some quarter of a mile long, he rushed with an activity I could not have dreamed of seeing in one so aged, and which put me to much trouble in pursuit. A few minutes brought us to a large and busy bazaar, with the localities of which the stranger appeared well acquainted, and where his original demeanor again became apparent, as he forced his way to and fro, without aim, among the host of buyers and sellers.

During the hour and a half, or thereabouts, which we passed in this place, it reqired much caution on my part to keep him within reach without attracting his observation. Luckily I wore a pair of caoutchouc overshoes, and could move about in perfect silence. At no moment did he see that I watched him. He entered shop after shop, priced nothing, spoke no word, and looked at all objects with a wild and vacant stare. I was now utterly amazed at his behavior, and firmly resolved that we should not part until I had satisfied myself in some measure respecting him.

A loud-toned clock stuck eleven, and the company were fast deserting the bazaar. A shop-keeper, in putting up a shutter, jostled the old man, and at the instant I saw a strong shudder come over his frame. He hurried into the street, looked anxiously around him for an instant, and then ran with incredible swiftness through many crooked and peopleless lanes, until we emerged once more upon the great thorough-fare whence we had started—the street of the D—— Hotel. It no longer wore, however, the same aspect. It was still brilliant with gas; but the rain fell fiercely, and there were few persons to be seen. The stranger grew pale. He walked moodily some paces up the once populous avenue, then, with a heavy sigh, turned in the direction of the river, and, plunging through a great variety of devious ways, came out, at length, in view of one of the principal theatres. It was about being closed, and the audience were thronging from the doors. I saw the old man gasp as if for breath while he threw himself amid the crowd; but I thought that the intense agony of his countenance had, in some measure, abated. His head again fell upon his breast; he appeared as I had seen him at first. I observed that he now took the course in which had gone the greater number of the audience—but, upon the whole, I was at a loss to comprehend the waywardness of his actions.

As he proceeded, the company grew more scattered, and his old uneasiness and vacillation were resumed. For some time he followed closely a party of some ten or twelve roisterers; but from this number one by one dropped off, until three only remained together, in a narrow and gloomy lane, little frequented. The stranger paused, and, for a moment, seemed lost in thought; then, with every mark of agitation, pursued rapidly a route which brought us to the verge of the city, amid regions very different from those we had hitherto traversed. It was the most noisome quarter of London, where every thing wore the worst impress of the most deplorable poverty, and of the most desperate crime. By the dim light of an accidental lamp, tall, antique, worm-eaten, wooden **23** tenements were seen tottering to their fall, in directions so many and capricious, that scarce the semblance of a passage was discernible between them. The paving-stones lay at random, displaced from their beds by the rankly-growing grass. Horrible filth festered in the dammed-up gutters. The whole atmosphere teemed with desolation. Yet, as we pro- **24** ceeded, the sounds of human life revived by sure degrees, and at length large bands of the most abandoned of a London populace were seen reeling to and fro. The spirits of the old man again flickered up, as a lamp which is near its death-hour. Once more he strode onward with elastic tread. Suddenly a corner was turned, a blaze of light burst upon our sight, and we stood before one of the huge suburban temples of Intemperance—one of the palaces of the fiend, Gin. **25**

It was now nearly daybreak; but a number of wretched inebriates still pressed in and out of the flaunting entrance. With a half shriek of joy the old man forced a passage within, resumed at once his original bearing, and stalked backward and forward, without apparent object, among the throng. He had not been thus long occupied, however, before a rush to the doors gave token that the host was closing them for the night. It was something even more intense than despair that I then observed upon the countenance of the singular being whom I had watched so pertinaciously. Yet he did not hesitate in his career, but, with a mad energy, retraced his steps at once, to the heart of the mighty London. Long and swiftly he fled, while I followed him in the wildest amazement, resolute not to abandon a scrutiny in which I now felt an interest all-absorbing. The sun arose while we proceeded, and, when we had once again reached that most thronged mart of the populous town, the street of the D—— Hotel, it presented an appearance of human bustle and activity scarcely inferior to what I had seen on the evening before. And here, long,

23 Occasional

24 Compare this with the description of the city in "King Pest."

25 In "Gin-Shops," which Poe not only read but reprinted in parts for a review, Dickens writes of "Wretched houses, with broken windows patched with rags and paper, every room let to a different family, and in many instances to two, or even three . . . filth everywhere—a gutter before the houses and a drain behind them—clothes drying at the windows, slops emptying from the ditto; girls of fourteen or fifteen, with matted hair, walking about bare-footed, and in old white great coats, almost their only covering; boys of all ages, in coats of all sizes, and no coats at all; men and women, in every variety of scanty and dirty apparel, lounging about, scolding, drinking, smoking, squabbling, fighting, and swearing.

"You turn the corner. What a change! All is light and brilliancy. The hum of many voices issues from that splendid gin-shop. . . ."

26 "And the lynx . . . lay down at the feet of the Demon, and looked at him steadily in the face" (Poe's "Silence").

The narrator hopes that, in the words of the old saw, he will be able to read the man's face like a book.

27 Aside from any moral or philosophical or symbolic reasons for the man's behavior, his constant movement in crowds is a symptom of an obsessive-compulsive neurosis, a psychoneurosis characterized by persistent and often unwanted ideas (obsessions) and impulses to carry out irrational, stereotyped, and ritualistic acts in an attempt to overcome anxiety or to assuage guilt feelings.

"Some clinicians believe that obsessive-compulsive reactions may be the first sign of a complete breakdown. Furthermore, many practitioners believe that obsessive-compulsive patients are the most difficult individuals to treat successfully, and it is not unusual to find the pattern intact or even intensified after extensive treatment." (*Abnormal Psychology*, CRM/Random House, 1972; p. 163)

The man of the crowd may also suffer from agoraphobia, or fear of open places.

Marie Bonaparte sees him as symbolic of Poe's hated foster father, John Allan, "who is banished from the mother and home and forced to walk the streets—peopled, as Poe politely disguises it, by prostitutes" (p. 425).

The mysterious wanderer may also represent the narrator's shadow, that submerged personality which figures so strongly in "William Wilson." One need only point out the strong affinity the narrator has for the stranger—a feeling that seems totally unexpected and irrational—and his own "obsessive" need to follow the man. In this Jungian interpretation, the narrator sees his shadow self in the old man, but when he comes close (literally) to an understanding of what the man symbolizes, he retreats, offering as an excuse that there is nothing left to be learned. There may indeed be much more to learn, but the narrator may not be ready for it.

28 "The '*Hortulus Animae cum Oratiunculis Aliquibus Superadditis*' of Grünninger" (Poe's note).

Poe means the *Ortulus anime cum oratiunculis*, published by Johann Reinhard Grüninger in 1500. Poe's spelling of the title and printer match those of Isaac D'Israeli's "Religious Nouvelettes," in his *Curiosities of Literature*.

The meaning of the German phrase is actually that a story is "too shocking to read," but in his collection of miscellany, "Marginalia" XLVI, Poe uses it once again to mean that something is too obscure to be understood.

Here Poe reinforces the idea that certain secrets of the soul are buried too deep to be uncovered, and that we may never fully understand the motives of any individual. Since Poe's time we have learned that repression is the most basic of all defense mechanisms, in which unacceptable or anxiety-producing mental contents are actively barred from the consciousness. We have also learned that a therapist can help the neurotic individual bring the unconscious impulses and inhibitions into his consciousness, and while there is no guarantee that the patient will be relieved of his obsessive behavior, such a change *is* possible.

The very uncertainty inherent in the psychoanalytic process keeps alive the mystery of the unconscious self, and thus Poe's "The Man of the Crowd" remains a haunting portrait of a man driven by inner forces that neither he nor we can fully understand.

"This old man . . . is the type and the genius of deep crime." *Illustration by F. S. Coburn, 1903*

amid the momently increasing confusion, did I persist in my pursuit of the stranger. But, as usual, he walked to and fro, and during the day did not pass from out the turmoil of that street. And, as the shades of the second evening came on, I grew wearied unto death, and, stopping fully in front of the **26** wanderer, gazed at him steadfastly in the face. He noticed me not, but resumed his solemn walk, while I, ceasing to follow, remained absorbed in contemplation. "This old man," I said at length, "is the type and the genius of deep crime. He **27** refuses to be alone. *He is the man of the crowd.* It will be in vain to follow; for I shall learn no more of him, nor of his deeds. The worst heart of the world is a grosser book than the 'Hortulus Animæ,' and perhaps it is but one of the great **28** mercies of God that '*er lasst sich nicht lesen.*'"

THE MURDERS IN THE RUE MORGUE

First published in *Graham's Magazine*, April 1841, this tale is a literary landmark: the first modern detective story.

True, nowhere is C. Auguste Dupin referred to as a "detective"—the word wasn't applied to a police specialist until 1843, and not to a private citizen until 1856—but there is no doubt that he is the forerunner of almost every fictional detective since, from Sherlock Holmes to Hercule Poirot.

Poe's success in his three tales of ratiocination, as he called them, stems from three basic innovations.

The first is, of course, the analytical detective himself, a man who is an intellectual, a true genius (complete, as all geniuses should be, with eccentricities) whose deductive powers allow him to seize upon almost invisible clues and thread them together into a solution.

"One likes in a detective story to have the pleasure of following the workings of one keen mind," says T. S. Eliot. "In real keenness of wit and the way in which this keenness is exhibited, no one has ever surpassed Poe's Monsieur Dupin." (*The Criterion*, 1927; Vol. 5, p. 362)

Poe's second innovation is the narrator who is as mystified as the reader by the intracacies of the plot and the actions of the detective, and who allows for the continued mystery and suspense. This is important, for as Poe observes, "The design of *mystery* . . . being once determined by the author, it becomes imperative, first, that no undue or inartistical means be employed to conceal the secret of the plot; and secondly, that the secret be well kept . . ." (Poe, "Charles Dickens").

In Poe's "Thou Art the Man," we see the difficulty that arises when the detective is also the narrator: in order to keep us in the dark, he has to withhold evidence, and we feel cheated.

But by introducing an intermediary as narrator, the problem is solved. As Poe points out in a letter to Philip Pendleton Cooke (August 9, 1846), ". . . where is the ingenuity of unravelling a web which you [the author] have woven for the express purpose of unravelling? The reader is made to confound the ingenuity of the suppositious Dupin with that of the writer of the story."

The third innovation is Poe's establishment, once and for all, of the focus of the detective story. As J. Brander Matthews puts it, "It is not in the mystery itself that the author seeks to interest the reader, but rather in the successive steps whereby his analytical observer is enabled to solve a problem that might well be dismissed as beyond human elucidation. Attention is centered on the unravelling of the tangled skein rather than on the knot itself. The emotion is not mere surprise, it is recognition of the unsuspected capabilities of the human brain; it is not a wondering curiosity as to an airless mechanism, but a heightening admiration for the analytic acumen capable of working out an acceptable answer to the puzzle propounded. In other words, Poe, while he availed himself of the obvious advantages of keeping a secret from his readers and of leaving them guessing as long as he pleased, shifted the point of attack and succeeded in giving a human interest to his tale of wonder. And by this shift Poe transported the detective story from the group of tales of adventure to the group of portrayals of character. By bestowing upon it a human interest, he raised it in the literary scale." (*Scribner's Magazine*, September 1907, pp. 287–93, Section III)

Poe seems to have drawn Dupin's character partly from Voltaire's *Zadig* (1748), which is mentioned in "Hop-Frog." Voltaire's hero manages to describe perfectly a dog he has never seen, explaining, "I saw an animal's tracks on the sand, and I judged . . . they were . . . of a dog. The long shallow furrows printed on the little ridges of sand between the tracks of the paws informed me that the animal was a bitch with pendant dugs, who hence had puppies recently. Other tracks . . . which seemed . . . to have scraped the surface of the sand beside the forepaws, gave me the idea that the bitch had very long ears; and [since] the sand was always less hollowed by one paw than by the three others, I concluded that our . . . bitch was somewhat lame." (Chapter 3)

Poe's rationalist side is represented as well, for Dupin is that ideal mix of reason and imagination which Poe often praises. In his essay, "Fancy and the Imagination" Poe writes, "All novel conceptions are merely unusual combinations. The mind of man can *imagine* nothing which has not already existed. . . . Thus with all which seems to be *new*—which appears to be a *creation* of intellect, it is resolvable into the old." Dupin's prowess lies in his ability to trace a series of "new" (that is, unusual or odd) circumstances back to their origin.

We note that Dupin is not only well-read in the sciences and mathematics but is a poet as well, once again underscoring the marriage of reason and imagination and perhaps explaining why, in all of Poe's fiction, Dupin is the only one who actively undertakes to understand his environment and succeeds without trauma or destruction.

As for the ape in the tale, Poe very likely saw an article, "New Mode of Thieving," in the *Annual Register for* 1834, or in its original form in the Ipswich *Shrewsbury Chronicle* (August 22, 1834), which tells of "an extra-ordinary burglary":

"Mrs. S. retired to her bed-room, and before her husband had desisted from his supper enjoyments, some of the family was alarmed by a scream from her bedroom, and one of the inmates (a female) proceeding thither, was attacked on entering the door, by a Monkey (or a Ribbed-face Baboon) which threw her down, and placing his feet upon her breast, held her pinned firmly to the ground. The screams of Mrs. Smith brought up her husband, who, seeing the condition of the prostrate female, assailed the monkey, and compelled him to quit his hold on the female, and thereby drew all his vengeance upon himself. The brute took up his position on the wash-basin stand; and every attempt to dislodge him brought to the ground some fragile articles of furniture . . . till, on Mr. Smith attempting to go into another room for his pistols, the monkey leaped on his back with the speed of lightning, made various attempts to reach his throat, broke his watch guard asunder in rage, and, dropping to the ground, bit his leg, and again fled to the basin-stand. . . . But where did this Baboon come from? The animal had been danced through this town two or three days by itinerant showmen; and had either escaped from them or been let loose for the sake of his plundering. . . . It appears he had dropped from the eaves of the house to the windowsill of Mrs. Smith's chamber, and got into the room through the window, which was left partly open. The owner recovered the animal from the housetops next morning, and escaped to Ludlow."

Another possible source is an early nineteenth-century story, circulating at the time, of a barber's pet monkey, which while the owner was away managed to shave an unwary customer—with traumatic results. When the customer began to shout in anger, the monkey ran up into the chimney until the somewhat worse-for-the-wear customer left.

In Duyckinck's *Cyclopaedia of American Literature*, I, p. 378, there is a poem by David Humphreys entitled *The Monkey*, which details how a pet ape, copying its master, attempts to shave itself and cuts its own throat. And in Scott's *Count Robert of Paris* (1831), a character is strangled by an orangutan.

Poe wrote "The Murders in the Rue Morgue" very quickly, for there are more changes in the manuscript than in most of his other stories. Seldom one to underestimate his own work, Poe spoke rather lightly of his tales of ratiocination, and even hinted that they had been overpraised. Perhaps because they were easier to write, and demanded less time, energy, and revision over the years than some of his other tales, he did not consider them as significant as "Ligeia" or "The Fall of the House of Usher." Sherlock Holmes's creator felt much the same. "He disliked the situation that so much of his finer work tended to be obscured by his lesser," says Adrian Conan Doyle of his celebrated father. "To write a historical novel with that degree of accuracy that his craftsmanship demanded called for research and long study. It called for work. To write a Holmes story required little or nothing from him, and the only explanation that I can offer for this is that he had so much of Holmes in his own make-up that no great effort was required." (*A Treasury of Sherlock Holmes*, Doubleday, 1955; p. xiii)

But both men showed an obvious affection for mystery tales, perhaps because of the very identification each felt with his detective hero. Arthur Conan Doyle summed up his debt to Poe in these words: "Edgar Allan Poe, who, in his carelessly prodigal fashion, threw out the seeds from which so many of our present forms of literature have sprung, was the father of the detective tale, and covered its limits so completely that I fail to see how his followers can find any fresh ground which they can confidently call their own. For the secret of the thinness and also of the intensity of the detective story is that the writer is left with only one quality, that of intellectual acuteness, with which to endow his hero. Everything else is outside the picture and weakens the effect. The problem and its solution must form the theme, and the character-drawing is limited and subordinate. On this narrow path the writer must walk, and he sees the footmarks of Poe always in front of him. He is happy if he ever finds the means of breaking away and striking out on some little side-track of his own." (In Matthews, Section IV. This article is reprinted in full in Eric W. Carlson, ed., *The Recognition of Edgar Allan Poe*, University of Michigan, 1966; pp. 81–94.)

It is fitting, then, that the annual awards for mystery stories have been dubbed "Edgars."

"The Murders in the Rue Morgue" has been a popular source of a number of films. Parts of the tale appear in the 1912 silent movie *The Raven*, but the first full-scale treatment came in 1932, directed by Robert Florey and starring Bela Lugosi, Sidney Fox, Leon Ames (Leon Waycoff), and Arlene Francis. In this version, a women is found dead with traces of gorilla blood in her veins. Lugosi delivers his lines in florid prose, but the film dies when he is offscreen. A 1971 version, directed by Gordon Hessler, starred Jason Robards, Christine Kaufmann, Herbert Lom, Lilli Palmer, and Michael Dunn. While closer to the spirit of the original, it still takes a great many liberties with Poe's story, sensationalizing even further the lurid events of the murders.

Elements of the tale appear in *Phantom of the Rue Morgue*, a 1954 film directed by Roy Del Ruth, with Karl Malden, Claude Dauphin, Patricia Medina, Steve Forrest, and Merv Griffin. Here the screenplay changes the ape to a mad killer on the loose in Paris, and throws in the obligatory romance that is part of almost all Poe films.

A much earlier borrowing is the Danish silent film *Sherlock Holmes in the Great Murder Mystery* (1908). A blend of Doyle and Poe, the story tells how, in a trance, Holmes discovers a murderer is a gorilla.

Michael Harrison (1907–) wrote a good series of pastiches about Dupin for *Ellery Queen's Mystery Magazine*, collected in *the Exploits of the Chevalier Dupin* (Sauk City, Wis: Mycroft & Moran, 1968). The British edition, *Murders in the Rue Royale* (1972), contains five more stories.

What song the Syrens sang, or what name Achilles assumed when he hid himself among women, although puzzling questions are not beyond all conjecture.

—*Sir Thomas Browne*. **1**

The mental features discoursed of as the analytical are, in themselves, but little susceptible of analysis. We appreciate **2** them only in their effects. We know of them, among other things, that they are always to their possessor, when inordinately possessed, a source of the liveliest enjoyment. As the strong man exults in his physical ability, delighting in such exercises as call his muscles into action, so glories the analyst in that moral activity which *disentangles*. He derives pleasure from even the most trivial occupations bringing his talents into play. He is fond of enigmas, of conundrums, of hiero- **3** glyphics; exhibiting in his solutions of each a degree of *acumen* which appears to the ordinary apprehension preternatural. His results, brought about by the very soul and essence of method, have, in truth, the whole air of intuition. **4**

The faculty of re-solution is possibly much invigorated by mathematical study, and especially by that highest branch of it which, unjustly, and merely on account of its retrograde

1 From *Urn-Burial*, Chapter V, by Sir Thomas Browne (1605–82). The sirens sang so loudly and seductively that sailors drove their ships onto the rocks in their madness. Ulysses stopped his sailors' ears with wax so they could sail by in safety. Achilles lived among women at the court of Lycomedes to avert a prophecy that he would die at Troy.

Browne, in a note, mentions that Tiberius enjoyed posing such impossible questions to the literary scholars of his day.

2 In the original version of the story, the following paragraph preceded what is now the opening of the story: "It is not improbable that a few farther steps in phrenological science will lead to a belief in the existence, if not to the actual discovery and location, of an organ of *analysis*. If this power (which may be described, although not defined, as the capacity for resolving thought into its elements) be not, in fact, an essential portion of what late philosophers term ideality, then there are indeed many good reasons for supposing it a primitive faculty. . . . That it may be a constituent of ideality is here suggested to the vulgar dictum (founded, however, upon the assumptions of grave authority), that the calculating and discriminating powers (causality and comparison) are at variance with the imaginative—that the three, in short, can hardly coexist. But, although thus opposed to received opinion, the idea will not appear ill-founded when we observe that the processes of invention and creation are strictly akin with the processes of resolution—the former being nearly, if not absolutely, the latter conversed."

This deletion perhaps reflects Poe's disenchantment with phrenology.

3 Riddles whose answers involve wordplay

4 In other words, he is a bit of a showman, making it seem that he knows the truth or some fact independent of any reasoning process.

5 Strictly speaking, mathematical analysis is; an investigation based on the properties of numbers, a discussion of a problem using algebra instead of geometry, calculus (and its higher developments), or a system of calculation such as vector analysis.

6 "Analysis" comes from a word meaning to loosen— that is, take apart—while "calculate" is based on a word meaning to reckon, or put together.

7 Checkers

8 Sought out with care, although a Frenchman would not use it that way. In French the word implies studied refinement or elegance.

9 A card game played by four players, two against two, with fifty-two cards.

10 Edmond Hoyle (1672–1769) was the great English authority and writer on card games.

5 operations, has been called, as if *par excellence,* analysis. Yet
6 to calculate is not in itself to analyze. A chess-player, for example, does the one without effort at the other. It follows that the game of chess, in its effects upon mental character, is greatly misunderstood. I am not now writing a treatise, but simply prefacing a somewhat peculiar narrative by observations very much at random; I will, therefore, take occasion to assert that the higher powers of the reflective intellect are more decidedly and more usefully tasked by the unostentatious
7 game of draughts than by all the elaborate frivolity of chess. In this latter, where the pieces have different and *bizarre* motions, with various and variable values, what is only complex is mistaken (a not unusual error) for what is profound. The *attention* is here called powerfully into play. If it flag for an instant, an oversight is committed, resulting in injury or defeat. The possible moves being not only manifold but involute, the chances of such oversights are multiplied; and in nine cases out of ten it is the more concentrative rather than the more acute player who conquers. In draughts, on the contrary, where the moves are *unique* and have but little variation, the probabilities of inadvertence are diminished, and the mere attention being left comparatively unemployed, what advantages are obtained by either party are obtained by superior *acumen.* To be less abstract—Let us suppose a game of draughts where the pieces are reduced to four kings, and where, of course, no oversight is to be expected. It is obvious that here the victory can be decided (the players being at all
8 equal) only by some *recherché* movement, the result of some strong exertion of the intellect. Deprived of ordinary resources, the analyst throws himself into the spirit of his opponent, identifies himself therewith, and not unfrequently sees thus, at a glance, the sole methods (sometimes indeed absurdly simple ones) by which he may seduce into error or hurry into miscalculation.
9   Whist has long been noted for its influence upon what is termed calculating power; and men of the highest order of intellect have been known to take an apparently unaccountable delight in it, while eschewing chess as frivolous. Beyond doubt there is nothing of a similar nature so greatly tasking the faculty of analysis. The best chess-player in Christendom *may* be little more than the best player of chess; but proficiency in whist implies capacity for success in all these more important undertakings where mind struggles with mind. When I say proficiency, I mean that perfection in the game which includes a comprehension of *all* the sources whence legitimate advantage may be derived. These are not only manifold but multiform, and lie frequently among recesses of thought altogether inaccessible to the ordinary understanding. To observe attentively is to remember distinctly; and, so far, the concentrative chess-player will do very well at whist; while
10 the rules of Hoyle (themselves based upon the mere mechanism of the game) are sufficiently and generally comprehensible. Thus to have a retentive memory, and to proceed by "the book," are points commonly regarded as the sum total

of good playing. But it is in matters beyond the limits of mere rule that the skill of the analyst is evinced. He makes, in silence, a host of observations and inferences. So, perhaps, do his companions; and the difference in the extent of the information obtained lies not so much in the validity of the inference as in the quality of the observation. The necessary knowledge is that of *what* to observe. Our player confines himself not at all; nor, because the game is the object, does he reject deductions from things external to the game. He examines the countenance of his partner, comparing it carefully with that of each of his opponents. He considers the mode of assorting the cards in each hand; often counting trump by trump, and honor by honor, through the glances bestowed by their holders upon each. He notes every variation of face as the play progresses, gathering a fund of thought from the differences in the expression of certainty, of surprise, of triumph, or chagrin. From the manner of gathering up a trick he judges whether the person taking it can make another in the suit. He recognizes what is played through feint, by the air with which it is thrown upon the table. A casual or inadvertent word; the accidental dropping or turning of a card, with the accompanying anxiety or carelessness in regard to its concealment; the counting of the tricks, with the order of their arrangement; embarrassment, hesitation, eagerness or trepidation—all afford, to his apparently intuitive perception, indications of the true state of affairs. The first two or three rounds having been played, he is in full possession of the content of each hand, and thenceforward puts down his cards with as absolute a precision of purpose as if the rest of the party had turned outward the faces of their own.

The analytical power should not be confounded with simple ingenuity; for while the analyst is necessarily ingenious, the ingenious man is often remarkably incapable of analysis. The **11** constructive or combining power, by which ingenuity is usually manifested, and to which the phrenologists (I believe erroneously) have assigned a separate organ, supposing it a primitive faculty, has been so frequently seen in those whose intellect bordered otherwise upon idiocy, as to have attracted general observation among writers on morals. Between ingenuity and the analytic ability there exists a difference far greater, indeed, than that between the fancy and the imagination, but of a character very strictly analogous. It will be **12** found, in fact, that the ingenious are always fanciful, and the *truly* imaginative never otherwise than analytic. **13**

The narrative which follows will appear to the reader somewhat in the light of a commentary upon the propositions just advanced.

Residing in Paris during the spring and part of the summer of 18—, I there became acquainted with a Monsieur C. Auguste Dupin. This young gentleman was of an excellent— **14** indeed of an illustrious family, but, by a variety of untoward events, had been reduced to such poverty that the energy of his character succumbed beneath it, and he ceased to bestir himself in the world, or to care for the retrieval of his fortunes.

11 Analysis is, in Poe's definition, part of imagination. What Dupin is able to accomplish is by means of the synthesis of imagination and rational thought.

12 See "The Assignation," note 3.

13 "Ingenious" here becomes a synonym for ordinary rationality without the slightest hint of imagination.

14 César Auguste Dupin. Besides implying an aristocratic nature and heritage, Dupin's name recalls that of André-Marie-Jean-Jacques Dupin (1783–1865), a famous legal expert who was said to be a walking encyclopedia. (Other well-known Dupins of the era included Philippe Dupin (1795–1846), a lawyer, and Baron François Pierre Charles Dupin (André's brother, 1784–1873), an economist.

In September 1840, a Dr. Socrates Maupin (now, *there* is a name for you) wrote Poe mentioning a friend, C. Auguste Dubouchet, who was looking for a position as a French teacher.

15 The Faubourg St. Germain lies on the left bank of the Seine, and is not only an aristocratic area but a haven for students and artists, making it an ideal neighborhood for Dupin. It takes its name from the historic abbey and church of St.-Germain-des-Prés, founded in the sixth century by Childebert I (the present church dates from the eleventh century).

In France, "Faubourg St. Germain" has come to mean any aristocratic quarter, as well as the aristocrats themselves. *Faubourg*, incidentally, means "suburb," which the area originally was.

16 By withdrawing from the world, Dupin can sharpen his observational and analytical skills, a situation paralleled in the life-style of Sherlock Holmes.

John G. Cawelti astutely observes the "suggestive similarities between Poe's Dupin and Doyle's Holmes and two other characters with whom one would not at first think to associate them: the fictional figure of the gothic villain and the real character of Dr. Sigmund Freud, particularly as that character was articulated in the role of interpreter of dreams and items of neurotic behavior.

"When one thinks about it, the close resemblance between Dupin and the gothic villain is immediately clear. Both are demonically brilliant, night-loving figures, and both are involved in plotting out elaborate and complex stratagems. One might interpret Poe's invention of the detective as a means of bringing the terrifying potency of the gothic villain under the control of rationality and thereby directing it to beneficial ends.

"Though it has long been common to interpret popular formulas in Freudian terms, the odd analogies between the figure of the detective and that of Dr. Freud himself are rather fascinating and have often been noted [most recently, one notes, in Nicholas Meyer's *The Seven-percent Solution* (1974)].

"The great difference is that where the detective's solution always projects the guilt onto an external character, Freud's method exposes the conflicting motives in our own minds." (*Adventure, Mystery, and Romance*, University of Chicago, 1976; pp. 94–95)

And T. S. Eliot makes a comparison between the Gothic and the detective story by remarking that "Sherlock Holmes was deceiving Watson when he told him that he . . . bought his Stradivarius violin for a few shillings at a second-hand shop in the Tottenham Court Road. He found that violin in the ruins of the house of Usher. There is a close similarity between the musical exercises of Holmes and those of Roderick Usher: those wild and irregular improvisations which, although on one occasion they sent Watson off to sleep, must have been excruciating to any ear trained to music." ("From Poe to Valéry," in *The Recognition of Edgar Allan Poe*, University of Michigan, 1966; p. 208)

17 The narrator seems "possessed" by Dupin, in a way not unlike the relationship of Roderick Usher and his friend, although certainly far less hysterical in nature. Still, the narrator has no life of his own, existing only as a tool of the detective. In the Holmes stories, Doyle gives his narrator not only a name but a more definable personality (and a wife).

18 "Care-charmer Sleep, son of the sable Night" is from the sonnet sequence *Delia* (1592), by Samuel Daniel (1562–1619). "Night, sable goddess! from her ebon throne/In rayless majesty, now stretches forth/Her leaden scepter o'er a slumbering world" is from *Night Thoughts*, by Edward Young (1683–1765)

By courtesy of his creditors, there still remained in his possession a small remnant of his patrimony; and, upon the income arising from this, he managed, by means of rigorous economy, to procure the necessaries of life, without troubling himself about its superfluities. Books, indeed, were his sole luxuries, and in Paris these are easily obtained.

Our first meeting was at an obscure library in the Rue Montmartre, where the accident of our both being in search of the same very rare and very remarkable volume brought us into closer communion. We saw each other again and again. I was deeply interested in the little family history which he detailed to me with all that candour which a Frenchman indulges whenever mere self is the theme. I was astonished, too, at the vast extent of his reading; and, above all, I felt my soul enkindled within me by the wild fervor, and the vivid freshness of his imagination. Seeking in Paris the objects I then sought, I felt that the society of such a man would be to me a treasure beyond price; and this feeling I frankly confided to him. It was at length arranged that we should live together during my stay in the city; and as my worldly circumstances were somewhat less embarrassed than his own, I was permitted to be at the expense of renting, and furnishing in a style which suited the rather fantastic gloom of our common temper, a time-eaten and grotesque mansion, long deserted through superstitions into which we did not inquire, and tottering to its fall in a retired and desolate portion of the Faubourg St. **15** Germain.

Had the routine of our life at this place been known to the world, we should have been regarded as madmen—although, perhaps, as madmen of a harmless nature. Our seclusion was perfect. We admitted no visitors. Indeed the locality of our retirement had been carefully kept a secret from my own former associates; and it had been many years since Dupin had ceased to know or be known in Paris. We existed within **16** ourselves alone.

It was a freak of fancy in my friend (for what else shall I call it?) to be enamored of the Night for her own sake; and into this *bizarrerie*, as into all his others, I quietly fell; giving **17** myself up to his wild whims with a perfect *abandon*. The **18** sable divinity would not herself dwell with us always; but we could counterfeit her presence. At the first dawn of the morning we closed all the massy shutters of our old building, lighted a couple of tapers which, strongly perfumed, threw out only the ghastliest and feeblest of rays. By the aid of these **19** we then busied our souls in dreams—reading, writing, or conversing, until warned by the clock of the advent of the true Darkness. Then we sallied forth into the streets, arm and arm, continuing the topics of the day, or roaming far and wide until a late hour, seeking, amid the wild lights and shadows of the populous city, that infinity of mental excitement which **20** quiet observation can afford.

At such times I could not help remarking and admiring (although from his rich ideality I had been prepared to expect it) a peculiar analytic ability in Dupin. He seemed, too, to take an eager delight in its exercise—if not exactly in its display—and did not hesitate to confess the pleasure thus derived. He boasted to me, with a low chuckling laugh, that most men, in respect to himself, wore windows in their bosoms, and was wont to follow up such assertions by direct **21** and very startling proofs of his intimate knowledge of my own. His manner at these moments was frigid and abstract; his eyes were vacant in expression; while his voice, usually a rich tenor, rose into a treble which would have sounded petulantly but for the deliberateness and entire distinctness of the enunciation. Observing him in these moods, I often dwelt **22** meditatively upon the old philosophy of the Bi-Part Soul, and **23** amused myself with the fancy of a double Dupin—the creative and the resolvent.

Let it not be supposed, from what I have just said, that I am detailing any mystery, or penning any romance. What I have described in the Frenchman was merely the result of an excited, or perhaps of a diseased intelligence. But of the character of his remarks at the periods in question an example will best convey the idea.

We were strolling one night down a long dirty street, in the vicinity of the Palais Royal. Being both, apparently, occupied **24** with thought, neither of us had spoken a syllable for fifteen minutes at least. All at once Dupin broke forth with these words:

"He is a very little fellow, that's true, and would do better for the *Théâtre des Variétés*." **25**

"There can be no doubt of that," I replied unwittingly, and not at first observing (so much had I been absorbed in reflection) the extraordinary manner in which the speaker had chimed in with my meditations. In an instant afterward I recollected myself, and my astonishment was profound.

"Dupin," said I, gravely, "this is beyond my comprehension. I do not hesitate to say that I am amazed, and can scarcely credit my senses. How was it possible you should know what I was thinking of—?" Here I paused, to ascertain beyond a doubt whether he really knew of whom I thought.

"——of Chantilly," said he, "why do you pause? You were **26** remarking to yourself that his diminutive figure unfitted him for tragedy."

This was precisely what had formed the subject of my reflections. Chantilly was a *quondam* cobbler of the Rue St. **27** Denis, who, becoming stage-mad, had attempted the *rôle* of **28** Xerxes, in Crébillon's tragedy so called, and been notoriously **29** Pasquinaded for his pains. **30**

"Tell me, for Heaven's sake," I exclaimed, "the method—if method there is—by which you have been enabled to fathom my soul in this matter." In fact I was even more startled than I would have been willing to express.

"It was the fruiterer," replied my friend, "who brought you to the conclusion that the mender of soles was not of sufficient height for Xerxes *et id genus omne*." **31**

"The fruiterer!—you astonish me—I know no fruiterer whomsoever."

19 A further example of the connection between dream interpretation and detection mentioned in note 16.

20 François Eudes de Mézeray (1610–83), a French historian, was said to have turned night into day in similar fashion, as apparently did Edward Young, author of *Night Thoughts* (note 18).

Night, while it may seem to obscure truth, also shuts out the confusing and distracting world of daylight. In darkness one can concentrate fully, as Dupin makes obvious in his conversation with the Prefect early in "The Purloined Letter."

21 According to Horace Binney Wallace ("William Landor"), Momus was the god of laughter (*Stanley* [1838], II, pp. 237–42), who told Vulcan he should have forged humans as automatons with windows in their bosoms.

The original story, from Lucian's *Hermotimus*, tells how Momus, being asked to pass judgment on the relative merits of Neptune, Vulcan, and Minerva, railed at them all. He said the horns of a bull ought to have been placed in its shoulders, where they would have been of much greater force; as for man, he said Jupiter ought to have made him with a window in his breast, so that his real thoughts would be plain to see. Hence an unreasonable carper is sometimes called a "Momus."

22 From Doyle's *A Study in Scarlet*: "In height [Holmes] was rather over six feet, and so excessively lean that he seemed to be considerably taller. His eyes were sharp and piercing, save during those intervals of torpor to which I have alluded; and his thin, hawk-like nose gave his whole expression an air of alertness and decision. His chin, too, had the prominence and squareness which mark the man of determination."

23 Mentioned also in "The Fall of the House of Usher," "Lionizing," and "William Wilson," the rational soul is distinguished from the animal and vegetable soul. The rational soul is immortal and capable of union with God, while the other is not. Here Poe compares the imaginative or creative mind with the godhead, and the resolvent or rational with the earthbound portion of the human soul.

24 Built for Cardinal Richelieu between 1629 and 1634, the Palais Royal is a rectangular building with a large courtyard in the center, with gardens and galleries. By the 1840s it was a popular public visiting place, and somewhat the worse for wear.

25 A vaudeville house of the day

26 Chantilly, a city in northern France, is famous for its lace; it seems appropriate in connection with a man of delicate appearance.

27 At one time

28 The Boulevard St. Denis is about a mile north of the Seine, northwest of the Church of St. Denis. Poe uses this, as well as other Paris landmarks in the Dupin tales, with little regard for actual geography.

29 *Xerxes* is the best known of the nine tragedies written by Prosper Jolyot de Crébillon, born Sieur de Crais-Billon (1674–1762). Poe quotes Crébillon again at the conclusion of "The Purloined Letter."

30 A *pasquinade* is a lampoon or satirical work posted in some public place. The name comes from Pasquino, an Italian tailor of the fifteenth century noted for his caustic wit. Some time after his death, a mutilated statue was dug up representing either Ajax supporting Menelaos, or Menelaos carrying the dead body of Patroclos, or a gladiator, and was placed at the end of the Braschi Palace near the Piazza Navona in Rome. Since it wasn't clear just whom the statue represented, the Italians called it "Pasquino," because it stood opposite the tailor's former home. The Romans used the torso to post their political, religious, and personal satires, which were therefore called Pasquin Songs, or *pasquinate* (pasquinades). There was also a statue called *Marforio* in the Capitol, to which replies to the pasquinades were affixed.

31 The Cobbler in *Julius Caesar*, i, i, 15, speaks of himself as a "mender of bad soles."
    The Latin phrase means "and all that sort of thing."

32 Charlatanry, quackery

33 Meeting, encounter

34 Dr. John Pringle Nichol (1804–59) was the author of a popularized edition of William Herschel's theories and discoveries. For more on Herschel, see "Hans Pfaall."

35 Named after Alphonse Marie Louis de Lamartine (1790–1869), French poet, novelist, and statesman. Poe did not esteem Lamartine very highly, which accounts for his name adorning this fictional alley.

36 The science or art of cutting, or making sections of, solids, as well as the name of the branch of geometry that deals with sections of solid figures. Here the word refers to the art of cutting stone for masonry work, echoing the subject matter of an article on street paving that Poe wrote for the *Broadway Journal*, April 19, 1845.

37 Atoms

38 Epicurus (341–270 B.C.) deviated from the deterministic philosophies of his day by introducing the idea of spontanaeity, which allowed atoms to form the objects of the world by chance. Everything, he said, spiritual and material, is made of atoms.

39 Nebulae are enormous clouds of dust and gas, often thick enough to obscure more-distant glowing clouds of stars. Some are luminous, others dark. Sir William Herschel (1738–1822) and his son John (1792–1871) disagreed with their contemporaries that the nebulae were swarms of stars, saying instead that they were a continuous, fluid matter.
    William Huggins (1824–1910) proved this to be so in 1864 by examining the spectra of the nebulae, few of which can be seen with the naked eye (an exception being the great nebula in Orion, discovered in 1610).

40 *La Musée des familles*, a periodical founded in 1833, was full of instructional and elevating articles.

"The man who ran up against you as we entered the street—it may have been fifteen minutes ago."

I now remembered that, in fact, a fruiterer, carrying upon his head a large basket of apples, had nearly thrown me down, by accident, as we passed from the Rue C—— into the thoroughfare where we stood; but what this had to do with Chantilly I could not possibly understand.

32   There was not a particle of *charlatanerie* about Dupin. "I will explain," he said, "and that you may comprehend al' clearly, we will first retrace the course of your meditations, from the moment in which I spoke to you until that of the **33** *rencontre* with the fruiterer in question. The larger links of **34** the chain run thus—Chantilly, Orion, Dr. Nicholas, Epicurus, Stereotomy, the street stones, the fruiterer."

There are few persons who have not, at some period of their lives, amused themselves in retracing the steps by which particular conclusions of their own minds have been attained. The occupation is often full of interest; and he who attempts it for the first time is astonished by the apparently illimitable distance and incoherence between the starting-point and the goal. What, then, must have been my amazement when I heard the Frechman speak what he had just spoken? And when I could not help acknowledging that he had spoken the truth. He continued:

"We had been talking of horses, if I remember aright, just before leaving the Rue C——. This was the last subject we discussed. As we crossed into this street, a fruiterer, with a large basket upon his head, brushing quickly past us, thrust you upon a pile of paving-stones collected at a spot where the causeway is undergoing repair. You stepped upon one of the loose fragments, slipped, slightly strained your ankle, appeared vexed or sulky, muttered a few words, turned to look at the pile, and then proceeded in silence. I was not particularly attentive to what you did; but observation has become me, of late, a species of necessity.

"You kept your eyes upon the ground—glancing, with a petulant expression, at the holes and ruts in the pavement (so that I saw you were still thinking of the stones), until we **35** reached the little alley called Lamartine, which has been paved, by way of experiment, with the overlapping and riveted blocks. Here your countenance brightened up, and, perceiving your lips move, I could not doubt that you murmured the **36** word 'stereotomy,' a term very affectedly applied to this species of pavement. I knew that you could not say to yourself **37** 'stereotomy' without being brought to think of atomies, and **38** thus of the theories of Epicurus; and since, when we discussed this subject not very long ago, I mentioned to you how singularly, yet with how little notice, the vague guesses of that noble Greek had met with confirmation in the late nebular cosmogony, I felt that you could not avoid casting your eyes **39** upward to the great *nebula* in Orion, and I certainly expected that you would do so. You did look up; and I was now assured that I had correctly followed your steps. But in that bitter **40** *tirade* upon Chantilly, which appeared in yesterday's '*Musée*,' the satirist, making some disgraceful allusions to the cobbler's change of name upon assuming the buskin, quoted a Latin **41** line about which we have often conversed. I mean the line

Perdidit antiquum litera prima sonum. **42**

I had told you that this was in reference to Orion, formerly **43** written Urion; and, from certain pungencies connected with this explanation, I was aware that you could not have forgotten it. It was clear, therefore, that you would not fail to combine the two ideas of Orion and Chantilly. That you did combine them I saw by the character of the smile which passed over your lips. You thought of the poor cobbler's immolation. So far, you had been stooping in your gait; but now I saw you draw yourself up to your full height. I was then sure that you reflected upon the diminutive figure of Chantilly. At this point I interrupted your meditations to remark that as, in fact, he *was* a very little fellow—that Chantilly—he would do better at the *Théâtre des Variétés*." **44**

Not long after this, we were looking over an evening edition of the "Gazette des Tribunaux," when the following paragraphs **45** arrested our attention.

"EXTRAORDINARY MURDERS.—This morning, about three o'clock, the inhabitants of the Quartier St. Roch were aroused **46** from sleep by a succession of terrific shrieks, issuing, apparently, from the fourth story of a house in the Rue Morgue, **47** known to be in the sole occupancy of one Madame L'Espanaye, **48** and her daughter, Mademoiselle Camille L'Espanaye. After some delay, occasioned by a fruitless attempt to procure admission in the usual manner, the gateway was broken in with a crowbar, and eight or ten of the neighbors entered, accompanied by two *gendarmes*. By this time the cries had ceased; but, as the party rushed up the first flight of stairs, two or more rough voices, in angry contention, were distingushed, and seemed to proceed from the upper part of the house. As the second landing was reached, these sounds, also, had ceased, and everything remained perfectly quiet. The party spread themselves, and hurried from room to room. Upon arriving at a large back chamber in the forth story, (the door of which, being found locked, with the key inside, was forced open,) a spectacle presented itself which struck every **49** one present not less with horror than with astonishment.

"The apartment was in the wildest disorder—the furniture broken and thrown about in all directions. There was only one bedstead; and from this the bed had been removed, and thrown into the middle of the floor. On a chair lay a razor, besmeared with blood. On the hearth were two or three long and thick tresses of grey human hair, also dabled in blood, and seeming to have been pulled out by the roots. On the floor were found four Napoleons, an ear-ring of topaz, three **50** large silver spoons, three smaller of *métal d'Alger*, and two **51** bags containing nearly four thousand francs in gold. The drawers of a *bureau*, which stood in one corner, were open, and had been, apparently, rifled, although many articles still remained in them. A small iron safe was discovered under the *bed* (not under the bedstead). It was open, with the key still

41 A laced boot, usually theatrical

42 "The first letter has lost its original sound" (Ovid, *Fasti*, Book V, 493).

43 Orion was a giant of Boeotia (north of Attica and the Gulf of Corinth) who was famous for his beauty. Blinded, but later with sight restored, he was slain by Diana and made one of the constellations. "Urion" was an early spelling.

44 "Dupin's first exercise in reason," says James Cox, "is to 'read' the narrator's mind by means of a series of highly faked deductions. . . . Pretense is in fact part of the game, for Dupin's entire method ultimately comes down not only to the tenuous reason he exhibits, but to his capacity to identify with the situation. He reads the narrator's mind by means of identification, or inner impersonation, just as he understands Minister D—— in "The Purloined Letter" by imitating in the loneliness of his chambers the facial gestures and appearance of his antagonist." (*Virginia Quarterly*, Vol. 44, 1968; p. 85)

45 *La Gazette des Tribunaux*, founded in 1826, was one of several journals of jurisprudence and judiciary debates, as well as police actions.

46 From the street of the same name

47 Originally, Poe named the Street the Rue Trianon, but almost as an afterthought he changed it—and the title into the bargain—to the present "Rue Morgue."
Morgue, in French, means a mortuary, but as an adjective it also has the connotation of pompous, arrogant, or haughty.

48 The name does not appear in any of the various French works of biography, although "Espinay" does.

49 This is the precursor of the mystery-story gimmick called "the locked-door mystery." In John Dickson Carr's *The Hollow Man* [*The Three Coffins*] (1935), Dr. Gideon Fell delivers a classic lecture on the number and types of crimes that can be committed in a hermetically sealed room, borrowing some of the ideas from Israel Zangwill's *The Big Bow Mystery* (1892).
In Issac Asimov's "The Dying Night," extraterrologist Dr. Wendell Urth makes use of the locked-room convention to embarrass policemen—and the murderer—with his impeccable logic, as well as his vast knowledge of astronomical lore.

50 Since objects of obvious value are strewn on the floor, robbery is not the motive. A Napoleon was a 20-franc gold piece.

51 An inexpensive alloy of lead, tin, and antimony, used in place of silver in flatware

52 Abrasions

53 If one remembers the trouble some executioners had in severing the head of the condemned—which is why M. Guillotin invented a device to speed up the process and make it more certain—it seems hard to believe that anyone could cut all the way through the spinal cord with a razor.

54 "Affair" as a romantic intrigue dates back to 1702. The French prefer *affair du coeur*.

55 Dubourg means "of the borough or market town," an appropriate name for a lower-class laundress. However, Poe may have had in mind the school run by the Misses Dubourg in London, where he was sent as a small boy. That he gives a laundress their name may indicate his feelings about the experience.

56 Perhaps recalling Jean Victor Moreau (1763–1813), a hero of the French Revolution who opposed Napoleon and was exiled first to Spain and then to America, where he was a Philadelphia bookseller before returning to Europe to die in a battle against Napoleon's forces.

in the door. It had no contents beyond a few old letters, and other papers of little consequence.

"Of Madame L'Espanaye no traces were here seen; but an unusual quantity of soot being observed in the fireplace, a search was made in the chimney and (horrible to relate!) the corpse of the daughter, head downward, was dragged therefrom; it having been thus forced up the narrow aperture for a considerable distance. The body was quite warm. Upon **52** examining it, many excoriations were perceived, no doubt occasioned by the violence with which it had been thrust up and disengaged. Upon the face were many severe scratches, and, upon the throat, dark bruises, and deep indentations of finger nails, as if the deceased had been throttled to death.

"After a thorough investigation of every portion of the house, without farther discovery, the party made its way into a small paved yard in the rear of the building, where lay the corpse of the old lady, with her throat so entirely cut that, **53** upon an attempt to raise her, the head fell off. The body, as well as the head, was fearfully mutilated—the former so much so as scarcely to retain any semblance of humanity.

"To this horrible mystery there is not as yet, we believe, the slightest clew."

The next day's paper had these additional particulars.

"*The Tragedy in the Rue Morgue.* Many individuals have been examined in relation to this most extraordinary and frightful affair. [The word '*affaire*' has not yet, in France, that **54** levity of import which it conveys with us,] "but nothing whatever has transpired to throw light upon it. We give below all the material testimony elicited.

55 "*Pauline Dubourg,* laundress, deposes that she has known both the deceased for three years, having washed for them during that period. The old lady and her daughter seemed on good terms—very affectionate toward each other. They were excellent pay. Could not speak in regard to their mode or means of living. Believed that Madame L. told fortunes for a living. Was reputed to have money put by. Never met any persons in the house when she called for the clothes or took them home. Was sure that they had no servant in employ. There appeared to be no furniture in any part of the building except in the fourth story.

56 "*Pierre Moreau,* tobacconist, deposes that he has been in the habit of selling small quantities of tobacco and snuff to Madame L'Espanaye for nearly four years. Was born in the neighborhood, and has always resided there. The deceased and her daughter had occupied the house in which the corpses were found, for more than six years. It was formerly occupied by a jeweller, who under-let the upper rooms to various persons. The house was the property of Madame L. She became dissatisfied with the abuse of the premises by her tenant, and moved into them herself, refusing to let any portion. The old lady was childish. Witness had seen the daughter some five or six times during the six years. The two lived an exceedingly retired life—were reputed to have money. Had heard it said among the neighbors that Madame L. told fortunes—did not believe it. Had never seen any person enter the door except the old lady and her daughter, a porter once or twice, and a physician some eight or ten times.

"... in ... a small paved yard ... lay the corpse of the old lady. ..." *Illustration by F. S. Coburn, 1901*

"Many other persons, neighbors, gave evidence to the same effect. No one was spoken of as frequenting the house. It was not known whether there were any living connexions of Madame L. and her daughter. The shutters of the front windows were seldom opened. Those in the rear were always closed, with the exception of the large back room, fourth story. The house was a good house—not very old.

"*Isidor Musèt, gendarme,* deposes that he was called to the **57** house about three o'clock in the morning, and found some twenty or thirty persons at the gateway, endeavoring to gain admittance. Forced it open, at length, with a bayonet—not with a crowbar. Had but little difficulty in getting it open, on account of its being a double or folding gate, and bolted neither at bottom nor top. The shrieks were continued until the gate was forced—and then suddenly ceased. They seemed to be screams of some person (or persons) in great agony— were loud and drawn out, not short and quick. Witness led the way up stairs. Upon reaching the first landing, heard two voices in loud and angry contention—the one a gruff voice,

57 Perhaps after Alfred de Musset (1810–57), French poet, dramatist, and fiction writer.

58 i.e., "heavens" and "devil"

59 Claude Duval (1643–70) was an infamous robber, but Poe probably took the name from Peter S. Duval, who made the plates for *The Conchologist's First Book* (1838), to which Poe contributed the Preface.

60 William Henry Odenheimer (1817–79) was rector of St. Peter's Church, Philadelphia, after 1840 and author of many books beginning in 1841.

61 The family name here may come from the French *mignard*, meaning simpering or affected, or it could be derived from the Mignot family of Charleston (Mignot and Mignaud sound similar in French), or from historian and journalist François Mignet (1796–1884).

62 i.e., "From Lorraine," in northeastern France

63 Le Bon means literally "the good," and he is, ironically, the first man accused of the murder.

64 William Byrd was the Virginia writer, planter, and government official (1674–1744) and son of yet another Wiliam Byrd (1652–1704). The son's wit and refreshing writing style have earned him a firm place in American literature, particularly as a spokesman for the South.

---

the other much shriller—a very strange voice. Could distinguish some words of the former, which was that of a Frenchman. Was positive that it was not a woman's voice. Could **58** distinguish the words '*sacré*' and '*diable*.' The shrill voice was that of a foreigner. Could not be sure whether it was the voice of a man or of a woman. Could not make out what was said, but believed the language to be Spanish. The state of the room and of the bodies was described by this witness as we described them yesterday.

59   "*Henri Duval*, a neighbor, and by trade a silversmith, deposes that he was one of the party who first entered the house. Corroborates the testimony of Muset in general. As soon as they forced an entrance, they reclosed the door, to keep out the crowd, which collected very fast, notwithstanding the lateness of the hour. The shrill voice, the witness thinks, was that of an Italian. Was certain it was not French. Could not be sure that it was a man's voice. It might have been a woman's. Was not acquainted with the Italian language. Could not distinguish words, but was convinced by the intonation that the speaker was an Italian. Knew Madame L. and her daughter. Had conversed with both frequently. Was sure that the shrill voice was not that of either of the deceased.

60   "—— *Odenheimer, restaurateur*. This witness volunteered his testimony. Not speaking French, was examined through an interpreter. Is a native of Amsterdam. Was passing the house at the time of the shrieks. They lasted for several minutes—probably ten. They were long and loud—very awful and distressing. Was one of those who entered the building. Corroborated the previous evidence in every respect but one. Was sure the shrill voice was that of a man—of a Frenchman. Could not distinguish the words uttered. They were loud and quick—unequal—spoken apparently in fear as well as in anger. The voice was harsh—not so much shrill as harsh. Could not call it a shrill voice. The gruff voice said repeatedly '*sacré*,' '*diable*' and once '*mon Dieu*.'

61   "*Jules Mignaud*, banker, of the firm of Mignaud et Fils,
62 Rue Deloraine. Is the elder Mignaud. Madame L'Espanaye had some property. Had opened an account with his banking house in the spring of the year —— (eight years previously). Made frequent deposits in small sums. Had checked for nothing until the third day before her death, when she took out in person the sum of 4000 francs. This sum was paid in gold, and a clerk sent home with the money.

63   "*Adolphe Le Bon*, clerk to Mignaud et Fils, deposes that on the day in question, about noon, he accompanied Madame L'Espanaye to her residence with the 4000 francs, put up in two bags. Upon the door being opened, Mademoiselle L. appeared and took from his hands one of the bags, while the old lady relieved him of the other. He then bowed and departed. Did not see any person in the street at the time. It is a bye-street—very lonely.

64   "*William Bird*, tailor, deposes that he was one of the party who entered the house. Is an Englishman. Has lived in Paris two years. Was one of the first to ascend the stairs. Heard the voices in contention. The gruff voice was that of a Frenchman. Could make out several words, but cannot now remember all. Heard distinctly '*sacré*' and '*mon Dieu*.' There was a sound at the moment as if of several persons struggling—a scraping and scuffling sound. The shrill voice was very loud—louder than the gruff one. Is sure that it was not the voice of an Englishman. Appeared to be that of a German. Might have been a woman's voice. Does not understand German.

"Four of the above-named witnesses, being recalled, deposed that the door of the chamber in which was found the body of Mademoiselle L. was locked on the inside when the party reached it. Every thing was perfectly silent—no groans or noises of any kind. Upon forcing the door no person was seen. The windows, both of the back and front room, were down and firmly fastened from within. A door between the two rooms was closed, but not locked. The door leading from the front room into the passage was locked, with the key on the inside. A small room in the front of the house, on the fourth story, at the head of the passage, was open, the door being ajar. This room was crowded with old beds, boxes, and so forth. These were carefully removed and searched. There was not an inch of any portion of the house which was not carefully searched. Sweeps were sent up and down the chimneys. The house was a four story one, with garrets (*mansardes*). A trap-door on the roof was nailed down very **65** securely—did not appear to have been opened for years. The time elapsing between the hearing of the voices in contention and the breaking open of the room door, was variously stated by the witnesses. Some made it as short as three minutes—some as long as five. The door was opened with difficulty.

"*Alfonzo Garcio*, undertaker, deposes that he resides in the **66** Rue Morgue. Is a native of Spain. Was one of the party who entered the house. Did not proceed up stairs. Is nervous, and was apprehensive of the consequences of agitation. Heard the voices in contention. The gruff voice was that of a Frenchman. Could not distinguish what was said. The shrill voice was that of an Englishman—is sure of this. Does not understand the English language, but judges by the intonation.

"*Alberto Montani*, confectioner, deposes that he was among **67** the first to ascend the stairs. Heard the voices in question. The gruff voice was that of a Frenchman. Distinguished several words. The speaker appeared to be expostulating. Could not make out the words of the shrill voice. Spoke quick and unevenly. Thinks it the voice of a Russian. Corroborates the general testimony. Is an Italian. Never conversed with a native of Russia.

"Several witnesses, recalled, here testified that the chimneys of all the rooms on the fourth story were too narrow to admit the passage of a human being. By 'sweeps' were meant cylindrical sweeping-brushes, such as are employed by those who clean chimneys. These brushes were passed up and down every flue in the house. There is no back passage by which any one could have descended while the party proceeded up stairs. The body of Mademoiselle L'Espanaye was so firmly wedged in the chimney that it could not be got down until four or five of the party united their strength.

"*Paul Dumas*, physician, deposes that he was called to view **68** the bodies about day-break. They were both then lying on the sacking of the bedstead in the chamber where Mademoiselle L. was found. The corpse of the young lady was much bruised

---

65 Mansard roofs are named after François Mansart (1598–1666), the architect who popularized (but did not invent) them. The slope of a mansard roof from eaves to ridge is broken into two portions, with the lower built with a steep, almost vertical, pitch, while the upper slope lies nearly flat. The result is more usable space immediately under the roof.

66 García is the more common Spanish name; "Garcio" may be an error, or perhaps it is Italian.

67 Possibly an Italianization of Montaigne (1533–92), the French essayist who believed that life was good and that man must discover his own nature in order to live in harmony with others. (Is this the "confection" Poe alludes to?)

68 Dumas is the name of the great father-and-son French writers Alexandre Dumas (1802–70), author of *The Three Musketeers* (1844) and *The Count of Monte Cristo* (1845), and Alexandre Dumas (1824–95), known as Dumas Fils, who wrote *La Dame aux camélias* (*Camille*) (1852).

69 The shinbone

70 Since "Étienne" is French for "Stephen," this translates as "Alexander Stephen(s), which happens to be the name of a southern politician who eventually became Vice-President of the Confederacy. He had served in Congress from 1843 to 1859 and had been a member of the Georgia legislature prior to that.

71 At a loss or puzzled, from hunting jargon meaning a break in the trail or a lost scent.

and excoriated. The fact that it had been thrust up the chimney would sufficiently account for these appearances. The throat was greatly chafed. There were several deep scratches just below the chin, together with a series of livid spots which were evidently the impression of fingers. The face was fearfully discolored, and the eye-balls protruded. The tongue had been partially bitten through. A large bruise was discovered upon the pit of the stomach, produced, apparently, by the pressure of a knee. In the opinion of M. Dumas, Mademoiselle L'Espanaye had been throttled to death by some person or persons unknown. The corpse of the mother was horribly mutilated. All the bones of the right leg and arm were more **69** or less shattered. The left *tibia* much splintered, as well as all the ribs of the left side. Whole body dreadfully bruised and discolored. It was not possible to say how the injuries had been inflicted. A heavy club of wood, or a broad bar of iron— a chair—any large, heavy, and obtuse weapon would have produced such results, if wielded by the hands of a very powerful man. No woman could have inflicted the blows with any weapon. The head of the deceased, when seen by witness, was entirely separated from the body, and was also greatly shattered. The throat had evidently been cut with some very **70** sharp instrument—probably with a razor.

"*Alexandre Etienne*, surgeon, was called with M. Dumas to view the bodies. Corroborated the testimony, and the opinions of M. Dumas.

"Nothing farther of importance was elicited, although several other persons were examined. A murder so mysterious, and so perplexing in all its particulars, was never before committed in Paris—if indeed a murder has been committed at all. The **71** police are entirely at fault—an unusual occurrence in affairs of this nature. There is not, however, the shadow of a clew apparent."

The evening edition of the paper stated that the greatest excitement still continued in the Quartier St. Roch—that the premises in question had been carefully re-searched, and fresh examinations of witnesses instituted, but all to no purpose. A postscript, however, mentioned that Adolphe Le Bon had been arrested and imprisoned—although nothing appeared to criminate him, beyond the facts already detailed.

Dupin seemed singularly interested in the progress of this affair—at least so I judged from his manner, for he made no comments. It was only after the announcement that Le Bon had been imprisoned that he asked me my opinion respecting the murders.

I could merely agree with all Paris in considering them an insoluble mystery. I saw no means by which it would be possible to trace the murderer.

"We must not judge of the means," said Dupin, "by this shell of an examination. The Parisian police, so much extolled for *acumen*, are cunning, but no more. There is no method in their proceedings, beyond the method of the moment. They make a vast parade of measures; but, not unfrequently, these are so ill adapted to the objects proposed, as to put us in mind of Monsieur Jourdain's calling for his *robe-de-chambre—pour mieux entendre la musique*. The results at- **72** tained by them are not infrequently surprising, but, for the most part, are brought about by simple diligence and activity. When these qualities are unavailing, their schemes fail. Vidocq, for example, was a good guesser, and a persevering **73** man. But, without educated thought, he erred continually by the very intensity of his investigations. He impaired his vision by holding the object too close. He might see, perhaps, one or two points with unusual clearness, but in so doing he, necessarily, lost sight of the matter as a whole. Thus there is such a thing as being too profound. Truth is not always in a well. In fact, as regards the more important knowledge, I do believe that she is invariably superficial. The depth lies in the valleys where we seek her, and not upon the mountain-tops where she is found. The modes and sources of this kind of error are well typified in the contemplation of the heavenly bodies. To look at a star by glances—to view it in a sidelong way, by turning toward it the exterior portions of the *retina* (more susceptible of feeble impressions of light than the interior), is to behold the star distinctly—is to have the best appreciation of its lustre—a lustre which grows dim just in proportion as we turn our vision *fully* upon it. A greater **74** number of rays actually fall upon the eye in the latter case, but, in the former, there is the more refined capacity for comprehension. By undue profundity we perplex and enfeeble thought; and it is possible to make even Venus herself vanish from the firmament by a scrutiny too sustained, too concentrated, or too direct.

"As for these murders, let us enter into some examinations for ourselves, before we make up an opinion respecting them. An inquiry will afford us amusement" [I thought this an odd term, so applied, but said nothing], "and, besides, Le Bon once rendered me a service for which I am not ungrateful. **75** We will go and see the premises with our own eyes. I know G——, the Prefect of Police, and shall have no difficulty in **76** obtaining the necessary permission."

The permission was obtained, and we proceeded at once to the Rue Morgue. This is one of those miserable thoroughfares which intervene between the Rue Richelieu and the Rue St. Roch. It was late in the afternoon when we reached it; as this quarter is at a great distance from that in which we resided. The house was readily found; for there were still many persons gazing up at the closed shutters, with an objectless curiosity, from the opposite side of the way. It was an ordinary Parisian house, with a gateway, on one side of which was a glazed watch-box, with a sliding panel in the window, indicating a *loge de concierge*. Before going in we walked up the street, **77** turned down an alley, and then, again turning, passed in the rear of the building—Dupin, meanwhile, examining the whole neighborhood, as well as the house, with a minuteness of attention for which I could see no possible object.

72 In Molière's *Bourgeois Gentilhomme*, I, ii, Jourdain calls for his *robe de chambre* in order to better appreciate chamber music.

73 François Eugène Vidocq (1775–1857) was a French detective and author of crime books, as well as the founder of the Police de Sûreté. He began in the military, moved on to crime, spent time in prison, then opportunistically offered his services to Napoleon as an informer in 1809, and became the first chief of the French police.

His agents were also former prisoners, and their operations were highly suspect—so much so that Vidocq was eventually forced to resign. He then opened his own office as a private detective in 1832, but because of his less-than-ethical methods, was forced into bankruptcy by the authorities. He died penniless.

Memoirs of Vidocq, French Police Agent was a ghost-written, sensationalized account of his career. Some "unpublished passages" from this appeared in *Burton's* in 1838 and 1839, and two of these—"Maire Laurent" and "Doctor Arsac"—have been cited as sources for this tale.

For "truth in a well," see "Maelström," note 1.

74 In dim light, looking directly at a small object may make it seem vague or even invisible, because the object is focused on that portion of the retina where there are no rods and cones. Looking out of the corner of the eye may restore the object to sight. Poe mentions this again in his poem *Al Aaraaf*, II, 72–74: ". . . ponder,/With half closing eyes,/On the stars. . . ." In "The Island of the Fay," the narrator muses "with half-shut eyes."

Poe probably took the idea from *Letters on Natural Magic* (1832), by Sir David Brewster, who quotes this passage from a paper by John Herschel and James South: "The lateral portions of the retina, less fatigued by strong lights, and less exhausted by perpetual attention are probably more sensible to faint impressions than the central ones, which may serve to account for this phaenomenon." Poe mentions Brewster's book again in his essay "Maelzel's Chess-Player."

75 As in "The Purloined Letter," Dupin seems to be in some way personally involved in events here, but in neither story does Poe elaborate, denying us of any glimpse into the detective's personal life.

76 Henri-Joseph Gisquet was prefect of the Paris police from 1831 to 1836.

77 The *concierge*, now a disappearing part of French life, is a man or woman who admits or refuses admittance to people in a house, apartment, or public building.

78 It has been at least two, and possibly three, days since the murders. The bodies, which were already in a sad state, must be quite a sight by now.

79 *Ménager* means to humor or indulge, and there is really no problem in translation, despite the narrator's comment.

80 As with *recherché*, Poe uses *outré* in his own fashion. The most common meaning of the word is "exaggerated or extravagant," but Poe seems to mean "bizarre or outrageous."

Retracing our steps, we came again to the front of the dwelling, rang, and, having shown our credentials, were admitted by the agents in charge. We went upstairs—into the chamber where the body of Mademoiselle L'Espanaye had **78** been found, and where both the deceased still lay. The disorders of the room had, as usual, been suffered to exist. I saw nothing beyond what had been stated in the "Gazette des Tribunaux." Dupin scrutinized everything—not excepting the bodies of the victims. We then went into the other rooms, and into the yard; a *gendarme* accompanying us throughout. The examination occupied us until dark, when we took our departure. On our way home my companion stopped in for a moment at the office of one of the daily papers.

I have said that the whims of my friend were manifold, and that *je les ménageais:*—for this phrase there is no English **79** equivalent. It was his humor, now, to decline all conversation on the subject of the murder, until about noon the next day. He then asked me, suddenly, if I had observed anything *peculiar* at the scene of the atrocity.

There was something in his manner of emphasizing the word "peculiar" which caused me to shudder, without knowing why.

"No, nothing *peculiar*," I said; "nothing more, at least, than we both saw stated in the paper."

"The 'Gazette,'" he replied, "has not entered, I fear, into the unusual horror of the thing. But dismiss the idle opinions of this print. It appears to me that this mystery is considered insoluble, for the very reason which should cause it to be **80** regarded as easy of solution—I mean for the *outré* character of its features. The police are confounded by the seeming absence of motive—not for the murder itself—but for the atrocity of the murder. They are puzzled, too, by the seeming impossibility of reconciling the voices heard in contention with the facts that no one was discovered upstairs but the assassinated Mademoiselle L'Espanaye, and that there were no means of egress without the notice of the party ascending. The wild disorder of the room; the corpse thrust, with the head downward, up the chimney; the frightful mutilation of the body of the old lady; these considerations, with those just mentioned, and others which I need not mention, have sufficed to paralyze the powers, by putting completely at fault the boasted *acumen*, of the government agents. They have fallen into the gross but common error of confounding the unusual with the abstruse. But it is by these deviations from the plane of the ordinary that reason feels its way, if at all, in its search for the true. In investigations such as we are now pursuing, it should not be so much asked 'what has occurred,' as 'what has occurred that has never occurred before.' In fact, the facility with which I shall arrive, or have arrived, at the solution of this mystery is in the direct ratio of its apparent insolubility in the eyes of the police."

I stared at the speaker in mute astonishment.

"I am now awaiting," continued he, looking toward the door of our apartment—"I am now awaiting a person who, although perhaps not the perpetrator of these butcheries, must have been in some measure implicated in their perpetration. Of the worst portion of the crimes committed, it is probable that he is innocent. I hope that I am right in this supposition; for upon it I build my expectation of reading the entire riddle. I look for the man here—in this room—every moment. It is true that he may not arrive; but the probability is that he will. Should he come, it will be necessary to detain him. Here are pistols; and we both know how to use them when occasion demands their use."

I took the pistols, scarcely knowing what I did, or believing what I heard, while Dupin went on, very much as if in a soliloquy. I have already spoken of his abstract manner at such times. His discourse was addressed to myself; but his voice, although by no means loud, had that intonation which is commonly employed in speaking to some one at a great distance. His eyes, vacant in expression, regarded only the wall. **81**

81 He may be in a self-induced hypnotic trance or meditative state. Or could he, like Holmes, be a drug-user?

"That the voices heard in contention," he said, "by the party upon the stairs, were not the voices of the women themselves, was fully proved by the evidence. This relieves us of all doubt upon the question whether the old lady could have first destroyed the daughter, and afterward have committed suicide. I speak of this point chiefly for the sake of method; for the strength of Madame L'Espanaye would have been utterly unequal to the task of thrusting her daughter's corpse up the chimney as it was found; and the nature of the wounds upon her own person entirely preclude the idea of self-destruction. Murder, then, has been committed by some third party; and the voices of this third party were those heard in contention. Let me now advert—not to the whole testimony respecting **82** these voices—but to what was *peculiar* in that testimony. Did you observe anything peculiar about it?"

82 Heed, pay attention

I remarked that, while all the witnesses agreed in supposing the gruff voice to be that of a Frenchman, there was much disagreement in regard to the shrill, or, as one individual termed it, the harsh voice.

"That was the evidence itself," said Dupin, "but it was not the peculiarity of the evidence. You have observed nothing distinctive. Yet there *was* something to be observed. The witnesses, as you remark, agreed about the gruff voice; they were here unanimous. But in regard to the shrill voice, the peculiarity is—not that they disagreed—but that, while an Italian, an Englishman, a Spaniard, a Hollander, and a Frenchman attempted to describe it, each one spoke of it as that *of a foreigner*. Each is sure that it was not the voice of one of his own countrymen. Each likens it—not to the voice of an individual of any nation with whose language he is conversant—but the converse. The Frenchman supposes it the voice of a Spaniard, and 'might have distinguished some words *had he been acquainted with the Spanish.*' The Dutchman maintains it to have been that of a Frenchman; but we find it stated that '*not understanding French this witness was examined through an interpreter.*' The Englishman thinks it the voice of a German, and *'does not understand German.'* The Spaniard 'is sure' that it was that of an Englishman, but 'judges by the intonation' altogether, *'as he has no knowledge of the English.'* The Italian believes it the voice of a Russian, but *'has never conversed with a native of Russia.'* A second Frenchman differs, moreover, with the first, and is positive that the voice was that of an Italian; but, *not being cognizant of that tongue*, is, like the Spaniard, 'convinced by the intonation.' Now, how strangely unusual must that voice have really been, about which such testimony as this *could* have been elicited!—in whose *tones*, even, denizens of the five great divisions of Europe could recognize nothing familiar! You will say that it might have been the voice of an Asiatic— of an African. Neither Asiatics nor Africans abound in Paris; but, without denying the inference, I will now merely call your attention to three points. The voice is termed by one witness 'harsh rather than shrill.' It is represented by two others to have been 'quick and *unequal*.' No words—no sounds resembling words—were by any witness mentioned as distinguishable.

83 "I know not," continued Dupin, "what impression I may have made, so far, upon your own understanding; but I do not hesitate to say that legitimate deductions even from this portion of the testimony—the portion respecting the gruff and shrill voices—are in themselves sufficient to engender a suspicion which should give direction to all farther progress in the investigation of the mystery. I said 'legitimate deductions': but my meaning is not thus fully expressed. I designed to imply that the deductions are the *sole* proper ones, and that the suspicion arises *inevitably* from them as the single result. What the suspicion is, however, I will not say just yet. I merely wish you to bear in mind that, with myself, it was sufficiently forcible to give a definite form—a certain tendency—to my inquiries in the chamber.

"Let us now transport ourselves, in fancy, to this chamber. What shall we first seek here? The means of egress employed by the murderers. It is not too much to say that neither of us believe in præternatural events. Madame and Mademoiselle L'Espanaye were not destroyed by spirits. The doers of the deed were material and escaped materially. Then how? Fortunately, there is but one mode of reasoning upon the point, and that mode *must* lead us to a definite decision. Let us examine, each by each, the possible means of egress. It is clear that the assassins were in the room where Mademoiselle L'Espanaye was found, or at least in the room adjoining, when the party ascended the stairs. It is then only from these two apartments that we have to seek issues. The police have laid bare the floors, the ceilings, and the masonry of the walls, in every direction. No *secret* issues could have escaped their vigilance. But, not trusting to *their* eyes, I examined with my own. There were, then, *no* secret issues. Both doors leading from the rooms into the passage were securely locked, with the keys inside. Let us turn to the chimneys. These, although of ordinary width for some eight or ten feet above the hearths,

83 Dupin's strength is his ability to separate important clues from the mass of information that merely bogs everyone else down.

will not admit, throughout their extent, the body of a large cat. The impossibility of egress, by means already stated, being thus absolute, we are reduced to the windows. Through those of the front room no one could have escaped without notice from the crowd in the street. The murderers *must* have passed, then, through those of the back room. Now, brought to this conclusion in so unequivocal a manner as we are, it is not our part, as reasoners, to reject it on account of apparent impossibilities. It is only left for us to prove that these apparent 'impossibilities' are, in reality, not such.

"There are two windows in the chamber. One of them is unobstructed by furniture, and is wholly visible. The lower portion of the other is hidden from view by the head of the unwieldy bedstead which is thrust close up against it. The former was found securely fastened from within. It resisted the utmost force of those who endeavored to raise it. A large gimlet-hole had been pierced in its frame to the left, and a very stout nail was found fitted therein, nearly to the head. Upon examining the other window, a similar nail was seen similarly fitted in it; and a vigorous attempt to raise this sash, failed also. The police were now entirely satisfied that egress had not been in these directions. And, therefore, it was thought a matter of supererogation to withdraw the nails and **84** open the windows.

"My own examination was somewhat more particular, and was so for the reason I have just given—because here it was, I knew, that all apparent impossibilities *must* be proved to be not such in reality.

"I proceed to think thus—*à posteriori*. The murderers *did* **85** escape from one of these windows. This being so, they could not have re-fastened the sashes from the inside, as they were found fastened;—the consideration which put a stop, through its obviousness, to the scrutiny of the police in this quarter. Yet the sashes *were* fastened. They *must*, then, have the power of fastening themselves. There was no escape from this conclusion. I stepped to the unobstructed casement, withdrew the nail with some difficulty, and attempted to raise the sash. It resisted all my efforts, as I had anticipated. A concealed spring must, I now knew, exist; and this corroboration of my idea convinced me that my premises, at least, were correct, however mysterious still appeared the circumstances attending the nails. A careful search soon brought to light the hidden spring. I pressed it, and, satisfied with the discovery, forebore to upraise the sash.

"I now replaced the nail and regarded it attentively. A person passing out through this window might have reclosed it, and the spring would have caught—but the nail could not have been replaced. The conclusion was plain, and again narrowed in the field of my investigation. The assassins *must* have escaped through the other window. Supposing, then, the springs upon each sash to be the same, as was probable, there *must* be found a difference between the nails, or at least between the modes of their fixture. Getting upon the sacking of the bedstead, I looked over the head-board minutely at the

84 More than necessary

85 Inductive reasoning, literally "from the latter," meaning to derive by reasoning from observed facts.

second casement. Passing my hand down behind the board, I readily discovered and pressed the spring, which was, as I had supposed, identical in character with its neighbor. I now looked at the nail. It was as stout as the other, and apparently fitted in in the same manner—driven in nearly up to the head.

"You will say that I was puzzled; but, if you think so, you must have misunderstood the nature of the inductions. To use a sporting phrase, I had not been once 'at fault.' The scent had never for an instant been lost. There was no flaw in any link of the chain. I had traced the secret to its ultimate result,—and that result was *the nail*. It had, I say, in every respect, the appearance of its fellow in the other window; but this fact was an absolute nullity (conclusive as it might seem to be) when compared with the consideration that here, at this point, terminated the clew. 'There *must* be something wrong,' I said, 'about the nail.' I touched it; and the head, with about a quarter of an inch of the shank, came off in my fingers. The rest of the shank was in the gimlet-hole, where it had been broken off. The fracture was an old one (for its edges were incrusted with rust), and had apparently been accomplished by the blow of a hammer, which had partially imbedded, in the top of the bottom sash, the head portion of the nail. I now carefully replaced this head portion in the indentation whence I had taken it, and the resemblance to a perfect nail was complete—the fissure was invisible. Pressing the spring, I gently raised the sash for a few inches; the head went up with it, remaining firm in its bed. I closed the window, and the semblance of the whole nail was again perfect.

"The riddle, so far, was now unriddled. The assassin had escaped through the window which looked upon the bed. Dropping of its own accord upon his exit (or perhaps purposely closed), it had become fastened by the spring; and it was the retention of this spring which had been mistaken by the police for that of the nail,—farther inquiry being thus considered unnecessary.

"The next question is that of the mode of descent. Upon this point I had been satisfied in my walk with you around the building. About five feet and a half from the casement in question there runs a lightning-rod. From this rod it would have been impossible for any one to reach the window itself, to say nothing of entering it. I observed, however, that the shutters of the fourth story were of the peculiar kind called by Parisian carpenters *ferrades*—a kind rarely employed at the present day, but frequently seen upon very old mansions at Lyons and Bordeaux. They are in the form of an ordinary door, (a single, not a folding door) except that the upper half is latticed or worked in open trellis—thus affording an excellent hold for the hands. In the present instance these shutters are fully three feet and a half broad. When we saw them from the rear of the house, they were both about half open—that is to say, they stood off at right angles from the wall. It is probable that the police, as well as myself, examined the back of the tenement; but, if so, in looking at these *ferrades* in the line

86 A *ferrade* is a barred cattle brand, a southern (Provençal) word. Apparently the shutters have the appearance of such a brand.

of their breadth (as they must have done), they did not perceive this great breadth itself, or, at all events, failed to take it into due consideration. In fact, having once satisfied themselves that no egress could have been made in this quarter, they would naturally bestow here a very cursory examination. It was clear to me, however, that the shutter belonging to the window at the head of the bed, would, if swung fully back to the wall, reach to within two feet of the lightning-rod. It was also evident that, by exertion of a very unusual degree of activity and courage, an entrance into the window, from the rod, might have been thus effected.—By reaching to the distance of two feet and a half (we now suppose the shutter open to its whole extent) a robber might have taken a firm grasp upon the trellis-work. Letting go, then, his hold upon the rod, placing his feet securely against the wall, and springing boldly from it, he might have swung the shutter so as to close it, and, if we imagine the window open at the time, might even have swung himself into the room.

"I wish you to bear especially in mind that I have spoken of a *very* unusual degree of activity as requisite to success in so hazardous and so difficult a feat. It is my design to show you, first, that the thing might possibly have been accomplished:—but, secondly and *chiefly*, I wish to impress upon your understanding the *very extraordinary*—the almost præternatural character of that agility which could have accomplished it.

"You will say, no doubt, using the language of the law, that 'to make out my case' I should rather undervalue, than insist upon a full estimation of the activity required in this matter. This may be the practice in law, but it is not the usage of reason. My ultimate object is only the truth. My immediate purpose is to lead you to place in juxta-position that *very unusual* activity of which I have just spoken, with that *very peculiar* shrill (or harsh) and *unequal* voice, about whose nationality no two persons could be found to agree, and in whose utterance no syllabification could be detected."

At these words a vague and half-formed conception of the meaning of Dupin flitted over my mind. I seemed to be upon the verge of comprehension, without power to comprehend—as men, at times, find themselves upon the brink of remembrance, without being able, in the end, to remember. My [87] friend went on with his discourse.

"You will see," he said, "that I have shifted the question from the mode of egress to that of ingress. It was my design to suggest that both were effected in the same manner, at the same point. Let us now revert to the interior of the room. Let us survey the appearances here. The drawers of the bureau, it is said, had been rifled, although many articles of apparel still remained within them. The conclusion here is absurd. It is a mere guess—a very silly one—and no more. How are we to know that the articles found in the drawers were not all these drawers had originally contained? Madame L'Espanaye and her daughter lived an exceedingly retired life—saw no company—seldom went out—had little use for numerous

[87] Says James Cox: "The narrator is at the same point in relation to the comprehension of the crime that the narrator of 'Ligeia' occupied in relation to the memory of Ligeia. As Dupin re-creates the crime he draws forth from the recesses of the narrator's awareness the *knowledge* of the crime which he and all of Europe refuse to know. The form the narrative assumes throughout this phase of the story is quite rightly that of the Platonic dialogue, for Dupin is a Socratic mid-wife bringing to birth from his dense interlocutor the idea not of original sin but original crime." (P. 86)

changes of habiliment. Those found were at least of as good quality as any likely to be possessed by these ladies. If a thief had taken any, why did he not take the best—why did he not take all? In a word, why did he abandon four thousand francs in gold to encumber himself with a bundle of linen? The gold *was* abandoned. Nearly the whole sum mentioned by Monsieur Mignaud, the banker, was discovered, in bags, upon the floor. I wish you, therefore, to discard from your thoughts the blundering idea of *motive*, engendered in the brains of the police by that portion of the evidence which speaks of money delivered at the door of the house. Coincidences ten times as remarkable as this (the delivery of the money, and murder committed within three days upon the party receiving it), happen to all of us every hour of our lives, without attracting even momentary notice. Coincidences, in general, are great stumbling-blocks in the way of that class of thinkers who have been educated to know nothing of the theory of probabilities— that theory to which the most glorious objects of human research are indebted for the most glorious of illustration. In the present instance, had the gold been gone, the fact of its delivery three days before would have formed something more than a coincidence. It would have been corroborative of this idea of motive. But, under the real circumstances of the case, if we are to suppose gold the motive of this outrage, we must also imagine the perpetrator so vacillating an idiot as to have abandoned his gold and his motive together.

"Keeping now steadily in mind the points to which I have drawn your attention—that peculiar voice, that unusual agility, and that startling absence of motive in a murder so singularly atrocious as this—let us glance at the butchery itself. Here is a woman strangled to death by manual strength, and thrust up a chimney, head downward. Ordinary assassins employ no such modes of murder as this. Least of all, do they thus dispose of the murdered. In the manner of thrusting the corpse up the chimney, you will admit that there was something *excessively outré*—something altogether irreconcilable with our common notions of human action, even when we suppose the actors the most depraved of men. Think, too, how great must have been that strength which could have thrust the body *up* such an aperture so forcibly that the united vigor of several persons was found barely sufficient to drag it *down!*

"Turn, now, to other indications of the employment of a vigor most marvellous. On the hearth were thick tresses— very thick tresses—of grey human hair. These had been torn out by the roots. You are aware of the great force necessay in tearing thus from the head even twenty or thirty hairs together. You saw the locks in question as well as myself. Their roots (a hideous sight!) were clotted with fragments of the flesh of the scalp—sure token of the prodigious power which had been **88** exerted in uprooting perhaps half a million of hairs at a time. The throat of the old lady was not merely cut, but the head absolutely severed from the body: the instrument was a mere razor. I wish you also to look at the *brutal* ferocity of these

88 The human head has on the average only sixty thousand hairs.

deeds. Of the bruises upon the body of Madame L'Espanaye I do not speak. Monsieur Dumas, and his worthy coadjutor Monsieur Etienne, have pronounced that they were inflicted by some obtuse instrument; and so far these gentlemen are very correct. The obtuse instrument was clearly the stone pavement in the yard, upon which the victim had fallen from the window which looked in upon the bed. This idea, however simple it may now seem, escaped the police for the same reason that the breadth of the shutters escaped them—because by the affair of the nails, their perceptions had been hermetically sealed against the possibility of the windows having ever **89** been opened at all.

"If now, in addition to all these things, you have properly reflected upon the odd disorder of the chamber, we have gone so far as to combine the ideas of an agility astounding, a strength superhuman, a ferocity brutal, a butchery without motive, a *grotesquerie* in horror absolutely alien from humanity, and a voice foreign in tone to the ears of men of many nations, and devoid of all distinct of intelligible syllabification. What result, then, has ensued? What impression have I made upon your fancy?"

I felt a creeping of the flesh as Dupin asked me the question. "A madman," I said, "has done this deed—some raving maniac, escaped from a neighboring *Maison de Santé*." **90**

"In some respects," he replied, "your idea is not irrelevant. But the voices of madmen, even in their wildest paroxysms, **91** are never found to tally with that peculiar voice heard upon the stairs. Madmen are of some nation, and their language, however incoherent in its words, has always the coherence of syllabification. Besides, the hair of a madman is not such as I now hold in my hand. I disentangled this little tuft from the rigidly clutched fingers of Madame L'Espanaye. Tell me what you can make of it."

"Dupin!" I said, completely unnerved; "this hair is most unusual—this is no *human* hair."

"I have not asserted that it is," said he, "but, before we decide this point, I wish you to glance at the little sketch I have here traced upon this paper. It is a *fac-simile* drawing of what has been described in one portion of the testimony as 'dark bruises, and deep indentations of finger nails,' upon the throat of Mademoiselle L'Espanaye, and in another, (by Messrs. Dumas and Etienne,) as a 'series of livid spots, evidently the impression of fingers.'

"You will perceive," continued my friend, spreading out the paper upon the table before us, "that this drawing gives the idea of a firm and fixed hold. There is no *slipping* apparent. Each finger has retained—possibly until the death of the victim—the fearful grasp by which it originally imbedded itself. Attempt, now, to place all your fingers, at the same time, in the respective impressions as you see them."

I made the attempt in vain.

"We are possibly not giving this matter a fair trial," he said. "The paper is spread out upon a plane surface; but the human throat is cylindrical. Here is a billet of wood, the circumference

89 "Hermetically sealed" actually means airtight, but even by Poe's time it had come to mean "tightly closed."

90 An insane asylum

91 Sudden violent emotions or attacks

92 Baron Georges Léopold Chrétien Frédéric Dagobert Cuvier (1769–1832), aside from his lengthy name, was also known as a great naturalist and a pioneer of comparative anatomy. He describes the orangutan in his *Le Règne animal destribué d'après son organisation* (1817). While Dupin quite naturally quotes the French naturalist, Poe himself probably got his information from a more immediate source: Thomas Wyatt's *Synopsis of Natural History* (1839), which he helped edit.

The male orangutan stands about four-and-one-half feet tall and weighs about one hundred fifty pounds. It has long arms, used for swinging from tree to tree, and is a shy and peaceful vegetarian—a most unlikely candidate for the violent perpetrator of the two murders.

In *Native Son* (1940), Richard Wright has his character Bigger suffocate Mary Dalton, cut off her head with a hatchet, and shove her body into a furnace. The Chicago newspaper accounts of the murder liken Bigger to an ape. In "How Bigger Was Born" (1940), Wright says he used actual news accounts as the basis for the murder, adding, "These killings were accomplished with the ferocity of Poe's 'Murders in the Rue Morgue'—the work of a giant ape."

Marie Bonaparte takes a long look at this story and, although her reasoning is too complex to summarize here, makes a case for the events in Poe's tale as symbolic of Poe's belief that his mother had been unfaithful. She suggests that the very young Edgar may have seen his mother with a lover (Elizabeth's pregnancy with Poe's sister Rosalie was the object of much suspicion) and years later translated this into the "fierce ape, embodying those aggressive and bestial instincts which, as primitively conceived by the child, dominate his always sadistic concept of the sex act." (P. 455)

She notes that since Poe's tale was written, "what numbers of detective novels have entertained, mystified, and thrilled successive generations of readers! In all, as Freud first pointed out to me, the unconscious roots of their interest, for us, lies in the fact that the trail the detective follows repeats, though transformed to other activities, the infant's original sexual investigations." (P. 456)

93 Dupin never guesses. "The shrewd guess, the fertile hypothesis, the courageous leap to a tentative conclusion—these are the most valuable coin of the thinker at work. But in most schools guessing is heavily penalized and is associated somehow with laziness," writes Jerome Seymour Bruner in *The Process of Education* (1960), and Dupin apparently agrees with the latter belief.

94 The *Grand Dictionnaire Universel du XIX Siècle* (Paris, 1865) lists all important publications with the title *Le Monde*, but this one is not among them. It has no relationship to the present-day *Le Monde*.

95 A park in Paris bordering on the western suburb of Neuilly-sur-Seine; a favorite pleasure ground since the seventeenth century

96 From Borneo

97 Malta is the once-British-owned island in the Mediterranean south of Sicily, formerly of great strategic value. It has been a republic since 1974.

98 I.e., the fourth floor. In Europe, what Americans call the first floor is called the ground floor, and the European first floor is our second floor.

of which is about that of the throat. Wrap the drawing around it, and try the experiment again."

I did so; but the difficulty was even more obvious than before.

"This," I said, "is the mark of no human hand."

92 "Read now," replied Dupin, "this passage from Cuvier."

It was a minute anatomical and generally descriptive account of the large fulvous Ourang-Outang of the East Indian Islands. The gigantic stature, the prodigious strength and activity, the wild ferocity, and the imitative propensities of these mammalia are sufficiently well known to all. I understood the full horrors of the murder at once.

"The description of the digits," said I, as I made an end of the reading, "is in exact accordance with this drawing. I see that no animal but an Ourang-Outang, of the species here mentioned, could have impressed the indentations as you have traced them. This tuft of tawny hair, too, is identical in character with that of the beast of Cuvier. But I cannot possibly comprehend the particulars of this frightful mystery. Besides, there were *two* voices heard in contention, and one of them was unquestionably the voice of a Frenchman."

"True; and you will remember an expression attributed almost unanimously, by the evidence, to this voice,—the expression, '*mon Dieu!*' This, under the circumstances, has been justly characterized by one of the witnesses (Montani, the confectioner), as an expression of remonstrance or expostulation. Upon these two words, therefore, I have mainly built my hopes of a full solution of the riddle. A Frenchman was cognizant of the murder. It is possible—indeed it is far more than probable—that he was innocent of all participation in the bloody transactions which took place. The Ourang-Outang may have escaped from him. He may have traced it to the chamber; but, under the agitating circumstances which ensued, he could never have re-captured it. It is still at large. I will not pursue these guesses—for I have no right to call them more—since the shades of reflection upon which they are based are scarcely of sufficient depth to be appreciable by my own intellect, and since I could not pretend to make them intelligible to the understanding of another. We will call them

93 guesses then, and speak of them as such. If the Frenchman in question is indeed, as I suppose, innocent of this atrocity, this advertisement, which I left last night, upon our return home, at the office of 'Le Monde,' (a paper devoted to the

94 shipping interest, and much sought by sailors), will bring him to our residence."

95 CAUGHT—*In the Bois de Boulogne, early in the morning of the —— inst., (The morning of the murder,) a very large,*

96 *tawny Ourang-Outang of the Bornese species. The owner,*

97 *(who is ascertained to be a sailor, belonging to a Maltese vessel), may have the animal again, upon identifying it satisfactorily, and paying a few charges arising from its capture and keeping. Call at No. ——, Rue ——, Faubourg*

98 *St. Germain—au troisième.*

"How was it possible," I asked, "that you should know the man to be a sailor, and belonging to a Maltese vessel?"

"I do *not* know it," said Dupin. "I am not *sure* of it. Here, however, is a small piece of ribbon, which from its form, and from its greasy appearance, has evidently been used in tying the hair in one of those long *queues* of which sailors are so **99** fond. Moreover, this knot is one which few besides sailors can tie, and is peculiar to the Maltese. I picked the ribbon up at **100** the foot of the lightning-rod. It could not have belonged to either of the deceased. Now if, after all, I am wrong in my induction from this ribbon, that the Frenchman was a sailor belonging to a Maltese vessel, still I can have done no harm in saying what I did in the advertisement. If I am in error, he will merely suppose that I have been misled by some circumstance into which he will not take the trouble to inquire. But if I am right, a great point is gained. Cognizant although innocent of the murder, the Frenchman will naturally hesitate about replying to the advertisement—about demanding the Ourang-Outang. He will reason thus:—'I am innocent; I am poor; my Ourang-Outang is of great value—to one in my circumstances a fortune of itself—why should I lose it through idle apprehensions of danger? Here it is, within my grasp. It was found in the Bois de Boulogne—at a vast distance from the scene of that butchery. How can it ever be suspected that a brute beast should have done the deed? The police are at fault—they have failed to procure the slightest clew. Should they even trace the animal, it would be impossible to prove me cognizant of the murder, or to implicate me in guilt on account of that cognizance. Above all, *I am known*. The advertiser designates me as the possessor of the beast. I am not sure to what limit his knowledge may extend. Should I avoid claiming a property of so great value, which it is known that I possess, I will render the animal, at least, liable to suspicion. It is not my policy to attract attention either to myself or to the beast. I will answer the advertisement, get the Ourang-Outang, and keep it close until this matter has blown over.' "

At this moment we heard a step upon the stairs.

"Be ready," said Dupin, "with your pistols, but neither use them nor show them until at a signal from myself."

The front door of the house had been left open, and the visitor had entered, without ringing, and advanced several steps upon the staircase. Now, however, he seemed to hesitate. Presently we heard him descending. Dupin was moving quickly to the door, when we again heard him coming up. He did not turn back a second time, but stepped up with decision and rapped at the door of our chamber.

"Come in," said Dupin, in a cheerful and hearty tone.

A man entered. He was a sailor, evidently,—a tall, stout, and muscular-looking person, with a certain dare-devil expression of countenance, not altogether unprepossessing. His face, greatly sunburnt, was more than half hidden by whisker and *mustachio*. He had with him a huge oaken cudgel, but appeared to be otherwise unarmed. He bowed awkwardly, and bade us "good evening," in French accents, which, although somewhat Neufchatelish, were still sufficiently in- **101** dicative of a Parisian origin.

99 Pigtails

100 While Dupin displays this kind of knowledge only occasionally, it is a common characteristic of Sherlock Holmes.

101 Neufchâtel is an area of France whose population is Protestant and peasant, so that the word has come to mean "uncouth."

"Sit down, my friend," said Dupin. "I suppose you have called about the Ourang-Outang. Upon my word, I almost envy you the possession of him; a remarkably fine, and no doubt a very valuable animal. How old do you suppose him to be?"

The sailor drew a long breath, with the air of a man relieved of some intolerable burden, and then replied, in an assured tone:

"I have no way of telling—but he can't be more than four or five years old. Have you got him here?"

"Oh no; we had no conveniences for keeping him here. He is at a livery stable in the Rue Dubourg, just by. You can get him in the morning. Of course you are prepared to identify the property?"

"To be sure I am, sir."

"I shall be sorry to part with him," said Dupin.

"I don't mean that you should be at all this trouble for nothing, sir," said the man. "Couldn't expect it. Am very willing to pay a reward for the finding of the animal—that is to say, any thing in reason."

"Well," replied my friend, "that is all very fair, to be sure. Let me think!—what should I have? Oh! I will tell you. My reward shall be this. You shall give me all the information in your power about these murders in the Rue Morgue."

Dupin said the last words in a very low tone, and very quietly. Just as quietly, too, he walked toward the door, locked it, and put the key in his pocket. He then drew a pistol from his bosom and placed it, without the least flurry, upon the table.

The sailor's face flushed up as if he were struggling with suffocation. He started to his feet and grasped his cudgel; but the next moment he fell back into his seat, trembling violently, and with the countenance of death itself. He spoke not a word. I pitied him from the bottom of my heart.

"My friend," said Dupin, in a kind tone, "you are alarming yourself unnecessarily—you are indeed. We mean you no harm whatever. I pledge you the honor of a gentleman, and of a Frenchman, that we intend you no injury. I perfectly well know that you are innocent of the atrocities in the Rue Morgue. It will not do, however, to deny that you are in some measure implicated in them. From what I have already said, you must know that I have had means of information about this matter—means of which you could never have dreamed. Now the thing stands thus. You have done nothing which you could have avoided—nothing, certainly, which renders you **102** culpable. You were not even guilty of robbery, when you might have robbed with impunity. You have nothing to conceal. You have no reason for concealment. On the other hand, you are bound by every principle of honor to confess all you know. An innocent man is now imprisoned, charged with that crime of which you can point out the perpetrator."

The sailor had recovered his presence of mind, in a great measure, while Dupin uttered these words; but his original boldness of bearing was all gone.

102 Actually, he has concealed evidence in the case by not coming forth with his story—but perhaps French law is different in this regard.

"So help me God," said he, after a brief pause, "I *will* tell you all I know about this affair;—but I do not expect you to believe one half I say—I would be a fool indeed if I did. Still, I *am* innocent, and I will make a clean breast if I die for it."

What he stated was, in substance, this. He had lately made a voyage to the Indian Archipelago. A party, of which he **103** formed one, landed at Borneo, and passed into the interior on an excursion of pleasure. Himself and a companion had captured the Ourang-Outang. This companion dying, the animal fell into his own exclusive possession. After great trouble, occasioned by the intractable ferocity of his captive during the home voyage, he at length succeeded in lodging it safety at his own residence in Paris, where, not to attract toward himself the unpleasant curiosity of his neighbors, he kept it carefully secluded, until such time as it should recover from a wound in the foot, received from a splinter on board ship. His ultimate design was to sell it.

Returning home from some sailors' frolic on the night, or rather in the morning of the murder, he found the beast occupying his own bed-room, into which it had broken from a closet adjoining, where it had been, as was thought, securely confined. Razor in hand, and fully lathered, it was sitting before a looking-glass, attempting the operation of shaving, in which it had no doubt previously watched its master through the keyhole of the closet. Terrified at the sight of so dangerous a weapon in the possession of an animal so ferocious, and so well able to use it, the man, for some moments, was at a loss what to do. He had been accustomed, however, to quiet the creature, even in its fiercest moods, by the use of a whip, and to this he now resorted. Upon sight of it, the Ourang-Outang sprang at once through the door of the chamber, down the stairs, and thence, through a window, unfortunately open, into the street.

The Frenchman followed in despair; the ape, razor still in hand, occasionally stopping to look back and gesticulate at its pursuer, until the latter had nearly come up with it. It then again made off. In this manner the chase continued for a long time. The streets were profoundly quiet, as it was nearly three o'clock in the morning. In passing down an alley in the rear of the Rue Morgue, the fugitive's attention was arrested by a light gleaming from the open window of Madame L'Espanaye's chamber, in the fourth story of her house. Rushing to the building, it perceived the lightning-rod, clambered up with inconceivable agility, grasped the shutter, which was thrown fully back against the wall, and, by its means, swung itself directly upon the headboard of the bed. The whole feat did not occupy a minute. The shutter was kicked open again by the Ourang-Outang as it entered the room.

The sailor, in the meantime, was both rejoiced and perplexed. He had strong hopes of now recapturing the brute, as it could scarcely escape from the trap into which it had ventured, except by the rod, where it might be intercepted as it came down. On the other hand, there was much cause

103 The East Indies (Indonesia)

. . . the gigantic animal had seized Madame L'Espanaye by the hair, (which was loose, as she had been combing it,). . . . *Illustration by F. S. Coburn, 1901*

for anxiety as to what it might do in the house. This latter reflection urged the man still to follow the fugitive. A lightning-rod is ascended without difficulty, especially by a sailor; but, when he had arrived as high as the window, which lay far to his left, his career was stopped; the most that he could accomplish was to reach over so as to obtain a glimpse of the interior of the room. At this glimpse he nearly fell from his hold through excess of horror. Now it was that those hideous shrieks arose upon the night, which had startled from slumber the inmates of the Rue Morgue. Madame L'Espanaye and her daughter, habited in their night clothes, had apparently been arranging some papers in the iron chest already mentioned, which had been wheeled into the middle of the room. It was open, and its contents lay beside it on the floor. The victims must have been sitting with their backs toward the window; and, from the time elapsing between the ingress of the beast and the screams, it seems probable that it was not immediately perceived. The flapping-to of the shutter would naturally have been attributed to the wind.

As the sailor looked in, the gigantic animal had seized Madame L'Espanaye by the hair, (which was loose, as she had been combing it,) and was flourishing the razor about her face, in imitation of the motions of a barber. The daughter lay prostrate and motionless; she had swooned. The screams and struggles of the old lady (during which the hair was torn from her head) had the effect of changing the probably pacific purposes of the Ourang-Outang into those of wrath. With one determined sweep of its muscular arm it nearly severed her head from her body. The sight of blood inflamed its anger into phrenzy. Gnashing its teeth, and flashing fire from its eyes, it flew upon the body of the girl, and imbedded its fearful talons in her throat, retaining its grasp until she expired. Its wandering and wild glances fell at this moment upon the head of the bed, over which the face of its master, rigid with horror, was just discernible. The fury of the beast, who no doubt bore still in mind the dreaded whip, was instantly converted into fear. Conscious of having deserved punishment, it seemed desirous of concealing its bloody deeds, and skipped about the chamber in an agony of nervous agitation; throwing down and breaking the furniture as it moved, and dragging the bed from the bedstead. In conclusion, it seized first the corpse of the daughter, and thrust it up the chimney, as it was found; then that of the old lady, which it immediately hurled through the window headlong.

As the ape approached the casement with its mutilated burden, the sailor shrank aghast to the rod, and, rather gliding than clambering down it, hurried at once home—dreading the consequences of the butchery, and gladly abandoning, in his terror, all solicitude about the fate of the Ourang-Outang. The words heard by the party upon the staircase were the Frenchman's exclamations of horror and affright, commingled with the fiendish jabberings of the brute.

I have scarcely anything to add. The Ourang-Outang must have escaped from the chamber, by the rod, just before the

104

breaking of the door. It must have closed the window as it passed through it. It was subsequently caught by the owner himself, who obtained for it a very large sum at the *Jardin des Plantes*. Le Bon was instantly released, upon our narration of **105** the circumstances (with some comments from Dupin) at the *bureau* of the Prefect of Police. This functionary, however well disposed to my friend, could not altogether conceal his chagrin at the turn which affairs had taken, and was fain to indulge in a sarcasm or two, about the propriety of every person minding his own business.   **106**

"Let them talk," said Dupin, who had not thought it necessary to reply. "Let him discourse; it will ease his conscience. I am satisfied with having defeated him in his own castle. Nevertheless, that he failed in the solution of this **107** mystery, is by no means that matter for wonder which he supposes it; for, in truth, our friend the Prefect is somewhat too cunning to be profound. In his wisdom is no *stamen*. It **108** is all head and no body, like the pictures of the Goddess Laverna,—or, at best, all head and shoulders, like a codfish. **109** But he is a good creature after all. I like him especially for one master stroke of cant, by which he has attained his reputation for ingenuity. I mean the way he has *'de nier ce qui est, et d'expliquer ce qui n'est pas.'*"   **110**

105 The Paris botanical garden and zoo

106 Poe's bungling police are by now a fixture of the classic detective story. Holmes shares this low opinion of the force: "There is no crime to detect, or, at most, some bungling villainy with a motive so transparent that even a Scotland Yard official can see through it" ("A Study in Scarlet").

John Cawelti points out the importance of these "characters who are involved with the crime but need the detective's aid to solve it. . . . The special drama of crime in the classical detective story lies in the way it threatens the serene domestic circles of bourgeois life with anarchy and chaos. The official guardians of this order, the police, turn out to be inefficient bunglers, and the finger of suspicion points to everybody. The ordered rationality of society momentarily seems a flimsy surface over a seething pit of guilt and disorder. Then the detective intervenes and proves that the general suspicion is false. He proves the social order is not responsible for the crime because it was the act of a particular individual with his own private motives." (*Adventure, Mystery, and Romance*, p. 96)

Cawelti's book is must reading for anyone interested in the origins and development of the mystery story.

107 On his own territory, in his own area of expertise. "For a man's home is his castle, and one's home is the safest refuge to everyone," writes Sir Edward Coke (1552–1634, and "The house of everyone is to him as his castle and fortress, as well for his defense against injury and violence as for his repose" (*Third Institute* [1644] and *Semayne's Case*, 5, Report 91).

108 The stamen is the thread spun by the Fates at a person's birth, on whose length one's life-span is supposed to depend. The word has come to mean the measure of the capacity that a person is given at birth.

109 Laverna was the goddess of thieves and rogues, represented as a head without a body—stolen, perhaps, when she wasn't looking.

110 ". . . of denying what is, and explaining what isn't," from a footnote in Letter xi in Part VI of Rousseau's *La Nouvelle Héloïse* (1761): "It is a crotchet common to philosophers of all ages to deny what is, and explain what is not."

Poe missed another quote from Rousseau that might have been of use in one of the Dupin tales: "People who know little are usually great talkers, while men who know much say little," from *Émile* (1762), I.

. . . it seized first the corpse of the daughter, and thrust it up the chimney. . . . *Illustration by Aubrey Beardsley*

THE MYSTERY OF MARIE ROGÊT

A SEQUEL TO "THE MURDERS IN THE RUE MORGUE"

First published in Snowden's *Ladies' Companion*, November and December 1842 and February 1843, with manuscript revisions made for *Tales* (1845).

This is the least of the three Dupin tales both in popularity and critical interest, probably because there is little characterization or action. The mystery is described, analyzed, and solved by the detective while seated in the comfort of his home, from information supplied by the daily and weekly newspapers.

However, "The Mystery of Marie Rogêt" does have the distinction of being the first detective story to attempt to solve an actual crime, in this case the murder of Mary Rogers, a young woman who had worked in a New York City cigar store. Her murder and the efforts to uncover the motive and the murderer became *the* story of the day, with the press joining in an effort to milk the sensational crime for all it was worth. Poor Mary Rogers thus was the first American media star, a news-created celebrity in an era when American journalism was first realizing its power in manipulating public opinion to boost circulation.

In brief, here's what we know about Mary Rogers. She was born about 1820, the child of Daniel and Phoebe Rogers; her father died some years before her disappearance, the result of a steamboat explosion on the Mississippi. In 1837, she took a job with John Anderson's tobacco shop, on upper Broadway, working behind the counter—a daring move in those days, for women who worked in such a masculine milieu risked damage to their reputation.

The store was a favorite hangout for New York's reporters and editors, as well as Broadway gamblers. James Fenimore Cooper and Washington Irving may well have been customers, and even Poe might have known Mary, since he lived fairly close to the store, although there is no evidence that he did.

In October 1838, two and a half years before her death, Mary Rogers disappeared from her home, leaving a note that she was going to kill herself. The New York *Sun* reported:

"*Something mysterious*—a Mrs. Hays [Mary's aunt] yesterday evening brought to the coroner a letter which Miss Mary Cecilia Rogers, a young lady who recently attended Anderson's cigar store in Broadway, adjoining the hospital-yard, had yesterday left at the house of her mother, No. 114 Pitt Street, which letter informed her mother that she had left home forever, for the purpose of putting an end to her life, and bidding her mother an affectionate and final farewell. Alarmed by the appalling announcement, the terrified mother caused search to be made for her daughter in every place where she thought it possible she could have resorted either for the fullfillment of her dreadful purpose or for concealment; but no trace of her could be discovered up to yesterday morning. . . . The cause of this wayward freak of the young lady, is supposed by her friends to be disappointed love—she having recently received the addresses of a certain widower, who it is said, has deserted her and by his desertion has brought upon her a state of mind which has prompted her, it is feared, to commit self-destruction." (October 5, 1838)

The *Times and Commercial Intelligencer* the next day denied the story, saying that Mary had gone on a visit to a friend in Brooklyn, and was now at home with her mother.

A week later, the New York *Weekly Herald* reported: "The recent affair of the young girl in Anderson's cigar store must lead every reflecting person and every good member of the community

224

to desire that something should be done instantly to remedy the great evil consequent upon very beautiful young girls being placed in cigar and confectionary stores" (October 13).

The mystery of the first disappearance was "solved" several years later by the *Herald*: "This young girl, Mary Rogers, was missing from Anderson's store three years ago for two weeks. It is asserted that she was then seduced by an officer of the U. S. Navy and kept at Hoboken for two weeks." (August 3, 1841)

On July 25, 1841, after telling her fiancé, Daniel Payne, that she was off to visit an Aunt, Mary Rogers disappeared for the second and last time. Three days later her body was found floating in the Hudson River. The newspapers picked up the story on August 1.

Because the body had been bound, suspicion landed on the many gangs of toughs who were then reportedly causing much trouble in the city. Mary's employer, John Anderson, was questioned, as were her fiancé, Daniel Payne, and former boyfriend, Alfred Crommelin.

The newspapers continued to pursue every rumor and every suspect while the police tried to sift it all out. Even the mayor of New York talked personally with the physician who had performed the autopsy.

In October 1841, Daniel Payne's body was found near the site of Mary Rogers' murder, a suicide note nearby (see note 37).

By June 1842 Poe had finished his version of the story, and after attempting to interest several editors in the project, finally sold it to the *Ladies' Companion*. In its original form, the tale indicated that the culprit was a secret lover.

Said Poe, "I believe not only that I have demonstrated the fallacy of the general idea—that the girl was the victim of a gang of ruffians—but have *indicated the assassin* in a manner which will give renewed impetus to investigation. My main object, nevertheless, as you will readily understand, is an analysis of the true principles which should direct inquiry in similar cases." (Letter of June 4, 1842, to George Roberts)

A problem reared its inconvenient head in the person of Mrs. Frederica Loss, whose deathbed confession cast new light on the case. Said the New York *Tribune*:

"The terrible mystery . . . is at last explained. . . . Mrs. Loss, the woman who kept the refreshment house nearest the scene of her death . . . was accidentally wounded by the premature discharge of a gun in the hands of her son; the wound proved fatal; but before she died she sent for Justice Merritt of New Jersey, and told him the facts. On Sunday the 25th of July, 1841, Mary Rogers came to her house in company with a young physician, who undertook to procure for the unfortunate girl a premature delivery. While in the hands of the physician she died, and a consultation was then held as to the disposal of the body. It was finally taken at night by the son of Mrs. Loss and sunk in the river where it was found. Her clothes were first tied up up in a bundle and sunk in a pool on the land of Mr. Fames G. King in that neighborhood; but is was afterwards thought they were not safe there, and they were accordingly taken and scattered through the woods as they were afterwards found. The name of the physician is unknown, but Mayor Morris has been made acquainted with these facts . . . and we doubt not an immediate inquiry after the guilty wretch will be made." (November 26) See note 35.

Poe went to work on the story again, which explains the jump from December to February in the story's serialized appearance, in order to bring in this new evidence.

There has long been a story that John Anderson paid Poe to write "The Mystery of Marie Rogêt" in order to draw suspicion away from him. There is no proof one way or the other about this, although it is true that Poe and Anderson were good friends, and the latter bought space in Poe's magazine *The Broadway Journal* for three months, the only tobacconist to do so.

In 1891, Anderson's daughter, Laura V. Appleton, tried to break her late father's will in order to inherit some of the million dollars he had amassed in his lifetime. Felix McClosky, Anderson's business partner, testified that Anderson had told him that Mary had had an abortion "the year before the murder took place—or a year and a half—something of that kind—and that he got into some trouble about it—and outside of *that* there was no grounds on earth for anybody to suppose he had anything to do with the murder" (*American Literature*, November 1948).

Poe was confident he had indicated the murderer, even if he hadn't done so by name. (Irving Wallace, in *The Fabulous Originals* [1955], suggests that *Poe* may have been the murderer! [pp.

214–15].) He was pleased with the story, particularly because it created a stir, and because he needed more money—Virginia had suffered her first consumptive hemorrhage during January 1842 and would need even more care than before.

In his novel *Poe Must Die* (Charter Books, 1978), Marc Olden concocts an uneasy blend of fact, fiction, and the fantastic in an attempt to create something like the success of *The Seven-Per-Cent Solution* (1973). Six months after the publication of "Marie Rogêt," Poe is proved to be absolutely correct in his suppositions. Now recognized for his deductive genius, he is a threat to a group of spiritualists and grave robbers led by a man who calls on the legions of Hell to carry out his threat that Poe must die. Against the background of New York in the 1840s, Poe spars with his opponents, haunted by the memory of the dead Virginia and by his alcoholism. A good idea, the novel is marred by an awkward style and incoherent development.

The best book on the Mary Rogers/Marie Rogêt story is without a doubt John Walsh's *Poe the Detective* (Rutgers, 1968), must reading for anyone intrigued by the real murder mystery as well as the mechanics by which Poe turned it into fiction.

Universal filmed the tale in 1942 (alos known as *Phantom of Paris*), with Maria Montez, Patric Knowles, Maria Ouspenskaya and John Litel, with some additions from "The Murders in the Rue Morgue." A young woman's body is found, her face clawed off by some kind of animal; later her brain is snatched from her body while it lies in the city morgue. Misplaced comic relief and poor characterizations mar the film, which comes to life in the last reel—unfortunately, too late.

Poe appended this note to the 1845 edition:

"On the original publication of "Marie Rogêt," the foot-notes now appended were considered unnecessary; but the lapse of several years since the tragedy upon which the tale is based, renders it expedient to give them, and also to say a few words in explanation of the general design. A young girl, *Mary Cecilia Rogers*, was murdered in the vicinity of New York; and although her death occasioned an intense and long-enduring excitement, the mystery attending it had remained unsolved at the period when the present paper was written and published (November, 1842). Herein, under pretence of relating the fate of a Parisian *grisette*, the author has followed, in minute detail, the essential, while merely paralleling the inessential, facts of the real murder of Mary Rogers. Thus all argument founded upon the fiction is applicable to the truth: and the investigation of the truth was the object.

"The 'Mystery of Marie Rogêt' was composed at a distance from the scene of the atrocity, and with no other means of investigation than the newspapers afforded. Thus much escaped the writer of which he could have availed himself had he been on the spot and visited the localities. It may not be improper to record, nevertheless, that the confessions of *two* persons (one of them the Madame Deluc of the narrative), made, at different periods, long subsequent to the publication, confirmed, in full, not only the general conclusion, but absolutely *all* the chief hypothetical details by which that conclusion was attained."

Actually, Poe's tale departs from the facts in several instances and does *not* truly stand as a complete solution to the Mary Rogers case. In fact, the case was never solved to anyone's satisfaction.

---

1 "The *nom de plume* of Von Hardenburg," (Poe's note).
  Poe probably found this translation of the German in Sarah Austin's *Fragments from German Prose Writers*, which he reviewed in *Graham's*, December 1841, making some improvements in the translator's style as quoted here. The original is from "Moralische Ansichten," in *Novalis Schriften*, edited by Ludwig Tieck and Friedrich Schlegel (1802).
  Friedrich von Hardenburg (1772–1801) was one of the great German romantics, whose chief work was his novel *Heinrich von Ofterdingen* (1802), unfinished at his death from tuberculosis.

Es giebt eine Reihe idealischer Begebenheiten, die der Wirklichkeit parallel lauft. Selten fallen sie zusammen. Menschen und Züfalle modificiren gewöhnlich die idealische Begebenheit, so dass sie unvollkommen erscheint, und ihre Folgen gleichfalls unvollkommen sind. So bei der Reformation; statt des Protestantismus kam das Lutherthum hervor.

There are ideal series of events which run parallel with the real ones. They rarely coincide. Men and circumstances generally modify the ideal train of events, so that it seems imperfect, and its consequences are equally imperfect. Thus with the Reformation; instead of Protestantism came Lutheranism.

1

—*Novalis [Moralische] Ansichten.*

There are few persons, even among the calmest thinkers, who have not occasionally been startled into a vague yet thrilling half-credence in the supernatural, by *coincidences* of so seemingly marvellous a character that, as *mere* coincidences, the intellect has been unable to receive them. Such sentiments—for the half-credences of which I speak have never the full force of *thought*—such sentiments are seldom thoroughly stifled unless by reference to the doctrine of chance, or, as it is technically termed, the Calculus of Probabilities. **2** Now this Calculus is, in its essence, purely mathematical; and thus we have the anomaly of the most rigidly exact in science applied to the shadow and spirituality of the most intangible in speculation.

The extraordinary details which I am now called upon to make public, will be found to form, as regards sequence of time, the primary branch of a series of scarcely intelligible *coincidences*, whose secondary or concluding branch will be recognized by all readers in the late murder of MARY CECILIA ROGERS, at New York. **3**

When, in an article entitled *The Murders in the Rue Morgue*, I endeavored, about a year ago, to depict some very remarkable features in the mental character of my friend, the Chevalier C. Auguste Dupin, it did not occur to me that I should ever resume the subject. This depicting of character **4** constituted my design; and this design was thoroughly fulfilled in the wild train of circumstances brought to instance Dupin's idiosyncrasy. I might have adduced other examples, but I should have proven no more. Late events, however, in their surprising development, have startled me into some further details, which will carry with them the air of extorted confession. Hearing what I have lately heard, it would be indeed strange should I remain silent in regard to what I both heard and saw so long ago.

Upon the winding up of the tragedy involved in the deaths of Madame L'Espanaye and her daughter, the Chevalier dismissed the affair at once from his attention, and relapsed into his old habits of moody revery. Prone, at all times, to abstraction, I readily fell in with his humor; and continuing to occupy our chambers in the Faubourg Saint Germain, we gave the Future to the winds, and slumbered tranquilly in the Present, weaving the dull world around us into dreams. **5**

But these dreams were not altogether uninterrupted. It may readily be supposed that the part played by my friend, in the drama at the Rue Morgue, had not failed of its impression upon the fancies of the Parisian police. With its emissaries, the name of Dupin had grown into a household word. The simple character of those inductions by which he had disentangled the mystery never having been explained even to the Prefect, or to any other individual than myself, of course it is not surprising that the affair was regarded as little less than miraculous, or that the Chevalier's analytical **6** abilities acquired for him the credit of intuition. His frankness would have led him to disabuse every inquirer of such prejudice; but his indolent humor forbade all further agitation of a topic whose interest to himself had long ceased. It thus

2 The *Théorie analytique des probabilités* (1812) is a mathematical classic written by Pierre Simon, Marquis de Leplace (1749–1827). "Probability" means simply the assignment of a number as the measure of the "chance" that a given event will occur or reoccur.

3 The transformation of Mary to Marie is obvious, but Rogers to Rogêt may not be to readers unfamiliar with French. The final *-er* and *-et* endings would both be pronounced "ay." The circumflex, however, is unnecessary other than giving a French look to the name (it normally signals that an *s* has been dropped from the old spelling, as in *forêt*, forest).

4 Sequels, however, are inevitable when public demand is great enough and matched by the authors' need for money. Arthur Conan Doyle had thought of killing off Sherlock Holmes as early as 1891. "He takes my mind from better things," he said (John Dickson Carr, *The Life of Sir Arthur Conan Doyle*, Vintage, 1975; p. 100), although the protests of his wife and the sure-fire public response made him change his mind.

5 "We . . . busied ourselves in dreams," says the narrator in "Murders in the Rue Morgue," describing their habit of venturing forth only at night. Here it is the day-to-day, mundane activities of the world that seem dreamlike, unreal.

6 *Chevalier* means "knight," but that seems hardly appropriate, considering Dupin's lack of chivalry. The O.E.D. points out that in 1839 the word was used for "the cadets of the Old French noblesses, who embraced a military career."

"The Mystery of Marie Rogêt." *Illustration by Albert Edward Sterner for* Century Magazine, *1903*

7 Mary Rogers' mother was named Phoebe, which was another name for Artemis, Greek goddess of the moon. "Estelle" comes from a word meaning "star."

8 "Nassau Street" (Poe's note). The Rue Pavée St. André is on the Right Bank, off the Rue Rivoli. French readers were disturbed by Poe's freehanded use of Parisian locales, which often do not match the real thing.

9 A *pension* is a boardinghouse.

10 See "The Murders in the Rue Morgue," note 24.

11 "Anderson" (Poe's note). Le Blanc can be translated as "the pure" (innocent), recalling the long-standing rumor that Anderson paid Poe to make him look good in the case.

12 A young woman of the working class, usually a shop assistant

13 "The Hudson" (Poe's note). Poe changed "five months" to "three years" in the 1849 edition.

14 "Weehawken" (Poe's note). Weehawken is a township in northeast New Jersey, site of the famous duel between Aaron Burr and Alexander Hamilton.
 The *Barrières* of Paris were constructed in 1785 as entrances to the city, where taxes were collected on goods brought there. The Rue du Roule is east of the Louvre, on the Right Bank.

15 A New York *Herald* reporter, on the scene by coincidence, described the discovery of Mary Rogers' body: "The first look we had of her was most ghastly. Her forehead and face appeared to have been battered and butchered to a mummy. Her features were scarcely visible, so much violence had been done to her." (August 4, 1841) Three days in the Hudson didn't help, either.

happened that he found himself the cynosure of the policial eyes; and the cases were not few in which attempt was made to engage his services at the Prefecture. One of the most remarkable instances was that of the murder of a young girl named Marie Rogêt.

This event occurred about two years after the atrocity in the Rue Morgue. Marie, whose Christian and family name will at once arrest attention from their resemblance to those of the unfortunate "cigar-girl," was the only daughter of the

7 widow Estelle Rogêt. The father had died during the child's infancy, and from the period of his death, until within eighteen months before the assassination which forms the subject of our narrative, the mother and daughter had dwelt together in

8,9 the Rue Pavé Saint Andrée; Madame there keeping a *pension*, assisted by Marie. Affairs went on thus until the latter had attained her twenty-second year, when her great beauty attracted the notice of a perfumer, who occupied one of the

10 shops in the basement of the Palais Royal, and whose custom lay chiefly among the desperate adventures infesting that

11 neighborhood. Monsieur Le Blanc was not unaware of the advantages to be derived from the attendance of the fair Marie in his perfumery; and his liberal proposals were accepted eagerly by the girl, although with somewhat more of hesitation by Madame.

The anticipations of the shopkeeper were realized, and his rooms soon became notorious through the charms of the

12 sprightly *grisette*. She had been in his employ about a year, when her admirers were thrown into confusion by her sudden disappearance from the shop. Monsieur Le Blanc was unable to account for her absence, and Madame Rogêt was distracted with anxiety and terror. The public papers immediately took up the theme, and the police were upon the point of making serious investigations, when, one fine morning, after the lapse of a week, Marie, in good health, but with a somewhat saddened air, made her re-appearance at her usual counter in the perfumery. All inquiry, except that of a private character, was, of course, immediately hushed. Monsieur Le Blanc professed total ignorance, as before. Marie, with Madame, replied to all questions, that the last week had been spent at the house of a relation in the country. Thus the affair died away, and was generally forgotten; for the girl, ostensibly to relieve herself from the impertinence of curiosity, soon bade a final adieu to the perfumer, and sought the shelter of her mother's residence in the Rue Pavée Saint Andrée.

It was about five months after this return home, that her friends were alarmed by her sudden disappearance for the second time. Three days elapsed, and nothing was heard of

13 her. On the fourth her corpse was found floating in the Seine, near the shore which is opposite the Quartier of the Rue Saint Andrée, and at a point not very far distant from the secluded

14 neighborhood of the Barrière du Roule.

15 The atrocity of this murder (for it was at once evident that murder had been committed), the youth and beauty of the victim, and, above all, her previous notoriety, conspired to

produce intense excitement in the minds of the sensitive Parisians. I can call to mind no similar occurrence producing so general and so intense an effect. For several weeks, in the discussion of this one absorbing theme, even the momentous political topics of the day were forgotten. The Prefect made **16** unusual exertions; and the powers of the whole Parisian police were, of course, tasked to the utmost extent.

Upon the first discovery of the corpse, it was not supposed that the murderer would be able to elude, for more than a very brief period, the inquisition which was immediately set on foot. It was not until the expiration of a week that it was deemed necessary to offer a reward; and even than this reward was limited to a thousand francs. In the meantime the investigation proceeded with vigor, if not always with judgment, and numerous individuals were examined to no purpose; while, owing to the continual absence of all clew to the mystery, the popular excitement greatly increased. At the end of the tenth day it was thought advisable to double the sum originally proposed; and, at length, the second week having elapsed without leading to any discoveries, and the prejudice which always exists in Paris against the police having given vent to itself in several serious *émeutes*, the Prefect took it **17** upon himself to offer the sum of twenty thousand francs "for the conviction of the assassin," or, if more than one should prove to have been implicated, "for the conviction of any one of the assassins." In the proclamation setting forth this reward, a full pardon was promised to any accomplice who should come forward in evidence against his fellow; and to the whole was appended, wherever it appeared, the private placard of **18** a committee of citizens, offering ten thousand francs, in addition to the amount proposed by the Prefecture. The entire reward thus stood at no less than thirty thousand francs, which will be regarded as an extraordinary sum when we consider the humble condition of the girl, and the great frequency, in large cities, of such atrocities as the one described.

No one doubted now that the mystery of this murder would be immediately brought to light. But although, in one or two instances, arrests were made which promised elucidation, yet nothing was elicited which could implicate the parties suspected; and they were discharged forthwith. Strange as it may appear, the third week from the discovery of the body had passed, and passed without any light being thrown upon the subject, before even a rumor of the events which had so agitated the public mind reached the ears of Dupin and myself. Engaged in researches which had absorbed our whole attention, it had been nearly a month since either of us had gone abroad, or received a visitor, or more than glanced at the leading political articles in one of the daily papers. The first intelligence of the murder was brought us by G——, in person. He called upon us early in the afternoon of the thirteenth of July, 18—, and remained with us until late in the night. He had been piqued by the failure of all his endeavors to ferret out the assassins. His reputation—so he said with a peculiarly Parisian air—was at stake. Even his

16 The New York press gave the story its undivided attention for more than six weeks.

17 Literally, riots or insurrections

18 A small card or poster pasted over or next to the official reward poster

19 The prefect has apparently slipped Dupin some money as encouragement—and to bail himself out of public disgrace. Or it may be the reward mentioned earlier. In the actual case, a citizens group collected $445 as a reward leading to the arrest of the murderer, and Governor Seward offered $750 from the state of New York.

20 The prefect is long-winded indeed to keep it up for seven or eight hours. Dupin's slumber behind his dark glasses indicates how useful he expects the prefect's testimony to be in solving the case.

21 Poe here departs from his opening statement that he will stick to the facts. He substitutes June 22 for July 25.

22 "Payne" (Poe's note). St. Eustache (Eustathius, who died c. 360) was leader of the First Council of Nicaea and was deposed and exiled during the Arian reaction. The name is also that of a sixteenth-century church in Paris northeast of Les Halles, north of the Rue Pavée and Rue du Roule.

23 There is no Rue des Drômes in Paris. The real aunt lived on Jane Street.

24 Mary and her mother lived in a boardinghouse at 126 Nassau St.

honor was concerned. The eyes of the public were upon him; and there was really no sacrifice which he would not be willing to make for the development of the mystery. He concluded a somewhat droll speech with a compliment upon what he was pleased to term the *tact* of Dupin, and made him a direct and certainly a liberal proposition, the precise nature of which I do not feel myself at liberty to disclose, but which has no

19 bearing upon the proper subject of my narrative.

The compliment my friend rebutted as best he could, but the proposition he accepted at once, although its advantages were altogether provisional. This point being settled the Prefect broke forth at once into explanations of his own views, interspersing them with long comments upon the evidence; of which we were not yet in possession. He discoursed much and, beyond doubt, learnedly; while I hazarded an occasional suggestion as the night wore drowsily away. Dupin, sitting steadily in his accustomed armchair, was the embodiment of respectful attention. He wore spectacles, during the whole interview; and an occasional glance beneath their green glasses sufficed to convince me that he slept not the less soundly, because silently, throughout the seven or eight leaden-footed hours which immediately preceded the departure of the

20 Prefect.

In the morning, I procured, at the Prefecture, a full report of all the evidence elicited, and, at the various newspaper offices, a copy of every paper in which, from first to last, had been published any decisive information in regard to this sad affair. Freed from all that was positively disproved, this mass of information stood thus:

Marie Rogêt left the residence of her mother, in the Rue Pavée St. Andrée, about nine o'clock in the morning of

21 Sunday, June the twenty-second, 18–. In going out, she gave

22 notice to a Monsieur Jaques St. Eustache, and to him only, of her intention to spend the day with an aunt, who resided

23 in the Rue des Drômes. The Rue des Drômes is a short and narrow but populous thoroughfare, not far from the banks of the river, and at a distance of some two miles, in the most

24 direct course possible, from the *pension* of Madame Rogêt. St. Eustache was the accepted suitor of Marie, and lodged, as well as took his meals, at the *pension*. He was to have gone for his betrothed at dusk, and to have escorted her home. In the afternoon, however, it came on to rain heavily, and, supposing that she would remain all night at her aunt's (as she had done under similar circumstances before), he did not think it necessary to keep his promise. As night drew on, Madame Rogêt (who was an infirm old lady, seventy years of age) was heard to express a fear "that she should never see Marie again;" but this observation attracted little attention at the time.

On Monday it was ascertained that the girl had not been to the Rue des Drômes; and when the day elapsed without tidings of her, a tardy search was instituted at several points in the city and its environs. It was not, however, until the fourth day from the period of her disappearance that any thing satisfactory was ascertained respecting her. On this day (Wednesday, the twenty-fifth of June) a Monsieur Beauvais, **25** who, with a friend, had been making inquiries for Marie near the Barrière du Roule, on the shore of the Seine which is opposite the Rue Pavée St. Andrée, was informed that a **26** corpse had just been towed ashore by some fishermen, who had found it floating in the river. Upon seeing the body, Beauvais, after some hesitation, identified is as that of the perfumery-girl. His friend recognized it more promptly.

The face was suffused with dark blood, some of which issued from the mouth. No foam was seen, as in the case of the merely drowned. There was no discoloration in the cellular tissue. About the throat were bruises and impressions of fingers. The arms were bent over on the chest, and were rigid. The right hand was clenched; the left partially open. On the left wrist were two circular excoriations, apparently the effect of ropes, or of a rope in more than one volution. A part of the right wrist, also, was much chafed, as well as the back throughout its extent, but more especially at the shoulder-blades. In bringing the body to the shore the fishermen had attached to it a rope, but none of the excoriations had been affected by this. The flesh of the neck was much swollen. There were no cuts apparent, or bruises which appeared the effect of blows. A piece of lace was found tied so tightly around the neck as to be hidden from sight; it was completely buried in the flesh, and was fastened by a knot which lay just under the left ear. This alone would have sufficed to produce death. The medical testimony spoke confidently of the virtuous character of the deceased. She had been subjected, it said, to brutal violence. The corpse was in such condition when found, **27** that there could have been no difficluty in its recognition by friends.

The dress was much torn and otherwise disordered. In the outer garment, a slip, about a foot wide, had been torn upward from the bottom hem to the waist, but not torn off. It was wound three times around the waist, and secured by a sort of hitch in the back. The dress immediately beneath the frock was of fine muslin; and from this a slip eighteen inches wide had been torn entirely out—torn very evenly and with great care. It was found around her neck, fitting loosely, and secured with a hard knot. Over this muslin slip and the slip of lace the strings of a bonnet were attached, the bonnet being appended. The knot by which the strings of the bonnet were fastened was not a lady's, but a slip or sailor's knot.

After the recognition of the corpse, it was not, as usual, taken to the Morgue (this formality being superfluous), but hastily interred not far from the spot at which it was brought ashore. Through the exertions of Beauvais, the matter was industriously hushed up, as far as possible; and several days had elapsed before any public emotion resulted. A weekly paper, however, at length took up the theme; the corpse was **28** disinterred, and a re-examination instituted; but nothing was elicited beyond what has been already noted. The clothes, however, were now submitted to the mother and friends of

25 "Crommelin" (Poe's note). Alfred Crommelin discovered Mary's body, or, rather, happened on the scene when it was discovered, near Castle Point, and recognized it as that of one of his fellow boarders.

26 "French readers would be greatly astonished to find . . . the Barrière du Roule on the shore of the Seine on the bank opposite the rue Pavée-Saint André" (E. D. Forgues, *Revue des Deux Mondes*, October 1846).

27 According to John Walsh, "A Coroner's inquest, presided over by Justice Gilbert Merrit, was held the same evening the body was discovered in Hoboken, after a Dr. Richard Cook had examined the body. The jury needed no time to deliberate and promptly rendered a decision that the death was the result of "violence committed by some person or persons unknown."
Crommelin's deposition, according to the *Evening Post* (August 13), stated that "on the morning after the inquest was held on Mary's body it was deemed necessary, in consequence of the great heat of the weather to temporarily inter the body, which was done, at two feet from the surface of the earth and in a double coffin."

28 "The N.Y. *Mercury*" (Poe's note).

the deceased, and fully identified as those worn by the girl upon leaving home.

Meantime, the excitement increased hourly. Several individuals were arrested and discharged. St. Eustache fell especially under suspicion; and he failed, at first, to give an intelligible account of his whereabouts during the Sunday on which Marie left home. Subsequently, however, he submitted to Monsieur G——, affidavits, accounting satisfactorily for every hour of the day in question. As time passed and no discovery ensued, a thousand contradictory rumors were circulated, and journalists busied themselves in *suggestions*. Among these, the one which attracted the most notice, was the idea that Marie Rogêt still lived—that the corpse found in the Seine was that of some other unfortunate. It will be proper that I submit to the reader some passages which embody the suggestion alluded to. These passages are *literal* **29** translations from *L'Etoile* a paper conducted, in general, with much ability.

30 "Mademoiselle Rogêt left her mother's house on Sunday morning, June the twenty-second, 18—, with the ostensible purpose of going to see her aunt, or some other connection, in the Rue des Drômes. From that hour, nobody is proved to have seen her. There is no trace or tidings of her at all. * * * There has no person, whatever, come forward, so far, who saw her at all, on that day, after she left her mother's door. * * * Now, though we have no evidence that Marie Rogêt was in the land of the living after nine o'clock on Sunday, June the twenty-second, we have proof that, up to that hour, she was alive. On Wednesday noon, at twelve, a female body was discovered afloat on the shore of the Barrière de Roule. This was, even if we presume that Marie Rogêt was thrown into the river within three hours after she left her mother's house, only three days from the time she left her home—three days to an hour. But it is folly to suppose that the murder, if murder was committed on her body, could have been consummated soon enough to have enabled her murderers to throw the body into the river before midnight. Those who are guilty of such horrid crimes choose darkness rather than light. * * * Thus we see that if the body found in the river *was* that of Marie Rogêt, it could only have been in the water two and a half days, or three at the outside. All experience has shown that drowned bodies, or bodies thrown into the water immediately after death by violence, require from six to ten days for sufficient decomposition to take place to bring them to the top of the water. Even where a cannon is fired over a corpse, and it rises before at least five or six days' immersion, it sinks again, if let alone. Now, we ask, what was there in this case to cause a departure from the ordinary course of nature? * * * If the body had been kept in its mangled state on shore until Tuesday night, some trace would be found on shore of the murderers. It is a doubtful point, also, whether the body would be so soon afloat, even were it thrown in after having been dead two days. And, furthermore, it is exceedingly improbable that any villains who had committed such a murder as is here supposed, would have thrown the body in without weight to sink it, when such a precaution could have so easily been taken."

29 "The 'N.Y. *Brother Jonathan*,' edited by H. Hastings Weld, Esq." (Poe's note). The passages from *L'Etoile* are lifted almost verbatim from this paper. The real *L'Etoile* was a pro-government paper with a small circulation, of 2,749 readers at its height, in 1824.

30 Poe alters the time to suit his fictional purpose, but the rest of the quote from *Brother Jonathan* (August 28) provides much of the substance for Dupin's later comments.

The editor here proceeds to argue that the body must have been in the water "not three days merely, but, at least, five times three days," because it was so far decomposed that Beauvais had great difficulty in recognizing it. This latter point, however, was fully disproved. I continue the translation:

"What, then, are the facts on which M. Beauvais says that he has no doubt the body was that of Marie Rogêt? He ripped up the gown sleeve, and says he found marks which satisfied him of the identity. The public generally supposed those marks to have consisted of some description of scars. He rubbed the arm and found *hair* upon it—something as indefinite, we think, as can readily be imagined—as little conclusive as finding an arm in the sleeve. M. Beauvais did not return that night, but sent word to Madame Rogêt, at seven o'clock, on Wednesday evening, that an investigation was still in progress respecting her daughter. If we allow that Madame Rogêt, from her age and grief, could not go over (which is allowing a great deal), there certainly must have been some one who would have thought it worth while to go over and attend the investigation, if they thought the body was that of Marie. Nobody went over. There was nothing said or heard about the matter in the Rue Pavée St. Andrée, that reached even the occupants of the same building. M. St. Eustache, the lover and intended husband of Marie, who boarded in her mother's house, deposes that he did not hear of the discovery of the body of his intended until the next morning, when M. Beauvais came into his chamber and told him of it. For an item of news like this, it strikes us it was very coolly received."

In this was the journal endeavored to create the impression of an apathy on the part of the relatives of Marie, inconsistent with the supposition that these relatives believed the corpse to be hers. Its insinuations amount to this: that Marie, with the connivance of her friends, had absented herself from the city for reasons involving a charge against her chastity; and that these friends upon the discovery of a corpse in the Seine, somewhat resembling that of the girl, had availed themselves of the opportunity to impress the public with the belief of her death. But *L'Etoile* was again over-hasty. It was distinctly proved that no apathy, such as was imagined, existed; that the old lady was exceedingly feeble, and so agitated as to tbe unable to attend to any duty; that St. Eustache, so far from receiving the news coolly, was distracted with grief, and bore himself so frantically, that M. Beauvais prevailed upon a friend and relative to take charge of him, and prevent his attending the examination at the disinterment. Moreover, although it was stated by *L'Etoile*, that the corpse was re-interred at the public expense, that an advantageous offer of private sepulture was absolutely declined by the family, and that no member of the family attended the ceremonial;—although, I say, all this was asserted by *L'Etoile* in furtherance of the impression it designed to convey—yet *all* this was satisfactorily disproved. In a subsequent number of the paper, an attempt was made to throw suspicion upon Beauvais himself. The editor says:

"Now, then, a change comes over the matter. We are told that, on one occasion, while a Madame B—— was at

A weekly paper, however, at length took up the theme. *. . . Artist unknown*

Madame Rogêt's house, M. Beauvais, who was going put, told her that a *gendarme* was expected there, and that she, Madame B., must not say any thing to the *gendarme* until he returned, but let the matter be for him. * * * In the present posture of affairs, M. Beauvais appears to have the whole matter locked up in his head. A single step cannot be taken without M. Beauvais, for, go which way you will, you run against him. * * * For some reason he determined that nobody shall have any thing to do with the proceedings but himself, and he has elbowed the male relatives out of the way, according to thier representations, in a very singular manner. He seems to have been very much averse to permitting the relatives to see the body."

By the following fact, some color was given to the suspicion thus thrown upon Beauvais. A visitor at his office, a few days prior to the girl's disappearance, and during the absence of its occupant, had observed *a rose* in the key-hole of the door, and the name *"Marie"* inscribed upon a slate which hung near at hand.

The general impression, so far as we were enabled to glean it from the newspapers, seemed to be, that Marie had been the victim of *a gang* of desperadoes—that by these she had been borne across the river, maltreated, and murdered. *Le Commerciel*, however, a print of extensive influence, was **31** earnest in combating this popular idea. I quote a passage or two from its columns:

"We are persuaded that pursuit has hitherto been on a false scent, so far as it has been directed to the Barrière du Roule. It is impossible that a person so well known to thousands as this young woman was, should have passed three blocks without some one having seen her; and any one who saw her would have remembered it, for she interested all who knew her. It was when the streets were full of people, when she went out. * * * It is impossible that she could have gone to the Barrière du Roule, or to the Rue des Drômes, without being recognized by a dozen persons; yet no one has come forward who saw her outside her mother's door, and there is no evidence, except the testimony concerning her *expressed intentions*, that she did go out at all. Her gown was torn, bound round her, and tied; and by that the body was carried as a bundle. If the murder had been committed at the Barrière du Roule, there would have been no necessity for any such arrangement. The fact that the body was found floating near the Barrière, is no proof as to where it was thrown into the water. * * * A piece of one of the unfortunate girl's petticoats, two feet long and one foot wide, wa torn out and tied under her chin around the back of her head, probably to prevent screams. This was done by fellows who had no pocket-handkerchief."

A day or two before the Prefect called upon us, however, some important information reached the police, which seemed to overthrow, at least, the chief portion of *Le Commerciel's* argument. Two small boys, sons of a Madame Deluc, while roaming among the woods near the Barrière du Roule, chanced to penetrate a close thicket, within which were three or four

31 "N.Y. *'Journal of Commerce'* " (Poe's note), referring to the August 23 edition. There is no record of a Paris newspaper with this name, or of the more likely spelling, *Le Commercial*.

large stones, forming a kind of seat with a back and footstool. On the upper stone lay a white petticoat; on the second, a silk scarf. A parasol, gloves, and a pocket-handkerchief were also **32** here found. The handkerchief bore the name "Marie Rogêt." Fragments of dress were discovered on the brambles around. The earth was trampled, the bushes were broken, and there was every evidence of a struggle. Between the thicket and the river, the fences were found taken down, and the ground bore evidence of some heavy burthen having been dragged along it. **33**

A weekly paper, *Le Soleil*, had the following comments **34** upon this discovery—comments which merely echoed the sentiment of the whole Parisian press:

> "The things had all evidently been there at least three weeks; they were all mildewed down hard with the action of the rain, and stuck together from mildew. The grass had grown around and over some of them. The silk on the parasol was strong, but the threads of it were run together within. The upper part, where it had been doubled and folded, was all mildewed and rotten, and tore on its being opened. * * * The pieces of her frock torn out by the bushes were about three inches wide and six inches long. One part was the hem of the frock, and it had been mended; the other piece was part of the skirt, not the hem. They looked like strips torn off, and were on the thorn bush, about a foot from the ground. * * * There can be no doubt, therefore, that the spot of this appalling outrage has been discovered."

Consequent upon this discovery new evidence appeared. Madame Deluc testified that she keeps a roadside inn not far from the bank of the river, opposite the Barrière du Roule. **35** The neighborhood is secluded—particularly so. It is the usual Sunday resort of blackguards from the city, who cross the river in boats. About three o'clock, in the afternoon of the Sunday in question, a young girl arrived at the inn, accompanied by a young man of dark complexion. The two remained here for some time. On their departure, they took the road to some thick woods in the vicinity. Madame Deluc's attention was called to the dress worn by the girl, on ·account of its resemblance to one worn by a deceased relative. A scarf was particularly noticed. Soon after the departure of the couple, a gang of miscreants made their appearance, behaved boisterously, ate and drank without making payment, followed in the route of the young man and girl, returned to the inn about dusk, and re-crossed the river as if in great haste.

It was soon after dark, upon this same evening, that Madame Deluc, as well as her eldest son, heard the screams of a female in the vicinity of the inn. The screams were violent but brief. Madame D. recognized not only the scarf which was found in the thicket, but the dress which was discovered upon the corpse. An omnibus driver, Valence, now also testified that **36** he saw Marie Rogêt cross a ferry on the Seine, on the Sunday in question, in company with a young man of dark complexion. He, Valence, knew Marie, and could not be mistaken in her identity. The articles found in the thicket were fully identified by the relatives of Marie.

32 It is "pocket handkerchiefs" in the first version.

33 Poe here again changes the sequence of events. The narrator tells us later that the police had the information less than three weeks after Rogêt's death, while the discovery of Mary Rogers' possessions came on August 25, a full month after her death.

34 "Philadelphia '*Saturday Evening Post*,' edited by C. I. Peterson, Esq." (Poe's note), from the September 25, 1841, edition, which it copied from the New York *Herald* of September 17.
There was a *Le Soleil* in 1845, but the paper appeared only six times before it went defunct.

35 Mrs. Frederica Loss, who owned a roadhouse near the shore at Weehawken, originally told the local police that her sons had found some articles of woman's clothing in a dense thicket about three hundred yards from her place of business. She recognized the scarf as that of a young woman who had been at the inn on the same Sunday Mary Rogers had disappeared, in company, she said, with "a dark complexioned young man." About 9 P.M. that same evening she heard "a frightful screaming as of a young girl in great distress, partly choked and calling for assistance, and sounded like 'Oh! Oh! God' etc, uttered in great agony. So loud were the screams that her other son heard them down in the cellar. She thought the bull had gored her boy, and rushed out in terror, calling his name down the road to Ludlow's. As soon as she called out, there was a noise as of a struggling, and a stifled, suffering scream, and then all was still." (New York *Herald*, September 17)
Mrs. Loss's deathbed testimony (see introductory note) tells a far different story.

36 "Adam" (Poe's note). The *Herald* reported on September 17 that a stage driver named Adam had seen Mary Rogers leave the Hoboken ferry at 3 P.M.

37 Opium dissolved in alchohol. Payne actually died some six weeks after Mary Rogers. He was found unconscious on a bench not far from the place where his fiancée's body had been found, a mile from the point where she was thought to have been murdered. Investigators found an empty bottle of laudanum nearby. A note with the body read, "To the World, Here I am on the spot. God forgive me for my misfortune, or for my misspent time." On October 7 he had asked at the Loss Inn where the thicket was, drunk some brandy and left, although he was later seen that day and the next wandering aimlessly about the area, drinking heavily. His death was probably the result of a combination of laudanum and alcohol, although the coroner's jury said it was due to "congestion of the brain, supposed to be brought about by exposure and irregularity of living incident to aberration of mind."

The bottle, marked "Laudanum, Souillard & Delluc," may have been the source for the name of Madame Deluc.

38 Allies of Achilles in the Trojan War, they were an old Thessalian race who began when Zeus changed ants into people. The word means "brave men," here used ironically.

39 "See 'The Murders in the Rue Morgue'" (Poe's note).

The items of evidence and information thus collected by myself, from the newspapers, at the suggestion of Dupin, embraced only one more point—but this was a point of seemingly vast consequence. It appears that, immediately after the discovery of the clothes as above described, the lifeless or nearly lifeless body of St. Eustache, Marie's be-
37 trothed, was found in the vicinity of what all now supposed the scene of the outrage. A phial labelled "laudanum," and emptied, was found near him. His breath gave evidence of the poison. He died without speaking. Upon his person was found a letter, briefly stating his love for Marie, with his design of self-destruction.

"I need scarcely tell you," said Dupin, as he finished the perusal of my notes, "that this is a far more intricate case than that of the Rue Morgue; from which it differs in one important respect. This is an *ordinary*, although an atrocious, instance of crime. There is nothing peculiarly *outré* about it. You will observe that, for this reason, the mystery has been considered easy, when, for this reason, it should have been considered difficult, of solution. Thus, at first, it was thought unnecessary
38 to offer a reward. The myrmidons of G—— were able at once to comprehend how and why such an atrocity *might have been* committed. They could picture to their imaginations a mode— many modes,—and a motive—many motives; and because it was not impossible that either of these numerous modes and motives *could* have been the actual one, they have taken it for granted that one of them *must*. But the ease with which these variable fancies were entertained, and the very plausibility which each assumed, should have been understood as indicative rather of the difficulties than of the facilities which must attend elucidation. I have therefore observed that it is by prominences above the plane of the ordinary, that reason feels her way, if at all, in her search for the true, and that the proper question in cases such as this, is not so much 'what has occurred?' as 'what has occurred that has never occurred before?' In the investigations at the house of Madame
39 L'Espanaye, the agents of G—— were discouraged and confounded by that very *unusualness* which, to a properly regulated intellect, would have afforded the surest omen of success; while this same intellect might have been plunged in despair at the ordinary character of all that met the eye in the case of the perfumery-girl, and yet told of nothing but easy triumph to the functionaries of the Prefecture.

"In the case of Madame L'Espanaye and her daughter, there was, even at the beginning of our investigation, no doubt that murder had been committed. The idea of suicide was excluded at once. Here, too, we are freed, at the commencement, from all supposition of self-murder. The body found at the Barrière du Roule was found under such circumstances as to leave us no room for embarrassment upon this important point. But it has been suggested that the corpse discovered is not that of Marie Rogêt for the conviction of whose assassin, or assassins, the reward is offered, and respecting whom, solely, our agreement has been arranged with the Prefect. We both know this gentleman well. It will not do to trust him too far. If, dating our inquiries from the body found, and then tracing a murderer, we yet discover this body to be that of some other individual than Marie; or if, starting from the living Marie, we find her, yet find her unassassinated—in either case we lose our labor; since it is Monsieur G—— with whom we have to deal. For our own purpose, therefore, if not for the purpose of justice, it is indispensable that our first step should be the determination of the identity of the corpse with the Marie Rogêt who is missing.

"With the public the arguments of *L'Etoile* have had weight; and that the journal itself is convinced of their importance would appear from the manner in which it commences one of its essays upon the subject—'Several of the morning papers of the day,' it says, 'speak of the *conclusive* article in Monday's *L'Etoile*.' To me, this article appears conclusive of little beyond the zeal of its inditer. We should bear in mind that, in general, **40** it is the object of our newspapers rather to create a sensation—to make a point—than to further the cause of truth. The latter end is only pursued when it seems coincident with the former. The print which merely falls in with ordinary opinion (however well founded this opinion may be) earns for itself no credit with the mob. The mass of the people regard as profound only him who suggests *pungent contradictions* of the general idea. In ratiocination, not less than in literature, it is the *epigram* which is the most immediately and the most universally appreciated. In both, it is of the lowest order of merit. **41**

"What I mean to say is, that it is the mingled epigram and melodrame of the idea, that Marie Rogêt still lives, rather **42** than any true plausibility in this idea, which have suggested it to *L'Etoile*, and secured it a favorable reception with the public. Let us examine the heads of this journal's argument; endeavoring to avoid the incoherence with which it is originally set forth.

"The first aim of the writer is to show, from the brevity of the interval between Marie's disappearance and the finding of the floating corpse, that this corpse cannot be that of Marie. The reduction of this interval to its smallest possible dimension, becomes thus, at once, an object with the reasoner. In the rash pursuit of this object, he rushes into mere assumption at the outset. 'It is folly to suppose,' he says, 'that the murder, if murder was committed on her body, could have been consummated soon enough to have enabled her murderers to throw the body into the river before midnight.' We demand at once, and very naturally, *why?* Why is it folly to suppose that the murder was committed *within five minutes* after the girl's quitting her mother's house? Why is it folly to suppose that the murder was committed at any given period of the day? There have been assassinations at all hours. But, had the murder taken place at any moment between nine o'clock in the morning of Sunday and a quarter before midnight, there **43** would still have been time enough 'to throw the body into the river before midnight.' This assumption, then, amounts pre-

40 One who composes or dictates a literary work, speech, or letter; an author

41 Dupin puts down the common opinions of the masses again in "The Purloined Letter."

42 "Melodrame" was common usage in Poe's day.

43 Poe substitutes 9 A.M. for 10 A.M.

cisely to this—that the murder was not committed on Sunday at all—and, if we allow *L'Etoile* to assume this, we may permit it any liberties whatever. The paragraph beginning: 'It is folly to suppose that the murder, etc.,' however it appears as printed in *L'Etoile*, may be imagined to have existed actually *thus* in the brain of its inditer: 'It is folly to suppose that the murder, if murder was committed on the body, could have been committed soon enough to have enabled her murderers to throw the body into the river before midnight; it is folly, we say, to suppose all this, and to suppose at the same time (as we are resolved to suppose), that the body was *not* thrown in until *after* midnight'—a sentence sufficiently inconsequential in itself, but not so utterly preposterous as the one printed.

"Were it my purpose," continued Dupin, "merely to *make out a case* against this passage of *L'Etoile's* argument, I might safely leave it where it is. It is not, however, with *L'Etoile* that we have to do, but with the truth. The sentence in question has but one meaning, as it stands; and this meaning I have fairly stated; but it is material that we go behind the mere words, for an idea which these words have obviously intended, and failed to convey. It was the design of the journalists to say that at whatever period of the day or night of Sunday this murder was committed, it was improbable that the assassins would have ventured to bear the corpse to the river before midnight. And herein lies, really, the assumption of which I complain. It is assumed that the murder was committed at such a position, and under such circumstances, that *the bearing it* to the river became necessary. Now, the assassination might have taken place upon the river's brink, or on the river itself; and, thus, the throwing the corpse in the water might have been resorted to at any period of the day or night, as the most obvious and most immediate mode of disposal. You will understand that I suggest nothing here as probable, or as coincident with my own opinion. My design, so far, has no reference to the *facts* of the case. I wish merely to caution you against the whole tone of *L'Etoile's suggestion*, **44** by calling your attention to its *ex parte* character at the outset.

"Having prescribed thus a limit to suit its own preconceived notions; having assumed that, if this were the body of Marie, it could have been in the water but a very brief time, the journal goes on to say:

> "'All experience has shown that drowned bodies, or bodies thrown into the water immediately after death by violence, require from six to ten days for sufficient decomposition to take place to bring them to the top of the water. Even when a cannon is fired over a corpse, and it rises before at least five or six days' immersion, it sinks again if
> **45** let alone.'

"These assertions have been tacitly received by every paper **46** in Paris, with the exception of *Le Moniteur*. This latter print endeavors to combat that portion of the paragraph which has reference to 'drowned bodies' only, by citing some five or six instances in which the bodies of individuals known to be

44 On one side only; a one-sided, or partisan, point of view

45 Cannons were fired to jar the riverbed and loosen any dead bodies stuck in the mud, so they would float to the surface. Mark Twain describes the process in *Huckleberry Finn*, Chapter VIII, adding that loaves of bread filled with quicksilver were dropped into the water, "because they always go right to the drownded carcass and stop there."

46 "The 'N.Y. *Commercial Advertiser*,' edited by Col. Stone" (Poe's note). Far from agreeing on the length of time required for a body to surface, five New York newspapers argued over the question, notes William K. Wimsatt in *PMLA*, March 1941, p. 235.

Le Moniteur was the oldest newspaper in France after *La Gazette*, but it faded from prominence before mid-century and disappeared.

drowned were found floating after the lapse of less time than is insisted upon by *L'Etoile*. But there is something excessively unphilosophical in the attempt, on the part of *Le Moniteur*, to rebut the general assertion of *L'Etoile*, by a citation of particular instances militating against that assertion. Had it been possible to adduce fifty instead of five examples of bodies found floating at the end of two or three days, these fifty examples could still have been properly regarded only as exceptions to *L'Etoile's* rule, until such time as the rule itself should be confuted. Admitting the rule (and this *Le Moniteur* does not deny, insisting merely upon its exceptions), the argument of *L'Etoile* is suffered to remain in full force; for this argument does not pretend to involve more than a question of the *probability* of the body having risen to the surface in less than three days; and this probability will be in favor of *L'Etoile's* position until the instances so childishly adduced shall be sufficient in number to establish an antagonistical rule.

"You will see at once that all argument upon this head should be urged, if at all, against the rule itself; and for this end we must examine the *rationale* of the rule. Now the human body, in general, is neither much lighter nor much heavier than the water of the Seine; that is to say, the specific gravity of the human body, in its natural condition, is about equal to the bulk of fresh water which it displaces. The bodies of fat and fleshy persons, with small bones, and of women generally, are lighter than those of the lean and large-boned, and of men; and the specific gravity of the water of a river is somewhat influenced by the presence of the tide from the sea. But, leaving this tide out of question, it may be said that *very* few human bodies will sink at all, even in fresh water, *of their own accord*. Almost any one, falling into a river, will be enabled to float, if he suffer the specific gravity of the water fairly to be adduced in comparison with his own—that is to say, if he suffer his whole person to be immersed, with as little exception as possible. The proper position for one who cannot swim, is the upright position of the walker on land, with the head thrown fully back, and immersed; the mouth and nostrils alone remaining above the surface. Thus circumstanced, we shall find that we float without difficulty and without exertion. It is evident, however, that the gravities of the body, and of the bulk of water displaced, are very nicely balanced, and that a trifle will cause either to preponderate. An arm, for instance, uplifted from the water, and thus deprived of its support, is an additional weight sufficient to immerse the whole head, while the accidental aid of the smallest piece of timber will enable us to elevate the head so as to look about. Now, in the struggles of one unused to swimming, the arms are invariably thrown upward, while an attempt is made to keep the head in its usual perpendicular position. The result is the immersion of the mouth and nostrils, and the inception, during efforts to breathe while beneath the surface, of water into the lungs. Much is also received into the stomach, and the whole body becomes heavier by the

47 While Poe's source is not known, it agrees with a later work, *Principles and Practice of Medical Jurisprudence* (1873), by Alfred S. Taylor.

48 Mercuric chloride was in general use as a preservative of tissues for microscopic study, as well as for embalming. Because of its poisonous nature, as well as its interference with toxicological analysis, it was later superseded by formaldehyde.

difference between the weight of the air originally distending these cavities, and that of the fluid which now fills them. This difference is sufficient to cause the body to sink, as a general rule; but is insufficient in the cases of individuals with small bones and an abnormal quantity of flaccid or fatty matter. Such **47** individuals float even after drowning.

"The corpse, being supposed at the bottom of the river, will remain until, by some means, its specific gravity again becomes less than that of the bulk of water which it displaces. This effect is brought about by decomposition, or otherwise. The result of decomposition is the generation of gas, distending the cellular tissues and all the cavities, and giving the *puffed* appearance which is so horrible. When this distension has so far progressed that the bulk of the corpse is materially increased without a corresponding increase of *mass* or weight, its specific gravity becomes less than that of the water displaced, and it forthwith makes its appearance at the surface. But decomposition is modified by innumerable circumstances—is hastened or retarded by innumerable agencies; for example, by the heat or cold of the season, by the mineral impregnation or purity of the water, by its depth or shallowness, by its currency or stagnation, by the temperament of the body, by its infection or freedom from disease before death. Thus it is evident that we can assign no period, with any thing like accuracy, at which the corpse shall rise through decomposition. Under certain conditions this result would be brought about within an hour; under others it might not take place at all. There are chemical infusions by which the animal frame can be preserved *forever* from corruption; the bichloride **48** of mercury is one. But, apart from decomposition, there may be, and very usually is, a generation of gas within the stomach, from the acetous fermentation of vegetable matter (or within other cavities from other causes), sufficient to induce a distension which will bring the body to the surface. The effect produced by the firing of a cannon is that of simple vibration. This may either loosen the corpse from the soft mud or ooze in which it is imbedded, thus permitting it to rise when other agencies have already prepared it for so doing; or it may overcome the tenacity of some putrescent portions of the cellular tissue, allowing the cavities to distend under the influence of the gas.

"Having thus before us the whole philosophy of this subject, we can easily test by it the assertions of *L'Etoile*. 'All experience shows,' says this paper, 'that drowned bodies, or bodies thrown into the water immediately after death by violence, require from six to ten days for sufficient decomposition to take place to bring them to the top of the water. Even when a cannon is fired over a corpse, and it rises before at least five of six days' immersion, it sinks again if let alone.'

"The whole of this paragraph must now appear a tissue of inconsequence and incoherence. All experience does *not* show that 'drowned bodies' *require* from six to ten days for sufficient decomposition to take place to bring them to the surface. Both science and experience show that the period of their rising is, and necessarily must be, indeterminate. If, moreover, a body has risen to the surface through firing of cannon, it will *not* 'sink again if let alone,' until decomposition has so far progressed as to permit the escape of the generated gas. But I wish to call your attention to the distinction which is made between 'drowned bodies,' and 'bodies thrown into the water immediately after death by violence.' Although the writer admits the distinction, he yet includes them all in the same category. I have shown how it is that the body of a drowning man becomes specifically heavier than its bulk of water, and that he would not sink at all, except for the struggle by which he elevates his arms above the surface, and his gasps for breath while beneath the surface—gasps which supply by water the place of the original air in the lungs. But these struggles and these gasps would not occur in the body 'thrown into the water immediately after death by violence.' Thus, in the latter instance, *the body, as a general rule, would not sink at all*—a fact of which *L'Etoile* is evidently ignorant. When decomposition had proceeded to a very great extent—when the flesh had in a great measure left the bones—then, indeed, but not *till* then, should we lose sight of corpse.

"And now what are we to make of the argument, that the body found could not be that of Marie Rogêt, because, three days only have elapsed, this body was found floating? If drowned, being a woman, she might never have sunk; or, having sunk, might have re-appeared in twenty-four hours or less. But no one supposes her to have been drowned; and, dying before being thrown into the river, she might have been found floating at any period afterward whatever.

" 'But,' says *L'Etoile*, 'if the body had been kept in its mangled state on shore until Tuesday night, some trace would be found on shore of the murderers.' Here it is at first difficult to perceive the intention of the reasoner. He means to anticipate what he imagines would be an objection to this theory—viz.: that the body was kept on shore two days, suffering rapid decomposition—*more* rapid than if immersed in water. He supposes that, had this been the case, it *might* have appeared at the surface on the Wednesday, and thinks that *only* under such circumstances it could have so appeared. He is, accordingly, in haste to show that it *was not* kept on shore; for, if so, 'some trace would be found on shore of the murderers.' I presume you smile at the *sequitur*. You cannot be made to see how the mere *duration* of the corpse on the shore could operate to *multiply traces* of the assassins. Nor can I.

" 'And furthermore it is exceedingly improbable,' continues our journal, 'that any villains who had committed such a murder as is here supposed, would have thrown the body in without weight to sink it, when such a precaution could have so easily been taken.' Observe, here, the laughable confusion of thought! No one—not even *L'Etoile*—disputes the murder committed *on the body found*. The marks of violence are too obvious. It is our reasoner's object merely to show that this body is not Marie's. He wishes to prove that *Marie* is not

49 This is not from the *"L'Etoile"* passage quoted earlier but does appear in *Brother Jonathan* on August 28, reprinted from *The Tattler* of August 23. Poe uses it here to strengthen his point.

50 H. L. Mencken tells this story: "When Captain Frederick Marryat, the author of 'Mr. Midshipman Easy,' came to the United States in 1837, he got into trouble at Niagara Falls when a young woman acquaintance slipped and barked her shin. As she limped home, he asked, 'Did you hurt your *leg* much?' She turned from him 'evidently much shocked or much offended,' but presently recovered her composure and told him gently that *leg* was never mentioned before ladies; the proper term was *limb*. Even chickens ceased to have *legs*, and another British traveler, W. F. Goodmane, was 'not a little confused on being requested by a lady, at a public dinner-table, to furnish her with the *first and second joint*." (*The American Language*, Knopf, 1963; pp. 356–57)

Poe's discussion of this subject, complete with garters, thus seems rather racy for the period. It was news in 1936 when a poll taken in the Bible Belt showed that 72.3 percent of the men and 54.6 percent of the women reported they saw no impropriety in the word "garter" (Mencken, p. 365). The garter discussion comes from *Brother Jonathan* (August 28) and is not included in the excerpts that Poe actually quotes verbatim.

assassinated—not that the corpse was not. Yet his observation proves only the latter point. Here is a corpse without weight attached. Murderers, casting it in, would not have failed to attach a weight. Therefore it was not thrown in by murderers. This is all which is proved, if any thing is. The question of identity is not even approached, and *L'Etoile* has been at great pains merely to gainsay now what it has admitted only a moment before. 'We are perfectly convinced,' it says, 'that **49** the body found was that of a murdered female.'

"Nor is this the sole instance, even in this division of his subject, where our reasoner unwittingly reasons against himself. His evident object, I have already said, is to reduce, as much as possible, the interval between Marie's disappearance and the finding of the corpse. Yet we find him *urging* the point that no person saw the girl from the moment of her leaving her mother's house. 'We have no evidence,' he says, 'that Marie Rogêt was in the land of the living after nine o'clock on Sunday, June the twenty-second.' As his argument is obviously an *ex parte* one, he should, at least, have left this matter out of sight; for had any one been known to see Marie, say on Monday, or on Tuesday, the interval in question would have been much reduced, and, by his own ratiocination, the probability much diminished of the corpse being that of the *grisette*. It is, nevertheless, amusing to observe that *L'Etoile* insists upon its point in the full belief of its furthering its general argument.

"Reperuse now that portion of this argument which has reference to the identification of the corpse by Beauvais. In regard to the *hair* upon the arm, *L'Etoile* has been obviously disingenuous. M. Beauvais, not being an idiot, could never have urged in identification of the corpse, simply *hair upon its arm*. No arm is *without* hair. The *generality* of the expression of *L'Etoile* is a mere perversion of the witness' phraseology. He must have spoken of some *peculiarity* on this hair. It must have been a peculiarity of color, of quantity, of length, or of situation.

" 'Her foot,' says the journal, 'was small—so are thousands of feet. Her garter is no proof whatever—nor is her shoe—for shoes and garters are sold in packages. The same may be said of the flowers in her hat. One thing upon which M. Beauvais strongly insists is, that the clasp on the garter found had been set back to take it in. This amounts to nothing; for most women find it proper to take a pair of garters home and fit them to **50** the size of the limbs they are to encircle, rather than to try them in the store where they purchase.' Here it is difficult to suppose the reasoner in earnest. Had M. Beauvais, in his search for the body of Marie, discovered a corpse correspnding in general size and appearnace to the missing girl, he would have been warranted (without reference to the question of habiliment at all) in forming an opinion that his search had been successful. If, in addition to the point of general size and contour, he had found upon the arm a peculiar hairy appearance which he had observed upon the living Marie, his opinion might have been justly strengthened; and the increase of positiveness might well have been in the ratio of the peculiarity, or unusualness, of the hairy mark. If, the feet of Marie being small, those of the corpse were also small, the increase of probability that the body was that of Marie would not be an increase in a ratio merely arithmetical, but in one highly geometrical, or accumulative. Add to all this shoes such as she had been known to wear upon the day of her disappearance, and, although these shoes may be 'sold in packages,' you so far augment the probability as to verge upon the certain. What, of itself, would be no evidence of identity, becomes through its corroborative position, proof most sure. Give us, then, flowers in the hat corresponding to those worn by the missing girl, and we seek for nothing further—what then if two or three, or more? Each successive one is multiple evidence—proof not *added* to proof, but *multiplied* by hundreds or thousands. Let us now discover, upon the deceased, garters such as the living used, and it is almost folly to proceed. But these garters are found to be tightened, by the setting back of a clasp, in just a manner as her own had been tightened by Marie shortly previous to her leaving home. It is now madness or hypocrisy to doubt. What *L'Etoile* says in respect to this abbreviation of the garters being an unusual occurrence, shows nothing beyond its own pertinacity in error. The elastic nature of the clasp-garter is self-demonstration of the *unusualness* of the abbreviation. What is made to adjust itself, must of necessity require foreign adjustment but rarely. It must have been by an accident, in its strictest sense, that these garters of Marie needed the tightening described. They alone would have amply established her identity. But it is not that the corpse was found to have the garters of the missing girl, or found to have her shoes, or her bonnet, or the flowers of her bonnet, or her feet, or a peculiar mark upon the arm, or her general size and appearance—it is that the corpse had each, and *all collectively*. Could it be proved that the editor of *L'Etoile* really entertained a doubt, under the circumstances, there would be no need, in his case, of a commission *de lunatico inquirendo*. He has thought it sagacious to echo the **51** small talk of the lawyers, who, for the most part, content themselves with echoing the rectangular precepts of the courts. I would here observe that very much of what is rejected as evidence by a court, is the best of evidence to the intellect. For the court, guided itself by the general principles of evidence—the recognized and *booked* principles—is averse from swerving at particular instances. And this steadfast adherence to principle, with rigorous disregard of the conflicting exception, is a sure mode of attaining the *maximum* of attainable truth, in any long sequence of time. The practice, *in mass*, is therefore philosophical; but it is not the less certain that it engenders vast individual error. **52**

"In respect to the insinuations leveled at Beauvais, you will be willing to dismiss them in a breath. You have already fathomed the true character of this good gentleman. He is a *busybody*, with much of romance and little of wit. Any one so constituted will readily so conduct himself, upon occasion

51 Under common law, one could draw up a writ requesting a jury trial to determine sanity or insanity. *The Commissioner, or De Lunatico Inquirendo,* was also the name of a satirical romance published in 1842 by Wiley and Putnam.

52 " 'A theory based on the qualities of an object, will prevent its being unfolded according to its objects; and he who arranges topics in reference to their causes, will cease to value them according to their results. Thus the jurisprudence of every nation will show that, when law becomes a science and a system, it ceases to be justice. The errors into which a blind devotion to *principles* of classification has led the common law, will be seen by observing how often the legislature has been obliged to come forward to restore the equity its scheme had lost.'—*Landor*" (Poe's note).
From *Stanley* (1838), II, p. 78, by "William Landor" (Horace Binney Wallace).

of *real* excitement, as to render himself liable to suspicion on the part of the over-acute, or the ill-disposed. M. Beauvais (as it appears from your notes) had some personal interviews with the editor of *L'Etoile*, and offended him by venturing an opinion that the corpse, notwithstanding the theory of the editor, was, in sober fact, that of Marie. 'He persists,' says the paper, 'in asserting the corpse to be that of Marie, but cannot give a circumstance, in addition to those which we have commented upon, to make others believe.' Now, without re-adverting to the fact that stronger evidence 'to make others believe,' could *never* have been adduced, it may be remarked that a man may very well be understood to believe, in a case of this kind, without the ability to advance a single reason for the belief of a second party. Nothing is more vague than impressions of individual identity. Each man recognizes his neighbor, yet there are few instances in which any one is prepared to *give a reason* for his recognition. The editor of *L'Etoile* had no right to be offended at M. Beauvais' unreasoning belief.

"The suspicious circumstances which invest him, will be found to tally much better with my hypotheisis of *romantic busy-bodyism,* than with the reasoner's suggestion of guilt. Once adopting the more charitable interpretation, we shall find no difficulty in comprehending the rose in the keyhole; the 'Marie' upon the slate; the 'elbowing the male relatives out of the way'; the 'aversion to permitting them to see the body'; the caution given to Madame B——, that she must hold no conversation with a *gendarme* until his (Beauvais') return; and, lastly, his apparent determination 'that nobody should have any thing to do with the proceedings except himself.' It seems to me unquestionable that Beauvais was a suitor of Marie's; that she coquetted with him; and that he was ambitious of being thought to enjoy her fullest intimacy and confidence. I shall say nothing more upon this point; and, as the evidence fully rebuts the assertion of *L'Etoile,* touching the matter of *apathy* on the part of the mother and other relatives—an apathy inconsistent with the supposition of their believing the corpse to be that of the perfumery-girl—we shall now proceed as if the question of *identity* were settled to our perfect satisfaction."

"And what," I here demanded, "do you think of the opinions of *Le Commerciel?*"

"That, in spirit, they are far more worthy of attention than any which have been promulgated upon the subject. The deductions from the premises are philosophical and acute; but the premises, in two instances, at least, are founded in imperfect observation. *Le Commerciel* wishes to intimate that Marie was seized by some gang of low ruffians not far from her mother's door. 'It is impossible,' it urges, 'that a person so well known to thousands as this young woman was, should have passed three blocks without some one having seen her.' This is the idea of a man long resident in Paris—a public man—and one whose walks to and fro in the city have been mostly limited to the vicinity of the public offices. He is aware

53 Policeman, from *gens d'armes,* "men of arms"

that he seldom passes so far as a dozen blocks from his own *bureau*, without being recognized and accosted. And, knowing **54** the extent of his personal acquaintance with others, and of others with him, he compares his notoriety with that of the perfumery-girl, finds no great difference between them, and reaches at once the conclusion that she, in her walks, would be equally liable to recognition with himself in his. This could only be the case were her walks of the same unvarying, methodical character, and within the same *species* of limited region as are his own. He passes to and fro, at regular intervals, within a confined periphery, abounding in individuals who are led to observation of his person through interest in the kindred nature of his occupation with their own. But the walks of Marie may, in general, be supposed discursive. In this **55** particular instance, it will be understood as most probable, that she proceeded upon a route of more than average diversity from her accustomed ones. The parallel which we imagine to have existed in the mind of *Le Commerciel* would only be sustained in the event of the two individuals' traversing the whole city. In this case, granting the personal acquaintances to be equal, the chances would be also equal than an equal number of personal *rencontres* would be made. For my own part, I should hold it not only as possible, but as far more than probable, that Marie might have proceeded, at any given period, by any one of the many routes between her own residence and that of her aunt, without meeting a single individual whom she knew, or by whom she was known. In viewing this question in its full and proper light, we must hold steadily in mind the great disproportion between the personal acquaintances of even the most noted individual in Paris, and the entire population of Paris itself.

"But whatever force there may still appear to be in the suggestion of *Le Commerciel*, will be much diminished when we take into consideration *the hour* at which the girl went abroad. 'It was when the streets were full of people,' says *Le Commerciel*, 'that she went out.' But not so. It was at nine o'clock in the morning. Now at nine o'clock of every morning **56** in the week, *with the exception of Sunday*, the streets of the city are, it is true, thronged with people. At nine on Sunday, the populace are chiefly within doors *preparing for church*. No observing person can have failed to notice the peculiarly deserted air of the town, from about eight until ten on the morning of every Sabbath. Between ten and eleven the streets **57** are thronged, but not at so early a period as that designated.

"There is another point at which there seems a deficiency of *observation* on the part of *Le Commerciel*. 'A piece,' it says, 'of one of the unfortunate girl's petticoats, two feet long, and one foot wide, was torn out and tied under her chin, and around the back of her head, probably to prevent screams. This was done by fellows who had no pocket-handkerchiefs.' Whether this idea is or is not well founded, we will endeavor to see hereafter; but by 'fellows who have no pocket-hand-kerchiefs,' the editor intends the lowest class of ruffians. These, however, are the very description of people who will

54 Office

55 Running here and there, from one locality to another. The O.E.D. gives this meaning as "rare."

56 As before, Poe alters the time to 9 A.M. instead of 10 A.M.

57 In New York, perhaps, but in France, where anti-clericalism is, and has been, common for centuries, women and children make up the bulk of the churchgoing public. Of course, anyone not in church might still be in bed.

always be found to have handkerchiefs even when destitute of shirts. You must have had occasion to observe how absolutely indispensable, of late years, to the thorough blackguard, has become the pocket-handkerchief."

"And what are we to think," I asked, "of the article in *Le Soleil?*"

"That it is a pity its inditer was not born a parrot—in which case he would have been the most illustrious parrot of his race. He has merely repeated the individual items of the already published opinion; collecting them, with a laudable industry, from this paper and from that. 'The things had all *evidently* been there,' he says, 'at least three or four weeks, and there can be *no doubt* that the spot of this appalling outrage has been discovered.' The facts here re-stated by *Le Soleil*, are very far indeed from removing my own doubts upon this subject, and we will examine them more particularly hereafter in connection with another division of the theme.

"At present we must occupy ourselves with other investigations. You cannot fail to have remarked the extreme laxity of the examination of the corpse. To be sure, the question of identity was readily determined, or should have been; but there were other points to be ascertained. Had the body been in any respect *despoiled?* Had the deceased any articles of jewelry about her person upon leaving home? If so, had she any when found? These are important questions utterly untouched by the evidence; and there are others of equal moment, which have met with no attention. We must endeavor to satisfy ourselves by personal inquiry. The case of St. Eustache must be re-examined. I have no suspicion of this person; but let us proceed methodically. We will ascertain beyond a doubt the validity of the *affidavits* in regard to his whereabouts on the Sunday. Affidavits of this character are readily made matter of mystification. Should there be nothing wrong here, however, we will dismiss St. Eustache from our investigations. His suicide, however, coroborative of suspicion, were there found to be deceit in the affidavits, is, without such deceit, in no respect an unaccountable circumstance, or one which need cause us to deflect from the line of ordinary analysis.

"In that which I now propose, we will discard the interior points of this tragedy, and concentrate our attention upon its outskirts. Not the least usual error in investigations such as this is the limiting of inquiry to the immediate, with total disregard of the collateral or circumstantial events. It is the malpractice of the courts to confine evidence and discussion to the bounds of apparent relevancy. Yet experience has shown, and a true philosophy will always show, that a vast, perhaps the larger, portion of truth arises from the seemingly irrelevant. It is through the spirit of this principle, if not precisely through its letter, that modern science has resolved to *calculate upon the unforeseen*. But perhaps you do not comprehend me. The history of human knowledge has so uninterruptedly shown that to collateral, or incidental, or accidental events we are indebted for the most numerous and

58 Actually, it comes entirely from the New York *Herald* of September 17.

59 Robbed. Poe was apparently unaware of testimony that stated that the body was found without "rings, breastpin or any other jewelry on her person" (*Evening Post,* August 13).

60 Dupin touches upon this somewhat in "Murders," and it forms the basis for much of the rationale of detective fiction that followed Poe. It is the nature of Dupin, Holmes, Miss Marple, Poirot, Father Brown, and the rest to be able to withdraw slightly from the confusion around them in order to put the clues together.

most valuable discoveries, that it has at length become necessary, in prospective view of improvement, to make not only large, but the largest, allowances for inventions that shall arise by chance, and quite out of the range of ordinary expectation. It is no longer philosophical to base upon what has been a vision of what is to be. *Accident* is admitted as a portion of the substructure. We make chance a matter of absolute calculation. We subject the unlooked for and unimagined to the mathematical *formulæ* of the schools.

"I repeat that it is no more than fact that the *larger* portion of all truth has sprung from the collateral; and it is but in accordance with the spirit of the principle involved in this fact that I would divert inquiry, in the present case, from the trodden and hitherto unfruitful ground of the event itself to the contemporary circumstances which surround it. While you ascertain the validity of the affidavits, I will examine the newspapers more generally than you have as yet done. So far, we have only reconnoitred the field of investigation; but it will be strange, indeed, if a comprehensive survey, such as I propose, of the public prints will not afford us some minute points which shall establish a *direction* for inquiry."

In pursuance of Dupin's suggestion, I made scrupulous examination of the affair of the affidavits. The result was a firm conviction of their validity, and of the consequent innocence of St. Eustache. In the meantime my friend occupied himself, with what seemed to me a minuteness altogether objectless, in a scrutiny of the various newspaper files. At the end of a week he placed before me the following extracts: [61]

"About three years and a half ago, a disturbance very [62] similar to the present was caused by the disappearance of this same Marie Rogêt from the *parfumerie* of Monsieur Le Blanc, in the Palais Royal. At the end of a week, however, she re-appeared at her customary *comptoir*, as well as ever, [63] with the exception of a slight paleness not altogether usual. It was given out by Monsieur Le Blanc and her mother that she had merely been on a visit to some friend in the country; and the affair was speedily hushed up. We presume that the present absence is a freak of the same nature, and that, at the expiration of a week or, perhaps, of a month, we shall have her among us again."—*Evening Paper*, Monday, June 23. [64]

"An evening journal of yesterday refers to a former mysterious disappearance of Mademoiselle Rogêt. It is well known that, during the week of her absence from Le Blanc's *parfumerie*, she was in the company of a young naval officer much noted for his debaucheries. A quarrel, it is supposed, providentially led to her return home. We have the name of the Lothario in question, who is at present stationed in [65] Paris, but for obvious reasons forbear to make it public."— *Le Mercurie*, Tuesday Morning, June 24. [66]

"An outrage of the most atrocious character was perpetrated near this city the day before yesterday. A gentleman, with his wife and daughter, engaged, about dusk, the services of six young men, who were idly rowing a boat to and fro near the banks of the Seine, to convey him across the river. Upon reaching the opposite shore the three

[61] The six quotations here cannot be traced to their origins. Wimsatt points out that since the footnotes that Poe does give very likely came from memory, "the remarkable thing is not that some of the references cannot be found but that so many can be" (*PMLA*, March 1941).

[62] In the first version, "Two or three years since . . ."

[63] Counter

[64] "N.Y. *Express*" (Poe's note).

[65] A "Lothario" is mentioned in the *Times and Commercial Intelligencer*, October 5: "A gallant gay Lothario whose name did not transpire." The word means a libertine or rake, and comes from the name of one of the characters in Nicholas Rowe's *Fair Penitent* (1703).

[66] "N.Y. *Herald*" (Poe's note). *Le Mercure de France* was founded in 1672 and folded in 1825. *Le Mercure Français* appeared in 1837 only.

67 "N.Y. *Courier and Inquirer*" (Poe's note). This may have come from an article in that paper published August 16, two weeks after Mary Rogers disappeared, not on the day Poe cites here.

68 "Mennais was one of the parties originally suspected and arrested, but discharged through total lack of evidence" (Poe's note). The fictional name may derive from that of French philosopher Père Félicité Robert de Lamennais (1782–1854), but it stands for Joseph W. Morse, who had gone with a woman to Staten Island, quarreled with her, and fearing the wrath of his wife, fled to Worcester, Massachusetts. He was suspected, but the woman with whom he had fought spoke up and cleared his name. The *Courier and Inquirer* details all this in its issues of August 16–23, 1841, but Poe probably wrote what is printed here himself.

69 "N.Y. *Courier and Inquirer*" (Poe's note).

70 "N.Y. *Evening Post*" (Poe's note). The date is impossible.

71 "N.Y. *Standard*" (Poe's note). There is no record of any such story, and so it may be Poe's invention—as is the name of the French paper.

passengers stepped out, and had proceeded so far as to be beyond the view of the boat, when the daughter discovered that she had left in it her parasol. She returned for it, was seized by the gang, carried out into the stream, gagged, brutally treated, and finally taken to the shore at a point not far from that at which she had originally entered the boat with her parents. The villains have escaped for the time, but the police are upon their trail, and some of them will soon be taken."—*Morning Paper*, June 25. **67**

"We have received one or two communications, the object of which is to fasten the crime of the late atrocity upon Mennais: but as this gentleman has been fully exonerated by a legal inquiry, and as the arguments of our several correspondents appear to be more zealous than profound, we do not think it advisable to make them public."—*Morning Paper*, June 28. **68** **69**

"We have received several forcibly written communications, apparently from various sources, and which go far to render it a matter of certainty that the unfortunate Marie Rogêt has become a victim of one of the numerous bands of blackguards which infest the vicinity of the city upon Sunday. Our own opinion is decidedly in favor of this supposition. We shall endeavor to make room for some of these arguments hereafter."—*Evening Paper*, June 30. **70**

"On Monday, one of the bargemen connected with the revenue service saw an empty boat floating down the Seine. Sails were lying in the bottom of the boat. The bargeman towed it under the barge office. The next morning it was taken from thence without the knowledge of any of the officers. The rudder is now at the barge office."—*Le Diligence*, Thursday, June 26. **71**

Upon reading these various extracts, they not only seemed to me irrelevant, but I could perceive no mode in which any one of them could be brought to bear upon the matter in hand. I waited for some explanation from Dupin.

"It is not my present design," he said, "to *dwell* upon the first and second of these extracts. I have copied them chiefly to show you the extreme remissness of the police, who, as far as I can understand from the Prefect, have not troubled themselves, in any respect, with an examination of the naval officer alluded to. Yet it is mere folly to say that between the first and second disappearance of Marie there is no *supposable* connection. Let us admit the first elopement to have resulted in a quarrel between the lovers, and the return home of the betrayed. We are now prepared to view a second *elopement* (if we *know* that an elopement has again taken place) as indicating a renewal of the betrayer's advances, rather than as the result of new proposals by a second individual—we are prepared to regard it as a 'making up' of the old *amour*, rather than as the commencement of a new one. The chances are ten to one, that he who had once eloped with Marie would again propose an elopement, rather than that she to whom proposals of elopement had been made by one individual, should have them made to her by another. And here let me call your attention to the fact, that the time elapsing between the first ascertained and the second supposed elopement is a few months more than the general period of the cruises of our men-of-war. Had the lover been interrupted in his first villainy by the necessity of departure to sea, and had he seized the first moment of his return to renew the base designs not yet altogether accomplished—or not yet altogether accomplished *by him*? Of all these things we know nothing.

"You will say, however, that, in the second instance, there was *no* elopement as imagined. Certainly not—but are we prepared to say that there was not the frustrated design? Beyond St. Eustache, and perhaps Beauvais, we find no recognized, no open, no honorable suitors of Marie. Of none other is there any thing said. Who, then, is the secret lover, of whom the relatives (*at least most of them*) know nothing, but whom Marie meets upon the morning of Sunday, and who is so deeply in her confidence, that she hesitates not to remain with him until the shades of the evening descend, amid the solitary groves of the Barrière du Roule? Who is that secret lover, I ask, of whom, at least, *most* of the relatives know nothing? And what means the singular prophecy of Madame Rogêt on the morning of Marie's departure?—'I fear **72** that I shall never see Marie again.'

"But if we cannot imagine Madame Rogêt privy to the design of elopement, may we not at least suppose this design entertained by the girl? Upon quitting home, she gave it to be understood that she was about to visit her aunt in the Rue des Drômes, and St. Eustache was requested to call for her at dark. Now, at first glance, this fact strongly militates against my suggestion;—but let us reflect. That she *did* meet some companion, and proceed with him across the river, reaching the Barrière du Roule at so late an hour as three o'clock in the afternoon, is known. But in consenting so to accompany this individual (*for whatever purpose—to her mother known or unknown*), she must have thought of her expressed intention **73** when leaving home, and of the surprise and suspicion aroused in the bosom of her affianced suitor, St. Eustache, when, calling for her, at the hour appointed, in the Rue des Drômes, he should find that she had not been there, and when, moreover, upon returning to the *pension* with this alarming intelligence, he should become aware of her continued absence from home. She must have thought of these things, I say. She must have foreseen the chagrin of St. Eustache, the suspicion of all. She could not have thought of returning to brave this suspicion; but the suspicion becomes a point of trivial importance to her, if we suppose her *not* intending to return.

"We may imagine her thinking thus—'I am to meet a certain person for the purpose of elopement, or for certain other purposes known only to myself. It is necessary that there be no chance of interruption—there must be sufficient time given us to elude pursuit—I will give it to be understood that I shall visit and spend the day with my aunt at the Rue des Drômes— I will tell St. Eustache not to call for me until dark—in this way, my absence from home for the longest possible period, without causing suspicion or anxiety, will be accounted for, and I shall gain more time than in any other manner. If I bid

72 Earlier, the narrator says this comment by the mother came in the evening after the daughter left the house.

73 Poe added this rather important passage for the later, printed edition.

St. Eustache call for me at dark, he will be sure not to call before; but if I wholly neglect to bid him call, my time for escape will be diminished, since it will be expected that I return the earlier, and my absence will the sooner excite anxiety. Now, if it were my design to return *at all*—if I had in contemplation merely a stroll with the individual in question—it would not be my policy to bid St. Eustache call; for calling, he will be *sure* to ascertain that I have played him false—a fact of which I might keep him forever in ignorance, by leaving home without notifying him of my intention, by returning before dark, and by then stating that I had been to visit my aunt in the Rue des Drômes. But, as it is my design *never* to return—or not for some weeks—or not until certain concealments are effected—the gaining of time is the only

74 point about which I need give myself any concern.'

"You have observed, in your notes, that the most general opinion in relation to this sad affair is, and was from the first, that the girl had been the victim of *a gang* of blackguards. Now, the popular opinion, under certain conditions, is not to be disregarded. When arising of itself—when manifesting itself in a strictly spontaneous manner—we should look upon it as analogous with that *intuition* which is the idiosyncrasy of the individual man of genius. In ninety-nine cases from the hundred I would abide by its decision. But it is important that we find no palpable traces of *suggestion*. The opinion must be rigorously *the public's own;* and the distinction is often exceedingly difficult to perceive and to maintain. In the present instance, it appears to me that this 'public opinion,' in respect to *a gang,* has been superinduced by the collateral event which is detailed in the third of my extracts. All Paris is excited by the discovered corpse of Marie, a girl young, beautiful, and notorious. This corpse is found, bearing marks of violence, and floating in the river. But it is now made known that, at the very period, or about the very period, in which it is supposed that the girl was assassinated, an outrage similar in nature to that endured by the deceased, although less in extent, was perpetrated, by a gang of young ruffians, upon the person of a second young female. Is it wonderful that the one known atrocity should influence the popular judgment in regard to the other unknown? This judgment awaited direction, and the known outrage seemed so opportunely to afford it! Marie, too, was found in the river; and upon this very river was this known outrage committed. The connection of the two events had about it so much of the

75 palpable, that the true wonder would have been a *failure* of the populace to appreciate and to seize it. But, in fact, the one atrocity, known to be so committed, is, if any thing, evidence that the other, committed at a time nearly coincident, was *not* so committed. It would have been a miracle indeed, if, while a gang of ruffians were perpetrating, at a given locality, a most unheard-of wrong, there should have been another similar gang, in a similar locality, in the same city, under the same circumstances, with the same means and appliances, engaged in a wrong of precisely the same aspect,

74 In the original version, another paragraph followed: "Such thoughts as these we may imagine to have passed through the mind of Marie, but the point is one upon which I consider it necessary now to insist. I have reasoned thus, merely to call attention, as I said a minute ago, to the culpable remissness of the police."

Poe also added "or for certain other purposes known only to myself" in the first sentence and "—or not for some weeks—or not until certain concealments are effected—the . . ." in the last. Both alter the shape of the original tale, as he gathered more facts about the case from his reading.

75 Obvious

at precisely the same period of time! Yet in what, if not in this marvellous train of coincidence, does the accidentally *suggested* opinion of the populace call upon us to believe?　**76**

"Before proceeding further, let us consider the supposed scene of the assassination, in the thicket at the Barrière du Roule. This thicket, although dense, was in the close vicinity of a public road. Within were three or four large stones, forming a kind of seat with a back and a footstool. On the upper stone was discovered a white petticoat; on the second, a silk scarf. A parasol, gloves, and a pocket-handkerchief were also here found. The handkerchief bore the name 'Marie Rogêt.' Fragments of dress were seen on the branches around. The earth was trampled, the bushes were broken, and there was every evidence of a violent struggle.

"Notwithstanding the acclamation with which the discovery of this thicket was received by the press, and the unanimity with which it was supposed to indicate the precise scene of the outrage, it must be admitted that there was some very good reason for doubt. That it *was* the scene, I may or I may not believe—but there was excellent reason for doubt. Had **77** the *true* scene been, as *Le Commerciel* suggested, in the neighborhood of the Rue Pavée St. Andrée, the perpetrators of the crime, supposing them still resident in Paris, would naturally have been stricken with terror at the public attention thus acutely directed into the proper channel; and, in certain classes of minds, there would have arisen, at once, a sense of the necessity of some exertion to redivert this attention. And thus, the thicket of the Barriére du Roule having been already suspected, the idea of placing the articles where they were found, might have been naturally entertained. There is no real evidence, although *Le Soleil* so supposes, that the articles discovered had been more than a very few days in the thicket; while there is much circumstantial proof that they could not have remained there, without attracting attention, during the twenty days elapsing between the fatal Sunday and the afternoon upon which they were found by the boys. 'They **78** were all *mildewed* down hard,' says *Le Soleil*, adopting the opinions of its predecessors, 'with the action of the rain and stuck together from *mildew*. The grass had grown around and over some of them. The silk of the parasol was strong, but the threads of it were run together within. The upper part, where it had been doubled and folded, was all *mildewed* and rotten, and tore on being opened.' In respect to the grass having 'grown around and over some of them,' it is obvious that the fact could only have been ascertained from the words, and thus from the recollections, of two small boys; for these boys removed the articles and took them home before they had been seen by a third party. But the grass will grow, especially in warm and damp weather (such as was that of the period of the murder), as much as two or three inches in a single day. A parasol lying upon a newly turfed ground, might, in a week, be entirely concealed from sight by the upspringing grass. And touching that *mildew* upon which the editor of *Le Soleil* so pertinaciously insists, that he employs the word no less

76 Dupin goes out on a limb here. Says Wimsatt, "Here as again, flagrantly, at the end of his story, Poe has asserted the contrary of one of the principles of *a priori* probability" (*PMLA*, March 1941, p. 236). In other words, while the probability is low that two similar incidents would occur at the same time, the very fact that *one* has occurred does not rule out conclusively that the other also took place. Dupin later asserts that *many* gangs were in the vicinity.

77 Poe added the "may or I may not" to the later edition.

78 Actually, according to the testimony of Mrs. Loss, the boys found Mary Rogers' clothing a full month after her disappearance (New York *Herald*, September 17).

79 The powdery mildews individually have a short life-span, but they reproduce and spread quickly, so that mildew would not disappear from an object within twenty-four hours unless dried out by the sun's heat.

The Paris of Dupin

than three times in the brief paragraph just quoted, is he really unaware of the nature of this *mildew*? Is he to be told that it is one of the many classes of *fungus*, of which the most ordinary feature is its upspringing and decadence within **79** twenty-four hours?

"Thus we see, at a glance, that what has been most triumphantly adduced in support of the idea that the articles had been 'for at least three or four weeks' in the thicket, is most absurdly null as regards any evidence of that fact. On the other hand, it is exceedingly difficult to believe that these articles could have remained in the thicket specified for a longer period than a single week—for a longer period than from one Sunday to the next. Those who know any thing of the vicinity of Paris, know the extreme difficulty of finding *seclusion*, unless at a great distance from its suburbs. Such a thing as an unexplored or even an unfrequently visited recess, amid its woods or groves, is not for a moment to be imagined. Let any one who, being at heart a lover of nature, is yet chained by duty to the dust and heat of this great metropolis— let any such one attempt, even during the week-days, to slake his thirst for solitude amid the scenes of natural loveliness which immediately surround us. At every second step, he will find the growing charm dispelled by the voice and personal intrusion of some ruffian or party of carousing blackguards. He will seek privacy amid the densest foliage, all in vain. Here are the very nooks where the unwashed most abound— here are the temples most desecrate. With sickness of the heart the wanderer will flee back to the polluted Paris as to a less odious because less incongruous sink of pollution. But if the vicinity of the city is so beset during the working days of the week, how much more so on the Sabbath! It is now especially that, released from the claims of labor, or deprived of the customary opportunities of crime, the town blackguard seeks the precincts of the town, not through love of the rural, which in his heart he despises, but by way of escape from the restraints and conventionalities of society. He desires less the fresh air and the green trees, than the utter *license* of the country. Here, at the roadside inn, or beneath the foliage of the woods, he indulges unchecked by any eye except those of his boon companions, in all the mad excess of a counterfeit hilarity—the joint offspring of liberty and of rum. I say nothing more than what must be obvious to every dispassionate observer, when I repeat that the circumstance of the articles in question having remained undiscovered, for a longer period than from one Sunday to another, in *any* thicket in the immediate neighborhood of Paris, is to be looked upon as little less than miraculous.

"But there are not wanting other grounds for the suspicion that the articles were placed in the thicket with the view of diverting attention from the real scene of the outrage. And, first, let me direct your notice to the *date* of the discovery of the articles. Collate this with the date of the fifth extract made by myself from the newspapers. You will find that the discovery followed, almost immediately, the urgent communications sent to the evening paper. These communications, although various, and apparently from various sources, tended all to the same point—viz., the directing of attention to *a gang* as the perpetrators of the outrage, and to the neighborhood of the Barrière du Roule as its scene. Now, here, of course, the situation is not that, in consequence of these communications, or of the public attention by them directed, the articles were found by the boys; but the suspicion might and may well have been, that the articles were not *before* found by the boys, for the reason that the articles had not before been in the thicket; having been deposited there only at so late a period as at the date, or shortly prior to the date of the communications, by the guilty authors of these communications themselves.

"This thicket was a singular—an exceedingly singular one. It was unusually dense. Within its naturally walled enclosure were three extraordinary stones, *forming a seat with a back and a footstool*. And this thicket, so full of art, was in the immediate vicinity, *within a few rods*, of the dwelling of Madame Deluc, whose boys were in the habit of closely examining the shrubberies about them in search of the bark of the sassafras. Would it be a rash wager—a wager of one **80** thousand to one—that *a day* never passed over the heads of these boys without finding at least one of them ensconced in the umbrageous hall, and enthroned upon its natural throne? Those who would hesitate at such a wager, have either never been boys themselves, or have forgotten the boyish nature. **81** I repeat—it is exceedingly hard to comprehend how the articles could have remained in this thicket undiscovered, for a longer period than one or two days; and that thus there is good ground for suspicion, in spite of the dogmatic ignorance of *Le Soleil*, that they were, at a comparatively late date, deposited where found.

"But there are still other and stronger reasons for believing them so deposited, than any which I have as yet urged. And, now, let me beg your notice to the highly artificial arrangement of the articles. On the *upper* stone lay a white petticoat; on the *second*, a silk scarf; scattered around, were a parasol, gloves, and a pocket-handkerchief bearing the name 'Marie Rogêt.' Here is just such an arrangement as would *naturally* be made by a not-over-acute person wishing to dispose the articles *naturally*. But it is by no means a *really* natural arrangement. I should rather have looked to see the things *all* lying on the ground and trampled under foot. In the narrow limits of that bower, it would have been scarcely possible that the petticoat and scarf should have retained a position upon the stones, when subjected to the brushing to and fro of many struggling persons. 'There was evidence,' it is said, 'of a **82** struggle; and the earth was trampled, the bushes were broken,'—but the petticoat and the scarf are found deposited as if upon shelves. 'The pieces of the frock torn out by the bushes were about three inches wide and six inches long. One part was the hem of the frock and it had been mended. They *looked like strips torn off*.' Here, inadvertently, *Le Soleil* has employed an exceedingly suspicious phrase. The pieces, as

80 Sassafras is a tall eastern tree (*Sassafras albidum*) whose dried root bark is used in tea to reduce sweating in fever. This typically American tree would hardly be found in Paris, outside of a botanical garden.

81 In other words, some young, possibly unreliable witnesses are the only people to have seen the clothes arrayed on the rocks as Dupin describes them, making this a shaky piece of evidence at best.

82 Poe/Dupin at first says the disposition of Marie's garments is suspicious—they are arrayed too neatly upon the rocks, suggesting someone had doctored the scene of the crime. But he then drops this line of reasoning without further explanation and postulates that an individual did the work and then left the scene too terrified to return. His sudden departure, Dupin says, means that the arrangement of the clothes was natural! This is either sleight of hand on Poe's part or he has failed to notice the lack of logic in these comments.

described, do indeed 'look like strips torn off'; but purposely and by hand. It is one of the rarest of accidents that a piece is 'torn off,' from any garment such as is now in question, by the agency *of a thorn*. From the very nature of such fabrics, a thorn or nail becoming tangled in them, tears them rectangularly—divides them into two longitudinal rents, at right angles with each other, and meeting at an apex where the thorn enters—but it is scarcely possible to conceive the piece 'torn off.' I never so knew it, nor did you. To tear a piece *off* from such fabric, two distinct forces, in different directions, will be, in almost every case, required. If there be two edges to the fabric—if, for example, it be a pocket-handkerchief, and it is desired to tear from it a slip, then, and then only, will the one force serve the purpose. But in the present case the question is of a dress, presenting but one edge. To tear a piece from the interior, where no edge is presented, could only be effected by a miracle through the agency of thorns, and no *one* thorn could accomplish it. But, even where an edge is presented, two thorns will be necessary, operating, the one in two distinct directions, and the other in one. And this in the supposition that the edge is unhemmed. If hemmed, the matter is nearly out of the question. We thus see the numerous and great obstacles in the way of pieces being 'torn off' through the simple agency of 'thorns'; yet we are required to believe not only that one piece but that many have been so torn. 'And one part,' too, '*was the hem of the frock*'! Another piece was '*part of the skirt, not the hem,*'—that is to say, was torn completely out, through the agency of thorns, from the unedged interior of the dress! These, I say, are things which one may well be pardoned for disbelieving; yet, taken collectively, they form, perhaps, less of reasonable ground for suspicion, than the one startling circumstance of the articles having been left in this thicket at all, by any *murderers* who had enough precaution to think of removing the corpse. You will not have apprehended me rightly, however, if you suppose it my design to *deny* this thicket as the scene of the outrage. There might have been a wrong *here*, or, more possibly, an accident at Madame Deluc's. But, in fact, this is a point of minor importance. We are not engaged in an attempt to discover the scene, but to produce the perpetrators of the murder. What I have adduced, notwithstanding the minuteness with which I have adduced it, has been with the view, first, to show the folly of the positive and headlong assertions of *Le Soleil*, but secondly and chiefly, to bring you, by the most natural route, to a further contemplation of the doubt whether this assassination has, or has not, been the work of

83 a gang.

"We will resume this question by mere allusion to the
84 revolting details of the surgeon examined at the inquest. It is only necessary to say that his published *inferences*, in regard to the number of the ruffians, have been properly ridiculed as unjust and totally baseless, by all the reputable anatomists of Paris. Not that the matter *might not* have been as inferred, but that there was no ground for the inference:—was there not much for another?

83 This entire paragraph is more than a little confusing, with Dupin backtracking and sidestepping until one has difficulty following his logic. Just what *is* he trying to prove? Perhaps Poe, not wanting to commit himself to a solution until the actual murderer was caught, is treading carefully.

"Accident" here refers to the abortion (see introductory note).

84 According to *Brother Jonathan* (August 21), the medical testimony of Dr. Cook "enabled [him] to state positively that the poor girl had been brutally violated. The following, however, is the substance of what he did say on this subject. He said that previous to the shocking outrage, she had evidently been a person of chastity and correct habits; that her person was horribly violated *by more than two or three persons;* he gave sufficient reasons for coming to this conclusion. He also stated distinctly, that he examined fully on that point, and found that there was not the slightest trace of pregnancy."

Then, on September 4, the paper changed its viewpoint, calling the doctor's comments "disgustingly ridiculous" but giving no reason for the accustation and not being specific about what part of the doctor's opinion was unacceptable: the proof of Mary's virginity, the absence of pregnancy, or her gang rape.

"Let us reflect now upon 'the traces of a struggle'; and let me ask what these traces have been supposed to demonstrate. A gang. But do they not rather demonstrate the absence of a gang? What *struggle* could have taken place—what struggle so violent and so enduring as to have left its 'traces' in all directions—between a weak and defenceless girl and the *gang* of ruffians imagined? The silent grasp of a few rough arms and all would have been over. The victim must have been absolutely passive at their will. You will here bear in mind **85** that the arguments urged against the thicket as the scene, are applicable, in chief part, only against it as the scene of an outrage committed by *more than a single individual*. If we imagine but *one* violator, we can conceive, and thus only conceive, the struggle of so violent and so obstinate a nature as to have left the 'traces' apparent.

"And again. I have already mentioned the suspicion to be excited by the fact that the articles in question were suffered to remain *at all* in the thicket where discovered. It seems almost impossible that these evidences of guilt should have been accidentally left where found. There was sufficient presence of mind (it is supposed) to remove the corpse; and yet a more positive evidence than the corpse itself (whose features might have been quickly obliterated by decay), is allowed to lie conspicuously in the scene of the outrage—I allude to the handkerchief with the *name* of the deceased. If this was accident, it was not the accident *of a gang*. We can imagine it only the accident of an individual. Let us see. An individual has committed the murder. He is alone with the ghost of the departed. He is appalled by what lies motionless before him. The fury of his passion is over, and there is abundant room in his heart for the natural awe of the deed. His is none of that confidence which the presence of numbers inevitably inspires. He is *alone* with the dead. He trembles and is bewildered. Yet there is a necessity for disposing of the corpse. He bears it to the river, and leaves behind him the other evidences of his guilt; for it is difficult, if not impossible to carry all the burthen at once, and it will be easy to return for what is left. But in his toilsome journey to the water his fears redouble within him. The sounds of life encompass his path. A dozen times he hears or fancies he hears the step of an observer. Even the very lights from the city bewilder him. Yet, in time, and by long and frequent pauses of deep agony, he reaches the river's brink, and disposes of his ghastly charge—perhaps through the medium of a boat. But *now* what treasure does the world hold—what threat of vengeance could it hold out—which would have power to urge the return of that lonely murderer over that toilsome and perilous path, to the thicket and its blood-chilling recollections? He returns *not*, let the consequences be what they may. He *could* not return if he would. His sole thought is immediate escape. He turns his back *forever* upon those dreadful shrubberies, and flees as from the wrath to come.

"But how with a gang? Their number would have inspired them with confidence; if, indeed, confidence is ever wanting in the breast of the arrant blackguard; and of arrant blackguards

85 The first version begins, "You will bear in mind that I *admit* the thicket as the scene of the outrage; and you will immediately perceive that the arguments. . . ."

alone are the supposed *gangs* ever constituted. Their number, I say, would have prevented the bewildering and unreasoning terror which I have imagined to paralyze the single man. Could we suppose an oversight in one, or two, or three, this oversight would have been remedied by a fourth. They would have left nothing behind them; for their number would have enabled them to carry *all* at once. There would have been no need of *return*.

"Consider now the circumstance that, in the outer garment •of the corpse when found, 'a slip, about a foot wide, had been torn upward from the bottom hem to the waist, wound three times round the waist, and secured by a sort of hitch in the back.' This was done with the obvious design of affording *a handle* by which to carry the body. But would any *number* of men have dreamed of resorting to such an expedient? To three or four, the limbs of the corpse would have afforded not only a sufficient, but the best possible, hold. The device is that of a single individual; and this brings us to the fact that 'between the thicket and the river the rails of the fences were found taken down, and the ground bore evident traces of some heavy burden having been dragged along it!' But would a *number* of men have put themselves to the superfluous trouble of taking down a fence, for the purpose of dragging through it a corpse which they might have *lifted over* any fence in an instant? Would a *number* of men have so *dragged* a corpse at all as to have left evident *traces* of the dragging?

"And here we must refer to an observation of *Le Commerciel;* an observation upon which I have already, in some measure, commented. 'A piece,' says this journal, 'of one of the unfortunate girl's petticoats was torn out and tied under her chin, and around the back of her head, probably to prevent screams. This was done by fellows who had no pocket-handkerchiefs.'

"I have before suggested that a genuine blackguard is never *without* a pocket-handkerchief. But it is not to this fact that I now especially advert. That it was not through want of a handkerchief for the purpose imagined by *Le Commerciel,* that this bandage was employed, is rendered apparent by the handkerchief left in the thicket; and that the object was not 'to prevent screams' appears, also, from the bandage having been employed in preference to what would so much better have answered the purpose. But the language of the evidence speaks of the strip in question as 'found around the neck, fitting loosely, and secured with a hard knot.' These words are sufficiently vague, but differ materially from those of *Le Commerciel.* The slip was eighteen inches wide, and therefore, although of muslin, would form a strong band when folded or rumpled longitudinally. And thus rumpled it was discovered. My inference is this. The solitary murderer, having borne the corpse for some distance (whether from the thicket or else-where) by means of the bandage *hitched* around its middle, found the weight, in this mode of procedure, too much for his strength. He resolved to drag the burthen—the evidence goes to show that it *was* dragged. With this object in view, it

86 From the August 21 testimony of Dr. Cook

87 To use as a mask, one supposes

88 From Dr. Cook's account: "The dress immediately beneath the frock, and between the frock and the upper petticoat, was made of fine muslin; a piece was torn clean out of this garment, about a foot or eighteen inches in width; this piece was torn very evenly, and with great care, commencing at the bottom of the garment. This same piece was afterwards tied round her mouth, with a hard knot at the back part of the neck; I think this was done to smother her cries, and that it was probably held tight round her mouth by one of her ravishers: This same piece of muslin was found by me around her neck, fitting loosely to the neck with the knot remaining.—Over these were tied the hat and hat strings."

became necessary to attach something like a rope to one of the extremities. It could be best attached about the neck, where the head would prevent its slipping off. And now the murderer bethought him, unquestionably, of the bandage about the loins. He would have used this, but for its volution about the corpse, the *hitch* which embarrassed it, and the reflection that it had not been 'torn off' from the garment. It was easier to tear a new slip from the petticoat. He tore it, made it fast about the neck, and so *dragged* his victim to the brink of the river. That this 'bandage,' only attainable with trouble and delay, and but imperfectly answering its purpose— that this bandage was employed *at all*, demonstrates that the necessity for its employment sprang from circumstances arising at a period when the handkerchief was no longer attainable— that it to say, arising, as we have imagined, after quitting the thicket (if the thicket it was), and on the road between the thicket and the river.

"But the evidence, you will say, of Madame Deluc (!) points especially to the presence of *a gang* in the vicinity of the thicket, at or about the epoch of the murder. This I grant. I doubt if there were not a *dozen* gangs, such as described by Madame Deluc, in and about the vicinity of the Barrière du Roule at *or about* the period of this tragedy. But the gang which has drawn upon itself the pointed animadversion,[89] although the somewhat tardy and very suspicious evidence, of Madame Deluc, is the *only* gang which is represented by that honest and scrupulous old lady as having eaten her cakes and swallowed her brandy, without putting themselves to the trouble of making her payment. *Et hinc illae irae?*[90]

"But what *is* the precise evidence of Madame Deluc? 'A gang of miscreants made their appearance, behaved boisterously, ate and drank without making payment, followed in the route of the young man and the girl, returned to the inn *about dusk*, and re-crossed the river as if in great haste.'

"Now this 'great haste' very possibly seemed *greater* haste in the eyes of Madame Deluc, since she dwelt lingeringly and lamentingly upon her violated cakes and ale,—cakes and ale[91] for which she might still have entertained a faint hope of compensation. Why, otherwise, since it was *about dusk*, should she make a point of the *haste?* It is no cause for wonder, surely, that even a gang of blackguards should make *haste* to get home when a wide river is to be crossed in small boats, when storm impends, and when night *approaches*.

"I say *approaches;* for the night had *not yet arrived*. It was only *about dusk* that the indecent haste of these 'miscreants' offended the sober eyes of Madame Deluc. But we are told that it was upon this very evening that Madame Deluc, as well as her eldest son, 'heard the screams of a female in the vicinity of the inn.' And in what words does Madame Deluc designate the period of the evening at which these screams were heard? 'It was *soon after dark*,' she says. But 'soon *after* dark' is, at least, *dark;* and 'about dusk' is as certainly daylight. Thus it is abundantly clear that the gang quitted the Barrière du Roule *prior* to the screams overheard (?) by Madame

---

89 Observation or notice

90 "And hence this anger?" Dupin is calling into question Madame Deluc's testimony. The phrase seems to be a blend of *"tantaene animis caelestibus irae"* (Aeneid, I, ii) and *"hinc illae lacrimae"* (Horace, *Epistolae*, I, xix, 41).

91 "Dost thou think, because thou are virtuous, there shall be no more cakes and ale?" (*Twelfth Night*, II, iii, 109)

Deluc. And although, in all the many reports of the evidence, the relative expressions in question are distinctly and invariably employed just as I have employed them in this conversation with yourself, no notice whatever of the gross discrepancy has, as yet, been taken by any of the public journals, or by any of the myrmidons of police.

"I shall add but one to the arguments against *a gang;* but this *one* has, to my own understanding at least, a weight altogether irresistible. Under the circumstances of large reward offered, and full pardon to any king's evidence, it is not to be imagined, for a moment, that some member of *a gang* of low ruffians, or of any body of men, would not long ago have betrayed his accomplices. Each one of a gang, so placed, is not so much greedy of reward, or anxious for escape, as *fearful of betrayal*. He betrays eagerly and early that *he may not himself be betrayed*. That the secret has not been divulged is the very best of proof that it is, in fact, a secret. The horrors of this dark deed are known only to *one,* or two, living human beings, and to God.

"Let us sum up now the meagre yet certain fruits of our long analysis. We have attained the idea either of a fatal **92** accident under the roof of Madame Deluc, or of a murder perpetrated, in the thicket at the Barrière du Roule, by a lover, or at least by an intimate and secret associate of the deceased. This associate is of swarthy complexion. This complexion, the 'hitch' in the bandage, and the 'sailor's knot' with which the bonnet-ribbon is tied, point to a seaman. His companionship with the deceased—a gay but not an abject young girl—designates him as above the grade of the common sailor. Here the well-written and urgent communications to the journals are much in the way of corroboration. The circumstance of the first elopement, as mentioned by *Le Mercurie,* tends to blend the idea of this seaman with that of the 'naval officer' who is first known to have led the unfortunate into crime.

"And here, most fitly, comes the consideration of the continued absence of him of the dark complexion. Let me pause to observe that the complexion of this man is dark and swarthy; it was no common swarthiness which constituted the *sole* point of remembrance, both as regards Valence and Madame Deluc. But why is this man absent? Was he murdered by the gang? If so, why are there only *traces* of the assassinated *girl?* The scene of the two outrages will naturally be supposed identical. And where is his corpse? The assassins would most probably have disposed of both in the same way. But it may be said that this man lives, and is deterred from making himself known, through dread of being charged with the murder. This consideration might be supposed to operate upon him now—at this late period—since it has been given in evidence that he was seen with Marie, but it would have had no force at the period of the deed. The first impulse of an innocent man would have been to announce the outrage, and to aid in identifying the ruffians. This *policy* would have suggested. He had been seen with the girl. He had crossed

92 Poe added "either of a fatal accident under the roof of Madame Deluc, or . . ." to the later edition, acknowledging the possibility of a fatal abortion.

the river with her in an open ferry-boat. The denouncing of the assassins would have appeared, even to an idiot, the surest and sole means of relieving himself from suspicion. We cannot suppose him, on the night of the fatal Sunday, both innocent himself and incognizant of an outrage committed. Yet only under such circumstances is it possible to imagine that he would have failed, if alive, in the denouncement of the assassins.   **93**

"And what means are ours of attaining the truth? We shall find these means multiplying and gathering distinctness as we proceed. Let us sift to the bottom this affair of the first elopement. Let us know the full history of 'the officer,' with his present circumstances, and his whereabouts at the precise period of the murder. Let us carefully compare with each other the various communications sent to the evening paper, in which the object was to inculpate *a gang*. This done, let us compare these communications, both as regards style and MS., with those sent to the morning paper, at a previous period, and insisting so vehemently upon the guilt of Mennais. And, all this done, let us again compare these various communications with the known MSS. of the officer. Let us endeavor to ascertain, by repeated questionings of Madame Deluc and her boys, as well as of the omnibus-driver, Valence, something more of the personal appearance and bearing of the 'man of dark complexion.' Queries, skilfully directed, will not fail to elicit, from some of these parties, information on this particular point (or upon others)—information which the parties themselves may not even be aware of possessing. And let us now trace *the boat* picked up by the bargeman on the morning of Monday the twenty-third of June, and which was removed from the barge-office, without the cognizance of the officer in attendance, and *without the rudder*, at some period prior to the discovery of the corpse. With a proper caution and perseverance we shall infallibly trace this boat; for not only can the bargeman who picked it up identify it, but the *rudder is at hand*. The rudder *of a sail boat* would not have been abandoned, without inquiry, by one altogether at ease in heart. And here let me pause to insinuate a question. There was no *advertisement* of the picking up of this boat. It was silently taken to the barge-office, and as silently removed. But its owner or employer—how *happened* he, at so early a period as Tuesday morning, to be informed, without the agency of advertisement, of the locality of the boat taken up on Monday, unless we imagine some connection with the *navy*—some personal permanent connection leading to cognizance of its minute interests—its petty local news?

"In speaking of the lonely assassin dragging his burden to the shore, I have already suggested the probability of his availing himself *of a boat*. Now we are to understand that Marie Rogêt *was* precipitated from a boat. This would naturally have been the case. The corpse could not have been trusted to the shallow waters of the shore. The peculiar marks on the back and shoulders of the victim tell of the bottom ribs of a boat. That the body was found without weight is also corro-

93 Dupin sums up a number of clues here. The dark complexion comes from Madame Deluc's testimony, as well as that of the omnibus driver, Valence; the hitch in the bandage and the sailor's knot come from the doctor's examination of the body. The girl's beauty and popularity indicate to him that the man in question is probably an officer, since she could have had her pick of any man. The letters to the newspapers show a certain amount of intelligence on the part of the writer, whom Dupin practically identifies with the murderer. The naval officer was mentioned in the extract about the girl's earlier disappearance (see introductory note).

It is Dupin's supposition that Marie had been planning to elope with this officer, and the couple had been caught in the rain at the Barrière du Roule and forced to take shelter in the thicket. There the man had raped Marie in a moment of "passion," and then murdered her through guilt.

Importantly, Poe deletes from the first version: "We are not forced to suppose a premeditated design of murder or of violation. But there was the friendly shelter of the thicket, and the approach of rain—there was opportunity and strong temptation—and then a sudden and violent wrong to be concealed only by one of darker dye."

"There, at some obscure wharf, he would have leaped on land." *Illustration by F. S. Coburn, 1902*

94 I.e., it was not weighed down with a stone.

95 "Of the Magazine in which the article was originally published" (Poe's note). This is actually Poe's composition; he does the same thing in "Von Kempelen."

He later wrote to George Eveleth (January 4, 1848): "The 'naval officer' who committed the murder (or rather the accidental death arising from an attempt at abortion) *confessed* it; and the whole matter is now well understood—but, for the sake of relatives, this is a topic on which I must not speak further." Poe is fibbing again; there is no record of any such confession.

There was from the start an opinion that Mary could have died during an abortion, which prompted Dr. Cook's remark that "there was not the slightest trace of pregnancy."

Also, after the words "brought to pass," Poe deleted "that an individual assassin was convicted, upon his own confession, of the murder of Marie Rogêt," giving the one-man theory less impact—just in case?

96 There is a good possibility that Poe meant the story to end here, since the rest sounds very much like something tacked on to beg off any direct comparison with the actual murder case—especially since he has changed some of the facts to suit his tale. If so, this was done before the story was first published.

94 borative of the idea. If thrown from the shore a weight would have been attached. We can only account for its absence by supposing the murderer to have neglected the precaution of supplying himself with it before pushing off. In the act of consigning the corpse to the water, he would unquestionably have noticed his oversight; but then no remedy would have been at hand. Any risk would have been preferred to a return to that accursed shore. Having rid himself of his ghastly charge, the murderer would have hastened to the city. There, at some obscure wharf, he would have leaped on land. But the boat—would he have secured it? He would have been in too great haste for such things as securing a boat. Moreover, in fastening it to the wharf, he would have felt as if securing evidence against himself. His natural thought would have been to cast from him, as far as possible, all that had held connection with his crime. He would not only have fled from the wharf, but he would not have permitted *the boat* to remain. Assuredly he would have cast it adrift. Let us pursue our fancies.—In the morning, the wretch is stricken with unutterable horror at finding that the boat has been picked up and detained at a locality which he is in the daily habit of frequenting—at a locality, perhaps, which his duty compels him to frequent. The next night, *without daring to ask for the rudder*, he removes it. Now *where* is that rudderless boat? Let it be one of our first purposes to discover. With the first glimpse we obtain of it, the dawn of our success shall begin. This boat shall guide us, with a rapidity which will surprise even ourselves, to him who employed it in the midnight of the fatal Sabbath. Corroboration will rise upon corroboration, and the murderer will be traced."

[For reasons which we shall not specify, but which to many readers will appear obvious, we have taken the liberty of here omitting, from the MSS. placed in our hands, such portion as details the *following up* of the apparently slight clew obtained by Dupin. We feel it advisable only to state, in brief, that the result desired was brought to pass; and that the Prefect fulfilled punctually, although with reluctance, the terms of his compact with the Chevalier. Mr. Poe's article concludes with the

95 following words.—*Eds.*]

It will be understood that I speak of coincidences and *no more*. What I have said above upon this topic must suffice. In my own heart there dwells no faith in præter-nature. That Nature and its God are two, no man who thinks will deny. That the latter, creating the former, can, at will, control of modify it, is also unquestionable. I say "at will"; for the question is of will, and not, as the insanity of logic has assumed, of power. It is not that the Deity *cannot* modify his laws, but that we insult him in imagining a possible necessity for modification. In their origin these laws were fashioned to embrace *all* contingencies which *could* lie in the Future. With

96 God all is *Now*.

I repeat, then, that I speak of these things only as of coincidences. And further: in what I relate it will be seen that between the fate of the unhappy Mary Cecilia Rogers, so far as that fate is known, and the fate of one Marie Rogêt up to a certain epoch in her history, there has existed a parallel in the contemplation of whose wonderful exactitude the reason becomes embarrassed. I say all this will be seen. But let it not for a moment be supposed that, in proceeding with the sad narrative of Marie from the epoch just mentioned, and in tracing to its *dénouement* the mystery which enshrouded her, **97** it is my covert design to hint at an extension of the parallel, or even to suggest that the measures adopted in Paris for the discovery of the assassin of a *grisette*, or measures founded in any similar ratiocination, would produce any similar result.

For, in respect to the latter branch of the supposition, it should be considered that the most trifling variation in the facts of the two cases might give rise to the most important miscalculations, by diverting thoroughly the two courses of events; very much as, in arithmetic, an error which, in its own individuality, may be inappreciable, produces, at length, by dint of multiplication at all points of the process, a result enormously at variance with truth. And, in regard to the former branch, we must not fail to hold in view that the very Calculus of Probabilities to which I have referred, forbids all idea of the extension of the parallel,—forbids it with a positiveness strong and decided just in proportion as this parallel has already been long-drawn and exact. This is one of those anomalous propositions which, seemingly appealing to thought altogether apart from the mathematical, is yet one which only the mathematician can fully entertain. Nothing, for example, is more difficult than to convince the merely general reader that the fact of sixes having been thrown twice in succession by a player at dice, is sufficient cause for betting the largest odds that sixes will not be thrown in the third attempt. A suggestion to this effect is usually rejected by the **98** intellect at once. It does not appear that the two throws which have been completed, and which lie now absolutely in the Past, can have influence upon the throw which exists only in the Future. The chance for throwing sixes seems to be precisely as it was at any ordinary time—that it to say, subject only to the influence of the various other throws which may be made by the dice. And this is a reflection which appears so exceedingly obvious that attempts to controvert it are received more frequently with a derisive smile than with any thing like respectful attention. The error here involved—a gross error redolent of mischief—I cannot pretend to expose within the limits assigned me at present; and with the philosophical it needs no exposure. It may be sufficient here to say that it forms one of an infinite series of mistakes which arise in the path of Reason through her propensity for seeking truth *in detail*.   **99**

97 The final unraveling of the complications

98 Says Wimsatt: "Poe states a principle which he could have read in Laplace's *Probabilities* . . . that equally probable independent events (e.g. throws of a given number with dice) remain equally probable at any point in any series" and "on 'the error here involved,' it is hardly necessary to say that Poe stands almost alone among the 'philosophical.' "

99 Who *really* killed Mary Rogers? Most who have studied the matter say it was definitely not the naval officer. Anderson in later years admitted that Mary had had an abortion, but a year before her death. The murder investigation ended in confusion, and no one has solved it to this day.

Marie Bonaparte's analysis of the tale is not as plausible as some of her other interpretations (if one can accept those), because she does not take into account the fact that the events in the tale are those of an actual murder case and not dredged up from Poe's psyche. Thus her comment that underlying the tale is Poe's desire to rape Virginia, his dying wife, is hard to take seriously.

THE GOLD-BUG

This, Poe's most popular story during his lifetime, was written in 1842 and submitted as an entry in a contest sponsored by a new weekly, the *Dollar Newspaper*. It won first prize (one hundred dollars) and appeared in the June 21 and 28, 1843, issues. Although the *Dollar* copyrighted the story—an unusual practice in those days—publications across the country ignored the fact and reprinted the story without permission anyway.

An English pirated edition appeared in 1846 or 1847, and the story was translated into French as "*Le Scarabée d'or*" in the *Revue Britannique*, November 1845, and later in the *Démocratie Pacifique*, in 1848. In August 1843 a stage production was mounted in Philadelphia.

Sources for the tale are many, although not all are well documented. Some suggestions include Washington Irving's "Wolfert Webber," which includes in its hidden-treasure plot the possible prototypes of Poe's narrator, Legrand, and Jupiter. Robert M. Bird's novel *Shepard Lee*, which Poe reviewed, shows some similarities as well.

Another source could be *The Journal of Llewellin Penrose, A Seaman*, edited by John Eagles (1815), which has some scenes during the actual discovery of treasure that resemble those in "The Gold-Bug."

In the July 19, 1842, edition of the *Dollar Newspaper*, editor Joseph Sailer answers a charge made in the Philadelphia *Spirit of the Times* (July 1, 1843) that Poe's tale was very much like a story by a thirteen-year-old author, George Ann Humphreys Sherburne, entitled *Imogine*. The reply (probably co-written with Poe): "There is not a word about Kidd—not a word about secret writing—not a syllable about a Gold-Bug—not a syllable about anything that is found in Mr. Poe's story; the only point of coincidence being *the finding of money*—a subject which has been handled not only by Miss Sherburne, but by some fifty, if not by some five hundred talewriters; Mr. P. himself, in "The Gold-Bug," alluding to the multiplicity of stories upon this topic." Sailer's comments are quite correct: there are very few comparisons to be made between the two tales, certainly nothing that could be used to prove even a touch of plagiarism.

Poe's knowledge of natural history displayed in the tale came through his editing Professor Thomas Wyatt's book *A Synopsis of Natural History* (1839). Poe used this material elsewhere, too, including "The Tell-Tale Heart," "The Murders in the Rue Morgue," "The Thousand-and-Second Tale of Scheherazade," and "The Sphinx."

In England, the word "bug" has for a long time had the unpleasant meaning of "louse," and Poe's friend N. P. Willis wrote him in 1845 that Poe's title might hurt sales in that country, but apparently the teaming up with the word "gold" saved the day—and the title. However, one edition, published in 1852, did change it to "The Gold-Beetle." "Bug" also means a madman.

Poe is in part satirizing the mania for gold that has plagued man for thousands of years and would soon break out again in California (and which Poe would use as the basis for "Von Kempelen and His Discovery" as well as the poem *Eldorado*).

While "The Gold-Bug" is grouped here with Poe's tales of ratiocination, some critics have wondered whether this story is a detective story at all. There is no detective, they say, and the plot revolves around the simple solution of a cipher. It is a tale of hidden treasure, yes, but the "detective" Legrand doesn't play fair, keeping things from us in order to preserve the mystery. However, we should remember that Poe was a pioneer in the mystery field, and the rules hadn't yet been established. As for the second charge, Legrand actually hides no more from the readers than Dupin does—or Holmes, for that matter.

The tale—whatever its genre—was also inspiration for many mystery and adventure writers that followed Poe. John Dickson Carr, in *The Life of Sir Arthur Conan Doyle* (Vintage, 1975; p. 29), writes: "One book he received, not in the line of self-improvement, might have upset the studies of anyone less dogged. The book not only impressed Arthur; it electrified him. He confessed in later years that no author, with the exception of Macaulay and Scott, so much shaped his tastes or his literary bent. The author was Edgar Allan Poe, and the first story he encountered was *The Gold Bug*."

Doyle, says Carr, declared that Poe "was the supreme short-story writer of all time. And he stressed it again, with his tribute to the inventor of the detective-story among other things, when he took the chair at the Hotel Metropole dinner to honour the centenary year of Poe's birth." (Pp. 291–92)

In the *Musée des Familles* for April 1864, Jules Verne introduced a translation of Poe's tale thus: "This strange, disturbing story grips us through the use of techniques that no one tried before. It is crammed with observation and infallibly logical deductions; and it alone would suffice to make the writer his fame. To my mind, it is the most remarkable of all the *Tales*, the one in which is revealed to the highest degree the literary genre now known as Poe's own." In his *Journey to the Center of the Earth* (Chapters 2 and 3) we find a mysterious runic cryptograph, made by an Icelandic professor, which leads the protagonists to the secret entrance to the planet's interior.

Robert Louis Stevenson's *Treasure Island* (1883) owes much to Poe's scrap of paper left by Kidd and the lost treasure left on a strange island, as he admits in his own foreword to the novel.

A more recent use of Poe's materials is Isaac Asimov's "The Key" (1966), in which extraterrologist Dr. Wendell Urth solves what appears to be an unsoluble cryptogram by using a series of logical propositions and explanations of symbols strongly reminiscent of Legrand's. There is also mention of a buried treasure for which a murder has been committed, a human skull, and Urth's comment about "Carolina or some other outlandish place" to tip off the source. Asimov's story is collected in *Asimov's Mysteries* (Doubleday, 1968).

Surprisingly, no film has been made of "The Gold-Bug," but elements of the story do appear in *The Raven* (1912), and *Manfish* (1956), a story of a murder and treasure hunting in the Caribbean, with Victor Jory and Lon Chaney, Jr.

Vincent Price narrates the tale on disc (Caedmon 1449).

What ho! what ho! this fellow is dancing mad!
He hath been bitten by the Tarantula.
         —*All in the Wrong*.   **1**

Many years ago, I contracted an intimacy with a Mr. William Legrand. He was of an ancient Huguenot family, and had **2** once been wealthy; but a series of misfortunes had reduced him to want. To avoid the mortification consequent upon his disasters, he left New Orleans, the city of his forefathers, and took up his residence at Sullivan's Island, near Charleston, South Carolina. **3**

This island is a very singular one. It consists of little else than the sea sand, and is about three miles long. Its breadth at no point exceeds a quarter of a mile. It is separated from the mainland by a scarcely perceptible creek, oozing its way through a wilderness of reeds and slime, a favorite resort of the marsh-hen. The vegetation, as might be supposed, is scant, or at least dwarfish. No trees of any magnitude are to be seen. Near the western extremity, where Fort Moultrie stands, and where are some miserable frame buildings, tenanted, during the summer, by the fugitives from Charleston dust and fever, may be found, indeed, the bristly palmetto;

1 Poe the hoaxer strikes again: these lines do not come from Arthur Murphy's comedy *All in the Wrong* (1761); Poe made them up himself.

The tarantella, a folk dance of southern Italy that originated in the seventeenth century, was supposed to cure the bite of the tarantula (*Lycosa tarantula*), which was thought to be the cause of tarantism, a nervous disorder characterized by spasms and twitching. People thought the symptoms of the disease could, quite literally, be danced away.

2 There was a Huguenot family named Legrand living in Charleston at one time, but not when Poe was familiar with the area. He may have had in mind the Baltimore orator John C. Legrand.

The Huguenots were the Calvinist Protestants of France who, after a series of religious persecutions, were driven from France to England, the Netherlands, Germany, Switzerland, and America—where they settled in New York, Pennsylvania, and the Carolinas.

3 Poe was stationed at Fort Moultrie from November 1827 to December 1828 and thus knew well both Sullivan's Island and the Charleston area, even though he couldn't resist changing facts to suit his story's needs. Most of the descriptions here are accurate, however, including the myrtles mentioned in the next paragraph, which do indeed grow on the eastern end of Sullivan's Island.

Fort Moultrie stands at the entrance to the harbor of Charleston. It was originally named Fort Sullivan but was renamed after its builder, Colonel William Moultrie, successfully defended it against a British attack in June 1776. Fort Sumter, site of the opening engagement of the Civil War, is not far away. Fort Moultrie is also the burial site of Seminole chief Osceola, who was imprisoned there in 1831.

4 Compare with the description of Dupin—or of Sherlock Holmes.

5 Jan Swammerdam (1637–80) was a Dutch naturalist who specialized in insects. His *Biblia naturae, sive Historia insectorum*, published after his death, was translated into English in 1758 as *A General History of Insects*.

A pioneer in the use of the microscope, Swammerdam was probably the first to detect the red corpuscles (1658). He was also an early and influential supporter of the theory of evolution, contrary to the then current belief in spontaneous generation.

6 Like many black slaves, Jupiter has a somewhat grandiose Roman name. (One remembers that not too many years ago, another such name was changed from Cassius Marcellus to Muhammad Ali.)

Poe's attitude toward blacks is typical of southern thought at the time: Negroes were inferior, little more than childlike, and with all the affection (and intellect) of a family dog. Today this is probably the most embarrassing feature of Poe's prose, and we can only be thankful that it does not appear more often than it does—especially since the dialect is so thick it is almost undecipherable.

7 Scarabs are dung beetles (*Scarabaeus sacer*), whose periodic reappearance in the mud of the Nile led the ancient Egyptians to associate them with the worship of the sun god, Ra, and with resurrection and immortality.

There are over thirty thousand species of the scarab beetle, with over nine hundred in the United States alone.

but the whole island, with the exception of this western point, and a line of hard, white beach on the seacoast, is covered with a dense undergrowth of the sweet myrtle, so much prized by the horticulturists of England. The shrub here often attains the height of fifteen or twenty feet, and forms an almost impenetrable coppice, burthening the air with its fragrance.

In the inmost recesses of this coppice, not far from the eastern or more remote end of the island, Legrand had build himself a small hut, which he occupied when I first, by mere accident, made his acquaintance. This soon ripened into friendship—for there was much in the recluse to excite interest and esteem. I found him well educated, with unusual powers of mind, but infected with misanthropy, and subject to **4** perverse moods of alternate enthusiasm and melancholy. He had with him many books, but rarely employed them. His chief amusements were gunning and fishing, or sauntering along the beach and through the myrtles, in quest of shells or entomological specimens;—his collection of the latter might **5** have been envied by a Swammerdamm. In these excursions **6** he was usually accompanied by an old negro, called Jupiter, who had been manumitted before the reverses of the family, but who could be induced, neither by threats nor by promises, to abandon what he considered his right of attendance upon the footsteps of his young "Massa Will." It is not improbable that the relatives of Legrand, conceiving him to be somewhat unsettled in intellect, had contrived to instil this obstinacy into Jupiter, with a view of the supervision and guardianship of the wanderer.

The winters in the latitude of Sullivan's Island are seldom very severe, and in the fall of the year it is a rare event indeed when a fire is considered necessary. About the middle of October, 18—, there occurred, however, a day of remarkable chilliness. Just before sunset I scrambled my way through the evergreens to the hut of my friend, whom I had not visited for several weeks—my residence being, at that time, in Charleston, a distance of nine miles from the Island, while the facilities of passage and repassage were very far behind those of the present day. Upon reaching the hut I rapped, as was my custom, and getting no reply, sought for the key where I knew it was secreted, unlocked the door and went in. A fine fire was blazing upon the hearth. It was a novelty, and by no means an ungrateful one. I threw off an overcoat, took an arm-chair by the crackling logs, and awaited patiently the arrival of my hosts.

Soon after dark they arrived, and gave me a most cordial welcome. Jupiter, grinning from ear to ear, bustled about to prepare some marsh-hens for supper. Legrand was in one of his fits—how else shall I term them?—of enthusiasm. He had found an unknown bivalve, forming a new genus, and, more than this, he had hunted down and secured, with Jupiter's **7** assistance, a *scarabæus* which he believed to be totally new, but in respect to which he wished to have my opinion on the morrow.

"And why not to-night?" I asked, rubbing my hands over

the blaze, and wishing the whole tribe of *scarabæi* at the devil.

"Ah, if I had only known you were here!" said Legrand, "but it's so long since I saw you; and how could I foresee that you would pay me a visit this very night of all others? As I was coming home I met Lieutenant G——, from the fort, and, very foolishly, I lent him the bug; so it will be impossible for you to see it until morning. Stay here to-night, and I will send Jup down for it at sunrise. It is the loveliest thing in creation!" **8**

"What?—sunrise?"

"Nonsense! no!—the bug. It is of a brilliant gold color—about the size of a large hickory-nut—with two jet black spots near one extremity of the back, and another, somewhat longer, at the other. The *antennæ* are—" **9**

"Dey aint *no* tin in him, Massa Will, I keep a tellin on you," here interrupted Jupiter; "de bug is a goole bug, solid, ebery bit of him, inside and all, sep him wing—neber feel half so hebby a bug in my life."

"Well, suppose it is, Jup," replied Legrand, somewhat more earnestly, it seemed to me, than the case demanded, "is that any reason for your letting the birds burn? The color"—here he turned to me—"is really almost enough to warrant Jupiter's idea. You never saw a more brilliant metallic lustre than the scales emit—but of this you cannot judge till to-morrow. In the mean time I can give you some idea of the shape." Saying this, he seated himself at a small table, on which were a pen and ink, but no paper. He looked for some in a drawer, but found none.

"Never mind," said he at length, "this will answer"; and he drew from his waistcoat pocket a scrap of what I took to be very dirty foolscap, and made upon it a rough drawing with the pen. While he did this, I retained my seat by the fire, for I was still chilly. When the design was complete, he handed it to me without rising. As I received it, a loud growl was heard, succeeded by a scratching at the door. Jupiter opened it, and a large Newfoundland, belonging to Legrand, rushed in, leaped upon my shoulders, and loaded me with caresses; for I had shown him much attention during previous visits. When his gambols were over, I looked at the paper, and, to speak the truth, found myself not a little puzzled at what my friend had depicted.

"Well!" I said, after contemplating it for some minutes, "this *is* a strange *scarabæus*, I must confess: new to me; never saw anything like it before—unless it was a skull, or a death's-head—which it more nearly resembles than anything else that **10** has come under *my* observation."

"A death's-head!" echoed Legrand—"Oh—yes—well, it has something of that appearance upon paper, no doubt. The two upper black spots look like eyes, eh? and the longer one at the bottom like a mouth—and then the shape of the whole is oval."

"Perhaps so," said I; "but, Legrand, I fear you are no artist. I must wait until I see the beetle itself, if I am to form any idea of its personal appearance."

8 Captain Henry Griswold was one of Poe's officers at Fort Moultrie.

9 "Antennae" sounds like "an-tin-y" to Jupiter. Poe's reaching a bit with this one.

10 Poe uses the word "death's-head" for "skull" frequently in "The Gold-Bug," although the expression was not in common use in his day.

As for the "death's-head beetle," there is no such insect. But in Wyatt's *Synopsis of Natural History* (pp. 138–139), there is the following commentary on the death's-head moth: "The Death's-headed Sphinx has occasioned much terror in certain countries by the kind of cry which it utters, and the insignia of death upon its corselet." Poe borrowed the markings of the moth and perhaps combined these with personal recollections of beetles he must have seen while at Fort Moultrie.

"Well, I don't know," said he, a little nettled. "I draw tolerably—*should* do it at least—have had good masters, and flatter myself that I am not quite a blockhead."

"But, my dear fellow, you are joking then," said I, "this is a very passable *skull*—indeed, I may say that it is a very excellent skull, according to the vulgar notions about such specimens of physiology—and your *scarabæus* must be the queerest *scarabæus* in the world if it resembles it. Why, we may get up a very thrilling bit of superstition upon this hint.

11 I presume you will call the bug *scarabæus caput hominis,* or something of that kind—there are many similar titles in the Natural Histories. But where are the *antennæ* you spoke of?"

"The *antennæ!*" said Legrand, who seemed to be getting unaccountably warm upon the subject; "I am sure you must see the *antennæ*. I made them as distinct as they are in the original insect, and I presume that is sufficient."

"Well, well," I said, "perhaps you have—still I don't see them;" and I handed him the paper without additional remark, not wishing to ruffle his temper; but I was much surprised at the turn affairs had taken; his ill humor puzzled me—and, as for the drawing of the beetle, there were positively *no antennæ* visible, and the whole *did* bear a very close resemblance to the ordinary cuts of a death's-head.

He received the paper very peevishly, and was about to crumple it, apparently to throw it in the fire, when a casual glance at the design seemed suddenly to rivet his attention. In an instant his face grew violently red—in another as excessively pale. For some minutes he continued to scrutinize the drawing minutely where he sat. At length he arose, took a candle from the table, and proceeded to seat himself upon a sea-chest in the farthest corner of the room. Here again he made an anxious examination of the paper; turning it in all directions. He said nothing, however, and his conduct greatly astonished me; yet I thought it prudent not to exacerbate the

12 growing moodiness of his temper by any comment. Presently he took from his coat pocket a wallet, placed the paper carefully in it, and deposited both in a writing-desk, which he locked. He now grew more composed in his demeanor; but his original air of enthusiasm had quite disappeared. Yet he seemed not so much sulky as abstracted. As the evening wore away he became more and more absorbed in reverie, from which no sallies of mine could arouse him. It had been my intention to pass the night at the hut, as I had frequently done before, but, seeing my host in this mood, I deemed it proper to take leave. He did not press me to remain, but, as I departed, he shook my hand with even more than his usual cordiality.

It was about a month after this (and during the interval I had seen nothing of Legrand) when I received a visit, at Charleston, from his man, Jupiter. I had never seen the good old negro look so dispirited, and I feared that some serious disaster had befallen my friend.

"Well, Jup," said I, "what is the matter now?—how is your master?"

11 "Man's-head scarab"

12 Time and time again in his tales Poe makes a point that the true man of genius, a master of both reason and imagination, goes beyond our simple understanding. We think him mad, when it is we who are merely dense.

"Why, to speak de troof, massa, him not so berry well as mought be."

"Not well! I am truly sorry to hear it. What does he complain of?"

"Dar! dat's it!—him neber plain of notin—but him berry sick for all dat."

"*Very* sick, Jupiter!—why did n't you say so at once? Is he confined to bed?"

"No, dat he aint!—he aint find nowhar—dat's just whar de shoe pinch—my mind is got to be berry hebby bout poor Massa Will."

"Jupiter, I should like to understand what it is you are talking about. You say your master is sick. Hasn't he told you what ails him?"

"Why, massa, taint worf while for to git mad bout de matter—Massa Will say noffin at all aint de matter wid him— but den what make him go about looking dis here way, wid he head down and he soldiers up, and as white as a gose? And **13** den he keep a syphon all de time——"

"Keeps a what, Jupiter?"

"Keeps a syphon wid de figgurs on de slate—de queerest **14** figgurs I ebber did see. Ise gittin to be skeered, I tell you. Hab for to keep mighty tight eye pon him noovers. Todder **15** day he gib me slip fore de sun up and was gone de whole ob de blessed day. I had a big stick ready cut for to gib him d—d good beating when he did come—but Ise sich a fool dat I had n't **16** de heart arter all—he look so berry poorly."

"Eh?—what?—ah yes!—upon the whole I think you had better not be too severe with the poor fellow—don't flog him, Jupiter—he can't very well stand it—but can you form no idea of what has occasioned this illness, or rather this change of conduct? Has anything unpleasant happened since I saw you?"

"No, massa, dey aint bin noffin onpleasant *since* den—'t was *fore* den I'm feared—'t was de berry day you was dare."

"How? what do you mean?"

"Why, massa, I mean de bug—dare now."

"The what?"

"De bug—I'm berry sartain dat Massa Will bin bit somewhere bout de head by dat goole-bug."

"And what cause have you, Jupiter, for such a supposition?"

"Claws enuff, massa, and mouff too. I nebber did see sich a d—d bug—he kick and he bite ebery ting what cum near him. Massa Will cotch him fuss, but had for to let him go gin mighty quick, I tell you—den was de time he must ha got de bite. I did n't like de look ob de bug mouff, myself, no how, so I wouldn't take hold ob him wid my finger, but I cotch him wid a piece ob paper dat I found. I rap him up in de paper and stuff piece ob it in he mouff—dat was de way."

"And you think, then, that your master was really bitten by the beetle, and that the bite made him sick?"

"I don't tink noffin about it—I nose it. What make him dream bout de goole so much if taint cause he bit by de goole-bug? Ise heerd bout dem goole-bugs fore dis."

"But how do you know he dreams about gold?"

13 When Baudelaire translated "The Gold-Bug" into French, he understandably misunderstood the dialect spelling "gose" (ghost) for "goose," and so in the French version the sentence still reads "as white as a goose."

14 A blend of cypher and siphon, a joke at the expense of the uneducated Jupiter

15 "Maneuvers"

16 While the idea of a slave beating his master with a stick might seem farfetched, Jupiter could have gotten away with it, since beating was considered an effective form of shock treatment for incipient madness.

"How I know? why cause he talk about it in he sleep—dat's how I nose."

"Well, Jup, perhaps you are right; but to what fortunate circumstance am I to attribute the honor of a visit from you to-day?"

"What de matter, massa?"

"Did you bring any message from Mr. Legrand?"

17 "Epistle"

17   "No, massa, I bring dis here pissel"; and here Jupiter handed me a note which ran thus:

My Dear—

Why have I not seen you for so long a time? I hope you have not been so foolish as to take offence at any little *brusquerie* of mine; but no, that is improbable.

Since I saw you I have had great cause for anxiety. I have something to tell you, yet scarcely know how to tell it, or whether I should tell it at all.

I have not been quite well for some days past, and poor old Jup annoys me, almost beyond endurance, by his well-meant attentions. Would you believe it?—he had prepared a huge stick, the other day, with which to chastise me for giving him the slip, and spending the day, *solus*, among the hills on the main land. I verily believe that my ill looks alone saved me a flogging.

I have made no addition to my cabinet since we met.

If you can, in any way, make it convenient, come over with Jupiter. *Do* come. I wish to see you *to-night*, upon business of importance. I assure you that it is of the *highest* importance.

Ever yours,
William Legrand.

There was something in the tone of this note which gave me great uneasiness. Its whole style differed materially from that of Legrand. What could he be dreaming of? What new crotchet possessed his excitable brain? What "business of the highest importance" could *he* possibly have to transact? Jupiter's account of him boded no good. I dreaded lest the continued pressure of misfortune had, at length, fairly unsettled the reason of my friend. Without a moment's hesitation, therefore, I prepared to accompany the negro.

Upon reaching the wharf, I noticed a scythe and three spades, all apparently new, lying in the bottom of the boat in which we were to embark.

"What is the meaning of all this, Jup?" I inquired.

"Him syfe, massa, and spade."

"Very true; but what are they doing here?"

"Him de syfe and de spade what Massa Will sis pon my buying for him in de town, and de debbil's own lot of money I had to gib for em."

"But what, in the name of all that is mysterious, is your 'Massa Will' going to do with scythes and spades?"

"Dat's more dan *I* know, and debbil take me if I don't believe 't is more dan he know, too. But it's all cum ob de bug."

Finding that no satisfaction was to be obtained of Jupiter, whose whole intellect seemed to be absorbed by "de bug," I now stepped into the boat and made sail. With a fair and strong breeze we soon ran into the little cove to the northward of Fort Moultrie, and a walk of some two miles brought us to the hut. It was about three in the afternoon when we arrived. Legrand had been awaiting us in eager expectation. He grasped my hand with a nervous *empressement* which alarmed me and strengthened the suspicions already entertained. His countenance was pale even to ghastliness, and his deep-set eyes glared with unnatural lustre. After some inquiries respecting his health, I asked him, not knowing what better to say, if he had yet obtained the *scarabæus* from Lieutenant G——.

"Oh, yes," he replied, coloring violently, "I got it from him the next morning. Nothing should tempt me to part with that *scarabæus*. Do you know that Jupiter is quite right about it?"

"In what way?" I asked, with a sad foreboding at heart.

"In supposing it to be a bug of *real gold*." He said this with an air of profound seriousness, and I felt inexpressibly shocked.

"This bug is to make my fortune," he continued, with a triumphant smile, "to reinstate me in my family possessions. Is it any wonder, then, that I prize it? Since Fortune has thought fit to bestow it upon me, I have only to use it properly and I shall arrive at the gold of which it is the index. Jupiter, bring me that *scarabæus!*"

"What! de bug, massa? I'd rudder not go fer trubble dat bug—you mus git him for your own self." Hereupon Legrand arose, with a grave and stately air, and brought me the beetle from a glass case in which it was enclosed. It was a beautiful *scarabæus*, and, at that time, unknown to naturalists—of course a great prize in a scientific point of view. There were two round, black spots near one extremity of the back, and a long one near the other. The scales were exceedingly hard and glossy, with all the appearance of burnished gold. The **18** weight of the insect was very remarkable, and, taking all things into consideration, I could hardly blame Jupiter for his opinion respecting it; but what to make of Legrand's agreement with that opinion, I could not, for the life of me, tell.

"I sent for you," said he, in a grandiloquent tone, when I had completed my examination of the beetle, "I sent for you, that I might have your counsel and assistance in furthering the views of Fate and of the bug"——

"My dear Legrand," I cried, interrupting him, "you are certainly unwell, and had better use some little precautions. You shall go to bed, and I will remain with you a few days, until you get over this. You are feverish and"——

"Feel my pulse," said he.

I felt it, and, to say the truth, found not the slightest indication of fever.

"But you may be ill and yet have no fever. Allow me this once to prescribe for you. In the first place, go to bed. In the next"—— **19**

"You are mistaken," he interposed, "I am as well as I can expect to be under the excitement which I suffer. If you really wish me well, you will relieve this excitement."

18 Besides the markings of the death's-head moth, the Gold-Bug also seems to share a resemblance to the iridescent golden yellow insect *Callichroma splendidum* and to the click beetle, *Alaus oculatus*—both found on Sullivan's Island even today.

19 The narrator is both too rational and unimaginative, sharing that dubious distinction with the narrator of the Dupin tales.

"And how is this to be done?"

"Very easily. Jupiter and myself are going upon an expedition into the hills, upon the main land, and, in this expedition, we shall need the aid of some person in whom we can confide. You are the only one we can trust. Whether we succeed or fail, the excitement which you now perceive in me will be equally allayed."

"I am anxious to oblige you in any way," I replied; "but do you mean to say that this infernal beetle has any connection with your expedition into the hills?"

"It has."

"Then, Legrand, I can become a party to no such absurd proceeding."

"I am sorry—very sorry—for we shall have to try it by ourselves."

"Try it by yourselves! The man is surely mad!—but stay!—how long do you propose to be absent?"

"Probably all night. We shall start immediately, and be back, at all events, by sunrise."

"And will you promise me, upon your honor, that when this freak of yours is over, and the bug business (good God!) settled to your satisfaction, you will then return home and follow my advice implicitly, as that of your physician?"

"Yes; I promise; and now let us be off, for we have no time to lose."

With a heavy heart I accompanied my friend. We started about four o'clock—Legrand, Jupiter, the dog, and myself. Jupiter had with him the scythe and spades—the whole of which he insisted upon carrying—more through fear, it seemed to me, of trusting either of the implements within reach of his master, than from any excess of industry or complaisance. His demeanor was dogged in the extreme, and "dat d—d bug" were the sole words which escaped his lips during the journey.

20 For my own part, I had charge of a couple of dark lanterns, while Legrand contented himself with the *scarabæus*, which he carried attached to the end of a bit of whip-cord; twirling it to and fro, with the air of a conjuror, as he went. When I observed this last, plain evidence of my friend's aberration of mind, I could scarcely refrain from tears. I thought it best, however, to humor his fancy, at least for the present, or until I could adopt some more energetic measures with a chance of success. In the mean time I endeavored, but all in vain, to sound him in regard to the object of the expedition. Having succeeded in inducing me to accompany him, he seemed unwilling to hold conversation upon any topic of minor importance, and to all my questions vouchsafed no other reply than "we shall see!"

We crossed the creek at the head of the island by means of a skiff, and, ascending the high grounds on the shore of the main land, proceeded in a northwesterly direction, through a tract of country excessively wild and desolate, where no trace of a human footstep was to be seen. Legrand led the way with decision; pausing only for an instant, here and there, to consult what appeared to be certain landmarks of his own contrivance upon a former occasion.

20 See "The Tell-Tale Heart," note 5.

In this manner we journeyed for about two hours, and the sun was just setting when we entered a region infinitely more dreary than any yet seen. It was a species of table land, near the summit of an almost inaccessible hill, densely wooded from base to pinnacle, and interspersed with huge crags that appeared to lie loosely upon the soil, and in many cases were prevented from precipitating themselves into the valleys below, merely by the support of the trees against which they reclined. Deep ravines, in various directions, gave an air of still sterner solemnity to the scene.

The natural platform to which we had clambered was thickly overgrown with brambles, through which we soon discovered that it would have been impossible to force our way but for the scythe; and Jupiter, by direction of his master, proceeded to clear for us a path to the foot of an enormously tall tulip-tree, which stood, with some eight or ten oaks, upon the level, **21** and far surpassed them all, and all other trees which I had then ever seen, in the beauty of its foliage and form, in the wide spread of its branches, and in the general majesty of its appearance. When we reached this tree, Legrand turned to Jupiter, and asked him if he thought he could climb it. The old man seemed a little staggered by the question, and for some moments made no reply. At length he approached the huge tree, walked slowly around it, and examined it with minute attention. When he had completed his scrutiny, he merely said,

"Yes, massa, Jup climb any tree he ebber see in he life."

"Then up with you as soon as possible, for it will soon be too dark to see what we are about."

"How far mus go up, massa?" inquired Jupiter.

"Get up the main trunk first, and then I will tell you which way to go—and here—stop! take this beetle with you."

"De bug, Massa Will!—de goole bug!" cried the negro, drawing back in dismay—"what for mus tote de bug way up de tree?—d—n if I do!"

"If you are afraid, Jup, a great big negro like you, to take hold of a harmless little dead beetle, why you can carry it up by this string—but, if you do not take it up with you in some way, I shall be under the necessity to breaking your head with this shovel."

"What de matter now, massa?" said Jup, evidently shamed into compliance; "always want for to raise fuss wid old nigger. Was only funnin any how. *Me* feered de bug! what I keer for de bug?" Here he took cautiously hold of the exreme end of the string, and, maintaining the insect as far from his person as circumstances would permit, prepared to ascend the tree.

In youth, the tulip-tree, of *Liriodendron Tulipiferum*, the **22** most magnificent of American foresters, has a trunk peculiarly smooth, and often rises to a great height without lateral branches; but, in its riper age, the bark becomes gnarled and uneven, while many short limbs make their appearance on the stem. Thus the difficulty of ascension, in the present case, lay more in semblance than in reality. Embracing the huge cylinder, as closely as possible, with his arms and knees, seizing with his hands some projections, and resting his naked

21 No tulip trees (*Liriodendron tulipifera*) grow on Sullivan's Island, but Poe was very fond of them, mentioning them in several stories, including "Landor's Cottage."

A member of the Magnoliaceae (which include the southern magnolia and the umbrella tree), the tulip tree is a living relic, once widespread throughout North America and Europe but now native only to the eastern United States and China.

22 Poe changes the spelling of the second name to agree with *dendron*, which is a Greek neuter form.

Barton Lévi St. Armand says this "misspelling" (at least as far as botanical classification is concerned) is meant to be a pun on *ferrum*, which denotes the metal iron, a sword, or any iron implement. He notes the hard, smooth, almost metallic nature of the tulip tree in Poe's description of it as a "huge cylinder." This leads him to an alchemical interpretation of the tree—and ultimately the tale itself.

Jupiter hangs on the tree, and "Jupiter" was the symbolic name for tin, one of the seven planetary metals of alchemy. In alchemy books, St. Armand points out, we find the symbol of the Tree of Knowledge, with a figure climbing up or down it. Climbing up meant destructive knowledge (Melusina), while climbing down from heaven meant divine revelation (Mercurius). Jupiter climbs to the seventh limb up, and seven is the highest digit in the alchemical hierarchy, which ran in an ascending order from tin (Jupiter), through lead (Saturn), mercury (Mercury), iron (Mars), copper (Venus), silver (Moon) and gold (Sun). A detailed (and complex) explanation of this line of reasoning can be found in St. Armand's article in *Poe Studies*, Vol. IV, p. 1.

It seems bizarre, but one *is* struck, when reading the article, by recalling Jupiter's "Dey ain't *no* tin in him."

toes upon others, Jupiter, after one or two narrow escapes from falling, at length wriggled himself into the first great form, and seemed to consider the whole business as virtually accomplished. The *risk* of the achievement was, in fact, now over, although the climber was some sixty or seventy feet from the ground.

"Which way mus go now, Massa Will?" he asked.

"Keep up the largest branch—the one on this side," said Legrand. The negro obeyed him promptly, and apparently with but little trouble; ascending higher and higher, until no glimpse of his squat figure could be obtained through the dense foliage which enveloped it. Presently his voice was heard in a sort of halloo.

"How much fudder is got for go?"

"How high up are you?" asked Legrand.

"Ebber so fur," replied the negro, "can see de sky fru do top ob de tree."

"Never mind the sky, but attend to what I say. Look down the trunk and count the limbs below you on this side. How many limbs have you passed?"

"One, two, three, four, fibe—I done pass fibe big limb, massa, pon dis side."

"Then go one limb higher."

In a few minutes the voice was heard again, announcing that the seventh limb was attained.

"Now, Jup," cried Legrand, evidently much excited, "I want you to work you way out upon that limb as far as you can. If you see anything strange, let me know."

By this time what little doubt I might have entertained of my poor friend's insanity, was put finally at rest. I had no alternative but to conclude him stricken with lunacy, and I became seriously anxious about getting him home. While I was pondering upon what was best to be done, Jupiter's voice was again heard.

"Mos feered for to ventur pon dis limb berry far—tis dead limb putty much all de way."

"Did you say it was a *dead* limb, Jupiter?" cried Legrand in a quavering voice.

"Yes, massa, him dead as de door-nail—done up for sartain—done departed dis here life."

"What in the name of heaven shall I do?" asked Legrand, seemingly in the greatest distress.

"Do!" said I, glad of an opportunity to interpose a word, "why come home and go to bed. Come now!—that's a fine fellow. It's getting late, and, besides, you remember your promise."

"Jupiter," cried he, without heeding me in the least, "do you hear me?"

"Yes, Massa Will, here you ebber so plain."

"Try the wood well, then, with your knife, and see if you think it *very* rotten."

"Him rotten, massa, sure nuff," replied the negro in a few moments, "but not so berry rotten as mought be. Mought ventur out leetle way pon de limb by myself, dat's true."

". . . pon my word—dare's a great big nail in de skull, what fastens ob it on to de tree." *Illustration by Herpin, nineteenth century*

"By yourself!—what do you mean?"

"Why I mean de bug. 'T is *berry* hebby bug. Spose I drop him down fuss, and den de limb won't break wid just de weight ob one nigger."

"You infernal scoundrel!" cried Legrand, apparently much relieved, "what do you mean by telling me such nonsense as that? As sure as you let that beetle fall I'll break your neck. Look here, Jupiter! do you hear me?"

"Yes, massa, need n't hollo at poor nigger dat style."

"Well! now listen!—if you will venture out on the limb as far as you think safe, and not let go the beetle, I'll make you a present of a silver dollar as soon as you get down."

"I'm gwine, Massa Will—deed I is," replied the negro very promptly—"mos out to the eend now."

"*Out to the end*!" here fairly screamed Legrand, "do you say you are out to the end of that limb?"

"Soon to be de eend, massa,—o-o-o-o-oh! Lor-gol-a-marcy! what *is* dis here pon de tree?"

"Well!" cried Legrand, highly delighted, "what is it?"

"Why taint noffin but a skull—somebody bin lef him head up de tree, and de crows done gobble ebery bit ob de meat off."

"A skull, you say!—very well!—how is it fastened to the limb?—what holds it on?"

"Sure nuff, massa; mus look. Why dis berry curous sarcumstance, pon my word—dare's a great big nail in de skull, what fastens ob it on to de tree."

"Well now, Jupiter, do exactly as I tell you—do you hear?"

"Yes, massa."

"Pay attention, then!—find the left eye of the skull."

"Hum! hoo! dat's good! why dar aint no eye lef at all."

"Curse your stupidity! do you know your right hand from your left?"

"Yes, I nose dat—nose all bout dat—tis my left hand what I chops de wood wid."

"To be sure! you are left-handed; and your left eye is on the same side as your left hand. Now, I suppose, you can find the left eye of the skull, or the place where the left eye has been. Have you found it?"

Here was a long pause. At length the negro asked,

"Is de lef eye of de skull pon de same side as de lef hand of de skull, too?—cause de skull aint got not a bit ob a hand at all—nebber mind! I got de lef eye now—here the left eye! what mus do wid it?"

"Let the beetle drop through it, as far as the string will reach—but be careful and not let go your hold of the string."

"All dat done, Massa Will; mighty easy ting for to put de bug fru de hole—look out for him dar below!"

During this colloquy no portion of Jupiter's person could be seen; but the beetle, which he had suffered to descend, was now visible at the end of the string, and glistened, like a globe of burnished gold, in the last rays of the setting sun, some of which still faintly illumined the eminence upon which we stood. The *scarabæus* hung quite clear of any branches, and, if allowed to fall, would have fallen at our feet. Legrand immediately took the scythe, and cleared with it a circular space, three or four yards in diameter, just beneath the insect, and, having accomplished this, ordered Jupiter to let go the string and come down from the tree.

Driving a peg, with great nicety, into the ground, at the precise spot where the beetle fell, my friend now produced from his pocket a tape-measure. Fastening one end of this at that point of the trunk of the tree which was nearest the peg, he unrolled it till it reached the peg, and thence farther unrolled it, in the direction already established by the two points of the tree and the peg, for the distance of fifty feet—Jupiter clearing away the brambles with the scythe. At the spot thus attained a second peg was driven, and about this, as a centre, a rude circle, about four feet in diameter, described. Taking now a spade himself, and giving one to Jupiter and one to me, Legrand begged us to set about digging as quickly as possible.

To speak the truth, I had no special relish for such amusement at any time, and, at this particular moment, would most willingly have declined it; for the night was coming on, and I felt much fatigued with the exercise already taken; but I saw no mode of escape, and was fearful of disturbing my poor friend's equanimity by a refusal. Could I have depended, indeed, upon Jupiter's aid, I would have had no hesitation in attempting to get the lunatic home by force; but I was too well assured of the old negro's disposition, to hope that he would assist me under any circumstances, in a personal contest with his master. I made no doubt that the latter had been infected with some of the innumerable Southern superstitions about money buried, and that his phantasy had received confirmation by the finding of the *scarabæus*, or, perhaps, by Jupiter's obstinacy in maintaining it to be "a bug of real gold." A mind disposed to lunacy would readily be led away by such suggestions—especially if chiming in with favorite preconceived ideas—and then I called to mind the poor fellow's speech about the beetle's being "the index of his fortune." Upon the whole, I was sadly vexed and puzzled, but, at length, I concluded to make a virtue of necessity—to dig with a good will, and thus the sooner to convince the visionary, by ocular demonstration, of the fallacy of the opinions he entertained. **23**

The lanterns having been lit, we all fell to work with a zeal worthy a more rational cause; and, as the glare fell upon our persons and implements, I could not help thinking how picturesque a group we composed, and how strange and suspicious our labors must have appeared to any interloper who, by chance, might have stumbled upon our whereabouts.

We dug very steadily for two hours. Little was said; and our chief embarrassment lay in the yelpings of the dog, who took exceeding interest in our proceedings. He, at length, became so obstreperous that we grew fearful of his giving alarm to some stragglers in the vicinity;—or, rather, this was the apprehension of Legrand;—for myself, I should have rejoiced at any interruption which might have enabled me to get the wanderer home. The noise was, at length, very effectually silenced by Jupiter, who, getting out of the hole with a dogged air of deliberation, tied the brute's mouth up with one of his suspenders, and then returned, with a grave chuckle, to his task.

When the time mentioned had expired, we had reached a depth of five feet, and yet no signs of any treasure became manifest. A general pause ensured, and I began to hope that the farce was at an end. Legrand, however, although evidently much disconcerted, wiped his brow thoughtfully and recommenced. We had excavated the entire circle of four feet diameter, and now we slightly enlarged the limit, and went to the farther depth of two feet. Still nothing appeared. The goldseeker, whom I sincerely pitied, at length clambered from the pit, with the bitterest disappointment imprinted upon every feature, and proceeded, slowly and reluctantly, to put on his coat, which he had thrown off at the beginning of his labor. In the mean time I made no remark. Jupiter, at a signal from his master, began to gather up his tools. This done, and the dog having been unmuzzled, we turned in profound silence towards home.

We had taken, perhaps, a dozen steps in this direction, when, with a loud oath, Legrand strode up to Jupiter, and

23 The reader has as much information about Legrand as the narrator does, and so we come to see Legrand in the same way. When the truth is revealed, we find we have been blind to something that was really quite obvious. This is one of the tricks of the trade in detective fiction, but the trick in this case is fair, because the narrative viewpoint is consistent throughout.

24 Perverse insistence

25 A curvet is a prancing leap of a horse, in which first the forelegs and then the hind legs are raised so that for an instant all four legs are in the air. How Legrand accomplishes this feat is not clear.

A caracole is a halfturn to the right or left executed by a mounted horse, but also a turning or capering movement.

The terminology doesn't seem quite appropriate, but we get the idea. Perhaps the narrator is a horse fancier.

26 The light is dawning. The narrator begins to grasp something beyond the seemingly inexplicable behavior of Legrand. The allusion is to *Hamlet*, II, ii: "Though this be madness, yet there is method in 't."

27 The mathematical calculations in this paragraph are not accurate, but Poe probably didn't care, since it is the appearance of precision that is important.

seized him by the collar. The astonished negro opened his eyes and mouth to the fullest extent, let fall the spades, and fell upon his knees.

"You scoundrel," said Legrand, hissing out the syllables from between his clenched teeth—"you infernal black villain!—speak, I tell you!—answer me this instant, without prevarication!—which—which is your left eye?"

"Oh, my golly, Massa Will! aint dis here my lef eye for sartin?" roared the terrified Jupiter, placing his hand upon his *right* organ of vision, and holding it there with a desperate **24** pertinacity, as if in immediate dread of his master's attempt at a gouge.

"I thought so!—I knew it!—hurrah!" vociferated Legrand, letting the negro go, and executing a series of curvets and **25** caracols, much to the astonishment of his valet, who, arising from his knees, looked, mutely, from his master to myself, and then from myself to his master.

"Come! we must go back," said the latter, "the game's not up yet;" and he again led the way to the tulip-tree.

"Jupiter," said he, when we reached its foot, "come here! was the skull nailed to the limb with the face outward, or with the face to the limb?"

"De face was out, massa, so dat de crows could get at de eyes good, widout any trouble."

"Well, then, was it this eye or that through which you let fall the beetle?"—here Legrand touched each of Jupiter's eyes.

"T was dis eye, massa—de lef eye—jis as you tell me," and here it was his right eye that the negro indicated.

"That will do—we must try again."

Here my friend, about whose madness I now saw, or fancied **26** that I saw, certain indications of method, removed the peg which marked the spot where the beetle fell, to a spot about three inches to the west-ward of its former position. Taking, now, the tape-measure from the nearest point of the trunk to the peg, as before, and continuing the extension in a straight line to the distance of fifty feet, a spot was indicated, removed, **27** by several yards, from the point at which we had been digging.

Around the new position a circle, somewhat larger than in the former instance, was now described, and we again set to work with the spades. I was dreadfully weary, but, scarcely understanding what had occasioned the change in my thoughts, I felt no longer any great aversion from the labor imposed. I had become most unaccountably interested—nay, even excited. Perhaps there was something, amid all the extravagant demeanor of Legrand—some air of forethought, or of deliberation, which impressed me. I dug eagerly, and now and then caught myself actually looking, with something that very much resembled expectation, for the fancied treasure, the vision of which had demented my unfortunate companion. At a period when such vagaries of thought most fully possessed me, and when we had been at work perhaps an hour and a half, we were again interrupted by the violent howlings of the dog. His uneasiness, in the first instance, had been, evidently, but the result of playfulness or caprice, but he now assumed a bitter and serious tone. Upon Jupiter's again attempting to muzzle him, he made furious resistance, and, leaping into the hole, tore up the mould frantically with his claws. In a few seconds he had uncovered a mass of human bones, forming two complete skeletons, intermingled with several buttons of metal, and what appeared to be the dust of decayed woollen. One or two strokes of a spade upturned the blade of a large Spanish knife, and, as we dug farther, three or four loose pieces of gold and silver coin came to light.

At sight of these the joy of Jupiter could scarcely be restrained, but the countenance of his master wore an air of extreme disappointment. He urged us, however, to continue our exertions, and the words were hardly uttered when I stumbled and fell forward, having caught the toe of my boot in a large ring of iron that lay half buried in the loose earth.

We now worked in earnest, and never did I pass ten minutes of more intense excitement. During this interval we had fairly unearthed an oblong chest of wood, which, from its perfect preservation, and wonderful hardness, had plainly been subjected to some mineralizing process—perhaps that of the Bi-chloride of Mercury. This box was three feet and a **28** half long, three feet broad, and two and a half feet deep. It was firmly secured by bands of wrought iron, riveted, and forming a kind of trellis-work over the whole. On each side of the chest, near the top, were three rings of iron—six in all—by means of which a firm hold could be obtained by six persons. Our utmost united endeavors served only to disturb the coffer very slightly in its bed. We at once saw the impossibility of removing so great a weight. Luckily, the sole fastenings of the lid consisted of two sliding bolts. These we drew back—trembling and panting with anxiety. In an instant, a treasure of incalculable value lay gleaming before us. As the rays of the lanterns fell within the pit, there flashed upwards from a confused heap of gold and of jewels, a glow and a glare that absolutely dazzled our eyes.

I shall not pretend to describe the feelings with which I gazed. Amazement was, of course, predominant. Legrand appeared exhausted with excitement, and spoke very few words. Jupiter's countenance wore, for some minutes, as deadly a pallor as it is possible, in the nature of things, for any negro's visage to assume. He seemed stupefied—thunder-stricken. Presently he fell upon his knees in the pit, and, burying his naked arms up to the elbows in gold, let them there remain, as if enjoying the luxury of a bath. At length, with a deep sigh, he exclaimed, as if in a soliloquy,

"And dis all cum ob de goole-bug! de putty goole-bug! de poor little goole-bug, what I boosed in dat sabage kind ob **29** style! Aint you shamed ob yourself, nigger?—answer me dat!"

It became necessary, at last, that I should arouse both master and valet to the expediency of removing the treasure. It was growing late, and it behooved us to make exertion, that we might get every thing housed before daylight. It was difficult to say what should be done; and much time was spent in deliberation—so confused were the ideas of all. We, finally, lightened the box by removing two thirds of its contents, when

28 Bichloride of mercury, a deadly poison, was in common use as a preservative against rot until this century.

29 Abused

The chest had been full to the brim, and we spent the whole day, and the greater part of the next night, in a scrutiny of its contents. *Illustration by F. Darley for the original publication of the story in* Dollar Newspaper, *1843*

30 Previous agreement

31 Close to 2 million of today's inflated dollars

32 Tokens of value

33 From the medieval French, meaning "goods of weight." Avoirdupois weight is based on the pound of sixteen ounces and the ounce of sixteen drams.

we were enabled, with some trouble, to raise it from the hole. The articles taken out were deposited among the brambles, and the dog left to guard them, with strict orders from Jupiter neither, upon any pretence, to stir from the spot, not to open his mouth until our return. We then hurriedly made for home with the chest; reaching the hut in safety, but after excessive toil, at one o'clock in the morning. Worn out as we were, it was not in human nature to do more just then. We rested until two, and had supper; starting for the hills immediately afterwards, armed with three stout sacks, which, by good luck, were upon the premises. A little before four we arrived at the pit, divided the remainder of the booty, as equally as might be, among us, and, leaving the holes unfilled, again set out for the hut, at which, for the second time, we deposited our golden burthens, just as the first streaks of the dawn gleamed from over the tree-tops in the East.

We were now thoroughly broken down; but the intense excitement of the time denied us repose. After an unquiet slumber of some three or four hours' duration, we arose, as **30** if by preconcert, to make examination of our treasure.

The chest had been full to the brim and we spent the whole day, and the greater part of the next night, in a scrutiny of its contents. There had been nothing like order or arrangement. Every thing had been heaped in promiscuously. Having assorted all with care, we found ourselves possessed of even vaster wealth than we had at first supposed. In coin there was **31** rather more than four hundred and fifty thousand dollars— estimating the value of the pieces, as accurately as we could, by the tables of the period. There was not a particle of silver. All was gold of antique date and of great variety—French, Spanish, and German money, with a few English guineas, **32** and some counters, of which we had never seen specimens before. There were several very large and heavy coins, so worn that we could make nothing of their inscriptions. There was no American money. The value of the jewels we found more difficulty in estimating. There were diamonds—some of them exceedingly large and fine—a hundred and ten in all, and not one of them small; eighteen rubies of remarkable brilliancy;—three hundred and ten emeralds, all very beautiful; and twenty-one sapphires, with an opal. These stones had all been broken from their settings and thrown loose in the chest. The settings themselves, which we picked out from among the other gold, appeared to have been beaten up with hammers, as if to prevent identification. Besides all this, there was a vast quantity of solid gold ornaments;—nearly two hundred massive finger and ear rings;—rich chains—thirty of these, if I remember;—eighty-three very large and heavy crucifixes;—five gold censers of great value;—a prodigious golden punch-bowl, ornamented with richly chased vine-leaves and Bacchanalian figures; with two sword-handles exquisitely embossed, and many other smaller articles which I cannot recollect. The weight of these valuables exceeded **33** three hundred and fifty pounds avoirdupois; and in this estimate I have not included one hundred and ninety-seven superb gold watches; three of the number being worth each five hundred dollars, if one. Many of them were very old, and as time keepers valueless; the works having suffered, more or less, from corrosion—but all were richly jewelled and in cases of great worth. We estimated the entire contents of the chest, that night, at a million and a half of dollars; and, upon the **34** subsequent disposal of the trinkets and jewels (a few being retained for our own use), it was found that we had greatly undervalued the treasure.

When, at length, we had concluded our examination, and the intense excitement of the time had, in some measure, subsided, Legrand, who saw that I was dying with impatience for a solution of this most extraordinary riddle, entered into a full detail of all the circumstances connected with it. **35**

"You remember," said he, "the night when I handed you the rough sketch I had made of the *scarabæus*. You recollect also, that I became quite vexed at you for insisting that my drawing resembled a death's-head. When you first made this assertion I thought you were jesting; but afterwards I called to mind the peculiar spots on the back of the insect, and admitted to myself that your remark had some little foundation in fact. Still, the sneer at my graphic powers irritated me—for I am considered a good artist—and, therefore, when you handed me the scrap of parchment, I was about to crumple it up and throw it angrily into the fire."

"The scrap of paper, you mean," said I.

"No; it had much of the appearance of paper, and at first I supposed it to be such, but when I came to draw upon it, I discovered it, at once, to be a piece of very thin parchment. **36** It was quite dirty, you remember. Well, as I was in the very act of crumpling it up, my glance fell upon the sketch at which you had been looking, and you may imagine my astonishment when I perceived, in fact, the figure of a death's-head just where, it seemed to me, I had made the drawing of the beetle. For a moment I was too much amazed to think with accuracy. I knew that my design was very different in detail from this— although there was a certain similarity in general outline. Presently I took a candle, and seating myself at the other end of the room, proceeded to scrutinize the parchment more closely. Upon turning it over, I saw my own sketch upon the reverse, just as I had made it. My first idea, now, was mere surprise at the really remarkable similarity of outline—at the singular coincidence involved in the fact, that unknown to me, there should have been a skull upon the other side of the parchment, immediately beneath my figure of the *scarabæus*, and that this skull, not only in outline, but in size, should so closely resemble my drawing. I say the singularity of this coincidence absolutely stupefied me for a time. This is the usual effect of such coincidences. The mind struggles to establish a connection— a sequence of cause and effect—and, being unable to do so, suffers a species of temporary paralysis. **37** But, when I recovered from this stupor, there dawned upon me gradually a conviction which startled me even far more than the coincidence. I began distinctly, positively, to remem-

34 About $6.2 million in today's currency

35 Compare the form of "The Gold-Bug" with that of "The Purloined Letter." Both involve a mystery that is first described and then elaborated upon until no solution seems possible until made totally comprehensible by the simple explanation of the protagonist.

36 Parchment is made from the untanned skins of sheep, calves, or goats, and prepared for use as writing material. The name is a corruption of Pergamum, an ancient city of Asia Minor where parchment was first developed, in the second century B.C.

The skins were soaked in water, treated with lime to loosen the hair, scraped, washed, stretched, and dried, then rubbed with chalk and pumice. Today, while still in demand for special documents, parchment is used mostly for drumheads, tambourines, and banjos.

37 Legrand describes the sort of memory block that comes to all of us when we sense the sought-for fact or idea as it flutters almost into our consciousness and then just as quickly flits away. Trying to think of the idea seldom helps, but dropping it and going on to something else often seems to bring it into focus.

ber that there had been *no* drawing on the parchment when I made my sketch of the *scarabæus*. I became perfectly certain of this; for I recollected turning up first one side and then the other, in search of the cleanest spot. Had the skull been then there, of course I could not have failed to notice it. Here was indeed a mystery which I felt it impossible to explain; but, even at that early moment, there seemed to glimmer, faintly, within the most remote and secret chambers of my intellect, a glow-worm-like conception of that truth which last night's adventure brought to so magnificent a demonstration. I arose at once, and putting the parchment securely away, dismissed all farther reflection until I should be alone.

"When you had gone, and when Jupiter was fast asleep I betook myself to a more methodical investigation of the affair. In the first place I considered the manner in which the parchment had come into my possession. The spot where we discovered the *scarabæus* was on the coast of the main land, about a mile eastward of the island, and but a short distance above high water mark. Upon my taking hold of it, it gave me a sharp bite, which caused me to let it drop. Jupiter, with his accustomed caution, before seizing the insect, which had flown towards him, looked about him for a leaf, or something of that nature, by which to take hold of it. It was at this moment that his eyes, and mine also, fell upon the scrap of parchment, which I then supposed to be paper. It was lying half buried in the sand, a corner sticking up. Near the spot where we found it, I observed the remnants of the hull of what appeared to have been a ship's long boat. The wreck seemed to have been there for a very great while; for the resemblance to boat timbers could scarcely be traced.

"Well, Jupiter picked up the parchment, wrapped the beetle in it, and gave it to me. Soon afterwards we turned to go home, and on the way met Lieutenant G——. I showed him the insect, and he begged me to let him take it to the fort. On my consenting, he thrust it forthwith into his waistcoat pocket, without the parchment in which it had been wrapped, and which I had continued to hold in my hand during his inspection. Perhaps he dreaded my changing my mind, and thought it best to make sure of the prize at once—you know how enthusiastic he is on all subjects connected with Natural History. At the same time, without being conscious of it, I must have deposited the parchment in my own pocket.

"You remember that when I went to the table, for the purpose of making a sketch of the beetle, I found no paper where it was usually kept. I looked in the drawer, and found none there. I searched my pockets, hoping to find an old letter—and then my hand fell upon the parchment. I thus detail the precise mode in which it came into my possession; for the circumstances impressed me with peculiar force.

"No doubt you will think me fanciful—but I had already established a kind of *connection*. I had put together two links of a great chain. There was a boat lying on a sea-coast, and not far from the boat was a parchment—*not a paper*—with a skull depicted on it. You will, of course, ask 'where is the connection?' I reply that the skull, or death's-head, is the well-known emblem of the pirate. The flag of the death's-head is hoisted in all engagements. **38**

"I have said that the scrap was parchment, and not paper. Parchment is durable—almost imperishable. Matters of little moment are rarely consigned to parchment; since, for the mere ordinary purposes of drawing or writing, it is not nearly so well adapted as paper. This reflection suggested some meaning—some relevancy—in the death's-head. I did not fail to observe, also, the *form* of the parchment. Although one of its corners had been, by some accident, destroyed, it could be seen that the original form was oblong. It was just such a slip, indeed, as might have been chosen for a memorandum—for a record of something to be long remembered and carefully preserved."

"But," I interposed, "you say that the skull was *not* upon the parchment when you made the drawing of the beetle. How then do you trace any connection between the boat and the skull—since this latter, according to your own admission, must have been designed (God only knows how or by whom) at some period subsequent to your sketching the *scarabæus?*"

"Ah, hereupon turns the whole mystery; although the secret, at this point, I had comparatively little difficulty in solving. My steps were sure, and could afford but a single result. I reasoned, for example, thus: When I drew the *scarabæus*, there was no skull apparent on the parchment. When I had completed the drawing, I gave it to you, and observed you narrowly until you returned it. *You*, therefore, did not design the skull, and no one else was present to do it. Then it was not done by human agency. And nevertheless it was done.

"At this stage of my reflections I endeavored to remember, and *did* remember, with entire distinctness, every incident which occurred about the period in question. The weather **39** was chilly (oh rare and happy accident!), and a fire was blazing on the hearth. I was heated with exercise and sat near the table. You, however, had drawn a chair close to the chimney. Just as I placed the parchment in your hand, and as you were in the act of inspecting it, Wolf, the Newfoundland, entered, and leaped upon your shoulders. With your left hand you caressed him and kept him off, while your right, holding the parchment, was permitted to fall listlessly between your knees, and in close proximity to the fire. At one moment I thought the blaze had caught it, and was about to caution you, but, before I could speak, you had withdrawn it, and were engaged in its examination. When I considered all these particulars, I doubted not for a moment that *heat* had been the agent in bringing to light, on the parchment, the skull which I saw designed on it. You are well aware that chemical preparations exist, and have existed time out of mine, by means of which it is possible to write on either paper or vellum, so that the characters shall become visible only when subjected to the action of fire. Zaffre, digested in *aqua regia*, and diluted with four times its weight of water, is sometimes employed; a green tint results. The regulus of cobalt, dissolved in spirit of nitre, gives a red. These colors disappear at longer or shorter **40**

38 He is the man of genius *par excellence*, if a bit overbearing at the moment.

39 It is one of the marks of the true detective that he notices and remembers almost everything.

40 An article in Reese's Cyclopaedia on "ink" apparently supplied the information here. Zaffre is a blue pigment from cobalt ore, roasted with silica. Aqua regia is a mixture of nitric and hydrochloric acids that dissolves gold. A regulus is the more or less impure mass of metal formed beneath the slag in smelting and reducing ores. These latter terms are from alchemy, further boosting St. Armand's argument for an alchemical interpretation of the tale (note 22).

41 "Caloric" is an archaic word for heat.

42 William Kidd (1645?–1701) was born in Scotland and went to sea while still very young. He later settled in New York, where he married. He was commissioned by the governor of that colony to defend English ships from pirates in the Red Sea and the Indian Ocean, and in 1697 went to Madagascar. A series of events, including disease, mutiny, and a paucity of prizes, apparently decided him to take up piracy himself. He attempted later to clear himself of piracy charges in New York by pointing out that the ships he attacked were lawful prizes, but he was arrested in 1697 and sent to England, where he was tried on five charges of piracy and one of murder.

Some historians say the trial was unfair, and it *was* complicated by the fact that the four Whig peers who had backed him earlier were now politically embarrassed by his career and wanted him out of the way. He was convicted of murder and three charges of piracy, and hanged—twice. The first time, his luck held. The second time, the rope did.

The legends of Kidd's treasure are unsubstantiated but still very much with us. In the past twenty-five years alone, numerous attempts have been launched to uncover the horde of gold and jewels supposedly buried somewhere along the eastern seaboard.

43 He's aware, it seems, of the strain on our belief. Poe has him at least state the problem and then move on without comment, so the damage is blunted and we can't really say he's putting something over on us.

intervals after the material written on cools, but again become apparent upon the reapplication of heat.

"I now scrutinized the death's-head with care. Its outer edges—the edges of the drawing nearest the edge of the vellum—were far more *distinct* than the others. It was clear **41** that the action of the caloric had been imperfect or unequal. I immediately kindled a fire, and subjected every portion of the parchment to a glowing heat. At first, the only effect was the strengthening of the faint lines in the skull; but, on persevering in the experiment, there became visible, at the corner of the slip, diagonally opposite to the spot in which the death's-head was delineated, the figure of what I at first supposed to be a goat. A closer scrutiny, however, satisfied me that it was intended for a kid."

"Ha! ha!" said I, "to be sure I have no right to laugh at you—a million and a half of money is too serious a matter for mirth—but you are not about to establish a third link in your chain—you will not find any especial connexion between your pirates and a goat—pirates, you know, have nothing to do with goats; they appertain to the farming interest."

"But I have just said that the figure was *not* that of a goat."

"Well, a kid then—pretty much the same thing."

"Pretty much, but not altogether," said Legrand. "You may **42** have heard of one *Captain* Kidd. I at once looked on the figure of the animal as a kind of punning or hieroglyphical signature. I say signature; because its position on the vellum suggested this idea. The death's-head at the corner diagonally opposite, had, in the same manner, the air of a stamp, or seal. But I was sorely put out by the absence of all else—of the body to my imagined instrument—of the text for my context."

"I presume you expected to find a letter between the stamp and the signature."

"Something of that kind. The fact is, I felt irresistibly impressed with a presentiment of some vast good fortune impending. I can scarcely say why. Perhaps, after all, it was rather a desire than an actual belief;—but do you know that Jupiter's silly words, about the bug being of solid gold, had a remarkable effect on my fancy? And then the series of **43** accidents and coincidences—these were so *very* extraordinary. Do you observe how mere an accident it was that these events should have occurred on the *sole* day of all the year in which it has been, or may be, sufficiently cool for fire, and that without the fire, or without the intervention of the dog at the precise moment in which he appeared, I should never have become aware of the death's-head, and so never the possessor of the treasure?"

"But proceed—I am all impatience."

"Well; you have heard, of course, the many stories current—the thousand vague rumors afloat about money buried, somewhere on the Atlantic coast, by Kidd and his associates. These rumors must have had some foundation in fact. And that the rumors have existed so long and so continuously, could have resulted, it appeared to me, only from the circumstance of the buried treasure still *remaining* entombed. Had Kidd concealed his plunder for a time, and afterwards reclaimed it, the rumors would scarcely have reached us in their present unvarying form. You will observe that the stories told are all about money-seekers, not about money-finders. Had the pirate recovered his money, there the affair would have dropped. It seemed to me that some accident—say the loss of a memorandum indicating its locality—had deprived him of the means of recovering it, and that this accident had become known to his followers, who otherwise might never have heard that treasure had been concealed at all, and who, busying themselves in vain, because unguided attempts, to regain it, had given first birth, and then universal currency, to the reports which are now so common. Have you ever heard of any important treasure being unearthed along the coast?"

"Never."

"But that Kidd's accumulations were immense, is well known. I took it for granted, therefore, that the earth still held them; and you will scarcely be surprised when I tell you that I felt a hope, nearly amounting to certainty, that the parchment so strangely found, involved a lost record of the place of deposit."

"But how did you proceed?"

"I held the vellum again to the fire, after increasing the **44** heat; but nothing appeared. I now thought it possible that the coating of dirt might have something to do with the failure; so I carefully rinsed the parchment by pouring warm water over it, and, having done this, I placed it in a tin pan, with the skull downwards, and put the pan upon a furnace of lighted charcoal. In a few minutes, the pan having become thoroughly heated, I removed the slip, and, to my inexpressible joy, found it spotted, in several places, with what appeared to be figures arranged in lines. Again I placed it in the pan, and suffered it to remain another minute. On taking it off, the whole was just as you see it now."

Here Legrand, having re-heated the parchment, submitted it to my inspection. The following characters were rudely traced, in a red tint, between the death's-head and the goat:

53‡‡†305))6* ;4826)4‡.)4‡) ;806* ;48†8 ¶60))85;;]8* ;:‡
8†83(88) 5† ;46(;88*96*?;8) *‡(;485) ;5*†2:*‡(;4956*2(5*
—4) 8¶8* ;4069285) ;)6†8)4‡‡;1 (‡9;48081 ;8:8‡1 ;48†85;4)
485†528806*81 (‡9;48;(88;4 (‡?34;48)4‡;161;:188;‡?;

"But," said I, returning him the slip, "I am as much in the dark as ever. Were all the jewels of Golconda awaiting me on **45** my solution of this enigma, I am quite sure that I should be unable to earn them."

"And yet," said Legrand, "the solution is by no means so difficult as you might be led to imagine from the first hasty inspection of the characters. These characters, as any one might readily guess, form a cipher—that is to say, they convey a meaning; but then, from what is known of Kidd, I could not suppose him capable of constructing any of the more abstruse cryptographs. I made up my mind, at once, that this was of **46** a simple species—such, however, as would appear, to the

44 Vellum is an excellent grade of parchment.

45 An ancient, deserted city of southeast India, famous for its treasures, although its diamond troves are largely legendary.

46 Poe's use of the word is the first recorded by the O.E.D., although the word "cryptography" is found in David Arnold Conradus' article "*Cryptographica Denudata*," in the *Gentleman's Magazine* for 1742. Poe obviously knew the article, for his wording here is similar to that of Conradus.

crude intellect of the sailor, absolutely insoluble without the key."

"And you really solved it?"

"Readily; I have solved others of an abstruseness ten thousand times greater. Circumstances, and a certain bias of mind, have led me to take interest in such riddles, and it may well be doubted whether human ingenuity can construct an enigma of the kind which human ingenuity may not, by proper application, resolve. In fact, having once established connected and legible characters, I scarcely gave a thought to the mere difficulty of developing their import.

"In the present case—indeed in all cases of secret writing—the first question regards the *language* of the cipher; for the principles of solution, so far, especially, as the more simple ciphers are concerned, depend on, and are varied by, the genius of the particular idiom. In general, there is no alternative but experiment (directed by probabilities) of every tongue known to him who attempts the solution, until the true one be attained. But, with the cipher now before us, all difficulty is removed by the signature. The pun on the word 'Kidd' is appreciable in no other language than the English. But for this consideration I should have begun my attempts with the Spanish and French, as the tongues in which a secret of this kind would most naturally have been written by a pirate of the Spanish main. As it was, I assumed the cryptograph to be English.

"You observe there are no divisions between the words. Had there been divisions, the task would have been comparatively easy. In such case I should have commenced with a collation and analysis of the shorter words, and, had a word of a single letter occurred, as is most likely, (*a* or *I*, for example,) I should have considered the solution as assured. But, there being no division, my first step was to ascertain the predominant letters, as well as the least frequent. Counting all, I constructed a table, thus:

Of the character 8 there are 33.

;	"	26.
4	"	19.
‡)	"	16.
*	"	13.
5	"	12.
6	"	11.
† 1	"	8.
0	"	6.
9 2	"	5.
: 3	"	4.
?	"	3.
¶	"	2.
—.	"	1.

47 "Now, in English, the letter which most frequently occurs is *e*. Afterwards, the succession runs thus: *a o i d h n r s t u y c f g l m w b k p q x z*. E, however, predominates so remarkably that an individual sentence of any length is rarely seen, in which it is not the prevailing character.

---

47 Conradus also mentions the frequency of the letter *e*.

"Here, then, we have, in the very beginning, the ground-work for something more than a mere guess. The general use which may be made of the table is obvious—but, in this particular cipher, we shall only very partially require its aid. As our predominant character is 8, we will commence by assuming it as the *e* of the natural alphabet. To verify the supposition, let us observe if the 8 be seen often in couples—for *e* is doubled with great frequency in English—in such words, for example, as 'meet,' 'fleet,' 'speed,' 'seen,' 'been,' 'agree,' &c. In the present instance we see it doubled no less than five times, although the cryptograph is brief.

"Let us assume 8, then, as *e*. Now, of all *words* in the language, 'the' is most usual; let us see, therefore, whether there are not repetitions of any three characters, in the same order of collocation, the last of them being 8. If we discover repetitions of such letters, so arranged, they will most probably represent the word 'the.' On inspection we find no less than seven such arrangements, the characters being ;48. We may, therefore, assume that the semicolon represents *t*, that 4 represents *h*, and that 8 represents *e*—the last being now well confirmed. Thus a great step has been taken.

"But, having established a single word, we are enabled to establish a vastly important point; that is to say, several commencements and terminations of other words. Let us refer, for example, to the last instance but one, in which the combination ;48 occurs—not far from the end of the cipher. We know that the semicolon immediately ensuing is the commencement of a word, and, of the six characters succeeding this 'the,' we are cognizant of no less than five. Let us set these characters down, thus, by the letters we know them to represent, leaving a space for the unknown—

t eeth.

"Here we are enabled, at once, to discard the '*th*,' as forming no portion of the word commencing with the first *t*; since, by experiment of the entire alphabet for a letter adapted to the vacancy we perceive that no word can be formed of which this *th* can be a part. We are thus narrowed into

t ee,

and, going through the alphabet, if necessary, as before, we arrive at the word 'tree,' as the sole possible reading. We thus gain another letter, *r*, represented by (, with the words 'the tree' in juxtaposition.

"Looking beyond these words, for a short distance, we again see the combination of ;48, and employ it by way of *termination* to what immediately precedes. We have thus this arrangement:

the tree;4 (‡?34 the,

or, substituting the natural letters, where known, it reads thus:

the tree thr ‡?3h the.

"Now, if, in place of the unknown characters, we leave blank spaces, or substitute dots, we read thus:

the tree thr . . . h the,

when the word '*through*' makes itself evident at once. But this discovery gives us three new letters, *o*, *u* and *g*, represented by ‡? and 3.

"Looking now, narrowly, through the cipher for combinations of known characters, we find, not very far from the beginning, this arrangement,

83(88, or egree,

which, plainly, is the conclusion of the word 'degree,' and gives us another letter, *d*, represented by †.

"Four letters beyond the word 'degree,' we perceive the combination

;46(;88*

"Translating the known characters, and representing the unknown by dots, as before, we read thus:

th.rtee.

an arrangement immediately suggestive of the word 'thirteen,' and again furnishing us with two new characters, *i* and *n*, represented by 6 and *.

"Referring, now, to the beginning of the cryptograph, we find the combination,

53‡‡†.

"Translating, as before, we obtain

.good,

which assures us that the first letter is A, and that the first two words are 'A good.'

"To avoid confusion, it is now time that we arrange our key, as far as discovered, in a tabular form. It will stand thus:

5	represents	a
†	"	d
8	"	e
3	"	g
4	"	h
6	"	i
*	"	n
‡	"	o
(	"	r
;	"	t

"We have, therefore, no less than ten of the most important letters represented, and it will be unnecessary to proceed with the details of the solution. I have said enough to convince you that ciphers of this nature are readily soluble, and to give you some insight into the *rationale* of their development. But be assured that the specimen before us appertains to the very simplest species of cryptograph. It now only remains to give you the full translation of the characters upon the parchment, as unriddled. Here it is:

'*A good glass in the bishop's hostel in the devil's seat twenty-one degrees and thirteen minutes northeast and by north main branch seventh limb east side shoot from the left eye of the death's-head a bee line from the tree through the shot fifty feet out.*' "

"But," said I, "the enigma seems still in as bad a condition as ever. How is it possible to extort a meaning from all this jargon about 'devil's seats,' 'death's-heads,' and 'bishop's hotels?' "

"I confess," replied Legrand, "that the matter still wears a serious aspect, when regarded with a casual glance. My first endeavor was to divide the sentence into the natural division intended by the cryptographist."

"You mean, to punctuate it?"

"Something of that kind."

"But how was it possible to effect this?"

"I reflected that it had been a *point* with the writer to run his words together without division, so as to increase the difficulty of solution. Now, a not over-acute man, in pursuing such an object, would be nearly certain to overdo the matter. When, in the course of his composition, he arrived at a break in his subject which would naturally require a pause, or a point, he would be exceedingly apt to run his characters, at this place, more than usually close together. If you will observe the MS., in the present instance you will easily detect five such cases of unusual crowding. Acting on this hint, I made the division thus:

" '*A good glass in the Bishop's hostel in the Devil's seat— twenty-one degrees and thirteen minutes—northeast and by north—main branch seventh limb east side—shoot from the left eye of the death's-head—a bee-line from the tree through the shot fifty feet out.*' "

"Even this division," said I, "leaves me still in the dark."

"It left me also in the dark," replied Legrand, "for a few days; during which I made diligent inquiry, in the neighborhood of Sullivan's Island, for any building which went by the name of the 'Bishop's Hotel;' for, of course I dropped the obsolete word 'hostel.' Gaining no information on the subject, I was on the point of extending my sphere of search, and proceeding in a more systematic manner, when, one morning, it entered into my head, quite suddenly, that this 'Bishop's Hostel' might have some reference to an old family, of the name of Bessop, which, time out of mind, had held possession **48** of an ancient manor-house, about four miles to the northward of the Island. I accordingly went over to the plantation, and re-instituted my inquiries among the older negroes of the place. At length one of the most aged of the women said that she had heard of such a place as *Bessop's Castle*, and thought that she could guide me to it, but that it was not a castle, nor a tavern, but a high rock.

"I offered to pay her well for her trouble, and, after some demur, she consented to accompany me to the spot. We found it without much difficulty, when, dismissing her, I proceeded to examine the place. The 'castle' consisted of an irregular assemblage of cliffs and rocks—one of the latter being quite remarkable for its height as well as for its insulated and artificial appearance. I clambered to its apex, and then felt much at a loss as to what should be next done.

"While I was busied in reflection, my eyes fell upon a narrow ledge in the eastern face of the rock, perhaps a yard below the summit on which I stood. This ledge projected about eighteen inches, and was not more than a foot wide, while a niche in the cliff just above it, gave it a rude resemblance to one of the hollow-backed chairs used by our ancestors. I made no doubt that here was the 'devil's seat' **49**

48 Poe made the name up, no doubt, since no one has been able to trace any Bessop to South Carolina, Baltimore, Philadelphia, Richmond, or anywhere else.

49 Naming natural features after the Devil seems to be a pastime of long standing—e.g., the Devil's Postpile, Devil's Tower, Devil's Slide, Devil's Canyon, Devil's Island, Devil's Lake. Perhaps someone ought to investigate this phenomenon.

alluded to in the MS., and now I seemed to grasp the full secret of the riddle.

"The 'good glass,' I knew, could have reference to nothing but a telescope; for the word 'glass' is rarely employed in any other sense by seamen. Now here, I at once saw, was a telescope to be used, and a definite point of view, *admitting no variation*, from which to use it. Nor did I hesitate to believe that the phrases, 'twenty-one degrees and thirteen minutes,' and 'northeast and by north,' were intended as directions for the levelling of the glass. Greatly excited by these discoveries, I hurried home, procured a telescope, and returned to the rock.

"I let myself down to the ledge, and found that it was impossible to retain a seat on it unless in one particular position. This fact confirmed my preconceived idea. I proceeded to use the glass. Of course, the 'twenty-one degrees and thirteen minutes' could allude to nothing but elevation above the visible horizon, since the horizontal direction was clearly indicated by the words, 'northeast and by north.' This latter direction I at once established by means of a pocket-compass; then, pointing the glass as nearly at an angle of twenty-one degrees of elevation as I could do it by guess, I moved it cautiously up or down, until my attention was arested by a circular rift or opening in the foliage of a large tree that overtopped its fellows in the distance. In the centre of this rift I perceived a white spot, but could not, at first, distinguish what it was. Adjusting the focus of the telescope, I again looked, and now made it out to be a human skull.

"On this discovery I was so sanguine as to consider the enigma solved for the phrase 'main branch, seventh limb, east side,' could refer only to the position of the skull on the tree, while 'shoot from the left eye of the death's-head' admitted, also, of but one interpretation, in regard to a search for buried treasure. I perceived that the design was to drop a bullet from the left eye of the skull, and that a bee-line, or, in other words, a straight line, drawn from the nearest point of the trunk through 'the shot,' (or the spot where the bullet fell,) and thence extended to a distance of fifty feet, would indicate a definite point—and beneath this point I thought it at least possible that a deposit of value lay concealed."

"All this," I said, "is exceedingly clear, and, although ingenious, still simple and explicit. When you left the Bishop's Hotel, what then?"

"Why, having carefully taken the bearings of the tree, I turned homewards. The instant that I left 'the devil's seat,' however, the circular rift vanished; nor could I get a glimpse of it afterwards, turn as I would. What seems to me the chief ingenuity in this whole business, is the fact (for repeated experiment has convinced me it *is* a fact) that the circular opening in question is visible from no other attainable point of view than that afforded by the narrow ledge on the face of the rock.

"In this expedition to the 'Bishop's Hotel' I had been attended by Jupiter, who had, no doubt, observed, for some weeks past, the abstraction of my demeanor, and took especial care not to leave me alone. But, on the next day, getting up very early, I contrived to give him the slip, and went into the hills in search of the tree. After much toil I found it. When I came home at night my valet proposed to give me a flogging. With the rest of the adventure I believe you are as well acquainted as myself."

"I suppose," said I, "you missed the spot, in the first attempt at digging, through Jupiter's stupidity in letting the bug fall through the right instead of through the left eye of the skull."

"Precisely. This mistake made a difference of about two inches and a half in the 'shot'—that is to say, in the position of the peg nearest the tree; and had the treasure been *beneath* the 'shot,' the error would have been of little moment; but 'the shot,' together with the nearest point of the tree, were merely two points for the establishment of a line of direction; of course the error, however trivial in the beginning, increased as we proceeded with the line, and by the time we had gone fifty feet, threw us quite off the scent. But for my deep-seated conviction that treasure was here somewhere actually buried, we might have had all our labor in vain."

"I presume the fancy of *the skull*, of letting fall a bullet through the skull's eye—was suggested to Kidd by the piratical flag. No doubt he felt a kind of poetical consistency in recovering his money through this ominous insignium."

"Perhaps so; still I cannot help thinking that common-sense had quite as much to do with the matter as poetical consistency. To be visible from the devil's seat, it was necessary that the object, if small, should be white; and there is nothing like your human skull for retaining and even increasing its whiteness under exposure to all vicissitudes of weather."

"But your grandiloquence, and your conduct in swinging the beetle—how excessively odd! I was sure you were mad. And why did you insist on letting fall the bug, instead of a bullet, from the skull?"

"Why, to be frank, I felt somewhat annoyed by your evident suspicions touching my sanity, and so resolved to punish you quietly, in my own way, by a little bit of sober mystification. **50** For this reason I swung the beetle, and for this reason I let it fall from the tree. An observation of yours about its great weight suggested the latter idea."

"Yes, I perceive; and now there is only one point which puzzles me. What are we to make of the skeletons found in the hole?"

"That is a question I am no more able to answer than yourself. There seems, however, only one plausible way of accounting for them—and yet it is dreadful to believe in such atrocity as my suggestion would imply. It is clear that Kidd—if Kidd indeed secreted this treasure, which I doubt not—it is clear that he must have had assistance in the labor. But, the worst of this labor concluded, he may have thought it expedient to remove all participants in his secret. Perhaps a couple of blows with a mattock were sufficient, while his coadjutors **51** were busy in the pit; perhaps it required a dozen—who shall tell?"

50 Legrand, like Poe, is a showman at heart.

51 A digging tool with features of adz, ax, and pick.

THE OBLONG BOX

First published in *Godey's Lady's Book*, September 1844.

As a tale of terror, this is certainly one of Poe's less effective efforts, but if we read it as a mystery story it fares better. For the narrator is very much like that of the Dupin stories—except that he does not have the help of the superior mind of the French detective. The result is disastrous, much as might have been the case in "Murders" or "The Purloined Letter" had not Dupin been present to solve the mysteries.

The sources of "The Oblong Box" have been traced fairly readily. The ending is almost straight from *Geraldine*, a poem by Rufus Dawes, and none too good a poem at that. Poe reviewed Dawes's work, quoting from the last stanza of *Geraldine:* "He saw her, kissed her cheek, and wildly flung/His arms around her with a mad'ning throw—/Then plunged within the cold unfathomed deep/While sirens sang their victim to his sleep."

Poe called the poem "preposterous," but obviously the situation stuck in his mind, perhaps with a half-formed idea of how to build and improve upon it.

Some of the tale also involves a true case of the day, in which John C. Colt (brother of the revolver inventor) murdered a creditor, packed his body in salt, and shipped it to St. Louis by way of New Orleans. Colt was sentenced to hang but killed himself first.

Other sources include "The Picture," by John Frost, published in *Burton's Magazine* in June 1840, in which a man buys a picture of the Madonna for five dollars. After saving it from his sinking ship he discovers it to be worth a fortune. As for the title, Poe may have seen it in "A Tale of a Nose," by Edward Vernon Sparhawk, in the *Southern Literary Messenger*, April 1835, in this description of the berths in a packetboat: "Settees, cots, and a kind of oblong box, having thin mattresses spread over them, with a sheet and blanket perhaps, are wedged together, each calculated to hold the body of a human being by the most scanty and economical measurement."

In the 1969 British-American film *The Oblong Box*, directed by Gordon Hessler and starring Vincent Price and Christopher Lee, only the tile is the same—the new plot has to do with a witchdoctor whose medicine makes a madman appear dead. The results alternate between tepid and ridiculous.

Actor Ugo Toppo has recorded the tale (CMS 567).

---

1 Poe's familiarity with Charleston was also put to good use in "The Gold-Bug."

2 Packet boat, from the French *paquebot,* a boat or vessel sailing at regular intervals between two ports in order to carry mail, goods, and passengers. There was a packet boat *Independence,* launched in 1834, but it sailed between New York and Liverpool. No real Captain Hardy has been found.

3 Charlottesville University perhaps, although the hero of "The Picture" went to Cambridge.

1 Some years ago, I engaged passage from Charleston, S. C., to the city of New York, in the fine packet-ship "Independ-

2 ence," Captain Hardy. We were to sail on the fifteenth of the month (June), weather permitting; and, on the fourteenth, I went on board to arrange some matters in my state-room.

I found that we were to have a great many passengers, including a more than usual number of ladies. On the list were several of my acquaintances; and among other names, I was rejoiced to see that of Mr. Cornelius Wyatt, a young artist, for whom I entertained feelings of warm friendship. He

3 had been with me a fellow-student at C—— University, where we were very much together. He had the ordinary temperament of genius, and was a compound of misanthropy, sensi-

bility, and enthusiasm. To these qualities he united the warmest and truest heart which ever beat in a human bosom.

I observed that his name was carded upon *three* state-rooms: and, upon again referring to the list of passengers, I found that he had engaged passage for himself, wife, and two sisters—his own. The state-rooms were sufficiently roomy, and each had two berths, one above the other. These berths, to be sure, were so exceedingly narrow as to be insufficient for more than one person; still, I could not comprehend why there were *three* state-rooms for these four persons. I was, just at that epoch, in one of those moody frames of mind which make a man abnormally inquisitive about trifles: and I confess, with shame, that I busied myself in a variety of ill-bred and preposterous conjectures about this matter of the supernumerary state-room. It was no business of mine, to be sure; but **4** with none the less pertinacity did I occupy myself in attempts to resolve the enigma. At last I reached a conclusion which wrought in me great wonder why I had not arrived at it before. "It is a servant, of course," I said; "What a fool I am, not sooner to have thought of so obvious a solution!" And then I **5** again repaired to the list—but here I saw distinctly that *no* servant was to come with the party: although, in fact, it had been the original design to bring one—for the words "and servant" had been first written and then overscored. "Oh, extra baggage, to be sure," I now said to myself—"something he wishes not to be put in the hold—something to be kept under his own eye—ah, I have it—a painting or so—and this is what he has been bargaining about with Nicolino, the Italian **6** Jew." This idea satisfied me, and I dismissed my curiosity for the nonce.

Wyatt's two sisters I knew very well, and most amiable and clever girls they were. His wife he had newly married, and I had never yet seen her. He had often talked about her in my presence, however, and in his usual style of enthusiasm. He described her as of surpassing beauty, wit, and accomplishment. I was, therefore, quite anxious to make her acquaintance.

On the day in which I visited the ship (the fourteenth), Wyatt and party were also to visit it—so the captain informed me,—and I waited on board an hour longer than I had designed, in hope of being presented to the bride; but then an apology came. "Mrs. W. was a little indisposed, and would decline coming on board until to-morrow, at the hour of sailing."

The morrow having arrived, I was going from my hotel to the wharf, when Captain Hardy met me and said that, "owing to circumstances" (a stupid but convenient phrase), "he rather thought the 'Independence' would not sail for a day or two, and that when all was ready, he would send up and let me know." This I thought strange, for there was a stiff southerly breeze; but as "the circumstances" were not forthcoming, although I pumped for them with much perseverance, I had nothing to do but to return home and digest my impatience at leisure.

I did not receive the expected message from the captain for

4 The narrator is inquisitive and observant, but too quick to a conclusion. He also falls into the very trap explained by Dupin in "The Purloined Letter": confusing the artist's motives and actions with what he would do in the same situation. He should put himself in the artist's position—and in his mind.

5 He's still a fool; he just doesn't realize it yet.

6 Poe may have borrowed the name from Jose Nicolini (1788–1855), an Italian poet who translated Byron. Poe mentions him in a review in the *Southern Literary Messenger*, January 1836.

Captain Hardy. *Artist unknown*

nearly a week. It came at length, however, and I immediately went on board. The ship was crowded with passengers, and every thing was in the bustle attendant upon making sail. Wyatt's party arrived in about ten minutes after myself. There were the two sisters, the bride, and the artist—the latter in one of his customary fits of moody misanthropy, I was too well used to these, however, to pay them any special attention. He did not even introduce me to his wife;—this courtesy devolving, per force, upon his sister Marian—a very sweet and intelligent girl, who, in a few hurried words, made us acquainted.

Mrs. Wyatt had been closely veiled; and when she raised her veil, in acknowledging my bow, I confess that I was very profoundly astonished. I should have been much more so, however, had not long experience advised me not to trust, with too implicit a reliance, the enthusiastic descriptions of my friend, the artist, when indulging in comments upon the loveliness of woman. When beauty was the theme, I well knew with what facility he soared into the regions of the purely ideal.

The truth is, I could not help regarding Mrs. Wyatt as a decidedly plain-looking woman. If not positively ugly, she was not, I think, very far from it. She was dressed, however, in exquisite taste—and then I had no doubt that she had captivated my friend's heart by the more enduring graces of the intellect and soul. She said very few words, and passed at once into her state-room with Mr. W.

My old inquisitiveness now returned. There was *no* servant—*that* was a settled point. I looked, therefore, for the extra baggage. After some delay, a cart arrived at the wharf, with an oblong pine box, which was every thing that seemed to be expected. Immediately upon its arrival we made sail, and in a short time were safely over the bar and standing out to sea.

The box in question was, as I say, oblong. It was about six feet in length by two and a half in breadth;—I observed it attentively, and like to be precise. Now this shape was *peculiar*; and no sooner had I seen it, than I took credit to myself for the accuracy of my guessing. I had reached the conclusion, it will be remembered, that the extra baggage of my friend, the artist, would prove to be pictures, or at least a picture; for I knew he had been for several weeks in conference with Nicolino:—and now here was a box, which, from its shape, *could* possibly contain nothing in the world but a copy of Leonardo's "Last Supper"; and a copy of this very "Last Supper," done by Rubini the younger, at Florence, I had known, for some time, to be in the possession of Nicolino. This point, therefore, I considered as sufficiently settled. I chuckled excessively when I thought of my acumen. It was the first time I had ever known Wyatt to keep from me any of his artistical secrets; but here he evidently intended to steal a march upon me, and smuggle a fine picture to New York, under my very nose; expecting me to know nothing of the matter. I resolved to quiz him *well*, now and hereafter.

One thing, however, annoyed me not a little. The box did *not* go into the extra state-room. It was deposited in Wyatt's

7 Again note the similarity between his thought patterns and those of the narrator and the prefect in "The Purloined Letter" as they sift through the evidence.

8 Perhaps suggested by Giovanni Rubini (1794–1854), an Italian tenor whom he must have read about in the memoirs of Madame Malibran, noted in "The Spectacles."

9 Compare with "The Tell-Tale Heart": ". . . he did not even dream of my secret deeds or thoughts. I fairly chuckled at the idea."

own; and there, too, it remained, occupying very nearly the whole of the floor—no doubt to the exceeding discomfort of the artist and his wife;—this the more especially as the tar or paint with which it was lettered in sprawling capitals, emitted a strong, disagreeable, and, to *my* fancy, a peculiarly disgusting odor. On the lid were painted the words—"*Mrs. Adelaide Curtis, Albany, New York. Charge of Cornelius Wyatt, Esq. This side up. To be handled with care.*"

Now, I was aware that Mrs. Adelaide Curtis, of Albany, was the artist's wife's mother;—but then I looked upon the whole address as a mystification, intended especially for myself. I made up my mind, of course, that the box and contents would never get farther north than the studio of my misanthropic friend, in Chambers Street, New York. **10**

For the first three or four days we had fine weather, although the wind was dead ahead; having chopped round to the northward, immediately upon our losing sight of the coast. The passengers were, consequently, in high spirits and disposed to be social. I *must* except, however, Wyatt and his sisters, who behaved stiffly, and, I could not help thinking, uncourteously to the rest of the party. *Wyatt's* conduct I did not so much regard. He was gloomy, even beyond his usual habit—in fact he was *morose*—but in him I was prepared for eccentricity. For the sisters, however, I could make no excuse. They secluded themselves in their state-rooms during the greater part of the passage, and absolutely refused, although I repeatedly urged them, to hold communication with any person on board.

Mrs. Wyatt herself was far more agreeable. That is to say, she was *chatty*; and to be chatty is no slight recommendation at sea. She became *excessively* intimate with most of the ladies; and, to my profound astonishment, evinced no equivocal disposition to coquet with the men. She amused us all very much. I say "*amused*"—and scarcely know how to explain myself. The truth is, I soon found that Mrs. W. was far oftener laughed at than *with*. The gentlemen said little about her; but the ladies, in a little while, pronounced her "a good-hearted thing, rather indifferent-looking, totally uneducated, and decidedly vulgar." The great wonder was, how Wyatt had been entrapped into such a match. Wealth was the general solution—but this I knew to be no solution at all; for Wyatt had told me that she neither brought him a dollar nor had any expectations from any source whatever. "He had married," he said, "for love, and for love only; and his bride was far more than worthy of his love." When I thought of these expressions, on the part of my friend, I confess that I felt indescribably puzzled. Could it be possible that he was taking leave of his senses? What else could I think? *He*, so refined, so intellectual, so fastidious, with so exquisite a perception of the faulty, and so keen an appreciation of the beautiful! To be sure, the lady seemed especially fond of *him*—particularly so in his absence—when she made herself ridiculous by frequent quotations of what had been said by her "beloved husband, Mr. Wyatt." The word "husband" seemed forever—to use one of her own delicate expressions—forever "on the tip of her tongue." In

10 Although no Adelaide Curtis has been traced, Chambers Street in New York happens to be the one from which the box bearing the body of the creditor killed by Colt left New York.

. . . to my profound astonishment, [she] evinced no equivocal disposition to coquet with the men. *Artist unknown*

the meantime, it was observed by all on board, that he avoided *her* in the most pointed manner, and, for the most part, shut himself up alone in his state-room, where, in fact, he might have been said to live altogether, leaving his wife at full liberty to amuse herself as she thought best, in the public society of the main cabin.

My conclusion, from what I saw and heard, was, that the artist, by some unaccountable freak of fate, or perhaps in some fit of enthusiastic and fanciful passion, had been induced to unite himself with a person altogether beneath him, and that the natural result, entire and speedy disgust had ensued. I pitied him from the bottom of my heart—but could not, for that reason, quite forgive his incommunicativeness in the matter of the "Last Supper." For this I resolved to have my revenge.

One day he came upon deck, and, taking his arm as had been my wont, I sauntered with him backward and forward. His gloom, however (which I considered quite natural under the circumstances), seemed entirely unabated. He said little, and that moodily, and with evident effort. I ventured a jest or two, and he made a sickening attempt at a smile. Poor fellow!—as I thought of *his wife*, I wondered that he could have heart to put on even the semblance of mirth. At last I ventured a home thrust. I determined to commence a series of covert insinuations, or innuendoes, about the oblong box— just to let him perceive, gradually, that I was *not* altogether the butt, or victim, of his little bit of pleasant mystification.

11 My first observation was by way of opening a masked battery. I said something about the "peculiar shape of *that* box"; and, as I spoke the words, I smiled knowingly, winked, and touched him gently with my forefinger in the ribs.

The manner in which Wyatt received this harmless pleasantry convinced me, at once, that he was mad. At first he stared at me as if he found it impossible to comprehend the witticism of my remark; but as its point seemed slowly to make its way into his brain, his eyes, in the same proportion, seemed protruding from their sockets. Then he grew very red—then hideously pale—then, as if highly amused with what I had insinuated, he began a loud and boisterous laugh, which, to my astonishment, he kept up, with gradually increasing vigor, for ten minutes or more. In conclusion, he fell flat and heavily upon the deck. When I ran to uplift him, to all appearance he was *dead*.

I called assistance, and, with much difficulty, we brought him to himself. Upon reviving he spoke incoherently for some time. At length we bled him and put him to bed. The next morning he was quite recovered, so far as regarded his mere bodily health. Of his mind I say nothing, of course. I avoided him during the rest of the passage, by advice of the captain, who seemed to coincide with me altogether in my views of his insanity, but cautioned me to say nothing on this head to any person on board.

Several circumstances occurred immediately after this fit of Wyatt's, which contributed to heighten the curiosity with which I was already possessed. Among other things, this: I

11 A concealed cannon emplacement

had been nervous—drank too much strong green tea, and slept ill at night—in fact, for two nights I could not be properly said to sleep at all. Now, my state-room opened into the main cabin, or dining-room, as did those of all the single men on board. Wyatt's three rooms were in the after-cabin, which was separated from the main one by a slight sliding door, never locked even at night. As we were almost constantly on a wind, and the breeze was not a little stiff, the ship heeled to leeward very considerably; and whenever her starboard side was to leeward, the sliding door between the cabins slid open, and so remained, nobody taking the trouble to get up and shut it. But my berth was in such a position, that when my own state-room door was open, as well as the sliding door in question (and my own door was *always* open on account of the heat) I could see into the after-cabin quite distinctly, and just at that portion of it, too, where were situated the state-rooms of Mr. Wyatt. Well, during two nights (*not* consecutive) while I lay awake, I clearly saw Mrs. W., about eleven o'clock upon each night, steal cautiously from the state-room of Mr. W., and enter the extra room, where she remained until daybreak, when she was called by her husband and went back. That they were virtually separated was clear. They had separate apartments—no doubt in contemplation of a more permanent divorce; and here, after all, I thought was the mystery of the extra state-room.

There was another circumstance, too, which interested me much. During the two wakeful nights in question, and immediately after the disappearance of Mrs. Wyatt into the extra state-room, I was attracted by certain singular, cautious, subdued noises in that of her husband. After listening to them for some time, with thoughtful attention, I at length succeeded perfectly in translating their import. They were sounds occasioned by the artist in prying open the oblong box, by means of a chisel and mallet—the latter being apparently muffled, or deadened, by some soft woollen or cotton substance in which its head was enveloped.

In this manner I fancied I could distinguish the precise moment when he fairly disengaged the lid—also, that I could determine when he removed it altogether, and when he deposited it upon the lower berth in his room; this later point I knew, for example, by certain slight taps which the lid made in striking against the wooden edges of the berth, as he endeavored to lay it down *very* gently—there being no room for it on the floor. After this there was a dead stillness, and I heard nothing more, upon either occasion, until nearly daybreak; unless, perhaps, I may mention a low sobbing, or murmuring sound, so very much suppressed as to be nearly inaudible—if, indeed, the whole of this latter noise were not rather produced by my own imagination. I say it seemed to *resemble* sobbing or sighing—but, of course, it could not have been either. I rather think it was a ringing in my own ears. **12** Mr. Wyatt, no doubt, according to custom, was merely giving the rein to one of his hobbies—indulging in one of his fits of artistic enthusiasm. He had opened his oblong box, in order to feast his eyes on the pictorial treasure within. There was

12 Like the narrator of "The Gold-Bug," he assumes all the wrong things from the actions of his acquaintance.

nothing in this, however, to make him *sob*. I repeat, therefore, that it must have been simply a freak of my own fancy, distempered by good Captain Hardy's green tea. Just before dawn, on each of the two nights of which I speak, I distinctly heard Mr. Wyatt replace the lid upon the oblong box, and force the nails into their old places by means of the muffled mallet. Having done this, he issued from his state-room, fully dressed, and proceeded to call Mrs. W. from hers.

13 Cape Hatteras, a promontory on a low, sandy island off eastern North Carolina, is a point of danger to Atlantic shipping because of frequent storms. There has been a lighthouse on the cape since 1798, although the famous barber-pole-striped structure there now dates back only to 1870.

13 We had been at sea seven days, and were now off Cape Hatteras, when there came a tremendously heavy blow from the southwest. We were, in a measure, prepared for it, however, as the weather had been holding out threats for some time. Every thing was made snug, alow and aloft; and as the wind steadily freshened, we lay to, at length, under spanker and foretopsail, both double-reefed.

In this trim we rode safely enough for forty-eight hours— the ship proving herself an excellent sea-boat in many respects, and shipping no water of any consequence. At the end of this period, however, the gale had freshened into a hurricane, and our after-sail split into ribbons, bringing us so much in the trough of the water that we shipped several prodigious seas, one immediately after the other. By this accident we lost three

14 From the German and Dutch, meaning the cook room, or kitchen, of a ship. A spanker is a sail to the rear of a three-masted ship. Double-reefed means rolled and tied down. A foretopsail is the topsail on the mast nearest the bow. Larboard is portside (left). Bulwarks are a protective wall. The staysail is a triangular sail between two masts.

14 men overboard with the caboose, and nearly the whole of the larboard bulwarks. Scarcely had we recovered our senses, before the foretopsail went into shreds, when we got up a storm stay-sail, and with this did pretty well for some hours, the ship heading the sea much more steadily than before.

The gale still held on, however, and we saw no signs of its abating. The rigging was found to be ill-fitted, and greatly strained; and on the third day of the blow, about five in the afternoon, our mizzen-mast, in a heavy lurch to windward, went by the board. For an hour or more, we tried in vain to get rid of it, on account of the prodigious rolling of the ship; and, before we had succeeded, the carpenter came aft and announced four feet water in the hold. To add to our dilemma, we found the pumps choked and nearly useless.

All was now confusion and despair—but an effort was made to lighten the ship by throwing overboard as much of her cargo as could be reached, and by cutting away the two masts that remained. This we at last accomplished—but we were still unable to do any thing at the pumps: and, in the meantime, the leak gained on us very fast.

At sundown, the gale had sensibly diminished in violence, and, as the sea went down with it, we still entertained faint hopes of saving ourselves in the boats. At eight P.M., the clouds broke away to windward, and we had the advantage of a full moon—a piece of good fortune which served wonderfully to cheer our drooping spirits.

After incredible labor we succeeded, at length, in getting the long-boat over the side without material accident, and into this we crowded the whole of the crew and most of the passengers. This party made off immediately, and, after undergoing much suffering, finally arrived, in safety, at Ocra-

15 Ocracoke Inlet lies between Pamlico Sound and the Atlantic, about twenty-five miles southwest of Hatteras. In 1837, the *Home* went down there on its way from New York to Charleston, in one of the worst maritime disasters of the era.

15 coke Inlet, on the third day after the wreck.

Fourteen passengers, with the captain, remained on board, resolving to trust their fortunes to the jolly-boat at the stern. We lowered it without difficulty, although it was only by a miracle that we prevented it from swamping as it touched the water. It contained, when afloat, the captain and his wife, Mr. Wyatt and party, a Mexican officer, wife, four children, and myself, with a negro valet.

We had no room, of course, for any thing except a few positively necessary instruments, some provisions, and the clothes upon our backs. No one had thought of even attempting to save any thing more. What must have been the astonishment of all, then, when, having proceeded a few fathoms from the ship. Mr. Wyatt stood up in the stern-sheets, and coolly demanded of Captain Hardy that the boat should be put back for the purpose of taking in his oblong box!

"Sit down, Mr. Wyatt," replied the captain, somewhat sternly, "you will capsize us if you do not sit quite still. Our gunwale is almost in the water now."

"The box!" vociferated Mr. Wyatt, still standing—"the box I say! Captain Hardy, you cannot, you *will* not refuse me. Its weight will be but a trifle—it is nothing—mere nothing. By the mother who bore you—for the love of Heaven—by your hope of salvation, I *implore* you to put back for the box!" **16**

The captain, for a moment, seemed touched by the earnest appeal of the artist, but he regained his stern composure, and merely said:

"Mr. Wyatt, you are *mad*. I cannot listen to you. Sit down, I say, or you will swamp the boat. Stay—hold him—seize him!—he is about to spring overboard! There—I knew it—he is over!"

As the captain said this, Mr. Wyatt, in fact, spring from the boat, and, as we were yet in the lee of the wreck, succeeded, by almost superhuman exertion, in getting hold of a rope which hung from the fore-chains. In another moment he was on board, and rushing frantically down into the cabin.

In the meantime, we had been swept astern of the ship, and being quite out of her lee, were at the mercy of the tremendous sea which was still running. We made a determined effort to put back, but our little boat was like a feather in the breath of the tempest. We saw at a glance that the doom of the unfortunate artist was sealed.

As our distance from the wreck rapidly increased, the madman (for as such only could we regard him) was seen to emerge from the companionway, up which by dint of strength that appeared gigantic, he dragged, bodily, the oblong box. While we gazed in the extremity of astonishment, he passed, rapidly, several turns of a three-inch rope, first around the box and then around his body. In another instant both body and box were in the sea—disappearing suddenly, at once and forever.

We lingered awhile sadly upon our oars, with our eyes riveted upon the spot. At length we pulled away. The silence remained unbroken for an hour. Finally, I hazarded a remark.

"Did you observe, captain, how suddenly they sank? Was

16 "... tell me—tell me, I implore!/. . . By that Heaven that bends above us—by that God we both adore . . ." (*The Raven*).

In another instant both body and box were in the sea. . . . *Illustration by F. S. Coburn, 1902*

not that an exceedingly singular thing? I confess that I entertained some feeble hope of his final deliverance, when I saw him lash himself to the box, and commit himself to the sea."

"They sank as a matter of course," replied the captain, "and that like a shot. They will soon rise again, however—*but not* **17** *till the salt melts.*"

"The salt!" I ejaculated.

"Hush!" said the captain, pointing to the wife and sisters of the deceased. "We must talk of these things at some more appropriate time."

*   *   *

We suffered much, and made a narrow escape; but fortune befriended *us*, as well as our mates in the long-boat. We landed, in fine, more dead than alive, after four days of intense **18** distress, upon the beach opposite Roanoke Island. We remained here a week, were not ill-treated by the wreckers, and at length obtained a passage to New York.

About a month after the loss of the "Independence," I happened to meet Captain Hardy in Broadway. Our conversation turned, naturally, upon the disaster, and especially upon the sad fate of poor Wyatt. I thus learned the following particulars.

The artist had engaged passage for himself, wife, two sisters and a servant. His wife was, indeed, as she had been represented, a most lovely, and most accomplished woman. On the morning of the fourteenth of June (the day in which I first visited the ship), the lady suddenly sickened and died. The young husband was frantic with grief—but circumstances imperatively forbade the deferring his voyage to New York. It was necessary to take to her mother the corpse of his adored wife, and, on the other hand, the universal prejudice which would prevent his doing so openly was well known. Nine tenths of the passengers would have abandoned the ship rather **19** than take passage with a dead body.

In this dilemma, Captain Hardy arranged that the corpse, being first partially embalmed, and packed, with a large quantity of salt, in a box of suitable dimensions, should be conveyed on board as merchandise. Nothing was to be said of the lady's decease; and, and as it was well understood that Mr. Wyatt had engaged passage for his wife, it became necessary that some person should personate her during the voyage. This the deceased's lady's-maid was easily prevailed on to do. The extra state-room, originally engaged for this girl, during her mistress' life, was now merely retained. In this state-room the pseudo-wife slept, of course, every night. In the daytime she performed, to the best of her ability, the part of her mistress—whose person, it had been carefully ascertained, was unknown to any of the passengers on board.

My own mistake rose, naturally enough, through too care- **20** less, too inquisitive, and too impulsive a temperament. But of late, it is a rare thing that I sleep soundly at night. There is a countenance which haunts me, turn as I will. There is an hysterical laugh which will forever ring within my ears.

17 The body, we learn, was encased in salt to prevent its deterioration. Two things would happen when the salt melted: 1) the box would become lighter as the heavy salt, now dissolved, leaked out; and 2) the body would decompose, creating enough gas inside the coffin to bring it to the surface.

18 Roanoke Island is on the northern coast of North Carolina, in the Croatan Sound, between Albemarle and Pamlico sounds. In Poe's time, many of the island's residents made a living by salvaging wreckage from vessels lost in the area's many storms.

19 Because of putrefaction, or superstition?

20 Exactly the opposite of Dupin

"They will soon rise again, however—*but not till the salt melts.*" Artist unknown

THE PURLOINED LETTER

First published in the *Gift*, December 1844, although a shorter version appeared in Chambers'
Edinburgh Journal, perhaps without Poe's permission, in November 1844.

This is the third and most unified of Poe's tales of ratiocination. Unlike the other two Dupin
mysteries, no murder has been committed here. The crime is known and so is the criminal. The
problem that Dupin faces is that of locating a piece of incriminating evidence in order to protect the
good name of a well-known lady. It is a game of wits that leaves the police, the narrator, and the
reader perplexed, and underscores once again the superiority of Dupin's mind.

It is also (arguably) the most enjoyable of the mystery tales because of its bantering tone and the
complete absence of ghoulish details. The lighter quality adds to the game of cat and mouse between
Dupin and Minister M——, and when the letter has been found and a fake one put in its place, we
feel the distinct pleasure of seeing a smug and vicious man get his comeuppance.

Unlike most of Poe's tales, this one seems to be wholly his own, with no major sources to be
credited.

The story was very popular in France; Sardou wrote a play based on it and saw it performed to
great success at the Gymnase.

In a fairly direct steal, Wilkie Collins uses the basic idea behind "The Purloined Letter" in "The
Stolen Letter" (1854), not even bothering to disguise the title. A fairly trivial piece, it tells how the
son of a haughty squire finds his upcoming marriage to a governess imperiled by a blackmailer who
has in his possession a letter with some damaging information. A clever lawyer (who narrates the
whole piece in a relentlessly self-congratulatory and flippant fashion) manages to find the document
hidden under the carpet of the blackmailer's room. This passage from the tale gives a feeling for the
tone of the story:

" 'Mr. Frank,' says I, 'you came here to get my help and advice in this extremely ticklish business,
and you are ready, as I know without asking, to remunerate me for all and any of my services at the
usual professional rate. Now, I've made up my mind to act boldly—desperately, if you like,—on the
hit or miss, win all or lose all principle—in dealing with this matter. Here is my proposal. I'm going
to try if I can't do Mr. Davager out of his letter. If I don't succeed before tomorrow afternoon, you
hand him the money, and I charge you nothing for professional services. If I do succeed, I hand you
the letter instead of Mr. Davager, and you give me the money instead of giving it to him. It's a
precious risk for me, but I'm ready to run it. You must pay your five hundred anyway. . . ." *(Tales
of Suspense*, Folio Society, 1954; p. 34).

Since the detective is also the narrator, Collins finds it difficult to avoid both the self-congratulatory
air and the problem of arbitrarily withholding evidence, both of which hamper Poe's "Thou Art the
Man" but which he solves in the Dupin stories by using a narrator who is not the protagonist.

Arthur Conan Dlyle, while never copying any of Poe's tales, comes close to the mood and subject
of "The Purloined Letter" in "The Adventure of the Second Stain." In both tales a letter is missing,
a letter that can have serious consequences on matters of state. In each, too, blackmail is indicated.
And in both, the missing letter turns up right under everybody's nose.

1 "Nothing is more disagreeable to wisdom than too much cunning." No source in Seneca's writing has been found.

2 A literal translation of the French *à Paris*, perhaps to suggest the setting of the tale, for Poe uses several unidiomatic (in English) expressions throughout the tale. Unfortunately, they aren't always idiomatic in French, either, for Baudelaire, in his translation of the tales, changes this to "*J'étais à Paris en 18—*" ("I was living in Paris in 18—").

3 A pipe, from the German word for sea foam. Meerschaum is a mineral that looks like white clay, used chiefly for making pipes and cigar and cigarette holders. About as dense as water, lighter pieces of the material sometimes float to shore, giving rise to the mistaken belief that it is petrified sea foam. Before drying, it is relatively soft and can be carved into ornate forms. In French, it's called *écume de mer* (also "sea foam").

4 An American would say the fourth floor.

5 See "The Murders in the Rue Morgue," note 15.

6 Not since July 13, 18—, when the prefect admitted to Dupin that he could not solve the mystery of Marie Rogêt. The year is omitted, as was customary, to add to the feeling of authenticity—to protect the innocent, as it were.

7 Dupin is toying with the prefect, who doesn't seem to catch the play on "reflect" and "dark." Dupin may find it easier to think in the dark because there are fewer distractions. We recall that in "Murders," the narrator and the detective went out only at night.

Henri-Joseph Gisquet was chief of police in Paris from 1831 to 1836.

8 "And simple truth miscall'd simplicity" (Shakespeare, Sonnet 66, line 11).

---

1 Nil sapientiae odiosius acumine nimio.
—Seneca.

2 At Paris, just after dark one gusty evening in the autumn of 18—, I was enjoying the twofold luxury of meditation and a **3** meerschaum, in company with my friend C. Auguste Dupin, **4** in his little back library, or book-closet, *au troisième*, No. 33, **5** Rue Dunot, Faubourg St. Germain. For one hour at least we had maintained a profound silence; while each, to any casual observer, might have seemed intently and exclusively occupied with the curling eddies of smoke that oppressed the atmosphere of the chamber. For myself, however, I was mentally discussing certain topics which had formed matter for conversation between us at an earlier period of the evening; I mean the affair of the Rue Morgue, and the mystery attending the murder of Marie Rogêt. I looked upon it, therefore, as something of a coincidence, when the door of our apartment was thrown open and admitted our old acquaintance, Monsieur G——, the Prefect of the Parisian police.

We gave him a hearty welcome; for there was nearly half as much of the entertaining as of the contemptible about the **6** man, and we had not seen him for several years. We had been sitting in the dark, and Dupin now arose for the purpose of lighting a lamp, but sat down again, without doing so, upon G.'s saying that he had called to consult us, or rather to ask the opinion of my friend, about some official business which had occasioned a great deal of trouble.

"If it is any point requiring reflection," observed Dupin, as he forbore to enkindle the wick, "we shall examine it to better **7** purpose in the dark."

"That is another of your odd notions," said the Prefect, who had a fashion of calling every thing "odd" that was beyond his comprehension, and thus lived amid an absolute legion of "oddities."

"Very true," said Dupin, as he supplied his visiter with a pipe, and rolled towards him a comfortable chair.

"And what is the difficulty now?" I asked. "Nothing more in the assassination way, I hope?"

"Oh no; nothing of that nature. The fact is, the business is *very* simple indeed, and I make no doubt that we can manage it sufficiently well ourselves; but then I thought Dupin would like to hear the details of it, because it is so excessively odd."

"Simple and odd," said Dupin.

"Why, yes; and not exactly that, either. The fact is, we have all been a good deal puzzled because the affair *is* so simple, and yet baffles us altogether."

"Perhaps it is the very simplicity of the thing which puts **8** you at fault," said my friend.

"What nonsense you *do* talk!" replied the Prefect, laughing heartily.

"Perhaps the mystery is a little *too* plain," said Dupin.

"Oh, good heavens! who ever heard of such an idea?"

"A little *too* self-evident."

"Ha! ha! ha!—ha! ha! ha!—ho! ho! ho!"—roared our visiter,

profoundly amused, "oh, Dupin, you will be the death of me yet!"   **9**

"And what, after all, *is* the matter on hand?" I asked.

"Why, I will tell you," replied the Prefect, as he gave a long, steady, and contemplative puff, and settled himself in his chair. "I will tell you in a few words; but, before I begin, let me caution you that this is an affair demanding the greatest secrecy, and that I should most probably lose the position I now hold, were it known that I confided it to any one."

"Proceed," said I.

"Or not," said Dupin.

"Well, then; I have received personal information, from a very high quarter, that a certain document of the last importance, has been purloined from the royal apartments. The   **10** individual who purloined it is known; this beyond a doubt; he was seen to take it. It is known, also, that it still remains in his possession."

"How is this known?" asked Dupin.

"It is clearly inferred," replied the Prefect, "from the nature of the document, and from the non-appearance of certain results which would at once arise from its passing *out* of the robber's possession;—that is to say, from his employing it as he must design in the end to employ it."

"Be a little more explicit," I said.

"Well, I may venture so far as to say that the paper gives its holder a certain power in a certain quarter where such power is immensely valuable." The Prefect was fond of the cant of diplomacy.

"Still I do not quite understand," said Dupin.

"No? Well; the disclosure of the document to a third person, who shall be nameless, would bring in question the honor of a personage of most exalted station; and this fact gives the holder of the document an ascendancy over the illustrious personage whose honor and peace are so jeopardized."

"But this ascendancy," I interposed, "would depend upon the robber's knowledge of the loser's knowledge of the robber. Who would dare——"

"The thief," said G., "is the Minister D——, who dares all things, those unbecoming as well as those becoming a man. The method of the theft was not less ingenious than bold. The document in question—a letter, to be frank—had been received by the personage robbed while alone in the royal *boudoir*. During its perusal she was suddenly interrupted by the entrance of the other exalted personage from whom especially it was her wish to conceal it. After a hurried and vain endeavor to thrust it in a drawer, she was forced to place it, open as it was, upon a table. The address, however, was uppermost, and, the contents thus unexposed, the letter escaped notice. At this juncture enters the Minister D——. His lynx eye immediately perceives the paper, recognises the handwriting of the address, observes the confusion of the personage addressed, and fathoms her secret. After some business transactions, hurried through in his ordinary manner, he produces a letter somewhat similar to the one in question,

9 The interplay between Dupin and the prefect is particularly delightful, and the reader enjoys it all the more for the certainty that Dupin understands much more than do the police—or the narrator, for that matter.

A similar scene occurs in "The Adventure of the Second Stain":

"Holmes raised his eyebrows.

"'And yet you have sent for me?'

"'Ah, yes, that's another matter—a mere trifle, but the sort of thing you take an interest in—queer, you know, and what you might call freakish. It has nothing to do with the main fact—can't have, on the face of it.' "

Of course it *does* have something to do with "the main fact," just as in Poe's tale the mystery of the letter is indeed "a little *too* self-evident."

10 Although "purloin" is a perfectly good English word, Poe may have used it because it is of French origin (Old French *porloigner*, "to put away, do away with"). According to the O.E.D., the meaning of "to steal" is an English development.

opens it, pretends to read it, and then places it in close juxtaposition to the other. Again he converses, for some fifteen minutes, upon the public affairs. At length, in taking leave, he takes also from the table the letter to which he had no claim. Its rightful owner saw, but, of course, dared not call attention to the act, in the presence of the third personage who stood at her elbow. The minister decamped; leaving his own letter—one of no importance—upon the table."

"Here, then," said Dupin to me, "you have precisely what you demand to make the ascendancy complete—the robber's knowledge of the loser's knowledge of the robber."

"Yes," replied the Prefect; "and the power thus attained has, for some months past, been wielded, for political purposes, to a very dangerous extent. The personage robbed is more thoroughly convinced, every day, of the necessity of reclaiming her letter. But this, of course, cannot be done openly. In fine, driven to despair, she has committed the matter to me."

"Than whom," said Dupin, amid a perfect whirlwind of
11 smoke, "no more sagacious agent could, I suppose, be desired, or even imagined."

"You flatter me," replied the Prefect; "but it is possible that some such opinion may have been entertained."

"It is clear," said I, "as you observe, that the letter is still in possession of the minister; since it is this possession, and not any employment of the letter, which bestows the power. With the employment the power departs."

"True," said G.; "and upon this conviction I proceeded. My
12 first care was to make thorough search of the minister's hotel; and here my chief embarrassment lay in the necessity of searching without his knowledge. Beyond all things, I have been warned of the danger which would result from giving him reason to suspect our design."

13 But," said I, "you are quite *au fait* in these investigations. The Parisian police have done this thing often before."

"O yes; and for this reason I did not despair. The habits of the minister gave me, too, a great advantage. He is frequently absent from home all night. His servants are by no means numerous. They sleep at a distance from their master's apartment, and, being chiefly Neapolitans, are readily made
14 drunk. I have keys, as you know, with which I can open any chamber or cabinet in Paris. For three months a night has not passed, during the greater part of which I have not been engaged, personally, in ransacking the D——Hôtel. My honor is interested, and, to mention a great secret, the reward is enormous. So I did not abandon the search until I had become fully satisfied that the thief is a more astute man than myself. I fancy that I have investigated every nook and corner of the premises in which it is possible that the paper can be concealed."

"But is it not possible," I suggested, "that although the letter may be in possession of the minister, as it unquestionably is, he may have concealed it elsewhere than upon his own premises?"

"This is barely possible," said Dupin. "The present peculiar

11 "Sagacious" again. See "The Masque of the Red Death," note 5.

As we have seen in the earlier two tales, the police never come off too well in the detective story. Indeed, the traditional detective tale *depends* on the inadequacy of ordinary law-enforcement officials in order to sustain the element of mystery. There is no doubt some conscious or unconscious satisfaction in all this, for while we need the police to keep our streets safe, we also resent their authority and their restraints on our freedom to do as we please. Detective stories let us get back at the police as authority figures, in the smug belief that we know more than they do and wouldn't make such stupid mistakes.

It's an illusion, of course. For we are every bit as mystified as the police are, but our vicarious pleasure and our identification with the detective is still the main appeal of the detective story.

12 Town house

13 Well versed in something, knowing all about something. Baudelaire rewrites this as *"tout à fait"* ("all done, completed"), which doesn't convey Poe's meaning. Perhaps he assumed Poe was using *au fait* to mean "by the way, after all," which it can mean.

14 Naples has always come in for more than its share of insults, perhaps because it is primarily a fishing city surrounded by a peasant population. While it is known for songs, festivals, and gaiety, the slur here goes much further than mere celebrations. It may be typical of French chauvinism—or Poe's personal opinion.

condition of affairs at court, and especially of those intrigues in which D—— is known to be involved, would render the instant availability of the document—its susceptibility of being produced at a moment's notice—a point of nearly equal importance with its possession."

"Its susceptibility of being produced?" said I.

"That is to say, of being *destroyed*," said Dupin.

"True," I observed; "the paper is clearly then upon the premises. As for its being upon the person of the minister, we may consider that as out of the question."

"Entirely," said the Prefect. "He has been twice waylaid, as if by footpads, and his person rigorously searched under **15** my own inspection."

"You might have spared yourself this trouble," said Dupin. "D——, I presume, is not altogether a fool, and, if not, must have anticipated these waylayings, as a matter of course."

"Not *altogether* a fool," said G., "but then he's a poet, which I take to be only one remove from a fool."

"True," said Dupin, after a long and thoughtful whiff from his meerschaum, "although I have been guilty of certain doggerel myself." **16**

"Suppose you detail," said I, "the particulars of your search."

"Why the fact is, we took our time, and we searched *every where*. I have had long experience in these affairs. I took the **17** entire building, room by room; devoting the nights of a whole week to each. We examined, first, the furniture of each apartment. We opened every possible drawer; and I presume you know that, to a properly trained police agent, such a thing as a *secret* drawer is impossible. Any man is a dolt who permits a 'secret' drawer to escape him in a search of this kind. The thing is *so* plain. There is a certain amount of bulk—of space—to be accounted for in every cabinet. Then we have accurate rules. The fiftieth part of a line could not escape us. After the cabinets we took the chairs. The cushions we probed with the fine long needles you have seen me employ. From the tables we removed the tops."

"Why so?"

"Sometimes the top of a table, or other similarly arranged piece of furniture, is removed by the person wishing to conceal an article; then the leg is excavated, the article deposited within the cavity, and the top replaced. The bottoms and tops of bed-posts are employed in the same way."

"But could not the cavity be detected by sounding?" I asked.

"By no means, if, when the article is deposited, a sufficient wadding of cotton be placed around it. Besides, in our case, we were obliged to proceed without noise."

"But you could not have removed—you could not have taken to pieces *all* articles of furniture in which it would have been possible to make a deposit in the manner you mention. A letter may be compressed into a thin spiral roll, not differing much in shape or bulk from a large knitting-needle, and in this form it might be inserted into the rung of a chair, for example. You did not take to pieces all the chairs?"

15 Highwaymen who rob on foot

16 Poe the poet gets in a few licks here. In the course of the tale, he shows, through Dupin, that because the poet has Imagination as well as Reason, he is better equipped for solving mysteries than anyone else.

The notion of the poet as fool is an old one—usually expressed by other poets:

The lunatic, the lover and the poet
Are of imagination all compact: . . .
The poet's eye, in a fine frenzy rolling,
Doth glance from heaven to earth, from earth to heaven;
And as imagination bodies forth
The forms of things unknown, the poet's pen
Turns them to shapes, and gives to airy nothing
A local habitation and a name.
(*A Midsummer-Night's Dream*, V, i, 7)
"All poets are mad" (Robert Burton, *Anatomy of Melancholy*).

17 The irony is that their very *thoroughness* is what thwarts them. They cannot see the forest for the trees, to coin a phrase.

18 The term was used for both the hand-held magnifying glass and the compound microscope.

19 A gimlet is a kind of boring tool, hollow on one side of the curved blade, having a cross handle at one end and a worm, or screw, at the other.

20 Note that the preceding conversation has been almost entirely between the narrator and the prefect, allowing them to express every rational, logical argument likely to occur to the conventional mind. Dupin keeps to himself, preferring to let the other two go over all the basic facts of the situation. One wonders if he is even listening.

18
19
"Certainly not; but we did better—we examined the rungs of every chair in the hotel, and, indeed, the jointings of every description of furniture, by the aid of a most powerful microscope. Had there been any traces of recent disturbance we should not have failed to detect it instantly. A single grain of gimlet-dust, for example, would have been as obvious as an apple. Any disorder in the glueing—any unusual gaping in the joints—would have sufficed to insure detection."

"I presume you looked to the mirrors, between the boards and the plates, and you probed the beds and the bed-clothes, as well as the curtains and carpets."

"That of course; and when we had absolutely completed every particle of the furniture in this way, then we examined the house itself. We divided its entire surface into compartments, which we numbered, so that none might be missed; then we scrutinized each individual square inch throughout the premises, including the two houses immediately adjoining, with the microscope, as before."

"The two houses adjoining!" I exclaimed; "you must have had a great deal of trouble."

"We had; but the reward offered is prodigious."

"You include the *grounds* about the houses?"

"All the grounds are paved with brick. They gave us comparatively little trouble. We examined the moss between the bricks, and found it undisturbed."

"You looked among D——'s papers, of course, and into the books of the library?"

"Certainly; we opened every package and parcel; we not only opened every book, but we turned over every leaf in each volume, not contenting ourselves with a mere shake, according to the fashion of some of our police officers. We also measured the thickness of every book-*cover*, with the most accurate admeasurement, and applied to each the most jealous scrutiny of the microscope. Had any of the bindings been recently meddled with, it would have been utterly impossible that the fact should have escaped observation. Some five or six volumes, just from the hands of the binder, we carefully probed, longitudinally, with the needles."

"You explored the floors beneath the carpets?"

"Beyond doubt. We removed every carpet, and examined the boards with the microscope."

"And the paper on the walls?"

"Yes."

"You looked into the cellars?"

"We did."

"Then," I said, "you have been making a miscalculation, and the letter is *not* upon the premises, as you suppose."

20 "I fear you are right there," said the Prefect. "And now, Dupin, what would you advise me to do?"

"To make a thorough re-search of the premises."

"That is absolutely needless," replied G——. "I am not more sure that I breathe than I am that the letter is not at the Hôtel."

"I have no better advice to give you," said Dupin. "You have, of course, an accurate description of the letter?"

"Oh yes!"—And here the Prefect, producing a memorandum-book, proceeded to read aloud a minute account of the internal, and especially of the external appearance of the missing document. Soon after finishing the perusal of this description, he took his departure, more entirely depressed in spirits than I had ever known the good gentleman before.

In about a month afterwards he paid us another visit, and found us occupied very nearly as before. He took a pipe and a chair and entered into some ordinary conversation. At length I said,—

"Well, but G——, what of the purloined letter? I presume you have at last made up your mind that there is no such thing as overreaching the Minister?"

"Confound him, say I—yes; I made the re-examination, however, as Dupin suggested—but it was all labor lost, as I knew it would be."

"How much was the reward offered, did you say?" asked Dupin.

"Why, a very great deal—a *very* liberal reward—I don't like to say how much, precisely; but one thing I *will* say, that I would n't mind giving my individual check for fifty thousand francs to any one would could obtain me that letter. The fact is, it is becoming of more and more importance every day; and the reward has been lately doubled. If it were trebled, however, I could do not more than I have done."

"Why, yes," said Dupin, drawlingly, between the whiffs of his meerschaum, "I really—think, G——, you have not exerted yourself—to the utmost in this matter. You might— do a little more, I think, eh?"

"How?—in what way?"

"Why—puff, puff—you might—puff, puff—employ counsel in the matter, eh?—puff, puff, puff. Do you remember the story they tell of Abernethy?"

"No; hang Abernethy!"   **21**

"To be sure! hang him and welcome. But, once upon a time, a certain rich miser conceived the design of spunging upon this Abernethy for a medical opinion. Getting up, for this purpose, an ordinary conversation in a private company, he insinuated his case to the physician, as that of an imaginary individual.

" 'We will suppose,' said the miser, 'that his symptoms are such and such; now, doctor, what would *you* have directed him to take?'

" 'Take!' said Abernethy, 'why, take *advice*, to be sure.' "

"But," said the Prefect, a little discomposed, "I am *perfectly* willing to take advice, and to pay for it. I would *really* give fifty thousand francs to any one who would aid me in the matter."

"In that case," replied Dupin, opening a drawer, and producing a checkbook, "you may as well fill me up a check for the amount mentioned. When you have signed it, I will hand you the letter."

I was astounded. The Prefect appeared absolutely thunderstricken. For some minutes he remained speechless and motionless, looking incredulously at my friend with open

21 John Abernethy (1764–1831) was a great British surgeon, but another doctor, Sir Isaac Pennington (1745–1817) is the real subject of this story. Poe saw it in *Nuts to Crack* (1835), a jokebook he reviewed, and confused the names.

22 A writing desk, although the word is no longer in common use.

23 i.e., catching the common criminal. The implication is that the police can solve crimes only when the criminals think the same way they do.

24 Procrustes was the name of the giant Polypemon (not to be confused with the Cyclops Polyphemus) after he took up a criminal career. The legendary bandit seized travelers on the road to Eleusis (in Attica) and tied them to an iron bed. He would make his victims fit the bed by either stretching them if they were too short or by cutting off their legs if they were too tall. Theseus, figuring that turnabout is fair play, made the giant undergo the same treatment.

mouth, and eyes that seemed starting from their sockets; then, apparently recovering himself in some measure, he seized a pen, and after several pauses and vacant stares, finally filled up and signed a check for fifty thousand francs, and handed it across the table to Dupin. The latter examined it carefully and deposited it in his pocket-book; then, unlocking an **22** *escritoire*, took thence a letter and gave it to the Prefect. This functionary grasped it in a perfect agony of joy, opened it with a trembling hand, cast a rapid glance at its contents, and then, scrambling and struggling to the door, rushed at length unceremoniously from the room and from the house, without having uttered a syllable since Dupin had requested him to fill up the check.

When he had gone, my friend entered into some explanations.

"The Parisian police," he said, "are exceedingly able in their way. They are persevering, ingenious, cunning, and thoroughly versed in the knowledge which their duties seem **23** chiefly to demand. Thus, when G—— detailed to us his mode of searching the premises at the Hôtel D——, I felt entire confidence in his having made a satisfactory investigation—so far as his labors extended."

"So far as his labors extended?" said I.

"Yes," said Dupin. "The measures adopted were not only the best of their kind, but carried out to absolute perfection. Had the letter been deposited within the range of their search, these fellows would, beyond a question, have found it."

I merely laughed—but he seemed quite serious in all that he said.

"The measures, then," he continued, "were good in their kind, and well executed; their defect lay in their being inapplicable to the case, and to the man. A certain set of highly ingenious resources are, with the Prefect, a sort of Procrustean **24** bed, to which he forcibly adapts his designs. But he perpetually errs by being too deep or too shallow, for the matter in hand; and many a schoolboy is a better reasoner than he. I knew one about eight years of age, whose success at guessing in the game of 'even and odd' attracted universal admiration. This game is simple, and is played with marbles. One player holds in his hand a number of these toys, and demands of another whether that number is even or odd. If the guess is right, the guesser wins one; if wrong, he loses one. The boy to whom I allude won all the marbles of the school. Of course he had some principle of guessing; and this lay in mere observation and admeasurement of the astuteness of his opponents. For example, an arrant simpleton is his opponent, and, holding up his closed hand, asks, 'are they even or odd?' Our schoolboy replies, 'odd,' and loses; but upon the second trial he wins, for he then says to himself, 'the simpleton had them even upon the first trial, and his amount of cunning is just sufficient to make him have them odd upon the second; I will therefore guess odd;'—and he guesses odd, and wins. Now, with a simpleton a degree above the first, he would have reasoned thus: 'This fellow finds that in the first instance I guessed odd, and, in the second, he will propose to himself upon the first impulse, a simple variation from even to odd, as did the first simpleton; but then a second thought will suggest that this is too simple a variation, and finally he will decide upon putting it even as before. I will therefore guess even;'—he guesses even, and wins. Now this mode of reasoning in the schoolboy, whom his fellows termed 'lucky,'—what, in its last analysis, is it?"

"It is merely," I said, "an identification of the reasoner's intellect with that of his opponent." **25**

"It is," said Dupin; "and, upon inquiring of the boy by what means he effected the *thorough* identification in which his success consisted, I received answer as follows: "When I wish to find out how wise, or how stupid, or how good, or how wicked is any one, or what are his thoughts at the moment, I fashion the expression of my face, as accurately as possible, in accordance with the expression of his, and then wait to see what thoughts or sentiments arise in my mind or heart, as if to match or correspond with the expression.' This response of the schoolboy lies at the bottom of all the spurious profundity which has been attributed to Rochefoucauld, to La Bougive, to Machiavelli, and to Campanella." **26**

"And the identification," I said, "of the reasoner's intellect with that of his opponent, depends, if I understand you aright, upon the accuracy with which the opponent's intellect is admeasured."

"For its practical value it depends upon this," replied Dupin; "and the Prefect and his cohort fail so frequently, first, by default of this identification, and, secondly, by ill-admeasurement, or rather through non-admeasurement, of the intellect with which they are engaged. They consider only their *own* ideas of ingenuity; and, in searching for anything hidden, advert only to the modes in which *they* would have hidden it. they are right in this much—that their own ingenuity is a faithful representative of that of *the mass;* but when the cunning of the individual felon is diverse in character from their own, the felon foils them, of course. This always happens when it is above their own, and very usually when it is below. They have no variation of principle in their investigations; at best, when urged by some unusual emergency—by some extraordinary reward—they extend or exaggerate their old modes of *practice,* without touching their principles. What, for example, in this case of D——, has been done to vary the principle of action? What is all this boring, and probing, and sounding, and scrutinizing with the microscope, and dividing the surface of the building into registered square inches— what is it all but an exaggeration *of the application* of the one principle or set of principles of search, which are based upon the one set of notions regarding human ingenuity, to which the Prefect, in the long routine of his duty, has been accustomed? Do you not see he has taken it for granted that *all* men proceed to conceal a letter,—not exactly in a gimlet-hole bored in a chair-leg—but, at least, in *some* out-of-the-way hole or corner suggested by the same tenor of thought which

25 The deductive mind is in full sway. The person attuned to his place in the scheme of things—and that of others—can discern a great deal. Says Sherlock Holmes, as if in agreement: "So all life is a great chain, the nature of which is known whenever we are shown a single link of it. Like all other arts, the Science of Deduction and Analysis is one which can only be acquired by long and patient study, nor is life long enough to allow any mortal to attain the highest possible perfection in it" ("A Study in Scarlet")

26 François de la Rochefoucauld (1613–80) is best known for his maxims and reflective epigrams. He saw man as in a "deplorable state of nature, corrupted by sin"; his best-known saying is "The virtues join with self-interest as the rivers join with the sea."

"La Bougive" is most likely the result of a slip of the pen or a typesetter's error, for no one by that name is known; Baudelaire replaces it with La Bruyère. This seems a reasonable correction, for Jean de La Bruyère (1645–96) was, like Dupin, a detached observer, known for his strong moral views on the economy and social conditions of his country.

Niccolò Machiavelli (1469–1527) wrote *The Prince* (1532), which describes precisely the manner in which a prince may gain and maintain power.

Tommaso Campanella (1568–1639) was the philosopher and writer of the Italian Renaissance whose best-known work is *Civitas Solis* (1623). He was a man very much like Poe's Dupin:

"When he had a mind to penetrate into the inclinations of those he had to deal with, he composed his face, his gesture, and his whole body, as nearly as he could into the exact similitude of the person he intended to examine; and then carefully observed what turn of mind he seemed to acquire by this change. So that, says my author, he was able to enter into the dispositions and thoughts of people, as effectually as if he had been changed into the very men. I have often observed, that on mimicking the looks and gestures of angry, or placid, or frighted, or daring men, I have involuntarily found my mind turned to that passion whose appearance I endeavoured to imitate. . . ." (Edmund Burke, *Works*, Boston, Mass., 1826; I, 178–79)

Yet Dupin seems to feel that these men, as intelligent as they are, have only mastered the art of empathy, a skill with which any schoolboy is familiar. His comment is perhaps exaggerated, but he means to point out that at the heart of all great complexities is something quite simple and basic.

The key to solving a mystery thus lies in the ability to simplify detail. But the ordinary mind (the narrator, the prefect, or the reader) is so cluttered with extraneous matter that it cannot cut through its automatic responses. Says Sherlock Holmes:

"I consider that a man's brain originally is like a little empty attic, and you have to stock it with such furniture as you choose. A fool takes in all the lumber of every sort that he comes across, so that the knowledge which might be useful to him gets crowded out, or at best is jumbled up with a lot of other things, so that he has difficulty in laying his hands upon it. Now the skillful workman is very careful indeed as to what he takes into his brain-attic. He will have nothing but the tools which may help in doing his work, but of these he has a large assortment, and all in the most perfect order." ("A Study in Scarlet")

27 Poe's use of the word is appropriate in its English sense, but in France it means "affected," "elaborate," and so Baudelaire changes it to *tout à fait singulier* ("very odd," "peculiar").

28 "The undistributed middle." One of the rules of a syllogism is that the middle term must refer to all the individuals in the class it denotes.

All poets are fools, reasons the prefect. The minister is a poet. Therefore, the minister is a fool. He errs because the basic premise is faulty: "Fool" does *not* apply to *all* the individuals in the class "poet."

29 The mathematician has logic and reason, but not imagination. This the poet has in abundance. And it is his imagination that allows the detective to enter the mind of the criminal and re-create his thinking processes, and thus solve the crime. The police *guess* what the minister might do; Dupin *knows*.

30 "Philosophy is written in this grand book—I mean the universe—which stands continually open to our gaze, but it cannot be understood unless one first learns to comprehend the language and interpret the characters in which it is written. It is written in the language of mathematics, and its characters are triangles, circles, and other geometrical figures, without which it is humanly impossible to understand a single word of it; without these, one is wandering about in a dark labyrinth." (Galileo, *Il Saggiatore*, 1623)

31 "The odds are that every idea which is widely accepted, every received convention, is a stupidity, simply because it is acceptable to the masses."

Sebastien Roch Nicholas Chamfort (1740–94) was another French writer of maxims and epigrams, who was popular at court despite his republican leanings (perhaps because of epigrams like this one). During the Reign of Terror he was denounced and committed suicide.

32 Dupin's point seems to be that a word's original meaning should not be confused with words that derive from it. However, in mathematics, "analysis" means the resolving of problems into equations without in any way being related to the root of the word "algebra" (which is Arabic). Thus the point isn't made too well by the reciting of Latin roots and their modern descendants.

Ambitus means "a going around" as in a compass, and later took on the connotation of seeking office. *Religio*, meaning "superstition," is of doubtful etymology, but Cicero connected *religionem* with *relegere*, "to read over again," and later authors suggested *religare*, "to bind or relegate."

The Latin *honestus* does have the meaning of "honorable," as well as "respectable," "decent," "fine," and "handsome," but Cicero used *homines honesti* to mean members of his own party.

would urge a man to secrete a letter in a gimlet-hole bored **27** in a chair-leg? And do you not see also, that such *recherchés* nooks for concealment are adapted only for ordinary occasions, and would be adopted only by ordinary intellects; for, in all cases of concealment, a disposal of the article concealed—a disposal of it in this *recherché* manner,—is, in the very first instance, presumable and presumed; and thus its discovery depends, not at all upon the acumen, but altogether upon the mere care, patience, and determination of the seekers; and where the case is of importance—or, what amounts to the same thing in the *political* eyes, when the reward is of magnitude,—the qualities in question have *never* been known to fail. You will now understand what I meant in suggesting that, had the purloined letter been hidden any where within the limits of the Prefect's examination—in other words, had the principle of its concealment been comprehended within the principles of the Prefect—its discovery would have been a matter altogether beyond question. This functionary, however, has been thoroughly mystified; and the remote source of his defeat lies in the supposition that the Minister is a fool, because he has acquired renown as a poet. All fools are poets; this the Prefect *feels*; and he is merely guilty of a *non* **28** *distributio medii* in thence inferring that all poets are fools."

"But is this really the poet?" I asked. "There are two brothers, I now; and both have attained reputation in letters. The Minister I believe has written learnedly on the Differential **29** Calculus. He is a mathematician, and no poet."

"You are mistaken; I know him well; he is both. As poet *and* mathematician, he would reason well; as mere mathe- **30** matician, he could not have reasoned at all, and thus would have been at the mercy of the Prefect."

"You surprise me," I said, "by these opinions, which have been contradicted by the voice of the world. You do not mean to set at naught the well-digested idea of centuries. The mathematical reason has long been regarded as *the reason par excellence*."

" '*Il y a à parier*,' " replied Dupin, quoting from Chamfort, " '*que toute idée publique, toute convention reçue, est une* **31** *sottise, car elle a convenu au plus grand nombre.*' The mathematicians, I grant you, have done their best to promulgate the popular error to which you allude, and which is none the less an error for its promulgation as truth. With an art worthy a better cause, for example, they have insinuated the term 'analysis' into application to algebra. The French are the originators of this particular deception; but if a term is of any importance—if words derive any value from applicability— then 'analysis' conveys 'algebra' about as much as, in Latin, '*ambitus*' implies 'ambition,' '*religio*' 'religion,' or '*homines* **32** *honesti*,' a set of *honorable* men."

"You have a quarrel on hand, I see," said I, "with some of the algebraists of Paris; but proceed."

"I dispute the availability, and thus the value, of that reason which is cultivated in any especial form other than the abstractly logical. I dispute, in particular, the reason educed by mathematical study. The mathematics are the science of form and quantity; mathematical reasoning is merely logic applied to observation upon form and quantity. The great error lies in supposing that even the truths of what is called *pure* algebra, are abstract or general truths. And this error is so egregious that I am confounded at the universality with which it has been received. Mathematical axioms are *not* axioms of general truth. What is true of *relation*—of form and **33** quantity—is often grossly false in regard to morals, for example. In this latter science it is very usually *un*true that the aggregated parts are equal to the whole. In chemistry also the axiom fails. In the consideration of motive it fails; for two motives, each of a given value, have not, necessarily, a value when united, equal to the sum of their values apart. There are numerous other mathematical truths which are only truths within the limits of *relation*. But the mathematician argues, from his *finite truths*, through habit, as if they were of an absolutely general applicability—as the world indeed imagines them to be. Bryant, in his very learned 'Mythology,' mentions an analogous source of error, when he says that 'although the Pagan fables are not believed, yet we forget ourselves continually, and make inferences from them as existing realities.' **34** With the algebraists, however, who are Pagans themselves, the 'Pagan fables' *are* believed, and the inferences are made, not so much through lapse of memory, as through an unaccountable addling of the brains. In short, I never yet encountered the mere mathematician who could be trusted out of equal roots, or one who did not clandestinely hold it as a point of his faith that $x^2 + px$ was absolutely and unconditionally equal to q. Say to one of these gentlemen, by way of experiment, if you please, that you believe occasions may occur where $x^2 + px$ is *not* altogether equal to q, and, having made him understand what you mean, get out of his reach as speedily as convenient, for, beyond doubt, he will endeavor to knock you down.

"I mean to say," continued Dupin, while I merely laughed at his last observations, "that if the Minister had been no more than a mathematician, the Prefect would have been under no necessity of giving me this check. I knew him, however, as both mathematician and poet, and my measures were adapted to his capacity, with reference to the circumstances by which he was surrounded. I knew him as a courtier, too, and as a bold *intriguant*. Such a man, I considered, could not fail to be aware of the ordinary *policial* modes of action. He could not have failed to anticipate—and events have proved that he did not fail to anticipate—the waylayings to which he was subjected. He must have foreseen, I reflected, the secret investigations of his premises. His frequent absences from home at night, which were hailed by the Prefect as certain aids to his success, I regarded only as *ruses*, to afford opportunity for thorough search to the police, and thus the sooner to impress them with the conviction to which G——, in fact, did finally arrive—the conviction that the letter was not upon the premises. I felt, also, that the whole train of

33 Mathematics is an abstract science that proceeds from a body of explicitly stated assumptions, or axioms. Theoretical mathematics, unlike other forms, may deal with assumptions not drawn from the physical world. In any case, what Dupin says is, of course, true: mathematics is a specialized tool, not applicable to every situation.

"It may be true that people who are *merely* mathematicians have certain specific shortcomings; however, that is not the fault of mathematics, but is true of every exclusive occupation," writes Karl Friedrich Gauss (1777–1855) in a letter to H. C. Schumacher (1845).

34 Jacob Bryant, *A New System of Antient Mythology* (1807), II, 173.

35 The heart of the Dupin stories consists of the narrator's observations as the detective solves the crime. As Dupin does so, he draws from the narrator and the reader the solution that has been in front of them all the time. The form is the Socratic dialogue, with the detective in the role of philosopher-teacher.

Dupin, as we have noted, has been remarkably silent up to this point about his solution to the mystery. The great Holmes reflects on Dupin's technique in "A Study in Scarlet." Watson speaks first.

" 'It is simple enough as you expain it,' I said, smiling. 'You remind me of Edgar Allan Poe's Dupin. I had no idea that such individuals did exist outside of stories.'

"Sherlock Holmes rose and lit his pipe. 'No doubt you think that you are complimenting me in comparing be to Dupin,' he observed. 'Now in my opinion, Dupin was a very inferior fellow. That trick of his of breaking in on his friends' thoughts with an apropos remark after a quarter of an hour's silence is really very showy, and superficial. He had some analytical genius, no doubt, but he was by no means such a phenomenon as Poe appeared to imagine.' "

This is Holmes's opinion, however, not Doyle's (see "The Murders in the Rue Morgue" introduction note). Holmes speaks perhaps from a certain amount of professional jealousy, since in *The Hound of the Baskervilles* Watson reveals that he is hardly lacking in this respect:

"One of Sherlock Holmes' defects—if, indeed one may call it a defect—was that he was exceedingly loath to communicate his full plans to any other person until the instant of their fulfillment. Partly it came no doubt from his masterful nature, which loved to dominate and surprise those who were around him. Partly also from his professional caution, which urged him never to take any chances. The result, however, was very trying for those who were acting as his agents and assistants." (Ch. 14)

Psychologists have often noted that we tend to criticize in others what we know to be faults in ourselves.

thought, which I was at some pains in detailing to you just now, concerning the invariable principle of *policial* action in searches for articles concealed—I felt that this whole train of thought would necessarily pass through the mind of the Minister. It would imperatively lead him to despise all the ordinary *nooks* of concealment. *He* could not, I reflected, be so weak as not to see that the most intricate and remote recess of his hotel would be as open as his commonest closets to the eyes, to the probes, to the gimlets, and to the microscopes of the Prefect. I saw, in fine, that he would be driven, as a matter of course, to *simplicity*, if not deliberately induced to it as a matter of choice. You will remember, perhaps, how desperately the Prefect laughed when I suggested, upon our first interview, that it was just possible this mystery troubled him so much on account of its being so *very* self-evident."

"Yes," said I, "I remember his merriment well. I really thought he would have fallen into convulsions."

"The material world," continued Dupin, "abounds with very strict analogies to the immaterial; and thus some color of truth has been given to the rhetorical dogma, that metaphor, or simile, may be made to strengthen an argument, as well as to embellish a description. The principle of the *vis inertiæ*, for example, seems to be identical in physics and metaphysics. It is not more true in the former, that a large body is with more difficulty set in motion than a smaller one, and that its subsequent *momentum* is commensurate with this difficulty, than it is, in the latter, that intellects of the vaster capacity, while more forcible, more constant, and more eventful in their movements than those of inferior grade, are yet the less readily moved, and more embarrassed and full of hesitation in the first few steps of their progress. Again: have you ever noticed which of the street signs, over the shop doors, are the most attractive of attention?"

35   "I have never given the matter a thought," I said.

"There is a game of puzzles," he resumed, "which is played upon a map. One party playing requires another to find a given word—the name of town, river, state or empire—any word, in short, upon the motley and perplexed surface of the chart. A novice in the game generally seeks to embarrass his opponents by giving them the most minutely lettered names; but the adept selects such words as stretch, in large characters, from one end of the chart to the other. These, like the over-largely lettered signs and placards of the street, escape observation by dint of being excessively obvious; and here the physical oversight is precisely analogous with the inapprehension by which the intellect suffers to pass unnoticed those considerations which are too obtrusively and too palpably self-evident. But this is a point, it appears, somewhat above or beneath the understanding of the Prefect. He never once thought it probable, or possible, that the Minister had deposited the letter immediately beneath the nose of the whole world, by way of best preventing any portion of that world from perceiving it.

"But the more I reflected upon the daring, dashing, and

discriminating ingenuity of D——; upon the fact that the document must always have been *at hand*, if he intended to use it to good purpose; and upon the decisive evidence, obtained by the Prefect, that it was not hidden within the limits of that dignitary's ordinary search—the more satisfied I became that, to conceal this letter, the Minister had resorted to the comprehensive and sagacious expedient of not attempting to conceal it at all.

"Full of these ideas, I prepared myself with a pair of green spectacles, and called one fine morning, quite by accident, at the Ministerial hotel. I found D—— at home, yawning, lounging, and dawdling, as usual, and pretending to be in the last extremity of *ennui*. He is, perhaps, the most really energetic human being now alive—but that is only when nobody sees him.

"To be even with him, I complained of my weak eyes, and lamented the necessity of the spectacles, under cover of which I cautiously and thoroughly surveyed the apartment, while seemingly intent only upon the conversation of my host.

"I paid special attention to a large writing-table, near which he sat, and upon which lay confusedly, some miscellaneous letters and other papers, with one or two musical instruments and a few books. Here, however, after a long and very deliberate scrutiny, I saw nothing to excite particular suspicion.

"At length my eyes, in going the circuit of the room, fell upon a trumpery fillagree card-rack of paste-board, that hung dangling by a dirty blue ribbon, from a little brass knob just beneath the middle of the mantelpiece. In this rack, which had three or four compartments, were five or six visiting cards and a solitary letter. This last was much soiled and crumpled. It was torn nearly in two, across the middle—as if a design, in the first instance, to tear it entirely up as worthless, had been altered, or stayed, in the second. It had a large black seal, bearing the D—— cipher *very* conspicuously, and was addressed, in a diminutive female hand, to D——, the minister, himself. It was thrust carelessly, and even, as it seemed, contemptuously, into one of the upper divisions of the rack.

"No sooner had I glanced at this letter, than I concluded it to be that of which I was in search. To be sure, it was, to all appearance, radically different from the one of which the Prefect had read us so minute a description. Here the seal was large and black, with the D—— cipher; there it was small and red, with the ducal arms of the S—— family. Here, the address, to the Minister, was diminutive and feminine; there the superscription, to a certain royal personage, was markedly bold and decided; the size alone formed a point of correspondence. But, then, the *radicalness* of these differences, which was excessive; the dirt; the soiled and torn condition of the paper, so inconsistent with the *true* methodical habits of D——, and so suggestive of a design to delude the beholder into an idea of the worthlessness of the document; these things, together with the hyper-obtrusive situation of this document, full in the view of every visiter, and thus exactly

by Johann Friedrich Vogel, 1856

by F. S. Coburn, 1903

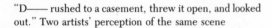

"D—— rushed to a casement, threw it open, and looked out." Two artists' perception of the same scene

in accordance with the conclusions to which I had previously arrived; these things, I say, were strongly corroborative of suspicion, in one who came with the intention to suspect.

"I protracted my visit as long as possible, and, while I maintained a most animated discussion with the Minister, on a topic which I knew well had never failed to interest and excite him, I kept my attention really riveted upon the letter. In this examination, I committed to memory its external appearance and arrangement in the rack; and also fell, at length, upon a discovery which set at rest whatever trivial doubt I might have entertained. In scrutinizing the edges of the paper, I observed them to be more *chafed* than seemed necessary. They presented the *broken* appearance which is manifested when a stiff paper, having been once folded and pressed with a folder, is refolded in a reversed direction, in the same creases or edges which had formed the original fold. This discovery was sufficient. It was clear to me that the letter had been turned, as a glove, inside out, re-directed, and re-sealed. I bade the minister good morning, and took my departure at once, leaving a gold snuff-box upon the table.

"The next morning I called for the snuff-box, when we resumed, quite eagerly, the conversation of the preceding day. While thus engaged, however, a loud report, as if of a pistol, was heard immediately beneath the windows of the hotel, and was succeeded by a series of fearful screams, and the shoutings of a mob. D—— rushed to a casement, threw it open, and looked out. In the meantime, I stepped to the card-rack, took the letter, put it in my pocket, and replaced it by a *fac-simile,* (so far as regards externals,) which I had carefully prepared at my lodgings; imitating the D—— cipher, very readily, by means of a seal formed of bread.

"The disturbance in the street had been occasioned by the frantic behavior of a man with a musket. He had fired it among a crowd of women and children. It proved, however, to have been without ball, and the fellow was suffered to go his way as a lunatic or a drunkard. When he had gone, D—— came from the window, whither I had followed him immediately upon securing the object in view. Soon afterwards I bade him farewell. The pretended lunatic was a man in my own pay."

"But what purpose had you," I asked, "in replacing the letter by a *fac-simile?* Would it not have been better, at the first visit, to have seized it openly, and departed?"

"D——," replied Dupin, "is a desperate man, and a man of nerve. His hotel, too, is not without attendants devoted to his interests. Had I made the wild attempt you suggest, I might never have left the Ministerial presence alive. The good people of Paris might have heard of me no more. But I had an object apart from these considerations. You know my political prepossessions. In this matter, I act as a partisan of the lady concerned. For eighteen months the Minister has **36** had her in his power. She has now him in hers; since, being unaware that the letter is not in his possession, he will proceed with his exactions as if it was. Thus will he inevitably commit himself, at once, to his political destruction. His downfall, too, will not be more precipitate than awkward. It is all very well to talk about the *facilis descensus Averni;* but in all kinds **37** of climbing, as Catalani said of singing, it is far more easy to **38** get up than to come down. In the present instance I have no sympathy—at least no pity—for him who descends. He is that *monstrum horrendum,* an unprincipled man of genius. I confess, however, that I should like very well to know the precise character of his thoughts, when, being defied by her whom the Prefect terms 'a certain personage,' he is reduced to opening the letter which I left for him in the card rack."

"How? did you put any thing particular in it?"

"Why—it did not seem altogether right to leave the interior blank—that would have been insulting. D——, at Vienna **39** once, did me an evil turn, which I told him, quite good-humoredly, that I should remember. So, as I knew he would **40** feel some curiosity in regard to the identity of the person who had outwitted him, I thought it a pity not to give him a clue. He is well acquainted with my MS., and I just copied into the **41** middle of the blank sheet the words—

——Un dessein si funeste,
S'il n'est digne d'Atrée, est digne de Thyeste.

They are to be found in Crébillon's 'Atrée.'"   **42**

36 Could it be that Dupin is somehow intimately connected with this mysterious lady? Unfortunately, Dupin's love life is even hazier than that of Sherlock Holmes.

37 "The easy to descent to Hell" is slightly misquoted from Vergil's *Aeneid,* VI, 126: "The gates of hell are open night and day;/Smooth the descent and easy is the way:/But to return, and view the cheerful skies,/In this the task and mighty labor lies" (translated by John Dryden).

38 Angelica Catalani (1779–1849) was an Italian opera star and teacher. Another possibility, Angelo Catalani, was a nineteenth-century music historian and teacher.

39 Dupin is not without a certain regard for his adversary.

40 So, Dupin and the minister know each other from times past. It seems a shame that Poe doesn't make more of this interesting—if last-minute—development. One thinks of Holmes's archenemy, Professor Moriarty, and wishes Poe had included such a character in further tales.

41 Handwriting (the literal translation of "manuscript")

42 "A design so deadly, even if not worthy of Atreus, is worthy of Thyestes," is from *Atrée et Thyeste* (1707), by Prosper Jolyot de Crébillon (1674–1762), based on the tragedy *Thyestes,* by Seneca.

The quotation refers to King Atreus of Mycenae, who murdered his nephews and served them up to their father, Thyestes, at dinner. Thyestes had seduced the wife of Atreus. After the meal, he pronounced a curse on the house of Atreus.

Dupin is saying that the minister's attempt at blackmail was good, but not as well executed as it could have been.

THOU ART THE MAN

First published in *Godey's Lady's Book*, November 1844.

In its own way, this is an important story, not because it is one of Poe's best but because it shows his experimentation with the form of the detective tale. It also points out how exceptional the three Dupin stories really are, for here Poe combines his detective and narrator in one character, and the result is as unsatisfying as Wilkie Collins' "The Stolen Letter" (see "The Purloined Letter," introductory note).

When the narrator is "personally involved in the events, his own fate is at stake," observes Leon Surmelian, "and his attitude toward the other characters will be a highly personal one and perhaps prejudiced; he cannot be neutral if they influence his fate in any way, he cannot regulate his distance from the secondary characters with the freedom enjoyed by the omniscient narrator" (*Techniques of Fiction Writing*, Doubleday, 1968; p. 74). Of course this is not a problem in most of Poe's tales—in fact, the narrator's imperfections actually add to the complexities of meaning. But the detective story is different, since we want to feel as though we are solving the mystery along with the detective; if he hides or covers up any clues, we feel cheated. And if we sense he is playing games with us, we feel put off.

"Thou Art the Man" at least has its moments, such as the use of "moral contrast in which Dickens was so adept," as A. H. Quinn points out, adding that although the story is not a great one, "we might think better of it had we not come to expect so much more from the author of "The Purloined Letter" (*Edgar Allan Poe*, Appleton-Century, 1941; p. 422).

Most of the story seems to be Poe's invention, although in William Leggett's "The Rifle" (1828), a man is also cleared of murder charges through a ballistics test, as with Poe's tale, several decades before police began using such methods. The use of ventriloquism as a plot device can be found in Charles Brockden Brown's *Wieland* (1798).

The title comes from II Samuel 12:7: "And Nathan said to David, Thou art the man. Thus saith the Lord God of Israel, I anointed thee king over Israel, and I delivered thee out of the hand of Saul." The words are the accusation of the prophet Nathan that David had conspired to have Bathsheba's husband killed in order to have her for his own.

---

1 Oedipus solved the riddle of the Sphinx, who had destroyed and eaten all those who had guessed wrong.

2 The name may be a wordplay on the meaning of "rattle" as moving or working quickly and noisily.

3 "For to be carnally minded is death" (Romans 8:6). It should be clear from this that while the story is serious, there is also an undercurrent of humor that should not be overlooked.

4 A good name for a New Englander, whose region's mills turned out the nation's supply of textiles.

1,2 I will now play the Œdipus to the Rattleborough enigma. I will expound to you—as I alone can—the secret of the enginery that effected the Rattleborough miracle—the one, the true, the admitted, the undisputed, the indisputable miracle, which put a definite end to infidelity among the Rattleburghers, and converted to the orthodoxy of the grandames all the carnal-**3** minded who had ventured to be skeptical before.

This event—which I should be sorry to discuss in a tone of unsuitable levity—occurred in the summer of 18—. Mr. **4** Barnabas Shuttleworthy—one of the wealthiest and most respectable citizens of the borough—had been missing for several days under circumstances which gave rise to suspicion of foul play. Mr. Shuttleworthy had set out from Rattleborough very early one Saturday morning, on horseback, with the avowed intention of proceeding to the city of ——, about fifteen miles distant, and of returning the night of the same day. Two hours after his departure, however, his horse returned without him, and without the saddle-bags which had been strapped on his back at starting. The animal was wounded, too, and covered with mud. These circumstances naturally gave rise to much alarm among the friends of the missing man; and when it was found, on Sunday morning, that he had not yet made his appearance, the whole borough arose *en masse* to go and look for his body.

The foremost and most energetic in instituting this search was the bosom friend of Mr. Shuttleworthy—a Mr. Charles Goodfellow, or, as he was universally called, "Charley Good-fellow," or "Old Charley Goodfellow." Now, whether it is a marvellous coincidence, or whether it is that the name itself has an imperceptible effect upon the character, I have never yet been able to ascertain; but the fact is unquestionable, that there never yet was any person named Charles who was not an open, manly, honest, good-natured, and frank-hearted fellow, with a rich, clear voice, that did you good to hear it, and an eye that looked you always straight in the face, as much as to say: "I have a clear conscience myself, am afraid of no man, and am altogether above doing a mean action." And thus all the hearty, careless, "walking gentlemen" of the stage are very certain to be called Charles.   5

Now, "Old Charley Goodfellow," although he had been in Rattleborough not longer than six months or thereabouts, and although nobody knew any thing about him before he came to settle in the neighborhood, had experienced no difficulty in the world in making the acquaintance of all the respectable people in the borough. Not a man of them but would have taken his bare word for a thousand at any moment; and as for the women, there is no saying what they would not have done to oblige him. And all this came of his having been christened Charles, and of his possessing, in consequence, that ingenuous face which is proverbially the very "best letter of recommendation."   6

I have already said that Mr. Shuttleworthy was one of the most respectable, and, undoubtedly, he was the most wealthy man in Rattleborough, while "Old Charley Goodfellow" was upon as intimate terms with him as if he had been his own brother. The two old gentlemen were next-door neighbors, and although Mr. Shuttleworthy seldom, if ever, visited "Old Charley," and never was known to take a meal in his house, still this did not prevent the two friends from being exceedingly intimate, as I have just observed; for "Old Charley" never let a day pass without stepping in three or four times to see how his neighbor came on, and very often he would stay to breakfast or tea, and almost always to dinner; and then the amount of wine that was made way with by the two cronies at a sitting, it would really be a difficult thing to ascertain. "Old Charley's" favorite berverage was *Château Margaux*,   7 and it appeared to do Mr. Shuttleworthy's heart good to see

5 Names *do* make a difference. A survey by Temple University's Thomas Busse showed that boys and girls who have "desirable" names achieve higher IQ scores. Names, the study suggests, give off specific connotations, and a child's self-image is reflective of how others see him. S. Gray Garwood, of Tulane University, corroborated the findings, showing that commonly used names usually create better, stronger, and more positive images than unusual ones. (*Science News*, January 8, 1977, p. 23; *Good Housekeeping*, June 1977, p. 219)

Robin Goodfellow is another name for Puck, the impish sprite who plays tricks on unwary travelers. A "walking gentleman of the stage" is an actor who plays "well-dressed parts of small importance" (Century Dictionary).

6 "Queen Isabella of Spain used to say 'Whosoever hath a good presence and a good fashion carries constantly letters of recommendation' " (Francis Bacon, *Apophthegms*, no. 99).

"You don't carry in your countenance a letter of recommendation" (Dickens, *Barnaby Rudge*, Ch. 2).

7 One of the choicest soils in the Médoc region of France is in the vineyards of Château Margaux, fifteen miles from Bordeaux. In Poe's time its wine was extremely expensive.

the old fellow swallow it, as he did, quart after quart; so that, one day, when the wine was *in* and the wit, as a natural consequence, somewhat *out*, he said to his crony, as he slapped him upon the back: "I tell you what it is, 'Old Charley,' you are, by all odds, the heartiest old fellow I ever came across in all my born days; and, since you love to guzzle the wine at that fashion, I'll be darned if I don't have to make thee a present of a big box of the Château Margaux. Od rot me,"—(Mr. Shuttleworth had a sad habit of swearing, although **8** he seldom went beyond "Od rot me," of "By gosh," or "By the jolly golly,")—"Od rot me," says he, "if I don't send an order to town this very afternoon for a double box of the best that can be got, and I'll make ye a present of it, I will!—ye needn't say a word now—I *will*, I tell ye, and there's an end of it; so look out for it—it will come to hand some of these fine **9** days, precisely when ye are looking for it the least!" I mention this little bit of liberality on the part of Mr. Shuttleworthy, just by way of showing you how *very* intimate an understanding existed between the two friends.

Well, on the Sunday morning in question, when it came to be fairly understood that Mr. Shuttleworthy had met with foul play, I never saw any one so profoundly affected as "Old Charley Goodfellow." When he first heard that the horse had come home without his master, and without his master's saddle-bags, and all bloody from a pistol-shot, that had gone clean through and through the poor animal's chest without quite killing him,—when he heard all this, he turned as pale as if the missing man had been his own dear brother or father, and shivered and shook all over as if he had had a fit of the **10** ague.

At first he was too much overpowered with grief to be able to do any thing at all, or to decide upon any plan of action; so that for a long time he endeavored to dissuade Mr. Shuttleworthy's other friends from making a stir about the matter, thinking it best to wait awhile—say for a week or two, or a month or two—to see if something wouldn't turn up, or if Mr. Shuttleworthy wouldn't come in the natural way, and explain his reasons for sending his horse on before. I dare say you have often observed this disposition to temporize, or to procrastinate, in people who are laboring under any very poignant sorrow. Their powers of mind seem to be rendered torpid, so that they have a horror of any thing like action, and like nothing in the world so well as to lie quietly in bed and "nurse their grief," as the old ladies express it—that is to say, ruminate over their trouble.

The people of Rattleborough had, indeed, so high an opinion of the wisdom and discretion of "Old Charley" that the greater part of them felt disposed to agree with him, and not make a stir in the business "until something should turn up," as the honest old gentleman worded it; and I believe that, after all, this would have been the general determination, but for the very suspicious interference of Mr. Shuttleworthy's nephew, a young man of very dissipated habits, and otherwise of rather bad character. This nephew, whose name was

Pennifeather, would listen to nothing like reason in the matter of "lying quiet," but insisted upon making immediate search for the "corpse of the murdered man." This was the expression he employed; and Mr. Goodfellow acutely remarked, at the time, that it was "a *singular* expression, to say no more." This remark of "Old Charley's," too had great effect upon the crowd; and one of the party was heard to ask, very impressively, "how it happened that young Mr. Pennifeather—was so intimately cognizant of all the circumstances connected with his wealthy uncle's disappearance, as to feel authorized to assert, distinctly and unequivocally, that his uncle *was* 'a murdered man.' " Hereupon some little squibbling and bickering occurred among various members of the crowd, and especially between "Old Charley" and Mr. Pennifeather— although this latter occurrence was, indeed, by no means a novelty, for little good-will had subsisted between the parties for the last three or four months; and matters had even gone so far that Mr. Pennifeather had actually knocked down his uncle's friend for some alleged excess of liberty that the latter had taken in the uncle's house, of which the nephew was an inmate. Upon this occasion "Old Charley" is said to have behaved with exemplary moderation and Christian charity. He arose from the blow, adjusted his clothes, and made no attempt at retaliation at all—merely muttering a few words about "taking summary vengeance at the first convenient opportunity,"—a natural and very justifiable ebullition of anger, which meant nothing, however, and, beyond doubt, was no sooner given vent to than forgotten.

However these matters may be (which have no reference to the point now at issue), it is quite certain that the people of Rattleborough, principally through the persuasion of Mr. Pennifeather, came at length to the determination of dispersing over the adjacent country in search of the missing Mr. Shuttleworthy. I say they came to this determination in the first instance. After it had been fully resolved that a search should be made, it was considered almost a matter of course that the seekers should disperse—that is to say, distribute themselves in parties—for the more thorough examination of the region round about. I forget, however, by what ingenious train of reasoning it was that "Old Charley" finally convinced the assembly that this was the most injudicious plan that could be pursued. Convince them, however, he did—all except Mr. Pennifeather, and, in the end, it was arranged that a search should be instituted, carefully and very thoroughly, by the burghers *en masse,* "Old Charley" himself leading the way.

As for the matter of that, there could have been no better pioneer than "Old Charley," whom everybody knew to have the eye of a lynx; but, although he led them into all manner of out-of-the-way holes and corners, by routes that nobody had ever suspected of existing in the neighborhood, and although the search was incessantly kept up day and night for nearly a week, still no trace of Mr. Shuttleworthy could be discovered. When I say no trace, however, I must not be understood to speak literally; for trace, to some extent, there certainly was. The poor gentleman had been tracked, by his horse's shoes (which were peculiar), to a spot about three miles to the east of the borough, on the main road leading to the city. Here the track made off into a by-path through a piece of woodland—the path coming out again into the main road, and cutting off about half a mile of the regular distance. Following the shoe-marks down this lane, the party came at length to a pool of stagnant water, half hidden by the brambles, to the right of the lane, and opposite this pool all vestige of the track was lost sight of. It appeared, however, that a struggle of some nature had here taken place, and it seemed as if some large and heavy body, much larger and heavier than a man, had been drawn from the by-path to the pool. This latter was carefully dragged twice, but nothing was found; and the party were upon the point of going away, in despair of coming to any result, when Providence suggested to Mr. Goodfellow the expediency of draining the water off altogether. This project was received with cheers, and many high compliments to "Old Charley" upon his sagacity and consideration. As many of the burghers had brought spades with them, supposing that they might possibly be called upon to disinter a corpse, the drain was easily and speedily effected; and no sooner was the bottom visible, than right in the middle of the mud that remained was discovered a black silk velvet waistcoat, which nearly every one present immediately recognized as the property of Mr. Pennifeather. This waistcoat was much torn and stained with blood, and there were several persons among the party who had a distinct remembrance of its having been worn by its owner on the very morning of Mr. Shuttleworthy's departure for the city; while there were others, again, ready to testify upon oath, if required, that Mr. P. did *not* wear the garment in question at any period during the *remainder* of that memorable day; nor could any one be found that he had seen it upon Mr. P.'s person at any period at all **11** subsequent to Mr. Shuttleworthy's disappearance.

Matters now wore a very serious aspect for Mr. Pennifeather, and it was observed, as an indubitable confirmation of the suspicions which were excited against him, that he grew exceedingly pale, and when asked what he had to say for himself, was utterly incapable of saying a word. Hereupon, the few friends his riotous mode of living had left him deserted him at once to a man, and were even more clamorous than his ancient and avowed enemies for his instantaneous arrest. But, on the other hand, the magnanimity of Mr. Goodfellow shone forth with only the more brilliant lustre through contrast. He made a warm and intensely eloquent defence of Mr. Pennifeather, in which he alluded more than once to his own sincere forgiveness of that wild young gentlemen—"the heir of the worthy Mr. Shuttleworthy"—for the insult which he (the young gentleman) had, no doubt in the heat of passion, thought proper to put upon him (Mr. Goodfellow). "He forgave him for it," he said, "from the very bottom of his heart; and for himself (Mr. Goodfellow), so far from pushing the suspicious circumstances to extremity, which, he was sorry to say, really

11 Typical witnesses, these people point up the problem of gathering facts as evidence—a situation that plagues the police in "The Murders in the Rue Morgue." Repeated studies show that eyewitnesses seldom remember correctly what they have seen.

"It is discouraging to note that the essential findings on the unreliability of eyewitness testimony were made 80 years ago, and yet the practice of basing a case on eyewitness testimony and trying to persuade a jury that such test is superior to circumstantial evidence continues to this day. The fact is both types of evidence involve areas of doubt," points out Robert Buckhout in *Scientific American* (December 1974, p. 31).

The sources of unreliability, Buckhout says, are 1) insignificance of the event at the time and to the witness; 2) length of the period of observation; 3) less-than-ideal observation conditions; 4) witness's mental state at the time; 5) witness's physical condition; and 6) the tendency to see what we want or need to see.

had arisen against Mr. Pennifeather, he (Mr. Goodfellow) would make every exertion in his power, would employ all the little eloquence in his position to—to—to—soften down, as much as he could conscientiously do so, the worst features of this really exceedingly perplexing piece of business."

Mr. Goodfellow went on for some half hour longer in this strain, very much to the credit both of his head and of his heart; but your warmhearted people are seldom apposite in their observations—they run into all sorts of blunders, *contre-temps* and *mal apropos-isms,* in the hotheadedness of their **12** zeal to serve a friend—thus, often with the kindest intentions in the world, doing infinitely more to prejudice his cause than to advance it.

So, in the present instance, it turned out with all the eloquence of "Old Charley"; for, although he labored earnestly in behalf of the suspected, yet it so happened, somehow or other, that every syllable he uttered of which the direct but unwitting tendency was not to exalt the speaker in the good opinion of his audience, had the effect of deepening the suspicion already attached to the individual whose cause he pleaded, and of arousing against him the fury of the mob.

One of the most unaccountable errors committed by the orator was his allusion to the suspected as "the heir of the worthy old gentleman Mr. Shuttleworthy." The people had really never thought of this before. They had only remembered certain threats of disinheritance uttered a year or two previously by the uncle (who had no living relative except the nephew), and they had, therefore, always looked upon this disinheritance as a matter that was settled—so single-minded a race of beings were the Rattleburghers; but the remark of "Old Charley" brought them at once to a consideration of this point, and thus gave them to see the possibility of the threats having been nothing *more* than a threat. And straightway, hereupon, arose the natural question of *cui bono?*—a question **13** that tended even more than the waistcoat to fasten the terrible crime upon the young man. And here, lest I be misunderstood, permit me to digress for one moment merely to observe that the exceedingly brief and simple Latin phrase which I have employed, is invariably mistranslated and misconceived. *"Cui bono?"* in all the crack novels and elsewhere,—in those of Mrs. Gore, for example, (the author of "Cecil,") a lady who **14** quotes all tongues from the Chaldæan to Chickasaw, and is **15,16** helped to her learning, "as needed," upon a systematic plan, **17,18,19** by Mr. Beckford,—in *all* the crack novels, I say, from those of Bulwer and Dickens to those of Turnapenny and Ainsworth, the two little Latin words *cui bono* are rendered "to what purpose," or, (as if *quo bono*) "to what good?" Their true meaning, nevertheless, is "for whose advantage." *Cui,* to whom; *bono,* is it for a benefit? It is a purely legal phrase, and applicable precisely in cases such as we have now under consideration, where the probability of the doer of a deed hinges upon the probability of the benefit accruing to this individual or to that from the deed's accomplishment. Now, in the present instance, the question *cui bono?* very pointedly

12 "Contretemps" means a mishap or disappointment. *"Mal à propos-isms"* is a bit recherché (to use Poe's term), since "malapropism" and "malapropos" are perfectly good English words. for an inappropriate term.

13 The explanation of the word is correct. It comes from Cicero's *Pro Roscio Amerino,* XXX, 84.

14 Catherine Grace Gore (1799–1861) was called "the novelist of fashionable life" by Thackeray. Her novel *Cecil* was published in 1841; *Mrs. Armytage, or Female Domination* (1836) is her nearest work to first rank.

15 The Chaldean Empire, in the southern part of the valley of the Tigris and Euphrates, flourished under Nebuchadnezzar II but came to an end in 539 B.C.

16 The Chickasaws were American Indians of the Hokan-Siouan linguistic stock, of what is now northern Mississippi.

17 Bulwer-Lytton wrote a series of books about interesting criminals, including *The Disowned* (1829), *Lucretia* (1846), *Paul Clifford* (1830), and *Eugene Aram* (1832). For Beckford, see "Landor's Cottage," note 22.

18 One who writes for money, although there is no listing of the word in the O.E.D.

19 English author William Harrison Ainsworth (1805–82) wrote a long list of historical novels (many with graphically horrifying pictures), mostly for the young, including *Jack Sheppard* (1839) and *The Tower of London* (1840). Poe complains of Ainsworth's errors in Latin in the *Democratic Review,* November 1844.

implicated Mr. Pennifeather. His uncle had threatened him, after making a will in his favor, with disinheritance. But the threat had not been actually kept; the original will, is appeared, had not been altered. *Had* it been altered, the only supposable motive for murder on the part of the suspected would have been the ordinary one for revenge; and even this would have been counteracted by the hope of reinstation into the good graces of the uncle. But the will being unaltered, while the threat to alter remained suspended over the nephew's head, there appears at once the very strongest possible inducement for the atrocity; and so concluded, very sagaciously, the worthy citizens of the borough of Rattle.

Mr Pennifeather was, accordingly, arrested upon the spot, and the crowd, after some further search, proceeded homeward, having him in custody. On the route, however, another circumstance occurred tending to confirm the suspicion entertained. Mr. Goodfellow, whose zeal led him to be always a little in advance of the party, was seen suddenly to run forward a few paces, stoop, and then apparently to pick up some small object from the grass. Having quickly examined it, he was observed, too, to make a sort of half attempt at concealing it in his coat pocket; but this action was noticed, as I say, and consequently prevented, when the object picked up was found to be a Spanish knife which a dozen persons at once recognized as belonging to Mr. Pennifeather. Moreover, his initials were engraved upon the handle. The blade of this knife was open and bloody.

No doubt now remained of the guilt of the nephew, and immediately upon reaching Rattleborough he was taken before a magistrate for examination.

Here matters again took a most unfavorable turn. The prisoner, being questioned as to his whereabouts on the morning of Mr. Shuttleworthy's disappearance, had absolutely the audacity to acknowledge that on that very morning he had been out with his rifle deer-stalking, in the immediate neighborhood of the pool where the bloodstained waistcoat had been discovered through the sagacity of Mr. Goodfellow.

This latter now came forward, and, with tears in his eyes, asked permission to be examined. He said that a stern sense of the duty he owed his Maker, not less than his fellow-men, would permit him no longer to remain silent. Hitherto, the sincerest affection for the young man (notwithstanding the latter's ill treatment of himself, Mr. Goodfellow) had induced him to make every hypothesis which imagination could suggest, by way of endeavoring to account for what appeared suspicious in the circumstances that told so seriously against Mr. Pennifeather; but these circumstances were now altogether *too* convincing—*too* damning; he would hesitate no longer—he would tell all he knew, although his heart (Mr. Goodfellow's) should absolutely burst asunder in the effort. He then went on to state that, on the afternoon of the day previous to Mr. Shuttleworthy's departure for the city, that worthy old gentleman had mentioned to his nephew, in *his* hearing (Mr. Goodfellow's), that his object in going to town

20 The nationality of the knife is of no importance other than marking it as Mr. Pennifeather's.

20

on the morrow was to make a deposit of an unusually large sum of money in the "Farmers' and Mechanics' Bank," and **21** that, then and there, the said Mr. Shuttleworthy had distinctly avowed to the said nephew his irrevocable determination of rescinding the will originally made, and of cutting him off with a shilling. He (the witness) now solemnly called upon the accused to state whether what he (the witness) had just stated was or was not the truth in every substantial particular. Much to the astonishment of every one present, Mr. Pennifeather frankly admitted that *it was*.

The magistrate now considered it his duty to send a couple of constables to search the chamber of the accused in the house of his uncle. From this search they almost immediately returned with the well-known steel-bound, russet leather pocket-book which the old gentleman had been in the habit of carrying for years. Its valuable contents, however, had been abstracted, and the magistrate in vain endeavored to extort from the prisoner the use which had been made of them, or the place of their concealment. Indeed, be obstinately denied all knowledge of the matter. The constables also discovered, between the bed and sacking of the unhappy man, a shirt and neck-handkerchief both marked with the initials of his name, and both hideously besmeared with the blood of the victim.

At this juncture, it was announced that the horse of the murdered man had just expired in the stable from the effects of the wound he had received, and it was proposed by Mr. Goodfellow that a *post-mortem* examination of the beast should be immediately made, with the view, if possible, of discovering the ball. This was accordingly done; and, as if to demonstrate beyond a question the guilt of the accused, Mr. Goodfellow, after considerable searching in the cavity of the chest, was enabled to detect and to pull forth a bullet of very extraordinary size, which, upon trial, was found to be exactly adapted to the bore of Mr. Pennifeather's rifle, while it was far too large for that of any other person in the borough or its vicinity. To render the matter even surer yet, however, this bullet was discovered to have a flaw or seam at right angles to the usual suture; and upon examination, this seam corresponded precisely with an accidental ridge or elevation in a pair of moulds acknowledged by the accused himself to be his own property. Upon the finding of this bullet, the examining magistrate refused to listen to any further testimony, and immediately committed the prisoner for trial—declining resolutely to take any bail in the case although against this severity Mr. Goodfellow very warmly remonstrated, and offered to become surety in whatever amount might be required. This generosity on the part of "Old Charley" was only in accordance with the whole tenor of his amiable and chivalrous conduct during the entire period of his sojourn in the borough of Rattle. In the present instance, the worthy man was so entirely carried away by the excessive warmth of his sympathy, that he seemed to have quite forgotten, when he offered to go bail for his young friend, that he himself (Mr. Goodfellow) did not possess a single dollar's worth of property upon the face of the earth.

21 The Farmers' and Mechanics' Bank opened in Philadelphia in 1824.

The result of the committal may be readily foreseen. Mr. Pennifeather, amid the loud execrations of all Rattleborough, was brought to trial at the next criminal sessions, when the chain of circumstantial evidence (strengthened as it was by some additional damning facts, which Mr. Goodfellow's sensitive conscientiousness forbade him to withhold from the court) was considered so unbroken and so thoroughly conclusive, that the jury, without leaving their seats, returned an immediate verdict of *"Guilty of murder in the first degree."* Soon afterward the unhappy wretch received sentence of death, and was remanded to the county jail to await the inexorable vengeance of the law.

In the meantime, the noble behavior of "Old Charley Goodfellow" had doubly endeared him to the honest citizens of the borough. He became ten times a greater favorite than ever; and, as a natural result of the hospitality with which he was treated, he relaxed, as it were, perforce, the extremely parsimonious habits which his poverty had hitherto impelled him to observe, and very frequently had little *réunions* at his own house, when wit and jollity reigned supreme—dampened a little, *of course*, by the occasional remembrance of the untoward and melancholy fate which impended over the nephew of the late lamented bosom friend of the generous host.

One fine day, this magnanimous old gentleman was agreeably surprised at the receipt of the following letter:—

> *"Charles Goodfellow, Esquire:*
> *"Dear Sir—In conformity with an order transmitted to our firm about two months since, by our esteemed correspondent, Mr. Barnabas Shuttleworthy, we have the honor of forwarding this morning, to your address, a double box of Château-Margaux, of the antelope brand, violet seal. Box numbered and marked as per margin.*
> 　　　　*"We remain, sir,*
> 　　　　　*"Your most ob'nt ser'ts,*
> 　　　　　　*"*Hoggs, Frogs, Bogs, & Co.
> *"City of——, June 21, 18—.*
> *"P.S.—The box will reach you, by wagon, on the day after your receipt of this letter. Our respects to Mr. Shuttleworthy.*
> 　　　　　　　*"*H., F., B., & Co.*"*

The fact is, that Mr. Goodfellow had, since the death of Mr. Shuttleworthy, given over all expectation of ever receiving the promised Château Margaux; and he, therefore, looked upon it *now* as a sort of especial dispensation of Providence in his behalf. He was highly delighted, of course, and in the exuberance of his joy invited a large party of friends to a *petit souper* on the morrow, for the purpose of broaching the good old Mr. Shuttleworthy's present. Not that he *said* any thing about "the good old Mr. Shuttleworthy" when he issued the invitations. The fact is, he thought much and concluded to say nothing at all. He did *not* mention to any one—if I remember aright—that he had received a *present* of Château Margaux. He merely asked his friends to come and help him drink some

22 "Bogs, Hogs, Logs, Frogs, & Co." appears in Poe's comic essay "Diddling."

23 Supper

of a remarkably fine quality and rich flavor that he ordered up from the city a couple of months ago, and of which he would be in the receipt upon the morrow. I have often puzzled myself to imagine *why* it was that "Old Charley" came to the conclusion to say nothing about having received the wine from his old friend, but I could never precisely understand his reason for the silence, although he had *some* excellent and very magnanimous reason, no doubt. **24**

The morrow at length arrived, and with it a very large and highly respectable company at Mr. Goodfellow's house. Indeed, half the borough was there,—I myself among the number,—but, much to the vexation of the host, the Château Margaux did not arrive until a late hour, and when the sumptuous supper supplied by "Old Charley" had been done very ample justice by the guests. It came at length, however— a monstrously big box of it there was, too,—and as the whole party were in excessively good humor, it was decided, *nem. con.*, that it should be lifted upon the table and its contents **25** disembowelled forthwith.

No sooner said than done. I lent a helping hand; and, in a trice, we had the box upon the table, in the midst of all the bottles and glasses, not a few of which were demolished in the scuffle. "Old Charley," who was pretty much intoxicated, and excessively red in the face, now took a seat, with an air of mock dignity, at the head of the board, and thumped furiously upon it with a decanter, calling upon the company to keep order "during the ceremony of disinterring the treasure."

After some vociferation, quiet was at length fully restored, and, as very often happens in similar cases, a profound and remarkable silence ensued. Being then requested to force open the lid, I complied, of course, "with an infinite deal of pleasure." I inserted a chisel, and giving it a few slight taps with a hammer, the top of the box flew suddenly off, and, at the same instant, there sprang up into a sitting position, directly facing the host, the bruised, bloody, and nearly putrid corpse of the murdered Mr. Shuttleworthy himself. It gazed for a few moments, fixedly and sorrowfully, with its decaying and lack-lustre eyes, full into the countenance of Mr. Good- fellow; uttered slowly, but clearly and impressively, the words—"Thou art the man!" and then, falling over the side of the chest as if thoroughly satisfied, stretched out its limbs quiveringly upon the table.

The scene that ensued is altogether beyond description. The rush for the doors and windows was terrific, and many of the most robust men in the room fainted outright through sheer horror. But after the first wild, shrieking burst of affright, all eyes were directed to Mr. Goodfellow. If I live a thousand years, I can never forget the more than mortal agony which was depicted in that ghastly face of his, so lately rubicund **26** with triumph and wine. For several minutes he sat rigidly as a statue of marble; his eyes seeming, in the intense vacancy of their gaze, to be turned inward and absorbed in the contemplation of his own miserable, murderous soul. At length their expression appeared to flash suddenly out into the

24 The narrator is playing games with us, since he already knows the truth and all this is merely for show. How much better the story would be if Dupin were the detective and his friend were describing the events that followed and the effect they had on him and the dinner guests. Instead, we have at the end something like "Oh, I forgot to tell you something that may clear up matters." In the Dupin stories, the evidence is always right there in front of us, awaiting only Dupin's explanation of what it all means.

25 *Nemine contradicente*, without opposition

26 "Red-faced with good living" (O.E.D.)

"Old Charley" *Artist unknown*

external world, when, with a quick leap, he sprang from his chair, and falling heavily with his head and shoulders upon the table, and in contact with the corpse, poured out rapidly and vehemently a detailed confession of the hideous crime for which Mr. Pennifeather was then imprisoned and doomed to die.

What he recounted was in substance this:—He followed his victim to the vicinity of the pool; there shot his horse with a pistol; despatched its rider with the butt end; possessed himself of the pocket-book; and, supposing the horse dead, dragged it with great labor to the brambles by the pond. Upon his own beast he slung the corpse of Mr. Shuttleworthy, and thus bore it to a secure place of concealment a long distance off through the woods.

The waistcoat, the knife, the pocket-book, and bullet, had been placed by himself where found, with the view of avenging himself upon Mr. Pennifeather. He had also contrived the discovery of the stained handkerchief and shirt.

Toward the end of the blood-chilling recital, the words of the guilty wretch faltered and grew hollow. When the record was finally exhausted, he arose, staggered backward from the table, and fell—*dead*.

The means by which this happily-timed confession was extorted, although efficient, were simple indeed. Mr. Goodfellow's excess of frankness had disgusted me, and excited my suspicions from the first. I was present when Mr. Pennifeather had struck him, and the fiendish expression which then arose upon his countenance, although momentary, assured me that his threat of vengeance would, if possible, be rigidly fulfilled. I was thus prepared to view the *manœuvring* of "Old Charley" in a very different light from that in which it was regarded by the good citizens of Rattleborough. I saw at once that all the criminating discoveries arose, either directly or indirectly, from himself. But the fact which clearly opened my eyes to the true state of the case, was the affair of the bullet, *found* by Mr. G. in the carcass of the horse. *I* had not forgotten, although the Rattleburghers *had*, that there was a hole where the ball had entered the horse, and another where it *went out*. If it were found in the animal then, after having made its exit, I saw clearly that it must have been deposited by the person who found it. The bloody shirt and handkerchief confirmed the idea suggested by the bullet; for the blood on examination proved to be capital claret, and no more. When I came to think of these things, and also of the late increase of liberality and expenditure on the part of Mr. Goodfellow, I entertained a suspicion which was none the less strong because I kept it altogether to myself.

In the meantime, I instituted a rigorous private search for the corpse of Mr. Shuttleworthy, and, for good reasons, searched in quarters as divergent as possible from those to which Mr. Goodfellow conducted his party. The result was that, after some days, I came across an old dry well, the mouth of which was nearly hidden by brambles; and here, at the bottom, I discovered what I sought.

Now it so happened that I had overheard the colloquy between the two cronies, when Mr. Goodfellow had contrived to cajole his host into the promise of a box of Château Margaux. Upon this hint I acted. I procured a stiff piece of whalebone, thrust it down the throat of the corpse, and deposited the latter in an old wine box—taking care so to double the body up as to double the whalebone with it. In this manner I had to press forcibly upon the lid to keep it down while I secured it with nails; and I anticipated, of course, that as soon as these latter were removed, the top would fly *off* and the body *up*. 27

Having thus arranged the box, I marked, numbered, and addressed it as already told; and then writing a letter in the name of the wine-merchants with whom Mr. Shuttleworthy dealt, I gave instructions to my servant to wheel the box to Mr. Goodfellow's door, in a barrow, at a given signal from myself. For the words which I intended the corpse to speak, I confidently depended upon my ventriloquial abilities; for 28 their effect, I counted upon the conscience of the murderous wretch.

I believe there is nothing more to be explained. Mr. Pennifeather was released upon the spot, inherited the fortune of his uncle, profited by the lessons of experience, turned over a new leaf, and led happily ever afterward a new life. 29

27 Neither Poe nor the narrator seems to have taken *rigor mortis* into account, or if that state had passed, the extensive decay and smell.

28 A convenient talent, one he has kept hidden from us until now

29 Marie Bonaparte points out that "the poor hack-writer, so appropriately named Mr. Pennifeather, is as innocent as the new-born babe of the murder of his rich uncle, Mr. Shuttleworthy, whose heir he is. Only a double of the latter, a rogue ironically called Old Charley Goodfellow, who likewise belongs to the series of 'fathers' or hypocritical John Allans, could have been capable of so heinous a deed!" (P. 499)

Humor and Satire

THE DUC DE L'OMELLETTE

First published in the Philadelphia *Saturday Courier*, March 3, 1832, and revised several times before appearing in its final form in the collected works of 1850.

Perhaps because it is short and simple, this is one of Poe's more successful comic tales. Too, the hero is more sympathetic than many of Poe's protagonists, in part because we tend to side with *any* man who attempts to beat the Devil.

"The Duc De L'Omelette" is apparently a comic appraisal of the career of writer N. P. Willis, whose literary death was constantly predicted by his humorless critics but who eventually became a popular success by means of the very conceits that had been pounced on by the literati.

Nathaniel Parker Willis (1806–67) has been described as an arrant sensationalist and something of a fop. His literary style is treated more fully in the notes that follow, but one incident involving Willis gives another side of his character. The editor of one magazine made a personal attack on Willis in his pages, and Willis challenged him to a duel (shots were fired, but neither man was seriously injured).

Today, Willis is a forgotten figure except for his association with Poe, whom he at first criticized (see "Lionizing") but later encouraged.

And stepped at once into a cooler clime.
—*Cowper*.   **1**

Keats fell by a criticism. Who was it died of "The Andromache?" **2,3**
Ignoble souls!—De L'Omelette perished of an ortolan. **4**
L'histoire en est brève. Assist me, Spirit of Apicius! **5**

A golden cage bore the little winged wanderer, enamored, melting, indolent, to the *Chaussée D'Antin*, from its home in **6** far Peru. From its queenly possessor La Bellissima, to the **7** Duc De L'Omelette, six peers of the empire conveyed the happy bird. **8**

That night the Duc was to sup alone. In the privacy of his **9** bureau he reclined languidly on that ottoman for which he sacrificed his loyalty in outbidding his king,—the notorious ottoman of Cadêt. **10**

He buries his face in the pillow. The clock strikes! Unable to restrain his feelings, his Grace swallows an olive. At this moment the door gently opens to the sound of soft music, and lo! the most delicate of birds is before the most enamored of men! But what inexpensive dismay now overshadows the countenance of the Duc?—"*Horreur!—chien!—Baptiste!— l'oiseau! ah, bon Dieu! cet oiseau modeste que tu as déshabillé de ses plumes, et que tu as servi sans papier!*" It is superfluous **11** to say more:—the Duc expired in a paroxysm of disgust. * * *

"Ha! ha! ha!" said his Grace on the third day after his decease.

1 From William Cowper (1731–1800), *The Task* I, 337. This long poem, written in 1785, foreshadows nineteenth-century romanticism in its descriptions of life in the country.

2 John Keats (1795–1821) returned from a walking tour of the Highlands to discover he had been critically attacked in an edition of *Blackwood's Magazine and Quarterly Review* (1818). It was a turning point in his career, and while popular accounts have it that he died of a broken heart, the real cause was tuberculosis, which he had contracted from nursing his dying brother, Tom, that same year. Keats died three years later in Italy.

3 "Montfleury. The author of the *Parnasse Réformé* makes him speak in Hades:—*L'homme donc qui voudrait savoir de dont je suis mort, qu'il ne demande pas s'il fût de fièvre ou de podagre ou d'autre chose, mais qu'il entende que ce fut de 'L'Andromache.'*" (Poe's note)

The quote comes from Isaac D'Israeli's article "Tragic Actors," in his *Curiosities of Literature*, where he translates the entire passage: "A thousand times have I been obliged to force myself to represent more passions than Le Brun ever painted or conceived . . . and consequently to strain all the parts of my body to render my gestures fitter to accompany those different impressions. The man then who would know of what I died, let him not ask if it were of a fever, the dropsy, or the gout; but let him know that it was of the Andromache!"

Montfleury was a French actor who supposedly died of overacting while performing in Racine's *Andromaque*. The *Parnasse Réformé*, from which this passage comes in its original form, was written by Gabriel Guéret (1641–88).

4 Ortolans are very small birds, much prized in France for their flavor when roasted and eaten whole in one mouthful, except for the legs, which are wrapped in paper. In Benjamin D'Israeli's *The Young Duke* (1831) we find, "Let me die eating ortolans to the sound of soft music." The French means, "The story of it is brief."

5 Marcus Gabius Apicius was a Roman gourmand of the first century A.D. who squandered most of his large fortune on feasts, and then, realizing he would have to economize in the future, committed suicide. The cookbook that bears his name is actually by some later author, possibly a man named Caelius.

6 The Chaussée d'Antin was a fashionable Paris street. As for the bird from "far Peru," this is really a swipe at Willis, who in his writings mentions his South American trulian, which flew freely from room to room in his home.

7 The Most Beautiful

8 As in a sacrificial ritual

9 Willis, in the *American Monthly Magazine*, wrote a column from what he described as a crimson-curtained room, seated at a rosewood desk with Chinese cupid ink holders and velvet butterfly pen wipers. The reader was invited to "lounge" on a nearby Turkish ottoman (while dodging the flying trulian, one supposes) and help himself to a plate of olives Willis kept on his desk.

"Have another olive, that large, green beauty—nay—you are quite welcome" is a typical line from Willis' column (*American Monthly*, October 1830).

10 Cadêt Rousselle was a theatrical character who burlesqued the great heroes of legend and history from the French Revolution through the first half of the nineteenth century (*Cadêt Rousselle au jardin Turc, Cadêt Rousselle chez le sultan Achmet*, etc.). Which play is referred to here is not certain, but "ottoman" does also mean "Turk."

11 "Horror! dog! Baptist! the bird—oh, good Lord! This little bird which you have stripped the feathers from, and which you have served without paper!" (See note 4)

12 Prince of Goose Liver (pâté)

13 Poems with the ending "-iad" were very popular in the eighteenth and early-nineteenth centuries (*The Dunciad, The Columbiad*). This one celebrates the mazurka, a Polish round dance that Chopin used as the basis for many of his piano works.

14 The Académie Française, which governs French arts and letters

15 There was a tailor in Paris by the name of Bourdon between 1831 and 1836.

16 No one has been able to trace the name to an actual tailor.

17 Curling papers. The comparison is clear between the ortolan, frying in its own grease and its legs encased in paper, and the Duc, roasting in Hell.

18 One of the Phoenician deities was a fly, called a *zebub*, and the name of the fly god was *Baal Zebub*, from which comes Beelzebub, sometimes used to mean Satan and at other times one of his lieutenants (Milton's *Paradise Lost*).

Nathaniel Parker Willis
Artist unknown

"He! he! he!" replied the Devil faintly, drawing himself up with an air of *hauteur*.

"Why, surely you are not serious," retorted De L'Omelette. "I have sinned—*c'est vrai*—but, my good sir, consider!—you have no actual intention of putting such—such—barbarous threats into execution."

"No *what?*" said his Majesty—"come, sir, strip!"

"Strip, indeed! very pretty i' faith! no, sir, I shall *not* strip. Who are you, pray, that I, Duc De L'Omelette, Prince de **12,13** Foie-Gras, just come of age, author of the 'Mazurkiad,' and **14** Member of the Academy, should divest myself at your bidding **15** of the sweetest pantaloons ever made by Bourdon, the dantiest **16** *robe-de-chambre* ever put together by Rombêrt—to say noth- **17** ing of the taking my hair out of paper—not to mention the trouble I should have in drawing off my gloves?"

18 "Who am I?—ah, true! I am Baal-Zebub, Prince of the Fly. I took thee, just now, from a rose-wood coffin inlaid with **19** ivory. Thou wast curiously scented, and labelled as per invoice. **20** Belial sent thee,—my Inspector of Cemeteries. The pantaloons, which thou sayest were made by Bourdon, are an excellent pair of linen drawers, and thy *robe-de-chambre* is a shroud of no scanty dimensions."

"Sir!" replied the Suc, "I am not to be insulted with **21** impunity!—Sir! I shall take the earliest opportunity of avenging this insult!—Sir! you shall hear from me! In the meantime *au revoir!*"—and the Duc was bowing himself out of the Satanic presence, when he was interrupted and brought back by a gentleman in waiting. Hereupon his Grace rubbed his eyes, yawned, shrugged his shoulders, reflected. Having become satisfied of his identity, he toook a bird's-eye view of his whereabouts.

The apartment was superb. Even De L'Omelette pro- **22** nounced it *bien comme il faut*. It was not its length nor its breadth,—but its height—ah, that was appalling!—There was no ceiling—certainly none—but a dense whirling mass of fiery-colored clouds. His Grace's brain reeled as he glanced upward. From above, hung a chain of an unknown blood-red metal—its upper end lost, like the city of Boston, *parmi les* **23** *nues.* From its nether extremity swung a large cresset. The **24,25** Duc knew it to be a ruby; but from it there poured a light so intense, so still, so terrible, Persia never worshipped such—Gheber never imagined such—Mussulman never dreamed of such when, drugged with opium, he has tottered to a bed of poppies, his back to the flowers, and his face to the God Apollo. The Duc muttered a slight oath, decidedly approba- **26** tory.

The corners of the room were rounded into niches. Three of these were filled with statues of gigantic proportions. Their beauty was Grecian, their deformity Egyptian, their *tout ensemble* French. In the fourth niche the statue was veiled; it was *not* colossal. But then there was a taper ankle, a sandalled foot. De L'Omelette pressed his hand upon his **27** heart, closed his eyes, raised them, and caught his Satanic Majesty—in a blush.

But the paintings!—Kupris! Astarte! Astoreth!—a thousand **28** and the same! And Rafael has beheld them! Yes, Rafael has **29** been here; for did he not paint the ——? and was he not consequently damned? The paintings!—the paintings! O luxury! O love!—who, gazing on those forbidden beauties, shall have eyes for the dainty devices of the golden frames that besprinkled, like stars, the hyacinth and the prophyry walls? **30**

But the Duc's heart is fainting within him. He is not, however, as you suppose, dizzy with magnificence, nor drunk with the estatic breath of those innumerable censers. *C'est vrai que de toutes ces choses il a pensé beaucoup—mais!* The **31** Duc De L'Omelette is terror-stricken; for, through the lurid vista which a single uncurtained window is affording, lo! gleams the most ghastly of all fires!

Le pauvre Duc! He could not help imagining that the glorious, the voluptuous, the never-dying melodies which pervaded that hall, as they passed filtered and transmuted through the alchemy of the enchanted window-panes, were the wailings and the howlings of the hopeless and the damned! And there, too!—there!—upon the ottoman!—who could *he* be?—he, the *petit-maître*—no, the Deity—who sat as if carved **32** in marble, *et qui sourit*, with his pale countenance, *si amérement?* **33**

Mais il faut agir—that is to say, a Frenchman never faints **34** outright. Besides, his Grace hated a scene—De L'Omelette is himself again. There were some foils upon a table—some points also. The Duc had studied under B——; *il avait tué ses* **35** *six hommes.* Now, then, *il peut s'échapper.* He measures two points, and, with a grace inimitable, offers his Majesty the choice. *Horreur!* his Majesty does not fence! **36**

Mais il joue!—how happy a thought!—but his Grace had always an excellent memory. He had dipped in the *"Diable"* of the Abbé Gualtier. Therein it is said *"que le Diable n'ose* **37** *pas refuser un jeu d'écarté."* **38**

19 Referring to Willis' rosewood desk and the bottle of perfumed Hungary water he kept there

20 Another name of a devil, from the Hebrew "shame" or "worthlessness"

21 Compare this with Fortunato's comment early in "The Cask of Amontillado."

22 As it should be

23 The blood-red metal was called *orichalcum* in Latin, and was supposedly from Atlantis, but it was also the name of the yellow brass used in Roman coins.
Compare the following, from Poe's *Al Aaraaf:* "Let down our golden everlasting chain / Whose strong embrace holds Heaven and Earth and Main."

24 "Among the clouds," the description of Mount Atlas in Pomponius Mela's *De Situ Orbis,* III, 10
In Poe's first version it is Coleridge who is lost, then Carlyle, and finally Boston in the *Broadway Journal* version (October 11, 1845), probably because Poe was speaking in that city shortly after the story appeared.

25 An iron vessel with a burning wick, suspended from a chain or cord to serve as a lantern

26 An allusion to sun worship or fire worship by various peoples. Ghebers are the Parsees of Bombay (fire worshipers). The god Apollo is also identified with the sun.

27 The Venus of Milo was discovered in 1820.

28 Kupris (from which Cypress takes its name) is one of the names for the Greek gooddess Aphrodite. The Phoenician Astarte is also identified with the goddess of love. Astoreth is here meant as another name for the goddess, but in the Bible it is given a more general usage (I Samuel 12:10). See also *The Meaning of Aphrodite,* by Paul Friedrich, Chicago, 1978.

29 Referring to Raphael, or Raffaello Sanzio (1483–1520), this comment has yet to be satisfactorily explained.

30 Porphyritic rock is a granite with crystals imbedded in it. "Hyacinth" apparently refers to jacinth, an expensive stone.

31 "It is true that he thought of all these things a good deal—but!" Willis had a habit of dropping French phrases in his writing (but then, so did Poe).

32 The little master

33 ". . . who smiled so bitterly"

34 "But something has to be done."

35 Fencing swords

36 ". . . he has killed six men. . . . He could escape."
"B——" is probably Joseph T. Buckingham, editor of the *Courier,* who had rebuked Willis for pretension.

37 The Abbé Louis Édouard Camille Gaultier (1746–1818) was well known for his theory that languages and geography could be taught through games. He wrote nothing by the title given here.

38 "The Devil does not dare refuse a game of cards." The tradition of beating the Devil at his own game recurs frequently in folklore and literature.

39 Charles Le Brun (1619–90) was the virtual dictator of the arts in France under Louis XIV, until the death of his protector, Colbert. For the French Academy, he laid down a strict system of rules, and even wrote a treatise on the expression of the passions.

40 Vingt-et-un, or blackjack, is a card game originating in French casinos about 1700.

41 "If I lose I will be twice damned; if I win, I will return to my ortolans—let the cards be readied!"

42 "Bresquet, jester to Francis the first of France, did keep a calendar of fools, wherewith he did use to make the king sport, telling him ever the reason why he put one into his calendar. When Charles the fifth, emperor, upon confidence of the noble nature of Francis, passed through France, for the appeasing of the rebellion of Gaunt, Bresquet put him into his calendar. The King asked him the cause. He answered, 'Because you having suffered at the hands of Charles the greatest bitterness . . . he would trust his person into your hands.' 'Why, Bresquet,' said the King, 'what wilt thou say, if thou seest him pass in as great safety?' Saith Bresquet, 'Why then I will put him out, and put in you.'" (Francis Bacon, *Apophthegms*, No. 200)

43 "It's your play."

44 Laying down the king

45 Alexander the Great once visited Diogenes of Sinope and asked him if he could do the philosopher a favor. "Get out of my sunlight," said Diogenes. Alexander later remarked that if he were to be anyone but Alexander, he would be Diogenes.

Poe refers to "Alexander the drunkard" in the first version of the tale.

46 "Had he not been De L'Omelette, he would have had no objection to being the Devil."

But the chances—the chances! True—desperate; but scarcely more desperate than the Duc. Besides, was he not **39** in the secret?—had he not skimmed over Père Le Brun?— **40** was he not a member of the Club Vingt-un? "*Si je perds,*" said he, "*je serai deux fois perdu*—I shall be doubly damned— *voilà tout!* (Here his Grace shrugged his shoulders.) *Si je gagne, je reviendrai à mes ortolans—que les cartes soient* **41** *préparées!*"

His Grace was all care, all attention—his Majesty all confidence. A spectator would have thought of Francis and **42** Charles. His Grace thought of his game. His Majesty did not think; he shuffled. The Duc cut.

The cards are dealt. The trump is turned—it is—it is—the king! No—it was the queen. His Majesty cursed her masculine habiliments. De L'Omelette placed his hand upon his heart.

They play. The Duc counts. The hand is out. His Majesty counts heavily, smiles, and is taking wine. The Duc slips a card.

43 "*C'est à vous à faire,*" said his Majesty, cutting. His Grace **44** bowed, dealt, and arose from the table *en presentant le Roi*.

His Majesty looked chagrined.

Had Alexander not been Alexander, he would have been **45** Diogenes; and the Duc assured his antagonist in taking leave, "*que s'il n'eût été De L'Omelette il n'aurait point d'objection* **46** *d'être le Diable.*"

His Majesty looked chagrined. *Illustration by F. S. Coburn, 1902*

A TALE OF JERUSALEM

First published in the Philadelphia *Saturday Courier*, June 9, 1832, revised and published in the present version in the *Broadway Journal*, September 20, 1845.

Although Poe pokes fun at the dietary laws of the Jews, this tale should not really be called anti-Semitic. True, the Romans come out the winner, but then, every practical joke must have a victim.

Poe's chief source is Horatio Smith's *Zillah, a Tale of the Holy City* (1828), including the sequence of events, the Hebraic allusions, and even some of the speech patterns of the characters.

In Chapter I, page 219, of *Zillah* we read, "When the Holy City was besieged, not many years agone, they let down in a basket, every day, over the walls, so much money as would buy lambs for the daily sacrifices, which lambs they drew up again in the same basket. But an Israelite, who spoke Greek, having acquainted the besiegers that so long as sacrifices were offered the city could not be taken, the profane villains popped a hog in the basket instead of the usual victim, and from that time we have been accustomed to curse every one that could speak Greek."

Ben-Zion Yedidiah translated Poe's tale into Hebrew for his anthology *Gaheleth-Ha-Esh* (Tel Aviv, 1950).

Intonsos rigidam in frontem ascendere canos
Passus erat——

             —LUCAN—*De Catone*.   **1**

——a bristly *bore*.

           —*Translation*.

"Let us hurry to the walls," said Abel-Phittim to Buzi-Ben- **2**
Levi and Simeon the Pharisee, on the tenth day of the month
Thammuz, in the year of the world three thousand nine **3**
hundred and forty-one—"let us hasten to the ramparts ad- **4**
joining the gate of Benjamin, which is in the city of David, **5**
and overlooking the camp of the uncircumcised; for it is the **6**
last hour of the fourth watch, being sunrise; and the idolaters,
in fulfilment of the promise of Pompey, should be awaiting us
with the lambs for the sacrifices." **7**

Simeon, Abel-Phittim, and Buzi-Ben-Levi, were the Gizbarim, or subcollectors of the offering, in the holy city of
Jerusalem. **8**

"Verily," replied the Pharisee, "let us hasten: for this
generosity in the heathen is unwonted; and fickle-mindedness
has ever been an attribute of the worshippers of Baal." **9**

"That they are fickle-minded and treacherous is as true as
the Pentateuch," said Buzi-Ben-Levi, "but that is only toward **10**
the people of Adonai. When was it ever known that the **11**
Ammonites proved wanting to their own interests? Methinks **12**

1 Poe has some fun here with the original quotation from Lucan's *Pharsalia*, II, 375–76, replacing *descendere* with *ascendere*, so that the line now reads "his uncut grey hair stood on end," instead of the original "He let his uncut grey hair hang down over his stern forehead." One late editor didn't get the joke and corrected the quotation.

2. Abel-Shittim in the first edition. It means a grove of acacia trees, as well as a spot on the Plain of Moab, although Poe no doubt relished the scatalogical connotation.

Buzi is close to the word *buz*, or "contempt," and was the name of Ezekiel's father (Ezekiel 1:3). His full name here means Buzi, son of Levi.

In ancient times the Levites served as priests. Of the twelve tribes, they alone received no allotment of land; instead they received revenue from certain cities, and each city had its quota of Levites to support.

"Simeon," or "Shimeon," means a "hearkening."

3 The tenth month of the Hebrew year

4 Poe is obviously referring to the siege of Jerusalem in 65 B.C. (or 63 B.C., depending on the reference source). But 65 B.C. was not the year 3941 in the Jewish calendar. The year 3941 would have been about A.D. 180. The correct year here would be 3695.

5 "They passed out by the gate of Benjamin, at the northeast corner of the city" (*Zillah*, IV, 276). See also Jeremiah 38:7.

The "City of David" meant the oldest portion of the city, where David set up his capital about 1000 B.C.

6 Circumcision among the Jews has always been a symbol of the Covenant with God made by Abraham. Here it is used only for comic effect in the voluminous verbiage of the speaker.

7 Gnaeus Pompeius Magnus, or Pompey (106–48 B.C.), was a Roman general and rival of Julius Caesar. He helped stop the slave revolt led by Spartacus, annexed Syria and Palestine, and began the Roman organization of the East. With Caesar and Crassus, he formed the First Triumvirate; then he married Caesar's daughter. Later (49 B.C.), Caesar broke with the Senate and crossed the Rubicon, starting civil war. Pompey fled to Egypt after being defeated at Pharsala (48 B.C.) and was assassinated there.

The sacrifices are dictated in Exodus 29:38: "Now this is that which thou shalt offer upon the altar; two lambs of the first year day by day continually. . . ."

8 From *Zillah*, I, 44, although Poe has thoughtfully corrected the spelling from Gizbarin to Gizbarim.

9 Baal is the name used throughout the Old Testament for the deity or deities of Canaan. Originally applied to any local god, by the fourteenth century B.C., Baal was the ruler of the universe. The cult of Baal found its way into Israel and merged with local beliefs.

The practices of holy prostitution and of child sacrifice were horrifying to the Hebrew prophets, who denounced the cult and its temples.

10 "As true as the Pentateuch" is from *Zillah*, I, 17. The Pentateuch is the first five books of the Old Testament.

11 "Lord." Adonai is the word used by pious Jews when they read from the Scriptures where the name of God, JHVH, or "Jehovah," is written.

12 From Ammon, east of the Dead Sea. The god of Ammon was Milcom, to whom Solomon built an altar. A Semitic people, the Ammonites flourished from the thirteenth to the eighteenth centuries B.C. and were then absorbed by the Arabs. They were hostile to the Hebrews, to whom they were supposedly related (the common ancestor was Lot's son).

13 From *Zillah*, I, 103: "The Jews reckoned five corners of their beards—one on either cheek, one on either lip, and one below on the chin,—all of which a priest was forbidden to shave." See also Leviticus 21:5.

14 "The Dashing Pharisee, so called, because he crawled along apart and in humility; the heel of one foot touching the great toe of the other, and neither foot being lifted from the ground, so that his toes dashed against the stones" (*Zillah*, IV, 144)

15 The Philistines were a non-Semitic people who came from the Aegean (probably Crete) in the twelfth century B.C. Their control of iron supplies and their close political organization of cities made them a rival of Israel for centuries—so much so that their name became a synonym for "barbarian."

16 "And the Lord went before them by day in a pillar of a cloud, to lead them the way; and by night in a pillar of fire, to give them light; to go by day and night" (Exodus 13:21).

In *Zillah*, I, 95 (note), we find that "It is maintained by the Talmudists, that the rain never put out the fire of the altar, not did the wind ever prevail over its pillar of smoke."

it is no great stretch of generosity to allow us lambs for the altar of the Lord, receiving in lieu thereof thirty silver shekels per head!"

"Thou forgettest, however, Ben-Levi," replied Abel-Phittim, "that the Roman Pompey, who is now impiously besieging the city of the Most High, has no assurity that we apply not the lambs thus purchased for the altar, to the sustenance of the body, rather than of the spirit."

13   "Now, by the five corners of my beard!" shouted the Pharisee, who belonged to the sect called The Dashers (that little knot of saints whose manner of *dashing* and lacerating the feet against the pavement was long a thorn and a reproach to less zealous devotees—a stumbling-block to less gifted

14 perambulators)—"by the five corners of that beard which, as a priest, I am forbidden to shave!—have we lived to see the day when a blaspheming and idolatrous upstart of Rome shall accuse us of appropriating to the appetites of the flesh the most holy and consecrated elements? Have we lived to see the day when——"

15   "Let us not question the motives of the Philistine," interrupted Abel-Phittim, "for to-day we profit for the first time by his avarice or by his generosity; but rather let us hurry to the ramparts, lest offerings should be wanting for that altar whose fire the rains of heaven cannot extinguish, and whose

16 pillars of smoke no tempest can turn aside."

That part of the city to which our worthy Gizbarim now hastened, and which bore the name of its architect, King David, was esteemed the most strongly-fortified district of

17 Jerusalem; being situated upon the steep and lofty hill of Zion.

18 Here, a broad, deep, circumvallatory trench, hewn from the solid rock, was defended by a wall of great strength erected upon its inner edge. This wall was adorned, at regular interspaces, by square towers of white marble; the lowest sixty, and the highest one hundred and twenty cubits in

19 height. But, in the vicinity of the gate of Benjamin, the wall

20 arose by no means from the margin of the fosse. On the contrary, between the level of the ditch and the basement of the rampart, sprang up a perpendicular cliff of two hundred

21 and fifty cubits, forming part of the precipitous Mount Moriah. So that when Simeon and his associated arrived on the summit

22 of the tower called Adoni-Bezek—the loftiest of all the turrets around about Jerusalem, and the usual place of conference with the besieging army—they looked down upon the camp of the enemy from an eminence excelling by many feet that

23 of the Pyramid of Cheops, and, by several, that of the temple of Belus.

"Verily," sighed the Pharisee, as he peered dizzily over the precipice, "the uncircumcised are as the sands by the sea-

24 shore—as the locusts in the wilderness! The valley of the King

25 hath become the valley of Adommin."

"And yet," added Ben-Levi, "thou canst not point me out a Philistine—no, not one—from Aleph to Tau—from the wilderness to the battlements—who seemeth any bigger than

26 the letter Jod!"

"Lower away the basket with the shekels of silver!" here shouted a Roman soldier in a hoarse, rough voice, which appeared to issue from the regions of Pluto—"lower away the **27** basket with the accursed coin which it has broken the jaw of a noble Roman to pronounce! Is it thus you evince your **28** gratitude to our master Pompeius, who, in his condescension, has thought fit to listen to your idolatrous importunities? The god Phœbus, who is a true god, has been charioted, for an hour—and were you not to be on the ramparts by sunrise? **29** Ædepol!—do you think that we, the conquerors of the world, **30** have nothing better to do than stand waiting by the walls of every kennel, to traffic with the dogs of the earth? Lower away! I say—and see that your trumpery be bright in color **31** and just in weight!"

"El Elohim!" ejaculated the Pharisee, as the discordant **32** tones of the centurion rattled up the crags of the precipice, and fainted away against the temple—"El Elohim!—*who* is the God Phœbus?—*whom* doth the blasphemer invoke? Thou, Buzi-Ben-Levi who art read in the laws of the Gentiles, and hast sojourned among them who dabble with the Teraphim!— **33** is it Nergal of whom the idolator speaketh?—or Ashimah?— or Nibhaz?—or Tartak?—or Adramalech?—or Anamalech?— or Succoth-Benith?—or Dagon?—or Belial?—or Baal-Perith?—or Baal-Peor?—or Baal-Zebub?" **34**

"Verily it is neither—but beware how thou lettest the rope slip too rapidly through thy fingers; for should the wicker-work chance to hang on the projecting of yonder crag, there will be a woful outpouring of the holy things of the sanctuary."

By the assistance of some rudely constructed machinery, the heavily laden basket was now carefully lowered down among the multitude; and, from the giddy pinnacle, the Romans were seen gathering confusedly round it; but owing to the vast height and the prevalence of a fog, no distinct view of their operations could be obtained.

Half an hour had already elapsed.

"We shall be too late!" sighed the Pharisee, as at the expiration of this period, he looked over into the abyss—"we shall be too late! we shall be turned out of office by the Katholim." **35**

"No more," responded Abel-Phittim,—"no more shall we **36** feast upon the fat of the land—no longer shall our beards be odorous with frankincense—our loins girded up with fine linen from the Temple."

"Raca!" swore Ben-Levi, "Raca! do they mean to defraud **37** us of the purchase money or, Holy Moses! are they weighing the shekels of the tabernacle?"

"They have given the signal at last!" cried the Pharisee— "they have given the signal at last!—pull away, Abel-Phittim!— and thou, Buzi-Ben-Levi, pull away!—for verily the Philistines have either still hold upon the basket, or the Lord hath softened their hearts to place therein a beast of good weight!" And the Gizbarim pulled away, while their burthen swung heavily upward through the still increasing mist.

* * *

17 "Yet have I set my king upon my holy hill of Zion" (Psalms 2:6). David conquered the city that later became Jerusalem from the Jebusites, and put up a great wall around it. "Zion" is defined in 2 Samuel 5:7 as the city of David. Christian tradition names the city's south-western hill as Zion, but there is still much controversy over its location. Originally the name referred to the Jebusite fortress on the southeastern hill.

The name became symbolic of Jerusalem, of the Promised Land, of the Messianic hopes of Israel (hence, Zionism), and among Christians, of Heaven.

18 "Circumvallate" means to surround with a rampart, but the O.E.D. does not give the varient Poe uses here.

19 A cubit is about eighteen inches, originally the length of the forearm from the elbow to the tip of the middle finger. The first tower is thus ninety feet high, while the second is one hundred eighty feet high.

20 A ditch or moat

21 The site of the Temple. The name means "chosen of God."

22 Adoni-bezek was the king of Bezek, who was captured by the Israelites and brought back to Jerusalem. In Judges 1:5–7 we read: "And they found Adoni-bezek in Bezek: and they fought against him, and they slew the Canaanites and the Perizzites. But Adoni-bezek fled; and they pursued after him, and caught him, and cut off his thumbs and his great toes. And Adoni-bezek said, Threescore and ten kings, having their thumbs and their great toes cut off, gathered their meat under my table: as I have done, so God hath requited me. And they brought him to Jerusalem, and there he died."

In *Zillah*, IV, 112, he is called "the lightning of the Lord," the literal translation of his name.

23 The Great Pyramid of Cheops is over 480 feet high, and while the temple of Belus at Babylon is no longer standing, it was also a mighty structure. The Sumerian god Bel (whose name means "Lord") was the god of the air, of nature, and master of man's fates to the people of Babylon. He is also known as Enlil.

24 The desert locust caused great suffering in biblical times: "And they shall cover the face of the earth, that one cannot be able to see the earth . . ." (Exodus 10:5).

25 Adommim, translated as "the Red," was a road cut through red soil which climbed from the plain of Jericho to the hills above Jerusalem. It was a point marking the frontier between Judah and Benjamin.

26 *Aleph* is the first letter of the Hebrew alphabet, *tau* (*tav*) the last. *Jod* is the smallest letter, from which we derive the phrase "no bigger than a jot."

27 Pluto was the Greek and Roman god of the under-world.

28 A shekel before 700 B.C. meant uncoined metal cast in ingots or bars of a fixed weight, or in ornaments, but by the period of this tale had evolved into a coin.

The difficulty the Roman soldier has in pronouncing "shekel" echoes the story in Judges 12:4–6, in which Jephthah uses the word *shibboleth* (meaning "stream in flood") as a password by which to distinguish the fleeing Ephraimites—who could not pronounce *sh*—from his own men, the Gileadites.

29 The sun has been up for an hour. Phoebus, or Phoebus Apollo, god of light, drove his chariot and flaming horses across the heavens.

30 "By the god Pollux."

31 Useless articles.

32 Literally "the gods" but used in the singular sense of "Good god" or "Good Lord." Elohim is related to the Arabic word Allah.

33 The Teraphim are idols mentioned in Judges 17:5 and Hosea 3:4. Ancient household idols of the Jews, they were probably similar to the lares and penates of Rome. They were used for divination. We know little of their form, but they were sometimes the size of a man. They are mentioned also in Judges 18:17, 18:20, Genesis 31:30, and elsewhere in the Old Testament.

34 These are the names of ancient heathen gods that would have been familiar to the Hebrews. Nergal, worshiped in Babylonia and Asyria, was the god of midsummer sun, of war, of the chase, and of the dead. He could be beneficent but was usually thought of in connection with pestilence and destruction. (See 2 Kings 17:30.)

Ashimah, a god whose cult flourished in Hamath (Hama), in northern Syria, at the northern boundary of the Israelite tribes, is also mentioned in 2 Kings 17:30.

Nibhaz and Tartak were worshiped in Samaria by the captive Avites (Avims), a people of southwestern Palestine who were probably assimilated by the Philistines (See 2 Kings 17:31, Joshua 13:3, Deuteronomy 2:23).

Adrammelech was possibly a god of the Sepharvim or Sippar, and may be another name for Samas, the sun god. Anammelech was a Babylonian deity whose worship was carried by the Sepharvites into Samaria. Rites included human sacrifice.

Succoth-Benoth was a deity worshiped by the Babylonian captives in Samaria (2 Kings 17:30). *Succoth* is possibly a Hebraic form of Sarpenitum, the consort of Marduk, or derived from Cush or Cuth, the "queen of heaven" worshiped by northern Arabians.

Dagon, the god of fertility, was widely worshiped in the Near East, particularly in Canaan. In the Old Testament he is mentioned as one of the chief deities of the Philistines (Judges 16:23). Poe fanatic H. P. Lovecraft used his name for the title of one of his grotesque tales, as well as drawing from other Hebraic names for the names and places of his world of the Old Ones. Dagon was half man, half fish.

Belial means "worthlessness" or "shame," but the name is not that of a god in ancient times, but rather, a name for wicked people. According to the Encyclopaedia Biblica (London, 1903), "In the interval between the Old Testament and New Testament, Belial was used as a synonym for arch-demon Satan (as Beliar or Berial)," as in 2 Corinthians 6:15. Belial may originally have been an angel of the abyss, from the Assyrian-Babylonian name for the underworld; in the Hebrew Psalms 18:4–5 the word means "the abyss."

Baal-Perith, or Ball-berith, means "Baal of the Covenant" and was the local god of Shechem, the town of central Palestine where Jacob lived (Judges 8:33, 9:4, 9:46).

Baal Peor was the local divinity of Peor, a mountain east of Jordan. One of the apostasies of Israel involved this god; apparently the cult was orgiastic, and the name became symbolic for all shameful perversions of the faith (Numbers 25, Deuteronomy 4:3, Psalms 106:28, Hosea 9:10). Under the form Belphegor or Belfagor, the name became that of a devil in the Middle Ages.

38 "Booshoh he!"—as, at the conclusion of an hour, some object at the extremity of the rope became indistinctly visible— "Booshoh he!" was the exclamation which burst from the lips of Ben-Levi.

"Booshoh he!—for shame!—it is a ram from the thickets of

39 Engedi, and as rugged as the valley of Jehoshaphat!"

40 "It is a firstling of the flock," said Abel-Phittim, "I know him by the bleating of his lips, and the innocent folding of his limbs. His eyes are more beautiful than the jewels of the

41 Pectoral, and his flesh is like the honey of Hebron."

42 "It is a fatted calf from the pastures of Bashan," said the Pharisee, "the heathen have dealt wonderfully with us!—let us raise up our voices in a psalm!—let us give thanks on the shawm and on the psaltery—on the harp and on the huggab—

43 on the cythern and on the sackbut!"

It was not until the basket had arrived within a few feet of the Gizbarim, that a low grunt betrayed to their perception a *hog* of no common size.

44 "Now El Emanu!" slowly, and with upturned eyes ejaculated the trio, as, letting go their hold, the emancipated porker tumbled headlong among the Philistines, "El Emanu!—God

45 be with us—*it is the unutterable flesh!*"

"It is a firstling of the flock," said Abel-Phittim. . . .
Illustration by F. S. Coburn

Baal-Zebub is the name of the god of Ekron, an important Philistine city southeast of Jaffa, not far from the sea (today called Akir). As "Lord of the Flies," he is the central symbol of William Golding's 1954 novel of the same name.

Lauran Paine points out in his fascinating book *The Hierarchy of Hell* (Hippocrene Books, 1972) that the major Phoenician gods have all evolved into Christian demons: Baal, Ashtoreth, Melkarth, Moloch, Dagon, Hadad, and more (pp. 38–39).

Poe mentions Ashimah in "Four Beasts in One," Belial in "Duc De L'Omelette," Beelzebub in "Duc" and also in "Loss of Breath."

35 "The two Katholikin, or overseers of the Treasury were comparing their accounts together" (*Zillah*, I, 43). Poe may have erred in transferring the name, or he may have had in mind a sly jab at Roman Catholics, for which modern Hebrew translates as Katholim.

36 For "the fat of the land," see Genesis 45:18. Some of the description here resembles the scene to which Jesus objects so violently in Matthew 21:12.

37 Apparently an offensive word, according to Matthew 5:22

38 "Shame on you!"

39 Also "Josaphat" or "Joshaphat," from the Hebrew word for "judges." It is mentioned in Joel 3 as a place of judgment, and identified by tradition with the northern extension of the vale of Kidron, on the east of Jerusalem. Jehoshaphat was king of Judah c.873–848 B.C.

Engedi, Hebrew for "well of the kid," was an oasis on the western side of the Dead Sea, famed for its vineyards, and the place where David hid from Saul.

40 "Abel . . . brought of the firstlings of his flock" (Genesis 4:4).

41 "And thou shalt make the breastplate of judgment with cunning work . . ." is from Exodus 28:15–30, also mentioned in *Zillah*, II, 161. The honey of Hebron appears in *Zillah*, I, 202, and refers to the site in south Palestine of the family tomb of Abraham, the home of David, and the place where Absalom began his revolt. The site of the city is still in question; the modern city of Hebron is situated elsewhere. Hebron is also sometimes confused with Abdon, another boundary town, in northwestern Palestine. For more on Hebron, see Genesis 13:18, Numbers 13:22, Joshua 10:36, and II Samuel 2.

42 "strong bulls of Bashan have beset me round" (Psalms 22:12). Bashan means "plain without stones" in Hebrew. Its ancient inhabitants, says the Bible, were giants. Scholars believe Bashan culture shows traces of Indo-Iranian influence. See also Deuteronomy 3:11, Numbers 21:33, 2 Kings 10:33, Psalms 68:15 and Amos 4:1, as well as *Zillah*, II, 40.

43 The shawm is the early ancestor of the modern oboe and in use until the seventeenth century, consisting of a single piece of wood curving in a bell.

The psaltery is a class of ancient instruments also called zithers, consisting of a flat soundboard over which a number of strings are stretched, and plucked with the fingers or a plectrum.

The *huggab* was an early wind instrument "resembling Pan's pipe," according to *Zillah*, I, 210. It is translated variously as "pipe" and "organ" in the Bible.

The cythern, or cithern, is derived from the Greek

kithara, which consisted of a square wooden soundbox and two curved arms connected by a crossbar, with strings stretched between the soundbox and crossbar; it was plucked.

The harplike device used by King David was actually the *kinnor,* which was a lyre not unlike the *kithara.* The Greek word comes from *Zillah,* I, 31.

The sackbut is the name given to the medieval trombone; the Hebrews would have used a ram's horn.

The list of instruments comes from Daniel 3:5, and of course reflects the terminology familiar to the translators of the King James Version of the Bible. The New English Bible (1970) translates the passage as "horn, pipe, zither, triangle, dulcimer, music, and singing of every kind."

44 Also Emanuel, "God with us" (Isaiah 7:14).

45 The same sentence appears in *Zillah,* III, 51.

"And the swine, because it divideth the hoof, yet cheweth not the cud, it is unclean unto you; ye shall not eat of their flesh, nor touch their dead carcase" (Deuteronomy 14:8). Hogs are probably susceptible to a greater number of diseases than any other domestic animal, and many of their ills are transmissible to man (brucellosis, trichinoisis, and cysticercosis). Muslims are also forbidden to eat pork.

The use of the pig in pagan sacrifices may have also contributed to the Hebrews' general abhorrence, but even though there may be a logical explanation for the dietary laws, the real reason they are observed, say some, is simply because the foods in question are forbidden by God.

BON-BON

First published as "The Bargain Lost," in the Philadelphia *Saturday Courier*, December 1, 1832, the tale was originally a shorter piece about a metaphysician named Pedro Garcia who lived in Venice and had a strange encounter with one of the Devil's messengers. The idea that the Devil eats souls was the spark for the story, possibly suggested by Canto 34 of Dante's *Inferno*, or perhaps by William Elliot's translation of *The Visions of Quevedo* (from *Sueños*, by Francisco Gómez de Quevedo y Villegas), published in 1831. The latter contains this comment on souls: "Lucifer is very fond of this meal, and the expression 'may the devil swallow me,' which tailors often use, is not inappropriate. . . ."

Poe revised the tale as "Bon-Bon," and it was published in the *Southern Literary Messenger* of August 1835. He changed the setting from Venice to France and made his chief character a cook as well as a philosopher, in order to expand the comic possibilities. It's likely that Poe took the idea from *Les Premiers Traits de l'érudition universelle* (1767) by Baron Bielfeld (1717–70), because in Book II, Chapter XVI, Section 10, we find: ". . . gourmets . . . value a chef as a divine mortal; [holding] by reasonable argument . . . that his art is more useful, and that he demands as much intellect and wisdom as the metaphysician."

As one of Poe's better successes in the comic vein, "Bon-Bon" was produced on the New York stage in 1920.

Quand un bon vin meuble mon estomac,
Je suis plus savant que Balzac—
Plus sage que Pibrac;
Mon bras seul faisant l'attaque
De la nation Cosaque,
La mettroit au sac:
De Charon je passerois le lac
En dormant dans son bac;
J'irois au fier Eac,
Sans que mon cœur fît tic ni tac,
Présenter du tabac.

— French Vaudeville. **1**

That Pierre Bon-Bon was a *restaurateur* of uncommon qual- **2** ifications, no man who, during the reign of ——, frequented the little café in the *cul-de-sac* Le Febvre at Rouen, will, I **3** imagine, feel himself at liberty to dispute. That Pierre Bon-Bon was, in an equal degree, skilled in the philosophy of that period is, I presume, still more especially undeniable. His *pâtés à la fois* were beyond doubt immaculate; but what pen **4** can do justice to his essays *sur la Nature*—his thoughts *sur l'Ame*—his observations *sur l'Esprit*? If his *omelettes*—if his **5** *fricandeaux* were inestimable, what *littérateur* of that day **6** would not have given twice as much for an *"Idée de Bon-Bon"*

1 The poem is from Bielfeld's *Erudition*, Book II, Chapter VII, Section 29.

> When a good wine fills my stomach
> I am more learned than Balzac—
> Wiser than Pibrac;
> My lone arm attacking
> The Cossack nation,
> Plunders it;
> I cross Charon's lake
> Asleep in his ferry;
> I would go to proud Aeacus,
> Without my heart beating hard
> To offer him some snuff.

Balzac here refers to Jean Louis Guez de Balzac (1597?–1654), whose clear and orderly style was a great influence in reforming French prose. Guy du Faur, Seigneur de Pibrac (1529–84) was a French jurist and poet. Aeacus, a son of Zeus, was the legendary king of Aegina. With others, he built the walls of Troy, and after his death became a judge of the dead in Hades.

2 A bonbon is a sweet or confection—an apt name for the rather insubstantial (in spirit, at least) philosopher of this tale.

3 Rouen, in northwestern France, was the ancient capital of Normandy. Situated on the Seine near its mouth on the English Channel, Rouen is the port of Paris and a commercial—not philosophic—center. LeFebvre is a street named after François Joseph Le-

Febvre (1755–1820), Duke of Danzig and a Marshal of France. By placing the story at Rouen, Poe further detracts from Pierre Bon-Bon's pretense of great intellect.

4 *Pâté de foie gras* is goose-liver pâté (*foie* is liver). *Pâté à la fois* is a nonsense phrase meaning "pâté at the same time." Like Bon-Bon, it is two things at once.

5 Essays on Nature, thoughts on the Soul, observations on the Spirit

6 Perhaps Poe means *fricandelles*—chopped-meat patties. In other words, Bon-Bon's philosophy is also chopped and mixed up (a fricandeau is glazed veal). A *litterateur* is a man of letters. The philosopher is a sort of literary sump hole, where ideas from other sources collect but who has never added any original thoughts of his own.

7 The Academy was a garden in Athens, named for the hero Academus; it was the place where Plato taught. As a school it continued until closed by the Byzantine emperor Justinian in A.D. 529. Over the centuries, the Academy became a synonym for the entire school of Platonic philosophy, just as the Lyceum—the gymnasium of ancient Athens, where Aristotle taught—came to stand for the school of Aristotelian thought.

8 Immanuel Kant (1724–1804), German metaphysician and one of the world's great philosophical figures. Kant proposed that objective reality is really only the creation of the knowing mind, that anything outside the senses, space, or time is unknowable, even though it may exist. Poe was not a fan of Kant.

9 Gottfried Wilhelm, Baron von Leibnitz (1646–1716), German philosopher and mathematician, was known for his work in logic, calculus—and the divine nature of the universe. Poe felt a kinship with Leibnitz, particularly in the latter subject.
A *fricassée* is meat sliced and fried (or stewed), then served with a sauce.

10 The Ionic (Greek) school of philosophy included Thales, Anaximander, and Heraclitus. The Italic, or Eleatic, school included Parmenides and Zeno.

11 Before the fact and after the fact

12 George of Trebizond in 1464 wrote a comparison of Plato and Aristotle, and Johannes Bessarion wrote an attack on George of Trebizond five years later. It would take an agile philosopher to agree with both of them. Trebizond, by the way, is the name of the last Greek empire, founded in 1204, when the Fourth Crusade overthrew the Byzantine Empire. Trebizond was annexed to the Ottoman Empire in 1461, up to which point it was the last refuge of Hellenistic civilization.

13 Poe's source for this information is unknown, but he mentions it again in "Marginalia," CCLXXXV.

14 "Φρενες." [Poe's note] Poe here gives the word *phrenes*, which in Greek means mind or will (not soul). The singular, *phren*, means diaphraghm or midriff. In many ancient languages, including Greek and Hebrew, the word for "soul" was also used for "breath." See "Loss of Breath."

15 High relief, as opposed to bas-relief, is a term used in sculpture to differentiate between two kinds of three-

as for all the trash of all the *"Idées"* of all the rest of the *savants?* Bon-Bon had ransacked libraries which no other man had ransacked—had read more than any other would have entertained a notion of reading—had understood more than any other would have conceived the possibility of understanding; and although, while he flourished, there were not wanting some authors at Rouen to assert "that his *dicta* evinced neither

7 the purity of the Academy, nor the depth of the Lyceum"— although, mark me, his doctrines were by no means very generally comprehended, still it did follow that they were difficult of comprehension. It was, I think, on account of their self-evidency that many persons were led to consider them abstruse. It is to Bon-Bon—but let this go no further—it is to

8 Bon-Bon that Kant himself is mainly indebted for his metaphysics. The former was indeed not a Platonist, nor strictly speaking an Aristotelian—nor did he, like the modern Leib-

9 nitz, waste those precious hours which might be employed in the invention of a *fricassée* or, *facili gradu*, the analysis of a sensation, in frivolous attempts at reconciling the obstinate oils and waters of ethical discussion. Not at all. Bon-Bon was

10 Ionic—Bon-Bon was equally Italic. He reasoned *à priori*—He

11 reasoned *à posteriori*. His ideas were innate—or otherwise. He believed in George of Trebizond—He believed in Bossa-

12 rion. Bon-Bon was emphatically a—Bon-Bonist.

I have spoken of the philosopher in his capacity of *restaurateur*. I would not, however, have any friend of mine imagine that, in fulfilling his hereditary duties in that time, our hero wanted a proper estimation of their dignity and importance. Far from it. It was impossible to say in which branch of his profession he took the greater pride. In his opinion the powers of the intellect held intimate connection with the capabilities of the stomach. I am not sure, indeed, that he greatly disagreed

13 with the Chinese, who hold that the soul lies in the abdomen. The Greeks at all events were right, he thought, who employed

14 the same word for the mind and the diaphragm. By this I do not mean to insinuate a charge of gluttony, or indeed any other serious charge to the prejudice of the metaphysician. If Pierre Bon-Bon had his failings—and what great man has not a thousand?—if Pierre Bon-Bon, I say, had his failings, they were failings of very little importance—faults indeed which, in other tempers, have often been looked upon rather in the light of virtues. As regards one of these foibles, I should not even have mentioned it in this history but for the remarkable

15 prominency—the extreme *alto rilievo*—in which it jutted out from the plane of his general disposition. He could never let slip an opportunity of making a bargain.

Not that he was avaricious—no. It was by no means necessary to the satisfaction of the philosopher, that the bargain should be to his own proper advantage. Provided a trade could be effected—a trade of any kind, upon any terms, or under any circumstances—a triumphant smile was seen for many days thereafter to enlighten his countenance, and a knowing wink of the eye to give evidence of his sagacity.

At any epoch it would not be very wonderful if a humor so

peculiar as the one I have just mentioned, should elicit attention and remark. At the epoch of our narrative, had this peculiarity *not* attracted observation, there would have been room for wonder indeed. It was soon reported that, upon all occasions of the kind, the smile of Bon-Bon was found to differ widely from the´downright grin with which he would laugh at his own jokes, or welcome an acquaintance. Hints were thrown out of an exciting nature; stories were told of perilous bargains made in a hurry and repented of at leisure; and instances were adduced of unaccountable capacities, vague longings, and unnatural inclinations implanted by the author of all evil for wise purposes of his own.

The philosopher had other weaknesses—but they are scarcely worthy our serious examination. For example, there are few men of extraordinary profundity who are found wanting in an inclination for the bottle. Whether this inclination be an exciting cause, or rather a valid proof, of such profundity, it is a nice thing to say. Bon-Bon, as far as I can learn, did not think the subject adapted to minute investigation;—nor do I. Yet in the indulgence of a propensity so truly classical, it is not to be supposed that the *restaurateur* would lose sight of that intuitive discrimination which was wont to characterize, at one and the same time, his *essais* and his *omelettes*. In his seclusions the Vin de Bourgogne had its allotted hour, and there were appropriate moments for the Côtes du Rhone. **16** With him Sauterne was to Médoc what Catulus was to Homer. **17** He would sport with a syllogism in sipping St. Péray, but unravel an argument over Clos de Vougêot, and upset a theory in a torrent of Chambertin. Well had it been if the same quick **18** sense of propriety had attended him in the peddling propensity to which I have formerly alluded—but this was by no means the case. Indeed to say the truth, *that* trait of mind in the philosophic Bon-Bon *did* begin at length to assume a character of strange intensity and mysticism, and appeared deeply tinctured with the *diablerie* of his favorite German studies. **19**

To enter the little *café* in the *cul-de-sac* Le Febvre was, at **20** the period of our tale, to enter the *sanctum* of a man of genius. Bon-Bon was a man of genius. There was not a *sous-cuisinier* **21** in Rouen, who could not have told you that Bon-Bon was a man of genius. His very cat knew it, and forbore to whisk her tail in the presence of the man of genius. His large water-dog was acquainted with the fact, and upon the approach of his master, betrayed his sense of inferiority by a sanctity of deportment, a debasement of the ears, and a dropping of the lower jaw not altogether unworthy of a dog. It is, however, **22** true that much of this habitual respect might have been attributed to the personal appearance of the metaphysician. A distinguished exterior will, I am constrained to say, have its way even with a beast; and I am willing to allow much in the outward man of the *restaurateur* calculated to impress the imagination of the quadruped. There is a peculiar majesty about the atmosphere of the little great—if I may be permitted so equivocal an expression—which mere physical bulk alone will be found at all times inefficient in creating. If, however,

dimensional projection from a flat background, such as on a frieze. *Alto rilievo* shows a great deal of protrusion—here compared with Bon-Bon's stomach.

16 Bourgogne, or Burgundy, is the ancient wine-grape center of France, predating even the arrival of the Romans. Côtes-du-Rhône is the wine region on the Rhône River from Lyon south to Avignon, which produces vintages of lesser quality that those of Burgundy.

17 Sauterne is a sweet, dessert wine from the area near Bordeaux, while Médoc is a dry red wine from the region on the Gironde River forty miles north of the city of Bordeaux.

Catullus (84?–54? B.C.), a Roman, was one of the world's greatest lyric poets. One might recall that Poe disliked long poems, such as the epics of Homer, and preferred the shorter, lyric form himself.

18 St.-Péray, a sparkling white wine whose proponents claim it was invented before champagne, comes from the town of St.-Péray, about sixty miles north of Avignon on the Rhône.

Clos de Vougeot, along with the other wines of the Clos (in Burgundy), have been long considered among the most desirable in all of France. French regiments that pass by are traditionally brought to a halt in order to salute these vineyards.

Chambertin, another Burgundy, takes its name from a long-ago real estate deal. The Benedictines, who controlled most of the nearby vineyards, subsidized a peasant named Bertin to rip up his vegetable crops and plant vines. The field kept the name *Champs de Bertin* (shortened to Chambertin) and soon outstripped its neighbors in fame. Chambertin was Napoleon's favorite wine.

For a thoroughly enjoyable account of the French wine-growing regions, try *The Great Wine Rivers*, by Creighton Churchill (Macmillan, 1971).

19 The early interest by the Germans in folktales of mystery and superstition gave rise to Gothic fiction such as *Frankenstein* and *The Castle of Otranto* in English. Poe's "The Fall of the House of Usher" and "The Masque of the Red Death" come very close to this style, and "Metzengerstein" is in direct imitation of the German style of Gothic fiction.

20 *Cul-de-sac* literally means "bottom of the bag" or "bag end" (I wonder if this is partially the origin of the name of Bilbo Baggins' home in *The Hobbit*). *Cul* alone is not considered polite usage in France, since it means "ass," or posterior.

Marshall LeFebvre's mother had been a washer-woman, and he himself had risen from lower-class obscurity to the right hand of Napoleon. Bon-Bon, an oafish philosopher, spends his time on a proletarian street in a spiritually proletarian city.

21 Under-cook, the second-in-command after the chef

22 Both animals are only doing what one would expect them to do when their master walks into the room.

... it was impossible to behold the rotundity of his stomach without a sense of magnificence nearly bordering upon the sublime. *Artist unknown*

23 Bon-Bon even *looks* like a round piece of candy, and his brains take second place to his body size.

24 His clothing resembles the motley of the traditional jester or clown, and his cap, a fool's cap.

25 Her name means "well met" or "welcome," and she apparently improvises all her poetry.

26 A folio is a book made of sheets of paper folded only once (four pages to a sheet), and so is fairly large.

27 Library

28 A polemic is a controversial argument, often religious.

29 Duodecimos are books whose sheets have been folded into twelve leaves each, so that the books are naturally quite small. Here the leaves seem to be part of a stew (*mélange*).

30 Eusebius of Caesarea (A.D. 260?–340), a theologian and father of ecclesiastical history, whose works include a history of the Church in ten books

23 Bon-Bon was barely three feet in height, and if his head was diminutively small, still it was impossible to behold the rotundity of his stomach without a sense of magnificence nearly bordering upon the sublime. In its size both dogs and men must have seen a type of his acquirements—in its immensity a fitting habitation of his immortal soul.

I might here—if it so pleased me—dilate upon the matter of habiliment, and other mere circumstances of the external metaphysician. I might hint that the hair of our hero was worn short, combed smoothly over his forehead, and surmounted **24** by a conical-shaped white flannel cap and tassels—that his pea-green jerkin was not after the fashion of those worn by the common class of *restaurateurs* at that day—that the sleeves were something fuller than the reigning costume permitted— that the cuffs were turned up, not as usual in that barbarous period, with cloth of the same quality and color as the garment, but faced in a more fanciful manner with the parti-colored velvet of Genoa—that his slippers were of a bright purple, curiously filigreed, and might have been manufactured in Japan, but for the exquisite pointing of the toes, and the brilliant tints of the binding and embroidery—that his breeches were of the yellow satin-like material called *aimable*—that his sky-blue cloak, resembling in form a dressing-wrapper, and richly bestudded all over with crimson devices, floated cavalierly upon his shoulders like a mist of the morning—and that his *tout ensemble* gave rise to the remarkable words of **25** Benevenuta, the Improvisatrice of Florence, that it was difficult to say whether Pierre Bon-Bon was indeed a bird of Paradise, or the rather a very Paradise of perfection." I might, I say, expatiate upon all these points if I pleased,—but I forbear; merely personal details may be left to historical novelists,—they are beneath the moral dignity of matter-of-fact.

I have said that "to enter the *café* in the *cul-de-sac* Le Febvre was to enter the *sanctum* of a man of genius"—but then it was only the man of genius who could duly estimate **26** the merits of the *sanctum*. A sign, consisting of a vast folio, swung before the entrance. On one side of the volume was painted a bottle; on the reverse a *pâté*. On the back were visible in large letters *Œuvres de Bon-Bon*. Thus was delicately shadowed forth the twofold occupation of the proprietor.

Upon stepping over the threshold, the whole interior of the building presented itself to view. A long, low-pitched room, of antique construction, was indeed all the accommodation afforded by the *café*. In a corner of the apartment stood the bed of the metaphysician. An array of curtains, together with a canopy *à la Grècque*, gave it an air at once classic and comfortable. In the corner diagonally opposite, appeared, in direct family communion, the properties of the kitchen and **27,28** the *bibliothèque*. A dish of polemics stood peacefully upon the dresser. Here lay an ovenful of the latest ethics—there a **29** kettle of duodecimo *mélanges*. Volumes of German morality were hand and glove with the gridiron—a toasting-fork might **30** be discovered by the side of Eusebius—Plato reclined at his ease in the frying-pan—and contemporary manuscripts were filed away upon the spit.

In other respects the *Café de Bon-Bon* might be said to differ little from the usual *restaurants* of the period. A large fireplace yawned opposite the door. On the right of the fireplace an open cupboard displayed a formidable array of labelled bottles.

It was here, about twelve o'clock one night, during the severe winter of ——, that Pierre Bon-Bon, after having listened for some time to the comments of his neighbors upon his singular propensity—that Pierre Bon-Bon, I say, having turned them all out of his house, locked the door upon them with an oath, and betook himself in no very pacific mood to the comforts of a leather-bottomed armchair, and a fire of blazing fagots.

It was one of those terrific nights which are only met with once or twice during a century. It snowed fiercely, and the house tottered to its centre with the floods of wind that, rushing through the crannies of the wall, and pouring impetuously down the chimney, shook awfully the curtains of the philosopher's bed, and disorganized the economy of his pâté-pans and papers. The huge folio sign that swung without, exposed to the fury of the tempest, creaked ominously, and gave out a moaning sound from its stanchions of solid oak.

It was in no placid temper, I say, that the metaphysician drew up his chair to its customary station by the hearth. Many circumstances of a perplexing nature had occurred during the day, to disturb the serenity of his meditations. In attempting *des œufs à la Princesse,* he had unfortunately perpetrated an *omelette à la Reine;* the discovery of a principle in ethics had **31** been frustrated by the overturning of a stew; and last, not least, he had been thwarted in one of those admirable bargains which he at all times took such especial delight in bringing to a successful termination. But in the chafing of his mind at these unaccountable vicissitudes, there did not fail to be mingled some degree of that nervous anxiety which the fury of a boisterous night is so well calculated to produce. Whistling to his more immediate vicinity the large black water-dog we **32** have spoken of before, and settling himself uneasily in his chair, he could not help casting a wary and unquiet eye toward those distant recesses of the apartment whose inexorable shadows not even the red fire-light itself could more than partially succeed in overcoming. Having completed a scrutiny whose exact purpose was perhaps unintelligible to himself, he drew close to his seat a small table covered with books and papers, and soon became absorbed in the task of retouching a voluminous manuscript, intended for publication on the morrow.

He had been thus occupied for some minutes, when "I am in no hurry, Monsieur Bon-Bon," suddenly whispered a whining voice in the apartment.

"The devil!" ejaculated our hero, starting to his feet, overturning the table at his side, and staring around him in astonishment.

31 Eggs "à la Princess" have become an omelette "à la Queen." The former includes asparagus tips, cream sauce, and truffles; the latter, a purée of chicken with sauce suprême, truffles, mushrooms, and olives. However, Poe seems to be using the names for the humorous effect alone.

32 Evidently a Labrador retriever

33 "Depended" here means "hung." Poe may have misunderstood the traditional belief that iron *repelled* supernatural forces.

34 He resembles Washington Irving's Ichabod Crane.

35 A stylus was a pointed instrument used to write on waxed tablets in ancient Rome and Greece; the blunt end was used to erase the marks. *The Stylus* was also the name of the publication that Poe attempted to start but abandoned in 1843.

36 The "Gentleman in Black" was a name given to the Devil, but it could just as easily have described a clergyman. In legend, the Devil often appeared in the guise of a monk. For example, there is a story that he appeared in this guise before Martin Luther; and in Marlowe's *Dr. Faustus* (1592), Mephistopholes appears as a Franciscan.

Another bit of folklore, especially among sailors, has it that it is unlucky to meet a clergyman.

"Very true," calmly replied the voice.

"Very true!—what is very true?—how came you here?" vociferated the metaphysician, as his eye fell upon something which lay stretched at full length upon the bed.

"I was saying," said the intruder, without attending to the interrogatories,—"I was saying that I am not at all pushed for time—that the business upon which I took the liberty of calling, is of no pressing importance—in short, that I can very well wait until you have finished your Exposition."

"My Exposition!—there now!—how do *you* know?—how came *you* to understand that I was writing an Exposition—good God!"

"Hush!" replied the figure, in a shrill undertone; and, arising quickly from the bed, he made a single step toward **33** our hero, while an iron lamp that depended overhead swung convulsively back from his approach.

The philosopher's amazement did not prevent a narrow scrutiny of the stranger's dress and appearance. The outlines of his figure, exceedingly lean, but much above the common height, were rendered minutely distinct by means of a faded suit of black cloth which fitted tight to the skin, but was **34** otherwise cut very much in the style of a century ago. These garments had evidently been intended for a much shorter person than their present owner. His ankles and wrists were left naked for several inches. In his shoes, however, a pair of very brilliant buckles gave the lie to the extreme poverty implied by the other portions of his dress. His head was bare, and entirely bald, with the exception of the hinder part, from which depended a *queue* of considerable length. A pair of green spectacles, with side glasses, protected his eyes from the influence of the light, and at the same time prevented our hero from ascertaining either their color or their conformation. About the entire person there was no evidence of a shirt; but a white cravat, of filthy appearance, was tied with extreme precision around the throat, and the ends, hanging down formally side by side gave (although I dare say unintentionally) the idea of an ecclesiastic. Indeed, many other points both in his appearance and demeanor might have very well sustained a conception of that nature. Over his left ear, he carried, after the fashion of a modern clerk, an instrument resembling the **35** *stylus* of the ancients. In a breastpocket of his coat appeared conspicuously a small black volume fastened with clasps of steel. This book, whether accidentally or not, was so turned outwardly from the person as to discover the words *"Rituel* **36** *Catholique"* in white letters upon the back. His entire physiognomy was interestingly saturnine—even cadaverously pale. The forehead was lofty, and deeply furrowed with the ridges of contemplation. The corners of the mouth were drawn down into an expression of the most submissive humility. There was also a clasping of the hands, as he stepped toward our hero—a deep sigh—and altogether a look of such utter sanctity as could not have failed to be unequivocally prepossessing. Every shadow of anger faded from the countenance of the metaphysician, as, having completed a satisfactory survey of his visitor's person, he shook him cordially by the hand, and conducted him to a seat.

There would however be a radical error in attributing this instantaneous transition of feeling in the philosopher, to any one of those causes which might naturally be supposed to have had an influence. Indeed, Pierre Bon-Bon, from what I have been able to understand of his disposition, was of all men the least likely to be imposed upon by any speciousness of exterior deportment. It was impossible that so accurate an observer of men and things should have failed to discover, upon the moment, the real character of the personage who had thus intruded upon his hospitality. To say no more, the conformation of his visitor's feet was sufficiently remarkable—he maintained lightly upon his head an inordinately tall hat—there was a tremulous swelling about the hinder part of his breeches—and the vibration of his coat tail was a palpable fact. Judge, then, with what feelings of satisfaction our hero found himself thrown thus at once into the society of a person for whom he had at all times entertained the most unqualified respect. He was, however, too much of the diplomatist to let escape him any intimation of his suspicions in regard to the true state of affairs. It was not his cue to appear at all conscious of the high honor he thus unexpectedly enjoyed; but, by leading his guest into conversation, to elicit some important ethical ideas, which might, in obtaining a place in his contemplated publication, enlighten the human race, and at the same time immortalize himself—ideas which, I should have added, his visitor's great age, and well-known proficiency in the science of morals, might very well have enabled him to afford.

Actuated by these enlightened views, our hero bade the gentleman sit down, while he himself took occasion to throw some faggots upon the fire, and place upon the now reestablished table some bottles of *Mousseux*. Having quickly **37** completed these operations, he drew his chair *vis-à-vis* to his companion's, and waited until the latter should open the conversation. But plans even the most skilfully matured are often thwarted in the outset of their application—and the *restaurateur* found himself *nonplussed* by the very first words **38** of his visitor's speech.

"I see you know me, Bon-Bon," said he; "ha! ha! ha!—he! he! he!—hi! hi! hi!—ho! ho! ho!—hu! hu! hu!"—and the Devil, dropping at once the sanctity of his demeanor, opened to its fullest extent a mouth from ear to ear, so as to display a set of jagged and fang-like teeth, and, throwing back his head, laughed long, loudly, wickedly, and uproariously, while the black dog, crouching down upon his haunches, joined lustily in the chorus, and the tabby cat, flying off at a tangent, stood up on end, and shrieked in the farthest corner of the apartment.

Not so the philosopher: he was too much a man of the world either to laugh like the dog, or by shrieks to betray the indecorous trepidation of the cat. It must be confessed, he felt a little astonishment to see the white letters which formed the words *"Rituel Catholique"* on the book in his guest's pocket, momently changing both their color and their import, and in

37 Wines of the Vouvray area of the Loire Valley, with a sparkle comparable to that of champagne.

38 Brought to a standstill, perplexed, embarrassed; From the Latin *non plus* (not more, no further)

39 Register of the Condemned

39 a few seconds, in place of the original title, the words *"Registre des Condamnés"* blaze forth in characters of red. This startling circumstance, when Bon-Bon replied to his visitor's remark, imparted to his manner an air of embarrassment which probably might not otherwise have been observed.

"Why, sir," said the philosopher, "why, sir, to speak sincerely—I believe you are—upon my word—the d—— dest—that is to say, I think—I imagine—I *have* some faint— some *very* faint idea—of the remarkable honor——"

"Oh!—ah!—yes!—very well!" interrupted his Majesty; "say no more—I see how it is." And hereupon, taking off his green spectacles, he wiped the glasses carefully with the sleeve of his coat, and deposited them in his pocket.

If Bon-Bon had been astonished at the incident of the book, his amazement was now much increased by the spectacle which here presented itself to view. In raising his eyes, with a strong feeling of curiosity to ascertain the color of his guest's, he found them by no means black, as he had anticipated—nor gray, as might have been imagined—nor yet hazel nor blue— nor indeed yellow nor red—nor purple—nor white—nor

And hereupon, taking off his green spectacles, he wiped the glasses carefully with the sleeve of his coat, and deposited them in his pocket. *Illustration by F. S. Coburn, 1903*

green—nor any other color in the heavens above, or in the earth beneath, or in the waters under the earth. In short, Pierre Bon-Bon not only saw plainly that his Majesty had no eyes whatsoever, but could discover no indications of their having existed at any previous period—for the space where eyes should naturally have been was, I am constrained to say, simply a dead level of flesh.

It was not in the nature of the metaphysician to forbear making some inquiry into the sources of so strange a phenomenon; and the reply of his Majesty was at once prompt, dignified, and satisfactory.

"Eyes! my dear Bon-Bon—eyes! did you say?—oh!—ah!— I perceive! The ridiculous prints, eh, which are in circulation, have given you a false idea of my personal appearance? Eyes!— true. Eyes, Pierre Bon-Bon, are very well in their proper place—*that*, you would say, is the head?—right—the head of a worm. To *you*, likewise, these optics are indispensable—yet I will convince you that my vision is more penetrating than your own. There is a cat I see in the corner—a pretty cat— look at her—observe her well. Now, Bon- Bon, do you behold the thoughts—the thoughts, I say—the ideas—the reflections—which are being engendered in her pericranium? There it is, now—you do not! She is thinking we admire the length of her tail and the profundity of her mind. She has just concluded that I am the most distinguished of ecclesiastics, and that you are the most superficial of metaphysicians. Thus you see I am not altogether blind; but to one of my profession, the eyes you speak of would be merely an incumbrance, liable at any time to be put out by a toasting-iron or a pitchfork. To you, I allow, these optical affairs are indispensable. Endeavor, Bon-Bon, to use them well;—*my* vision is the soul."

Hereupon the guest helped himself to the wine upon the table, and pouring out a bumper for Bon-Bon, requested him to drink it without scruple, and make himself perfectly at home.

"A clever book that of yours, Pierre," resumed his Majesty, tapping our friend knowingly upon the shoulder, as the latter put down his glass after a thorough compliance with his visitor's injunction. "A clever book that of yours, upon my honor. It's a work after my own heart. Your arrangement of the matter, I think, however, might be improved, and many of your notions remind me of Aristotle. That philosopher was one of my most intimate acquaintances. I liked him as much for his terrible ill temper, as for his happy knack at making a blunder. There is only one solid truth in all that he has written, and for that I gave him the hint out of pure compassion for his absurdity. I suppose, Pierre Bon-Bon, you very well know to what divine moral truth I am alluding?"

"Cannot say that I——"

"Indeed!—why it was I who told Aristotle that, by sneezing, men expelled superfluous ideas through the proboscis." **40**

"Which is—undoubtedly the case," said the metaphysician, while he poured out for himself another bumper of Mousseux, and offered his snuff-box to the fingers of his visitor.

40 "Sneezing comes from . . . the head . . . the seat of reasoning" (from Aristotle, *Problemata*, xxxiii, 9).

    Poe seems to have borrowed some of the traits of the Devil from a tale called "Metempsychosis," by Dr. Robert Macnish, which appeared in *Blackwood's*, May 1826. There the Devil sneezes, has a hooked nose, a brown face, and a well-powdered pigtail—and talks of philosophers of the past.

41 "Even so late as near the beginning of the sixteenth century, a certain priest, having met with this passage in some Greek author, *ho nous estin aulos, mens humana immaterialis est,* and finding, in his lexicon, that aulos signified a flute or pipe [as well as breath or wind], brought no less than fifteen arguments, in an academic exercise, to prove the human soul to be a whistle" (Richard Griffith, *Koran,* III, 152).

By inverting the lambda, it becomes a gamma, and thus the word aulos (breath) becomes *augos* (light) and the phrase reads "the mind is a light."

42 "Ils écrivaient sur la Philosophie (*Cicero, Lucretius, Seneca*) mais c'était la Philosophie Grecque.—*Condorcet*" (Poe's note). The phrase means: "They write on philosophy (the Romans Cicero, Lucretius, Seneca) but it is Greek philosophy," and comes from *Esquisse d'un tableau historique,* by Marie Jean Antoine Nicolas Caritat, Marquis de Condorcet (1743–94) (VI, 94 in the Paris edition of 1847 but written much earlier).

The anarchy mentioned earlier in the paragraph refers to the chaotic conditions in Rome between 86 and 82 B.C., between the death of Marius and the return of Sulla.

43 The Greek philosopher (340–270 B.C.) who founded the Epicurean school. His axiom waas that "Happiness or enjoyment is the greatest good in life." His disciples corrupted his doctrine into "Good living is the only object of life," and it seems to be that interpretation the Devil agrees with here.

44 Diogenes Laërtius (early-third century) was a Greek biographer whose ten books on the lives and opinions of philosophers from Thales to Epicurus are one of our major historical sources.

"There was Plato, too," continued his Majesty, modestly declining the snuff-box and the compliment it implied—"there was Plato, too, for whom I at one time, felt all the affection of a friend. You know Plato, Bon-Bon?—ah, no, I beg a thousand pardons. He met me at Athens, one day, in the Parthenon, and told me he was distressed for an idea. I bade **41** him write down that ο νους εστιν αυλος. He said that he would do so, and went home, while I stepped over to the pyramids. But my conscience smote me for having uttered a truth, even to aid a friend, and hastening back to Athens, I arrived behind the philosopher's chair as he was inditing the 'αυλος.' Giving the lambda a fillip with my finger, I turned it upside down. So the sentence now reads 'ο νους εστιν αυγος ,' and is, you perceive, the fundamental doctrine in his metaphysics."

"Were you ever at Rome?" asked the *restaurateur,* as he finished his second bottle of Mousseux, and drew from the closet a large supply of Chambertin.

"But once, Monsieur Bon-Bon, but once. There was a time," said the Devil, as if reciting some passage from a book—"there was a time when occurred an anarchy of five years, during which the republic, bereft of all its officers, had no magistracy besides the tribunes of the people, and these were not legally vested with any degree of executive power—at that time, Monsieur Bon-Bon—at that time *only* I was in Rome, and I have no earthly acquaintance, consequently, with **42** any of its philosophy."

"What do you think of—what do you think of—hiccup!— **43** Epicurus?

"What do I think of *whom?*" said the Devil, in astonishment; "you surely do not mean to find any fault with Epicurus! What do I think of Epricurus! Do you mean me, sir?—I am Epicurus! I am the same philosopher who wrote each of the three **44** hundred treatises commemorated by Diogenes Laertes."

"That's a lie!" said the metaphysician, for the wine had gotten a little into his head.

"Very well!—very well, sir!—very well, indeed, sir!" said his Majesty, apparently much flattered.

"That's a lie! repeated the *restaurateur,* dogmatically; "that's a—hiccup!—a lie!"

"Well, well, have it your own way!" said the Devil, pacifically, and Bon-Bon, having beaten his Majesty at an argument, thought it his duty to conclude a second bottle of Chambertin.

"As I was saying," resumed the visitor—"as I was observing a little while ago, there are some very *outré* notions in that book of yours, Monsieur Bon-Bon. What, for instance, do you mean by all that humbug about the soul? Pray, sir, what *is* the soul?"

"The—hiccup!—soul," replied the metaphysician, referring to his MS., "is undoubtedly——"

"No, sir!"

"Indubitably——"

"No, sir!"

"Indisputably——"

"No, sir!"

"Evidently——"

"No, sir!"

"Incontrovertibly——"

"No, sir!"

"Hiccup!——"

"No, sir!"

"And beyond all question, a——"

"No, sir, the soul is no such thing!" (Here the philosopher, looking daggers, took occasion to make an end, upon the spot, of his third bottle of Chambertin.)

"Then—hiccup!—pray, sir—what—what is it?"

"That is neither here nor there, Monsieur Bon-Bon," replied his Majesty, musingly. "I have tasted—that is to say, I have [45] known some very bad souls, and some too—pretty good ones." Here he smacked his lips, and, having unconsciously let fall his hand upon the volume in his pocket, was seized with a violent fit of sneezing.

He continued:

"There was the soul of Cratinus—passable: Aristophanes— [46,47] racy: Plato—exquisite—not *your* Plato, but Plato the comic poet; your Plato would have turned the stomach of Cerberus— [48] faugh! Then let me see! there were Nævius, and Adronicus, and Plautus, and Terentius. Then there were Lucilius, and [49] Catullus, and Naso, and Quintus Flaccus,—dear Quinty! as I called him when he sung a *seculare* for my amusement, while I toasted him, in pure good humor, on a fork. But they [50] want *flavor*, these Romans. One fat Greek is worth a dozen of them, and besides will *keep*, which cannot be said of a Quirite. Let us taste your Sauterne." [51]

Bon-Bon had by this time made up his mind to the *nil admirari*, and endeavored to hand down the bottles in ques- [52] tion. He was, however, conscious of a strange sound in the room like the wagging of a tail. Of this, although extremely indecent in his Majesty, the philosopher took no notice:— simply kicking the dog, and requesting him to be quiet. The visitor continued:

"I found that Horace tasted very much like Aristotle;—you know I am fond of variety. Terentius I could not have told [53] from Menander. Naso, to my astonishment, was Nicander in [54] disguise. Virgilius had a strong twang of Theocritus. Martial [55,56] put me much in mind of Archilochus—and Titus Livius was positively Polybius and none other." [57]

"Hiccup!" here replied Bon-Bon, and his Majesty proceeded:

"But if I *have* a *penchant*, Monsieur Bon-Bon—if I *have* a *penchant*, it is for a philosopher. Yet, let me tell you, sir, it is not every dev—I mean it is not every gentleman who knows how to *choose* a philosopher. Long ones are *not* good; and the best, if not carefully shelled, are apt to be a little rancid on account of the gall." [58]

"Shelled!!"

"I mean taken out of the carcass."

45 i.e., the soul is neither here nor there—an appropriate comment on its intangibility.

46 Cratinus (died c.419 B.C.) was an Athenian comic poet, of whose works only fragments survive today.

47 Greek comic dramatist (448?–380? B.C.) best known for *Lysistrata*, *The Clouds*, *The Birds* and *The Frogs*. All contain sexual innuendos that certainly would have seemed racy in Poe's time—particularly the first.

48 The three-headed dog that guarded the entrance to the infernal regions

49 Naevius (c.270–201 B.C.), early Roman poet and playwright. Livius Andronicus (fl. third century B.C.) was the Roman translator of the *Odyssey*. Titus Maccius Plautus (c.254–184 B.C.) and Terence (c.190–159 B.C.) were the great Roman comic dramatists, the first being a model for Shakespeare and Molière.

50 Gaius Lucilius (c.180–102 B.C.) was the founder of Latin satire and a great influence on Horace and Juvenal. Publius Ovidius Naso, or Ovid (43 B.C.–A.D.18), is the Latin poet who wrote the classic *Art of Love* and *Metamorphoses*. Quintus Horatius Flaccus wrote a *Secular Ode* in 53 B.C. for Rome's seven hundredth birthday. We learn, in his *Satire* (II, vi, 37) that he did not like to be addressed as "Quinte" by anyone but close friends.

51 A Roman citizen. The word comes from Quirinus, a Roman war god who was later identified with Romulus, the founder of Rome.

52 "Astonished at nothing" (Horace, Epistolae, I, vi, 1)

53 Quintus Horatius Flaccus, or Horace (65–8 B.C.), one of the greatest lyric poets, best known for his odes, satires, and epistles.

54 Menander (342?–291? B.C.), the Greek poet and comic playwright who first used the love plot as his central theme

55 Nicander, a grammarian and physician, authored works on beasts and poisons in the second century B.C.

56 Publius Vergilius Maro, or Vergil (70–19 B.C.), the greatest poet of ancient Rome and author of the *Aeneid*. Theocritus (third century B.C.) was the founder of pastoral poetry—certainly a far cry from Vergil's heroic verse.

57 Marcus Valerius Martialis, or Martial (first century A.D.) was famous for his witty and ribald epigrams on Roman manners and mores. Archilochus (714–676 B.C.) is the Greek writer known for his ill-natured satires, which in one case are supposed to have driven to suicide a women who rejected his love. Titus Patavinus Livius, or Livy (59 B.C.–A.D. 17), the great Roman historian, used as one source the earlier Greek historian Polybius (203?–120 B.C.)

58 Gall is the secretion of the liver—bile—which can spoil certain game if not carefully removed. It is intensely bitter. Here it also means self-assurance, impudence.

59 Greek physician (c.460–370 B.C.)

60 A combination of the Persian *aza* (mastic) and Latin *foetida* (stinking), a resinous gum with a strong odor used in medicine to treat spasms

61 "Acute disorder of the digestive organs, not epidemic, marked by vomiting, purging, colic and cramps in legs and abdominal walls, with considerable exhaustion, mostly confined to the hotter months and frequently due to erratic diet. Also called Sporadic Cholera . . ." (Century Dictionary and Cyclopedia, 1900)

62 Since taking God's name in vain is a sin, one would think that the Devil's reaction would be, at least, mixed.

63 In the living body. The traffic in souls is common stuff of legend, appearing in the Faust legend and in such tales as "The Devil and Daniel Webster" (by Stephen Vincent Benét).

64 Here we have a rogues' gallery of legendary and historical characters. Cain, Adam's son, killed his brother. Nimrod is mentioned in the Bible as a mighty hunter, but has been traditionally characterized as cruel and inhuman. Nero (A.D. 37–68) was not only blamed for the burning of Rome in A.D. 64 but for poisoning his adopted son. Caligula (A.D. 12–41), whose real name was Caius Caesar Germanicus, earned a name for ruthless and cruel autocracy, torture, and execution. Dionysius the Elder (c.430–367 B.C.) was the tyrant of Syracuse. Pisistratus (c.605–527 B.C.) was a Greek statesman and tyrant of Athens, whose power (like that of Dionysius) was founded on the support of rural citizens.

65 Niccolò Machiavelli (1469–1527) was an Italian author and statesman and one of the outstanding figures of the Renaissance. His love of liberty and his republican virtues are genuine—only in *The Prince* does he suggest tyranny as a political good. Still, the word "Machiavellian" has come to mean amoral cunning or justification of tyranny.

Jules Mazarin (1602–61) was the French statesman and cardinal of the Roman Church whose original name was Guilio Mazarini. He was an associate of Cardinal Richelieu and succeeded him as chief minister of France in 1642, and though he had never been ordained a priest was made a cardinal on the recommendation of Louis XIII (1641). He may have been secretly married to Anne of Austria, but he is remembered more for his financial abuses and centralizing policies.

Maximilien Marie Isidore de Robespierre (1758–94), one of the leading figures of the French Revolution, was considered by some as a ruthless dictator and by others the idealistic champion of social revolution. It is not surprising that Poe, with his anti-republican attitudes, includes in this list the names of several "tyrants" whose power derived from the lower classes.

George IV (1762–1830) of England led a dissipated society when he was still Prince of Wales, and as king was hated for his extravagance and dissolute habits. Poe satirizes him again in "Four Beasts in One." Actually, the previous George (III) wasn't much better, being stubborn and not too intelligent—and in later life, insane.

Elizabeth I (1533–1603) is mentioned here probably for her actions against Mary Queen of Scots.

"What do you think of a—hiccup!—physician?"

"*Don't* mention them!—ugh! ugh!" (Here his Majesty retched violently.) "I never tasted but one—that rascal Hippocrates!—smelt of asafœtida—ugh! ugh! ugh!—caught a wretched cold washing him in the Styx—and after all he gave me the cholera-morbus."

The—hiccup!—wretch!" ejaculated Bon-Bon, "the—hiccup!—abortion of a pill-box!"—and the philosopher dropped a tear.

"After all," continued the visitor, "after all, if a dev—if a gentleman wishes to *live*, he must have more talents than one or two; and with us a fat face is an evidence of diplomacy."

"How so?"

"Why we are sometimes exceedingly pushed for provisions. You must know that, in a climate so sultry as mine, it is frequently impossible to keep a spirit alive for more than two or three hours; and after death, unless pickled immediately (and a pickled spirit is *not* good), they will—smell—you understand, eh? Putrefaction is always to be apprehended when the souls are consigned to us in the usual way."

"Hiccup!—hiccup!—good God! how *do* you manage?"

Here the iron lamp commenced swinging with redoubled violence, and the Devil half started from his seat;—however, with a slight sigh, he recovered his composure, merely saying to our hero in a low tone: "I tell you what, Pierre Bon-Bon, we *must* have no more swearing."

The host swallowed another bumper, by way of denoting thorough comprehension and acquiescence, and the visitor continued:

"Why, there are *several* ways of managing. The most of us starve: some put up with the pickle: for my part I purchase my spirits *vivent corpore*, in which case I find they keep very well."

"But the body!—hiccup!—the body!!"

"The body, the body—well, what of the body?—oh! ah! I perceive. Why, sir, the body is not *at all* affected by the transaction. I have made innumerable purchases of the kind in my day, and the parties never experienced any inconvenience. There were Cain and Nimrod, and Nero, and Caligula, and Dionysius, and Pisistratus, and—and a thousand others, who never knew what it was to have a soul during the latter part of their lives; yet, sir, these men adorned society. Why isn't there A——, now, whom you know as well as I? Is *he* not in possession of all his faculties, mental and corporeal? Who writes a keener epigram? Who reasons more wittily? Who—but, stay! I have his agreement in my pocket-book."

Thus saying, he produced a red leather wallet, and took from it a number of papers. Upon some of these Bon-Bon caught a glimpse of the letters *Machi—Maza—Robesp*—with the words *Caligula, George, Elizabeth*. His Majesty selected a narrow slip of parchment, and from it read aloud the following words:

"In consideration of certain mental endowments which it is unnecessary to specify, and in further consideration of one thousand louis d'or, I being aged one year and one month, do hereby make over to the bearer of this agreement all my right, title, and appurtenance in the shadow called my soul. (Signed) A . . . . ." (Here his Majesty repeated a name which I do not **66** feel myself justified in indicating more unequivocally.)

"A clever fellow that," resumed he; "but, like you, Monsieur Bon-Bon, he was mistaken about the soul. The soul a shadow, truly! The soul a shadow! Ha! ha! ha!—he! he! he!—hu! hu! hu! Only think of a fricasséed shadow!" **67**

"*Only* think—hiccup!—of a fricasséed shadow!" exclaimed our hero, whose faculties were becoming much illuminated by the profundity of his Majesty's discourse.

"Only think of a—hiccup!—fricasséed shadow!! Now, damme!—hiccup!—humph! If *I* would have been such a—hiccup!—nincompoop! *My* soul, Mr.—humph!"

"*Your* soul, Monsieur Bon-Bon?"

"Yes, sir—hiccup!—*my* soul is——"

"What, sir?"

"*No* shadow, damme!"

"Did you mean to say——"

"Yes, sir, *my* soul is—hiccup!—humph!—yes, sir."

"Did you not intend to assert——"

"*My* soul is—hiccup!—peculiarly qualified for—hiccup!—a——"

"What, sir?"

"Stew."

"Ha!"

"Soufflée." **68**

"Eh!"

"Fricassée." **69**

"Indeed!"

"Ragout and fricandeau—and see here, my good fellow! I'll **70** let you have it—hiccup!—a bargain." Here the philosopher slapped his Majesty upon the back.

"Couldn't think of such a thing," said the latter calmly, at the same time rising from his seat. The metaphysician stared.

"Am supplied at present," said his Majesty.

"Hic-cup!—e-h?" said the philosopher.

"Have no funds on hand."

"What?"

"Besides, very unhandsome in me——"

"Sir!"

"To take advantage of——"

"Hic-cup!"

"Your present disgusting and ungentlemanly situation."

Here the visitor bowed and withdrew—in what manner could not precisely be ascertained—but in a well-concerted effort to discharge a bottle at "the villain," the slender chain was severed that depended from the ceiling, and the metaphysician prostrated by the downfall of the lamp. **71**

66 "Quere—Arouet" (Poe's note). The note is signed Arouet, the real name of Voltaire (1694–1778), French poet, dramatist, satirist, historian, and philosopher, famous for his skepticism, his fight against fanaticism, intolerance, and superstition—and his hostility towards organized religion.

67 "The early Israelites were metaphysically unable to conceive the body without psychical functions, or the soul without a certain corporeity. The departed were conceived, accordingly, as possessing not only a soul but a shadowy body. This appears in the use of the term 'shades' which was current in all ages." (Encyclopaedia Biblica, p. 1341)

68 A soufflé is a flavored sauce into which stiffly beaten egg whites are blended; turned into a mold and baked, it puffs up and browns at the top.

69 In *The Visions of Quevedo*, p. 146, we read that the Persian souls are "fricasseed with gravy de demon."

70 A ragout is a stew.

71 One assumes the lamp has fallen because the strong reaction to the Devil has gradually pulled it out of the wall. There is also some poetic justice here, since the lamp is a traditional symbol of learning and enlightenment, and Bon-Bon is a deserving recipient.

FOUR BEASTS IN ONE

THE HOMO-CAMELEOPARD

First published in the *Southern Literary Messenger*, March 1836, as "Epimanes," this is one of Poe's better comic efforts, although not widely read. It takes as its basis the history of Antiochus IV of Syria, and blends with it stories about George IV of England (see "Bon-Bon," note 66) and King Charles X of France.

"Homo-cameleopard" is an imaginary beast of Poe's creation, a combination of man, camel, lion (leo) and panther (pard), which seems to resemble a rather bizarre giraffe. The name comes from *kamelopardalis*, the Greek word for giraffe, with Poe making a few appropriate changes in the spelling to accommodate his four-beasts-in-one idea. Both George IV and Charles X owned giraffes.

The English word "camelopard," by the way, was used to mean "giraffe" from about 1400 to the early-nineteenth century.

---

1 "Each person has his virtues," is from *Xerxes* (IV, ii) (1714), a play by Prosper Jolyot de Crébillon. Poe also quotes the playwright at the end of "The Purloined Letter."

2 Antiochus IV, or Antiochus Epiphanes (d. 163 B.C.) was king of Syria from 175 to 163 B.C. A son of Antiochus III, he succeeded his brother Seleucus IV to the throne. He is best known for his attempt to Hellenize Judaea and rid the country of Judaism—a policy that resulted in the rebellion of the Maccabees.

Antiochus had taken advantage of factionalists among the Jews; he also stripped and desecrated the Temple and began a religious persecution. The priest Mattathias led the rebellion, and his son Judas Maccabeus took on the leadership at his father's death, in 166 B.C.

Antiochus, in 171 B.C., invaded Egypt, which was torn by strife between Ptolemy VI and his brother (later Ptolemy VII), and might have actually conquered it had not the Romans intervened in 168 B.C.

Antiochus was briefly succeeded by his son, Antiochus V, a boy king who was overthrown by Demetrius I. Antiochus called himself Epiphanes ("Illustrious") but was called Epimanes ("Madman") by others.

3 Gog appears in Ezekiel 38–39 as a leader who will attack Israel and be defeated. Magog is his homeland. Gog is often identified with the Scythians, and appears again in Revelation 20:8, where the assailants of Israel are Gog and Magog.

According to Caxton, Gog and Magog were the last of a race of giants that inhabited Albion (England) and were brought to London in chains, where they did duty as porters for Brute, the mythological first king of Britain. Their effigies hung at London's Guildhall until the Great Fire; the present ones, fourteen feet high, were carved in 1708 by Richard Saunders.

4 Cambyses (d. 521 B.C.) was king of ancient Persia (529–521 B.C.), the son and successor to Cyrus the Great.

1 Chacun a ses vertus.
—*Crébillon's*—*Xerxes*.

2 Antiochus Epiphanes is very generally looked upon as the Gog **3** of the prophet Ezekiel. This honor is, however, more properly **4** attributable to Cambyses, the son of Cyrus. And, indeed, the character of the Syrian monarch does by no means stand in need of any adventitious embellishment. His accession to the throne, or rather his usurpation of the sovereignty, a hundred and seventy-one years before the coming of Christ; his attempt **5** to plunder the temple of Diana at Ephesus; his implacable **6** hostility to the Jews; his pollution of the Holy of Holies; and **7,8** his miserable death at Taba, after a tumultuous reign of eleven years, are circumstances of a prominent kind, and therefore **9** more generally noticed by the historians of his time than the impious, dastardly, cruel, silly, and whimsical achievements which make up the sum total of his private life and reputation.

*   *   *

Let us suppose, gentle reader, that it is now the year of the **10** world three thousand eight hundred and thirty, and let us, for a few minutes, imagine ourselves at that most grotesque **11** habitation of man, the remarkable city of Antioch. To be sure there were, in Syria and other countries, sixteen cities of that appellation, besides the one to which I more particularly allude. But *ours* is that which went by the name of Antiochia Epidaphne, from its vicinity to the village of Daphne, where stood a temple to that divinity. It was built (although about **12** this matter there is some dispute) by Seleucus Nicanor, the first king of the country after Alexander the Great, in memory of his father Antiochus, and became immediately the residence of the Syrian monarchy. In the flourishing times of the Roman Empire it was the ordinary station of the prefect of the eastern provinces; and many of the emperors of the queen city (among whom may be mentioned especially, Verus and Valens) spent here the greater part of their time. But I perceive we have **13** arrived at the city itself. Let us ascend this battlement, and throw our eyes upon the town and neighboring country.

"What broad and rapid river is that which forces its way, with innumerable falls, through the mountainous wilderness, and finally through the wilderness of buildings?"   **14**

That is the Orontes, and it is the only water in sight, with the exception of the Mediterranean, which stretches, like a broad mirror, about twelve miles off to the southward. Every one has seen the Mediterranean; but let me tell you, there are few who have had a peep at Antioch. By few, I mean, few who, like you and me, have had, at the same time, the advantages of a modern education. Therefore cease to regard that sea, and give your whole attention to the mass of houses that lie beneath us. You will remember that it is now the year of the world three thousand eight hundred and thirty. Were it later—for example, were it the year of our Lord eighteen hundred and forty-five—we should be deprived of this extraordinary spectacle. In the nineteenth century Antioch is— that is to say, Antioch *will be*—in a lamentable state of decay. It will have been, by that time, totally destroyed, at three different periods, by three successive earthquakes. Indeed, **15** to say the truth, what little of its former self may then remain, will be found in so desolate and ruinous a state that the patriarch shall have removed his residence to Damascus. This **16** is well. I see you profit by my advice, and are making the most of your time in inspecting the premises—in

—satisfying your eyes
With the memorials and the things of fame
That most renown this city.—   **17**

I beg pardon: I had forgotten that Shakespeare will not flourish for seventeen hundred and fifty years to come. But does not the appearance of Epidaphne justify me in calling it *grotesque*?

"It is well fortified, and in this respect is as much indebted to nature as to art."

Very true.

"There are a prodigious number of stately palaces."

There are.

"And the numerous temples, sumptuous and magnificent, may bear comparison with the most lauded of antiquity."

All this I must acknowledge. Still there is an infinity of mud huts, and abominable hovels. We cannot help perceiving abundance of filth in every kennel, and, were it not for the **18** overpowering fumes of idolatrous incense, I have no doubt we should find a most intolerable stench. Did you ever behold streets so insufferably narrow, or houses so miraculously tall? What a gloom their shadows cast upon the ground! It is well the swinging lamps in those endless colonnades are kept

He disposed of his brother, Smerdis, to take unchallenged control of the country. He invaded Egypt, but further plans of conquest came to a halt when an imposter claiming to be Smerdis led an insurrection at home. Cambyses died mysteriously—some say by suicide— while attempting to put down the uprising, and Darius I succeeded him to the throne. He is the subject of a tragedy, *Cambises* (c. 1560–70), by Thomas Preston (1537–98), about whom nothing is known. The play, which mixed passion and horror with scenes of low comedy (provided by peasants), was highly popular. Shakespeare spoofs its histrionics in the words of Falstaff, 1 *Henry IV*, II, 4, 425.

5 Poe's summary of Antiochus' history is accurate, possibly the result of his reading of Charles Anthon's edition of Lemprière (1827), or of John Lemprière's own Classical Dictionary (American ed., 1809). He takes as the date for the creation of the world 4004 B.C. and the birth of Christ as 4 B.C., as does Lemprière.

6 From what few historical accounts we have, it is generally accepted that Antiochus IV's attempted attack was aimed at the temple of Diana at Elymaïs or Persepolis, in Persia—not Ephesus.

7 See the two books of the Maccabees, the last two books in the Western canon of the Apocrypha. I Maccabees begins with the struggle against Antiochus IV by Mattathias (c. 167 B.C.) and ends with the murder of Simon (135 B.C.). II Maccabees is a later work (I Maccabees is usually dated about 100 B.C.), one of five books by Jason of Cyrene written in Greek in the first century B.C. It deals with the purification of the Temple, the battles with Antiochus Epiphanes and with his son, Eupator, and the recapture of Jerusalem by the Hebrews. Both books are printed in The New English Bible with the Apocrypha (Oxford/Cambridge, 1970).

8 i.e., the innermost chamber of the Temple in Jerusalem

9 As written by Greek historian Polybius (203?–120? B.C.), 31:9

10 The year 175 B.C. See note 5.

11 Antioch (modern Turkey's Antakya), situated on the Orontes River at the foot of Mt. Silpius and near the sea, was founded about 300 B.C. by Seleucus I near two already existing Greek colonies, and named for his father. Lying, as it did, at the crossing of trade routes from the Euphrates to the Mediterranean Sea, and from Al-Bika to Asia Minor, it soon grew into one of the great commercial centers and most sumptuous cities of the world.

Earthquakes have long been a problem, and there have been far more than Poe's three, the last in 1872. Modern Antioch covers only a fraction of the ancient city, of which little is visible today.

Daphne was the city's resort area, named after the daughter of the river god Ladon (or Peneus).

12 The correct spelling is Seleucus Nicator (d. 280 B.C.), but Poe follows the spelling of the early editions of Lemprière.

Seleucus I was an able general of Alexander who tried harder than any of the other Macedonian generals to set up a kingdom based on Alexander's ideas. He was murdered when he grew powerful enough to seize the vacant throne of Macedonia; he was succeeded by Antiochus I.

The death of Antiochus IV, by Doré

13 Antioch was occupied by the Roman general Pompey in 64 B.C. and soon became the largest and most important Roman city in the region. Various emperors built great temples, a forum, a theater, baths, aqueducts, and other important structures.

Valens was the brother of Roman emperor Flavius Valentinianus I (b. A.D. 321) and made by him co-Augustus in the eastern empire in 364. Verus (b. A.D. 130) was the adopted son of Antoninus Pius (b. 86) and shared in the imperial powers in full equality with Marcus Aurelius (b. 121). He was sent by Marcus to command in the east against Parthia, but his troops brought back a terrible plague, which seriously depopulated the empire (166–67).

19 burning throughout the day; we should otherwise have the darkness of Egypt in the time of her desolation.

"It is certainly a strange place! What is the meaning of yonder singular building? See! it towers above all others, and lies to the eastward of what I take to be the royal palace!"

20 That is the new Temple of the Sun, who is adored in Syria under the title of Elah Gabalah. Hereafter a very notorious Roman emperor will institute this worship in Rome, and **21** thence derive a cognomen. Heliogabalus. I dare say you would like to take a peep at the divinity of the temple. You need not look up at the heavens; his Sunship is not there—at least not the Sunship adored by the Syrians. *That* deity will be found in the interior of yonder building. He is worshipped under the figure of a large stone pillar terminating at the summit in a cone or *pyramid*, whereby is denoted Fire.   **22**

"Hark!—behold!—who *can* those ridiculous beings be, half naked, with their faces painted, shouting and gesticulating to the rabble?"

Some few are mountebanks. Others more particularly belong **23** to the race of philosophers. The greatest portion, however— those especially who belabor the populace with clubs—are the principal courtiers of the palace, executing, as in duty bound, some laudable comicality of the king's.

"But what have we here? Heavens! the town is swarming with wild beasts! How terrible a spectacle!—how dangerous a peculiarity!"

Terrible if you please; but not in the least degree dangerous. Each animal, if you will take the pains to observe, is following, very quietly, in the wake of its master. Some few, to be sure, are led with a rope about the neck, but these are chiefly the lesser or timid species. The lion, the tiger, and the leopard are entirely without restraint. They have been trained without difficulty to their present profession, and attend upon their respective owners in the capacity of *valets-de-chambre*. It is true, there are occasions when Nature asserts her violated dominion;—but then the devouring of a man-at-arms, or the throttling of a consecrated bull, is a circumstance of too little moment to be more than hinted at in Epidaphne.

"But what extraordinary tumult do I hear? Surely this is a loud noise even for Antioch! It argues some commotion of unusual interest."

Yes—undoubtedly. The king has ordered some novel spectacle—some gladiatorial exhibition at the Hippodrome—or perhaps the massacre of the Scythian prisoners—or the con- **24** flagration of his new palace—or the tearing down of a handsome temple—or, indeed, a bonfire of a few Jews. The uproar increases. Shouts of laughter ascend the skies. The air becomes dissonant with wind instruments, and horrible with the clamor of a million throats. Let us descend, for the love of fun, and see what is going on! This way—be careful! Here we are in the principal street, which is called the street of Timarchus. **25** The sea of people is coming this way, and we shall find a difficulty in stemming the tide. They are pouring through the alley of Heraclides, which leads directly from the palace— therefore the king is most probably among the rioters. Yes— I hear the shouts of the herald proclaiming his approach in the pompous phraseology of the East. We shall have a glimpse of his person as he passes by the temple of Ashimah. Let us **26** ensconce ourselves in the vestibule of the sanctuary; he will be here anon. In the meantime let us survey this image. What is it? Oh! it is the god Ashimah in proper person. You perceive, however, that he is neither a lamb, nor a goat, nor a satyr; neither has he much resemblance to the Pan of the Arcadians. **27** Yet all these appearances have been given—I beg pardon— *will* be given—by the learned of future ages, to the Ashimah of the Syrians. Put on your spectacles, and tell me what it is. What is it?

14 The Orontes begins in the valley of Al-Bika, in Lebanon, and flows about 250 miles north through Syria before turning southwest into Turkey for a short course past Antioch into the Mediterranean. It is unnavigable.

15 See note 11.

16 It was at Antioch that the followers of Jesus were first called Christians, after they separated themselves from the synagogue (Acts 11:26, 13:1), and is the location of one of the three original patriarchates. It was a great center of Christian learning and played a significant role in the theological controversies of the early Christian church.

Damascus was not the seat of a patriarch. It fell to the Muslims in 635, and the Crusaders failed in their attempt to annex the city. In the Middle Ages, however, Damascus did become more important than Antioch in terms of commerce.

The five patriarchates were Rome, Jerusalem, Antioch, Alexandria, and Constantinople.

17 *Twelfth Night*, III, iii.

18 Gutter

19 "And the Lord said unto Moses, Stretch out thine hand toward heaven, that there may be darkness over the land of Egypt, even darkness which may be felt" (Exodus 10:21).

20 Ela Gabal, or Elagabalus, a Syrian sun god, represented in the form of a huge cone-shaped stone

21 Or Elagabalus (c. 205–22), Roman emperor (218–22). He was a priest of the sun god Elagabalus at Emesa and was named Varius Avitus Bassianus. He was a cousin of Caracalla and falsely claimed to be the emperor's son by Varius' mother and grandmother, both of whom were highly ambitious. He was chosen by the troops in Syria as emperor in opposition to the legitimate heir, Macrinus, and when Macrinus was defeated and slain at Antioch, Heliogabalus became emperor as Marcus Aurelius Antoninus.

His reign was a tragic farce. He imported the cult of which he was a priest, and Rome was shocked and disgusted by the indecency of the rites, as well as by the private life of the emperor, who gave high offices to an actor, a charioteer, and a barber.

His grandmother induced him to adopt his cousin Alexander Severus, but Heliogabalus later tried to have the boy killed. To no one's great sorrow, Heliogabalus and his mother were both murdered during an uprising of the Praetorian Guard, and Alexander Severus succeeded to the throne.

According to one story, Heliogabalus invited the principal men of Rome to a banquet and smothered them in a shower of roses.

In Gilbert and Sullivan's *The Pirates of Penzance*, the patter song "I am the very model of a modern major-general" mentions "the crimes of Heliogabalus," managing the feat of rhyming the king's name with "peculiarities parabolous."

22 See note 20.

23 Ones who resort to degrading means to obtain notoriety. The word comes from the Italian word meaning "mount on a bench" and referred originally to an itinerant quack who spoke to his audience from a portable stage, entertaining them with stories and tricks in order to sell them some nostrum.

24 Scythia was a region extending from the Danube on the west to the borders of China on the east. The Scythians flourished from the eighth to the fourth centuries B.C. The Greeks thought them barbarians, and Alexander the Great sent an expedition against them in 325 B.C. The Scythians destroyed the Greek force but were driven out of the Balkans by the Celts after 300 B.C.

25 Timarchus and Heracleides were brothers, and close associates of Antiochus IV. They built his council chamber at Miletus, the ancient seaport of western Asia Minor.

26 Ashima was a god whose cult flourished in Hamath (or Hama), northeast of Damascus. An ancient city, the Bible places it as the northern boundary of the Israelite tribes.

27 Pan, the pastoral god of fertility, was worshiped for the most part in Arcadia, a region in the middle of the Peloponnesus, where there is no seaboard and the land is surrounded and dissected by mountains. He was said to be the son of Hermes, another Arcadian gift to the Greek pantheon.

28 There is no proof of any such connection between the Greek and Semitic names.

29 A form dating back to the sixteenth century

30 "Flavius Vopiscus says, that the hymn here introduced was sung by the rabble upon the occasion of Aurelian, in the Sarmatic war, having slain, with his own hand, nine hundred and fifty of the enemy" (Poe's note).

The Latin verses come from *Scriptores Historiae Augustae*, "Divus Aurelianus," VI, attributed to Flavius Vopiscus of Syracuse. Poe probably saw them in Claudius Salmasius' edition of *Scriptores*, published in 1620. The song means, "We, one man, have beheaded a thousand. Long live the man who slew a thousand. No one has tasted as much wine as he has spilled blood."

The Sarmatians replaced the Scythians north of the Black Sea after the first century B.C. They were a kindred group from the east, and in A.D. 172 they attacked the lower Danube frontier, setting off the Sarmatian War. The Aurelian mentioned here is Marcus Aurelius Antoninus.

31 "Nor must you raise your eyes to the heavens and look up to the sun, the moon, and the stars, all the hosts of heaven, and be led on to bow down to them and worship them; the Lord your God assigned these for the worship of the various people under heaven" (Deuteronomy 4:19).

"Bless me! it is an ape!"

True—a baboon; but by no means the less a deity. His name **28** is a derivation of the Greek *Simia*—what great fools are antiquarians! But see!—see!—yonder scampers a ragged little urchin. Where is he going? What is he bawling about? What does he say? Oh! he says the king is coming in triumph; that he is dressed in state; that he has just finished putting to **29** death, with his own hand, a thousand chained Israelitish prisoners! For this exploit the ragamuffin is lauding him to the skies! Hark! here comes a troop of a similar description. They have made a Latin hymn upon the valor of the king, and are singing it as they go:

> Mille, mille, mille,
> Mille, mille, mille,
> Decollavimus, unus homo!
> Mille, mille, mille, mille, decollavimus!
>
> Mille, mille, mille,
> Vivat qui mille mille occidit!
> Tantum vini habet nemo
> **30** Quantum sanguinis effudit!

Which may be thus paraphrased:

> A thousand, a thousand, a thousand,
> A thousand, a thousand, a thousand,
> We, with one warrior, have slain!
> A thousand, a thousand, a thousand, a thousand.
> Sing a thousand over again!
> Soho!—let us sing
> Long life to our king,
> Who knocked over a thousand so fine!
> Soho!—let us roar,
> He has given us more
> Red gallons of gore
> Than all Syria can furnish of wine!

"Do you hear that flourish of trumpets?"

Yes—the king is coming! See! the people are aghast with **31** admiration, and lift up their eyes to the heavens in reverence! He comes!—he is coming!—there he is!

"Who?—where?—the king?—I do not behold him;—cannot say that I perceive him."

Then you must be blind.

"Very possible. Still I see nothing but a tumultuous mob of idiots and madmen, who are busy in prostrating themselves before a gigantic cameleopard, and endeavoring to obtain a kiss of the animal's hoofs. See! the beast has very justly kicked one of the rabble over—and another—and another—and another. Indeed, I cannot help admiring the animal for the excellent use he is making of his feet."

Rabble, indeed!—why these are the noble and free citizens of Epidaphne! Beast, did you say?—take care that you are not overheard. Do you not perceive that the animal has the visage of a man? Why, my dear sir, that cameleopard is no other than Antiochus Epiphanes—Antiochus the Illustrious, King of Syria, and the most potent of all the autocrats of the East!

It is true, that he is entitled, at times, Antiochus Epimanes—
Antiochus the madman—but that is because all people have
not the capacity to appreciate his merits. It is also certain that
he is at present ensconced in the hide of a beast, and is doing
his best to play the part of a cameleopard; but this is done for
the better sustaining of his dignity as king. Besides, the
monarch is of gigantic stature, and the dress is therefore
neither unbecoming nor over large. We may, however,
presume he would not have adopted it but for some occasion
of especial state. Such, you will allow, is the massacre of a
thousand Jews. With how superior a dignity the monarch
perambulates on all fours! His tail, you perceive, is held aloft
by his two principal concubines, Ellinë and Argelaïs; and his **32**
whole appearance would be infinitely prepossessing, were it
not for the protuberance of his eyes, which will certainly start
out of his head, and the queer color of his face, which has
become nondescript from the quantity of wine he has swallowed. Let us follow him to the hippodrome, whither he is
proceeding, and listen to the song of triumph which he is
commencing:

> Who is king but Epiphanes?
>   Say—do you know?
> Who is king but Epiphanes?
>   Bravo!—bravo!
> There is none but Epiphanes,
>   No—there is none:
> So tear down the temples,
>   And put out the sun!   **33**

Well and strenuously sung! The populace are hailing him
"Prince of Poets," as well as "Glory of the East," "Delight of
the Universe," and "Most Remarkable of Cameleopards."
They have *encored* his effusion, and—do you hear?—he is
singing it over again. When he arrives at the hippodrome, he
will be crowned with the poetic wreath, in anticipation of his
victory at the approaching Olympics.

"But, good Jupiter! what is the matter in the crowd behind
us?"

Behind us, did you say?—oh! ah!—I perceive. My friend,
it is well that you spoke in time. Let us get into a place of
safety as soon as possible. Here!—let us conceal ourselves in
the arch of this aqueduct, and I will inform you presently of
the origin of the commotion. It has turned out as I have been
anticipating. The singular appearance of the cameleopard with
the head of a man, has, it seems, given offence to the notions
of propriety entertained in general by the wild animals
domesticated in the city. A mutiny has been the result; and,
as is usual upon such occasions, all human efforts will be of
no avail in quelling the mob. Several of the Syrians have
already been devoured; but the general voice of the four-
footed patriots seems to be for eating up the cameleopard.
"The Prince of Poets," therefore, is upon his hinder legs
running for his life. His courtiers have left him in the lurch,
and his concubines have followed so excellent an example.
"Delight of the Universe," thou art in a sad predicament!

32 Ellinë and Argelaïs have not been identified; they may be inventions of Poe.

33 In the original version the third and fourth lines read, "Who is God but Epiphanes?/Say do you know?" which Poe changed to the present "Who is king . . ." apparently to soothe the feelings of sensitive church-goers. Unfortunately, this dims the satire on this Seleucid king who claimed, as did Alexander, that he was of a divine nature.

"Glory of the East," thou art in danger of mastication! Therefore never regard so piteously thy tail; it will undoubtedly be draggled in the mud, and for this there is no help. Look not behind thee, then, at its unavoidable degradation; but take courage, ply thy legs with vigor, and scud for the hippodrome! Remember that thou art Antiochus Epiphanes. Antiochus the Illustrious!—also "Prince of Poets," "Glory of the East," "Delight of the Universe," and "Most Remarkable of Cameleopards!" Heavens! what a power of speed thou art displaying! What a capacity for leg-bail thou art developing! Run, Prince!—Bravo, Epiphanes!—Well done, Cameleopard!—Glorious Antiochus!—He runs!—he leaps!—he flies! Like an arrow from a catapult he approaches the hippodrome! He leaps!—he shrieks!—he is there! This is well; for hadst thou, "Glory of the East," been half a second longer in reaching the gates of the amphitheatre, there is not a bear's cub in Epidaphne that would not have had a nibble at thy carcass. Let us be off—let us take our departure!—for we shall find our delicate modern ears unable to endure the vast uproar which is about to commence in celebration of the king's escape! Listen! it has already commenced. See!—the whole town is topsy-turvy.

"Surely this is the most populous city of the East! What a wilderness of people! What a jumble of all ranks and ages! What a multiplicity of sects and nations! what a variety of costumes! what a Babel of languages! what a screaming of beasts! what a tinkling of instruments! what a parcel of philosophers!"

Come let us be off.

"Stay a moment! I see a vast hubbub in the hippodrome; what is the meaning of it, I beseech you?"

That?—oh, nothing! The noble and free citizens of Epidaphne being, as they declare, well satisfied of the faith, valor, wisdom, and divinity of their king, and having, moreover, been eye-witnesses of his late superhuman agility, do think it no more than their duty to invest his brows (in addition to the poetic crown) with the wreath of victory in the foot-race—a wreath which it is evident he *must* obtain at the celebration of the next Olympiad, and which, therefore, they now give him in advance.

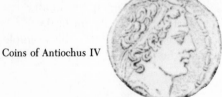

Coins of Antiochus IV

LIONIZING

First published in the *Southern Literary Messenger*, May 1835, then revised for *Tales* (1845) in the form given here.

Often considered one of Poe's best comic efforts, "Lionizing" is a spoof on Nathaniel Parker Willis (see introductory note to "Duc De L'omelette"), whom Poe later came to admire. Many readers find the humor brittle and overdone, but there are some good moments in it.

Willis went to Europe in 1831 and wrote about his experiences in a series of articles, which he later collected as *Pencillings by the Way* (1835). In them we read of his duel with a Captain Marryat, his friendship with Lady Blessington, and his meetings with the British literati. Willis has been described as an arrant sentimentalist and something of a fop, who often embellished his works with words of his own invention and was involved in many of the hot-tempered literary quarrels of the day.

Another source of the tale is Bulwer-Lytton's "Too Handsome for Anything," which is part of his *Conversations with an Ambitious Student in Ill Health, with Other Pieces* (1832).

In the issue in which "Lionizing" first appeared, Poe wrote (anonymously) that it "is an admirable piece of burlesque which displays much reading, a lively humor, and an ability to afford amusement or instruction." Poe was never at a loss to sell one of his works to an audience.

In a letter to J. P. Kennedy (February 11, 1836), Poe wrote that "Lionizing" is a satire "properly speaking—at least so meant— . . . of the rage for Lions and the facility of becoming one." A "lion" is a person of note or celebrity who is much sought after. Thackeray, in 1826, writes, "What is a lion? A lion is a man or woman one must have at one's parties." (*Works*, XXIV, 251)

"The lions of a place are sights worth seeing, or the celebrities; so called from the ancient custom of showing strangers, as chief of London sights, the lions at the Tower" (Brewer's Dictionary of Phrase and Fable [1894]). In the *Pickwick Papers*, the aptly named Mrs. Leo Hunter is one who hunts up celebrities to adorn or give prestige to parties.

This kind of social milieu is given full comic treatment as Poe points out the importance of playing the games by the rules. The narrator makes the mistake of not humoring everyone else's "expertise," thereby incurring their wrath—and society's.

Freudian critic Marie Bonaparte, not surprisingly, sees the hero's pride in a huge nose as a "substitute for the penis" (p. 397).

—— all people went
Upon their ten toes in wild wonderment.
      —Bishop Hall's Satires.   **1**

I am—that is to say, I *was*—a great man; but I am neither the author of Junius nor the man in the mask; for my name, I **2,3** believe, is Robert Jones, and I was born somewhere in the city of Fum-Fudge.   **4**

The first action of my life was the taking hold of my nose with both hands. My mother saw this and called me a genius— my father wept for joy and presented me with a treatise on Nosology. This I mastered before I was breeched.   **5,6**

1 Borrowed (and altered) from Bishop Joseph Hall (1574–1656) in his *Satires* (1597), II, iii, 19–20: "Genus and Species long since barefoote went/Upon their ten-toes in wilde wonderment." Hall, who became Bishop of Norwich, claimed the honor of being the first English satirist; later he came under attack from Milton for the book *Episcopacy by Divine Right, Asserted by J. H.* (1640).

2 The author of a series of political letters published in the London *Public Advertiser* from 1769 to 1772, probably Sir Philip Francis (1740–1818), although the identity of "Junius" is still the best-kept secret in the history of journalism.

3 The Man in the Iron Mask was probably Count Ercolo Antonio Mattioli, a senator of Mantua and private agent of Ferdinand Charles, Duke of Mantua. He suffered imprisonment for twenty-four years for having deceived Louis XIV in a secret treaty for the purchase of the fortress of Casale, the key to Italy. The agents of Spain and Austria bribed him by outbidding the Grande Monarque. The secrecy observed was inviolate, because the infamy of the transaction would not bear daylight.

Voltaire reasoned that the Man in the Iron Mask was actually the illegitimate son of Anne of Austria and thus an older half brother to Louis XIV. Dumas, in his *Vicomte de Bragelonne* (1848–50), described him as a twin brother to the king, and other, wilder suggestions have filled many books and essays on the subject.

The "iron" mask was actually of black velvet, and the man, whoever he was, was buried in the cemetery of St. Paul, Paris, in 1703 under the name of Marchioly.

4 "Fum" means to beat, strum, or thump. "Fudge" means a made-up story, a deceit, or contemptible nonsense.

5 "Nosology" is a real word, but it refers to the classification, combination, or collection of diseases, or the branch of medicine that classifies diseases. Poe's pun on the word is not original. In *Blackwood's*, V, 157 (1819), we find "Noseology, a dissertation on the Intellectual Faculties, as manifested by the various configurations of the Nose," and in XI, 427 (1822), "If ever we should posses a classified nosology, my nose must be ranked in the order which shall comprise the pitch-delighting olfactories."

Johann Casper Laueter in 1775 developed a system of divining character by noses, ears, eyes, and chins.

As for nose literature, there is an amazing amount, from O. Basselin's ode to his nose ("Oh nose, I am as proud of thee/As any mountain of its snow") to Sterne's *Tristram Shandy* (1760). Others include: *On the Dignity, Gravity, and Authority of Noses*, by Tagliacozzi or Tagliacozzo (1597); *The Noses of Adam and Eve*, by Antoinette Bourignon (1616–80); *Pious Meditations on the Nose of the Virgin Mary*, by J. Petit; *Review of Noses*, by Théophile Raynaud; and *Sermon on Noses (La Diceria de'Nasi)* by Annibale Caro (1584).

6 Put in long pants

7 The personality of a lion (used as a mock title)

8 Small servings of a cordial or other liquor

9 Casparus Bartholinus, or Kaspar Bartholin (1585–1629), Danish physician, was born in Sweden and became professor of medicine and later of theology. He was the author of a textbook on anatomy, *Institutiones anatomicae* (1611). His grandson, also named Kaspar (1655–1738) was a medical expert on the respiratory system.

10 "Afflatus" means a breathing upon, but more often refers to a miraculous communication of supernatural knowledge or divine inspiration.

11 Poe here lists the names of the principal reviews of his day.

12 i.e., "bluestocking." The word originated in the gatherings in mid-eighteenth-century London at the homes of Mrs. Montagu, Mrs. Vesey, and Mrs. Ord, who, instead of card games, featured conversations on

I now began to feel my way in the science, and soon came to understand that, provided a man had a nose sufficiently conspicuous, he might, by merely following it, arrive at a **7** Lionship. But my attention was not confined to theories alone. Every morning I gave my proboscis a couple of pulls and **8** swallowed a half dozen of drams.

When I came of age my father asked me, one day, if I would step with him into his study.

"My son," said he, when we were seated, "what is the chief end of your existence?"

"My father," I answered, "it is the study of Nosology."

"And what, Robert," he inquired, "is Nosology?"

"Sir," I said, "it is the science of Noses."

"And can you tell me," he demanded, "what is the meaning of a nose?"

"A nose, my father," I replied, greatly softened, "has been variously defined by about a thousand different authors." [Here I pulled out my watch.] "It is now noon, or thereabouts—we shall have time enough to get through with them all before midnight. To commence then:—The nose, according to Bar-**9** tholinus, is that protuberance—that bump—that excrescence—that—"

"Will do, Robert," interrupted the good old gentleman. "I am thunderstruck at the extent of your information—I am positively—upon my soul." [Here he closed his eyes and placed his hand upon his heart.] "Come here!" [Here he took me by the arm.] "Your education may now be considered as finished—it is high time you should scuffle for yourself—and you cannot do a better thing than merely follow your nose—so—so—so—" [Here he kicked me down stairs and out of the door.]—"So get out of my house, and God bless you!"

10 As I felt within me the divine *afflatus*, I considered this accident rather fortunate than otherwise. I resolved to be guided by the paternal advice. I determined to follow my nose. I gave it a pull or two upon the spot, and wrote a pamphlet on Nosology forthwith.

All Fum-Fudge was in an uproar.

11 "Wonderful genius!" said the *Quarterly*.

"Superb physiologist!" said the *Westminster*.

"Clever fellow!" said the *Foreign*.

"Fine writer!" said the *Edinburgh*.

"Profound thinker!" said the *Dublin*.

"Great man!" said *Bentley*.

"Divine soul!" said *Fraser*.

"One of us!" said *Blackwood*.

12 "Who can he be?" said Mrs. Bas-Bleu.

"What can he be?" said big Miss Bas-Bleu.

"Where can he be?" said little Miss Bas-Bleu.—But I paid these people no attention whatever—I just stepped into the shop of an artist.

13 The Duchess of Bless-my-Soul was sitting for her portrait; the Marquis of So-and-So was holding the Duchess' poodle; the Earl of This-and-That was flirting with her salts; and his

Royal Highness of Touch-me-Not was leaning upon the back of her chair.

I approached the artist and turned up my nose.

"Oh, beautiful!" sighed her Grace.

"Oh my!" lisped the Marquis.

"Oh, shocking!" groaned the Earl.

"Oh, abominable!" growled his Royal Highness.

"What will you take for it?" asked the artist.

"For his *nose!*" shouted her Grace.

"A thousand pounds," said I, sitting down.

"A thousand pounds?" inquired the artist, musingly.

"A thousand pounds," said I.

"Beautiful!" said he, entranced.

"A thousand pounds," said I.

"Do you warrant it?" he asked, turning the nose to the light.

"I do," said I, blowing it well.

"Is it *quite* original?" he inquired, touching it with reverence.

"Humph!" said I, twisting it to one side.

"Has *no* copy been taken?" he demanded, surveying it through a microscope.

"None," said I, turning it up.

"*Admirable!*" he ejaculated, thrown quite off his guard by the beauty of the manœuvre.

"A thousand pounds," said I.

"A thousand pounds," said I. *Illustration by F. S. Coburn, 1902*

literary topics, in which eminent men of letters often took part. These were likened to the *Società della calza,* a fifteenth-century society in Venice whose members were distinguished by the color of their stockings.

Another version has it that many of those who attended the London gatherings came in less than full dress, and that Benjamin Stillingfleet habitually wore gray, or "blue," worsted stockings instead of black silk.

At any rate, the coterie was quickly dubbed the Blue Stocking Society, and the word came to mean a person who affects literary tastes.

13 Lady Blessington is mentioned by Willis in his description of her salon in *Pencillings by the Way,* Chapter XCVI: "A German prince, with a star at his breast, trying with all his might, but from his embarrassed look, quite unsuccessfully, to comprehend the drift of the argument; the Duke of de Richelieu, whom I had seen at the court of France, the inheritor of nothing but the name of his great ancestor, a dandy and a fool, making no attempt to listen; a famous traveller, just returned from Constantinople; and the splendid person of Count D'Orsay in a careless attitude upon the ottoman, completed the cordon."

14 In Latin, *virtu(s)* means manhood, or virility, leading Marie Bonaparte and others to conclude that the "nose" of the tale is actually the penis, turning the whole thing into a sort of dirty joke. Although it's possible that Poe may himself have understood this joke, it doesn't seem necessary to an understanding or appreciation of the tale.

15 Jermyn Street was a fashionable area of London where many literary greats lived, and where a number of clubs were situated.

16 "His majesty" in the original version, but Poe changed it after the coronation of Victoria, who succeeded William IV to the throne in 1837. Likewise, he added "Prince of Wales" in the 1845 version, since the future Edward VII had received that title in 1842.

17 The modern Platonist is perhaps Thomas Taylor, who, according to Benjamin Disraeli, was turned out of his London home for sacrificing a bull to Jupiter in the back parlor (mentioned in *Pencillings,* CXXI). The other names come from Disraeli's *Vivian Grey* (1826), Chapter 6: "Father! I wish to make myself master of the latter Platonists. I want Plotinus, and Porphyry, and Iamblichus, and Syrianus, and Maximum Tyrius, and Proclus, and Hierocles, and Sallustius, and Damascius."

Platonism involves the doctrine of preexisting eternal ideas, and teaches the immortality and preexistence of the soul, the dependence of virtue upon discipline, and the trustworthiness of knowledge.

Plotinus (c.205–70) was the teacher of Porphyry (233?–c.304), and Iamblichus (d. c.330) was a pupil of Porphyry; Syrianus was a fifth-century Greek teacher of philosophy, as was Proclus (410?–485). Maximum Tyrius was a rhetorician and philosopher of the second century, and Hierocles of Alexandria was the fifth-century Neoplatonist who was also the first to search out and compile jokes.

18 Anne Robert Jacques Turgot, Baron de l'Aulne (1727–81), French economist and philosopher. Richard Price (1723–91), English noncomformist minister and political philosopher. Joseph Priestly (1733–1804), English scientist and theologian, whose *Essay on Government* (1768) suggested the idea of "the greatest happiness of the greatest number" to Jeremy Bentham. Marie Jean Antoine Nicholas de Caritat, Marquis de Condorcet (1743–94), French mathematician, philosopher, and political leader. Germaine de Staël (1766–1817), French-Swiss woman of letters, whose full name was Anne Louise Germaine Necker, Baronne de Staël-Holstein. Most of the above were political activists because their belief in the perfectability of man made any acceptance of the status quo a cardinal sin. Poe mentions them again in "The Domain of Arnheim."

Conversations with an Ambitious Student in Ill Health, with Other Pieces (1832), by Bulwer-Lytton, is mentioned in "Loss of Breath." (Also see introductory note.)

19 The prefect of police in "The Purloined Letter" says something similar.

20 This paragraph has to do with Newtonian theories of attraction and repulsion, and similar matters. Fire for a long time was a mystery. What caused it? Did it have a material body, or was it ethereal? What bound matter together? What caused gravity? There was a great deal of overlap between philosophy and science in those pre-specialization days, with comparisons made between the properties of matter and ether on the one hand, and spirit and soul on the other.

The bipart soul was the name given to the notion that every person's soul was made up of a true spiritual and eternal soul—and a material and mortal one. Because one soul was immortal, it was then supposed that this one also existed before the material body was born. The study of primitive intelligence, many thought, might give some clue to the nature of the material versus the ethereal soul.

Poe also brings up the subject of the bipart soul in "William Wilson," "The Murders in the Rue Morgue," and "The Fall of the House of Usher."

As for "homoömeria" (homoeomery), it refers to the belief of Anaxagoras that the ultimate particles of matter are all of the same kind.

21 Eusebius of Caesarea, or Eusebius Pamphili (c.263?–339?) was a church historian and bishop. His relative Eusebius of Nicomedia was bishop of that city (d. 342). Arius was the proponent of the idea that Christ was less than God, instead of one with Him—strongly condemned at the Council of Nicaea in 325.

In the controversy over Arianism, Eusebius of Caesarea seemed to favor the semi-Arian views of Eusebius of Nicomedia, and he once gave refuge to Arius. Eusebius of Nicomedia also sheltered Arius and fought his condemnation at Nicaea. He was patriarch of Constantinople from 339 to 342.

"Puseyism" refers to Edward Bouverie Pusey (1800–82), who advocated the doctrine of the Real Presence, which holds that the body and blood of Christ are actually (not merely symbolically) present in the sacrament, and who established the first Anglican sisterhood. Poe didn't think much of him.

"*Homousios*" and "*Homouioisios*" usually appear in English as "homoousian" and "homoiousian" and refer to the question of whether Christ is the same as, like, or less than, the Father.

22 The Rocher de Cancale was the name of a well-known Paris restaurant that Willis mentions in his *Pencillings*.

"A *thousand* pounds?" said he.

"Precisely," said I.

"A thousand *pounds?*" said he.

"Just so," said I.

14 "You shall have them," said he. "What a piece of *virtu!*" So he drew me a check upon the spot, and took a sketch of my **15,16** nose. I engaged rooms in Jermyn street, and sent her Majesty the ninety-ninth edition of the "Nosology," with a portrait of the proboscis.—That sad little rake, the Prince of Wales, invited me to dinner.

We were all lions and *recherchés*.

There was a modern Platonist. He quoted Porphyry, Iamblicus, Plotinus, Proclus, Hierocles, Maximum Tyrius, and **17** Syrianus.

There was a human-perfectibility man. He quoted Turgot, Price, Priestley, Condorcet, De Staël, and the "Ambitious **18** Student in Ill-Health."

There was Sir Positive Paradox. He observed that all fools **19** were philosophers, and that all philosophers were fools.

There was Æstheticus Ethix. He spoke of fire, unity, and atoms; bipart and pre-existent soul; affinity and discord; **20** primitive intelligence and homoömeria.

There was Theologos Theology. He talked of Eusebius and Arianus; heresy and the Council of Nice; Puseyism and **21** consubtantialism; Homousios and Homouioisios.

There was Fricassée from the Rocher de Cancale. He mentioned Muriton of red tongue; cauliflowers and *velouté* sauce; veal *à la* St. Menehoult; marinade *à la* St. Florentin; **22** and orange jellies *en mosaïques*.

There was Bibulus O'Bumper. He touched upon Latour and Markbrünnen; upon Mousseux and Chambertin; upon Richbourg and St. George; upon Haubrion, Leonville, and Medoc; upon Barac and Preignac; upon Grâve, upon Sauterne, upon Lafitte, and upon St. Peray. He shook his head at Clos de Vougeot, and told, with his eyes shut, the difference between **23** Sherry and Amontillado.

There was Signor Tintontintino from Florence. He discoursed of Cimabue, Arpino, Carpaccio, and Argostino—of the gloom of Caravaggio, of the amenity of Albano, of the colors of Titian, of the frows of Rubens, and of the waggeries **24** of Jan Steen.

There was the President of the Fum-Fudge University. He was of opinion that the moon was called Bendis in Thrace, **25** Bubastis in Egypt, Dian in Rome, and Artemis in Greece.

There was a Grand Turk from Stamboul. He could not help thinking that the angels were horses, cocks, and bulls; that somebody in the sixth heaven had seventy thousand heads; and that the earth was supported by a sky-blue cow with an **26** incalculable number of green horns.

There was Delphinus Polyglott. He told us what had become of the eighty-three lost tragedies of Æschylus; of the fifty-four orations of Isæus; of the three hundred and ninety-one speeches of Lysias; of the hundred and eighty treatises of Theophrastus; of the eighth book of the conic sections of

Apollonius; of Pindar's hymns and dithyrambics; and of the five and forty tragedies of Homer Junior. **27**

There was Ferdinand Fitz-Fossillus Feltspar. He informed us all about internal fires and tertiary formations; about aëriforms, fluidiforms, and solidiforms; about quartz and marl; about schist and schorl; about gypsum and trap; about talc and calc; about blende and horn-blende; about mica-slate and pudding-stone; about cyanite and lepidolite; about hæmatite and tremolite; about antimony and calcedony; about manganese and whatever you please. **28**

There was myself. I spoke of myself;—of myself, of myself, of myself;—of Nosology, of my pamphlet, and of myself. I turned up my nose, and I spoke of myself.

"Marvellous clever man!" said the Prince.

"Superb!" said his guests;—and next morning her Grace of Bless-my-Soul paid me a visit.

"Will you go to Almack's, pretty creature?" she said, tapping **29** me under the chin.

"Upon honor," said I.

"Nose and all?" she asked.

"As I live," I replied.

"Here then is a card, my life. Shall I say you *will* be there?"

"Dear Duchess, with all my heart."

"Pshaw, no!—but with all your nose?"

"Every bit of it, my love," said I:—so I gave it a twist or two, and found myself at Almack's.

The rooms were crowded to suffocation.

"He is coming!" said somebody on the staircase.

"He is coming!" said somebody farther up.

"He is coming!" said somebody farther still.

"He is come!" exclaimed the Duchess. "He is come, the little love!"—and, seizing me firmly by both hands, she kissed me thrice upon the nose.

A marked sensation immediately ensued.

"*Diavolo!*" cried Count Capricornutti. **30**

"*Dios guarda!*" muttered Don Stiletto. **31**

"*Mille tonnerres!*" ejaculated the Prince de Grenouille. **32**

"*Tousand Teufel!*" growled the Elector of Bluddennuff. **33**

It was not to be borne. I grew angry. I turned short upon Bluddennuff.

"Sir!" said I to him, "you are a baboon."

"Sir," he replied, after a pause, *"Donner und Blitzen!"* **34**

This was all that could be desired. We exchanged cards, At Chalk-Farm, the next morning, I shot off his nose—and then **35** called upon my friends.

"*Bête!*" said the first.

"Fool!" said the second.

"Dolt!" said the third.

"Ass!" said the fourth.

"Ninny!" said the fifth.

"Noodle!" said the sixth.

"Be off !" said the seventh.

At all this I felt mortified, and so called upon my father.

"Father," I asked, "what is the chief end of my existence?"

The dishes listed are real ones, and for the adventurous, the recipes are in *Larousse Gastronomique* (New York, 1961).

23 This paragraph is packed with names of famous wine châteaux.

Château Latour is one of the great wine estates of the Haut-Médoc, just north of Bordeaux. Mousseux is undistinguished, the poor Frenchman's substitute for champagne. Chambertin is one of the greatest red burgundies, from the Côte de Nuits area in eastern France (See "Bon-Bon", note 19). Richebourg, also in the Côtes de Nuits area, produces one of the greatest burgundies, and certainly one of the fullest.

St. Georges is the name of several châteaux: Les Saint-Georges in the Côtes de Nuits, home of sparkling burgundy; Saint-Georges in the Midi, the home of good red table wines; Saint-Georges-Saint-Emilion, in the near South.

Château Haut-Brion is in the Graves district of the Bordeaux region, and in Poe's time produced only red wines of great distinction. "Leonville" is probably Léoville, in the Médoc, which includes Châteaux Léoville-Lascases, Léoville-Poyferré, and Léoville-Barton.

"Barac" is Barsac, an area in southwestern France near Graves and the Sauterne region, where white wines abound. Preignac is in the Sauterne region near Bordeaux.

Château Lafite (formerly Laffitte) is in the Médoc, where great light wines, famed for their finesse, are produced in nearly every good year. The Château Mouton-Rothschild is nearby.

St.-Péray is in the Rhône Valley, north of Avignon, where the white wines are small and rarely distinguished. Clos de Vougeot is in the Côtes de Nuits area; it produces a fine burgundy.

For the differences among sherries, see "The Cask of Amontillado," note 9.

24 Cimabue (c. 1240–1302?) is considered one of the first painters of the modern era; he was the teacher of Giotto.

Giuseppe Cesari Arpino, called Cavaliere d'Arpino (1568–1640) was the last melancholy champion of conservative mannerism; he opposed Caravaggio's naturalist revolution. Vittore Carpaccio (c. 1460–1523) was probably a pupil, and certainly a follower, of Giovanni Bellini (c. 1430–1516).

Agostino di Duccio (1418–81) was a sculptor, while Agostino dalle Prospettive (fl. early 1500s) was a painter. The former was by far the better known.

Michelangelo Merisi da Caravaggio (d. 1610) is known for his vivid realism, his use of contemporary costumes and settings, his rejection of idealism, the immediacy and simplicity of his approach, and his use of light and shadow.

Francesco Albani (1578–1660) was a Bolognese painter. Titian, or Tiziano Vecelli (c. 1487–1576), was the greatest of the Venetian painters and, in some senses a founder of modern painting. The "fraus" of Peter Paul Rubens (1577–1640) refer to the somewhat fleshy (by modern standards) nude women for which the painter is well known. Jan Steen (1626–79) was a Dutch painter of humorous subjects from the life of the peasantry and middle classes.

In his review of Longfellow in *Graham's* (April 1842), Poe writes, "If truth is the highest aim of . . . painting . . . Jan Steen was a greater artist than [Michel] Angelo," but in the same magazine a month earlier, Poe says, "For one Angelo there are five hundred Jan Steens."

25 "Queen of Night! in whatever name thou most delightest! Or Bendis, as they hail thee in rugged Thrace;

or Bubastis, as they howled to thee in mysterious Egypt; or Dian, as they sacrificed to thee in gorgeous Rome; or Artemis, as they sighed to thee on the bright plains of ever glorious Greece" (Disraeli, *Vivian Grey*, III, vi).

26 See "The Thousand-and-Second Tale of Scheherazade," note 46.

27 "Delphinius" refers to the Delphin edition of the Latin classics prepared for the Dauphin by order of Louis XIV and edited by thirty-nine scholars.

Aeschylus (525–456 B.C.), Athenian tragic poet and playwright, is best known for *The Seven Against Thebes*, *Prometheus Bound*, and *Agamemnon*. He wrote perhaps ninety plays, but only seven survive intact.

Isaeus (fl. early-fourth century B.C.) was one of the Ten Attic Orators and a teacher of Demosthenes. Of his twelve surviving orations, eleven deal with legal cases of inheritance.

Lysias (c.459–c.380B.C.), whose oration against Eratosthenes is a model of Greek oratory, was hounded by his government and took to writing speeches for a living. Only thirty-four of his speeches remain complete.

Theophrastus (c.372–c.287 B.C.) was Aristotle's successor as head of the Peripatetics. His *Characters*, a series of sketches of various ethical types, provides us with a valuable picture of his time.

Apollonius of Tyana (fl. A.D. 100?) was a philosopher and leading exponent of Neo-Pythagoreanism. Of his works, only fragments of a biography of Pythagoras and a treatise on sacrifice are extant.

Pindar (518?–c.438 B.C.) is generally regarded as the greatest Greek lyric poet. Of his complete works, forty-five odes survive, one of the greatest collection of poems by a single author in Greek.

A dithyramb is an irregular short poem or chant in a wild, inspired, or enthusiastic style.

As for Homer Junior, his apocryphal lost forty-five tragedies are mentioned in the 1806 edition of John Lemprière's *Bibliotheca Classica*.

28 Geology is the subject here. "Feltspar" is feldspar, a crystalline mineral of silica and other substances. "Tertiary" is an outdated term first applied to a layer of sedimentary and unconsolidated deposits, geologically younger than the underlying deposits, which were called Primary and Secondary.

"Aeriform" means gaseous; "fluidiform" means fluid, but also refers to an ethereal "double" of the human body, or astral soul; the O.E.D. does not list "solidiform." Marl is a kind of soil of clay mixed with carbonate of lime; it is used as a fertilizer; marl also refers to a kind of sandstone, and manure.

Schist is a recrystallized rock, but in Poe's day the word commonly meant a slatelike rock. Schorl is a rock composed of tourmaline and quartz. Gypsum is a form of hydrated sulphate of calcium.

"Trap" is a word for igneous rocks other than granite, including basalt. Talc is hydrated silicate of magnesium, while calc is a prefix meaning limy; calc-flint is lime-silicate rock and calc-alkali is lime and alkali rock.

Blende is zinc-sulphide igneous rock. Hornblende is any dark-colored prismatic crystals found with metallic ores, but with no metal. ("Blende" means "deceiver.") "Mica-slate" is another term for mica-silicates of aluminum and potassium which split into thin plates.

Cyanite (kyanite) is another mineral, as is lepidolite (of the mica group). Haematite is a principal ore of iron, while tremolite is one of the common rock-forming minerals (as is hornblende). Antimony is a tin-white mineral, a blend of magnesium and calcium. Chalcedony is a hard, glassy mineral which includes agate, jasper, and flint. Manganese is a mineral that resembles iron but is not magnetic.

"My son," he replied, "it is still the study of Nosology; but in hitting the Elector upon the nose you have overshot your mark. You have a fine nose, it is true; but then Bluddennuff has none. You are damned, and he has become the hero of the day. I grant you that in Fum-Fudge the greatness of a lion is in proportion to the size of his proboscis—but, good heavens! there is no competing with a lion who has no proboscis at all."

29 Almack's was a suite of assembly rooms in King Street, St. James's, London, built in 1765 by a Scotsman named MacAll, who inverted his name to remove any possible prejudice and hide his origin (to understand the depth of the prejudice against the Scotch, one need only note Samuel Johnson's definition of oats in his Dictionary as a substance used to feed horses in England but which is the mainstay of the Scottish population).

Balls, presided over by a committee of ladies of the highest rank, were given in these rooms, and to be admitted was as great a distinction as to be presented at court.

The rooms were closed in 1890.

30 The Devil!

31 God protect us!

32 *Milles tonnéres* means "a thousand thunders." *Grenouille* means frog.

33 *"Tousand Teufel"* means "a thousand devils." "Bluddennuff " (blood enough) may translate as "sufficiently stupid" (*blöd* means "stupid")

34 Thunder and lightning

35 North of Regent's Park; a well-known dueling site

MYSTIFICATION

First published as "Von Jung, the Mystific," in the New York *American Monthly Magazine*, June 1837, "Mystification" is a humorous blend of dueling, secret writing, and the *Doppelgänger*, or double.

Burton Pollin (*Mississippi Quarterly*, Spring 1972) suggests that the tale is a satire on Theodore S. Fay (1807–98), editor of the New York *Mirror* and author of *Norman Leslie* (1835), a novel based on an actual murder case. Part of that novel, "The German Student's Story," appeared in the *Mirror* in June 1835, and later that year Poe reviewed the novel as "bepuffed, beplastered, and be-Mirrored."

Large portions of the original were deleted in subsequent editions, but Mabbott includes the deletions in *Collected Works* (1978), Vol. II, pp. 291–304.

---

1 Edward Knowell is a character in Ben Jonson's *Every Man in His Humour* (1616 ed.), IV, vii, 145–46.

2 In German, *Ritz* means "crack," while *jung* means young, fresh, or new. The name suggests that this young man is fond of cracking jokes.

3 Johann Ludwig Tieck (1773–1853) was the voluminous writer of the German romantic period mentioned in several of Poe's other tales as well.

4 Göttingen

Slid, if these be your "passados" and "montantes," I'll have none o'them.

1

—NED KNOWLES.

2 The Baron Ritzner Von Jung was of a noble Hungarian family, every member of which (at least as far back into antiquity as any certain records extend) was more or less remarkable for talent of some description—the majority for that species of 3 *grotesquerie* in conception of which Tieck, a scion of the house, has given a vivid, although by no means the most vivid exemplification. My acquaintance with Ritzner commenced at the magnificent Chateau Jung, into which a train of droll adventures, not to be made public, threw me during the summer months of the year 18—. Here it was that I obtained a place in his regard, and here, with somewhat more difficulty, a partial insight into his mental conformation. In later days this insight grew more clear, as the intimacy which had at first permitted it became more close; and when, after three years' 4 separation, we met at G——n, I knew all that it was necessary to know of the character of the Baron Ritzner Von Jung.

I remember the buzz of curiosity which his advent excited within the college precincts on the night of the twenty-fifth of June. I remember still more distinctly, that while he was pronounced by all parties at first sight "the most remarkable man in the world," no person made any attempt at accounting for his opinion. That he was *unique* appeared so undeniable, that it was deemed impertinent to inquire wherein the uniquity consisted. But, letting this matter pass for the present, I will merely observe that, from the first moment of his setting foot within the limits of the university, he began to exercise over the habits, manners, persons, purses, and propensities of the whole community which surrounded him, an influence the most extensive and despotic, yet at the same time the most indefinite and altogether unaccountable. Thus the brief period of his residence at the university forms an era in its annals, and is characterized by all classes of people appertaining to it or its dependencies as "that very extraordinary epoch forming the domination of the Baron Ritzner Von Jung."

Upon his advent to G——n, he sought me out in my apartments. He was then of no particular age, by which I mean that it was impossible to form a guess respecting his age by any data personally afforded. He might have been fifteen or fifty, and *was* twenty-one years and seven months. He was by no means a handsome man—perhaps the reverse. The contour of his face was somewhat angular and harsh. His forehead was lofty and very fair; his nose a snub; his eyes large, heavy, glassy and meaningless. About the mouth there was more to be observed. The lips were gently protruded, and rested the one upon the other, after such fashion that it is impossible to conceive any, even the most complex, combination of features, conveying so entirely, and so singly, the idea of unmitigated gravity, solemnity and repose.

It will be perceived, no doubt, from what I have already said, that the Baron was one of those human anomalies now and then to be found, who make the science of *mystification* **5** the study and the business of their lives. For this science a peculiar turn of mind gave him instinctively the cue, while his physical appearance afforded him unusual facilities for carrying his projects into effect. I firmly believe that no student at G——n, during that renowned epoch so quaintly termed the domination of the Baron Ritzner Von Jung, ever rightly entered into the mystery which overshadowed his character. I truly think that no person at the university, with the

5 "The action of mystifying a person, playing upon his credulity, or throwing dust in his eyes" (O.E.D.)

. . . the most egregious and unpardonable of all conceivable tricks, whimsicalities and buffooneries were brought about, if not directly by him, at least plainly through his intermediate agency or connivance. *Artist unknown*

6 Heraclitus (c.540–475 B.C.) was the Greek philosopher from Ephesus known as "the Weeping Philosopher." He was one of the first metaphysicians.

7 Poe's invented word

8 in Latin, "fostering mother," the university at which one was a student, but also, in ancient Rome, the title of several goddesses, including Cybele and Ceres

9 "Sweetness of doing nothing," which some trace back to Pliny the Younger's *Epistolae*, vii, 9: "For some time past I have not known the meaning of leisure, of repose, of that indolent yet delightful doing nothing, being nothing."

11 An evil spirit that descends upon a person during sleep; a nightmare

11 German students were notorious for their duels. This form of combat dates back to the wager of battle, in which an accused person fought his accuser under judicial supervision. Pope Stephen VI prohibited the judicial ordeal, and wager of battle was abolished in France in the 1600s, when the duel came into its own as a sort of replacement. The object of a duel, by the way, was not necessarily to kill one's opponent, and duels were often stopped after a prescribed number of shots or the drawing of blood.

exception of myself, ever suspected him to be capable of a joke, verbal or practical:—the old bull-dog at the garden-gate

6 would sooner have been accused,—the ghost of Heraclitus,— or the wig of the Emeritus Professor of Theology. This, too, when it was evident that the most egregious and unpardonable of all conceivable tricks, whimsicalities and buffooneries were brought about, if not directly by him, at least plainly through his intermediate agency or connivance. The beauty, if I may

7 so call it, of his *art mystifique*, lay in that consummate ability (resulting from an almost intuitive knowledge of human nature, and a most wonderful self-possession,) by means of which he never failed to make it appear that the drolleries he was occupied in bringing to a point, arose partly in spite, and partly in consequence of the laudable efforts he was making for their prevention, and for the preservation of the good

8 order and dignity of Alma Mater. The deep, the poignant, the overwhelming mortification, which upon each such failure of his praiseworthy endeavors, would suffuse every lineament of his countenance, left not the slightest room for doubt of his sincerity in the bosoms of even his most skepticle companions. The adroitness, too, was no less worthy of observation by which he contrived to shift the sense of the grotesque from the creator to the created—from his own person to the absurdities to which he had given rise. In no instance before that of which I speak, have I known the habitual mystific escape the natural consequence of his manœuvres—an attachment of the ludicrous to his own character and person. Continually developed in an atmosphere of whim, my friend appeared to live only for the severities of society; and not even his own household have for a moment associated other ideas than those of the rigid and august with the memory of the Baron Ritzner Von Jung.

During the epoch of his residence at G———n it really

9
10 appeared that the demon of the *dolce far niente* lay like an incubus upon the university. Nothing, at least, was done beyond eating and drinking and making merry. The apartments of the students were converted into so many pot-houses, and there was no pot-house of them all more famous or more frequented than that of the Baron. Our carousals here were many, and boisterous, and long, and never unfruitful of events.

Upon one occasion we had protracted our sitting until nearly daybreak, and an unusual quantity of wine had been drunk. The company consisted of seven or eight individuals besides the Baron and myself. Most of these were young men of wealth, of high connection, of great family pride, and all alive with an exaggerated sense of honor. They abounded in the

11 most ultra German opinions respecting the *duello*. To these Quixotic notions some recent Parisian publications, backed by three or four desperate and fatal rencounters at G———n, had given new vigor and impulse; and thus the conversation, during the greater part of the night, had run wild upon the all-engrossing topic of the times. The Baron, who had been unusually silent and abstracted in the earlier portion of the evening, at length seemed to be aroused from his apathy, took a leading part in the discourse, and dwelt upon the benefits, and more especially upon the beauties, of the received code of etiquette in passages of arms with an ardor, an eloquence, an impressiveness, and an affectionateness of manner, which elicite the warmest enthusiasm from his hearers in general, and absolutely staggered even myself, who well knew him to be at heart a ridiculer of those very points for which he contended, and especially to hold the entire *fanfaronnade* of duelling etiquette in the sovereign contempt which **12** it deserves.

Looking around me during a pause in the Baron's discourse (of which my readers may gather some faint idea when I say that it bore resemblance to the fervid, chanting, monotonous, yet musical, sermonic manner of Coleridge), I perceived **13** symptoms of even more than the general interest in the countenance of one of the party. This gentleman, whom I shall call Hermann, was an original in every respect—except, perhaps, in the single particular that he was a very great fool. He contrived to bear, however, among a particular set at the university, a reputation for deep metaphysical thinking, and, I believe, for some logical talent. As a duellist he had acquired great renown, even at G——n. I forget the precise number of victims who had fallen at his hands; but they were many. He was a man of courage undoubtedly. But it was upon his minute acquaintance with the etiquette of the *duello,* and the *nicety* of his sense of honor, that he most especially prided himself. These things were a hobby which he rode to the death. To Ritzner, ever upon the lookout for the grotesque, his peculiarities had for a long time past afforded food for mystification. Of this, however, I was not aware; although, in the present instance, I saw clearly that something of a whimsical nature was upon the *tapis* with my friend, and that Hermann was its especial object.

As the former proceeded in his discourse, or rather monologue, I perceived the excitement of the latter momently increasing. At length he spoke; offering some objection to a point insisted upon by R., and giving his reasons in detail. To these the Baron replied at length (still maintaining his exaggerated tone of sentiment) and concluding, in what I thought very bad taste, with a sarcasm and a sneer. The hobby of Hermann now took the bit in his teeth. This I could discern **14** by the studied hair-splitting *farrago* of his rejoinder. His last **15** words I distinctly remember. "Your opinions, allow me to say, Baron Von Jung, although in the main correct, are, in many nice points, discreditable to yourself and to the university of which you are a member. In a few respects they are even unworthy of serious refutation. I would say more than this, sir, were it not for the fear of giving you offence (here the speaker smiled blandly), I would say, sir, that your opinions are not the opinions to be expected from a gentleman."

As Herman completed this equivocal sentence, all eyes were turned upon the Baron. He became pale, then excessively red; then, dropping his pocket-handkerchief, stopped to recover it, when I caught a glimpse of his countenance, while

12 *Fanfaronnade* means bragging or boasting.

13 Coleridge was at one time a lay preacher. "Did you ever hear me preach?" he once asked Charles Lamb. "I never heard you do anything else," Lamb replied.

14 In the first version of the tale, there is a long description of Hermann, with a reference to the Farnesian Hercules, a sculpture at Naples.

15 A confused group, a hodgepodge, from the Latin *farrago,* a mixed fodder for cattle

16 *Mynheer* is Dutch (*Mijnheer*); *mein Herr* is the German equivalent.

17 Compare with the climax of "William Wilson." It also recalls an old joke: "An Irishman, having resolved on suicide, caught sight of himself in a large mirror and discarged his pistol at the image. His landlady cried out, 'I am ruined and undone forever!' 'And so am I,' says Paddy, 'for I have just now killed the handsomest man in the world!' " The story appears in *Democritus, or the Laughing Philosopher* (1770).

18 Philip the Fair was Philip IV of France (1268–1314), who issued many laws, which were often identical to older ones. The book, however, is by Jean Savaron, entitled *Traicte contre les Duels, Avec l'Édict de Phillippes le Bel . . .* (1610).
The Theater of Honour and Knighthood (1623) is the English version of André Favyn's 1620 French book.
Le Vray et ancien Usage des duels . . . (1617) is by Sieur Vital d'Audiguier.

it could be seen by no one else at the table. It was radiant with the quizzical expression which was its natural character, but which I had never seen it assume except when we were alone together, and when he unbent himself freely. In an instant afterward he stood erect, confronting Hermann; and so total an alteration of countenance in so short a period I certainly never saw before. For a moment I even fancied that I had misconceived him, and that he was in sober earnest. He appeared to be stifling with passion, and his face was cadaverously white. For a short time he remained silent, apparently striving to master his emotion. Having at length seemingly succeeded, he reached a decanter which stood near him, saying as he held it firmly clenched—"The language you have

16 thought proper to employ, Mynheer Hermann, in addressing yourself to me, is objectionable in so many particular, that I have neither temper nor time for specification. That my opinion, however, are not the opinions to be expected from a gentleman, is an observation so directly offensive as to allow me but one line of conduct. Some courtesy, nevertheless, is due to the presence of this company, and to yourself, at this moment, as my guest. You will pardon me, therefore, if, upon this consideration, I deviate slightly from the general usage among gentlemen in similar cases of personal affront. You will forgive me for the moderate tax I shall make upon your imagination, and endeavor to consider, for an instant, the reflection of your person in yonder mirror as the living Mynheer Hermann himself. This being done, there will be no difficulty whatever. I shall discharge this decanter of wine at your image in yonder mirror, and thus fulfil all the spirit, if not the exact letter, of resentment for your insult, while the necessity of physical violence to your real person will be obviated."

With these words he hurled the decanter, full of wine, against the mirror which hung directly opposite Hermann; striking the reflection of his person with great precision, and

17 of course shattering the glass into fragments. The whole company at once started to their feet, and, with the exception of myself and Ritzner, took their departure. As Hermann went out, the Baron whispered me that I should follow him and make an offer of my services. To this I agreed; not knowing precisely what to make of so ridiculous a piece of business.

The duellist accepted my aid with his usual stiff and *ultra recherché* air, and, taking my arm, led me to his apartment. I could hardly forbear laughing in his face while he proceeded to discuss, with the profoundest gravity, what he termed "the refinedly peculiar character" of the insult he had received. After a tiresome harangue in his ordinary style, he took down from his bookshelves a number of musty volumes on the subject of the *duello*, and entertained me for a long time with their contents; reading aloud, and commenting earnestly as he read. I can just remember the titles of some of the works. There were the "Ordonnance of Philip le Bel on Single Combat"; the "Theatre of Honor," by Favyn, and a treatise

18 "On the Permission of Duels," by Audiguier. He displayed, also, with much pomposity, Brantôme's "memoirs of Duels," published at Cologne, 1666, in the types of Elzevir—a precious and unique vellum-paper volume, with a fine margin, and bound by Derôme. But he requested my attention particularly, **19** and with an air of mysterious sagacity, to a thick octavo, written in barbarous Latin by one Hedelin, a Frenchman, and having the quaint title, "*Duelli Lex scripta, et non, aliterque.*" From this he read me one of the drollest chapters **20** in the world concerning "*Injuriæ per applicationem, per constructionem, et per se,*" about half of which, he averred, **21** was strictly applicable to his own "refinedly peculiar" case although not one syllable of the whole matter could I understand for the life of me. Having finished the chapter, he closed the book, and demanded what I thought necessary to be done. I replied that I had entire confidence in his superior delicacy of feeling, and would aide by what he proposed. With this answer he seemed flattered, and sat down to write a note to the Baron. It ran thus:

"SIR—My friend, M. P——, will hand you this note. I find it incumbent upon me to request, at your earliest convenience, an explanation of this evening's occurrences at your chambers. In the event of your declining this request, Mr. P. will be happy to arrange, with any friend whom you may appoint, the steps preliminary to a meeting.
"With sentiments of perfect respect,
       "Your most humble servant,
                           "JOHAN HERMANN"
"*To the Baron Ritzner Von Jung,*
    August 18th, 18—."

Not knowing what better to do, I called upon Ritzner with this epistle. He bowed as I presented it; then, with a grave countenance, motioned me to a seat. Having perused the cartel he wrote the following reply, which I carried to Hermann.

"SIR,—Through our common friend, Mr. P., I have received your note of this evening. Upon due reflection I frankly admit the propriety of the explanation you suggest. This being admitted, I still find great difficulty, (owing to the *refinedly peculiar* nature of our disagreement, and of the personal affront offered on my part,) in so wording what I have to say by way of apology, as to meet all the minute exigencies, and all the variable shadows of the case. I have great reliance, however, on that extreme delicacy of discrimination, in matters appertaining to the rules of etiquette, for which you have been so long and so preëminently distinguished. With perfect certainty, therefore, of being comprehended, I beg leave, in lieu of offering any sentiments of my own, to refer you to the opinions of the Sieur Hedelin, as set forth in the ninth paragraph of the chapter of '*Injuriæ per applicationem, per constructionem, et per se,*' in his '*Duelli Lex scripta, et non, aliterque.*' The nicety of your discernment in all the matters here treated, will be sufficient, I am assured, to convince you *that the mere circumstance of me referring you* to this admirable passage,

19 *Anecdotes de la cour de France, touchant les duels* is by Pierre de Bourdeilles, Seigneur de Brantôme (1540–1614), courtier, soldier, and author of a lengthy, gossipy memoir. The Elzevir edition appeared in 1665–66. Derôme was the name of the great family of French bookbinders. Elzevir is the name of the family of Dutch publishers and printers in the seventeenth century whose style of type bears their name, and whose books are of special value.

20 "The Law of Dueling, Written, and not Written, and otherwise" is an imaginary work. Hédelin, however, was real. He was the Abbé of Aubignac; he lived from 1604 to 1676 but has no connection with this tale.

21 "Of injuries by application, by arrangement, and by themselves"

Hermann would have died a thousand deaths rather than acknowledge his inability to understand anything and everything in the universe that had ever been written about the *duello*. *Artist unknown*

22 Guillaume de Salluste du Bartas (1544–90) was a French poet and Huguenot soldier under Henry IV, known chiefly for his epics. He wrote no nonsense poetry at all, and therefore Poe must have misread a section of Isaac D'Israeli's *Curiosities of Literature* (1791, second series 1823) entitled "Literary Follies." D'Israeli writes that Du Bartas tried to imitate the song of a lark in verse, and then immediately goes on to discuss some French nonsense poems called "Amphigouries," none of which are attributed to Du Bartas.

Considering Poe's work schedule and his need to keep writing to bring in money for his beleaguered household, it is understandable why such errors creep into his work from time to time.

ought to satisfy your request, as a man of honor, for explanation.

"With sentiments of profound respect,
"Your most obedient servant,
"VON JUNG"

"*The Herr Johan Hermann,
August 18th, 18—.*"

Hermann commenced the perusal of this epistle with a scowl, which, however, was converted into a smile of the most ludicrous self-complacency as he came to the rigmarole about *Injuriæ per applicationem, per constructionem, et per se.* Having finished reading, he begged me, with the blandest of all possible smiles, to be seated, while he made reference to the treatise in question. Turning to the passage specified, he read it with great care to himself, the closed the book, and desired me, in my character of confidential acquaintance, to express to the Baron Von Jung his exalted sense of his chivalrous behavior, and, in that of second, to assure him that the explanation offered was of the fullest, the most honorable, and the most unequivocally satisfactory nature.

Somewhat amazed at all this, I made my retreat to the Baron. He seemed to receive Hermann's amicable letter as a matter of course, and after a few words of general conversation, went to an inner room and brought out the everlasting treatise "*Duelli Lex scripta, et non, aliterque.*" He handed me the volume and asked me to look over some portion of it. I did so, but to little purpose, not being able to gather the least particle of meaning. He then took the book himself, and read me a chapter aloud. To my surprise, what he read proved to be a most horribly absurd account of a duel between two baboons. He now explained the mystery; showing that the volume, as it appeared *prima facie*, was written upon the plan 22 of the nonsense verses of Du Bartas; that is to say, the language was ingeniously framed so as to present to the ear all the outward signs of intelligibility, and even of profundity, while in fact not a shadow of meaning existed. The key to the whole was found in leaving out every second and third word alternately, when there appeared a series of ludicrous quizzes upon a single combat as practised in modern times.

The Baron afterwards informed me that he had purposely thrown the treatise in Hermann's way two or three weeks before the adventure, and that he was satisfied, from the general tenor of his conversation, that he had studied it with the deepest attention, and firmly believed it to be a work of unusual merit. Upon this hint he proceeded. Hermann would have died a thousand deaths rather than acknowledge his inability to understand anything and everything in the universe that had ever been written about the *duello*.

HOW TO WRITE A BLACKWOOD ARTICLE

First published in the Baltimore *American Museum*, November 1838, as "The Psyche Zenobia."

Usually treated as two separate stories, "How to Write a Blackwood Article" and "A Predicament" are really one piece and appeared as such in their first two outings. The two-part setup dates from the Lea and Blanchard edition of *Tales of the Grotesque and Arabesque* (1840).

This is one of Poe's best comic ventures, as well as a source of insight into his writing methods. For Zenobia, like Poe, selects incidents to heighten the effect of her tale, but as we shall see, falls far short of his results.

Through his only female narrator, Poe both pays homage to and yet also satirizes *Blackwood's Edinburgh Magazine*, founded in the early-nineteenth century by the Scottish publisher William Blackwood (1776–1834) to be a Tory rival to the Liberal *Edinburgh* magazine, and to promote his own publishing house. After an initial failure, Blackwood moved into the sensational, scathing, and satirical, and the magazine's fortune was made.

"Of the British magazines reprinted and circulated in America in the earlier nineteenth century, *Blackwood's* was of paramount importance and was only equalled by the great Reviews," says Michael Allen in his *Poe and the British Magazine Tradition* (Oxford University Press, 1969; p. 28). Poe was certainly not anti-*Blackwood's*, but found much to praise in its pages: ". . . here it will be seen how full of prejudice are the usual animadversions against those *tales of effect* many fine examples of which were found in the earlier numbers of Blackwood. The impressions produced were wrought in a legitimate sphere of action, and constituted a legitimate, although sometimes an exaggerated interest. They were relished by every man of genius; although there were found many men of genius who condemned them without just ground." (Poe, "Nathaniel Hawthorne," *Works*, Fred de Fau Co., 1902; III, pp. 296–97)

What Poe satirizes here is the mindless copying of the Blackwood style of fiction—the Gothic tale of sensation—by inept writers. The Blackwood tale typically elaborated its central effect with philosophical or psychological mannerisms and a great show of learning, and was centered around a protagonist isolated by some bizarre turn of events, with his predicament milked for all its possible effect on the reader.

While Poe also followed the formula to some degree, "How to Write a Blackwood Article" and "A Predicament" are instructive in just how far he had progressed beyond the simple tale of sensation.

"In the name of the Prophet—figs!!"
—*Cry of the Turkish fig-pedler*.   **1**

I presume everybody has heard of me. My name is the Signora Psyche Zenobia. This I know to be a fact. Nobody but my **2** enemies ever calls me Suky Snobbs. I have been assured that Suky is but a vulgar corruption of Psyche, which is good Greek, and means "the soul" (that's me, I'm *all* soul) and sometimes "a butterfly," which latter meaning undoubtedly alludes to my appearance in my new crimson satin dress, with the sky-blue Arabian *mantelet*, and the trimmings of green **3** *agraffas*, and the seven flounces of orange-colored *auriculas*. **4,5**

1 A burlesque of the solemn language employed in Eastern countries in the common business of everyday life. The line occurs in the parody of Samuel Johnson's pompous style in *Rejected Addresses*, by James and Horace Smith, published in 1812. A series of pieces in the manner of the best (and worst) writers of the day, it has hardly been surpassed as a complete book of parodies:

"He that is most assured of success will make the fewest appeals to favor, and where nothing is claimed that is undue, nothing that is due will be withheld. A swelling opening is too often succeeded by an insignificant conclusion. Parturient mountains have ere now produced muscipular abortions; and the auditor who compares incipient grandeur with final vulgarity is reminded of the pious hawkers of Constantinople, who

373

solemnly perambulate her streets, exclaiming, "In the name of the Prophet—figs!"

In the *Broadway Journal*, August 30, 1845, Poe writes, "If *primitive* meanings are to be adhered to, we might maintain that Mr. T——is no sycophant merely because he is not in the habit of discovering figs."

"Sycophant" comes from the Greek *sykophantes*, or fig shower, which referred to an obscene gesture. Poe seems to have been unaware of this, although "In a Blackwood article nothing makes so fine a show as your Greek," says Blackwood to Zenobia.

2 "Psyche" is Greek for soul, which leads the narrator to the appropriate comment that she is *all* soul. It is also the name of Cupid's love in the late-born myth of Cupid and Psyche (Apuleius, second century A.D.).

"Suk(e)y" is a nickname for Susanna—and a common term for a teakettle.

Poe is here poking fun at Sarah Green's *Romance Readers and Romance Writers* (1810), in which a character named Margaret Marsham begins, "What then? To add to my earthly miseries am I to be called Peggy? My name is Margaritta! I am sure that if I am called Peggy again, I shall go into a fit."

3 A loose, sleeveless cape covering the shoulders

4 Agra gauze (from the Indian city of Agra) is a silk gauze with a stiff finish; it is used for trimming.

5 A yellow cloth, named after the *Primula auricula*, a Swiss wildflower that was domesticated and widely planted in gardens both in Europe and the United States

6 Zenobia (died c.272) was queen of Palmyra, a city of central Syria. She was an Arab and the wife of Septimus Odenathus. He was murdered, probably through her doing, and she became ruler of his lands in the name of her son. Her machinations and dealings with allies and enemies alike brought her more notoriety than her fabled beauty, and her name has come down to us as a symbol of ruthless arrogance.

In 1837, William Ware (1797–1852) published his very popular novel *Zenobia* (originally called *Letters of Lucius M. Piso from Palmyra, to His Friend Marcus Curtius at Rome*), and so the name was familiar to most of Poe's readers.

7 A "Greek" in nineteenth-century parlance meant a cunning or wily person, a cheat (especially at cards), a person of loose habits—and, as here, no doubt, an Irishman.

8 Henry Peter Brougham (1778–1868) was a contributor to the *Edinburgh Review* in its early years, and in part responsible for its success. He founded the Society for the Diffusion of Useful Knowledge in 1825 and became Lord Chancellor of England in 1830. He was the author of *Discourses of Natural Theology* (1835), and his outspoken comments on social and political issues never failed to stir controversy.

The club's name is a word play on "blue stocking" (see "Lionizing," note 12).

9 Syllabub, or sillabub, is a drink made from milk or cream, mixed with cider or wine, then sweetened and flavored. The milk curdles in the process and the whole mixture is usually whipped to a froth before drinking.

11 See "Bon-Bon", note 8.

As for Snobbs—any person who should look at me would be instantly aware that my name wasn't Snobbs. Miss Tabitha Turnip propagated that report through sheer envy. Tabitha Turnip indeed! Oh the little wretch! But what can we expect from a turnip? Wonder if she remembers the old adage about "blood out of a turnip, &c." [Mem: put her in mind of it the first opportunity.] [Mem again—pull her nose.] Where was I? Ah! I have been assured that Snobbs is a mere corruption **6** of Zenobia, and that Zenobia was a queen—(So am I. Dr. Moneypenny always calls me the Queen of Hearts)—and that Zenobia, as well as Psyche, is good Greek, and that my father **7** was "a Greek," and that consequently I have a right to our patronymic, which is Zenobia, and not by any means Snobbs. Nobody but Tabitha Turnip calls me Suky Snobbs. I am the Signora Psyche Zenobia.

As I said before, everybody has heard of me. I am that very Signora Psyche Zenobia, so justly celebrated as corresponding secretary to the "*Philadelphia, Regular, Exchange, Tea, Total, Young, Belles, Lettres, Universal, Experimental, Bibliographical, Association, To, Civilize, Humanity*." Dr. Moneypenny made the title for us, and says he chose it because it sounded big like an empty rum-puncheon. (A vulgar man that sometimes—but he's deep.) We all sign the initials of the society after our names, in the fashion of the R. S. A., Royal Society of Arts—the S. D. U. K., Society for the Diffusion of Useful Knowledge, &c., &c. Dr. Moneypenny says that S stands for *stale*, and that D. U. K. spells duck, (but it don't) and that S. D. U. K. stands for Stale Duck, and not for Lord Brougham's **8** society—but then Dr. Moneypenny is such a queer man that I am never sure when he is telling me the truth. At any rate we always add to our names the initials P. R. E. T. T. Y. B. L. U. E. B. A. T. C. H.—that is to say, Philadelphia, Regular, Exchange, Tea, Total, Young, Belles, Lettres, Universal, Experimental, Bibliographical, Association, To, Civilize, Humanity—one letter for each word, which is a decided improvement upon Lord Brougham. Dr. Moneypenny will have it that our initials give our true character—but for my life I can't see what he means.

Notwithstanding the good offices of the Doctor, and the strenuous exertions of the association to get itself into notice, it met with no very great success until I joined it. The truth is, the members indulged in too flippant a tone of discussion. The papers read every Saturday evening were characterized **9** less by depth than buffoonery. They were all whipped syllabub. There was no investigation of first causes, first principles. There was no investigation of anything at all. There was no attention paid to that great point, the "fitness of things." In short there was no fine writing like this. It was all low—very! No profundity, no reading, no metaphysics—nothing which the learned call spirituality, and which the unlearned choose to stigmatize as cant. [Dr. M. says I ought to spell "cant" with **10** a capital K—but I know better.]

When I joined the society it was my endeavor to introduce a better style of thinking and writing, and all the world knows how well I have succeeded. We get up as good papers now in the P. R. E. T. T. Y. B. L. U. E. B. A. T. C. H. as any to be found even in *Blackwood.* I say, *Blackwood,* because I have been assured that the finest writing, upon every subject, is to be discovered in the pages of that justly celebrated Magazine. We now take it for our model upon all themes, and are getting into rapid notice accordingly. And, after all, it's not so very difficult a matter to compose an article of the genuine *Blackwood* stamp, if one only goes properly about it. Of course I don't speak of the political articles. Everybody knows how *they* are managed, since Dr. Moneypenny explained it. Mr. Blackwood has a pair of tailor's-shears, and three apprentices who stand by him for orders. One hands him the *Times,* another the *Examiner* and a third a "Gulley's New Compendium of Slang-Whang." Mr. B. merely cuts out **11** and intersperses. It is soon done—nothing but *Examiner,* "Slang-Whang," and *Times*—then *Times,* "Slang-Whang," and *Examiner*—and then *Times, Examiner,* and "Slang-Whang."

But the chief merit of the Magazine lies in its miscellaneous articles; and the best of these come under the head of what Dr. Moneypenny calls the *bizarreries* (whatever that may **12** mean) and what everybody else calls the *intensities.* This is a species of writing which I have long known how to appreciate, although it is only since my late visit to Mr. Blackwood (deputed by the society) that I have been made aware of the exact method of composition. This method is very simple, but not so much so as the politics. Upon my calling at Mr. B.'s, and making known to him the wishes of the society, he received me with great civility, took me into his study, and gave me a clear explanation of the whole process.

"My dear madam," said he, evidently struck with my majestic appearance, for I had on the crimson satin, with the green *agraffas,* and orange-colored *auriculas.* "My *dear* madam," said he, "sit down. The matter stands thus: In the first place your writer of intensities must have very black ink, and a very big pen, with a very blunt nib. And, mark me, Miss Psyche Zenobia!" he continued, after a pause, with the most expressive energy and solemnity of manner, "mark me!— *that pen—must—never be mended!* Herein, madam, lies the secret, the soul, of intensity. I assume upon myself to say, that no individual, of however great genius ever wrote with a good pen,—understand me,—a good article. You may take it for granted, that when manuscript can be read it is never worth reading. This is a leading principle in our faith, to which if you cannot readily assent, our conference is at an end."

He paused. But, of course, as I had no wish to put an end to the conference, I assented to a proposition so very obvious, and one, too, of whose truth I had all along been sufficiently aware. He seemed pleased, and went on with his instructions.

"It may appear invidious in me, Miss Psyche Zenobia, to refer you to any article, or set of articles, in the way of model or study; yet perhaps I may as well call your attention to a few cases. Let me see. There was 'The Dead Alive,' a capital **13** thing!—the record of a gentleman's sensations when entombed

11 The two papers are London publications. "Slang-whang" meant abusive talk; John Gully (1783–1863) was a prizefighter who became a member of Parliament. Poe misspells his name in the tale.

12 Poe uses the word "bizarreries" to describe some of his tales. "Intensities," however, is not much used in this way, and the O.E.D. gives Poe as one of its two citations.

13 Actually, "Buried Alive"; this was an article in the October 1821 edition of *Blackwood's,* and a source for Poe's "The Premature Burial."

14 *Confessions of an English Opium-Eater* (1822), by Thomas De Quincey, (1785–1859), gives an account of the poet's early life and describes the growth and effects of his drug habit. He was a prolific contributor to *Blackwood's* after 1825.

15 Of Welsh origin, the word originally meant a soft jelly or porridge made of flour or oatmeal, but by extension, has come to mean flattery or empty compliment, nonsense or humbug.

16 A rummer is a large drinking glass, "Hollands" is gin, and the baboon is aptly named after the berries that give gin its distinctive taste. Coleridge supposedly wrote *Kubla Khan* under the influence of opium.

17 This story appeared in the *Blackwood's* October 1837 edition. The story actually concerns a boiler, not an oven. See "The Pit and the Pendulum," note 32.

18 A tale by Samuel Warren that appeared in August 1830

19 Written by William Maginn, the story appeared in November 1821.

20 Informed; here, "put you wise"

21 An earthquake swallows the hero of Poe's *Narrative of Arthur Gordon Pym*, the narrator of "Mellonta Tauta" falls out of a balloon, and a chimney plays a role in "Murders in the Rue Morgue."

Poe was no stranger to the tale of effect. However, he believed that a story should also make sense—that is, have a basis in reality—and suggest more than the mere situation in which the protagonist finds himself. It is the placing of improbable people in even more improbable situations, simply for the purpose of raising the hair on the reader's neck, which Poe objects to.

22 "Tis strange—but true; for truth is always strange;/ Stranger than fiction" (Byron, *Don Juan*, XIV, ci).

23 "The Unfortunate Miss Bailey," an old folk tune, recalls the tale of a maid who, after being seduced by a captain from Halifax, hanged herself by her garters, only to return as a ghost to haunt her seducer.

24 Sold to rid one of "acrimonious humors" at twenty-five cents a box. In the earliest version of the tale, Poe mentions Morrison's Pills instead, which, like Brandreth's, were heavily advertised in his day. Brandreth's are mentioned again in "Some Words with a Mummy."

25 This style seems to have been taken over By Madison Avenue. Advertising. Of today, that is.

26 A spinning top with a reed device that hums when air is forced through it.

before the breath was out of his body—full of taste, terror, sentiment, metaphysics, and erudition. You would have sworn that the writer had been born and brought up in a coffin.

14 Then we had the 'Confessions of an Opium-eater'—fine, very fine!—glorious imagination—deep philosophy—acute speculation—plenty of fire and fury, and a good spicing of the

15 decidedly unintelligible. That was a nice bit of flummery, and went down the throats of the people delightfully. They would have it that Coleridge wrote the paper—but not so. It was composed by my pet baboon, Juniper, over a rummer of

16 Hollands and water, 'hot, without sugar.' " [This I could scarcely have believed had it been anybody but Mr. Blackwood, who assured me of it.] "Then there was '*The Involuntary Experimentalist*,' all about a gentleman who got baked in an

17 oven, and came out alive and well, although certainly done

18 to a turn. And then there was '*The Diary of a Late Physician*,' where the merit lay in good rant, and indifferent Greek—both of them, taking things with the public. And then there

19 was '*The Man in the Bell*,' a paper by-the-by, Miss Zenobia, which I cannot sufficiently recommend to your attention. It is the history of a young person who goes to sleep under the clapper of a church bell, and is awakened by its tolling for a funeral. The sound drives him mad, and, accordingly, pulling out his tablets, he gives a record of his sensations. Sensations are the great things after all. Should you ever be drowned or hung, be sure and make a note of your sensations—they will be worth to you ten guineas a sheet. If you wish to write forcibly, Miss Zenobia, pay minute attention to the sensations."

"That I certainly will, Mr. Backwood," said I.

"Good!" he replied. "I see you are a pupil after my own

20 heart. But I must put you *au fait* to the details necessary in composing what may be denominated a genuine Blackwood article of the sensation stamp—the kind which you will understand me to say I consider the best for all purposes.

"The first thing requisite is to get yourself into such a scrape as no one ever got into before. The oven, for instance,—that was a good hit. But if you have no oven, or big bell, at hand, and if you cannot conveniently tumble out of a balloon, or be swallowed up in an earthquake, or get stuck fast in a chimney, you will have to be contented with simply imagining some

21 similar misadventure. I should prefer, however, that you have the actual fact to bear you out. Nothing so well assists the fancy, as an experimental knowledge of the matter in hand. 'Truth is strange,' you know, 'stranger than fiction'—besides

22 being more to the purpose."

Here I assured him I had an excellent pair of garters, and

23 would go and hang myself forthwith.

"Good!" he replied, "do so;—although hanging is somewhat hackneyed. Perhaps you might do better. Take a dose of

24 Brandreth's pills, and then give us your sensations. However, my instructions will apply equally well to any variety of misadventure, and on your way home you may easily get knocked in the head, or run over by an omnibus, or bitten by a mad dog, or drowned in a gutter. But to proceed.

"Having determined upon your subject, you must next

consider the tone, or manner, of your narration. There is the tone didactic, the tone enthusiastic, the tone natural—all commonplace enough. But then there is the tone laconic, or curt, which has lately come much into use. It consists in short sentences. Somehow thus: Can't be too brief. Can't be too snappish. Always a full stop. And never a paragrah.   **25**

"Then there is the tone elevated, diffusive, and interjectional. Some of our best novelists patronize this tone. The words must be all in a whirl, like a humming-top, and make   **26** a noise very similar, which answers remarkably well instead of meaning. This is the best of all possible styles where the writer is in too great a hurry to think.

"The tone metaphysical is also a good one. If you know any   **27** big words this is your chance for them. Talk of the Ionic and Eleatic schools—of Archytas, Gorgias, and Alcmæon. Say   **28** something about objectivity and subjectivity. Be sure and abuse a man called Locke. Turn up your nose at things in   **29** general, and when you let slip any thing a little *too* absurd, you need not be at the trouble of scratching it out, but just add a foot-note and say that you are indebted for the above profound observation to the '*Kritik der reinen Vernunft*,' or to the '*Metaphysische Anfangsgründe der Naturwissenschaft*.'   **30** This will look erudite and—and—and frank.

"There are various other tones of equal celebrity, but I shall mention only two more—the tone transcendental and the tone heterogeneous. In the former the merit consists in seeing into the nature of affairs a very great deal farther than anybody else. This second sight is very efficient when properly managed. A little reading of the *Dial* will carry your a great way.   **31** Eschew, in this case, big words; get them as small as possible, and write them upside down. Look over Channing's poems and quote what he says about a 'fat little man with a delusive show of Can.' Put in something about the Supernal Oneness.   **32,33** Don't say a syllable about the Infernal Twoness. Above all,   **34** study innuendo. Hint everything—assert nothing. If you feel inclined to say 'bread and butter,' do not by any means say it outright. You may say any thing and every thing *approaching* to 'bread and butter.' You may hint at buck-wheat cake, or you may even go so far as to insinuate oat-meal porridge, but if bread and butter be your real meaning, be cautious, my *dear* Miss Psyche, not on any account to say 'bread and butter!' "

I assured him that I should never say it again as long as I lived. He kissed me and continued:

"As for the tone heterogeneous, it is merely a judicious mixture, in equal proportions, of all the other tones in the world, and is consequently made up of every thing deep, great, odd, piquant, pertinent, and pretty.

"Let us suppose now you have determined upon your incidents and tone. The most important portion—in fact, the soul of the whole business, is yet to be attended to,—I allude to *the filling up*. It is not to be supposed that a lady, or gentleman either, has been leading the life of a book-worm. And yet above all things it is necessary that your article have an air of erudition, or at least afford evidence of extensive

27 Metaphysics has to do with the study of the ultimate nature of existence and is a constant concern of Poe's writing.

28 See "Bon-Bon," note 10. The Eleatic school was the pre-Socratic philosophical school at Elea (Lucania), in Italy. It was founded by Parmenides, who denied the reality of change, arguing that things either exist or do not.

Archytas of Tarentum was a contemporary of Plato. Gorgias (c.485–380 B.C.) was the Greek Sophist who pursued the negative aspects of the Eleatic school and asserted that nothing exists—or if it does, it cannot be known—and therefore objective truth is impossible. Alcmaeon was a pupil of Pythagoras.

29 John Locke (1632–1704) repudiated the traditional doctrine of innate ideas, saying that the mind is born a blank, upon which the world describes itself through the senses. Knowledge from the senses is perfected through reflection.

Such logical thinking would not sit well with the more mystical thought of the metaphysicians.

30 The *Critique of Pure Reason* (1781) and *Metaphysical Foundations of Natural Science* (1786), both by Kant. See "Bon-Bon," note 8.

31 The Transcendentalist review of the day, founded in 1840 by Theodore Parker, Bronson Alcott, Orestes Brownson, Margaret Fuller, and Ralph Waldo Emerson. This reference first appears in the tale in the 1845 version.

32 William Ellery Channing (1780–1841) was considered the apostle of Unitarianism; he prepared the way for the Transcendentalists. He denied the Puritan tenet that human nature is essentially depraved. Poe gave his poetry an unfavorable review in *Graham's*, August 1843.

The reference is to Channing's poem *Thoughts*: "Thou meetest a common man/With a delusive show of *can*."

33 Transcendentalism was a reaction against eighteenth-century rationalism, the skeptical philosophy of Locke, and the Puritan tradition of New England. It was at the same time romantic, idealistic, mystical, and highly individualistic. At the center, however, was the belief that there was a unity of the world and God, that God was spiritually present in all aspects of the world:

"Man may fulfil his divine potentialities either through a rapt, mystifical state, in which the divine is infused into the human, or through coming into contact with the truth, beauty, and goodness embodied in nature, and originating in the Over-Soul. Thus occurs the doctrine of correspondence between the tangible world and the human mind, and the identity of moral and physical laws." (*Oxford Companion to American Literature* [1956], p. 773)

While Poe would have protested, there *are* elements in his writings that share something with Emerson, and even the Puritan tradition. It would have been almost impossible to escape such influences and still be an American.

34 i.e., the existence of evil as well as good. The number two was the symbol of evil to Pythagoras, and "deuce" also means the Devil.

In ancient times, the second day of the second month of the year was sacred to Pluto and was thought to be very unlucky. Witness also that Ethelred II, Harold II, William II, Henry II, Edward II, Richard II, Charles II, James II, and George II were all English monarchs with more than their share of problems.

35 Meaning "witticism," it is a bastardization of the French with an English suffix.

36 There were three sets of Greek muses: the Camenae (Calliope, Cleio, Erato, Euterpe, Melpomene, Polyhymnia, Thalia, Terpsichore, and Urania); the Delphic (Hypate, Mese, and Nete); and the Boeotian, (Aoide or Aoede, Melete, and Mneme). The latter, mentioned by Poe, were worshiped at Helicon, and were the daughters of Uranus and Gaea. They are considered older than the nine more famous muses. (Aoide was the muse of song, Melete of practice, and Mneme of memory.)

37 In Greek legend a youthful hunter named Alpheus was turned into a river in Arcadia in order to pursue his love, the nymph Arethusa, into the sea. He followed her under the sea, underground and back to Arcadia to the source of the river in Ortygia, a fountain called Arethusa. The myth explains why the river Alpheus runs underground for some distance.
   "In Xanadu did Kubla Khan/A stately pleasure-dome decree:/Where Alph, the sacred river, ran/Through caverns measureless to man/Down to a sunless sea" (Coleridge, *Kubla Khan*).

38 The source of this quote is unknown. The *Iris persica*, a fragrant iris, is not grown in many gardens today.

39 *Epidendron* is an orchid mentioned in Patrick Keith's *System of Physiological Botany* (1816), II, 429. It is mentioned again in "The Thousand-and-Second Tale of Scheherazade."

40 *Yu Chiao Li* (The Beautiful Couple) was translated into English in 1827 from the French version of a year earlier. Poe may have heard of it through Philip Pendleton Cooke's "Leaves from My Scrapbook," in the *Southern Literary Messenger*, April 1836.

41 See "Thou Art the Man," note 16.

42 Zaïre (or Zara) is the title and heroine of a tragedy by Voltaire (1732), and no relation to the river Zaïre of "Silence." She was the daughter of the King of Jerusalem and was killed by a jealous lover, who mistook her meeting with her brother as a romantic rendezvous. When he learned the truth, he killed himself.

general reading. Now I'll put you in the way of accomplishing this point. See here!" (pulling down some three or four ordinary-looking volumes, and opening them at random). "By casting your eye down almost any page of any book in the world, you will be able to perceive at once a host of little 35 scraps of either learning or *bel-esprit-ism*, which are the very thing for the spicing of a Blackwood article. You might as well note down a few while I read them to you. I shall make two divisions: first, *Piquant Facts for the Manufacture of Similes*; and second, *Piquant Expressions to be introduced as occasion may require*. Write now!—" and I wrote as he dictated.
   "PIQUANT FACTS FOR SIMILES. 'There were originally but 36 three Muses—Melete, Mneme, and Aœde—meditation, memory, and singing.' You may make a good deal of that little fact if properly worked. You see it is not generally known, and looks *recherché*. You must be careful and give the thing with a downright improviso air.
   "Again. 'The river Alpheus passed beneath the sea, and emerged without injury to the purity of its waters.' Rather stale that, to be sure, but, if properly dressed and dished up, 37 will look quite as fresh as ever.
   "Here is something better. 'The Persian Iris appears to some persons to possess a sweet and very powerful perfume, 38 while to others it is perfectly scentless.' Fine that, and very delicate! Turn it about a little, and it will do wonders. We'll have some thing else in the botanical line. There's nothing goes down so well, especially with the help of a little Latin. Write!
   " *'The Epidendrum Flos Aeris*, of Java, bears a very beautiful flower, and will live when pulled up by the roots. The natives suspend it by a cord from the ceiling, and enjoy its fragrance 39 for years.' That's capital! That will do for the similes. Now for the Piquant Expressions.
   "PIQUANT EXPRESSIONS. *'The Venerable Chinese novel Ju-* 40 *Kiao-Li.'* Good! By introducing these few words with dexterity you will evince your intimate acquaintance with the language and literature of the Chinese. With the aid of this you may possibly get along without either Arabic, or Sanscrit, or 41 Chickasaw. There is no passing muster, however, without Spanish, Italian, German, Latin, and Greek. I must look you out a little specimen of each. Any scrap will answer, because you must depend upon your own ingenuity to make it fit into your article. Now write!
   " *'Aussi tendre que Zaïre'*—as tender as Zaire—French. Alludes to the frequent repetition of the phrase, *la tendre* 42 *Zaïre*, in the French tragedy of that name. Properly introduced, will show not only your knowledge of the language, but your general reading and wit. You can say, for instance, that the chicken you were eating (write an article about being choked to death by a chicken-bone) was not altogether *aussi tendre que Zaïre*. Write!

> *'Ven muerte tan escondida,*
> *Que no te sienta venir,*
> *Porque el plazer del morir,*
> *No me torne a dar la vida.'*

"That's Spanish—from Miguel de Cervantes. 'Come quickly, **43**
O death! but be sure and don't let me see you coming, lest
the pleasure I shall feel at your appearance should unfortunately bring me back again to life.' This you may slip in quite
á propos when you are struggling in the last agonies with the
chicken-bone. Write

> *'Il pover' huomo che non se'n era accorto,*
> *Andava combattendo, e era morto.'*

"That's Italian, you perceive—from Ariosto. It means that a **44**
great hero, in the heat of combat, not perceiving that he had
been fairly killed, continued to fight valiantly, dead as he was.
The application of this to your own case is obvious—for I trust,
Miss Psyche, that you will not neglect to kick for at least an
hour and a half after you have been choked to death by that
chicken-bone. Please to write!

> *'Und sterb' ich doch, so sterb' ich denn*
> *Durch sie—durch sie!'*

"That's German—from Schiller. 'And if I die, at least I die— **45**
for thee—for thee!' Here it is clear that you are apostrophising
the *cause* of your disaster, the chicken. Indeed what gentleman
(or lady either) of sense, *wouldn't* die, I should like to know,
for a well fattened capon of the right Molucca breed, stuffed **46**
with capers and mushrooms, and served up in a salad-bowl,
with orange-jellies *en mosaïques*. Write! (You can get them
that way at Tortoni's.)—Write, if you please!   **47**
"Here is a nice little Latin phrase, and rare too (one can't
be too *recherché* or brief in one's Latin, it's getting so common)
ignoratio elenchi. He has committed an *ignoratio elenchi*— **48**
that is to say, he has understood the words of your proposition,
but not the ideas. The man was *a fool*, you see. Some poor
fellow whom you addressed while choking with that chicken-
bone, and who therefore didn't precisely understand what you
were talking about. Throw the *ignoratio elenchi* in his teeth,
and, at once, you have him annihilated. If he dares to reply,
you can tell him from Lucan (here it is) that speeches are **49**
mere *anemonæ verborum*, anemone words. The anemone, **50**
with great brilliancy, has no smell. Or, if he begins to bluster,
you may be down upon him with *insomnia Jovis*, reveries of
Jupiter—a phrase which Silius Italicus (see here!) applies to
thoughts pompous and inflated. This will be sure and cut him **51**
to the heart. He can do nothing but roll over and die. Will
you be kind enough to write?
"In Greek we must have some thing pretty—from Demosthenes, for example. Ανηρ ο φευγων και παλιν μαχησεται. **52**
[Aner o pheugon kai palin makesetai.] There is a tolerably
good translation of it in Hudibras—   **53**

> *'For he that flies may fight again,*
> *Which he can never do that's slain.'*

In a *Blackwood* article nothing makes so fine a show as your
Greek. The very letters have an air of profundity about them. **54**
Only observe, madam, the astute look of that Epsilon! That
Phi ought certainly to be a bishop! Was ever there a smarter **55**

43 *Don Quixote,* II, xxxviii

44 Ariosto (1474–1533) was one of the greatest of Italian
poets; his masterpiece was *Orlando Furioso,* written in
1516. However, the lines quoted here come from Matteo
Maria Boiardo's *Orlando Innamorato* (1506), II, xxiv, 60.
Poe's source is Father Dominique Bouhours's *La Manière
de bien penser dans les ouvrages d'esprit* (1687), which
mistakenly attributes them to Ariosto.

45 Johann Christoph Friedrich von Schiller (1759–1805),
a major figure of early romanticism. Beethoven's Ninth
Symphony utilizes one of his poems.
  Poe originally began "The Assignation" with this
quote.

46 The Moluccas are islands in eastern Indonesia.

47 The name of restaurants both in Paris and New York

48 An irrelevant conclusion

49 Marcus Annaeus Lucanus, or Lucan (A.D. 39–65),
was a Roman poet and writer of prose of whose works
only *Pharsalia,* an epic in ten books, remains intact.

50 Not in Lucan, but in Lucian's (second century A.D.)
Lexiphanes, Section 23

51 The real source is Longinus' (third century A.D.) *On
the Sublime,* IX, 14.

52 Again the attribution is incorrect. The line is from
Menander's (343?–291? B.C.) *Monosticha,* although Francis Bacon ascribes it to Demosthenes (*Apophthegms*
169).

53 *Hudibras* is a satirical poem by Samuel Butler
(1612–80), named after its hero; it satirizes the Puritans.
The correct reading is: "For those that fly, may fight
again,/Which he can never do that's slain" (Part III,
Chapter 3, line 245).

54 And in Poe as well, much to the annoyance of
Greekless modern readers

55 A chess bishop

fellow than that Omicron? Just twig that Tau! In short, there is nothing like Greek for a genuine sensation-paper. In the present case your application is the most obvious thing in the world. Rap out the sentence, with a huge oath, and by way of *ultimatum* at the good-for-nothing dunder-headed villain who couldn't understand your plain English in relation to the chicken-bone. He'll take the hint and be off, you may depend upon it."

These were all the instructions Mr. B. could afford me upon the topic in question, but I felt they would be entirely sufficient. I was, at length, able to write a genuine *Blackwood* article, and determined to do it forthwith. In taking leave of me, Mr. B. made a proposition for the purchase of the paper when written; but as he could offer me only fifty guineas a sheet, I thought it better to let our society have it, than sacrifice it for so paltry a sum. Notwithstanding this niggardly spirit, however, the gentleman showed his consideration for me in all other respects, and indeed treated me with the greatest civility. His parting words made a deep impression upon my heart, and I hope I shall always remember them with gratitude.

"My dear Miss Zenobia," he said, while the tears stood in his eyes, "is there *any*thing else I can do to promote the success of your laudable undertaking? Let me reflect! It is just possible that you may not be able, so soon as convenient, to— to—get yourself drowned, or—choked with a chicken-bone, or—or hung,—or—bitten by a—but stay! Now I think me of it, there are a couple of very excellent bull-dogs in the yard— fine fellows, I assure you—savage, and all that—indeed just the thing for your money—they'll have you eaten up, *auriculas* and all, in less than five minutes (here's my watch!)—and then only think of the sensations! Here! I say—Tom!—Peter!— Dick, you villain!—let out those"—but as I was really in a great hurry, and had not another moment to spare, I was reluctantly forced to expedite my departure, and accordingly took leave *at once*—somewhat more abruptly, I admit, than strict courtesy would have otherwise allowed.

It was my primary object upon quitting Mr. Blackwood, to get into some immediate difficulty, pursuant to his advice, and with this view I spent the greater part of the day in wandering about Edinburgh, seeking for desperate adventures—adventures adequate to the intensity of my feelings, and adapted to the vast character of the article I intended to write. In this excursion I was attended by my negro-servant, Pompey, and my little lap-dog Diana, whom I had brought with me from Philadelphia. It was not, however, until late in the afternoon that I fully succeeded in my arduous undertaking. An important event then happened of which the following *Blackwood* article, in the tone heterogeneous, is the substance and result.

56 Edinburgh was the home of *Blackwood's*. "Burgh" for "burrough" became obsolete in England in the seventeenth century but lingers on in Scotland.

57 Black servants were often given classical names (Jupiter in "The Gold Bug" is another example). The original Pompey (Gnaeus Pompeius Magnus) was a Roman general and member of the First Triumvirate with Julius Caesar and Crassus. The name pops up again in "The Man Who Was Used Up" and "The Business Man."

58 The goddess of the moon and of the hunt; the protector of women

A PREDICAMENT

59

59 Originally titled "The Scythe of Time," perhaps recalling *Paradise Lost*, X, 606

What chance, good lady, hath bereft you thus? **60**
                                            —COMUS.

60 From Milton's *Comus*, line 277

It was a quiet and still afternoon when I strolled forth in the goodly city of Edina. The confusion and bustle in the streets **61** were terrible. Men were talking. Women were screaming. Children were choking. Pigs were whistling. Carts they rattled. Bulls they bellowed. Cows they lowed. Horses they **62** neighed. Cats they caterwauled. Dogs they danced. *Danced!* **63** Could it then be possible? *Danced!* Alas, thought I, *my* dancing days are over! Thus it is ever. What a host of gloomy recollections will ever and anon be awakened in the mind of genius and imaginative contemplation, especially of a genius doomed to the everlasting, and eternal, and continual, and, as one might say, the—*continued*—yes, the *continued and continuous*, bitter, harassing, disturbing, and, if I may be allowed the expression, the *very* disturbing influence of the serene, and god-like, and heavenly, and exalting, and elevated, and purifying effect of what may be rightly termed the most enviable, the most *truly* enviable—nay! the most benignly beautiful, the most deliciously ethereal, and, as it were, the most *pretty* (if I may use so bold an expression) *thing* (pardon me, gentle reader!) in the world—but I am led away by my feelings. In *such* a mind, I repeat, what a host of recollections are stirred up by a trifle! The dogs danced! *I—could* not! They frisked—I wept. They capered—I sobbed aloud. Touching circumstances! which cannot fail to bring to the recollection of the classical reader that exquisite passage in relation to the fitness of things, which is to be found in the commencement of the third volume of that admirable and venerable Chinese novel the *Jo-Go-Slow*. **64**

In my solitary walk through the city I had two humble but faithful companions. Diana, my poodle! sweetest of creatures! She had a quantity of hair over her one eye, and a blue riband tied fashionably around her neck. Diana was not more than five inches in height, but her head was somewhat bigger than her body, and her tail being cut off exceedingly close, gave an air of injured innocence to the interesting animal which rendered her a favorite with all.

And Pompey, my negro!—sweet Pompey! how shall I ever forget thee? I had taken Pompey's arm. He was three feet in height (I like to be particular) and about seventy, or perhaps eighty, years of age. He had bowlegs and was corpulent. His mouth should not be called small, nor his ears short. His

61 Edinburgh

62 Poetic license allows a poet the freedom to tamper with normal sentence structure in order to meet the demands of rhyme and meter. In prose, however, such inversions seem merely stilted, and worthy of ridicule.

63 "Caterwaul" means to make a noise like a cat at rutting time.

64 Although the opening paragraph is not so different in tone from some of Poe's serious work, the difference (and this Poe would emphasize strongly) is that Zenobia's rhetoric, the emotion, the literary effect, are all for nothing, because the subject matter itself is inconsequential.

65 A reference to large feet.

66 A stocking

67 "Fiddling" also means acting idly or frivolously.

68 That's quite a trick if he's only three feet tall—but then, we don't know *her* height.

teeth, however, were like pearl, and his large full eyes were deliciously white. Nature had endowed him with no neck, and had placed his ankles (as usual with that race) in the

65 middle of the upper portion of the feet. He was clad with a
66 striking simplicity. His sole garments were a stock of nine inches in height, and a nearly-new drab overcoat which had formerly been in the service of the tall, stately, and illustrious Dr. Moneypenny. It was a good overcoat. It was well cut. It was well made. The coat was nearly new. Pompey held it up out of the dirt with both hands.

There were three persons in our party, and two of them have already been the subject of remark. There was a third—that person was myself. I am the Signora Psyche Zenobia. I am *not* Suky Snobbs. My appearance is commanding. On the memorable occasion of which I speak I was habited in a crimson satin dress, with a sky-blue Arabian *mantelet*. And the dress had trimmings of green *agraffas*, and seven graceful flounces of the orange-colored *auricula*. I thus formed the third of the party. There was the poodle. There was Pompey. There was myself. We were *three*. Thus it is said there were originally but three Furies—Melty, Nimmy, and Hetty—

67 Meditation, Memory, and Fiddling.
68   Leaning upon the arm of the gallant Pompey, and attended at a respectable distance by Diana, I proceeded down one of the populous and very pleasant streets of the now deserted Edina. On a sudden, there presented itself to view a church—a Gothic cathedral—vast, venerable, and with a tall steeple, which towered into the sky. What madness now possessed me? Why did I rush upon my fate? I was seized with an uncontrollable desire to ascend the giddy pinnacle, and thence survey the immense extent of the city. The door of the cathedral stood invitingly open. My destiny prevailed. I entered the ominous archway. Where then was my guardian angel?—if indeed such angels there be. *If!* Distressing monosyllable! what a world of mystery, and meaning, and doubt, and uncertainty is there involved in thy two letters! I entered the ominous archway! I entered; and, without injury to my orange-colored *auriculas*, I passed beneath the portal, and emerged within the vestibule. Thus it is said the immense river Alfred passed, unscathed, and unwetted, beneath the sea.

I thought the staircase would never have an end. *Round!* Yes, they went round and up, and round and up and round and up, until I could not help surmising, with the sagacious Pompey, upon whose supporting arm I leaned in all the confidence of early affection—I *could* not help surmising that the upper end of the continuous spiral ladder had been accidentally, or perhaps designedly, removed. I paused for breath; and, in the meantime, an accident occurred of too momentous a nature in a moral, and also in a metaphysical point of view, to be passed over without notice. It appeared to me—indeed I was quite confident of the fact—I could not be mistaken—no! I had, for some moments, carefully and anxiously observed the motions of my Diana—I say that *I could not be* mistaken—Diana *smelt a rat!* At once I called Pompey's attention to the subject, and he—he agreed with me. There was then no longer any reasonable room for doubt. The rat had been smelled—and by Diana. Heavens! shall I ever forget the intense excitement of the moment? The rat!—it was there—that is to say, it was somewhere. Diana smelled the rat. I—*I could* not! Thus it is said the Prussian Isis has, for some persons, a sweet and very powerful perfume, while to others it is perfectly scentless.

The staircase had been surmounted, and there were now only three or four more upward steps intervening between us and the summit. We still ascended, and now only one step remained. One step! One little, little step! Upon one such little step in the great staircase of human life how vast a sum of human happiness or misery depends! I thought of myself, then of Pompey, and then of the mysterious and inexplicable destiny which surrounded us. I thought of Pompey!—alas, I thought of love! I thought of my many false *steps* which have been taken, and may be taken again. I resolved to be more cautious, more reserved. I abandoned the arm of Pompey, and, without his assistance, surmounted the one remaining step, and gained the chamber of the belfry. I was followed immediately afterward by my poodle. Pompey alone remained behind. I stood at the head of the staircase, and encouraged him to ascend. He stretched forth to me his hand, and unfortunately in so doing was forced to abandon his firm hold upon the overcoat. Will the gods never cease their persecution? The overcoat is dropped, and, with one of his feet, Pompey stepped upon the long and trailing skirt of the overcoat. He stumbled and fell—this consequence was inevitable. He fell forward, and, with his accursed head, striking me full in the—in the breast, precipitated me headlong, together with himself, upon the hard, filthy, and detestable floor of the belfry. But my revenge was sure, sudden, and complete. Seizing him furiously by the wool with both hands, I tore out a vast quantity of black, and crisp, and curling material, and tossed it from me with every manifestation of disdain. It fell among the ropes of the belfry and remained. Pompey arose, and said no word. But he regarded me piteously with his large eyes and—sighed. Ye Gods—that sigh! It sunk into my heart. And the hair—the wool! Could I have reached that wool I would have bathed it with my tears, in testimony of regret. But alas! it was now far beyond my grasp. As it dangled among the cordage of the bell, I fancied it alive. I fancied that it stood on end with indignation. Thus the *happy dandy Flos Aeris* of Java, bears, it is said, a beautiful flower, which will live when pulled up by the roots. The natives suspend it by a cord from the ceiling and enjoy its fragrance for years.

Our quarrel was now made up, and we looked about the room for an aperture through which to survey the city of Edina. Windows there were none. The sole light admitted into the gloomy chamber proceeded from a square opening, about a foot in diameter, at a height of about seven feet from the floor. Yet what will the energy of true genius not effect?

69 "Quoth Hudibras, I smell a rat" (*Hudibras,* I, 815).

70 Isis was the Egyptian goddess identified with the moon.

71 Does Zenobia show a sexual interest in Pompey? Poe does not elaborate, but knowing his southern attitude, this supposition may be another implicit attack on the Psyche Zenobia—and her type.

72 A most compromising position, and one charged with sexual innuendo for Poe's day.

I resolved to clamber up to this hole. A vast quantity of wheels, pinions, and other cabalistic-looking machinery stood opposite the hole, close to it; and through the hole there passed an iron rod from the machinery. Between the wheels and the wall where the hole lay there was barely room for my body—yet I was desperate, and determined to persevere. I called Pompey to my side.

"You perceive that aperture, Pompey. I wish to look through it. You will stand here just beneath the hole—so. Now, hold out one of your hands, Pompey, and let me step upon it— thus. Now, the other hand, Pompey, and with its aid I will get upon your shoulders."

He did everything I wished, and I found, upon getting up, that I could easily pass my head and neck through the aperture. The prospect was sublime. Nothing could be more magnificent. I merely paused a moment to bid Diana behave herself, and assure Pompey that I would be considerate and bear as lightly as possible upon his shoulders. I told him I would be tender of his feelings—*ossi tender que beefsteak*. Having done this justice to my faithful friend, I gave myself up with great zest and enthusiasm to the enjoyment of the scene which so obligingly spread itself out before my eyes.

Upon this subject, however, I shall forbear to dilate. I will not describe the city of Edinburgh—the classic Edina. I will confine myself to the momentous details of my own lamentable adventure. Having, in some measure, satisfied my curiosity in regard to the extent, situation, and general appearance of the city, I had leisure to survey the church in which I was, and the delicate architecture of the steeple. I observed that the aperture through which I had thrust my head was an opening in the dial-plate of a gigantic clock, and must have appeared, from the street, as a large key-hole, such as we see in the face of the French watches. No doubt the true object was to admit the arm of an attendant, to adjust, when necessary, the hands of the clock from within. I observed also, with surprise, the immense size of these hands, the longest of which could not have been less than ten feet in length, and, where broadest, eight or nine inches in breadth. They were of solid steel apparently, and their edges appeared to be sharp. Having noticed these particulars, and some others, I again turned my eyes upon the glorious prospect below, and soon became absorbed in contemplation.

From this, after some minutes, I was aroused by the voice of Pompey, who declared that he could stand it no longer, and requested that I would be so kind as to come down. This was unreasonable, and I told him so in a speech of some length. He replied but with an evident misunderstanding of my ideas upon the subject. I accordingly grew angry, and told him in plain words, that he was a fool, that he had committed an *ignoramus e-clench-eye*, that his notions were mere *insommary Bovis*, and his words little better than *an enemy-werrybor'em*. With this he appeared satisfied, and I resumed my contemplations.

It might have been half an hour after this altercation when, as I was deeply absorbed in the heavenly scenery beneath

73 An accepted usage, meaning to expand, amplify, or discourse at large

73

me, I was startled by something very cold which pressed with a gentle pressure on the back of my neck. It is needless to say that I felt inexpressibly alarmed. I knew that Pompey was beneath my feet, and that Diana was sitting, according to my explicit directions, upon her hind legs, in the farthest corner of the room. What could it be? Alas! I but too soon discovered. Turning my head gently to one side, I perceived, to my extreme horror, that the huge, glittering, scimitar-like minute-hand of the clock had, in the course of its hourly revolution, *descended upon my neck*. There was, I knew, not a second to be lost. I pulled back at once—but it was too late. There was no chance of forcing my head through the mouth of that terrible trap in which it was so fairly caught, and which grew narrower and narrower with a rapidity too horrible to be conceived. The agony of that moment is not to be imagined. I threw up my hands and endeavored, with all my strength, to force upwards the ponderous iron bar. I might as well have tried to lift the cathedral itself. Down, down, down it came, closer and yet closer. I screamed to Pompey for aid; but he said that I had hurt his feelings by calling him "an ignorant old squint-eye." I yelled to Diana; but she only said "bow-wow-wow," and that I had told her "on no account to stir from the corner." Thus I had no relief to expect from my associates.

Meantime the ponderous and terrific *Scythe of Time* (for I now discovered the literal import of that classical phrase) had not stopped, nor was it likely to stop, in its career. Down and still down, it came. It had already buried its sharp edge a full inch in my flesh, and my sensations grew indistinct and confused. At one time I fancied myself in Philadelphia with **74** the stately Dr. Moneypenny, at another in the back parlor of Mr. Blackwood receiving his invaluable instructions. And then again the sweet recollection of better and earlier times came over me, and I thought of that happy period when the world was not all a desert, and Pompey not altogether cruel.

The ticking of the machinery amused me. *Amused me*, I say, for my sensations now bordered upon perfect happiness, and the most trifling circumstances afforded me pleasure. The eternal *click-clack, click-clack, click-clack* of the clock was the

74 Compare with the pendulum in "The Pit and the Pendulum."

. . . I perceived, to my extreme horror, that the huge, glittering, scimitar-like minute-hand of the clock had . . . *descended upon my neck*. *Illustration by Albert Edward Sterner for* Century Magazine, *1903*

75 Dr. Ollapod is a character in a farce by George Colman the Younger (1762–1836), *The Poor Gentleman*— an apothecary always trying to say witty things and looking for wit in the conversation of others.

In March 1835, a new column appeared in the *Knickerbocker Magazine*, signed "Ollapod" and written by editor Lewis Gaylord Clark's twin brother, Willis Gaylord Clark. Lewis Clark was famous for his "puffing" of stories, and the Colman character suggested presumption, self-complacency, heavy humor, and long-winded charlatanism.

76 A lively Polish dance, much like the polka, in triple time. The dancing "V" may be Victoria.

77 Martin Van Buren (1782–1862), eighth President of the United States (1837–41), who lost the Democratic nomination in 1844 because he flatly opposed the annexation of Texas, on antislavery grounds.

78 Think this one over a bit . . .

most melodious of music in my ears, and occasionally even put me in mind of the graceful sermonic harangues of Dr. **75** Ollapod. Then there were the great figures upon the dial-plate—how intelligent, how intellectual, they all looked! And **76** presently they took to dancing the Mazurka, and I think it was the figure V. who performed the most to my satisfaction. She was evidently a lady of breeding. None of your swaggerers, and nothing at all indelicate in her motions. She did the pirouette to admiration—whirling round upon her apex. I made an endeavor to hand her a chair, for I saw that she appeared fatigued with her exertions—and it was not until then that I fully perceived my lamentable situation. Lamentable indeed! The bar had buried itself two inches in my neck. I was aroused to a sense of exquisite pain. I prayed for death, and, in the agony of the moment, could not help repeating those exquisite verses of the poet Miguel De Cervantes:

77
> *Vanny Buren, tan escondida*
> *Query no te senty venny*
> *Pork and pleasure, delly morry*
> *Nommy, torny, darry, widdy!*

But now a new horror presented itself, and one indeed sufficient to startle the strongest nerves. My eyes, from the cruel pressure of the machine, were absolutely starting from their sockets. While I was thinking how I should possibly manage without them, one actually tumbled out of my head, and, rolling down the steep side of the steeple, lodged in the rain gutter which ran along the eaves of the main building. The loss of the eye was not so much as the insolent air of independence and contempt with which it regarded me after it was out. There it lay in the gutter just under my nose, and the airs it gave itself would have been ridiculous had they not been disgusting. Such a winking and blinking were never **78** before seen. This behavior on the part of my eye in the gutter was not only irritating on account of its manifest insolence and shameful ingratitude, but was also exceedingly inconvenient on account of the sympathy which always exists·between two eyes of the same head, however far apart. I was forced, in a manner, to wink and to blink, whether I would or not, in exact concert with the scoundrelly thing that lay just under my nose. I was presently relieved, however, by the dropping out of the other eye. In falling it took the same direction (possibly a concerted plot) as its fellow. Both rolled out of the gutter together, and in truth I was very glad to get rid of them.

The bar was now four inches and a half deep in my neck, and there was only a little bit of skin to cut through. My sensations were those of entire happiness, for I felt that in a few minutes, at farthest, I should be relieved from my disagreeable situation. And in this expectation I was not at all deceived. At twenty-five minutes past five in the afternoon, precisely, the huge minute-hand had proceeded sufficiently far on its terrible revolution to sever the small remainder of my neck. I was not sorry to see the head which had occasioned me so much embarrassment at length make a final separation from my body. It first rolled down the side of the steeple, then lodged, for a few seconds, in the gutter, and then made its way, with a plunge, into the middle of the street.

I will candidly confess that my feelings were now of the most singular—nay, of the most mysterious, the most perplexing and incomprehensible character. My senses were here and there at one and the same moment. With my head I imagined, at one time, that I the head, was the real Signora Psyche Zenobia—at another I felt convinced that myself, the body, was the proper identity. To clear my ideas on this topic I felt in my pocket for my snuff-box, but, upon getting it, and endeavoring to apply a pinch of its grateful contents in the ordinary manner, I became immediately aware of my peculiar deficiency, and threw the box at once down to my head. It took a pinch with great satisfaction, and smiled me an acknowledgement in return. Shortly afterward it made me a speech, which I could hear but indistinctly without ears. I gathered enough, however, to know that it was astonished at my wishing to remain alive under such circumstances. In the concluding sentences it quoted the noble words of Ariosto—

> *Il pover hommy che non sera corty*
> *And have a combat tenty erry morty;*   **79**

79 See note 44.

thus comparing me to the hero who, in the heat of the combat, not perceiving that he was dead, continued to contest the battle with inextinguishable valor. There was nothing now to prevent my getting down from my elevation, and I did so. What it was that Pompey saw so *very* peculiar in my appearance I have never yet been able to find out. The fellow opened his mouth from ear to ear and shut his two eyes as if he were endeavoring to crack nuts between the lids. Finally, throwing off his overcoat, he made one spring for the staircase and disappeared. I hurled after the scoundrel these vehement words of Demosthenes—

> *Andrew O'Phlegethon, you really make haste to fly.*   **80**

80 Phlegethon was the river of fire, one of the five rivers of Hades, which flowed into the river Acheron.

and then turned to the darling of my heart, to the one-eyed! the shaggy-haired Diana. Alas! what horrible vision affronted my eyes? *Was* that a rat I saw skulking into his hole? *Are* these the picked bones of the little angel who has been cruelly devoured by the monster? Ye Gods! and what *do* I behold— *is* that the departed spirit, the shade, the ghost of my beloved puppy, which I perceive sitting with a grace so melancholy, in the corner? Harken! for she speaks, and, heavens! it is in **81** the German of Schiller—

81 Compare with the climax of "Ligeia."

> *Unt stubby duk, so stubby dun*
> *Duk she! duk she!*

Alas! and are not her words too true?

> And if I died at least I died
> For thee—for thee.

Sweet creature! she *too* has sacrificed herself in my behalf. Dogless, niggerless, headless, what *now* remains for the unhappy Signora Psyche Zenobia? Alas—*nothing!* I have done. **82**

82 Most critics are content to leave this tale as a pure satire on the *Blackwood* formula for writing fiction, but Marie Bonaparte sees the clock as a castration symbol (p. 588), without explaining how this applies to Zenobia, unfortunately.

THE DEVIL IN THE BELFRY

First published in the Philadelphia *Saturday Chronicle and Mirror of the Times*, May 18, 1839, "The Devil in the Belfry" is a true grotesque (in Poe's use of the term) and one with more than mere comic effect. In it, Poe deals both with German intellectualism of the day and the effect of discordant bells on the listener—a theme he would take up again in his poem *The Bells*.

One probable source for the tale is Thomas Carlyle's *Sartor Resartus* (The Tailor Retailored), published in *Fraser's Magazine* in 1833–34. In Book II, Chapter ix, we find:

"Beautiful it was to sit there, as in my Skyey Tent, musing and meditating; on the high table-land, in front of the Mountains. . . . And then to fancy . . . the straw-roofed Cottages, wherein stood many a Mother baking bread, with her children round her:—all hidden and protectingly folded up in the valley-folds; yet there and alive, as sure as if I beheld them. Or to see, as well as fancy, the nine Towns and Villages, that lay around my mountain-seat, which, in still weather, were wont to speak to me (by their steeple-bells) with metal tongue; and, in almost all weather, proclaimed their vitality by repeated Smoke-clouds; whereon, as in a culinary horologe, I might read the hour of the day. For it was the smoke of cookery, as kind housewives, at morning, midday, eventide, were boiling their husbands' kettles; and ever a blue pillar rose up into the air, successively or simultaneously, from each of the nine, saying, as plainly as smoke could say: Such and such a man is getting ready here. Not uninteresting! For you have the whole Borough, with all its love-makings and scandal-mongeries, contentions and contentments, as in miniature, and could cover it all with your hat."

Poe mentions reading *Sartor Resartus* in "Marginalia," No. 135.

Poe may also have had in mind "The Man in the Bell," by William Maginn, which appeared in *Blackwood's*, November 1821 (and is mentioned in "How to Write a Blackwood Article"). In that tale a man shut inside a bell tower is driven mad by the sound of the chimes, whereupon he begins to see demons in the belfry. Still another possible source might be "The Barber of Gottingen," in *Blackwood's*, October 1826, wherein the Devil forces a barber to give him a shave and then climbs a high tower to pull someone's nose. Finally, in Dickens' *Nicholas Nickleby*, there is a Baron von Koeldwethout, of Grogzwig, in Germany. Poe's place name here is Grogswigg, and the story seems to be set in the German settlements of Pennsylvania.

The word "belfry," by the way, does not come from the word *bell*. The Middle English word was *berfrey*, but by association with bell tower the word changed its spelling and pronunciation in the fifteenth century. *Berfrey* originally meant a penthouse, then a movable tower used by besiegers, then a tower to protect watchmen, a watchtower, a beacon tower, an alarm-bell tower, and finally a place where a bell is hung. The modern French word is *beffroi*.

Claude Debussy worked on an opera based on Poe's tale from 1902 to 1907 but was unable to complete it before his death. "Debussy planned for the devil to whistle rather than sing; he planned a chorus composed of many interwoven parts for the individual burghers, *vrouwen* and urchins," says William Austin in *Music in the Twentieth Century* (Norton, 1966; p. 3).

What o'clock is it?
—*Old Saying.* **1**

Everybody knows, in a general way, that the finest place in the world is—or, alas, *was*—the Dutch borough of Vondervotteimittiss. Yet, as it lies some distance from any of the **2** main roads, being in a somewhat out-of-the-way situation, there are, perhaps, very few of my readers who have ever paid it a visit. For the benefit of those who have *not*, therefore, it will be only proper that I should enter into some account of it. And this is, indeed, the more necessary, as with the hope of enlisting public sympathy in behalf of the inhabitants, I design here to give a history of the calamitous events which have so lately occurred within its limits. No one who knows me will doubt that the duty thus self-imposed will be executed to the best of my ability, with all that rigid impartiality, all that cautious examination into facts, and diligent collation of authorities, which should ever distinguish him who aspires to the title of historian.

By the united aid of medals, manuscripts, and inscriptions. I am enabled to say, positively, that the borough of Vondervotteimittiss has existed, from its origin, in precisely the same condition which it at present preserves. Of the date of this **3** origin, however, I grieve that I can only speak with that species of indefinite definiteness which mathematicians are, at times, force to put up with in certain algebraic formulæ. The date, I may thus say, in regard to the remoteness of its antiquity, cannot be less than any assignable quantity whatsoever.

Touching the derivation of the name Vondervotteimittiss, I confess myself, with sorrow, equally at fault. Among a multitude of opinions upon this delicate point—some acute, some learned, some sufficiently the reverse—I am able to select nothing which ought to be considered satisfactory. Perhaps the idea of Grogswigg—nearly coincident with that **4** of Kroutaplenttey—is to be cautiously preferred:—It runs:— **5** *Vondervotteimittiss—Vonder, lege Donder—Votteimittiss, quasi und Bleitziz—Bleitziz obsol: pro Blitzen.*" This deriva- **6** tion, to say the truth, is still countenanced by some traces of the electric fluid evident on the summit of the steeple of the **7** House of the Town Council. I do not choose, however, to commit myself on a theme of such importance, and must refer the reader desirous of information, to the "*Oratiunculæ de Rebus Præter-Veteris*," of Dundergutz. See, also, Blunder- **8** buzzard "*De Derivationibus*," pp. 27 to 5010, Folio, Gothic edit., Red and Black character, Catch-word and No Cypher; **9** —wherein consult, also, marginal notes in the autograph of Stuffundpuff, with the Sub-Commentaries of Gruntundguzzell. **10**

Notwithstanding the obscurity which thus envelops the date of the foundation of Vondervotteimittiss, and the derivation of its name, there can be no doubt, as I said before, that it has always existed as we find it at this epoch. The oldest man in the borough can remember not the slightest difference in the

---

1 Here, as elsewhere in the tale (and in "A Predicament"), Poe burlesques the citations of "learned" writers who dredge up obscure quotes to beef up their prose.

2 In earlier versions of the tale, Poe adds the helpful footnote "Vonder vaat time it is."

3 The stagnation of the village seems to echo Washington Irving's description of New Amsterdam under the reign of Governor Wouter van Twiller and his council in "Knickerbocker's" *History of New York* (1809).

4 See introductory note for "Grogswigg." Poe reviewed *Nicholas Nickleby* in 1839.

5 Kraut-a-plenty, or "lots of Krauts." The O.E.D. does not give the origin of the word "Kraut" meaning German, although it obviously comes from sauerkraut, the well-known German cabbage dish. *A Dictionary of Slang and Unconventional English* (Macmillan, 1970) cites only a 20th-century origin and meaning, although the word is clearly much older than that.

6 This kind of etymological claptrap is not uncommon. Too often, people assume the origins of a word by its similarity to another word, but as we see in the case of *belfry* (introductory note), this is often misleading.
  The nonsense etymology reads something like this: "For *Vonder*, read 'thunder'; for *Votteimittiss*, like a *Bleitziz*—obsolete for *Blitzen*, lightning."
  "Thunder and lightning" is a mild German oath used also in "Lionizing."

7 i.e., lightning. In Poe's time, the word "fluid" was used for electricity or magnetic force, like our familiar "current."

8 "Little Discussions of the Most Ancient Things." "Dundergutz" is related to "dunderhead."

9 This sort of bibliographical citation is antique but nonetheless correct.

10 "Stuff and puff" (referring to pipe-smoking) and "grunt and guzzle"

11 The town's inhabitants believe only what they see and are perfectly content with that, making them materialists to an extreme degree.

12 French critic Jean-Paul Weber sees the tale as an allegory, with the whole village built like a clock, surrounded by hills like a clock case. There are sixty houses (minutes), and each house has twenty-four cabbages (hours). The seven faces of the huge clock represent the days of the week. "The grotesque visitor looks like a minute hand, with his big hat and skinny body, and he covers up the slow-moving hour hand at noon." ("Edgar Poe or The Theme of the Clock," in *Poe, A Collection of Critical Essays* [Prentice-Hall, 1967], pp. 79–83)

13 A clock is both the symbol of the mundane world and a symbol of life and death (as in "The Masque of The Red Death").

The cabbage is about the lowliest of vegetables, and in many countries it is considered fit only for the poor, or for animal fodder. It was also a schoolboy term for a literary crib or other petty theft, and of course, as *kraut*, which is a slang expression for a German.

14 A coarse, sturdy fabric made of wool, linen, or cotton

appearance of any portion of it; and, indeed, the very suggestion of such a possibility is considered an insult. The site of the village is in a perfectly circular valley, about a quarter of a mile in circumference, and entirely surrounded by gentle hills, over whose summit the people have never yet ventured to pass. For this they assign the very good reason that they **11** do not believe there is any thing at all on the other side.

Round the skirts of the valley (which is quite level, and paved throughout with flat tiles), extends a continuous row of sixty little houses. These, having their backs on the hills, must look, of course, to the centre of the plain, which is just sixty yards from the front of each dwelling. Every house has a small garden before it, with a circular path, a sun-dial, and twenty- **12** four cabbages. The buildings themselves are so precisely alike, that one can in no manner be distinguished from the other. Owing to the vast antiquity, the style of architecture is somewhat odd, but it is not for that reason the less strikingly picturesque. They are fashioned of hard-burned little bricks, red, with black ends, so that the walls look like a chessboard upon a great scale. The gables are turned to the front, and there are cornices, as big as all the rest of the house, over the eaves and over the main doors. The windows are narrow and deep, with very tiny panes and a great deal of sash. On the roof is a vast quantity of tiles with long curly ears. The woodwork, throughout, is of a dark hue, and there is much carving about it, with but a trifling variety of pattern; for, time out of mind, the carvers of Vondervotteimittiss have never been able to carve more than two objects—a timepiece **13** and a cabbage. But these they do exceedingly well, and intersperse them, with singular ingenuity, wherever they find room for the chisel.

The dwellings are as much alike inside as out, and the furniture is all upon one plan. The floors are of square tiles, the chairs and tables of black-looking wood with thin crooked legs and puppy feet. The mantel-pieces are wide and high, and have not only timepieces and cabbages sculptured over the front, but a real timepiece, which makes a prodigious ticking, on the top in the middle, with a flower-pot containing a cabbage standing on each extremity by way of outrider. Between each cabbage and the timepiece, again, is a little China man having a large stomach with a great round hole in it, through which is seen the dial-plate of a watch.

The fireplaces are large and deep, with fierce crooked-looking fire-dogs. There is constantly a rousing fire, and a huge pot over it, full of sauerkraut and pork, to which the good woman of the house is always busy in attending. She is a little fat old lady, with blue eyes and a red face, and wears a huge cap like a sugar-loaf, ornamented with purple and **14** yellow ribbons. Her dress is of orange-colored linsey-woolsey, made very full behind and very short in the waist—and indeed very short in other respects, not reaching below the middle of her leg. This is somewhat thick, and so are her ankles, but she has a fine pair of green stockings to cover them. Her shoes—of pink leather—are fastened each with a bunch of yellow ribbons puckered up in the shape of a cabbage. In her left hand she has a little heavy Dutch watch; in her right she wields a ladle for the sauerkraut and pork. By her side there stands a fat tabby cat, with a gilt toy-repeater tied to its tail **15** which "the boys" have there fastened by way of a quiz.

The boys themselves are, all three of them, in the garden attending the pig. They are each two feet in height. They have three-cornered cocked hats, purple waistcoats reaching down to their thighs, buckskin knee-breeches, red woollen stockings, heavy shoes with big silver buckles, and long surtout coats with large buttons of mother-of-pearl. Each, too, has a pipe in his mouth, and a little dumpy watch in his right hand. He takes a puff and a look, and then a look and a puff. The pig—which is corpulent and lazy—is occupied now in picking up the stray leaves that fall from the cabbages, and now in giving a kick behind at the gilt repeater, which the urchins have also tied to *his* tail, in order to make him look as handsome as the cat.

Right at the front door, in a high-backed leather-bottomed armed chair, with crooked legs and puppy feet like the tables, is seated the old man of the house himself. He is an exceedingly puffy little old gentleman, with big circular eyes and a huge double chin. His dress resembles that of the boys—and I need say nothing further about it. All the difference is, that his pipe is somewhat bigger than theirs, and he can make a greater smoke. Like them, he has a watch, but he carries his watch in his pocket. To say the truth, he has something of more importance than a watch to attend to—and what that is, I shall presently explain. He sits with his right leg upon his left knee, wears a grave countenance, and always keeps one of his eyes, at least, resolutely bent upon a certain remarkable object in the centre of the plain.

This object is situated in the steeple of the House of the Town Council. The Town Council are all very little, round, oily, intelligent men, with big saucer eyes and fat double chins, and have their coats much longer and their shoe-buckles much bigger than the ordinary inhabitants of Vondervotteim-ittiss. Since my sojourn in the borough, they have had several special meetings, and have adopted these three important resolutions:—

"That it is wrong to alter the good old course of things:"

"That there is nothing tolerable out of Vondervotteimittiss:" and—

"That we will stick by our clocks and our cabbages."

Above the session-room of the Council is the steeple, and in the steeple is the belfry, where exists, and has existed time out of mind, the pride and wonder of the village—the great clock of the borough of Vondervotteimittiss. And this is the object to which the eyes of the old gentlemen are turned who sit in the leather-bottomed arm-chairs.

The great clock has seven faces—one in each of the seven sides of the steeple—so that it can be readily seen from all quarters. Its faces are large and white, and its hands heavy and black. There is a belfry-man whose sole duty is to attend to it; but this duty is the most perfect of sinecures—for the clock of Vondervotteimittiss was never yet known to have any thing the matter with it. Until lately, the bare supposition of such a thing was considered heretical. From the remotest period of antiquity to which the archives have reference, the hours have been regularly struck by the big bell. And, indeed, the case was just the same with all the other locks and watches in the borough. Never was such a place for keeping the true time. When the large clapper thought proper to say "Twelve o'clock!" all its obedient followers opened their throats simultaneously, and responded like a very echo. In short, the good burghers were fond of their sauerkraut, but then they were proud of their clocks.

All people who hold sinecure offices are held in more or less respect, and as the belfry-man of Vondervotteimittiss has the most perfect of sinecures, he is the most perfectly respected of any man in the world. He is the chief dignitary of the borough, and the very pigs look up to him with a sentiment of reverence. His coat-tail is *very* far longer—his pipe, his shoe-buckles, his eyes, and his stomach, *very* far bigger—than those of any other old gentleman in the village; and as to his chin, it is not only double, but triple.

I have thus painted the happy estate of Vondervotteimittiss: alas, that so fair a picture should ever experience a reverse!

There has been long a saying among the wisest inhabitants, **16** that "no good can come from over the hills;" and it really seemed that the words had in them something of the spirit of prophecy. It wanted five minutes of noon, on the day before yesterday, when there appeared a very odd-looking object on the summit of the ridge to the eastward. Such an occurrence, of course, attracted universal attention, and every little old gentleman who sat in a leather-bottomed arm-chair turned one of his eyes with a stare of dismay upon the phenomenon, still keeping the other upon the clock in the steeple.

By the time that it wanted only three minutes to noon, the droll object in question was perceived to be a very diminutive foreign-looking man. He descended the hills at a great rate, so that everybody had soon a good look at him. He was really the most finicky little personage that had ever been seen in Vondervotteimittiss. His countenance was of a dark snuff-color, and he had a long hooked nose, pea eyes, a wide mouth, and an excellent set of teeth, which latter he seemed anxious of displaying, as he was grinning from ear to ear. What with mustachios and whiskers, there was none of the rest of his face to be seen. His head was uncovered, and his hair neatly **17** done up in *papillotes*. His dress was a tight-fitting swallow-tailed black coat (from one of whose pockets dangled a vast length of white handkerchief), black kerseymere knee-breeches, black stockings, and stumpy-looking pumps, with huge bunches of black satin ribbon for bows. Under one arm **18** he carried a huge *chapeau-de-bras*, and under the other a fiddle nearly five times as big as himself. In his left hand was a gold snuff-box, from which, as he capered down the hill, cutting all manner of fantastic steps, he took snuff incessantly with an air of the greatest possible self-satisfaction. God bless me!—here was a sight for the honest burghers of Vondervotteimittiss!

16 Especially since they think there's nothing there, according to the fourth paragraph

17 Curling papers

18 A three-cornered silk hat worn in the eighteenth century (also known as *chapeau-bras*).

To speak plainly, the fellow had, in spite of his grinning, an audacious and sinister kind of face; and as he curvetted right into the village, the old stumpy appearance of his pumps excited no little suspicion; and many a burgher who beheld him that day would have given a trifle for a peep beneath the white cambric handkerchief which hung so obtrusively from the pocket of his swallow-tailed coat. But what mainly occasioned a righteous indignation was, that the scoundrelly popinjay, while he cut a fandango here, and a whirligig there, **19** did not seem to have the remotest idea in the world of such a thing as *keeping time* in his steps.

The good people of the borough had scarcely a chance, however, to get their eyes thoroughly open, when, just as it wanted half a minute of noon, the rascal bounced, as I say, right into the midst of them; gave a *chassez* here, and a *balancez* there; and then, after a *pirouette* and a *pas-de-zéphyr*, pigeon-winged himself right up into the belfry of the **20** House of the Town Council, where the wonder-stricken belfry-man sat smoking in a state of dignity and dismay. But the little chap seized him at once by the nose; gave it a swing and a pull; clapped the big *chapeau-de-bras* upon his head; knocked it down over his eyes and mouth; and then, lifting up the big fiddle, beat him with it so long and so soundly, that what with the belfry-man being so fat, and the fiddle being so hollow, you would have sworn that there was a regiment of double-bass drummers all beating the devil's tattoo up in **21** the belfry of the steeple of Vondervotteimittiss.

There is no knowing to what desperate act of vengeance this unprincipled attack might have aroused the inhabitants, but for the important fact that it now wanted only half a second of noon. The bell was about to strike, and it was a matter of absolute and pre-eminent necessity that everybody should look well at his watch. It was evident, however, that just at this moment the fellow in the steeple was doing something that he had no business to do with the clock. But as it now began to strike, nobody had any time to attend to his manœuvres, for they had all to count the strokes of the bell as it sounded.

"One!" said the clock.

"Von!" echoed every little old gentleman in every leather-bottomed armchair in Vondervotteimittiss. "Von!" said his watch also; "von!" said the watch of his vrow; and "von!" said the watches of the boys, and the little gilt repeaters on the tails of the cat and pig.

"Two!" continued the big bell; and

"Doo!" repeated all the repeaters.

"Three! Four! Five! Six! Seven! Eight! Nine! Ten!" said the bell.

"Dree! Vour! Fibe! Sax! Seben! Aight! Noin! Den!" answered the others.

"Eleven!" said the big one.

"Eleben!" assented the little ones.

"Twelve!" said the bell.

"Dvelf!" they replied, perfectly satisfied, and dropping their voices.

19 A vain and fancy dresser, from the French *papegai*, which traces its origins to Arabic. The *-gai* ending was confused with the European "jay," and the word came to mean a parrot.

20 A *chaser* is a sliding dance step (not *chassez*); *balancer* means to rock or sway; a *pirouette* is a rapid turn; and a *pas de zéphyr* is a light-footed dance step. A pigeonwing is a fancy step.

21 Nervous drumming of one's fingers on a table

22 "When the clock strikes thirteen" means "never." When a clock actually does strike thirteen—which *is* possible—it is usually taken as an ill omen. Here, however, the townspeople only think of the extra hour that has struck, meaning that sixty minutes have "passed" since the twelfth chime. Their lives are ruled by the clock.

St. Paul's clock once supposedly struck thirteen. John Hatfield, a soldier in the reign of William III (1689–1702), was brought before a court martial for falling asleep on duty at Windsor Terrace. In proof of his innocence he asserted that he had heard St. Paul's clock strike thirteen, which was confirmed by several witnesses. Hatfield was freed; he died in 1770 at age 102.

23 "Old Nick" is an English term for the Devil, possibly from the name of the Scandinavian evil spirit Neken or Nikken. Samuel Butler implies the word is derived from Nicholas Machiavelli, but the term existed many years before the birth of that Florentine: "Nick Machiavel had ne'er a trick/(Though he gives name to our old Nick)," in *Hudibras*, iii, 1.

24 A fool or blockhead, but of unknown derivation

25 The first song begins: "Good Luck, Judy O'Flanagan/ Dearly she loved nate Looney McTwoulter." Thomas Moore borrowed the tune and set to it his words: "Sing, sing—music was given."

"Paddy O'Rafferty" is mentioned in Washington Irving's "The Bold Dragoon" (1824), in which the Devil is requested to play it. Beethoven set it to music (Opus 224).

26 The moral to this story might well be "He who isolates himself from Truth is bound to go to the Devil."

On his lap lay the big fiddle, at which he was scraping, out of all time and tune, with both hands, making a great show, the nincompoop! of playing "Judy O'Flannagan and Paddy O'Rafferty." *Illustration by H. Church, 1903*

THE DEVIL IN THE BELFRY

CHURCH NY

"Und dvelf it iss!" said all the little old gentlemen, putting up their watches. But the big bell had not done with them yet.

"*Thirteen!*" said he.

"Der Teufel!" gasped the little old gentlemen, turning pale, dropping their pipes, and putting down all their right legs from over their left knees.

"Der Teufel!" groaned they, "Dirteen! Dirteen!!—Mein
22 Gott, it is Dirteen o'clock!!"

Why attempt to describe the terrible scene which ensued? All Vondervotteimittis flew at once into a lamentable state of uproar.

"Vot is cum'd do mein pelly?" roared all the boys,—"I've been ongry for dis hour!"

"Vot is cum'd to mein kraut?" scramed all the vrows, "It has been done to rags for dis hour!"

"Vot is cum'd to mein pipe?" swore all the little old gentlemen, "Donder and Blitzen! it has been smoked out for dis hour!"—and they filled them up again in a great rage, and, sinking back in their arm-chairs, puffed away so fast and so fiercely that the whole valley was immediately filled with impenetrable smoke.

Meantime the cabbages all turned very red in the face, and
23 it seemed as if old Nick himself had taken possession of every thing in the shape of a timepiece. The clocks carved upon the furniture took to dancing as if bewitched, while those upon the mantel-pieces could scarcely contain themselves for fury, and kept such a continual striking of thirteen, and such a frisking and wriggling of their pendulums as was really horrible to see. But, worse than all, neither the cats nor the pigs could put up any longer with the behavior of the little repeaters tied to their tails, and resented it by scampering all over the place, scratching and poking, and squeaking and screeching, and caterwauling and squalling, and flying into the faces, and running under the petticoats of the people, and creating altogether the most abominable din and confusion which it is possible for a reasonable person to conceive. And to make matters still more distressing, the rascally little scapegrace in the steeple was evidently exerting himself to the utmost. Every now and then one might catch a glimpse of the scoundrel through the smoke. There he sat in the belfry upon the belfry-man, who was lying flat upon his back. In his teeth the villain held the bell-rope, which he kept jerking about with his head, raising such a clatter that my ears ring again even to think of it. On his lap lay the big fiddle, at which he was scraping, out of all time and tune, with both hands, making a great show,
24 the nincompoop! of playing "Judy O'Flannagan" and "Paddy
25 O'Rafferty."

Affairs being thus miserably situated, I left the place in disgust, and now appeal for aid to all lovers of correct time and fine kraut. Let us proceed in a body to the borough, and restore the ancient order of things in Vondervotteimittiss by
26 ejecting that little fellow from the steeple.

WHY THE LITTLE FRENCHMAN WEARS HIS HAND IN A SLING

First published in 1837–39 in a periodical still unknown, then in *Tales of the Grotesque and Arabesque* (1840), this tale is apt to give a modern reader a headache—all that supposed Irish dialect is as tough going as translating a foreign language. It is also about as insignificant as anything Poe ever wrote, even though it was the first of Poe's tales to be pirated in London (*Bentley's Miscellany*, July 1840).

The source is clearly General George Pope Morris' "The Little Frenchman and his Water Lots," which appeared in the New York *Mirror*. December 31, 1836. Morris (1802–64) was an editor, poet, and playwright, whose "Little Frenchman" stories were immediately popular and whose *The Deserted Bride and Other Poems* (1838) included the well-known *Woodman, Spare That Tree!*

Poe took from Morris' tale the chief character and his Irish brogue, but little else. The American vogue for dialect humor reached its peak in the late-nineteenth and early-twentieth centuries and included Josh Billings (Henry Wheeler Shaw, 1818–85), whose humor was in part the result of odd spelling, unorthodox grammar, and outrageous puns; John Phoenix (George Horatio Derby, 1823–61); Artemus Ward (Charles Farrar Browne, 1834–67); and "Mr. Dooley," the Chicago Irishman of thickest brogue who, from behind his bar, dispensed wit and wisdom on the events of the world (written by Finley Peter Dunne, 1867–1936). The latter's most famous utterance: "Whether th' Constitution follows th' flag or not, th' Supreme Court follows th' illiction returns."

The narrator's home is Connaught (or Connacht), the most westerly province of Ireland, which comprises the counties of Mayo, Sligo, Leitrim, Roscommon, and Galway. It was one of the ancient kingdoms of Ireland, whose rulers, the O'Connors, were supplanted by the Anglo-Norman De Burghs in the thirteenth century; its people have long been considered the most pugnacious of the island.

It's on my visiting cards sure enough (and it's them that's all o' pink satin paper) that inny gintleman that plases may behould the intheristhin words, "Sir Pathrick O'Grandison, [1] Barronitt, 39 Southampton Row, Russell Square, Parish o' Bloomsbury." And shud ye be wantin to diskiver who is the pink of purliteness quite, and the laider of the hot tun in the [2] houl city o' Lonon—why it's jist mesilf. And fait that same is no wonder at all at all (so be plased to stop curlin your nose), for every inch o' the six wakes that I've been a gintleman, and left aff wid the bog-throthing to take up wid the Barronissy, it's Pathrick that's been living like a houly imperor, and gitting the iddication and the graces. Och! and wouldn't it be a blessed thing for your sperrits if ye cud lay your two peepers jist, upon Sir Pathrick O'Grandison, Barronitt, when he is all riddy drissed for the hopperer, or stipping into the Brisky for [3] the drive into the Hyde Park. But it's the illegant big figgur

1 The narrator seems to be named after Samuel Richardson's novel *Sir Charles Grandison* (1753). His home in London shares the address of the house where John Allan and his family lived for a short while.

2 *Haut ton;* high-toned, or upper class

3 A britska is a light, four-wheeled carriage with a folding top, originally from Poland.

. . . the little ould furrener Frinchman that lives jist over the way, and that's a-oggling and a-goggling the houl day . . . at the purty widdy Misthress Tracle that's my own nixt-door neighbor. . . . *Artist unknown*

4 Treacle (syrup)

5 A lad or small boy, from the Irish *spailpin*.

6 In northwestern Ireland. The people of Connaught have long been referred to as the most argument- and fight-loving of the Irish.

7 Darling or dear, from the Irish Gaelic *mo mhuirnin*.

8 A pratie is a potato.

9 Frederick Lucchesi (d. 1869) was a native of Lucca, Italy, but lived in Baltimore for thirty-five years, where he was a musician and teacher and professor of music. Another character by this name is mentioned in "The Cask of Amontillado."

that I ave, for the rason o' which all the ladies fall in love wid me. Isn't it my own swate silf now that'll missure the six fut, and the three inches more nor that, in me stockings, and that am excadingly will proportioned all over to match? And is it ralelly more than three fut and a bit that there is, inny how, of the little ould furrener Frinchman that lives jist over the way, and that's a-oggling and a-goggling the houl day (and bad **4** luck to him) at the purty widdy Misthress Tracle that's my own nixt-door neighbor (God bliss her!) and a most particuller **5** frind and acquaintance? You percave the little spalpeen is summat down in the mouth, and wears his lift hand in a sling; and it's for that same thing, by yur lave, that I'm going to give you the good rason.

The truth of the houl matter is jist simple enough; for the **6** very first day that I com'd from Connaught, and showd my swate little silf in the strait to the widdy, who was looking through the windy, it was a gone case althegither wid the heart o' the purty Misthress Tracle. I percaved it, ye see, all at once, and no mistake, and that's God's truth. First of all it was up wid the windy in a jiffy, and thin she threw open her two peepers to the itmost, and thin it was a little gould spy-glass that she clapped tight to one o' them, and divil may burn me if it didn't spake to me as plain as a peeper cud spake, and says it, through the spy-glass: "Och! the tip o' the mornin' to **7** ye, Sir Pathrick O'Grandison, Barronitt, mavourneen; and it's a nate gintleman that ye are, sure enough, and it's mesilf and me forten jist that'll be at yur sarvice, dear, inny time o' day at all at all for the asking." And it's not mesilf ye wud have to be bate in the purliteness; so I made her a bow that wud ha' broken yur heart althegither to behould, and thin I pulled aff me hat with a flourish, and thin I winked at her hard wid both eyes, as much as to say: "True for you, yer a swate little crature, Mrs. Tracle, me darlint, and I wish I may be drownthed dead in a bog, if it's not mesilf, Sir Pathrick O'Grandison, Barronitt, that'll make a houl bushel o' love to yur leddyship, in the twinkling o' the eye of a Londonderry **8** purraty."

And it was the nixt mornin, sure, jist as I was making up me mind whither it wouldn't be the purlite thing to sind a bit o' writin to the widdy by way of a love-litter, when up com'd the delivery servant wid an illegant card, and he tould me that the name on it (for I niver could rade the copper-plate printin' on account of being lift-handed) was all about Moun-**9** seer, the Count, A Goose, Look-aisy, Maiter-di-dauns, and that the houl of the divilish lingo was the spalpeeny long name of the little ould furrener Frinchman as lived over the way.

And jist wid that in com'd the little willain himself, and thin he made me a broth of a bow, and thin he said he had ounly taken the liberty of doing me the honor of the giving me a call, and thin he went on to palaver at a great rate, and divil the bit did I comprehind what he wud be afther the tilling me at all at all, excepting and saving that he said "parley wou, woolly wou," and tould me, among a bushel o' lies, bad luck to him, that he was mad for the love o' my widdy Misthress

Tracle, and that my widdy Mrs. Tracle had a puncheon for **10** *him*.

At the hearin of this, ye may swear, though, I was as mad as a grasshopper, but I remimbered that I was Sir Pathrick O'Grandison, Barronitt, and that it wasn't althegither gentaal to lit the anger git the upper hand o' the purliteness, so I made light o' the matter and kipt dark, and got quite sociable wid the little chap, and afther a while what did he do but ask me to go wid him to the widdy's, saying he wud give me the feshionable inthroduction to her leddyship.

"Is it there ye are?" said I thin to mesilf, "and it's thrue for you, Pathrick, that ye're the fortunittest mortal in life. We'll soon see now whither it's your swate silf, or whither it's little Mounseer Maiter-di-dauns, that Misthress Tracle is head and ears in the love wid."

Wid that we wint aff to the widdy's, next door, and ye may well say it was an illegant place; so it was. There was a carpet all over the floor, and in one corner there was a forty-pinny **11** and a jews-harp and the divil knows what ilse, and in another corner was a sofy, the beautifullest thing in all natur, and sitting on the sofy, sure enough, there was the swate little angel, Misthress Tracle.

"The tip o' the mornin' to ye," says I, "Mrs. Tracle," and thin I made sich an illegant obaysance that it wud ha quite althegither bewildered the brain o' ye.

"Wully woo, parley woo, plump in the mud," says the little **12** furrener Frinchman, "and sure Mrs. Tracle," says he, that he did, "isn't this gintleman here jist his reverence Sir Pathrick O'Grandison, Barronitt, and isn't he althegither and entirely the most purticular frind and acquaintance that I have in the houl world?"

And wid that the widdy, she gits up from the sofy, and makes the swatest curtchy nor iver was seen; and thin down she sits like an angel; and thin, by the powers, it was that little spalpeen Mounseer Maiter-di-dauns that plumped his silf right down by the right side of her. Och hon! I ixpicted the two eyes o' me wud ha com'd out of me head on the spot, I was so disperate mad! Howiver, "Bait who!" says I, after a while. "Is it there ye are, Mounseer Maiter-di-dauns?" and so down I plumped on the lift side of her leddyship, to be aven with the willain. Botheration! it wud ha done your heart good to percave the illegant double wink that I gived her jist thin right in the face wid both eyes.

But the little ould Frinchman he niver beginned to suspict me at all at all, and disperate hard it was he made the love to her leddyship. "Woully wou," says he, "Parley wou," says he, "Plump in the mud," says he.

"That's all to no use, Mounseer Frog, mavourneen," thinks I; and I talked as hard and as fast as I could all the while, and throth it was mesilf jist that divarted her leddyship complately and intirely, by rason of the illegant conversation that I kipt up wid her all about the dear bogs of Connaught. And by and by she gived me such a swate smile, from one ind of her mouth to the ither, that it made me as bould as a pig, and I jist took hould of the ind of her little finger in the most dilikittest manner in natur, looking at her all the while out o' the whites of my eyes.

And then ounly percave the cuteness of the swate angel, for no sooner did she obsarve that I was afther the squazing of **13** her flipper, than she up wid it in a jiffy, and put it away behind her back, jist as much as to say, "Now thin, Sir Pathrick O'Grandison, there's bitther chance for ye, mavourneen, for it's not althegither the gentaal thing to be afther the squazing of my flipper right full in the sight of that little furrener Frinchman, Mounseer Maiter-di-dauns."

Wid that I giv'd her a big wink jist to say, "lit Sir Pathrick alone for the likes o' them thricks," and thin I wint aisy to work, and you'd have died wid the divarsion to behould how cliverly I slipped my right arm betwane the back o' the sofy, and the back of her leddyship, and there, sure enough, I found a swate little flipper all a waiting to say, "the tip o' the mornin' to ye, Sir Pathrick O'Grandison Barronitt." And wasn't it mesilf, sure, that jist giv'd it the laste little bit of a squaze in the world, all in the way of a commincement, and not to be too rough wid her leddyship? and och, botheration, wasn't it the gentaalest and dilikittest of all the little squazes that I got in return? "Blood and thunder, Sir Pathrick, mavourneen," thinks I to mesilf, "fait it's jist the mother's son of you, and nobody else at all at all, that's the handsomest and the fortunittest young bog-throtter that ever com'd out of Connaught!" And wid that I giv'd the flipper a big squaze, and a big squaze it was, by the powers, that her leddyship giv'd to me back. But it would ha split the seven sides of you wid the laffin' to behould jist then all at once, the consated behavior of Mounseer Maiter-di-dauns. The likes o' sich a jabbering, and a smirking, and a parley-wouing as he begin'd wid her leddyship, niver was known before upon arth; and divil may burn me if it wasn't me own very two peepers that cotch'd him tipping her the wink out of one eye. Och, hon! if it wasn't **14** mesilf thin that was mad as a Kilkenny cat I shud like to be tould who it was!

"Let me infarm you, Mounseer Maiter-di-dauns," said I, as purlite as iver ye seed, "that it's not the gentaal thing at all at all, and not for the likes o' you inny how, to be afther the oggling and a-goggling at her leddyship in that fashion," and jist wid that such another squaze as it was I giv'd her flipper, all as much as to say: "isn't it Sir Pathrick now, my jewel, that'll be able to the protectin' o' you, my darlint?" and then there com'd another squaze back, all by way of the answer. "Thrue for you, Sir Pathrick," it said as plain as iver a squaze said in the world. "Thrue for you, Sir Pathrick, mavourneen, and it's a proper nate gintleman ye are—that's God's truth," and with that she opened her two beautiful peepers till I belaved they wud ha' com'd out of her hid althegither and intirely, and she looked first as mad as a cat at Mounseer Frog, and thin as smiling as all out o' doors at mesilf.

"Thin," says he, the willain, "Och hon! and a wolly-wou, parley-wou," and then wid that he shoved up his two shoulders

---

13 Slang for the hand; not much used any more

14 During the Irish Rebellion, Kilkenny was garrisoned by a troop of Hessian soldiers who amused themselves by tying two cats together by their tails and throwing them across a clothesline to fight. The officers, hearing of this, decided to put a stop to it. The lookout man, intent on the sport, did not hear the officer of duty approach the barracks, but one of the troopers, a bit more quick-sighted, seized a sword and cut the two tails, allowing the cats to escape. When the officer inquired about the two bleeding tails left on the scene, he was coolly informed that two cats had been fighting and had devoured each other, leaving only their tails behind.

Whatever the true story, it is certain that the towns of Kilkenny and Irishtown were such rivals about their respective boundaries and rights to the end of the seventeenth century that they mutually improverished the other, leaving little else than "two tails" behind.

till the divil the bit of his hid was to be diskivered, and then he let down the two corners of his purraty-trap, and thin not **15**   **15** Mouth
a haporth more of the satisfaction could I git out o' the spalpeen.

Belave me, my jewel, it was Sir Pathrick that was unreasonable mad thin, and the more by token that the Frinchman kipt an wid his winking at the widdy; and the widdy she kipt an wid the squazing of my flipper, as much as to say: "At him again Sir Pathrick O'Grandison, mavourneen;" so I just ripped out wid a big oath, and says I,

"Ye little spalpeeny frog of a bog-throtting son of a bloody noun!"—and jist thin what d'ye think it was that her leddyship did? Troth she jumped up from the sofy as if she was bit, and made off through the door, while I turned my head round afther her, in a complete bewilderment and botheration, and followed her wid me two peepers. You percave I had a reason of my own for knowing that she couldn't git down the stares althegither and intirely; for I knew very well that I had hould of her hand, for divil the bit had I iver lit it go. And says I,

"Isn't it the laste little bit of a mistake in the world that ye've been afther the making, yer leddyship? Come back now, that's a darlint, and I'll give ye yur flipper." But aff she wint down the stares like a shot, and thin I turned round to the little Frinch furrener. Och hon! if it wasn't his spalpeeny little paw that I had hould of in my own—why thin—it wasn't—that's all.

And maybe it wasn't mesilf that jist died then outright wid the laffin', to behold the little chap when he found out that it wasn't the widdy at all at all that he had hould of all the time, but only Sir Pathrick O'Grandison. The ould divil himself niver behild sich a long face as he pet an! As for Sir Pathrick O'Grandison, Barronitt, it wasn't for the likes of his riverence to be afther the minding of a thrifle of a mistake. Ye may jist say though (for it's God's thruth), that afore I left hould of the flipper of the spalpeen (which was not till afther her leddyship's futman had kicked us both down the stares), I gived it such a nate little broth of a squaze, as made it all up into a raspberry jam.

"Wouly-wou," said he, "parley-wou," says he—"Cot tam!"

And that's jist the thruth of the rason why he wears his lift hand in a sling.

THE BUSINESS MAN

First published in *Burton's Gentleman's Magazine*, February 1840, as "Peter Pendulum, the Business Man."

"The Business Man" is a parody of the then popular *Charcoal Sketches* (1838), by Joseph C. Neal (1807–47), which, according to E. A. Duyckinck, dealt with that "peculiar class of citizens falling under the social history description of the genus 'loafer.'" Neal "interpreted their ailments, repeated their slang," and through his "alliterative and extravagant titles" helped take the stories out of their harsh reality, where "it would be painful to . . . laugh at real misery while we may be amused with comic exaggeration." (Cyclopaedia of American Literature, 1855, II; p. 456).

The name "Peter Pendulum" came from sketches by Joseph Dennie in the *Farmer's Museum* (Walpole, N.H., 1795–99), according to Duyckinck (I, p. 562).

1 "Despatch is the soul of business" is from a letter by Lord Chesterfield, February 5, 1750. See also " . . . brevity is the soul of wit," in *Hamlet* (II, ii).

2 II Corinthians 3:6: ". . . not of the letter, but of the spirit," and Romans 7:6: "But now we are delivered from the law, that being dead wherein we were held; that we should serve in newness of spirit, and not in the oldness of the letter."

3 A jack-a-dandy is a pert or conceited person, while a will-o'-the-wisp is an apparition (often glowing marsh gas) that leads a person astray by its fugitive appearance.

4 A scamp or rascal, from the Irish *spailpin*

5 The front part of the head

6 A satirical reference to phrenology. See "Ligeia," notes 10 and 12, and "The Fall of the House of Usher," note 25.

Method is the soul of business.
—*Old Saying*.

1

I am a business man. I am a methodical man. Method is *the* thing, after all. But there are no people I more heartily despise than your eccentric fools who prate about method without understanding it; attending strictly to its letter, and violating **2** its spirit. These fellows are always doing the most out-of-the-way things in what they call an orderly manner. Now here, I conceive, is a positive paradox. True method appertains to the ordinary and the obvious alone, and cannot be applied to the *outré*. What definite idea can a body attach to such expressions as "methodical Jack o' Dandy," or "a systematical **3** Will o' the Wisp?"

My notions upon this head might not have been so clear as they are, but for a fortunate accident which happened to me when I was a very little boy. A good-hearted old Irish nurse (whom I shall not forget in my will) took me up one day by the heels, when I was making more noise than was necessary, and swinging me round two or three times, d—d my eyes for **4** "a skreeking little spalpeen," and then knocked my head into a cocked hat against the bedpost. This, I say, decided my fate, **5** and made my fortune. A bump arose at once on my sinciput, **6** and turned out to be as pretty an organ of *order* as one shall see on a summer's day. Hence that positive appetite for system and regularity which has made me the distinguished man of business that I am.

If there is any thing on earth I hate, it is a genius. Your geniuses are all arrant asses—the greater the genius the greater the ass—and to this rule there is no exception whatever. Especially, you cannot make a man of business out of a genius, any more than money out of a Jew, or the best nutmegs out of pine-knots. The creatures are always going off at a tangent into some fantastic employment, or ridiculous speculation, entirely at variance with the "fitness of things," and having no business whatever to be considered as a business at all. Thus you may tell these characters immediately by the nature of their occupations. If you ever perceive a man setting up as a merchant or a manufacturer; or going into the cotton or tobacco trade, or any of those eccentric pursuits; or getting to be a dry-goods dealer, or soapboiler, or something of that **7** kind; or pretending to be a lawyer, or a blacksmith, or a physician—any thing out of the usual way—you may set him down at once as a genius, and then, according to the rule-of-three, he's an ass.

Now I am not in any respect a genius, but a regular business man. My day-book and ledger will evince this in a minute. **8** They are well kept, though I say it myself; and, in my general habits of accuracy and punctuality, I am not to be beat by a clock. Moreover, my occupations have been always made to chime in with the ordinary habitudes of my fellow-men. Not that I feel the least indebted, upon this score, to my exceedingly weak-minded parents, who, beyond doubt, would have made an arrant genius of me at least, if my guardian angel had not come, in good time, to the rescue. In biography the truth is everything, and in autobiography it is especially so—yet I scarcely hope to be believed when I state, however solemnly, that my poor father put me, when I was about fifteen years of age, into the counting-house of what he termed "a respectable hardware and commission merchant doing a capital bit of business!" A capital bit of fiddlestick! However, the consequence of this folly was, that in two or three days, I had to be sent home to my button-headed family in a high state of fever, and with a most violent and dangerous pain in the sinciput, all round about my organ of order. It was nearly a gone case with me then—just touch-and-go for six weeks—the physicians giving me up and all that sort of thing. But, although I suffered much, I was a thankful boy in the main. I was saved from being a "respectable hardware and commission merchant, doing a capital bit of business," and I felt grateful to the protuberance which had been the means of my salvation, as well as to the kind-hearted female who had originally put these means within my reach.

The most of boys run away from home at ten or twelve years of age, but I waited till I was sixteen. I don't know that I should have gone even then, if I had not happened to hear my old mother talk about setting me up on my own hook in the grocery way. The *grocery* way!—only think of that! I resolved to be off forthwith, and try and establish myself in some *decent* occupation, without dancing attendance any longer upon the caprices of these eccentric old people, and running the risk of being made a genius of in the end. In this project I succeeded perfectly well at the first effort, and by the time I was fairly eighteen, found myself doing an extensive

7 Soap is made by boiling fats and oils in a kettle, then adding alkali and salt.

8 A book in which are recorded the commercial transactions of the day as they occur.

"The Business Man." *Artist unknown*

9 The idea was to have a well-dressed model wear a shop's clothes and encourage prospective customers to look the same by shopping there themselves.

10 A Dr. Kutankumagen appears in Dickens' *Mudfrog Papers* (1838). His specialty is bleeding his patients.

11 Satinet is an imitation satin, woven in silk, or in silk and cotton, while broadcloth is a plain-woven material used mainly in men's suits.

12 The solution to the problem of ring-around-the-collar in 1840 was the disposable paper collar. A Petersham is a heavy overcoat, named after Viscount Petersham.

13 A short-tailed coat

14 The O.E.D. gives the first citation for the word "pants" as 1846—six years after it had appeared here.

9 and profitable business in the Tailor's Walking-Advertisement line.

I was enabled to discharge the onerous duties of this profession, only by that rigid adherence to system which formed the leading feature of my mind. A scrupulous *method* characterized my actions as well as my accounts. In my case, it was method—not money—which made the man—at least all of him that was not made by the tailor whom I served. At nine, every morning, I called upon that individual for the clothes of the day. Ten o'clock found me in some fashionable promenade or other place of public amusement. The precise regularity with which I turned my handsome person about, so as to bring successively into view every portion of the suit upon my back, was the admiration of all the knowing men in the trade. Noon never passed without my bringing home a customer to the house of my employers, Messrs. Cut & **10** Comeagain. I say this proudly, but with tears in my eyes—for the firm proved themselves the basest of ingrates. The little account, about which we quarrelled and finally parted, cannot, in any item, be thought overcharged, by gentlemen really conversant with the nature of the business. Upon this point, however, I feel a degree of proud satisfaction in permitting the reader to judge for himself. My bill ran thus:

Messrs. Cut & Comeagain, Merchant Tailors.

		To Peter Profitt, Walking Advertiser,	Drs.
July 10.		To promenade, as usual, and customer brought home,	$00 25
July 11.		To do do do do	25
July 12.		To one lie, second class; damaged black cloth sold for invisible green,	25
11 July 13.		To one lie, first class, extra quality and size; recommending milled satinet as broadcloth,	75
12 July 20.		To purchasing bran new paper shirt collar or dickey, to set off gray Petersham,	2
13 Aug. 15.		To wearing double-padded bobtail frock (thermometer 70° in the shade),	25
14 Aug. 16.		Standing on one leg three hours, to show off new-style strapped pants at 12½ cents per leg per hour,	37½
Aug. 17.		To promenade, as usual, and large customer brought home (fat man),	50
Aug. 18.		To do do (medium size),	50
Aug. 19.		To do do (small man and bad pay,)	6
			$2 96½

The item chiefly disputed in this bill was the very moderate charge of two pennies for the dickey. Upon my word of honor, this *was not* an unreasonable price for that dickey. It was one of the cleanest and prettiest little dickeys I ever saw; and I have good reason to believe that it effected the sale of three Petershams. The elder partner of the firm, however, would allow me only one penny of the charge, and took it upon himself to show in what manner four of the same-sized conveniences could be got out of a sheet of foolscap. But it is needless to say that I stood upon the *principle* of the thing.

Business is business, and should be done in a business way. There was no *system* whatever in swindling me out of a penny—a clear fraud of fifty per cent.—no *method* in any respect. I left at once the employment of Messrs. Cut & Comeagain, and set up in the Eye-Sore line by myself—one of the most lucrative, respectable, and independent of the ordinary occupations.

My strict integrity, economy, and rigorous business habits, here again came into play. I found myself driving a flourishing trade, and soon became a marked man upon 'Change.' The truth is, I never dabbled in flashy matters, but jogged on in the good old sober routine of the calling—a calling in which I should, no doubt, have remained to the present hour, but for a little accident which happened to me in the prosecution of one of the usual business operations of the profession. Whenever a rich old hunks, or prodigal heir, or bankrupt **15** corporation gets into the notion of putting up a palace, there is no such thing in the world as stopping either of them, and this every intelligent person knows. The fact in question is indeed the basis of the Eye-Sore trade. As soon, therefore, as a building project is fairly afoot by one of these parties, we merchants secure a nice corner of the lot in contemplation, or a prime little situation just adjoining, or right in front. This done we wait until the palace is halfway up, and then we pay some tasty architect to run us up an ornamental mud hovel, right against it; or a Down-East or Dutch pagoda, or a pig-sty, **16** or an ingenious little bit of fancy work, either Esquimau, Kickapoo, or Hottentot. Of course we can't afford to take these structures down under a bonus of five hundred per cent. upon the prime cost of our lot and plaster. *Can* we? I ask the question. I ask it of business men. It would be irrational to suppose that we can. And yet there was a rascally corporation which asked me to do this very thing—this *very thing!* I did not reply to their absurd proposition, of course; but I felt it a duty to go that same night, and lamp-black the whole of **17** their palace. For this the unreasonable villains clapped me into jail; and the gentlemen of the Eye-Sore trade could not well avoid cutting my connection when I came out.

The Assault-and-Battery business, into which I was now **18** forced to adventure for a livelihood, was somewhat ill-adapted to the delicate nature of my constitution; but I went to work in it with a good heart, and found my account here, as heretofore, in those stern habits of methodical accuracy which had been thumped into me by that delightful old nurse—I would indeed be the basest of men not to remember her well in my will. By observing, as I say, the strictest system in all my dealings, and keeping a well-regulated set of books, I was enabled to get over many serious difficulties, and, in the end, to establish myself very decently in the profession. The truth is, that few individuals, in any line, did a snugger little business than I. I will just copy a page or so out of my day-book; and this will save me the necessity of blowing my own trumpet—a contemptible practice of which no high-minded man will be guilty. Now, the day-book is a thing that don't lie.

15 A surly, crusty old man

16 "Down-East" means the seacoast of New England, particularly Maine. "Dutch" may refer to New York. "Pagoda" here means a temple or decorative structure.

17 The carbon deposit on the inside of a lantern chimney, often used as a black pigment

18 A protection racket. One sells "protection," but all the money buys is protection from the seller.

"Jan. 1.—New-Year's-Day. Met Snap in the street, groggy. Mem—he'll do. Met Gruff shortly afterward, blind drunk. Mem—he'll answer too. Entered both gentlemen in my ledger, and opened a running account with each.

"Jan. 2.—Saw Snap at the Exchange, and went up and trod on his toe. Doubled his fist and knocked me down. Good!—got up again. Some trifling difficulty with Bag, my attorney. I want the damages at a thousand, but he says that for so simple a knock-down we can't lay them at more than five hundred. Mem—must get rid of Bag—no *system* at all.

"Jan. 3.—Went to the theatre, to look for Gruff. Saw him sitting in a side box, in the second tier, between a fat lady and a lean one. Quizzed the whole party through an opera-glass, till I saw the fat lady blush and whisper to G. Went round, then, into the box, and put my nose within reach of his hand. Wouldn't pull it—no go. Blew it, and tried again—no go. Sat down then, and winked at the lean lady, when I had the high satisfaction of finding him lift me up by the nape of the neck, and fling me over into the pit. Neck dislocated, and right leg capitally splintered, Went home in high glee, drank a bottle of champagne, and booked the young man for five thousand. Bag says it'll do.

"Feb. 15.—Compromised the case of Mr. Snap. Amount entered in journal—fifty cents—which see.

"Feb. 16.—Cast by that ruffian, Gruff, who made me a present of five dollars. Costs of suit, four dollars and twenty-five cents. Net profit,—see journal,—seventy-five cents."

Now, here is a clear gain, in a very brief period, of no less than one dollar and twenty-five cents—this is in the mere cases of Snap and Gruff; and I solemnly assure the reader that these extracts are taken at random from my Day-Book.

It's an old saying, and a true one, however, that money is **19** nothing in comparison with health. I found the exactions of the profession somewhat too much for my delicate state of body; and, discovering, at last, that I was knocked all out of shape, so that I didn't know very well what to make of the matter, and so that my friends, when they met me in the street, couldn't tell that I was Peter Proffit at all, it occurred to me that the best expedient I could adopt, was to alter my line of business. I turned my attention, therefore, to Mud-**20** Dabbling, and continued it for some years.

The worst of this occupation is that too many people take a fancy to it, and the competition is in consequence excessive. Every ignoramus of a fellow who finds that he hasn't brains in sufficient quantity to make his way as a walking advertiser, **21** or an eye-sore prig, or a salt-and-batter man, thinks, of course, that he'll answer very well as a dabbler of mud. But there never was entertained a more erroneous idea than that it requires no brains to mud-dabble. Especially, there is nothing to be made in this way without *method*. I did only a retail business myself, but my old habits of *system* carried me swimmingly along. I selected my street-crossing, in the first place, with great deliberation, and I never put down a broom in any part of the town *but that*. I took care, too, to have a

19 "Look to your health; and if you have it, praise God, and value it next to a good conscience; for health is the second blessing that we mortals are capable of; a blessing that money cannot buy" (Izaak Walton (1593–1683), *The Compleat Angler*, Chapter 21).

20 Another sort of protection racket

21 A "walking advertiser" is a sandwich-board man or a leaflet distributor. An "eye-sore prig" is explained in the text, but "prig" often meant a thief. "Salt-and-batter" means assault and battery.

nice little puddle at hand, which I could get at in a minute. By these means I got to be well known as a man to be trusted; and this is one-half the battle, let me tell you, in trade. Nobody ever failed to pitch *me* a copper, and got over *my* crossing with a clean pair of pantaloons. And, as my business habits, in this respect, were sufficiently understood, I never met with any attempt at imposition. I wouldn't have put up with it, if I had. Never imposing upon any one myself, I suffered no one to play the possum with me. The frauds of the banks of course I couldn't help. Their suspension put me to **22** ruinous inconvenience. These, however, are not individuals, but corporations; and corporations, it is very well known, have neither bodies to be kicked nor souls to be damned.

I was making money at this business when, in an evil moment, I was induced to merge in the Cur-Spattering—a **23** somewhat analogous, but, by no means, so respectable a profession. My location, to be sure, was an excellent one, being central, and I had capital blacking and brushes. My little dog, too, was quite fat and up to all varieties of snuff. He had been in the trade a long time, and, I may say, understood it. Our general routine was this;—Pompey, having rolled **24** himself well in the mud, sat upon end at the shop door, until he observed a dandy approaching in bright boots. He then proceeded to meet him, and gave the Wellingtons a rub or **25** two with his wool. Then the dandy swore very much, and looked about for a bootblack. There I was, full in his view, with blacking and brushes. It was only a minute's work, and then came a sixpence. This did moderately well for a time;—in fact, I was not avaricious, but my dog was. I allowed him a third of the profit, but he was advised to insist upon half. This I couldn't stand—so we quarrelled and parted.

I next tried my hand at the Organ-Grinding for a while, and may say that I made out pretty well. It is a plain, straightforward business, and requires no particular abilities. You can get a music-mill for a mere song, and to put it in order, you have but to open the works, and give them three or four smart raps with a hammer. It improves the tone of the thing, for business purposes, more than you can imagine. This done, you have only to stroll along, with the mill on your back, until you see tanbark in the street, and a knocker wrapped up in buckskin. **26,27** Then you stop and grind; looking as if you meant to stop and grind till doomsday. Presently a window opens, and somebody pitches you a sixpence, with a request to "Hush up and go on," &c. I am aware that some grinders have actually afforded to "go on" for this sum; but for my part, I found the necessary outlay of capital too great to permit of my "going on" under a shilling.

At this occupation I did a good deal; but, somehow, I was not quite satisfied, and so finally abandoned it. The truth is, I labored under the disadvantage of having no monkey—and American streets are *so* muddy, and a Democratic rabble is *so* obtrusive, and so full of demnition mischievous little boys.

I was now out of employment for some months, but at length succeeded, by dint of great interest, in procuring a

22 There were many bank closings in Jackson's and Van Buren's terms as President.

23 Actually, its the cur that does the spattering.

24 Pompey is the name of a black servant in "The Man That Was Used Up" and "A Predicament."

25 High boots covering the knees in front and cut away behind; named after the Duke of Wellington (1769–1852), who defeated Napoleon at Waterloo.

26 Tanbark was sometimes used to cover a dirt street in order to keep down dust and noise.

27 Apparently to keep the occupants from being disturbed because of illness or death

28 Postage stamps were not used in the United States until 1847, and there was no city delivery of mail until 1867, so that one paid a fee to have a letter delivered by a private firm. Such swindles can be found in an article in the *Saturday Evening Post*, November 12, 1842, and since this section of the tale does not appear in the 1840 version, Poe very likely read it there.

29 Bengal is the region on the Bay of Bengal, today divided between India and Bangladesh. Botany Bay is the name of an Australian bay, but also of that country's first penal colony (whose actual site was nearby Sydney Harbor).

30 There is a great deal of wordplay going on in this paragraph. First, the word "cat" in early-nineteenth-century America meant a harlot. A cathead is the projecting beam of a ship (used in raising the anchor) and because of this became a sailor's term for a woman's breasts. "Tail" was a term for a woman's sexual parts, but also for the posterior, and sailors called the inner end of the beam mentioned above a "cat's tail."

The double meaning here allows Poe to get away with the indecent connotation, which, he could say, was only in the mind of the reader.

31 *Nemine contradicente*—without opposition

32 Genesis 1:22. God later gives the same encouragement to man in Genesis 1:28.

33 An unguent for the hair, heavily advertised at the time by its maker, Rowland & Son, and supposedly made from ingredients from Macassar, in present-day Indonesia.

34 The seat of many elegant homes in the nineteenth century, including that of Washington Irving. See "The Domain of Arnheim."

28 situation in the Sham-Post. The duties, here, are simple, and not altogether unprofitable. For example:—very early in the morning I had to make up my packet of sham letters. Upon the inside of each of these I had to scrawl a few lines—on any subject which occurred to me as sufficiently mysterious— signing all the epistles Tom Dobson, or Bobby Tompkins, or anything in that way. Having folded and sealed all, and **29** stamped them with sham postmarks—New Orleans, Bengal, Botany Bay, or any other place a great way off—I set out, forthwith, upon my daily route, as if in a very great hurry. I always called at the big houses to deliver the letters, and receive the postage. Nobody hesitates at paying for a letter— especially for a double one—people are *such* fools—and it was no trouble to get round a corner before there was time to open the epistles. The worst of this profession was, that I had to walk so much and so fast; and so frequently to vary my route. Besides, I had serious scruples of conscience. I can't bear to hear innocent individuals abused—and the way the whole town took to cursing Tom Dobson and Bobby Tompkins was really awful to hear. I washed my hands of the matter in disgust.

My eighth and last speculation has been in the Cat-Growing way. I have found this a most pleasant and lucrative business, and, really, no trouble at all. The country, it is well known, has become infested with cats—so much so of late, that a petition for relief, most numerously and respectably signed, was brought before the Legislature at its late memorable session. The Assembly, at this epoch, was unusually well-informed, and, having passed many other wise and wholesome enactments, it crowned all with the Cat-Act. In its original form, this law offered a premium for cat-*heads* (four-pence a-piece), but the Senate succeeded in amending the main **30** clause, so as to substitute the word "*tails*" for "heads." This amendment was so obviously proper, that the House concurred **31** in it *nem. con.*

As soon as the governor had signed the bill, I invested my whole estate in the purchase of Toms and Tabbies. At first I could only afford to feed them upon mice (which are cheap), **32** but they fulfilled the scriptural injunction at so marvellous a rate, that I at length considered it my best policy to be liberal, and so indulged them in oysters and turtle. Their tails, at a legislative price, now bring me in a good income; for I have **33** discovered a way, in which, by means of Macassar oil, I can force three crops in a year. It delights me to find, too, that the animals soon get accustomed to the thing, and would rather have the appendages cut off than otherwise. I consider, myself, therefore, a made man, and am bargaining for a country seat **34** on the Hudson.

NEVER BET THE DEVIL YOUR HEAD

A TALE WITH A MORAL

First published in *Graham's Magazine*, September 1841, this is one of the more blatant examples we have of Poe's theory of humor as "the witty exaggerated into the burlesque." It seems to be a satire on literary pedanticism, transcendentalism, and in particular the transcendentalist magazine *The Dial*, although Poe denies this in a letter, saying instead that "The tale in question is a mere Extravaganza levelled at no one in particular, but hitting right and left at things in general" (September 19, 1841). One would think Poe would rather admit to aiming *squarely* at a target.

The climax of the tale has a parallel in Chapter two of *The Posthumous Papers of the Pickwick Club*, where Pickwick and his friends are warned of a low archway as they ride in a coach: "Terrible place—dangerous work; other day, five children—mother—tall lady, eating sandwiches—forgot the arch—crash, knock—children look round, mother's head off . . . head of a family off; shocking, shocking." Poe reviewed Dickens' book in the *Southern Literary Messenger*, November 1836.

As "Toby Dammit," the table is incorporated into the film *Tales of Mystery and Imagination* (1968); the sequence was directed by Federico Fellini.

"Con tal que las costumbres de un autor," says Don Thomas De Las Torres, in the preface to his "Amatory Poems," *"sean puras y castas, importa muy poco que no sean igualmente severas sus obras"*—meaning, in plain English, that, provided the morals of an author are pure, personally, it signifies nothing what are the morals of his books. We presume that **1** Don Thomas is now in Purgatory for the assertion. It would be a clever thing, too, in the way of poetical justice, to keep him there until his "Amatory Poems" get out of print, or are laid definitely upon the shelf through lack of readers. Every fiction *should have* a moral; and what is more to the purpose, the critics have discovered that every fiction *has*. Philip **2** Melancthon, some time ago, wrote a commentary upon the "Batrachomyomachia," and proved that the poet's object was to excite a distaste for sedition. Pierre La Seine, going a step **3** farther, shows that the intention was to recommend to young men temperance in eating and drinking. Just so, too, Jacobus **4** Hugo has satisfied himself that, by Euenis, Homer meant to insinuate John Calvin; by Antinöus, Martin Luther; by the Lotophagi, Protestants in general; and, by the Harpies, the Dutch. Our more modern Scholiasts are equally acute. These **5,6** fellows demonstrate a hidden meaning in "The Antediluvians," a parable in "Powhatan," new views in "Cock Robin," and transcendentalism in "Hop O' My Thumb." In short, it has **7** been shown that no man can sit down to write without a very

1 "As long as the habits of an author are pure and chaste, it matters very little if his works are less austere," from *Cuentos en verso castellano* (1828), by Tomás Hermenegildo de las Torres. Poe quotes it again in "Fifty Suggestions," XIX, adding, "For so unprincipled an idea, Don Tomas, no doubt, is still having a hard time of it in Purgatory; and, by way of most pointedly manifesting their disgust at his philosophy on the topic in question, many modern theologians and divines are now busily swearing their conduct by his proposition exactly *conversal*."

2 Just as Poe spoofs contemporary literature in the subtitle of his tale, which may or may not have a moral, here he satirizes those critics who claim to see a moral as the end-all of all literary creations. For Poe, didacticism was the archenemy of imagination.

He also lambastes the practice of reading into a work all manner of interpretations, depending on the reader's bias or interest. Perhaps we would do well to heed Poe's message.

3 "Philip Melanchthon wrote a commentary on the Battle of the Frogs and Mice, and conceived the scope of the poet to have been to excite a hatred of tumults and seditions in the minds of the readers" (H. N. Colerdige, *Introductions to the Study of the Classic Poets*, 1831; p. 189n.). Philip Melanchthon (1497–1560) was second only to Luther as a scholar and humanist during the Reformation.

4 "Pierre la Seine thought the object was to recommend to young men temperance in eating and drinking;—

407

Why, I do not find written" (from H. N. Coleridge; see note 3).

5 "Jacobus Hugo was of opinion that Homer under divine influence prophesized the destruction of Jerusalem under that of Troy; the life, miracles and passion of our Savior, and the history of the Church under the Emperors in the Iliad. He thinks Homer secretly meant the Dutch by the Harpies, John Calvin by *Euenis*, Martin Luther by Antinous . . . and the Lutherans generally by the Lotophagi." (Coleridge, p. 89n.)

Euenis is probably Eumaios, the swineherd whom Odysseus visits in the guise of a beggar; he is compared to John Calvin (1509–64), French Protestant theologian. Antinoüs was the son of Eupeithes; he was the most brutal and arrogant of Penelope's suitors and the first to be killed by Odysseus on his return to Ithaca. The Lotophagi are the lotus eaters of North Africa, visited by Odysseus on his return from Troy. Eating their food made people lose any desire to leave. The Harpies were ugly, birdlike monsters, with large claws, which stank and were perpetually hungry. Jacobus Hugo (Jacques Hugues) is best known for his *True History of Rome* (1655).

6 Those who write explanatory notes on authors or works

7 *The Antediluvians, or The World Destroyed,* by Dr. James McHenry (1785–1845), a narrative poem in ten books, published in 1839–40. McHenry was also a critic who came down hard on Bryant and Willis, as well as American literature in general. The resulting uproar was squelched by Willis Gaylord Clark in 1834, in an article effectively destroying McHenry's critical position.

Powhatan: A Metrical Romance is by Seba Smith (1792–1868), a teacher, editor, humorist, poet, and teller of folktales (often under the name of Major Jack Downing). His *Powhatan* got a negative review from Poe in the July 1841 *Graham's.*

"Cock Robin" and "Hop O' My Thumb,' of course, are children's stories.

8 *The Dial,* in Poe's time, was the organ of the transcendentalist movement. (see "How to Write a Blackwood Article," note 31 and 33).

The "Down-Easter" is an imaginary publication. In New England parlance, "Down-East" means the Atlantic seaboard.

9 While "ignoramus" means an ignorant person in current usage, the Latin word originally meant "we do not know," or "we take no notice," and was the endorsement made by a grand jury upon a bill or indictment presented to them when they considered the evidence for the prosecution insufficient to warrant the case going to a petit jury. The word then came to mean admitting ignorance of the point in question, and finally the modern meaning by about 1616.

10 This imaginary title appears again in "The Literary Life of Thingum Bob, Esq." and in the essay "Autography."

11 Jean de La Fontaine (1621–95), French poet, author of the celebrated *Fables,* which were drawn largely from Aesop.

12 Originally the last part of a bolt of cloth that hangs loose, "fag end" came to mean the last part or remnant of anything, after the best has been used.

profound design. Thus to authors in general much trouble is spared. A novelist, for example, need have no care of his moral. It is there—that is to say, it is somewhere—and the moral and the critics can take care of themselves. When the proper time arrives, all that the gentleman intended, and all that he did not intend, will be brought to light, in the *Dial,* **8** or the *Down-Easter,* together with all that he ought to have intended, and the rest that he clearly meant to intend:—so that it will all come very straight in the end.

There is no just ground, therefore, for the charge brought **9** against me by certain ignoramuses—that I have never written a moral tale, or, in more precise words, a tale with a moral. They are not the critics predestined to bring me out, and *develop* my morals:—that is the secret. By and by the *North* **10** *American Quarterly Humdrum* will make them ashamed of their stupidity. In the meantime, by way of staying execution— by way of mitigating the accusations against me—I offer the sad history appended,—a history about whose obvious moral there can be no question whatever, since he who runs may read it in the large capitals which form the title of the tale. I should have credit for this arrangement—a far wiser one than **11** that of La Fontaine and others, who reserve the impression to be conveyed until the last moment, and thus sneak it in at **12** the fag end of their fables.

Defuncti injuriâ ne afficiantur was a law of the twelve tables, and *De mortuis nil nisi bonum* is an excellent injunc- **13** tion—even if the dead in question be nothing but dead small beer. It is not my design, therefore, to vituperate my deceased **14** friend, Toby Dammit. He was a sad dog, it is true, and a dog's death it was that he died; but he himself was not to blame for his vices. They grew out of a personal defect in his mother. She did her best in the way of flogging him while an infant— for duties to her well-regulated mind were always pleasures, and babies like tough steaks, or the modern Greek olive trees, **15** are invariably the better for beating—but, poor woman! she had the misfortune to be left-handed, and a child flogged left-handedly had better be left unflogged. The world revolves from right to left. It will not do to whip a baby from left to right. If each blow in the proper direction drives an evil propensity out, it follows that every thump in an opposite one knocks its quota of wickedness in. I was often present at Toby's chastisements, and, even by the way in which he kicked, I could perceive that he was getting worse and worse every day. At last I saw, through the tears in my eyes, that there was no hope of the villain at all, and one day when he had been cuffed until he grew so black in the face that one might have mistaken him for a little African, and no effect had been produced beyond that of making him wriggle himself into a fit, I could stand it no longer, but went down upon my knees forthwith, and, uplifting my voice, made prophecy of his ruin.

The fact is that his precocity in vice was awful. At five months of age he used to get into such passions that he was unable to articulate. At six months, I caught him gnawing a pack of cards. At seven months he was in the constant habit of catching and kissing the female babies. At eight months he peremptorily refused to put his signature to the Temperance pledge. Thus he went on increasing in iniquity, month after month, until, at the close of the first year, he not only insisted upon wearing *moustaches*, but had contracted a propensity for cursing and swearing, and for backing his assertions by bets.

Through this latter most ungentlemanly practice, the ruin which I had predicted to Toby Dammit overtook him at last. The fashion had "grown with his growth and strengthened with his strength," so that, when he came to be a man, he **16** could scarcely utter a sentence without interlarding it with a proposition to gamble. Not that he actually *laid* wagers—no. I will do my friend the justice to say that he would as soon have laid eggs. With him the thing was a mere formula— nothing more. His expressions on this head had no meaning attached to them whatever. They were simple if not altogether innocent expletives—imaginative phrases wherewith to round off a sentence. When he said "I'll bet you so and so," nobody ever thought of taking him up; but still I could not help thinking it my duty to put him down. The habit was an immoral one, and so I told him. It was a vulgar one—this I begged him to believe. It was discountenanced by society— here I said nothing but the truth. It was forbidden by act of Congress—here I had not the slightest intention of telling a lie. I remonstrated—but to no purpose. I demonstrated—in vain. I entreated—he smiled. I implored—he laughed. I preached—he sneered. I threatened—he swore. I kicked him—he called for the police. I pulled his nose—he blew it, and offered to bet the Devil his head that I would not venture to try that experiment again.

Poverty was another vice which the peculiar physical deficiency of Dammit's mother had entailed upon her son. He was detestably poor; and this was the reason, no doubt, that his expletive expressions about betting seldom took a pecuniary turn. I will not be bound to say that I ever heard him make use of such a figure of speech as "I'll bet you a dollar." It was usually "I'll bet you what you please," or "I'll bet you what you dare," or "I'll bet you a trifle," or else, more significantly still, *"I'll bet the Devil my head."* **17**

This latter form seemed to please him best:—perhaps because it involved the least risk; for Dammit had become excessively parsimonious. Had any one taken him up, his head was small, and thus his loss would have been small too. But these are my own reflections, and I am by no means sure that I am right in attributing them to him. At all events the phrase in question grew daily in favor, notwithstanding the gross impropriety of a man betting his brains like bank-notes:—but this was a point which my friend's perversity of disposition would not permit him to comprehend. In the end, he abandoned all other forms of wager, and gave himself up to *"I'll bet the Devil my head,"* with a pertinacity and exclusiveness of devotion that displeased not less than it surprised me. I am always displeased by circumstances for which I cannot

13 "Let the dead suffer no injury" does not appear in the twelve tables of early Roman law; its origin is unknown. To speak "nothing but good of the dead" is from Chilo, a Greek philosopher mentioned in *Lives of the Philosophers*, I, "Chilo," 2, by Diogenes Laërtius; it appears in Plutarch as one of the laws of Solon (*Lives*, Solon, Sec. 21).

In "Fifty Suggestions," IX, Poe writes, "The injunction *not to do ill* to the dead—seems, at a first glance, scarcely susceptible of improvement in the delicate respect of its terms," but later mentions James Puckle's maxim *"When speaking of the dead . . . so fold up your discourse that their virtues may be outwardly shown, while their vices are wrapped up in silence."*

14 The name, as one might expect, is a play on words. "Toby" was a term for the posterior. "Toby Dammit" may also be a play on "to be damnéd."

15 "Children are never too tender to be whipped:—like tough beef-steaks, the more you beat them the more tender they become ("Fifty Suggestions," XX).

"Some schoolmasters seem to think of their pupils as the modern Greeks do of their olive trees, that the more they are beaten the more they thrive" ("Sweepings from a Drawer," by William Landor, *Burton's*, November 1839).

16 Adapted from Pope's *Essay on Man*, II, 136, this appears also in "The Black Cat."

17 A reference to trafficking with the Devil for one's soul

18 Poe critizes these men for engaging in obscurantism, a charge that critic Yvor Winters has leveled against Poe in "Edgar Allan Poe: a Crisis in the History of American Obscurantism," *American Literature*, January 1937.

19 ". . . it is only as the politician is about being 'turned out' that —like the snake of the Irish Chronicle when touched by St. Patrick—he 'awakens to a sense of his *situation*'" ("Fifty Suggestions," XII).

account. Mysteries force a man to think, and so injure his health. The truth is, there was something in *the air* with which Mr. Dammit was wont to give utterance to his offensive expression—something in his *manner* of enunciation—which at first interested, and afterward made me very uneasy— something which, for want of a more definite term at present, I must be permitted to call *queer;* but which Mr. Coleridge would have called mystical, Mr. Kant pantheistical, Mr. **18** Carlyle twistical, and Mr. Emerson hyperquizzitistical. I began not to like it at all. Mr. Dammit's soul was in a perilous state. I resolved to bring all my eloquence into play to save it. I vowed to serve him as St. Patrick, in the Irish chronicle, is said to have served the toad,—that is to say, "awaken him **19** to a sense of his situation." I addressed myself to the task forthwith. Once more I betook myself to remonstrance. Again I collected my energies for a final attempt at expostulation.

When I had made an end of my lecture, Mr. Dammit indulged himself in some very equivocal behavior. For some moments he remained silent, merely looking me inquisitively in the face. But presently he threw his head to one side, and elevated his eyebrows to a great extent. Then he spread out the palms of his hands and shrugged up his shoulders. Then he winked with the right eye. Then he repeated the operation with the left. Then he shut them both up very tight. Then he opened them both so very wide that I became seriously alarmed for the consequences. Then, applying his thumb to his nose, he thought proper to make an indescribable movement with the rest of his fingers. Finally, setting his arms a-kimbo, he condescended to reply.

I can call to mind only the heads of his discourse. He would be obliged to me if I would hold my tongue. He wished none of my advice. He despised all my insinuations. He was old enough to take care of himself. Did I still think him baby Dammit? Did I mean to say anything against his character? Did I intend to insult him? Was I a fool? Was my maternal parent aware, in a word, of my absence from the domiciliary residence? He would put this latter question to me as to a man of veracity, and he would bind himself to abide by my reply. Once more he would demand explicitly if my mother knew that I was out. My confusion, he said, betrayed me, and he would be willing to bet the Devil his head that she did not.

Mr. Dammit did not pause for my rejoinder. Turning upon his heel he left my presence with undignified precipitation. It was well for him that he did so. My feelings had been wounded. Even my anger had been aroused. For once I would have taken him up upon his insulting wager. I would have won for the Arch-Enemy Mr. Dammit's little head—for the fact is, my mamma *was* very well aware of my merely temporary absence from home.

But *Khoda shefa midêhed*—Heaven gives relief—as the Mussulmen say when you tread upon their toes. It was in pursuance of my duty that I had been insulted, and I bore the insult like a man. It now seemed to me, however, that I had done all that could be required of me, in the case of this miserable individual, and I resolved to trouble him no longer with my counsel, but to leave him to his conscience and himself. But although I forbore to intrude with my advice, I would not bring myself to give up his society altogether. I even went so far as to humor some of his less reprehensible propensities; and there were times when I found myself lauding his wicked jokes, as epicures do mustard, with tears in my eyes:—so profoundly did it grieve me to hear his evil talk.

One fine day, having strolled out together, arm in arm, our route led us in the direction of a river. There was a bridge, and we resolved to cross it. It was roofed over, by way of protection from the weather, and the archway, having but few windows, was thus very uncomfortably dark. As we entered the passage, the contrast between the external glare and the interior gloom struck heavily upon my spirits. Not so upon those of the unhappy Dammit, who offered to bet the Devil his head that I was hipped.**20** He seemed to be in an unusual good humor. He was excessively lively—so much so that I entertained I know not what of uneasy suspicion. It is not impossible that he was affected with the transcendentals. I am not well enough versed, however, in the diagnosis of this disease to speak with decision upon the point; and unhappily there were none of my friends of the *Dial* present. I suggest the idea, nevertheless, because of a certain species of austere Merry-Andrewism**21** which seemed to beset my poor friend, and caused him to make quite a Tom-Fool of himself.**22** Nothing would serve him but wriggling and skipping about under and over everything that came in his way; now shouting out, and now lisping out,**23** all manner of odd little and big words, yet preserving the gravest face in the world all the time. I really could not make up my mind whether to kick or to pity him. At length, having passed nearly across the bridge, we approached the termination of the footway, when our progress was impeded by a turnstile of some height. Through this I made my way quietly, pushing it around as usual. But this turn would not serve the turn of Mr. Dammit. He insisted upon leaping the stile, and said he could cut a pigeon-wing**24** over it in the air. Now this, conscientiously speaking, I did not think he could do. The best pigeon-winger over all kinds of style was my friend Mr. Carlyle, and as I knew *he* could not do it, I would not believe that it could be done by Toby Dammit. I therefore told him, in so many words, that he was a braggadocio,**25** and could not do what he said. For this I had reason to be sorry afterward;—for he straightway offered to *bet the Devil his head* that he could.

I was about to reply, notwithstanding my previous resolutions, with some remonstrance against his impiety, when I heard, close at my elbow, a slight cough, which sounded very much like the ejaculation "*ahem!*" I started, and looked about me in surprise. My glance at length fell into a nook of the framework of the bridge, and upon the figure of a little lame old gentleman of venerable aspect. Nothing could be more reverend than his whole appearance; for he not only had on

20 Depressed, affected with hypochondria (as Roderick Usher is)

21 The origin of "Merry Andrew" is in doubt, but it means a clown or buffoon. A 1958 Danny Kaye film bears this title.

22 A buffoon or clown, but also a mentally deficient person or halfwit.

23 "Imperfect utterance" [O.E.D.]

24 A fancy dance step or figure in skating. For Carlyle, see "The Literary Life of Thingum Bob, Esq.," note 46.

25 An empty, idle boaster. The word is pure English, based on an Italian model.

26 A portrait of poetaster Robert Montgomery (1807–55) made him look "like a hero of a French cookery-book—with his hair parted in the middle like a girl's, and tumbled up in huge masses at the temples," according to critic John Neal in the December 1829 edition of the *Yankee*.

A drawing of the poet by Daniel Maclise is labeled "the author of Satan," because Montgomery's poem *Satan, or Intellect Without God* (1830) was his most popular work. Macaulay called Montgomery the author of "some volumes of detestable verses on religious subjects, which by mere puffing in magazines and newspapers have had an immense sale" (Dictionary of National Biography, Oxford Press, 1922).

27 James Russell Lowell satirized Poe in the same way in *A Fable for Critics* (1848): "There comes Poe, with his raven, like Barnaby Rudge,/Three-fifths of him genius and two-fifths sheer fudge."

28 Named after General Henri Joseph Paixhans (1783–1854), who designed a gun for throwing explosive shells.

29 Rufus Griswold's *Poets and Poetry of America* (1842) was called "The Big Book" because of its unwieldy size.

30 Indeed.

a full suit of black, but his shirt was perfectly clean and the collar turned very neatly down over a white cravat, while his hair was parted in front like a girl's. His hands were clasped pensively together over his stomach, and his two eyes were **26** carefully rolled up into the top of his head.

Upon observing him more closely, I perceived that he wore a black silk apron over his small-clothes; and this was a thing which I thought very odd. Before I had time to make any remark, however, upon so singular a circumstance, he interrupted me with a second "*ahem!*"

To this observation I was not immediately prepared to reply. The fact is, remarks of this laconic nature are nearly unanswerable. I have known a Quarterly Review *non-plused* **27** by the word "*Fudge!*" I am not ashamed to say, therefore, that I turned to Mr. Dammit for assistance.

"Dammit," said I, "what are you about? don't you hear?—the gentleman says '*ahem!*'" I looked sternly at my friend while I thus addressed him; for, to say the truth, I felt particularly puzzled, and when a man is particularly puzzled he must knit his brows and look savage, or else he is pretty sure to look like a fool.

"Dammit," observed I—although this sounded very much like an oath, than which nothing was further from my thoughts—"Dammit," I suggested—"the gentleman says '*ahem!*'"

I do not attempt to defend my remark on the score of profundity; I did not think it profound myself; but I have noticed that the effect of our speeches is not always proportionate with their importance in our own eyes; and if I had **28** shot Mr. D. through and through with a Paixhan bomb, or knocked him on the head with the "Poets and Poetry of **29** America," he could hardly have been more discomfited than when I addressed him with those simple words—"Dammit, what are you about?—don't you hear?—the gentleman says '*ahem!*'"

"You don't say so?" gasped he at length, after turning more colors than a pirate runs up, one after the other, when chased by a man-of-war. "Are you quite sure he said *that?* Well, at all events I am in for it now, and may as well put a bold face upon the matter. Here goes, then—*ahem!*"

At this the little old gentleman seemed pleased—God only **30** knows why. He left his station at the nook of the bridge, limped forward with a gracious air, took Dammit by the hand and shook it cordially, looking all the while straight up in his face with an air of the most unadulterated benignity which it is possible for the mind of man to imagine.

"I am quite sure you will win it, Dammit," said he, with the frankest of all smiles, "but we are obliged to have a trial, you know, for the sake of mere form."

"Ahem!" replied my friend, taking off his coat, with a deep sigh, tying a pocket-handkerchief around his waist, and producing an unaccountable alteration in his countenance by twisting up his eyes and bringing down the corners of his mouth—"ahem!" And "ahem!" said he again, after a pause; and not another word more than "ahem!" did I ever know him to say after that. "Aha!" thought I, without expressing myself aloud—"this is quite a remarkable silence on the part of Toby Dammit, and is no doubt a consequence of his verbosity upon a previous occasion. One extreme induces another. I wonder if he has forgotten the many unanswerable questions which he propounded to me so fluently on the day when I gave him my last lecture? At all events, he is cured of the transcendentals." **31**

"Ahem!" here replied Toby, just as if he had been reading my thoughts, and looking like a very old sheep in a reverie.

The old gentleman now took him by the arm, and led him more into the shade of the bridge—a few paces back from the turnstile. "My good fellow," said he, "I make it a point of conscience to allow you this much run. Wait here, till I take my place by the stile, so that I may see whether you go over it handsomely, and transcendentally, and don't omit any flourishes of the pigeon-wing. A mere form, you know. I will say 'one, two, three, and away.' Mind you start at the word 'away.' " Here he took his position by the stile, paused a moment as if in profound reflection, then *looked up* and, I thought, smiled very slightly, then tightened the strings of his apron, then took a long look at Dammit, and finally gave the word as agreed upon—

One—two—three—and away!

Punctually at the word "away," my poor friend set off in a strong gallop. The style was not very high, like Mr. Lord's—nor yet very low, like that of Mr. Lord's reviewers, but upon the whole I made sure that he would clear it. And then what **32** if he did not?—ah, that was the question—what if he did not? "What right," said I, "had the old gentleman to make any other gentleman jump? The little old dot-and-carry-one! who **33** is *he*? If he asks *me* to jump, I won't do it, that's flat, and I don't care who *the devil he is*." The bridge, as I say, was arched and covered in, in a very ridiculous manner, and there was a most uncomfortable echo about it at all times—an echo which I never before so particularly observed as when I uttered the four last words of my remark.

But what I said, or what I thought, or what I heard, occupied only an instant. In less than five seconds from his starting, my poor Toby had taken the leap. I saw him run nimbly, and spring grandly from the floor of the bridge, cutting the most awful flourishes with his legs as he went up. I saw him high in the air, pigeon-winging it to admiration just over the top of the stile; and of course I thought it an unusually singular thing that he did not *continue* to go over. But the whole leap was the affair of a moment, and, before I had a chance to make any profound reflections, down came Mr. Dammit on the flat of his back, on the same side of the stile from which he had started. At the same instant I saw the old gentleman limping off at the top of his speed, having caught and wrapped up in his apron something that fell heavily into it from the darkness of the arch just over the turnstile. At all this I was much astonished; but I had no leisure to think, for Mr. Dammit lay particularly still, and I concluded that his

31 Poe turns the word into a kind of disease.

32 Willam Wilberforce Lord (1819–1907), clergyman and poet, was hailed as "The American Milton" when he published his *Poems* in 1845, in spite of a devastatingly negative review by Poe, who was infuriated by Lord's burlesque of *The Raven*.

33 "Dot-and-carry" refers to a person with a wooden, shorter, or lame leg.

34 Homeopathy is a system of medicine whose fundamental principle is the law of similars—that like is cured by like. It was first given practical application by Samuel Hahnemann, of Leipzig, Germany, at the start of the nineteenth century. When a drug was shown to produce the same symptoms as did a certain disease, it was then used in small doses to treat that disease. Schools of homeopathic medicine are recognized in both the United States and Europe.

35 *Ouch!* A "bar sinister" is actually a sign of illegitimacy on a family coat of arms, here given a punning from which it may never recover.

36 The rather startling ending is somewhat crude for Poe but looks ahead to the even more startling humor of Ambrose Bierce (1842–1914?), who pushed Poe's subject matter and style even farther into the bizarre and grotesque.

Marie Bonaparte, noting that Freudian analysis has established a connection between the symbol of the bridge and "the father's penis as one which serves to connect two bodies, two stretches of country" (p. 529), takes the idea farther, suggesting that the covered bridge is the mother's vagina and Toby Dammit is the father's penis. The Devil is the castrator. In this somewhat bewildering analysis, Toby also "accomplishes the coveted return to the womb symbolized by river bank, water and death" (p. 534).

If one is interested in bridge symbolism, it should be noted that the bridge also represents the communication between heaven and earth, uniting man with the divinity. If the tale is truly a satire on transcendentalism, which proclaimed that God and Earth, spirit and nature, were already One, the events on Poe's covered bridge may simply be a warning against that New England philosophy, which Poe felt was too quick to go flying off into the unknown.

feelings had been hurt, and that he stood in need of my assistance. I hurried up to him and found that he had received what might be termed a serious injury. The truth is, he had been deprived of his head, which after a close search I could not find anywhere;—so I determined to take him home, and **34** send for the homœopathists. In the meantime, a thought struck me, and I threw open an adjacent window of the bridge; when the sad truth flashed upon me at once. About five feet just above the top of the turnstile, and crossing the arch of the footpath so as to constitute a brace, there extended a flat iron bar, lying with its breadth horizontally, and forming one of a series that served to strengthen the structure throughout its extent. With the edge of this brace it appeared evident that the neck of my unfortunate friend had come precisely in contact.

He did not long survive his terrible loss. The homœopathists did not give him little enough physic, and what little they did give him he hesitated to take. So in the end he grew worse, and at length died, a lesson to all riotous livers. I bedewed his **35** grave with my tears, worked a *bar* sinister on his family escutcheon, and for the general expenses of his funeral sent in my very moderate bill to the transcendentalists. The scoundrels refused to pay, so I had Mr. Dammit dug up at **36** once, and sold him for dog's meat.

I saw him high in the air, pigeon-winging it to admiration just over the top of the stile. . . . *Illustration by F. S. Coburn, 1902*

THE SPECTACLES

First published in the Philadelphia *Dollar Newspaper*, March 27, 1844, this occasionally amusing story has the telltale air of one written for payment by the word. It is not only much too long (particularly in the Opera sequence), but the punch line is telegraphed long before the climax. Still, there are some good things here, and also some interesting parallels between this comic tale and some of Poe's more serious efforts.

As for a source, Poe may have read "The Mysterious Portrait," in *The New Monthly Belle Assemblée* for July 1836. In that tale, a young Frenchman falls in love with a woman whose face he sees in a miniature portrait dropped on the Champs Élysées. The woman turns out to be his grandmother, and the portrait was of course painted while she was still young. Ultimately she matches him up with her young ward, and the two are married.

Another source could be "The Blunderer," which appeared in *Knickerbocker Magazine*, February 1837, and was reprinted in the *New Yorker* that same month. In this tale we find the elements of the nearsighted young man, some odd French dialect, and several similar incidents.

Poe may also have been familiar with *You Can't Marry Your Grandmother*, a farce by Thomas Haynes Bayly, first produced in 1838; it, too, contains some of the plot elements of Poe's tale.

That the story was simply too long was obvious to Poe, for when it was reprinted in the *Broadway Journal*, in 1845, he added a note apologizing "for the insufficient variety" in the tale, saying that he was "not aware of the great length of 'The Spectacles' until too late to remedy the evil." Of course it was not too late to remedy "the evil" a year after its first publication, but Poe, who scrupulously rewrote and refined other stories, apparently felt this one just wasn't worth the effort. Most modern readers would probably agree.

In 1938, *Liberty* magazine (September 24) announced it has found a long-hidden first version of the tale but withheld the name of the publication in which the piece was allegedly discovered "for a short time to permit of additional research and of copyright protection." Nothing was heard of the matter again.

Many years ago, it was the fashion to ridicule the idea of "love at first sight;" but those who think, not less than those who feel deeply, have always advocated its existence. Modern **1** discoveries, indeed, in what may be termed ethical magnetism or magnetoaesthetics, render it probable that the most **2** natural, and, consequently, the truest and most intense of the human affections are those which arise in the heart as if by electric sympathy—in a word, that the brightest and most enduring of the psychal fetters are those which are riveted by a glance. The confession I am about to make will add another to the already almost innumerable instances of the truth of the position.

My story requires that I should be somewhat minute. I am **3** still a very young man—not yet twenty-two years of age. My name, at present, is a very usual and rather plebeian one—

1 Marlowe's *Hero and Leander* (1598), I, 176. Note also Kipling's comment: "It takes a great deal of Christianity to wipe out uncivilized Eastern instincts, such as falling in love at first sight," in *Plain Tales from the Hills*, "Lispeth" (1888).

2 Neither word is in the commonly used encyclopedias or dictionaries of the time. Both seem to be derived from the idea of magnetic influence proposed by Mesmer. Magneto-aesthetics might thus be aesthetic feelings or tendencies that flow from a person or object. Ethical magnetism might be a magnetic influence on the ethos, or spirit, of a people or community.

3 This, as we find out, is not to be the case.

4 A Christian name is the first name, as distinct from the family name, so that the narrator's Christian name is Napoleon, not Bonaparte.

5 Jean Froissart (c. 1337–1410?) is the French chronicler whom Poe uses as one source for "Hop-Frog." Froissart never married.

Another possibility is that the name comes from the French *froisser,* "to crumple"; Poe sees great humor in this series of rhyming names.

6 The standard English translation of the chronicles was by John Bourchier, Lord Berners, who published them in 1523–25; they are still available in editions today. Barbara Tuchman makes great use of Froissart in *A Distant Mirror* (Knopf, 1978).

7 *Croisser* means "to fold."

8 The root word may be *voir,* "to see."

9 The root word may be *moi* ("me"), *mois* ("month") or *moiser* ("to brace").

10 "Sanguine" means hot-blooded, or easy to anger. Aside from these various character traits, the narrator is also impossibly vain.

11 Perhaps the Park Theater, in New York, although Poe could be referring to the Palais-Royal Theatre, where vaudevilles and farces of broad character were performed, according to Karl Baedeker's *Paris and Environs* (1896).

12 Possibly after William Henry Fox Talbot (1800–77), English inventor of photographic processes.

Simpson. I say "at present;" for it is only lately that I have been so called—having legislatively adopted this surname within the last year, in order to receive a large inheritance left me by a distant male relative, Adolphus Simpson, Esq. The bequest was conditioned upon my taking the name of the testator—the family, not the Christian name; my Christian name is Napoleon Bonaparte—or, more properly, these are **4** my first and middle appellations.

I assumed the name, Simpson, with some reluctance, as in **5** my true patronym, Froissart, I felt a very pardonable pride—believing that I could trace a descent from the immortal author **6** of the "Chronicles." While on the subject of names, by the by, I may mention a singular coincidence of sound attending the names of some of my immediate predecessors. My father was a Monsieur Froissart, of Paris. His wife—my mother, **7** whom he married at fifteen—was a Mademoiselle Croissart, eldest daughter of Croissart the banker; whose wife, again, being only sixteen when married, was the eldest daughter of **8** one Victor Voissart. Monsieur Voissart, very singularly, had **9** married a lady of similar name—a Mademoiselle Moissart. She, too, was quite a child when married; and her mother, also, Madame Moissart, was only fourteen when led to the altar. These early marriages are usual in France. Here, however, are Moissart, Voissart, Croissart, and Froissart, all in the direct line of descent. My own name, though, as I say, became Simpson, by act of Legislature, and with so much repugnance on my part, that, at one period, I actually hesitated about accepting the legacy with the useless and annoying *proviso* attached.

As to personal endowments, I am by no means deficient. On the contrary, I believe that I am well made, and possess what nine-tenths of the world would call a handsome face. In height I am five feet eleven. My hair is black and curling. My nose is sufficiently good. My eyes are large and gray; although, in fact, they are weak to a very inconvenient degree, still no defect in this regard would be suspected from their appearance. The weakness itself, however, has always much annoyed me, and I have resorted to every remedy—short of wearing glasses. Being youthful and good-looking, I naturally dislike these, and have resolutely refused to employ them. I know nothing, indeed, which so disfigures the countenance of a young person, or so impresses every feature with an air of demureness, if not altogether of sanctimoniousness and of age. An eye-glass, on the other hand, has a savor of downright foppery and affectation. I have hitherto managed as well as I could without either. But something too much of these merely personal details, which, after all, are of little importance. I will content myself with saying, in addition, that my temperament is **10** sanguine, rash, ardent, enthusiastic—and that all my life I have been a devoted admirer of the women.

11   One night last winter I entered a box at the P—— Theatre, **12** in company with a friend, Mr. Talbot. It was an opera night, and the bills presented a very rare attraction, so that the house was excessively crowded. We were in time, however, to obtain the front seats which had been reserved for us, and into which, with some little difficulty, we elbowed our way.

For two hours my companion, who was a musical *fanatico*, gave his undivided attention to the stage; and, in the meantime, I amused myself by observing the audience, which consisted, in chief part, of the very *élite* of the city. Having satisfied myself upon this point, I was about turning my eyes to the *prima donna*, when they were arrested and riveted by a figure in one of the private boxes which had escaped my observation.

If I lived a thousand years I can never forget the intense emotion with which I regarded this figure. It was that of a female, the most exquisite I had ever beheld. The face was so far turned toward the stage that, for some minutes, I could not obtain a view of it—but the form was *divine;* no other words can sufficiently express its magnificent proportion—and even the term "divine" seems ridiculously feeble as I write it.

The magic of a lovely form in woman—the necromancy of **13** female gracefulness—was always a power which I had found it impossible to resist; but here was grace personified, incarnate, the *beau idéal* of my wildest and most enthusiastic visions. The figure, almost all of which the construction of the box permitted to be seen, was somewhat above the medium height, and nearly approached, without positively reaching, the majestic. Its perfect fulness and *tournure* were delicious. **14** The head, of which only the back was visible, rivalled in outline that of the Greek Psyche, and was rather displayed **15** than concealed by an elegant cap of *gaze aérienne*, which put **16** me in mind of the *ventum textilem* of Apuleius. The right arm **17** hung over the balustrade of the box, and thrilled every nerve of my frame with its exquisite symmetry. Its upper portion was draperied by one of the loose open sleeves now in fashion. This extended but little below the elbow. Beneath it was worn an under one of some frail material, close-fitting, and terminated by a cuff of rich lace, which fell gracefully over the top of the hand, revealing only the delicate fingers, upon one of which sparkled a diamond ring, which I at once saw was of extraordinary value. The admirable roundness of the wrist was well set off by a bracelet which encircled it, and which also was ornamented and clasped by a magnificent *aigrette* of **18** jewels,—telling, in words that could not be mistaken, at once of the wealth and fastidious taste of the wearer.

I gazed at this queenly apparition for at least half an hour, as if I had been suddenly converted to stone; and during this period, I felt the full force and truth of all that has been said or sung concerning "love at first sight." My feelings were totally different from any which I had hitherto experienced, in the presence of even the most celebrated specimens of female loveliness. An unaccountable, and what I am compelled to consider a *magnetic*, sympathy of soul for soul, seemed to rivet, not only my vision, but my whole powers of thought and feeling, upon the admirable object before me. I saw—I felt—I knew that I was deeply, madly, irrevocably in love—and this even before seeing the face of the person beloved.

13 Necromancy has to do with communication with the dead; but it also means enchantment or conjuration.

14 Figure, appearance

15 A head and torso of Psyche was on display at a museum in Naples.

16 Airy silk veiling

17 While *ventum textilem* (airy cloth) is mentioned in Petronius' *Satyricon* (first century A.D.), 55, it also appears, attributed to Apuleius in D'Israeli's *Curiosities of Literature*, under "Some Ingenious Thoughts.".

18 A spray of gems. The hero of "The Business Man" also stares at a theater party.

So intense, indeed, was the passion that consumed me, that I really believe it would have received little if any abatement had the features, yet unseen, proved of merely ordinary character; so anomalous is the nature of the only true love—of the love at first sight—and so little really dependent is it upon the external conditions which only seem to create and control it.

While I was thus wrapped in admiration of this lovely vision, a sudden disturbance among the audience caused her to turn her head partially toward me, so that I beheld the entire profile of the face. Its beauty even exceeded my anticipations—and yet there was something about it which disappointed me without my being able to tell exactly what it was. I said "disappointed," but this is not altogether the word. My sentiments were at once quieted and exalted. They partook less of transport and more of calm enthusiasm—of enthusiastic repose. This state of feeling arose, perhaps, from the Madonna-like and matronly air of the face; and yet I at once understood that it could not have arisen entirely from this. There was something else—some mystery which I could not develop—some expression about the countenance which slightly disturbed me while it greatly heightened my interest. In fact, I was just in that condition of mind which prepares a young and susceptible man for any act of extravagance. Had the lady been alone, I should undoubtedly have entered her box and accosted her at all hazards; but, fortunately, she was attended by two companions—a gentleman, and a strikingly beautiful woman, to all appearance a few years younger than herself.

I revolved in my mind a thousand schemes by which I might obtain, hereafter, an introduction to the elder lady, or, for the present, at all events, a more distinct view of her beauty. I would have removed my position to one nearer her own, but the crowded state of the theatre rendered this impossible; and the stern decrees of Fashion had, of late, imperatively prohibited the use of the opera-glass, in a case such as this, even had I been so fortunate as to have one with me—but I had not—and was thus in despair.

At length I bethought me of applying to my companion.

"Talbot," I said, "*you* have an opera-glass. Let me have it."

"An opera-glass!—no!—what do you suppose *I* would be doing with an opera-glass?" Here he turned impatiently toward the stage.

"But, Talbot," I continued, pulling him by the shoulder, "listen to me, will you? Do you see the stage-box?—there!—no, the next.—Did you ever behold as lovely a woman?"

"She is very beautiful, no doubt," he said.

"I wonder who she can be?"

"Why, in the name of all that is angelic, don't you *know* who she is? 'Not to know her argues yourself unknown.' She is the celebrated Madame Lalande—the beauty of the day *par excellence*, and the talk of the whole town. Immensely wealthy too—a widow—and a great match—has just arrived from Paris."

"Do you know her?"

19 In other words, she looks like someone's mother, which should be a tip-off to the narrator.

20 "Not to know me argues yourselves unknown" is from *Paradise Lost*, IV, 830.

21 Henriette Lalande (1797–1867) was a famous opera star, whom Poe heard about through a book he reviewed in *Burton's*, May 1840, entitled *Memoirs and Letters of Madame Malibran*, by the Countess de Merlin.

"Yes—I have the honor."

"Will you introduce me?"

"Assuredly—with the greatest pleasure; when shall it be?"

"To-morrow, at one, I will call upon you at B——'s."

"Very good; and now *do* hold your tongue, *if* you can."

In this latter respect I was forced to take Talbot's advice; for he remained obstinately deaf to every further question or suggestion, and occupied himself exclusively for the rest of the evening with what was transacting upon the stage.

In the meantime I kept my eyes riveted on Madame Lalande, and at length had the good fortune to obtain a full front view of her face. It was exquisitely lovely: this, of course, my heart had told me before, even had not Talbot fully satisfied me upon the point—but still the unintelligible something disturbed me. I finally concluded that my senses were impressed by a certain air of gravity, sadness, or, still more properly, of weariness, which took something from the youth and freshness of the countenance, only to endow it with a seraphic tenderness and majesty, and thus, of course, to my enthusiastic and romantic temperament, with an interest tenfold.

While I thus feasted my eyes, I perceived, at last, to my great trepidation, by an almost imperceptible start on the part of the lady, that she had become suddenly aware of the intensity of my gaze. Still, I was absolutely fascinated, and could not withdraw it, even for an instant. She turned aside her face, and again I saw only the chiselled contour of the back portion of the head. After some minutes, as if urged by curiosity to see if I was still looking, she gradually brought her face again around and again encountered my burning gaze. Her large dark eyes fell instantly, and a deep blush mantled her cheek. But what was my astonishment at perceiving that she not only did not a second time avert her head, but that she actually took from her girdle a double eye-glass—elevated it—adjusted it—and then regarded me through it, intently and deliberately, for the space of several minutes.

Had a thunderbolt fallen at my feet I could not have been more thoroughly astounded—astounded *only*—not offended or disgusted in the slightest degree; although an action so bold in any other woman would have been likely to offend or disgust. But the whole thing was done with so much quietude—so much *nonchalance*—so much repose—with so evident an air of the highest breeding, in short—that nothing of mere effrontery was perceptible, and my sole sentiments were those of admiration and surprise.

I observed that, upon her first elevation of the glass, she had seemed satisfied with a momentary inspection of my person, and was withdrawing the instrument, when, as if struck by a second thought, she resumed it, and so continued to regard me with fixed attention for the space of several minutes—for five minutes, at the very least, I am sure.

This action, so remarkable in an American theatre, attracted very general observation, and gave rise to an indefinite movement, or *buzz*, among the audience, which for a moment filled me with confusion, but produced no visible effect upon the countenance of Madame Lalande.

Having satisfied her curiosity—if such it was—she dropped the glass, and quietly gave her attention again to the stage; her profile now being turned toward myself, as before. I continued to watch her unremittingly, although I was fully conscious of my rudeness in so doing. Presently I saw the head slowly and slightly change its position; and soon I became convinced that the lady, while pretending to look at the stage was, in fact, attentively regarding myself. It is needless to say what effect this conduct, on the part of so fascinating a woman, had upon my excitable mind.

Having thus scrutinized me for perhaps a quarter of an hour, the fair object of my passion addressed the gentleman who attended her, and, while she spoke, I saw distinctly, by the glances of both, that the conversation had reference to myself.

Upon its conclusion, Madame Lalande again turned toward the stage, and, for a few minutes, seemed absorbed in the performances. At the expiration of this period, however, I was thrown into an extremity of agitation by seeing her unfold, for the second time, the eye-glass which hung at her side, fully confront me as before, and, disregarding the renewed buzz of the audience, survey me, from head to foot, with the same miraculous composure which had previously so delighted and confounded my soul.

This extraordinary behavior, by throwing me into a perfect fever of excitement—into an absolute delirium of love—served rather to embolden than to disconcert me. In the mad intensity of my devotion, I forgot everything but the presence and the majestic loveliness of the vision which confronted my gaze. Watching my opportunity, when I thought the audience were fully engaged with the opera, I at length caught the eyes of Madame Lalande, and, upon the instant, made a slight but unmistakable bow.

She blushed very deeply—then averted her eyes—then slowly and cautiously looked around, apparently to see if my rash action had been noticed—then leaned over toward the gentleman who sat by her side.

I now felt a burning sense of the impropriety I had committed, and expected nothing less than instant exposure; while a vision of pistols upon the morrow floated rapidly and uncomfortably through my brain. I was greatly and immediately relieved, however, when I saw the lady merely hand the gentleman a play-bill, without speaking; but the reader may form some feeble conception of my astonishment—of my *profound* amazement—my delirious bewilderment of heart and soul—when, instantly afterward, having again glanced furtively around, she allowed her bright eyes to set fully and steadily upon my own, and then, with a faint smile, disclosing a bright line of her pearly teeth, made two distinct, pointed, and unequivocal affirmative inclinations of the head.

It is useless, of course, to dwell upon my joy—upon my transport—upon my illimitable ecstasy of heart. If ever man was mad with excess of happiness, it was myself at that moment. I loved. This was my *first* love—so I felt it to be. It was love supreme—indescribable. It was "love at first sight;" and at first sight, too, it had been appreciated and *returned*.

Yes, returned. How and why should I doubt it for an instant? What other construction could I possibly put upon such conduct, on the part of a lady so beautiful—so wealthy— evidently so accomplished—of so high breeding—of so lofty a position in society—in every regard so entirely respectable as I felt assured was Madame Lalande? Yes, she loved me— she returned the enthusiasm of my love, with an enthusiasm as blind—as uncompromising—as uncalculating—as aban- doned—and as utterly unbounded as my own! These delicious fancies and reflections, however, were now interrupted by the falling of the drop-curtain. The audience arose; and the usual tumult immediately supervened. Quitting Talbot ab- ruptly, I made every effort to force my way into closer proximity with Madame Lalande. Having failed in this, on account of the crowd, I at length gave up the chase, and bent my steps homeward; consoling myself for my disappointment in not having been able to touch even the hem of her robe, **22** by the reflection that I should be introduced by Talbot, in due form, upon the morrow.

This morrow at last came; that is to say, a day finally dawned upon a long and weary night of impatience; and then the hours until "one" were snail-paced, dreary, and innumerable. But even Stamboul, it is said, shall have an end, and there came **23** an end to this long delay. The clock struck. As the last echo ceased, I stepped into B——'s and inquired of Talbot.

"Out," said the footman—Talbot's own.

"Out!" I replied, staggering back half a dozen paces—"let me tell you, my fine fellow, that this thing is thoroughly impossible and impracticable; Mr. Talbot is *not* out. What do you mean?"

"Nothing, sir; only Mr. Talbot is not in. That's all. He rode over to S——, immediately after breakfast, and left word that he would not be in town again for a week."

I stood petrified with horror and rage. I endeavored to reply, but my tongue refused its office. At length I turned on my heel, livid with wrath, and inwardly consigning the whole tribe of the Talbots to the innermost regions of Erebus. It was **24** evident that my considerate friend, *il fanatico*, had quite forgotten his appointment with myself—had forgotten it as soon as it was made. At no time was he a very scrupulous man of his word. There was no help for it; so smothering my vexation as well as I could, I strolled moodily up the street, propounding futile inquiries about Madame Lalande to every male acquaintance I met. By report she was known, I found, to all—to many by sight—but she had been in town only a few weeks, and there were very few, therefore, who claimed her personal acquaintance. These few, being still comparatively strangers, could not, or would not, take the liberty of intro- ducing me through the formality of a morning call. While I stood thus, in despair, conversing with a trio of friends upon

22 "And besought him that they might only touch the hem of his garment: and as many as touched were made perfectly whole." (Matthew 14:36)

23 This proverb about Istanbul (Constantinople) pops up again in Poe's "A Letter to Mr. ——" (1831). Its origin is uncertain.

24 Hades

the all-absorbing subject of my heart, it so happened that the subject itself passed by.

"As I live, there she is!" cried one.

"Surprisingly beautiful" exclaimed a second.

"An angel upon earth!" ejaculated a third.

I looked; and in an open carriage which approached us, passing slowly down the street, sat the enchanting vision of the opera, accompanied by the younger lady who had occupied a portion of her box.

"Her companion also wears remarkably well," said the one of my trio who had spoken first.

"Astonishingly," said the second; "still quite a brilliant air; but art will do wonders. Upon my word, she looks better than she did at Paris five years ago. A beautiful woman still;—don't you think so, Froissart?—Simpson, I mean."

"*Still!*" said I, "and why shouldn't she be? But compared with her friend she is as a rushlight to the evening star—a **25** glowworm to Antares."

"Ha! ha! ha!—why, Simpson, you have an astonishing tact at making discoveries—original ones, I mean." And here we separated, while one of the trio began humming a gay **26** *vaudeville*, of which I caught only the lines—

> Ninon, Ninon, Ninon á bas—
> A bas Ninon De L'Enclos!

During this little scene, however, one thing had served greatly to console me, although it fed the passion by which I was consumed. As the carriage of Madame Lalande rolled by our group, I had observed that she recognized me; and more than this, she had blessed me, by the most seraphic of all imaginable smiles, with no equivocal mark of recognition.

As for an introduction, I was obliged to abandon all hope of it, until such time as Talbot should think proper to return from the country. In the meantime I perseveringly frequented every reputable place of public amusement; and, at length, at the theatre, where I first saw her, I had the supreme bliss of meeting her, and of exchanging glances with her once again. This did not occur, however, until the lapse of a fortnight. Every day, in the *interim*, I had inquired for Talbot at his hotel, and every day had been thrown into a spasm of wrath by the everlasting "Not come home yet" of his footman.

Upon the evening in question, therefore, I was in a condition little short of madness. Madame Lalande, I had been told, was a Parisian—had lately arrived from Paris—might she not suddenly return?—return before Talbot came back—and might she not be thus lost to me forever? The thought was too terrible to bear. Since my future happiness was at issue. I resolved to act with a manly decision. In a word, upon the breaking up of the play, I traced the lady to her residence, noted the address, and the next morning sent her a full and elaborate letter, in which I poured out my whole heart.

I spoke boldly, freely—in a word, I spoke with passion. I concealed nothing—nothing even of my weakness. I alluded to the romantic circumstances of our first meeting—even to

25 A red star of the first magnitude

26 Poe may have had in mind the derivation of the word in *chanson du Vau de Vire*, a song of the valley of Vire (Normandy). The name is said to have been given to songs composed by Olivier Basselin in the fifteenth century.

Ninon de Lenclos, of L'Enclos, was a seventeenth-century Frenchwoman (1620–1705) known for her beauty and wit, who numbered among her lovers and friends the Great Condé, La Rochefoucauld and Saint-Évremond. She gathered in her Paris salon a circle of literary figures and reputedly had men falling at her feet well into her nineties.

the glances which had passed between us. I went so far as to say that I felt assured of her love; while I offered this assurance, and my own intensity of devotion, as two excuses for my otherwise unpardonable conduct. As a third, I spoke of my fear that she might quit the city before I could have the opportunity of a formal introduction. I concluded the most wildly enthusiastic epistle ever penned, with a frank declaration of my worldly circumstances—of my affluence—and with an offer of my heart and of my hand.

In an agony of expectation I awaited the reply. After what seemed the lapse of a century it came.

Yes, *actually came*. Romantic as all this may appear, I really received a letter from Madame Lalande—the beautiful, the wealthy, the idolized Madame Lalande. Her eyes—her magnificent eyes, had not belied her noble heart. Like a true Frenchwoman, as she was, she had obeyed the frank dictates of her reason—the generous impulses of her nature—despising the conventional pruderies of the world. She had *not* scorned my proposals. She had *not* sheltered herself in silence. She had *not* returned my letter unopened. She had even sent me, in reply, one penned by her own exquisite fingers. It ran thus:

> "Monsieur Simpson vill pardonne me for not compose de butefulle tong of his contrée so vell as might. It is only de late dat I am arrive, and not yet ave de opportunité for to—l'étudier.
>
> "Vid dis apologie for the manière, I vill now say dat, hélas!—Monsieur Simpson ave guess but de too true. Need I say de more? Hélas! am I not ready speak de too moshe?
>
> "Eugénie Lalande" **27**

This noble-spirited note I kissed a million times, and committed, no doubt, on its account, a thousand other extravagances that have now escaped my memory. Still Talbot *would* not return. Alas! could he have formed even the vaguest idea of the suffering his absence had occasioned his friend, would not his sympathizing nature have flown immediately to my relief? Still, however, he came *not*. I wrote. He replied. He was detained by urgent business—but would shortly return. He begged me not to be impatient—to moderate my transports—to read soothing books—to drink nothing stronger than Hock—and to bring the consolations of philosophy to my **28** aid. The fool! if he could not come himself, why, in the name of everything rational, could he not have enclosed me a letter of presentation? I wrote him again, entreating him to forward one forthwith. My letter was returned by *that* footman, with the following endorsement in pencil. The scoundrel had joined his master in the country:

> "Left S—— yesterday, for parts unknown—did not say where—or when be back—so thought best to return letter, knowing your handwriting, and as how you is always more or less, in a hurry.
>
> "Yours sincerely,   Stubbs"

27 The name of the empress of the French (1853–70) and escort to Napoleon III, who married her in 1853, two years after meeting her.

The dialect here is strange French indeed, since an educated French speaker would not use the sound "v" to replace "w" and certainly would not write English in such a "phonetic" manner. This is merely comic spelling, an unfortunate humorous bent of the mid-nineteenth century. See "Why the Little Frenchman Wears His Hand in a Sling," introductory note.

28 Rhine wine. The word is the English form of Hochheimer, under which name most sweet, white wines were imported into England and the United States in the eighteenth century.

After this, it is needless to say, that I devoted to the infernal deities both master and valet;—but there was little use in anger, and no consolation at all in complaint.

But I had yet a resource left, in my constitutional audacity. Hitherto it had served me well, and I now resolved to make it avail me to the end. Besides, after the correspondence which had passed between us, what act of mere informality *could* I commit, within bounds, that ought to be regarded as indecorous by Madame Lalande? Since the affair of the letter, I had been in the habit of watching her house, and thus discovered that, about twilight, it was her custom to promenade, attended only by a negro in livery, in a public square overlooked by her windows. Here, amid the luxuriant and shadowing groves, in the gray gloom of a sweet midsummer evening, I observed my opportunity and accosted her.

The better to deceive the servant in attendance, I did this with the assured air of an old and familiar acquaintance. With a presence of mind truly Parisian, she took the cue at once, and, to greet me, held out the most bewitchingly little of hands. The valet at once fell into the rear; and now, with hearts full to overflowing, we discoursed long and unreservedly of our love.

As Madame Lalande spoke English even less fluently than she wrote it, our conversation was necessarily in French. In this sweet tongue, so adapted to passion, I gave loose to the impetuous enthusiasm of my nature, and, with all the eloquence I could command, besought her to consent to an immediate marriage.

At this impatience she smiled. She urged the old story of decorum—that bug-bear [29] which deters so many from bliss until the opportunity for bliss has forever gone by. I had most imprudently made it known among my friends, she observed, that I desired her acquaintance—thus that I did not possess it—thus, again, there was no possibility of concealing the date of our first knowledge of each other. And then she adverted, with a blush, to the extreme recency of this date. To wed immediately would be improper—would be indecorous—would be *outré*. All this she said with a charming air of *naïveté* which enraptured while it grieved and convinced me. She went even so far as to accuse me, laughingly, of rashness—of imprudence. She bade me remember that I really even knew not who she was—what were her prospects, her connections, her standing in society. She begged me, but with a sigh, to reconsider my proposal, and termed my love an infatuation—a will o' the wisp—a fancy or fantasy of the moment—a baseless and unstable creation rather of the imagination than of the heart. These things she uttered as the shadows of the sweet twilight gathered darkly and more darkly around us—and then, with a gentle pressure of her fairy-like hand, overthrew, in a single sweet instant, all the argumentative fabric she had reared.

I replied as best I could—as only a true lover can. I spoke at length, and perseveringly of my devotion, of my passion—of her exceeding beauty, and of my own enthusiastic admi-

29 Originally a sort of hobgoblin supposed to devour naughty children, it has since come to mean any imaginary being of terror ("bug" once meant an object of terror).

ration. In conclusion, I dwelt, with a convincing energy, upon the perils that encompass the course of love—that course of true love that never did run smooth, and thus deduced the manifest danger of rendering that course unnecessarily long. **30**

30 *A Midsummer-Night's Dream*, I, i, 134

This latter argument seemed finally to soften the rigor of her determination. She relented; but there was yet an obstacle, she said, which she felt assured I had not properly considered. This was a delicate point—for a woman to urge, especially so; in mentioning it, she saw that she must make a sacrifice of her feelings; still, for *me*, every sacrifice should be made. She alluded to the topic of *age*. Was I aware—was I fully aware of the discrepancy between us? That the age of the husband should surpass by a few years—even by fifteen or twenty— the age of the wife, was regarded by the world as admissible, and indeed, as even proper; but she had always entertained the belief that the years of the wife should *never* exceed in number those of the husband. A discrepancy of this unnatural kind gave rise, too frequently, alas! to a life of unhappiness. Now she was aware that my own age did not exceed two and twenty; and I, on the contrary, perhaps, was *not* aware that the years of my Eugénie extended very considerably beyond that sum.

About all this there was a nobility of soul—a dignity of candor—which delighted—which enchanted me—which eternally riveted my chains. I could scarcely restrain the excessive transport which possessed me.

"My sweetest Eugénie," I cried, "what is all this about which you are discoursing? Your years surpass in some measure my own. But what then? The customs of the world are so many conventional follies. To those who love as ourselves, in what respect differs a year from an hour? I am twenty-two, you say; granted: indeed, you may as well call me, at once, twenty-three. Now you yourself, my dearest Eugénie, can have numbered no more than—can have numbered no more than—no more than—than—than—than—"

Here I paused for an instant, in the expectation that Madame Lalande would interrupt me by supplying her true age. But a Frenchwoman is seldom direct, and has always, by way of answer to an embarrassing query, some little practical reply of her own. In the present instance, Eugénie, who for a few moments past had seemed to be searching for something in her bosom, at length let fall upon the grass a miniature, which I immediately picked up and presented to her.

"Keep it!" she said, with one of her most ravishing smiles. "Keep it for my sake—for the sake of her whom it too flatteringly represents. Besides, upon the back of the trinket you may discover, perhaps, the very information you seem to desire. It is now, to be sure, growing rather dark—but you can examine it at your leisure in the morning. In the meantime, you shall be my escort home to-night. My friends are about holding a little musical *levée*. I can promise you, too, some **31** good singing. We French are not nearly so punctilious as you Americans, and I shall have no difficulty in smuggling you in, in the character of an old acquaintance."

31 In French, *levée* means a collection (of people). *Soirée* is the more familiar term for an evening get-together.

32 The astral, or solar, lamp had the oil contained in a flattened metal ring; it was made so that uninterrupted light was thrown on the table below.

With this, she took my arm, and I attended her home. The mansion was quite a fine one, and, I believe, furnished in good taste. Of this latter point, however, I am scarcely qualified to judge; for it was just dark as we arrived; and in American mansions of the better sort lights seldom, during the heat of summer, make their appearance at this, the most pleasant period of the day. In about an hour after my arrival,
32 to be sure, a single shaded solar lamp was lit in the principal drawing-room; and this apartment, I could thus see, was arranged with unusual good taste and even splendor; but two other rooms of the suite, and in which the company chiefly assembled, remained, during the whole evening, in a very agreeable shadow. This is a well-conceived custom, giving the party at least a choice of light or shade, and one which our friends over the water could not do better than immediately adopt.

The evening thus spent was unquestionably the most delicious of my life. Madame Lalande had not overrated the musical abilities of her friends; and the singing I here heard I had never heard excelled in any private circle out of Vienna. The instrumental performers were many and of superior talents. The vocalists were chiefly ladies, and no individual sang less than well. At length, upon a peremptory call for "Madame Lalande," she arose at once, without affectation or demur, from the *chaise longue* upon which she had sat by my side, and, accompanied by one or two gentlemen and her female friend of the opera, repaired to the piano in the main drawing-room. I would have escorted her myself, but felt that, under the circumstances of my introduction to the house, I had better remain unobserved where I was. I was thus deprived of the pleasure of seeing, although not of hearing, her sing.

The impression she produced upon the company seemed electrical—but the effect upon myself was something even more. I know not how adequately to describe it. It arose in part, no doubt, from the sentiment of love with which I was imbued; but chiefly from my conviction of the extreme sensibility of the singer. It is beyond the reach of art to endow either air or recitative with more impassioned *expression* than was hers. Her utterance of the romance in Otello—the tone with which she gave the words *"Sul mio sasso,"* in the
33 Capuletti—is ringing in my memory yet. Her lower tones were absolutely miraculous. Her voice embraced three complete octaves, extending from the contralto D to the D upper soprano, and, though sufficiently powerful to have filled the
34 San Carlos, executed, with the minutest precision, every difficulty of vocal composition—ascending and descending
35,36 scales, cadences, or *fioriture*. In the finale of the Sonnambula, she brought about a most remarkable effect at the words—

33 *Otello*, by Rossini (1816), III, 1, and Bellini's *I Capuletti ed i Montecchi* (1830), IV, 1

34 A Neapolitan opera house

35 Vocal ornamentation

36 Bellini's *La Sonnambula* (1831): "Oh, recall not one earthly sorrow/With the blisses of heav'n around us/An illusion it was that bound us" (Schirmer, 1901 edition).

37 Madame Malibran (see note 21) was a well-known singer of the day. The anecdote comes from the Countess de Merlin's *Memoirs*, II, 110. What all this has to do with the plot is uncertain.

> Ah! non giunge uman pensiero
> Al contento ond 'io son piena.

37   Here, in imitation of Malibran, she modified the original phrase of Bellini, so as to let her voice descend to the tenor

G, when, by a rapid transition, she struck the G above the treble stave, springing over an interval of two octaves.

Upon rising from the piano after these miracles of vocal execution, she resumed her seat by my side; when I expressed to her, in terms of the deepest enthusiasm, my delight at her performance. Of my surprise I said nothing, and yet was I most unfeignedly surprised; for a certain feebleness, or rather a certain tremulous indecision of voice in ordinary conversation, had prepared me to anticipate that, in singing, she would not acquit herself with any remarkable ability.

Our conversation was now long, earnest, uninterrupted, and totally unreserved. She made me relate many of the earlier passages of my life, and listened with breathless attention to every word of the narrative. I concealed nothing—felt that I had a right to conceal nothing—from her confiding affection. Encouraged by her candor upon the delicate point of her age, I entered, with perfect frankness, not only into a detail of my many minor vices, but made full confession of those moral and even of those physical infirmities, the disclosure of which, in demanding so much higher a degree of courage, is so much surer an evidence of love. I touched upon my college indiscretions—upon my extravagances—upon my carousals—upon my debts—upon my flirtations. I even went so far as to speak of a slightly hectic cough with which, at one time, I had been troubled—of a chronic rheumatism—of a twinge of hereditary gout—and, in conclusion, of the disagreeable and inconvenient, but hitherto carefully concealed, weakness of my eyes.

"Upon this latter point," said Madame Lalande, laughingly, "you have been surely injudicious in coming to confession; for, without the confession, I take it for granted that no one would have accused you of the crime. By the by," she continued, "have you any recollection—" and here I fancied that a blush, even through the gloom of the apartment, became distinctly visible upon her cheek—"have you any recollection, *mon cher ami,* of this little ocular assistant which now depends from my neck?"

As she spoke she twirled in her fingers the identical double eye-glass, which had so overwhelmed me with confusion at the opera.

"Full well—alas! do I remember it," I exclaimed, pressing passionately the delicate hand which offered the glasses for my inspection. They formed a complex and magnificent toy, richly chased and filigreed, and gleaming with jewels which, even in the deficient light, I could not help perceiving were of high value.

"*Eh bien! mon ami,*" she resumed with a certain *empressement* of manner that rather surprised me—"*Eh bien! mon ami,* you have earnestly besought of me a favor which you have been pleased to denominate priceless. You have demanded of my my hand upon the morrow. Should I yield to your entreaties—and, I may add, to the pleadings of my own bosom—would I not be entitled to demand of you a very—a very little boon in return?"

"Name it!" I exclaimed with an energy that had nearly drawn upon us the observation of the company, and restrained by their presence alone from throwing myself impetuously at her feet. "Name it, my beloved, my Eugénie, my own!—name it!—but, alas! it is already yielded ere named."

"You shall conquer then, *mon ami*," she said, "for the sake of the Eugénie whom you love, this little weakness which you have at last confessed—this weakness more moral than physical—and which, let me assure you, is so unbecoming the nobility of your real nature—so inconsistent with the candor of your usual character—and which, if permitted further control, will assuredly involve you, sooner or later, in some very disagreeable scrape. You shall conquer, for my sake, this affectation which leads you, as you yourself acknowledge, to the tacit or implied denial of your infirmity of vision. For, this infirmity you virtually deny, in refusing to employ the customary means for its relief. You will understand me to say, then, that I wish you to wear spectacles:—ah, hush!—you have already consented to wear them, *for my sake*. You shall accept the little toy which I now hold in my hand, and which, though admirable as an aid to vision, is really of no very immense value as a gem. You perceive that, by a trifling modification thus—or thus—it can be adapted to the eyes in the form of spectacles, or worn in the waistcoat pocket as an eye-glass. It is in the former mode, however, and habitually, that you have already consented to wear it *for my sake*."

This request—must I confess it?—confused me in no little degree. But the condition with which it was coupled rendered hesitation, of course, a matter altogether out of the question.

"It is done!" I cried, with all the enthusiasm that I could muster at the moment. "It is done—it is most cheerfully agreed. I sacrifice every feeling for your sake. To-night I wear this dear eye-glass, *as* an eye-glass, and upon my heart; but with the earliest dawn of that morning which gives me the pleasure of calling you wife, I will place it upon my—upon my nose—and there wear it ever afterward, in the less romantic, and less fashionable, but certainly in the more serviceable form which you desire."

Our conversation now turned upon the details of our arrangements for the morrow. Talbot, I learned from my betrothed, had just arrived in town. I was to see him at once, and procure a carriage. The *soirée* would scarcely break up before two; and by this hour the vehicle was to be at the door; when, in the confusion occasioned by the departure of the company, Madame L. could easily enter it unobserved. We were then to call at the house of a clergyman who would be in waiting; there be married, drop Talbot, and proceed on a short tour to the East; leaving the fashionable world at home to make whatever comments upon the matter it thought best.

Having planned all this, I immediately took leave, and went in search of Talbot, but, on the way, I could not refrain from stepping into a hotel, for the purpose of inspecting the miniature; and this I did by the powerful aid of the glasses.

The countenance was a surpassingly beautiful one! Those large luminous eyes!—that proud Grecian nose!—those dark luxuriant curls!—"Ah!" said I, exultingly to myself, "this is indeed the speaking image of my beloved!" I turned the reverse, and discovered the words—"Eugénie Lalande—aged twenty-seven years and seven months."

I found Talbot at home, and proceeded at once to acquaint him with my good fortune. He professed excessive astonishment, of course, but congratulated me most cordially, and proffered every assistance in his power. In a word, we carried out our arrangement to the letter; and, at two in the morning, just ten minutes after the ceremony, I found myself in a close carriage with Madame Lalande—with Mrs. Simpson, I should say—and driving at a great rate out of town, in a direction North-east by North, half-North.

It had been determined for us by Talbot, that, as we were to be up all night, we should make our first stop at C——, a village about twenty miles from the city, and there get an early breakfast and some repose, before proceeding upon our route. At four precisely, therefore, the carriage drew up at the door of the principal inn. I handed my adored wife out, and ordered breakfast forthwith. In the meantime we were shown into a small parlor, and sat down.

It was now nearly if not altogether daylight; and, as I gazed, enraptured, at the angel by my side, the singular idea came, all at once, into my head, that this was really the very first moment since my acquaintance with the celebrated loveliness of Madame Lalande, that I had enjoyed a near inspection of that loveliness by daylight at all.

"And now, *mon ami*," said she, taking my hand, and so interrupting this train of reflection, "and now, *mon cher ami*, since we are indissolubly one—since I have yielded to your passionate entreaties, and performed my portion of our agreement—I presume you have not forgotten that you also have a little favor to bestow—a little promise which it is your intention to keep. Ah! let me see! Let me remember! Yes; full easily do I call to mind the precise words of the dear promise you made to Eugénie last night. Listen! You spoke thus: 'It is done!—it is most cheerfully agreed! I sacrifice every feeling for your sake. To-night I wear this dear eye-glass *as* an eye-glass, and upon my heart; but with the earliest dawn of that morning which gives me the privilege of calling you wife, I will place it upon my—upon my nose,—and there wear it ever afterward, in the less romantic, and less fashionable, but certainly in the more serviceable, form which you desire.' These were the exact words, my beloved husband, were they not?"

"They were," I said; "you have an excellent memory; and assuredly, my beautiful Eugénie, there is no disposition on my part to evade the performance of the trivial promise they imply. See! Behold! They are becoming—rather—are they not?" And here, having arranged the glasses in the ordinary form of spectacles, I applied them gingerly in their proper position; while Madame Simpson, adjusting her cap, and folding her arms, sat bolt upright in her chair, in a somewhat stiff and prim, and indeed, in a somewhat undignified position.

"Goodness gracious me!" I exclaimed, almost at the very instant that the rim of the spectacles had settled upon my nose—"*My!* goodness gracious me!—why what *can* be the matter with these glasses?" and taking them quickly off, I wiped them carefully with a silk handkerchief and adjusted them again.

But if, in the first instance, there had occurred something which occasioned me surprise, in the second, this surprise became elevated into astonishment; and this astonishment was profound—was extreme—indeed I may say it was horrific. What, in the name of everything hideous, did this mean? Could I believe my eyes?—*could* I?—that was the question. Was that—was that—was that *rouge?* And were those—and were those—were those *wrinkles*, upon the visage of Eugénie Lalande? And oh, Jupiter! and every one of the gods and goddesses, little and big!—what—what—what—*what* had become of her teeth? I dashed the spectacles violently to the ground, and, leaping to my feet, stood erect in the middle of the floor, confronting Mrs. Simpson, with my arms set **38** a-kimbo, and grinning and foaming, but, at the same time, utterly speechless with terror and with rage.

Now I have already said that Madame Eugénie Lalande—that is to say, Simpson—spoke the English language but very little better than she wrote it; and for this reason she very properly never attempted to speak it upon ordinary occasions. But rage will carry a lady to any extreme; and in the present case it carried Mrs. Simpson to the very extraordinary extreme of attempting to hold a conversation in a tongue that she did not altogether understand.

"Vell, Monsieur," said she, after surveying me, in great apparent astonishment, for some moments—"Vell, Monsieur!—and vat den?—vat de matter now? Is it de dance of de **39** Saint Vitusse dat you ave? If not like me; vat for vy buy de pig in de poke?"

"You wretch!" said I, catching my breath—"you—you—you **40** villainous old hag!"

"Ag?—ole?—me not so *ver* ole, after all! me not one single day more dan de eighty-doo."

"Eighty-two!" I ejaculated, staggering to the wall—"eighty-two hundred thousand baboons! The miniature said twenty-seven years and seven months!"

"To be sure!—dat is so!—ver true! but den de portraite has been take for dese fifty-five year. Ven I go marry my segonde usbande, Monsieur Lalande, at dat time I had de portraite take for my daughter by my first usbande, Monsieur Moissart."

"Moissart!" said I.

"Yes, Moissart," said she, mimicking my pronunciation, which, to speak the truth, was none of the best; "and vat den? Vat *you* know about de Moissart?"

"Nothing, you old fright!—I know nothing about him at all; only I had an ancestor of that name, once upon a time."

38 A word of disputed origin, meaning a position in which the hands rest on the hips and the elbows are turned outward.

39 St. Vitus' dance, or chorea, is an acute disturbance of the central nervous system in which the victim has involuntary muscular contractions of the face, arms, and legs. In French, however, it is *St. Vite*, another indication of the problems of "phonetic" dialect spelling as humor.

40 He is not only vain and nearsighted, he is insulting. Even if Poe wants us to believe at the end that his vanity is cured by the lesson he learns, he is still thoroughly unpleasant most of the time, and here, downright cruel.

Meantime I sank aghast into the chair which she had vacated. *Illustration by F. S. Coburn, 1902*

"Dat name! and vat you ave for say to dat name? 'Tis ver *goot* name; and so is Voissart—dat is ver goot name too. My daughter, Mademoiselle Moissart, she marry von Monsieur Voissart; and de name is both *ver* respectaable name."

"Moissart?" I exclaimed, "and Voissart! why what is it you mean?"

"Vat I mean?—I mean Moissart and Voissart; and for de matter of dat, I mean Croissart and Froissart, too, if I only tink proper to mean it. My daughter's daughter, Mademoiselle Voissart, she marry von Monsieur Croissart, and den agin, my daughter's grande daughter, Mademoiselle Croissart, she marry von Monsieur Froissart; and I suppose you say dat *dat* is not von *ver* respectaable name."

"Froissart!" said I, beginning to faint, "why surely you don't say Moissart, and Voissart, and Croissart, and Froissart?"

"Yes," she replied, leaning fully back in her chair, and stretching out her lower limbs at great length; "yes, Moissart, and Voissart, and Croissart, and Froissart. But Monsieur Froissart, he vas von *ver* big vat you call fool—he vas von ver great big donce like yourself—for he lef *la belle France* for come to dis stupide Amérique—and ven he get here he vent and ave von *ver* stupide, von *ver, ver* stupide sonn, so I hear, dough I not yet av de plaisir to meet vid him—neither me nor my companion, de Madame Stéphanie Lalande. He is name de Napoleon Bonaparte Froissart, and I suppose you say dat *dat*, too, is not von *ver* respectaable name."

Either the length or the nature of this speech, had the effect of working up Mrs. Simpson into a very extraordinary passion indeed: and as she made an end of it, with great labor, she jumped up from her chair like somebody bewitched, dropping upon the floor an entire universe of bustle as she jumped. Once upon her feet, she gnashed her gums, brandished her arms, rolled up her sleeves, shook her fist in my face, and concluded the performance by tearing the cap from her head, and with it an immense wig of the most valuable and beautiful black hair, the whole of which she dashed upon the ground with a yell, and there trampled and danced a fandango upon it, in an absolute ecstasy and agony of rage.

Meantime I sank aghast into the chair which she had vacated. "Moissart and Voissart!" I repeated, thoughtfully, as she cut one of her pigeon-wings, and "Croissart and Froissart!" as she completed another—"Moissart and Voissart and Croissart and Napoleon Bonaparte Froissart!—why, you eneffable old serpent, that's *me*—that's *me*—d'ye hear?—that's *me*—here I screamed at the top of my voice—"that's *me-e-e! I* am Napoleon Bonaparte Froissart! and if I haven't married my great, great, grandmother, I wish I may be everlastingly confounded!"

41 Madame Eugénie Lalande, *quasi* Simpson—formerly Moissart—was, in sober fact, my great, great grandmother. In her youth she had been beautiful, and even at eighty-two, retained the majestic height, the sculptural contour of head, the fine eyes and the Grecian nose of her girlhood. By the aid of these, **42** of pearl-powder, of rouge, of false hair, false teeth, and false *tournure*, as well as of the most skilful modistes of Paris, she contrived to hold a respectable footing among the beauties *un peu passées* of the French metropolis. In this respect, indeed, she might have been regarded as little less than the equal of the celebrated Ninon de L'Enclos.

She was immensely wealthy, and being left, for the second time, a widow without children, she bethought herself of my existence in America, and for the purpose of making me her heir, paid a visit to the United States, in company with a distant and exceedingly lovely relative of her second husband's—a Madame Stéphanie Lalande.

At the opera, my great, great, grandmother's attention was arrested by my notice; and, upon surveying me through her eye-glass, she was struck with a certain family resemblance to herself. Thus interested, and knowing that the heir she sought was actually in the city, she made inquiries of her party respecting me. The gentleman who attended her knew my person, and told her who I was. The information thus obtained induced her to renew her scrutiny; and this scrutiny it was which so emboldened me that I behaved in the absurd manner already detailed. She returned my bow, however, under the impression that, by some odd accident, I had discovered her identity. When, deceived by my weakness of vision, and the arts of the toilet, in respect to the age and charms of the strange lady, I demanded so enthusiastically of Talbot who she was, he concluded that I meant the younger beauty, as a matter of course, and so informed me, with perfect truth, that she was "the celebrated widow, Madame Lalande."

41 Almost; as it were

42 A milk-white face powder, the color of pearls. *Un peu passé* means past one's prime.

In the street, next morning, my great, great, grandmother encountered Talbot, an old Parisian acquaintance; and the conversation, very naturally, turned upon myself. My deficiencies of vision were then explained, for these were notorious, although I was entirely ignorant of their notoriety; and my good old relative discovered, much to her chagrin, that she had been deceived in supposing me aware of her identity, and that I had been merely making a fool of myself in making open love, in a theatre, to an old woman unknown. By way of punishing me for this imprudence, she concocted with Talbot a plot. He purposely kept out of my way to avoid giving me the introduction. My street inquiries about "the lovely widow, Madame Lalande," were supposed to refer to the younger lady, of course; and thus the conversation with the three gentlemen whom I encountered shortly after leaving Talbot's hotel will be easily explained, as also their allusion to Ninon de L'Enclos. I had no opportunity of seeing Madame Lalande closely during daylight, and, at her musical *soirée*, my silly weakness in refusing the aid of glasses effectually prevented me from making a discovery of her age. When "Madame Lalande" was called upon to sing, the younger lady was intended; and it was she who arose to obey the call; my great, great, grandmother, to further the deception, arising at the same moment and accompanying her to the piano in the main drawing-room. Had I decided upon escorting her thither, it had been her design to suggest the propriety of my remaining where I was; but my own prudential views rendered this unnecessary. The songs which I so much admired, and which so confirmed my impression of the youth of my mistress, were executed by Madame Stéphanie Lalande. The eye-glass was presented by way of adding a reproof to the hoax—a sting to the epigram of the deception. Its presentation afforded an opportunity for the lecture upon affectation with which I was so especially edified. It is almost superfluous to add that the glasses of the instrument, as worn by the old lady, had been exchanged by her for a pair better adapted to my years. They suited me, in fact to a T.

The clergyman, who merely pretended to tie the fatal knot, was a boon companion of Talbot's, and no priest. He was an **43** excellent "whip," however; and having doffed his cassock to **44** put on a great-coat, he drove the hack which conveyed the "happy couple" out of town. Talbot took a seat at his side. The two scoundrels were thus "in at the death," and through a half-open window of the back parlor of the inn, amused themselves in grinning at the *dénouement* of the drama. I believe I shall be forced to call them both out.

Nevertheless, I am *not* the husband of my great, great grandmother; and this is a reflection which affords me infinite relief;—but I *am* the husband of Madame Lalande—of Madame Stéphanie Lalande—with whom my good old relative, besides making me her sole heir when she dies—if she ever does—has been at the trouble of concocting me a match. In conclusion: I am done forever with *billets doux,* and am never **45** to be met without SPECTACLES. **46**

43 Close

44 Coachman

45 Love letters

46 "None so blind as those that will not see," in the words of Mathew Henry (1662–1714), *Commentaries,* on Jeremiah 5:21.

The ending here is surprisingly didactic for Poe, but the narrator's nasty disposition and vanity make the change difficult to swallow. Since it is his admitted "deficiencies of vision" that cause his problems, the optimistic finale suggests that one can alter one's vision of the world—a point that Poe makes more seriously in such tales as "A Descent into the Maelström" and "The Pit and the Pendulum."

The emptiness of the tale is underscored by the fact that it is one of the few on which Marie Bonaparte does *not* turn her Freudian microscope. Perhaps it is just as well.

THE SYSTEM OF DOCTOR TARR
AND PROFESSOR FETHER

First published in *Graham's Magazine*, November 1845, this is (along with "How to Write a Blackwood Article"/"A Predicament") Poe's best comic tale. Much of the fun stems from the fact that while the inmates are mad, the narrator is a fool who does not realize that the lunatics have taken over the asylum.

Sources include two separate articles by N. P. Willis that recount his visit to a madhouse in Palermo, Sicily, in 1832. There he saw that patients were allowed a great deal of freedom within its walls, and took the responsibility of cooking, washing, and decorating the place. The Sicilian baron in charge of the asylum explains that his secret is "employment and constant kindness." The baron's first words to Willis are *"Je suis le premier fou"* ("I am the head madman").

Willis describes some of the patients, many of whom turn up in Poe's tale. The factual description, and a story called "The Madhouse of Palermo" are included in Willis' *Prose Works* (1845), pp. 103 and 457.

As for the "soothing system" of treatment for the mentally disturbed, Charles Dickens mentions it in his *American Notes for General Circulation* (1842), Vol. I, Chapters 3 and 5, in a description of asylums in South Boston and Hartford. According to the English author, the doctor in charge wanted to show "some confidence, and repose some trust, even in mad people." Many of Dickens' descriptions of patients also seem to have influenced Poe's tale.

With all three authors, a visitor to an asylum narrates his experience, and the asylums have adopted the "Moral Treatment," as it was termed in the early-nineteenth century. Patients have almost complete freedom to go as they please, and their whims are tolerated and delusions humored. The narrator in each definitely approves of the situation.

In the Dickens article, we find the observation that the mentally disturbed see through the delusions of their fellows but not through their own. We also find the physician trying to treat the delusions of the insane by appealing to their sense of the ridiculous. Willis' asylum is private, a converted château, as is Poe's, and is also in a southern (European) setting.

This last point has made some critics suggest that Poe's tale is a symbolic telling of the dangers of allowing slaves too much freedom. The Abolitionists attacked the plantation owners for not treating their slaves humanely; the plantation owners responded that their system was the only one that worked. The slave economy was dependent upon harsh treatment and strict control. Poe's story could be seen as a warning, by a Southerner, of what would happen if blacks were allowed as much freedom as the Abolitionists demanded. While this may sound farfetched, the title of the tale recalls that tarring and feathering was a punishment for Abolitionists caught in the South. See also note 43.

"Tarr and Fether" may also be read as a self-parody of "The Fall of the House of Usher." In both tales, a somewhat complacent narrator arrives on horseback, approaching a forbidding old mansion that causes vague feelings of dread. In both, the inmates attempt to bury sanity beneath the house. And in both, the climax is one of noise and violence.

Three generally forgotten films have been made from the tale. The first, a 1912 French version, *Le Système du Docteur Goudron et du Professeur Plume*, was directed by Robert Saidreau (perhaps a pseudonym for Maurice Tourneur), and added a scene in which the inmates perform as "operation" on the director of the asylum. The second version, *Five Tales of Horror*, was a 1919 German film that also included "The Black Cat"; it starred Conrad Veidt and Anita Berber. The German *Histoires Extraordinaires/Fünf Unheimliche Geschichten* (1931) was essentially a remake of the 1919 film.

During the autumn of 18—, while on a tour through the extreme southern provinces of France, my route led me within **1** a few miles of a certain *Maison de Santé* or private Mad **2** House, about which I had heard much, in Paris, from my medical friends. As I had never visited a place of the kind, I thought the opportunity too good to be lost; and so proposed to my travelling companion (a gentleman with whom I had made casual acquaintance a few days before), that we should turn aside, for an hour or so, and look through the establishment. To this he objected—pleading haste, in the first place, and, in the second, a very usual horror at the sight of a lunatic. He begged of me, however, not to let any mere courtesy toward himself interfere with the gratification of my curiosity, **3** and said that he would ride on leisurely, so that I might overtake him during the day, or, at all events, during the next. As he bade me good-by, I bethought me that there might be some difficulty in obtaining access to the premises, and mentioned my fears on this point. He replied that, in fact, unless I had personal knowledge of the superintendent, Monsieur Maillard, or some credential in the way of a letter, **4** a difficulty might be found to exist, as the regulations of these private mad-houses were more rigid than the public hospital laws. For himself, he added, he had, some years since, made the acquaintance of Maillard, and would so far assist me as to ride up to the door and introduce me; although his feelings on the subject of lunacy would not permit of his entering the house.

I thanked him, and, turning from the main road, we entered a grassgrown by-path, which, in half an hour, nearly lost itself in a dense forest, clothing the base of a mountain. Through this dank and gloomy wood we rode some two miles, when the *Maison de Santé* came in view. It was a fantastic *château*, **5** much dilapidated, and indeed scarcely tenantable through age and neglect. Its aspect inspired me with absolute dread, and, checking my horse, I half resolved to turn back. I soon, however, grew ashamed of my weakness, and proceeded.

As we rode up to the gate-way, I perceived it slightly open, and the visage of a man peering through. In an instant afterward, this man came forth, accosted my companion by name, shook him cordially by the hand, and begged him to alight. It was Monsieur Maillard himself. He was a portly, fine-looking gentleman of the old school, with a polished manner, and a certain air of gravity, dignity, and authority which was very impressive.

My friend, having presented me, mentioned my desire to inspect the establishment, and received Monsieur Maillard's assurance that he would show me all attention, now took leave, and I saw him no more.

When he had gone, the superintendent ushered me into a small and exceedingly neat parlor, containing, among other indications of refined taste, many books, drawings, pots of flowers, and musical instruments. A cheerful fire blazed upon the hearth. At a piano, singing an aria from Bellini, sat a young **6** and very beautiful woman, who, at my entrance, paused in her song, and received me with graceful courtesy. Her voice

1 Provence, the region and former province of southern France, which took its name from the Roman *provincia*. Marseille, Toulon, Avignon, Arles, and Aix-en-Provence (the historic capital) are the chief cities of the area.

2 Literally, "house of health," meaning either a private hospital (sanatorium) or an insane asylum. Vincent van Gogh (1853–90) spent time in such a place in the South of France (Arles Hospital) as well as an asylum in Saint-Rémy.

3 At one time, viewing the insane was a popular leisure-time diversion. However, the narrator seems to be a more scientific-minded sort.

4 From the French, meaning a chain, net, or mesh

5 Compare this passage with the early part of "The Fall of the House of Usher."

6 Vincenzo Bellini (1801–35) came from a Sicilian musical family; his first experience was in church music. Six years after moving to Naples, his first successful opera was staged, *Bianca e Fernando* (1826). A profusely melodic series of operas followed, including *Norma*, *La Sonnambula*, and *I Puritani*. See also "The Spectacles," notes 33 and 36.

7 The antecedent of the "soothing system" was probably the work of Philippe Pinel (1745–1826), chief physician at La Bicêtre Hospital in Paris, who began the practice of talking with his patients and assembling case histories for later study. He scored many successes by treating his patients with kindness and consideration; they were left unchained and allowed to walk the hospital grounds. His pupil Esquirol (1772–1840) continued the work and established a new system of mental hospitals in France.

In England, the Quaker William Tuke (1732–1822) established York Retreat, a private estate where, again, the mentally ill could escape the harsher measures of the asylum. Despite his work and that of Pinel and Esquirol, public opinion toward mental illness was slow to change, and more humane treatment in institutions remained a dream well into the twentieth century.

8 Originally the word (dating back to 1400) meant "mental derangement, characterized by great excitement, extravagant delusions and hallucinations, and, in its acute stage by great violence" (O.E.D.).

9 From the Latin *liberata*, meaning that which a manor lord gave to his servants, such as food or clothing. Later it came to mean the uniform he gave them to identify them as his own.

10 An inopportune occurrence

was low, and her whole manner subdued. I thought, too, that I perceived the traces of sorrow in her countenance, which was excessively, although to my taste, not unpleasingly, pale. She was attired in deep mourning, and excited in my bosom a feeling of mingled respect, interest, and admiration.

I had heard, at Paris, that the institution of Monsieur Maillard was managed upon what is vulgarly termed the "system of soothing"—that all punishments were avoided—that even confinement was seldom resorted to—that the patients, while secretly watched, were left much apparent liberty, and that most of them were permitted to roam about the house and grounds in the ordinary apparel of persons in **7** right mind.

Keeping these impressions in view, I was cautious in what I said before the young lady; for I could not be sure that she was sane; and, in fact, there was a certain restless brilliancy about her eyes which half led me to imagine she was not. I confined my remarks, therefore, to general topics, and to such as I thought would not be displeasing or exciting even to a lunatic. She replied in a perfectly rational manner to all that I said; and even her original observations were marked with the soundest good sense; but a long acquaintance with the **8** metaphysics of *mania*, had taught me to put no faith in such evidence of sanity, and I continued to practise, throughout the interview, the caution with which I commenced it.

9 Presently a smart footman in livery brought in a tray with fruit, wine, and other refreshments, of which I partook, the lady soon afterward leaving the room. As she departed I turned my eyes in an inquiring manner toward my host.

"No," he said, "oh, no—a member of my family—my niece, and a most accomplished woman."

"I beg a thousand pardons for the suspicion," I replied, "but of course you will know how to excuse me. The excellent administration of your affairs here is well understood in Paris, and I thought it just possible, you know—"

"Yes, yes—say no more—or rather it is myself who should thank you for the commendable prudence you have displayed. We seldom find so much of forethought in young men; and, **10** more than once, some unhappy *contre-temps* has occurred in consequence of thoughtlessness on the part of our visitors. While my former system was in operation, and my patients were permitted the privilege of roaming to and fro at will, they were often aroused to a dangerous frenzy by injudicious persons who called to inspect the house. Hence I was obliged to enforce a rigid system of exclusion; and none obtained access to the premises upon whose discretion I could not rely."

"While your *former* system was in operation!" I said, repeating his words—"do I understand you, then, to say that the 'soothing system' of which I have heard so much is no longer in force?"

"It is now," he replied, "several weeks since we have concluded to renounce it forever."

"Indeed! you astonish me!"

"We found it, sir," he said, with a sigh, "absolutely necessary to return to the old usages. The *danger* of the soothing system was, at all times, appalling; and its advantages have been much overrated. I believe, sir, that in this house it has been given a fair trial, if ever in any. We did every thing that rational humanity could suggest. I am sorry that you could not have paid us a visit at an earlier period, that you might have judged for yourself. But I presume you are conversant with the soothing practice—with its details."

"Not altogether. What I have heard has been at third or fourth hand."

"I may state the system, then, in general terms, as one in which the patients were *ménagés*, humored. We contradicted **11** *no* fancies which entered the brains of the mad. On the contrary, we not only indulged but encouraged them; and many of our most permanent cures have been thus effected. There is no argument which so touches the feeble reason of the madman as the *reductio ad absurdum*. We have had men, **12** for example, who fancied themselves chickens. The cure was, to insist upon the thing as a fact—to accuse the patient of stupidity in not sufficiently perceiving it to be a fact—and thus to refuse him any other diet for a week than that which properly appertains to a chicken. In this manner a little corn and gravel were made to perform wonders."

"But was this species of acquiescence all?"

"By no means. We put much faith in amusements of a simple kind, such as music, dancing, gymnastic exercises generally, cards, certain classes of books, and so forth. We affected to treat each individual as if for some ordinary physical disorder; and the word 'lunacy' was never employed. A great **13** point was to set each lunatic to guard the actions of all the others. To repose confidence in the understanding or discretion of a madman, is to gain him body and soul. In this way we were enabled to dispense with an expensive body of keepers."

"And you had no punishments of any kind?"

"None."

"And you never confined your patients?"

"Very rarely. Now and then, the malady of some inidividual growing to a crisis, or taking a sudden turn to fury, we conveyed him to a secret cell, lest his disorder should infect the rest, and there kept him until we could dismiss him to his friends—for with the raging maniac we have nothing to do. He is usually removed to the public hospitals."

"And you have now changed all this—and you think for the better?"

"Decidedly. The system had its disadvantages, and even its dangers. It is now, happily, exploded throughout all the **14** *Maisons de Santé* of France."

"I am very much surprised," I said, "at what you tell me; for I made sure that, at this moment, no other method of treatment for mania existed in any portion of the country."

"You are young yet, my friend," replied my host, "but the time will arrive when you will learn to judge for yourself of what is going on in the world, without trusting to the gossip

11 Members of the household or family

12 Reducing to absurdity; that is, taking a point to its logical extreme to show its fallacy.

13 From the Latin *luna*, "moon." A belief common among the Greeks and Romans was that the mind was affected by the moon and that "lunatics" were more and more frenzied as the moon increased to its full. Recent studies have once again opened up the possibility that the phases of the moon may indeed have something to do with affecting mental states. Certain crimes, for example, rise in frequency during the period of the full moon.
"Demoniac frenzy, moping melancholy,/And moon-struck madness" (*Paradise Lost*, XI, 485)
For more on historical attitudes on madness, see George Rosen's *Madness in Society* (University of Chicago, 1968).

14 Held in contempt, discovered, or revealed

of others. Believe nothing you hear, and only one half that you see. Now about our *Maisons de Santé,* it is clear that some ignoramus has misled you. After dinner, however, when you have sufficiently recovered from the fatigue of your ride, I will be happy to take you over the house, and introduce to you a system which, in my opinion, and in that of every one who has witnessed its operation, is incomparably the most effectual as yet devised."

"Your own?" I inquired—"one of your own invention?"

"I am proud," he replied, "to acknowledge that it is—at least in some measure."

In this manner I conversed with Monsieur Maillard for an hour or two, during which he showed me the gardens and conservatories of the place.

"I cannot let you see my patients," he said, "just at present. To a sensitive mind there is always more or less of the shocking in such exhibitions; and I do not wish to spoil your appetite for dinner. We will dine. I can give you some veal *à la St.* **15,16** *Menehoult,* with cauliflowers in *velouté* sauce—after that a **17** glass of *Clos de Vougeôt*—then your nerves will be sufficiently steadied."

At six, dinner was announced; and my host conducted me **18** into a large *salle à manger,* where a very numerous company were assembled—twenty-five or thirty in all. They were, apparently, people of rank—certainly of high breeding—although their habiliments, I thought, were extravagantly rich, partaking somewhat too much of the ostentatious finery of the **19** *vieille cour.* I noticed that at least two-thirds of these guests were ladies; and some of the latter were by no means accoutred in what a Parisian would consider good taste at the present day. Many females, for example, whose age could not have been less than seventy, were bedecked with a profusion of jewelry, such as rings, bracelets, and ear-rings, and wore their bosoms and arms shamefully bare. I observed, too, that very few of the dresses were well made—or, at least, that very few of them fitted the wearers. In looking about, I discovered the interesting girl to whom Monsieur Maillard had presented me in the little parlor; but my surprise was great to see her **20** wearing a hoop and farthingale, with high-heeled shoes, and a dirty cap of Brussels lace, so much too large for her that it gave her face a ridiculously diminutive expression. When I had first seen her, she was attired, most becomingly, in deep mourning. There was an air of oddity, in short, about the dress of the whole party, which, at first, caused me to recur to my original idea of the "soothing system," and to fancy that Monsieur Maillard had been willing to deceive me until after dinner, that I might experience no uncomfortable feelings during the repast, at finding myself dining with lunatics; but I remembered having been informed, in Paris, that the southern provincialists were a peculiarly eccentric people, **21** with a vast number of antiquated notions; and then, too, upon conversing with several members of the company, my apprehensions were immediately and fully dispelled.

The dining-room itself, although perhaps sufficiently com-

15 Veal *à la Mènehoult* is coated with butter and breadcrumbs, then grilled.

16 Velouté is a white sauce that uses a flour and butter *roux* as a thickening agent and is moistened with white stock from poultry, veal, or fish.

17 See "Bon-Bon," note 18.

18 Dining room

19 The old court, i.e., of Louis XIV–XVI.

20 A farthingale was a hooped petticoat.

21 Provence had until the nineteenth cèntury kept pretty much to itself. It was the home of the troubadors and courtly-love tradition in the eleventh and twelfth centuries and even had its own language (Provençal, or Langue d'Oc), which was later replaced by French but underwent occasional revivals—including one in the nineteenth century.

fortable and of good dimensions, had nothing too much of elegance about it. For example, the floor was uncarpeted; in France, however, a carpet is frequently dispensed with. The windows, too, were without curtains; the shutters, being shut, were securely fastened with iron bars, applied diagonally, after the fashion of our shop-shutters. The apartment, I observed, formed, in itself, a wing of the *château*, and thus the windows were on three sides of the parallelogram, the door being at the other. There were no less than ten windows in all.

The table was superbly set out. It was loaded with plate, and more than loaded with delicacies. The profusion was absolutely barbaric. There were meats enough to have feasted the Anakim. Never, in all my life, had I witnessed so lavish, **22** so wasteful an expenditure of the good things of life. There seemed very little taste, however, in the arrangements; and my eyes, accustomed to quiet lights, were sadly offended by the prodigious glare of a multitude of wax candles, which, in silver *candelabra*, were deposited upon the table, and all about the room, wherever it was possible to find a place. There were several active servants in attendance; and, upon a large table, at the farther end of the apartment, were seated seven or eight people with fiddles, fifes, trombones, and a drum. These fellows annoyed me very much, at intervals, during the repast, by an infinite variety of noises, which were intended for music, and which appeared to afford much entertainment to all present, with the exception of myself.

Upon the whole, I could not help thinking that there was much of the *bizarre* about every thing I saw—but then the world is made up of all kinds of persons, with all modes of thought, and all sorts of conventional customs. I had travelled, too, so much, as to be quite an adept at the *nil admirari;* so **23** I took my seat very coolly at the right hand of my host, and, having an excellent appetite, did justice to the good cheer set before me.

The conversation, in the meantime, was spirited and general. The ladies, as usual, talked a great deal. I soon found that nearly all the company were well educated; and my host was a world of good-humored anecdote in himself. He seemed quite willing to speak of his position as superintendent of a *Maison de Santé;* and, indeed, the topic of lunacy was, much to my surprise, a favorite one with all present. A great many amusing stories were told, having reference to the *whims* of the patients.

"We had a fellow here once," said a fat little gentleman, who sat at my right—"a fellow that fancied himself a tea-pot; and by the way, is it not especially singular how often this particular crotchet has entered the brain of the lunatic? There is scarcely an insane asylum in France which cannot supply a human tea-pot. *Our* gentleman was a Britannia-ware tea-pot, and was careful to polish himself every morning with buckskin and whiting." **24**

"And then," said a tall man just opposite, "we had here, not long ago, a person who had taken it into his head that he was

22 Anak was a Palestinian giant in the Old Testament, whose descendants were also of large proportions. Hebrew spies said they themselves were mere grasshoppers by comparison.

"And there we saw the giants, the sons of Anak" (Numbers 13:33).

23 Blasé, showing no surprise

24 Whiting is a preparation of finely powdered chalk used for cleaning and whitewashing.

A human teapot also apppears in Pope's *The Rape of the Lock*, IV, 49–50: "Here living Teapots stand, one arm held out,/One bent; the handle this, and that the spout."

a donkey—which, allegorically speaking, you will say, was quite true. He was a troublesome patient; and we had much ado to keep him within bounds. For a long time he would eat nothing but thistles; but of this idea we soon cured him by insisting upon his eating nothing else. Then he was perpetually kicking out his heels—so—so—"

25 "Mr. De Kock! I will thank you to behave yourself!" here interrupted an old lady, who sat next to the speaker. "Please keep your feet to yourself! You have spoiled my brocade! Is it necessary, pray, to illustrate a remark in so practical a style? Our friend here can surely comprehend you without all this. Upon my word, you are nearly as great a donkey as the poor unfortunate imagined himself. Your acting is very natural, as I live."

"*Mille pardons! Ma'm'selle!*" replied Monsieur De Kock, thus addressed—"a thousand pardons! I had no intention of
26 offending. Ma'm'selle Laplace—Monsieur De Kock will do himself the honor of taking wine with you."

Here Monsieur De Kock bowed low, kissed his hand with much ceremony, and took wine with Ma'm'selle Laplace.

"Allow me, *mon ami*," now said Monsieur Maillard, addressing myself, "allow me to send you a morsel of this veal *à la St. Menehoult*—you will find it particularly fine."

At this instant three sturdy waiters had just succeeded in depositing safely upon the table an enormous dish, or trencher, containing what I supposed to be the "*monstrum, horrendum,*
27 *informe, ingens, cui lumen ademptum.*" A closer scrutiny assured me, however, that it was only a small calf roasted whole, and set upon its knees, with an apple in its mouth, as is the English fashion of dressing a hare.

"Thank you, no," I replied; "to say the truth, I am not particularly partial to veal *à la St.* —— what is it?—for I do not find that it altogether agrees with me. I will change my plate, however, and try some of the rabbit."

There were several side-dishes on the table, containing what appeared to be the ordinary French rabbit—a very delicious *morceau*, which I can recommend.

"Pierre," cried the host, "change this gentleman's plate,
28 and give him a side-piece of this rabbit *au-chat.*"

"This what?" said I.

"This rabbit *au-chat.*"

"Why, thank you—upon second thoughts, no. I will just help myself to some of the ham."

There is no knowing what one eats, thought I to myself, at the tables of these people of the province. I will have none of their rabbit *au-chat*—and, for the matter of that, none of their *cat-au-rabbit* either.

"And then," said a cadaverous-looking personage, near the foot of the table, taking up the thread of the conversation where it had been broken off—"and then, among other oddities, we had a patient, once upon a time, who very
29 pertinaciously maintained himself to be a Cordova cheese, and went about, with a knife in his hand, soliciting his friends to try a small slice from the middle of his leg."

25 Paul de Kock (1794–1871) wrote sensational novels about Parisian life.

26 Pierre Simon, Marquis de Laplace (1749–1827), was famous for his observations of the moon.

27 From the *Aeneid*, III, 658.: "a horrible deformed huge monster," referring to the Cyclops. Poe also used the Latin phrase in "The Purloined Letter."

28 "In the manner of a cat"

29 Córdova, or Córdoba, in Andalusian Spain, was a center of Moslem and Jewish culture during the Middle Ages.

Here the speaker, very rudely,
as I thought, put his right
thumb in his left cheek, withdrew it with a sound resembling
the popping of a cork. . . .
Illustration by F. S. Coburn, 1903

"He was a great fool, beyond doubt," interposed some one, "but not to be compared with a certain individual whom we all know, with the exception of this strange gentleman. I mean the man who took himself for a bottle of champagne, and always went off with a pop and a fizz, in this fashion."

Here the speaker, very rudely, as I thought, put his right thumb in his left cheek, withdrew it with a sound resembling the popping of a cork, and then, by a dexterous movement of the tongue upon the teeth, created a sharp hissing and fizzing, which lasted for several minutes, in imitation of the frothing of champagne. This behavior, I saw plainly, was not very pleasing to Monsieur Maillard; but that gentleman said nothing, and the conversation was resumed by a very lean little man in a big wig.

"And then there was an ignoramus," said he, "who mistook himself for a frog; which, by the way, he resembled in no little degree. I wish you could have seen him, sir,"—here the speaker addressed myself—"it would have done your heart good to see the natural airs that he put on. Sir, if that man was *not* a frog, I can only observe that it is a pity he was not. His **30** croak thus—o-o-o-o-gh!—o-o-o-o-gh! was the finest note in the world—B flat; and when he put his elbows upon the table thus—after taking a glass or two of wine—and distended his mouth, thus, and rolled up his eyes, thus, and winked them with excessive rapidity, thus, why then, sir, I take it upon myself to say, positively, that you would have been lost in admiration of the genius of the man."

"I have no doubt of it," I said.

"And then," said somebody else, "then there was Petit Gaillard, who thought himself a pinch of snuff, and was truly **31** distressed because he could not take himself between his own finger and thumb."

"And then there was Jules Desoulières, who was a very **32** singular genius, indeed, and went mad with the idea that he

30 "Frog," referring to a Parisian, dates back to at least the eighteenth century, and stems from their ancient heraldic device, which was three frogs or toads. "Frogs" was a common court phrase at Versailles. The origin may have been the situation of Paris in its early years, when it was little more than a quagmire called *Lutetia* (mud land), and its inhabitants lived like frogs or toads in the mud.

The Dictionary of Slang and Unconventional English says that "Frog" meaning a Frenchman did not come into common use until after 1870, adding that, in the seventeenth century, the word also meant a Dutchman. Poe again uses the word "Frog" to mean Frenchman in "Why the Little Frenchman Wears His Hand in a Sling."

31 A gaillard (or galliard) was a sprightly dance from the early-sixteenth century.

32 Possibly meaning a pie made of shoes, since *soulier* is French for "shoe." *Dessouler* means to sober up, or sleep it off.

33 Literally, "the great clown," but probably a reference to Georges Louis Leclerc de Buffon (1707–88), the French naturalist who devoted his life to the monumental *Histoire Naturelle*, in forty-four volumes.

34 Marcus Tullius Cicero (100–43 B.C.), the great Roman orator and politician; Demosthenes (384?–322 B.C.), the famous Greek orator who placed pebbles in his mouth and forced himself to be heard over the roar of the sea; Henry Peter Brougham (1778–1868), liberal leader in the House of Commons and one of the founders of the *Edinburgh Review*, as well as one of the great orators of the day.

35 A tee-totum is a spinning top. The name Boullard may be a form of either *boule* (ball) or *bouler* (to swell).

36 Her name means "joyful." She seems to be drawn from a character in *Charles O'Malley* (1842), by Charles Lever (1806–72). In that novel a young man falls in love, unknowingly, with a madwoman whose behavior is very similar to that of Madame Joyeuse, particularly the rooster crow.

was a pumpkin. He persecuted the cook to make him up into pies—a thing which the cook indignantly refused to do. For my part, I am by no means sure that a pumpkin pie *à la Desoulières* would not have been very capital eating indeed!"

"You astonish me!" said I; and I looked inquisitively at Monsieur Maillard.

"Ha! ha! ha!" said that gentleman—"he! he! he!—hi! hi! hi!—ho! ho! ho!—hu! hu! hu!—very good indeed! You must not be astonished, *mon ami;* our friend here is a wit—a *drôle*—you must not understand him to the letter."

"And then," said some other one of the party, "then there was Bouffon Le Grand—another extraordinary personage in his way. He grew deranged through love, and fancied himself possessed of two heads. One of these he maintained to be the head of Cicero; the other he imagined a composite one, being Demosthenes' from the top of the forehead to the mouth, and Lord Brougham's from the mouth to the chin. It is not impossible that he was wrong; but he would have convinced you of his being in the right; for he was a man of great eloquence. He had an absolute passion for oratory, and could not refrain from display. For example, he used to leap upon the dinner-table thus, and—and—"

Here a friend, at the side of the speaker, put a hand upon his shoulder and whispered a few words in his ear; upon which he ceased talking with great suddenness, and sank back within his chair.

"And then," said the friend who had whispered, "there was Boullard, the tee-totum. I call him the tee-totum because, in fact, he was seized with the droll, but not altogether irrational, crotchet, that he had been converted into a tee-totum. You would have roared with laughter to see him spin. He would turn round upon one heel by the hour, in this manner—so—"

Here the friend whom he had just interrupted by a whisper, performed an exactly similar office for himself.

"But then," cried an old lady, at the top of her voice, "your Monsieur Boullard was a madman, and a very silly madman at best; for who, allow me to ask you, ever heard of a human tee-totum? The thing is absurd. Madame Joyeuse was a more sensible person, as you know. She had a crotchet, but it was instinct with common sense, and gave pleasure to all who had the honor of her acquaintance. She found, upon mature deliberation, that, by some accident, she had been turned into a chicken-cock; but, as such, she behaved with propriety. She flapped her wings with prodigious effect—so—so—so—and, as for her crow, it was delicious! Cock-a-doodle-doo!—cock-a-doodle-doo!—cock-a-doodle-de-doo-doo-dooo-do-o-o-o-o-o-o!"

"Madame Joyeuse, I will thank you to behave yourself!" here interrupted our host, very angrily. "You can either conduct yourself as a lady should do, or you can quit the table forthwith—take your choice."

The lady (whom I was much astonished to hear addressed as Madame Joyeuse, after the description of Madame Joyeuse she had just given) blushed up to the eyebrows, and seemed exceedingly abashed at the reproof. She hung down her head, and said not a syllable in reply. But another and younger lady resumed the theme. It was my beautiful girl of the little parlor!

"Oh, Madame Joyeuse *was* a fool!" she exclaimed, "but there was really much sound sense, after all, in the opinion of Eugénie Salsafette. She was a very beautiful and painfully **37** modest young lady, who thought the ordinary mode of habiliment indecent, and wished to dress herself, always, by getting outside instead of inside of her clothes. It is a thing very easily done, after all. You have only to do so—and then so—so—so and then so—so—so—and then—"

"*Mon dieu!* Ma'm'selle Salsafette!" here cried a dozen voices at once. "What *are* you about?—forbear!—that is sufficient!—we see, very plainly, how it is done!—hold! hold!" and several persons were already leaping from their seats to withhold Ma'm'selle Salsafette from putting herself upon a par with the Medicean Venus, when the point was very effectually and **38** suddenly accomplished by a series of loud screams, or yells, from some portion of the main body of the *château*.

My nerves were very much affected, indeed, by these yells; but the rest of the company I really pitied. I never saw any set of reasonable people so thoroughly frightened in my life. They all grew as pale as so many corpses, and, shrinking within their seats, sat quivering and gibbering with terror, and listening for a repetition of the sound. It came again—louder and seemingly nearer—and then a third time *very* loud, and then a fourth time with a vigor evidently diminished. At this apparent dying away of the noise, the spirits of the company were immediately regained, and all was life and anecdote as before. I now ventured to inquire the cause of the disturbance.

"A mere *bagatelle*," said Monsieur Maillard. "We are used **39** to these things, and care really very little about them. The lunatics, every now and then, get up a howl in concert; one starting another, as is sometimes the case with a bevy of dogs at night. It occasionally happens, however, that the *concerto* yells are succeeded by a simultaneous effort at breaking loose; when, of course, some little danger is to be apprehended."

"And how many have you in charge?"

"At present we have not more than ten, all together."

"Principally females, I presume?"

"Oh, no—every one of them men, and stout fellows, too, I can tell you."

"Indeed! I have always understood that the majority of lunatics were of the gentler sex."   **40**

"It is generally so, but not always. Some time ago, there were about twenty-seven patients here; and, of that number, no less than eighteen were women; but, lately, matters have changed very much, as you see."

"Yes—have changed very much, as you see," here interrupted the gentleman who had broken the shins of Ma'm'selle Laplace.

37 The name comes from salsify, an edible root, which has nothing to do with her impromptu striptease.

38 The Venus of the Medici, the most celebrated nude of Poe's day, was on display at the Uffizi, in Florence. Poe also mentions it in "The Assignation."

39 A trifle, of no importance. The word's origin is uncertain, but it seems to share an ancestor with "baggage."

40 The notion that women are somehow more susceptible to mental disturbance probably arose because women in Western society have traditionally had to meet much more rigid codes of behavior than men. In his book *Satanism and Witchcraft* (1939), Jules Michelet suggests that societal pressures on women in the Middle Ages manifested themselves in odd behavior, and ultimately, charges of witchcraft (pp. 21–54).

"Yes—have changed very much, as you see!" chimed in the whole company at once.

"Hold your tongues, every one of you!" said my host, in a great rage. Whereupon the whole company maintained a dead silence for nearly a minute. As for one lady, she obeyed Monsieur Maillard to the letter, and thrusting out her tongue, which was an excessively long one, held it very resignedly, with both hands, until the end of the entertainment.

"And this gentlewoman," said I, to Monsieur Maillard, bending over and addressing him in a whisper—"this good lady who has just spoken, and who gives us the cock-a-doodle-de-doo—she, I presume, is harmless—quite harmless, eh?"

"Harmless!" ejaculated he, in unfeigned surprise, "why—why, what *can* you mean?"

"Only slightly touched?" said I, touching my head. "I take it for granted that she is not particularly—not dangerously affected, eh?"

"*Mon dieu!* what *is* it you imagine? This lady, my particular old friend, Madame Joyeuse, is as absolutely sane as myself. She has her little eccentricities, to be sure—but then, you know, all old women—all *very* old women—are more or less eccentric!"

"To be sure," said I—"to be sure—and then the rest of these ladies and gentlemen—"

"Are my friends and keepers," interrupted Monsieur Maillard, drawing himself up with *hauteur*—"my very good friends and assistants."

"What! all of them?" I asked—"the women and all?"

"Assuredly," he said—"we could not do at all without the women; they are the best lunatic nurses in the world; they have a way of their own, you know; their bright eyes have a marvellous effect—something like the fascination of the snake, you know."

"To be sure," said I—"to be sure! They behave a little odd, eh?—they are a little *queer*, eh?—don't you think so?"

"Odd!—queer!—why, do you *really* think so? We are not very prudish, to be sure, here in the South—do pretty much as we please—enjoy life, and all that sort of thing, you know—"

"To be sure," said I—"to be sure."

"And then, perhaps, this *Clos de Vougeôt* is a little heady, you know—a little *strong*—you understand, eh?"

"To be sure," said I—"to be sure. By the by, Monsieur, did I understand you to say that the system you have adopted, in place of the celebrated soothing system, was one of very rigorous severity?"

"By no means. Our confinement is necessarily close; but the treatment—the medical treatment, I mean—is rather agreeable to the patients than otherwise."

"And the new system is one of your own invention?"

"Not altogether. Some portions of it are referable to Professor Tarr, of whom you have, necessarily heard; and, again, there are modifications in my plan which I am happy to acknowledge as belonging of right to the celebrated Fether, with whom, if I mistake not, you have the honor of an intimate acquaintance."

"I am quite ashamed to confess," I replied, "that I have never even heard the names of either gentleman before."

"Good heavens!" ejaculated my host, drawing back his chair abruptly, and uplifting his hands. "I surely do not hear you aright! You did not intend to say, eh? that you had never *heard* either of the learned Doctor Tarr, or of the celebrated Professor Fether?"

"I am forced to acknowledge my ignorance," I replied; "but the truth should be held inviolate above all things. Nevertheless, I feel humbled to the dust, not to be acquainted with the works of these, no doubt, extraordinary men. I will seek out their writings forthwith, and peruse them with deliberate care. Monsieur Maillard, you have really—I must confess it— you have *really*—made me ashamed of myself!"

And this was the fact.

"Say no more, my good young friend," he said kindly, pressing my hand—"join me now in a glass of Sauterne."

We drank. The company followed our example without stint. They chatted—they jested—they laughed—they perpetrated a thousand absurdities—the fiddles shrieked—the drum row-de-dowed—the trombones bellowed like so many brazen bulls of Phalaris—and the whole scene, growing **41** gradually worse and worse, as the wines gained the ascendancy, became at length a sort of pandemonium *in petto*. In the **42** meantime, Monsieur Maillard and myself, with some bottles of Sauterne and Vougeôt between us, continued our conversation at the top of the voice. A word spoken in an ordinary key stood no more chance of being heard than the voice of a fish from the bottom of Niagara Falls.

"And, sir," said I, screaming in his ear, "you mentioned something before dinner about the danger incurred in the old system of soothing. How is that?"

"Yes," he replied, "there was, occasionally, very great danger indeed. There is no accounting for the caprices of madmen; and, in my opinion, as well as in that of Dr. Tarr and Professor Fether, it is *never* safe to permit them to run at large unattended. A lunatic may be 'soothed,' as it is called, for a time, but, in the end, he is very apt to become obstreperous. His cunning, too, is proverbial and great. If he has a project in view, he conceals his design with a marvellous wisdom; and the dexterity with which he counterfeits sanity, presents, to the metaphysician, one of the most singular problems in the study of mind. When a madman appears *thoroughly* sane, indeed, it is high time to put him in a straight-jacket."

"But the *danger*, my dear sir, of which you were speaking— in your own experience—during your control of this house— have you had practical reason to think liberty hazardous in the case of a lunatic?"

"Here?—in my own experience?—why, I may say, yes. For example:—no *very* long while ago, a singular circumstance occurred in this very house. The 'soothing system,' you know,

41 (C. 570–554 B.C.), the tyrant of Agrigentum, Sicily, notorious for his cruelty. See "Loss of Breath," note 20, for his roaring success as an unpopular monarch.

42 Pandemonium is the parliament of hell in Milton's *Paradise Lost*, Book I—from the Greek *pan daimon*, "every demon."
In petto means "in secrecy," from the Italian, meaning "in the breast."

was then in operation, and the patients were at large. They behaved remarkably well—especially so—any one of sense might have known that some devilish scheme was brewing from that particular fact, that the fellow behaved so *remarkably* well. And, sure enough, one fine morning the keepers found themselves pinioned hand and foot, and thrown into the cells, where they were attended, as if *they* were the lunatics, by the lunatics themselves, who had usurped the offices of the keepers."

"You don't tell me so! I never heard of any thing so absurd in my life!"

"Fact—it all came to pass by means of a stupid fellow—a lunatic—who, by some means, had taken it into his head that he had invented a better system of government than any ever heard of before—of lunatic government, I mean. He wished to give his invention a trial, I suppose, and so he persuaded the rest of the patients to join him a conspiracy for the overthrow of the reigning powers."

"And he really succeeded?"

"No doubt of it. The keepers and kept were soon made to exchange places. Not that exactly either, for the madmen had been free, but the keepers were shut up in cells forthwith, and treated, I am sorry to say, in a very cavalier manner."

"But I presume a counter-revolution was soon effected. This condition of things could not have long existed. The country people in the neighborhood—visitors coming to see the establishment—would have given the alarm."

"There you are out. The head rebel was too cunning for that. He admitted no visitors at all—with the exception, one day, of a very stupid-looking young gentleman of whom he had no reason to be afraid. He let him in to see the place— just by way of variety—to have a little fun with him. As soon as he had gammoned him sufficiently, he let him out, and sent him about his business."

"And *how* long, then, did the madmen reign?"

"Oh, a very long time, indeed—a month certainly—how much longer I can't precisely say. In the meantime, the lunatics had a jolly season of it—that you may swear. They doffed their own shabby clothes, and made free with the family wardrobe and jewels. The cellars of the *château* were well stocked with wine; and these madmen are just the devils that know how to drink it. They lived well, I can tell you."

"And the treatment—what was the particular species of treatment which the leader of the rebels put into operation?"

"Why, as for that, a madman is not necessarily a fool, as I have already observed; and it is my honest opinion that his treatment was a much better treatment than that which it superseded. It was a very capital system indeed—simple— neat—no trouble at all—in fact it was delicious—it was—"

Here my host's observations were cut short by another series of yells, of the same character as those which had previously disconcerted us. This time, however, they seemed to proceed from persons rapidly approaching.

"Gracious heavens!" I ejaculated—"the lunatics have most undoubtedly broken loose."

"I very much fear it is so," replied Monsieur Maillard, now becoming excessively pale. He had scarcely finished the sentence, before loud shouts and imprecations were heard beneath the windows; and, immediately afterward, it became evident that some persons outside were endeavoring to gain entrance into the room. The door was beaten with what appeared to be a sledge-hammer, and the shutters were wrenched and shaken with prodigious violence.

A scene of the most terrible confusion ensued. Monsieur Maillard, to my excessive astonishment, threw himself under the sideboard. I had expected more resolution at his hands. The members of the orchestra, who, for the last fifteen minutes, had been seemingly too much intoxicated to do duty, now sprang all at once to their feet and to their instruments, and, scrambling upon their table, broke out, with one accord, into, "Yankee Doodle," which they performed, if not exactly **43** in tune, at least with an energy superhuman, during the whole of the uproar.

Meantime, upon the main dining-table, among the bottles and glasses, leaped the gentleman who, with such difficulty, had been restrained from leaping there before. As soon as he fairly settled himself, he commenced an oration, which, no doubt, was a very capital one, if it could only have been heard. At the same moment, the man with the tee-totum predilection, set himself to spinning around the apartment, with immense energy, and with arms outstretched at right angles with his body; so that he had all the air of a tee-totum in fact, and knocked everybody down that happened to get in his way. And now, too, hearing an incredible popping and fizzing of champagne, I discovered at length, that it proceeded from the person who performed the bottle of that delicate drink during dinner. And then, again, the frog-man croaked away as if the salvation of his soul depended upon every note that he uttered. And, in the midst of all this, the continuous braying of a donkey arose over all. As for my old friend, Madame Joyeuse, I really could have wept for the poor lady, she appeared so terribly perplexed. All she did, however, was to stand up in a corner, by the fireplace, and sing out incessantly at the top of her voice, "Cock-a-doodle-de-dooooooh!"

And now came the climax—the catastrophe of the drama. As no resistance, beyond whooping and yelling and cock-a-doodling, was offered to the encroachments of the party without, the ten windows were very speedily, and almost simultaneously, broken in. But I shall never forget the emotions of wonder and horror with which I gazed, when, leaping through these windows, and down among us *pêle-mêle*, fighting, stamping, scratching, and howling, there rushed a perfect army of what I took to be chimpanzees, ourang-outangs, or big black baboons of the Cape of Good Hope. **44**

43 Why Frenchmen should be playing "Yankee Doodle" is a hard one to answer. Poe may be taking a swipe at the North (they are mad), or it may be taken as evidence of the interpretation that the tale is a warning against allowing slaves freedom (introductory note).

44 Orang-utans appear in "Hop-Frog" and "Murders in the Rue Morgue." As for baboons, most are yellowish or brown, and none live near the Cape of Good Hope, in South Africa. He may mean a chimpanzee, which can reach five feet, or some other ape.

As for my old friend, Madame Joyeuse, I really could have wept for the poor lady. . . . All she did, however, was to stand up in a corner, by the fireplace, and sing out incessantly at the top of her voice, "Cock-a-doodle-de-dooooooh!" *Illustration by Johann Friedrich Vogel*

I received a terrible beating—after which I rolled under a sofa and lay still. After lying there some fifteen minutes, however, during which time I listened with all my ears to what was going on in the room, I came to some satisfactory *dénouement* of this tragedy. Monsieur Maillard, it appeared, in giving me the account of the lunatic who had excited his fellows to rebellion, had been merely relating his own exploits. This gentleman had, indeed, some two or three years before, been the superintendent of the establishment; but grew crazy himself, and so became a patient. This fact was unknown to the travelling companion who introduced me. The keepers, ten in number, having been suddenly overpowered, were first well tarred, then carefully feathered, and then shut up in underground cells. They had been so imprisoned for more than a month, during which period Monsieur Maillard had generously allowed them not only the tar and feathers (which **45** constituted his "system"), but some bread and abundance of water. The latter was pumped on them daily. At length, one escaping through a sewer, gave freedom to all the rest.

The "soothing system," with important modifications, has been resumed at the *château;* yet I cannot help agreeing with Monsieur Maillard, that his own "treatment" was a very capital one of its kind. As he justly observed, it was "simple—neat—and gave no trouble at all—not the least."

I have only to add that, although I have searched every library in Europe for the works of Doctor *Tarr* and Professor *Fether,* I have, up to the present day, utterly failed in my endeavors at procuring an edition.

45 While tarring and feathering was a common punishment afflicted on Abolitionists in the South, it is an old idea, dating back to the Crusades, as a kind of mob vengeance applied to obnoxious persons of all sorts.

". . . a thiefe or felon that hath stollen, being lawfully convicted, shal have his head shorne, and boyling pitch poured upon his head, and feathers or downe strawed upon the same, whereby he may be knowen . . ." (Richard Hakluyt, *Voyages,* 1582; II, 21).

And now came the climax. . . . *Illustration by F. S. Coburn, 1903*

THE LITERARY LIFE OF THINGUM BOB, ESQ.

LATE EDITOR OF THE "GOOSETHERUMFOODLE." BY HIMSELF.[1]

First published in the *Southern Literary Messenger*, December 1844, this tale pokes fun at the publishing profession, a world that Poe knew at first hand. The main target is *Graham's Lady's and Gentleman's Magazine*, but Lewis Gaylord Clark and his brother Willis also come in for their share of satire as publishers of *Knickerbocker Magazine*.

I am now growing in years, and—since I understand that Shakespeare and Mr. Emmons are deceased—it is not im- [2] possible that I may even die. It has occurred to me, therefore, that I may as well retire from the field of Letters and repose upon my laurels. But I am ambitious of signalizing my abdication of the literary sceptre by some important bequest to posterity; and, perhaps, I cannot do a better thing than just pen for it an account of my earlier career. My name, indeed, has been so long and so constantly before the public eye, that I am not only willing to admit the naturalness of the interest which it has everywhere excited, but ready to satisfy the extreme curiosity which it has inspired. In fact, it is no more than the duty of him who achieves greatness to leave behind [3] him, in his ascent, such landmarks as may guide others to be great. I propose, therefore, in the present paper (which I had some idea of calling "Memoranda to Serve for the Literary History of America") to give a detail of those important, yet feeble and tottering, first steps, by which, at length, I attained the high road to the pinnacle of human renown.

Of one's *very* remote ancestors it is superfluous to say much. My father, Thomas Bob, Esq., stood for many years at the summit of his profession, which was that of a merchant-barber, [4] in the city of Smug. His warehouse was the resort of all the principal people of the place, and especially of the editorial corps—a body which inspires all about it with profound veneration and awe. For my own part, I regarded them as gods, and drank in with avidity the rich wit and wisdom which continuously flowed from their august mouths during the process of what is styled "lather." My first moment of positive inspiration must be dated from that ever-memorable epoch, when the brilliant conductor of the *Gad-Fly*, in the intervals [5] of the important process just mentioned, recited aloud, before a conclave of our apprentices, an inimitable poem in honor of the "Only Genuine Oil-of-Bob" (so called from its talented [6]

1 One could break this puzzling word down this way: "Goose," to condemn by hissing; "rum," odd, disreputable; and "fuddle," mental fuzziness, muddlement, a drunken bout, a drunk.

2 Richard Emmons (b. 1788), doctor and poet, wrote *The Fredoniad, or Independence Preserved* (1827) and *The Battle of Bunker Hill* (1839), both of which are maudlin, and sometimes laughable, attempts at epic poetry.

3 *Twelfth Night*, II, v.

4 Having his own business

5 A gadfly is one that bites and goads cattle, and thus the word has come to mean a person who irritates, torments, or worries another.

6 "Oil of" usually means "oil made from"—which is obviously not the case here—and refers to a medication or emollient. In the nineteenth century, it was also used humorously, as in "oil of angel" (bribes), "oil of palms" (money), "oil of malt" (malt liquor), and "oil of fool" (flattery used to trick someone).

7 To run from, or be off

8 "Thingumbob" dates back to at least 1751, although "thingum" can be traced to 1680. Both refer to a certain thing that can't quite be named, a what-have-you, a whatchamacallit.

9 A first-rate person, from the trump card of bridge or whist

10 Poe was both editor and poet—but so were Bryant, Willis, William Gilmore Simms, W. G. Clark, and Griswold.

11 William Cecil, Lord Burleigh (1520–98), was ordered to give the poet Spenser a one hundred pound pension by Elizabeth I, and replied in shock, "What! all this for a song!" (Birch, *Life of Spenser*, xiii)

12 Dante Alighieri (1265–1321), author of the *Commedia* (better known, incorrectly, as *The Divine Comedy*), whose "Inferno" is the first, and most intriguing, section of the monumental work.

13 Ugolino della Gherardesca (d. 1289), Count of Pisa, who in about 1270 deserted his party and formed an alliance with Giovanni Visconti, the head of the opposition. The plot failed and Giovanni died. Ugolino joined the Florentines and forced Pisa to restore his property, but died when a conspiracy was launched against him and he and his two sons were starved to death in the tower of Gualandi. Dante makes mention of it in the *Inferno*, canto 33.

14 Slightly altered from *Hamlet*, I, iv.

"Angels and ministers of grace defend us!
Be thou a spirit of health or goblin damn'd,
Bring with thee airs from heaven or blasts from hell,
By thy intents wicked or charitable,
Thou com'st in such a questionable shape
That I will speak to thee. . . ."

inventor, my father), and for which effusion the editor of the *Fly* was remunerated with a regal liberality by the firm of Thomas Bob & Company, merchant-barbers.

The genius of the stanzas of the "Oil-of-Bob" first breathed into me, I say, the divine *afflatus*. I resolved at once to become a great man, and to commence by becoming a great poet. That very evening I fell upon my knees at the feet of my father.

"Father," I said, "pardon me!—but I have a soul above **7** lather. It is my firm intention to cut the shop. I would be an editor—I would be a poet—I would pen stanzas to the 'Oil-of-Bob.' Pardon me and aid me to be great!"

8 "My dear Thingum," replied my father (I had been christened Thingum after a wealthy relative so surnamed). "My dear Thingum," he said, raising me from my knees by the **9** ears—"Thingum, my boy, you're a trump, and take after your father in having a soul. You have an immense head, too, and it must hold a great many brains. This I have long seen, and therefore had thoughts of making you a lawyer. The business, however, has grown ungenteel, and that of politician don't pay. Upon the whole you judge wisely;—the trade of editor is best:—and if you can be a poet at the same time,—as most **10** of the editors are, by the by,—why you will kill two birds with one stone. To encourage you in the beginning of things, I will allow you a garret; pen, ink, and paper; a rhyming dictionary; and a copy of the *Gad-Fly*. I suppose you would scarely demand any more."

"I would be an ungrateful villain if I did," I replied with enthusiasm. "Your generosity is boundless. I will repay it by making you the father of a genius."

Thus ended my conference with the best of men, and immediately upon its termination I betook myself with zeal to my poetical labors; as upon these, chiefly, I founded my hopes of ultimate elevation to the editorial chair.

In my first attempts at composition I found the stanzas to "The Oil-of-Bob" rather a drawback than otherwise. Their splendor more dazzled than enlightened me. The contemplation of their excellence tended, naturally, to discourage me by comparison with my own abortions; so that for a long time I labored in vain. At length there came into my head one of those exquisitely original ideas which now and then *will* permeate the brain of a man of genius. It was this:—or, rather, thus was it carried into execution. From the rubbish of an old book-stall, in a very remote corner of the town, I got together several antique and altogether unknown or forgotten volumes.
11 The bookseller sold them to me for a song. From one of these,
12 which purported to be a translation of one Dante's "Inferno," I copied with remarkable neatness a long passage about a man
13 named Ugolino, who had a parcel of brats. From another, which contained a good many old plays by some person whose name I forget, I extracted in the same manner, and with the same care, a great number of lines about "angels" and "ministers saying grace," and "goblins damned," and more
14 besides of that sort. From a third, which was the composition

of some blind man or other, either a Greek or a Choctaw—I cannot be at the pains of remembering every trifle exactly—I took about fifty verses beginning with "Achilles' wrath," and "grease," and something else. From a fourth, which I recollect **15** was also the work of a blind man, I selected a page or two all about "hail" and "holy light;" and, although a blind man has no business to write about light, still the verses were sufficiently good in their way. **16**

Having made fair copies of these poems, I signed every one of them "Oppodeldoc" (a fine sonorous name), and, doing each **17** up nicely in a separate envelope, I dispatched one to each of the four principal magazines, with a request for speedy insertion and prompt pay. The result of this well-conceived plan, however (the success of which would have saved me much trouble in after-life), served to convince me that some editors are not to be bamboozled, and gave the *coup-de-grâce* **18,19** (as they say in France) to my nascent hopes (as they say in the city of the transcendentals). **20**

The fact is, that each and every one of the magazines in question gave Mr. "Oppodeldoc" a complete using-up, in the "Monthly Notices to Correspondents." The *Hum-Drum* gave him a dressing after this fashion:

" 'Oppodeldoc' (whoever he is) has sent us a long *tirade* concerning a bedlamite whom he styles 'Ugolino,' who had **21** a great many children that should have been all whipped and sent to bed without their suppers. The whole affair is exceedingly tame—not to say *flat*. 'Oppodeldoc' (whoever he is) is entirely devoid of imagination—and imagination, in our humble opinion, is not only the soul of POESY, but also its very heart. 'Oppodeldoc' (whoever he is) has the audacity to demand of us, for his twattle, a 'speedy insertion and prompt pay.' We neither insert nor purchase any stuff of the sort. There can be no doubt, however, that he would meet with a ready sale for all the balderdash he can scribble, at the office of either the *Rowdy-Dow*, the *Lollipop*, or the **22** *Goosetherumfoodle*."

All this, it must be acknowledged, was very severe upon "Oppodeldoc,"—but the unkindest cut was putting the word POESY in small caps. In those five pre-eminent letters what a world of bitterness is there not involved!

But "Oppodeldoc" was punished with equal severity in the *Rowdy-Dow*, which spoke thus:

"We have received a most singular and insolent communication from a person (whoever he is) signing himself 'Oppodeldoc,'—thus desecrating the greatness of the illustrious Roman emperor so named. Accompanying the letter of 'Oppodeldoc' (whoever he is) we find sundry lines of most disgusting and unmeaning rant about 'angels and ministers of grace,'—rant such as no madman short of a Nat Lee, or **23** an 'Oppodeldoc' could possible perpetrate. And for this trash of trash, we are modestly requested to 'pay promptly.' No sir—no! We pay for nothing of *that* sort. Apply to the *Hum-Drum*, the *Lollipop*, or the *Goosetherumfoodle*. These *periodicals* will undoubtedly accept any literary offal you may send them—and as undoubtedly *promise* to pay for it."

15 "The wrath of Peleus's son [Achilles], the direful spring/Of all the Grecian woes, O Goddess, sing!" (*Iliad*, I, i) Homer was blind.

The Choctaw Indians formerly occupied central and southern Mississippi, with some outlying groups in Alabama and Georgia (see Irvin Peithmann, *The Choctaw Indians of Mississippi*, Southern Illinois University, 1961).

Could Poe have known that a town called Homerville would be founded in Georgia in the 1850s?

16 Milton, *Paradise Lost* (Book 3, line 1):

"Hail, holy light, offspring of Heaven first-born,
Or of th' Eternal co-eternal beam,
May I express the unblamed? Since God is light,
And never but in approached light
Dwelt from eternity."

Milton became blind in 1652, and until his death, in 1674, dictated his poetry to his daughters.

17 Oppodeldoc was a patent medicine made from soap, alcohol, camphor, and essential oils, used as a rub by barbers and horse doctors. The word dates back to 1541, when Paracelsus coined it from three ingredients for his medicinal plaster—*opo*panax, b*dell*ium, aristolochia—but later added ammonia to the mixture. It was on the list of the eight most popular patent remedies drawn up in 1824 by the Philadelphia College of Pharmacy, according to Burton R. Pollin (*Poe News*, Vol. V, pp. 30–32), who also cites this 1810 advertisement: "This incomparable Oppodeldoc . . . is warm, penetrating, attenuating, and is therefore an excellent embrocation for the Gout and Rheumatism. . . . Long contracted Sprains are removed by it, and it is of the utmost service for Weak or Rickety children . . . for Burns and Scalds . . . for Horses that are strained in the back Sinews, wrung in the Withers, or have their back galled with the saddle . . . for a fresh Cut . . . for the sting of Wasps . . . for sudden Head-Aches. . . ."

18 *Bamboozled*, meaning "tricked or deceived," first appeared about 1700 and is mentioned in the *Tatler*, no. 230, as an example of "the continual Corruption of our English Tongue," along with such words as banter, kidney, sham, mop, bubble, and bully.

19 Literally, "stroke of grace"; the blow by which a condemned or mortally wounded person is put out of his misery

20 Boston

21 A madman, after Bedlam (St. Mary of Bethlehem) Hospital, London, since the fifteenth century an asylum for the mentally ill

22 The O.E.D. incorrectly gives the first use to Lowell (as "row-de-dow"), in 1848; the word means a noise, din, or uproar. "Lollipop" as a "lucious" literary composition is given a first citation of 1849. Both words appear here earlier.

23 Nathaniel Lee (1653–92), English dramatist, whose *The Rival Queens* (1677) tells of the jealousy between the wives of Alexander the Great, is today considered bombastic and extravagant. He died insane.

This was bitter indeed upon poor "Oppodeldoc;" but, in this instance, the weight of the satire falls upon the *Hum-Drum*, the *Lollipop*, and the *Goosetherumfoodle*, who are pungently styled *"periodicals"*—in italics, too—a thing that must have cut them to the heart.

Scarcely less savage was the *Lollipop*, which thus discoursed:

"Some *individual*, who rejoices in the appellation 'Oppodeldoc' (to what low uses are the names of the illustrious dead too often applied!) has enclosed us some fifty or sixty *verses* commencing after this fashion:

> Achilles' wrath, to Greece the direful spring
> Of woes unnumbered, &c., &c., &c., &c.

" 'Oppodeldoc' (whoever he is) is respectfully informed that there is not a printer's devil in our office who is not in the daily habit of composing better *lines*. Those of 'Oppodeldoc' will not *scan*. 'Oppodeldoc' should learn to *count*. But why he should have conceived the idea that *we* (of all others, *we!*) would disgrace our pages with his ineffable nonsense is utterly beyond comprehension. Why, the absurd twattle is scarcely good enough for the *Hum-Drum*, the *Rowdy-Dow*, the *Goosetherumfoodle*,—things that are in the practice of publishing 'Mother Goose's Melodies' as original lyrics. And 'Oppodeldoc' (whoever he is) has even the assurance to demand *pay* for this drivel. Does 'Oppodeldoc' (whoever he is) know—is he aware that we could not be paid to insert it?"

As I perused this I felt myself growing gradually smaller and smaller, and when I came to the point at which the editor sneered at the poem as *"verses,"* there was little more than an ounce of me left. As for "Oppodeldoc," I began to experience *compassion* for the poor fellow. But the *Goosetherumfoodle* showed, if possible, less mercy than the *Lollipop*. It was the *Goosetherumfoodle* that said:

24 "A wretched poetaster, who signs himself 'Oppodeldoc,' is silly enough to fancy that *we* will print and *pay for* a medley of incoherent and ungrammatical bombast which he has transmitted to us, and which commences with the following most *intelligible* line:

> 'Hail, Holy Light! Offspring of Heaven, first born.'

"We say, 'most *intelligible*.' 'Oppodeldoc' (whoever he is) will be kind enough to tell us, perhaps, how '*hail*' can be '*holy light*.' We always regarded it as *frozen rain*. Will he inform us, also, how frozen rain can be, at one and the same time, both 'holy light' (whatever that is) and an 'offspring'?—which latter term (if we understand any thing about English) is only employed, with propriety, in reference to small babies of about six weeks old. But it is preposterous to descant upon such absurdity—although 'Oppodeldoc' (whoever he is) has the unparalleled effrontery to suppose that we will not only 'insert' his ignorant ravings, but (absolutely) *pay for them!*

"Now this is fine—it is rich!—and we have half a mind to punish this young scribbler for his egotism by really **25** publishing his effusion *verbatim et literatim*, as he has

---

24 A poor poet, or at least a rank amateur

25 Word for word and letter for letter

written it. We could inflict no punishment so severe, and we *would* inflict it, but for the boredom which we should cause our readers in so doing.

"Let 'Oppodeldoc' (whoever he is) send any future *composition* of like character to the *Hum-Drum,* the *Lollipop,* or the *Rowdy-Dow. They* will 'insert' it. *They* 'insert' every month just such stuff. Send it to them. WE are not to be insulted with impunity."   **26**

This made an end of me; and as for the *Hum-Drum,* the *Rowdy-Dow,* and the *Lollipop,* I never could comprehend how they survived it. The putting *them* in the smallest possible *minion* (that was the rub—thereby insinuating their lowness— **27** their baseness), while WE stood looking down upon them in gigantic capitals!—oh it was *too* bitter!—it was wormwood— it was gall. Had I been either of these periodicals I would **28** have spared no pains to have the *Goosetherumfoodle* prosecuted. It might have been done under the Act for the "Prevention of Cruelty to Animals." As for Oppodeldoc **29** (whoever he was), I had by this time lost all patience with the fellow, and sympathized with him no longer. He was a fool, beyond doubt (whoever he was) and got not a kick more than he deserved.

The result of my experiment with the old books convinced me, in the first place, that "honesty is the best policy," and, in the second, that if I could not write better than Mr. Dante, and the two blind men, and the rest of the old set, it would, at least, be a difficult matter to write worse. I took heart, therefore, and determined to prosecute the "entirely original" (as they say on the covers of the magazines), at whatever cost of study and pains. I again placed before my eyes, as a model, the brilliant stanzas on "The Oil-of-Bob" by the editor of the *Gad-Fly* and resolved to construct an ode on the same sublime theme, in rivalry of what had already been done.

With my first line I had no material difficulty. It ran thus:

To pen an Ode upon the "Oil-of-Bob."

Having carefully looked out, however, all the legitimate rhymes to "Bob," I found it impossible to proceed. In this dilemma I had recourse to paternal aid; and, after some hours of mature thought, my father and myself thus constructed the poem:

To pen an Ode upon the "Oil-of-Bob"
Is all sorts of a job.
            (Signed)   SNOB.

To be sure, this composition was of no very great length,— but I "have yet to learn," as they say in the *Edinburgh Review,* **30** that the mere extent of a literary work has any thing to do with its merit. As for the Quarterly cant about "sustained effort," it is impossible to see the sense of it. Upon the whole, therefore, I was satisfied with the success of my maiden attempt, and now the only question regarded the disposal I should make of it. My father suggested that I should send it to the *Gad-Fly*—but there were two reasons which operated

26 Montresor's family motto in "The Cask of Amontillado"

27 Very small print

28 i.e., bitter. Lamentations 3:19: "The memory of my distress and my wanderings is wormwood and gall."

29 The Act for the Prevention of Cruelty to Animals was passed in England in 1822.

30 See the introductory note to "How to Write a Blackwood Article."

to prevent me from so doing. I dreaded the jealousy of the editor—and I had ascertained that he did not pay for original contributions. I therefore, after due deliberation, consigned the article to the more dignified pages of the *Lollipop* and awaited the event in anxiety, but with resignation.

In the very next published number I had the proud satisfaction of seeing my poem printed at length, as the leading article, with the following significant words, prefixed in italics and between brackets:

> [*We call the attention of our readers to the subjoined admirable stanzas on "The Oil-of-Bob." We need say nothing of their sublimity, or of their pathos:—it is impossible to peruse them without tears. Those who have been nauseated with a sad dose on the same august topic from the goose-quill of the editor of the "Gad-Fly," will do well to compare the two compositions.*
>
> *P. S.—We are consumed with anxiety to probe the mystery which envelops the evident pseudonym "Snob." May we hope for a personal interview?*]

All this was scarcely more than justice, but it was, I confess, rather more than I had expected:—I acknowledged this, be it observed, to the everlasting disgrace of my country and of mankind. I lost no time, however, in calling upon the editor of the *Lollipop* and had the good fortune to find this gentleman at home. He saluted me with an air of profound respect, slightly blended with a fatherly and patronizing admiration, wrought in him, no doubt, by my appearance of extreme youth and inexperience. Begging me to be seated, he entered at once upon the subject of my poem;—but modesty will ever forbid me to repeat the thousand compliments which he lavished upon me. The eulogies of Mr. Crab (such was the editor's name) were, however, by no means fulsomely indiscriminate. He analyzed my composition with much freedom and great ability—not hesitating to point out a few trivial defects—a circumstance which elevated him highly in my esteem. The *Gad-Fly* was, of course, brought upon the *tapis,* and I hope never to be subjected to a criticism so searching, or to rebukes so withering, as were bestowed by Mr. Crab upon that unhappy effusion. I had been accustomed to regard the editor of the *Gad-Fly* as something superhuman; but Mr. Crab soon disabused me of that idea. He set the literary as well as the personal character of the Fly (so Mr. C. satirically designated the rival editor), in its true light. He, the Fly, was very little better than he should be. He had written infamous things. He was a penny-a-liner, and a buffoon. He was a villain. He had composed a tragedy which set the whole country in a guffaw, and a farce which deluged the universe in tears. Besides all this, he had the impudence to pen what he meant for a lampoon upon himself (Mr. Crab), and the temerity to style him "an ass." Should I at any time wish to express my opinion of Mr. Fly, the pages of the *Lollipop,* Mr. Crab assured me, were at my unlimited disposal. In the meantime, as it was very certain that I would be attacked in the *Fly* for my attempt at composing a rival poem on the "Oil-of-Bob," he (Mr. Crab) would take it upon himself to attend, pointedly, to my private and personal interests. If I were not made a man of at once, it should not be the fault of himself (Mr. Crab).

Mr. Crab having now paused in his discourse (the latter portion of which I found it impossible to comprehend), I ventured to suggest something about the remuneration which I had been taught to expect for my poem, by an announcement on the cover of the *Lollipop*, declaring that it (the *Lollipop*) "insisted upon being permitted to pay exorbitant prices for all accepted contributions;—frequently expending more money for a single brief poem than the whole annual cost of the *Hum-Drum*, the *Rowdy-Dow*, and the *Goosetherumfoodle* combined."

As I mentioned the word "remuneration," Mr. Crab first opened his eyes, and then his mouth, to quite a remarkable extent, causing his personal appearance to resemble that of a highly agitated elderly duck in the act of quacking; and in this condition he remained (even and anon pressing his hands tightly to his forehead, as if in a state of desperate bewilderment) until I had nearly made an end of what I had to say.

Upon my conclusion, he sank back into his seat, as if much overcome, letting his arms fall lifelessly by his side, but keeping his mouth still rigorously open, after the fashion of the duck. While I remained in speechless astonishment at behavior so alarming, he suddenly leaped to his feet and made a rush at the bell-rope; but just as he reached this, he appeared to have altered his intention, whatever it was, for he dived under a table and immediately re-appeared with a cudgel. This he was in the act of uplifting (for what purpose I am at a loss to imagine), when, all at once, there came a benign smile over his features, and he sank placidly back in his chair.

"Mr. Bob," he said (for I had sent up my card before ascending myself). "Mr. Bob, you are a young man, I presume—*very?*"

I assented; adding that I had not yet concluded my third lustrum.

"Ah!" he replied, "very good! I see how it is—say no more! Touching this matter of compensation, what you observe is very just: in fact it is excessively so. But ah—ah—the *first* contribution—the *first*, I say—it is never the magazine custom to pay for—you comprehend, eh? The truth is, we are usually the *recipients* in such case." [Mr. Crab smiled blandly as he emphasized the word "recipients."] "For the most part, we are *paid* for the insertion of a maiden attempt—especially in verse. In the second place, Mr. Bob, the magazine rule is **31** never to disburse what we term in France the *argent comptant:*—I have no doubt you understand. In a quarter or two **32** after publication of the article—or in a year or two—we make no objection to giving our note at nine months; provided, always, that we can so arrange our affairs as to be quite certain of a 'burst up' in six. I really *do* hope, Mr. Bob, that you will

31 Poe was constantly frustrated in his attempts to earn a living through writing.

32 Cash. A "Burst-up" means a bankruptcy.

33 "As [Lord Byron] himself briefly described it in his Memoranda, 'I awoke one morning and found myself famous' " (Moore's *Life of Byron*, 1830, I, p. 347), a reference to the instantaneous success of *Childe Harold* (1809). The notation at the end of the paragraph indicates this is an advertisement paid for by the narrator.

34 *Hamlet*, I, ii, 140

35 *Graham's Magazine* was the largest in circulation of its day with over thirty-five thousand subscribers. Poe's *Broadway Journal* had fewer than a thousand.

36 Possibly Bryant, whom Poe thought overrated.

37 A nom de plume is a pen name, while a *nom de guerre* is a name assumed by, or given to, a person in a profession or other enterprise. Meaning "war name," it dates back to the time when it was customary for everyone who entered the French Army to assume a name, as knights did when they went by the device of their shields or some other distinctive part of their armor (e.g., the Red-Cross Knight in Spenser's *Faerie Queene*).

look upon this explanation as satisfactory." Here Mr. Crab concluded, and the tears stood in his eyes.

Grieved to the soul at having been, however innocently, the cause of pain to so eminent and so sensitive a man, I hastened to apologize, and to reassure him, by expressing my perfect coincidence with his views, as well as my entire appreciation of the delicacy of his position. Having done all this in a neat speech, I took leave.

One fine morning, very shortly afterward, "I awoke and **33** found myself famous." The extent of my renown will be best estimated by reference to the editorial opinions of the day. These opinions, it will be seen, were embodied in critical notices of the number of the *Lollipop* containing my poem, and are perfectly satisfactory, conclusive, and clear with the exception, perhaps, of the hieroglyphical marks, "*Sep*. 15—1 *t*." appended to each of the critiques.

The *Owl*, a journal of profound sagacity, and well known for the deliberate gravity of its literary decisions—the *Owl*, I say, spoke as follows:

> "The *Lollipop!* The October number of this delicious magazine surpasses its predecessors, and sets competition at defiance. In the beauty of its typography and paper—in the number and excellence of its steel plates—as well as in the literary merit of its contributions—the *Lollipop* com- **34** pares with its slow-paced rivals as Hyperion with a Satyr. The *Hum-Drum*, the *Rowdy-Dow*, and the *Goosetherum-foodle*, excel, it is true, in braggadocio, but in all other points, give us the *Lollipop!* How this celebrated journal can sustain its evidently tremendous expenses, is more than we can understand. To be sure, it has a circulation of 100,000, and its subscription list has increased one fourth during the last month; but, on the other hand, the sums it **35** disburses constantly for contributions are inconceivable. It **36** is reported that Mr. Slyass received no less than thirty-seven and a half cents for his inimitable paper on 'Pigs.' With Mr. CRAB, as editor, and with such names upon the list of contributors as SNOB and Slyass, there can be no such word as 'fail' for the *Lollipop*. Go and subscribe. *Sep*. 15—1 *t*."

I must say that I was gratified with this high-toned notice from a paper so respectable as the *Owl*. The placing my **37** name—that is to say, my *nom de guerre*—in priority of station to that of the great Slyass, was a compliment as happy as I felt it to be deserved.

My attention was next arrested by these paragraphs in the *Toad*—a print highly distinguished for its uprightness and independence—from its entire freedom from sycophancy and subservience to the givers of dinners:

> "The *Lollipop* for October is out in advance of all its contemporaries, and infinitely surpasses them, of course, in the splendor of its embellishments, as well as in the richness of its contents. The *Hum-Drum*, the *Rowdy-Dow*, and the *Goosetherumfoodle* excel, we admit, in braggadocio, but, in all other points, give us the *Lollipop*. How this

celebrated magazine can sustain its evidently tremendous expenses is more than we can understand. To be sure, it has a circulation of 200,000, and its subscription list has increased one third during the last fortnight, but, on the other hand, the sums it disburses, monthly, for contributions, are fearfully great. We learn that Mr. Mumblethumb received no less than fifty cents for his late 'Monody in a Mud-Puddle.'   **38**

"Among the original contributors to the present number we notice (besides the eminent editor, Mr. CRAB), such men as SNOB, Sylass, and Mumblethumb. Apart from the editorial matter, the most valuable paper, nevertheless, is, we think, a poetical gem by SNOB, on the 'Oil-of-Bob'—but our readers must not suppose from the title of this incomparable *bijou,* that it bears any similitude to some balderdash on the same subject by a certain contemptible individual whose name is unmentionable to ears polite. The *present* poem 'On the Oil-of-Bob,' has excited universal anxiety and curiosity in respect to the owner of the evident pseudonym, 'Snob'—a curiosity which, happily, we have it in our power to satisfy. 'Snob' is the *nom de plume* of Mr. Thingum Bob, of this city,—a relative of the great Mr. Thingum (after whom he is named), and otherwise connected with the most illustrious families of the State. His father, Thomas Bob, Esq., is an opulent merchant in Smug. *Sep.* 15—1 *t.*"

This generous approbation touched me to the heart—the more especially as it emanated from a source so avowedly— so proverbially pure as the *Toad.* The word "balderdash," as **39** applied to the "Oil-of-Bob" of the *Fly,* I considered singularly pungent and appropriate. The words "gem" and "*bijou,*" however, used in reference to my composition, struck me as being, in some degree, feeble. They seemed to me to be deficient in force. They were not sufficiently *prononcés* (as we **40** have it in France).

I had hardly finished reading the *Toad,* when a friend placed in my hands a copy of the *Mole,* a daily, enjoying high reputation for the keenness of its perception about matters in general, and for the open, honest, above-ground style of its editorials. The *Mole* spoke of the *Lollipop* as follows:

"We have just received the *Lollipop* for October, and *must* say that never before have we perused any single number of any periodical which afforded us a felicity so supreme. We speak advisedly. The *Hum-Drum,* the *Rowdy-Dow,* and the *Goosetherumfoodle* must look well to their laurels. These prints, no doubt, surpass every thing in loudness of pretension, but, in all other points, give us the *Lollipop!* How this celebrated magazine can sustain its evidently tremendous expenses, is more than we can comprehend. To be sure, it has a circulation of 300,000; and its subscription list has increased one half within the last week, but then the sum it disburses, monthly, for contributions, is astonishingly enormous. We have it upon good authority that Mr. Fatquack received no less than sixty-two cents and a half for his late Domestic Nouvelette, the 'Dish-Clout.'   **41**

"The contributors to the number before us are Mr. CRAB (the eminent editor), SNOB, Mumblethumb, Fatquack, and

38 Coleridge wrote *Monody on a Teakettle,* but *Knickerbocker Magazine* was also known for its odd titles.

39 The origin of the word is unknown, but it originally meant a froth or frothy liquid, then a jumbled mixture of liquors, and finally a senseless jumble of words, or nonsense.

40 Pronounced, strong

41 A dishcloth, but also a type of limpness or weakness. Cooper's "Autobiography of a Pocket-Handkerchief" was published in *Graham's* in 1843.

others; but, after the inimitable compositions of the editor himself, we prefer a diamond-like effusion from the pen of a rising poet who writes over the signature 'Snob'—a *nom de guerre* which we predict will one day extinguish the radiance of 'Boz.' 'Snob,' we learn, is a Mr. Thingum Bob, Esq., sole heir of a wealthy merchant of this city, Thomas Bob, Esq., and a near relative of the distinguished Mr. Thingum. The title of Mr. B.'s admirable poem is the 'Oil-of-Bob'—a somewhat unfortunate name, by-the-by, as some contemptible vagabond connected with the penny press has already disgusted the town with a great deal of drivel upon the same topic. There will be no danger, however, of confounding the compositions. *Sep*. 15—1 *t*."

The generous approbation of so clear-sighted a journal as the *Mole* penetrated my soul with delight. The only objection which occurred to me was, that the terms "contemptible vagabond" might have been better written "*odious and* contemptible *wretch, villain,* and vagabond." This would have sounded more gracefully, I think. "Diamond-like," also, was scarcely, it will be admitted, of sufficient intensity to express what the *Mole* evidently *thought* of the brilliancy of the "Oil-of-Bob."

On the same afternoon in which I saw these notices in the *Owl*, the *Toad*, and the *Mole*, I happened to meet with a copy **42** of the *Daddy-Long-Legs*, a periodical proverbial for the extreme extent of its understanding. And it was the *Daddy-Long-Legs* which spoke thus:

> "The *Lollipop!!* This gorgeous magazine is already before the public for October. The question of pre-eminence is forever put to rest, and hereafter it will be excessively preposterous in the *Hum-Drum*, the *Rowdy-Dow*, or the *Goosetherumfoodle* to make any further spasmodic attempts at competition. These journals may excel the *Lollipop* in outcry, but, in all other points, give us the *Lollipop!* How this celebrated magazine can sustain its evidently tremendous expenses, is past comprehension. To be sure it has a circulation of precisely half a million, and its subscription list has increased seventy-five per cent, within the last couple of days, but then the sums it disburses, monthly, for contributions, are scarcely credible; we are cognizant of the fact, that Mademoiselle Cribalittle received no less than eighty-seven cents and a half for her late valuable Revolutionary Tale, entitled 'The York-Town Katy-Did, and the **43** Bunker-Hill Katy-Didn't.'
>
> "The most able papers in the present number are, of course, those furnished by the editor (the eminent Mr. Crab), but there are numerous magnificent contributions from such names as Snob, Mademoiselle Cribalittle, Slyass, Mrs. Fibalittle, Mumblethumb, Mrs. Squibalittle, and last, though not least, Fatquack. The world may well be challenged to produce so rich a galaxy of genius.
>
> "The poem over the signature 'Snob' is, we find, attracting universal commendation, and, we are constrained to say, deserves, if possible, even more applause than it has received. The 'Oil-of-Bob' is the title of this masterpiece of eloquence and art. One or two of our readers *may* have a

42 The owl is a predator, the mole an underground pest, and daddy longlegs is the name for the pesky crane fly as well as an arachnid—all appropriately uncomplimentary titles.

43 A katydid is a kind of grasshopper, so called from the sound it makes. Yorktown was the site of the decisive American victory over the British in 1781, while Bunker Hill was the site of an American defeat (actually at nearby Breed's Hill), but the British win failed to break the 1775 siege of Boston by the Americans.

very faint, although sufficiently disgusting recollection of a poem (?) similarly entitled, the perpetration of a miserable penny-a-liner, mendicant, and cut-throat, connected in the capacity of scullion, we believe, with one of the indecent prints about the purlieus of the city; we beg them, for God's sake, not to confound the compositions. The author of *the* 'Oil-of-Bob' is, we hear, THINGUM BOB, Esq., a gentleman of high genius, and a scholar 'Snob' is merely a *nom de guerre. Sep.* 15—1 *t.*"

I could scarcely restrain my indignation while I perused the concluding portions of this diatribe. It was clear to me that the yea-nay manner—not to say the gentleness—the positive forbearance—with which the *Daddy-Long-Legs* spoke of that pig, the editor of the *Gad-Fly*—it was evident to me, I say, that this gentleness of speech could proceed from nothing else than a partiality for the *Fly*—whom it was clearly the intention of the *Daddy-Long-Legs* to elevate into reputation at my expense. Any one, indeed, might perceive, with half an eye, that, had the real design of the *Daddy* been what it wished to appear, it (the *Daddy*) might have expressed itself in terms more direct, more pungent, and altogether more to the purpose. The words "penny-a-liner," "mendicant," "scullion," and "cut-throat," were epithets so intentionally inexpressive and equivocal, as to be worse than nothing when applied to the author of the very worst stanzas ever penned by one of the human race. We all know what is meant by "damning with faint praise," and, on the other hand, who could fail **44** seeing through the covert purpose of the *Daddy,*—that of glorifying with feeble abuse?

44 From Pope's *Epistle to Dr. Arbuthnot*, line 201

What the *Daddy* chose to say to the *Fly*, however, was no business of mine. What it said of myself *was*. After the noble manner in which the *Owl*, the *Toad*, the *Mole*, had expressed themselves in respect to my ability, it was rather too much to be coolly spoken of by a thing like the *Daddy-Long-Legs*, as merely "a gentleman of high genius and a scholar." Gentleman indeed! I made up my mind at once either to get a written apology from the *Daddy-Long-Legs,* or to call it out.

Full of this purpose, I looked about me to find a friend whom I could entrust with a message to his Daddyship, and as the editor of the *Lollipop* had given me marked tokens of regard, I at length concluded to seek assistance upon the present occasion.

I have never yet been able to account, in a manner satisfactory to my own understanding, for the *very* peculiar countenance and demeanor with which Mr. Crab listened to me, as I unfolded to him my design. He again went through the scene of the bell-rope and cudgel, and did not omit the duck. At one period I thought he really intended to quack. His fit, nevertheless, finally subsided as before, and he began to act and speak in a rational way. He declined bearing the cartel, however, and in fact, dissuaded me from sending it at all; but was candid enough to admit that the *Daddy-Long-Legs* had been disgracefully in the wrong—more especially in what related to the epithets "gentleman and scholar."

Toward the end of this interview with Mr. Crab, who really appeared to take a paternal interest in my welfare, he suggested to me that I might turn an honest penny, and at the same time, advance my reputation, by occasionally playing Thomas Hawk for the *Lollipop*.

I begged Mr. Crab to inform me who was Mr. Thomas Hawk, and how it was expected that I should play him.

45 Here Mr. Crab again "made great eyes" (as we say in Germany), but at length, recovering himself from a profound attack of astonishment, he assured me that he employed the words "Thomas Hawk" to avoid the colloquialism, Tommy, which was low—but that the true idea was Tommy Hawk—or tomahawk—and that by "playing tomahawk" he referred to scalping, brow-beating, and otherwise using up the herd of poor-devil authors.

I assured my patron that, if this was all, I was perfectly resigned to the task of playing Thomas Hawk. Hereupon Mr. Crab desired me to use up the editor of the *Gad-Fly* forthwith, in the fiercest style within the scope of my ability, and as a specimen of my powers. This I did, upon the spot, in a review of the original "Oil-of-Bob," occupying thirty-six pages of the *Lollipop*. I found playing Thomas Hawk, indeed, a far less onerous occupation than poetizing; for I went upon *system* altogether, and thus it was easy to do the thing thoroughly well. My practice was this. I bought auction copies (cheap) of "Lord Brougham's Speeches," "Cobbett's Complete Works," the "New Slang-Syllabus," the "Whole Art of Snubbing," "Prentice's Billingsgate" (folio edition), and "Lewis G. Clarke

46 on Tongue." These works I cut up thoroughly with a curry-
47 comb, and then, throwing the shreds into a sieve, sifted out carefully all that might be thought decent (a mere trifle); reserving the hard phrases, which I threw into a large tin pepper-castor with longitudinal holes, so that an entire sentence could get through without material injury. The mixture was then ready for use. When called upon to play Thomas Hawk, I anointed a sheet of foolscap with the white of a
48 gander's egg; then, shredding the thing to be reviewed as I had previously shredded the books—only with more care, so as to get every word separate—I threw the latter shreds in with the former, screwed on the lid of the castor, gave it a shake, and so dusted out the mixture upon the egged foolscap; where it stuck. The effect was beautiful to behold. It was captivating. Indeed, the reviews I brought to pass by this simple expedient have never been approached, and were the wonder of the world. At first, through bashfulness—the result of inexperience—I was a little put out by a certain inconsistency—a certain air of the *bizarre* (as we say in France), worn by the composition as a whole. All the phrases did not *fit* (as we say in the Anglo-Saxon). Many were quite awry. Some, even, were upside-down; and there were none of them which were not, in some measure, injured in regard to effect, by this latter species of accident, when it occurred—with the exception of Mr. Lewis Clarke's paragraphs, which were so vigorous and altogether stout, that they seemed not particularly

45 Wide-open disbelief

46 A list of highly critical writers:
  Miss Cribalittle is Mrs. E. F. Ellet, who was a notorious plagiarist, especially of Revolutionary War stories.
  Lord Brougham's speeches were delivered in Parliament after 1810; he was well known for his use of ridicule and sarcasm.
  William Cobbett (1762–1835) is best known for his pro-British pamphlets written in the United States under the pseudonym of Peter Porcupine.
  George Dennison Prentice (1802–70) said Poe was "a better judge of asses than men like Carlyle" after Poe called Carlyle an ass.
  Billingsgate is a term for foul or abusive language, after the London fish market.
  Lewis Gaylord Clark, coeditor of the *Knickerbocker*, reprinted Prentice's comment on Poe and Carlyle.

47 A currycomb is used to groom a horse, but "curry" also means to engage in flattery, as "curry favor."

48 Foolscap is a kind of paper, but the wordplay should be clear, as should be the impossibility of a gander's laying an egg.

disconcerted by any extreme of position, but looked equally happy and satisfactory, whether on their heads, or on their heels.

What became of the editor of the *Gad-Fly*, after the publication of my criticism on his "Oil-of-Bob," it is somewhat difficult to determine. The most reasonable conclusion is, that he wept himself to death. At all events he disappeared instantaneously from the face of the earth, and no man has seen even the ghost of him since.

This matter having been properly accomplished, and the Furies appeased, I grew at once into high favor with Mr. Crab. He took me into his confidence, gave me a permanent situation as Thomas Hawk of the *Lollipop*, and, as for the present, he could afford me no salary, allowed me to profit, at discretion, by his advice.

"My dear Thingum," said he to me one day after dinner, "I respect your abilities and love you as a son. You shall be my heir. When I die I will bequeath you the *Lollipop*. In the meantime I will make a man of you—I *will*—provided always that you follow my counsel. The first thing to do is to get rid of the old bore."

"Boar?" said I inquiringly—"pig, eh?—*aper?* (as we say in **49** Latin)—who?—where?"

"Your father," said he.

"Precisely," I replied,—"pig."

"You have your fortune to make, Thingum," resumed Mr. Crab, "and that governor of yours is a millstone about your neck. We must cut him at once." [Here I took out my knife.] "We must cut him," continued Mr. Crab, "decidedly and forever. He won't do—he *won't*. Upon second thoughts, you had better kick him, or cane him, or something of that kind."

"What do you say," I suggested modestly, "to my kicking him in the first instance, caning him afterward, and winding up by tweaking his nose?"

Mr. Crab looked at me musingly for some moments, and then answered:

"I think, Mr. Bob, that what you propose would answer sufficiently well—indeed remarkably well—that is to say, as far as it went—but barbers are exceedingly hard to cut, and I think, upon the whole, that, having performed upon Thomas Bob the operations you suggest, it would be advisable to blacken, with your fists, both his eyes, very carefully and thoroughly, to prevent his ever seeing you again in fashionable promenades. After doing this, I really do not perceive that you can do any more. However—it might be just as well to roll him once or twice in the gutter, and then put him in charge of the police. Any time the next morning you can call at the watchhouse and swear an assault."

I was much affected by the kindness of feeling toward me personally, which was evinced in this excellent advice of Mr. Crab, and I did not fail to profit by it forthwith. The result was, that I got rid of the old bore, and began to feel a little independent and gentleman-like. The want of money, however, was, for a few weeks, a source of some discomfort; but

49 A wild boar

50 "*Rem facias . . . quocumque modo,*" meaning to make money in any way, comes from Horace, *Epistles I*, i, 65–66.

"The Literary Life of Thingum Bob, Esq." *Illustration by F. S. Coburn, 1903*

at length, by carefully putting to use my two eyes, and observing how matters went just in front of my nose, I perceived how the thing was to be brought about. I say "thing"—be it observed—for they tell me the Latin for it is *rem*. By the way, talking of Latin, can any one tell me the **50** meaning of *quocunque*—or what is the meaning of *modo?*

My plan was exceedingly simple. I bought, for a song, a sixteenth of the *Snapping-Turtle:*—that was all. The thing was *done*, and I put money in my purse. There were some trivial arrangements afterward, to be sure; but these formed no portion of the plan. They were a consequence—a result. For example, I bought pen, ink, and paper, and put them into furious activity. Having thus completed a Magazine article, I gave it, for appellation, "FOL LOL, *by the Author of* 'THE OIL-OF-BOB,' " and enveloped it to the *Goosetherumfoodle*. That journal, however, having pronounced it "twattle" in the "Monthly Notices to Correspondents," I reheaded the paper " 'Hey-Diddle-Diddle,' by THINGUM BOB, Esq., Author of the Ode on 'The Oil-of-Bob,' *and* Editor of the *Snapping-Turtle*." With this amendment, I re-enclosed it to the *Goosetherumfoodle*, and, while I awaited a reply, published daily, in the *Turtle*, six columns of what may be termed philosophical and analytical investigation of the literary merits of the *Goosetherumfoodle*, as well as of the personal character of the editor of the *Goosetherumfoodle*. At the end of a week the *Goosetherumfoodle* discovered that it had, by some odd mistake, "confounded a stupid article, headed, 'Hey-Diddle-Diddle,' and composed by some unknown ignoramus, with a gem of resplendent lustre similarly entitled, the work of Thingum Bob, Esq., the celebrated author of 'The Oil-of-Bob.' " The *Goosetherumfoodle* deeply "regretted this very natural accident," and promised, moreover, an insertion of the *genuine* "Hey-Diddle-Diddle" in the very next number of the Magazine.

The fact is, I *thought*—I *really* thought—I thought at the time—I thought *then*—and have no reason for thinking otherwise *now*—that the *Goosetherumfoodle did* make a mistake. With the best intentions in the world, I never knew any thing that made as many singular mistakes as the *Goosetherumfoodle*. From that day I took a liking to the *Goosetherumfoodle*, and the result was I soon saw into the very depths of its literary merits, and did not fail to expatiate upon them, in the *Turtle*, whenever a fitting opportunity occurred. And it is to be regarded as a very peculiar coincidence—as one of those positively *remarkable* coincidences which set a man to serious thinking—that just such a total revolution of opinion—just such entire *bouleversement* (as we say in French),—just such thorough *topsiturviness* (if I may be permitted to employ a rather forcible term of the Choctaws), as happened, *pro* and *con*, between myself on the one part, and the *Goosetherumfoodle* on the other, did actually again happen, in a brief period afterwards, and with precisely similar circumstances, in the case of myself and the *Rowdy-Dow*, and in the case of myself and the *Hum-Drum*.

Thus it was that, by a master-stroke of genius, I at length consummated my triumphs by "putting money in my purse," **51** and thus may be said really and fairly to have commenced that brilliant and eventful career which rendered me illustrious, and which now enables me to say with Chateaubriand: "I have made history—*J'ai fait l'histoire*." **52**

I have indeed "made history." From the bright epoch which I now record, my actions—my works—are the property of mankind. They are familiar to the world. It is, then, needless for me to detail how, soaring rapidly, I fell heir to the *Lollipop*—how I merged this journal in the *Hum-Drum*—how again I made purchase of the *Rowdy-Dow*, thus combining the three periodicals—how lastly, I effected a bargain for the sole remaining rival, and united all the literature of the country in one magnificent Magazine known everywhere as the

Rowdy-Dow, Lollipop, Hum-Drum,
and
GOOSETHERUMFOODLE

Yes; I have made history. My fame is universal. It extends to the uttermost ends of the earth. You cannot take up a common newspaper in which you shall not see some allusion to the immortal THINGUM BOB. It is Mr. Thingum Bob said so, and Mr. Thingum Bob wrote this, and Mr. Thingum Bob did that. But I am meek and expire with an humble heart. After all, what is it?—this indescribable something which men will persist in terming "genius"? I agree with Buffon—with **53** Hogarth—it is but *diligence* after all. **54**

Look at *me!*—how I labored—how I toiled—how I wrote! Ye Gods, did I *not* write? I knew not the word "ease." By day I adhered to my desk, and at night, a pale student, I consumed the midnight oil. You should have seen me—you *should*. I **55** leaned to the right. I leaned to the left. I sat forward. I sat backward. I sat *tête baissée* (as they have it in the Kickapoo), **56** bowing my head close to the alabaster page. And, through all, I—*wrote*. Through joy and through sorrow, I—*wrote*. Through hunger and through thirst, I—*wrote*. Through good report and through ill report, I—*wrote*. Through sunshine and through moonshine, I—*wrote*. *What* I wrote it is unnecessary to say. The *style!*—that was the thing. I caught it from Fatquack—whizz!—fizz!—and I am giving you a specimen of it now.

51 *Othello* I, iii, 347: "Put money in thy purse."

52 Chateaubriand's *Mémoires d'outre-tombe* was published in part in the New York *Mirror*, May 24, 1834. The complete edition was published in 1860.

53 "Mr. Poe has that indescribable something which men have agreed to call genius" (James Russell Lowell in *Graham's*, February 1845), from which apparently comes Poe's title—"Thingumbob" means "indescribable something."

54 "*Le génie, c'est la patience*," Georges de Buffon (1707–88), *Discours sur la Style* (1753). "Genius is but labor and diligence," William Hogarth (1697–1764), in William Seward's *Biographiana* (1799), II, 293.

55 ". . . hath thy toil/O'er books consumed the midnight oil?," by John Gay, *Fables* (1727) "Introduction."

56 Head hung

THE THOUSAND-AND-SECOND TALE
OF SCHEHERAZADE

First published in *Godey's Magazine and Lady's Book,* February 1845.

This is one of Poe's more successful attempts at humor, a skillful blend of satire, fact, hyperbole, and understatement, all to prove that truth is indeed stranger than fiction.

The Thousand and One Nights, better known today as the *Arabian Nights,* is a series of oriental tales cleverly strung together by means of the continuing story of Scheherazade, daughter of the Grand Vizier of the Indies. The Sultan Shahriyah (or Schariar) of Samarkand, having discovered that his sultana had been unfaithful, resolved to marry a fresh wife every night and have her strangled at daybreak. Scheherazade married him, and so beguiled him with her tales (which she could never quite finish each night, forcing her husband to let her live until the next) that after 1,001 nights he revoked his cruel decree, gave his affection completely to her, and called her "the liberator of the sex."

The best-known of the tales, at least to Westerners, are "Ali Baba and the 40 Thieves," "Sinbad the Sailor," and "Aladdin." Not much is known about the origin of the collection, although many of the tales are obviously of Indian origin. The book as we know it today is essentially Moslem in spirit and is native either to Persia or to one of the Arabic-speaking countries. The first European translation was by Antoine Galland in French (1704–17), and most subsequent Western editions lean heavily on Galland's rather freehanded translation.

Galland also added a number of tales to the original, as told to him by a Syrian friend in 1790, including "The Enchanted Horse," "Ali Baba," and Aladdin."

In the *Southern Literary Messenger,* August 1836, Poe quotes James Montgomery: "Who does not turn with absolute contempt from the rings and gems, glitter, and caves and genii of Eastern Tales as from the trinkets of a toyshop, and the trumpery of a raree-show?" Poe answers, "What man of genius but must answer, 'Not I.' "

Poe's affection for the tales may have led to the writing of this story after reading an article by a friend, Joseph M. Field, in the St. Louis *Weekly Reveille* (November 18, 1844). "The Petrified Forest" tells of a trading party in the West, and of one member who blunts his hatchet on a petrified tree. One of the party has been entertaining the group by reading aloud some of the Arabian Nights stories around the campfire, and the petrified-tree experience now makes the first member "believe, implicitly, in all the stories he had ever read before from the Arabian Nights. And nothing ever after could convince him that the flying palaces of Aladdin, the wonderful caverns and transcendent gardens, the abodes of the Genii, and the wonderful floral extravagances of the fairies, was anything but most solemn truth, set down in a book."

Much of Poe's information was taken from newspaper accounts and books of the day, most prominently Dr. Dionysius Lardner's *Course of Lectures* (1842), which Poe criticizes in "Three Sundays in a Week" but finds useful here.

One thing his sources did not tell him, and that makes it clear that Poe was not familiar with the *Thousand and One Nights* as a whole, is that while there are 1,001 nights, there are only 264 tales, since the clever princess managed to stretch out many for several nights each.

Truth is stranger than fiction.
—*Old Saying.*   1

Having had occasion, lately, in the course of some Oriental investigations, to consult the "Tellmenow Isitsöornot," work **2** which (like the "Zohar" of Simeon Jochaides) is scarcely known **3** at all, even in Europe; and which has never been quoted, to my knowledge, by any American—if we except, perhaps, the author of the "Curiosities of American Literature";—having **4** had occasion, I say, to turn over some pages of the first-mentioned very remarkable work, I was not a little astonished to discover that the literary world has hitherto been strangely in error respecting the fate of the vizier's daughter, Scheherazade, as that fate is depicted in the "Arabian Nights"; and **5,6** that the *dénouement* there given, if not altogether inaccurate, as far as it goes, is at least to blame in not having gone very much farther.

For full information on this interesting topic, I must refer the inquisitive reader to the "Isitsöornot" itself; but, in the meantime, I shall be pardoned for giving a summary of what I there discovered.

It will be remembered, that, in the usual version of the tales, a certain monarch, having good cause to be jealous of his queen, not only puts her to death, but makes a vow, by his beard and the prophet, to espouse each night the most **7** beautiful maiden in his dominions, and the next morning to deliver her up to the executioner.

Having fulfilled this vow for many years to the letter, and with a religious punctuality and method that conferred great credit upon him as a man of devout feeling and excellent sense, he was interrupted one afternoon (no doubt at his prayers) by a visit from his grand vizier, to whose daughter, **8** it appears, there had occurred an idea.

Her name was Scheherazade, and her idea was, that she would either redeem the land from the depopulating tax upon its beauty, or perish, after the approved fashion of all heroines, in the attempt.

Accordingly, and although we do not find it to be leap-year **9** (which makes the sacrifice more meritorious), she deputes her father, the grand vizier, to make an offer to the king of her hand. This hand the king eagerly accepts—(he had intended to take it at all events, and had put off the matter from day to day, only through fear of the vizier),—but, in accepting it **10** now, he gives all parties very distinctly to understand, that, grand vizier or no grand vizier, he has not the slightest design of giving up one iota of his vow or of his privileges. When, therefore, the fair Scheherazade insisted upon marrying the king, and did actually marry him despite her father's excellent advice not to do anything of the kind—when she would and did marry him, I say, will I nill I, it was with her beautiful **11** black eyes as thoroughly open as the nature of the case would allow.

It seems, however, that this politic damsel (who had been **12** reading Machiavelli, beyond doubt), had a very ingenious **13**

1 See also Poe's use of this in "Von Kempelen and his Discovery" and "A Tale of the Ragged Mountains." Byron makes use of it as well, in *Don Juan*, XIV.

2 A fictional title (try reading it aloud, slowly)

3 The *Zohar* is an actual work, attributed to Rabbi Simeon ben Jochai (first century A.D.), one of the sources of the Kabbala. It is a commentary on the Pentateuch (Mosaic books), which many scholars now argue was actually written in the thirteenth century. Washington Irving mentions it in similar words in his *History of New York by Dietrich Knickerbocker* (1809), Chapter 4, Book IV.

4 Rufus Griswold published an American edition of D'Israeli's *Curiosities of Literature* (1844).

5 It seems appropriate that Poe should find the character of Scheherazade intriguing, since Joseph Campbell calls her "a priestess of the psyche secure in her science" (*Portable Arabian Nights*, Viking, 1952).

6 One of Galland's editions was called *Arabian Nights' Entertainments*, giving rise to the popular title.

7 The beard was extremely important; the Turks thought it a dire disgrace to have it cut, and slaves in the harem have clean chins, as a sign of their servitude.

8 Poe expresses the general attitude of his day toward anything not specifically Christian, as he does in "A Tale of Jerusalem."

9 Leap year has traditionally been a time when women could turn the tables and ask a man to marry, rather than the other way around.

A legend has it that St. Patrick began the custom, but there is also preserved an Act of the Scottish Parliament, passed in 1228: "Ordonit that during the reign of her maist blessed majestie, Margaret, ilka maiden, ladee of baith high and lowe estait, shall hae libertie to speak the man she likes. Gif he refuses to tak hir to bee his wyf, he shale be mulct in the sum of ane hundridty pundes, or less, as his estait may bee, except and alwais gif he can make it appeare that he is bethrohit to anither woman, then he schal be free." The year 1228, by the way, was a leap year.

10 A high executive officer, from the Turkish *vezir* and Arabic *wazir*

11 Whether one likes it or not

12 Prudent, shrewd

13 The word is a synonym for amoral cunning and justification of power, after Niccolò Machiavelli (1469–1527), whose *The Prince* is one of the great works of the Renaissance. Ironically, Machiavelli was not himself "Machiavellian."

Poe seems to be paraphrasing Samuel Butler (1612–80) here, for in that author's *Hudibras* (1663) we find: "There is a Machiavelian plot,/Tho' ev'ry nare olfact it not."

little plot in her mind. On the night of the wedding, she contrived, upon I forget what specious pretence, to have her sister occupy a couch sufficiently near that of the royal pair to admit of easy conversation from bed to bed; and, a little before cock-crowing, she took care to awaken the good monarch, her husband (who bore her none the worse will because he intended to wring her neck on the morrow),—she managed to awaken him, I say, (although on account of a capital conscience and an easy digestion, he slept well,) by the profound interest of a story (about a rat and a black cat, I think) which she was narrating (all in an undertone, of course) to her sister. When the day broke, it so happened that this history was not altogether finished, and that Scheherazade, in the nature of things could not finish it just then, since it was

14 high time for her to get up and be bowstrung—a thing very little more pleasant than hanging, only a trifle more genteel!

The king's curiosity, however, prevailing, I am sorry to say, even over his sound religious principles, induced him for this once to postpone the fulfilment of his vow until next morning, for the purpose and with the hope of hearing that night how it fared in the end with the black cat (a black cat, I think it was) and the rat.

The night having arrived, however, the lady Scheherazade not only put the finishing stroke to the black cat and the rat (the rat was blue) but before she well knew what she was about, found herself deep in the intricacies of a narration, having reference (if I am not altogether mistaken) to a pink horse (with green wings) that went, in a violent manner, by clockwork, and was wound up with an indigo key. With this history the king was even more profoundly interested than with the other—and, as the day broke before its conclusion (notwithstanding all the queen's endeavors to get through with it in time for the bowstringing), there was again no resource but to postpone that ceremony as before, for twenty-four hours. The next night there happened a·similar accident with a similar result; and then the next—and then again the next; so that, in the end, the good monarch, having been unavoidably deprived of all opportunity to keep his vow during a period of no less than one thousand and one nights, either forgets it altogether by the expiration of this time, or gets himself absolved of it in the regular way, or (what is more probable) breaks it outright, as well as the head of his father confessor. At all events, Scheherazade, who, being lineally descended from Eve, fell heir, perhaps, to the whole seven baskets of talk, which the latter lady, we all know, picked up from under

15 the trees in the garden of Eden; Scheherazade, I say, finally triumphed, and the tariff upon beauty was repealed.

Now, this conclusion (which is that of the story as we have it upon record) is, no doubt, excessively proper and pleasant—but alas! like a great many pleasant things, is more pleasant than true; and I am indebted altogether to the "Isitsöornot" for the means of correcting the error. *"Le mieux,"* says a

16 French proverb, *"est l'ennemi du bien,"* and, in mentioning

14 Strangled with a bowstring

15 "The Rabbins ought to be ashamed of themselves for their scandalous libel, in saying that ten baskets of chatter were let down from heaven, and that the women appropriated nine of them" (New York *Mirror*, May 30, 1835). The story was apparently making the rounds of the periodicals of the time.

17 "The better is the enemy of the good" from Voltaire's *Contes Moreaux* (1772), quoting an Italian proverb.

that Scheherazade had inherited the seven baskets of talk, I should have added that she put them out at compound interest until they amounted to seventy-seven.

"My dear sister," said she, on the thousand-and-second night (I quote the language of the "Isitsöornot" at this point, *verbatim*), "my dear sister," said she, "now that all this little difficulty about the bowstring has blown over, and that this odious tax is so happily repealed, I feel that I have been guilty of great indiscretion in withholding from you and the king (who, I am sorry to say, snores—a thing no gentleman would do) the full conclusion of Sinbad the sailor. This person went through numerous other and more interesting adventures than those which I related; but the truth is, I felt sleepy on the particular night of their narration, and so was seduced into cutting them short—a grievous piece of misconduct, for which I only trust that Allah will forgive me. But even yet it is not too late to remedy my great neglect—and as soon as I have given the king a pinch or two in order to wake him up so far that he may stop making that horrible noise, I will forthwith entertain you (and him if he pleases) with the sequel of this very remarkable story."

Hereupon the sister of Scheherazade, as I have it from the "Isitsöornot," expressed no very particular intensity of gratification; but the king, having been sufficiently pinched, at length ceased snoring, and finally said, "Hum!" and then "Hoo!" when the queen, understanding these words (which are no doubt Arabic) to signify that he was all attention, and would do his best not to snore any more—the queen, I say, having arranged these matters to her satisfaction, re-entered thus, at once, into the history of Sinbad, the sailor:

" 'At length, in my old age,' (these are the words of Sinbad himself, as retailed by Scheherazade)—'at length, in my old age, and after enjoying many years of tranquillity at home, I became once more possessed of a desire of visiting foreign countries; and one day, without acquainting any of my family with my design, I packed up some bundles of such merchandise as was most precious and least bulky, and, engaging a porter to carry them, went with him down to the sea-shore, to await the arrival of any chance vessel that might convey me out of the kingdom into some region which I had not as yet explored.

" 'Having deposited the packages upon the sands, we sat down beneath some trees, and looked out into the ocean in the hope of perceiving a ship, but during several hours we saw none whatever. At length I fancied that I could hear a singular buzzing or humming sound—and the porter, after listening awhile, declared that he also could distinguish it. Presently it grew louder, and then still louder, so that we could have no doubt that the object which caused it was approaching us. At length, on the edge of the horizon, we discovered a black speck, which rapidly increased in size until we made it out to be a vast monster, swimming with a great part of its body above the surface of the sea. It came toward us with inconceivable swiftness, throwing up huge waves of

. . . we sat down beneath some trees, and looked out into the ocean in the hope of perceiving a ship.
. . . *Illustration by F. S. Coburn, 1902*

17 Steam-powered warships were still new on the scene. The first, the *Princeton*, was launched in 1844.

18 Successors of Mohammed as temporal and spiritual head of Islam (Arabic *khalifah*)

19 Generally, the art of revealing future events by means of communicating with the dead, but now meaning all magic conjuration

foam around its breast, and illuminating all that part of the sea through which it passed, with a long line of fire that extended **17** far off into the distance.

" 'As the thing drew near we saw it very distinctly. Its length was equal to that of three of the loftiest trees that grow, and it was as wide as the great hall of audience in your palace, **18** O most sublime and munificent of the caliphs. Its body, which was unlike that of ordinary fishes, was as solid as a rock, and of a jetty blackness throughout all that portion of it which floated above the water, with the exception of a narrow blood-red streak that completely begirdled it. The belly, which floated beneath the surface, and of which we could get only a glimpse now and then as the monster rose and fell with the billows, was entirely covered with metallic scales, of a color like that of the moon in misty weather. The back was flat and nearly white, and from it there extended upwards of six spines, about half the length of the whole body.

" 'This horrible creature had no mouth that we could perceive; but, as if to make up for this deficiency, it was provided with at least four score of eyes, that protruded from their sockets like those of the green dragon-fly, and were arranged all around the body in two rows, one above the other, and parallel to the blood-red streak, which seemed to answer the purpose of an eyebrow. Two or three of these dreadful eyes were much larger than others, and had the appearance of solid gold.

" 'Although this beast approached us, as I have before said, with the greatest rapidity, it must have been moved altogether **19** by necromancy—for it had neither fins like a fish nor web-feet like a duck, nor wings like the sea-shell which is blown along in the manner of a vessel; not yet did it writhe itself forward [20] as do the eels. Its head and its tail were shaped precisely alike, only, not far from the latter, were two small holes that served for nostrils, and through which the monster puffed out its thick breath with prodigious violence, and with a shrieking, disagreeable noise.

" 'Our terror at beholding this hideous thing was very great, but it was even surpassed by our astonishment, when upon getting a nearer look, we perceived upon the creature's back a vast number of animals about the size and shape of men, and altogether much resembling them, except that they wore no garments (as men do), being supplied (by nature, no doubt,) with an ugly uncomfortable covering, a good deal like cloth, but fitting so tight to the skin, as to render the poor wretches laughably awkward, and put them apparently to severe pain. On the very tips of their heads were certain square-looking boxes, which, at first sight, I thought might have been intended to answer as turbans, but I soon discovered that they were excessively heavy and solid, and I therefore concluded they were contrivances designed, by their great weight, to keep the heads of the animals steady and safe upon their shoulders. Around the necks of the creatures were fastened black collars, (badges of servitude, no doubt,) such as we keep on our dogs, only much wider and infinitely stiffer—so that it was quite impossible for these poor victims to move their heads in any direction without moving the body at the same time; and thus they were doomed to perpetual contemplation of their noses—a view puggish and snubby in a wonderful if not positively in an awful degree.

" 'When the monster had nearly reached the shore where we stood, it suddenly pushed out one of its eyes to a great extent, and emitted from it a terrible flash of fire, accompanied by a dense cloud of smoke, and a noise that I can compare to nothing but thunder. As the smoke cleared away, we saw one of the odd man-animals standing near the head of the large beast with a trumpet in his hand, through which (putting it to his mouth) he presently addressed us in loud, harsh, and disagreeable accents, that, perhaps, we should have mistaken for language, had they not come altogether through the nose.

" 'Being thus evidently spoken to, I was at a loss how to reply, as I could in no manner understand what was said; and in this difficulty I turned to the porter, who was near swooning through affright, and demanded of him his opinion as to what species of monster it was, what it wanted, and what kind of creatures those were that so swarmed upon its back. To this the porter replied, as well as he could for trepidation, that he had once before heard of this sea-beast; that it was a cruel demon, with bowels of sulphur and blood of fire, created by evil genii as the means of inflicting misery upon mankind; that [21] the things upon its back were vermin, such as sometimes [22] infest cats and dogs, only a little larger and more savage; and that these vermin had their uses, however evil—for, through the torture they caused the beast by their nibblings and

[20] The paper nautilus, a cephalopod mollusk (genus *Argonauta*), has a delicate, papery shell in the form of a spiral.

[21] Genies, the djinn

[22] i.e., marines or navy men. There may be some sour grapes surfacing here, considering Poe's bad experiences is the military (See Introduction).

23 Pure gibberish

24 London Cockney, which Poe apparently thinks sounds dreadful enough to be a cross between the sound of a horse and that of a rooster.

25 "The coralites" (Poe's note). A corallite is the skeleton of an individual coral polyp, which together with others build up the great coral reefs of the seas.

26 " 'One of the most remarkable natural curiosities in Texas is a petrified forest, near the head of Pasigono river. It consists of several hundred trees, in an erect position, all turned to stone. Some trees, now growing, are partly petrified. This is a startling fact for natural philosophers, and must cause them to modify the existing theory of petrification.'—*Kennedy*.

"This account, at first discredited, has since been corroborated by the discovery of a completely petrified forest, near the head waters of the Cheyenne, or Chienne river, which has its source in the Black Hills of the rocky chain.

"There is scarcely, perhaps, a spectacle on the surface of the globe more remarkable, either in a geological or picturesque point of view than that presented by the petrified forest, near Cairo. The traveller, having passed the tombs of the caliphs, just beyond the gates of the city, proceeds to the southward, nearly at right angles to the road across the desert to Suez, and after having travelled some ten miles up a low barren valley, covered with sand, gravel, and sea shells, fresh as if the tide had retired but yesterday, crosses a low range of sandhills, which has for some distance run parallel to his path. The scene now presented to him is beyond conception singular and desolate. A mass of fragments of trees, all converted into stone, and when struck by his horse's hoof ringing like cast iron, is seen to extend itself for miles and miles around him, in the form of a decayed and prostrate forest. The wood is of a dark brown hue, but retains its form in perfection, the pieces being from one to fifteen feet in length, and from half a foot to three feet in thickness, strewed so closely together, as far as the eye can reach, that an Egyptian donkey can scarcely thread its way through amongst them, and so natural that, were it in Scotland or Ireland, it might pass without remark for some enormous drained bog, on which the exhumed trees lay rotting in the sun. The roots and rudiments of the branches are, in many cases, nearly perfect, and in some the worm-holes eaten under the bark are readily recognizable. The most delicate of the sap vessels, and all the finer portions of the centre of the wood, are perfectly entire, and bear to be examined with the strongest magnifiers. The whole are so thoroughly silicified as to scratch glass and be capable of receiving the highest polish.—*Asiatic Magazine*." (Poe's note)

The first paragraph comes from the St. Louis *Weekly Reveille* article mentioned in the introductory note, but the ultimate source is *Texas* (London, 1841), page 69 in the 1844 New York reprint.

Paragraph two was added after the first publication of the story and is from the same source, while the third paragraph (again, added later) is the only one from the *Asiatic Journal* (August 1844) article "Petrified Forest near Cairo."

27 "The Mammoth Cave of Kentucky" (Poe's note). Mammoth Cave, one of the largest known caves in the world, was discovered by white men in 1799, but was known long before by the Indians. During the War of 1812, settlers mined saltpeter for gunpowder there. The full extent of the cave is still unexplored, but the known

stingings, it was goaded into that degree of wrath which was requisite to make it roar and commit ill, and so fulfil the vengeful and malicious designs of the wicked genii.

" 'This account determined me to take to my heels, and, without once even looking behind me, I ran at full speed up into the hills, while the porter ran equally fast, although nearly in an opposite direction, so that by these means, he finally made his escape with my bundles, of which I have no doubt he took excellent care—although this is a point I cannot determine, as I do not remember that I ever beheld him again.

" 'For myself, I was so hotly pursued by a swarm of the men-vermin (who had come to the shore in boats) that I was very soon overtaken, bound hand and foot, and conveyed to the beast, which immediately swam out again into the middle of the sea.

" 'I now bitterly repented my folly in quitting a comfortable home to peril my life in such adventures as this; but regret being useless, I made the best of my condition, and exerted myself to secure the good-will of the man-animal that owned the trumpet, and who appeared to exercise authority over his fellows. I succeeded so well in this endeavor that, in a few days, the creature bestowed upon me various tokens of his favor, and in the end even went to the trouble of teaching me the rudiments of what it was vain enough to denominate its language; so that, at length, I was enabled to converse with it readily, and came to make it comprehend the ardent desire I had of seeing the world.

" ' "*Washish squashish squeak, Sinbad, hey-diddle diddle,*
23 *grunt unt grumble, hiss, fiss, whiss,*" said he to me, one day after dinner'—but I beg a thousand pardons, I had forgotten that your majesty is not conversant with the dialect of the Cock-neighs (so the man-animals were called; I presume because their language formed the connecting link between
24 that of the horse and that of the rooster). With your permission, I will translate. '*Washish squashish,*' and so forth:—that is to say, 'I am happy to find, my dear Sinbad, that you are really a very excellent fellow; we are now about doing a thing which is called circumnavigating the globe; and since you are so desirous of seeing the world, I will strain a point and give you a free passage upon the back of the beast.' ' "

When the Lady Scheherazade had proceeded thus far, relates the "Isitsöornot," the king turned over from his left side to his right, and said:

"It is, in fact, *very* surprising, my dear queen, that you omitted, hitherto, these latter adventures of Sinbad. Do you know I think them exceedingly entertaining and strange?"

The king having thus expressed himself, we are told, the fair Scheherazade resumed her history in the following words:

"Sinbad went on in this manner with his narrative—'I thanked the man-animal for its kindness, and soon found myself very much at home on the beast, which swam at a prodigious rate through the ocean; although the surface of the latter is, in that part of the world, by no means flat, but round like a pomegranate, so that we went—so to say—either up hill or down hill all the time.' "

"That, I think, was very singular," interrupted the king.

"Nevertheless, it is quite true," replied Scheherazade.

"I have my doubts," rejoined the king; "but, pray, be so good as to go on with the story."

"I will," said the queen. " 'The beast,' continued Sinbad, 'swam, as I have related, up hill and down hill, until, at length, we arrived at an island, many hundreds of miles in circumference, but which, nevertheless, had been built in the middle of the sea by a colony of little things like caterpillars.' " 25

"Hum!" said the king.

" 'Leaving this island,' said Sinbad—(for Scheherazade, it must be understood, took no notice of her husband's ill-mannered ejaculation)—'leaving this island, we came to another where the forests were of solid stone, and so hard that they shivered to pieces the finest-tempered axes with which we endeavored to cut them down.' " 26

"Hum!" said the king, again; but Scheherazade, paying him no attention, continued in the language of Sinbad.

" 'Passing beyond this last island, we reached a country where there was a cave that ran to the distance of thirty or forty miles within the bowels of the earth, and that contained a greater number of far more spacious and more magnificent palaces than are to be found in all Damascus and Bagdad. From the roofs of these palaces there hung myriads of gems, like diamonds, but larger than men; and in among the streets of towers and pyramids and temples, there flowed immense rivers as black as ebony, and swarming with fish that had no eyes.' " 27

"Hum!" said the king.

" 'We then swam into a region of the sea where we found a lofty mountain, down whose sides there streamed torrents of melted metal, some of which were twelve miles wide and sixty miles long; while from an abyss on the summit, issued 28 so vast a quantity of ashes that the sum was entirely blotted out from the heavens, and it became darker than the darkest midnight; so that when we were even at the distance of a hundred and fifty miles from the mountain, it was impossible to see the whitest object, however close we held it to our eyes.' " 29

"Hum!" said the king.

" 'After quitting this coast, the beast continued his voyage until we met with a land in which the nature of things seemed reversed—for we here saw a great lake, at the bottom of which, more than a hundred feet beneath the surface of the water, there flourished in full leaf a forest of tall and luxuriant trees.' " 30

"Hoo!" said the king.

" 'Some hundred miles farther on brought us to a climate where the atmosphere was so dense as to sustain iron or steel, just as our own does feathers.' " 31

"Fiddle de dee," said the king.

" 'Proceeding still in the same direction, we presently

passages extend more than 150 miles. Eyeless fish, bats, and insects make their home there, and the cave is today a national park.

Poe may have read of the cave in books by Alexander Bullett, Nahum Ward, and/or Edmund F. Lee, all published between 1816 and 1844.

28 "In Iceland, 1783" (Poe's note). The Laki fissure is considered by most geologists the site of the greatest lava flow in history. Fissure eruptions such as this one put out a great deal of lava because there is little loss of heat through explosive activity. Poe's information is probably from the Encyclopaedia of Geography (1836), by Hugh Murray, I, 215, 217, 221.

29 " 'During the eruption of Hecla, in 1766, clouds of this kind produced such a degree of darkness that, at Glaumba, which is more than fifty leagues from the mountain, people could only find their way by groping. During the eruption of Vesuvius, in 1794, at Caserta, four leagues distant, people could only walk by the light of torches. On the first of May, 1812, a cloud of volcanic ashes and sand, coming from a volcano in the island of St. Vincent, covered the whole of Barbadoes, spreading over it so intense a darkness that, at mid-day, in the open air, one could not perceive the trees or other objects near him, or even a white handkerchief placed at the distance of six inches from the eye.'—*Murray*, p. 215, *Phil. edit.*" (Poe's note)

30 " 'In the year 1790, in the Caraccas, during an earthquake a portion of the granite soil sank and left a lake eight hundred yards in diameter, and from eighty to a hundred feet deep. It was a part of the forest of Aripao which sank, and the trees remained green for several months under the water.'—*Murray*, p. 221." (Poe's note)

31 "The hardest steel ever manufactured may, under the action of a blowpipe, be reduced to an impalpable powder, which will float readily in the atmospheric air" (Poe's note). Poe added this note when the story was included in *Tales*, but no one has been able to track down his source for the steel powder.

32 "The region of the Niger. See *Simmond's 'Colonial Magazine'*." (Poe's note) The Niger is twenty-six hundred miles long. Poe's source is Richard Mouat's article in *Simmond's Colonial Magazine*, "A Narrative of the Niger Expedition," June–September 1844.

33 "The *Myrmeleon*—lion-ant. The term 'monster' is equally applicable to small abnormal things and to great, while such epithets as 'vast' are merely comparative. The cavern of the myrmeleon is *vast* in comparison with the hole of the common red ant. A grain of silex is, also, a 'rock.' " (Poe's note) Poe's source is Thomas Wyatt's *Synopsis of Natural History*, p. 135.

The ant lion, as it is known today, is the voracious larva of the insect *Dendroleon obsoletum*. Widely distributed throughout the world in dry, dusty regions, it uses its huge jaws to dig into crumbly soil and excavate a circular pit, where it waits at the bottom for its prey to tumble in. It then seizes its meal-to-be in its long, sharply toothed jaws and sucks the blood.

34 "The *Epidendron, Flos Aeris*, of the family of the *Orchideæ*, grows with merely the surface of its roots attached to a tree or other object, from which it derives no nutriment—subsisting altogether on air." (Poe's note)

The source is *The System of Physiological Botany* (1816), by Patrick Keith, II, p. 429. Poe also mentions the *Epidendron* in "How to Write a Blackwood Article" and "Eleonora."

These orchids, known as epiphytic, have a stem swollen at the base to form a pseudobulb (for food storage) and hanging aerial roots, which gather moisture from the air, and in some cases, manufacture chlorophyll.

35 "The *Parasites*, such as the wonderful *Rafflesia Arnoldi*." (Poe's note) This parasitic plant has no stalk or leaves and measures up to three feet across. It had been discovered about twenty-five years earlier, in Sumatra.

36 "*Schouw* advocates a class of plants that grow upon living animals—the *Plantae Epizoœ*. Of this class are the *Fuci* and *Algae*." (Poe's note).

Joachim Frederik Schouw (1789–1852) was a Danish botanist, but Poe's source is Murray's Encyclopaedia, from which the note is taken verbatim.

The above classifications do not exist today. *Fucus* is a form of alga. Epizoon today refers only to an animal that lives on the surface of another animal, such as a barnacle on a whale.

"*Mr. J. B. Williams, of Salem, Mass.*, presented the 'National Institute,' with an insect from New Zealand, with the following description:—' "*The Hotte*," a decided caterpillar, or worm, is found growing at the foot of the *Rata* tree, with a plant growing out of its head. This most peculiar and most extraordinary insect travels up both the *Rata* and *Perriri* trees, and entering into the top, eats its way, perforating the trunk of the tree until it reaches the root, it then comes out of the root, and dies, or remains dormant, and the plant propagates out of its head; the body remains perfect and entire, of a harder substance than when alive. From this insect the natives make a coloring for tattooing." (Poe's note) This comes from the third *Bulletin of the National Institute* (1845), p. 369. John B. Williams was a U.S. consul in Auckland, New Zealand. "Perriri" should be *Puriri*.

37 "In mines and natural caves we find a species of cryptogamous *fungus* that emits an intense phosphorescence." (Poe's note) *Cryptogamia* was an older classification of the group that includes plants not producing true flowers or seeds, such as mosses and ferns. See also "The Fall of the House of Usher" for phosphorescent fungi.

38 "The orchis, scabius and vallisneria." (Poe's note) Added to the book edition, this is a reference to the orchids, the Scabiosa (teasel family) and Vallisneria, or eel-grass. The first grows in trees (but is not a parasite), the second is known for its ability to spread rapidly, and the third spreads by means of underground runners.

39 " 'The corolla of this flower (*Aristolochia Clematitis*), which is tubular, but terminating upwards in a ligulate limb, is inflated into a globular figure at the base. The tubular part is internally beset with a stuff hairs, pointing downwards. The globular part contains the pistil, which consists merely of a germen and stigma, together with the surrounding stamens. But the stamens, being shorter than even the germen, cannot discharge the pollen so as to throw it upon the stigma, as the flower stands always upright till after impregnation. And hence, without some additional and peculiar aid, the pollen must necessarily fall down to the bottom of the flower. Now, the aid that nature had furnished in this case, is that of the *Tipula Pennicornis*, a small insect, which entering the tube of the corolla in quest of honey, descends to the bottom, and rummages about till it becomes quite

arrived at the most magnificent region in the whole world. Through it there meandered a glorious river for several thousands of miles. This river was of unspeakable depth, and of a transparency richer than that of amber. It was from three to six miles in width; and its banks which arose on either side to twelve hundred feet in perpendicular height, were crowned with everblossoming trees, and perpetual sweet-scented flowers, that made the whole territory one gorgeous garden; but the name of this luxuriant land was the kingdom of Horror, **32** and to enter it was inevitable death.' "

"Humph!" said the king.

" 'We left this kingdom in great haste, and, after some days, came to another, where we were astonished to perceive myriads of monstrous animals with horns resembling scythes upon their heads. These hideous beasts dig for themselves vast caverns in the soil, of a funnel shape, and line the sides of them with rocks, so disposed one upon the other that they fall instantly, when trodden upon by other animals, thus precipitating them into the monster's dens, where their blood is immediately sucked, and their carcasses afterwards hurled contemptuously out to an immense distance from the caverns **33** of death.' "

"Pooh!" said the king.

" 'Continuing our progress, we perceived a district with **34** vegetables that grew not upon any soil, but in the air. There **35** were others that sprang from the substance of other vegetables; others that derived their substance from the bodies of living **36** animals; and then again, there were others that glowed all **37** over with intense fire; others that moved from place to place **38** at pleasure, and what was still more wonderful, we discovered flowers that lived and beathed and moved their limbs at will, and had, moreover, the detestable passion of mankind for enslaving other creatures, and confining them in horrid and **39** solitary prisons until the fulfillment of appointed tasks.' "

"Pshaw!" said the king.

" 'Quitting this land, we soon arrived at another in which the bees and the birds are mathematicians of such genius and erudition, that they give daily instructions in the science of geometry to the wise men of the empire. The king of the place having offered a reward for the solution of two very difficult problems, they were solved upon the spot—the one by the bees, and the other by the birds; but the king keeping their solution a secret, it was only after the most profound researches and labor, and the writing of an infinity of big books, during a long series of years, that the men-mathematicians at length arrived at the identical solutions which had **40** been given upon the spot by the bees and by the birds.' "

"Oh my!" said the king.

" 'We had scarcely lost sight of this empire when we found ourselves close upon another, from whose shores there flew over our heads a flock of fowls a mile in breadth, and two hundred and forty miles long; so that, although they flew a mile during every minute, it required no less than four hours for the whole flock to pass over us—in which there were **41** several millions of millions of fowls.' "

"Oh fy!" said the king.

" 'No sooner had we got rid of these birds, which occasioned us great annoyance, than we were terrified by the appearance of a fowl of another kind, and infinitely larger than even the rocs which I met in my former voyages; for it was bigger than **42** the biggest of the domes on your seraglio, oh, most Munificent **43** of Caliphs. This terrible fowl had no head that we could perceive, but was fashioned entirely of belly, which was of a prodigious fatness and roundness, of a soft-looking substance, smooth, shining and striped with various colors. In its talons, the monster was bearing away to his eyrie in the heavens, a house from which it had knocked off the roof, and in the interior of which we distinctly saw human beings, who, beyond doubt, were in a state of frightful despair at the horrible fate which awaited them. We shouted with all our might, in the hope of frightening the bird into letting go of its prey; but it merely gave a snort or puff, as if of rage and then let fall upon our heads a heavy sack which proved to be filled with sand!' " **44**

"Stuff!" said the king.

" 'It was just after this adventure that we encountered a continent of immense extent and prodigious solidity, but which, nevertheless, was supported entirely upon the back of a sky-blue cow that had no fewer than four hundred horns.' " **45**

"*That*, now, I believe," said the king, "because I have read something of the kind before, in a book."

" 'We passed immediately beneath this continent (swimming in between the legs of the cow), and, after some hours, found ourselves in a wonderful country indeed, which, I was informed by the man-animal, was his own native land, inhabited by things of his own species, This elevated the man-animal very much in my esteem, and in fact, I now began to feel ashamed of the contemptuous familiarity with which I had treated him; for I found that the man-animals in general were a nation of the most powerful magicians, who lived with worms in their brain, which, no doubt, served to stimulate them by their **46** painful writhings and wrigglings to the most miraculous efforts of imagination.' "

"Nonsense!" said the king.

" 'Among the magicians, were domesticated several animals of very singular kinds; for example, there was a huge horse whose bones were iron and whose blood was boiling water. In place of corn, he had black stones for his usual food; and yet, in spite of so hard a diet, he was so strong and swift that he could drag a load more weighty than the grandest temple in this city, at a rate surpassing that of the flight of most birds.' " **47**

"Twattle!" said the king.

" 'I saw, also, among these people a hen without feathers, but bigger than a camel; instead of flesh and bone she had iron and brick; her blood, like that of the horse (to whom, in fact, she was nearly related), was boiling water; and like him she ate nothing but wood or stones. This hen brought forth very frequently, a hundred chickens in the day; and, after birth, they took up residence for several weeks within the stomach of their mother.' " **48**

covered with pollen; but, not being able to force its way out again, owing to the downward position of the hairs, which converge to a point like the wires of a mousetrap, and being somewhat impatient of its confinement, it brushes backwards and forwards, trying every corner, till, after repeatedly traversing the stigma, it covers it with pollen sufficient for its impregnation, in consequence of which the flower soon begins to droop, and the hairs to shrink to the side of the tube, effecting an easy passage for the escape of the insect' *Rev. P. Keith—System of Physiological Botany.* " (Poe's note) Vol. II, p. 354.

40 "The bees—ever since bees were—have been constructing their cells with just such sides, in just such number, and at just such inclinations, as it has been demonstrated (in a problem involving the profoundest mathematical principles) are the very sides, in the very number, and at the very angles, which will afford the creatures the most room that is compatible with the greatest stability of structure.

During the latter part of the last century, the question arose among mathematicians—'to determine the best form that can be given to the sails of a windmill, according to their varying distances from the revolving vanes, and likewise from the centres of revolution.' This is an excessively complex problem; for it is, in other words, to find the best possible position at an infinity of varied distances, and at an infinity of points on the arm. There were a thousand futile attempts to answer the query on the part of the most illustrious mathematicians; and when, at length, an undeniable solution was discovered, men found that the wings of a bird had given it with absolute precision ever since the first bird had traversed the air." (Poe's note)

41 "He observed a flock of pigeons passing betwixt Frankfort and the Indiana territory, one mile at least in breadth; it took up four hours in passing; which, at the rate of one mile per minute, gives a length of 240 miles; and, supposing three pigeons to each square yard, gives 2,230,272,000 pigeons.—'*Travels in Canada and the United States,*' *by Lieut. F. Hall.*" (Poe's note)

The American passenger pigeon was slaughtered indiscriminately and became extinct in 1914, when the last bird died in a zoo, the solitary remnant of the vast flocks that once did literally darken the sky during their flight and migrations.

42 The roc was a giant bird of Arabian mythology. In "The Second Voyage of Sinbad the Sailor," Sinbad lands on a deserted island. "Climbing a tall tree, I spied a white dome in the interior of the island. Approaching, I found it of vast compass yet without an entrance. The sun darkened when a prodigious bird arrived: this was the Roc, which feeds its young on elephants; the dome was its egg. . . ." (*The Portable Arabian Nights*, 1952; p. 424)

43 Harem

44 Sinbad has seen a balloon with its wicker car, or gondola. Compare with this passage from "The Fourth Voyage of Sinbad the Sailor": "We hurried to the sea, but the birds dropped prodigious stones on us. These broke the rudder, and the ship foundered with all aboard. Seizing a plank, I was washed to a beautiful island." (*Portable Arabian Nights*, p. 428)

45 " 'The earth is upheld by a cow of a blue color, having horns four hundred in number.'—*Sale's Koran.*" (Poe's note)

This does not come from the Koran, although it does

appear in the mythology of the Middle East. In ancient Egyptian tales, the goddess Hathor was often represented as a cow (her sacred animal) with the solar disk between her horns. Neith (Neit), whom the Greeks identified with their Pallas Athene, was the great weaver who wove the world with her shuttle as a woman weaves cloth. Under the name Mehueret she was the Celestial Cow who gave birth to the sky when nothing existed.

46 " 'The *Entozoa*, or intestinal worms, have repeatedly been observed in the muscles, and in the cerebral substance of men.'—See *Wyatt's Physiology*, p. 143. (Poe's note)

Poe is mistaken—he means Wyatt's *Synopsis of Natural History* (p. 143). John Morgan of Philadelphia first observed these parasites, and published a paper in *Transactions of the American Philosophical Society* in 1787. Poe mentions the phenomenon again in "The Island of the Fay" and in several articles. An Entozoon is merely a parasite that lives in the body of another animal.

47 "On the great Western Railway, between London and Exeter, a speed of 71 miles per hour has been attained. A train weighing 90 tons was whirled from Puddington to Didcot (53 miles), in 51 minutes." (Poe's note)

This parallels an article entitled "Oriental Incredulity," which appeared in the Philadelphia *Saturday Evening Post*, September 4, 1841, in which an Englishman tells a Turk the speed of the train between Manchester and Liverpool. "It's a lie," says the Turk. The Englishman assures him that he himself has seen the train travel this fast. "I don't believe it a bit more for that," the unruffled Turk replies.

48 "The *Eccaleobion*." (Poe's note) The "Eccaleobion"— from the Greek, meaning "life-invoking"—was an egg-hatching device first demonstrated in New York in 1844 but that had been shown in London five years before. It was the first incubator to use artificial heat.

"The greatest curiosity that was ever in the United States is the wonderful Eccaleobion, 285 Broadway, displaying the laws established by the creator for the production of life. The idea of producing life by machinery is certainly worthy of attention. The curious and reflecting mind may have food for his thoughts. And no person can go from the Eccaleobion dissatisfied. What would our forefathers have thought had they been told that for 25¢ they could see *chickens hatched by steam?* Their first thought would be, 'We'll go and see it.' " (New York *Tribune*, June 10, 1844)

49 "Maelzel's Automation Chess-player." (Poe's note) Maelzel had claimed that this was a mechanical chess-playing man, but Poe proved it was a fake in his essay "Maezel's Chess-player." Here he satirizes the decision by the hidden assistant inside the contraption not to defeat Charles Carroll of Carrollton, in order to prevent trouble—and possible exposure.

50 The Magi were members of the ancient Persian priestly class, but the word came to mean anyone skilled in magic, astrology or sorcery.

51 "Babbage's Calculating Machine." (Poe's note) Charles Babbage was a professor of mathematics at Cambridge who, after eighteen years of work to perfect a machine that would produce logarithm tables, instead came up with a model that would add, subtract, multiply, and divide (1834).

"Fal lal!" said the king.

" 'One of this nation of mighty conjurers created a man out of brass and wood, and leather, and endowed him with such ingenuity that he would have beaten at chess, all the race of mankind with the exception of the great Caliph, Haroun **49,50** Alraschid. Another of these magi constructed (of like material) a creature that put to shame even the genius of him who made it; for so great were its reasoning powers that, in a second, it performed calculations of so vast an extent that they would have required the united labor of fifty thousand fleshy **51** men for a year. But a still more wonderful conjurer fashioned for himself a mighty thing that was neither man nor beast, but which had brains of lead, intermixed with a black matter like pitch, and fingers that employed with such incredible speed and dexterity that it would have had no trouble in writing out twenty thousand copies of the Koran in an hour; and this with so exquisite a precision, that in all the copies there should not be found one to vary from another by the breadth of the finest **52** hair. This thing was of prodigious strength, so that it erected or overthrew the mightiest empires at a breath; but its powers were exercised equally for evil and for good.' "

"Ridiculous!" said the king.

" 'Among this nation of necromancers there was also one who had in his veins the blood of the salamanders; for he made no scruple of sitting down to smoke his chibouc in a red-hot oven until his dinner was thoroughly roasted upon its **53** floor. Another had the faculty of converting the common metals into gold, without even looking at them during the **54** process. Another had such a delicacy of touch that he made **55** a wire so fine as to be invisible. Another had such quickness of perception that he counted all the separate motions of an elastic body, while it was springing backward and forward at **56** the rate of nine hundred millions of times in a second.' "

"Absurd!" said the king.

" 'Another of these magicians, by means of a fluid that nobody ever yet saw, could make the corpses of his friends brandish their arms, kick out their legs, fight, or even get up **57** and dance at his will. Another had cultivated his voice to so great an extent that he could have made himself heard from **58** one end of the world to the other. Another had so long an arm that he could sit down in Damascus and indite a letter at **59** Bagdad—or indeed at any distance whatsoever. Another commanded the lightning to come down to him out of heavens, and it came at his call; and served him for a plaything when **60** it came. Another took two loud sounds and out of them made a silence. Another constructed a deep darkness out of two **61,62** brilliant lights. Another made ice in a red-hot furnace. Another **63** directed the sun to paint his portrait, and the sun did. Another took this luminary with the moon and the planets, and having first weighed them with scrupulous accuracy, probed into their depths and found out the solidity of the substance of which they are made. But the whole nation is, indeed, of so surprising a necromantic ability, that not even their infants, nor their commonest cats and dogs have any difficulty in seeing objects that do not exist at all, or that for twenty millions of years before the birth of the nation itself had been blotted out from the face of creation.' " **64**

"Preposterous!" said the king.

" 'The wives and daughters of these incomparably great and wise magi,' "continued Scheherazade, without being in any manner disturbed by these frequent and most ungentlemanly interruptions on the part of her husband—" 'the wives and daughters of these eminent conjurers are every thing that is accomplished and refined; and would be every thing that is interesting and beautiful, but for an unhappy fatality that besets them, and from which not even the miraculous powers of their husbands and fathers has, hitherto, been adequate to save. Some fatalities come in certain shapes, and some in others—but this of which I speak has come in the shape of a crotchet.' " **65**

"A what?" said the king.

" 'A crotchet,' " said Scheherazade. " 'One of the evil genii, who are perpetually upon the watch to inflict ill, has put it into the heads of these accomplished ladies that the thing which we describe as personal beauty consists altogether in the protuberance of the region which lies not very far below the small of the back. Perfection of loveliness, they say, is in **66** the direct ratio of the extent of this lump. Having been long possessed of this idea, and bolsters being cheap in that country, the days have long gone by since it was possible to distinguish a woman from a dromedary——' "

"Stop!" said the king—"I can't stand that, and I won't. You have already given me a dreadful headache with your lies. The day, too, I perceive, is beginning to break. How long have we been married?——my conscience is getting to be troublesome again. And then that dromedary touch—do you take me for a fool? Upon the whole, you might as well get up and be throttled."

These words, as I learn from the "Isitsöornot," both grieved and astonished Scheherazade; but, as she knew the king to be a man of scrupulous integrity, and quite unlikely to forfeit his word, she submitted to her fate with a good grace. She derived, however, great consolation (during the tightening of the bowstring), from the reflection that much of the history remained still untold, and that the petulance of her brute of a husband had reaped for him a most righteous reward, in **67** depriving him of many inconceivable adventures.

52 The Hoe press, developed in the early 1840s, gave the printing business a much-needed boost and opened the floodgates of American periodical literature. N. P. Willis, in a style not unlike Sinbad's, says, "Now (thanks to Mr. Hoe), we have a steam press, which *puts up three fingers for a sheet of white paper, pulls it down into its bosom, gives it a squeeze that makes an impression, and then lays it into the palm of an iron hand which deposits it evenly on a heap—at the rate of two thousand an hour!*" (*Complete Works*, 1846; p. 725)

53 "*Chabert,* and since him, a hundred others." (Poe's note) John Xavier Chabert sat in an oven, according to Dionysius Lardner's *Course of Lectures,* 1842, p. 25, but was protected from the hot floor, where he broiled a steak. A *chibouk,* or *chibouque,* is a Turkish tobacco pipe.

54 "The Electrotype." (Poe's note) The electrotype process involves depositing a metal film (by means of electrolysis) on an engraved surface to form a printing plate. Copper or nickel is normally used, and the mold is wax, lead, or (today) plastic. The plating *could* be gold, (but unlikely), and this suggests alchemy to Poe.

55 "*Wollaston* made of platinum for the field of views in a telescope a wire one eighteen-thousandth part of an inch in thickness. It could be seen only by means of the microscope." (Poe's note) William Hyde Wollaston (1766–1828) discovered the method to make platinum malleable. He also discovered the dark lines in the solar spectrum, and the elements palladium and rhodium.

56 "Newton demonstrated that the retina beneath the influence of the violet ray of the spectrum, vibrated 900,000,000 times in a second." (Poe's note)

Although Lardner discusses the vibrations of the retina (pp. 40–41), he doesn't give the figure Poe does. Poe's source for the figure is unknown; he may have deduced it himself from his reading. The retina is the network of nerve fibers that fan out from the optic nerve and contains the sensory receptors of light.

57 "The Voltaic pile." (Poe's note) Lardner mentions the Voltaic Pile, or battery, on pp. 11–12, and Poe uses it often in his tales, including "Loss of Breath," "Some Words with a Mummy," and "The Premature Burial." See "Loss of Breath," note 25.

58 "The Electro Telegraph Printing Apparatus." (Poe's note) One of Morse's ideas, actually conceived before the telegraph, was a machine something like our modern Teletype. By 1844, Morse had managed to send a message over a wire 153 miles long.

59 "The Electro Telegraph transmits intelligence instantaneously—at least so far as regards any distance upon the earth." (Poe's note) Samuel Morse had made his well-publicized transmission from Washington to Baltimore in May 1844.

60 Franklin's kite experiment. The phenomenon of electricity interested him greatly, and in 1748 he turned his printing business over to his foreman, intending to devote his life to science. His spectacular experiment of flying a kite in a thunderstorm (which could have cost him his life, as it had others—about whom he did not know) proved the identity of the electricity in lightning and won him recognition from the leading scientists in England and on the Continent.

61 "Common experiments in Natural Philosophy. If two red rays from two luminous points be admitted into a dark chamber so as to fall on a white surface, and differ in their length by 0.0000258 of an inch, their intensity is doubled. So also if the difference in length be any whole-number multiple of that fraction. A multiple by 2 1/4, 3 1/4, &c., gives an intensity equal to one ray only; but a multiple by 2 1/2, 3 1/2, &c., gives the result of total darkness. In violet rays similar effects arise when the difference in length is 0.000157 of an inch; and with all other rays the results are the same—the difference varying with a uniform increase from the violet to the red.

"Analogous experiments in respect to sound produce analogous results." (Poe's note)

Two light waves (or two sound waves) can indeed cancel each other's power. Sir David Brewster (1781–1868), in *Letters on Natural Magic* (1832), first described this red-ray process. He was also the inventor of the kaleidoscope and improved greatly on the light–houses of the day.

62 "Place a platina crucible over a spirit lamp, and keep it at red heat; pour in some sulphuric acid, which, though the most volatile of bodies at a common temperature, will be found to become completely fixed in a hot crucible, and not a drop evaporates—being surrounded by an atmosphere of its own, it does not, in fact, touch the sides. A few drops of water are now introduced, when the acid, immediately comimg in contact with the heated sides of the crucible, flies off in sulphurous acid vapor, and so rapid is its progress, that the caloric of the water passes off with it, which falls a lump of ice to the bottom; by taking advantage of the moment before it is allowed to remelt, it may be turned out a lump of ice from a red-hot vessel." (Poe's note)

This comes, practically verbatim, from a *Weekly Reveille* article, "Production of Ice in a Red-Hot Crucible," November 18, 1844.

63 "The Daguerreotype." (Poe's note) This invention of Louis Jacques Mandé Daguerre (1787–1851) was first announced in 1839. A photograph produced on a silver-coated copper plate treated with iodine vapor through the light of the sun, it was introduced into the United States by J. W. Draper and Samuel Morse.

64 "Although light travels 167,000 miles in a second, the distance of 61 Cygni (the only star whose distance is ascertained) is so inconceivably great, that its rays would require more than ten years to reach the earth. For stars beyond this, 20—or even 1000 years—would be a moderate estimate. Thus, if they had been annihilated 20, or 1000 years ago, we might still see them to-day, by the light which *started* from their surfaces 20 or 1000 years in the past time. That many which we see daily are really extinct, is not impossible—not even improbable." (Poe's note)

Poe made many important changes from the first version of the tale to the last, since astronomy was also changing its views. The figure "167,000 miles in a second" was originally "200,000," and "Cygni" was "Sirius." "More than ten" was "at least three."

Between the 1845 edition of the tale and its appearance in the complete *Works* of 1850, Poe added new information to this note, which was included by Poe's editor, Griswold, in the posthumous edition. The new material: "The elder Herschel maintains that the light of the faintest nebulæ seen through his great telescope must have taken 3,000,000 years in reaching the earth. Some, made visible by Lord Ross' instrument, must, then, have required at least 20,000,000." See "Hans Pfaall," introductory note, for more on Herschel. The discovery of the makeup of the sun, moon, and planets may refer to the work of Wollaston and of Bavarian physicist Joseph von Fraunhofer (1787–1826), who first mapped the dark lines that appear when a beam of sunlight passes through a glass prism and spreads its rainbowlike spectrum across a piece of white paper. The dark lines amid the color represent the particular atomic constituents absorbed by the somewhat cooler outer atmospheric layers of the sun. By comparing the sun's spectrum with lab spectra of incandescent elements, scientists could identify most of the sun's own elements.

65 A "crotchet" is a perverse conceit or fancy on some point, which a person holds contrary to common opinion; it also means a hook or quarter note. All apply here (see next note).

66 The bustle, a late-eighteenth-century development, first meant the projecting part of the dress itself, but soon came to mean the stuffed pad or cushion worn beneath the skirt. Ostensibly to improve the line of the drape, one wonders whether it was Victorian woman's way of reminding Victorian man just what was under the voluminous garments she was forced to wear. Poe didn't like it, and also ridiculed it in "The Spectacles" and "Mellonta Tauta."

67 "He that receiveth a prophet in the name of a prophet shall receive a prophet's reward; and he that receiveth a righteous man in the name of a righteous man shall receive a righteous man's reward" (Matthew 10:41).

Compare this tale's conclusion with that of the original Scheherazade story: "On the morrow the king rose, full of joy and contentment, and, summoning all his troops, bestowed on his vizier, Scheherazade's father, a rich and splendid robe of honor and said to him, 'God protect thee, for that thou gavest me to wife thy noble daughter, who hath been the means of my repentence from slaying the daughters of the people. Indeed, I have found her noble, pure, chaste, and virtuous, and God hath vouchsafed me three male children by her; wherefore praised be He for this exceeding bounty!'"

One wonders what the king in Poe's tale would have said if Scheherazade had also had possession of a crystal ball, had looked into the future, and told him what she saw there!

SOME WORDS WITH A MUMMY

First published in the *American Review: A Whig Journal*, April 1845, this tale takes as its jumping-off point the contemporary craze for things Egyptian (thanks to the recently deciphered hieroglyphics made possible by the discovery of the Rosetta Stone, in 1799) and moves on to take a few pokes at the Altar of Progress and to deflate the ideal of Democracy.

Sources include *Ancient Egypt*, by George Robins Gliddon, published in the *New World* in April 1843; an article in the New York *Tribune* (December 21, 1841) that discussed John Gardner Wilkinson's *Manners and Customs of the Ancient Egyptians* (1837–41); a similar book by Ippolito Rosellini (1840), and the anonymously written *Egyptian History deduced from Monuments still in existence* (1841); as well as the articles on embalming and mummies in the Encyclopaedia Americana.

1 A *symposium* originally meant a party with drinking, conversation, and intellectual entertainment.

2 Supposedly indigestible, Welsh rarebit/rabbit is a cheese sauce over toast, said to produce nightmares. The word was originally "Welsh *rabbit*," an English jab at the comparitively poorer inhabitants of Wales, who could not afford the meat that graced many English tables and ate this meat substitute instead. As time went by, the joke was lost and speakers decided that the word must be "rarebit," since there was obviously no rabbit involved.

3 An Edison silent film (1906), *Dreams of a Rarebit Fiend*, depicts a man in the throes of a nightmare brought on by too much rarebit. His bed flies out the window, taking him on a whirlwind, aerial tour of the city.

4 Stout is a strong, dark ale, darker and maltier than porter, with a more pronounced hop aroma and with an alcoholic content of 6 to 7 per cent.

5 " 'Pon honor.' " (Upon my honor!)

6 A sabretash (*sabretache*) is a leather satchel that hangs from the sword belt of a cavalry officer. The word was used as a person's name in a series of articles that appeared in *Fraser's Magazine* in 1838–39, and a column in the New York *Mirror*, November 12, 1842, is signed "Captain Sabretash."

1 The *symposium* of the preceding evening had been a little too much for my nerves. I had a wretched headache, and was desperately drowsy. Instead of going out, therefore, to spend the evening, as I had proposed, it occurred to me that I could not do a wiser thing than just eat a mouthful of supper and go immediately to bed.

A *light* supper, of course. I am exceedingly fond of Welsh-
2 rabbit. More than a pound at once, however, may not at all
3 times be advisable. Still, there can be no material objection to two. And really between two and three, there is merely a single unit of difference. I ventured, perhaps, upon four. My wife will have it five;—but, clearly, she has confounded two very distinct affairs. The abstact number, five, I am willing to admit; but, concretely, it has reference to bottles of Brown
4 Stout, without which, in the way of condiment, Welsh-rabbit is to be eschewed.

Having thus concluded a frugal meal, and donned my nightcap, with the sincere hope of enjoying it till noon the next day, I placed my head upon the pillow, and, through the aid of a capital conscience, fell into a profound slumber forthwith.

But when were the hopes of humanity fulfilled? I could not have completed my third snore when there came a furious ringing at the street-door bell, and then an impatient thumping at the knocker, which awakened me at once. In a minute afterward, and while I was still rubbing my eyes, my wife thrust in my face a note, from my old friend, Doctor Ponnon-
5 ner. It ran thus:

Come to me, by all means, my dear good friend, as soon as you receive this. Come and help us to rejoice. At last, by long persevering diplomacy, I have gained the assent of the Directors of the City Museum, to my examination of the Mummy—you know the one I mean. I have permission to unswathe it and open it, if desirable. A few friends only will be present—you, of course. The Mummy is now at my house, and we shall begin to unroll it at eleven to-night.

"Yours, ever,

PONNONNER

By the time I had reached the "Ponnonner," it struck me that I was as wide awake as a man need be. I leaped out of bed in an ecstasy, overthrowing all in my way; dressed myself with a rapidity truly marvellous; and set off, at the top of my speed, for the Doctor's.

There I found a very eager company assembled. They had been awaiting me with much impatience; the Mummy was extended upon the dining-table; and the moment I entered, its examination was commenced.

It was one of a pair brought, several years previously, by Captain Arthur Sabretash, a cousin of Ponnonner's, from a **6** tomb near Eleithias, in the Libyan mountains, a considerable distance above Thebes on the Nile. The grottos at this point, **7** although less magnificent than the Theban sepulchres, are of higher interest, on account of affording more numerous illustrations of the private life of the Egyptians. The chamber from which our specimen was taken, was said to be very rich in such illustrations—the walls being completely covered with fresco paintings and bas-reliefs, while statues, vases, and Mosaic work of rich patterns, indicated the vast wealth of the **8** deceased.

The treasure had been deposited in the museum precisely in the same condition in which Captain Sabretash had found it—that is to say, the coffin had not been disturbed. For eight years it had thus stood, subject only externally to public inspection. We had now, therefore, the complete Mummy at our disposal; and to those who are aware how very rarely the unransacked antique reaches our shores, it will be evident, at once, that we had great reason to congratulate ourselves upon our good fortune.

Approaching the table, I saw on it a large box, or case, nearly seven feet long, and perhaps three feet wide, by two feet and a half deep. It was oblong—not coffin-shaped. The material was at first supposed to be the wood of the sycamore (*platanus*), but, upon cutting into it, we found it to be pasteboard, or, more properly, *papier mâché*, composed of papyrus. It was thickly ornamented with paintings, repre- **9** senting funeral scenes, and other mournful subjects—interspersed among which, in every variety of position, were certain series of hieroglyphical characters intended, no doubt, for the name of the departed. By good luck, Mr. Gliddon formed one of our party; and he had no difficulty in translating the letters, which were simply phonetic, and represented the word, *Allamistakeo*. **10**

We had some difficulty in getting this case open without injury; but, having at length accomplished the task, we came to a second, coffin-shaped, and very considerably less in size

7 Eleithias, or Eileithyia, was an ancient Egyptian city called Nuben by the Egyptians; the site is presently occupied by El Kab. The Lybian mountains are the hills near Thebes.

This information and much of what follows come from the Encyclopaedia Americana (1836) article on "Mummies": "Numerous caves or grottoes are found in the two mountainous ridges which run nearly parallel with the Nile from Cairo to Syene. Some of the most remarkable of these tombs are those in the vicinity of ancient Thebes, in the Lybian mountains, many of which were first examined by Belzoni, and those near Eleithias (described by Hamilton) farther up the river, which though less splendid than Theban sepulchres, contain more illustrations of the private life of the Egyptians."

8 The word was capitalized until the end of the nineteenth century, perhaps by association with the "Mosaic" referring to Moses, even though the art term came from the same root as our "muse."

9 It would seem difficult to make *papier-mâché* from papyrus, since the latter was made into writing material by virtue of its long fibers, and *papier-mâché* is a chopped or ground-up pulp. The *Americana* mentions pasteboard as the substance in question.

10 "All a mistake"

Interest in mummies and Egypt was still high in Poe's time because of recent finds and the deciphering of the Rosetta Stone. This period engraving is of the actual mummy of Ramses II.

11 "The coffin is usually of sycamore, cedar, or paste-board; the case is entire, and covered, within and without, by paintings, representing funeral scenes, and a great variety of other subjects. . . ." (*Americana*)

12 The body was rubbed with a mixture of cedar oil, cumin, wax, natron (a compound to produce dehydration), gum, and possibly milk and wine, then dusted with spices.

13 Giddon's *Ancient Egypt*, pp. 6–7.
While the Egyptians never gave up pictograms, they had phonetic symbols and did use them.

14 "Embalmers of different ranks and duties extracted the brain through the nostril, and the entrails though an incision in the side . . ." (*Americana*). For a fascinating glimpse into the process, with many revealing photographs, see *X-Raying the Pharaohs*, by James E. Harris and Kent R. Weeks, Scribners, 1978.

than the exterior one, but resembling it precisely in every other respect. The interval between the two was filled with resin, which had, in some degree, defaced the colors of the **11** interior box.

Upon opening this latter (which we did quite easily), we arrived at a third case, also coffin-shaped, and varying from the second one in no particular, except in that of its material, which was cedar, and still emitted the peculiar and highly **12** aromatic odor of that wood. Between the second and the third case there was no interval—the one fitting accurately within the other.

Removing the third case, we discovered and took out the body itself. We had expected to find it, as usual, enveloped in frequent rolls, or bandages, of linen; but, in place of these, we found a sort of sheath, made of papyrus, and coated with a layer of plaster, thickly gilded and painted. The paintings represented subjects connected with the various supposed duties of the soul, and its presentation to different divinities, with numerous identical human figures, intended, very probably, as portraits of the person embalmed. Extending from head to foot was a columnar, or perpendicular, inscription, in **13** phonetic hieroglyphics, giving again his name and titles, and the names and titles of his relations.

Around the neck thus ensheathed, was a collar of cylindrical glass beads, diverse in color, and so arranged as to form images of deities, of the scarabæus, etc., with the winged globe. Around the small of the waist was a similar collar or belt.

Stripping off the papyrus, we found the flesh in excellent preservation, with no perceptible odor. The color was reddish. The skin was hard, smooth, and glossy. The teeth and hair were in good condition. The eyes (it seemed) had been removed, and glass ones substituted, which were very beautiful and wonderfully life-like, with the exception of somewhat too determined a stare. The finger and toe nails were brilliantly gilded.

Mr. Gliddon was of opinion, from the redness of the epidermis, that the embalmment had been effected altogether by asphaltum; but, on scraping the surface with a steel instrument. and throwing into the fire some of the powder thus obtained, the flavor of camphor and other sweet-scented gums became apparent.

We searched the corpse very carefully for the usual openings **14** through which the entrails are extracted, but, to our surprise, we could discover none. No member of the party was at that period aware that entire or unopened mummies are not unfrequently met. The brain it was customary to withdraw through the nose; the intestines through an incision in the side; the body was then shaved, washed, and salted; then, laid aside for several weeks, when the operation of embalming, properly so called, began.

As no trace of an opening could be found, Doctor Ponnonner was preparing his instruments for dissection, when I observed that it was then past two o'clock. Hereupon it was agreed to postpone the internal examination until the next evening; and we were about to separate for the present, when some one suggested an experiment or two with the Voltaic pile. **15**

The application of electricity to a Mummy three or four thousand years old at the least, was an idea, if not very sage, still sufficiently original, and we all caught at it at once. About one tenth in earnest and nine tenths in jest, we arranged a battery in the Doctor's study, and conveyed thither the Egyptian.

It was only after much trouble that we succeeded in laying bare some portions of the temporal muscle which appeared of less stony rigidity than other parts of the frame, but which, as we had anticipated, of course, gave no indication of galvanic susceptibility when brought in contact with the wire. This, the first trial, indeed, seemed decisive, and, with a hearty laugh at our own absurdity, we were bidding each other good night, when my eyes, happening to fall upon those of the Mummy, were there immediately riveted in amazement. My brief glance, in fact, had sufficed to assure me that the orbs we had all supposed to be glass, and which were originally noticeable for a certain wild stare, were now so far covered by the lids, that only a small portion of the *tunica albuginea* **16** remained visible.

With a shout I called attention to the fact, and it became immediately obvious to all.

I cannot say that I was *alarmed* at the phenomenon, because "alarmed" is, in my case, not exactly the word. It is possible, however, that, but for the Brown Stout, I might have been a little nervous. As for the rest of the company, they really made no attempt at concealing the downright fright which possessed them. Doctor Ponnonner was a man to be pitied. Mr. Gliddon, by some peculiar process, rendered himself invisible. Mr. Silk Buckingham, I fancy, will scarcely be so **17** bold as to deny that he made his way, upon all fours, under the table.

After the first shock of astonishment, however, we resolved, as a matter of course, upon further experiment forthwith. Our operations were now directed against the great toe of the right foot. We made an incision over the outside of the exterior *os sesamoideum pollicis pedis*, and thus got at the root of the **18** *abductor* muscle. Readjusting the battery, we now applied **19** the fluid to the bisected nerves—when, with a movement of **20** exceeding lifelikeness, the Mummy first drew up its right knee so as to bring it nearly in contact with the abdomen, and then, straightening the limb with inconceivable force, bestowed a kick upon Doctor Ponnonner, which had the effect of discharging that gentleman, like an arrow from a catapult, through a window into the street below. **21**

We rushed out *en masse* to bring in the mangled remains of the victim, but had the happiness to meet him upon the staircase, coming up in an unaccountable hurry, brimful of the most ardent philosophy, and more than ever impressed with the necessity of prosecuting our experiment with vigor and with zeal.

15 Another appearance of the voltaic pile, or galvanic battery; see "Loss of Breath," note 25.

16 The whites of the eyes

17 James Silk Buckingham (1786–1855), a writer of travel books, especially on the East. His series of books on the United States was critical of slavery and the South, and Poe turned against him.

18 The sesamoid bones are small, rounded masses of bone embedded in tendons or joint capsules subjected to compression as well as tensile stresses.

19 A muscle producing movement away from the body

20 Electric current

21 According to *The Medical Repository*, January 1820, when Dr. Andrew Ure, of Glasgow, applied an electrical charge to a recently hanged man, one leg kicked an assistant, nearly knocking him over. Another person fainted, and several others ran out of the room (Robert Lee Rhea, *University of Texas Studies*, 1930; Vol. 10, p. 145).

22 John Barnes was an established theatrical comic who made a reputation for himself by exaggerated humor and stage business.

23 "But to my mind, though I am native here/And to the manner born, it is a custom/More honour'd in the breach than the observance" (*Hamlet*, I, iv, 14–16).

According to the Century Dictionary (1900), "*Manner* here is sometimes understood as *manor* (which was formerly spelled *manner*), and is often changed to *manor* to make the phrase applicable to locality."

Mr. Gliddon replied at great length, in phonetics. . . .
Illustration by Johann Friedrich Vogel, 1856

It was by advice, accordingly, that we made, upon the spot, a profound incision into the tip of the subject's nose, while the Doctor himself, laying violent hands upon it, pulled it into vehement contact with the wire.

Morally and physically—figuratively and literally—was the effect electric. In the first place, the corpse opened its eyes and winked very rapidly for several minutes as does Mr. **22** Barnes in the pantomime; in the second place, it sneezed; in the third, it sat upon end; in the fourth, it shook its fist in Doctor Ponnonner's face; in the fifth, turning to Messieurs Gliddon and Buckingham, it addressed them, in very capital Egyptian, thus:

"I must say, gentlemen, that I am much surprised as I am mortified at your behavior. Of Doctor Ponnonner nothing better was to be expected. He is a poor little fat fool who *knows* no better. I pity and forgive him. But you, Mr. Gliddon—and you, Silk—who have travelled and resided in **23** Egypt until one might imagine you to the manor born—you, I say, who have been so much among us that you speak Egyptian fully as well, I think, as you write your mother-tongue—you, whom I have always been led to regard as the firm friend of the mummies—I really did anticipate more gentlemanly conduct from *you*. What am I to think of your standing quietly by and seeing me thus unhandsomely used? What am I to suppose by your permitting Tom, Dick, and Harry to strip me of my coffins, and my clothes, in this wretchedly cold climate? In what light (to come to the point) am I to regard your aiding and abetting that miserable little villain, Doctor Ponnonner, in pulling me by the nose?"

It will be taken for granted, no doubt, that upon hearing this speech under the circumstances, we all either made for the door, or fell into violent hysterics, or went off in a general swoon. One of these three things was, I say, to be expected. Indeed each and all of these lines of conduct might have been very plausibly pursued. And, upon my word, I am at a loss to kow how or why it was that we pursued neither the one nor the other. But, perhaps, the true reason is to be sought in the spirit of the age, which proceeds by the rule of contraries altogether, and is now usually admitted as the solution of everything in the way of paradox and impossibility. Or, perhaps, after all, it was only the Mummy's exceedingly natural and matter-of-course air that divested his words of the terrible. However this may be, the facts are clear, and no member of our party betrayed any very particular trepidation, or seemed to consider that any thing had gone very especially wrong.

For my part I was convinced it was all right, and merely stepped aside, out of the range of the Egyptian's fist. Doctor Ponnonner thrust his hands into his breeches' pockets, looked hard at the Mummy, and grew excessively red in the face. Mr. Gliddon stroked his whiskers and drew up the collar of his shirt. Mr. Buckingham hung down his head, and put his right thumb into the left corner of his mouth.

The Egyptian regarded him with a severe countenance for some minutes, and at length, with a sneer, said:

"Why don't you speak, Mr. Buckingham? Did you hear what I asked you, or not? *Do* take your thumb out of your mouth!"

Mr. Buckingham, hereupon, gave a slight start, took his right thumb out of the left corner of his mouth, and, by way of indemnification, inserted his left thumb in the right corner of the aperture above-mentioned.

Not being able to get an answer from Mr. B., the figure turned peevishly to Mr. Gliddon, and, in a peremptory tone, demanded in general terms what we all meant.

Mr. Gliddon replied at great length, in phonetics; and but for the deficiency of American printing-offices in hieroglyphical type, it would afford me much pleasure to record here, in the original, the whole of his very excellent speech.

I may as well take this occasion to remark, that all the subsequent conversation in which the Mummy took a part, was carried on in primitive Egyptian, through the medium (so far as concerned myself and other untravelled members of the company)—through the medium, I say, of Messieurs Gliddon and Buckingham, as interpreters. These gentlemen spoke the mother tongue of the Mummy with inimitable fluency and grace; but I could not help observing that (owing, no doubt, to the introduction of images entirely modern, and, of course, entirely novel to the stranger) the two travellers were reduced, occasionally, to the employment of sensible forms for the purpose of conveying a particular meaning. Mr. Gliddon, at one period, for example, could not make the Egyptian comprehend the term "politics," until he sketched upon the wall, with a bit of charcoal, a little carbuncle-nosed gentleman, out at elbows, standing upon a stump, with his **24** left leg drawn back, his right arm thrown forward, with the fist shut, the eyes rolled up toward Heaven, and the mouth open at an angle of ninety degrees. Just in the same way Mr. Buckingham failed to convey the absolutely modern idea, "wig," until (at Doctor Ponnonner's suggestion) he grew very **25** pale in the face, and consented to take off his own.

It will be readily understood that Mr. Gliddon's discourse turned chiefly upon the vast benefits accruing to science from the unrolling and disembowelling of mummies; apologizing, upon this score, for any disturbance that might have been occasioned *him,* in particular, the individual Mummy called Allamistakeo; and concluding with a mere hint (for it could scarcely be considered more) that, as these little matters were now explained, it might be as well to proceed with the investigation intended. Here Doctor Ponnonner made ready his instruments.

In regard to the latter suggestions of the orator, it appears that Allamistakeo had certain scruples of conscience, the nature of which I did not distinctly learn; but he expressed himself satisfied with the apologies tendered, and, getting down from the table, shook hands with the company all round.

Mr. Gliddon . . . could not make the Egyptian comprehend the term "politics," until he sketched upon the wall, with a bit of charcoal, a little carbuncle-nosed gentleman, out at elbows, standing upon a stump. . . . *Illustration by F. S. Coburn, 1902*

24 A politician "stumping" it. The O.E.D. says "to make stump speeches" was an Americanism as early as 1838, and R. M. Bird's *Peter Pilgrim* (1839), which Poe probably knew, has "I stumped through my district, and my fellow-citizens sent me to Congress!"

25 This is *wig* in Poe's versions, but has been *whig* in most editions since Griswold's. Either Griswold was mistaken, or he thought that Poe meant it as a pun.

An article in the New York *Tribune,* December 21, 1841, reprinted from a London paper, refers to a wig in the British Museum from Thebes "of immense size; as large as those worn by fashionable gallants in the time of Charles II, or by our learned judges (often to their great annoyance) at the present time."

26 Perhaps a healing plaster made form tar and wax; an "iron plaster."

27 Often called simply a "waterfall," it is a "neckcloth, scarf, or tie with long pendant ends," according to the O.E.D.

28 An echo of the long-lived personages of the Old Testament

29 This places the mummy's burial in 3204 B.C.

30 Asphaltum is a brownish-black substance found in nature where petroleum has evaporated. The tarry substance would possibly make a preservative, but the Egyptians commonly used pitch or resin.

31 "Impregnation of the animal body with corrosive sublimate appears to be the most effectual means of preserving it, excepting immersion in spirits. The impregnation is performed by the injection of a strong solution, consisting of about four ounces of bichloride of mercury to a pint of alcohol, into the three blood-vessels, and, after the viscera are removed, the body is immersed, for three months, in the same solution, after which it dries easily, and is almost imperishable." (*Encyclopaedia Americana*, "Mummies")

While bichloride of mercury was in common use by undertakers in Poe's time, there is no evidence that the

When this ceremony was at an end, we immediately busied ourselves in repairing the damages which our subject had sustained from the scalpel. We sewed up the wound in his temple, bandaged his foot, and applied a square inch of black **26** plaster to the tip of his nose.

It was now observed that the Count (this was the title, it seems, of Allamistakeo) had a slight fit of shivering—no doubt from the cold. The Doctor immediately repaired to his wardrobe, and soon returned with a black dress coat, made in Jennings' best manner, a pair of sky-blue plaid pantaloons with straps, a pink gingham *chemise,* a flapped vest of brocade, a white sack overcoat, a walking cane with a hook, a hat with no brim, patent-leather boots, straw-colored kid gloves, an **27** eye-glass, a pair of whiskers, and a waterfall cravat. Owing to the disparity of size between the Count and Doctor (the proportion being as two to one), there was some little difficulty in adjusting these habiliments upon the person of the Egyptian; but when all was arranged, he might have been said to be dressed. Mr. Gliddon, therefore, gave him his arm, and led him to a comfortable chair by the fire, while the Doctor rang the bell upon the spot and ordered a supply of cigars and wine.

The conversation soon grew animated. Much curiosity was, of course, expressed in regard to the somewhat remarkable fact of Allamistakeo's still remaining alive.

"I should have thought," observed Mr. Buckingham, "that it is high time you were dead."

"Why," replied the Count, very much astonished, "I am little more than seven hundred years old! My father lived a **28** thousand, and was by no means in his dotage when he died."

Here ensued a brisk series of questions and computations, by means of which it became evident that the antiquity of the Mummy had been grossly misjudged. It had been five thousand and fifty years and some months since he had been consigned **29** to the catacombs at Eleithias.

"But my remark," resumed Mr. Buckingham, "had no reference to your age at the period of interment (I am willing to grant, in fact, that you are still a young man), and my allusion was to the immensity of time during which, by your **30** own showing, you must have been done up in asphaltum."

"In what?" said the Count.

"In asphaltum," persisted Mr. B.

"Ah, yes; I have some faint notion of what you mean; it might be made to answer, no doubt,—but in my time we employed scarcely any thing else than the Bichloride of **31** Mercury."

"But what we are especially at a loss to understand," said Doctor Ponnonner, "is how it happens that, having been dead and buried in Egypt five thousand years ago, you are here to-day all alive and looking so delightfully well."

"Had I been, as you say, *dead,*" replied the Count, "it is more than probable that dead I should still be; for I perceive you are yet in the infancy of Galvanism, and cannot accomplish with it what was a common thing among us in the old days.

But the fact is, I fell into catalepsy, and it was considered by my best friends that I was either dead or should be; they accordingly embalmed me at once—I presume you are aware of the chief principle of the embalming process?"

"Why, not altogether."

"Ah, I perceive;—a deplorable condition of ignorance! Well, I cannot enter into details just now: but it is necessary to explain that to embalm (properly speaking), in Egypt, was to arrest indefinitely *all* the animal functions subjected to the process. I use the word 'animal' in its widest sense, as including the physical not more than the moral and *vital* being. I repeat that the leading principle of embalmment consisted, with us, in the immediately arresting, and holding in perpetual *abeyance*, *all* the animal functions subjected to the process. To be brief, in whatever condition the individual was, at the period of embalmment, in that condition he remained. Now, as it is my good fortune to be of the blood of the Scarabæus, I was embalmed *alive*, as you see me at present."

"The blood of the Scarabæus!" exclaimed Doctor Ponnonner.

"Yes. The Scarabæus was the *insignium*, or the 'arms,' of a very distinguished and a very rare patrician family. To be 'of the blood of the Scarabæus,' is merely to be one of that family of which the Scarabæus is the *insignium*. I speak figuratively."

32

"But what has this to do with your being alive?"

"Why, it is the general custom in Egypt to deprive a corpse, before embalmment, of its bowels and brains; the race of the Scarabæi alone did not coincide with the custom. Had I not been a Scarabæus, therefore, I should have been without bowels and brains; and without either it is inconvenient to live."

"I perceive that," said Mr. Buckingham, "and I presume that all the *entire* mummies that come to hand are of the race of Scarabæi."

"Beyond doubt."

"I thought," said Mr. Gliddon, very meekly, "that the Scarabæus was one of the Egyptian gods."

"One of the Egyptian *what?*" exclaimed the Mummy, starting to its feet.

"Gods!" repeated the traveller.

"Mr. Gliddon, I really am astonished to hear you talk in this style," said the Count, resuming his chair. "No nation upon the face of the earth has ever acknowledged more than *one god*. The Scarabæus, the Ibis, etc., were with us (as **33** similar creatures have been with others) the symbols, or *media*, through which we offered worship to a Creator too august to be more directly approached."

There was here a pause. At length the colloquy was renewed by Doctor Ponnonner.

"It is not improbable, then, from what you have explained," said he, "that among the catacombs near the Nile there may exist other mummies of the Scarabæus tribe, in a condition of vitality."

"There can be no question of it," replied the Count; "all the

Egyptians used this extremely dangerous substance. Rather, according to Harris and Weeks, a substance called "natron," a naturally occurring compound of sodium bicarbonate and sodium chloride or sodium sulphate, was used to dry out the body. After the internal organs were removed, the body cavity was washed, then stuffed with sand, straw, resin, rags, or dried vegetable fibers. Then the body was placed on a sloping board and covered with the dried natron. After about forty days, the stuffing was removed, and the body was washed and dried. Resin or resin-soaked linen went into the cranial cavity, and sawdust and other material was stuffed into the abdomen, and the incision into the stomach was sewn up. (*X-Raying the Pharaohs*, pp. 82–91)

32 The Scarabaeus, or scarab beetle, was known to the Egyptians for its habit of rolling a ball of dung to its nest, seen as a parallel to the sun god Khepri, who rolled the sun across the heavens. The *kheper* beetle, as it was called, was the hieroglyphic inspiration for the sun god's name, and stone figures of the scarab were in common use as amulets. Poe also makes use of the beetle in "The Gold-Bug."

Note that the Egyptian has been buried alive through catalepsy, a typically Poesque fate.

33 In Egypt's early days, the people worshiped local gods, such as Osiris (at Busiris), Ptah (at Emphis), Amun-Re (or Ra, at Thebes), and Atum-Re (or Ra, at On). Atum-Re was a sun deity, and by the beginning of the Middle Kingdom (2445 B.C., he was identified with many of the local deities, and so moved the country toward a monotheistic system. However, it was not until Amenophis IV ascended the throne in 1375 B.C., that a state religion worshiping only one god was established: that of the Sun Disk, Re-horakhte. Five years into his reign, the king changed his name to Akhenaten ("Useful to the Sun Disk") and ordered that the temples of Amun-Re in Karnak be closed and the god's name removed.

Egypt's monotheistic period lasted only about thirty years. After the death of Tutankhamen ("Living Image of Amon," 1357–1347 B.C.), during the reign of Horemheb (1344–1315 B.C.), the country was returned to the worship of Amun-Re and his local variations. The temples of Akhenaten's sun-god cult were systematically pulled down and obliterated.

Much of this information was unknown in Poe's time, and in fact much has been learned in only the past few years. For an excellent summary of Akhenaten and his temple at Karnak, see "The Razed Temple of Akhenaten," by Donald B. Redford, in *Scientific American*, December 1978; pp. 136–47.

34 Just waiting for Hollywood to discover them. The series of mummy films (at least six major productions, beginning in 1932) was inspired by the curse that supposedly haunted the group who first opened the tomb of Tutankhamen, but one can see some of the reasoning for the reawakening of those cinematic mummies in Poe's tale.

35 A similar complaint is registered in "Never Bet the Devil Your Head."

The lamp may be a reference to Diogenes, who, according to popular legend, used it to seek an honest man, but who in reality was merely looking for someone who could truthfully be called a "man."

36 The Kabbala, or Cabala, was an esoteric system of interpretation of the Scriptures, based on a tradition claimed to come from Abraham but actually a product of the Middle Ages, as a reaction to the formalism of rabbinical Judaism. It reached its height of popularity in the twelfth century, based on the belief that every word, letter, number, and even diacritical mark contained mysteries interpretable by those who knew the secret.

Scarabæi embalmed accidentally while alive, are alive now. Even some of those *purposely* so embalmed, may have been **34** overlooked by their executors, and still remain in the tomb."

"Will you be kind enough to explain," I said, "what you mean by 'purposely so embalmed'?"

"With great pleasure," answered the Mummy, after surveying me leisurely through his eye-glass—for it was the first time I had ventured to address him a direct question.

"With great pleasure," said he. "The usual duration of man's life, in my time, was about eight hundred years. Few men died, unless by most extraordinary accident, before the age of six hundred; few lived longer than a decade of centuries; but eight were considered the natural term. After the discovery of the embalming principle, as I have already described it to you, it occurred to our philosophers that a laudable curiosity might be gratified, and, at the same time, the interests of science much advanced, by living this natural term in instalments. In the case of history, indeed, experience demonstrated that something of this kind was indispensable. An historian, for example, having attained the age of five hundred, would write a book with great labor and then get himself carefully embalmed; leaving instructions to his executors *pro tem.*, that they should cause him to be revivified after the lapse of a certain period—say five or six hundred years. Resuming existence at the expiration of this term, he would invariably find his great work converted into a species of hap-hazard note-book—that is to say, into a kind of literary arena for the conflicting guesses, riddles, and personal squabbles of whole herds of exasperated commentators. These guesses, etc., which passed under the name of annotations, or emendations, were found so completely to have enveloped, distorted, and overwhelmed the text, that the author had to go about with **35** a lantern to discover his own book. When he discovered, it was never worth the trouble of the search. After re-writing it throughout, it was regarded as the bounden duty of the historian to set himself to work immediately in correcting, from his own private knowledge and experience, the traditions of the day concerning the epoch at which he had originally lived. Now this process of re-scription and personal rectification, pursued by various individual sages from time to time, had the effect of preventing our history from degenerating into absolute fable."

"I beg your pardon," said Doctor Ponnonner at this point, laying his hand gently upon the arm of the Egyptian—"I beg your pardon, sir, but may I presume to interrupt you for one moment?"

"By all means, *sir*," replied the Count, drawing up.

"I merely wished to ask you a question," said the Doctor. "You mentioned the historian's personal correction of *traditions* respecting his own epoch. Pray, sir, upon an average, **36** what proportions of these Kabbala were usually found to be right?"

"The Kabbala, as you properly term them, sir, were generally discovered to be precisely on a par with the facts

recorded in the un-re-written histories themselves;—that is
to say, not one individual iota of either was ever known, under
any circumstances, to be not totally and radically wrong."

"But since it is quite clear," resumed the Doctor, "that at
least five thousand years have elapsed since your entombment,
I take it for granted that your histories at that period, if not
your traditions, were sufficiently explicit on that one topic of
universal interest, the Creation, which took place, as I presume
you are aware, only about ten centuries before."   **37**

"Sir!" said Count Allamistakeo.

The Doctor repeated his remarks, but it was only after
much additional explanation that the foreigner could be made
to comprehend them. The latter at length said, hesitatingly:

"The ideas you have suggested are to me, I confess, utterly
novel. During my time I never knew any one to entertain so
singular a fancy as that the universe (or this world if you will
have it so) ever had a beginning at all. I remember once, and
once only, hearing something remotely hinted, by a man of
many speculations, concerning the origin *of the human race;*
and by this individual, the very word *Adam* (or Red Earth), **38**
which you make use of, was employed. He employed it,
however, in a generical sense, with reference to the spontaneous germination from rank soil (just as a thousand of the
lower *genera* of creatures are germinated)—the spontaneous **39**
germination, I say, of five vast hordes of men, simultaneously
upspringing in five distinct and nearly equal divisions of the
globe."

Here, in general, the company shrugged their shoulders,
and one or two of us touched our foreheads with a very
significant air. Mr. Silk Buckingham, first glancing slightly at
the occiput and then at the sinciput of Allamistakeo, spoke as
follows:

"The long duration of human life in your time, together
with the occasional practice of passing it, as you have explained,
in instalments, must have had, indeed, a strong tendency to
the general development and conglomeration of knowledge.
I presume, therefore, that we are to attribute the marked
inferiority of the old Egyptians in all particulars of science,
when compared with the moderns, and more especially with
the Yankees, altogether to the superior solidity of the Egyptian
skull."

"I confess again," replied the Count, with much suavity,
"that I am somewhat at a loss to comprehend you; pray, to
what particulars of science do you allude?"

Here our whole party, joining voices, detailed, at great
length, the assumptions of phrenology and the marvels of
animal magnetism.

Having heard us to an end, the Count proceeded to relate
a few anecdotes, which rendered it evident that prototypes of
Gall and Spurzheim had flourished and faded in Egypt so long
ago as to have been nearly forgotten, and that the manœuvres
of Mesmer were really very contemptible tricks when put in
collation with the positive miracles of the Theban *savants,*
who created lice and a great many other similar things.   **40**

37 Referring to Bishop Ussher's placing of the date of creation at 4004 B.C. Ussher's (1581–1656) belief held sway for several hundred years, but the discoveries in Egypt were beginning to challenge that view. Gliddon, in *Ancient Egypt*, p. 33, points out that Ussher's is only one of a myriad of published opinions on dates of the Old Testament, and so hardly sacrosanct.

38 Adam means "man," in the generic sense, in Hebrew, and is related to the Assyrian *admu*, meaning a child, one made by God. Byron gives the derivation of "red earth" in *The Deformed Transformed*, I, i, 385, and in *Ancient Egypt*, Gliddon says, "in Hebrew, ADAM, the first man, meaning both *man* and *red earth*, or clay" (pp. 28–29).

39 Spontaneous generation, or abiogenesis, dates back to the ancient Greeks, who, without the microscope, could find no other explanation for the appearance of certain life-forms. Even long afterward, people believed that mice came from grain or a dirty shirt left in a box in the dark, that maggots could be produced in decaying meat, and that cockroaches sprang from decaying food without benefit of parents. Pasteur demonstrated that even microbes did not originate without preexisting microbes, and so scotched the whole notion once and for all.

The only "spontaneous generation" now considered possible is the theory that the first primitive life forms on earth came from organic compounds formed by the effect of electricity (lightning) on the earth's early atmosphere.

40 Gall and Spurzheim were phrenologists, and Mesmer was the father of "animal magnetism." Poe, who seems to give them some credence elsewhere, here indicates they are perhaps not to be completely trusted.

As for the Theban savants who created lice, Poe may be referring obliquely to the Egyptian magicians who attempted to "bring forth lice, but . . . could not," in Exodus 8:18, after Aaron had "smote the dust of the earth" with his rod "and it became lice in man, and in beast; all the dust of the land became lice throughout all the land of Egypt."

It wasn't easy being an Egyptian in those days.

41 "Ptolemy describes an astrolabe; they calculated eclipses; they said that the moon was diversified by sea and land. . . ." (New York *Tribune*, December 21, 1841)

In Egypt, basic astronomical knowledge was in the hands of the astrologer-priests, who controlled the calendar and who established rites for the worship of the heavenly bodies. Such knowledge was closely guarded, but we do know that they mapped the heavens, identified stars, and developed instruments for determining the positions of heavenly bodies before the rise of the Old Kingdom (before 3200 B.C.).

42 Claudius Ptolemaeus (fl. A.D. 127–141 or 151) was the celebrated Greco-Egyptian mathematician, astronomer, and geographer who made his observations in Alexandria and was the last great astronomer of ancient times. His works were the standard textbooks until the acceptance of the teachings of Copernicus. The Ptolemaic system has the sun and other heavenly bodies revolving around the earth.

De facie lunae (on the face of the moon) is mentioned in the *Tribune* article, *supra*, as the source of information about the eighteenth Theban dynasty and its scientific knowledge.

Plutarch, the Roman historian, lived from about A.D. 46 to 120.

43 Diodorus Siculus (d. after 21 B.C.), was a Sicilian historian who wrote in Greek a forty-volume history of the world, which is today considered unreliable. The *Tribune* article mentions him as the source for its information on Egyptian glassmaking.

44 Poe considered this structure a prime example of bad taste. Built by Aaron P. Price in 1843, it was illuminated at night by gas lights. Poe ridiculed it on a number of occasions, including a review of George Jones's *Ancient America* in March 1845.

45 A made-up name (shades of H. P. Lovecraft!)

46 Karnak, one mile east of Luxor, occupying part of the site of Thebes. Remnants of the pharaohs abound, most notably in the Great Temple of Amon.

I here asked the Count if his people were able to calculate eclipses. He smiled rather contemptuously, and said they **41** were.

This put me a little out, but I began to make other inquiries in regard to his astronomical knowledge, when a member of the company, who had never as yet opened his mouth, whispered in my ear, that for information on this head, I had better consult Ptolemy (whoever Ptolemy is), as well as one **42** Plutarch *de facie lunæ*.

I then questioned the Mummy about burning-glasses and lenses, and, in general, about the manufacture of glass; but I had not made an end of my queries before the silent member again touched me quietly on the elbow, and begged me for **43** God's sake to take a peep at Diodorus Siculus. As for the Count, he merely asked me, in the way of reply, if we moderns possessed any such microscopes as would enable us to cut cameos in the style of the Egyptians. While I was thinking how I should answer this question, little Doctor Ponnonner committed himself in a very extraordinary way.

"Look at our architecture!" he exclaimed, greatly to the indignation of both the travellers, who pinched him black and blue to no purpose.

"Look," he cried with enthusiasm, "at the Bowling-Green **44** Fountain in New York! or if this be too vast a contemplation, regard for a moment the Capitol at Washington, D. C.!"— and the good little medical man went on to detail, very minutely, the proportions of the fabric to which he referred. He explained that the portico alone was adorned with no less than four and twenty columns, five feet in diameter, and ten feet apart.

The Count said that he regretted not being able to remember, just at that moment, the precise dimensions of any one **45** of the principal buildings of the city of Aznac, whose foundations were laid in the night of Time, but the ruins of which were still standing, at the epoch of his entombment, in a vast plain of sand to the westward of Thebes. He recollected, however (talking of the porticos), that one affixed to an inferior **46** palace in a kind of suburb called Carnac, consisted of a hundred and forty-four columns, thirty-seven feet in circumference, and twenty-five feet apart. The approach to this portico, from the Nile, was through an avenue two miles long, composed of sphynxes, statues, and obelisks, twenty, sixty, and a hundred feet in height. The palace itself (as well as he could remember) was, in one direction, two miles long, and might have been altogether about seven in circuit. Its walls were richly painted all over, within and without, with hieroglyphics. He would not pretend to *assert* that even fifty or sixty of the Doctor's Capitols might have been built within these walls, but he was by no means sure that two or three hundred of them might not have been squeezed in with some trouble. That palace at Carnac was an insignificant little building after all. He (the Count), however, could not conscientiously refuse to admit the ingenuity, magnificence, and superiority of the Fountain at the Bowling Green, as described by the Doctor. Nothing like it, he was forced to allow, had ever been seen in Egypt or elsewhere.

I here asked the Count what he had to say to our railroads.

"Nothing," he replied, "in particular." They were rather slight, rather ill-conceived, and clumsily put together. They could not be compared, of course, with the vast, level, direct, iron-grooved causeways upon which the Egyptians conveyed entire temples and solid obelisks of a hundred and fifty feet in altitude.   **47**

I spoke of our gigantic mechanical forces.

He agreed that we knew something in that way, but inquired how I should have gone to work in getting up the imposts on the lintels of even the little palace at Carnac.

This question I concluded not to hear, and demanded if he had any idea of Artesian wells; but he simply raised his eyebrows; while Mr. Gliddon winked at me very hard and said, in a low tone, that one had been recently discovered by the engineers employed to bore for water in the Great Oasis.

I then mentioned our steel; but the foreigner elevated his nose, and asked me if our steel could have executed the sharp carved work seen on the obelisks, and which was wrought altogether by edge-tools of copper.

This disconcerted us so greatly that we thought it advisable to vary the attack to Metaphysics. We sent for a copy of a book called the "Dial," and read out of it a chapter or two about something which is not very clear, but which the Bostonians call the Great Movement of Progress.

The Count merely said that Great Movements were awfully common things in his day, and as for Progress, it was at one time quite a nuisance, but it never progressed.

We then spoke of the great beauty and importance of Democracy, and were at much trouble in impressing the Count with a due sense of the advantages we enjoyed in living where there was suffrage *ad libitum*, and no king.

He listened with marked interest, and in fact seemed not a little amused. When we had done, he said that, a great while ago, there had occurred something of a very similar sort. Thirteen Egyptian provinces determined all at once to be free, and to set a magnificent example to the rest of mankind. They assembled their wise men, and concocted the most ingenious constitution it is possible to conceive. For a while they managed remarkably well; only their habit of bragging was prodigious. The thing ended, however, in the consolidation of the thirteen states, with some fifteen or twenty others, into the most odious and insupportable despotism that was ever heard of upon the face of the Earth.   **48**

I asked what was the name of the usurping tyrant.

As well as the Count could recollect, it was *Mob*.   **49**

Not knowing what to say to this, I raised my voice, and deplored the Egyptian ignorance of steam.

The Count looked at me with much astonishment, but made no answer. The silent gentleman, however, gave me a violent nudge in the ribs with his elbows—told me I had sufficiently exposed myself for once—and demanded if I was really such

47 "That they were acquainted with the principle of the railroad is obvious, that is to say, they had artificial causeways, levelled, direct and grooved (the grooves being anointed with oil), for the conveyance from great distances of enormous blocks of stone, entire stone temples, and colossal statues half the height of the monument. Remnants of iron, it is said, have been found in these grooves." (*Tribune*)

This supposition has since been disproved.

48 "The modern reformist Philosophy which annihilates the individual by way of aiding the mass; and the late reformist Legislation, which prohibits pleasure with the view of advancing happiness, seems to be chips of that old block of a French feudal law which, to prevent young partridges from being disturbed, imposed penalties upon hoeing and weeding" ("Marginalia," LXXVIII).

Poe was not overly fond of the effects of democracy, which placed power in the hands of the "mob."

49 "The nose of a mob is its imagination. By this, at any time, it can be quietly led" ("Marginalia," XXVII). Poe's antidemocratic beliefs, personified in the "mob," turn up again in "Mellonta Tauta."

50 Hero, or Heron, of Alexandria (second and third centuries A.D.) is remembered for his study of mechanics and pneumatics. He invented many contrivances operated by water, steam, and compressed air, including a fountain, a fire engine, siphons, and an engine in which the recoil of steam revolved a ball or a wheel.

Salomon de Caus, or Caux (1576–1626), was a French engineer and physicist who, in *Les Raisons des forces mouvantes avec diverses machines* (1615), shows an early prototype of the steam engine, leading some to call him its inventor. Others give the credit to Giambattista della Porta (c. 1538–1615), an Italian physicist who improved the camera obscura and wrote *Magia naturalis* (1558).

51 Worthless and often dangerous patent medicines were big business in the nineteenth century, and in fact right up to the passage of the Pure Food and Drug Act of 1906. A look at the Sears, Roebuck catalog of 1900 (reprinted in 1970 by DBI Books), pp. 14–25, is instructive of the kind of pills, powders, elixirs, and nostrums sold to cure almost any ailment.

Ponnonner's Lozenges are fictitious, but Brandreth's Pills were well known; Poe mentions them also in "How to Write a Blackwood Article," note 24.

52 After trying to make a case for the superiority of the nineteenth century and its debt to Progress, the narrator and his friends can really claim only two advances over the ancient Egyptians: the voluminous clothing and patent medicines of the day. Poe's irony is straight to the point.

53 An idea carried further in Edward Bellamy's *Looking Backward: 2000–1887* (1888), in which the author paints a future utopia, and, again, in H. G. Wells's *When the Sleeper Wakes* (1899), in which a man, like Bellamy's hero, wakens after two centuries of sleep. Wells's theme, like Poe's, is the relative and ambivalent nature of progress.

a fool as not to know that the modern steam engine is derived
50 from the invention of Hero, through Solomon de Caus.

We were now in imminent danger of being discomfited; but, as good luck would have it, Doctor Ponnonner, having rallied, returned to our rescue, and inquired if the people of Egypt would seriously pretend to rival the moderns in the all-important particular of dress.

The Count, at this, glanced downward to the straps of his pantaloons, and then taking hold of the end of one of his coat-tails, held it up close to his eyes for some minutes. Letting it fall, at last, his mouth extended itself very gradually from ear to ear; but I do not remember that he said anything in the way of reply.

Hereupon we recovered our spirits, and the Doctor, approaching the Mummy with great dignity, desired it to say candidly, upon its honor as a gentleman, if the Egyptians had comprehended, at *any* period, the manufacture of either
51 Ponnonner's lozenges or Brandreth's pills.

We looked, with profound anxiety, for an answer;— but in vain. It was not forthcoming. The Egyptian blushed and hung down his head. Never was triumph more consummate; never was defeat borne with so ill a grace. Indeed, I could not endure the spectacle of the poor Mummy's mortification. I
52 reached my hat, bowed to him stiffly, and took leave.

Upon getting home I found it past four o'clock, and went immediately to bed. It was now ten A.M. I have been up since seven, penning these memoranda for the benefit of my family and of mankind. The former I shall behold no more. My wife is a shrew. The truth is, I am heartily sick of this life and of the nineteenth century in general. I am convinced that everything is going wrong. Besides, I am anxious to know who will be President in 2045. As soon, therefore, as I shave and swallow a cup of coffee, I shall just step over to Ponnonner's
53 and get embalmed for a couple of hundred years.

X-ING A PARAGRAB

First published in *The Flag of Our Union*, May 12, 1849, this comic tale springs from an apparently frequent problem among printers of Poe's day, of running out of a certain letter while typesetting and having to substitute *x* in its place.

The subject is also treated in "Xtraordinary Play upon Xes," in the New York *Mirror*, September 12, 1840, and in an earlier story in the same publication, "No O's," March 5, 1836. Poe may have been familiar with either or both of them.

As it is well known that the "wise men" came "from the East," and as Mr. Touch-and-go Bullet-head came from the East, it **1** follows that Mr. Bullet-head was a wise man; and if collateral proof of the matter be needed, here we have it—Mr. B. was an editor. Irascibility was his sole foible; for in fact the obstinacy of which men accused him was anything but his *foible*, since he justly considered it his *forte*. It was his strong point—his virtue; and it would have required all the logic of a Brownson to convince him that it was "anything else." **2**

I have shown that Touch-and-go Bullet-head was a wise man; and the only occasion on which he did not prove infallible was when, abandoning that legitimate home for all wise men, the East, he migrated to the city of Alexander-the-Great-o-nopolis, or some place of a similar title, out West. **3**

I must do him the justice to say, however, that when he made up his mind finally to settle in that town, it was under the impression that no newspaper, and consequently no editor, existed in that particular section of the country. In establishing the *Tea-Pot* he expected to have the field all to himself. I feel **4** confident he never would have dreamed of taking up his residence in Alexander-the-Great-o-nopolis had he been aware that, in Alexander-the-Great-o-nopolis, there lived a gentleman named John Smith (if I rightly remember), who for many years had there quietly grown fat in editing and publishing the *Alexander-the-Great-o-noplis Gazette*. It was solely, therefore, on account of having been misinformed, that Mr. Bullet-head found himself in Alex—— suppose we call it Nopolis, **5** "for short"—but, as he *did* find himself there, he determined to keep up his character for obst—— for firmness, and remain. So remain he did; and he did more; he unpacked his press, type, etc., etc., rented an office exactly opposite to that of the *Gazette*, and, on the third morning after his arrival, issued the first number of the *Alexan——* that is to say, of the *Nopolis*

1 "Bullethead" means dull or foolish. "Touchandgo" as a name appears in Thomas Love Peacock's *Crotchet Castle* (1831). The "East," or "Down-East," means the northern Atlantic seaboard, which was the home of transcendentalism, the Puritan ethic, the Abolitionists, and the self-proclaimed intellectual elite of America. Poe had few kind words for the New England mind. In a letter to F. W. Thomas, February 14, 1849, Poe writes: "That conceited booby, the East—which is by no means the East out of which came the wise men mentioned in Scripture!"

2 New Englander Orestes Augustus Brownson (1803–76) was the most influential writer on social and religious questions of the day.

3 In an article in the *Evening Mirror*, January 11, 1845, Poe satirizes the city of Alphadelphia, Michigan, asking "What on earth is the meaning of Alphadelphia?"

4 As in "a tempest in a teapot"

5 "No city"

6 According to legend, salamanders were supposed to live in fire, which, however, they quenched with the chill of their body. Pliny tells how he tried the experiment once, but the poor creature was soon burnt to a powder (*Natural History*, 67, XXIX, 4).

7 He means, *"O tempora, O mores!"* (Oh what times, what customs!), from Cicero's *Orations in Catilinum*, I, 2. Mr. Bullet-head's way with a phrase reminds one of the Psyche Zenobia in "How to Write a Blackwood Article"/"A Predicament."

8 A severe scolding, after the original *Philippics*, a series of nine orations by Demosthenes against King Philip of Macedonia.

9 From Thomas Hood's *The Bridge of Sighs* (1844), line 46

10 "Everyone has to skin his own eels" is an old saying, apparently meaning each person must do things his own way; although it may relate to the unpleasant aspect of eel-skinning, meaning that no one will do the job for you.

11 An upstart. The word first appeared as an insulting name for the Duke of Suffolk (murdered in 1450), whose badge was a clog and chain such as was attached to a tame ape. The word by 1522 meant a tame ape or monkey, and then a person who acts like one.

12 Boston

Tea-Pot:—as nearly as I can recollect, this was the name of the new paper.

The leading article, I must admit, was brilliant—not to say severe. It was especially bitter about things in general—and as for the editor of the *Gazette*, he was torn all to pieces in particular. Some of Bullet-head's remarks were really so fiery that I have always, since that time, been forced to look upon **6** John Smith, who is still alive, in the light of a salamander. I cannot pretend to give *all* the *Tea-Pot's* parargraphs *verbatim*, but one of them runs thus:

"Oh, yes!—Oh, we perceive! Oh, no doubt! The editor over the way is a genius—Oh, my! Oh, goodness, gracious!—what **7** *is* this world coming to? *Oh, tempora! Oh, Moses!*"

8 A philippic at once so caustic and so classical, alighted like a bombshell among the hitherto peaceful citizens of Nopolis. Groups of excited individuals gathered at the corners of the streets. Every one awaited, with heartfelt anxiety, the reply of the dignified Smith. Next morning it appeared as follows:

"We quote from the *Tea-Pot* of yesterday the subjoined paragraph: '*Oh*, yes! *Oh*, we perceive! *Oh*, no doubt! *Oh*, my! *Oh*, goodness! *Oh*, tempora! *Oh*, Moses!' Why, the fellow is all O! That accounts for his reasoning in a circle, and explains why there is neither beginning nor end to him, not to any thing he says. We really do not believe the vagabond can write a word that hasn't an O in it. Wonder if this O-ing is a habit of his? By-the-by, he came away from Down-East in a great hurry. Wonder if he *O's* as much there as he does **9** here? '*O!* it is pitiful.' "

The indignation of Mr. Bullet-head at these scandalous insinuations, I shall not attempt to describe. On the eel-**10** skinning principle, however, he did not seem to be so much incensed at the attack upon his integrity as one might have imagined. It was the sneer at his *style* that drove him to desperation. What!—*he*, Touch-and-go Bullet-head!—not able to write a word without an O in it! He would soon let the **11** jackanapes see that he was mistaken. Yes! he would let him see how *much* he was mistaken, the puppy! He, Touch-and-**12** go Bullet-head, of Frogpondium, would let Mr. John Smith perceive that he, Bullet-head, could indite, if it so pleased him, a whole paragraph—ay! a whole article—in which that contemptible vowel should not *once*—not even *once*—make its appearance. But no;—that would be yielding a point to the said John Smith. *He*, Bullet-head, would make *no* alteration in his style, to suit the caprices of any Mr. Smith in Christendom. Perish so vile a thought! The O forever! He would persist in the O. He would be as O-wy as O-wy could be.

Burning with the chivalry of this determination, the great Touch-and-go, in the next *Tea-Pot,* came out merely wih this simple but resolute paragraph, in reference to this unhappy affair:

"The editor of the *Tea-Pot* has the *honor* of advising the editor of the *Gazette* that he (the *Tea-Pot*) will take an opportunity, in to-morrow morning's paper, of convincing him (the *Gazette*) that he (the *Tea-Pot*) both can and will be *his own master*, as regards style;—he (the *Tea-Pot*) intending to show him (the *Gazette*) the supreme, and indeed the withering contempt with which the criticism of him (the *Gazette*) inspires the independent bosom of him (the *Tea-Pot*) by composing for the especial gratification (?) of him (the *Gazette*) a leading article, of some extent, in which the beautiful vowel—the emblem of Eternity—yet so offensive to the hyper-exquisite delicacy of him (the *Gazette*) shall most certainly *not be avoided* by his (the *Gazette*'s) most obedient, humble servant, the *Tea-Pot*. 'So much for Buckingham!'"   **13**

In fulfilment of the awful threat, thus darkly intimated rather than decidedly enunciated, the great Bullet-head turning a deaf ear to all entreaties for "copy," and simply requesting his foreman to "go to the d——l," when he (the foreman) assured him (the *Tea-Pot!*) that it was high time to "go to press": turning a deaf ear to everything, I say, the great Bullet-head sat up until day-break, consuming the midnight oil, and absorbed in the composition of the really unparalleled paragraph, which follows:—

"So ho, John! how now? Told you so, you know. Don't crow, **14** another time, before you're out of the woods! Does your mother *know* you're out? Oh, no, no!—so go home at once, now, John, to your odious old woods of Concord! Go home to **15** your woods, old owl,—go! You won't? Oh, poh, poh, John, don't do so! You've *got* to go, you know! So go at once, and don't go slow; for nobody owns you here, you know. Oh! John, John, if you *don't* go you're no *homo*—no! You're only a fowl, an owl; a cow, a sow; a doll, a poll; a poor, old, good-for- **16** nothing-to-nobody, log, dog,, hog, or frog, come out of a Concord bog. Cool, now—cool! *Do* be cool, you fool! None of your crowing, old cock! Don't frown so—don't! Don't hollo, nor howl, nor growl, nor bow-wow-wow! Good Lord, John, how you *do* look! Told you so, you know—but stop rolling your goose of an old poll about so, and go and drown your sorrows in a bowl!"

Exhausted, very naturally, by so stupendous an effort, the great Touch-and-go could attend to nothing farther that night. Firmly, composedly, yet with an air of conscious power, he handed his MS. to the devil in waiting, and then, walking **17** leisurely home, retired, with ineffable dignity to bed.

Meantime the devil, to whom the copy was entrusted, ran up stairs to his "case," in an unutterable hurry, and forthwith made a commencement at "setting" the MS. "up."

In the first place, of course,—as the opening word was "So"—he made a plunge into the capital S hole and came out in triumph with a capital S. Elated by this success, he immediately threw himself upon the little-*o* box with a blindfold impetuosity—but who shall describe his horror when his fingers came up without the anticipated letter in their clutch? who shall paint his astonishment and rage at perceiving, as he rubbed his knuckles, that he had been only thumping them to no purpose, against the bottom of an *empty* box. Not a single little-*o* was in the little-*o* hole; and, glancing fearfully at the capital-O partition, he found *that*, to his extreme terror,

13 "Off with his head—so much for Buckingham!" is from a comic version of *Richard III* written by Colley Cibber (1671–1757), IV, iii.

14 Note that this passage is rhymed verse in prose form.

15 The home of the transcendentalists Emerson and Thoreau

16 An ox

17 i.e., a printer's devil, an errand boy so called because he would become black with ink in a precisely similar predicament. Awe-stricken, his first impulse was to rush to the foreman.

"Sir!" said he gasping for breath, "I can't never set up nothing without no o's."

"*What* do you mean by that?" growled the foreman, who was in a very ill humor at being kept up so late.

"Why, sir, there beant an *o* in the office, neither a big un nor a little un!"

"What—what the d——l has become of all that were in the case?"

"*I* don't know, sir," said the boy, "but one of them ere *G'zette* devils is bin prowling 'bout here all night, and I spect *he's* gone and cabbaged em every one."

18   "Dod rot him! I haven't a doubt of it," replied the foreman, getting purple with rage—"but I tell you what you do, Bob, that's a good boy—you go over the first chance you get and hook every one of their i's and (d——n them!) their izzards."

"Jist so," replied Bob, with a wink and a frown—"*I'll* be into em, *I'll* let em know a thing or two; but in de meantime, that ere paragrab? *Mus* go in to-night, you know—else there'll be the d——l to pay, and—"

19   "And not a *bit* of pitch hot," interrupted the foreman, with a deep sigh, and an emphasis on the "bit." "Is it a *very* long paragraph, Bob?"

"Shouldn't call it a *wery* long paragrab," said Bob.

"Ah, well, then! do the best you can with it! we *must* get to press," said the foreman, who was over head and ears in work, "just stick in some other letter for *o*, nobody's going to read the fellow's trash anyhow."

"*Wery* well," replied Bob, "here goes it!" and off he hurried to his case; muttering as he went: "Considdeble vell, them ere expressions, perticcler for a man as doesn't swar. So I's to gouge out all their eyes, eh? and d——n all their gizzards! Vell! this here's the chap as is just able *for* to do it." The fact is that although Bob was but twelve years old and four feet high, he was equal to any amount of fight, in a small way.

The exigency here described is by no means of rare occurrence in printing-offices; and I cannot tell how to account for it but the fact is indisputable, that when the exigency *does* occur, it almost always happens that *x* is adopted as a substitute for the letter deficient. The true reason, perhaps, is that *x* is rather the most superabundant letter in the cases, or at least *was* so in the old times long enough to render the substitution in question an habitual thing with printers. As for Bob, he would have considered it heretical to employ any other character, in a case of this kind, than the *x* to which he had been accustomed.

"I *shell* have to *x* this ere paragrab," said he to himself, as he read it over in astonishment, "but it's jest about the awfulest *o*-wy paragrab I ever *did* see:" so *x* it he did, unflinchingly, and to press it went *x-ed*.

Next morning, the population of Nopolis were taken all aback by reading in the *Tea-Pot*, the following extraordinary leader:

---

18 Like "Dad" in "Dad blame it," "Dod" as a euphemism for God dates back to the 1600s.

19 "The devil to pay and no pitch hot" is an old saying meaning inevitable trouble, possibly from "pitch and pay," meaning to pitch down one's money and pay at once. Sailors also "payed" (caulked with pitch) the "devil" (the seam near the keel)

"Sx hx, Jxhn! hxw nxw? Txld yxu sx, yxu knxw. Dxn't crxw, anxther time, befxre yxu're xut xf the wxxds! Dxes yxur mxther *knxw* yxu're xut? Xh, nx, nx!—sx gx hxme at xnce, nxw, Jxhn, tx yxur xdixus xld wxxds xf Cxncxrd! Gx hxme tx yxur wxxds, xld xwl,—gx! Yxu wxn't? Xh, pxh, pxh, Jxhn, dxn't dx sx! Yxu've *gxt* tx gx, yxu knxw! Sx gx at xnce, and dxn't gx slxw; fxr nxbxdy xwns yxu here, yxu knxw. Xh, Jxhn, Jxhn, if yxu *dxn't* gx yxu're nx *hxmx*—nx! Yxu're xnly a fxwl, an xwl; a cxw, a sxw; a dxll, a pxll; a pxxr xld gxxd-fxr-nxthing-tx-nxbxdy, lxg, dxg, hxg, xr frxg, cxme xut xf a Cxncxrd bxg. Cxxl, nxw—cxxl! *Dx* be cxxl, yxu fxxl! Nxne xf yxur crxwing, xld cxck! Dxn't frxwn sx—dxn't! Dxn't hxllx, nxr hxwl, nxr grxwl, nxr bxw-wxw-wxw! Gxxd Lxrd, Jxhn, hxw yxu *dx* lxxk! Txld yxu sx, yxu knxw—but stxp rxlling yxur gxxse xf an xld pxll abxut sx, and gx and drxwn yxur sxrrxws in a bxwl!"

The uproar occasioned by this mystical and cabalistical [20] article, is not to be conceived. The first definite idea entertained by the populace was, that some diabolical treason lay concealed in the hieroglyphics; and there was a general rush to Bullet-head's residence, for the purpose of riding him on a rail; but that gentleman was nowhere to be found. He had [21] vanished, no one could tell how; and not even the ghost of him has ever been seen since.

Unable to discover its legitimate object, the popular fury at length subsided; leaving behind it, by way of sediment, quite a medley of opinion about this unhappy affair.

One gentleman thought the whole an X-ellent joke.

Another said that, indeed, Bullet-head had shown much X-uberance of fancy.

[20] See "Some Words with a Mummy," note 36.

[21] In the West, unwelcome strangers were often placed on a fence rail, their feet and hands bound, and carried out of town to the jeers and laughter of the citizenry. Tar and feathers were sometimes an added attraction.

An early printing press *Artist unknown*

A third admitted him X-entric, but no more.

A fourth could only suppose it the Yankee's design to X-press, in a general way, his X-asperation.

"Say, rather, to set an X-ample to posterity," suggested a fifth.

That Bullet-head had been driven to an extremity, was clear to all; and in fact, since *that* editor could not be found, there was some talk about lynching the other one.

The more common conclusion, however, was that the affair was, simply, X-traordinary and in-X-plicable. Even the town mathematician confessed that he could make nothing of so dark a problem. X, everybody knew, was an unknown quantity; but in this case (as he properly observed), there was an unknown quantity of X.

The opinion of Bob, the devil (who kept dark about his having "X-ed the paragrab"), did not meet with so much attention as I think it deserved, although it was very openly and very fearlessly expressed. He said that, for his part, he had no doubt about the matter at all, that it was a clear case, that Mr. Bullet-head never *could* be persvaded fur to drink like other folks, but vas *con*tinually a-svigging o' that ere

22 blessed XXX ale, and, as a naiteral consekvence, it just puffed him up savage, and made him X (cross) in the X-treme.

---

22 In designating brands of ale, stout, or porter, double X means a medium quality, while XXX, or treble X, means the strongest, adding to the already overtaxed pun level of the paragraph.

Flights and Fantasies

"... the range of Imagination is unlimited. Its materials extend throughout the universe."

—"Marginalia," XXXI

LOSS OF BREATH

First published as "A Decided Loss," in the Philadelphia *Saturday Courier,* November 10, 1832, then revised and published as "Loss of Breath" in the *Southern Literary Messenger,* September 1835.

Although it has its moments, "Loss of Breath" cannot be counted as one of Poe's best tales, perhaps because of its now dated satire aimed at the transcendentalism of Friedrich Wilhelm Joseph von Schelling (1775–1854). Schelling held that nature could not be subordinated to the intellect, and if we are able to understand nature at all it is because the principle of mind must also exist in nature. This led him to the opinion that the difference between mind and nature was only a matter of degree.

Poe's sources are fewer here but include *Peter Schlemihl* (1814), by Adelbert von Chamisso (1781–1838), a tale of a man who sells his shadow to the Devil (the word "Schlemihl" came to mean a person who makes a desperate and silly bargain), and an episode in Voltaire's *Candide* (1759), in which Dr. Pangloss, having been hanged, comes to life when a surgeon begins to dissect him.

See Mabbott's second volume of Poe's collected works (pp. 77–81) for twenty-six paragraphs that Poe either discarded or replaced.

There has been little critical interpretation of this tale. Marie Bonaparte, never one to let one of Poe's tales slip through her Freudian fingers, spends *thirty-seven pages* on "Loss of Breath" as an unconscious parable about impotence and Poe's castration fears (i.e., "loss of breath" equals psychological castration; pp. 373–410).

Another possibility is that the story has to do with another meaning of "breath": the soul. Originally "spirit" and "soul" were synonyms meaning "breath" or "wind," for when breath left the body, the body died. The soul or spirit was thus the principle of life. Considering Poe's interest in the soul elsewhere, there is some reason to believe he might be treating the concept humorously here. Note that the heroine of "How to Write a Blackwood Article," Psyche Zenobia, is "all soul" and that "Psyche" means spirit or soul. Note, too, that she is all wind as well.

O breathe not, *&c.*
—MOORE'S MELODIES.   **1**

The most notorious ill-fortune must, in the end, yield to the untiring courage of philosophy—as the most stubborn city to the ceaseless vigilance of an enemy. Shalmanezer, as we have **2** it in the holy writings, lay three years before Samaria; yet it fell. Sardanapalus—see Diodorus—maintained himself seven in Nineveh; but to no purpose. Troy expired at the close of **3** the second lustrum; and Azoth, as Aristæus declares upon his **4** honor as a gentleman, opened at last her gates to Psammitticus, after having barred them for the fifth part of a century. **5**
* * *

"Thou wretch!—thou vixen!—thou shrew!" said I to my wife on the morning after our wedding, "thou witch!—thou hag!— thou whipper-snapper!—thou sink of iniquity!—thou fiery- **6**

1 "Oh! breathe not his name," *Irish Melodies,* by Thomas Moore (1779–1852). Moore wrote a great deal of verse in many forms and was very popular but is not read much these days. His *Irish Melodies* (1820) are full of beautiful lyrics, and his *The Fudge Family in Paris* (1818) is a light and kindly satire that is still fun to read. Moore edited Byron's works by the personal request of the dying poet, although he consented to the destruction of Byron's own memoirs.

2 Shalmanezer (or Shalmaneser) was king of Assyria, the monarch who "took Samaria, and carried Israel away into Assyria" (II Kings 17:6) in 722 B.C. Samaria was the ancient city of central Palestine considered a place of iniquity by the Jews. Destroyed in 120 B.C., it was rebuilt in later years by Herod the Great and renamed Sebaste, after the Roman emperor Augustus (in Greek, Sebastos).

3 Sardanapalus was the king of Nineveh and Assyria, noted for his luxury and sensual life-style. His "effeminacy induced Arba'ces, the Mede, to consipre against him. Myrra, an Ionian slave, and his favourite concubine, roused him from his lethargy, and induced him to appear at the head of his armies. He won three successive battles, but being then defeated, was induced by Myrra to place himself on a funeral pile, which she herself set fire to, and then jumping into the flames, perished with her beloved master. (Died B.C. 817)." (Brewer, *The Dictionary of Phrase and Fable*, 1894 ed.)

Another version has it that after being besieged by the Medes for two years, he set fire to his palace and burned himself and his court to death. Byron wrote a tragedy on the theme. The identity of Sardanapalus is still a mystery, even though some have tried to identify him with Assur-bani-pal (d. 626 B.C.?), the last of the great kings of Assyria. What little we know of him comes from the *Persica*, of Ctesias (fl. 400 B.C.), a Greek historian.

Diodorus Siculus (d. after 21 B.C.) was a Sicilian historian who wrote in Greek a world history in forty books ending with Caesar's Gallic wars.

4 Troy, the ancient city made famous by Homer, was also called Ilion or Ilium; it stood in what is now Asiatic Turkey, four miles from the mouth of the Dardanelles. Little was known of its true history in Poe's time, since Heinrich Schliemann (1822–90) did not start excavations there until 1871.

A lustrum is five years and in Homer's epic, Troy fell at the end of ten years of war with the Greeks—the period covered by the *Iliad*.

5 The siege of Azoth by Psammetichos I (Egyptian *Psamtik*), the king of Egypt who died in 609 B.C., is recorded by Herodotus in his *Histories*, II, 157, but his source was supposedly the poet Aristaeus of Proconnesus. Psammetichos was the founder of the XXVIth dynasty, a king who shook off his Assyrian allegiance and encouraged the settling of Greek soldiers and traders in Egypt.

6 "Whippersnapper," of course, means an impertinent or insignificant person; it derives from "whip-snapper," a cracker of whips.

7 In "The Man That Was Used Up" also, Poe takes a turn of phrase and treats it as a literal possibility. This kind of bizarre wordplay doesn't seem as funny to us today—and as a matter of fact, was not that greatly appreciated in Poe's time, either. It is obvious from his letters and essays that for Poe humor is often merely a matter of pushing an idea as far as it will go.

8 "And the way of passions took me to the true philosophy" is from Jean Jacques Rousseau's *Julie, ou la Nouvelle Héloïse*, Part II, letter iii, where it is better translated as "The road of the passions has led me to true philosophy."

9 A *pas de zéphyr* is a dance step, but a zephyr is also the name of a gentle breeze (from Zephyrus, the god of the west wind), and *pas* also means "no" or "not." Thus, *pas de zéphyr* can also be translated as "no breath."

10 Breath is necessary for speech, since it is the passage of air that vibrates the vocal cords. However, this *is* a fantastic tale. Note, too, that in another tale the dead Valdemar manages to speak without breathing—perhaps not unlike those whose larynx has been removed—by learning to gulp air and forcing it out, using that "certain spasmodic action of the muscles of the throat."

faced quintessence of all that is abominable!—thou—thou—" here standing upon tiptoe, seizing her by the throat, and placing my mouth close to her ear, I was preparing to launch forth a new and more decided epithet of opprobrium, which should not fail, if ejaculated, to convince her of her insignificance, when, to my extreme horror and astonishment, I discovered that *I had lost my breath*.

The phrases "I am out of breath," "I have lost my breath," &c., are often enough repeated in common conversation; but it had never occurred to me that the terrible accident of which I speak could *bona fide* and actually happen! Imagine—that is if you have a fanciful turn—imagine, I say, my wonder—my **7** consternation—my despair!

There is a good genius, however, which has never entirely deserted me. In my most ungovernable moods I still retain a sense of propriety, *et le chemin des passions me conduit*—as Lord Edouard in the "Julie" says it did him—*à la philosophie* **8** *véritable*.

Although I could not at first precisely ascertain to what degree the occurrence had affected me, I determined at all events to conceal the matter from my wife, until further experience should discover to me the extent of this my unheard of calamity. Altering my countenance, therefore, in a moment, from its bepuffed and distorted appearance, to an expression of arch and coquettish benignity, I gave my lady a pat on the one cheek, and a kiss on the other, and without saying one syllable (Furies! I could not), left her astonished at my drollery, as I pirouetted out of the room in a *pas de* **9** *zéphyr*.

Behold me then safely ensconced in my private *boudoir,* a fearful instance of the ill consequences attending upon irascibility—alive, with the qualifications of the dead—dead, with the propensities of the living—an anomaly on the face of the earth—being very calm, yet breathless.

Yes! breathless. I am serious in asserting that my breath was entirely gone. I could not have stirred with it a feather if my life had been at issue, or sullied even the delicacy of a mirror. Hard fate!—yet there was some alleviation to the first overwhelming paroxysm of my sorrow. I found, upon trial, that the powers of utterance which, upon my inability to proceed in the conversation with my wife, I then concluded to be totally destroyed, were in fact only partially impeded, and I discovered that had I, at that interesting crisis, dropped my voice to a singularly deep guttural, I might still have continued to her the communication of my sentiments; this pitch of voice (the guttural) depending, I find, not upon the current of the breath, but upon a certain spasmodic action of **10** the muscles of the throat.

Throwing myself upon a chair, I remained for some time absorbed in meditation. My reflections, be sure, were of no consolatory kind. A thousand vague and lachrymatory fancies took possession of my soul—and even the idea of suicide flitted across my brain; but it is a trait in the perversity of human nature to reject the obvious and the ready, for the far-distant and equivocal. Thus I shuddered at self-murder as the most decided of atrocities while the tabby-cat purred strenuously upon the rug, and the very water-dog wheezed assiduously under the table; each taking to itself much merit for the strength of its lungs, and all obviously done in derision of my own pulmonary incapacity. **11**

Oppressed with a tumult of vague hopes and fears, I at length heard the footsteps of my wife descending the staircase. Being now assured of her absence, I returned with a palpitating heart to the scene of my disaster.

Carefully locking the door on the inside, I commenced a vigorous search. It was possible, I thought, that, concealed in some obscure corner, or lurking in some closet or drawer, might be found the lost object of my inquiry. It might have a vapory—it might even have a tangible form. Most philosophers, upon many points of philosophy, are still very unphilosophical. William Godwin, however, says in his "Mande- **12** ville," that "invisible things are the only realities," and this, all will allow, is a case in point. I would have the judicious reader pause before accusing such asseverations of an undue quantum of absurdity. Anaxagoras, it will be remembered, maintained that snow is black, and this I have since found to be the case. **13**

Long and earnestly did I continue the investigation: but the contemptible reward of my industry and perseverance proved to be only a set of false teeth, two pair of hips, an eye, and a number of *billets-doux* from Mr. Windenough to my wife. **14** I might as well here observe that this confirmation of my lady's partiality for Mr. W. occasioned me little uneasiness. That Mrs. Lackobreath should admire anything so dissimilar to myself was a natural and necessary evil. I am, it is well known, of a robust and corpulent appearance, and at the same time somewhat diminutive in stature. What wonder, then, that the lath-like tenuity of my acquaintance, and his altitude, which **15** has grown into a proverb, should have met with all due estimation in the eyes of Mrs. Lackobreath. But to return.

My exertions, as I have before said, proved fruitless. Closet after closet—drawer after drawer—corner after corner—were scrutinized to no purpose. At one time, however, I thought myself sure of my prize, having, in rummaging a dressing-case, accidentally demolished a bottle of Grandjean's Oil of Archangels—which, as an agreeable perfume, I here take the **16** liberty of recommending.

With a heavy heart I return to my *boudoir*—there to ponder upon some method of eluding my wife's penetration, until I could make arrangements prior to my leaving the country, for to this I had already made up my mind. In foreign climate, being unknown, I might, with some probability of success, endeavor to conceal my unhappy calamity—a calamity calculated, even more than beggary, to estrange the affections of the multitude, and to draw down upon the wretch the well-merited indignation of the virtuous and the happy. I was not long in hesitation. Being naturally quick, I committed to memory the entire tragedy of "Metamora." I had the good **17**

11 A "water-dog" and a cat also appear in "The Duc De L'Omelette."

12 William Godwin (1756–1836), the English author and political philosopher, is best known as the author of a book of startling opinions, *Political Justice* (1793), and for being the father of Mary Wollstonecraft, author of *Frankenstein* and wife of the poet Shelley.

13 Anaxagoras (c.500–428 B.C.), the Greek philosopher, is credited with taking the seat of philosophy to Athens. His beliefs that the sun was a white-hot stone and that the moon was made of earth that reflected the sun's rays resulted in a charge of atheism and blasphemy, and he had to flee the city.

He never said that snow was black, but, rather, that there must be blackness in snow, which would explain why it turned into dark water. Unfortunately, Pierre Bayle, in his 1696 Dictionnaire, either willfully or mistakenly translated his comments, and the snow-is-black attribution stuck.

14 A rather bizarre inventory—and a bit risqué, since *billets-doux* are love letters.

15 i.e., thin and weak

16 Auguste Grandjean was a New York hair-compound maker around 1844. He appears again in "The Angel of the Odd."

17 *Metamora* (1829) was a play by John Augustus Stone (1800–34), about the American Indian chief known as King Philip. No complete version exists today.

18 The orator Demosthenes stuffed pebbles in his mouth and tried to make himself heard over the roar of the sea.

19 Straitjacket or strait-waistcoat (not "straight").

20 According to legend, Perillos, a brass maker of Athens, proposed to Phalaris, Tyrant of Agrigentum, to invent for him a new kind of punishment. And so he did—with a vengeance. He cast a bronze bull with a door in its side. The victim was shut up in the bull and roasted to death, but the throat of the device was so contrived that the groans and screams of the sufferer resembled the bellowings of a mad bull.

Phalaris liked the idea (a jolly sort, he) and ordered it to be tested by Perillos himself.

21 Shirt collars were separate from the shirt itself well into the 1920s.

22 To see if the victim's breath would condense upon it as a proof of life. With medical instruments still fairly crude, it was often difficult to tell if a person was alive or dead, especially if the pulse was very weak or seemingly absent. It's no wonder that the possibility of accidental live burial seemed very real to most readers of Poe's time (see "The Premature Burial" for more).

fortune to recollect that in the accentuation of this drama, or at least of such portion of it as is allotted to the hero, the tones of voice in which I found myself deficient were altogether unnecessary, and that the deep guttural was expected to reign monotonously throughout.

18 I practised for some time by the borders of a well-frequented marsh;—herein, however, having no reference to a similar proceeding of Demosthenes, but from a design peculiarly and conscientiously my own. Thus armed at all points, I determined to make my wife believe that I was suddenly smitten with a passion for the stage. In this, I succeeded to a miracle; and to every question or suggestion found myself at liberty to reply in my most frog-like and sepulchral tones with some passage from the tragedy—any portion of which, as I soon took great pleasure in observing, would apply equally well to any particular subject. It is not to be supposed, however, that in the delivery of such passages I was found at all deficient in the looking asquint—the showing my teeth—the working my knees—the shuffling my feet—or in any of those unmention-able graces which are now justly considered the characteristics of a popular performer. To be sure they spoke of confining me **19** in a straight-jacket—but, good God! they never suspected me of having lost my breath.

Having at length put my affairs in order, I took my seat very early one morning in the mail stage for ——, giving it to be understood, among my acquaintances, that business of the last importance required my immediate personal attend-ance in that city.

The coach was crammed to repletion; but in the uncertain twilight the features of my companions could not be distin-guished. Without making any effectual resistance, I suffered myself to be placed between two gentlemen of colossal dimensions; while a third, of a size larger, requesting pardon for the liberty he was about to take, threw himself upon my body at full length, and falling asleep in an instant, drowned all my guttural ejaculations for relief, in a snore which would **20** have put to blush the roarings of the bull of Phalaris. Happily the state of my respiratory faculties rendered suffocation an accident entirely out of the question.

As, however, the day broke more distinctly in our approach to the outskirts of the city, my tormentor, arising and adjusting **21** his shirt-collar, thanked me in a very friendly manner for my civility. Seeing that I remained motionless (all my limbs were dislocated and my head twisted on one side), his apprehensions began to be excited; and arousing the rest of the passengers, he communicated, in a very decided manner, his opinion that a dead man had been palmed upon them during the night for a living and responsible fellow-traveller; here giving me a thump on the right eye, by way of demonstrating the truth of his suggestion.

Hereupon all, one after another (there were nine in com-pany), believed it their duty to pull me by the ear. A young practising physician, too, having applied a pocket-mirror to **22** my mouth, and found me without breath, the assertion of my persecutor was pronounced a true bill; and the whole party expressed a determination to endure tamely no such impositions for the future, and to proceed no farther with any such carcasses for the present.

I was here, accordingly, thrown out at the sign of the "Crow" (by which tavern the coach happened to be passing), without meeting with any further accident than the breaking of both my arms, under the left hind wheel of the vehicle. I must besides do the driver the justice to state that he did not forget to throw after me the largest of my trunks, which, unfortunately falling on my head, fractured my skull in a manner at once interesting and extraordinary.

The landlord of the "Crow," who is a hospitable man, finding that my trunk contained sufficient to indemnify him for any little trouble he might take in my behalf, sent forthwith for a surgeon of his acquaintance, and delivered me to his care with a bill and receipt for ten dollars.

The purchaser took me to his apartments and commenced operations immediately. Having cut off my ears, however, he discovered signs of animation. He now rang the bell, and sent for a neighboring apothecary with whom to consult in the **23** emergency. In case of his suspicions with regard to my existence proving ultimately correct, he, in the meantime, made an incision in my stomach, and removed several of my viscera for private dissection. **24**

The apothecary had an idea I was actually dead. This idea I endeavored to confute, kicking and plunging with all my might, and making the most furious contortions—for the operations of the surgeon had, in a measure, restored me to the possession of my faculties. All, however, was attributed to the effects of a new galvanic battery, wherewith the **25** apothecary, who is really a man of information, performed several curious experiments, in which, from my personal share in their fulfilment, I could not help feeling deeply interested. It was a source of mortification to me nevertheless, that although I made several attempts at conversation, my powers of speech were so entirely in abeyance, that I could not even open my mouth; much less, then, make reply to some ingenious but fanciful theories of which, under other circumstances, my minute acquaintance with the Hippocratian pathology would have afforded me a ready confutation.

Not being able to arrive at a conclusion, the practitioners remanded me for further examination. I was taken up into a garret; and the surgeon's lady having accommodated me with drawers and stockings, the surgeon himself fastened my hands, and tied up my jaws with a pocket-handkerchief—then bolted the door on the outside as he hurried to his dinner, leaving me alone to silence and to meditation.

I now discovered to my extreme delight that I could have spoken had not my mouth been tied up with the pocket-handkerchief. Consoling myself with this reflection, I was mentally repeating some passages of the "Omnipresence of the Deity," as is my custom before resigning myself to sleep, **26** when two cats, of a greedy and vituperative turn, entering at

23 Apothecaries, or druggists, were often consulted as physicians, usually for their knowledge of drugs. Indeed, outside of delicate surgery, they were interchangeable with doctors in many communities in England, where after 1700 they became general medical practitioners by law.

24 The use of cadavers for medical research was still a distasteful and distrusted affair (it remains so for many people), and since bodies were hard to come by, a black-market trade sprang up. Bodies were sometimes stolen from crypts or graves (see "The Fall of the House of Usher"), but more frequently, doctors and medical students used unidentified bodies from city morgues or those of paupers assigned to the potter's field.

25 The galvanic battery is named after Luigi Galvani (1737–98), Italian physician. During experiments on muscle and nerve preparations of frogs, he noticed the contraction of a frog's leg when touched with charged metal. He devised an arc of two metals with which contractions could be induced and in 1791 published his results, attributing the source of electricity to the animal tissue. Alessandro, Conte Volta (1745–1827), disagreed, correctly supposing that the electricity originated in the metallic arc. The controversy focused attention on electricity in animals and stimulated research in electrotherapy and on electric currents.

26 A popular moralistic poem (1828), by Robert Montgomery, that Poe disliked intensely

27 Angelica Catalani (1782–1849) was a well-known opera star of the day, known for her perfect musicianship. She was also manager of the Italian Opera in Paris (1814–17).

28 The Persian Magian was Gaumata, the imposter who posed as the elder son of Cyrus the Great, usurping the throne after the murder of the real son (Smerdis) by Cambyses. He lost his ears (not his nose) because of an affront to Cyrus.

The story of Zopyrus appears in Herodotus, *Histories*, III, 153–60.

29 George Wilson of Philadelphia, who was reprieved from hanging, imprisoned, then pardoned in 1841

30 "I have . . . written a treatise on drunkenness," says Antony in Horace Smith's *Zillah*, III, 40, which was also the chief source for "A Tale of Jerusalem."

For more on authors' unusual experiences, see "How to Write a Blackwood Article"/"A Predicament."

31 Hanging usually kills by breaking the victim's neck, not by choking him.

27 a hole in the wall, leaped up with a flourish *à la Catalani,* and alighting opposite one another on my visage, betook themselves to indecorous contention for the paltry consideration of my nose.

But, as the loss of his ears proved the means of elevating **28** to the throne of Cyrus, the Magian or Mige-Gush of Persia, and as the cutting off his nose gave Zopyrus possession of Babylon, so the loss of a few ounces of my countenance proved the salvation of my body. Aroused by the pain, the burning with indignation, I burst, at a single effort, the fastenings and the bandage. Stalking across the room I cast a glance of contempt at the belligerents, and throwing open the sash to their extreme horror and disappointment, precipitated myself, very dexterously, from the window.

29   The mail-robber W——, to whom I bore a singular resemblance, was at this moment passing from the city jail to the scaffold erected for his execution in the suburbs. His extreme infirmity and long-continued ill-health had obtained him the privilege of remaining unmanacled; and habited in his gallows costume—one very similar to my own—he lay at full length in the bottom of the hangman's cart (which happened to be under the windows of the surgeon at the moment of my precipitation) without any other guard than the driver, who was asleep, and two recruits of the sixth infantry, who were drunk.

As ill-luck would have it, I alit upon my feet within the vehicle. W——, who was an acute fellow, perceived his opportunity. Leaping up immediately, he bolted out behind, and turning down an alley, was out of sight in the twinkling of an eye. The recruits, aroused by the bustle, could not exactly comprehend the merits of the transaction. Seeing, however, a man, the precise counterpart of the felon, standing upright in the cart before their eyes, they were of the opinion that the rascal (meaning W——) was after making his escape (so they expressed themselves), and, having communicated this opinion to one another, they took each a dram, and then knocked me down with the butt-ends of their muskets.

It was not long ere we arrived at the place of destination. Of course nothing could be said in my defence. Hanging was my inevitable fate. I resigned myself thereto with a feeling half stupid, half acrimonious. Being little of a cynic, I had all the sentiments of a dog. The hangman, however, adjusted the noose about my neck. The drop fell.

I forbear to depict my sensations upon the gallows; although here, undoubtedly, I could speak to the point, and it is a topic upon which nothing has been well said. In fact, to write upon such a theme it is necessary to have been hanged. Every author should confine himself to matters of experience. Thus **30** Mark Antony composed a treatise upon getting drunk.

I may just mention, however, that die I did not. My body **31** *was,* but I had no breath *to be,* suspended; and but for the knot under my left ear (which had the feel of a military stock) I dare say that I should have experienced very little inconvenience. As for the jerk given to my neck upon the falling of the drop, it merely proved a corrective to the twist afforded me by the fat gentleman in the coach.

For good reasons, however, I did my best to give the crowd the worth of their trouble. My convulsions were said to be **32** extraordinary. My spasms it would have been difficult to beat. The populace *encored*. Several gentlemen swooned; and a multitude of ladies were carried home in hysterics. Pinxit **33** availed himself of the opportunity to retouch, from a sketch taken upon the spot, his admirable painting of the Marsyas flayed alive.

When I had afforded sufficient amusement, it was thought proper to remove my body from the gallows—this the more especially as the real culprit had in the meantime been retaken and recognized, a fact which I was so unlucky as not to know.

Much sympathy was, of course, exercised in my behalf, and as no one made claim to my corpse, it was ordered that I should be interred in a public vault.

Here, after due interval, I was deposited. The sexton departed, and I was left alone. A line of Marston's "Malcontent"—   **34**

    Death's a good fellow and keeps open house—

struck me at that moment as a palpable lie.

I knocked off, however, the lid of my coffin, and stepped out. The place was dreadfully dreary and damp, and I became troubled with *ennui*. By way of amusement, I felt my way among the numerous coffins ranged in order around. I lifted them down, one by one, and breaking open their lids, busied myself in speculations about the mortality within.

"This," I soliloquized, tumbling over a carcass, puffy, bloated, and rotund—"this has been, no doubt, in every sense of the word, an unhappy—an unfortunate man. It has been his terrible lot not to walk but to waddle—to pass through life not like a human being, but like an elephant—not like a man, but like a rhinoceros.

"His attempts at getting on have been mere abortions, and his circumgyratory proceedings a palpable failure. Taking a step forward, it has been his misfortune to take two toward the right, and three toward the left. His studies have been confined to the poetry of Crabbe. He can have no idea of the **35** wonder of a *pirouette*. To him a *pas de papillon* has been an **36** abstract conception. He has never ascended the summit of a hill. He has never viewed from any steeple the glories of a metropolis. Heat has been his mortal enemy. In the dog-days **37** his days have been the days of a dog. Therein, he has dreamed of flames and suffocation—of mountains upon mountains—of Pelion upon Ossa. He was short of breath—to say all in a **38** word, he was short of breath. He thought it extravagant to play upon wind-instruments. He was the inventor of self-moving fans, wind-sails, and ventilators. He patronized Du Pont the bellows-maker, and died miserably in attempting to **39** smoke a cigar. His was a case in which I feel a deep interest—a lot in which I sincerely sympathize.

32 Public executions were commonplace well into the nineteenth century (and in some states, into the twentieth), sometimes being a major source of entertainment for the multitudes, who often had little else to cheer them (one assumes they were cheered in this case because they weren't the one being hanged).

33 i.e., "he painted"; an artist's mark
Marsyas was the Phrygian flute player who challenged Apollo to a contest of skill, and, being beaten by the god, was flayed alive for his presumption. The river Marsyas sprang from his blood. The story is apparently symbolic of the rivalry between the Dorian mode, employed in the worship of Apollo and performed on the lute, and the Phrygian mode, employed in the rites of Cybele and played on the flute.
The painter Raphael (1483–1520) portrayed the flaying of Marsyas.

34 John Marston (1575?–1634), Elizabethan dramatist and satirist, is known for his entertaining comedies such as *The Malcontent* (1604) and his melodramatic tragedies such as *The Wonder of Women* (1606).
The quote, however, is from Marston's *Antonio and Mellida*, Part 1, III, ii.

35 Crabs cannot walk forward. Poe alludes to nothing about the real George Crabbe (1754–1832).

36 A dance step (*papillon* is French for butterfly)

37 From the Latin *dies caniculares*, the days about the time of the helical rising of the dog star (Sirius), which in ancient times were the hottest and most unwholesome time of year (July 3 to August 11).

38 "Heaping Pelion upon Ossa" means adding difficulty to difficulty, or embarrassment to embarrassment. According to myth, when the giants attempted to climb to heaven, they stacked Mount Pelion upon Mount Ossa (both in Thessaly) to make a scaling ladder. (Also "heaping Ossa upon Pelion")

39 No such-named bellows maker is known, but there was Éleuthère Irénée Du Pont (1772–1834), the American gunpowder manufacturer and founder of the chemical company that bears his name.

40 Rigor mortis sets in from ten minutes to several hours after death, then passes in about twenty-four hours, when bacterial decomposition and acid formation dissolve the coagulated body proteins that cause the initial rigidity.

41 A shot tower is a tall, round tower in which molten lead is dropped into water below, to make gunshot.

42 *Populus nigra italica*, a tree that grows quickly to 40–100 feet tall, in a beautiful columnar form with upward-reaching branches. It's most commonly used in country driveways and for windbreaks.

43 An appropriately lugubrious subject

44 Alternative title of John Flint South's *A Short Description of the Bones* (1825).

45 The branch of physics that deals with the mechanical properties (density, elasticity, pressure) of fluids

46 From Captain Robert Barclay-Allardyce, who walked one thousand miles in one thousand hours, at one mile each hour, in 1809.

47 While William Windham (1750–1810) was a British statesmen, no Allbreath existed—he is another Poe pun. As for Phiz, this was the pen name of English illustrator Hablot Knight Browne (1815–82), who drew the illustrations for Dickens' *Pickwick Papers* at age twenty-one, went on to illustrate more of that author's works, and contributed cartoons to *Punch*.

48 "*Tenera res in feminis fama pudicitiae, et quasi flos pulcherrimus, cito ad levem marcescit auram, levique flatu corrumpitur, maxime, etc.—Hieronymus ad Salvinam.*" (Poe's note)
"A reputation for modesty among women is a delicate thing, and as if a most beautiful flower, as soon as it is exposed to the light air, is greatly damaged by a slight breeze," from St. Jerome's seventy-ninth letter to Salvina. Sophronius Eusebius Hieronymus, or St. Jerome (c.347–420?), Christian scholar, criticized the secular clergy, translated biblical books from the Hebrew, and sometimes quarreled with St. Augustine, with whom he kept correspondence. He was also suspicious of women, following one Church line that, because they were descendents of Eve, women were not to be trusted, and in fact, dragged men into sin. The Wife of Bath, in Chaucer's *The Canterbury Tales*, ridicules medieval antifeminism, which traced its roots to Jerome.

49 Epilepsy, although the O.E.D. gives no such variant of the word

"But here,"—said I—"here"—and I dragged spitefully from its receptacle a gaunt, tall, and peculiar-looking form, whose remarkable appearance struck me with a sense of unwelcome familiarity—"here is a wretch entitled to no earthly commiseration."Thus saying, in order to obtain a more distinct view of my subject, I applied my thumb and forefinger to its nose,

40 and causing it to assume a sitting position upon the ground, held it thus, at the length of my arm, while I continued my soliloquy.

—"Entitled," I repeated, "to no earthly commiseration. Who indeed would think of compassionating a shadow? Besides, has he not had his full share of the blessings of mortality? He was the

41 originator of tall monuments—shot-towers—lightning-rods—

42,43 Lombardy poplars. His treatise upon "Shades and Shadows" has immortalized him. He edited with distinguished ability the last

44 edition of "South on the Bones." He went early to college and

45 studied pneumatics. He then came home, talked eternally, and played upon the French horn. He patronized the bagpipes. Captain Barclay, who walked against Time, would not walk against

46 *him*. Windham and Allbreath were his favorite writers; his fa-

47 vorite artist, Phiz. He died gloriously while inhaling gas—*levique*

48 *flatu corrumpitur*, like the *fama pudicitiæ* in Hieronymus. He was indubitably a——"

"How *can* you?—how—*can*—you?"—interrupted the object of my animadversions, gasping for breath, and tearing off, with a desperate exertion, the bandage around its jaws—"how *can* you, Mr. Lackobreath, be so infernally cruel as to pinch me in that manner by the nose? Did you not see how they had fastened up my mouth—and you *must* know—if you know any thing—how vast a superfluity of breath I have to dispose of ! If you do *not* know, however, sit down and you shall see. In my situation it is really a great relief to be able to open one's mouth—to be able to expatiate—to be able to communicate with a person like yourself, who do not think yourself called upon at every period to interrupt the thread of a gentleman's discourse. Interruptions are annoying and should undoubtedly be abolished—don't you think so?—no reply, I beg you,—one person is enough to be speaking at a time.—I shall be done by and by, and then you may begin.—How the devil, sir, did you get into this place?—not a word I beseech you—been here some time myself—terrible accident!—heard of it, I suppose?—awful calamity!—walking under your windows—some short while ago—about the time you were stagestruck—horrible occurrence!—heard of 'catching one's breath,' eh?—hold your tongue I tell you!—I caught somebody else's!—had always too much of my own—met Blab at the corner of the street—wouldn't give me a chance for a word—couldn't get in a syllable edgeways—attacked, consequently, with epi-

49 lepsis—Blab made his escape—damn all fools!—they took me up for dead, and put me in this place—pretty doings all of them!—heard all you said about me—every word a lie—horrible!—wonderful!—outrageous!—hideous! —incomprehensible!—et cetera—et cetera—et cetera—et cetera——"

It is impossible to conceive my astonishment at so unexpected a discourse; or the joy with which I became gradually convinced that the breath so fortunately caught by the gentleman (whom I soon recognized as my neighbor Windenough) was, in fact, the identical expiration mislaid by myself in the conversation with my wife. Time, place, and circumstance rendered it a matter beyond question. I did not, however, immediately release my hold upon Mr. W.'s proboscis—not at least during the long period in which the inventor of Lombardy poplars continued to favor me with his explanations.

In this repect I was actuated by that habitual prudence which has ever been my predominating trait. I reflected that many difficulties might still lie in the path of my preservation which only extreme exertion on my part would be able to surmount. Many persons, I considered, are prone to estimate commodities in their possession—however valueless to the then proprietor—however troublesome, or distressing—in direct ratio with the advantages to be derived by others from their attainment, or by themselves from their abandonment. Might not this be the case with Mr. Windenough? In displaying anxiety for the breath of which he was at present so willing to get rid, might I not lay myself open to the exactions of his avarice? There are scoundrels in this world, I remembered with a sigh, who will not scruple to take unfair opportunities with even a next-door neighbor, and (this remark is from Epictetus) it is precisely at that time when men are most **50** anxious to throw off the burden of their own calamities that they feel the least desirous of relieving them in others.

Upon considerations similar to these, and still retaining my grasp upon the nose of Mr. W., I accordingly thought proper to model my reply.

"Monster!" I began in a tone of the deepest indignation—"monster and double-winded idiot!—dost *thou*, whom for thine iniquities it has pleased heaven to accurse with a twofold respiration—dost *thou*, I say, presume to address me in the familiar language of an old acquaintance?—'I lie,' forsooth! and 'hold my tongue,' to be sure!—pretty conversation, indeed, to a gentleman with a single breath!—all this, too, when I have it in my power to relieve the calamity under which thou dost so justly suffer—to curtail the superfluities of thine unhappy respiration." **51**

Like Brutus, I paused for a reply—with which, like a tornado, Mr. Windenough immediately overwhelmed me. Protestation followed upon protestation, and apology upon apology. There were no terms with which he was unwilling to comply, and there were none of which I failed to take the fullest advantage.

Preliminaries being at length arranged, my acquaintance delivered me the respiration; for which (having carefully examined it) I gave him afterward a receipt.

I am aware that by many I shall be held to blame for speaking, in a manner so cursory, of a transaction so impalpable. It will be thought that I should have entered more minutely into the details of an occurrence by which—and this

"Monster!" I began in a tone of the deepest indignation—"monster and double-winded idiot!" *Illustration by F. S. Coburn, 1903*

50 "In prosperity it is very easy to find a friend; in adversity, nothing is so difficult" (Epictetus 122).

51 *Julius Caesar*, III, ii. Brutus, after engineering the assassination of Caesar, addresses the Roman crowd, persuading them that his action was just and ending with a series of questions as to whom he may have offended: "I pause for a reply."

52 "Whig" is an abbreviation for Whiggamore (from "whig," to drive, and "a mare"), the name first given to the Covenanters in western Scotland in the mid-1600s; first formally organized in America in 1836, after the Anti-Masonic and National Republican parties combined with other dissidents in supporting the candidacy of Henry Clay in 1832. After this high point, the party slowly faded until 1852, when it disappeared altogether.

53 The Democratic party originated as the Jeffersonian, anti-Federalist Democratic Republican party, but became known as the Democrats early in the 1800s (and no wonder, with a name like that). The Democrats remained in power until 1849.

When Jackson, leader of the frontier faction, received the party's endorsement, the conservatives split to form the Whig party. Their only President was William Henry Harrison (1840–41), a very temporary victory at best.

54 From *Zillah*, I, 151. See also Tennyson's *St. Simeon Stylites*, 1:7: "Battering the gates of heaven with storms of prayer."

55 Epimenides was a Cretan prophet of the seventh or sixth century B.C., who fell asleep in a cave when he was a boy and did not wake for fifty-seven years—when he found himself endowed with miraculous wisdom. When the Athenians were struck by war and pestilence, and the oracle declared they had brought on divine anger through profaning the temple in which the followers of Cylon had been put to death, they were told to expiate their offense. They sent for Epimenides to purify the temple. When he was finished, he refused to accept any presents, asking instead for the friendship of the Athenians on behalf of Knossos, his home.

Diogenes Laërtius (fl. early-third century B.C.), the Greek biographer, comes down to us in ten books on the philosophers from Thales to Epicurus.

56 A pen name apparently derived from "Barry Cornwall," the pseudonym of songwriter Bryan Waller Procter, and "Mark Littleton," J. P. Kennedy's pseudonym in his novel *Horse-Shoe Robinson* (1835). Poe may also have had in mind the hero of Thackeray's *Barry Lyndon* (1844). He used the name to sign the original versions of "King Pest," "Mystification," "Why the Little Frenchman Wears His Hand in a Sling," and "The Duc De L'Omelette," but only this tale now bears the pseudonym.

is very true—much new light might be thrown upon a highly interesting branch of physical philosophy.

To all this I am sorry that I cannot reply. A hint is the only answer which I am permitted to make. There were *circumstances*—but I think it much safer upon consideration to say as little as possible about an affair so delicate—*so delicate*, I repeat, and at the time involving the interests of a third party whose sulphurous resentment I have not the least desire, at this moment, of incurring.

We were not long after this necessary arrangement in effecting an escape from the dungeons of the sepulchre. The united strength of our resuscitated voices was soon sufficiently **52** apparent. Scissors, the Whig editor, republished a treatise upon "the nature and origin of subterranean noises." A reply—rejoinder—confutation—and justification—followed in the col- **53** umns of a Democratic gazette. It was not until the opening of the vault to decide the controversy, that the appearance of Mr. Windenough and myself proved both parties to have been decidedly in the wrong.

I cannot conclude these details of some very singular passages in a life at all times sufficiently eventful, without again recalling to the attention of the reader the merits of that indiscriminate philosophy which is a sure and ready shield against those shafts of calamity which can neither be seen, felt, nor fully understood. It was in the spirit of this wisdom that, among the ancient Hebrews, it was believed the gates of Heaven would be inevitably opened to that sinner, or saint, who, with good lungs and implicit confidence, should voci- **54** ferate the word "*Amen!*" It was in the spirit of this wisdom that, when a great plague raged at Athens, and every means **55** had been in vain attempted for its removal, Epimenides, as Laertius relates, in his second book, of that philosopher, advised the erection of a shrine and temple "to the proper God."

56   LYTTLETON BARRY.

SHADOW–A PARABLE

First published in the *Southern Literary Messenger*, September 1835, this short piece is one of Poe's best. Its style is a blend of the King James Bible, Bulwer-Lytton, De Quincey, Macpherson's *Ossian*, and Coleridge's *Wanderings of Cain*.

The word "shadow" is a particular favorite of Poe, and he uses it elsewhere to mean, variously, a ghost, darkness, fear, death, and the unknown. His poem *El Dorado* is perhaps his most virtuosic use of the word, as well as one of his superior works in verse.

"Shadow" is read by actor Ugo Toppo on disc (CMS 567).

Yea! though I walk through the valley of the Shadow.
　　　　　　　　　　　　　　　　—*Psalm of David*. **1**

Ye who read are still among the living; but I who write shall have long since gone my way into the region of shadows. For indeed strange things shall happen, and secret things be known, and many centuries shall pass away, ere these memorials be seen of men. And, when seen, there will be some to disbelieve, and some to doubt, and yet a few who will find much to ponder upon in the characters here graven with a stylus of iron. **2**

The year had been a year of terror, and of feelings more intense than terror for which there is no name upon the earth. For many prodigies and signs had taken place, and far and wide, over sea and land, the black wings of the Pestilence were spread abroad. To those, nevertheless, cunning in the **3** stars, it was not unknown that the heavens wore an aspect of ill; and to me, the Greek Oinos, among others, it was evident **4,5** that now had arrived the alternation of that seven hundred and ninety-fourth year when, at the entrance of Aries, the planet Jupiter is conjoined with the red ring of the terrible Saturnus. The peculiar spirit of the skies, if I mistake not **6** greatly, made itself manifest, not only in the physical orb of the earth, but in the souls, imaginations, and meditations of mankind.

Over some flasks of the red Chian wine, within the walls **7** of a noble hall, in a dim city called Ptolemais, we sat, at night, **8** a company of seven. And to our chamber there was no **9** entrance save by a lofty door of brass: and the door was fashioned by the artisan Corinnos, and, being of rare work- **10** manship, was fastened from within. Black draperies, likewise, in the gloomy room, shut out from our view the moon, the lurid stars, and the peopleless streets—but the boding and the memory of Evil, they would not be so excluded. There

1 The King James Version of the Bible uses "valley of the shadow of death," as does the Septuagint (the pre-Christian Greek Old Testament), the Aramaic Targum, and the Vulgate—yet "valley of the shadow" and "valley of darkness" are just as correct as translations of the Hebrew. The problem is that the Old Testament was written before the development of the Masoretic punctuation, which indicates vowel placement. Thus the Hebrew word in question may be a combination of *tsel* (shadow) and *maveth* (death), or a single word, *salmuth* (darkness).

2 Immediately, the scene is set: long ago and far away, in a culture whose records are recorded on stone. The actual setting seems to be the twilight of Ptolemaic Egypt, named after the Ptolemies, Greeks who, after the death of Alexander (323 B.C.), ruled the country until Caesar Augustus put an end to the dynasty by the death of the son of Julius Caesar and Cleopatra, and annexed Egypt to Rome.

3 Poe probably means bubonic plague, and there may be some justification for this, since something very much like it appeared in Egypt in the third century B.C., if sources are to be believed, but it disappeared until A.D. 542, when the first documented cases of bubonic plague appeared at the port of Pelusium, on the Nile.

The diseases of the Bible, usually referred to as "plague," could have been an early, virulent form of measles—or smallpox, influenza, typhoid, or dysentery. The Antonine Plague, of A.D. 165–80, wiped out large numbers of people, but we cannot say what the cause was.

For a fascinating account of such matters, see William H. McNeill's *Plagues and Peoples* (Anchor Press, 1976).

4 The ancients considered the world as a living being; the sun and moon being its two eyes, the earth its body, the ether its intellect, and the sky its wings. Man was looked on as the world in miniature, so it was natural to assume that the movements of the world and of man corresponded. And if one could ascertain one, the other was sure to follow. So rose the system of astrology, which professes to interpret the events of a person's life by the corresponding movements of the stars.

5 Oinos means "wine."

6 A conjunction of the planets Jupiter and Saturn was considered an omen, a warning of change, and the sign of the Ram foreshadowed violence and misfortune. Such a conjunction was said to occur every 794 years, according to the section "Les Mathématiques," in Bielfeld's *Encylopaedia*, Book I, xlix, 78, a book Poe referred to often.

7 Khios or Chios, an island in the Aegean just west of Asia Minor, claims to be the birthplace of Homer. During the Hellenistic era it was renowned for its wine and maintained its independence because of its importance. "From Chios or Thasos is imported a Greek light wine not inferior in quality to the Aminean vintages," writes Pliny in his *Natural History*, XIV, 25.

8 Ptolemais Theron, on the western coast of the Red Sea, where, Pliny writes, the sun cast no shadow at noon "for 45 days before and 45 days after midsummer" (*Natural History*, II, lxxv, 183).

9 See "The Masque of the Red Death," note 12.

10 Corinnos was the name of a poet who lived at the time of the Trojan War, but not the name of any known artist. Poe perhaps meant to suggest a connection between Corinnos and Corinth, for in that city brass making was an art, and Corinthian brass contained gold and silver.

11 More sevens. Seven lamps appear also in "The Masque of the Red Death." And in *Paradise Lost* we read, "Sev'n Lamps as in a Zodiac representing/The Heav'nly fires" (XII, 255). Compare the "revel" here with that in "The Masque of the Red Death."

12 Anacreon (fl. 521 B.C.), born in Teos, in Ionia, wrote graceful, elegant poetry celebrating the pleasures of wine and love. Little of his work survives.

Poe refers to him as "the Teian" in "Morella," note 21.

13 The relationship between blood and wine is not restricted to the Christian sacrament. Red wine has for centuries symbolized blood and sacrifice, as well as youth and eternal life—the latter in the "divine" intoxication which enables man to share, for a fleeting moment, the feelings of the gods.

14 Zoïlus, or Zoïlos (c.400–c.320 B.C.) was a Greek rhetorician and philosopher, shrewd, witty, and spiteful. He was nicknamed Homeromastix (Homer's scourge), because he mercilessly attacked the epics of Homer, calling the poet a purveyor of fables, and the companions of Ulysses on the island of Circe "weeping porkers." He also took shots at Plato, Isocrates, and other big game.

Poe may also have based the name on the Greek word *zoë*, or "life."

were things around us and about of which I can render no distinct account—things material and spiritual—heaviness in the atmosphere—a sense of suffocation—anxiety—and, above all, that terrible state of existence which the nervous experience when the senses are keenly living and awake, and meanwhile the powers of thought lie dormant. A dead weight hung upon us. It hung upon our limbs—upon the household furniture—upon the goblets from which we drank; and all things were depressed, and borne down thereby—all things save only the flames of the seven iron lamps which illumined **11** our revel. Uprearing themselves in tall slender lines of light, they thus remained burning all pallid and motionless; and in the mirror which their lustre formed upon the round table of ebony at which we sat, each of us there assembled beheld the pallor of his own countenance, and the unquiet glare in the downcast eyes of his companions. Yet we laughed and were merry in our proper way—which was hysterical; and sang the **12** songs of Anacreon—which are madness; and drank deeply— **13** although the purple wine reminded us of blood. For there was yet another tenant of our chamber in the person of young **14** Zoilus. Dead, and at full length he lay, enshrouded;—the genius and the demon of the scene. Alas! he bore no portion in our mirth, save that his countenance, distorted with the

Dead, and at full length he lay, enshrouded.— *Illustration by Johann Friedrich Vogel, 1856*

plague, and his eyes, in which Death had but half extinguished the fire of the pestilence, seemed to take such interest in our merriment as the dead may haply take in the merriment of those who are to die. But although I Oinos, felt that the eyes of the departed were upon me, still I forced myself not to perceive the bitterness of their expression, and, gazing down steadily into the depths of the ebony mirror, sang with a loud **15** and sonorous voice the songs of the son of Teios. But gradually **16** my songs they ceased, and their echoes, rolling afar off among the sable draperies of the chamber, became weak, and undistinguishable, and so faded away. And lo! from among those sable draperies where the sounds of the song departed, there came forth a dark and undefined shadow—a shadow such as the moon, when low in heaven, might fashion from the figure of a man: but it was the shadow neither of man nor of God, nor of any familiar thing. And quivering awhile among the draperies of the room, it at length rested in full view upon the surface of the door of brass. But the shadow was vague, **17** and formless, and indefinite, and was the shadow neither of man nor God—neither God of Greece, nor God of Chaldæa, **18** nor any Egyptian God. And the shadow rested upon the brazen doorway, and under the arch of the entablature of the door, and moved not, nor spoke any word, but there became stationary and remained. And the door whereupon the shadow rested was, if I remember aright, over against the feet of the young Zoilus enshrouded. But we, the seven there assembled, having seen the shadow as it came out from among the draperies, dared not steadily behold it, but cast down our eyes, and gazed continually into the depths of the mirror of ebony. And at length I, Oinos, speaking some low words, demanded of the shadow its dwelling and its appellation. And **19** the shadow answered, "I am SHADOW, and my dwelling is near to the Catacombs of Ptolemais, and hard by those dim plains of Helusion which border upon the foul Charonian **20** canal." And then did we, the seven, start from our seats in horror, and stand trembling, and shuddering, and aghast, for the tones in the voice of the shadow were not the tones of any one being, but of a multitude of beings, and, varying in their cadences from syllable to syllable, fell duskly upon our ears in the well-remembered and familiar accents of many thousand departed friends.   **21**

15 Mirrors are an ambivalent symbol, often invested with a magic quality.

"For now we see through a glass, darkly; but then face to face: now I know in part; but then shall I know even as also I am known" (I Corinthians 13:12).

16 See note 12.

17 Compare with the bedroom scene in "Ligeia."

Among primitive peoples, the notion that the shadow is the *alter ego* or soul is firmly established; it is also reflected in the folklore and literature of some advanced cultures. . . . 'Shadow' is the term given by Jung to the primitive and instinctive side of the individual" (J. E. Cirlot, *A Dictionary of Symbols* [1962], pp. 290–91).

According to Frazer's *Golden Bough*, shadow and mirror are both symbols of the soul (Macmillan [1958 ed.], pp. 220–25).

18 The southernmost portion of the valley of the Tigris and Euphrates rivers. The Chaldeans were a Semitic people whose empire flourished under Nebuchadnezzar II but declined rapidly afterward and came to an end when Babylon fell to Cyrus the Great, in 539 B.C.

There was no one god of the Chaldeans. Their four great gods were Anu, who reigned over the heavens; Enlil, or Bel, who ruled the earth; Ea, who ruled the waters; and Marduk, who absorbed all the others in time and took over all their various functions and prerogatives. It may be Marduk who is referred to here. Asshur, an Assyrian god, took first place when the might of Babylon faded before that of Nineveh.

19 The Egyptians believed that their names were a reflection of their souls and that a name could have a magical effect upon some other person.

Names are important in "Ligeia" and "Morella."

20 "The Elysian plain, near the Catacombs in Egypt, stood upon the foul Charonian canal" (Jacob Bryant, *A New System . . . of Antient Mythology*, 3rd ed. [1817], I, 34). There is little information on the burial practices of the Ptolemies, who, being Greek, may not have practiced traditional mummification. On the other hand, it is well known that Egyptians mummified bodies up through the fourth century A.D. There are catacombs near Alexandria and Cairo, but they are not specifically Ptolemeian.

Poe may also have chosen the Ptolemies because they were known for their wickedness and poor government.

"Helusion" is Poe's transliteration of the Greek word we transliterate as Elysium or the Elysian Fields, the abode of the dead. Charon was the ferryman of the dead across the river Styx into Hades. For a fare of one silver *obol*, placed in the mouth of the corpse at burial, Charon would ferry the soul across Styx and Acheron.

The canal is mentioned in Pliny (VI, xxxiii, 165–66): ". . . a canal made by Ptolemy II, 100 feet wide and 40 deep, for 37½ miles."

21 In the *Odyssey*, IV, 277–79, Helen of Troy speaks with the voices of the wives of dead Greek heroes. In some mythologies, including the Norse, souls of the dead wandered with the winds, and their voices mingled with the sound of the wind (an idea echoed in Truman Capote's *The Grass Harp*).

"The deep/Moans round with many voices." (Tennyson, *Ulysses*, 1, 55)

"And 'mid this tumult Kubla heard from far/Ancestral voices. . . ." (Coleridge, *Kubla Khan*)

"The Voice of the dead was a living voice to me." (Tennyson, *In the Valley of Cauteretz*)

SILENCE - A FABLE

First published as "Siope—a Fable" in the *Baltimore Book*, 1838, this is surely one of Poe's most baffling tales, for while it reads well, moves smoothly, and seems to tell a story, the ending leaves one with a mystery still unsolved.

However, Poe has left some clues. One is his poem *Sonnet—Silence:*

> There are some qualities—some incorporate things,
>   That have a double life, which thus is made
> A type of that twin entity which springs
>   From matter and light, evinced in solid and shade.
> There is a two-fold *Silence*—sea and shore—
>   Body and soul. One dwells in lonely places,
>   Newly with grass o'ergrown; some solemn graces,
> Some human memories and tearful lore,
> Render him terrorless: his name's "No more."
> He is the corporate Silence: dread him not!
>   No power hath he of evil in himself;
> But should some urgent fate (untimely lot!)
>   Bring thee to meet his shadow (nameless elf,
> That haunteth the lone regions where hath trod
> No foot of man,) commend thyself to God!
>
>   (1839–45)

This poem in turn seems to owe something to two sonnets by Thomas Hood (1799–1845), *Silence* and *Sonnet:—Death*.

Poe originally began his tale with a line from his poem *Al Aaraaf:* "Ours is a world of words: Quiet we call/'*Silence*'—which is the merest word of all."

The tale's theme, then, seems to be that man clings to reality—any reality, no matter how impossible or horrible it may be—because the alternative is too terrifying to live with.

Poe's source seems to be in part "Monos and Daimonos, a Legend," a story by Bulwer-Lytton, which appeared in the London *New Monthly*, May 1830, and which he praised in a review of the author's *Rienzi* in the *Southern Literary Messenger*, February 1836. From it he borrowed the rock, the solitary human, the demon, the wild beasts, and even some of the wording: "As the Lord liveth, I believe the tale that I shall tell you will have sufficient claim on your attention." However, as is often the case, Poe's use of the material outstrips the original, which is overlong and rambling.

Nikolai Miaskovsky (1881–1950), the Russian composer, wrote a symphonic poem based on the tale. A reading of the story by Martin Donegan is available on records (CMS 626).

Ἔνδουσιν δ ορεων κορυφαι τε και φαραγγες
Πρώνές τε καὶ χαράδραι

—ALCMAN.

*"The mountain pinnacles slumber; valleys,
crags, and caves are silent."*   **1**

"Listen to *me*," said the Demon, as he placed his hand upon **2**
my head. "The region of which I speak is a dreary region in
Libya, by the borders of the river Zaïre, and there is no quiet **3**
there, nor silence.

"The waters of the river have a saffron and sickly hue; and
they flow not onward to the sea, but palpitate forever and
forever beneath the red eye of the sun with a tumultuous and
convulsive motion. For many miles on either side of the river's **4**
oozy bed is a pale desert of gigantic water-lilies. They sigh **5**
one unto the other in that solitude, and stretch toward the **6**
heavens their long and ghastly necks, and nod to and fro their
everlasting heads. And there is an indistinct murmur which
cometh out from among them like the rushing of subterrene
water. And they sigh one unto the other.

"But there is a boundary to their realm—the boundary of
the dark, horrible, lofty forest. There, like the waves about
the Hebrides, the low underwood is agitated continually. But **7**
there is no wind throughout the heaven. And the tall primeval
trees rock eternally hither and thither with a crashing and
mighty sound. And from their high summits, one by one, drop **8**
everlasting dews. And at the roots strange poisonous flowers
lie writhing in perturbed slumber. And overhead, with a
rustling and loud noise, the gray clouds rush westwardly
forever, until they roll, a cataract, over the fiery wall of the
horizon. But there is no wind throughout the heaven. And by
the shores of the river Zaïre there is neither quiet nor silence.

"It was night, and the rain fell; and, falling, it was rain, but,
having fallen, it was blood. And I stood in the morass among **9**
the tall lilies, and the rain fell upon my head—and the lilies
sighed one unto the other in the solemnity of their desolation.

"And, all at once, the moon arose through the thin ghastly
mist, and was crimson in color. And mine eyes fell upon a **10**
huge gray rock which stood by the shore of the river, and was
lighted by the light of the moon. And the rock was gray, and
ghastly, and tall,—and the rock was gray. Upon its front were
characters engraven in the stone; and I walked through the **11**
morass of water-lilies, until I came close unto the shore, that
I might read the characters upon the stone. But I could not
decipher them. And I was going back into the morass, when
the moon shone with a fuller red, and I turned and looked
again upon the rock, and upon the characters;—and the
characters were DESOLATION.   **12**

"And I looked upward, and there stood a man upon the
summit of the rock; and I hid myself among the water-lilies
that I might discover the actions of the man. And the man was
tall and stately in form, and was wrapped up from his shoulders
to his feet in the toga of old Rome. And the outlines of his **13**

1 From a fragment of Alcman (fl. before 600 B.C.), poet of Sparta and founder of the Dorian school of choral lyric poetry. His verse—simple, clear, and musical—was often sung at festivals. The verse here is quoted by Apollonius of Rhodes in his *Homeric Lexicon*.

2 Some have interpreted this as the Demon of the Imagination.
Poe's first version begins: "There is a spot upon this accursed earth which thou hast never yet beheld. And if by any chance thou *hast* beheld it, it must have been in one of those vigorous dreams which come like the Simoom upon the brain of the sleeper who hath lain down to sleep among the forbidden sunbeams—among the sunbeams, I say, which slide from off the solemn columns of the melancholy temples in the wilderness. The region of which I speak. . . ."

3 The Congo. Zaire is an old African name for the Congo River, and today it is the name for the nation created from the Belgian Congo after independence in 1960. The Portuguese arrived at the mouth of the Congo River in the fifteenth century.
"Libya" was the name the ancient Greeks used for Africa in general. The Romans sometimes used the words to mean Africa and sometimes to mean the fringe containing Carthage.

4 A 1670 map of the region (which remained almost unchanged until the nineteenth century) shows the Nile, Congo, and "Coanza" rivers rising in Lakes "Zaire" and "Zemba," in the center of southern Africa. Most of the inland details, however, are fictional. (John Ogilby, "Africa," in *The Story of Africa and Its Explorers*, by Robert Brown [London, no date])
Although it wasn't discovered by Europeans until the 1870s, Stanley Pool (a lakelike expanse of the Congo about 350 miles from its mouth and covering 320 square miles) fits the description given here.

5 Poe probably means the white Egyptian lotus (*Nymphaea caerulea*), sacred from ancient times and the national emblem of old Egypt. It is a common design in Egyptian art and architecture. Or he may have had in mind an American variety, *Nelumbo lutea*, which is yellow and found along the Atlantic seaboard in his time.

6 "Nature from her seat,/Sighing through all her works,/gave signs of woe/That all was lost" (*Paradise Lost*, IX, 780), referring to the reality of the fall from grace.

7 The Hebrides, or Western Islands, off west and northwest Scotland, number more than five hundred, but fewer than a fifth are inhabited. The stories of Sir Walter Scott did much to make these islands famous. The climate is mild and makes the area popular with visitors, but as might be expected from the location, the rocky coasts are turbulent and often hazardous.
Poe uses the same image in *The Valley Nis* (1831): "There the vague and dream trees/Do roll like seas in northern breeze/Around the stormy Hebrides" (lines 35–37), and in *The Valley of Unrest* (1836). The source, again, seems to be Milton: "Whether beyond the stormy Hebrides" (*Lycidas*, 156); or James Thomson (1700–48): "Or where the Northern ocean, in vast whirls/Boils round the naked melancholy isles/Of farthest Thule, and th'Atlantic surge/Pours in among the stormy Hebrides" (*The Seasons*, 871).

8 Trees that move when there is no wind to stir them add an eerie touch to many fantasy and horror tales, but in Poe they take on an added meaning: that of "senti-

The region of which I speak is a dreary region in Libya, by the borders of the river Zaïre. *Artist unknown*

figure were indistinct—but his features were the features of a deity; for the mantle of the night, and of the mist, and of the moon, and of the dew, had left uncovered the features of his face. And his brow was lofty with thought, and his eye wild with care; and in the few furrows upon his cheek I read the fables of sorrow, and weariness, and disgust with mankind, and a longing after solitude.

"And the man sat upon the rock, and leaned his head upon his hand, and looked out upon the desolation. He looked down into the low unquiet shrubbery, and up into the tall primeval trees, and up higher at the rustling heaven, and into the crimson moon. And I lay close within shelter of the lilies, and observed the actions of the man. And the man trembled in the solitude;—but the night waned, and he sat upon the rock.

"And the man turned his attention from the heaven, and looked out upon the dreary river Zaïre, and upon the yellow ghastly waters, and upon the pale legions of the water-lilies. And the man listened to the sighs of the water-lilies, and to the murmur that came up from among them. And I lay close within my covert and observed the actions of the man. And **14** the man trembled in the solitude;—but the night waned and he sat upon the rock.

"Then I went down into the recesses of the morass and waded afar in among the wilderness of lilies, and called upon the hippopotami which dwelt among the fens in the recesses of the morass. And the hippopotami heard my call, and came, with the behemoth, unto the foot of the rock, and roared **15** loudly and fearfully beneath the moon. And I lay close within my covert and observed the actions of the man. And the man trembled in the solitude;—but the night waned and he sat upon the rock.

"Then I cursed the elements with the curse of tumult; and a frightful tempest gathered in the heaven where, before, there had been no wind. And the heaven became livid with the violence of the tempest—and the rain beat upon the head of the man—and the floods of the river came down—and the river was tormented into foam—and the water-lilies shrieked within their beds—and the forest crumbled before the wind—and the thunder rolled—and the lightning fell—and the rock rocked to its foundation. And I lay close within my covert and observed the actions of the man. And the man trembled in the solitude;—but the night waned and he sat upon the rock.

"Then I grew angry and cursed, with the curse of *silence*, the river, and the lilies, and the wind, and the forest, and the

ence," a word that Poe coined (although "sentient" already existed) meaning consciousness, capability of feeling and perception. This idea is exploited to its fullest in "The Fall of the House of Usher."

Another possibility, suggested by the fact that the clouds in the sky also rush by without benefit of a breeze, is that the spot here is somehow not of the earth, that it shares an identity with some other, faraway place.

9 Red rain has been documented, usually as the result of dust, red algae, or even tiny brine shrimp. Red, however, is also the color of magic, and of blood—and death.

10 A blood-red moon also appears in the last lines of "The Fall of the House of Usher." A symbol of death and destruction, Poe probably borrowed it from Revelation 6:12; ". . . and the moon became as blood."

11 Characters carved in stone also appear in Poe's novel *The Narrative of Arthur Gordon Pym*, but so large that Pym walks through them, thinking they are only passages in the rock.

12 The "abomination of desolation" comes from Matthew 24:14–16: ". . . and then shall the end come. When ye therefore shall see the abomination of desolation, spoken of by Daniel the prophet, stand in the holy place. . . . Then let them which be in Judaea flee into the mountains. . . ." In Poe's *The Coliseum* (1833), stanza 2, we find "Silence! and Desolation! and dim Night!"

"The seat of desolation, void of light" is from *Paradise Lost* (I, 181), and in Proverbs 1:27–28, we read: "When your fear cometh as desolation, and your destruction cometh as a whirlwind; when distress and anguish cometh upon you. Then shall they call upon me, but I will not answer; they shall seek me early, but they shall not find me. . . ."

"Desolation" here means both a bleak and forbidding landscape and the biblical meaning of shunned or wasted by God. Poe's point is that, as terrible as desolation may be, absolute silence is worse.

13 Pliny, in *Natural History* (V, 1), reports that many important Romans claimed to have explored Africa as far inland as Mount Atlas. A merchant named Diogenes boasted of having made his way inland as far as what we know today as Mount Kilimanjaro, in Tanzania.

14 A hiding place

15 "Behold now behemoth, which I made with thee; he eateth grass as an ox. . . . He lieth under the shady trees, in the covert of the reed, and fens. . . . Behold, he drinketh up a river, and hasteth not; he trusteth that he can draw up Jordan into his mouth. (Job 40:15–24)

The behemoth is probably the hippopotamus, but the word has been translated as elephant, which accounts for Poe's usage here. According to the O.E.D., the word may be a plural of the Hebrew word for beast, or it may be the Hebrew pronunciation of the Egyptian *p-che-mau*, or water ox.

Although most people pronounce it with the accent on the first syllable, the stress properly belongs on the second.

. . . his features were the features of a deity; for the mantle of the night, and of the mist, and of the moon, and of the dew, had left uncovered the features of his face. *Illustration by Fortune Louis Meaulle, 1856*

16 In *Vathek* (1786), the Gothic novel by William Beckford (1760–1844), there is a cliff on which are engraved letters illuminated "by the splendor of the moon, which streamed full on the place . . . like those on the sabres of the Giaour, and which possessed the same virtue of changing every minute" (*Three Gothic Novels*, Penguin Books, 1968; p. 244).

"There is a silence where hath been no sound,/There is a silence where no sound may be,/In the cold grave—under the deep, deep sea,/Or in wide desert where no life is found" (*Silence*, by Thomas Hood [1827]).

17 "The voice of him that crieth in the wilderness" (Isaiah 40:3); also, "She is empty, and void, and waste. . . ." (Nahum 2:10)

18 Persian priests, probably Median (now Iranian) in origin, who, according to Herodotus, were a tribe rather than a priestly family (Zoroaster was probably a Magus). Although some historians credit them with forming a pre-Zoroastrian religion, we actually know nothing about them except through inference. The word "magic" stems from their name, for they were supposed to have power over demons. The most famous Magi were, of course, the Wise Men of the Gospels. There are no "volumes of the Magi."

19 "Genii" is the plural of "genius," in the sense of a spirit, and is also the English approximation of the Arabian *djinn*, or genie.

The Persian and Indian genii had a corporeal form, which they could change at their pleasure. There were not guardian or attendant spirits but fallen angels who dwelled in Ginnistan under the dominion of Eblis. They were hostile to man but sometimes compelled to serve him as slaves (as in the tale of Aladdin).

20 For more on the sibyls, see "MS. Found in a Bottle," note 45.

"Day of wrath and doom impending,/David's word with Sibyl's blending,/Heaven and earth in ashes ending!" (*Dies Irae* of Tommaso di Celano [1185–1255])

21 Dodona was the most ancient oracle of Zeus in Greece, built by Deucalion after the flood and centered around an oak tree. It was situated in Epirus, on the Ionian Sea west of Macedon and Thessaly. Priests and priestesses interpreted the sound of the wind through the leaves as messages from the god.

Another version has it that plates of brass were suspended from the oak trees of Dodona which, when struck with thongs moved by the wind, gave out various sounds from which prophecies were derived. The Greek phrase *Kalkos Dodones* (brass of Dodona) means a babbler, or one who talks a great deal about nothing.

22 The lynx was sacred to Apollo, the god of divination and prophecy (among other things). Proverbial for its piercing eyesight, the ancient lynx was a mythical beast, half dog and half panther, but not like either in character. The catlike animal now called a lynx is not known for keen-sightedness.

23 See the ending of "The Man of the Crowd": "I grew wearied . . . and . . . gazed at him steadfastly in the face."

Poe may have had in mind this quote from Pindar (518–438 B.C.): "Not every truth is the better for showing its face undisguised; and often silence is the wisest thing for a man to heed" (*Nemean Odes*, V, 30).

heaven, and the thunder, and the sighs of the water-lilies. And they became accursed, and *were still*. And the moon ceased to totter up its pathway to heaven—and the thunder died away—and the lightning did not flash—and the clouds hung motionless—and the waters sunk to their level and remained—and the trees ceased to rock—and the water-lilies sighed no more—and the murmur was heard no longer from among them, nor any shadow of sound throughout the vast illimitable desert. And I looked upon the characters of the rock, and they were changed; and the characters were SI-**16** LENCE.

"And mine eyes fell upon the countenance of the man, and his countenance was wan with terror. And, hurriedly, he raised his head from his hand, and stood forth upon the rock and listened. But there was no voice throughout the vast **17** illimitable desert, and the characters upon the rock were SILENCE. And the man shuddered, and turned his face away, and fled afar off, in haste, so that I beheld him no more."

* * *

18 Now there are fine tales in the volumes of the Magi—in the iron-bound, melancholy volumes of the Magi. Therein, I say, are glorious histories of the Heaven, and of the Earth, and of **19** the mighty sea—and of the Genii that overruled the sea, and the earth, and the lofty heaven. There was much lore too in **20** the sayings which were said by the Sibyls; and holy, holy things were heard of old by the dim leaves that trembled **21** around Dodona—but, as Allah liveth, that fable which the Demon told me as he sat by my side in the shadow of the tomb, I hold to be the most wonderful of all! And as the Demon made an end of his story, he fell back within the cavity of the tomb and laughed. And I could not laugh with the Demon, and he cursed me because I could not laugh. And **22** the lynx which dwelleth forever in the tomb, came out therefrom, and lay down at the feet of the Demon, and looked **23** at him steadily in the face.

THE UNPARALLELED ADVENTURE OF ONE HANS PFAALL

First published in the *Southern Literary Messenger*, June 1835, "Hans Pfaall" is sometimes considered one of the first true science-fiction tales, but the quality of hoax is also strong, and ultimately works against the fantastic elements of the story.

On a literal level, "Hans Pfaall" tells about a bankrupt bellows mender who fakes a trip to the moon in an elaborate ruse to shake off his creditors. On another level, it is a dream voyage, a much different kind of escape from those same problems. On still another level, it may be a satire on the kind of metaphysical speculation that sends one into rarified regions—here in a balloon appropriately filled with hot air and shaped like a foolscap.

One offbeat interpretation, that of Allen H. Greer, is that "Hans Pfaall" is at least partly an allegorical parody on the life and times of President Andrew Jackson, whom Poe thought was a rather crude and untrustworthy politician (*Emerson Society Quarterly* [*ESQ*], Fall 1970, pp. 67–73).

Poe was interested in astronomy most of his life, as one can see from the number of references to stars in his works and the complicated cosmology of *Eureka* (1848). The principal source material for "Hans Pfaall" is Sir John Herschel's *Treatise on Astronomy* (1834). Herschel (1792–1871), the son of William Herschel (1738–1822), who was also a celebrated astronomer, confirmed his father's observations of double stars, was able to add new ones to those previously recognized, and extended his study to the nebulae. Of the two, the father was perhaps the greater, if only for his pioneering work, but the two of them together gave birth to modern astronomy.

Another possible source is George Tucker (1775–1861), who under the name of Joseph Atterley wrote *A Voyage to the Moon* (1827), one of the first modern books to suggest that a traveler could cross the cold, airless void to the moon.

Three weeks after Poe's tale was published, there appeared in the New York *Sun* a story by Richard Adams Locke entitled "Discoveries in the Moon." Supposedly reprinted from the Edinburgh *Courant and Journal of Science*, it contained some very specific echoes of Poe's tale.

"Have you seen the 'Discoveries in the Moon'?" Poe wrote to John P. Kennedy in September 1835. "Do you not think it altogether suggested by *Hans Phaal*? [Poe changed the spelling of his character's name several times.] It is very singular—but when I proposed writing a Tale concerning the Moon, the idea of *Telescope* discoveries suggested itself to me—but I afterwards abandoned it [Locke's tale was of Moon landscapes, cities and inhabitants all seen through a telescope]. I had however spoken of it freely, & from many little incidents & apparently trivial remarks in those *Discoveries* I am convinced that the idea was stolen from myself."

Poe, however, was so obsessed by the notion of plagiarism throughout his career that one wonders how true his suspicions were. Locke's tale is not at all concerned with a space voyage, as is "Hans Pfaall," but it may have stolen Poe's thunder in regard to the sequel promised at the end of the tale. At any rate, Poe did not press the charge further.

However, we do know that "Hans Pfaall" was meant to be a longer work. "The chief design in carrying my hero to the moon was to afford him an opportunity of describing the lunar scenery, but I found that he could add very little to the minute and authentic account of Sir John Herschel. The first part of 'Hans Phaall,' occupying about eighteen pages of 'the Messenger,' embraced merely a journal of the passage between the two orbs and a few words of general observation on the most obvious features of the satellite; the second part will most probably never appear. I did not think it advisable even to bring my voyager back to his parent earth. He remains where I left him, and is still, I believe, 'the man in the moon.' "

1 From *Wit and Drollery* (1661), but the title comes from Isaac D'Israeli's chapter on "Tom o'Bedlams" in *Curiosities of Literature* (1832). The complete stanza runs:

> With a heart of furious fancies
> Whereof I am commander;
> With a burning spear,
> And a horse of air,
> To the wilderness I wander;
> With a knight of ghosts and shadows;
> I summoned am to Tourney;
> Ten leagues beyond
> The wide world's end;
> Methinks it is no journey!

Poe echoes this idea in *Eldorado*.

A "Tom o'Bedlam" is a beggar who asks for alms on the basis of insanity. "Bedlam" is a contraction for Bethlehem (St. Mary's of Bethlehem), an institution for the insane in London, which was originally set up to accommodate six inmates but admitted forty-four in 1644 and had to dismiss many patients "half-cured." These "ticket-of-leave" men used to wander about as vagrants, singing mad songs and dressed in fantastic costumes in order to excite pity. Soon, however, a street-wise group of vagrants began impersonating these Tom o'Bedlams in order to extract money out of unwary passersby.

2 Rotterdam was a commercial center, not an intellectual one. Poe uses a similar touch in "Bon-Bon."

3 "Together by the ears" means full of ill will—i.e., quarreling and pulling each other's ears.

4 The market square

5 Rotterdam was indeed "well-conditioned" (well off), because of the separation in 1830 of Belgium from the Netherlands, which diverted trade from Antwerp to the Dutch city. However, its greatest growth took place in the latter half of the nineteenth century, when a new waterway made the port accessible to seagoing ships. The entire center of the city was destroyed by German air bombardment in 1940.

6 The atmosphere and the humor here owe much to Washington Irving, whose tales of the Dutch in America are chronicled in *Knickerbocker's History of New York* (1809). Even the phrasing here is more typical of Irving than of Poe.

7 The Dutch were great pipe smokers, accounting for the great clouds of smoke in Poe's description of the city. "He smoked and doubted eight hours, and he slept the remaining twelve of the four-and-twenty," says Irving of Wouter Van Twiller.

> *With a heart of furious fancies,*
> *Whereof I am commander,*
> *With a burning spear and a horse of air,*
> *To the wilderness I wander.*
> Tom O'Bedlam's Song
> *Artist unknown*

> With a heart of furious fancies,
> Whereof I am commander,
> With a burning spear and a horse of air,
> To the wilderness I wander.
> —*Tom O'Bedlam's Song*.

1

2 By late accounts from Rotterdam, that city seems to be in a high state of philosophical excitement. Indeed, phenomena have there occurred of a nature so completely unexpected—so entirely novel—so utterly at variance with preconceived opinions—as to leave no doubt on my mind that long ere this all Europe is in an uproar, all physics in a ferment, all reason **3** and astronomy together by the ears.

It appears that on the —— day of ——, (I am not positive about the date,) a vast crowd of people, for purposes not specifically mentioned, were assembled in the great square of **4,5** the Exchange in the well-conditioned city of Rotterdam. The day was warm—unusually so for the season—there was hardly a breath of air stirring; and the multitude were in no bad humor at being now and then besprinkled with friendly showers of momentary duration, that fell from large white masses of clouds profusely distributed about the blue vault of the firmament. Nevertheless, about noon, a slight but remarkable agitation became apparent in the assembly: the clattering of ten thousand tongues succeeded; and, in an instant afterward, ten thousand faces were upturned toward **6,7** the heavens, ten thousand pipes descended simultaneously from the corners of ten thousand mouths, and a shout, which could be compared to nothing but the roaring of Niagara, resounded long, loudly, and furiously, through all the city and through all the environs of Rotterdam.

The origin of this hubbub soon became sufficiently evident.

From behind the huge bulk of one of those sharply defined masses of cloud already mentioned, was seen slowly to emerge into an open area of blue space, a queer, heterogeneous, but apparently solid substance, so oddly shaped, so whimsically put together, as not to be in any manner comprehended, and never to be sufficiently admired, by the host of sturdy burghers who stood open-mouthed below. What could it be? In the name of all the devils in Rotterdam, what could it possibly portend? No one knew; no one could imagine; no one—not even the burgomaster Mynheer Superbus Von Underduk—had the slightest clew by which to unravel the mystery; so, as nothing more reasonable could be done, every one to a man replaced his pipe carefully in the corner of his mouth, and maintaining an eye steadily upon the phenomenon, puffed, paused, waddled about, and grunted significantly—then waddled back, grunted, paused, and finally—puffed again.

In the meantime, however, lower and still lower toward the goodly city, came the object of so much curiosity, and the cause of so much smoke. In a very few minutes it arrived near enough to be accurately discerned. It appeared to be—yes! it *was* undoubtedly a species of balloon; but surely no *such* balloon had ever been seen in Rotterdam before. For who, let me ask, ever heard of a balloon manufactured entirely of dirty newspapers? No man in Holland certainly; yet here, under **8** the very noses of the people, or rather at some distance *above* their noses, was the identical thing in question, and composed, I have it on the very best authority, of the precise material which no one had ever before known to be used for a similar purpose. It was an egregious insult to the good sense of the burghers of Rotterdam. As to the shape of the phenomenon, it was even still more reprehensible. Being little or nothing better than a huge fool's-cap turned upside down. And this **9** similitude was regarded as by no means lessened when, upon nearer inspection, the crowd saw a large tassel depending from its apex, and, around the upper rim or base of the cone, a circle of little instruments, resembling sheep-bells, which kept up a continual tinkling to the tune of Betty Martin. But **10** still worse.—Suspended by blue ribbons to the end of this fantastic machine, there hung, by way of car, an enormous drab beaver hat, with a brim superlatively broad, and a **11** hemispherical crown with a black band and a silver buckle. It is, however, somewhat remarkable that many citizens of Rotterdam swore to having seen the same hat repeatedly before; and indeed the whole assembly seemed to regard it with eyes of familiarity; while the vrow Grettel Pfaall, upon sight of it, uttered an exclamation of joyful surprise, and declared it to be the identical hat of her good man himself. **12** Now this was a circumstance the more to be observed, as Pfaall, with three companions, had actually disappeared from Rotterdam about five years before, in a very sudden and unaccountable manner, and up to the date of this narrative all attempts at obtaining intelligence concerning them had failed. To be sure, some bones which were thought to be human, mixed up with a quantity of odd-looking rubbish, had been

. . . a vast crowd of people . . . were assembled in the great square of the Exchange in the well-conditioned city of Rotterdam. *Illustration by F. S. Coburn, 1902*

8 This is an oblique reference to the shoddy practice of newspapers publishing hoaxes as actual fact—something that Poe had no compunction about in his "The Balloon-Hoax."

9 A fool's cap is conical in shape and usually garnished with bells, but in the nineteenth century it was made of paper and, as the dunce cap, was used to brand lazy or troublesome young students.

The word also defines a sixteen-by-thirteen-inch piece of paper specifically designed for manuscript writing (from the fool's cap watermark design once applied to the paper).

Given the first meaning of the word, the balloon can be seen as a practical joke, or hoax, but the second sense of "fool's cap" has led some scholars to suggest that the tale satirizes the hack writer's flight of fancy.

10 There is no known song of this title, but there is an old English proverb: "That's all my eye, and Betty Martin!" meaning something is nonsense or ridiculous. "Martin" has in the past referred to a drunkard, a fool, and a jackass.

11 In Poe's day, beaver pelts were used chiefly in the making of men's hats, since they were warm and soft to the touch. Such hats were not "fur hats" as we know them, but lightweight and crisp-looking.

12 Another echo of Washington Irving, specifically Rip Van Winkle, who disappeared for twenty years, leaving behind a nagging wife.

Poe's couple are named Hans and Grettel—one more hint to the fairytale nature of the story.

Marie Bonaparte makes a case for the hero's last name as "phallus," particularly in its earlier spelling ("Phaall"). There is the German word *pfahl*, "stake," which also hints at a Freudian sexual interpretation, but one could just as easily point to the Latin *follis*, or bellows, which in Late Latin became a word for "windbag," and eventually turned into the French *fou* and the English "fool."

13 Referring to the late-eighteenth-century style of pulling the hair back and tying it with a ribbon

14 Inflamed

15 Literally, "overall," meaning a long, close-fitting overcoat

16 Short trousers covering the hips and thighs, and fitting snugly at the lower edges, just below the knee

17 "Taffety" is another form of "taffeta," a crisp, plain-woven, lustrous cloth (Persian *taftah*).

18 The first sign that he has returned from space, where there is no gravity

19 Superbus Von Underduk's name means "best of the cringers."

20 "Aeronaut" was in common use by 1784.

lately discovered in a retired situation to the east of the city; and some people went so far as to imagine that in this spot a foul murder had been committed, and that the sufferers were in all probability Hans Pfaall and his associates. But to return.

The balloon (for such no doubt it was) had now descended to within a hundred feet of the earth, allowing the crowd below a sufficiently distinct view of the person of its occupant. This was in truth a very singular somebody. He could not have been more than two feet in height; but this altitude, little as it was, would have been sufficient to destroy his *equilibrium*, and tilt him over the edge of his tiny car, but for the intervention of a circular rim reaching as high as the breast, and rigged on to the cords of the balloon. The body of the little man was more than proportionally broad, giving to his entire figure a rotundity highly absurd. His feet, of course, could not be seen at all. His hands were enormously

13 large. His hair was gray, and collected into a *queue* behind.

14 His nose was prodigiously long, crooked, and inflammatory, his eyes full, brilliant, and acute; his chin and cheeks, although wrinkled with age, were broad, puffy, and double; but of ears of any kind there was not a semblance to be discovered upon any portion of his head. This odd little gentleman was dressed

15,16 in a loose surtout of sky-blue satin, with tight breeches to match, fastened with silver buckles at the knees. His vest was

17 of some bright yellow material; a white taffety cap was set jauntily on one side of his head; and, to complete his equipment, a blood-red silk handkerchief enveloped his throat, and fell down, in a dainty manner, upon his bosom, in a fantastic bow-knot of super-eminent dimensions.

Having descended, as I said before, to about one hundred feet from the surface of the earth, the little old gentleman was suddenly seized with a fit of trepidation, and appeared disinclined to make any nearer approach to *terra firma*. Throwing out, therefore, a quantity of sand from a canvas bag, which he lifted with great difficulty, he became stationary in an instant. He then proceeded, in a hurried and agitated manner, to extract from a side-pocket in his surtout a large morocco pocket-book. This he poised suspiciously in his hand, then eyed it with an air of extreme surprise, and was evidently

18 astonished at its weight. He at length opened it, and drawing therefrom a huge letter sealed with red sealing-wax and tied carefully with red tape, let it fall precisely at the feet of the

19 burgomaster, Superbus Von Underduk. His Excellency

20 stooped to take it up. But the æronaut, still greatly discomposed, and having apparently no further business to detain him in Rotterdam, began at this moment to make busy preparations for departure; and it being necessary to discharge a portion of ballast to enable him to reascend, the half dozen bags which he threw out, one after another, without taking the trouble to empty their contents, tumbled, every one of them, most unfortunately upon the back of the burgomaster, and rolled him over and over no less than half a dozen times, in the face of every individual in Rotterdam. It is not to be supposed, however, that the great Underduk suffered this impertinence on the part of the little old man to pass off with impunity. It is said, on the contrary, that during each of his half dozen circumvolutions, he emitted no less than half a dozen distinct and furious whiffs from his pipe, to which he held fast the whole time with all his might, and to which he intends holding fast (God willing) until the day of his decease.

In the meantime the balloon arose like a lark, and, soaring **21** far away above the city, at length drifted quietly behind a cloud similar to that from which it had so oddly emerged, and was thus lost forever to the wondering eyes of the good citizens of Rotterdam. All attention was now directed to the letter, the descent of which, and the consequences attending thereupon, had proved so fatally subversive of both person and personal dignity to his Excellency, Von Underduk. That functionary, however, had not failed, during his circumgyratory move- **22** ments, too bestow a thought upon the important object of securing the epistle, which was seen, upon inspection, to have fallen into the most proper hands, being actually addressed to himself and Professor Rubadub, in their official capacities **23** of President and Vice-President of the Rotterdam College of Astronomy. It was accordingly opened by those dignitaries upon the spot, and found to contain the following extraordinary and indeed very serious, communication:—

"To their Excellencies Von Underduk and Rubadub, President and Vice-President of the States' College of Astronomers, in the city of Rotterdam.

"Your Excellencies may perhaps be able to remember an humble artizan, by name Hans Pfaall, and by occupation a mender of bellows, who, with three others, disappeared from Rotterdam, about five years ago, in a manner which must have been considered unaccountable. If, however, it so please your Excellencies, I, the writer of this communication, am the identical Hans Pfaall himself. It is well known to most of my fellow-citizens, that for the period of forty years I continued to occupy the little square brick building, at the head of the alley called Sauerkraut, in which I resided at the time of my disappearance. My ancestors have also resided therein time out of mind—they, as well as myself, steadily following the respectable and indeed lucrative profession of mending of bellows: for, to speak the truth, until of late years, that the heads of all the people have been set agog with politics, no better business than my own could an honest citizen of Rotterdam either desire or deserve. Credit was good, employment was never wanting, and there was no lack of either money or good-will. But, as I was saying, we soon began to feel the effects of liberty and long speeches, and radicalism, and all that sort of thing. People who were formerly the best customers in the world, had now not a moment of time to think of us at all. They had as much as they could do to read about the revolutions, and keep up with the march of intellect and the spirit of the age. If a fire wanted fanning, it could **24** readily be fanned with a newspaper; and as the government **25** grew weaker, I have no doubt that leather and iron acquired

21 In Elizabeth Barrett Browning's *Aurora Leigh* (1857), a lark is "sucked up out of sight / In vortices of glory and blue air."

22 Poe coined this word, although "circumgyration" dates to 1603 and "circumgyre" to 1583.

23 In the nursery rhyme "Rub-a-dub-dub, Three Men in a Tub," the men are "knaves all three."

24 Once improvements in printing made newspapers cheap enough for the general populace, there was an explosion of new titles, with newspapers surfacing (and sinking) regularly. At the same time, political tracts and broadsides continued in their efforts to persuade and convince the better-educated.

25 Journalism in the 1800s was a far cry from the objective stance preferred today. Newspaper articles were a jumble of fact, fancy, and personal opinion.

. . . it being necessary to discharge . . . the half dozen bags which he threw out, one after another, without taking the trouble to empty their contents, tumbled, every one of them, most unfortunately upon the back of the burgomaster. . . . *Artist unknown*

26 A short firearm with a large bore and usually a flaring muzzle to make it effective at close quarters when loaded with a number of balls. The origin of the name seems to be the old Dutch word *donderbus* ("thunder gun").

27 Johann Franz Encke (1791–1865) was a German astronomer who was director of the observatory at Seeberg and later director of the Berlin observatory. He is best known for his study of the orbit of the comet of 1680 and for calculations, based on transits of Venus, of the earth's distance from the sun.

The Frenchman is probably J. L. Pons, of Marseilles, who named the comet after Encke.

28 A trace, a smattering

29 Pneumatics is the branch of mechanics that deals with the mechanical properties of gases.

30 Nantes is a busy city on the Loire, in western France.

31 The 1835 text continued: "In other words, I believed, and still do believe, that truth is frequently, of its own essence, superficial, and that, in many cases, the depth lies more in the abysses where we seek her, than in the actual situations wherein she may be found. . . ." This and the rest of the paragraph that follows can be found, somewhat altered, in the mouth of Dupin in "The Murders in the Rue Morgue."

durability in proportion—for, in a very short time, there was not a pair of bellows in all Rotterdam that ever stood in need of a stitch or required the assistance of a hammer. This was a state of things not to be endured. I soon grew as poor as a rat, and, having a wife and children to provide for, my burdens at length became intolerable, and I spent hour after hour in reflecting upon the most convenient method of putting an end to my life. Duns, in the meantime, left me little leisure for contemplation. My house was literally besieged from morning till night. There were three fellows in particular who worried me beyond endurance, keeping watch continually about my door, and threatening me with the law. Upon these three I vowed the bitterest revenge, if ever I should be so happy as to get them within my clutches; and I believe nothing in the world but the pleasure of this anticipation prevented me from putting my plan of suicide into immediate execution, by **26** blowing my brains out with a blunderbuss. I thought it best, however, to dissemble my wrath, and to treat them with promises and fair words, until, by some good turn of fate, an opportunity of vengeance should be afforded me.

"One day, having given them the slip, and feeling more than usually dejected, I continued for a long time to wander about the most obscure streets without object, until at length I chanced to stumble against the corner of a bookseller's stall. Seeing a chair close at hand, for the use of customers, I threw myself doggedly into it, and, hardly knowing why, opened the pages of the first volume which came within my reach. It proved to be a small pamphlet treatise on Speculative Astronomy, written either by Professor Encke of Berlin or by a **27** Frenchman of somewhat similar name. I had some little **28** tincture of information on matters of this nature, and soon became more and more absorbed in the contents of the book— reading it actually through twice before I awoke to a recollection of what was passing around me. By this time it began to grow dark, and I directed my steps toward home. But the **29** treatise (in conjunction with a discovery in pneumatics, lately communicated to me as an important secret, by a cousin from **30** Nantz) had made an indelible impression on my mind, and, as I sauntered along the dusky streets, I revolved carefully over in my memory the wild and sometimes unintelligible reasonings of the writer. There are some particular passages which affected my imagination in an extraordinary manner. The longer I meditated upon these, the more intense grew the interest which had been excited within me. The limited nature of my education in general, and more especially my ignorance on subjects connected with natural philosophy, so far from rendering me diffident of my own ability to comprehend what I had read, or inducing me to mistrust the many vague notions which had arisen in consequence, merely served as a farther stimulus to imagination; and I was vain enough, or perhaps reasonable enough, to doubt whether those crude ideas which, arising in ill-regulated minds, have all the appearance, may not often in effect possess all the force, the **31** reality, and other inherent properties, of instinct or intuition.

"It was late when I reached home, and I went immediately to bed. My mind, however, was too much occupied to sleep, and I lay the whole night buried in meditation. Arising early in the morning, I repaired eagerly to the bookseller's stall, and laid out what little ready money I possessed, in the purchase of some volumes of Mechanics and Practical Astronomy. Having arrived at home safely with these, I devoted every spare moment to their perusal, and soon made such proficiency in studies of this nature as I thought sufficient for the execution of a certain design with which either the devil or my better genius had inspired me. In the intervals of this period, I made every endeavor to conciliate the three creditors who had given me so much annoyance. In this I finally succeeded—partly by selling enough of my household furniture to satisfy a moiety of their claim; and partly by a promise **32** of paying the balance upon completion of a little project which I told them I had in view, and for assistance in which I solicited their services. By these means (for they were ignorant men) I found little difficulty in gaining them over to my purpose.

"Matters being thus arranged, I contrived, by the aid of my wife and with the greatest secrecy and caution, to dispose of what property I had remaining, and to borrow, in small sums, under various pretences, and without giving any attention (I am ashamed to say) to my future means of repayment, no inconsiderable quantity of ready money. With the means thus accruing I proceeded to procure at intervals, cambric muslin, **33** very fine, in pieces of twelve yards each; twine; a lot of the varnish of caoutchouc, a large and deep basket of wicker-work, **34** made to order; and several other articles necessary in the construction and equipment of a balloon of extraordinary dimensions. This I directed my wife to make up as soon as possible, and gave her all requisite information as to the particular method of proceeding. In the meantime I worked up the twine into net-work of sufficient dimensions; rigged it with a hoop and the necessary cords; and made purchase of numerous instruments and materials for experiment in the upper regions of the upper atmosphere. I then took opportunities of conveying by night, to a retired situation east of Rotterdam, five iron-bound casks, to contain about fifty gallons each, and one of a larger size; six tin tubes, three inches in diameter, properly shaped, and ten feet in length; a quantity of a *particular metallic substance, or semi-metal*, which I shall not name, and a dozen demijohns of *a very common acid*. The **35** gas to be formed from these latter materials is a gas never yet generated by any other person than myself—or at least never applied to any similar purpose. I can only venture to say here, that it is *a constituent of azote*, so long considered irreducible, and that its density is about 37.4 times *less than that of hydrogen*. It is tasteless, but not odorless; burns, when pure, with a greenish flame; and is instantaneously fatal to animal life. Its full secret I would make no difficulty in disclosing, but **36** that it of right belongs (as I have before hinted) to a citizen of Nantz, in France, by whom it was conditionally commu- **37**

32 One of two equal parts

33 A fine, white linen fabric, although the term is here applied to a cotton fabric that resembles cambric.

34 Rubber, from the old Spanish word *cauchuc*, which in turn came from the *Quechua* Indian word *cauchu*. Ainé and Cadêt Robert, eighteenth-century French balloonists, first claimed to have made fine silk impermeable to hydrogen leaks by coating it with a solution of rubber.

35 Narrow-necked glass bottles or stoneware enclosed in wickerwork and holding up to ten gallons, often used for corrosive liquids. The word comes from the popular name for the container, "Dame Jeanne."

36 In *Symzonia* (1820), by John Cleves Symmes, inhabitants of the hollow, inner earth fly in large cylindrical balloons filled with "an elastic gas, which was readily made by putting a small quantity of a very dense substance into some fluid, which disengaged a vast quantity of this light gas."

In the late-eighteenth century, Jacques Alexandre César Charles (1746–1823) generated hydrogen gas for his balloon ascents by the action of sulphuric acid on iron filings, using 498 pounds of acid and 1,000 pounds of iron. The first gas generator looked something like a chest of drawers, the iron and acid fed into a series of lead-lined compartments linked by a pipe to a main valve at the neck of the balloon. So much heat was generated by the process, however, that water had to be poured over the balloon to cool it. The water vapor began condensing inside and accumulated above the neck, causing more problems. (L. T. C. Rolt, *The Aeronauts*, Walker, 1966; p. 32)

37 The city is best known for the Edict of Nantes (1598), in which Henry IV of France gave religious freedom to all Protestants; it was repealed by Louis XIV in 1685.

38 The name of the animal is not mentioned, probably because there is no such membrane that could prevent gas from escaping in the vacuum of space.

39 A fuse meant a loosely twisted hemp cord steeped in a solution of saltpeter (potassium chloride) and lime water. It burns at a rate of one yard in three hours. A "quick match" was cotton impregnated with the same solution, then coated with gum and mealed gunpowder for much faster action.

40 The air pump devised by Joseph Priestley (1733–1804) was well known in Poe's time and appeared in numerous books on physics. It could be used to pump air out of a container in order to form a vacuum, or to increase the pressure in a container by reversing the mechanism.

The Grimm mentioned here is unidentified.

41 Rip Van Winkle's wife also accused her husband of being shiftless, and scolded him mercilessly. When he disappeared, she apparently did just fine without him.

nicated to myself. The same individual submitted to me, without being at all aware of my intentions, a method of constructing balloons from the membrane of a certain animal, through which substance any escape of gas was nearly an **38** impossibility. I found it however altogether too expensive, and was not sure, upon the whole, whether cambric muslin with a coating of gum caoutchouc, was not equally as good. I mention this circumstance, because I think it probable that hereafter the individual in question may attempt a balloon ascension with the novel gas and material I have spoken of, and I do not wish to deprive him of the honor of a very singular invention.

"On the spot which I intended each of the smaller casks to occupy respectively during the inflation of the balloon, I privately dug a small hole; the holes forming in this manner a circle twenty-five feet in diameter. In the centre of this circle, being the station designed for the large cask, I also dug a hole of greater depth. In each of the five smaller holes, I deposited a canister containing fifty pounds, and in the larger one a keg holding one hundred and fifty pounds, of cannon powder. These—the keg and canisters—I connected in a proper manner with covered trains; and having let into one **39** of the canisters the end of about four feet of slow-match, I covered up the hole, and placed the cask over it, leaving the other end of the match protruding about an inch, and barely visible beyond the cask. I then filled up the remaining holes, and placed the barrels over them in their destined situation!

"Besides the articles above enumerated, I conveyed to the *dépôt,* and there secreted, one of M. Grimm's improvements **40** upon the apparatus for condensation of the atmospheric air. I found this machine, however, to require considerable alteration before it could be adapted to the purposes to which I intended making it applicable. But, with severe labor and unremitting perseverance, I at length met with entire success in all my preparations. My balloon was soon completed. It would contain more than forty thousand cubic feet of gas; would take me up easily, I calculated, with all my implements, and, if I managed rightly, with one hundred and seventy-five pounds of ballast into the bargain. It had received three coats of varnish, and I found the cambric muslin to answer all the purposes of silk itself, being quite as strong and a good deal less expensive.

"Everything being now ready, I exacted from my wife an oath of secrecy in relation to all my actions from the day of my first visit to the bookseller's stall; and promising, on my part, to return as soon as circumstances would permit, I gave her what little money I had left, and bade her farewell. Indeed I had no fear on her account. She was what people call a notable woman, and could manage matters in the world without my assistance. I believe, to tell the truth, she always looked upon me as an idle body—a mere make-weight—good for nothing but building castles in the air,—and was rather **41** glad to get rid of me. It was a dark night when I bade her goodbye, and taking with me, as *aides-de-camp,* the three creditors who had given me so much trouble, we carried the balloon, with the car and accoutrements, by a roundabout way, to the station where the other articles were deposited. We there found them all unmolested, and I proceeded immediately to business.

"It was the first of April. The night, as I said before, was dark; there was not a star to be seen; and a drizzling rain, falling at intervals, rendered us very uncomfortable. But my chief anxiety was concerning the balloon, which, in spite of the varnish with which it was defended, began to grow rather heavy with the moisture; the powder also was liable to damage. I therefore kept my three duns working with great diligence, pounding down ice around the central cask, and stirring the acid in the others. They did not cease, however, importuning me with questions as to what I intended to do with all this apparatus, and expressed much dissatisfaction at the terrible labor I made them undergo. They could not perceive (so they said) what good was likely to result from their getting wet to the skin, merely to take a part in such horrible incantations. I began to get uneasy, and worked away with all my might, for I verily believe the idiots supposed that I had entered into a compact with the devil, and that, in short what I was now doing was nothing better than it should be. I was, therefore, in great fear of their leaving me altogether. I contrived, however, to pacify them by promises of payment of all scores **42** in full, as soon as I could bring the present business to a termination. To these speeches they gave, of course, their own interpretation; fancying, no doubt, that at all events I should come into possession of vast quantities of ready money; and provided I paid them all I owed, and a trifle more, in consideration of their services, I dare say they cared very little what became of either my soul or my carcass.

"In about four hours and a half I found the balloon sufficiently inflated. I attached the car, therefore, and put all my implements in it: a telescope; a barometer, with some important modifications; a thermometer; an electrometer; a compass; a **43,44** magnetic needle; a seconds watch; a bell; a speaking-trumpet, **45,46** etc., etc., etc.—also a globe of glass, exhausted of air, and carefully closed with a stopper—not forgetting the condensing apparatus, some unslacked lime, a stick of sealing-wax, a copious supply of water, and a large quantity of provisions, such as pemmican, in which much nutriment is contained in **47** comparatively little bulk. I also secured in the car a pair of pigeons and a cat.

"It was now nearly daybreak, and I thought it high time to take my departure. Dropping a lighted cigar on the ground, as if by accident, I took the opportunity, in stooping to pick it up, of igniting privately the piece of slow-match, the end of which as I said before, protruded a little beyond the lower rim of one of the smaller casks. This manœuvre was totally unperceived on the part of the three duns; and, jumping into the car, I immediately cut the single cord which held me to the earth, and was pleased to find that I shot upward with inconceivable rapidity, carrying with all ease one hundred and

42 "Score" meant a customer's debt, but to "settle," "clear," or "pay" a score meant to revenge an injury, as early as 1617.

43 An instrument for measuring the quantity and quality of electricity in an electrified body (1749); often two gold leaves, attached to a metal plate, that separate in the presence of an electrical charge

44 The "compass" here may refer to an instrument for fixing the constellation Pyxis, also called the "mariner's compass," since it was used to determine one's location. The "magnetic needle" is what we normally call a compass today.

45 Stopwatch

46 Megaphone

47 A concentrated food used by North American Indians, made of deer meat dried, pounded fine, and mixed with melted fat. It seems unlikely that a Dutchman would use the word.

48 Balloon flights date to 1773, when the Montgolfier brothers experimented with inverted paper bags filled with hot air. In 1783 they managed to get a linen bag about one hundred feet in diameter off the ground. That same year, Pilâtre de Rozier made the first manned ascent, to a height of eighty-four feet.

Hydrogen was first used, in 1783, by J. A. C. Charles, who with the brothers Robert, traveled twenty-seven miles from his starting point. The first sea voyage was made by Dr. John Jeffries across the English Channel in 1785.

49 W. W. Sadler in 1824 was thrown out of his balloon car during an ascent and was suspended by one leg for a short time. (*Scot's Magazine*, 1824, Vol. 94, p. 631.)

50 Like the narrators of "The Pit and the Pendulum" and "A Descent into the Maelström," Pfaall is calm and deliberate about his situation, trying to come to grips with the new environment he finds himself in. But the tone is different. He is *too* deliberate, *too* calm, *too* rational, and the tone becomes one of burlesque, rather than terror.

---

48 seventy-five pounds of leaden ballast, and able to have carried up as many more. As I left the earth, the barometer stood at thirty inches, and the centigrade thermometer at 19°.

"Scarcely, however, had I attained the height of fifty yards, when, roaring and rumbling up after me in the most tumultous and terrible manner, came so dense a hurricane of fire, and gravel, and burning wood, and blazing metal, and mangled limbs, that my very heart sunk within me, and I fell down in the bottom of the car, trembling with terror. Indeed, I now perceived that I had entirely overdone the business, and that the main consequences of the shock were yet to be experienced. Accordingly, in less than a second, I felt all the blood in my body rushing to my temples, and immediately thereupon, a concussion, which I shall never forget, burst abruptly through the night, and seemed to rip the very firmament asunder. When I afterward had time for reflection, I did not fail to attribute the extreme violence of the explosion, as regarded myself, to its proper cause—my situation directly above it, and in the line of its greatest power. But at the time, I thought only of preserving my life. The balloon at first collapsed, then furiously expanded, then whirled round and round with sickening velocity, and finally, reeling and staggering like a drunken man, hurled me over the rim of the car, and left me dangling, at a terrific height, with my head downward, and my face outward, by a piece of slender cord about three feet in length, which hung accidentally through a crevice near the bottom of the wicker-work, and in which, **49** as I fell, my left foot became most providentially entangled. It is impossible—utterly impossible—to form any adequate idea of the horror of my situation. I gasped convulsively for breath—a shudder resembling a fit of the ague agitated every nerve and muscle in my frame—I felt my eyes starting from their sockets—a horrible nausea overwhelmed me—and at length I lost all consciousness in a swoon.

"How long I remained in this state it is impossible to say. It must, however, have been no inconsiderable time, for when I partially recovered the sense of existence, I found the day breaking, the balloon at a prodigious height over a wilderness of ocean, and not a trace of land to be discovered far and wide within the limits of the vast horizon. My sensations, however, upon thus recovering, were by no means so replete with agony as might have been anticipated. Indeed, there was much of madness in the calm survey which I began to take of my **50** situation. I drew up to my eyes each of my hands, one after the other, and wondered what occurrence could have given rise to the swelling of the veins, and the horrible blackness of the finger-nails. I afterward carefully examined my head, shaking it repeatedly, and feeling it with minute attention, until I succeeded in satisfying myself that it was not, as I had more than half suspected, larger than my balloon. Then, in a knowing manner, I felt in both my breeches pockets, and, missing therefrom a set of tablets and a tooth-pick case, endeavored to account for their disappearance, and not being able to do so, felt inexpressibly chagrined. It now occurred to me that I suffered great uneasiness in the joint of my left ankle, and a dim consciousness of my situation began to glimmer through my mind. But, strange to say! I was neither astonished nor horror-stricken. If I felt any emotion at all, it was a kind of chuckling satisfaction at the cleverness I was about to display in extricating myself from this dilemma; and never, for a moment, did I look upon my ultimate safety as a question susceptible of doubt. For a few minutes I remained wrapped in the profoundest meditation. I have a distinct recollection of frequently compressing my lips, putting my fore-finger to the side of my nose, and making use of other gesticulations and grimaces common to men who, at ease in their arm-chairs, meditate upon matters of intricacy or importance. Having, as I thought, sufficiently collected my ideas, I now, with great caution and deliberation, put my hands behind my back, and unfastened the large iron buckle which belonged to the waistband of my pantaloons. This buckle had three teeth, which, being somewhat rusty, turned with great difficulty on their axis. I brought them, however, after some trouble, at right angles to the body of the buckle, and was glad to find them remain firm in that position. Holding within my teeth the instrument thus obtained, I now proceeded to untie the knot of my cravat. I had to rest several times before I could accomplish this manœuvre; but it was at length accomplished. To one end of the cravat I then made fast the buckle, and the other end I tied, for greater security, tightly around my wrist. Drawing now my body upward, with a prodigious exertion of muscular force, I succeeded, at the very first trial, in throwing the buckle over the car, and entangling it, as I had anticipated, in the circular rim of the wicker-work.

"My body was now inclined toward the side of the car, at an angle of about forty-five degrees; but it must not be understood that I was therefore only forty-five degrees below the perpendicular. So far from it, I still lay nearly level with the plane of the horizon; for the change of situation which I had acquired, had forced the bottom of the car considerably outward from my position, which was accordingly one of the most imminent peril. It should be remembered, however, that when I fell, in the first instance, from the car, if I had fallen with my face turned toward the balloon, instead of turned outwardly from it, as it actually was; or if, in the second place, the cord by which I was suspended had chanced to hang over the upper edge, instead of through a crevice near the bottom of the car—I say it may readily be conceived that, in either of these supposed cases, I should have been unable to accomplish even as much as I had now accomplished, and the disclosures now made would have been utterly lost to posterity. I had therefore every reason to be grateful; although, in point of fact, I was still too stupid to be anything at all, and hung for, perhaps, a quarter of an hour, in that extraordinary manner, without making the slightest farther exertion, and in a singularly tranquil state of idiotic enjoyment. But this feeling did not fail to die rapidly away, and thereunto succeeded horror, and dismay, and a sense of utter helplessness and ruin.

51 Or 19,800 feet. About the highest ascent in Poe's day was that of Charles Ferson Durant, who reached 8,000 feet in his ascent from Boston Common in 1837. Auguste and Jean Piccard made ascents in a sealed gondola to 55,000 and 58,000 feet, respectively, in the 1930s. In 1960, Joseph W. Kittinger soared to 102,000 feet, or a height of 19.3 miles.

52 A large man-of-war, or warship

53 A strong fascination for many romantic writers was imagining that one's spirit could soar out of this world into the Ideal. Some tried drugs or Mesmerism, while others analyzed dreams or daydreams as clues to this realm of the Sublime. This same interest is evident in most of Poe's serious tales, from "A Tale of the Ragged Mountains" and "Ligeia" to "Mesmeric Revelation."

54 The first story of a trip to the moon was written by Lucian of Samosata, A.D. 165. In *Icaromenippus*, he describes how a philosopher, using a feather from an eagle and another from a vulture, sailed into space in order to prove that the world was round.

So many stories have been written since about such flights that Marjorie Hope Nicholson wrote an entire book, *Vogages to the Moon* (1948) on the subject. She notes that it was another thirteen centuries after Lucian before someone else took up the theme, however. This was Ariosto's epic *Orlando Furioso* (1532), in which the hero travels to the moon in a chariot in search of his wife and finds the satellite complete with cities and towns, as well as what appears to be a huge lost-and-found department where all missing articles from the earth eventually wind up.

Jules Verne's *From the Earth to the Moon* (1865) is the most famous nineteenth-century story of a moon voyage.

55 All of these calculations, mistakes included, are lifted from Sir John Herschel's *Treatise on Astronomy*, which was published in Philadelphia in 1834. In 1846, Poe writes: "The Harpers had issued an American edition of Sir John Herschel's 'Treatise on Astronomy,' and I had been much interested in what is there said respecting the possibility of future investigations. The theme excited my fancy, and I longed to give free rein to it in depicting my day-dreams about the scenery of the moon. (*Godey's*, 1846)

Herschel and Poe both err in their description of an ellipse as a fraction of the "major semi-axis".

In fact, the blood so long accumulating in the vessels of my head and throat, and which had hitherto buoyed up my spirits with delirium, had now begun to retire within their proper channels, and the distinctness which was thus added to my perception of the danger, merely served to deprive me of the self-possession and courage to encounter it. But this weakness was, luckily for me, of no very long duration. In good time came to my rescue the spirit of despair, and, with frantic cries and struggles, I jerked my way bodily upward, till at length, clutching with a vise-like grip the long-desired rim, I writhed my person over it, and fell headlong and shuddering within the car.

"It was not until some time afterward that I recovered myself sufficiently to attend to the ordinary cares of the balloon. I then, however, examined it with attention, and found it, to my great relief, uninjured. My implements were all safe, and, fortunately, I had lost neither ballast nor provisions. Indeed, I had so well secured them in their places, that such an accident was entirely out of the question. Looking at my watch, I found it six o'clock. I was still rapidly ascending, and the barometer gave a present altitude of three and three-**51** quarter miles. Immediately beneath me in the ocean, lay a small black object, slightly oblong in shape, seemingly about the size of a domino, and in every respect bearing a great resemblance to one of those toys. Bringing my telescope to bear upon it, I plainly discerned it to be a British ninety-four-**52** gun ship, close-hauled, and pitching heavily in the sea with her head to the W. S. W. Besides this ship, I saw nothing but the ocean and the sky, and the sun, which had long arisen.

"It is now high time that I should explain to your Excellencies the object of my voyage. Your Excellencies will bear in mind that distressed circumstances in Rotterdam had at length driven me to the resolution of commiting suicide. It was not, however, that to life itself I had any positive disgust, but that I was harassed beyond endurance by the adventitious miseries attending my situation. In this state of mind, wishing to live, yet wearied with life, the treatise at the stall of the bookseller, backed by the opportune discovery of my cousin of Nantz, opened a resource to my imagination. I then finally made up my mind. I determined to depart, yet live—to leave the **53** world, yet continue to exist—in short, to drop enigmas, I resolved, let what would ensue, to force a passage, if I could, **54** *to the moon*. Now, lest I should be supposed more of a madman than I actually am, I will detail, as well as I am able, the considerations which led me to believe that an achievement of this nature, although without doubt difficult, and full of danger, was not absolutely, to a bold spirit, beyond the confines of the possible.

"The moon's actual distance from the earth was the first thing to be attended to. Now, the mean or average interval between the *centres* of the two planets is 59.9643 of the earth's **55** equatorial *radii*, or about only 237,000 miles. I say the mean or average interval; but it must be borne in mind that the form of the moon's orbit being an ellipse of eccentricity amounting to no less than 0.05484 of the major semi-axis of the ellipse itself, and the earth's centre being situated in its focus, if I could, in any manner, contrive to meet the moon in its perigee, the above-mentioned distance would be materially diminished. But, to say nothing at present of this possibility, it was very certain that, at all events, from the 237,000 miles I would have to deduct the *radius* of the earth, say 4,000, and the *radius* of the moon, say 1,080, in all 5,080, leaving an actual interval to be traversed, under average circumstances, of 231,920 miles. Now this, I reflected, was no very extraordinary distance. Travelling on the land has been repeatedly accomplished at the rate of sixty miles per hour; and indeed a much greater speed may be anticipated. But even at this velocity, it would take me no more than 161 days to reach the surface of the moon. There were, however, many particulars inducing me to believe that my average rate of travelling might possibly very much exceed that of sixty miles per hour, and, as these considerations did not fail to make a deep impression upon my mind, I will mention them more fully hereafter.

"The next point to be regarded was one of far greater importance. From indications afforded by the barometer, we find that, in ascensions from the surface of the earth we have, at the height of 1,000 feet, left below us about one-thirtieth of the entire mass of atmospheric air; that at 10,600 we have ascended through nearly one-third; and that at 18,000, which is not far from the elevation of Cotopaxi, we have surmounted one-half the material, or, at all events, one-half the *ponderable,* **56** body of air incumbent upon our globe. It is also calculated that at an altitude not exceeding the hundredth part of the earth's diameter—that is, not exceeding eighty miles—the rarefaction would be so excessive that animal life could in no manner be sustained, and, moreover, that the most delicate means we possess of ascertaining the presence of the atmosphere would be inadequate to assure us of its existence. But I did not fail to perceive that these latter calculations are founded altogether on our experimental knowledge of the properties of air, and the mechanical laws regulating its dilation and compression, in what may be called, comparatively speaking, *the immediate vicinity* of the earth itself; and, at the same time, it is taken for granted that animal life is and must be essentially *incapable of modification* at any given unattainable distance from the surface. Now, all such reasoning and from such *data* must, of course, be simply analogical. The greatest height ever reached by man was that of 25,000 feet, attained in the œronautic expedition of Messieurs Gay-Lussac and Biot. This is a moderate altitude, even when compared **57** with the eighty miles in question; and I could not help thinking that the subject admitted room for doubt and great latitude for speculation.

"But, in point of fact, an ascension being made to any given altitude, the ponderable quantity of air surmounted in any *farther* ascension is by no means in proportion to the additional height ascended (as may be plainly seen from what has been

56 Capable of being weighed. Cotopaxi, the highest active volcano in the world (19,498 feet), is in the Ecuadorian Andes.

57 Actually, Biot and Gay-Lussac reached only about 3,000 feet in 1804, but, that same year, Gay-Lussac ascended alone to a height of more than 23,000 feet. In a trip from Paris to Rouen, he performed experiments on the earth's magnetic field and on the composition of the atmosphere at various altitudes.

The highest ascent without oxygen was probably that of James Glaisher and Henry Coxwell in 1862. Since the two lost consciousness shortly after reaching 30,000 feet, there is no way of knowing exactly how high they went. They avoided death by one last, desperate attempt to open a stuck valve, which succeeded, plunging them 2,000 feet per minute until they regained consciousness and closed it again (Rolt, pp. 193–97).

stated before), but in a *ratio* constantly decreasing. It is therefore evident that, ascend as high as we may, we cannot, literally speaking, arrive at a limit beyond which *no* atmosphere is to be found. It *must exist*, I argued; although it *may* exist in a state of infinite rarefaction.

"On the other hand, I was aware that arguments have not been wanting to prove the existence of a real and definite limit to the atmosphere, beyond which there is absolutely no air whatsoever. But a circumstance which has been left out of view by those who contend for such a limit, seemed to me, although no positive refutation of their creed, still a point worthy very serious investigation. On comparing the intervals

58 between the successive arrivals of Encke's comet at its perihelion, after giving credit, in the most exact manner, for all the disturbances due to the attractions of the planets, it appears that the periods are gradually diminishing; that is to say, the major axis of the comet's ellipse is growing shorter, in a slow but perfectly regular decrease. Now, this is precisely what ought to be the case, if we suppose a resistance experienced from the comet from an extremely *rare ethereal medium* pervading the regions of its orbit. For it is evident that such a medium must, in retarding the comet's velocity, increase its centripetal, by weakening its centrifugal, force. In other words, the sun's attraction would be constantly attaining greater power, and the comet would be drawn nearer at every revolution. Indeed, there is no other way of accounting for the variation in question. But again:—The real diameter of the same comet's nebulosity is observed to contract rapidly as it approaches the sun, and dilate with equal rapidity in its departure toward its aphelion. Was I not justified in supposing,

59 with M. Valz, that this apparent condensation of volume has its origin in the compression of the same ethereal medium I have spoken of before, and which is dense in proportion to its

60 vicinity to the sun? The lenticular-shaped phenomenon, also called the zodiacal light, was a matter worthy of attention. This radiance, so apparent in the tropics, and which cannot be mistaken for any meteoric lustre, extends from the horizon obliquely upward, and follows generally the direction of the sun's equator. It appeared to me evidently in the nature of a rare atmosphere extending from the sun outward, beyond the

61 orbit of Venus at least, and I believed indefinitely farther. Indeed, this medium I could not suppose confined to the path of the comet's ellipse, or to the immediate neighborhood of the sun. It was easy, on the contrary, to imagine it pervading the entire regions of our planetary system, condensed into what we call atmosphere at the planets themselves, and perhaps at some of them modified by considerations purely geological; that is to say, modified, or varied in its proportions (or absolute nature) by matters volatilized from the respective orbs.

"Having adopted this view of the subject, I had little farther hesitation. Granting that on my passage I should meet with atmosphere *essentially* the same as at the surface of the earth, I conceived that, by means of the very ingenious apparatus of

---

58 Encke's comet, discovered in 1818, was named for him because he had calculated its orbit, finding the period of its recurrence to be 3.3 years and accurately predicting the date of its return (see note 27).

Perihelion is the point in the path of a planet or other celestial body that is nearest to the sun. Aphelion is the most distant point.

59 Valz's theory is mentioned in Herschel's *Treatise*, pp. 291–93.

60 "Lenticular" means shaped like a lentil, as in an double-convex lens. Herschel uses the term in his *Treatise*, p. 380.

61 "The zodical light is probably what the ancients called Trabes. *Emicant Trabes quos docos vocant.*—Pliny lib. 2, p. 26." (Poe's note)

According to Rees's Cyclopedia (1819), the apparent path of the sun across the sky is called the ecliptic; it was traditionally defined by the twelve constellations of the zodiac. This zodiacal path is about 10° wide and is centered on the ecliptic. Mercury's orbit is tilted 7° and the Moon's 5° to the ecliptic, and so the moving heavenly bodies are always found in the zodiacal belt.

Trabes is Latin for "beams."

M. Grimm, I should readily be enabled to condense it in sufficient quantity for the purposes of respiration. This would remove the chief obstacle in a journey to the moon. I had indeed spent some money and great labor in adapting the apparatus to the object intended, and confidently looked forward to its successful application, if I could manage to complete the voyage within any reasonable period. This brings me back to the *rate* at which it would be possible to travel.

"It is true that balloons, in the first stage of their ascensions from the earth, are known to rise with a velocity comparatively moderate. Now, the power of elevation lies altogether in the superior gravity of the atmospheric air compared with the gas in the balloon; and, at first sight, it does not appear probable that, as the balloon acquires altitude, and consequently arrives successively in atmospheric *strata* of densities rapidly diminishing—I say, it does not appear at all reasonable that, in this its progress upward, the original velocity should be accelerated. On the other hand, I was not aware that, in any recorded ascension, a *diminution* had been proved to be apparent in the absolute rate of ascent; although such should have been the case, if on account of nothing else, on account of the escape of gas through balloons ill-constructed, and varnished with no better material than the ordinary varnish. It seemed, therefore, that the effect of such escape was only sufficient to counterbalance the effect of the acceleration attained in the diminishing of the balloon's distance from the gravitating centre. I now considered that, provided in my passage I found the *medium* I had imagined, and provided that it should prove to be *essentially* what we denominate atmospheric air, it could make comparatively little difference at what extreme state of rarefaction I should discover it—that is to say, in regard to my power of ascending—for the gas in the balloon would not only be itself subject to similar rarefaction (in proportion to the occurrence of which, I could suffer an escape of so much as would be requisite to prevent explosion), but, *being what it was*, would, at all events, continue specifically lighter than any compound whatever of mere nitrogen and oxygen. Thus there was a chance—in fact there was a strong probability—that, *at no epoch of my ascent, I should reach a point where the united weights of my immense balloon, the inconceivably rare gas within it, the car, and its contents, should equal the weight of the mass of the surrounding atmosphere displaced;* and this will be readily understood as the sole condition upon which my upward flight would be arrested. But, if this point were even attained, I could dispense with ballast and other weight to the amount of nearly three hundred pounds. In the meantime, the force of gravitation would be constantly diminishing, in proportion to the squares of the distances, and so, with a velocity prodigiously accelerating, I should at length arrive in those distant regions where the force of the earth's attraction would be superseded by that of the moon. **62**

"There was another difficulty, however, which occasioned me some little disquietude. It has been observed, that, in balloon ascensions to any considerable height, besides the

62 While it is true that an object that breaks away from the earth's gravitational pull will then be affected by any strong gravitation from another source, the moon would not affect it until the object draws quite close. A gas-filled balloon would also not be able to generate sufficient momentum to escape the earth's pull: 25,000 mph, or seven miles per second. Even if it could make it out of the atmosphere, anything less than escape velocity would result in an elliptical orbit around the earth. A gas-filled balloon, however, rises only because it is lighter than the surrounding air. In space it would be useless.

63 "Since the original publication of Hans Pfaall, I find that Mr. Green, of Nassau-balloon notoriety, and other late aeronauts, deny the assertions of Humboldt, in this respect, and speak of a *decreasing* inconvenience,—precisely in accordance with the theory here urged." (Poe's note)

Charles Green made two ascents, to 19,335 and 27,146 feet; he is discussed in more detail in "The Balloon-Hoax."

Alexander von Humboldt (1769–1859), the great naturalist, also studied meteorology and atmospheric science.

64 At high altitudes, the air pressure is considerably less, and oxygen is less concentrated as well, so that the lungs must work harder to sustain life. At the same time, the gases within the body cells and in the bloodstream expand and cause painful swelling in the joints—a high-altitude case of the bends. Of course, given oxygen through a tightly sealed breathing apparatus, a person can exist easily in a vacuum. However, the rapid drop in air *pressure* would still cause problems (see n. 70).

pain attending respiration, great uneasiness is experienced about the head and body, often accompanied with bleeding at the nose, and other symptoms of an alarming kind, and growing more and more inconvenient in proportion to the

63 altitude attained. This was a reflection of a nature somewhat startling. Was it not probable that there symptoms would increase until terminated by death itself? I finally thought not. Their origin was to be looked for in the progressive removal of the *customary* atmospheric pressure upon the surface of the body, and consequent distention of the superficial blood-vessels—not in any positive disorganization of the animal system, as in the case of difficulty in breathing, where the atmospheric density is *chemically insufficient* for the due

64 renovation of blood in a ventricle of the heart. Unless for default of this renovation, I could see no reason, therefore, why life could not be sustained even in a *vacuum;* for the expansion and compression of chest, commonly called breathing, is action purely muscular, and the *cause*, not the *effect*, of respiration. In a word, I conceived that, as the body should become habituated to the want of atmospheric pressure, the sensations of pain would gradually diminish—and to endure them while they continued, I relied with confidence upon the iron hardihood of my constitution.

"Thus, may it please your Excellencies, I have detailed some, though by no means all, the considerations which led me to form the project of a lunar voyage. I shall not proceed to lay before you the result of an attempt so apparently audacious in conception, and, at all events, so utterly unparalleled in the annals of mankind.

"Having attained the altitude before mentioned—that is to say three miles and three quarters—I threw out from the car a quantity of feathers, and found that I still ascended with sufficient rapidity; there was, therefore, no necessity for discharging any ballast. I was glad of this, for I wished to retain with me as much weight as I could carry, for the obvious reason that I could not be *positive* either about the gravitation or the atmospheric density of the moon. I as yet suffered no bodily inconvenience, breathing with great freedom, and feeling no pain whatever in the head. The cat was lying very demurely upon my coat, which I had taken off, and eyeing the pigeons with an air of *nonchalance*. These latter being tied by the leg, to prevent their escape, were busily employed in picking up some grains of rice scattered for them in the bottom of the car.

"At twenty minutes past six o'clock, the barometer showed an elevation of 26,400 feet, or five miles to a fraction. The prospect seemed unbounded. Indeed, it is very easily calculated by means of spherical geometry, how great an extent of the earth's area I beheld. The convex surface of any segment of a sphere is, to the entire surface of the sphere itself, as the versed sine of the segment to the diameter of the sphere. Now, in my case, the versed sine—that is to say, the *thickness* of the segment beneath me—was about equal to my elevation, or the elevation of the point of sight above the surface. 'As five miles, then, to eight thousand,' would express the proportion of the earth's area seen by me. In other words, I beheld as much as a sixteen-hundredth part of the whole surface of the globe. The sea appeared unruffled as a mirror, although, by means of the telescope, I could perceive it to be in a state of violent agitation. The ship was no longer visible, having drifted away, apparently to the eastward. I now began to experience, at intervals, severe pain in the head, especially about the ears—still, however, breathing with tolerable freedom. The cat and pigeons seemed to suffer no inconvenience whatsoever.

"At twenty minutes before seven, the balloon entered a long series of dense cloud, which put me to great trouble, by damaging my condensing apparatus, and wetting me to the skin; this was, to be sure, a singular *rencontre*, for I had not believed it possible that a cloud of this nature could be sustained at so great an elevation. I thought it best, however, to throw out two five-pound pieces of ballast, reserving still a weight of one hundred and sixty-five pounds. Upon so doing, I soon rose above the difficulty, and perceived immediately, that I had obtained a great increase in my rate of ascent. In a few seconds after my leaving the cloud, a flash of vivid lightning shot from one end of it to the other, and caused it to kindle up, throughout its vast extent, like a mass of ignited charcoal. This, it must be remembered, was in the broad light of day. No fancy may picture the sublimity which might have been exhibited by a similar phenomenon taking place amid the darkness of the night. Hell itself might have been found a fitting image. Even as it was, my hair stood on end, while I gazed afar down within the yawning abysses, letting imagination descend, and stalk about in the strange vaulted halls, and ruddy gulfs, and red ghastly chasms of the hideous and unfathomable fire. I had indeed made a narrow escape. Has the balloon remained a very short while longer within the could—that is to say, had not the inconvenience of getting wet, determined me to discharge the ballast—my destruction might, and probably would, have been the consequence. Such perils, although little considered, are perhaps the greatest which must be encountered in balloons. I had by this time, however, attained too great an elevation to be any longer uneasy on this head.

"I was now rising rapidly, and by seven o'clock the barometer indicated an altitude of no less than nine miles and a half. I began to find great difficulty in drawing my breath. My head, too, was excessively painful; and, having felt for some time a moisture about my cheeks, I at length discovered it to be blood, which was oozing quite fast from the drums of my ears. My eyes, also, gave me great uneasiness. Upon passing the hand over them they seemed to have protruded from their sockets in no inconsiderable degree; and all objects in the car, and even the balloon itself, appeared distorted to my vision. These symptoms were more than I had expected, and occasioned me some alarm. At this juncture, very imprudently, and without consideration, I threw out from the car three

65 Herschel, pp. 27–28

66 The stratosphere is a warm layer which extends from 25,000 to 59,000 feet above the surface of the earth and effectively puts a lid on clouds—and weather. The dense clouds at this high elevation might be cloud clusters, which are often densely packed and 250 miles across. They travel westward at about twelve knots and are the birthplace of rain and thunderstorms.

67 Although we usually think of lightning as an electrical discharge between a cloud and the earth, it can also occur between two clouds, or between one part of a cloud and another.

68 James Glaisher, in 1862, writes of the effect of high altitude (29,000 feet): "Shortly after, I laid my arm upon the table, possessed of its full vigor, but on being desirous of using it I found it powerless. . . . Then I tried to shake myself, and succeeded, but I seemed to have no limbs. . . . I dimly saw Mr. Coxwell, and endeavoured to speak, but could not. In an instant intense darkness overcame me, so that the optic nerve lost power suddenly, but I was still conscious. . . . I thought I had been seized with asphyxia, and believed I should experience nothing more, as death would come unless we speedily descended. . . ." (Quoted in Rolt, pp. 195–96)

In 1875, Gaston Tissandier, along with two scientists named Sivel and Croce-Spinelli, ascended in a balloon from Paris with what they thought was a viable breathing apparatus. Even so, after 22,800 feet, Tissandier briefly lost consciousness. An unfortunate jettisoning of ballast made the balloon climb even higher, and he again lost consciousness. When he awoke, the balloon was descending very fast, and his two companions were dead. Their faces were black; blood had run from their mouths and noses. The two had not been wearing masks but had been inhaling oxygen from a hand-held container.

five-pound pieces of ballast. The accelerated rate of ascent thus obtained carried me too rapidly, and without sufficient gradation, into a highly rarefied *stratum* of the atmosphere, and the result had nearly proved fatal to my expedition and to myself. I was suddenly seized with a spasm which lasted for more than five minutes, and even when this, in a measure, ceased, I could catch my breath only at long intervals, and in a gasping manner,—bleeding all the while copiously at the nose and ears, and even slightly at the eyes. The pigeons appeared distressed in the extreme, and struggled to escape; while the cat mewed piteously, and, with her tongue hanging out of her mouth, staggered to and fro in the car as if under the influence of poison. I now too late discovered the great rashness of which I had been guilty in discharging the ballast, and my agitation was excessive. I anticipated nothing less than death, and death in a few minutes. The physical suffering I underwent contributed also to render me nearly incapable of making any exertion for the preservation of my life. I had, indeed, little power of reflection left, and the violence of the pain in my head seemed to be greatly on the increase. Thus I found that my senses would shortly give way altogether, and I had already clutched one of the valve ropes with the view of attempting a descent, when the recollection of the trick I had played the three creditors, and the possible consequences to myself, should I return, operated to deter me for the moment. I lay down in the bottom of the car, and endeavored to collect my faculties. In this I so far succeeded as to determine upon the experiment of losing blood. Having no lancet, however, I was constrained to perform the operation in the best manner I was able, and finally succeeded in opening a vein in my left arm, with the blade of my penknife. The blood had hardly commenced flowing when I experienced a sensible relief, and by the time I had lost about half a moderate basin-full, most of the worst symptoms had aban-

69 doned me entirely. I nevertheless did not think it expedient to attempt getting on my feet immediately; but having tied up my arm as well as I could, I lay still for about a quarter of an hour. At the end of this time I arose, and found myself freer from absolute *pain* of any kind than I had been during the last hour and a quarter of my ascension. The difficulty of breathing, however, was diminished in a very slight degree, and I found that it would soon be positively necessary to make use of any condenser. In the meantime, looking toward the cat, who was again snugly stowed away upon my coat, I discovered to my infinite surprise, that she had taken the opportunity of my indisposition to bring into light a litter of three little kittens. This was an addition to the number of passengers on my part altogether unexpected; but I was pleased at the occurrence. It would afford me a chance of bringing to a kind of test the truth of a surmise, which, more than anything else, had influenced me in attempting this ascension. I had imagined that the *habitual* endurance of the atmospheric pressure at the surface of the earth was the cause, or nearly so, of the pain attending animal existence at a distance above the surface.

69 Theoretically, removing some blood would allow more room for the gases trapped inside the body to expand, but in actual practice, it would only weaken a person, lowering blood pressure and reducing the number of oxygen-carrying red corpuscles vital to survival. Also, gas bubbles in the bloodstream would eventually lodge in a narrow vessel, cutting off oxygen to that area and causing excruciating pain.

Should the kittens be found to suffer uneasiness *in an equal degree with their mother*, I must consider my theory in fault, but a failure to do so I should look upon as a strong confirmation of my idea.   **70**

"By eight o'clock I had actually attained an elevation of seventeen miles above the surface of the earth. Thus it seemed to me evident that my rate of ascent was not only on the increase, but that the progression would have been apparent in a slight degree even had I not discharged the ballast which I did. The pains in my head and ears returned, at intervals, with violence, and I still continued to bleed occasionally at the nose; but, upon the whole, I suffered much less than might have been expected. I breathed, however, at every moment, with more and more difficulty, and each inhalation was attended with a troublesome spasmodic action of the chest. I now unpacked the condensing apparatus, and got it ready for immediate use.

"The view of the earth, at this period of my ascension, was beautiful indeed. To the westward, the northward, and the **71** southward, as far as I could see, lay a boundless sheet of apparently unruffled ocean, which every moment gained a deeper and deeper tint of blue. At a vast distance to the eastward, although perfectly discernible, extended the islands of Great Britain, the entire Atlantic coasts of France and Spain, with a small portion of the northern part of the continent of Africa. Of individual edifices not a trace could be discovered, and the proudest cities of mankind had utterly faded away from the face of the earth.

"What mainly astonished me, in the appearance of things below, was the seeming concavity of the surface of the globe. **72** I had, thoughtlessly enough, expected to see its real *convexity* become evident as I ascended; but a very little reflection sufficed to explain the discrepancy. A line, dropped from my position perpendicularly to the earth, would have formed the perpendicular of a right-angled triangle, of which the base would have extended from the right-angle to the horizon, and the hypothenuse from the horizon to my position. But my height was little or nothing in comparison with my prospect. In other words, the base and hypothenuse of the supposed triangle would, in my case, have been so long, when compared to the perpendicular, that the two former might have been regarded as nearly parallel. In this manner the horizon of the æronaut appears always to be *upon a level* with the car. But as the point immediately beneath him seems, and is, at a great distance below him, it seems of course, also at a great distance below the horizon. Hence the impression of concavity; and this impression must remain, until the elevation shall bear so great a proportion to the prospect, that the apparent parallelism of the base and hypothenuse disappears.   **73**

"The pigeons about this time seeming to undergo much suffering, I determined upon giving them their liberty. I first untied one of them, a beautiful gray-mottled pigeon, and placed him upon the rim of the wicker-work. He appeared extremely uneasy, looking anxiously around him, fluttering

70 The ability to tolerate high altitude is for the most part an inherited trait. For example, the Andean Indian has a large chest capacity and a short, stocky body, in order to make most efficient use of available oxygen. But a mother cat would pass along to her babies the same traits as her own, and so what is described here is highly unlikely, as is the possibility that the babies have somehow managed to acquire high-altitude adaptation since they were born.

71 Michael Collins, from his Apollo 11 capsule in 1969, expressed much the same feeling:
"It's really a fantastic sight through the sextant. A minute ago, during the automaneuver, the reticle swept across the Mediterranean. You could see all of North Africa absolutely clear, all of Portugal, Spain, southern France, all of Italy absolutely clear. Just a beautiful sight." (Norman Mailer, *A Fire on the Moon*, 1970; p. 257)

72 Mark Twain, in *Roughing It* (1872), Chapter 76: "It was curious; and not only curious, but aggravating; for it was having our trouble all for nothing, to climb ten thousand feet toward heaven and then have to look *up* at our scenery. . . . Formerly, when I had read an article in which Poe treated of this singular fraud perpetrated upon the eye by isolated great altitudes, I had looked upon the matter as an invention of his own fancy."

73 The optical illusion that turns concave into convex has often been noted, particulaly in unfamiliar scenery, such as photographs sent back from the moon, which seem to show craters when looked at in one way and mountains when the photographs are turned upside down.

his wings, and making a loud cooing noise, but could not be persuaded to trust himself from the car. I took him up at last, and threw him to about half a dozen yards from the balloon. He made, however, no attempt to descend as I had expected, but struggled with great vehemence to get back, uttering at the same time very shrill and piercing cries. He at length succeeded in regaining his former station on the rim, but had hardly done so when his head dropped upon his breast, and he fell dead within the car. The other one did not prove so unfortunate. To prevent his following the example of his companion, and accomplishing a return, I threw him down-ward with all my force, and was pleased to find him continue his descent, with great velocity, making use of his wings with

74 ease, and in a perfectly natural manner. In a very short time he was out of sight, and I have no doubt he reached home in safety. Puss, who seemed in a great measure recovered from her illness, now made a hearty meal of the dead bird, and then went to sleep with much apparent satisfaction. Her kittens were quite lively, and so far envinced not the slightest sign of any uneasiness.

"At a quarter past eight, being able no longer to draw breath without the most intolerable pain, I proceeded forthwith to adjust around the car the apparatus belonging to the condenser. This apparatus will require some little explanation, and your Excellencies will please to bear in mind that my object, in the first place, was to surround myself and car entirely with a barricade against the highly rarefied atmosphere in which I was existing, with the intention of introducing within this barricade, by means of my condenser, a quantity of this same atmosphere sufficiently condensed for the purposes of respiration. With this object in view I had prepared a very strong,

75 perfectly air-tight, but flexible gum-elastic bag. In this bag, which was of sufficient dimensions, the entire car was in a manner placed. That is to say, it (the bag) was drawn over the whole bottom of the car, up its sides, and so on, along the outside of the ropes, to the upper rim or hoop where the net-work is attached. Having pulled the bag up in this way, and formed a complete enclosure on all sides, and at bottom, it was now necessary to fasten up its top or mouth, by passing its material over the hoop of the net-work,—in other words, between the net-work and the hoop. But if the net-work were separated from the hoop to admit this passage, what was to sustain the car in the meantime? Now the net-work was not permanently fastened to the hoop, but attached by a series of running loops or nooses. I therefore undid only a few of these loops at one time, leaving the car suspended by the remainder. Having thus inserted a portion of the cloth forming the upper part of the bag, I refastened the loops—not to the loop, for that would have been impossible, since the cloth now inter-vened,—but to a series of large buttons, affixed to the cloth itself, about three feet below the mouth of the bag; the intervals between the buttons having been made to correspond to the intervals between the loops. This done, a few more of the loops were unfastened from the rim, a farther portion of

74 Considering the sparse atmosphere at this altitude, the first pigeon should have dropped like a stone; there certainly would not be enough air resistance to enable it to flap its wings and fly back to the balloon. The second bird's departure is more plausible, resembling in prin-ciple the space shuttle, which acts as a rocket until it encounters sufficient atmosphere for its wings to take over and let it glide to the ground.

75 A gum-elastic bag would certainly hold air, but as our recent space experiences have shown, the multitude of tiny meteorites and other space flotsam and jetsam would soon puncture it.

the cloth introduced and the disengaged loops then connected with their proper buttons. In this way it was possible to insert the whole upper part of the bag between the net-work and the hoop. It is evident that the hoop would now drop down within the car, while the whole weight of the car itself, with all its contents, would be held up merely by the strength of the buttons. This, at first sight, would seem an inadequate dependence; but it was by no means so, for the buttons were not only very strong in themselves, but so close together that a very slight portion of the whole weight was supported by any one of them. Indeed, had the car and contents been three times heavier than they were, I should not have been at all uneasy. I now raised up the hoop again within the covering of gum-elastic, and propped it at nearly its former height by means of three light poles.prepared for the occasion. This was done, of course, to keep the bag distended at the top, and to preserve the lower part of the net-work in its proper situation. All that now remained was to fasten up the mouth of the enclosure; and this was readily accomplished by gathering the folds of the material together, and twisting them up very tightly on the inside by means of a kind of stationary *tourniquet*.

"In the sides of the covering thus adjusted round the car, had been inserted three circular panes of thick but clear glass, through which I could see without difficulty around me in every horizontal direction. In that portion of the cloth forming the bottom, was likewise a fourth window, of the same kind, and corresponding with a small aperture in the floor of the car itself. This enabled me to see perpendicularly down, but having found it impossible to place any similar contrivance overhead, on account of the peculiar manner of closing up the opening there, and the consequent wrinkles on the cloth, I could expect to see no objects situated directly in my zenith. This, of course, was a matter of little consequence; for, had I even been able to place a window at top, the balloon itself would prevented my making any use of it.

"About a foot below one of the side windows was a circular opening, three inches in diameter, and fitted with a brass rim adapted in its inner edge to the windings of a screw. In this rim was screwed the large tube of the condenser, the body of the machine being, of course, within the chamber of gum-elastic. Through this tube a quantity of the rare atmosphere circumjacent being drawn by means of a *vacuum* created in **76** the body of the machine was thence discharged, in a state of condensation, to mingle with the thin air already in the chamber. This operation being repeated several times, at length filled the chamber with atmosphere proper for all the purposes of respiration; but in so confined a space it would, in a short time, necessarily become foul, and unfit for use from frequent contact with the lungs. It was then ejected by a small valve at the bottom of the car;—the dense air readily sinking into the thinner atmosphere below. To avoid the **77** inconvenience of making a total *vacuum* at any moment within the chamber, this purification was never accomplished all at once, but in a gradual manner,—the valve being opened only

76 Surrounding; adjacent on all sides

77 At this altitude, and under pressure, the air within would not "sink"—it would escape at high velocity. Poe seems unaware that a condenser increases air *pressure* inside, or that oxygen-depleted air does *not* necessarily sink. At any rate, the "capsule" would collapse almost immediately, just as his balloon would if it had a leak.

for a few seconds, then closed again, until one or two strokes from the pump of the condenser had supplied the place of the atmosphere ejected. For the sake of experiment I had put the cat and kittens in a small basket, and suspended it outside the car to a button at the bottom, close by the valve, through which I could feed them at any moment when necessary. I did this at some little risk, and before closing the mouth of the chamber, by reaching under the car with one of the poles before mentioned to which a hook had been attached. As soon as dense air was admitted in the chamber, the hoop and poles became unnecessary; the expansion of the enclosed atmosphere powerfully distending the gum-elastic.

"By the time I had fully completed these arrangements and filled the chamber as explained, it wanted only ten minutes of nine o'clock. During the whole period of my being thus employed, I endured the most terrible distress from difficulty of respiration, and bitterly did I repent the negligence, or rather fool-hardiness, of which I had been guilty, of putting off to the last moment a matter of so much importance. But having at length accomplished it, I soon began to reap the benefit of my invention. Once again I breathed with perfect freedom and ease—and indeed why should I not? I was also agreeably surprised to find myself, in a great measure, relieved from the violent pains which had hitherto tormented me. A slight headache, accompanied with a sensation of fulness or distention about the wrists, the ankles, and the throat, was nearly all of which I had now to complain. Thus it seemed evident that a greater part of the uneasiness attending the removal of atmospheric pressure had actually *worn off*, as I had expected, and that much of the pain endured for the last two hours should have been attributed altogether to the effects of a deficient respiration.

"At twenty minutes before nine o'clock—that is to say, a short time prior to my closing up the mouth of the chamber, the mercury attained its limit, or ran down, in the barometer, which, as I mentioned before, was one of an extended construction. It then indicated an altitude on my part of 132,000 feet, or five-and-twenty miles, and I consequently surveyed at that time an extent of the earth's area amounting to no less than the three-hundred-and-twentieth part of its entire superficies. At nine o'clock I had again lost sight of land to the eastward, but not before I became aware that the balloon was drifting rapidly to the N. N. W. The ocean beneath me still retained its apparent concavity, although my view was often interrupted by the masses of cloud which floated to and fro.

"At half past nine I tried the experiment of throwing out a handful of feathers through the valve. They did not float as I had expected; but dropped down perpendicularly, like a bullet, *en masse*, and with the greatest velocity,—being out of sight in a very few seconds. I did not at first know what to make of this extraordinary phenomenon; not being able to believe that my rate of ascent had, of a sudden, met with so prodigious an acceleration. But it soon occurred to me that the atmosphere was now far too rare to sustain even the feathers; that they actually fell, as they appeared to do, with great rapidity; and that I had been surprised by the united velocities of their descent and my own elevation.   **78**

"By ten o'clock I found that I had very little to occupy my immediate attention. Affairs went on swimmingly, and I believed the balloon to be going upward with a speed increasing momently, although I had no longer any means of ascertaining the progression of the increase. I suffered no pain or uneasiness of any kind, and enjoyed better spirits than I had at any period since my departure from Rotterdam; busying myself now in examining the state of my various apparatus, and now in regenerating the atmosphere within the chamber. This latter point I determined to attend to at regular intervals of forty minutes, more on account of the preservation of my health, then from so frequent a renovation being absolutely necessary. In the meanwhile I could not help making anticipations. Fancy revelled in the wild and dreamy regions of the moon. Imagination, feeling herself for once unshackled, roamed at will among the ever-changing wonders of a shadowy and unstable land. Now there were hoary and time-honored forests, and craggy precipices, and waterfalls tumbling with a loud noise into abysses without a bottom. Then I came **79** suddenly into still noonday solitudes, where no wind of heaven ever intruded, and where vast meadows of poppies, and slender, lily-looking flowers spread themselves out a weary distance, all silent and motionless for ever. Then again I journeyed far down away into another country where it was all one dim and vague lake, with a boundary line of clouds. **80** But fancies such as these were not the sole possessors of my brain. Horrors of a nature most stern and most appalling would too frequently obtrude themselves upon my mind, and shake the innermost depths of my soul with the bare supposition of their possibility. Yet I would not suffer my thoughts for any length of time to dwell upon these latter speculations, rightly judging the real and palpable dangers of the voyage sufficient for my undivided attention.

"At five o'clock, P.M., being engaged in regenerating the atmosphere within the chamber, I took that opportunity of observing the cat and kittens through the valve. The cat herself appeared to suffer again very much, and I had no hesitation in attributing her uneasiness chiefly to a difficulty in breathing; but my experiment with the kittens had resulted very strangely. I had expected, of course, to see them betray a sense of pain, although in a less degree than their mother; and this would have been sufficient to confirm my opinion concerning the habitual endurance of atmospheric pressure. But I was not prepared to find them, upon close examination, evidently enjoying a high degree of health, breathing with the greatest ease and perfect regularity, and evincing not the slightest sign of any uneasiness. I could only account for all this by extending my theory, and supposing that the highly rarefied atmosphere around might perhaps not be, as I had taken for granted, chemically insufficient for the purposes of

78 At ground level, a feather falls more slowly than a cannon ball because of air resistance. Galileo proved the factor of air resistance when he dropped cannon balls of different mass and volume—but all heavy enough to make the effect of air resistance unnoticeable—at the same time from the leaning tower of Pisa. In a vacuum, a feather and a lead ball would theoretically fall at the same rate. However, the acceleration of gravity does differ at various places on earth, although the differences are quite small. The acceleration of gravity is usually 32 feet (980 cm) per second per second at sea level. (A body starting from rest and falling freely would have a velocity of 32 feet per second at the end of the first second, of 64 feet per second at the end of the second second, of 96 feet per second at the end of the third, and so on.)

79 The first version of the tale contained some gloomier aspects, which Poe removed. At this point was this passage, full of dreamlike imagery, which wound up eventually (in altered form) in "The Island of the Fay": "And out of this melancholy water arose a forest of tall eastern trees, like a wilderness of dreams. And I bore in mind that the shadow of the trees which fell upon the lake remained not on the surface where they fell—but sank slowly and steadily down, and commingled with the waves, while from the trunks of the trees other shadows were continually coming out, and taking the place of their brothers thus entombed. 'This, then,' I said, thoughtfully, 'is the very reason why the waters of this lake grow blacker with age, and more melancholy as the hours run on.'"

The passage is hauntingly beautiful but totally out of place in "Hans Pfaall."

80 This view of the moon dates back to Ariosto (see note 54). Locke's moon hoax (introductory note) claims that Sir John Herschel has perfected a telescope that magnifies 40,000 times and through which objects as small as eighteen inches in diameter can be seen on the moon. Among the "discoveries": winged, manlike creatures, temples, and animals that resemble the American buffalo, but with eye flaps to protect them from the extremes of light and darkness.

life, and that a person born in such a *medium* might, possibly, be unaware of any inconvenience attending its inhalation, while, upon removal to the denser *strata* near the earth, he might endure tortures of a similar nature to those I had so lately experienced. It has since been to me a matter of deep regret that an awkward accident, at this time, occasioned me the loss of my little family of cats, and deprived me of the insight into this matter which a continued experiment might have afforded. In passing my hand through the valve, with a cup of water for the old puss, the sleeve of my shirt became entangled in the loop which sustained the basket, and thus, in a moment, loosened it from the button. Had the whole actually vanished into air, it could not have shot from my sight in a more abrupt and instantaneous manner. Positively, there could not have intervened the tenth part of a second between the disengagement of the basket and its absolute disappearance with all that it contained. My good wishes followed it to the earth, but of course, I had no hope that either cat or kittens would ever live to tell the tale of their misfortune.

81

"At six o'clock, I perceived a great portion of the earth's visible area to the eastward involved in thick shadow, which continued to advance with great rapidity, until, at five minutes before seven, the whole surface in view was enveloped in the darkness of night. It was not, however, until long after this

82

time that the rays of the setting sun ceased to illumine the balloon; and this circumstance, although of course fully anticipated, did not fail to give me an infinite deal of pleasure. It was evident that, in the morning, I should behold the rising luminary many hours at least before the citizens of Rotterdam, in spite of their situation so much farther to the eastward, and thus, day after day, in proportion to the height ascended, would I enjoy the light of the sun for a longer and a longer period. I now determined to keep a journal of my passage, reckoning the days from one to twenty-four hours continuously, without taking into consideration the intervals of darkness.

"At ten o'clock, feeling sleepy, I determined to lie down for the rest of the night; but here a difficulty presented itself, which, obvious as it may appear, had escaped my attention up to the very moment of which I am now speaking. If I went to sleep as I proposed, how could the atmosphere in the chamber be regenerated in the *interim?* To breathe it for more than an hour, at the farthest, would be a matter of impossibility; or, if even this term could be extended to an hour and a quarter, the most ruinous consequences might ensue. The consideration of this dilemma gave me no little disquietude; and it will hardly be believed, that, after the dangers I had undergone, I should look upon this business in so serious a light, as to give up all hope of accomplishing my ultimate design, and finally make up my mind to the necessity of a descent. But this hesitation was only momentary. I reflected that man is the veriest slave of custom, and that many points in the routine of his existence are deemed *essentially* important, which are only so *at all* by his having rendered them habitual. It was

81 This passage is a good example of the tale's uneasy blend of comedy, adventure, science, and sensationalism.

82 At this height there would be no "sunset."

very certain that I could not do without sleep; but I might easily bring myself to feel no inconvenience from being awakened at intervals of an hour during the whole period of my repose. It would require but five minutes at most to **83** regenerate the atmosphere in the fullest manner—and the only real difficulty was to contrive a method of arousing myself at the proper moment for so doing. But this was a question which, I am willing to confess, occasioned me no little trouble in its solution. To be sure, I had heard of the student who, to prevent his falling asleep over his books, held in one hand a ball of copper, the din of whose descent into a basin of the same metal on the floor beside his chair, served effectually to startle him up, if, at any moment, he should be overcome with drowsiness. My own case, however, was very different indeed, and left me no room for any similar idea; for I did not wish to keep awake, but to be aroused from slumber at regular intervals of time. I at length hit upon the following expedient, which, simple as it may seem, was hailed by me, at the moment of discovery, as an invention fully equal to that of the telescope, the steam-engine, or the art of printing itself.

"It is necessary to premise, that the balloon, at the elevation now attained, continued its course upward with an even and undeviating ascent, and the car consequently followed with a steadiness so perfect that it would have been impossible to detect in it the slightest vacillation. This circumstance favored me greatly in the project I now determined to adopt. My supply of water had been put on board in kegs containing five gallons each, and ranged very securely around the interior of the car. I unfastened one of these, and taking two ropes, tied them tightly across the rim of the wicker-work from one side to the other; placing them about a foot apart and parallel, so as to form a kind of shelf, upon which I placed the keg, and steadied it in a horizontal position. About eight inches immediately below these ropes, and four feet from the bottom of the car I fastened another shelf—but made of thin plank, being the only similar piece of wood I had. Upon this latter shelf, and exactly beneath one of the rims of the keg, a small earthen pitcher was deposited. I now bored a hole in the end of the keg over the pitcher, and fitted in a plug of soft wood, cut in a tapering or conical shape. This plug I pushed in or pulled out as might happen, until, after a few experiments, it arrived at that exact degree of tightness, at which the water, oozing from the hole, and falling into the pitcher below, would fill the latter to the brim in the period of sixty minutes. This, of course, was a matter briefly and easily ascertained, by noticing the proportion of the pitcher filled in any given time. **84** Having arranged all this, the rest of the plan is obvious. My bed was so contrived upon the floor of the car, as to bring my head, in lying down, immediately below the mouth of the pitcher. It was evident, that, at the expiration of an hour, the pitcher, getting full, would be forced to run over, and to run over at the mouth, which was somewhat lower than the rim. It was also evident, that the water thus falling from a height of more than four feet, could not do otherwise than fall upon

83 Recent research on sleep patterns refutes this. Subjects in experiments were attached to sensitive electronic devices and watched while they drifted off to sleep. If they were awakened often, and not allowed to have any sustained periods of deep sleep, most exhibited signs of stress, such as disorientation, grogginess.

84 This Rube Goldberg-like device is the clepsydra, or water clock, an earthenware vessel with a small opening that lets water out drop by drop. If the size of the container and the hole are such that the water passed can be marked off into twenty-four divisions, the device serves to measure time fairly well. Clepsydras date back to 2000 B.C.; later models sometimes used wheels, floats, and gears.

my face, and that the sure consequence would be, to waken me up instantaneously, even from the soundest slumber in the world.

"It was fully eleven by the time I had completed these arrangements, and I immediately betook myself to bed, with full confidence in the efficiency of my invention. Nor in this matter was I disappointed. Punctually every sixty minutes was I aroused by my trusty chronometer, when, having emptied the pitcher into the bung-hole of the keg, and performed the duties of the condenser, I retired again to bed. These regular interruptions to my slumber caused me even less discomfort than I had anticipated; and when I finally arose for the day, it was seven o'clock, and the sun had attained many degrees above the line of my horizon.

"*April 3d*. I found the balloon at an immense height indeed, and the earth's convexity had now become strikingly manifest. Below me in the ocean lay a cluster of black specks, which undoubtedly were islands. Overhead, the sky was a jetty black, and the stars were brilliantly visible; indeed they had been so constantly since the first day of ascent. Far away to the northward I perceived a thin, white, and exceedingly brilliant line, or streak, on the edge of the horizon, and I had no hesitation in supposing it to be the southern disc of the ices of the Polar sea. My curiosity was greatly excited, for I had hopes of passing on much farther to the north, and might possibly, at some period, find myself placed directly above the Pole itself. I now lamented that my great elevation would, in this case, prevent my taking as accurate a survey as I could wish. Much, however, might be ascertained.

"Nothing else of an extraordinary nature occurred during the day. My apparatus all continued in good order, and the balloon still ascended without any perceptible vacillation. The cold was intense, and obliged me to wrap up closely in an overcoat. When darkness came over the earth, I betook myself to bed, although it was for many hours afterward broad daylight all around my immediate situation. The water-clock was punctual in its duty, and I slept until next morning soundly, with the exception of the periodical interruption.

"*April 4th*. Arose in good health and spirits, and was astonished at the singular change which had taken place in the appearance of the sea. It had lost, in a great measure, the deep tint of blue it had hitherto worn, being now of a grayish-white, and of a lustre dazzling to the eye. The convexity of the ocean had become so evident, that the entire mass of the distant water seemed to be tumbling headlong over the abyss of the horizon, and I found myself listening on tiptoe for the echoes of the mighty cataract. The islands were no longer visible; whether they had passed down the horizon to the southeast, or whether my increasing elevation had left them out of sight, it is impossible to say. I was inclined, however, to the latter opinion. The rim of ice to the northward was growing more and more apparent. Cold by no means so intense. Nothing of importance occurred, and I passed the day in reading, having taken care to supply myself with books.

85 The blueness of the earth from space is caused by our atmosphere, which scatters blue light and absorbs red.

"*April 5th*. Beheld the singular phenomenon of the sun rising while nearly the whole visible surface of the earth continued to be involved in darkness. In time, however, the light spread itself over all, and I again saw the line of ice to the northward. It was now very distinct, and appeared of a much darker hue than the waters of the ocean. I was evidently approaching it, and with great rapidity. Fancied I could again distinguish a strip of land to the eastward, and one also to the westward, but could not be certain. Weather moderate. Nothing of any consequence happened during the day. Went early to bed.

"*April 6th*. Was surprised at finding the rim of ice at a very moderate distance, and an immense field of the same material stretching away off to the horizon in the north. It was evident that if the balloon held its present course, it would soon arrive above the Frozen Ocean, and I had now little doubt of ultimately seeing the Pole. During the whole of the day I continued to near the ice. Toward night the limits of my horizon very suddenly and materially increased, owing undoubtedly to the earth's form being that of an oblate spheroid, and my arriving above the flattened regions in the vicinity of the Arctic circle. When darkness at length overtook me, I went to bed in great anxiety, fearing to pass over the object of so much curiosity when I should have no opportunity of observing it.

"*April 7th*. Arose early, and, to my great joy, at length beheld what there could be no hesitation in supposing the northern Pole itself. It was there, beyond a doubt, and immediately beneath my feet; but, alas! I had now ascended to so vast a distance, that nothing could with accuracy be discerned. Indeed, to judge from the progression of the numbers indicating my various altitudes, respectively, at different periods, between six A.M. on the second of April, and twenty minutes before nine A.M. of the same day (at which time the barometer ran down), it might be fairly inferred that the balloon had now, at four o'clock in the morning of April the seventh, reached a height of *not less*, certainly, than 7254 miles above the surface of the sea. This elevation may appear immense, but the estimate upon which it is calculated gave a result in all probability far inferior to the truth. At all events I undoubtedly beheld the whole of the earth's major diameter; **86** the entire northern hemisphere lay beneath me like a chart orthographically projected; and the great circle of the equator itself formed the boundary line of my horizon. Your Excellencies may, however, readily imagine that the confined regions hitherto unexplored within the limits of the Arctic circle, although situated directly beneath me, and therefore seen without any appearance of being foreshortened, were still, in themselves, comparatively too diminutive, and at too great a distance from the point of sight, to admit of any very accurate examination. Nevertheless, what could be seen was of a nature singular and exciting. Northwardly from that huge rim before mentioned, and which, with slight qualification, may be called the limit of human discovery in these regions, one unbroken,

86 There is *no* finite distance from which one can see as much as half the surface of *any* sphere.

87 While we would expect the polar regions to appear a dazzling white, we must remember that in Poe's day nobody had actually seen the poles. According to one theory of the time, at each pole was a tremendous cataract, a whirlpool into which the oceans flowed and circulated to the opposite pole (see "MS. Found in a Bottle" and "A Descent into the Maelström").

It is probably this theory that accounts for the "dusky hue" of the pole and the "absolute blackness" of its center.

88 All space voyages, manned or not, must take into account not only the orbiting movement of a planet but also the shape of that orbit. Poe correctly considers that problem here.

or nearly unbroken, sheet of ice continues to extend. In the first few degrees of this its progress, its surface is very sensibly flattened, farther on depressed into a plane, and finally, becoming *not a little concave*, it terminates, at the Pole itself, in a circular centre, sharply defined, whose apparent diameter subtended at the balloon an angle of about sixty-five seconds, and whose dusky hue, varying in intensity, was, at all times, darker than any other spot upon the visible hemisphere, and **87** occasionally deepened into the most absolute blackness. Farther than this, little could be ascertained. By twelve o'clock the circular centre had materially decreased in circumference, and by seven, P.M. I lost sight of it entirely; the balloon passing over the western limb of the ice, and floating away rapidly in the direction of the equator.

"*April 8th.* Found a sensible diminution in the earth's apparent diameter, besides a material alteration in its general color and appearance. The whole visible area partook in different degrees of a tint of pale yellow, and in some portions had acquired a brilliancy even painful to the eye. My view downward was also considerably impeded by the dense atmosphere in the vicinity of the surface being loaded with clouds, between whose masses I could only now and then obtain a glimpse of the earth itself. This difficulty of direct vision had troubled me more or less for the last forty-eight hours; but my present enormous elevation brought closer together, as it were, the floating bodies of vapor, and the inconvenience became, of course, more and more palpable in proportion to my ascent. Nevertheless, I could easily perceive that the balloon now hovered above the range of great lakes in the continent of North America, and was holding a course, due south, which would soon bring me to the tropics. This circumstance did not fail to give me the most heartfelt satisfaction, and I hailed it as a happy omen of ultimate success. Indeed, the direction I had hitherto taken, had filled me with uneasiness; for it was evident that, had I continued it much longer, there would have been no possibility of my arriving at the moon at all, whose orbit is inclined to the ecliptic at only the small angle of 5° 8′ 48″. Strange as it may seem, it was only at this late period that I began to understand the great error I had committed, in not taking my departure **88** from earth at some point *in the plane of the lunar ellipse*.

"*April 9th.* To-day, the earth's diameter was greatly diminished, and the color of the surface assumed hourly a deeper tint of yellow. The balloon kept steadily on her course to the southward, and arrived, at nine, P.M., over the northern edge of the Mexican Gulf.

"*April 10th.* I was suddenly aroused from slumber, about five o'clock this morning, by a loud, crackling, and terrific sound, for which I could in no manner account. It was of very brief duration, but, while it lasted, resembled nothing in the world of which I had any previous experience. It is needless to say that I became excessively alarmed, having, in the first instance, attributed the noise to the bursting of the balloon. I examined all my apparatus, however, with great attention, and could discover nothing out of order. Spent a great part of the day in meditating upon an occurrence so extraordinary, but could find no means whatever of accounting for it. Went to bed dissatisfied, and in a state of great anxiety and agitation.

"*April 11th*. Found a startling diminution in the apparent diameter of the earth, and a considerable increase, now observable for the first time, in that of the moon itself, which wanted only a few days of being full. It now required long and excessive labor to condense within the chamber sufficient atmospheric air for the sustenance of life.

"*April 12th*. A singular alteration took place in regard to the direction of the balloon, and although fully anticipated, afforded me the most unequivocal delight. Having reached, in its former course, about the twentieth parallel of southern latitude, it turned off suddenly, at an acute angle, to the eastward, and thus proceeded throughout the day, keeping nearly, if not altogether, *in the exact plane of the lunar ellipse*. What was worthy of remark, a very perceptible vacillation in the car was a consequence of this change of route,—a vacillation which prevailed, in a more or less degree, for a period of many hours. **89**

"*April 13th*. Was again very much alarmed by a repetition of the loud crackling noise which terrified me on the tenth. Thought long upon the subject, but was unable to form any satisfactory conclusion. Great decrease in the earth's apparent diameter, which now subtended from the balloon an angle of very little more than twenty-five degrees. The moon could not be seen at all, being nearly in my zenith. I still continued in the plane of the ellipse, but made little progress to the eastward.

"*April 14th*. Extremely rapid decrease in the diameter of the earth. Today I became strongly impressed with the idea, that the balloon was now actually running up the line of apsides to the point of perigree,—in other words, holding the **90** direct course which would bring it immediately to the moon in that part of its orbit the nearest to the earth. The moon itself was directly overhead, and consequently hidden from my view. Great and long-continued labor necessary for the condensation of the atmosphere.

"*April 15th*. Not even the outlines of continents and seas could now be traced upon the earth with distinctness. About twelve o'clock I became aware, for the third time, of that appalling sound which had so astonished me before. It now, however, continued for some moments, and gathered intensity as it continued. At length, while, stupefied and terror-stricken, I stood in expectation of I knew not what hideous destruction, the car vibrated with excessive violence, and a gigantic and flaming mass of some material which I could not distinguish, came with a voice of a thousand thunders, roaring and booming by the balloon. When my fears and astonishment had in some degree subsided, I had little difficulty in supposing it to be some mighty volcanic fragment ejected from that world to which I was so rapidly approaching, and, in all probability, one of that singular class of substances occasionally picked up

89 The point where the gravity of the moon becomes stronger—relative to the balloon—than that of the earth

90 The plural of *apsis*, the point in an orbit at which the distance of the body from the center of attraction is either greatest or least. The *perigee* is the point in the orbit that is nearest the earth.

91 The concept that meteorites are volcanic rocks thrown from lunar eruptions seems to be Poe's invention. Today we know that the moon has been inactive for millions of years and that even when active its gravity would have prevented any expelled matter from hurtling earthward.

on the earth, and termed meteoric stones for want of a better **91** appellation.

"*April 16th*. To-day, looking upward as well as I could, through each of the side windows alternately, I beheld, to my great delight, a very small portion of the moon's disc protruding, as it were, on all sides beyond the huge circumference of the balloon. My agitation was extreme; for I had now little doubt of soon reaching the end of my perilous voyage. Indeed, the labor now required by the condenser, had increased to a most oppressive degree, and allowed me scarcely any respite from exertion. Sleep was a matter nearly out of the question. I became quite ill, and my frame trembled with exhaustion. It was impossible that human nature could endure this state of intense suffering much longer. During the now brief interval of darkness a meteoric stone again passed in my vicinity, and the frequency of these phenomena began to occasion me much apprehension.

"*April 17th*. This morning proved an epoch in my voyage. It will be remembered that, on the thirteenth, the earth subtended an angular breadth of twenty-five degrees. On the fourteenth this had greatly diminished; on the fifteenth a still more remarkable decrease was observable; and, on retiring on the night of the sixteenth, I had noticed an angle of no more than about seven degrees and fifteen minutes. What, therefore must have been my amazement, on awakening from a brief and disturbed slumber, on the morning of this day, the seventeenth, at finding the surface beneath me so suddenly and wonderfully *augmented* in volume, as to subtend no less than thirty-nine degrees in apparent angular diameter! I was thunderstruck! No words can give any adequate idea of the extreme, the absolute horror and astonishment, with which I was seized, possessed, and altogether overwhelmed. My knees tottered beneath me—my teeth chattered—my hair started up on end. 'The balloon, then, had actually burst!' These were the first tumultuous ideas that hurried through my mind: 'The balloon had positively burst!—I was falling— falling with the most impetuous, the most unparalleled velocity! To judge by the immense distance already so quickly passed over, it could not be more than ten minutes, at the farthest, before I should reach the surface of the earth, and be hurled into annihilation!' But at length reflection came to my relief. I paused; I considered; and I began to doubt. The matter was impossible. I could not in any reason have so rapidly come down. Besides, although I was evidently approaching the surface below me, it was with a speed by no means commensurate with the velocity I had at first conceived. This consideration served to calm the perturbation of my mind, and I finally succeeded in regarding the phenomenon in its proper point of view. In fact, amazement must have fairly deprived me of my senses, when I could not see the vast difference, in appearance, between the surface below me, and the surface of my mother earth. The latter was indeed over my head, and completely hidden by the balloon, while the moon—the moon itself in all its glory—lay beneath me, and at my feet.

"The stupor and surprise produced in my mind by this extraordinary change in the posture of affairs, was, perhaps, after all, that part of the adventure least susceptible of explanation. For the *bouleversement* in itself was not only natural and inevitable, but had been long actually anticipated as a circumstance to be expected whenever I should arrive at that exact point of my voyage where the attraction of the planet should be superseded by the attraction of the satellite— or, more precisely, where the gravitation of the balloon toward the earth should be less powerful than its gravitation toward the moon. To be sure I arose from a sound slumber, with all **92** my senses in confusion, to the contemplation of a very startling phenomenon, and one which, although expected, was not expected at the moment. The revolution itself must, of course, have taken place in an easy and gradual manner, and it is by no means clear that, had I even been awake at the time of the occurrence, I should have been made aware of it by any *internal* evidence of an inversion—that is to say, by any inconvenience of disarrangement, either about my person or about my apparatus. **93**

"It is almost needless to say that, upon coming to a due sense of my situation, and emerging from the terror which had absorbed every faculty of my soul, my attention was, in the first place, wholly directed to the contemplation of the general physical appearance of the moon. It lay beneath me like a chart—and although I judged it to be still at no inconsiderable distance, the indentures of its surface were defined to my vision with a most striking and altogether unaccountable distinctness. The entire absence of ocean or sea, and indeed of any lake or river, or body of water whatsoever, struck me, at first glance, as the most extraordinary feature in its geological condition. Yet, strange to say, I **94** beheld vast level regions of a character decidedly alluvial, although by far the greater portion of the hemisphere in sight was covered with innumerable volcanic mountains, conical in shape, and having more the appearance of artificial than of natural protuberances. The highest among them does not exceed three and three-quarter miles in perpendicular elevation; but a map of the volcanic districts of the Campi Phlegræi would afford to your Excellencies a better idea of **95** their general surface than any unworthy description I might think proper to attempt. The greater part of them were in a state of evident eruption, and gave me fearfully to understand their fury and their power, by the repeated thunders of the mis-called meteoric stones, which now rushed upward by the balloon with a frequency more and more appalling.

"*April 18th.* To-day I found an enormous increase in the moon's apparent bulk—and the evidently accelerated velocity of my descent began to fill me with alarm. It will be remembered, that, in the earliest stage of my speculations upon the possibility of a passage to the moon, the existence,

92 Poe does not explain how a balloon strong enough to escape the earth's gravity is affected by that of the moon, which has less mass and thus a lower gravitational pull, or how the balloon escapes the moon's gravity and returns to earth.
Bouleversement means an upset or upheaval.

93 The balloon, which was headed bag-first toward the moon, has now shifted around, with the car—the portion of the craft with the greatest mass—being more strongly affected by the moon's gravitational pull.

94 Although our exploration of the moon has shown this description to be false, it is interesting to recall the shock when Mariner 9's cameras showed alluvial plains on the planet Mars, caused by water flowing two to three miles wide in ages past.

95 A "sulphurous plain between Puteoli and Naples," according to Herschel, and the site of modern Solfatara. Coincidentally, perhaps, the date of Pfaall's landing on the moon—April 19—is also the date for this Poe squib: "Ap. 19, 1787, Dr. Herschel discovered 3 volcanos in the dark part of the moon. 2 of them seemed to be almost extinct, but the 3rd showed an active eruption of fire, or luminous matter, resembling a small piece of burning charcoal covered by a very thin coat of white ashes: it had a degree of brightness about as strong as that with which such a coal would be seen to glow in faint daylight. The adjacent parts of the mountain seemed faintly illuminated by the eruption." (*Works*, Fred de Fau Co., 1902, Vol. 16; p. 353)
Herschel could not have seen an eruption; it might have been a meteor striking the surface, however.

96 While John Jerome Schröter did deal with many of these observations in his *Philosophical Transactions of the Royal Society of London*, Vol. 82, Part 2, article 16, the material here is actually paraphrased from Abraham Rees's Cyclopaedia: "Nature and Furniture of the Moon."

97 "Hevelius writes that he has several times found, in skies perfectly clear, when even stars of the sixth and seventh magnitude were conspicuous, that, at the same altitude of the moon, at the same elongation from the earth, and with one and the same excellent telescope, the moon and its maculae did not appear equally lucid at all times. From the circumstances of the observation, it is evident that the cause of this phenomenon is not either in our air, in the tube, in the moon, or in the eye of the spectator, but must be looked for in something (an atmosphere?) existing about the moon.

"Cassini frequently observed Saturn, Jupiter, and the fixed stars, when approaching the moon to occultation, to have their circular figure changed into an oval one; and, in other occultations, he found no alteration of figure at all. Hence it might be supposed, that *at some times,* and not at others, there is a dense matter encompassing the moon wherein the rays of the stars are refracted." (Poe's note)

"Maculae" means spots, and occultation is the passage of one celestial body in front of a second, thus hiding the second from view.

Jean D. Cassini (1625–1712), a French astronomer, was the first to observe the Great Red Spot, on Jupiter, which we have seen up close only since the Mariner photographs of March 1978. Johannes Hevelius (1611–87), a Danzig-based German astronomer, made valuable observations on the moon's surface, discovered four comets, and collected data for his catalogue of more than fifteen hundred stars.

in its vicinity, of an atmosphere, dense in proportion to the bulk of the planet, had entered largely into my calculations; this too in spite of many theories to the contrary, and, it may be added, in spite of a general disbelief in the existence of any lunar atmosphere at all. But, in addition to what I have already urged in regard to Encke's comet and the zodiacal light, I had been strengthened in my opinion by certain observations of **96** Mr. Schroeter, of Lilienthal. He observed the moon when two days and a half old, in the evening soon after sunset, before the dark part was visible, and continued to watch it until it became visible. The two cusps appeared tapering in a very sharp faint prolongation, each exhibiting its farthest extremity faintly illuminated by the solar rays, before any part of the dark hemisphere was visible. Soon afterward, the whole dark limb became illuminated. This prolongation of the cusps beyond the semicircle, I thought, must have arisen from the refraction of the sun's rays by the moon's atmosphere. I computed, also, the height of the atmosphere (which could refract light enough into its dark hemisphere to produce a twilight more luminous than the light reflected from the earth when the moon is about 32° from the new) to be 1356 Paris feet; in this view, I supposed the greatest height capable of refracting the solar ray, to be 5376 feet. My ideas on this topic had also received confirmation by a passage in the eighty-second volume of the Philosophical Transactions, in which it is stated, that, at an occultation of Jupiter's satellites, the third disappeared after having been about 1″ or 2″ of time indistinct, **97** and the fourth became indiscernible near the limb.

"Upon the resistance or, more properly, upon the support of an atmosphere, existing in the state of density imagined, I had, of course, entirely depended for the safety of my ultimate descent. Should I then, after all, prove to have been mistaken, I had in consequence nothing better to expect, as a *finale* to my adventure, than being dashed into atoms against the rugged surface of the satellite. And, indeed, I had now every reason to be terrified. My distance from the moon was comparatively trifling, while the labor required by the condenser was diminished not at all, and I could discover no indication whatever of a decreasing rarity in the air.

"*April 19th.* This morning, to my great joy, about nine o'clock, the surface of the moon being frightfully near, and my apprehensions excited to the utmost, the pump of my condenser at length gave evident tokens of an alteration in the atmosphere. By ten, I had reason to believe its density considerably increased. By eleven, very little labor was necessary at the apparatus; and at twelve o'clock, with some hesitation, I ventured to unscrew the *tourniquet,* when, finding no inconvenience from having done so, I finally threw open the gum-elastic chamber, and unrigged it from around the car. As might have been expected, spasms and violent headache were the immediate consequences of an experiment so precipitate and full of danger. But these and other difficulties attending respiration, as they were by no means so great as to put me in peril of my life, I determined to endure as I best could, in consideration of my leaving them behind me momently in my approach to the denser *strata* near the moon. This approach, however, was still impetuous in the extreme; and it soon became alarmingly certain that, although I had probably not been deceived in the expectation of an atmosphere dense in proportion to the mass of the satellite, still I had been wrong in supposing this density, even at the surface, at all adequate to the support of the great weight contained in the car of my balloon. Yet this *should* have been the case, and in an equal degree as at the surface of the earth, the actual gravity of bodies at either planet supposed in the ratio of the atmospheric condensation. That it *was not* the case, however, my precipitous downfall gave testimony enough; *why* it was not so, can only be explained by a reference to those possible geological disturbances to which I have formerly alluded. At all events I was now close upon the planet, and coming down with the most terrible impetuosity. I lost not a moment, accordingly, in trhowing overboard first my ballast, then my water-kegs, then my condensing apparatus and gumelastic chamber, and finally every article within the car. But it was all to no purpose. I still fell with horrible rapidity, and was now not more than half a mile from the surface. As a last resource, therefore, having got rid of my coat, hat, and boots, I cut loose from the balloon *the car itself*, which was of no inconsiderable weight, and thus, clinging with both hands to the net-work, I had barely time to observe that the whole country, as far as the eye could reach, was thickly interspersed with diminutive habitations, ere I tumbled headlong into the very heart of a fantastical-looking city, and into the middle of a vast crowd of ugly little people, who none of them uttered a single syllable, or gave themselves the least trouble to render me assistance, but stood, like a parcel of idiots, grinning in a ludicrous manner, and eyeing me and my balloon askant, with their arms set a-kimbo. I turned from them in contempt, and, **98** gazing upward at the earth so lately left, and left perhaps forever, beheld it like a huge, dull, copper shield, about two degrees in diameter, fixed immovably in the heavens overhead, **99** and tipped on one of its edges with a crescent border of the most brilliant gold. No traces of land or water could be discovered, and the whole was clouded with variable spots, and belted with tropical and equatorial zones.

"Thus, may it please your Excellencies, after a series of great anxieties, unheard-of dangers, and unparalleled escapes, **100** I had, at length, on the nineteenth day of my departure from Rotterdam, arrived in safety at the conclusion of a voyage undoubtedly the most extraordinary, and the most momentous, ever accomplished, undertaken, or conceived by any denizen of earth. But my adventures yet remain to be related. And indeed your Excellencies may well imagine that, after a residence of five years upon a planet not only deeply interesting in its own peculiar character, but rendered doubly so by its intimate connection, in capacity of satellite, with the world inhabited by man, I may have intelligence for the private ear of the States' College of Astronomers of far more importance

. . . after a series of great anxieties, unheard-of dangers, and unparalleled escapes, I had, at length, on the nineteenth day of my departure from Rotterdam, arrived in safety at the conclusion of a voyage undoubtedly the most extraordinary, and the most momentous, ever accomplished, undertaken, or conceived by any denizen of earth. *Artist unknown*

98 Poe may have followed the example of a book by German astronomer Johannes Kepler (1571–1630). In *Somnium*, published posthumously in 1634, two characters reach the moon, a planet with air and water, and burning days and frozen nights equal to fourteen earth days each.

99 "If there be inhabitants in the moon, the earth must present to them the extraordinary appearance of a moon of nearly 2° in diameter, exhibiting the same phases as we see the moon to do, but *immoveably fixed in their sky* . . ." (Herschel, p. 220).

100 These would have been included in the next episodes of the story, but the appearance of "The Moon Hoax" ended that plan. The brief commentary on the moon that follows is, again, from Herschel.

than the details, however wonderful, of the mere *voyage* which so happily concluded. This is, in fact, the case. I have much—very much which it would give me the greatest pleasure to communicate. I have much to say of the climate of the planet; of its wonderful alternations of heat and cold; of unmitigated and burning sunshine for one fortnight, and more than polar frigidity for the next; of a constant transfer of moisture, by distillation like that *in vacuo*, from the point beneath the sun to the point the farthest from it; of a variable zone of running water; of the people themselves; of their manners, customs, and political institutions; of their peculiar physical construction; of their ugliness; of their want of ears, those useless appendages in an atmosphere so peculiarly modified; of their consequent ignorance of the use and properties of speech; of their substitute for speech in a singular method of inter-communication; of the incomprehensible connection between each particular individual in the moon with some particular individual on the earth—a connection analogous with, and depending upon, that of the orbs of the planet and the satellite, and by means of which the lives and destinies of the inhabitants of the one are interwoven with the

101 lives and destinies of the inhabitants of the other; and above all, if it so please your Excellencies—above all, of those dark and hideous mysteries which lie in the outer regions of the moon,—regions which, owing to the almost miraculous accordance of the satellite's rotation on its own axis with its sidereal revolution about the earth, have never yet been turned, and, by God's mercy, never shall be turned, to the scrutiny of the telescopes of man. All this, and more—much more—would I most willingly detail. But, to be brief, I must have my reward. I am pining for a return to my family and to my home; and as the price of any farther communication on my part—in consideration of the light which I have it in my power to throw upon many very important branches of physical and metaphysical science—I must solicit, through the influence of your honorable body, a pardon for the crime of which I have been guilty in the death of the creditors upon by departure from Rotterdam. This, then, is the object of the present paper. Its bearer, an inhabitant of the moon, whom I have prevailed upon, and properly instructed, to be my messenger to the earth, will await your Excellencies' pleasure, and return to me with the pardon in question, if it can, in any manner, be obtained.

"I have the honor to be, &c, your Excellencies' very humble servant,

HANS PFAALL"

Upon finishing the perusal of this very extraordinary document, Professor Rubadub, it is said, dropped his pipe upon the ground in the extremity of his surprise, and Mynheer Superbus Von Underduk having taken off his spectacles, wiped them, and deposited them in his pocket, so far forgot both himself and his dignity, as to turn round three times upon his heel in the quintessence of astonishment and admiration.

101 A reference to "lunacy," the notion that mental illness is caused by the effect of the moon on certain people (see "The System of Doctor Tarr and Professor Fether," note 13).

The letter, having been published, gave rise to a variety of gossip. . . . *Illustration by John Friedrich Vogel*

There was no doubt about the matter—the pardon should be obtained. So at least swore, with a round oath, Professor Rubadub, and so finally thought the illustrious Von Underduk, as he took the arm of his brother in science, and without saying a word, began to make the best of his way home to deliberate upon the measures to be adopted. Having reached the door, however, of the burgomaster's dwelling, the professor ventured to suggest that as the messenger had thought proper to disappear—no doubt frightened to death by the savage appearance of the burghers of Rotterdam—the pardon would be of little use, as no one but a man of the moon would undertake a voyage to so vast a distance. To the truth of this observation the burgomaster assented, and the matter was therefore at an end. Not so, however, rumors and speculations. The letter, having been published, gave rise to a variety of gossip and opinion. Some of the over-wise even made themselves ridiculous by decrying the whole business as nothing better than a hoax. But hoax, with these sort of people, is, I believe, a general term for all matters above their comprehension. For my part, I cannot conceive upon what data they have founded such an accusation. Let us see what they say:

Imprimis. That certain wags in Rotterdam have certain especial antipathies to certain burgomasters and astronomers. **102**

Secondly. That an odd little dwarf and bottle conjurer, both of whose ears, for some misdemeanor, have been cut off close to his head, has been missing for several days from the neighboring city of Bruges. **103**

Thirdly. That the newspapers which were stuck all over the little balloon were newspapers of Holland, and therefore could not have been made in the moon. They were dirty papers—very dirty—and Gluck, the printer, would take his Bible oath to their having been printed in Rotterdam.

Fourthly. That Hans Pfaall himself, the drunken villain, and the three very idle gentlemen styled his creditors, were all **104** seen, no longer than two or three days ago, in a tippling house in the suburbs, having just returned, with money in their pockets, from a trip beyond the sea.

Lastly. That it is an opinion very generally received, or which ought to be generally received, that the College of Astronomers in the city of Rotterdam, as well as all other colleges in all other parts of the world,—not to mention colleges and astronomers in general,—are, to say the least of the matter, not a whit better, nor greater, nor wiser than they ought to be. **105**

102 As usual, Poe provides a logical explanation for the fantastic events, in case one is necessary.

The point here seems to be that both politicians and theoreticians are by nature the butt of practical jokers.

103 The "moon creature" that the Rotterdam crowd thought they had seen

104 Poe seems to provide a hint of plot at the last. Their money was in turn borrowed from someone else, so that Pfaall provided both an excuse for their disappearance and a means for gathering a large sum of money.

105 In other words, they are as easily caught by a practical joke as the next man.

[Poe's note follows]
"Strictly speaking, there is but little similarity between the above sketchy trifle and the celebrated 'Moon-Story' of Mr. Locke; but as both have the character of *hoaxes* (although the one is in a tone of banter, the other of downright earnest) and as both hoaxes are on the same subject, the moon,—moreover, as both attempt to give plausibility by scientific detail,—the author of 'Hans Pfaall' thinks it necessary to say, in *self-defence*, that his own *jeu d'esprit* was published, in the *Southern Literary Messenger*, about three weeks before the commencement of Mr. L's in the *New York Sun*. Fancying a likeness which, perhaps, does not exist, some of the New York papers copied 'Hans Pfaall,' and collated it with the 'Moon-Hoax,' by way of detecting the writer of the one in the writer of the other.

"As many more persons were actually gulled by the 'Moon-Hoax' than would be willing to acknowledge the fact, it may here afford some little amusement to show why no one should have been deceived—to point out those particulars of the story which should have been sufficient to establish its real character. Indeed, however rich the imagination displayed in this ingenious fiction, it wanted much of the force which might have been given it by a more scrupulous attention to facts and to general analogy. That the public were misled, even for an instant, merely proves the gross ignorance which is so generally prevalent upon subjects of an astronomical nature.

[Poe writes elsewhere: "Immediately on the completion of the 'Moon Story' (it was three or four days in getting finished), I wrote an examination of its claims to credit, showing distinctly its fictitious character, but was astonished at finding that I could obtain few listeners, so really eager were all to be deceived, so magical were the charms of a style that served as the vehicle of an exceedingly clumsy invention" (*Godey's*, 1846). This public gullibility probably prompted him to try a similar trick in "The Balloon-Hoax."]

"The moon's distance from the earth is, in round numbers, 240,000 miles. If we desire to ascertain how near, apparently, a lens would bring the satellite (or any distant object), we, of course, have but to divide the distance by the magnifying or, more strictly, by the space-penetrating power of the glass. Mr. L. makes his lens have a power of 42,000 times. By this divide 240,000 (the moon's real distance), and we have five miles and five sevenths, as the apparent distance. No animal at all could be seen so far; much less the minute points particularized in the story. Mr. L. speaks about Sir John Herschel's perceiving flowers (the Papaver rheas, etc.), and even detecting the color and the shape of the eyes of small birds. Shortly before, too, he has himself observed that the lens would not render perceptible objects of less than eighteen inches in diameter; but even this, as I have said, is giving the glass by far too great power. It may be observed, in passing, that this prodigious glass is said to have been moulded at the glass-house of Messrs. Hartley and Grant, in Dumbarton; but Messrs. H. and G.'s establishment had ceased operations for many years previous to the publication of the hoax.

"On page 13, pamphlet edition, speaking of 'a hairy veil' over the eyes of a species of bison, the author says: 'It immediately occurred to the acute mind of Dr. Herschel that this was a providential contrivance to protect the eyes of the animal from the great extremes of light and darkness to which all the inhabitants of our side of the moon are periodically subjected.' But this cannot be thought a very 'acute' observation of the Doctor's. The inhabitants of our side of the moon have, evidently, no darkness at all, so there can be nothing of the 'extremes' mentioned. In the absence of the sun they have a light from the earth equal to that of thirteen full unclouded moons.

"The topography throughout, even when professing to accord with Blunt's Lunar Chart, is entirely at variance with that or any other lunar chart, and even grossly at variance with itself. The points of the compass, too, are in inextricable confusion; the writer appearing to be ignorant that, on a lunar map, these are not in accordance with terrestial points; the east being to the left, etc.

"Deceived, perhaps, by the vague titles, *Mare Nubium, Mare Tranquillitatis, Mare Fœcunditatis*, etc., given to the dark spots by former astronomers, Mr. L. has entered into details regarding oceans and other large bodies of water in the moon; whereas there is no astronomical point more positively ascertained than that no such bodies exist there. In examining the boundary between light and darkness (in the crescent or gibbous moon) where this boundary crosses any of the dark places, the line of division is found to be rough and jagged; but, were these dark places liquid, it would evidently be seen.

"The description of the wings of the man-bat, on page 21, is but a literal copy of Peter Wilkins' account of the wings of his flying islanders. This simple fact should have induced suspicion, at least, it might be thought. [*The Life and Adventures of Peter Wilkins: a Cornish Man* (1751), by Robert Paltock; it was turned into a play for the New York stage in 1840.]

"On page 23, we have the following: 'What a prodigious influence must our thirteen times larger globe have exercised upon this satellite when an embryo in the womb of time, the passive subject of chemical affinity!' This is very fine; but it should be observed that no astronomer would have made such remark, especially to any Journal of Science; for the earth, in the sense intended, is not only thirteen, but forty-nine times *larger* than the moon. A similar objection applies to the whole of the concluding pages, where, by way of introduction to some discoveries in Saturn, the philosophical correspondent enters into a minute school-boy account of that planet:—this to the *Edinburgh Journal of Science!*

"But there is one point, in particular, which should have betrayed the fiction. Let us imagine the power actually possessed of seeing animals upon the moon's surface;—what would *first* arrest the attention of an observer from the earth? Certainly neither their shape, size, nor any other such peculiarity, so soon as their remarkable *situation*. They would appear to be walking, with heels up and head down, in the manner of flies on a ceiling. The *real* observer would have uttered an instant ejaculation of surprise (however prepared by previous knowledge) at the singularity of their position; the *fictitious* observer has not even mentioned the subject, but speaks of seeing the entire bodies of such creatures, when it is demonstrable that he could have seen only the diameter of their heads! [Only if he were looking head-on]

"It might as well be remarked, in conclusion, that the size, and particularly the powers of the man-bats (for example, their ability to fly in so rare an atmosphere—if, indeed, the moon have any), with most of the other fancies in regard to animal and vegetable existence, are at variance, generally, with all analogical reasoning on these themes; and that analogy here will often amount to conclusive demonstration. It is, perhaps, scarcely necessary to add, that all the suggestions attributed to Brewster and Herschel, in the beginning of the article, about 'a transfusion of artificial light through the focal object of vision,' etc., etc., belong to that species of figurative writing which comes, most properly, under the denomination of rigmarole. [David Brewster (1781–1868) was the Scottish physicist and natural philosopher noted for his research into the polarization of light and for the invention of a kaleidoscope.]

"There is a real and very definite limit to optical discovery among the stars—a limit whose nature need only be stated to be understood. If, indeed, the casting of large lenses were all that is required, man's ingenuity would ultimately prove equal to the task, and we might have them of any size demanded. But, unhappily, in proportion to the increase of size in the lens, and consequently, of space-penetrating power, is the diminution of light from the object, by diffusion of its rays. And for this evil there is no remedy within human ability; for an object is seen by means of that light alone which proceeds from itself, whether direct or reflected. Thus the only 'artificial' light which could avail Mr. Locke, would be some artificial light which he should be able to throw—not upon the 'focal object of vision,' but upon the real object to be viewed—to wit: *upon the moon*. It has been easily calculated that, when the light proceeding from a star becomes so diffused as to be as weak as the natural light proceeding from the whole of the stars, in a clear and moonless night, then the star is no longer visible for any practical purpose.

"The Earl of Ross telescope, lately constructed in England, has a *speculum* with a reflecting surface of 4071 square inches; the Herschel telescope having one of only 1811. The metal of the Earl of Ross' is 6 feet in diameter; it is 5½ inches thick at the edges, and 5 at the centre. The weight is 3 tons. The focal length is 50 feet. [The Earl of Rosse's telescope was the largest of the day. Observations, which began in 1845 in Ireland, were centered on the nebulae. William Parsons, Earl of Rosse (1800–67) overcame defects caused by warping and cracking of glass surfaces in the cooling process, and counteracted to a considerable degree other defects that had hindered telescopic observation in the past. The telescope to which Poe refers had a speculum six feet in diameter.]

"I have lately read a singular and somewhat ingenious little book, whose title-page runs thus:—'L'Homme dans la lvne, ou le Voyage Chimerique fait au Monde de la Lvne, nouuellement decouuert par Dominique Gonzales, Aduanturier Espagnol, autremèt dit le Courier volant. Mis en notre langve par J. B. D. A. Paris, chez François Piot, pres la Fontaine de Saint Benoist. Et chez J. Goignard, au premier pilier de la grand' salle du Palais, proche les Consultations, MDCXLVII.' Pp. 176. [The book is actually *The Man in the Moon; or a Discourse of a Voyager thither, by Domingo Gonsales the Speedy Messenger* (1638), by Bishop Francis Godwin. The French edition was translated by Jean Baudoin; the initials should be J. B. A., not J. B. D. A. Jules Verne was also under the impression that the 1648 version was the original, and not a translation.]

"The writer professes to have translated his work from

the English of one Mr. D'Avisson (Davidson?) although
there is a terrible ambiguity in the statement. 'J'en ai
eu,' says he, 'l'original de Monsieur D'Avisson, medecin
des mieux versez qui soient aujourd'huy dans la
cònoissance des Belles Lettres, et sur tout de la Philosophie Naturelle. Je lui ai cette obligation entre les
autres, de m'auoir non seulement mis en main ce Livre
en anglois, mais encore le Manuscrit du Sieur Thomas
D'Anan, gentilhomme Eccossois, recommandable par sa
vertu, sur la version duquel j'advoue que j'ay tire le plan
de la mienne.' ["I have had the original of Mr. Davisson,
a doctor who writes better verses than can be understood
today by the *Belles Lettres* and above all, Natural
Philosophy. I have felt obligated to have at hand not
only the book in English, but also the manuscript of Sir
Thomas D'Anan, a Scottish gentleman (estimable because of his honesty), from which I acknowledge that I
have derived mine."]

"After some irrelevant adventures, much in the manner of Gil Blas [the hero of Lesage's novel of the same
name], and which occupy the first thirty pages, the
author related that, being ill during a sea voyage, the
crew abandoned him, together with a negro servant, on
the island of St. Helena. To increase the chances of
obtaining food, the two separate, and live as far apart as
possible. This brings about a training of birds, to serve
the purpose of carrier-pigeons between them. By and
by these are taught to carry parcels of some weight—
and this weight is gradually increased. At length the idea
is entertained of uniting the force of a great number of
the birds, with a view to raising the author himself. A
machine is contrived for the purpose, and we have a
minute description of it, which is materially helped out
by a steel engraving. Here we perceive the Signor
Gonzales, with point ruffles and a huge periwig, seated
astride something which resembles very closely a broom-
stick, and borne aloft by a multitude of wild swans
(*ganzas*) who had strings reaching from their tails to the
machine.

"The main event detailed in the Signor's narrative
depends upon a very important fact, of which the reader
is kept in ignorance until near the end of the book. The
ganzas, with whom he had become so familiar, were not
really denizens of St. Helena, but of the moon. Thence
it had been their custom, time out of mind, to migrate
annually to some portion of the earth. In proper season,
of course, they would return home; and the author,
happening, one day, to require their services for a short
voyage, is unexpectedly carried straight up, and in a
very brief period arrives at the satellite. Here he finds,
among other odd things, that the people enjoy extreme
happiness; that they have no *law;* that they die without
pain; that they are from ten to thirty feet in height; that
they live five thousand years; that they have an emperor
called Irdonozur; and that they can jump sixty feet high,
when, being out of the gravitating influence, they fly
about with fans.

"I cannot forbear giving a specimen of the general
philosophy of the volume.

" 'I must now declare to you,' says the Signor Gonzales,
'the nature of the place in which I found myself. All the
clouds were beneath my feet, or, if you please, spread
between me and the earth. As to the stars, *since there
was no night where I was, they always had the same
appearance; not brilliant, as usual, but pale, and very
nearly like the moon of a morning*. But few of them
were visible, and these ten times larger (as well as I
could judge), than they seem to the inhabitants of the
earth. The moon which wanted two days of being full,
was of a terrible bigness.

" 'I must not forget here, that the stars appeared only
on that side of the globe turned toward the moon, and

that the closer they were to it the larger they seemed. I have also to inform you that, whether it was calm weather or stormy, I found *myself always immediately between the moon and the earth*. I was convinced of this for two reasons—because my birds always flew in a straight line; and because whenever we attempted to rest, *we were carried insensibly around the globe of the earth*. For I admit the opinion of Copernicus, who maintains that it never ceases to revolve *from the east to the west*, not upon the poles of the Equinoctial, commonly called the poles of the world, but upon those of the Zodiac, a question of which I propose to speak more at length hereafter, when I shall have leisure to refresh my memory in regard to the astrology which I learned at Salamanca when young, and have since forgotten.'

"Notwithstanding the blunders italicized, the book is not without some claim to attention, as affording a naïve specimen of the current astronomical notions of the time. One of these assumed, that the 'gravitating power' extended but a short distance from the earth's surface, and, accordingly, we find our voyager 'carried insensibly around the globe,' etc.

"There have been other 'voyages to the moon,' but none of higher merit than the one just mentioned. That of Bergerac is utterly meaningless. [Cyrano de Bergerac wrote *Histoire comique des Etats et Empires de la Lune*, although the first edition (1650) was entitled *Histoire comique du Voyage dans la Lune*.] In the third volume of the *American Quarterly Review* will be found quite an elaborate criticism upon a certain 'Journey' of the kind in question;—a criticism in which it is difficult to say whether the critic most exposes the stupidity of the book, or his own absurd ignorance of astronomy. I forget the title of the work [*A Voyage to the Moon* (1827), by Joseph Atterley, a pseudonym for George Tucker, one of Poe's professors at Virginia]; but the *means* of the voyage are more deplorably ill conceived than are even the *ganzas* of our friend the Signor Gonzales. The adventurer, in digging the earth, happens to discover a peculiar metal for which the moon has a strong attraction, and straightaway constructs of it a box, which when cast loose from its terrestrial fastenings, flies with him, forthwith, to the satellite. The 'Flight of Thomas O'Rourke,' is a *jeu d'esprit* not altogether contemptible, and has been translated into German. Thomas, the hero, was, in fact, the gamekeeper of an Irish peer, whose eccentricities gave rise to the tale. The 'flight' is made on an eagle's back, from Hungry Hill, a lofty mountain at the end of Bantry Bay.

"In these various *brochures* the aim is always satirical; the theme being a description of Lunarian customs as compared with ours. In none, is there any effort at *plausibility* in the details of the voyage itself. The writers seem, in each instance, to be utterly uninformed in respect to astronomy. In 'Hans Pfaall' the design is original, inasmuch as regards an attempt at *verisimilitude*, in the application of scientific principles (so far as the whimsical nature of the subject would permit), to the actual passage between the earth and the moon." [Poe's note, added to the version that appeared in the Griswold-edited *Works* (1850)]

KING PEST

A TALE CONTAINING AN ALLEGORY [1]

First published in the *Southern Literary Messenger*, September 1835, then revised for the *Broadway Journal*, October 18, 1845, and revised again for the 1850 edition of *Works*, "King Pest" is one of Poe's more bewildering pieces, a jarring combination of humor and horror that has puzzled and bothered most readers since it first appeared. Poe must have felt strongly about it, for he reworked it several times, but despite occasional resemblances to "The Masque of the Red Death," it must rank as one of Poe's failures—albeit a fascinating one.

Sources for the tale include a story in the *London Naval Chronicle*, April 1811, which says in part: "Anno 1779, one Mr. Constable of Woolwich, passing through the church-yard of that place, at 12 o'clock at night, was surprised to hear a loud noise like that of several persons singing; at first he thought it proceeded from the church, but on going to the church doors, found them fast shut, and within silent. The noise continuing, he looked round the church-yard, and observed a light in one of the large family tombs; going up to it, he found some drunken sailors, who had got into a vault, and were regaling themselves with bread, cheese, and tobacco, and strong beer. . . . In their jollity, they had opened some of the coffins, and crammed the mouth of one of the bodies full of bread, cheese, and beer. Mr. Constable, with much difficulty, prevailed on them to return to their ship. In their way thither one of them being much in liquor, fell down, and was suffocated in the mud. On which his comrades took him up on their shoulders, bringing him back to sleep in company with the *honest gemmen* with whom he passed the evening."

There are two other possible sources: an article by N. P. Willis on a Parisian revel quoted and discussed in the notes to "Masque of the Red Death"; and the first chapter of Book VI of Benjamin Disraeli's *Vivian Grey* (1826), in which guests at a party have odd features, and a gate-crasher is held down and made to drink a large amount of liquor. Some other details in Disraeli's novel, including the language, also resemble Poe's tale.

---

1 Poe disliked allegory, or so he said at several points in his career, because it allowed no subtlety (see his review of Hawthorne's *Twice-Told Tales*). It may be that this tale is an attempt to spoof the allegory form, but if so, it meets with as little success as Poe claims for the serious allegorists. See note 30.

2 From *Gorboduc* (1561), by Thomas Norton and Thomas Sackville, Lord Buckhurst, the earliest English tragedy in blank verse. The subtitle of the play is "Ferrex and Porrex," after the two sons of the mythical English king Gorboduc. Porrex drove his brother from Britain, and when Ferrex returned with an army he was slain, but Porrex was shortly after put to death by his mother.

3 Edward III (1312–77) was king of England from 1327 to 1377, during which time the Black Death struck several times, killing 1.5 million people and changing the course of English (and modern) history. For more

The gods do bear and well allow in kings
The things which they abhor in rascal routes.
2   *—Buckhurst's Tragedy of Ferrex and Porrex.*

About twelve o'clock, one night in the month of October, and
3 during the chivalrous reign of the third Edward, two seaman belonging to the crew of the "Free and Easy," a trading
4 schooner plying between Sluys and the Thames, and then at anchor in that river, were much astonished to find themselves seated in the tap-room of an ale-house in the parish of St.
5 Andrews, London—which ale-house bore for sign the portraiture of a "Jolly Tar."

The room, although ill-contrived, smoke-blackened, low-pitched, and in every other respect agreeing with the general character of such places at the period—was, nevertheless, in the opinion of the grotesque groups scattered here and there within it, sufficiently well adapted to its purpose.

Of these groups our two seamen formed, I think, the most interesting, if not the most conspicuous.

The one who appeared to be the elder, and whom his companion addressed by the characteristic appellation of "Legs," was at the same time much the taller of the two. He might have measured six feet and a half, and an habitual stoop in the shoulders seemed to have been the necessary consequence of an altitude so enormous.—Superfluities in height were, however, more than accounted for by deficiencies in other respects. He was exceedingly thin; and might, as his associates asserted, have answered, when drunk, for a pennant at the mast-head, or, when sober, have served for a jib-boom. **6** But these jests, and others of a similar nature, had evidently produced, at no time, any effect upon the cachinnatory muscles of the tar. With high cheek-bones, a large hawk-nose, retreating chin, fallen underjaw, and huge protruding white eyes, the expression of his countenance, although tinged with a species of dogged indifference to matters and things in general, was not the less utterly solemn and serious beyond all attempts at imitation or description.

The younger seaman was, in all outward appearance, the converse of his companion. His stature could not have exceeded four feet. A pair of stumpy bow-legs supported his squat, unwieldy figure, while his unusually short and thick arms, with no ordinary fists at their extremities, swung off dangling from his sides like the fins of a sea-turtle. Small eyes, of no particular color, twinkled far back in his head. His nose remained buried in the mass of flesh which enveloped his round, full, and purple face; and his thick upper-lip rested upon the still thicker one beneath with an air of complacent self-satisfaction, much heightened by the owner's habit of licking them at intervals. He evidently regarded his tall shipmate with a feeling half-wondrous, half-quizzical; and stared up occasionally in his face as the red setting sun stares up at the crags of Ben Nevis. **7**

Various and eventful, however, had been the peregrinations **8** of the worthy couple in and about the different tap-houses of the neighbourhood during the earlier hours of the night. Funds even the most ample, are not always everlasting: and it was with empty pockets our friends had ventured upon the present hostelrie.

At the precise period, then, when this history properly commences, Legs, and his fellow, Hugh Tarpaulin, sat, each with both elbows resting upon the large oaken table in the middle of the floor, and with a hand upon either cheek. They were eyeing, from behind a huge flagon of unpaid-for "humming-stuff," the portentous words, "No Chalk," which to their **9** indignation and astonishment were scored over the doorway by means of that very mineral whose presence they purported to deny. Not that the gift of deciphering written characters— **10** a gift among the commonalty of that day considered little less cabalistical than the art of inditing—could, in strict justice, **11**

on the far-reaching effects of the plague on the development of modern society, see *Disease and History*, by Frederick F. Cartwright and Michael D. Biddiss (Crowell, 1972; pp. 38–46).

4 Sluis is a Dutch city founded in the thirteenth century as an additional port for the city of Bruges. In 1340 Edward III defeated the fleet of Philip VI of France just offshore, the first important engagement in the Hundred Years' War.

5 St. Andrew's Parish is in Holborn. Today the borough includes part of Bloomsbury, the British Museum, the University of London, and the Royal College of Surgeons.

6 A spar that serves as an extension of the bowsprit (the spar that projects straight out from the stem of a ship). "Cachinnatory," in the next sentence, means laughter-producing.

7 Ben Nevis is the highest mountain in Great Britain—4,406 feet high—in Inverness-shire, West Scotland.

8 Travels, wanderings

9 Alcohol

10 i.e., "no credit." It was the custom in alehouses to write up on a chalkboard an account, or "score," of credit given. Gradually the word "chalk" came to mean credit. "Chalk it up" meant to put something on one's account.

11 Writing

12 A lurch to the lee, or sheltered, side of a ship; here, a stagger

13 "Pump ship" means to pump out water and raise a ship in the water in preparation for sailing. "Clew up all sail" refers to drawing up the lower ends of sails (the "clews") to the upper or yard mast before furling them. "Scud" means to move swiftly in the water, especially before a gale.

14 St. Andrew's Stair is the approach to St. Andrew's Church, London. Poe's guardian, John Allan, had his English place of business not far away.

15 The plague first struck England in 1348–49, diminishing the population by somewhere between 20 and 45 percent. The Great Plague of London (1665) was the last important outbreak of the disease in Europe. In Poe's first versions, he used the word "pest."

. . . tales so blood-chilling were hourly told, that the whole mass of forbidden buildings was, at length, enveloped in terror as in a shroud . . . leaving the entire vast circuit of prohibited district to gloom, silence, pestilence, and death. *Illustration by Albert Edward Sterner for* Century Magazine, *1903*

12

13

14

15

have been laid to the charge of either disciple of the sea; but there was, to say the truth, a certain twist in the formation of the letters—an indescribable lee-lurch about the whole—which foreboded, in the opinion of both seamen, a long run of dirty weather; and determined them at once, in the allegorical words of Legs himself, to "pump ship, clew up all sail, and scud before the wind."

Having accordingly disposed of what remained of the ale, and looped up the points of their short doublets, they finally made a bolt for the street. Although Tarpaulin rolled twice into the fire-place, mistaking it for the door, yet their escape was at length happily effected—and half after twelve o'clock found our heroes ripe for mischief, and running for life down a dark alley in the direction of St. Andrew's Stair, hotly pursued by the landlady of the "Jolly Tar."

At the epoch of this eventful tale, and periodically, for many years before and after, all England, but more especially the metropolis, resounded with the fearful cry of "Plague!" The city was in a great measure depopulated—and in those horrible regions, in the vicinity of the Thames, where amid the dark, narrow, and filthy lanes and alleys, the Demon of Disease was supposed to have had his nativity, Awe, Terror, and Superstition were alone to be found stalking abroad.

By authority of the king such districts were placed *under ban*, and all persons forbidden, under pain of death, to intrude upon their dismal solitude. Yet neither the mandate of the monarch, nor the huge barriers erected at the entrances of the streets, nor the prospect of that loathsome death which, with almost absolute certainty, overwhelmed the wretch whom no peril could deter from the adventure, prevented the unfurnished and untenated dwellings from being stripped, by the hand of nightly rapine, of every article, such as iron, brass, or lead-work, which could in any manner be turned to a profitable account.

Above all, it was usually found, upon the annual winter opening of the barriers, that locks, bolts, and secret cellars, had proved but slender protection to those rich stores of wines and liquors which, in consideration of the risk and trouble of removal, many of the numerous dealers having shops in the neighborhood had consented to trust, during the period of exile, to so insufficient a security.

But there were very few of the terror-stricken people who attributed these doings to the agency of human hands. Pest-spirits, plague-goblins, and fever-demons, were the popular imps of mischief; and tales so blood-chilling were hourly told, that the whole mass of forbidden buildings was, at length, enveloped in terror as in a shroud, and the plunderer himself was often scared away by the horrors his own depredations had created; leaving the entire vast circuit of prohibited district to gloom, silence, pestilence, and death.

It was by one of the terrific barriers already mentioned, and which indicated the region beyond to be under the Pest-ban, that, in scrambling down an alley, Legs and the worthy Hugh Tarpaulin found their progress suddenly impeded. To return was out of the question, and no time was to be lost, as their pursuers were close upon their heels. With thorough-bred seamen to clamber up the roughly fashioned plank-work was a trifle; and, maddened with the twofold excitement of exercise and liquor, they leaped unhesitatingly down within the closure, and holding on their drunken course with shouts and yellings, were soon bewildered in its noisome and intricate recesses.

Had they not, indeed, been intoxicated beyond moral sense, their reeling footsteps must have been palsied by the horrors of their situation. The air was cold and misty. The paving-stones, loosened from their beds, lay in wild disorder amid the tall, rank grass, which sprang up around the feet and ankles. Fallen houses choked up the streets. The most fetid and poisonous smells everywhere prevailed;—and by the aid of that ghastly light which, even at midnight, never fails to emanate from a vapory and pestilential atmosphere, might be discerned lying in the by-paths and alleys, or rotting in the windowless habitations, the carcass of many a nocturnal plunderer arrested by the hand of the plague in the very perpetration of his robbery. **16**

But it lay not in the power of images, or sensations, or impediments such as these, to stay the course of men who, naturally brave, and at that time especially, brimful of courage and of "humming-stuff!" would have reeled, as straight as their condition might have permitted, undauntedly into the very jaws of Death. Onward—still onward stalked the grim Legs, making the desolate solemnity echo and re-echo with yells like the terrific war-whoop of the Indian: and onward, still onward rolled the dumpy Tarpaulin, hanging on to the doublet of his more active companion, and far surpassing the latter's most strenuous exertions in the way of vocal music, by bull-roarings *in basso*, from the profundity of his stentorian lungs. **17**

They had now evidently reached the strong hold of the pestilence. Their way at every step or plunge grew more noisome and more horrible—the paths more narrow and more intricate. Huge stones and beams falling momently from the decaying roofs above them, gave evidence, by their sullen and heavy descent, of the vast height of the surrounding houses; and while actual exertion became necessary to force a passage through frequent heaps of rubbish, it was by no means seldom that the hand fell upon a skeleton or rested upon a more fleshly corpse.

Suddenly, as the seamen stumbled against the entrance of a tall and ghastly-looking building, a yell more than usually shrill from the throat of the excited Legs, was replied to from within, in a rapid succession of wild, laughter-like, and fiendish shrieks. Nothing daunted at sounds which, of such a nature, at such a time, and in such a place, might have curdled the very blood in hearts less irrevocably on fire, the drunken couple rushed headlong against the door, burst it open, and staggered into the midst of things with a volley of curses.

The room within which they found themselves proved to be the shop of an undertaker; but an open trap-door, in a corner of the floor near the entrance, looked down upon a

16 The slapstick atmosphere is suddenly supplanted by a deadly serious tone with overtones of horror. The effect is jarring, especially since Poe does not follow up on it, moving on to the grotesque comedy that follows.

A similar description appears in "The Man of the Crowd": "The paving stones lay at random, displaced from their beds by the rankly growing grass. Horrible filth festered in the dammed-up gutters. The whole atmosphere teemed with desolation." The description there, however, is of a slum area.

17 Stentor was a Greek participant in the Trojan War who supposedly had a voice fifty times more powerful than normal but who died after losing a shouting match with the god Hermes. The stentorophonic tube, invented by Sir Samuel Morland, was a speaking trumpet, or megaphone, designed to be used at sea.

Onward—still onward stalked the grim Legs, making the desolate solemnity echo and re-echo with yells like the terrific war-whoop of the Indian: and onward, still onward rolled the dumpy Tarpaulin, hanging onto the doublet of his more active companion. . . . *Illustration by F. S. Coburn, 1901*

Overhead was suspended a human skeleton. . . . In the cranium of this hideous thing lay a quantity of ignited charcoal, which threw a fitful but vivid light over the entire scene. . . . *Illustration by Albert Edward Sterner for* Century Magazine, *1903*

long range of wine-cellars, whose depths the occasional sound of bursting bottles proclaimed to be well stored with their appropriate contents. In the middle of the room stood a table—in the centre of which again arose a huge tub of what appeared to be punch. Bottles of various wines and cordials, together with jugs, pitchers, and flagons of every shape and quality, were scattered profusely upon the board. Around it, **19** upon coffin-tressels, was seated a company of six. This company I will endeavor to delineate one by one.

Fronting the entrance, and elevated a little above his companions, sat a personage who appeared to be the president **20** of the table. His stature was gaunt and tall, and Legs was confounded to behold in him a figure more emaciated than himself. His face was as yellow as saffron—but no feature excepting one alone, was sufficiently marked to merit a particular description. This one consisted in a forehead so unusually and hideously lofty, as to have the appearance of a bonnet or crown of flesh superadded upon the natural head. His mouth was puckered and dimpled into an expression of ghastly affability, and his eyes, as indeed the eyes of all at table, were glazed over with the fumes of intoxication. This gentleman was clothed from head to foot in a richly-embroidered black silk-velvet pall, wrapped negligently around his form after the fashion of a Spanish cloak. His head was stuck full of sable hearse-plumes, which he nodded to and fro with a jaunty and knowing air; and, in his right hand, he held a huge human thigh-bone, with which he appeared to have been just knocking down some member of the company for a song.

Opposite him, and with her back to the door, was a lady of no whit the less extraordinary character. Although quite as tall as the person just described, she had no right to complain of his unnatural emaciation. She was evidently in the last stage **21** of a dropsy; and her figure resembled nearly that of the huge **22** puncheon of October beer which stood, with the head driven in, close by her side, in a corner of the chamber. Her face was exceedingly round, red, and full; and the same peculiarity, or rather want of peculiarity, attached itself to her countenance, which I before mentioned in the case of the president—that is to say, only one feature of her face was sufficiently distinguished to need a separate characterization: indeed the acute Tarpaulin immediately observed that the same remark might have applied to each individual person of the party; every one of whom seemed to possess a monopoly of some particular portion of physiognomy. With the lady in question this portion proved to be the mouth. Commencing at the right ear, it swept with a terrific chasm to the left—the short pendants which she wore in either auricle continually bobbing into the aperture. She made, however, every exertion to keep her mouth closed and look dignified, in a dress consisting of a newly starched and ironed shroud coming up close under her **23** chin, with a crimpled ruffle of cambric muslin.

At her right hand sat a diminutive young lady whom she appeared to patronise. This delicate little creature, in the

18 Wine bottles do not normally burst, since the fermentation is completed before they are sealed. However, in sparkling wines (such as champagne) a secondary fermentation is introduced into the bottle to produce carbonation, and in the early days of champagne making, bursting was a real problem.

19 A trestle, the support for a coffin, looks like two sawhorses.

20 This comic death figure is in some ways similar to the figure of the Red Death.

21 Dropsy, or edema, is an abnormal accumulation of fluid in the tissues, causing swelling, or distention. It sometimes accompanies nutritional deficiencies, such as with a loss of protein during severe starvation, or in kidney or other diseases.

Appropriately, "dropsy" was also a word meaning an unquenchable thirst.

22 Ale brewed in October

23 A fine linen resembling cambric. Lawn, in the next paragraph, refers to a sheer linen or cotton.

trembling of her wasted fingers, in the livid hue of her lips, and in the slight hectic spot which tinged her otherwise leaden complexion, gave evident indications of a galloping consumption. An air of extreme *haut ton,* however, pervaded her whole appearance; she wore in a graceful and *dégagé* manner, a large and beautiful winding-sheet of the finest India lawn; her hair hung in ringlets over her neck; a soft smile played about her mouth; but her nose, extremely long, thin, sinuous, flexible and pimpled, hung down far below her under lip, and in spite of the delicate manner in which she now and then moved it to one side or the other with her tongue, gave to her countenance a somewhat equivocal expression.

Over against her, and upon the left of the dropsical lady, was seated a little puffy, wheezing, and gouty old man, whose cheeks reposed upon the shoulders of their owner, like two huge bladders of Oporto wine. With his arms folded, and with **24** one bandaged leg deposited upon the table, he seemed to think himself entitled to some consideration. He evidently prided himself much upon every inch of his personal appearance, but took more especial delight in calling attention to his gaudy-colored surtout. This, to say the truth, must have cost **25** him no little money, and was made to fit him exceedingly well—being fashioned from one of the curiously embroidered silken covers appertaining to those glorious escutcheons which, in England and elsewhere, are customarily hung up, in some conspicuous place, upon the dwellings of departed aristocracy.

Next to him, and at the right hand of the president, was a gentleman in long white hose and cotton drawers. His frame shook, in a ridiculous manner, with a fit of what Tarpaulin called "the horrors." His jaws, which had been newly shaved, **26** were tightly tied up by a bandage of muslin; and his arms being fastened in a similar way at the wrists, prevented him from helping himself too freely to the liquors upon the table; a precaution rendered necessary, in the opinion of Legs, by the peculiarly sottish and wine-bibbing cast of his visage. A pair of prodigious ears, nevertheless, which it was no doubt found impossible to confine, towered away into the atmosphere of the apartment, and were occasionally pricked up in a spasm, at the sound of the drawing of a cork.

Fronting him, sixthly and lastly, was situated a singularly stiff-looking personage, who, being afflicted with paralysis, must, to speak seriously, have felt very ill at ease in his unaccommodating habiliments. He was habited, somewhat uniquely, in a new and handsome mahogany coffin. Its top or head-piece pressed upon the skull of the wearer, and extended over it in the fashion of a hood, giving to the entire face an air of indescribable interest. Arm-holes had been cut in the sides, for the sake not more of elegance than of convenience; but the dress, nevertheless, prevented its proprietor from sitting as erect as his associates; and as he lay reclining against his tressel, at an angle of forty-five degrees, a pair of huge goggle eyes rolled up their awful whites towards the ceiling in absolute amazement at their own enormity.

Before each of the party lay a portion of a skull, which was

24 Port is a strong dark red wine with a sweet and slightly astringent taste, named after the city of "O Porto" (The Port), Portugal. An English version, invented by Lord Pembroke (d. 1219) calls for twenty-seven gallons of rough cider, thirteen gallons of wine, and three gallons of brandy to make a hogshead of port.

25 A man's overcoat, but one that dates from much later than the reign of Edward III.

26 The DTs, or delirium tremens, is an acute alcoholic condition characterized by tremors, anxiety, hallucinations, and delusions.

used as a drinking cup. Overhead was suspended a human skeleton, by means of a rope tied round one of the legs and fastened to a ring in the ceiling. The other limb confined by no such fetter, stuck off from the body at right angles, causing the whole loose and rattling frame to dangle and twirl about at the caprice of every occasional puff of wind which found its way into the apartment. In the cranium of this hideous thing lay a quantity of ignited charcoal, which threw a fitful but vivid light over the entire scene; while coffins, and other wares appertaining to the shop of an undertaker, were piled high up around the room, and against the windows, preventing any ray from escaping into the street.

At sight of this extraordinary assembly, and of their still more extraordinary paraphernalia, our two seamen did not conduct themselves with that degree of decorum which might have been expected. Legs, leaning against the wall near which he happened to be standing, dropped his lower jaw still lower than usual, and spread open his eyes to their fullest extent: while Hugh Tarpaulin, stooping down so as to bring his nose upon a level with the table, and spreading out a palm upon either knee, burst into a long, loud, and obstreperous roar of very ill-timed and immoderate laughter.

Without, however, taking offence at behaviour so excessively rude, the tall president smiled very graciously upon the intruders—nodded to them in a dignified manner with his head of sable plumes—and, arising, took each by an arm, and led him to a seat which some others of the company had placed in the meantime for his accommodation. Legs to all this offered not the slightest resistance, but sat down as he was directed; while the gallant Hugh, removing his coffin tressel from its station near the head of the table, to the vicinity of the little consumptive lady in the winding-sheet, plumped down by her side in high glee, and pouring out a skull of red wine, quaffed it to their better acquaintance. But at this presumption the stiff gentleman in the coffin seemed exceedingly nettled; and serious consequences might have ensued, had not the president, rapping upon the table with his truncheon, diverted the attention of all present to the following speech:

"It becomes our duty upon the present happy occasion"—

"Avast there!" interrupted Legs, looking very serious, "avast there a bit, I say, and tell us who the devil ye all are, and what business ye have here, rigged off like the foul fiends, and swilling the snug blue ruin stowed away for the winter by my honest shipmate, Will Wimble the undertaker!"

At this unpardonable piece of ill-breeding, all the original company half started to their feet, and uttered the same rapid succession of wild fiendish shrieks which had before caught the attention of the seamen. The president, however, was the first to recover his composure, and at length, turning to Legs with great dignity, recommenced:

"Most willingly will we gratify any reasonable curiosity on the part of guests so illustrious, unbidden though they be. Know then that in these dominions I am monarch, and here

27 Meaning "Hold!" or "Halt!" A nautical word dating back to the 1600s, it is probably a corruption of the Dutch *jou-vast* or *houd vast*, meaning "hold fast."

28 Cheap gin

29 Mentioned in Addison and Steele's *Spectator*, no. 108, Will Wimble was the youngest son of a nobleman who could not enter a trade and so wasted his time in various ways.

rule with undivided empire under the title of 'King Pest the First.'

"This apartment, which you no doubt profanely suppose to be the shop of Will Wimble the undertaker—a man whom we know not, and whose plebeian appellation has never before this night thwarted our royal ears—this apartment, I say, is the Dais-Chamber of our Palace, devoted to the councils of our kingdom, and to other sacred and lofty purposes.

"The noble lady who sits opposite is Queen Pest, our Serene Consort. The other exalted personages whom you behold are all of our family, and wear the insignia of the blood royal under the respective titles of 'His Grace the Arch Duke Pest-Iferous'—'His Grace the Duke Pest-Ilential'—'His Grace the Duke Tem-Pest'—and 'Her Serene Highness the Arch Duchess Ana-Pest.'

"As regards," continued he, "your demand of the business upon which we sit here in council, we might be pardoned for replying that it concerns, and concerns *alone*, our own private and regal interest, and is in no manner important to any other than ourself. But in consideration of those rights to which as guests and strangers you may feel yourselves entitled, we will furthermore explain that we are here this night, prepared by deep research and accurate investigation, to examine, analyze, and thoroughly determine the indefinable spirit—the incomprehensible qualities and nature—of those inestimable treasures of the palate, the wines, ales, and liqueurs of this goodly metropolis: by so doing to advance not more our own designs than the true welfare of that unearthly sovereign whose reign is over us all, whose dominions are unlimited, and whose name is 'Death.' "

"Whose name is Davy Jones!" ejaculated Tarpaulin, helping the lady by his side to a skull of liqueur, and pouring out a second for himself.

"Profane varlet!" said the president, now turning his attention to the worthy Hugh, "profane and execrable wretch!—we have said, that in consideration of those rights which, even in thy filthy person, we feel no inclination to violate, we have condescended to make reply to thy rude and unseasonable inquiries. We, nevertheless, for your unhallowed intrusion upon our councils, believe it our duty to mulct thee and thy companion in each gallon of Black Strap—having imbibed which to the prosperity of our kingdom—at a single draught— and upon your bended knees—ye shall be forthwith free either to proceed upon your way, or remain and be admitted to the privileges of our table, according to your respective and individual pleasures."

"It would be a matter of utter impossibility," replied Legs, whom the assumptions and dignity of King Pest the First had evidently inspired with some feelings of respect, and who arose and steadied himself by the table as he spoke—"it would, please your majesty, be a matter of utter impossibility to stow away in my hold even one-fourth part of that same liquor which your majesty has just mentioned. To say nothing of the stuffs placed on board in the forenoon by way of ballast,

30

31

30 Poe apparently means an elaborate allegory based on the word *pest*, with each character a different sort of lifeless pest. King Pest is the intellectual (complete with swollen head), who produces nothing original. Queen Pest is a constant talker who says nothing of importance. Arch duchess Ana-Pest (an anapest is a metrical foot consisting of two short syllables followed by one long, or two unstressed syllables followed by one stressed) is a poet who noses her way into every aspect of life but who, again, creates nothing on her own. Arch Duke Tem-Pest is a man with nothing more than his position and appearance to recommend him. Duke Pest–Iferous is a drunkard. Duke Pest-Ilential is a frightened man who has withdrawn from the world around him.

31 An inferior, thick port, here likened to blackstrap molasses. "Mulct" means to punish.

and not to mention the various ales and liqueurs shipped this evening at different sea-ports, I have, at present, a full cargo of 'humming-stuff' taken in and duly paid for at the sign of the 'Jolly Tar.' You will, therefore, please your majesty, be so good as to take the will for the deed—for by no manner of means either can I or will I swallow another drop—least of all a drop of that villanous bilge-water that answers to the hail of 'Black Strap.' "

"Belay that!" interrupted Tarpaulin, astonished not more at the length of his companion's speech than at the nature of his refusal—"Belay that you lubber!—and I say, Legs, none of

32 An appropriate nautical term meaning a discussion, it comes from the Portuguese, who first used it on the African coast to mean a talk or colloquy (*palavra*). English sailors picked it up in the 1700s and passed the word on to general colloquial use.

32 your palaver! *My* hull is still light, although I confess you yourself seem to be a little top-heavy; and as for the matter of your share of the cargo, why rather than raise a squall I would find stowage-room for it myself, but"——

"This proceeding," interposed the president, "is by no means in accordance with the terms of the mulct or sentence, which is in its nature Median, and not to be altered or recalled. The conditions we have imposed must be fulfilled to the letter, and that without a moment's hesitation—in failure of

33 Unchangeable, from the "law of the Medes and the Persians, which altereth not" (Esther 1:19, Daniel 6:8).

33 which fulfillment we decree that you do here be tied neck and heels together, and duly drowned as rebels in yon hogshead of October beer!"

"A sentence!—a sentence!—a righteous and just sentence!—a glorious decree!—a most worthy and upright, and holy condemnation!" shouted the Pest family altogether. The king elevated his forehead into innumerable wrinkles; the gouty little old man puffed like a pair of bellows; the lady of the winding-sheet waved her nose to and fro; the gentleman in the cotton drawers pricked up his ears; she of the shroud gasped like a dying fish; and he of the coffin looked stiff and rolled up his eyes.

34 In "The Cask of Amontillado," "ugh-ugh" is a cough instead of a chuckle. "Assoilzie" means "absolves."

34 "Ugh! ugh! ugh!" chuckled Tarpaulin without heeding the general excitement, "ugh! ugh! ugh!—ugh! ugh! ugh! ugh!—ugh! ugh! ugh!—I was saying," said he, "I was saying when Mr. King Pest poked in his marlin-spike, that as for the matter of two or three gallons more or less of Black Strap, it was a trifle to a tight sea-boat like myself not overstowed—but when it comes to drinking the health of the Devil (whom God assoilzie) and going down upon my marrow bones to his ill-favored majesty there, whom I know, as well as I know myself to be a sinner, to be nobody in the whole world, but Tim

35 Also hurdy-gurdy, a street organ (as well as the person who plays the instrument). In the first draft of the tale, King Pest was an organ-grinder.

35 Hurlygurly the stage-player—why! it's quite another guess sort of a thing, and utterly and altogether past my comprehension."

He was not allowed to finish this speech in tranquillity. At the name of Tim Hurlygurly the whole assembly leaped from their seats.

"Treason!" shouted his Majesty King Pest the First.

"Treason!" said the little man with the gout.

"Treason!" screamed the Arch Duchess Ana-Pest.

"Treason!" muttered the gentleman with his jaws tied up.

"Treason!" growled he of the coffin.

"Treason! treason!" shrieked her majesty of the mouth; and,

seizing by the hinder part of his breeches the unfortunate Tarpaulin, who had just commenced pouring out for himself a skull of liqueur, she lifted him high into the air, and let him fall without ceremony into the huge open puncheon of his beloved ale. Bobbing up and down, for a few seconds, like an apple in a bowl of toddy, he, at length, finally disappeared amid the whirlpool of foam which, in the already effervescent liquor, his struggles easily succeeded in creating.

Not tamely, however, did the tall seaman behold the discomfiture of his companion. Jostling King Pest through the open trap, the valiant Legs slammed the door down upon him with an oath, and strode towards the centre of the room. Here tearing down the skeleton which swung over the table, he laid it about him with so much energy and good will, that, as the last glimpses of light died away within the apartment, he succeeded in knocking out the brains of the little gentleman with the gout. Rushing then with all his force against the fatal hogshead full of October ale and Hugh Tarpaulin, he rolled it over and over in an instant. Out burst a deluge of liquor so fierce—so impetuous—so overwhelming—that the room was flooded from wall to wall—the loaded table was overturned—the tressels were thrown upon their backs—the tub of punch into the fireplace—and the ladies into hysterics. Piles of death-furniture floundered about. Jugs, pitchers, and carboys min- **36** gled promiscuously in the *mêlée*, and wicker flagons encoun- **37** tered desperately with bottles of junk. The man with the horrors was drowned upon the spot—the little stiff gentleman floated off in his coffin—and the victorious Legs, seizing by the waist the fat lady in the shroud, rushed out with her into the street, and made a bee-line for the "Free and Easy," followed under easy sail by the redoubtable Hugh Tarpaulin, who, having sneezed three or four times, panted and puffed after him with the Arch Duchess Ana-Pest. **38**

36 Large flagons, from the Persian *qarabah*, but later used to mean globe-shaped bottles covered with basketwork for protection, most often used for holding acids or other corrosive liquids.

37 A junk bottle is made of thick green or black glass. The word dated to early-nineteenth-century America.

38 Marie Bonaparte sees the ending of the tale as a clear case of patricide that goes unpunished. "What matters is that *King Pest*—symbolically enough, again disguised as a bad actor—dies under a trap door, or that the two princes, his doubles, meet a grotesque death in enabling two carousing sailors to carry off Queen Pest, and the Archduchess Ana-Pest, her double." (P. 510)

THE MAN THAT WAS USED UP

A TALE OF THE LATE BUGABOO AND KICKAPOO CAMPAIGN

First published in *Burton's Gentleman's Magazine*, August 1839, this tale was one of Poe's favorites, taking to its logical extreme Shakespeare's "What a piece of work is a man" (*Hamlet*, II, ii).

The source may be in part *Asmodeus, or the Devil upon Two Sticks* (1707, revised 1727), by Alain-René Le Sage, in which two characters are put together much as General Smith is here. Inspiration could also have come from recent developments in both prosthesis manufacture and cosmetic rejuvenation.

Or Poe may have meant the entire tale as a burlesque on the expression "to be used up," which meant talked about, discussed, or written up. Poe's idea of humor was "the ludicrous heightened into the grotesque and the witty exaggerated into the burlesque." "When . . . Fantasy seeks . . . incongruous or antagonistical elements . . . we laugh outright in recognizing Humor . . . but when either Fancy or Humor is expressed to gain an end . . . it becomes, also, pure Wit or Sarcasm, just as the purpose is well-intended or malevolent" ("N.P. Willis," *Broadway Journal*, January 18, 1845).

---

1 "Weep, weep, my eyes, and float yourself in tears!/ The better half of my life has laid the other to rest" is by Pierre Corneille (1606–84), French classic dramatist (*Le Cid*, III, iii, 7–8).

2 A brevet officer is one who is raised to a nominal rank, without increase in pay, by a sovereign or government action.

Although the meaning didn't come into use until after Poe's death, he no doubt would have enjoyed the fact that "ABC" later referred to a process for making artificial manure (an acronym of Alum, Blood, and Clay, the three chief ingredients).

3 The narrator of "The Man That Was Used Up" resembles that of "The Oblong Box." Both are less-than-perfect detectives and each suffers a shock when he discovers the truth.

Pleurez, pleurez, mes yeux, et fondez-vous en eau!
La moitié de ma vie a mis l'autre au tombeau.

1

—CORNEILLE.

I cannot just now remember when or where I first made the acquaintance of that truly fine-looking fellow, Brevet Brigadier **2** General John A. B. C. Smith. Some one *did* introduce me to the gentleman, I am sure—at some public meeting, I know very well—held about something of great importance, no doubt—at some place or other, I feel convinced,—whose name I have unaccountably forgotten. The truth is—that the introduction was attended, upon my part, with a degree of anxious embarrassment which operated to prevent any definite impressions of either time or place. I am constitutionally nervous—this, with me, is a family failing, and I can't help it. In especial, the slightest appearance of mystery—of any point I cannot exactly comprehend—puts me at once into a pitiable **3** state of agitation.

There was something, as it were, remarkable—yes, *remarkable*, although this is but a feeble term to express my full meaning—about the entire individuality of the personage in question. He was, perhaps, six feet in height, and of a presence singularly commanding. There was an *air distingué* pervading the whole man, which spoke of high breeding, and hinted at high birth. Upon this topic—the topic of Smith's personal appearance—I have a kind of melancholy satisfaction in being

minute. His head of hair would have done honor to a Brutus; **4**
nothing could be more richly flowing, or possess a brighter
gloss. It was of a jetty black; which was also the color, or more
properly the no color, of his unimaginable whiskers. You
perceive I cannot speak of these latter without enthusiasm; it
is not too much to say that they were the handsomest pair of
whiskers under the sun. At all events, they encircled, and at
times partially overshadowed, a mouth utterly unequalled.
Here were the most entirely even, and the most brilliantly
white of all conceivable teeth. From between them, upon
every proper occasion, issued a voice of surpassing clearness,
melody, and strength. In the matter of eyes, also, my acquaintance was pre-eminently endowed. Either one of such
a pair was worth a couple of the ordinary ocular organs. They
were of a deep hazel exceedingly large and lustrous; and there
was perceptible about them, ever and anon, just that amount
of interesting obliquity which gives pregnancy to expression. **5**

The bust of the General was unquestionably the finest bust
I ever saw. For your life you could not have found a fault with
its wonderful proportion. This rare peculiarity set off to great
advantage a pair of shoulders which would have called up a
blush of conscious inferiority into the countenance of the
marble Apollo. I have a passion for fine shoulders, and may **6**
say that I never beheld them in perfection before. The arms
altogether were admirably modelled. Nor were the lower
limbs less superb. These were, indeed, the *ne plus ultra* of **7**
good legs. Every connoisseur in such matters admitted the
legs to be good. There was neither too much flesh nor too
little,—neither rudeness nor fragility. I could not imagine a
more graceful curve than that of the *os femoris*, and there was **8**
just that due gentle prominence in the rear of the *fibula* which **9**
goes to the conformation of a properly proportioned calf. I
wish to God my young and talented friend Chiponchipino, **10**
the sculptor, had but seen the legs of Brevet Brigadier General
John A. B. C. Smith.

But although men so absolutely fine-looking are neither as
plenty as reasons or blackberries, still I could not bring myself
to believe that *the remarkable* something to which I alluded
just now,—that the odd air of *je ne sais quoi* which hung **11**
about my new acquaintance,—lay altogether, or indeed at all,
in the supreme excellence of his bodily endowments. Perhaps
it might be traced to the *manner;*—yet here again I could not
pretend to be positive. There *was* a primness, not to say
stiffness, in his carriage—a degree of measured and, it I may
so express it, of rectangular precision attending his every
movement, which, observed in a more diminutive figure,
would have had the least little savor in the world of affectation,
pomposity, or constraint, but which, noticed in a gentleman
of his undoubted dimensions, was readily placed to the account
of reserve, *hauteur*—of a commendable sense, in short, of
what is due to the dignity of colossal proportion.

The kind friend who presented me to General Smith
whispered in my ear some few words of comment upon the
man. He was a *remarkable* man—a *very* remarkable man—

4 It was actually the hero Cincinnatus who was famed for his beautiful hair.

5 Descartes suggests a connection between obliquity of vision and beauty in *Oeuvres*, X, 53.

6 God of music, poetry, and the healing art, as well as the sun, Apollo is represented in art as the perfection of youthful manhood. The Apollo Belvedere is the most famous of such representations, supposed to be from the chisel of the Greek sculptor Calamis (fifth century B.C.). It represents the god holding a bow in his left hand; it is called Belvedere after the gallery in the Vatican where it stands. It was discovered in 1503 and purchased by Pope Julius II.

7 The best (literally, nothing greater or more)

8 The femur is the longest and largest bone in the body, extending from the hip to the knee; the thighbone.

9 The fibula is the slenderest bone of the body in proportion to its length, situated on the front part of the leg below the knee.

10 "Chip on little chip"

11 An indescribable something

"A downright fire-eater, and *no* mistake. Showed *that* . . . in the late tremendous swamp-fight, away down South, with the Bugaboo and Kickapoo Indians."
Artist unknown

12 Gunfire is meant here, not flames.

13 The Kickapoos lived in what is now southwestern Wisconsin in the early-seventeenth century, then moved south into central Illinois after 1769, and from there to Missouri and Kansas in the early-nineteenth century. A large band, dissatisfied with conditions there, migrated to Mexico in 1852. Today, Kickapoos live in Chihuahua, Mexico, and on reservations in Kansas and Oklahoma.

"Bugaboo" is a form of "bugbear," a fanciful creature that was supposed to come for children in the dark of the night (also "bogeyman"), but more generally used to mean a strong, usually unprovoked, fear.

indeed one of the *most* remarkable men of the age. He was an especial favorite, too, with the ladies—chiefly on account of his high reputation for courage.

"In *that* point he is unrivalled—indeed he is a perfect **12** desperado—a downright fire-eater, and no mistake," said my friend, here dropping his voice excessively low, and thrilling me with the mystery of his tone.

"A downright fire-eater, and *no* mistake. Showed *that*, I should say, to some purpose, in the late tremendous swamp-fight, away down South, with the Bugaboo and Kickapoo **13** Indians." [Here my friend opened his eyes to some extent.] "Bless my soul!—blood and thunder, and all that!—*prodigies* of valor!—heard of him of course?—you know he's the man——"

"Man alive, how *do* you do? why, how *are ye? very* glad to see ye, indeed!" here interrupted the General himself, seizing my companion by the hand as he drew near, and bowing stiffly but profoundly, as I was presented. I then thought (and I think so still) that I never heard a clearer nor a stronger voice, nor beheld a finer set of teeth: but I *must* say that I was sorry for the interruption just at that moment, as, owing to the whispers and insinuations aforesaid, my interest had been greatly excited in the hero of the Bugaboo and Kickapoo campaign.

However, the delightfully luminous conversation of Brevet Brigadier General John A. B. C. Smith soon completely dissipated this chagrin. My friend leaving us immediately, we had quite a long *tête-à-tête*, and I was not only pleased but *really*—instructed. I never heard a more fluent talker, or a man of greater general information. With becoming modesty, he forbore, nevertheless, to touch upon the theme I had just then most at heart—I mean the mysterious circumstances attending the Bugaboo war—and, on my own part, what I conceive to be a proper sense of delicacy forbade me to broach the subject; although, in truth, I was exceedingly tempted to do so. I perceived, too, that the gallant soldier preferred topics of philosophical interest, and that he delighted, especially, in commenting upon the rapid march of mechanical invention. Indeed, lead him where I would, this was a point to which he invariably came back.

"There is nothing at all like it," he would say; "we are a wonderful people, and live in a wonderful age. Parachutes and railroads—man-traps and spring-guns! Our steam-boats **14** are upon every sea, and the Nassau balloon packet is about **15** to run regular trips (fare either way only twenty pounds sterling) between London and Timbuctoo. And who shall **16** calculate the immense influence upon social life—upon arts— upon commerce—upon literature—which will be the immediate result of the great principles of electromagnetics! Nor, **17** is this all, let me assure you! There is really no end to the march of invention. The most wonderful—the most ingenious—and let me add, Mr.—Mr.—Thompson, I believe, is your name—let me add, I say the most *useful*—the most truly *useful*—mechanical contrivances are daily springing up like mushrooms, if I may so express myself, or, more figuratively, like—ah—grasshoppers—like grasshoppers, Mr. Thompson— about us and ah—ah—ah—around us!"

Thompson, to be sure, is not my name; but it is needless to say that I left General Smith with a heightened interest in the man, with an exalted opinion of his conversational powers, and a deep sense of the valuable privileges we enjoy in living in this age of mechanical invention. My curiosity, however, had not been altogether satisfied, and I resolved to prosecute immediate inquiry among my acquaintances touching the Brevet Brigadier General himself, and particularly respecting the tremendous events *quorum pars magna fuit*, during the **18** Bugaboo and Kickapoo campaign.

The first opportunity which presented itself, and (*horresco referens*) I did not in the least scruple to seize, occurred at **19** the Church of the Reverend Doctor Drummummupp, where **20** I found myself established, one Sunday, just at sermon time, not only in the pew, but by the side of that worthy and communicative little friend of mine, Miss Tabitha T. Thus **21** seated, I congratulated myself, and with much reason, upon the very flattering state of affairs. If any person knew any thing about Brevet Brigadier General John A. B. C. Smith, that person, it was clear to me, was Miss Tabitha T. We telegraphed a few signals and then commenced, *sotto voce*, a brisk *tête-à-tête*.

"Smith!" said she, in reply to my very earnest inquiry; "Smith!—why, not General A. B. C.? Bless me, I thought you *knew* all about *him!* This is a wonderfully inventive age! Horrid affair that!—a bloody set of wretches, those Kickapoos!— fought like a hero—prodigies of valor—immortal renown. Smith!—Brevet Brigadier General John A. B. C.!—why, you know he's the man——"

"Man," here broke in Doctor Drummummupp, at the top of his voice, and with a thump that came near knocking the pulpit about our ears—"man that is born of a woman hath but a short time to live; he cometh up and is cut down like a flower!" I started to the extremity of the pew, and perceived **22**

---

14 Man-traps were quite literally traps set out for humans, while spring-guns were automatic devices to fire on anyone who stepped on a hidden trigger. Both were commonly used to protect property from intruders.

Samuel Johnson's use of the terms is more inspired: "He should have warned us of our danger, before we entered his garden of flowery eloquence, by advertising 'Spring-guns and man-traps set here'" (Boswell, *Johnson*, 20 March 1776).

15 Nassau here refers to the former duchy north and east of the Main and Rhine rivers, famous for its white wines. In 1836, in a balloon called the *Great Nassau*, Thomas Monck Mason and Charles Green sailed from London to Weilburg, Germany. For more on the historic flight, see "The Balloon-Hoax."

16 Timbuctu is a city, now in central Mali near the Niger, a center of the Moslem faith in West Africa. Settled in 1087 by the Tuareg (Berbers of the Sahara), its fame as a center of trade in gold soon spread as far away as Europe. It was supposed to be unreachable by Westerners, and thus became a synonym for the far end of the earth.

17 Electromagnets, in which magnetism is produced by means of an electric current, were first made a practical reality by William Sturgeon in the early-nineteenth century. Today they are an important part of telephone and telegraph apparatus, as well as of induction coils. Learning in 1832 of Ampère's idea for an electric telegraph, Samuel Morse (1791–1872) worked for the next twelve months on his own version, finally demonstrating it in 1844 by transmitting WHAT HATH GOD WROUGHT over a wire from Washington to Baltimore.

In Poe's day, only the telegraph was a reality, but ambitious plans were already afoot for using electromagnets to drive vehicles. The electric motor was developed in rudimentary form in the 1820s by Michael Faraday, but it was not until 1856 that the first generator driven by steam went into service at a lighthouse.

18 *Aeneid*, II, 6: ". . . of which things he was a great part."

19 *Aeneid*, II, 204: "I shudder recalling it."

20 "Drum" here refers not only to drumming up customers but to driving a person into a frenzy by persistent repetition of admonition or other comment.

21 Apparently Tabitha Turnip, who in "How to Write a Blackwood Article" was the arch-social and literary rival of the Psyche Zenobia.

22 "Man that is born of a woman is of few days, and full of trouble. He cometh forth like a flower, and is cut down: he fleeth also as a shadow, and continueth not." (Job 14:1–2) by the animated looks of the divine, that the wrath which had nearly proved fatal to the pulpit had been excited by the whispers of the lady and myself. There was no help for it; so I submitted with a good grace, and listened, in all the martyrdom of dignified silence, to the balance of that very capital discourse.

Next evening found me a somewhat late visitor at the Rantipole theatre, where I felt sure of satisfying my curiosity at once, by merely stepping into the box of those exquisite specimens of affability and omniscience, the Misses Arabella and Miranda Cognoscenti. That fine tragedian, Climax, was doing Iago to a very crowded house, and I experienced some little difficulty in making my wishes understood; especially as our box was next the slips, and completely overlooked the stage.

"Smith?" said Miss Arabella, as she at length comprehended the purport of my query; "Smith?—why, not General John A. B. C.?"

"Smith?" inquired Miranda, musingly. "God bless me, did you ever behold a finer figure?"

"Never, madam, but *do* tell me——"

"Or so inimitable grace?"

"Never, upon my word! But pray, inform me——"

"Or so just an appreciation of stage effect?"

"Madam!"

"Or a more delicate sense of the true beauties of Shake-speare? Be so good as to look at that leg!"

"The devil!" and I turned again to her sister.

"Smith?" said she, "why, not General John A. B. C.? Horrid affair that, wasn't it?—great wretches, those Bugaboos—savage and so on—but we live in a wonderfully inventive age!—Smith!—O yes! great man!—perfect desperado!—immortal renown!—prodigies of valor! *Never heard!*" [This was given in a scream.] "Bless my soul!—why, he's the man——"

> "——mandragora
> Nor all the drowsy syrups of the world
> Shall ever medicine thee to that sweet sleep
> Which thou ow'dst yesterday!"

here roared out Climax just in my ear, and shaking his fist in my face all the time, in a way that I *couldn't* stand, and I *wouldn't*. I left the Misses Cognoscenti immediately, went behind the scenes forthwith, and gave the beggarly scoundrel such a thrashing as I trust he will remember till the day of his death.

At the *soirée* of the lovely widow, Mrs. Kathleen O'Trump, I was confident that I should meet with no similar disappointment. Accordingly, I was no sooner seated at the card-table, with my pretty hostess for a *vis-à-vis*, than I propounded those questions the solution of which had become a matter so essential to my peace.

"Smith?" said my partner, "why, not General John A. B. C.? Horrid affair that, wasn't it?—diamonds did you say?—terrible wretches those Kickapoos!—we are playing *whist*, if you please, Mr. Tattle—however, this is the age of invention,

---

23 The wise, the knowing

24 A rhetorical device in which the sense rises gradually in a series of images, each exceeding the one before it in force or dignity—as here the actor must continuously raise his voice in order to drown out the conversation of the narrator and the two women.

25 *Othello*, III, iii.

26 As in trump card, but perhaps also a reference to a trumpet (loud like a trumpet) or meaning a hindrance or obstacle.

27 He had a tête-à-tête (head-to-head) with Tabitha, but apparently a vis-à-vis (face-to-face) will do for Mrs. O'Trump.

23,24

25

26

27

most certainly *the* age, one may say—*the age par excellence*—speak French?—oh, quite a hero—perfect desperado!—*no hearts*, Mr. Tattle? I don't believe it.—immortal renown and all that!—prodigies of valor! *Never heard!!*—why, bless me, he's the man——"

"Mann?—*Captain* Mann?" here screamed some little feminine interloper from the farthest corner of the room. "Are you talking about Captain Mann and the duel?—oh, I *must* hear—do tell—go on, Mrs. O'Trump!—do now go on!" And go on Mrs. O'Trump did—all about a certain Captain Mann, who was either shot or hung, or should have been both shot and hung. Yes! Mrs. O'Trump, she went on, and I—I went off. There was no chance of hearing any thing further that evening in regard to Brevet Brigadier General John A. B. C. Smith.

Still I consoled myself with the reflection that the tide of ill-luck would not run against me forever, and so determined to make a bold push for information at the rout of that bewitching little angel, the graceful Mrs. Pirouette.

"Smith?" said Mrs. P., as we twirled about together in a *pas de zéphyr*, "Smith?—why, not General John A. B. C.? **28** Dreadful business that of the Bugaboos, wasn't it?—dreadful creatures, those Indians!—*do* turn out your toes! I really am ashamed of you—man of great courage, poor fellow!—but this is a wonderful age for invention—O dear me, I'm out of breath—quite a desperado—prodigies of valor—*never heard!*—can't believe it—I shall have to sit down and enlighten you—Smith! why, he's the man——"

"Man-*Fred*, I tell you!" here bawled out Miss Bas-Bleu, as **29,30** I led Mrs. Pirouette to a seat. "Did ever anybody hear the like? It's Man-*Fred*, I say, and not at all by any means Man-*Friday*." Here Miss Bas-Bleu beckoned to me in a very **31** peremptory manner; and I was obliged, will I nill I, to leave Mrs. P. for the purpose of deciding a dispute touching the title of a certain poetical drama of Lord Byron's. Although I pronounced, with great promptness, that the true title was Man-*Friday*, and not by any means Man-*Fred*, yet when I returned to seek Mrs. Pirouette she was not to be discovered, and I made my retreat from the house in a very bitter spirit of animosity against the whole race of the Bas-Bleus. **32**

Matters had now assumed a really serious aspect, and I resolved to call at once upon my particular friend, Mr. Theodore Sinivate; for I knew that here at least I should get **33** something like definite information.

"Smith?" said he, in his well-known peculiar way of drawing out his syllables; "Smith?—why, not General John A. B. C.? Savage affair that with the Kickapo-o-o-os, wasn't it? Say, don't you think so?—perfect despera-a-ado—great pity, 'pon my honor!—wonderfully inventive age!—pro-o-odigies of valor! By the by, did you ever hear about Captain Ma-a-a-n?"

"Captain Mann be d—d!" said I; "please to go on with your story."

"Hem!—oh well!—quite *la même cho-o-ose*, as we say in France. Smith, eh? Brigadier General John A—B—C.? I say"—[here Mr. S. thought proper to put his finger to the side of his nose]—"I say, you don't mean to insinuate now,

". . . I shall have to sit down and enlighten you—Smith! why, he's the man—" *Artist unknown*

28 Either these were exceptionally popular steps in Poe's day, or he was unfamiliar with any other dance terms, for he uses them again and again.

29 Manfred is the hero of Byron's dramatic poem *Manfred* (1817), who sells himself to the Prince of Darkness and lives in splendid solitude in the Alps; as well as the name of the Prince of Otranto, the central figure in Horace Walpole's Gothic novel *The Castle of Otranto* (1764). *Man-Fred* (1834) was a theatrical parody by Gilbert à Beckett (1811–56).

30 For more on bluestockings, see "Lionizing," note 12.

31 Man Friday is the young savage who becomes Robinson Crusoe's faithful attendant in Defoe's novel of 1719.

32 Apparently, the competition at this gathering of literary "experts" is too much to take sitting down. People were getting the "blues" as early as the sixteenth century, according to the O.E.D.

33 A Cockney pronunciation of "insinuate."

really and truly, and conscientiously, that you don't know all about that affair of Smith's, as well as I do, eh? Smith? John A—B—C.? Why, bless me, he's the ma-a-an——"

"*Mr.* Sinivate," said I, imploringly, "*is* he the man in the mask?"

"No-o-o!" said he, looking wise, "nor the man in the mo-o-on."

This reply I considered a pointed and positive insult, and so left the house at once in high dudgeon, with a firm resolve to call my friend, Mr. Sinivate, to a speedy account for his ungentlemanly conduct and ill-breeding.

In the meantime, however, I had no notion of being thwarted touching the information I desired. There was one resource left me yet. I would go to the fountain-head. I would call forthwith upon the General himself, and demand, in explicit terms, a solution of this abominable piece of mystery. Here, at least, there should be no chance for equivocation. I would be plain, positive, peremptory—as short as pie-crust— **34** as concise as Tacitus or Montesquieu.

It was early when I called, and the General was dressing, but I pleaded urgent business, and was shown at once into his bedroom by an old negro valet, who remained in attendance during my visit. As I entered the chamber, I looked about, of course, for the occupant, but did not immediately perceive him. There was a large and exceedingly odd-looking bundle of something which lay close by my feet on the floor, and, as I was not in the best humor in the world, I gave it a kick out of the way.

"Hem! ahem! rather civil that, I should say!" said the bundle, in one of the smallest, and altogether the funniest little voices, between a squeak and a whistle, that I ever heard in all the days of my existence.

"Ahem! rather civil that, I should observe."

I fairly shouted with terror, and made off, at a tangent, into the farthest extremity of the room.

"God bless me, my dear fellow!" here again whistled the bundle, "what—what—what—why, what *is* the matter? I really believe you don't know me at all."·

What *could* I say to all this—what *could* I? I staggered into an armchair, and, with staring eyes and open mouth, awaited the solution of the wonder.

"Strange you shouldn't know me though, isn't it?" presently re-squeaked the nondescript, which I now perceived was performing upon the floor some inexplicable evolution, very analogous to the drawing on of a stocking. There was only a single leg, however, apparent.

"Strange you shouldn't know me though, isn't it? Pompey, bring me that leg!" Here Pompey handed the bundle a very capital cork leg, already dressed, which it screwed on in a trice; and then it stood up before my eyes.

"And a bloody action it *was*," continued the thing, as if in a soliloquy; "but then one mustn't fight with the Bugaboos and Kickapoos, and think of coming off with a mere scratch. **35** Pompey, I'll thank you now for that arm. Thomas" [turning

34 Cornelius Tacitus (A.D. 55?–117?) was a Roman historian, while Charles de Secondat, Baron de La Brède et de Montesquieu (1689–1755) was a French philosopher and man of letters. Both are known for their conciseness; Tacitus in his history of Rome, and Montesquieu in his letters and analyses of the relation between human and natural law.

35 John F. Thomas was a maker of artificial limbs in Philadelphia. Joaquin Bishop was a Philadelphia chemical instrument maker. Nicholas Pettitt was a tailor in the same city. Andrew Ducrow was a London horse trainer and showman. *De l'Orme* (1830) was a novel by G. P. R. James. Parmly was the name of a whole family of dentists.

to me] "is decidedly the best hand at a cork leg; but if you should ever want an arm, my dear fellow, you must really let me recommend you to Bishop." Here Pompey screwed on an arm.

"We had rather hot work of it, that you may say. Now, you dog, slip on my shoulders and bosom. Pettitt makes the best shoulders, but for a bosom you will have to go to Ducrow."

"Bosom!" said I.

"Pompey, will you *never* be ready with that wig? Scalping is a rough process, after all; but then you can procure such a capital scratch at De L'Orme's."

"Scratch!"

"Now, you nigger, my teeth! For a *good* set of these you had better go to Parmly's at once; high prices, but excellent work. I swallowed some very capital articles, though, when the big Bugaboo rammed me down with the butt end of this rifle."

"Butt end! ram down!! my eye!!"

"O yes, by the by, my eye—here, Pompey, you scamp, screw it in! Those Kickapoos are not so very slow at a gouge; but he's a belied man, that Dr. Williams, after all; you can't imagine how well I see with the eyes of his make."   **36**

I now began very clearly to perceive that the object before me was nothing more nor less than my new acquaintance, Brevet Brigadier General John A. B. C. Smith. The manipulations of Pompey had made, I must confess, a very striking difference in the personal appearance of the man. The voice, however, still puzzled me no little; but even this apparent mystery was speedily cleared up.

"Pompey, you black rascal," squeaked the General, "I really do believe you would let me go out without my palate."

Hereupon, the negro, grumbling out an apology, went up to his master, opened his mouth with the knowing air of a horse-jockey, and adjusted therein a somewhat singular-looking machine, in a very dexterous manner, that I could not altogether comprehend. The alteration, however, in the entire expression of the General's countenance was instantaneous and surprising. When he again spoke, his voice had resumed all that rich melody and strength which I had noticed upon our original introduction.

"D——n the vagabonds!" said he, in so clear a tone that I positively started at the change, "D——n the vagabonds! they not only knocked in the roof of my mouth, but took the trouble to cut off at least seven eighths of my tongue. There isn't Bonfanti's equal, however, in America, for really good articles of this description. I can recommend you to him with confidence," [here the General bowed,] "and assure you that I have the greatest pleasure in so doing."   **37**

I acknowledged his kindness in my best manner, and took leave of him at once, with a perfect understanding of the true state of affairs—with a full comprehension of the mystery which had troubled me so long. It was evident. It was a clear case. Brevet Brigadier General John A. B. C. Smith was the man—was *the man that was used up*.   **38**

36 Dr. John Williams was sued in 1839 by a patient who had lost the sight of one eye while under his care. Three other Dr. Williamses (Eleaser, John, and Roger) were all religious men connected, in one way or the other, with the Indians.

37 Joseph Bonfanti sold talking dolls in New York and was well known for his rhyming advertisements.

"A Chronicle of 1675 relates how Captain Mosely with sixty men faced three hundred Indians in battle; the captain plucked off his periwig and tucked it in his breeches, preparatory to fighting, whereupon the red men turned tail and fled, crying out, "Umhm Umh, me no stay more fight Engismon, Engismon got two head, if me cut off un head he got noder a put on beder as dis." This theme persisted across the frontier, and we hear of a Yankee on the western plains, confronted with hostile Indians, pulling out his false teeth and unstrapping his cork leg, then making a move as if to unscrew his head, the while informing the braves he could similarly dismember them; they fled in terror." (Richard Dorson, *American Folklore* [1959], p. 21)

38 "Used up" means talked about, discussed, written about, worn out, rendered useless, consumed. All meanings apply in this grotesque play on words.

Marie Bonaparte writes: "The cardinal mutilation, however, is not mentioned, but we may well imagine it included, for the Kickapoos and Bugaboos who so generously relieved him of leg, arm, shoulders, pectoral muscles, scalp, teeth, eye, palate and seven-eighths tongue, would surely not have left him the penis! The castration of prisoners, moreover, holds high place among tribes quite as savage as were the Kickapoos and Bugaboos!" (p. 502) Her comment makes one wonder whom the General went to see to have a replacement made.

Certainly one would also be justified in interpreting the tale as a send-up of heroes, who often not only have feet of clay but bodies (and minds) of wood and cork.

THE ISLAND OF THE FAY

First published in *Graham's Magazine*, June 1841, this beautiful piece was written to accompany an engraving by John Sartain after English artist John Martin (1789–1854). Nicknamed "Mad" Martin, he was the most spectacularly melodramatic painter of historical subjects of the early-nineteenth century and developed a type of enormous canvas crowded with tiny figures set in fantastic architectural and natural settings.

The combination of a steel engraving with a poem or prose piece was a common practice in nineteenth-century magazines. Burton R. Pollin says that Martin's original was a fairly simple etching taken from one of his pamphlets on a new water supply for the city of London (1828) and that Sartain elaborated on it greatly with the help of Poe, so that the final engraving and the tale worked together to provide a strong effect on the reader (*Mystery and Detection Annual*, 1972).

A source for the tale may be a story about English poet William Blake that appeared in the New York *Mirror*, June 21, 1834:

" 'Did you ever see a fairy's funeral, madam?' he once said to a lady. . . . 'Never, sir,' was the answer. 'I have,' said Blake, 'but not before last night. I was walking alone in my garden; there was great stillness among the branches and flowers, and more than common sweetness in the air; I heard a low and pleasant sound, and knew not whence it came. At last I saw the broad leaf of a flower move, and underneath I saw a procession of creatures of the size and color of green and gray grasshoppers, bearing a body laid out on a rose-leaf, which they buried with songs, and then disappeared. It was a *fairy funeral*.' "

Despite the possible connection, Poe's story seems very much his own creation. It was written hastily, which accounts for its lack of unity in the first half. He used the scenery and mood later in "Eleonora" and in "Hans Pfaal" (1835 and 1840 versions only); there is a passage that echoes the present tale but which he removed from "Pfaall" in later editions (see "Pfaall" note 79).

Henry Gilbert (1868–1928), the American composer best known for his use of Negro tunes for his thematic material, wrote a piano piece after Poe's title.

---

1 In his first version, Poe used here his *Sonnet—to Science* as an "anonymous" poem, changing the ending of the poem to match the tale. The original poem ends: "Hast thou not dragged Diana from her car?/And driven the Hamadryad from the wood/To seek a shelter in some happier star?/Has thou not torn the Naiad from her flood,/The Elfin from the green grass, and from me/The summer dream beneath the tamarind tree?"

The changed final two lines read: "The elfin from the grass?—the dainty *fay*,/The witch, the sprite, the goblin—where are they?"

The present quotation means, "No place is without its genius"; it is from Servius' commentary on Virgil's *Aeneid*, V, 95, but Poe probably saw it in Victor Hugo's *Notre-Dame de Paris* (1831), Book VII, Chapter V.

2 "Moraux is here derived from *moeurs*, and its meaning is '*fashionable*,' or, more strictly, 'of manners.' " (Poe's note) "Music is the only one of the talents which gives

1

Nullus enim locus sine genio est.
   —*Servius*.

2 "*La musique*," says Marmontel, in those "Contes Moraux" which, in all our translations, we have insisted upon calling "Moral Tales," as if in mockery of their spirit—"*la musique est le seul des talents qui jouissent de lui-même; tous les autres veulent des témoins.*" He here confounds the pleasure derivable from sweet sounds with the capacity of creating them. No more than any other *talent*, is that for music susceptible of complete enjoyment, where there is no second party to appreciate its exercise. And it is only in common with other talents that it produces *effects* which may be fully enjoyed in solitude. The idea which the *raconteur* has either failed to entertain clearly, or has sacrificed in its expression to his national love of *point*, is, doubtless, the very tenable one that the higher order of music is the most thoroughly estimated when we are exclusively alone. The proposition, in this form, will be admitted at once by those who love the lyre for its own sake, and for its spiritual uses. But there is one pleasure still **3** within the reach of fallen mortality—and perhaps only one—which owes even more than does music to the accessory sentiment of seclusion. I mean the happiness experienced in the contemplation of natural scenery. In truth, the man who would behold aright the glory of God upon earth must in **4** solitude behold that glory. To me, at least, the presence—not of human life only, but of life in any other form than that of the green things which grow upon the soil and are voiceless—is a stain upon the landscape—is at war with the genius of the scene. I love, indeed, to regard the dark valleys, and the gray rocks, and the waters that silently smile, and the forests that **5** sigh in uneasy slumbers, and the proud watchful mountains that look down upon all—I love to regard these as themselves but the colossal members of one vast animate and sentient **6** whole—a whole whose form (that of the sphere) is the most perfect and most inclusive of all; whose path is among associate planets; whose meek handmaiden is the moon, whose mediate sovereign is the sun; whose life is eternity; whose thought is that of a God; whose enjoyment is knowledge; whose destinies are lost in immensity; whose cognizance of ourselves is akin with our own cognizance of the *animalculæ* which infest the brain—a being which we, in consequence, regard as purely inanimate and material, much in the same manner as these *animalculæ* must regard us.

Our telescopes, and our mathematical investigations assure us on every hand—notwithstanding the cant of the more ignorant of the priesthood—that space, and therefore that bulk, is an important consideration in the eyes of the Almighty. The cycles in which the stars move are those best adapted for the evolution, without collision, of the greatest possible number of bodies. The forms of those bodies are accurately such as, within a given surface, to include the greatest possible amount of matter;—while the surfaces themselves are so disposed as to accommodate a denser population than could be accommodated on the same surfaces otherwise arranged. Nor is it any argument against bulk being an object with God, that space itself is infinite; for there may be an infinity of matter to fill it. And since we see clearly that the endowment of matter with vitality is a principle—indeed, as far as our judgments extend, the *leading* principle in the operations of Deity—it is scarcely logical to imagine it confined to the regions of the minute, where we daily trace it, and not extending to those of the august. As we find cycle within cycle without end—yet all revolving around one far-distant centre which is the Godhead, may we not analogically suppose in the same manner, life within life, the less within the greater, and all within the Spirit Divine? In short, we are madly erring, **7** through self-esteem, in believing man, in either his temporal or future destinies, to be of more moment in the universe

pleasure by itself; all the others need witnesses" is by Jean François Marmontel (1723–99), in his *Contes Moraux* ("La Bergère des Alpes"). Poe, again, did not in all likelihood read the original but probably borrowed it from Bulwer-Lyttton's *Ernest Maltravers* (1837), Book VII, Chapter Two.

3 The lyre is the traditional instrument of the poet.

4 This is one of the basic tenets of the romantic movement. "To the Eyes of the Man of Imagination, Nature is Imagination itself," says William Blake (letter to Revd. Dr. Trusler, 1799), and William Wordsworth extolled the rural life "because in that situation the passions of men are incorporated with the beautiful and permanent forms of nature" (Preface to *Lyrical Ballads*, 1802).

5 See "To lone lake that smiles,/In its dream of deep rest," in Poe's "Al Aaraaf," II, 132–33.

6 "Sentient" means having feelings. See "The Fall of the House of Usher," note 49. For *animalculae* that infest the brain, see "Scheherazade," note 47.

7 ". . . all is Life—Life—Life within Life—the less within the greater, and all within the *Spirit Divine*." (Poe's *Eureka*, 1848)

8 "The clods of the valley shall be sweet unto him.
. . ." (Job 21:33)

9 "Speaking of the tides, Pomponius Mela, in his treatise
'De Situ Orbis,' says 'either the world is a great animal,
or &c.' " (Poe's note)

The quote probably came from Hugh Murray's *Encyclopaedia of Geography* (1834), in which the first-
century Roman geographer suggests that the tides are
the result of either the world being "a great animal
whose breathings excite the alternate movements" or of
"deep caves, into which the waters are alternately
absorbed and ejected."

10 "Balzac—in substance—I do not remember the
words." (Poe's note)

Zimmerman's *Solitude* (1756) was not the cause of
Jean Louis Guez de Balzac's comment in *Les Entretiens*
that "solitude is a fine thing; but it is necessary that
there be someone for you to tell that solitude is a good
thing," since the Balzac work predates Zimmerman's by
ninety-seven years. Poe apparently quotes from memory.

8 than that vast "clod of the valley" which he tills and contemns,
and to which he denies a soul for no more profound reason
9 that that he does not behold it in operation.

These fancies, and such as these, have always given to my
meditations among the mountains and the forests, by the
rivers and the ocean, a tinge of what the everyday world would
not fail to term fantastic. My wanderings amid such scenes
have been many, and far-searching, and often solitary; and
the interest with which I have strayed through many a dim,
deep valley, or gazed into the reflected heaven of many a
bright lake, has been an interest greatly deepened by the
thought that I have strayed and gazed *alone*. What flippant
10 Frenchman was it who said, in allusion to the well-known
work of Zimmerman, that, *"la solitude est une belle chose;
mais il faut quelqu'un pour vous dire que la solitude est une
belle chose"?* The epigram cannot be gainsayed; but the
necessity is a thing that does not exist.

It was during one of my lonely journeyings, amid a far-
distant region of mountain locked within mountain, and sad
rivers and melancholy tarns writhing or sleeping within all—
that I chanced upon a certain rivulet and island. I came upon
them suddenly in the leafy June, and threw myself upon the
turf, beneath the branches of an unknown odorous shrub, that
I might doze as I contemplated the scene. I felt that thus only
should I look upon it—such was the character of phantasm
which it wore.

A somber, yet beautiful and peaceful gloom here pervaded all things. *Artist unknown*

On all sides—save to the west, where the sun was about sinking—arose the verdant walls of the forest. The little river which turned sharply in its course, and was thus immediately lost to sight, seemed to have no exit from its prison, but to be absorbed by the deep-green foliage of the trees to the east— while in the opposite quarter (so it appeared to me as I lay at length and glanced upward) there poured down noiselessly and continuously into the valley, a rich golden and crimson water-fall from the sunset fountains of the sky.

About midway in the short vista which my dreamy vision took in, one small circular island, profusely verdured, reposed upon the bosom of the stream.

> So blended bank and shadow there
> That each seemed pendulous in air—   **11**

so mirror-like was the glassy water, that it was scarcely possible to say at what point upon the slope of the emerald turf its crystal dominion began.

My position enabled me to include in a single view both the eastern and western extremities of the islet, and I observed a singularly marked difference in their aspects. The latter was all one radiant harem of garden beauties. It glowed and blushed beneath the eye of the slant sunlight, and fairly laughed with flowers. The grass was short, springy, sweet-scented, and asphodel-interspersed. The trees were lithe, **12** mirthful, erect—bright, slender, and graceful—of Eastern figure and foliage, with bark smooth, glossy, and parti-colored. There seemed a deep sense of life and joy about all; and although no airs blew from out the heavens, yet every thing had motion through the gentle sweepings to and fro of innumerable butterflies, that might have been mistaken for tulips with wings.   **13**

The other or eastern end of the isle was whelmed in the blackest shade. A sombre, yet beautiful and peaceful gloom here pervaded all things. The trees were dark in color, and mournful in form and attitude, wreathing themselves into sad, solemn, and spectral shapes that conveyed ideas of mortal sorrow and untimely death. The grass wore the deep tint of the cypress, and the heads of its blades hung droopingly, and hither and thither among it were many small unsightly hillocks, low and narrow, and not very long, that had the aspect of graves, but were not; although over and all about them the rue and the rosemary clambered. The shade of the trees fell **14** heavily upon the water, and seemed to bury itself therein, impregnating the depths of the element with darkness. I fancied that each shadow, as the sun descended lower and lower, separated itself sullenly from the trunk that gave it birth, and thus became absorbed by the stream; while other shadows issued momently from the trees, taking the place of their predecessors thus entombed.   **15**

This idea, having once seized upon my fancy, greatly excited it, and I lost myself forthwith in revery. "If ever island were enchanted," said I to myself, "this is it. This is the haunt of the few gentle Fays who remain from the wreck of the race. **16**

"If ever island were enchanted," said I to myself, "this is it." *Illustrated by F. S. Coburn, 1902*

11 This is a slightly altered version of a part of Poe's poem *The City in the Sea* (1831). In "Landor's Cottage" we find the same idea of a shoreline blending invisibly with the water.

12 Asphodels appear in "Berenice" as a symbol of death. Here and in "Eleonora" they seem to represent life and vitality.

13 *"Florem putares nare per liquidum æthera.—P. Commire."* (Poe's note)
The words are from Père Jean Commire's "Papillo et Apis," which Poe no doubt found in D'Israeli's *Curiosities of Literature* under "Some Ingenious Thoughts": "P. Commire, a pleasing writer of Latin verse, says of the flight of a butterfly, '. . . IT FLIES, and swims a flower in liquid air!' "

14 "There's rosemary, that's for remembrance . . . and there is pansies, that's for thoughts" (*Hamlet*, IV, v, 174). Rue is a traditional symbol of grief.

15 Compare the canceled paragraph of "Hans Pfaall," note 79.

16 Fairies. "Fay" is also spelled "fey"; it comes from the French. "Fay," and "faerie" ("fayre") replaced the English word "elf" during the Tudor era.

17 "Canoe" is from the Spanish equivalent of a Caribbean word first brought back by Columbus; it meant (contrary to current usage) any small, light skiff propelled by paddling.

18 One might compare the Fay's life cycle with that of the *Ephemera*, immortalized in Benjamin Franklin's tale of that name (1778), or with an example out of Einstein's Theory of Relativity—watching one time sequence from a much different one.

19 One is reminded of the hypnogogic state, which Poe refers to from time to time, in which one sees unusual things in the half-light of consciousness.

20 Marie Bonaparte suggests that the tale is but another reference to "the advancing illness of his beloved mother. She it was who at every passage, 'through her winter and through her summer,' grew steadily weaker: she it was who vanished in that final December when 'darkness fell over all things,' a darkness, for the small boy, of lifelong grief and infantile amnesia. We may be sure, however, that she was destined to re-emerge from it, though this could not consciously be known to Poe. For, with the deep, the indelible memory of the unconscious, from which what was repressed returns in symbols and substitutions, he was to remember. And it was, verily, with the shadowed hues that fell from his dying mother that he was thenceforth to paint his landscapes. To him, all nature would wear the mortal hues of her cheeks, and they would colour his vision of earth and sea and sky." (Pp. 288–89)

In all fairness to Bonaparte (with whom I frequently disagree), the above wording is not really hers; it is the translation from the original French by John Rodker.

According to Jung, women who are fairy-like characters are strong projections of the cruder aspect of the anima (the female part of a man's psyche), when a man's feeling attitude toward life has remained infantile (M.-L. von Franz, in *Man and His Symbols*, pp. 186–97).

Are these green tombs theirs?—or do they yield up their sweet lives as man-kind yield up their own? In dying, do they not rather waste away mournfully, rendering unto God, little by little, their existence, as these trees render up shadow after shadow, exhausting their substance unto dissolution? What the wasting tree is to the water that imbibes its shade, growing thus blacker by what it preys upon, may not the life of the Fay be to the death which engulfs it?"

As I thus mused, with half-shut eyes, while the sun sank rapidly to rest, and eddying currents careered round and round the island, bearing upon their bosom large, dazzling, white flakes of the bark of the sycamore—flakes which, in their multiform positions upon the water, a quick imagination might have converted into any thing it pleased—while I thus mused, it appeared to me that the form of one of those very Fays about whom I had been pondering made its way slowly into the darkness from out the light at the western end of the **17** island. She stood erect in a singularly fragile canoe, and urged it with the mere phantom of an oar. While within the influence of the lingering sunbeams, her attitude seemed indicative of joy—but sorrow deformed it as she passed within the shade. Slowly she glided along, and at length rounded the islet and re-entered the region of light. "The revolution which has just been made by the Fay," continued I, musingly, "is the cycle **18** of the brief year of her life. She has floated through her winter and through her summer. She is a year nearer unto death; for I did not fail to see that, as she came into the shade, her shadow fell from her, and was swallowed up in the dark water, making its blackness more black."

And again the boat appeared, and the Fay; but about the attitude of the latter there was more of care and uncertainty, and less of elastic joy. She floated again from out the light, and into the gloom (which deepened momently), and again her shadow fell from her into the ebony water, and became absorbed into its blackness. And again and again she made the circuit of the island (while the sun rushed down to his slumbers), and at each issuing into the light, there was more sorrow about her person, while it grew feebler, and far fainter, and more indistinct; and at each passage into the gloom, there fell from her a darker shade, which became whelmed in a **19** shadow more black. But at length, when the sun had utterly departed, the Fay, now the mere ghost of her former self, went disconsolately with her boat into the region of the ebony flood—and that she issued thence at all I cannot say, for darkness fell over all things, and I beheld her magical figure **20** no more.

ELEONORA

First published in *The Gift*, 1841, "Eleonora" is Poe's most unabashedly romantic tale, written in the style of his prose poems (*Silence, Shadow, The Island of the Fay*). He was dissatisfied with the ending, which he felt needed more work—"a good subject spoiled by hurry in the handling" (*Graham's*, November 1841). Still, critics have been kind to "Eleonora," sensing in it honest emotions of love, "unblemished" by the more morbid aspects of Poe's other stories of male-female relationships.

The setting may be modeled after the "Happy Valley" of Samuel Johnson's *Rasselas* (1759), but Poe uses nothing else from that tale. There is also a parallel with *Paul et Virginie* (1788), by Bernardin de Saint-Pierre, in which a similar couple grow up together on the tropical island of Mauritius, fall in love, separate, and are reunited, only to have the woman die. Poe may also have had in mind D'Israeli's "Mejnoun and Leila" (*Romances*, 1803), for some of the more exotic elements of "Eleonora" seem to echo that oriental fable.

Too, many of the details of the story are clearly autobiographical, most of them described in the notes.

Sub conservatione formæ specificæ salva anima.
—*Raymond Lully*. **1**

I am come of a race noted for vigor of fancy and ardor of passion. Men have called me mad; but the question is not yet settled, whether madness is or is not the loftiest intelligence— whether much that is glorious—whether all that is profound— does not spring from disease of thought—from *moods* of mind exalted at the expense of the general intellect. They who **2** dream by day are cognizant of many things which escape those who dream only by night. In their grey visions they obtain glimpses of eternity, and thrill, in awaking, to find that they have been upon the verge of the great secret. In snatches, **3** they learn something of the wisdom which is of good, and more of the mere knowledge which is of evil. They penetrate, however, rudderless or compassless, into the vast ocean of the "light ineffable" and again, like the adventurers of the **4** Nubian geographer, *"agressi sunt mare tenebrarum, quid in eo esset exploraturi."* **5**
We will say, then, that I am mad. I grant, at least, that **6** there are two distinct conditions of my mental existence—the condition of a lucid reason, not to be disputed, and belonging to the memory of events forming the first epoch of my life— and a condition of shadow and doubt, appertaining to the present, and to the recollection of what constitutes the second great era of my being. Therefore, what I shall tell of the earlier period, believe; and to what I may relate of the later time,

1 "Under the protection of a specific form the soul is safe" is from Raymond Lully (1235–1315), but more likely Poe found it in Victor Hugo's *Notre-Dame de Paris*, Book VII, Chapter vi.

2 "What the world calls 'genius' is the state of mental disease arising from the undue predominance of some of the faculties. The works of such genius are never sound in themselves, and, in especial, always betray the general mental insanity." (Poe, "Fifty Suggestions," XXIII)
Likewise Dryden: "Great wits are sure to madness near allied" (*Absolom and Achitophel*, line 163); and Seneca: "There is no great genius without some touch of madness" (*On Tranquillity of the Mind*, 17, 10).

3 The state of being on the verge of some great secret is a perilous one, as proved in "Ligeia," "Morella," and "MS. Found in a Bottle."

4 "Lightning Divine, ineffable" (*Paradise Lost*, V, 734)

5 See "A Descent into the Maelström," note 5.

6 His fear of madness is a probable sign that he is *not* insane, since truly mentally disturbed people seldom recognize that their perspective is distorted. Most of Poe's insane or unbalanced narrators are quick to deny any such possibility.

7 The Sphinx, a monster whose upper part was a woman and whose lower part a dog with the tail of a snake, wings of a bird, paws of a lion, and the voice of a human, ate all Thebans who could not answer her riddle, but killed herself when Oedipus solved it. The riddle: "What is it that walks on four legs in the morning, two legs at noon and three legs in the evening? The answer is man, who crawls on hands and knees as a baby, walks on two legs in his prime, and uses a cane in his old age. Poe also mentions Oedipus and the riddle in "Thou Art the Man."

8 The narrator seems to be following the romantic dictate of Wordsworth that poetry is "the spontaneous overflow of powerful feelings: it takes its origin from emotion recollected in tranquillity . . . ," in *Preface to Lyrical Ballads*, 1802.

9 Eleonora is a variation on the name "Helen," as is the Lenore of "The Raven." All three are representative of Poe's ideal woman. He may have been reminded of the name by Dryden's *Eleonora* (1692), about a countess who dies young, or by the *Eléonore* of the poetry of Jean-Pierre-Jacques-Auguste de Labouïsse-Rochefort (1778–1852).

In the first version of the tale, the narrator also has a name: Pyrros, which means "ardent."

10 Compare with Shelley, "Life, like a dome of many-colored glass," in *Adonais*, line 462.

Valleys traditionally symbolize life itself and are the mystic dwelling places of shepherds and priests. Here, the two lovers in their idyllic surroundings are like the happy shepherd and shepherdess of the pastroal poem, while the narrator's worship of Eleonora approaches the mystical.

11 Poe had married his thirteen-year-old cousin, Virginia Clemm, in 1836, and the couple at first lived as brother and sister, with Virginia's mother (Edgar and Virginia were actually first cousins).

12 This reminds one of Alph, the sacred river of Coleridge's *Kubla Khan*, as well as of these lines from Milton's *Paradise Lost*, Book II, line 582: "Far off from these a slow and silent stream,/Lethe the river of oblivion rolls."

Dead souls drank from the river Lethe to forget their past lives before reincarnation, according to mythology, certainly an apt comparison to the narrator's wishes here. Rivers in general often symbolize "the irreversible passage of time, and in consequence, . . . a sense of loss and oblivion," says J. E. Cirlot in A Dictionary of Symbols.

7 give only such credit as may seem due; or doubt it altogether; or, if doubt it ye cannot, then play unto its riddle the Oedipus.

8
9 She whom I loved in youth, and of whom I now pen calmly and distinctly these remembrances, was the sole daughter of the only sister of my mother long departed. Eleonora was the name of my cousin. We had always dwelled together, beneath
10 a tropical sun, in the Valley of the Many-Colored Grass. No unguided footstep ever came upon that vale; for it lay far away up among a range of giant hills that hung beetling around about it, shutting out the sunlight from its sweetest recesses. No path was trodden in its vicinity; and, to reach our happy home, there was need of putting back, with force, the foliage of many thousands of forest trees, and of crushing to death the glories of many millions of fragrant flowers. Thus it was that we lived all alone, knowing nothing of the world without the
11 valley,—I, and my cousin, and her mother.

From the dim regions beyond the mountains at the upper end of our encircled domain, here crept out a narrow and deep river, brighter than all save the eyes of Eleonora; and, winding stealthily about in mazy courses, it passed away, at length, through a shadowy gorge, among hills still dimmer than those whence it had issued. We called it the "River of Silence:" for there seemed to be a hushing influence in its
12 flow. No murmur arose from its bed, and so gently it wandered along, that the pearly pebbles upon which we loved to gaze, far down within its bosom, stirred not at all, but lay in a motionless content, each in its own old station, shining on gloriously forever.

The margin of the river, and of the many dazzling rivulets

We had always dwelled together, beneath a tropical sun, in the Valley of the Many-Colored Grass. *Artist unknown*

that glided, through devious ways, into its channel, as well as **13**
the spaces that extended from the margins away down into
the depths of the streams until they reached the bed of
pebbles at the bottom,—these spots, not less than the whole
surface of the valley, from the river to the mountains that
girdled it in, were carpted all by a soft green grass, thick,
short, perfectly even, and vanilla-perfumed, but so besprinkled
throughout with the yellow buttercup, the white daisy, the
purple violet, and the ruby-red asphodel, that its exceeding
beauty spoke to our hearts, in loud tones, of the love and of
the glory of God. **14**

And, here and there, in groves about this grass, like
wildernesses of dreams, sprang up fantastic trees, whose tall
slender stems stood not upright, but slanted gracefully towards
the light that peered at noon-day into the centre of the valley.
Their bark was speckled with the vivid alternate splendor of
ebony and silver, and was smoother than all save the cheeks
of Eleonora; so that but for the brilliant green of the huge
leaves that spread from their summits in long tremulous lines, **15**
dallying with the Zephyrs, one might have fancied them giant **16**
serpents of Syria doing homage to their Sovereign the Sun. **17**

Hand in hand about this valley, for fifteen years, roamed
I with Eleonora before Love entered within our hearts. It was
one evening at the close of the third lustrum of her life, and
of the fourth of my own, that we sat, locked in each other's **18**
embrace, beneath the serpent-like trees, and looked down **19**
within the waters of the River of Silence at our images therein.
We spoke no words during the rest of that sweet day; and our
words even upon the morrow were tremulous and few. We
had drawn the god Eros from that wave, and now we felt that **20**
he had enkindled within us the fiery souls of our forefathers.
The passions which had for centuries distinguished our race,
came thronging with the fancies for which they had been
equally noted, and together breathed a delirious bliss over
the Valley of the Many-Colored Grass. A change fell upon all
things. Strange brilliant flowers, star-shaped, burst out upon
the trees where no flowers had been known before. The tints
of the green carpet deepened; and when, one by one, the
white daisies shrank away, there sprang up, in place of them,
ten by ten of the ruby-red asphodel. And life arose in our
paths; for the tall flamingo, hitherto unseen, with all gay
glowing birds, flaunted his scarlet plumage before us. The **21**
golden and silver fish haunted the river, out of the bosom of
which issued, little by little, a murmur that swelled, as length,
into a lulling melody more divine than that of the harp of
Æolus—sweeter than all save the voice of Eleonora. And now, **22**
too, a voluminous cloud, which we had long watched in the
regions of Hesper, floated out thence, all gorgeous in crimson
and gold, and settling in peace above us, sank, day by day,
lower and lower, until its edges rested upon the tops of the
mountains, turning all their dimness into magnificence, and
shutting us up, as if forever, within a magic prison-house of
grandeur and of glory.

The loveliness of Eleonora was that of the Seraphim; but **23**

13 A winding, straying course

14 The narrator describes a sort of Eden, with himself
and Eleonora as Adam and Eve.

The short, "perfectly even" grass is seen again in the
idyllic "Landor's Cottage."

The asphodel, or king's spear, was sacred to Persephone and is thus associated with the fields of the dead.
Its scientific name is *Asphodeline lutea*. The buttercup,
a ranunculus, is often associated with young love, and
the violet has long been considered a symbol of modesty.

15 And there were gardens bright with sinuous rills
Where blossomed many an incense-bearing tree;
And here were forests ancient as the hills,
Enfolding sunny spots of greenery.

(*Kubla Khan*)

Compare also with "The Island of the Fay": "The trees
were lithe . . . bright, slender, and graceful . . . with
bark smooth, glossy, and parti-colored."

16 Zephyrs are gentle western winds. Zephyr was the
child of Eos, goddess of dawn. His brothers were Notus,
the south wind, and Boreas, the north wind.

"Fair laughs the morn, and soft the zephyr blows"
(Gray, *The Bard*, II, 2)

17 The ancient Assyro-Babylonian sun god was named
Shamash, but there is no obvious connection between
the god and the giant snakes Poe mentions. Serpents,
however, do relate to the image of the Garden of Eden.

18 Eleonora is fifteen, the narrator twenty.

19 The serpentlike trees again conjure up images of
Eden, with the suggestion that the narrator and Eleonora, like Adam and Eve, must confront the real world
of good and evil, or life and death.

20 Eros, the god of love, was born of Chaos, but was
later known as the son of Aphrodite (Venus). Anteros
was the god of passion, son of Ares and Aphrodite, and
also the god of mutual love and tenderness, as opposed
to the erotic love represented by Eros.

21 The south Asian and African flamingo is scarlet,
unlike the more familiar American pink bird.

22 Aeolus was the god who lived on the island of Aeolia,
where he kept the winds in a cave. It is the sound of the
wind referred to here. It was a nineteenth-century notion
that the Aeolian harp, or wind chime, was the most
sublime of instruments, because through it Nature spoke
directly to man.

23 The Seraphim are angels who surround God's heavenly court, usually portrayed as more graceful and
beautiful than the Cherubim, and in art with a surrounding red color. There is irony in the narrator's calling
Eleonora "an angel" while at the same time emphasizing
her otherworldliness.

We called it the "River of Silence," for there seemed to be a hushing influence on its flow. . . . so gently it wandered along, that the pearly pebbles upon which we loved to gaze, far down within its bosom, stirred not at all, but lay in a motionless content, each in its own old station, shining on gloriously forever. *Illustration by Albert Edward Sterner for* Century Magazine *1903*

24 i.e., death. Eating of the forbidden fruit, which caused Adam and Eve to be expelled from Paradise and know death.

25 Shams ud-din Mahomet, also known as Hafiz, was the bard of Shiraz, Persia. He died about 1389, after a career of extolling wine and women.

26 An insect that lives only one day. See "The Island of the Fay," note 18.

27 The key word here is "entombed." While the narrator means the actual burial of Eleonora, in a very real way he has already entombed her, keeping her to himself, hidden away from the world.

In real life, Poe's wife was always frail, and after bursting a vein in her throat while singing in 1842, fell prey to tuberculosis, from which she died in January 1847 at age twenty-four.

28 Elysium, the Elysian Fields, home of the blessed after death

29 Compare "perfumed from an unseen censer/Swung by seraphim," *The Raven*, 79–80. A censer is the metal vessel in which incense is burnt; the smoke that rises is symbolic of prayers to heaven.

she was a maiden artless and innocent as the brief life she had led among the flowers. No guile disguised the fervor of love which animated her heart, and she examined with me its inmost recesses as we walked together in the Valley of the Many-Colored Grass, and discoursed of the mighty changes which had lately taken place therein.

At length, having spoken one day, in tears, of the last sad **24** change which must befall Humanity, she thenceforward dwelt only upon this one sorrowful theme, interweaving it into all **25** our converse, as, in the songs of the bard of Schiraz, the same images are found occurring, again and again, in every impressive variation of phrase.

She had seen that the finger of Death was upon her bosom— **26** that, like the ephemeron, she had been made perfect in loveliness only to die; but the terrors of the grave, to her, lay solely in a consideration which she revealed to me, one evening at twilight, by the banks of the River of Silence. She grieved to think that, having entombed her in the Valley of the Many-Colored Grass, I would quit forever its happy recesses, transferring the love which now was so passionately **27** her own to some maiden of the outer and every-day world. And, then and there, I threw myself hurriedly at the feet of Eleonora, and offered up a vow, to herself and to Heaven, that I would never bind myself in marriage to any daughter of Earth—that I would in no manner prove recreant to her dear memory, or to the memory of the devout affection with which she had blessed me. And I call the Mighty Ruler of the Universe to witness the pious solemnity of my vow. And the **28** curse which I invoked of *Him* and of her, a saint in Helusion, should I prove traitorous to that promise, involved a penalty the exceeding great horror of which will not permit me to make record of it here. And the bright eyes of Eleonora grew brighter at my words; and she sighed as if a deadly burthen had been taken from her breast; and she trembled and very bitterly wept; but she made acceptance of the vow, (for what was she but a child?) and it made easy to her the bed of her death. And she said to me, not many days afterwards, tranquilly dying, that, because of what I had done for the comfort of her spirit, she would watch over me in that spirit when departed, and, if so it were permitted her, return to me visibly in the watches of the night; but, if this thing were, indeed, beyond the power of the souls in Paradise, that she would, at least, give me frequent indications of her presence; sighing upon me in the evening winds, or filling the air which I breathed **29** with perfume from the censers of the angels. And, with these words upon her lips, she yielded up her innocent life, putting an end to the first epoch of my own.

Thus far I have faithfully said. But as I pass the barrier in Time's path formed by the death of my beloved, and proceed with the second era of my existence, I feel that a shadow gathers over my brain, and I mistrust the perfect sanity of the record. But let me on.—Years dragged themselves along heavily, and still I dwelled within the Valley of the Many-Colored Grass;—but a second change had come upon all things. The star-shaped flowers shrank into the stems of the trees, and appeared no more. The tints of the green carpet faded; and, one by one, the ruby-red asphodels withered away; and there sprang up, in place of them, ten by ten, dark eye-like violets that writhed uneasily and were ever encumbered with dew. And Life departed from our paths; for the **30** tall flamingo flaunted no longer his scarlet plumage before us, but flew sadly from the vale into the hills, with all the gay glowing birds that had arrived in his company. And the golden and silver fish swam down through the gorge at the lower end of our domain and bedecked the sweet river never again. And the lulling melody that had been softer than the wind-harp of Æolus and more divine than all save the voice of Eleonora, it died little by little away, in murmurs growing lower and lower, until the stream returned, at length, utterly, into the solemnity of its original silence. And then, lastly the voluminous cloud uprose, and, abandoning the tops of the mountains to the dimness of old, fell back into the regions of Hesper, **31** and took away all its manifold golden and gorgeous glories from the Valley of the Many-Colored Grass.

Yet the promises of Eleonora were not forgotten; for I heard the sounds of the swinging of the censers of the angels; and streams of a holy perfume floated ever and ever about the valley; and at lone hours, when my heart beat heavily, the winds that bathed my brow came unto me laden with soft sighs; and indistinct murmurs filled often the night air; and once—oh, but once only! I was awakened from a slumber like the slumber of death by the pressing of spiritual lips upon my own.

But the void within my heart refused, even thus, to be filled. I longed for the love which had before filled it to overflowing. At length the valley *pained* me through its memories of Eleonora, and I left it forever for the vanities and the turbulent triumphs of the world.

* * *

I found myself within a strange city, where all things might have served to blot from recollection the sweet dreams I had dreamed so long in the Valley of the Many-Colored Grass. The pomps and pageantries of a stately court, and the mad

30 Since asphodels are traditional symbols of immortality (by association with the Elysian Fields), their disappearance and replacement by the more earthly violets signals a major change in the valley.

That the flowers "writhe" may be the result of strong winds that once never touched the valley, or that the valley as it once was is in its death throes, or that Nature is grieving with the narrator (the dew on the flowers might be tears)—or simply that the narrator's vision is colored by his great loss.

In *The Valley Nis* (1831), Poe writes, "Helen, like thy human eye/There th' uneasy violets lie" (lines 29–30)

Poe's imagery in this passage is not unusual. In *The Hour of Death*, Felicia Dorothea Hemans (1793–1835) writes:

> Leaves have their time to fall,
> And flowers to wither at the north-wind's breath,
> And stars to set,—but all,
> Thou hast all seasons for thine own, O Death!

An interesting parallel, but no doubt unknown to Poe, is a poem by the Japanese Ono No Komachi (ninth century):

> The flowers withered,
> Their color faded away.
> While meaninglessly
> I spent my days in the world
> And the long rains were falling.

31 Hesperus, or Vesper, was carried away by the wind to become the evening star; his name is often applied to the planet Venus.

"Ere twice in murk and occidental damp/Moist Hesperus hath quench'd his sleepy lamp" (*All's Well That Ends Well*, II, i, 164–65)

Hand in hand about this valley, for fifteen years, roamed I with Eleanora. . . . *Artist unknown*

32 Ermengarde was the twelfth-century Countess of Narbonne, a patron of the troubadours. She was also the inspiration for several poems by Poe's friend N. P. Willis in *Melanie and Other Poems* (1837).

33 I.e., that awaken memory

34 The entire section that begins "Oh bright was the seraph Ermengarde!" and continues to the end of the tale is an invocation, a prose poem that gives a mystical, almost religious quality to the conclusion of this most unusual story.

Some readers have seen the ending of "Eleonora" in terms of that of "Morella," with the heroine reincarnated in the body of Ermengarde. But if this were so, Poe surely would have made it clear, and the voice in the night would not have been necessary.

Another possibility is that the narrator is insane and that Ermengarde is merely a hallucination. Again, this seems unlikely, since Poe is careful to delineate madness when necessary.

The most likely interpretation is the most obvious: that Eleonora forgives the narrator for his love for Ermengarde. God is love, and therefore all love is God-given, and God-directed, and the narrator's love for Ermengarde is a divine love in which the spirit of Eleonora shares. Note, too, that the "curse" was the narrator's own, not Eleonora's, and so he actually has little to fear from her departed soul. Besides, as a liberated spirit, she is free from the earthy concerns of jealousy.

Compare "They that love beyond the world cannot be separated from it. Death is but crossing the world, as friends do the seas; they live in one another still" (William Penn [1644–1718], *Some Fruits of Solitude*); and "For love is heaven, and heaven is love" (Scott, *The Lay of the Last Minstrel*, III, 2).

The autobiographical allusions are very strong. Poe was hard hit by the death of his young wife; he was both feverish and delirious for some weeks after Virginia's burial. Toward the end of 1847 he recovered his spirits and began to rebuild his life—and soon began his romantic entanglements with Helen Whitman, Annie Richmond, and Elmira Shelton. It would not be far-fetched to see in "Eleonora" Poe's working out of his own guilt feelings when his need for women in his life warred with his grief for the dead Virginia.

Marie Bonaparte suggests that the tale actually reflects Poe's feelings toward his mother, whom he had sought in all the women he loved. The bereavement of the narrator, like that of Poe for his dead wife, "would leave him, once more, with that same sense of loss, that some yearning for comfort. Once more the ardent longing for love would awake and, with it, the conflict between fidelity to a cherished memory and love of a new object in which the 'abiding soul' would dwell under a changed exterior. But this conflict he was not to resolve so successfully in his life, as in the story of *Eleonora*, which so supremely expresses the phantasy of wish-fulfillment and reconciliation." (P. 257)

Whichever, there is no doubt that "Eleonora" remains Poe's most lyric and subdued tale of love and that its tone is far different from his other studies of man and woman.

clangor of arms, and the radiant loveliness of woman, bewildered and intoxicated my brain. But as yet my soul had proved true to its vows, and the indications of the presence of Eleonora were still given me in the silent hours of the night. Suddenly, these manifestations they ceased; and the world grew dark before mine eyes; and I stood aghast at the burning thoughts which possessed—at the terrible temptations which beset me; for there came from some far, far distant and unknown land, into the gay court of the king I served, a maiden to whose beauty my whole recreant heart yielded at once—at whose footstool I bowed down without a struggle, in the most ardent, in the most abject worship of love. What indeed was my passion for the young girl of the valley in comparison with the fervor, and the delirium, and the spirit-lifting ecstasy of adoration with which I poured out my whole

32 soul in tears at the feet of the ethereal Ermengarde?—Oh bright was the seraph Ermengarde! and in that knowledge I had room for none other.—Oh divine was the angel Ermen-

33 garde! and as I looked down into the depths of her memorial eyes I thought only of them—and *of her*.

I wedded;—nor dreaded the curse I had invoked; and its bitterness was not visited upon me. And once—but once again in the silence of the night, there came through my lattice the soft sighs which had forsaken me; and they modelled themselves into familiar and sweet voice, saying:

"Sleep in peace!—for the Spirit of Love reigneth and ruleth, and, in taking to thy passionate heart her who is Ermengarde, thou art absolved, for reasons which shall be made known to

34 thee in Heaven, of thy vows unto Eleonora."

The loveliness of Eleanora was that of the Seraphim; but she was a maiden artless and innocent as the brief life she had led among the flowers. *Artist unknown*

THREE SUNDAYS IN A WEEK

First published as "A Succession of Sundays," in the Philadelphia *Saturday Evening Post*, November 27, 1841, and heavily revised for the *Broadway Journal*, May 10, 1845.

If Poe could be said ever to have written a *simple* love story, this would be it. An unassuming piece, without much beyond the movement toward the punch line, the story has never been highly regarded by critics, or read much by the public, who prefer the melodramatic side of Poe's talent.

The idea for the story probably came from "Three Thursdays in One Week," in the Philadelphia *Public Ledger*, October 29, 1841, or an untitled article that appeared in the same paper a month later (November 17), both based on the time phenomenon that motivates Poe's tale.

"Three Sundays in a Week" has the honor of being the first Poe tale translated into Spanish, in *El Museo Universal* (Madrid), February 15, 1857, although Poe's authorship is not mentioned.

The tale in turn may have sparked an idea in Jules Verne's *Around the World in Eighty Days* (1873), for that novel's surprise *dénouement* is based on the same geographical convention: that a day is lost when one goes west around the world, and a day gained when one goes east.

"You hard-hearted, dunder-headed, obstinate, rusty, crusty, musty, fusty, old savage!" said I, in fancy, one afternoon, to my grand-uncle Rumgudgeon—shaking my fist at him in imagination. **1**

Only in imagination. The fact is, some trivial discrepancy *did* exist, just then, between what I said and what I had not the courage to say—between what I did and what I had half a mind to do.

The old porpoise, as I opened the drawing-room door, was sitting with his feet upon the mantel-piece, and a bumper of port in his paw, making strenuous efforts to accomplish the ditty.

> *Remplis ton verre vide!*
> *Vide ton verre plein!* **2**

"My *dear* uncle," said I, closing the door gently, and approaching him with the blandest of smiles, "you are always so *very* kind and considerate, and have evinced your benevolence in so many—so *very* many ways—that I feel I have only to suggest this little point to you once more to make sure of your full acquiescence."

"Hem!" said he, "good boy! go on!"

"I am sure, my dearest uncle [you confounded old rascal!], that you have no design really, seriously, to oppose my union with Kate. This is merely a joke of yours, I know—ha! ha! ha!—how *very* pleasant you are at times." **3**

"Ha! ha! ha!" said he, "curse you! yes!"

"To be sure—of course! I *knew* you were jesting. Now,

1 Tennyson's "To Christopher North" contains a similar series of epithets, as does, in a slightly different vein, Poe's own "Loss of Breath."

A gudgeon is a small European freshwater fish used for bait; the word has come to mean a person that will bite at any bait, or swallow anything. By tacking "rum" on, Poe makes clear just what the uncle swallows most often.

2 "Refill your empty glass/Empty your full glass" is a popular old French drinking song.

3 Note the similarity between the straight-faced fibbing here and the more serious kind in both "The Cask of Amontillado" and "The Tell-Tale Heart."

"You hard-hearted, dunder-headed, obstinate, rusty, crusty, musty, fusty, old savage!" *Artist unknown*

4 One of the annoyances of literature is that no one has yet come up with a way to indicate laughter that doesn't seem— well, so literary. At least this one is better than "ugh-ugh-ugh-ugh," which Poe uses for both laughing *and* coughing.

5 One hundred thousand pounds.

6 A large glass

7 Having a full purse, rich—but also meaning to have puckers, puckered (drawn together like a purse's mouth)

8 Having a heavy or long purse means to be rich.

uncle, all that Kate and myself wish at present, is that you would oblige us with your advice as—as regards the *time—you* know, uncle—in short, when will it be most convenient for yourself, that the wedding shall—shall—come off, you know?"

"Come off, you scoundrel!—what do you mean by that?—Better wait till it goes on."

"Ha! ha! ha!—he! he! he!—hi! hi! hi!—ho! ho! ho!—hu! hu!

4 hu!—oh, that's good!—oh, that's capital—*such* a wit! But all we want just *now*, you know, uncle, is that you would indicate the time precisely."

"Ah!—precisely?"

"Yes, uncle—that is, if it would be quite agreeable to yourself."

"Wouldn't it answer, Bobby, if I were to leave it at random—some time within a year or so, for example?—*must* I say precisely?"

"*If* you please, uncle—precisely."

"Well, then, Bobby, my boy—you're a fine fellow aren't you?—since you *will* have the exact time I'll—why I'll oblige you for once."

"Dear uncle!"

"Hush, sir!" [drowning my voice]—"I'll oblige you for once.

5 You shall have my consent—and the *plum*, we mustn't forget the plum—let me see! when shall it be? To-day's Sunday—isn't it? Well, then, you shall be married precisely—*precisely*, now mind!—*when three Sundays come together in a week!* Do you hear me, sir! *What* are you gaping at? I say, you shall have Kate and her plum when three Sundays come together in a week—but not *till* then—you young scapegrace—not *till* then, if I die for it. You know me—*I'm a man of my word*—

6 now be off!" Here he swallowed his bumper of port, while I rushed from the room in despair.

A very "fine old English gentleman," was my grand-uncle Rumgudgeon, but unlike him of the song, he had his weak

7 points. He was a little, pursy, pompous, passionate, semicir-

8 cular somebody, with a red nose, a thick skull, a long purse, and a strong sense of is own consequence. With the best heart in the world, he contrived, through a predominant whim of *contradiction*, to earn for himself, among those who only knew him superficially, the character of a curmudgeon. Like many excellent people, he seemed possessed with a spirit of *tantalization*, which might easily, at a casual glance, have been mistaken for malevolence. To every request, a positive "No!" was his immediate answer; but in the end—in the long, long end—there were exceedingly few requests which he refused. Against all attacks upon his purse he made the most sturdy defence; but the amount extorted from him, at last, was generally in direct ratio with the length of the siege and the stubbornness of the resistance. In charity no one gave more liberally or with a worse grace.

For the fine arts, and especially for the belles-lettres, he entertained a profound contempt. With this he had been inspired by Casimir Périer, whose pert little query "À quoi

un poète est-il bon?" he was in the habit of quoting, with a **9**
very droll pronunciation, as the *ne plus ultra* of logical wit.
Thus my own inkling for the Muses had excited his entire **10**
displeasure. He assured me one day, when I asked him for a
new copy of Horace, that the translation of "*Poeta nascitur
non fit*" was "a nasty poet for nothing fit"—a remark which I
took in high dudgeon. His repugnance to "the humanities" **11**
had, also, much increased of late, by an accidental bias in
favor of what he supposed to be natural science. Somebody
had accosted him in the street, mistaking him for no less a
personage than Doctor Dubble L. Dee, the lecturer on quack
physics. This set him off at a tangent; and just at the epoch **12**
of this story—for story it is getting to be after all—my grand-
uncle Rumgudgeon was accessible and pacific only upon points
which happened to chime in with the caprioles of the hobby **13**
he was riding. For the rest, he laughed with his arms and
legs, and his politics were stubborn and easily understood.
He thought, with Horsley, that "the people have nothing to
do with the laws but to obey them." **14**

I had lived with the old gentleman all my life. My parents,
in dying, had bequeathed me to him as a rich legacy. I believe
the old villain loved me as his own child—nearly if not quite
as well as he loved Kate—but it was a dog's existence that he
led me, after all. From my first year until my fifth, he obliged
me with very regular floggings. From five to fifteen, he
threatened me, hourly, with the House of Correction. From
fifteen to twenty, not a day passed in which he did not promise
to cut me off with a shilling. I was a sad dog, it is true—but
then it was a part of my nature—a point of my faith. In Kate,
however, I had a firm friend, and I knew it. She was a good
girl, and told me very sweetly that I might have her (plum
and all) whenever I could badger my grand-uncle Rumgudgeon
into the necessary consent. Poor girl!—she was barely fifteen,
and without this consent, her little amount in the funds was
not come-at-able until five immeasurable summers had
"dragged their slow length along." What, then, to do? At **15**
fifteen, or even at twenty-one (for I had now passed my fifth
olympiad) five years in prospect are very much the same as **16**
five hundred. In vain we besieged the old gentleman with
importunities. Here was a *pièce de résistance* (as Messieurs
Ude and Carene would say) which suited his perverse fancy **17**
to a T. It would have stirred the indignation of Job himself, **18**
to see how much like an old mouser he behaved to us two
poor wretched little mice. In his heart he wished for nothing
more ardently than our union. He had made up his mind to
this all along. In fact, he would have given ten thousand
pounds from his own pocket (Kate's plum was *her own*) if he
could have invented anything like an excuse for complying
with our very natural wishes. But then we had been so
imprudent as to broach the subject *ourselves*. Not to oppose
it under such circumstances,. I sincerely believe, was not in
his power.

I have said already that he had his weak points; but, in
speaking of these, I must not be understood as referring to his

9 "What's a poet good for?" is from Casimir Pierre
Périer (1777–1832), French statesman. *Ne plus ultra*
means "nothing greater."

10 Inclination

11 "A poet is born, not made" comes not from Horace
but from Florus (fl. A.D. 125), *De Qualitate Vitae*
(fragment 8): "Each year new consuls and proconsuls are
made; but not every year is a king or a poet born."
Florus' statement soon took on a life of its own as the
proverb that Poe quotes here.

12 Dionysius Lardner (1793–1859) was a former professor of natural philosophy and astronomy at the University
of London who came to the United States in 1840 to
give a series of lectures on scientific subjects to much
popular interest and acclaim. Poe apparently thought
the Englishman was a quack.

13 The capering of a horse. Here the uncle rides a
hobbyhorse, perhaps an allusion to My Uncle Toby, of
Laurence Sterne's delightful *Tristram Shandy* (1767).

14 Samuel Horsley (1733–1806), Bishop of Rochester,
is quoted as saying this during a debate in the House of
Lords in 1795. Poe mentions it again in "Fifty Suggestions," XLV.

15 "A needless Alexandrine ends the song/That, like a
wounded snake, drags its slow length along" (Pope,
Essay on Criticism, II, 157).

16 A period of four years, based on the cycle of the
ancient Olympic Games.

17 Louis-Eustache Ude and Marie-Antoine Carême
were the authors of cookbooks of the period. Says the
Southern Literary Messenger of December 1835: "[An
article in a London periodical reviewing Ude's book] is
written in the most exquisite spirit of banter and is
irresistibly amusing"; and later, "*Pièces de résistance*,
says Lady Morgan on Carême's authority, came in with
the National Convention."

18 "To a T" is of uncertain origin but may come from
"to a tittle," meaning the same thing.

19 "Assuredly, it was not his weakness." Poe uses an early form of the French *faible*, from which we get our word "foible."

20 "And all that sort of thing" is the Latin phrase here. "Rigmarole" is apparently a variation of "ragman roll," or "rig-my-roll," meaning nonsense.

"Ragman" was a game of chance played with a rolled-up piece of cloth with strings attached to various items contained inside it, one of which the player selected or drew at random.

21 Prefatory remarks

22 Daughters of Night, or of Zeus and Themis, the Fates are the spirits of birth, allotting each person his portion of life. They are usually represented as three old women—Clotho, Lachesis, and Atropos—carrying staffs or spinning at a wheel, breaking the thread when a life is measured.

23 October 10, 1841, was a Sunday.

24 "Jade" is a term of insult aimed toward a woman, often used in place of "hussy."

---

obstinacy: which was one of his strong points—"*assurément*

19 *ce n'était pas sa foible*." When I mention his weakness I have allusion to a *bizarre* old-womanish superstition which beset him. He was great in dreams, portents, *et id genus omne* of

20 rigmarole. He was excessively punctilious, too, upon small points of honor, and, after his own fashion, was a man of his word, beyond doubt. This was, in fact, one of his hobbies. The *spirit* of his vows he made no scruple of setting at naught, but the *letter* was a bond inviolable. Now it was this latter peculiarity in his disposition, of which Kate's ingenuity enabled us one fine day, not long after our interview in the dining-room, to take a very unexpected advantage, and, having thus, in the fashion of all modern bards and orators, exhausted in

21 *prolegomena*, all the time at my command, and nearby all the room at my disposal. I will sum up in a few words what constitutes the whole pith of the story.

22   It happened then—so the Fates ordered it—that among the naval acquaintances of my betrothed, were two gentlemen who had just set foot upon the shores of England, after a year's absence, each, in foreign travel. In company with these gentlemen, my cousin and I, preconcertedly, paid uncle Rumgudgeon a visit on the afternoon of Sunday, October the

23 tenth, just three weeks after the memorable decision which had so cruelly defeated our hopes. For about half an hour the conversation ran upon ordinary topics; but at last, we contrived, quite naturally to give it the following turn:

Capt. Pratt. "Well, I have been absent just one year. Just one year today, as I live—let me see! yes!—this is October the tenth. You remember, Mr. Rumgudgeon, I called, this day year, to bid you good-bye. And by the way, it *does* seem something like a coincidence, does it not—that our friend, Captain Smitherton, here, has been absent exactly a year also—a year to-day?"

Smitherton. "Yes! just one year to a fraction. You will remember, Mr. Rumgudgeon, that I called with Captain Pratt on this very day, last year, to pay my parting respects."

Uncle. "Yes, yes, yes—I remember it very well—very queer indeed! Both of you gone just one year. A very strange coincidence, indeed! Just what Doctor Dubble L. Dee would denominate an extraordinary concurrence of events. Doctor Dub—"

Kate. [*Interrupting.*] "To be sure, papa, it *is* something strange; but then Captain Pratt and Captain Smitherton didn't go altogether the same route, and that makes a difference, you know."

Uncle. "I don't know any such thing, you huzzy! How should I? I think it only makes the matter more remarkable. Doctor Dubble L. Dee—"

Kate. "Why, papa, Captain Pratt went round Cape Horn, and Captain Smitherton doubled the Cape of Good Hope."

Uncle. "Precisely!—the one went east and the other went

24 west, you jade, and they both have gone quite round the world. By the by, Doctor Dubble L. Dee—"

Myself, [*Hurriedly.*] "Captain Pratt, you must come and

spend the evening with us to-morrow—you and Smitherton—you can tell us all about your voyage, and we'll have a game of whist, and—"

Pratt. "Whist, my dear fellow—you forget. To-morrow will be Sunday. Some other evening—"

Kate. "Oh, no, fie!—Robert's not *quite* so bad as that. *To-day's* Sunday."

Uncle. "To be sure—to be sure!"

Pratt. "I beg both your pardons—but I can't be so much mistaken. I know to-morrow's Sunday, because—"

Smitherton. (*Much surprised.*) "What *are* you all thinking about? Wasn't *yesterday* Sunday, I should like to know?"

All. "Yesterday, indeed! you *are* out!"

Uncle. "To-day's Sunday, I say—don't *I* know?"

Pratt. "Oh no!—to-morrow's Sunday."

Smitherton. "You are *all* mad—every one of you. I am as positive that yesterday was Sunday as I am that I sit upon this chair."

Kate, (*Jumping up eagerly.*) "I see it—I see it all. Papa, this is a judgment upon you, about—about you know what. Let me alone, and I'll explain it all in a minute. It's a very simple thing, indeed. Captain Smitherton says that yesterday was Sunday: so it was; he is right. Cousin Bobby, and uncle and I, say that to-day is Sunday: so it is; we are right. Captain Pratt maintains that to-morrow will be Sunday: so it will; he is right, too. The fact is, we are all right, and thus *three Sundays have come together in a week.*"

Smitherton, (*After a pause.*) "By the by, Pratt, Kate has us completely. What fools we two are! Mr. Rumgudgeon, the matter stands thus: the earth, you know, is twenty-four thousand miles in circumference. Now this globe of the earth

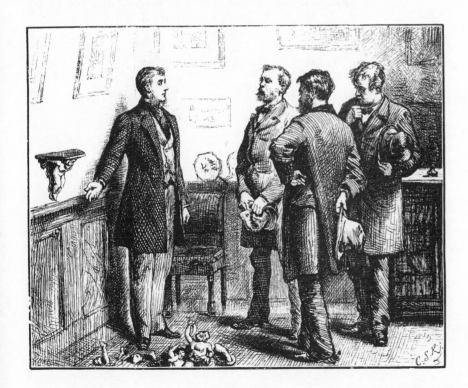

Captain Pratt . . . when he had sailed a thousand miles west of this position, was an hour, and when he had sailed twenty-four thousand miles west, was twenty-four hours, or one day, *behind* the time at London.
Artist unknown

turns upon its own axis—revolves—spins round—these twenty-four thousands miles of extent, going from west to east, in precisely twenty-four hours. Do you understand, Mr. Rumgudgeon?"

Uncle. "To be sure—to be sure—Doctor Dub—."

Smitherton, (*Drowning his voice.*) "Well, sir; that is at the rate of one thousand miles per hour. Now, suppose that I sail from this position a thousand miles east. Of course I anticipate the rising of the sun here at London by just one hour. I see the sun rise one hour before you do. Proceeding, in the same direction, yet another thousand miles, I anticipate the rising by two hours—another thousand, and I anticipate it by three hours, and so on, until I go entirely round the globe, and back to this spot, when, having gone twenty-four thousand miles east, I anticipate the rising of the London sun by no less than twenty-four hours; that is to say, I am a day *in advance* of your time. Understand, eh?"

Uncle. "But Dubble L. Dee—"

Smitherton, (*Speaking very loud.*) "Captain Pratt, on the contrary, when he had sailed a thousand miles west of this position, was an hour, and when he had sailed twenty-four thousand miles west, was twenty-four hours, or one day, *behind* the time at London. Thus, with me, yesterday was Sunday—thus, with you, to-day is Sunday—and thus, with Pratt, to-morrow will be Sunday. And what is more, Mr. Rumgudgeon, it is postitvely clear that we are *all right;* for there can be no philosophical reason assigned why the idea of one of us should have preference over that of the other."

Uncle. "My eyes!—well, Kate—well, Bobby!—this *is* a judgment upon me, as you say. But I am a man of my word—*mark that!* you shall have her, boy (plum and all), when you please. Done up, by Jove! Three Sundays all in a row! I'll go, and take Dubble L. Dee's opinion upon *that.*"

25 The international date line is a hypothetical line that follows the meridian of 180°, although it diverges to include the Aleutian Islands with Alaska and some of the South Sea Islands with Australia. This arbitrary line was adopted by mariners as the most convenient place for changing dates. Sailing west, ships lost a day, and sailing east, gained a day, because twenty-four hours (one hour for every 15°) is gained or lost when circling the globe.

A TALE OF THE RAGGED MOUNTAINS

Originally published in *Godey's Magazine and Lady's Book*, April 1844, "A Tale of the Ragged Mountains" revolves around one of Poe's favorite topics, metempsychosis, or reincarnation—here with an added dash of Mesmerism, which was causing great interest at the time the story was written: 1843. The result is somewhat ambiguous, if rather nicely so, since the point of the story could be either that one can recall a previous existence through hypnosis or that a historical incident can somehow be transferred to a patient's memory through a doctor's telepathic powers.

Sources include T. B. Macaulay's essay on G. R. Gleig's *Memoirs of the Life of Warren Hastings,* as well as the memoirs themselves, which contain the details on the riots in Benares. Poe's "frantic sally from the kiosk" comes from Gleig, although the sally in reality suffered neither annihilation nor the loss of its commander, Lieutenant David Birrell.

There are also parallels between Poe's tale and such diverse works as Charles Brockden Brown's *Edgar Huntly,* Washington Irving's "Rip Van Winkle," and Sir William Temple's essay "Of Ancient and Modern Learning." This latter work links Hindu belief in the transmigration of souls with the philosophy of Plato: "They held the transmigration of souls, and some used discourses of infernal mansion, in many things like those of Plato. Their moral philosophy consisted chiefly in preventing all diseases or distempers of the body, from which they esteemed the perturbation of mind, in great measure, to arise; then, in composing the mind, and exempting it from all anxious causes, esteeming the troublesome and solicitous thoughts, about past and future, to be like so many dreams, and no more to be regarded." (*Works of Sir William Temple,* 1814; III, 452–53)

During the fall of the year 1827, while residing near Charlottesville, Virginia, I casually made the acquaintance of Mr. **1** Augustus Bedloe. This young gentleman was remarkable in every respect, and excited in me a profound interest and curiosity. I found it impossible to comprehend him either in his moral or his physical relations. Of his family I could obtain no satisfactory account. Whence he came, I never ascertained. Even about his age—although I call him a young gentleman— there was something which perplexed me in no little degree. **2** He certainly *seemed* young—and he made a point of speaking about his youth—yet there were moments when I should have had little trouble in imagining him a hundred years of age. But in no regard was he more peculiar than in his personal appearance. He was singularly tall and thin. He stooped much. His limbs were exceedingly long and emaciated. His forehead was broad and low. His complexion was absolutely **3** bloodless. His mouth was large and flexible, and his teeth were more wildly uneven, although sound, than I had ever before seen teeth in a human head. The expression of his smile, however, was by no means unpleasing, as might be supposed; but it had no variation whatever. It was one of

1 Poe was in Charlottesville in 1826, and while there did take walks into the nearby Ragged Mountains.

Poe may have taken the name Bedlo(e) from the family who gave its name to the island in New York Harbor where the Statue of Liberty now stands, or from the Macaulay essay on Warren Hastings—for there we find mentioned a William Bedloe, an Englishman who informed on Papists in the seventeenth century.

2 The narrator knows as much about Bedloe as the narrators of "Ligeia" and "Morella" know about those women.

3 The low, sloping forehead may indicate a phrenological lack of memory (Eventuality), analysis (Comparison), and observation (Individuality). The pale complexion is an appropriately deathlike trait, as is his emaciated appearance.

4 Cats have the ability to see in the dark, and Bedloe's unusual eyesight seems to give him the ability to see things too dim for most human eyes to see.

5 "Facial neuralgia was one of the ailments commonly relieved not only by Mesmerism, but by real galvanic current. A patient . . . could apply the electrodes from a simple galvanic pile or Cruickshank's 'crown of cups' to his temples. The 'luminous rays' from Bedloe's eyes are a further hint to the 'electromagnetic' nature of his animating force." (Doris V. Falk, *PMLA*, Vol. 84, 1969; p. 541)

6 Templeton may be a fictionalization of Nathaniel Middleton, who was linked with the alleged wrongdoings of Hastings, and who in the sensational trial of the latter was called "the second-half of Mr. Hastings" (Muktar Ali Isani, *Poe Studies*, December 1972; p. 42).

On the other hand, Poe could be engaging in some phrenological wordplay, since the temple is supposedly the site of memory, among other attributes.

7 Saratoga Springs, in New York State north of Albany, was a popular resort area of the nineteenth century because of its mineral baths and horce racing (after 1850). In Poe's time it was primarily a curative spa, and he visited it in 1843. Tradition has it that he composed *The Raven* there.

8 Franz Anton Mesmer (1733–1815), an Austrian physician, studied in Vienna, where his interest in "animal magnetism" developed into a system of treatment through hypnotism, which was later called mesmerism. After his refusal to reveal the secret of his magnetic cures, his large and fashionable Parisian practice was curtailed by government investigation, and he retired.

9 "Rapport" was a term in general use in the early development of hypnosis and today is still used to describe a comfortable atmosphere between patient and hypnotist. In mesmerism, it was held to be the result of magnetic current moving from hypnotist to patient, inducing the latter into a trance. Today we know that rapport is the result of a patient's trust in his therapist, making it easier for him to be hypnotized.

"When mesmerist and patient were *en rapport*," says Doris V. Falk, "they both became conductors of the magnetic fluid or, as some practitioners held, of a newly discovered 'imponderable' comparable to—or perhaps identical with—electricity, light or electromagnetism. In fact, before he accomplished some famous 'cures' using actual magnets, Mesmer himself had considered the force to be electrical. . . ." (P. 536)

profound melancholy—of a phaseless and unceasing gloom.
4 His eyes were abnormally large, and round like those of a cat. The pupils, too, upon any accession or diminution of light, underwent contraction or dilation, just such as is observed in the feline tribe. In moments of excitement the orbs grew bright to a degree almost inconceivable; seeming to emit luminous rays, not of a reflected but of an intrinsic lustre, as does a candle or the sun; yet their ordinary condition was so totally vapid, filmy, and dull, as to convey the idea of the eyes of a long-interred corpse.

These peculiarities of person appeared to cause him much annoyance, and he was continually alluding to them in a sort of half explanatory, half apologetic strain, which, when I first heard it, impressed me very painfully. I soon, however, grew accustomed to it, and my uneasiness wore off. It seemed to be his design rather to insinuate than directly to assert that, physically, he had not always been what he was—that a long series of neuralgic attacks had reduced him from a condition
5 of more than usual personal beauty, to that which I saw. For many years past he had been attended by a physician, named
6 Templeton—an old gentleman, perhaps seventy years of age—
7 whom he had first encountered at Saratoga, and from whose attention, while there, he either received, or fancied that he received, great benefit. The result was that Bedloe, who was wealthy, had made an arrangement with Dr. Templeton, by which the latter, in consideration of a liberal annual allowance, had consented to devote his time and medical experience exclusively to the care of the invalid.

Doctor Templeton had been a traveller in his younger days, and at Paris had become a convert, in great measure, to the
8 doctrine of Mesmer. It was altogether by means of magnetic remedies that he had succeeded in alleviating the acute pains of his patient; and this success had very naturally inspired the latter with a certain degree of confidence in the opinions from which the remedies had been educed. The Doctor, however, like all enthusiasts, had struggled hard to make a thorough convert of his pupil, and finally so far gained his point as to induce the sufferer to submit to numerous experiments. By a frequent repetition of these, a result had arisen, which of late days has become so common as to attract little or no attention, but which, at the period of which I write, had very rarely been known in America. I mean to say, that between Doctor Templeton and Bedloe there had grown up, little by
9 little, a very distinct and strongly marked *rapport*, or magnetic relation. I am not prepared to assert, however, that this *rappor* extended beyond the limits of the simple sleep-producing power; but this power itself had attained great intensity. At the first attempt to induce the magnetic somnolency, the mesmerist entirely failed. In the fifth or sixth he succeeded very partially, and after long-continued effort. Only at the twelfth was the triumph complete. After this the will of the patient succumbed rapidly to that of the physician, so that, when I first became acquainted with the two, sleep was brought about almost instantaneously by the mere volition of

the operator, even when the invalid was unaware of his presence. It is only now, in the year 1845, when similar miracles are witnessed daily by thousands, that I dare venture to record this apparent impossibility as a matter of serious fact.

The temperament of Bedloe was, in the highest degree **10** sensitive, excitable, enthusiastic. His imagination was singularly vigorous and creative; and no doubt it derived additional force from the habitual use of morphine, which he swallowed **11** in great quantity, and without which he would have found it impossible to exist. It was his practice to take a very large dose of it immediately after breakfast each morning—or, rather, immediately after a cup of strong coffee, for he ate nothing in the forenoon—and then set forth alone, or attended only by a dog, upon a long ramble among the chain of wild and dreary hills that lie westward and southward of Charlottesville, and are there dignified by the title of the Ragged Mountains. **12**

Upon a dim, warm, misty day, toward the close of November, and during the strange *interregnum* of the seasons which in America is termed the Indian Summer, Mr. Bedloe departed **13** as usual for the hills. The day passed, and still he did not return.

About eight o'clock at night, having become seriously alarmed at his protracted absence, we were about setting out in search of him, when he unexpectedly made his appearance, in health no worse than usual, and in rather more than ordinary spirits. The account which he gave of his expedition, and of the events which had detained him, was a singular one indeed.

"You will remember," said he, "that it was about nine in the morning when I left Charlottesville. I bent my steps immediately to the mountains, and, about ten, entered a gorge which was entirely new to me. I followed the windings of this pass with much interest. The scenery which presented itself on all sides, although scarcely entitled to be called grand, had about it an indescribable and to me a delicious aspect of dreary desolation. The solitude seemed absolutely virgin. I **14** could not help believing that the green sods and the gray rocks upon which I trod had been trodden never before by the foot of a human being. So entirely secluded, and in fact inaccessible, except through a series of accidents, is the entrance of the ravine, that it is by no means impossible that I was indeed the first adventurer—the very first and sole adventurer who had ever penetrated its recesses.

"The thick and peculiar mist, or smoke, which distinguishes the Indian Summer, and which now hung heavily over all objects, served, no doubt, to deepen the vague impressions which these objects created. So dense was this pleasant fog **15** that I could at no time see more than a dozen yards of the path before me. This path was excessively sinuous, and as the sun could not be seen, I soon lost all idea of the direction in which I journeyed. In the meantime the morphine had its customary effect—that of enduing all the external world with

10 "Temperature" in some editions

11 The use of morphine, like the use of drugs in other tales, gives us a logical explanation for the mysterious events to come—if we want one.

Morphine in small doses induces sleep, but in larger quantities causes coma or convulsions and even death. Even small amounts must be used with caution. Bedloe is hardly cautious.

12 Bedloe's walks through the hills with his dog echo those of the narrator of "Landor's Cottage," as well as those of Rip Van Winkle.

The Ragged Mountains, outside Charlottesville, are part of the Blue Ridge chain. It is a local name only, and is not found much in books and articles on the area, although we do find that in 1774 one Micajah Chiles, Jr., patented land "on the side of one of the Ragged Mountains, and on the head of the East branches of Mechums River" (*Virginia Magazine of History and Biography*, XIX [1911]; p. 325).

13 Indian summer is that part of the fall when days are warm, giving an illusion of warmth and life just before the onslaught of winter. The term comes from the once common attitude that Indians were cunning, sneaky, and deceitful (as in "Indian giver"). This time of year is also the setting of "Landor's Cottage."

14 The romantics were a varied lot, but among many of them was a preoccupation with ruins, and with the more untamed and disorderly aspects of nature, as in the opening of "The Fall of the House of Usher: ". . . that half-pleasurable, because poetic, sentiment, with which the mind usually receives even the sternest natural images of the desolate or terrible."

15 There are two possibilities here. For the skeptic, the hazy air coupled with the morphine dose would cast doubt on the narrator's experience. For the romantic, who believed at one point that drugs could loose the soul to wander at will, the haze would signal the move from one sphere to another.

16 Three-leaved plants, such as clover, bird's-foot trefoil, and the shrubby trefoil (hop tree)

17 "The aboriginal inhabitants had no motives to lead them into caves like this and ponder on the verge of such a precipice. Their successors were still less likely to have wandered hither." (*Edgar Huntly*, Chapter 10)

Charles Brockden Brown's *Edgar Huntly* and *Wieland* are, as previously mentioned, must reading for Poe lovers.

18 "It was a mystery all insoluble; nor could I grapple with the shadowy fancies that crowded upon me as I pondered" ("The Fall of the House of Usher").

19 "For the Lord . . . shall descend from heaven with a shout, with the voice of the archangel, and with the trump . . ." (I Thessalonians 4:16).

20 ". . . the lonely courier shakes his bunch of iron rings to scare away the hyaenas" (Macaulay's essay on Warren Hastings, *Edinburgh Review*, October 1841).

21 The sentence is meant to bring the reader up short, since there are no hyenas in the New World.

"There came a wild . . . jingling sound, as if of a bunch of large keys, and upon the instant a dusky-visaged and half-naked man rushed passed me with a shriek." *Illustration by F. S. Coburn, 1903*

an intensity of interest. In the quivering of a leaf—in the hue **16** of a blade of grass—in the shape of a trefoil—in the humming of a bee—in the gleaming of a dew-drop—in the breathing of the wind—in the faint odors that came from the forest—there came a whole universe of suggestion—a gay and motley train of rhapsodical and immethodical thought.

"Busied in this, I walked on for several hours, during which the mist deepened around me to so great an extent that at length I was reduced to an absolute groping of the way. And now an indescribable uneasiness possessed me—a species of nervous hesitation and tremor. I feared to tread, lest I should be precipitated into some abyss. I remembered, too, strange stories told about these Ragged Hills, and of the uncouth and **17** fierce races of men who tenanted their groves and caverns. A thousand vague fancies oppressed and disconcerted me— **18** fancies the more distressing because vague. Very suddenly my attention was arrested by the loud beating of a drum.

"My amazement was, of course, extreme. A drum in these hills was a thing unknown. I could not have been more **19** surprised at the sound of the trump of the Archangel. But a new and still more astounding source of interest and perplexity **20** arose. There came a wild rattling or jingling sound, as if of a bunch of large keys, and upon the instant a dusky-visaged and half-naked man rushed past me with a shriek. He came so close to my person that I felt his hot breath upon my face. He bore in one hand an instrument composed of an assemblage of steel rings, and shook them vigorously as he ran. Scarcely had he disappeared in the mist, before, panting after him, with open mouth and glaring eyes, there darted a huge beast, **21** I could not be mistaken in its character. It was a hyena.

"The sight of this monster rather relieved than heightened my terrors—for I now made sure that I dreamed, and endeavored to arouse myself to waking consciousness. I stepped boldly and briskly forward. I rubbed my eyes. I called aloud. I pinched my limbs. A small spring of water presented itself to my view, and here, stooping, I bathed my hands and my head and neck. This seemed to dissipate the equivocal sensations which had hitherto annoyed me. I arose, as I thought, a new man, and proceeded steadily and complacently on my unknown way.

"At length, quite overcome by exertion, and by a certain oppressive closeness of the atmosphere, I seated myself beneath a tree. Presently there came a feeble gleam of sunshine, and the shadow of the leaves of the tree fell faintly but definitely upon the grass. At this shadow I gazed wonderingly for many minutes. Its character stupefied me with astonishment. I looked upward. The tree was a palm.

"I now arose hurriedly, and in a state of fearful agitation—for the fancy that I dreamed would serve me no longer. I saw—I felt that I had perfect command of my senses—and these senses now brought to my soul a world of novel and singular sensation. The heat became all at once intolerable. A strange odor loaded the breeze. A low, continuous murmur, like that arising from a full, but gently flowing river, came to

On the margin of this river stood an Eastern-looking city, such as we read of in the Arabian Tales, but of a character even more singular than any there described.
Illustration by R. P. Leitch

my ears, intermingled with the peculiar hum of multitudinous human voices. **22**

"While I listened in an extremity of astonishment which I need not attempt to describe, a strong and brief gust of wind bore off the incumbent fog as if by the wand of an enchanter.

"I found myself at the foot of a high mountain, and looking down into a vast plain, through which wound a majestic river. On the margin of this river stood an Eastern-looking city, such as we read of in the Arabian Tales, but of a character even more singular than any there described. From my position, which was far above the level of the town, I could perceive its every nook and corner, as if delineated on a map. The streets seemed innumerable, and crossed each other irregularly in all directions, but were rather long winding alleys than streets, and absolutely swarmed with inhabitants. The houses were wildly picturesque. On every hand was a wilderness of balconies, of verandahs, of minarets, of shrines, and fantastically carved oriels. Bazaars abounded; and in these **23** were displayed rich wares in infinite variety and profusion— silks, muslins, the most dazzling cutlery, the most magnificent jewels and gems. Besides these things, were seen, on all sides, banners and palanquins, litters with stately dames close-veiled, elephants gorgeously caparisoned, idols grotesquely hewn, drums, banners and gongs, spears, silver and gilded maces, And amid the crowd, and the clamor, and the general intricacy and confusion—amid the million of black and yellow men, turbaned and robed, and of flowing beard, there roamed a countless multitude of holy filleted bulls, while vast legions of the filthy but sacred ape clambered, chattering and shrieking, about the cornices of the mosques, or clung to the minarets and oriels. From the swarming streets to the banks **24**

22 ". . . his voice as the sound of many waters" (Revelation 1:15). Poe uses variations on this passage many times in his tales.

23 Projecting, or bay, windows in an upper story. Actually this is a Western term for this architectural feature, but Macaulay also uses it in his essay.

24 "It was commonly believed that half a million of human beings was crowded into the labyrinth of lofty alleys, rich with shrines, and minarets, and balconies, and carved oriels, to which the sacred apes clung by hundreds" (Macaulay's essay).

The hanuman monkey is sacred in this part of India, while the Muslim appearance of the city reflects the taste of the Mogul emperor Aurungzebe, son of Shah Jehan, who built the Taj Mahal. Ruler from 1678 to 1707, the emperor built the great mosque of Benares as a permanent barb in the side of the Hindus in their most holy city. The Mogul, or Moslem, empire of India lasted from 1526 to 1857, but was weakened by the end of the eighteenth century, and was merely a puppet under the British.

Mogul architecture evolved from the Persian, with its fantastic use of towers, archways, and elegant façades surmounted by cupolas, kiosks, and pinnacles.

of the river, there descended innumerable flights of steps leading to bathing places, while the river itself seemed to force a passage with difficulty through the vast fleets of deeply burdened ships that far and wide encountered its surface. Beyond the limits of the city arose, in frequent majestic groups, the palm and the cocoa, with other gigantic and weird trees of vast age; and here and there might be seen a field of rice, the thatched hut of a peasant, a tank, a stray temple, a gypsy camp, or a solitary graceful maiden taking her way, with a pitcher upon her head, to the banks of the magnificent river.

"You will say now, of couse, that I dreamed; but not so. What I saw—what I heard—what I felt—what I thought—had about it nothing of the unmistakable idiosyncrasy of the dream. All was rigorously self-consistent. At first, doubting that I was really awake, I entered into a series of tests, which soon convinced me that I really was. Now, when one dreams, and, in the dream, suspects that he dreams, the suspicion *never fails to confirm itself*, and the sleeper is almost immediately aroused. Thus Novalis errs not in saying that 'we are

25 near waking when we dream that we dream.' Had the vision occurred to me as I describe it, without my suspecting it as a dream, then a dream it might absolutely have been, but, occurring as it did, and suspected and tested as it was, I am forced to class it among other phenomena."

"In this I am not sure that you are wrong," observed Dr. Templeton, "but proceed. You arose and descended into the city."

"I arose," continued Bedloe, regarding the Doctor with an air of profound astonishment, "I arose, as you say, and descended into the city. On my way I fell in with an immense populace, crowding through every avenue, all in the same direction, and exhibiting in every action the wildest excitement. Very suddenly, and by some inconceivable impulse, I became intensely imbued with personal interest in what was going on. I seemed to feel that I had an important part to play, without exactly understanding what it was. Against the crowd which environed me, however, I experienced a deep sentiment of animosity. I shrank from amid them, and, swiftly, by a circuitous path, reached and entered the city. Here all was the wildest tumult and contention. A small party of men, clad in garments half Indian, half European, and officered by gentlemen in a uniform partly British, were engaged, at great odds, with the swarming rabble of the alleys. I joined the weaker party, arming myself with the weapons of a fallen officer, and fighting I knew not whom with the nervous ferocity of despair. We were soon overpowered by numbers, and driven to seek refuge in a species of kiosk. Here we barricaded ourselves, and, for the present, were secure. From a loop-

26 hole near the summit of the kiosk, I perceived a vast crowd, in furious agitation, surrounding and assaulting a gay palace that overhung the river. Presently, from an upper window of this palace, there descended an effeminate-looking person, by means of a string made of the turbans of his attendants. A boat

25 The quote comes from a book Poe reviewed in *Graham's*, December 1841, entitled *Fragments from German Prose Writers* (see "Marie Rogêt," note 1).

26 "Kiosk" comes from the Turkish word meaning pavilion and the Persian word meaning portico, and here means an open pavilion.

Macaulay writes: "The burning sun; the strange vegetation of the palm and the cocoa-tree; the rice-field and the tank; the huge trees, older than the Mogul empire . . . the thatched roof of the peasant's hut, and the rich tracery of the mosque . . . the drums, and banners, and gaudy idols . . . the graceful maiden, with the pitcher on her head, descending the steps to the river-side; the black faces, the long beards, the yellow streaks of sect; the turbans and the flowing robes. . . . All India was present . . . from the halls where suitors laid gold and perfumes at the feet of sovereigns, to the wild moor where the gipsy-camp was pitched—from the bazaars, humming like bee-hives with the crowd of buyers and sellers. . . ."

was at hand, in which he escaped to the opposite bank of the river. **27**

"And now a new object took possession of my soul. I spoke a few hurried but energetic words to my companions, and, having succeeded in gaining over a few of them to my purpose, made a frantic sally from the kiosk. We rushed amid the crowd that surrounded it. They retreated, at first, before us. They rallied, fought madly, and retreated again. In the meantime we were borne far from the kiosk, and became bewildered and entangled among the narrow streets of tall, overhanging houses, into the recesses of which the sun had never been able to shine. The rabble pressed impetuously upon us, harassing us with their spears, and overwhelming us with flights of arrows. These latter were very remarkable, and resembled in some respects the writhing creese of the Malay. **28** They were made to imitate the body of a creeping serpent, and were long and black, with a poisoned barb. One of them struck me upon the right temple. I reeled and fell. An instantaneous and dreadful sickness seized me. I struggled—I gasped—I died."

"You will hardly persist *now*," said I, smiling, "that the whole of your adventure was not a dream. You are not prepared to maintain that you are dead?"

When I said these words, I of course expected some lively sally from Bedloe in reply; but, to my astonishment, he hesitated, trembled, became fearfully pallid, and remained silent. I looked toward Templeton. He sat erect and rigid in his chair—his teeth chattered, and his eyes were starting from their sockets. "Proceed!" he at length said hoarsely to Bedloe.

"For many minutes," continued the latter, "my sole sentiment—my sole feeling—was that of darkness and nonentity, with the consciousness of death. At length there seemed to pass a violent and sudden shock through my soul, as if of electricity. With it came the sense of elasticity and of light. This latter I felt—not saw. In an instant I seemed to rise from the ground. But I had no bodily, no visible, audible, or palpable presence. The crowd had departed. The tumult had ceased. The city was in comparative repose. Beneath me lay my corpse, with the arrow in my temple, the whole head greatly swollen and disfigured. But all these things I felt—not saw. I took interest in nothing. Even the corpse seemed a matter in which I had no concern. Volition I had none, but appeared to be impelled into motion, and flitted buoyantly out of the city, retracing the circuitous path by which I had entered it. When I had attained that point of the ravine in the **29** mountains at which I had encountered the hyena, I again experienced a shock as of a galvanic battery; the sense of weight, of volition, of substance, returned. I became my original self, and bent my steps eagerly homeward—but the past had not lost the vividness of the real—and not now, even for an instant, can I compel my understanding to regard it as a dream."

"Nor was it," said Templeton, with an air of deep solemnity, "yet it would be difficult to say how otherwise it should be

27 "The captive prince, neglected by his jailers during the confusion, discovered an outlet which opened on the precipitous bank of the Ganges, let himself down to the water by a string made of the turbans of his attendants, found a boat, and escaped to the opposite shore" (Macaulay).

By "effeminate," Poe may mean either diminutive or bejeweled.

28 The *kris* or *creese* is a short sword or heavy dagger with a wavy blade, which does a maximum of damage both going in and coming out of a victim. The arrowheads mentioned appear to be Poe's invention, since they do not appear in Macaulay or in other accounts of India. Their serpentine shape, however, underscores their poisonous nature.

29 Poe may have been thinking of a passage from *Sheppard Lee*, which he quoted in a review of Robert M. Bird's novel in the September 1836 issue of the *Southern Literary Messenger:* "He feels exceedingly light and buoyant, with the power of moving without exertion. He sweeps along without putting his feet to the ground. . . . Mr. Lee . . . flies, instinctively to the nearest hut for assistance."

This echoes the experience of many who have lost consciousness or who have "died" (to be brought back to life by doctors), in which they feel themselves detached from their bodies, able to see and hear everything that takes place around them, viewing their own body from the outside.

Flight or floating also traditionally symbolizes thought, imagination, an escape from the worldly sphere and a move toward godlike attributes. The Neoplatonists believed that if the soul could shuck off its encumbering body, it might soar to realize the true existence beyond its earthly one.

30 Mesmerism was resurfacing with a vengeance at this time, although it soon peaked and withered, only to be resurrected again in the 1880s by the psychological movement. In Poe's day, German chemist Karl von Reichenbach was publishing books demonstrating the existence of a natural energy in matter and living things which he called *od* but which was more or less another version of Mesmer's magnetic fluid.

31 Warren Hastings (1732–1818), first governor-general of British India, began as a clerk with the East India Company, rose in the business, and later became governor of Bengal (1771), and three years later, governor-general of India. His aggressive policy of judicial and financial reform, law codification, and the suppression of banditry reestablished British prestige in India, but later he met with resistance to his methods. He resigned in 1784 and returned to England, where he was charged with high crimes and misdemeanors by Edmund Burke and Sir Philip Francis. (He had wounded the latter in a duel in India.) He was impeached in 1787, and the trial dragged on until his acquittal, in 1795. He regained popularity and was made a privy counselor in 1814.

32 Benares, or Banaras, on the Ganges, is one of the holiest cities of India. Buddha preached a sermon nearby in 500 B.C. There are temples to Siva and the mosque of Aurangzeb. Hindus believe that one who dies in Benares achieves salvation, and today a million pilgrims a year visit the city to make a circuit of fifty miles on its outskirts and bathe in the Ganges.

33 Cheyte Sing, or Chait Singh, the Rajah of Benares, led a revolt in 1781 against Hastings' ever-increasing demand for money to support British rule—*not* in 1780. The incident is treated at length in Hastings' own book *A Narrative of the Insurrection which happened in the Zemeedary of Benaris, in the Month of August 1781* (published in 1782).

34 Sepoys were native soldiers in the Bengal army of the East India Company, who a decade later (1857–58) rebelled because of insensitivity to local customs and government, more specifically triggered by the British providing them with cartridges coated with grease said to be the fat of cows (sacred to Hindus) and of pigs (anathema to Muslims).

35 Poisoned arrows are not used in India, but are in Africa, South America, and parts of the Far East.

36 This seems to indicate a telephathic transference of Dr. Templeton's thoughts to Bedloe, rather than a hypnotic regression. Mesmer's magnetic fluid, one recalls, was supposed to travel great distances if the rapport between patient and practitioner was strong enough. In this case, Bedloe's drug-induced stupor has apparently made him highly susceptible to the mesmeric influence. We might also read this as a sign of actual time travel by Bedloe's soul, perhaps given impetus by Templeton's influence. The spirit that is released, however, seems to be neither that of Bedloe nor that of Oldeb, but a force of its own.

37 Neuralgia is acute pain along the outer sensory nerve, very commonly occurring in the face. One doesn't die of neuralgia, however, since it is a symptom, rather than a disease—among other things, of the later effects of syphilis. But in 1845 "neuralgia" was a vague term describing a painful "degenerative nervous disease."

38 A medical term meaning a great flow of blood to the head, which was thought to cause pressure, leading to other problems and even death

"Here is a water-color drawing, which I should have shown you before, but which an unaccountable sentiment of horror has hitherto prevented me from showing."
Illustration by Johann Friedrich Vogel, 1856

termed. Let us suppose only, that the soul of the man of to-**30** day is upon the verge of some stupendous psychal discoveries. Let us content ourselves with this supposition. For the rest I have some explanation to make. Here is a water-colour drawing, which I should have shown you before, but which an unaccountable sentiment of horror has hitherto prevented me from showing."

We looked at the picture which he presented. I saw nothing in it of an extraordinary character; but its effect upon Bedloe was prodigious. He nearly fainted as he gazed. And yet it was but a miniature portrait—a miraculously accurate one, to be sure—of his own very remarkable features. At least this was my thought as I regarded it.

"You will perceive," said Templeton, "the date of this picture—it is here, scarcely visible, in this corner—1780. In this year was the portrait taken. It is the likeness of a dead friend—a Mr. Oldeb—to whom I became much attached at **31** Calcutta, during the administration of Warren Hastings. I was then only twenty years old. When I first saw you, Mr. Bedloe, at Saratoga, it was the miraculous similarity which existed between yourself and the painting which induced me to accost you, to seek your friendship, and to bring about those arrangements which resulted in my becoming your constant companion. In accomplishing this point, I was urged partly, and perhaps principally, by a regretful memory of the deceased, but also, in part by an uneasy, and not altogether horrorless curiosity respecting yourself.

"In your detail of the vision which presented itself to you amid the hills, you have described, with the minutest accuracy,

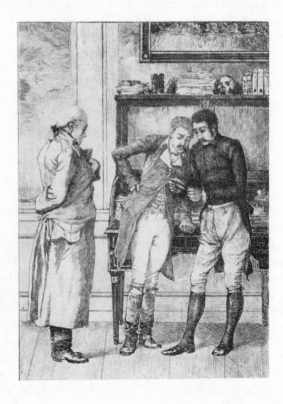

the Indian city of Benares, upon the Holy River. The riots, **32** the combat, the massacre, were the actual events of the insurrection of Cheyte Sing, which took place in 1780, when **33** Hastings was put in imminent peril of his life. The man escaping by the string of turbans was Cheyte Sing himself. The party in the kiosk were sepoys and British officers, headed **34** by Hastings. Of this party I was one, and did all I could to prevent the rash and fatal sally of the officer who fell, in the crowded alleys, by the poisoned arrow of a Bengalee. That **35** officer was my dearest friend. It was Oldeb. You will perceive by these manuscripts," (here the speaker produced a note-book in which several pages appeared to have been freshly written) "that at the very period in which you fancied these things amid the hills, I was engaged in detailing them upon paper here at home." **36**

In about a week after this conversation, the following paragraphs appeared in a Charlottesville paper:

"We have the painful duty of announcing the death of Mr. Augustus Bedlo, a gentleman whose amiable manners and many virtues have long endeared him to the citizens of Charlottesville.

"Mr. B., for some years past, has been subject to neuralgia, which has often threatened to terminate fatally; but this can be regarded only as the mediate cause of his decease. The **37** proximate cause was one of especial singularity. In an excursion to the Ragged Mountains, a few days since, a slight cold and fever were contracted, attended with great determination of blood to the head. To relieve this, Dr. Templeton resorted to **38** topical bleeding. Leeches were applied to the temples. In a fearfully brief period the patient died, when it appeared that, in the jar containing the leeches, had been introduced, by accident, one of the venomous vermicular sangsues which are now and then found in the neighboring ponds. This creature **39** fastened itself upon a small artery in the right temple. Its close resemblance to the medicinal leech caused the mistake **40** to be overlooked until too late.

"N.B. The poisonous sangsue of Charlottesville may always be distinguished from the medicinal leech by its blackness, and especially by its writhing or vermicular motions, which very nearly resemble those of a snake."

I was speaking with the editor of the paper in question, upon the topic of this remarkable accident, when it occurred to me to ask how it happened that the name of the deceased had been given as Bedlo.

"I presume," said I, "you have authority for this spelling, but I have always supposed the name to be written with an *e* at the end."

"Authority?—no," he replied. "It is a mere typographical error. The name is Bedloe with an *e*, all the world over, and I never knew it to be spelt otherwise in my life."

"Then," said I mutteringly, as I turned upon my heel, "then indeed has it come to pass that one truth is stranger than any fiction—for Bedlo, without the *e*, what is it but Oldeb conversed! And this man tells me it is a typographical error." **41**

39 There are no poisonous leeches or sangsues, although there was a tradition of their lethal nature giving rise to their former name, *Hirudo lethalis*. Burton R. Pollin says that an article in the *Cambridge Natural History* attributes to them the power to kill a man, but he calls it a "secondhand and rather unscientific account. Poe's use of the Hindu setting in his tale, based on Macaulay, may have stirred in his memory just such a tale of virulent Asiatic leeches. Soldiers fighting in Southeast Asia have attested to their ferocity, if not their venomousness. It is difficult to think of their resembling a black snake in appearance or in motion." (*Discoveries in Poe*, University of Notre Dame, 1970; pp. 27–28)

On the basis of Poe's usage, some dictionaries give "sangsue" as an English word for leech, even though the O.E.D. cites only this tale as a reference. The word actually comes from Victor Hugo's *Nôtre-Dame de Paris*, where Poe no doubt found it.

40 The leech is an annelid worm that sucks blood from living creatures to obtain food. Once used by physicians to bleed patients suffering from almost any ailment, they are now chiefly used in the treatment of bruises.

The idea behind bleeding was to overcome an "excess of blood" or to remove "poisonous elements" from the patient's body. Although the resultant lowering of blood pressure might help some, the general weakening of patients through loss of blood was often fatal.

41 The implication is that Bedloe is a kind of mirror image to Oldeb. As for the last line, it is the realization by the narrator of the all-important place of Fate in the scheme of things. The spelling of the name is no error, but part of some greater plan, of which the Oldeb-Bedloe-Templeton story is only a part. Oldeb *equals* Bedloe; they *are* the same.

Truth is indeed stranger than fiction, the tale seems to be saying, and indeed, it is this apparent truthfulness that makes the story work. In his discussion of Bird's *Sheppard Lee*, which also deals with metempsychosis, Poe calls attention to that novel's chief fault, its "*directness* of expression." It is far better, he points out, to write "as if the author were firmly impressed with the truth, yet astonished at the immensity of the wonders he relates, and for which, professedly, he neither claims nor anticipates credence," and to use a "minuteness of detail, especially upon points which have no immediate bearing upon the general story." This gives the tale "the character and luminousness of truth," he says, drawing the reader firmly into the tale.

One wonders if "A Tale of the Ragged Mountains" may not be about Bedloe at all, but, rather, about Templeton, who has lost his "dearest friend" in the Benares uprising and who now may be attempting to bring him back in the person of Bedloe. Templeton seems to feel remorse over the death of Oldeb because he failed to prevent the "rash and fatal sally" that ended his life. Now he has the chance to "resurrect" his friend but, through the leech he applies to Bedloe's temple, causes Bedloe to die as well (there may, then, be some significance that the leeches are placed on the temples, since they are the seat of the phrenological traits of Ideality, Sublimity, and Spirituality; not to mention the temple/Templeton parallel).

Marie Bonaparte points out that Hervey Allen, in his biography of Poe (*Israfel*, 1927; p. 569), states that at the time this story was written Poe had delusions of being persecuted. Such paranoia, she says, especially "in this tendency in men to believe, or wish, themselves persecuted by others," can be seen as "a conversion into its opposite of a homosexual attraction to men, projected on the imagined persecutor" (p. 567). She sees Bedloe as having a "homosexual fixation on Templeton." Thus, the "doctor pierces the young man first by his magnetic 'effluvia,' acting like erotic-stimuli on the nerves and, finally, by his penis-leech-serpent and its poison-semen. In the same way, Oldeb was killed and later Bedloe, in his effigy, by an enemy's poisoned, snake-like arrow, and we know how frequently, in the unconscious, *enemy* represents the father. We have here a classic delineation, in sado-phallic terms, of a passive homosexual relation to the father, which all small boys experience at some time and which persists in many men's unconscious. The poison enters by the temple, owing to the usual *displacement* upwards imposed by the moral censor. The enemy with poisoned arrow is linked with Dr. Templeton by as close as a body of identity, paternal in nature, as the 'brother' bond which likens Oldeb and Bedloe, elder and younger brothers, both of whom fall victims to the doctor's ill-starred love." (Pp. 567–68)

In Jung's view, "No psychic value can disappear without being replaced by another of equivalent intensity" (*Modern Man in Search of a Soul*, Kegan Paul, 1933; p. 242). "The idea of energy and its conservation," he writes, "must be a primordial image that was dormant in the collective unconscious. Such a conclusion naturally obliges us to prove that a primordial image of this kind really did exist in the mental history of mankind and was operative through the ages. As a matter of fact, this proof can be produced without much difficulty; the most primitive religions in the most widely separated parts of the earth are founded upon this image. These are the so-called dynamistic religions whose sole and determining thought is that there exists a universal magic power about which everything revolves. . . . According to the old view, the soul itself is this power; in the idea of the soul's immortality there is implicit its conservation, and in the Buddhist and primitive notion of metempsychosis—transmigration of souls—is implicit its unlimited changeability together with its constant preservation." (*The Psychology of C. G. Jung*, Yale, 1968; p. 55)

Thus the Jungian interpretation might be closer to what would be a literal interpretation of Poe's tale—that the soul of Oldeb did indeed manifest itself in the person of Bedloe.

In an article in the conservative *Journal of Nervous and Mental Disease* (1977), Dr. Ian Stevenson writes: "I prefer only to record my conviction that the evidence of human survival after death is strong enough to permit a belief in survival on the basis of the evidence. On the other hand, this evidence—imperfect as it remains—certainly does not compel such a belief. . . . If results in this field of inquiry have been small and remain indecisive, that is because the laborers have been few. When more scientists understand the theoretical issues involved in studying the question of survival after death, and when more of us agree that, despite formidable difficulties, the question is amenable to empirical investigation, then we can expect much more rapid progress."

Stevenson and his co-researchers believe that the experiences of persons who have undergone clinical death, particularly in their reports when revived of leaving their bodies, may provide a clue to the possibility of the survival of something that might be called "soul" or "spirit" after bodily death. He has also studied the appearance of certain inexplicable human traits such as genius, xenoglossy (the ability to speak in a language that one has not learned), and gender-identity confusion, in which a person firmly believes that he or she is trapped in the body of the opposite sex.

For a well-written overview of Stevenson's work, see "Intimations of a Former Life," by Tom Buckley, in *Quest/78*, September–October 1978; pp. 42–98.

MESMERIC REVELATION

First published in *Columbian Magazine*, August 1844.

Mesmerism, or hypnosis, first touched on in "A Tale of the Ragged Mountains," is here expanded and developed as the central theme of the tale.

Friedrich Anton Mesmer (1733?–1815) was basically a scientific man, who viewed the magnetic principle as a purely physical fact, free of any spiritual overtones. "There exists a mutual influence between the Heavenly Bodies, the Earth and Animate Bodies," he wrote. "A universally distributed and continuous fluid, which is . . . of an incomparably rarefied nature, and which by its nature is capable of receiving, propagating and communicating all the impressions of movement, is the means of this influence. . . . It is particularly manifest in the human body that the agent has properties similar to those of the magnet. . . . This property of the animal body, which brings it under the influence of the heavenly bodies and the reciprocal action of those surrounding it, as shown by its analogy with the Magnet, induced me to term it ANIMAL MAGNETISM. . . . With this knowledge, the physician will determine reliably the origin, nature, and progress of illnesses, even the most complicated; he will prevent them from gaining ground and will succeed in curing them without ever exposing the patient to dangerous effects or unfortunate consequences." (*Mesmerism*, a translation of *Mémoire sur le découverte du Magnétisme Animal*, 1779; translated by Gilbert Frankau, MacDonald, 1948; pp. 30–32)

Most of Mesmer's hopes for medical use were swept away when others saw in the hypnotic trance a sort of halfway house to the Other Side, a chance to peer into that unknown region beyond this mortal world.

This rush of interest in mesmerism unfortunately made it suspect in the eyes of the scientific community, and it wasn't until the latter part of the century that hypnosis was revived as a tool by Jean Martin Charcot (1825–93), who in turn passed it on (along with his insights into the nature of hysteria) to his pupil Sigmund Freud.

By Poe's time, mesmerism had already split, or rather, developed, into three distinct schools of thought, each claiming a scientific basis: the *fluidic theory*, which supposed that the magnetic influences from either a person or from natural sources could influence a susceptible person, even at great distances; the *mental healing* movement, which spawned several religious sects; and *spiritualism*, in which the physical theories of animal magnetism were broadened to accept clairvoyance, prevision, and other faculties that point to a world outside our own.

The introduction of mesmerism to the United States came in 1838, when French magnetist Charles Poyen gave lectures in New England. Poe attended a series of similar lectures in 1845, given by nineteen-year-old Andrew Jackson Davis in New York. Accompanied by his hypnotist and a reporter, Davis dictated from a trance a rambling discourse that would later be edited and compiled under the title *Principles of Nature, Her Divine Revelations, and a Voice to Mankind* (1847).

Although Davis spoke well of Poe on several occasions, Poe did not return the compliment, poking fun at him in "Mellonta Tauta" as "Martin Van Buren Mavis (sometimes called the 'Poughkeepsie Seer')." Davis lived in Poughkeepsie after 1839, and it was then that he began to hear the interior voices that dictated his life and career. In 1843, a Professor Grimes, "a well-known lecturer on Mesmerism, gave a performance at Poughkeepsie. After his departure, a tailor, William Livingstone, operated on [that is, hypnotised] young Davis and sent him into the trance. It soon appeared that the youth possessed clairvoyant powers; he read a newspaper placed to his forehead, told the time on the watches of those present, and diagnosed diseases. . . . In the clairvoyant state Davis claimed that not only the human body but the whole of nature became transparent to his spiritual vision." (Podmore, *From Mesmer to Christian Science*, University Books, 1963; p. 223)

Poe was intrigued by the prospects of mesmerism, but he was not a wholehearted believer in some of the more spiritualistic aspects of the "science." Perhaps, as a hoaxer himself, he understood human gullibility enough to be fairly skeptical. Despite his affinity for the romantic movement, there was always a part of Poe firmly embedded in the Age of Reason. In a letter to James Russell Lowell, July 2, 1844, he outlines some of his beliefs about life and the afterlife:

"The unparticled matter, permeating and impelling all things, is God. Its activity is the thought of God—which creates. Man, and other thinking beings, are individualizations of the unparticled matter. Man exists as a 'person' by being clothed with matter (the particled matter) which individualizes him. Thus habited, his life is rudimental. What we call 'death' is the painful metamorphosis. . . . At death the worm is the butterfly—still material, but of a matter unrecognized by our organism—recognized, occasionally, perhaps, by the sleep-waker, directly—without organs—through the mesmeric medium. Thus a sleep-waker may see ghosts. Divested of the rudimental covering, the being inhabits *space*—what we suppose to be the immaterial universe—passing every where, and acting on all things, by mere volition—the motion, or activity, of the unparticled matter."

Poe's rather rational mysticism carried over into "Mesmeric Revelation," and convinced many editors, reviewers, and readers that it was factual proof of the spiritual powers of mesmerism. In *Godey's*, August 1845, Poe says that the Swedenborgians—followers of Emanuel Swedenborg (1688–1772), who believed he had received direct insight into the spiritual world through angels and spirits—have informed him that the "findings" of "Mesmeric Revelation" are "absolutely true, although at first they were inclined to doubt my veracity—a thing which, in this particular instance, I never dreamed of not doing myself. The story is pure fiction from beginning to end."

Poe apparently enjoyed the furor over the tale, particularly the arguments over whether or not it was factual. "People seem to think there is something uncanny about him," wrote a friend, "and the strangest stories are told, what is more, *believed*, about his mesmeric experiences, at the mention of which he always smiles" (E. L. Didier, *Life and Poems of Edgar Allan Poe*,1877; p.13).

No direct sources have been found, although there is a case somewhat like the one Poe describes here in DuPotet's *An Introduction to the Study of Animal Magnetism* (London,1838; reprinted 1976 by Arno Press). A mesmerist named Chardel puts into a trance a woman patient, who apparently dies under the influence. He "magnetizes the plexus" and then gives her mouth-to-mouth rescucitation, for her heartbeat is undetectable, her gums are discolored, and her skin has "assumed a livid and yellowish hue." She eventually comes to.

DuPotet later comments: " 'Why do you call me back to life?' said a somnambulist in her magnetic exaltation; 'if you would only go away, this body which oppresses me would grow cold, and my soul would no longer be here on your return. I should then be perfectly happy.' " (P. 166)

1 These words seem to echo those of Rev. Chauncey Hare Townshend's *Facts in Mesmerism* (London, 1840), which point out that the ridicule of mesmerism by its critics is no proof or denial of its truth, and that "important deductions might be drawn from" a close look at mesmeric experiments and might provide some insight into "disputed questions of the highest interest to man, connected with the three great mysteries of being—life, death and immortality" (p. 51).

The opening sentences of Poe's tale serve several functions: they establish a prevailing mood of scientific study, they help bring the reader to at least a monentary acceptance (a willing suspension of disbelief) of the effects of mesmerism, and they give the fictional tale the appearance and feel of an actual case history.

2 The narrator refers here to the aspects of the hypnotic trance that produce a sleep from which a person cannot be easily awakened except by the hypnotist. The subject is sometimes deaf to everything except the voice of the therapist, sometimes insensitive to pain, and with the proper suggestion can make his body absolutely rigid.

Whatever doubt may still envelop the *rationale* of mesmerism,
1 its startling *facts* are now almost universally admitted. Of these latter, those who doubt, are your mere doubters by profession—an unprofitable and disreputable tribe. There can be no more absolute waste of time than the attempt to *prove*, at the present day, that man, by mere exercise of will, can so impress his fellow, as to cast him into an abnormal condition, of which the phenomena resemble very closely those of *death*, or at least resemble them more nearly than they do the phenomena of any other normal condition within our cogni-
2 zance; that, while in this state, the person so impressed
3 employs only with effort, and then feebly, the external organs of sense, yet perceives, with keenly refined perception, and through channels supposed unknown, matters beyond the scope of the physical organs; that, moreover, his intellectual faculties are wonderfully exalted and invigorated; that his sympathies with the person so impressing him are profound;

and, finally, that his susceptibility to the impression increases with its frequency, while, in the same proportion, the peculiar phenomena elicited are more extended and more *pronounced*.

I say that these—which are the laws of mesmerism in its general features—it would be supererogation to demonstrate; nor shall I inflict upon my readers so needless a demonstration to-day. My purpose at present is a very different one indeed. I am impelled, even in the teeth of a world of prejudice, to detail, without comment, the very remarkable substance of a colloquy occurring between a sleep-waker and myself. **4**

I had been long in the habit of mesmerizing the person in question (Mr. Vankirk), and the usual acute susceptibility and **5,6** exaltation of the mesmeric perception had supervened. For many months he had been laboring under confirmed phthisis, **7** the more distressing effects of which had been relieved by my manipulations; and on the night of Wednesday, the fifteenth instant, I was summoned to his bedside. **8**

The invalid was suffering with acute pain in the region of the heart, and breathed with great difficulty, having all the ordinary symptoms of asthma. In spasms such as these he had usually found relief from the application of mustard to the nervous centres, but to-night this had been attempted in vain.

As I entered his room he greeted me with a cheerful smile, and although evidently in much bodily pain, appeared to be, mentally, quite at ease.

"I sent for you to-night," he said, "not so much to administer to my bodily ailment, as to satisfy me concerning certain psychal impressions which, of late, have occasioned me much **9** anxiety and surprise. I need not tell you how sceptical I have hitherto been on the topic of the soul's immortality. I cannot deny that there has always existed, as if in that very soul which I have been denying, a vague half-sentiment of its own existence. But this half-sentiment at no time amounted to **10** conviction. With it my reason had nothing to do. All attempts as logical inquiry resulted, indeed, in leaving me more sceptical than before. I had been advised to study Cousin. I **11** studied him in his own works as well as in those of his European and American echoes. The 'Charles Elwood' of Mr. Brownson, for example, was placed in my hands. I read it **12** with profound attention. Throughout I found it logical, but the portions which were not *merely* logical were unhappily the initial arguments of the disbelieving hero of the book. In his summing up it seemed evident to me that the reasoner had not even succeeded in convincing himself. His end had plainly forgotten his beginning, like the government of Trinculo. In short, I was not long in perceiving that if man is to **13** be intellectually convinced of his own immortality, he will never be so convinced by the mere abstractions which have been so long the fashion of the moralists of England, of France, and of Germany. Abstractions may amuse and exercise, but **14** take no hold on the mind. Here upon earth, at least, philosophy, I am persuaded, will always in vain call upon us to look upon qualities as things. The will may assent—the soul—the intellect, never.

"I repeat, then, that I only half felt, and never intellectually

3 "The sleeper, with closed eyes, yet often speaks as if he saw certain objects, when his attention is directed to them. He even makes an apparent effort to see, or to look at them, while his eyes are only more firmly closed. . . . In fact, we have here the dawning of clairvoyance, which only reaches its noon-day brightness in the highest stages of sleep." (William Gregory, *Animal Magnetism, or Mesmerism and Its Phenomena*, 1909; reprinted by Arno Press, 1975; p. 6).

DuPotet defines the following aspects of the trance: 1) physical insensibility, "but whether persons in such apparent states . . . may not possess some internal consciousness, cannot possibly be determined"; 2) clairvoyance, "or vision without eyes," although patients sometimes declare that their sensations are more "of *feeling* than of *sight*"; 3) transference of the senses, in which the patients "sense" the appearance of an object with various parts of the body; 4) exaltation of knowledge, by which hypnotized patients "possess a knowledge beyond that which they possess in their waking state"; 5) prevision, or the ability to foresee the future; and 6) continuity of memory between trances, so that patients forget what occurred in the trance when they awake, yet remember it clearly when hypnotized again later (pp. 116–20).

Actually, patients under hypnosis may undergo fantasy experiences or hypnotic hallucinations, which can be very far from actual truth, according to Peter W. Sheehan in "Hypnosis and the Manifestations of 'Imagination' " (in *Hypnosis: Research Development and Perspectives*, Chicago, 1972; pp. 293–319).

4 Note that the word is "sleep-*waker*," not "sleep-*walker*." Townshend uses the same term, instead of the more common "somnambule," since the latter has the connotation of someone who walks in his sleep.

When the London *Popular Record of Modern Science* reprinted Poe's tale—pirated it, actually—Poe pointed out that the unauthorized new title, "The Last Conversation of a Somnambule," was "a phrase that is nothing at all to the purpose, since the person who 'converses' is not a Somnambule. He is a sleep-waker—*not* a sleep-walker; but I presume that 'The Record' thought it was only the difference of an *l*." (*Graham's*, March 1848)

5 His name means "of a church."

6 Once a patient has been successfully hypnotized and feels confident in the hypnotist, he usually falls into the trance much more easily, and often deeper than previously.

7 i.e., tuberculosis. Valdemar, in Poe's later story along similar lines, is also afflicted with the disease, as was Poe's wife.

8 "Instant" means "of the current month."

9 The O.E.D. cites this as the first use of the word meaning or pertaining to the soul.

10 J. P. F. Deleuze, in the early-nineteenth century, suggested that the mesmeric trance proved the spiritual nature of the soul, the division between the soul and the body, and that the soul, "though it generally makes use of the sense organs, can in certain states receive ideas and sensations without the mediation of those organs. . . . In short, it [has] incontrovertibly established that the soul can feel, think, know, and reason without the aid of the bodily organs; and that those organs, which in its ordinary state it uses as instruments, often prove obstacles to the knowledge which it can acquire by immediate apprehension unstained by transmission

A few passes threw Mr. Vankirk into the mesmeric sleep.
Illustration by F. S. Coburn, 1902

through the organs of sense." (*Bibliothèque du Magnétisme animal*, V, p. 14)

Poe found the inability to comprehend the soul, and its relation to the real world beyond that of sensory perception, almost a tragic truth. In "The Poetic Principle" (1848), he describes the importance of music and poetry, which bring tears to our eyes "not through excess of pleasure, but through a certain petulant, impatient sorrow at our inability to grasp *now*, wholly here on earth, at once and for ever, those divine and rapturous joys, of which *through* the poem, or *through* the music, we attain to but brief and indeterminate glimpses."

These "brief glimpses" haunt Poe's characters again and again, and it is their ability or inability to cope with their imperfection that determines their fate.

11 Victor Cousin (1792–1867) was the chief arbiter of philosophy in France during Poe's lifetime. Vankirk is probably referring to the *Cours de l'histoire de la philosophie* (1815–29), an eight-volume encyclopedia of philosophy.

In a review of *Orion*, a quasi-epic poem by Richard Henry Horne (1803–84) (*Graham's*, March 1844), Poe refers to "that divine sixth sense which is yet so faintly understood—that sense which phrenology has attempted to embody in its organ of *ideality*—that sense which is the basis of all Cousin's dreams—that sense which speaks of God through his purest, if not his *sole* attribute—which proves, and which alone proves his existence."

What "dreams" of Cousin's Poe means is not clear, since the French philosopher did not deal precisely with the subject discussed here. Poe may have simply been dropping a name. As for the phrenologists, Ideality meant "Taste; refinement; imagination; perception and admiration of the beautiful and perfect; purity of feeling; sense of propriety; polish; love of perfection; purity, poetry, flowers, beauty, elegance, gentility, the fine arts, etc.; personal neatness; finish"—according to O. F. Fowler's *The Practical Phrenologist* (1869), p. 127.

12 *Charles Elwood, or the Infidel Converted* (1840), is the work of Orestes Augustus Brownson (1803–76),

believed. But latterly there has been a certain deepening of the feeling, until it has come so nearly to resemble the acquiescence of reason, that I find it difficult to distinguish between the two. I am enabled, too, plainly to trace this effect to the mesmeric influence. I cannot better explain my meaning than by the hypothesis that the mesmeric exaltation enables me to perceive a train of ratiocination which, in my abnormal existence, convinces, but which, in full accordance with the mesmeric phenomena, does not extend, except through its *effect*, into my normal condition. In sleep-waking, the reasoning and its conclusion—the cause and its effect—are present together. In my natural state, the cause vanishing, the effect

15 only, and perhaps only partially, remains.

"These considerations have led me to think that some good results might ensue from a series of well-directed questions propounded to me while mesmerized. You have often observed the profound self-cognizance evinced by the sleep-waker—the extensive knowledge he displays upon all points relating to the mesmeric condition itself; and from this self-cognizance may be deduced hints for the proper conduct of a catechism."

I consented of course to make this experiment. A few passes threw Mr. Vankirk into the mesmeric sleep. His breathing became immediately more easy, and he seemed to suffer no physical uneasiness. The following conversation then ensued:—V. in the dialogue representing the patient, and P. myself.

P. Are you asleep?

16 *V.* Yes—no; I would rather sleep more soundly.

P. [*After a few more passes.*] Do you sleep now?

V. Yes.

P. How do you think your present illness will result?

V. [*After a long hesitation and speaking as if with effort.*] I must die.

P. Does the idea of death afflict you?

V. [*Very quickly.*] No—no!

P. Are you pleased with the prospect?

V. If I were awake I should like to die, but now it is no matter. The mesmeric condition is so near death as to content me.

P. I wish you would explain yourself, Mr. Vankirk.

V. I am willing to do so, but it requires more effort than I

17 feel able to make. You do not question me properly.

P. What then shall I ask?

V. You must begin at the beginning.

P. The beginning! But where is the beginning?

18 *V.* You know that the beginning is GOD. [*This was said in a low, fluctuating tone, and with every sign of the most profound veneration.*]

P. What, then, is God?

V. [*Hesitating for many minutes.*] I cannot tell.

19 *P.* Is not God spirit?

V. While I was awake I knew what you meant by "spirit," but now it seems only a word—such, for instance, as truth, beauty—a quality, I mean.

P. Is not God immaterial?

V. There is no immateriality; it is a mere word. That which is not matter, is not at all—unless qualities are things.

P. Is God, then, material?

V. No. [*This reply startled me very much*.]

P. What, then, is he?

V. [*After a long pause, and mutteringly*.] I see—but it is a thing difficult to tell. [*Another long pause*.] He is not spirit, for he exists. Nor is he matter, *as you understand it*. But there are *gradations* of matter of which man knows nothing; the grosser impelling the finer, the finer pervading the grosser. The atmosphere, for example, impels the electric principle, while the electric principle permeates the atmosphere. These gradations of matter increase in rarity or fineness, until we arrive at a matter *unparticled*—without particles—indivisible—*one*; and here the law of impulsion and permeation is modified. The ultimate or unparticled matter not only permeates all things, but impels all things; and thus *is* all things within itself. This matter is God. What men attempt to embody in the word "thought," is this matter in motion.

P. The metaphysicians maintain that all action is reducible to motion and thinking, and that the latter is the origin of the former.

V. Yes; and I now see the confusion of idea. Motion is the action of *mind*, not of *thinking*. The unparticled matter, or God, in quiescence, is (as nearly as we can conceive it) what men call mind. And the power of self-movement (equivalent in effect to human volition) is, in the unparticled matter, the result of its unity and omniprevalence; *how*, I know not, and now clearly see that I shall never know. But the unparticled matter, set in motion by a law or quality existing within itself, is thinking.

P. Can you give me no more precise idea of what you term the unparticled matter?

V. The matters of which man is cognizant escape the senses in gradation. We have, for example, a metal, a piece of wood, a drop of water, the atmosphere, a gas, caloric, electricity, the luminiferous ether. Now, we call all these things matter, and embrace all matter in one general definition; but in spite of this, there can be no two ideas more essentially distinct than that which we attach to a metal, and that which we attach to the luminiferous ether. When we reach the latter, we feel an almost irresistible inclination to class it with spirit, or with nihility. The only consideration which restrains us is our conception of its atomic constitution; and here, even, we have to seek aid from our notion of an atom, as something possessing in infinite minuteness, solidity, palpability, weight. Destroy the idea of the atomic constitution and we should no longer be able to regard the ether as an entity, or, at least, as matter. For want of a better word we might term it spirit. Take, now, a step beyond the luminiferous ether; conceive a matter as much more rare than the ether, as this ether is more rare than the metal, and we arrive at once (in spite of all the school dogmas) at a unique mass—an unparticled matter. For although we may admit infinite littleness in the atoms themselves, the infinitude of littleness in the spaces between them

20

Presbyterian, then Unitarian, then transcendentalist, and finally Roman Catholic in 1844. He was "one of the most attractive and commanding figures in the periodical history of the times," according to Frank Luther Mott's *History of American Magazines* (Harvard, 1940; I, 367–68).

In *Charles Elwood*, the "infidel" hero converts to Unitarianism, and the book underscores Brownson's belief in a Divine Order, with leaders who would pursue the general welfare *of* the people but would have little or nothing done *by* the people.

13 Poe seems to have gotten his allusions mixed. In *The Tempest*, it is Antonio who says, "The latter end of his commonwealth forgets the beginning," not about Trinculo but about Gonzago.

14 Vankirk is talking about the philosophical discourses of the early romantic period, which were indeed vague, as the Enlightenment began to lose its luster and philosophers and poets began to attempt a new way of viewing the self and the universe.

For the reader who would know more about the making of nineteenth-century thought, there is Morse Peckham's outstanding (and sometimes mind-boggling) *Beyond the Tragic Vision* (Braziller, 1962). It is sometimes rough going but well worth the effort.

15 DuPotet, in 1838, writes that patients in the hypnotic trance "suggest the idea of the soul being partially disencumbered of the coils of its mortality— seeing, hearing, feeling, taking cognizance of all things past, present, and future, through some other channels than the physical organs of its subordinate manifestations. All, too, agree in enjoying, in this state, a sort of exquisite elysium of repose from which they dread to be disturbed; the soul, apparently half set free, shrinks from being again brought back and entangled in the chains which bind it down to the narrow sphere of suffering humanity. It is impossible to contemplate a somnambulist in this state without a feeling of awe, not unmixed with anxious wonder; he is a being who appears to belong more to the world that is to come, than to that in which, as finite beings, we exist; he already appears half disrobed of his carnal nature, and participating in the sense, if not in the actual enjoyment, of his immortality; it is impossible to divine what views of infinity may now open before him." (Pp. 166–67)

This state is what early mesmerists referred to as "Prevision." DuPotet quotes Hippocrates: "When the body is at rest, the soul begins to move of her own accord, and, receding gradually from the different parts of the body, retires and concentrates herself in her own seat. . . . it is then the soul that wakes, knows, sees what is to be seen, hears what is to be heard, feels, grieves, and reasons more readily, and with greater facility." (P. 124)

16 The Abbé Faria, in his *De la cause du sommeil lucide* (1819), was the first to refer to the hypnotic state as "lucid sleep," as since that time there has been much discussion over the parallels between trance and normal sleep.

M. Brennan, in "The Phenomena of Hypnosis" (*Problems of Consciousness*, 1951; p. 125), thinks that, up to a certain point, the two states are psychologically comparable, and L. Bellak, in "An Ego-psychological Theory of Hypnosis" (*International Journal of Psycho-Analysis*, 1955; pp. 373–79), says that there *is* no fundamental difference, in terms of psychodynamics, between hypnosis and sleep, other than some quantitative differences in the degree of exclusion of the ego. The Russians have claimed to demonstrate through EEG readings the similarity between hypnosis and sleep, but other scientists have not agreed with their findings. Many American experts feel that respiration, pulse, and all other physiological aspects of hypnosis are essentially the same as they are in the waking state.

The use of mesmeric passes to bring on a trance was the common practice: "If you will try the experiment of drawing the points of the fingers of your right hand, without contact, but very near, over the hands of several persons, downwards from the wrist, the hands being held with the palms upwards, and your fingers either all abreast, or one following the other, and repeat this, slowly, several times, you will most probably find one or more who distinctly perceive a peculiar sensation, which is not always the same in different persons. Some will feel a slight warmth, others a slight coolness, others a pricking; some a tingling, others a numbness." (William Gregory, *Animal Magnetism, supra*)

This is essentially the basis for the passes described here, although Mesmer and the other magnetists overlooked the possibility that it is the fixation on the movement by the subject which brings on the trance, and not any transference of the "magnetic fluid" from the hypnotist.

The speed with which Vankirk goes under indicates both his past experience with hypnosis and his willingness to be placed in a trance. Many hypnotists find that by placing a posthypnotic suggestion with the subject while he is in a trance, a word or phrase will act as a "switch" to produce the hypnotic state in the future.

17 In *The Nature of Hypnosis* (1956), Paul Schilder says that ". . . the psychological state in hypnosis constitutes a return to an undifferentiated state; a return to a more primitive stage of development, psychoanalytically speaking, a regression." He points out that ". . . hypnosis affects the old layers of instinctual life and revitalizes them; consequently it is not surprising that new perceptual experiences are driven to the surface." (Pp. 37–38)

18 "In the beginning was the Word, and the Word was with God, and the Word was God" (John 1:1).

19 "God is a spirit . . ." (John 4:24).

20 In a letter to Dr. Thomas H. Chivers (July 10, 1844), Poe restates his belief that "God is material; yet the matter of God has all the qualities which we attribute to spirit: thus the difference is scarcely more than of words. There is a matter without particles—of no atomic composition: this is God. It permeates and impels all things, and thus *is* all things in itself. Its agitation is the thought of God. . . ." The wording here is practically the same as in his letter to Lowell (introductory note)

21 This and the next paragraph were added to the original version for *Tales* (1845). "Sidereal," in the next paragraph, means starry, or stellar.

22 Much of this material, in somewhat altered and expanded form, appears in Poe's *Eureka* (1848).

is an absurdity. There will be a point—there will be a degree of rarity at which, if the atoms are sufficiently numerous, the interspaces must vanish, and the mass absolutely coalesce. But the consideration of the atomic constitution being now taken away, the nature of the mass inevitably glides into what we conceive of spirit. It is clear, however, that it is as fully matter as before. The truth is, it is impossible to conceive spirit, since it is impossible to imagine what is not. When we flatter ourselves that we have formed its conception, we have merely deceived our understanding by the consideration of infinitely rarefied matter.

P. There seems to me an insurmountable objection to the idea of absolute coalescence;—and that in the very slight resistance experienced by the heavenly bodies in their revolutions through space—a resistance now ascertained, it is true, to exist in *some* degree, but which is, nevertheless, so slight as to have been quite overlooked by the sagacity even of Newton. We know that the resistance of bodies is, chiefly, in proportion to their density. Absolute coalescence is absolute density. Where there are no interspaces, there can be no yielding. An ether, absolutely dense, would put an infinitely more effectual stop to the progress of a star than would an **21** ether of adamant or of iron.

V. Your objection is answered with an ease which is nearly in the ratio of its apparent unanswerability.—As regards the progress of the star, it can make no difference whether the star passes through the ether *or the ether through it*. There is no astronomical error more unaccountable than that which reconciles the known retardation of the comets with the idea of their passage through an ether; for, however rare this ether be supposed, it would put a stop to all sidereal revolution in a very far briefer period than has been admitted by those astronomers who have endeavored to slur over a point which they found it impossible to comprehend. The retardation actually experienced is, on the other hand, about that which might be expected from the *friction* of the ether in the instantaneous passage through the orb. In the case, the retarding force is momentary and complete within itself—in the other it is endlessly accumulative.

P. But in all this—in this identification of mere matter with God—is there nothing of irreverence? [*I was forced to repeat this question before the sleep-waker fully comprehended my meaning.*]

V. Can you say *why* matter should be less reverenced than mind? But you forget that the matter of which I speak is, in all respects, the very "mind" or "spirit" of the schools, so far as regards its high capacities, and is, moreover, the "matter" of these schools at the same time. God, with all the powers attributed to spirit, is but the perfection of matter.

P. You assert, then, that the unparticled matter, in motion, is thought.

V. In general, this motion is the universal thought of the universal mind. This thought creates. All created things are **22** but the thoughts of God.

P. You say, "in general."

V. Yes. The universal mind is God. For new individualities, *matter* is necessary.

P. But you now speak of "mind" and "matter" as do the metaphysicians.

V. Yes—to avoid confusion. When I say "mind," I mean the unparticled or ultimate matter; by "matter," I intend all else.

P. You were saying that "for new individualities matter is necessary."

V. Yes; for mind, existing unincorporate, is merely God. To create individual, thinking beings, it was necessary to incarnate portions of the divine mind. Thus man is individualized. Divested of corporate investiture, he were God. Now the particular motion of the incarnated portions of the unparticled matter is the thought of man; as the motion of the whole is that of God.

P. You say that divested of the body man will be God?

V. [*After much hesitation*.] I could not have said this; it is an absurdity.

P. [*Referring to my notes*.] You *did* say that "divested of corporate investiture man were God."

V. And this is true. Man thus divested *would be* God— would be unindividualized. But he can never be thus divested—at least never *will be*—else we must imagine an action of God returning upon itself—a purposeless and futile action. Man is a creature. Creatures are thoughts of God. It is the nature of thought to be irrevocable.

P. I do not comprehend. You say that man will never put off the body?

V. I say that he will never be bodiless.

P. Explain.

V. There are two bodies—the rudimental and the complete, **23** corresponding with the two conditions of the worm and the butterfly. What we call "death," is but the painful metamor- **24** phosis. Our present incarnation is progressive, preparatory, temporary. Our future is perfected, ultimate, immortal. The ultimate life is the full design.

P. But of the worm's metamorphosis we are palpably cognizant.

V. *We*, certainly—but not the worm. The matter of which our rudimental body is composed, is within the ken of the organs of that body; or, more distinctly, our rudimental organs are adapted to the matter of which is formed the rudimental body; but not to that of which the ultimate is composed. The ultimate body thus escapes our rudimental senses, and we perceive only the shell which falls, in decaying, from the inner form; not that inner form itself; but this inner form, as well as the shell, is appreciable by those who have already acquired the ultimate life.

P. You have often said that the mesmeric state very nearly resembles death. How is this?

V. When I say that it resembles death, I mean that it resembles the ultimate life; for when I am entranced the senses of my rudimental life are in abeyance, and I perceive

23 Compare with this passage from I Corinthians 15:35–44:

"But some man will say, how are the dead raised up? and with what body do they come? . . . God giveth it a body as it hath pleased him, and to every seed his own body. All flesh is not the same flesh: but there is one kind of flesh of men, another flesh of beasts, another of fishes, and another of birds. There are also celestial bodies, and bodies terrestrial: but the glory of the celestial is one, and the glory of the terrestrial is another. . . . So also is the resurrection of the dead. It is sown in corruption; it is raised in incorruption: It is sown in dishonour; it is raised in glory: it is sown in weakness; it is raised in power: It is sown a natural body; it is raised a spiritual body. There is a natural body, and there is a spiritual body."

24 "The wings that form/The butterfly lie folded in the worm" (in Townshend, p. 355). In Greek, *psyche* meant both "soul" and "butterfly."

external things directly, without organs, through a medium which I shall employ in the ultimate, unorganized life.

P. Unorganized?

V. Yes; organs are contrivances by which the individual is brought into sensible relation with particular classes and forms of matter, to the exclusion of other classes and forms. The organs of man are adapted to his rudimental condition, and to that only; his ultimate condition, being unorganized, is of unlimited comprehension in all points but one—the nature of the volition of God—that is to say, the motion of the unparticled matter. You will have a distinct idea of the ultimate body by conceiving it to be entire brain. This it is *not*; but a conception of this nature will bring you near a comprehension of what it *is*. A luminous body imparts vibration to the luminiferous ether. The vibrations generate similar ones within the retina; these again communicate similar ones to the optic nerve. The nerve conveys similar ones to the brain; the brain, also, similar ones to the unparticled matter which permeates it. The motion of this latter is thought, of which perception is the first undulation. This is the mode by which the mind of the rudimental life communicates with the external world; and this external world is, to the rudimental life, limited, through the idiosyncrasy of its organs. But in the ultimate, unorganized life, the external world reaches the whole body, (which is of a substance having affinity to brain, as I have said,) with no other intervention than that of an infinitely rarer ether than even the luminiferous; and to this ether—in unison with it— the whole body vibrates, setting in motion the unparticled matter which permeates it. It is to the absence of idiosyncratic organs, therefore, that we must attribute the nearly unlimited perception of the ultimate life. To rudimental beings, organs are the cages necessary to confine them until fledged.

P. You speak of rudimental "beings." Are there other rudimental thinking beings than man?

V. The multitudinous conglomeration of rare matter into nebulæ, planets, suns, and other bodies which are neither nebulæ, suns, nor planets, is for the sole purpose of supplying *pabulum* for the idiosyncrasy of the organs of an infinity of rudimental beings. But for the necessity of the rudimental, prior to the ultimate life, there would have been no bodies such as these. Each of these is tenanted by a distinct variety of organic, rudimental, thinking creatures. In all, the organs vary with the features of the place tenanted. At death, or metamorphosis, these creatures, enjoying the ultimate life— immortality—and cognizant of all secrets but *the one*, act all things and pass everywhere by mere volition:—in-dwelling, not the stars, which to us seem the sole palpabilities, and for the accommodation of which we blindly deem space created— but that SPACE itself—that infinity of which the truly substantive vastness swallows up the star-shadows—blotting them out **25** as non-entities from the perception of the angels.

P. You say that "but for the *necessity* of the rudimental life, there would have been no stars." But why this necessity?

V. In the inorganic life, as well as in the inorganic matter

25 The next seven paragraphs were added for the 1845 edition of *Tales*.

generally, there is nothing to impede the action of one simple *unique* law—the Divine Volition. With the view of producing impediment, the organic life and matter (complex, substantial, and law-encumbered) were contrived.

P. But again—why need this impediment have been produced?

V. The result of law inviolate is perfection—right—negative happiness. The result of law violate is imperfection, wrong, positive pain. Through the impediments afforded by the number, complexity, and substantiality of the laws of organic life and matter, the violation of law is rendered, to a certain extent, practicable. Thus pain, which in the inorganic life is impossible, is possible in the organic.

P. But to what good end is pain thus rendered possible?

V. All things are either good or bad by comparison. A sufficient analysis will show that pleasure, in all cases, is but the contrast of pain. *Positive* pleasure is a mere idea. To be happy at any one point we must have suffered at the same. Never to suffer would have been never to have been blessed. But it has been shown that, in the inorganic life, pain cannot be; thus the necessity for the organic. The pain of the primitive life of Earth, is the sole basis of the bliss of the ultimate life of Heaven.

P. Still, there is one of your expressions which I find it impossible to comprehend—"the truly *substantive* vastness of infinity."

V. This, probably, is because you have no sufficiently generic conception of the term *"substantive"* itself. We must not regard it as a quality, but as a sentiment:—it is the perception, in thinking beings, of the adaptation of matter to their organization. There are many things on the Earth, which would be nihility to the inhabitants of Venus—many things visible and tangible in Venus, which we could not be brought to appreciate as existing at all. But to the inorganic beings—to the angels—the whole of the unparticled matter is substance; that is to say, the whole of what we term "space," is to them the truest substantiality;—the stars, meantime, through what we consider their materiality, escaping the angelic sense, just in proportion as the unparticled matter, through what we consider its immateriality, eludes the organic.

As the sleep-waker pronounced these latter words, in a feeble tone, I observed on his countenance a singular expression, which somewhat alarmed me, and induced me to awake him at once. No sooner had I done this, than, with a bright **26** smile irradiating all his features, he fell back upon his pillow and expired. I noticed that in less than a minute afterward his corpse had all the stern rigidity of stone. His brow was of the **27** coldness of ice. Thus, ordinarily, should it have appeared, only after long pressure from Azrael's hand. Had the sleep- **28** waker, indeed, during the latter portion of his discourse, been addressing me from out the region of the shadows?

26 Says DuPotet: "In most treatises on animal magnetism, it is stated that the magnetisers can at pleasure restore their patients to the ordinary, or waking state. This is an error. I have often, in a few minutes, brought on sleep, and could not for hours afterwards awaken the patient, notwithstanding that I have energetically applied all the processes usually prescribed in such cases. In vain have I exerted my abilities to the utmost; the more I have wished and willed to induce the waking state, the more has the intensity of the sleep increased." (Pp. 169–70)

27 Poe probably added the last few sentences after this, the original ending of the first published version, as another escape for the doubtful reader.

28 In both Judaic and Moslem tradition, Azrael is the angel of death, who severs the soul from the body.

THE BALLOON-HOAX

First published in *The Extra Sun*, April 13, 1844, then reprinted in the New York *Sunday Times*, April 14. The present text has a few revisions by Poe.

"The Balloon-Hoax" is such an entertaining yarn that it seems a shame Poe did not make it longer. The initial hours of the flight are fascinating, with an expert blend of technical description and fictional narrative, comparing favorably with Jules Verne.

After 1836 there was a steady interest in manned balloon flights, with balloonist after balloonist attempting new records for height, speed, and distance. For this tale (which was originally published as a bona fide newspaper article under a typically sensational headline), Poe borrows heavily from Monck Mason's *Account of the Late Aeronautical Expedition from London to Weilburg, accomplished by Robert Hollond, Esq., Monck Mason, Esq., and Charles Green, Aeronaut* (1836). *Burton's Gentleman's Magazine* in 1840 made mention of Green's belief that balloon travel across the Atlantic was feasible, even though the feat was not accomplished until the twentieth century.

Another probable source is an article in the *Dollar Newspaper*, June 21, 1843 (the same issue in which Poe's "The Gold-Bug" first appeared), describing the plan of American John Wise to use a hydrogen-filled balloon to cross the Atlantic, by means of an easterly current, in only three days.

"A Flight in the Aerial," which appeared in *The Spirit of the Times*, July 1843, tells of a highly unlikely trip over Europe and Africa, and includes as passengers Henson and Ainsworth, who also appear in Poe's tale. The piece was written by William Edmonstoune Aytoun under the pseudonym of Bon Gaultier, shortly before he became one of the editors of *Blackwood's*.

In *Alexander's Express Messenger*, February 21, 1844, an article appeared entitled "Another Aerial Machine," which described Monck Mason's latest model, which had just been put on display in the Adelaide Gallery. The *Express* article was cribbed from a pamphlet written anonymously by Mason, called *Remarks on the Ellipsoidal Balloon propelled by the Archimedean Screw, described as the New Aerial Machine* (1843). Poe may have used either the article or the pamphlet, or both, although he paraphrases freely.

In the *Columbia Spy*, May 1844, Poe writes: "The 'Balloon-Hoax' made a far more intense sensation than anything of that character since the 'Moon-Story' of Locke [see "Hans Pfaall"]. On the morning (Saturday) of its announcement, the whole square surrounding the 'Sun' building was literally besieged, blocked up—ingress and egress being alike impossible, from a period soon after sunrise until about two o'clock P.M. In Saturday's regular issue, it was stated that the news had been just received, and that an 'Extra' was then in preparation, which would be ready at ten. It was not delivered, however, until nearly noon. In the meantime I never witnessed more intense excitement to get possession of a newspaper. As soon as the first few copies made their way into the streets, they were bought up, at almost any price, from the news-boys, who made a profitable speculation beyond doubt. I saw a half-dollar given, in one instance, for a single paper, and a shilling was a frequent price. I tried, in vain, during the whole day, to get possession of a copy. It was excessively amusing, however, to hear the comments of those who had read the 'Extra.' "

We get a far different story from Thomas Low Nichols: "One day he sold an ingenious scientific hoax to a newspaper publisher for fifty dollars. The publisher brought it out as an extra; and Poe, crazed by a glass of wine, stood on the walk before the publisher's door, and told the assembled crowd that the extra was a hoax, as he personally knew, for he had written it himself. The crowd scattered, the sales fell off, and the publisher, on going to the door, to ascertain the cause of failure, saw his author making what he conceived to be the necessary explanations." (*Poe Studies*, 1972, Vol.

5; pp. 48–49) Poe in his version omits the self-sabotage, but instead projects a self-image of a chatty, witty, and superior sort.

Whichever version is correct, the realization by publishers that it was indeed Poe who wrote the hoax "seems to have reinforced a feeling that he was not entirely trustworthy. The *Sun* had known exactly what it was doing, but it may have been in other editors' minds that Poe was capable of playing a joke on them, as well as on their readers." (Julian Symons, *The Tell-Tale Heart*, Harper, 1978; p. 89) As a result, Poe seemed to be in less demand than before.

The hoax may not have been as successful as Poe had hoped, because the *Sun* had already printed the "Moon Hoax" and because readers may have found it hard to believe that a private express from Charleston could arrive ahead of the mail boat which would be "confirming" the story. When the *Sun* printed its retraction, it seemed to carry with it the feelings, if not the words, of Poe: "BALLOON— The mails from the South last Saturday night not having brought a confirmation of the arrival of the Balloon from England, the particulars of which from our correspondent we detailed in our Extra, we are inclined to believe that the intelligence is erroneous. The description of the Balloon, and the voyage was written with a minuteness and scientific ability calculated to obtain credit everywhere, and was read with great pleasure and satifaction. We by no means think such a project impossible." (April 15)

The first airship (a balloon with both a power plant and directional control) to cross the Atlantic was the *R34*, a British-built dirigible, which took seventy-five hours in 1919.

While Jules Verne wrote of such a crossing in *Five Weeks in a Balloon* (1863), the first successful manned crossing of the Atlantic by free-floating balloon took place on August 17, 1978, when three Americans floated over South Wales, headed toward northern France. For a well-written description of the successful voyage, see *Newsweek*, August 22, 1978, pp. 52–59.

[Astounding News by Express, via Norfolk!—The Atlantic Crossed in Three Days! Signal Triumph of Mr. Monck Mason's Flying Machine!—Arrival at Sullivan's Island, near Charleston, S. C., of Mr. Mason, Mr. Robert Holland, Mr. Henson, Mr. Harrison Ainsworth, and four others, in the Steering Balloon, "Victoria," after a passage of Seventy-five Hours from Land to Land! Full Particulars of the Voyage! **1**

The subjoined *jeu d'esprit* with he preceding heading in **2** magnificent capitals, well interspersed with notes of admiration, was originally published, as matter of fact, in the *New-York Sun*, a daily newspaper, and therein fully subserved the purpose of creating indigestible aliment for the quidnuncs **3** during the few hours intervening between a couple of the Charleston mails. The rush for the "sole paper which had the news," was something beyond even the prodigious; and, in fact, if (as some assert) the "Victoria" *did* not absolutely accomplish the voyage recorded, it will be difficult to assign a reason why she *should* not have accomplished it.] **4**

The great problem is at length solved! The air, as well as the earth and the ocean, has been subdued by science, and will become a common and convenient highway for mankind. *The Atlantic has been actually crossed in a Balloon!* and this too without difficulty—without any great apparent danger— with thorough control of the machine—and in the inconceivably brief period of seventy-five hours from shore to shore! By

1 The original *Sun* headline was as follows:
"Astounding Intelligence by Private Express from Charleston via Norfolk!—The Atlantic Ocean crossed in three days!!—Arrival at Sullivan's Island of a Steering Balloon invented by Mr. Monck Mason.

"We stop the press at a late hour to announce that by a Private Express from Charleston, S.C., we are just put in possession of full details of the most extraordinary adventure ever accomplished by man. *The Atlantic Ocean has been actually traversed in a balloon and in the incredibly brief period of Three Days!* Eight persons have crossed in the machine—among others Sir Everard Bringhurst and Mr. Monck Mason. We have barely time now to announce this most novel and unexpected intelligence; but we hope by 10 this morning to have ready an Extra with a detailed account of the voyage." (April 13, 1844)

The next day, the New York *Mercury* printed a story with the following headline: "By Express/Astounding Intelligence from the Man in the/Moon/Boundless space travelled in the/Twinkling of a Bed Post/Arrival in New York, of a/Moon-Beam,/With extraordinary and exclusive intelligence/for the Sunday Mercury."

2 Witticism

3 Persons who constantly ask, "What's new?"—gossips.

4 Poe seems to be attempting to justify his deception by pointing out the plausibility of the story.

5 Robert Hollond was a member of Parliament who backed Charles Green's ballooning venture. William Samuel Henson organized the Aerial Steam Transportation Company in 1842, but his plans failed and he moved to the United States—and obscurity—in 1849. William Harrison Ainsworth (1805–82) was an English novelist who had no connection with balloon flights but whose name allows Poe to add some literary flourishes to the tale. Poe reviewed his work favorably on several occasions. Bringhurst and Osborne are fictitious; Lord William George Bentinck (1802–48) had nephews, but not by that name.

Thomas Monck Mason (1803–89) was the only son of historian William Monck Mason (1775–1859). Educated at Trinity College, Dublin, he spent several years abroad studying music, and became one of the best flute players of the day. He leased Her Majesty's Theatre, in London, in 1832 and introduced may noted artists, but lost £60,000 in one year.

How he came to join forces with Charles Green (1785–1870) is still a question. The son of a London fruiterer, Green made his first ascent from Green Park, London, in July 1821, by request of the government, for the coronation of George IV. He later made 526 more ascents.

In 1836 he constructed the *Great Nassau* balloon for Gye and Hughes, proprietors of the Vauxhall Gardens (the probable meeting ground with impresario Mason), and made several ascents from there. On November 7, 1836, Green and Mason left Vauxhall at 1:30 P.M., crossed the Straits from Dover that evening, and descended the next day at 7 A.M. in Weilburg, in Nassau, Germany. The five hundred-mile trip took just eighteen hours. The success of the voyage made Green consider regularly scheduled flights, and the possibility of a propeller-driven balloon to cross the Atlantic by 1846.

His exploits naturally led to many harrowing experiences, including one in which some unknown person maliciously cut the ropes that tied his car to the balloon, so that after lift-off, the aeronauts had to take refuge on the hoop from which the car had been suspended, a perilous journey that ended in injuries to both Green and his co-pilot. (Dictionary of National Biography, Oxford, 1921–22)

6 No one by this name is listed in the Charleston directories of the day.

7 Sir George Cayley (1773–1857) is known in England as the Father of British Aeronautics for his work with balloons in the early-nineteenth century.

8 The Royal Adelaide Gallery was in the Strand, London, an area of hotels, theaters, and offices. It was a series of assembly rooms sometimes used for exhibits.

9 Compare this passage from one ·in both Mason's pamphlet and "Another Aerial Machine":

"Mr. Henson's scheme of flight is founded upon the principle of an inclined plane, started from an eminence by an extrinsic force, applied and *continued* by the revolution of impinging vanes, in form and number resembling the sails of a windmill. In the experiments which were made in this gallery with several models . . . it was found that so far from *aiding* the machine in its flight, the operation of these vanes actually *impeded* its progress; inasmuch as it was always found to proceed to a greater distance by the mere force of acquired velocity (which is the only force it ever displayed) than when the vanes were set in motion to aid it. . . . It is to the agency of this cause, namely the broken continuity of surface, that, I have no doubt, is also to be ascribed

the energy of an agent at Charleston, S. C., we are enabled to be the first to furnish the public with a detailed account of this most extraordinary voyage, which was performed between Saturday, the 6th instant, at 11 A.M. and 2 P.M., on Tuesday, the 9th instant, by Sir Everard Bringhurst; Mr. Osborne, a nephew of Lord Bentinck's; Mr. Monck Mason and Mr. Robert Holland, the well-known æronauts; Mr. Harrison Ainsworth, author of "Jack Sheppard," &c.; and Mr. Henson, the projector of the late unsuccessful flying machine—with **5** two seamen from Woolwich—in all, eight persons. The particulars furnished below may be relied on as authentic and accurate in every respect, as, with a slight exception, they are copied *verbatim* from the joint diaries of Mr. Monck Mason and Mr. Harrison Ainsworth, to whose politeness our agent is also indebted for much verbal information respecting the balloon itself, its construction, and other matters of interest. The only alteration in the MS. received, has been made for the purpose of throwing the hurried account of our agent, Mr. **6** Forsyth, in a connected and intelligible form.

THE BALLOON

Two very decided failures, of late—those of Mr. Henson **7** and Sir George Cayley,—had much weakened the public interest in the subject of aerial navigation. Mr. Henson's scheme (which at first was considered very feasible even by men of science) was founded upon the principle of an inclined plane, started from an eminence by an extrinsic force, applied and continued by the revolution of impinging vanes, in form and number resembling the vanes of a windmill. But, in all **8** the experiments made with models at the Adelaide Gallery, it was found that the operation of these fans not only did not propel the machine, but actually impeded its flight. The only propelling force it ever exhibited, was the mere *impetus* acquired from the descent of the inclined plane; and this *impetus* carried the machine farther when the vanes were at rest, than when they were in motion—a fact which sufficiently demonstrates their inutility; and in the absence of the propelling, which was also the *sustaining*, power, the whole fabric would necessarily descend. This consideration led Sir George Cayley to think only of adapting a propeller to some machine having of itself an independent power of support—in a word, to a balloon, the idea, however, being novel, or original, with Sir George, only so far as regards the mode of its application to practice. He exhibited a model of his invention at the Polytechnic Institution. The propelling principle, or power, was here, also, applied to interrupted surfaces, or vanes, put in revolution. These vanes were four in number, but were found entirely ineffectual in moving the balloon, or in aiding its ascending power. The whole project was thus a complete **9** failure.

It was at this juncture that Mr. Monck Mason (whose voyage **10** from Dover to Weilburg in the balloon, "Nassau," occasioned so much excitement in 1837) conceived the idea of employing the principle of the Archimedean screw for the **11** purpose of propulsion through the air—rightly attributing the failure of Mr. Henson's scheme, and of Sir George Cayley's, to the interruption of surface in the dependent vanes. He made the first public experiment at Willis's Rooms, but **12** afterward removed his model to the Adelaide Gallery. **13**

Like Sir George Cayley's balloon, his own was an ellipsoid. Its length was thirteen feet six inches—height, six feet eight inches. It contained about three hundred and twenty cubic feet of gas, which, if pure hydrogen, would support twenty-one pounds upon its first inflation, before the gas has time to deteriorate or escape. The weight of the whole machine and apparatus was seventeen pounds—leaving about four pounds to spare. Beneath the centre of the balloon, was a frame of light wood, about nine feet long, and rigged on to the balloon itself with a network in the customary manner. From this framework was suspended a wicker basket or car.

The screw consists of an axis of hollow brass tube, eighteen inches in length, through which, upon a semi-spiral inclined at fifteen degrees, pass a series of steel-wire radii, two feet long, and thus projecting a foot on either side. These radii are **14** connected at the outer extremities by two bands of flattened wire—the whole in this manner forming the framework of the screw, which is completed by a covering of oiled silk cut into gores, and tightened so as to present a tolerably uniform surface. At each end of its axis this screw is supported by pillars of hollow brass tube descending from the hoop. In the lower ends of these tubes are holes in which the pivots of the axis revolve. From the end of the axis which is next the car, proceeds a shaft of steel, connecting the screw with the pinion of a piece of spring machinery fixed in the car. By the operation of this spring, the screw is made to revolve with great rapidity, communicating a progressive motion to the whole. By means of the rudder, the machine was readily turned in any direction. The spring was of great power, compared with its dimensions, being capable of raising forty-five pounds upon a barrel of four inches diameter, after the first turn, and gradually increasing as it was wound up. It weighed, altogether, eight pounds six ounces. The rudder was a light frame of cane covered with silk, shaped somewhat like a battledoor, and was about three **15** feet long, and at the widest, one foot. Its weight was about two ounces. It could be turned *flat*, and directed upward or downward, as well as to the right or left; and thus enabled the æronaut to transfer the resistance of the air which in an inclined position it must generate in its passage, to any side upon which he might desire to act; thus determining the balloon in the opposite direction.

This model (which, through want of time, we have necessarily described in an imperfect manner) was put in action at the Adelaide Gallery, where it accomplished a velocity of five miles per hour; although, strange to say, it excited very little interest in comparison with the previous complex machine of Mr. Henson—so resolute is the world to despise anything which carries with it an air of simplicity. To accom-

the failure of the attempt of Sir George Cayley to propel a Balloon of a somewhat similar shape to the present, which he made at the Polytechnic Institution a short while since, when he employed a series of revolving vanes, four in number, disposed at proper intervals around, but which were found ineffectual to move it."

10 Weilburg is in Nassau, an area in Germany north and east of the Main and Rhine rivers, now part of the state of Hesse. The region gave its name to the balloon that Green commanded; but, interestingly enough, the New York *Sun* office was situated on Nassau Street.

11 Archimedes (287–212 B.C.) is famous for his work in geometry, mechanics, physics, and hydrostatics, as well as for yelling "Eureka!" and illustrating the principle of the lever by saying, "Give me place to stand and I will move the world."

The Archimedean screw is a cylinder inside of which a continuous screw, extending the length of the cylinder, forms a spiral chamber. By placing the lower end in water and revolving the screw, water can be raised. Its use in flight would be negligible, for it would hardly generate sufficient force to propel a balloon. What is being described here, as well as in Mason's pamphlet, is a prototype of the propeller.

12 Willis' Rooms, previously Almack's (see "Lionizing"), were assembly and meeting rooms.

13 Although his design was never put into use, the father of the ellipsoidal balloon was probably Lieutenant (later General) Jean Baptiste-Marie Meusnier (1754–93), who in 1784 described a propeller-driven balloon two hundred sixty feet long with a capacity of sixty thousand cubic feet of hydrogen. The propellers were to be driven, from the car, by means of ropes and pulleys, making this the first fully developed design for a propeller-driven aircraft. Some of Meusnier's ideas were later used by Charles and the brothers Robert in 1784 (see note 19).

The importance of the ellipsoidal balloon was that it offered less air resistance, and a longer car or basket could be suspended underneath. The same basic design was later incorporated into the dirigible and the blimp.

Readers who find the history of ballooning fascinating should read L. T. C. Rolt's *The Aeronauts* (Walker & Co., 1966), a highly readable account with many fine illustrations.

14 Compare with Mason's pamphlet:
"The Balloon is, as before stated, an ellipsoid or solid oval; in length, 13 feet 6 inches, and in height, 6 feet 8 inches. It contains, accordingly, a volume of gas equal to about 320 cubic feet, which, in pure hydrogen, would enable it to support a weight of twenty-one pounds, which is about its real power when recently inflated, and before the gas has had time to become deteriorated. . . .

"Beneath the centre of the Balloon, and about two-thirds of its length, is a frame of light wood, answering to the hoop of an ordinary Balloon; to which are attached the cords of the net which encloses the suspending vessel, and which serves to distribute the pressure of the appended weight equally over its whole surface, as well as to form an intermediate means of attachment for the rest of the apparatus. This consists of a car or basket in the centre. . . ."

15 A wooden bat or paddle used in washing, or a utensil used for placing loaves of bread into an oven, usually spelled "battledore."

16 The art of raising and guiding balloons, or aerial navigation. It can also mean the science of weighing air, known also as aerostatics.

17 A fictional location

18 Did someone *plan* on an ocean crossing?

19 Rubber. Jacques Alexandre César Charles (1746–1823) and the Robert brothers produced the first balloon of silk cloth made impermeable to hydrogen leaks by coating it with a solution of rubber.

20 Coal gas is obtained as a by-product of coke production. Its composition varies but is normally hydrogen and methane with small amounts of other gases, including carbon monoxide, carbon dioxide, and nitrogen. Usually used as a fuel or illuminating gas, it had, according to Green, four advantages over hydrogen. First, it was easy and quick as a means of inflation. Second, it was cheap; Green calculated that in 1821 he could inflate a balloon six times with coal gas for the cost of one filling with hydrogen. Third, he claimed that coal gas was less damaging to the silk fabric. Fourth, he believed it did not penetrate the fabric as readily as hydrogen.

Another advantage, which Green failed to understand, is that coal gas is less susceptible to changes in temperature, far less likely to expand or contract suddenly, so that a balloon filled with it will fly farther than one filled with hydrogen. Unfortunately, it takes far more coal gas to get the lift of hydrogen, and so coal-gas balloons were huge by comparison. (Rolt, pp. 118–19)

Hydrogen is the lightest and most readily available gas for balloons, but in the presence of oxygen it is highly explosive. American dirigibles and blimps were filled with helium, which has slightly less lifting power but is perfectly safe. The explosiveness of hydrogen was made abundantly clear in the *Hindenburg* disaster of 1937.

In *Burton's Gentleman's Magazine*, March 1840, Poe may have read: "Pure hydrogen must be discarded, as too subtle for our present means of retention. Balloons inflated with carburetted hydrogen (common coal gas) will retain a good inflation for a great length of time. Mr. G. states that he has had gas of this kind brought in small balloons, to fill his large one, from a distance of five or six miles; and we observe (what Mr. G. has not) that in Vienna, according to a simple method invented by M. F. Derionet, the gas is conveyed in hermetically sealed bags . . . from the factory to all parts of the town daily."

21 Hydrogen combines readily with many other elements, particularly oxygen, and the balloon membrane could not prevent the hydrogen atoms (being the smallest of all) from leaking out.

plish the great desideratum of ærial navigation, it was very generally supposed that some exceedingly complicated application must be made of some unusually profound principle in dynamics.

So well satisfied, however, was Mr. Mason of the ultimate success of his invention, that he determined to construct immediately, if possible, a balloon of sufficent capacity to test the question by a voyage of some extent—the original design being to cross the British Channel, as before, in the Nassau balloon. To carry out his views, he solicited and obtained the patronage of Sir Everard Bringhurst and Mr. Osborne, two gentlemen well known for scientific acquirement, and especially for the interest they have exhibited in the progress of

16 ærostation. The project, at the desire of Mr. Osborne, was kept a profound secret from the public—the only persons entrusted with the design being those actually engaged in the construction of the machine, which was built (under the superintendence of Mr. Mason, Mr. Holland, Sir Everard Bringhurst, and Mr. Osborne) at the seat of the latter gentle-

17 man near Penstruthal in Wales. Mr. Henson, accompanied by his friend Mr. Ainsworth, was admitted to a private view of the balloon, on Saturday last—when the two gentlemen made final arrangements to be included in the adventure. We are not informed for what reason the two seamen were also

18 included in the party—but, in the course of a day or two, we shall put our readers in possession of the minutest particulars respecting this extraordinary voyage.

The balloon is composed of silk, varnished with the liquid

19 gum caoutchouc. It is of vast dimensions, containing more than 40,000 cubic feet of gas; but as coal-gas was employed in place of the more expensive and inconvenient hydrogen, the supporting power of the machine, when fully inflated, and immediately after inflation, is not more than about 2500 pounds. The coal-gas is not only much less costly, but is easily

20 procured and managed.

For its introduction into common use for purposes of ærostation, we are indebted to Mr. Charles Green. Up to his discovery, the process of inflation was not only exceedingly expensive, but uncertain. Two and even three days have frequently been wasted in futile attempts to procure a sufficency of hydrogen to fill a balloon, from which it had great tendency to escape, owing to its extreme subtlety, and its affinity for the surrounding atmosphere. In a balloon sufficiently perfect to retain its contents of coal gas unaltered, in quality or amount, for six months, an equal quantity of hydrogen could not be maintained in equal purity for six

21 weeks.

The supporting power being estimated at 2500 pounds, and the united weights of the party amounting only to about 1200, there was left a surplus of 1300, of which again 1200 was exhausted by ballast, arranged in bags of different sizes, with therir respective weights marked upon them—by cordage, barometers, telescopes, barrels containing provision for a fortnight, water-casks, cloaks, carpet-bags, and various other indispensable matters, including a coffee-warmer, contrived for warming coffee by means of slack-lime, so as to dispense **22** altogether with fire, if it should be judged prudent to do so. All these articles, with the exception of the ballast, and a few trifles, were suspended from the hoop overhead. The car is **23** much smaller and lighter, in proportion, than the one appended to the model. It is formed of a light wicker, and is wonderfully strong, for so frail-looking a machine. Its rim is about four feet deep. The rudder is also very much larger, in proportion, than that of the model; and the screw is considerably smaller. The balloon is furnished besides with a grapnel, **24** and a guide-rope; which latter is of the most indispensable importance. A few words, in explanation, will here be necessary for such of our readers as are not conversant with the details of ærostation.

As soon as the balloon quits the earth, it is subjected to the influence of many circumstances tending to create a difference in its weight; augmenting or diminishing its ascending power. For example, there may be a deposition of dew upon the silk, to the extent, even, of several hundred pounds; ballast has then to be thrown out, or the machine may descend. This ballast being discarded, and a clear sunshine evaporating the dew, and at the same time expanding the gas in the silk, the whole will again rapidly ascend. To check this ascent, the only resource is (or rather *was*, until Mr. Green's invention of the guide-rope) the permission of the escape of gas from the valve; but, in the loss of gas, is a proportionate general loss of ascending power; so that, in a comparatively brief period, the best-constructed balloon must necessarily exhaust all its resources, and come to the earth. This was the great obstacle to voyages of length. **25**

The guide-rope remedies the difficulty in the simplest manner conceivable. It is merely a very long rope which is suffered to trail from the car, and the effect of which is to prevent the balloon from changing its level in any material degree. If, for example, there should be a deposition of moisture upon the silk, and the machine begins to descend in consequence, there will be no necessity for discharging ballast to remedy the increase of weight, for it is remedied, or counteracted, in an exactly just proportion, by the deposit on the ground of just so much of the end of the rope as is necessary. If, on the other hand, any circumstances should cause undue levity, and consequent ascent, this levity is immediately counteracted by the additional weight of rope upraised from the earth. Thus, the balloon can neither ascend nor descend, except within very narrow limits, and its resources, either in gas or ballast, remain comparatively unimpaired. When passing over an expanse of water, it becomes neccessary to employ small kegs of copper or wood, filled with liquid ballast of a lighter nature than water. These float, and serve all the purposes of a mere rope on land. Another most important office of the guide-rope, is to point out the *direction* of the balloon. The rope *drags*, either on land or sea, while the balloon is free; the latter, consequently, is always in advance, when any progress whatever is made: a comparison, therefore, by means of the compass, of the relative positions

Green's *Great Nassau. Artist unknown*

22 Lime disintegrating from moisture, producing heat

23 From Monck Mason's *Account of the Late Aeronautical Expedition:* "Provisions which had been calculated for a fortnight's consumption in case of emergency; ballast to the amount of upwards of a ton in weight, disposed in bags of different sizes, duly registered and marked, together with an unusual supply of cordage, implements, and other accessories to an aerial excursion, occupied the bottom of the car; while all around the hoop and elsewhere appended, hung cloaks, carpet-bags, barrels of wood and copper, coffee-warmer, barometers, telescopes, lamps, wine jars and spirit flasks, with many other articles designed to serve the purposes of a voyage to regions where once forgotten, nothing could be again supplied." (P. 11)

24 A small anchor with four or five hooks which dig into the ground when it is dragged along

25 Mason: "When a balloon ascends to navigate the atmosphere, independent of the loss of power occasioned by its own imperfections, an incessant waste of its resources in gas and ballast becomes the inevitable consequence of the situation. No sooner has it quitted the earth than it is immediately subjected to the influence of a variety of circumstances tending to create a difference in its weight; augmenting or diminishing, as the case may be, the power, by the means of which it is supported and scarcely a moment passes without some call for [the balloonist's] interposition, either to check the descent of the balloon by the rejection of ballast, or to control its ascent by the proportionate discharge of gas; a process by which, it is unnecessary to observe, the whole power of the balloon, however great its dimensions, must in time be exhausted, and sooner or later terminate its career by succumbing to the laws of terrestrial gravitation." (P. 9)

26 Mason: "By the simple contrivance of a rope of the requisite magnitude and extent, trailing on the ground beneath, (and if over the sea, with a sufficient quantity of liquid ballast contained in vessels floating on the surface,) have all these difficulties . . . been overcome." (Pp. 8–10).

It is this invention which, Mason suggests, opened the way for long-distance—and especially transoceanic—balloon crossings. The credit for the invention, or discovery, usually goes to Green, but Rolt gives the credit to Thomas Baldwin, who, in his account of aerial voyages, called *Aeropaidia* (1785), mentions the use of such a trailing rope to control the altitude of a balloon. Green was the first to actually use it, as far as we know. He may have read Baldwin, or he may have heard of a similar device invented by engineer John Woodhouse, which was used to balance caisson and counterweights on the first canal boat lift.

27 The first flight over the Straits of Dover was made by Pierre Blanchard (1753–1809) and an American, Dr. John Jeffries (1744–1819), from Dover to France. The car of the balloon is still on display in the museum at Calais, and a monument stands at the site of their landing. Blanchard received all the credit, plus twelve thousand livres and a life pension from Louis XVI, while Jeffries received only a few wisps of fleeting glory, even though he had been as important as anything else in the success of the flight. The two feuded, mostly because Blanchard was unwilling to share the glory. Shortly before takeoff, the Frenchman secretly strapped lead weights on himself to cause the balloon to appear overweight and thus force Jeffries to remain behind, but the American saw through the ruse. (Rolt, pp. 85–88).

28 "Instant" here means "of the current month."

29 As befits the imaginary Mr. Osborne, his home is also fictional. "Weal-Vor House" means "four-wheel house"—in other words, a wagon.

30 Manuscripts

31 To encumber, hamper, or impede. All the difficult work has been done before the launching so they can get off to a quick start.

32 The Bristol Channel lies between South Wales and the southwesternmost point of England.

of the two objects, will always indicate the *course*. In the same way, the angle formed by the rope with the vertical axis of the machine, indicates the *velocity*. When there is *no* angle—in other words, when the rope hangs perpendicularly, the whole apparatus is stationary; but the larger the angle, that is to say, the farther the balloon precedes the end of the **26** rope, the greater the velocity; and the converse.

27 As the original design was to cross the British Channel, and alight as near Paris as possible, the voyagers had taken the precaution to prepare themselves with passports directed to all parts of the Continent, specifying the nature of the expedition, as in the case of the Nassau voyage, and entitling the adventurers to exemption from the usual formalities of office; unexpected events, however, rendered these passports superfluous.

The inflation was commenced very quietly at daybreak, on **28** Saturday morning, the 6th instant, in the courtyard of Weal-**29** Vor House, Mr. Osborne's seat, about a mile from Penstruthal, in North Wales; and at seven minutes past eleven, every thing being ready for departure, the balloon was set free, rising gently but steadily, in a direction nearly south; no use being made, for the first half hour, of either the screw or the rudder. We proceed now with the journal, as transcribed by Mr. **30** Forsyth from the joint MSS. of Mr. Monck Mason and Mr. Ainsworth. The body of the journal, as given, is in the handwriting of Mr. Mason, and a P.S. is appended, each day, by Mr. Ainsworth, who has in preparation, and will shortly give the public a more minute, and, no doubt, a thrillingly interesting account of the voyage.

THE JOURNAL

Saturday, April the 6th.—Every preparation likely to em-**31** barrass us having been made over night, we commenced the inflation this morning at daybreak; but owing to a thick fog, which encumbered the folds of the silk and rendered it unmanageable, we did not get through before nearly eleven o'clock. Cut loose, then, in high spirits, and rose gently but steadily, with a light breeze at north, which bore us in the **32** direction of the Bristol Channel. Found the ascending force greater than we had expected; and as we arose higher and so got clear of the cliffs, and more in the sun's rays, our ascent became very rapid. I did not wish, however, to lose gas at so early a period of the adventure, and so concluded to ascend for the present. We soon ran out our guide-rope; but even when we had raised it clear of the earth, we still went up very rapidly. The balloon was unusually steady, and looked beautiful. In about ten minutes after starting, the barometer indicated an altitude of 15,000 feet. The weather was remarkably fine, and the view of the subjacent country—a most romantic one when seen from any point—was now especially sublime. The numerous deep gorges presented the appearance of lakes, on account of the dense vapors with which they were filled, and the pinnacles and crags to the southeast, piled in inextricable confusion, resembling nothing so much as the giant cities of Eastern fable. We were rapidly approaching the mountains in the south, but our elevation was more than sufficient to enable us to pass them in safety. In a few minutes we soared over them in fine style; and Mr. Ainsworth, with the seamen, was surprised at their apparent want of altitude when viewed from the car, the tendency of great elevation in a balloon being to reduce inequalities of the surface below, to nearly a dead level. At half-past eleven still proceeding nearly south, we obtained our first view of the Bristol Channel; and, in fifteen minutes afterward, the line of breakers on the coast appeared immediately beneath us, and we were fairly out at sea. We now resolved to let off enough gas to bring our guide-rope, with the buoys affixed, into the water. This was im- **33** mediately done, and we commenced a gradual descent. In about twenty minutes our first buoy dipped, and at the touch of the second soon afterward, we remained stationary as to elevation. We were all now anxious to test the efficiency of the rudder and screw, and we put them both into requisition forthwith, for the purpose of altering our direction more to the eastward, and in a line for Paris. By means of the rudder we instantly effected the necessary change of direction, and our course was brought nearly at right angles to that of the wind; when we set in motion the spring of the screw, and were rejoiced to find it propel us readily as desired. Upon this we gave nine hearty cheers, and dropped in the sea a bottle, **34** inclosing a slip of parchment with a brief account of the principle of the invention. Hardly, however, had we done with our rejoicings, when an unforeseen accident occurred which discouraged us in no little degree. The steel rod connecting the spring with the propeller was suddenly jerked out of place, at the car end, (by a swaying of the car through some movement of one of the two seamen we had taken up,) and in an instant hung dangling out of reach, from the pivot of the axis of the screw. While we were endeavoring to regain it, our attention being completely absorbed, we became involved in a strong current of wind from the east, which bore us, with rapidly increasing force, toward the Atlantic. We soon **35** found ourselves driving out to sea at the rate of not less, certainly, than fifty or sixty miles an hour, so that we came up with Cape Clear, at some forty miles to our north, before we **36** had secured the rod, and had time to think what we were about. It was now that Mr. Ainsworth made an extraordinary but, to my fancy, a by no means unreasonable or chimerical proposition, in which he was instantly seconded by Mr. Holland—viz.: that we should take advantage of the strong **37** gale which bore us on, and in place of beating back to Paris, make an attempt to reach the coast of North America. After **38** slight reflection I gave a willing assent to this bold proposition, which (strange to say) met with objection from the two seamen only. As the stronger party, however, we overruled their fears, and kept resolutely upon our course. We steered due west; but as the trailing of the buoys materially impeded our progress, and we had the balloon abundantly at command,

33 As did Monck over the Dover Straits in 1836 and over the Bristol Channel in 1844.

34 Although "three cheers" is the more common salute, there is a well-known toast called "three times three," for those most highly honored.

35 In Mason's account, this same change of wind interferes with the voyage, but the crew overcomes it by rising to a current traveling in the right direction. Here the current becomes the basis for the voyage to America.

36 Cape Clear lies on the southernmost tip of Ireland, to the east of Bantry Bay.

37 "Viz." is the medieval Latin contraction for *videlicet*, "namely," and pronounced as the English word.

38 This sudden, rash decision to cross the Atlantic in a balloon seems a bit unbelievable, but one should remember that there had been much talk in those years of just such a crossing. In 1835, an American, Richard Clayton, was constructing a mammoth balloon to be called *Star of the West*, but the project never got off the ground, so to speak. In 1843, John Wise launched an unsuccessful attempt to raise money for a balloon voyage to Europe, but it wasn't until 1859 that wealthy O. A. Gager financed the construction of the 50,000-cubic-foot *Atlantic*. The airship managed an 809-mile flight from St. Louis to New York in 19 hours 50 minutes, but problems forced a cancellation of an ocean crossing.

Poe was most probably influenced by Green's comment in 1840 that a crossing of the Atlantic was possible, particularly a low-altitude flight with a clockwork propeller.

39 "To beat up or about" means to make way in any direction against the wind, or to tack. "Lying to" means coming almost to a standstill, with a ship's head as near to the wind as possible, by backing or shortening sail.

40 Gin, from Old French *genèvre*, or juniper berries, which flavor the alchohol

41 This is highly improbable, considering the balloon's altitude. Poe, who has once again borrowed from Mason's account, has overlooked that the description there is based on a low-altitude flight—over land (Mason, pp. 13–14).

42 The phosphorescence described is a common sight at sea, produced by plankton that collect on the surface. The glow is produced by luciferin, a substance produced by the microscopic organisms, which when oxidized yields light energy.

43 While "whirl" may seem a poor word choice here, because of its usual connotation of circular movement, the O.E.D. also gives a meaning of being hurled or flung, and to rush. Dickens, in *American Notes* (1842), takes the latter meaning when he speaks of a "whirl of carriages."

44 Mason: ". . . the sea, unless perhaps under circumstances of the most extraordinary agitation, does not in itself appear to be the parent of the slightest sound; unopposed by any material obstacle, an awful stillness seems to reign over its motions" (p. 16 n.).

either for ascent or descent, we first threw out fifty pounds of ballast, and then wound up (by means of a windlass) so much of the rope as brought it quite clear of the sea. We perceived the effect of this manœuvre immediately, in a vastly increased rate of progress; and, as the gale freshened, we flew with a velocity nearly inconceivable; the guide-rope flying out behind the car, like a streamer from a vessel. It is needless to say that a very short time sufficed us to lose sight of the coast. We passed over innumerable vessels of all kinds, a few of which were endeavoring to beat up, but the most of them **39** lying to. We occasioned the greatest excitement on board all— an excitement greatly relished by ourselves, and especially by our two men, who, now under the influence of a dram of **40** Geneva, seemed resolved to give all scruple, or fear, to the wind. Many of the vessels fired signal guns; and in all we were saluted with loud cheers (which we heard with surprising **41** distinctness) and the waving of caps and handkerchiefs. We kept on in this manner throughout the day with no material incident, and, as the shades of night closed around us, we made a rough estimate of the distance traversed. It could not have been less than five hundred miles, and was probably much more. The propeller was kept in constant operation, and, no doubt, aided our progress materially. As the sun went down, the gale freshened into an absolute hurricane, and the ocean beneath was clearly visible on account of its phospho- **42** rescence. The wind was from the east all night, and gave us the brightest omen of success. We suffered no little from cold, and the dampness of the atmosphere was most unpleasant; but the ample space in the car enabled us to lie down, and by means of cloaks and a few blankets we did sufficiently well.

P.S. [By Mr. Ainsworth.] The last nine hours have been unquestionably the most exciting of my life. I can conceive nothing more sublimating than the strange peril and novelty of an adventure such as this. May God grant that we succeed! I ask not success for mere safety to my insignificant person, but for the sake of human knowledge and—for the vastness of the triumph. And yet the feat is only so evidently feasible that the sole wonder is why men have scrupled to attempt it before. One single gale such as now befriends us—let such a **43** tempest whirl forward a balloon for four or five days (these gales often last longer) and the voyager will be easily borne, in that period, from coast to coast. In view of such a gale the broad Atlantic becomes a mere lake. I am more struck, just now, with the supreme silence which reigns in the sea beneath us, notwithstanding its agitation, than with any other phenom- enon presenting itself. The waters give up no voice to the **44** heavens. The immense flaming ocean writhes and is tortured uncomplainingly. The mountainous surges suggest the idea of innumerable dumb gigantic fiends struggling in impotent agony. In a night such as is this to me, a man *lives*—lives a whole century of ordinary life—nor would I forego this rapturous delight for that of a whole century of ordinary existence.

Sunday, the 7th. [Mr. Mason's MS.] This morning the gale,

by ten, had subsided to an eight or nine knot breeze (for a vessel at sea), and bears us, perhaps, thirty miles per hour, or more. It has veered, however, very considerably to the north; and now, at sundown, we are holding our course due west, principally by the screw and rudder, which answer their purposes to admiration. I regard the project as thoroughly successful, and the easy navigation of the air in any direction (not exactly in the teeth of a gale) as no longer problematical. We could not have made head against the strong wind of yesterday; but, by ascending, we might have got out of its influence, if requisite. Against a pretty stiff breeze, I feel convinced, we can make our way with the propeller. At noon, to-day, ascended to an elevation of nearly 25,000 feet, by discharging ballast. Did this to search for a more direct current, but found none so favorable as the one we are now in. We have an abundance of gas to take us across this small **45** pond, even should the voyage last three weeks. I have not the slightest fear for the result. The difficulty has been strangely exaggerated and misapprehended. I can choose my current, and should I find *all* currents against me, I can make very tolerable headway with the propeller. We have had no incidents worth recording. The night promises fair.

P.S. [By Mr. Ainsworth.] I have little to record, except the fact (to me quite a surprising one) that, at an elevation equal to that of Cotopaxi, I experienced neither very intense **46** cold, nor headache, nor difficulty of breathing; neither, I find, **47** did Mr. Mason, nor Mr. Holland, nor Sir Everard. Mr. Osborne complained of constriction of the chest—but this soon wore off. We have flown at a great rate during the day, and we must be more than half way across the Atlantic. We have passed over some twenty or thirty vessels of various kinds, and all seem to be delightfully astonished. Crossing the **48** ocean in a balloon is not so difficult a feat after all. *Omne ignotum pro magnifico. Mem.*: at 25,000 feet elevation the sky **49** appears nearly black, and the stars are distinctly visible; while the sea does not seem convex (as one might suppose) but absolutely and more unequivocally *concave*. **50**

"*Monday, the 8th*. [Mr. Mason's MS.] This morning we had again some little trouble with the rod of the propeller, which must be entirely remodelled, for fear of serious accident—I mean the steel rod, not the vanes. The latter could not be improved. The wind has been blowing steadily and strongly from the northeast all day; and so far fortune seems bent upon favoring us. Just before day, we were all somewhat alarmed at some odd noises and concussions in the balloon, accompanied with the apparent rapid subsidence of the whole machine. These phenomena were occasioned by the expansion of the gas, through increase of heat in the atmosphere, and the consequent disruption of the minute particles of ice with which the network had become encrusted during the night. **51** Threw down several bottles to the vessels below. See one of them picked up by a large ship—seemingly one of the New York line packets. Endeavored to make out her name, but **52** could not be sure of it. Mr. Osborne's telescope made it out

45 Mason's party used this as a way to find an opposing wind to carry them back toward France.

One tricky area of ballooning is the shifting of altitude in order to encounter winds heading in the direction in which one wants to go. George Hadley in 1735 reasoned that close to the equator warm air rises, and in colder air it sinks. To keep up this movement, air must flow toward the equator on the surface, and return from the equator high above the surface, then cool and sink to begin the process once more. Air currents are affected by the spinning of the earth, the deflection of the northerly and southerly winds, and the jet stream, so that finding the proper current is, at best, difficult.

46 A mountain in Ecuador which, at 19,550 feet, was one of the highest known peaks at the time. In "Hans Pfaall," Poe gives its height as 18,000 feet.

47 Mason: ". . . we frequently rose to an elevation of about twelve thousand feet, occasionally higher. At no time, however, did we experience the *slightest* effect upon our bodies, proceeding from the diminished pressure of the atmosphere." (P. 34 n.) For more on atmospheric pressure, see "Hans Pfaall," note 68.

48 How they can tell this at their altitude is not explained.

49 "Everything unknown is taken for marvelous" (Tacitus, *Agricola*, section 30).

50 "Mr. Ainsworth has not attempted to account for this phenomenon, which, however, is quite susceptible of explanation. A line dropped from an elevation of 25,000 feet, perpendicularly to the surface of the earth (or sea), would form the perpendicular of a right-angled triangle, of which the base would extend from the right angle to the horizon, and the hypothenuse from the horizon to the balloon. But the 25,000 feet of altitude is little or nothing, in comparison with the extent of the prospect. In other words, the base and hypothenuse of the supposed triangle would be so long when compared with the perpendicular, that the two former may be regarded as nearly parallel. In this manner the horizon of the æronaut would appear to be *on a level* with the car. But, as the point immediately beneath him seems, and is, at a great distance below him, it seems, of course, also, at a great distance below the horizon. Hence the impression of *concavity*; and this impression must remain, until the elevation shall bear so great a proportion to the extent of the prospect, that the apparent parallelism of the base and hypothenuse disappears—when the earth's real convexity must become apparent." (Poe's note)

Mason also remarks on the utter blackness of the sky, and on the stars, which have "redoubled in their lustre" (p. 21). As for the concavity of the sea's appearance, see "Hans Pfaall," note 73.

51 Mason, p. 23.

52 See "The Oblong Box," note 2.

53 A packet from Liverpool docked in New York on April 13, but it was the *Sheridan*.

54 There is a definite feeling of anticlimax here. The tale began well and sustained itself well, but it is simply too short. There is so much more to be said, so many more situations and incidents that could be mentioned. And, of course, it could easily have been fleshed out with characterizations of the party on board, some of whom (the two sailors, for example) we would like to know more about.

Poe's intent, however, is to mimic a newspaper article. He also completed the piece in a rush, and may have intended to continue the story at a later time. What a shame he did not expand it into a longer story, or even a novel, such as Verne would do in *Five Weeks in a Balloon*. Unfortunately, Poe worked best in short spurts, and only managed to write one novel-length piece, *The Narrative of Arthur Gordon Pym* (which itself reads like a series of interrelated short stories).

55 Fort Moultrie and Sullivan's Island, in Charleston Harbor, figure prominently in the plot of "The Gold-Bug." Poe was stationed there in 1827–28.

53 something like 'Atalanta.' It is now 12, at night, and we are still going nearly west, at a rapid pace. The sea is peculiarly phosphorescent.

P.S. [By Mr. Ainsworth.] It is now 2, A.M., and nearly calm, as well as I can judge—but it is very difficult to determine this point, since we move *with* the air so completely. I have not slept since quitting Weal-Vor, but can stand it no longer, and must take a nap. We cannot be far from the American coast.

Tuesday, the 9th. [Mr. Ainsworth's MS.] *One,* P.M. *We are in full view of the low coast of South Carolina.* The great problem is accomplished. We have crossed the Atlantic—fairly and *easily* crossed it in a balloon! God be praised! Who **54** shall say that anything is impossible hereafter?

*   *   *

The Journal here ceases. Some particulars of the descent were communicated, however, by Mr. Ainsworth to Mr. Forsyth. It was nearly dead calm when the voyagers first came in view of the coast, which was immediately recognized by both the seamen, and by Mr. Osborne. The latter gentleman **55** having acquaintances at Fort Moultrie, it was immediately resolved to descend in its vicinity. The balloon was brought over the beach (the tide being out and the sand hard, smooth, and admirably adapted for a descent), and the grapnel let go, which took firm hold at once. The inhabitants of the island, and of the fort, thronged out, of course, to see the balloon; but it was with the greatest difficulty that any one could be made to credit the actual voyage—*the crossing of the Atlantic*. The grapnel caught at 2, P.M. precisely; and thus the whole voyage was completed in seventy-five hours; or rather less, counting from shore to shore. No serious accident occurred. No real danger was at any time apprehended. The balloon was exhausted and secured without trouble; and when the MS. from which this narrative is compiled was despatched from Charleston, the party were still at Fort Moultrie. Their further intentions were not ascertained; but we can safely promise our readers some additional information either on Monday or in the course of the next day, at farthest.

This is unquestionably the most stupendous, the most interesting, and the most important undertaking ever accomplished or even attempted by man. What magnificent events may ensue, it would be useless now to think of determining.

THE ANGEL OF THE ODD

AN EXTRAVAGANZA

First published in the *Columbian Magazine*, October 1844, this is still a rather enjoyable piece, although the satire on the philosophy of human perfectibility is over the heads of most modern readers. Sources include "It's Very Odd," in *Blackwood's*, January 1829; "Progress of Social Questions," in the New York *Tribune*, June 8, 1844; and Cornelius Webbe's *The Man About Town* (1839). The resemblances are minor, except for Webbe, who echoes Pope's dictum that a little learning can be a dangerous thing and features a tailor whose German dialect is similar to that which Poe uses here.

It was a chilly November afternoon. I had just consummated an unusually hearty dinner, of which the dyspeptic *truffé* **1** formed not the least important item, and was sitting alone in the dining-room, with my feet upon the fender, and at my **2** elbow a small table which I had rolled up to the fire, and upon which were some apologies for dessert, with some miscellaneous bottles of wine, spirit and *liqueur*. In the morning I had been reading Glover's "Leonidas," Wilkie's "Epigoniad," Lamartine's "Pilgrimage," Barlow's "Columbiad," Tuckerman's "Sicily," and Griswold's "Curiosities"; I **3** am willing to confess, therefore, that I now felt a little stupid. **4** I made effort to arouse myself by aid of frequent Lafitte, and, all failing, I betook myself to a stray newspaper in despair. Having carefully perused the column of "houses to let," and the column of "dogs lost," and then the two columns of "wives and apprentices runaway," I attacked with great resolution the editorial matter, and, reading it from beginning to end without understanding a syllable, conceived the possibility of its being Chinese, and so re-read it from the end to the beginning, but with no more satisfactory result. I was about throwing away, in disgust,

> This folio of four pages, happy work
> Which not even poets criticise, **5**

when I felt my attention somewhat aroused by the paragraph which follows:

"The avenues to death are numerous and strange. A London paper mentions the decease of a person from a singular cause. He was playing at 'puff the dart,' which is played with a long needle inserted in some worsted, and blown at a target through a tin tube. He placed the needle at the wrong end of the tube, and drawing his breath

---

1 A truffle, that edible subterranean fungus, which here apparently causes indigestion (dyspepsia)

2 A metal bar that keeps coals from falling onto the floor from a fireplace or stove

3 These works are, in Poe's opinion, overlong, boring, and indigestible.
　　Richard Glover (1712–85) was the English poet whose *Leonidas* (1737, enlarged 1770) was an epic poem that owed its success in part to the use made of it by Prime Minister Walpole's opponents.
　　William Wilkie's (the "Scotch Homer") *The Epigoniad* was published in 1757.
　　Alphonse de Lamartine (1790–1869), French poet and statesman, was preoccupied with nature, religion, and love, and wrote in a subjective style that made him the first truly romantic French poet. His *Pilgrimage to the Holy Land* was published in 1835. See "The Murders in the Rue Morgue," n. 35.
　　Joel Barlow (1754–1812) had a lifelong ambition to write the great American epic, which he finally published in 1807 as *The Columbiad*. Unfortunately, it is a tedious and turgid work, modeled after Milton, and today read only by graduate students of American literature.
　　Henry Theodore Tuckerman (1813–71) was an American writer who authored serenely sympathetic books of criticism and a series of romantic travel books such as *Isabel, or Sicily* (1839). He had disliked "The Tell-Tale Heart."
　　Rufus W. Griswold (1815–57) was not only the executor of Poe's estate (and his malicious biographer) but the editor of *Curiosities of Literature* (1844), that gargantuan volume which, despite its pedantry, was for Poe a constant source of quotations and facts for his tales.

4 In a state of stupor

5 From Cowper's *Task*, IV, 50–51

---

6 In recent years, several manufacturers of toys have been accused of producing playthings that have done the same thing to unsuspecting children.

7 The dregs

8 Cockaigne, or Cockayne, was a legendary country described in medieval tales, where delicacies of food and drink were to be had for the taking, a land of idleness and luxury. London is sometimes called by this name, especially Cockney London, because the French once called the English *cocagne* men (i.e., *bons vivants*).

9 *Lafitte* (1836) was a novel by "Professor" Joseph Holt Ingraham, which Poe disliked for its many odd words, its bad construction, and its lack of unity. The pun is here on the French wine Château Lafite-Rothschild.

10 Wine-pipes and rum-puncheons are bulk containers for liquor. "Falstaffian" of course refers to Shakespeare's portly character in the Henry IV plays and *The Merry Wives of Windsor*.

11 A cylindrical iron flask with a spout in the top center, apparently of German origin

12 The large, broad-brimmed hat of the Cavaliers, who supported Charles I in the English civil war in the mid-seventeenth century

6 strongly to puff the dart forward with force, drew the needle into his throat. It entered the lungs, and in a few days killed him."

Upon seeing this I fell into a great rage, without exactly knowing why. "This thing," I exclaimed, "is a contemptible **7** falsehood—a poor hoax—the lees of the invention of some pitiable penny-a-liner—of some wretched concoctor of acci- **8** dents in Cocaigne. These fellows, knowing the extravagant gullibility of the age, set their wits to work in the imagination of improbably possibilities—of odd accidents, as they term them; but to a reflecting intellect (like mine," I added, in parentheses, putting my forefinger unconsciously to the side of my nose), "to a contemplative understanding such as I myself possess, it seems evident at once that the marvellous increase of late in these 'odd accidents' is by far the oddest accident of all. For my own part, I intend to believe nothing henceforward that has any thing of the 'singular' about it."

"Mein Gott, den, vat a vool you bees for dat!" replied one of the most remarkable voices I ever heard. At first I took it for a rumbling in my ears—such as a man sometimes experiences when getting very drunk—but, upon second thought, I considered the sound as more nearly resembling that which proceeds from an empty barrel beaten with a big stick; and, in fact, this I should have concluded it to be, but for the articulation of the syllables and words. I am by no means **9** naturally nervous, and the very few glasses of Lafitte which I had sipped served to embolden me a little, so that I felt nothing of trepidation, but merely uplifted my eyes with a leisurely movement, and looked carefully around the room for the intruder. I could not, however, perceive any one at all.

"Humph!" resumed the voice, as I continued my survey, "you mus pe so dronk as de pig, den, for not zee me as I zit here at your zide."

Hereupon I bethought me of looking immediately before my nose, and there, sure enough, confronting me at the table sat a personage nondescript, although not altogether inde- scribable. His body was a wine-pipe, or a rum-puncheon, or **10** something of that character, and had a truly Falstaffian air. In its nether extremity were inserted two kegs, which seemed to answer all the purposes of legs. For arms there dangled from the upper portion of the carcass two tolerably long bottles, with the necks outward for hands. All the head that **11** I saw the monster possessed of was like a Hessian canteen which resembles a large snuff-box with a hole in the middle of the lid. This canteen (with a funnel on its top, like a cavalier **12** cap slouched over the eyes) was set on edge upon the puncheon, with the hole toward myself; and through this hole, which seemed puckered up like the mouth of a very precise old maid, the creature was emitting certain rumbling and grumbling noises which he evidently intended for intelligible talk.

"I zay," said he, "you mos pe dronk as de pig, vor zit dare and not zee me zit ere; and I zay, doo, you most pe pigger vool as de goose, vor to dispelief vat iz print in de print. 'Tis de troof—dat it iz—eberry vord ob it."

"Who are you, pray?" said I, with much dignity, although somewhat puzzled; "how did you get here? and what is it you are talking about?"

"As vor ow I com'd ere," replied the figure, "dat iz none of your pizzness; and as vor vat I be talking apout, I be talk apout vat I tink proper; and as vor who I be, vy dat is de very ting I com'd here for to let you zee for yourzelf."

"You are a drunken vagabond," said I, "and I shall ring the bell and order my footman to kick you into the street."

"He! he! he!" said the fellow, "hu! hu! hu! dat you can't do."

"Can't do!" said I, "what do you mean?—I can't do what?"

"Ring de pell," he replied, attempting a grin with his little villainous mouth.

Upon this I made an effort to get up, in order to put my threat into execution; but the ruffian just reached across the table very deliberately, and hitting me a tap on the forehead with the neck of one of the long bottles, knocked me back into the arm-chair from which I had half arisen. I was utterly astounded; and, for a moment, was quite at a loss what to do. In the meantime, he continued his talk.

"You zee," said he, "it iz te bess vor zit still; and now you shall know who I pe. Look at me! I am te *Angel ov te Odd*."

"And odd enough, too," I ventured to reply; "but I was always under the impression that an angel had wings."

"Te wing!" he cried, highly incensed, "vat I pe do mit te wing? Mein Gott! do you take me vor a shicken?"

"No—oh, no!" I replied, much alarmed, "you are no chicken—certainly not."

"Well, den, zit still and pehabe yourself, or I'll rap you again mid me vist. It iz te shicken ab te wing, und te owl ab te wing, und te imp ab de wing, und te head-teuffel ab te **13** wing. Te angel ab *not* te wing, and I am te *Angel ov te Odd*."

"And your business with me at present is—is—"

"My pizzness!" ejaculated the thing, "vy vot a low-bred puppy you mos pe vor to ask a gentleman und an angel apout his pizzness!"

This language was rather more than I could bear, even from an angel; so, plucking up courage, I seized a salt-cellar which lay within reach, and hurled it at the head of the intruder. Either he dodged, however, or my aim was inaccurate; for all I accomplished was the demolition of the crystal which protected the dial of the clock upon the mantle-piece. As for the Angel, he evinced his sense of my assault by giving me two or three hard consecutive raps upon the forehead as before. These reduced me at once to submission, and I am almost ashamed to confess that, either through pain or vexation, there came a few tears into my eyes.

"Mein Gott!" said the Angel of the Odd, apparently much softened at my distress; "mein Gott, te man is eder ferry dronk or ferry sorry. You mos not trink it so strong—you mos put

13 Head devil

14 Literally, "cherrywater," a colorless cherry brandy. Poe may have intended a pun on *Kirch* (church), or merely on "water."

15 Gil Blas is the hero of Alain René Lesage's picaresque novel of the same name. Timid but audacious, well disposed but easily led astray, good-natured but without moral principles, Gil Blas is a delightful portrait of the weaknesses and foibles of human nature. Lesage (1668–1747) probably derived his story from an earlier, Spanish romance.

"A great deal of happiness and a little more of good sense" is the translation.

de water in te wine. Here, trink dis, like a goot veller, und don't gry now—don't!"

Hereupon the Angel of the Odd replenished my goblet (which was about a third full of Port) with a colorless fluid that he poured from one of his hand bottles. I observed that these bottles had labels about their necks, and that these labels were **14** inscribed "Kirschenwasser."

The considerate kindness of the Angel mollified me in no little measure; and, aided by the water with which he diluted my Port more than once, I at length regained sufficient temper to listen to his very extraordinary discourse. I cannot pretend to recount all that he told me, but I gleaned from what he said that he was the genius who presided over the *contretemps* of mankind, and whose business it was to bring about the *odd accidents* which are continually astonishing the skeptic. Once or twice, upon my venturing to express my total incredulity in respect to his pretensions, he grew very angry indeed, so that at length I considered it the wiser policy to say nothing at all, and let him have his own way. He talked on, therefore, at great length, while I merely leaned back in my chair with my eyes shut, and amused myself with munching raisins and filliping the stems about the room. But, by-and-by, the Angel suddenly construed this behavior of mine into contempt. He arose in a terrible passion, slouched his funnel down over his eyes, swore a vast oath, uttered a threat of some character which I did not precisely comprehend, and finally made me a low bow and departed, wishing me, in the language of the archbishop in Gil-Blas, *"beaucoup de bonheur et un peu plus* **15** *de bon sens."*

His departure afforded me relief. The *very* few glasses of Lafitte that I had sipped had the effect of rendering me drowsy, and I felt inclined to take a nap of some fifteen or twenty minutes, as is my custom after dinner. At six I had an appointment of consequence, which it was quite indispensable that I should keep. The policy of insurance for my dwelling-house had expired the day before; and, some dispute having arisen, it was agreed that, at six, I should meet the board of directors of the company and settle the terms of a renewal. Glancing upward at the clock on the mantel-piece (for I felt too drowsy to take out my watch), I had the pleasure to find that I had still twenty-five minutes to spare. It was half-past five; I could easily walk to the insurance office in five minutes; and my usual siestas had never been known to exceed five and twenty. I felt sufficiently safe, therefore, and composed myself to my slumbers forthwith.

Having completed them to my satisfaction, I again looked toward the time-piece, and was half inclined to believe in the possibility of odd accidents when I found that, instead of my ordinary fifteen or twenty minutes, I had been dozing only three; for it still wanted seven and twenty of the appointed hour. I betook myself again to my nap, and at length a second time awoke, when, to my utter amazement, it *still* wanted twenty-seven minutes of six. I jumped up to examine the clock, and found that it had ceased running. My watch informed me that it was half past seven; and, of course, having slept two hours, I was too late for my appointment. "It will make no difference," I said: "I can call at the office in the morning and apologize; in the meantime what can be the matter with the clock?" Upon examining it I discovered that one of the raisin-stems which I had been filliping about the room during the discourse of the Angel of the Odd had flown through the fractured crystal, and lodging, singularly enough, in the key-hole, with an end projecting outward, had thus arrested the revolution of the minute hand.

"Ah!" said I; "I see how it is. This thing speaks for itself. A natural accident, such as *will* happen now and then!"

I gave the matter no further consideration, and at my usual hour retired to bed. Here, having placed a candle upon a reading stand at the bed head, and having made an attempt to peruse some pages of the "Omnipresence of the Deity," I **16** unfortunately fell asleep in less than twenty seconds, leaving the light burning as it was.

My dreams were terrifically disturbed by visions of the Angel of the Odd. Methought he stood at the foot of the couch, drew aside the curtains, and in the hollow, detestable tones of a rum-puncheon, menaced me with the bitterest vengeance for the contempt with which I had treated him. He concluded a long harangue by taking off his funnel-cap, inserting the tube into my gullet, and thus deluging me with an ocean of Kirschenwasser, which he poured, in a continuous flood, from one of the long-necked bottles that stood him instead of an arm. My agony was at length insufferable, and I awoke just in time to perceive that a rat had run off with the lighted candle from the stand, but *not* in season to prevent his making his escape with it through the hole. Very soon, a strong suffocating odor assailed my nostrils; the house, I clearly perceived, was on fire. In a few minutes the blaze broke forth with violence, and in an incredibly brief period the entire building was wrapped in flames. All egress from my chamber, except through a window, was cut off. The crowd, however, quickly procured and raised a long ladder. By means of this I was descending rapidly, and in apparent safety, when a huge hog, about whose rotund stomach, and indeed about whose whole air and physiognomy, there was something which reminded me of the Angel of the Odd—when this hog, I say, which hitherto had been quietly slumbering in the mud, took it suddenly into his head that his left shoulder needed scratching, and could find no more convenient rubbing-post than that afforded by the foot of the ladder. In an instant I was precipitated, and had the misfortune to fracture my arm.

This accident, with the loss of my insurance, and with the more serious loss of my hair, the whole of which had been singed off by the fire, predisposed me to serious impressions, so that, finally, I made up my mind to take a wife. There was a rich widow disconsolate for the loss of her seventh husband, and to her wounded spirit I offered the balm of my vows. She yielded a reluctant consent to my prayers. I knelt at her feet in gratitude and adoration. She blushed, and bowed her

16 See "Loss of Breath," note 26.

17 A hair preparation; see "Loss of Breath," note 16.

18 "To have a drop in one's eye" means to be visibly inebriated; "to take one's drops" means to drink heavily.

19 A method of catching crows. When they were thoroughly stupefied, the farmer could walk up to them and hit them over the head.

20 See "The Balloon-Hoax," note 26.

17 luxuriant tresses into close contact with those supplied me, temporarily, by Grandjean. I know not how the entanglement took place, but so it was. I rose with a shining pate, wigless; she in disdain and wrath, half buried in alien hair. Thus ended my hopes of the widow by an accident which could not have been anticipated, to be sure, but which the natural sequence of events had brought about.

Without despairing, however, I undertook the siege of a less implacable heart. The fates were again propitious for a brief period; but again a trivial incident interfered. Meeting my betrothed in an avenue thronged with the *élite* of the city, I was hastening to greet her with one of my best-considered bows, when a small particle of some foreign matter, lodging in the corner of my eye, rendered me, for the moment, completely blind. Before I could recover my sight, the lady of my love had disappeared—irreparably affronted at what she chose to consider my premeditated rudeness in passing her by ungreeted. While I stood bewildered at the suddenness of this accident (which might have happened, nevertheless, to any one under the sun), and while I still continued incapable of sight, I was accosted by the Angel of the Odd, who proffered me his aid with a civility which I had no reason to expect. He examined my disordered eye with much gentleness and skill, informed me that I had a drop in it, and (whatever a "drop"
18 was) took it out, and afforded me relief.

I now considered it high time to die (since fortune had so determined to persecute me) and accordingly made my way to the nearest river. Here, divesting myself of my clothes (for there is no reason why we cannot die as we were born), I threw myself headlong into the current; the sole witness of my fate being a solitary crow that had been seduced into the
19 eating of brandy-saturated corn, and so had staggered away from his fellows. No sooner had I entered the water than this bird took it into its head to fly away with the most indispensable portion of my apparel. Postponing, therefore, for the present, my suicidal design, I just slipped my nether extremities into the sleeves of my coat, and betook myself to a pursuit of the felon with all the nimbleness which the case required and its circumstances would admit. But my evil destiny attended me still. As I ran at full speed, with my nose up in the atmosphere, and intent only upon the purloiner of my property, I suddenly perceived that my feet rested no longer upon *terra firma;* the fact is, I had thrown myself over a precipice, and should inevitably have been dashed to pieces but for my good fortune
20 in grasping the end of a long guide-rope, which depended from a passing balloon.

As soon as I sufficiently recovered my senses to comprehend the terrific predicament in which I stood or rather hung, I exerted all the power of my lungs to make that predicament known to the æronaut overhead. But for a long time I exerted myself in vain. Either the fool could not, or the villian would not perceive me. Meantime the machine rapidly soared, while my strength even more rapidly failed. I was soon upon the point of resigning myself to my fate, and dropping quietly into the sea, when my spirits were suddenly revived by hearing

". . . I had thrown myself over a precipice, and should inevitably have been dashed to pieces but for my good fortune in grasping the end of a long guide-rope, which depended from a passing balloon. *Artist unknown*

a hollow voice from above, which seemed to be lazily humming an opera air. Looking up, I perceived the Angel of the Odd. He was leaning with his arms folded, over the rim of the car; and with a pipe in his mouth, at which he puffed leisurely, seemed to be upon excellent terms with himself and the universe. I was too much exhausted to speak, so I merely regarded him with an imploring air.

For several minutes, although he looked me full in the face, he said nothing. At length removing carefully his meerschaum from the right to the left corner of his mouth, he condescended to speak.

"Who pe you," he asked, "und what der teuffel you pe do dare?"

To this piece of impudence, cruelty, and affectation, I could reply only by ejaculating the monosyllable "Help!"

"Elp!" echoed the ruffian—"not I. Dare iz te pottle—elp yourself, und pe tam'd!"

With these worda he let fall a heavy bottle of Kirschenwasser which, dropping precisely upon the crown of my head, caused me to imagine that my brains were entirely knocked out. Impressed with this idea, I was about to relinquish my hold and give up the ghost with a good grace, when I was arrested by the cry of the Angel, who bade me hold on.

"Old on!" he said; "don't pe in te urry—don't. Will you pe take de odder pottle, or ave you pe got zober yet and come to your zenzes?"

I made haste, hereupon, to nod my head twice—once in the negative, meaning thereby that I would prefer not taking the other bottle at present—and once in the affirmative, intending thus to imply that I *was* sober and *had* positively come to my senses. By these means I somewhat softened the Angel.

"Und you pelief, ten," he inquired, "at te last? You pelief, ten, in te possibility of te odd?"

I again nodded my head in assent.

"Und you are pelief in *me*, te Angel ov te Odd?"

I nodded again.

"Und you acknowledge tat you pe te blind dronk and te vool?"

I nodded once more.

"Put your right hand into your left hand preeches pocket, ten, in token ov your vull zubmizzion unto te Angel ov te Odd."

This thing, for very obvious reasons, I found it quite impossible to do. In the first place, my left arm had been broken in my fall from the ladder, and, therefore, had I let go my hold with the right hand, I must have let go altogether. In the second place, I could have no breeches until I came across the crow. I was therefore obliged, much to my regret, to shake my head in the negative—intending thus to give the Angel to understand that I found it inconvenient, just at that moment, to comply with his very reasonable demand! No sooner, however, had I ceased shaking my head than—

"Go to der teuffel, ten!" roared the Angel of the Odd.

In pronouncing these words, he drew a sharp knife across the guide-rope by which I was suspended, and as we then happened to be precisely over my own house (which, during my peregrinations, had been handsomely rebuilt), it so occurred that I tumbled headlong down the ample chimney and alit upon the dining-room hearth.

Upon coming to my senses (for the fall had very thoroughly stunned me), I found it about four o'clock in the morning. I lay outstretched where I had fallen from the balloon. My head grovelled in the ashes of an extinguished fire, while my feet reposed upon the wreck of a small table, overthrown, and amid the fragments of a miscellaneous dessert, intermingled with a newspaper, some broken glass and shattered bottles, and an empty jug of the Schiedam Kirschenwasser. Thus revenged himself the Angel of the Odd.

21 Schiedam, in the Netherlands west of Rotterdam, is famous for its gin.

THE FACTS IN THE CASE OF M. VALDEMAR

First published in the *American Review*, December 1845.

At least one editor rejected the story before it was finally published, which is not surprising, considering the nature of the subject. Poe revised the manuscript slightly, correcting several misprints after its appearance in 1845, but it was never published by itself again.

Poe was surprised that many readers believed the story to be true, since he had not intended it as a hoax, but given both the realistic tone of the narrative and the beliefs of the period, it should not be surprising that the fiction was regarded as fact.

The story itself is in part a continuation of "Mesmeric Revelation." To the basic theme of hypnosis stalling the onset of death, Poe adds material suggested by several sources familiar to him. One of these is a letter by Dr. Sidney Doane, of New York, printed in the *Broadway Journal* in February 1845, which tells of the removal of a tumor from a woman who had been hypnotized. Another source is Chauncey Hare Townshend's *Facts in Mesmerism* (London, 1844), which asserts that, in one case, a man's life was prolonged two months through hypnosis.

Still another source is Justinus Andreas Kerner's *The Seeress of Prevorst*, in its translation by Catherine Crowe (1845), which details the death of a woman while under mesmeric influence.

To a critic in the New York *Daily Tribune* who charged that, while the story was a good one it was far too fantastic to be taken literally, Poe replies in the *Broadway Journal*, December 13, 1845: "For our part we find it difficult to understand how any dispassionate transcendentalist can doubt the facts as we state them; they are by no means so incredible as the marvels which are hourly narrated, and believed, on the topic of Mesmerism. *Why* cannot a man's death be postponed indefinitely by Mesmerism? *Why* cannot a man talk after he is dead? *Why?*—*Why?*—that is the question; and as soon as the Tribune has answered it to our satisfaction we will talk to it farther." Poe's comments echo his reaction after "The Balloon Hoax."

A Boston mesmerist, Robert H. Collyer, wrote to Poe: "Your account of M. Valdemar's case has been universally copied in this city, and has created a very great sensation. . . . I have not the least doubt of the *possibility* of such a phenomenon; for I did actually restore to active animation a person who died from excessive drinking of ardent spirits. . . . I will give you the detailed account on your reply to this, which I require for publication, in order to put at rest the growing impression that your account is merely a *splendid creation* of your own brain, not having any truth in fact." Poe printed the letter in the *Broadway Journal*, December 27, 1845, emphasizing once again that while the story was not based on fact, it very well could have been. One would like to hear more about Collyer's amazing feat.

The story was taken up and reprinted several times, sometimes as fiction, sometimes as fact. Elizabeth Barrett Browning, in a letter to Poe, tells him, "There is a tale of yours which I do not find in this volume [*The Raven and Other Poems* (1845), which Poe dedicated to her], but which is going the rounds of the newspapers, about Mesmerism, throwing us all into—dreadful doubts as to whether it can be true, as the children say of ghost stories. The certain thing in the tale in question is the power of the writer, and the faculty he has of making horrible improbilities seem near and familiar."

Two stories that seem to have been influenced by Poe's tale are Jules Verne's *Mathias Sandorf*, in which a doctor uses mesmerism to attempt a delay in the death of a young man, and H. P. Lovecraft's "Cool Air" (1928), about a scientist who keeps himself alive after death through a refrigeration device. The plot in the Lovecraft tale is different, but the tone and dialogue are remarkably similar:

" 'The end,' ran that noisome scrawl, 'is here. No more ice—the man looked and ran away. Warmer every minute, and the tissues can't last. I fancy you know—what I said about the will and the nerves and the preserved body after the organs ceased to work. It was a good theory, but couldn't keep up indefinitely. There was a gradual deterioration. . . . And the organs never would work again. It had to be done my way—artificial preservation—*for you see I died that time eighteen years ago.*' "

"Valdemar" appeared in the first issue of *Amazing Stories* (1926), where the story was dubbed a work of "scientifiction." "Science fiction" had not yet been coined.

Although the resemblance is slight, C. S. Lewis admits that his third novel of the Perelandra trilogy, *That Hideous Strength* (1946), had its basis in a dream that was "inspired" by Poe's tale:

"In his diary of 12 September 1923: 'I had a most horrible dream. By a certain poetic justice it turned on the idea Jenkin and I were going to use in our shocker play; namely that of a scientist discovering how to keep consciousness and some motor nerves alive in a corpse, at the same time arresting decay, so that you really had an immortal dead man. I dreamed that the horrible thing was sent to us—in a coffin of course—to take care of. . . . It escaped and I fancy ran amok. I am not sure that the idea of the play did not originate in another dream I had some years ago—unless the whole thing comes from Edgar Allan Poe.' " (*C. S. Lewis: a Biography,* by Roger Lancelyn Green and Walter Hooper, Harcourt, 1974; p. 175)

Film versions include *Master of Horror* (*Masterpieces of Horror* or *Masterworks of Horror*), an Argentinian production from 1960, but released in the United States in 1965; and *Tales of Terror* (*Poe's Tales of Terror*), in part drawn from "Valdemar," directed by Roger Corman in 1962. The mesmerism sequence, with Basil Rathbone, Debra Paget, and Vincent Price, has its moments.

Basil Rathbone reads a spine-tingling version on disc (Caedmon TC 1115). If one wants to buy a recording of Poe, this is by far the best (also included are "The Pit and the Pendulum" and "The Cask of Amontillado").

---

1 It isn't surprising that many readers thought this was a factual case, so carefully crafted is the opening. The incident, the narrator tells us, has created extensive discussion, and heated argument. An unwary reader of the time, coming across this in a newspaper, might easily have been taken in.

At the same time, the opening paragraph works in more subtle ways. The narrator here sounds somewhat defensive about the entire matter. But is he objecting more to the "unpleasant misrepresentations," or to the "great deal of disbelief"? In other words, does he fear the repercussions from the distorted impression that is making the rounds—or is he merely concerned that nobody will acknowledge his achievement of keeping a man alive through hypnosis?

Whichever view one accepts, it is clear that he is defending his experiment, and that it is a position he finds difficult to maintain. One also wonders just what the *exaggerated* accounts have been, since what he relates here is clearly fantastic.

2 For more on Mesmer, see "Mesmeric Revelation," introductory note, and "A Tale of the Ragged Mountains," note 30.

3 At the very point of death; also *in extremis*

4 As is often the case, Poe's sly humor invades even the most serious of tales. Valdemar is a Danish-surnamed gentleman who lives in Harlem (a Dutch-named area of New York), who speaks and writes Polish, and who translates the works of Schiller and Rabelais under a Jewish pseudonym. Angeline Legrasso suggests that Poe may have had in mind Piero Maroncelli (1795–1846), a translator who in Poe's words was "suffering from severe illness, and from this it can scarcely be expected that he

Of course I shall not pretend to consider it any matter for wonder, that the extraordinary case of M. Valdemar has **1** excited discussion. It would have been a miracle had it not—especially under the circumstances. Through the desire of all parties concerned, to keep the affair from the public, at least for the present, or until we had farther opportunities for investigation—through our endeavors to effect this—a garbled or exaggerated account made its way into society, and became the source of many unpleasant misrepresentations, and, very naturally, of a great deal of disbelief.

It is now rendered necessary that I give the *facts*—as far as I comprehend them myself. They are, succinctly, these:

My attention, for the last three years, had been repeatedly **2** drawn to the subject of Mesmerism; and, about nine months ago, it occurred to me, quite suddenly, that in the series of experiments made hitherto, there had been a very remarkable and most unaccountable omission:—no person had as yet been **3** mesmerized *in articulo mortis.* It remained to be seen, first, whether, in such condition, there existed in the patient any susceptibility to the magnetic influence; secondly, whether, if any existed, it was impaired or increased by the condition; thirdly, to what extent, or for how long a period, the encroachments of Death might be arrested by the process. There were other points to be ascertained, but these most excited my curiosity—the last in especial, from the immensely important character of its consequences.

In looking around me for some subject by whose means I

might test these particulars, I was brought to think of my friend, M. Ernest Valdemar, the well-known compiler of the **4** "Bibliotheca Forensica," and author (under the *nom de plume* **5** of Issachar Marx) of the Polish versions of "Wallenstein" and **6** "Gargantua." M. Valdemar, who has resided principally at **7** Harlem, N. Y., since the year 1839, is (or was) particularly **8** noticeable for the extreme spareness of his person—his lower limbs much resembling those of John Randolph, and, also, for **9** the whiteness of his whiskers, in violent contrast to the blackness of his hair—the latter, in consequence, being very generally mistaken for a wig. His temperament was markedly nervous, and rendered him a good subject for mesmeric experiment. On two or three occasions I had put him to sleep **10** with little difficulty, but was disappointed in other results which his peculiar constitution had naturally led me to anticipate. His will was at no period positively, or thoroughly, under my control, and in regard to *clairvoyance*, I could **11** accomplish with him nothing to be relied upon. I always attributed my failure at these points to the disordered state of his health. For some months previous to my becoming acquainted with him, his physicians had declared him in a confirmed phthisis. It was his custom, indeed, to speak calmly **12** of his approaching dissolution, as of a matter neither to be **13** avoided nor regretted.

When the ideas to which I have alluded first occurred to me, it was of course very natural that I should think of M. Valdemar. I knew the steady philosophy of the man too well to apprehend any scruples from *him;* and he had no relatives in America who would be likely to interfere. I spoke to him frankly upon the subject; and, to my surprise, his interest seemed vividly excited. I say to my surprise; for, although he **14** had always yielded his person freely to my experiments, he had never before given me any tokens of sympathy with what I did. His disease was of that character which would admit of exact calculation in respect to the epoch of its termination in death; and it was finally arranged between us that he would send for me about twenty-four hours before the period announced by his physicians as that of his decease.

It is now rather more than seven months since I received, from M. Valdemar himself, the subjoined note:

MY DEAR P——, **15**
You may as well come *now*. D—— and F—— are agreed that I cannot hold out beyond to-morrow midnight; and I think they have hit the time very nearly.

VALDEMAR.

I received this note within half an hour after it was written, and in fifteen minutes more I was in the dying man's chamber. I had not seen him for ten days, and was appalled by the fearful alteration which the brief interval had wrought in him. His face wore a leaden hue; the eyes were utterly lustreless; and the emaciation was so extreme that the skin had been broken through by the cheek-bones. His expectoration was excessive. The pulse was barely perceptible. He retained,

will recover" (*Godey's Lady's Book*, June 1846; quoted in *PMLA*, September 1943).

"Waldemar" (but pronounced Valdemar) is the name of a series of Danish kings. However, Poe may have used it as a pun on the phrase *val de mort*, "valley of death." And since a friend once asked me if the "M" of "M. Valdemar" stood for Michael, let me add that it stands for "Monsieur."

5 A fictitious title

6 More humor: in Genesis 49:14, we read that "Issachar is a strong ass crouching down between two burdens." Samuel Butler, in *Hudibras*, writes, "Is't possible that you, whose ears/Are of the tribe of Issachar's . . ./Should yet be deaf against a noise/So roaring as the public voice?"

7 *Wallenstein* is a dramatic trilogy by Johann Christoph Friedrich von Schiller (1759–1805), which reflects his labor on a historical study of the Thirty Years' War, written in 1798–99. All Schiller's plays emphasize his idealism, high ethical principles, and insistence on freedom and the nobility of the spirit.

Gargantua, or actually, *Les grandes et inestimables cronicques du grand et énorme géant Gargantua* (1532), is a collection of legends about the giant by François Rabelais (c. 1490–1553). A remarkably successful book, it prompted Rabelais to write a history of Pantagruel, son of Gargantua, the same year.

8 In Poe's time, Harlem was a separate city, in fact a rural area until improved transportation facilities linked it with the rest of Manhattan. Named after the North Holland city, the Dutch settlement of Nieuw Haarlem was established by Peter Stuyvesant in 1658. It was a fashionable residential section in the decades following Poe's death.

9 John Randolph (1773–1833), a fellow Virginian, had died twelve years earlier. Known as "John Randolph of Roanoke," he served in the House of Representatives but lost his leadership after his break with Jefferson over the acquisition of Florida. His philosophy is best summed up in his own words: "I am an aristocrat. I love liberty: I hate equality"—a sentiment Poe could share completely.

In later years, however, he was a bizarre figure, known for his eccentricities and spells of dementia. Poe may have seen him under these conditions, since he was in Richmond a great deal and the allusion to Randolph could be a clue to Valdemar's own mental state.

10 There was a general belief that a high-strung person was more susceptible to the hypnotic state. Today, the consensus seems to be that a subject's susceptibility is more closely linked with his or her ability to concentrate and a lack of fear of or defenses against the process—neither a trait of a nervous disposition.

11 The O.E.D. gives 1847 for the first use of this word, even though it appeared in "Valdemar" two years before. In French, it means "keenness of perception; insight into things beyond the range of ordinary perception." In Poe's time, however, it came to mean the ability by some persons to perceive objects at a distance or concealed from sight, whether or not under mesmeric influence.

The narrator is treading on dangerous ground here, for he is trying to see what the "Other Side" is like—a knowledge granted only those who have actually died.

12 Pulmonary tuberculosis, a progressively wasting or consumptive condition, which afflicts the patient of "Mesmeric Revelation" and which took the life of Poe's wife (and perhaps his mother).

13 Perhaps a telegraphic pun referring to the tale's climax, since "dissolution" means both death and dissolving.

14 This is surprising, since the last line of the preceding paragraph tells us that Valdemar views death as "a matter neither to be avoided nor regretted." However, it may be that as long as there was no hope, he was resigned to his fate, but now that there is a chance to stave off death, he has changed his attitude.

15 "P——," of course, can be read as "Poe," but there is no reason to assume this is anything other than a ploy to lend plausibility to the first-person narrative. "D——" could be Dr. John W. Draper, a well-known professor at the New York University Medical School; Poe did not like him very much, as is obvious from the swipe in "Von Kempelen." "F——" could be Dr. John W. Francis, Poe's own physician as well as president of the Academy of Medicine.

16 A notebook

17 The reference here is to the stage of tuberculosis at which calcified deposits have built up in the lungs. Oftentimes, this calcification of the primary lesions arrests the disease by encapsulating the bacteria. In this case, however, the patient has developed a severe infection in which the lungs can no longer function. Only a quarter of Valdemar's lungs are capable of inhaling and exhaling. There are holes in the tissue, and at one point, the lung is actually "glued" to the ribcage.

Poe's descriptions here are quite accurate; he may have had access to some postmortem reports of consumption victims.

18 Not one to keep things simple, Poe gives Valdemar the finishing touch: a possible weakening of the arterial wall, which could rupture at any time, hemorrhage, and cause sudden death. Poor Valdemar is going to go—and soon.

19 Nurses in Poe's day were seldom the highly trained professionals we know. Florence Nightingale, founder of modern nursing, did not open her first school until 1860.

20 Mr. L——l has not been identified.

nevertheless, in a very remarkable manner, both his mental power and a certain degree of physical strength. He spoke with distinctness—took some palliative medicines without aid—and, when I entered the room, was occupied in penciling

16 memoranda in a pocket-book. He was propped up in the bed by pillows. Doctors D—— and F—— were in attendance.

After pressing Valdemar's hand, I took these gentlemen aside, and obtained from them a minute account of the patient's condition. The left lung had been for eighteen months in a semi-osseous or cartilaginous state, and was, of course, entirely useless for all purposes of vitality. The right, in its upper portion, was also partially, if not thoroughly ossified, while the lower region was merely a mass of purulent tubercles, running one into another. Several extensive perforations existed; and, at one point, permanent adhesion to the ribs had taken place. These appearances in the right lobe were of comparatively recent date. The ossification had proceeded with very unusual rapidity; no sign of it had been discovered a month before, and the adhesion had only been observed

17 during the three previous days. Independently of the phthisis,

18 the patient was suspected of aneurism of the aorta; but on this point the osseous symptoms rendered an exact diagnosis impossible. It was the opinion of both physicians that M. Valdemar would die about midnight on the morrow (Sunday). It was then seven o'clock on Saturday evening.

On quitting the invalid's bed-side to hold conversation with myself, Doctors D—— and F—— had bidden him a final farewell. It had not been their intention to return; but, at my request, they agreed to look in upon the patient about ten the next night.

When they had gone, I spoke freely with M. Valdemar on the subject of his approaching dissolution, as well as, more particularly, of the experiment proposed. He still professed himself quite willing and even anxious to have it made, and urged me to commence it at once. A male and a female nurse were in attendance; but I did not feel myself altogether at liberty to engage in a task of this character with no more reliable witnesses than these people, in case of sudden

19 accident, might prove. I therefore postponed operations until about eight the next night, when the arrival of a medical student with whom I had some acquaintance, (Mr. Theodore

20 L——l,) relieved me from farther embarrassment. It had been my design, originally, to wait for the physicians; but I was induced to proceed, first, by the urgent entreaties of M. Valdemar, and secondly, by my conviction that I had not a moment to lose, as he was evidently sinking fast.

Mr. L——l was so kind as to accede to my desire that he would take notes of all that occurred; and it is from his memoranda that what I now have to relate is, for the most part, either condensed or copied *verbatim*.

It wanted about five minutes of eight when, taking the patient's hand, I begged him to state, as dictinctly as he could, to Mr. L——l, whether he (M. Valdemar) was entirely willing that I should make the experiment of mesmerizing him in his then condition.

He replied feebly, yet quite audibly, "Yes, I wish to be mesmerized"—adding immediately afterwards, "I fear you have deferred it too long." **21**

While he spoke thus, I commenced the passes which I had already found most effectual in subduing him. He was evidently **22** influenced with the first lateral stroke of my hand across his forehead; but although I exerted all my powers, no farther perceptible effect was induced until some minutes after ten o'clock, when Doctors D—— and F—— called, according to appointment. I explained to them, in a few words, what I designed, and as they opposed no objection, saying that the patient was already in the death agony, I proceeded without hesitation—exchanging, however, the lateral passes for downward ones, and directing my gaze entirely into the right eye of the sufferer.

By this time his pulse was imperceptible and his breathing was stertorous, and at intervals of half a minute. **23**

This condition was nearly unaltered for a quarter of an hour. At the expiration of this period, however, a natural although a very deep sigh escaped the bosom of the dying man, and the stertorous breathing ceased—that is to say, its stertorousness was no longer apparent; the intervals were undiminished. The patient's extremities were of an icy coldness.

At five minutes before eleven I perceived unequivocal signs of the mesmeric influence. The glassy roll of the eyes was changed for that expression of uneasy *inward* examination **24** which is never seen except in cases of sleep-waking, and which it is quite impossible to mistake. With a few rapid lateral passes I made the lids quiver, as in incipient sleep, and with a few more I closed them altogether. I was not satisfied, however, with this, but continued the manipulations vigorously, and with the fullest exertion of the will, until I had completely stiffened the limbs of the slumberer, after placing them in a seemingly easy position. The legs were at full length; the arms were nearly so, and reposed on the bed at a moderate distance from the loins. The head was very slightly elevated.

When I had accomplished this, it was fully midnight, and I requested the gentlemen present to examine M. Valdemar's condition. After a few experiments, they admitted him to be in an unusually perfect state of mesmeric trance. The curiosity of both the physicians was greatly excited. Dr. D—— resolved at once to remain with the patient all night, while Dr. F—— took leave with a promise to return at daybreak. Mr. L——l and the nurses remained.

We left M. Valdemar entirely undisturbed until about three o'clock in the morning, when I approached him and found him in precisely the same condition as when Dr. F—— went away—that is to say, he lay in the same position; the pulse was imperceptible; the breathing was gentle (scarcely noticeable, unless through the application of a mirror to the lips);

21 Apparently Valdemar knows he is nearing death, but it would seem that as long as he is still breathing, it is not "too late" to put him in the mesmeric trance. Or does he have an inkling of things to come?

22 For an explanation of the "mesmeric pass," see "Mesmeric Revelation," note 16.

23 i.e., gasping

24 Hypnotized patients do not normally focus on objects or people immediately in front of them. See "Mesmeric Revelation," note 3.

the eyes were closed naturally; and the limbs were as rigid and as cold as marble. Still, the general appearance was certainly not that of death.

As I approached M. Valdemar I made a kind of half effort to influence his right arm into pursuit of my own, as I passed the latter gently to and fro above his person. In such experiments with this patient I had never perfectly succeeded before, and assuredly I had little thought of succeeding now; but to my astonishment, his arm very readily, although feebly, followed every direction I assigned it with mine. I determined to hazard a few words of conversation.

"M. Valdemar," I said, "are you asleep?" He made no answer, but I peceived a tremor about the lips, and was thus induced to repeat the question, again and again. At its third repetition, his whole frame was agitated by a very slight shivering; the eye-lids unclosed themselves so far as to display a white line of the ball; the lips moved sluggishly, and from between them, in a barely audible whisper, issued the words:

25 "Yes;—asleep now. Do not wake me!—let me die so!"

I here felt the limbs and found them as rigid as ever. The right arm, as before, obeyed the direction of my hand. I questioned the sleep-waker again:

"Do you still feel pain in the breast, M. Valdemar?"

25 This recalls the question asked by a patient of the French mesmerist DuPotet: "Why do you call me back to life? If you would only go away, this body which oppresses me would grow cold, and my soul would no longer be here on your return. I should then be perfectly happy."

"Yes; —asleep now. Do not wake me!—let me die so!"
Illustration by Johann Friedrich Vogel

The answer now was immediate, but even less audible than before:

"No pain—I am dying."

I did not think it advisable to disturb him farther just then, and nothing more was said or done until the arrival of Dr. F——, who came a little before sunrise, and expressed unbounded astonishment at finding the patient still alive. After feeling the pulse and applying a mirror to the lips, he requested me to speak to the sleep-waker again. I did so, saying:

"M. Valdemar, do you still sleep?"

As before, some minutes elapsed ere a reply was made; and during the interval the dying man seemed to be collecting his energies to speak. At my fourth repetition of the question, he said very faintly, almost inaudibly:

"Yes; still asleep—dying."

It was now the opinion, or rather the wish, of the physicians, that M. Valdemar should be suffered to remain undisturbed in his present apparently tranquil condition, until death should supervene—and this, it was generally agreed, must now take place within a few minutes. I concluded, however, to speak to him once more, and merely repeated my previous question.

While I spoke, there came a marked change over the countenance of the sleep-waker. The eyes rolled themselves slowly open, the pupils disappearing upwardly; the skin generally assumed a cadaverous hue, resembling, not so much parchment as white paper; and the circular hectic spots which, **26** hitherto, had been strongly defined in the centre of each cheek, *went out* at once. I use this expression, because the suddenness of their departure put me in mind of nothing so much as the extinguishment of a candle by a puff of the breath. The upper lip, at the same time, writhed itself away from the teeth, which it had previously covered completely; while the lower jaw fell with an inaudible jerk, leaving the mouth widely extended, and disclosing in full view the swollen and blackened tongue. I presume that no member of the party then present **27** had been unaccustomed to death-bed horrors; but so hideous beyond conception was the appearance of M. Valdemar at this moment, that there was a general shrinking back from the region of the bed.

I now feel that I have reached a point of this narrative at which every reader will be startled into positive disbelief. It is my business, however, simply to proceed. **28**

There was no longer the faintest sign of vitality in M. Valdemar; and concluding him to be dead, we were consigning him to the charge of the nurses, when a strong vibratory motion was observable in the tongue. This continued for perhaps a minute. At the expiration of this period, there issued from the distended and motionless jaws a voice—such as it would be madness in me to attempt describing. There are, indeed, two or three epithets which might be considered as applicable to it in part; I might say, for example, that the sound was harsh, and broken and hollow; but the hideous whole is indescribable, for the simple reason that no similar

26 Flushed, red, feverish

27 The swollen, blackened tongue may be the result of losing body fluids and blood through his coughing earlier, or it may be a sign that despite the mesmeric trance, decay has already begun to set in.

28 A nice touch; the narrator's comments add both a feeling of truth and a sense of something horrible yet to come.

29 The voice must have a hollow, faraway sound. The cavernous quality suggests the underground tomb, such as the one in which Roderick Usher buries his sister, or the catacombs of "The Cask of Amontillado."

In Jules Verne's *Mathias Sandorf*, a doctor produces "one of these physiological effects in which *will* plays such a large part . . . endowed with an amazing power of suggestion, he was able by the penetration of his look, unaided by magnesium flare or shining focus, to provoke in the young man, at that moment dying, a hypnotic state and substitute his will for that of the sufferer. . . ."

30 The "gelatinous" voice is another fine touch, particularly in light of the climax of the story.

31 A glance at *Bartlett's Familiar Quotations* shows that almost half of the allusions to sleep are actually about death. For the physiological similarities between the mesmeric state and sleep, see "Mesmeric Revelation," note 16.

32 Another comic element, even while the story approaches its shocking conclusion

33 Valdemar's refusal to speak shows that the narrator is no longer in control and that anything can happen from now on.

34 From Justinus Kerner's *The Seeress of Prevorst* (1845): "Once, when she appeared dead, some one having uttered my name, she started into life again, and seemed unable to die—the magnetic relation between us not yet broken. She was, indeed, susceptible to magnetic influence to the last; for, when she was already cold, and her jaws stiff, her mother having made three passes over her face, she lifted her eyelids and moved her lips. At ten o'clock her sister saw a tall bright form enter the chamber, and at the same instant, the dying woman uttered a loud cry of joy; her spirit seemed then to be set free. After a short interval, her soul also departed, leaving behind it a totally irrecognizable husk—not a single trace of her features remaining."

This sounds a bit like "Ligeia," as well.

sounds have ever jarred upon the ear of humanity. There were two particulars, nevertheless, which I thought then, and still think, might fairly be stated as characteristic of the intonation—as well adapted to convey some idea of its unearthly peculiarity. In the first place, the voice seemed to reach our ears—at least mine—from a vast distance, or from some deep cavern within **29** the earth. In the second place, it impressed me (I fear, indeed, that it will be impossible to make myself comprehended) as **30** gelatinous or glutinous matters impress the sense of touch.

I have spoken both of "sound" and of "voice." I mean to say that the sound was one of distinct—of even wonderfully, thrilling distinct—syllabification. M. Valdemar *spoke*—obviously in reply to the question I had propounded to him a few minutes before. I had asked him, it will be remembered, if he still slept. He now said:

"Yes;—no;—I *have been* sleeping—and now—now—*I am* **31** dead."

No person present even affected to deny, or attempted to repress, the unutterable, shuddering horror which these few words, thus uttered, were so well calculated to convey. Mr. **32** L——l (the student) swooned. The nurses immediately left the chamber, and could not be induced to return. My own impressions I would not pretend to render intelligible to the reader. For nearly an hour, we busied ourselves, silently—without the utterance of a word—in endeavors to revive Mr. L——l. When he came to himself, we addressed ourselves again to an investigation of M. Valdemar's condition.

It remained in all respects as I have last described it, with the exception that the mirror no longer afforded evidence of respiration. An attempt to draw blood from the arm failed. I should mention, too, that this limb was no farther subject to my will. I endeavored in vain to make it follow the direction of my hand. The only real indication, indeed, of the mesmeric influence, was now found in the vibratory movement of the tongue, whenever I addressed M. Valdemar a question. He seemed to be making an effort to reply, but had no longer **33** sufficient volition. To queries put to him by any other person than myself he seemed utterly insensible—although I endeavored to place each member of the company in mesmeric *rapport* with him. I believe that I have now related all that is necessary to an understanding of the sleep-waker's state at this epoch. Other nurses were procured; and at ten o'clock I left the house in company with the two physicians and Mr. L——l.

In the afternoon we all called again to see the patient. His condition remained precisely the same. We had now some discussion as to the propriety and feasibility of awakening him; but we had little difficulty in agreeing that no good purpose would be served by so doing. It was evident that, so far, death (or what is usually termed death) had been arrested by the **34** mesmeric process. It seemed clear to us all that to awaken M. Valdemar would be merely to insure his instant, or at least his speedy dissolution.

From this period until the close of last week—*an interval*

of nearly seven months—we continued to make daily calls at M. Valdemar's house, accompanied, now and then, by medical and other friends. All this time the sleep-waker remained *exactly* as I have last described him. The nurses' attentions were continual.

It was on Friday last that we finally resolved to make the experiment of awakening, or attempting to awaken him; and it is the (perhaps) unfortunate result of this latter experiment which has given rise to so much discussion in private circles— to so much of what I cannot help thinking unwarranted popular feeling. **35**

For the purpose of relieving M. Valdemar from the mesmeric trance, I made use of the customary passes. These, for a time, were unsuccessful. The first indication of revival was afforded by a partial descent of the iris. It was observed, as especially remarkable, that this lowering of the pupil was accompanied by the profuse out-flowing of a yellowish ichor (from beneath the lids) of a pungent and highly offensive odor.

It was now suggested that I should attempt to influence the patient's arm, as heretofore. I made the attempt and failed. Dr. F—— then intimated a desire to have me put a question. I did so, as follows:

"M. Valdemar, can you explain to us what are your feelings or wishes now?"

There was an instant return of the hectic circles on the cheeks; the tongue quivered, or rather rolled violently in the mouth (although the jaws and lips remained rigid as before;) and at length the same hideous voice which I have already described, broke forth:

"For God's sake!—quick!—quick!—put me to sleep—or, quick!—waken me!—quick!—*I say to you that I am dead!*" **36**

I was thoroughly unnerved, and for an instant remained undecided what to do. At first I made an endeavor to re-compose the patient; but, failing in this through total abeyance of the will, I retraced my steps and as earnestly struggled to awaken him. In this attempt I soon saw that I should be successful—or at least I soon fancied that my success would be complete—and I am sure that all in the room were prepared to see the patient awaken.

For what really occurred, however, it is quite impossible that any human being could have been prepared.

As I rapidly made the mesmeric passes, amid ejaculations of "dead! dead!" absolutely *bursting* from the tongue and not from the lips of the sufferer, his whole frame at once—within the space of a single minute, or even less, shrunk—crumbled— absolutely *rotted* away beneath my hands. Upon the bed, before that whole company, there lay a nearly liquid mass of loathsome—of detestable putridity **37**

35 While the narrator considers this a purely scientific experiment, others regard it as a blasphemous meddling in matters he has no business with. The same attitudes prevail in Mary Shelley's *Frankenstein* (1818).

36 Valdemar hangs in a limbo between life and death, and he naturally wants to be allowed to go one way or the other. The narrator is playing God, dangling his friend by a promise of immortality that he cannot really keep.

37 Poe's final manuscript substitutes "putridity" for "putrescence." Somehow "putridity" isn't as effective as "putrescence"—it sounds a bit too clinical. But "*putrescence*"—now, *there's* a word. Basil Rathbone, in his recording of the tale, uses "putrescence," endowing it with all the disgust his mellifluous voice can summon up.

THE SPHINX

First published in *Arthur's Ladies' Magazine*, January 1846, this tale is seldom read or critically discussed. Inspired—if that is the word—by Poe's work with Thomas Wyatt on the latter's *Synopsis of Natural History* (as a complier) in 1839, the tale points out once again that things are not always what they seem.

1 Cholera had been endemic in the Ganges area for centuries, but in 1817 a particularly severe epidemic began to spread outside India by means of the English ships and troops that were now on the scene. The disease moved slowly overland, but ships quickly carried cholera to the East by 1822. War and troop movements carried the disease into the Baltic by 1831, and then to England. In the next year, it hit Ireland, and Irish immigrants took it with them to Canada, where it filtered southward into the United States in 1832 and Mexico in 1833. By 1874, it had burned itself out in both Western Europe and North America.

For more on cholera, see McNeill, *Plagues and Peoples*, Anchor/Doubleday, 1976; pp. 261–76.

2 A product of the picturesque cult of the late-eighteenth and early-nineteenth centuries in England, this was an artfully rustic building with a thatched roof and rough-hewn wooden timbers.

3 "And earth, and stars, and sea, and sky/Are redolent of sleep. . . ." (Poe's *Seranade*, lines 14–15)

It was common opinion that diseases such as cholera and yellow fever were caused by "bad air" (the meaning of malaria in Italian). In some cases, cannons were fired to create air movement, in the belief that the "miasma" would dissipate, as in a memorable scene in the Bette Davis film *Jezebel* (1938).

4 " 'Now the popular opinion, under certain conditions, is not to be disregarded. When arising of itself—when manifesting itself in a strictly spontaneous manner—we should look upon it as analogous with that *intuition* which is the idiosyncrasy of the individual man of genius.' " (Dupin, in "The Mystery of Marie Rogêt")

1 During the dread reign of cholera in New York, I had accepted the invitation of a relative to spend a fortnight with him in the
2 retirement of his *cottage orné* on the banks of the Hudson. We had here around us all the ordinary means of summer amusement; and what with rambling in the woods, sketching, boating, fishing, bathing, music, and books, we should have passed the time pleasantly enough, but for the fearful intelligence which reached us every morning from the populous city. Not a day elapsed which did not bring us news of the decease of some acquaintance. Then, as the fatality increased, we learned to expect daily the loss of some friend. At length we trembled at the approach of every messenger. The very
3 air from the South seemed to us redolent with death. That palsying thought, indeed, took entire possession of my soul. I could neither speak, think, nor dream of anything else. My host was of a less excitable temperament, and, although greatly depressed in spirits, exerted himself to sustain my own. His richly philosophical intellect was not at any time affected by unrealities. To the substances of terror he was sufficiently
4 alive, but of its shadows he had no apprehension.

His endeavors to arouse me from the condition of abnormal gloom into which I had fallen, were frustrated, in great measure, by certain volumes which I had found in his library. These were of a character to force into germination whatever seeds of hereditary superstition lay latent in my bosom. I had been reading these books without his knowledge, and thus he was often at a loss to account for the forcible impressions which had been made upon my fancy.

A favorite topic with me was the popular belief in omens—a belief which, at this one epoch of my life, I was almost seriously disposed to defend. On this subject we had long and animated discussions; he maintaining the utter groundlessness of faith in such matters, I contending that a popular sentiment arising with absolute spontaneity—that is to say, without apparent traces of suggestion—had in itself the unmistakable elements of truth, and was entitled to much respect.

The fact is, that soon after my arrival at the cottage there had occurred to myself an incident so entirely inexplicable, and which had in it so much of the portentous character, that I might well have been excused for regarding it as an omen. It appalled, and at the same time so confounded and bewildered me, that many days elapsed before I could make up my mind to communicate the circumstance to my friend.

Near the close of an exceedingly warm day, I was sitting, book in hand, at an open window, commanding, through a long vista of the river banks, a view of a distant hill, the face of which nearest my position had been denuded by what is termed a land-slide, of the principal portion of its trees. My thoughts had been long wandering from the volume before me to the gloom and desolation of the neighboring city. Uplifting my eyes from the page, they fell upon the naked face of the hill, and upon an object—upon some living monster of hideous conformation, which very rapidly made its way from the summit to the bottom, disappearing finally in the dense forest below. As this creature first came in sight, I doubted my own sanity—or at least the evidence of my own eyes—and many minutes passed before I succeeded in convincing myself that I was neither mad nor in a dream. Yet when I describe the monster (which I distinctly saw, and calmly surveyed through the whole period of its progress), my readers, I fear, will feel more difficulty in being convinced of these points than even I did myself.

Estimating the size of the creature by comparison with the diameter of the large trees near which it passed—the few giants of the forests which had escaped the fury of the land-slide—I concluded it to be far larger than any ship of the line in existence. I say ship of the line, because the shape of the monster suggested the idea—the hull of one of our seventy-fours might convey a very tolerable conception of the general **5** outline. The mouth of the animal was situated at the extremity of a proboscis some sixty or seventy feet in length, and about as thick as the body of an ordinary elephant. Near the root of this trunk was an immense quantity of black shaggy hair—more than could have been supplied by the coats of a score of buffaloes; and projecting from this hair downwardly and laterally, sprang two gleaming tusks not unlike those of the wild boar, but of infinitely greater dimension. Extending forward, parallel with the proboscis, and on each side of it, was a gigantic staff, thirty of forty feet in length, formed seemingly of pure crystal, and in shape a perfect prism:—it reflected in the most gorgeous manner the rays of the declining sun. The trunk was fashioned like a wedge with the apex to the earth. From it there were outspread two pairs of wings—each wing nearly one hundred yards in length—one pair being placed above the other, and all thickly covered with metal scales; each scale apparently some ten or twelve feet in diameter. I observed that the upper and lower tiers of wings were connected by a strong chain. But the chief peculiarity of this horrible thing was the representation of a *Death's Head,* which covered nearly the whole surface of its breast, **6**

5 Warships with seventy-four guns

6 Poe borrows the death's-head for his scarab in "The Gold-Bug."

and which was as accurately traced in glaring white, upon the dark ground of the body, as if it had been there carefully designed by an artist. While I regarded this terrific animal, and more especially the appearance on its breast, with a feeling of horror and awe—with a sentiment of forthcoming evil, which I found it impossible to quell by any effort of the reason, I perceived the huge jaws at the extremity of the proboscis suddenly expand themselves, and from them there proceeded a sound so loud and so expressive of woe, that it struck upon my nerves like a knell, and as the monster disappeared at the foot of the hill, I fell at once, fainting, to the floor.

Upon recovering, my first impulse, of course, was to inform my friend of what I had seen and heard—and I can scarcely explain what feeling of repugnance it was which, in the end, operated to prevent me.

At length, one evening, some three of four days after the occurrence, we were sitting together in the room in which I had seen the apparition—I occupying the same seat at the same window, and he lounging on a sofa near at hand. The association of the place and time impelled me to give him an account of the phenomenon. He heard me to the end—at first laughed heartily—and then lapsed into an excessively grave demeanor, as if my insanity was a thing beyond suspicion. At this instant I again had a distinct view of the monster—to which, with a shout of absolute terror, I now directed his attention. He looked eagerly—but maintained that he saw nothing—although I designated minutely the course of the creature, as it made its way down the naked face of the hill.

I was now immeasurably alarmed, for I considered the vision either as an omen of my death, or, worse, as the forerunner of an attack of mania. I threw myself passionately back in my chair, and for some moments buried my face in my hands. When I uncovered my eyes, the apparition was no longer visible.

My host, however, had in some degree resumed the calmness of his demeanor, and questioned me very rigorously in respect to the conformation of the visionary creature. When I had fully satisfied him on his head, he sighed deeply, as if relieved of some intolerable burden, and went on to talk, with what I thought a cruel calmness, of various points of speculative philosophy, which had heretofore formed subject of discussion between us. I remember his insisting very especially (among other things) upon the idea that the principal source of error in all human investigations lay in the liability of the understanding to under-rate or to over-value the importance of an object, through mere misadmeasurement of its propinquity. "To estimate properly, for example," he said, "the influence to be exercised on mankind at large by the thorough diffusion of Democracy, the distance of the epoch at which such diffusion may possibly be accomplished should not fail to form an item in the estimate. Yet can you tell me one writer on the subject of government who has ever thought this particular **7** branch of the subject worthy of discussion at all?"

7 While in "Some Words with a Mummy" and "Mellonta Tauta" Poe seems to have grave doubts about democracy, here he merely suggests that we are too close to it to judge it properly.

He here paused for a moment, stepped to a book-case, and brought forth one of the ordinary synopses of Natural History. Requesting me then to exchange seats with him, that he might the better distinguish the fine print of the volume, he took my arm-chair at the window, and, opening the book, resumed his discourse very much in the same tone as before.

"But for your exceeding minuteness," he said, "in describing the monster, I might never have had it in my power to demonstrate to you what it was. In the first place, let me read to you a school-boy account of the genus *Sphinx*, of the family *Crepuscularia*, of the order *Lepidoptera*, of the class of *Insecta*—or insects. The account runs thus: **8**

" 'Four membranous wings covered with little colored scales of metallic appearance; mouth forming a rolled proboscis, produced by an elongation of the jaws, upon the sides of which are found the rudiments of mandibles and downy palpi; the inferior wings retained to the superior by a stiff hair, antennæ in the form of an elongated club, prismatic; abdomen pointed. The Death's-headed Sphinx has occasioned much terror among the vulgar, at times, by the melancholy kind of cry which it utters, and the insignia of death which it wears upon its corslet.' " **9**

He here closed the book and leaned forward in the chair, placing himself accurately in the position which I had occupied at the moment of beholding "the monster."

"Ah, here it is," he presently exclaimed—"it is reascending the face of the hill, and a very remarkable looking creature I admit it to be. Still, it is by no means so large or so distant as you imagined it; for the fact is that, as it wriggles its way up this thread, which some spider has wrought along the window-sash, I find it to be about the sixteenth of an inch in its extreme length, and also about the sixteenth of an inch distant from the pupil of my eye."

8 The sphinx moth is a hawkmoth, of the family Sphingidae, which hovers over flowers, sucking their nectar through its long proboscis (through which it can also produce a rhythmic, muted squeek, according to the *Dictionary of Butterflies and Moths*, London, 1975).

9 This is quoted practically verbatim from Wyatt.

The Carolina Sphinx. *Artist unknown*

THE DOMAIN OF ARNHEIM

First published in *Columbian Lady's and Gentleman's Magazine*, March 1847, this is an expansion of "The Landscape Garden," published in Snowden's *Ladies' Companion*, October 1842. The earlier tale is omitted in this collection, since it is essentially the same as the first fifteen paragraphs of "The Domain of Arnheim."

Both tales represent an effort to combine the essay form with that of the tale, but the later version is much more readable than the first. The sources include Prince Hermann von Pückler-Muskau's (1785–1871) *Tour in England, Ireland and France* (1833) and a review of Andrew J. Downing's *A Treatise on the Theory and Practice of Landscape Gardening* (1841). Downing (1815–52), the son of a nurseryman and from the beginning an enthusiast for landscape and plants, became America's leading writer on landscape gardening, cottages, and country houses (see Hitchcock, *Architecture: Nineteenth and Twentieth Centuries*, Pelican Books, 1971).

In "The Poetic Principle," Poe writes: "The Poetic sentiment, of course, may develop itself in various modes—in Painting, in Sculpture, in Architecture, in the Dance, very especially in Music—and very peculiarly, and with a wide field, in the composition of the Landscape Garden."

It is obvious from his comments, and from the two stories (as well as "Landor's Cottage"), that Poe was impressed with the notion of improving on nature. He may have been inspired to enlarge and alter his earlier "Landscape Garden" after reading articles on William Beckford's Fonthill Abbey, in England, and on Edwin Forrest's villa "Fonthill Castle," overlooking the Hudson (and not far from Poe's own Fordham cottage), built in 1846. Forrest's home still stands, as the library of the College of Mount St. Vincent, in the Bronx.

Arnheim is the name of the ancestral home of the heroine of Walter Scott's *Ann of Geierstein* (1829)—as well as the name of a port on the lower Rhine, now in the Netherlands. Poe's attaching the name to the magical atmosphere of his tale is appropriate, for in Scott's novel, the Arnheim family is involved in sorcery.

"The Domain of Arnheim" remains a marvelous prose poem, similar in its beauty to the description of the early part of "Eleonora" and coming closer to that musical element which Poe so prized and strove so mightily to achieve in his poetry.

---

1 From "Christ's Victorie and Triumph in Heaven and Earth" (1610), by Giles Fletcher the Younger (1588–1623)), stanza 42. Poe may have found the lines in Samuel Carter Hall's *Book of Gems* (1836), which he reviewed in the *Southern Literary Messenger*, August 1836, or in an article on landscape gardening in *Arcturus*, June 1841.

2 When he was a boy, Poe often visited the home of John Allan's partner, Charles Ellis, which had a beautiful garden. Poe's invented name could be a combination of "Ellis" and "Thelluson" (of which more later on), although one could also make a psychological case for a wish by the young boy to be Ellis's son, instead of Allan's.

The garden like a lady fair was cut,
  That lay as if she slumbered in delight,
And to the open skies her eyes did shut.
  The azure fields of Heaven were 'sembled right
  In a large round set with the flowers of light.
The flowers de luce and the round sparks of dew
That hung from their azure leaves did shew
Like twinkling stars that sparkle in the evening blue.

1
                       —Giles Fletcher.

From his cradle to his grave a gale of prosperity bore my
2 friend Ellison along. Nor do I use the word prosperity in its mere worldly sense. I mean it as synonymous with happiness.

The person of whom I speak seemed born for the purpose of foreshadowing the doctrines of Turgot, Price, Priestley, and Condorcet—of exemplifying by individual instance what has **3** been deemed the chimera of the perfectionists. In the brief existence of Ellison I fancy that I have seen refuted the dogma, that in man's very nature lies some hidden principle, the antagonist of bliss. An anxious examination of his career has given me to understand that, in general, from the violation of a few simple laws of humanity arises the wretchedness of mankind—that as a species we have in our possession the as yet unwrought elements of content—and that, even now in the present darkness and madness of all thought on the great question of the social condition, it is not impossible that man, the individual, under certain unusual and highly fortuitous conditions, may be happy.

With opinions such as these my young friend, too, was fully imbued, and thus it is worthy of observation that the uninterrupted enjoyment which distinguished his life was, in great measure, the result of preconcert. It is indeed evident that with less of the instinctive philosophy which, now and then, stands so well in the stead of experience, Mr. Ellison would have found himself precipitated, by the very extraordinary success of his life, into the common vortex of unhappiness which yawns for those of preeminent endowments. But it is by no means my object to pen an essay on happiness. The ideas of my friend may be summed up in a few words. He admitted but four elementary principles, or more strictly, conditions, of bliss. That which he considered chief was (strange to say!) the simple and purely physical one of free exercise in the open air. "The health," he said, "attainable by other means is scarcely worth the name." He instanced the ecstasies of the fox-hunter, and pointed to the tillers of the earth, the only people who, as a class, can be fairly considered happier than others. His second condition was the love of woman. His third, and most difficult of realization, was the contempt of ambition. His fourth was an object of unceasing pursuit; and he held that, other things being equal, the extent of attainable happiness was in proportion to the spirituality of this object.

Ellison was remarkable in the continuous profession of good gifts lavished upon him by fortune. In personal grace and beauty he exceeded all men. His intellect was of that order to which the acquisition of knowledge is less a labor than an intuition and a necessity. His family was one of the most illustrious of the empire. His bride was the loveliest and most devoted of women. His possessions had been always ample; but on the attainment of his majority, it was discovered that one of those extraordinary freaks of fate had been played in his behalf which startle the whole social world amid which they occur, and seldom fail radically to alter the moral constitution of those who are their objects.

It appears that about a hundred years before Mr. Ellison's coming of age, there had died, in a remote province, one Mr. Seabright Ellison. This gentleman had amassed a princely

3 In "Lionizing," these authors are named in the section satirizing the human-perfectability philosophers (note 17), and in a review of *Lecture on the Study of History,* by Alexander Dimitry, in *Burton's,* July 1839, Poe calls them authors of "eloquent madness."

fortune, and, having no immediate connections, conceived the whim of suffering his wealth to accumulate for a century after his decease. Minutely and sagaciously directing the various modes of investment, he bequeathed the aggregate amount to the nearest of blood, bearing the name of Ellison, who should be alive at the end of the hundred years. Many attempts had been made to set aside this singular bequest; their *ex post facto* character rendered them abortive; but the attention of a jealous government was aroused, and a legislative act finally obtained, forbidding all similar accumulations. This act, however, did not prevent young Ellison from entering into possession, on his twenty-first birth-day, as the heir of his ancestor Seabright, a fortune of *four hundred and fifty millions* **4** *of dollars*.

When it had become known that such was the enormous wealth inherited, there were, of course, many speculations as to the mode of its disposal. The magnitude and the immediate availability of the sum bewildered all who thought on the topic. The possessor of any *appreciable* amount of money might have been imagined to perform any one of a thousand things. With riches merely surpassing those of any citizen, it would have been easy to suppose him engaging to supreme excess in the fashionable extravagances of his time—or busying himself with political intrigue—or aiming at ministerial power—or purchasing increase of nobility—or collecting large museums of *virtu*—or playing the munificent patron of letters, of science, of art—or endowing, and bestowing his name upon extensive institutions of charity. But for the inconceivable wealth in the actual possession of the heir, these objects and all ordinary objects were felt to afford too limited a field. Recourse was had to figures, and these but sufficed to confound. It was seen that, even at three per cent., the annual income of the inheritance amounted to no less than thirteen millions and five hundred thousand dollars; which was one million and one hundred and twenty-five thousand per month; or thirty-six thousand nine hundred and eight-six per day; or one thousand five hundred and forty-one per hour; or six and twenty dollars for every minute that flew. Thus the usual track of supposition was thoroughly broken up. Men knew not what to imagine. There were some who even conceived that Mr. Ellison would divest himself of at least one half of his fortune, as of utterly superfluous opulence—enriching whole troops of his relatives by division of his superabundance. To the nearest of these he did, in fact, abandon the very unusual wealth **5** which was his own before the inheritance.

I was not surprised, however, to perceive that he had long made up his mind on a point which had occasioned so much discussion to his friends. Nor was I greatly astonished at the nature of his decision. In regard to individual charities he had satisfied his conscience. In the possibility of any improvement, properly so called, being effected by man himself in the general condition of man, he had (I am sorry to confess it) little faith. Upon the whole, whether happily or unhappily, he was thrown back, in very great measure, upon self.

4 "An incident, similar in outline to the one here imagined, occurred, not very long ago, in England. The name of the fortunate heir was Thelluson. I first saw an account of this matter in the 'Tour' of Prince Puckler Muskau, who makes the sum inherited *ninety millions of pounds*, and justly observes that 'in the contemplation of so vast a sum, and of the services to which it might be applied, there is something even of the sublime.' To suit the views of this article I have followed the Prince's statement, although a grossly exaggerated one. The germ, and in fact, the commencement of the present paper was published many years ago—previous to the issue of the first number of Sue's admirable "*Juif Errant*," which may possibly have been suggested to him by Muskau's account." (Poe's note)

Poe added this note, as well as the last sentence of the paragraph, to the "Landscape Garden" text. Eugène Sue, the French novelist, published his *Wandering Jew* in 1844–45, while Poe's tale had appeared in 1842.

Thelluson's case was a famous one in the annals of English law, for it settled once and for all the question of whether testators could dispose of their estates so that the income could accumulate and form a large fortune, limited in favor of certain descendants. The litigation lasted nearly fifty years, and resembles that in Dickens' *Bleak House* (1852).

5 Poe, who was himself always just one step ahead of his creditors, must have found it ironic that some people could come by so much wealth so easily, and with so little work. At the same time, there is no denying his own wishful identification with Ellison.

In the widest and noblest sense he was a poet. He comprehended, moreover, the true character, the august aims, the supreme majesty and dignity of the poetic sentiment. The fullest, if not the sole proper satisfaction of this sentiment he instinctively felt to lie in the creation of novel forms of beauty. Some peculiarities, either in his early eduction, or in the nature of his intellect, had tinged with what is termed materialism all his ethical speculations; and it was this bias, perhaps, which led him to believe that the most advantageous at least, if not the sole legitimate field for the poetic exercise, lies in the creation of novel moods of purely *physical* loveliness. Thus it happened he became neither musician nor poet—if we use this latter term in its every-day acceptation. Or it might have been that he neglected to become either, merely in pursuance of his idea that in contempt of ambition is to be found one of the essential principles of happiness on earth. Is it not indeed, possible that, while a high order of genius is necessarily ambitious, the highest is above that which is termed ambition? And may it not thus happen that many far greater than Milton have contentedly remained "mute and inglorious"? I believe that the world has never seen—and **6** that, unless through some series of accidents goading the noblest order of mind into distasteful exertion, the world will never see—that full extent of triumphant execution, in the richer domains of art, of which the human nature is absolutely capable.

Ellison became neither musician nor poet; although no man lived more profoundly enamored of music and poetry. Under other circumstances than those which invested him, it is not impossible that he would have become a painter. Sculpture, although in its nature rigorously poetical, was too limited in its extent and consequences, to have occupied, at any time, much of his attention. And I have now mentioned all the provinces in which the common understanding of the poetic sentiment has declared it capable of expatiating. But Ellison maintained that the richest, the truest, and most natural, if not altogether the most extensive province, had been unaccountably neglected. No definition had spoken of the landscape-gardener as of the poet; yet it seemed to my friend that the creation of the landscape-garden offered to the proper Muse the most magnificent of opportunities. Here, indeed, was the fairest field for the display of imagination in the endless combining of forms of novel beauty; the elements to enter into combination being, by a vast superiority, the most glorious which the earth could afford. In the multiform and multicolor of the flower and the trees, he recognized the most direct and energetic efforts of Nature at physical loveliness. And in the direction or concentration of this effort—or, more properly, in its adaptation to the eyes which were to behold it on earth—he perceived that he should be employing the **7** best means—laboring to the greatest advantage—in the fulfilment, not only of his own destiny as poet, but of the august purposes for which the Deity had implanted the poetic sentiment in man.

6 "Some mute inglorious Milton here may rest,/Some Cromwell guiltless of his country's blood" (Thomas Gray, *Elegy Written in a Country Churchyard*, stanza 15).

7 "Beholding beauty with the eye of the mind, he will be enabled to bring forth, not images of beauty, but realities (for he has hold not of an image but of a reality), and bringing forth and nourishing virtue to become the friend of God and be immortal, if mortal man may" (Plato, *Dialogues*, "Symposium," 212).

8 Claude Gellée (1600–82, known professionally as Claude Lorrain) had a reputation as a landscape painter that long outlived him. His sources lie chiefly in the romanticized poetic landscapes of the later Mannerists, using the division of the picture into areas of dark greenish brown foreground, light green middle distance, and blue far distance, with trees treated as feathery fronds in silhouette. His chief effect is that of sunlight shimmering on water, or of the direct rays of the sun illuminating the picture.

9 "[The poet] will feel that there is no necessity to trick out or to elevate nature; and the more industriously he applies this principle, the deeper will be his faith that no words, which his fancy or imagination can suggest, will be compared with those which are the emanations of reality and truth" (Wordsworth, Preface to *Lyrical Ballads*, 1800).

"Consider, for one example, this peculiarity of Modern Literature, the sin that has been named View-hunting. In our elder writers, there are no paintings of scenery for its own sake; no euphuistic gallantries with Nature, but a constant heartlove of her, a constant dwelling in communion with her. View-hunting, with so much else that is of kin to it, first came decisively into action through the *Sorrows of Werther* [Goethe, 1774]. . . . Scarcely ever, til that late epoch, did any worshipper of Nature become entirely aware that he was worshipping, much to his own credit; and think of saying to himself: Come, let us make a description! Intolerable enough: when every puny whipster plucks out his pencil, and insists on painting you a sentence. . . ." (Carlyle, "Characteristics," 1831)

"Its adaptation to the eyes which were to behold it on earth." In his explanation of this phraseology, Mr. Ellison did much toward solving what has always seemed to me an enigma:—I mean the fact (which none but the ignorant dispute) that no such combination of scenery exists in nature as the painter of genius may produce. No such paradises are **8** to be found in reality as have glowed on the canvas of Claude. In the most enchanting of natural landscapes, there will always be found a defect or an excess—many excesses and defects. While the component parts may defy, individually, the highest skill of the artist, the arrangement of these parts will always be susceptible of improvement. In short, no position can be attained on the wide surface of the *natural* earth, from which an artistical eye, looking steadily, will not find matter of offence in what is termed the "composition" of the landscape. And yet how unintelligible is this! In all other matters we are justly instructed to regard nature as supreme. With her details we shrink from competition. Who shall presume to imitate the colors of the tulip, or to improve the proportions of the lily of the valley? The criticism which says, of sculpture or portraiture, that here nature is to be exalted or idealized rather than imitated, is in error. No pictorial or sculptural combinations of points of human loveliness do more than approach the living and breathing beauty. In landscape alone is the principle of the critic true, and, having felt its truth here, it is but the headlong spirit of generalization which has led him to pronounce it true throughout all the domains of **9** art. Having, I say, *felt* its truth here; for the feeling is no affectation or chimera. The mathematics afford no more absolute demonstrations than the sentiment of his art yields the artist. He not only believes, but positively knows, that such and such apparently arbitrary arrangements of matter constitute and alone constitute the true beauty. His reasons, however, have not yet been matured into expression. It remains for a more profound analysis than the world has yet seen, fully to investigate and express them. Nevertheless he is confirmed in his instinctive opinions by the voice of all his brethern. Let a "composition" be defective; let an emendation be wrought in its mere arrangement of form; let this emendation be submitted to every artist in the world; by each will its necessity be admitted. And even far more than this; in remedy of the defective composition, each insulated member of the fraternity would have suggested the identical emendation.

I repeat that in landscape arrangements alone is the phsyical nature susceptible of exaltation, and that, therefore, her susceptibility of improvement at this one point, was a mystery I had been unable to solve. My own thoughts on the subject had rested in the idea that the primitive intention of nature would have so arranged the earth's surface as to have fulfilled at all points man's sense of perfection in the beautiful, the sublime, or the picturesque; but that this primitive intention had been frustrated by the known geological disturbances— disturbances of form and color-grouping, in the correction or allaying of which lies the soul of art. The force of this idea was much weakened, however, by the necessity which it involved of considering the disturbances abnormal and unadapted to any purpose. It was Ellison who suggested that they are prognostic of *death*. He thus explained:—Admit the earthly immortality of man to have been the first intention. We have then the primitive arrangement of the earth's surface adapted to his blissful estate, as not existent but designed. The disturbances were the preparations for his subsequently conceived deathful condition.

"Now," said my friend, "what we regard as exaltation of the landscape may be really such, as respects only the mortal or human *point of view*. Each alteration of the natural scenery may possibly effect a blemish in the picture, if we can suppose this picture viewed at large—in mass—from some point distant from the earth's surface, although not beyond the limits of its atmosphere. It is easily understood that what might improve a closely scrutinized detail, may at the same time injure a general or more distinctly observed effect. There *may* be a class of beings, human once, but now invisible to humanity, to whom, from afar, our disorder may seem order—our unpicturesqueness picturesque; in a word, the earth-angels, for whose scrutiny more especially than our own, and for whose death-refined appreciation of the beautiful, may have been set in array by God the wide landscape-gardens of the hemispheres."

In the course of discussion, my friend quoted some passages from a writer on landscape-gardening, who has been supposed to have well treated his theme:

"There are properly but two styles of landscape-gardening, the natural and the artificial. One seeks to recall the original beauty of the country, by adapting its means to the surrounding scenery; cultivating trees in harmony with the hills or plains of the neighboring land; detecting and bringing into practice those nice relations of size, proportion and color which, hid from the common observer, are revealed everywhere to the experienced student of nature. The result of the natural style of gardening is seen rather in the absence of all defects and incongruities—in the prevalence of a healthy harmony and order—than in the creation of any special wonders or miracles. The artificial style has as many varieties as there are different tastes to gratify. It has a certain general relation to the various styles of building. There are the stately avenues and retirements of Versailles; Italian terraces; and a various mixed old English style, which bears some relation to the domestic Gothic or English Elizabethan architecture. Whatever may be said against the abuses of the artificial landscape-gardening, a mixture of pure art in the garden scene adds to it a great beauty. This is partly pleasing to the eye, by the show of order and design, and partly moral. A terrace, with an old moss-covered balustrade, calls up at once to the eye the fair forms that have passed there in other days. The slightest exhibition of art is an evidence of care and human interest."

"From what I have already observed," said Ellison, "you

10 A wordplay on the name of Lancelot "Capability" Brown (1716–83), English landscape gardener and architect, who received his nickname from his discussing the "capabilities" of a particular area he was working on. He is mentioned in the *Arcturus* article, from which also comes the quotation above. See "Landor's Cottage," note 9.

11 Poe uses a different list in "The Landscape Garden," with the exception of the "Inferno." *Cato* (1713) is a moralistic tragedy by Joseph Addison (1672–1719), which was successful primarily because of the political mood of the time. "To say it is dead is too much, for it was never alive" (*Concise Cambridge History of English Literature*, 1972; p. 383).

will understand that I reject the idea, here expressed, of recalling the original beauty of the country. The original beauty is never so great as that which may be introduced. Of course, everything depends on the selection of a spot with **10** capabilities. What is said about detecting and bringing into practice nice relations of size, proportion, and color, is one of those mere vaguenesses of speech which serve to veil inaccuracy of thought. The phrase quoted may mean anything, or nothing, and guides in no degree. That the true result of the natural style of gardening is seen rather in the absence of all defects and incongruities than in the creation of any special wonders or miracles, is a proposition better suited to the grovelling apprehension of the herd than to the fervid dreams of the man of genius. The negative merit suggested appertains to that hobbling criticism which, in letters, would elevate Addison into apotheosis. In truth, while that virtue which consists in the mere avoidance of vice appeals directly to the understanding, and can thus be circumscribed in *rule*, the loftier virtue, which flames in creation, can be apprehended in its results alone. Rule applies but to the merits of denial— to the excellencies which refrain. Beyond these the critical art can but suggest. We may be instructed to build a 'Cato,' but **11** we are in vain told *how* to conceive a Parthenon or an 'Inferno.' The thing done, however; the wonder accomplished; and the capacity for apprehension becomes universal. The sophists of the negative school who, through inability to create, have scoffed at creation, are now found the loudest in applause. What, in its chrysalis condition of principle, affronted their demure reason, never fails, in its maturity of accomplishment, to extort admiration from their instinct of beauty.

"The author's observations on the artificial style," continued Ellison, "are less objectionable. A mixture of pure art in a garden scene adds to it a great beauty. This is just; as also is the reference to the sense of human interest. The principle expressed is incontrovertible—but there *may* be something beyond it. There may be an object in keeping with the principle—an object unattainable by the means ordinarily possessed by individuals, yet which, if attained, would lend a charm to the landscape-garden far surpassing that which a sense of merely human interest could bestow. A poet, having very unusual pecuniary resources, might, while retaining the necessary idea of art or culture, or, as our author expresses it, of interest, so imbue his designs at once with extent and novelty of beauty, as to convey the sentiment of spiritual interference. It will be seen that, in bringing about such result, he secures all the advantages of interest or *design*, while relieving his work of the harshness or technicality of the worldly *art*. In the most rugged of wildernesses—in the most savage of the scenes of pure nature—there is apparent the *art* of a creator; yet this art is apparent to reflection only; in no respect has it the obvious force of a feeling. Now let us suppose this sense of the Almighty design to be *one step depressed*— to be brought into something like harmony or consistency with the sense of human art—to form an intermedium between the two:—let us imagine, for example, a landscape whose combined vastness and definitiveness—whose united beauty, magnificence, and *strangeness*, shall convey the idea of care, or culture, or superintendence, on the part of beings superior, yet akin to humanity—then the sentiment of *interest* is preserved, while the art intervolved is made to assume the air of an intermediate or secondary nature—a nature which is not God, nor an emanation from God, but which still is nature in the sense of the handiwork of the angels that hover between man and God."

It was in devoting his enormous wealth to the embodiment of a vision such as this—in the free exercise in the open air ensured by the personal superintendence of his plans—in the unceasing object which these plans afforded—in the high spirituality of the object—in the contempt of ambition which it enabled him truly to feel—in the perennial springs with which it gratified, without possibility of satiating, that one master passion of his soul, the thirst for beauty; above all, it was in the sympathy of a woman, not unwomanly, whose loveliness and love enveloped his existence in the purple atmosphere of Paradise, that Ellison thought to find, *and found*, exemption from the ordinary cases of humanity, with a far greater amount of positive happiness than ever glowed in the rapt daydreams of De Staël. **12**

I despair of conveying to the reader any distinct conception of the marvels which my friend did actually accomplish. I wish **13** to describe, but am disheartened by the difficulty of description, and hesitate between detail and generality. Perhaps the better course will be to unite the two in their extremes.

Mr. Ellison's first step regarded, of course, the choice of a locality; and scarcely had he commenced thinking on this point, when the luxuriant nature of the Pacific Islands arrested his attention. In fact, he had made up his mind for a voyage to the South Seas, when a night's reflection induced him to abandon the idea. "Were I misanthropic," he said, "such a *locale* would suit me. The thoroughness of its insulation and seclusion, and the difficulty of ingress and egress, would in such case be the charm of charms; but as yet I am not Timon. **14** I wish the composure but not the depression of solitude. There must remain with me a certain control over the extent and duration of my repose. There will be frequent hours in which I shall need, too, the sympathy of the poetic in what I have done. Let me seek, then, a spot not far from a populous city—whose vicinity, also, will best enable me to execute my plans."

In search of a suitable place so situated, Ellison travelled for several years, and I was permitted to accompany him. A thousand spots with which I was enraptured he rejected without hesitation, for reasons which satisfied me, in the end, that he was right. We came at length to an elevated tableland of wonderful fertility and beauty, affording a panoramic prospect very little less in extent than that of Ætna, and, in **15**

12 The German romantic (see "Lionizing," note 17).

13 With this sentence begins the entirely new portion Poe wrote for the 1847 version.

14 In Shakespeare's *Timon of Athens*, Timon leaves society to live alone in a cave.

15 Mount Etna, 10,700 feet high, sits on the eastern coast of Sicily; it is the highest active volcano in Europe. The view from the top has always been considered awe-inspiring; it is mentioned in Patrick Brydone's *Tour Through Sicily and Malta* (1773).

Ellison's opinion as well as my own, surpassing the far-famed view from that mountain in all the true elements of the picturesque.

"I am aware," said the traveller, as he drew a sigh of deep delight after gazing on this scene, entranced, for nearly an hour, "I know that here, in my circumstances, nine-tenths of the most fastidious of men would rest content. This panorama is indeed glorious, and I should rejoice in it but for the excess of its glory. The taste of all the architects I have ever known leads them, for the sake of 'prospects,' to put up buildings on hill-tops. The error is obvious. Grandeur in any of its moods, but especially in that of extent, startles, excites—and then fatigues, depresses. For the occasional scene nothing can be better—for the constant view nothing worse. And, in the constant view, the most objectionable phase of grandeur is that of extent; the worst phase of extent, that of distance. It is at war with the sentiment and with the sense of *seclusion*—the sentiment and sense which we seek to humor in 'retiring to the country.' In looking from the summit of a mountain we cannot help feeling *abroad* in the world. The heart-sick avoid distant prospects as a pestilence."

It was not until toward the close of the fourth year of our search that we found a locality with which Ellison professed himself satisfied. It is, of course, needless to say *where* was the locality. The late death of my friend, in causing his domain to be thrown open to certain classes of visitors, has given to *Arnheim* a species of secret and subdued if not solemn celebrity, similar in kind, although infinitely superior in **16** degree, to that which so long distinguished Fonthill.

The usual approach to Arnheim was by the river. The visitor left the city in the early morning. During the forenoon he passed between shores of a tranquil and domestic beauty, on which grazed innumerable sheep, their white fleeces spotting the vivid green of rolling meadows. By degrees the idea of cultivation subsided into that of merely pastoral care. This slowly became merged in a sense of retirement—this again in a consciousness of solitude. As the evening approached, the channel grew more narrow; the banks more and more precipitous; and these latter were clothed in richer, more profuse, and more sombre foliage. The water increased in transparency. The stream took a thousand turns, so that at no moment could its gleaming surface be seen for a greater distance than a furlong. At every instant the vessel seemed imprisoned within an enchanted circle, having insuperable and impenetrable walls of foliage, a roof of ultra-marine satin, and *no* floor—the keel balancing itself with admirable nicety on that of a phantom bark which, by some accident having been turned upside down, floated in constant company with the substantial one, for the purpose of sustaining it. The channel now became a *gorge*—although the term is somewhat inapplicable, and I employ it merely because the language has no word which better represents the most striking—not the most distinctive—feature of the scene. The character of gorge was maintained

16 Fonthill Abbey, in Wiltshire, England, was a Gothic castle built in the 1790s for William Beckford, author of *Vathek*. The building fell into ruin after Beckford's death.

only in the height and parallelism of the shores; it was lost altogether in their other traits. The walls of the ravine (through which the clear water still tranquilly flowed) arose to an elevation of a hundred and occasionally of a hundred and fifty feet, and inclined so much toward each other as, in a great measure, to shut out the light of the day; while the long plume-like moss which depended densely from the intertwining shrubberies overhead, gave the whole chasm an air of funereal gloom. The windings became more frequent and intricate, and seemed often as if returning in upon themselves, so that the voyager had long lost all idea of direction. He was, moreover, enwrapt in an exquisite sense of the strange. The thought of nature still remained, but her character seemed to have undergone modification, there was a weird symmetry, a thrilling uniformity, a wizard propriety in these her works. Not a dead branch—not a withered leaf—not a stray pebble— not a path of the brown earth was anywhere visible. The crystal water welled up against the clean granite, or the unblemished moss, with a sharpness of outline that delighted while it bewildered the eye. **17**

Having threaded the mazes of this channel for some hours, the gloom deepening every moment, a sharp and unexpected turn of the vessel brought it suddenly, as if dropped from heaven, into a circular basin of very considerable extent when compared with the width of the gorge. It was about two hundred yards in diameter, and girt in at all points but one— that immediately fronting the vessel as it entered—by hills equal in general height to the walls of the chasm, although of a thoroughly different character. Their sides sloped from the water's edge at an angle of some forty-five degrees, and they were clothed from base to summit—not of a perceptible point escaping—in a drapery of the most gorgeous flower-blossoms; scarcely a green leaf being visible among the sea of odorous and fluctuating color. This basin was of great depth, but so transparent was the water that the bottom, which seemed to consist of a thick mass of small round alabaster pebbles, was distinctly visible by glimpses—that is to say, whenever the eye could permit itself *not* to see, far down in the inverted heaven, the duplicate blooming of the hills. On these latter there were no trees, nor even shrubs of any size. The impressions wrought on the observer were those of richness, warmth, color, quietude, uniformity, softness, delicacy, daintiness, voluptuousness, and miraculous extremeness of culture that suggested dreams of a new race of fairies, laborious, tasteful, magnificent, and fastidious; but as the eye traced upward the myriad-tinted slope, from its sharp junction with the water to its vague termination amid the folds of overhanging cloud, it became, indeed, difficult not to fancy a panoramic cataract of rubies, sapphires, opals, and golden onyxes, rolling silently out of the sky. **18**

The visitor, shooting suddenly into this bay from out of the gloom of the ravine, is delighted but astounded by the full orb of the declining sun, which he had supposed to be already far

17 Poe seems to have based much of his description on the paintings of Thomas Cole (1801–48), a series the artist titled *"The Voyage of Life"* and exhibited in Boston and New York in the early 1840s. Cole wrote extensive notes for the series, to which Poe may have had access. Cole was the original painter of the Hudson River school of American landscape painting.

There is a definite musical development in this last portion of the tale, a gradual crescendo in both rhythm and tempo, building to the climax and release of the last sentence. If Poe truly believed music was the art closest to the Sublime, then here he comes very close to the sort of effect that music can create.

18 "May thy billows roll ashore/The beryl and the golden ore" (Milton, *Coumus*, lines 1932–33).

by Albert Edward Sterner, 1903

. . . the whole Paradise of Arnheim bursts upon the view.
Three visions of Arnheim

19 Christ reassures his disciples after his resurrection:
"Be of good cheer; it is I; be not afraid." (Matthew 14:27)

20 "The house of Winstanley . . . must have been the
wonder of the age. . . . There was an arbor in the
garden, by the side of a canal; you had scarcely seated
yourself when you were sent out afloat to the middle of
the canal—from whence you could not escape till this
man of art and science wound you up to the arbor."
(D'Israeli, *Curiosities of Literature*, "Dreams at the
Dawn of Philosophy")
Henry Winstanley built the first Eddystone Light
("Winstanley's Tower"); he was killed when a storm
carried it away, in 1703.

below the horizon, but which now confronts him, and forms
the sole termination of an otherwise limitless vista seen
through another chasm-like rift in the hills.

But here the voyager quits the vessel which has borne him
so far, and descends into a light canoe of ivory, stained with
arabesque devices in vivid scarlet, both within and without.
The poop and beak of this boat arise high above the water,
with sharp points, so that the general form is that of an
irregular crescent. It lies on the surface of the bay with the
proud grace of a swan. On its ermined floor reposes a single
feathery paddle of satin-wood; but no oarsman or attendant is
19 to be seen. The guest is bidden to be good cheer—that the
fates will take care of him. The larger vessel disappears, and
he is left alone in the canoe, which lies apparently motionless
in the middle of the lake. While he considers what course to
pursue, however, he becomes aware of a gentle movement in
the fairy bark. It slowly swings itself around until its prow
points toward the sun. It advances with a gentle but gradually
accelerated velocity, while the slight ripples it creates seem
to break about the ivory side in divinest melody—seem to
offer the only possible explanation of the soothing yet melancholy music for whose unseen origin the bewildered voyager
20 looks around him in vain.

The canoe steadily proceeds, and the rocky gate of the vista
is approached, so that its depths can be more distinctly seen.

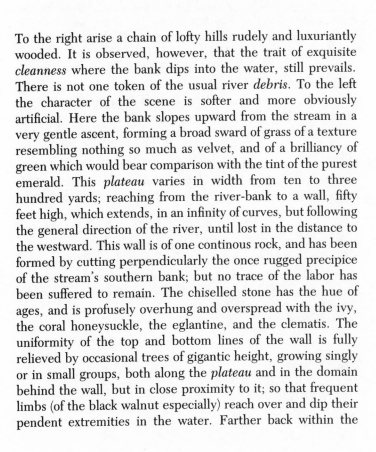

by F. S. Coburn, 1902.

by C. A. Stoddard

To the right arise a chain of lofty hills rudely and luxuriantly wooded. It is observed, however, that the trait of exquisite *cleanness* where the bank dips into the water, still prevails. There is not one token of the usual river *debris*. To the left the character of the scene is softer and more obviously artificial. Here the bank slopes upward from the stream in a very gentle ascent, forming a broad sward of grass of a texture resembling nothing so much as velvet, and of a brilliancy of green which would bear comparison with the tint of the purest emerald. This *plateau* varies in width from ten to three hundred yards; reaching from the river-bank to a wall, fifty feet high, which extends, in an infinity of curves, but following the general direction of the river, until lost in the distance to the westward. This wall is of one continous rock, and has been formed by cutting perpendicularly the once rugged precipice of the stream's southern bank; but no trace of the labor has been suffered to remain. The chiselled stone has the hue of ages, and is profusely overhung and overspread with the ivy, the coral honeysuckle, the eglantine, and the clematis. The uniformity of the top and bottom lines of the wall is fully relieved by occasional trees of gigantic height, growing singly or in small groups, both along the *plateau* and in the domain behind the wall, but in close proximity to it; so that frequent limbs (of the black walnut especially) reach over and dip their pendent extremities in the water. Farther back within the domain, the vision is impeded by an impenetrable screen of foliage.

These things are observed during the canoe's gradual approach to what I have called the gate of the vista. On drawing nearer to this, however, its chasm-like appearance vanishes; a new outlet from the bay is discovered to the left— in which direction the wall is also seen to sweep, still following the general course of the stream. Down this new opening the eye cannot penetrate very far; for the stream, accompanied by the wall, still bends to the left, until both are swallowed up by the leaves.

The boat, nevertheless, glides magically into the winding channel; and here the shore opposite the wall is found to resemble that opposite the wall in the straight vista. Lofty hills, rising occasionally into mountains, and covered with vegetation in wild luxuriance, still shut in the scene.

Floating gently onward, but with a velocity slightly augmented, the voyager, after many short turns, finds his progress apparently barred by a gigantic gate or rather door of burnished gold, elaborately carved and fretted, and reflecting the direct rays of the now fast-sinking sun with an effulgence that seems to wreathe the whole surrounding forest in flames. This gate is inserted in the lofty wall; which here appears to cross the river at right angles. In a few moments, however, it is seen that the main body of the water still sweeps in a gentle and extensive curve to the left, the wall following it as before, while a stream of considerable volume diverging from the principal one, makes it way, with a slight ripple, under the door, and is thus hidden from sight. The canoe falls into the lesser channel and approaches the gate. Its ponderous wings are slowly and musically expanded. The boat glides between them, and commences a rapid descent into a vast amphitheatre entirely begirt with purple mountains, whose bases are laved by a gleaming river throughout the full extent of their circuit. Meantime the whole Paradise of Arnheim bursts upon the view. There is a gush of entrancing melody; there is an oppressive sense of strange sweet odor;—there is a dream-like intermingling to the eye of tall slender Eastern trees— bosky shrubberies—flocks of golden and crimson birds—lily-fringed lakes—meadows of violets, tulips, poppies, hyacinths, and tuberoses—long intertangled lines of silver streamlets— and, upspringing confusedly from amid all, a mass of semi-Gothic, semi-Saracenic architecture, sustaining itself by miracle in mid-air; glittering in the red sunlight with a hundred oriels, minarets, and pinnacles; and seeming the phantom handiwork, conjointly, of the Sylphs, of the Fairies, of the Genii, and of the Gnomes.

21 Poe mentions "Eastern" trees in "The Island of the Fay" and "The Poetic Principle." The allusion is more poetic than botanic, although here they sound like (and are sometimes pictured as) European cypresses, such as one sees in Rome.

22 According to the belief commonly held in the Middle Ages, sylphs are the elemental spirits of air, named by the Rosicrucians and Cabalists from the Greek *silphe* (butterfly or moth). Mortals who had preserved their chastity were supposed to enjoy intimate familiarity with these gentle spirits, and according to some, all coquettes at death became sylphs.

MELLONTA TAUTA

First published in *Godey's Lady's Book*, February 1849, although written in early 1848; while *Godey's* delayed publication, Poe rewrote the tale as "A Remarkable Letter" and appended it to *Eureka* (1848).

If parts of the tale seem familiar, it is simply because Poe is here covering familiar territory. The degeneration of democracy into mob rule, for example, echoes "The Angel of the Odd" and "Scheherazade." The balloon voyage expands on the information Poe used as the basis for "The Balloon-Hoax." Poe once again mocks the general American worship of Progress, as he had done for several years ("Man is now only more active, not wiser, nor more happy, than he was 6000 years ago," he wrote Dr. Thomas Holley Chivers in 1844).

Many readers find this a tedious bit of forced humor, a sort of comic stew into which Poe seems to have thrown in anything he found lying around. If nothing else, "Mellonta Tauta" is a prime example of the wide range of Poe's thought and reading.

He encloses a note, in *Godey's Lady's Book*, saying that the tale is a translation by "Martin Van Buren Mavis, (sometimes known as the 'Poughkeepsie Seer')," referring to Andrew Jackson Davis [see "Mesmeric Revelation," introductory note].

The title of the piece means "These things are in the future"; it comes from Sophocles' *Antigone* by way of a quotation in the opening of Book IX of Bulwer-Lytton's *Ernest Maltravers* (1837). In *Eureka*, Poe once again gives the Greek words, adding, "I am but pausing, for a moment, on the awful threshold of *the Future*."

Poe may have been familiar with several French looks into the future, including *L'An deux mille quatre cent quarante* (*The Year 2440*), by Sébastien Mercier, published in 1770, but translated for some reason as *Memoirs of the Year 2500* in Richmond in 1799; *L'An Deux Mille* (1790), by Restif de la Bretonne; and *Mémoires d'un industriel de l'an 2240* (1829), by Barthélemy Enfantin.

ON BOARD BALLOON "SKYLARK"
APRIL 1, 2848 **1**

Now, my dear friend—now, for your sins, you are to suffer the infliction of a long gossiping letter. I tell you distinctly that I am going to punish you for all your impertinences by being as tedious, as discursive, as incoherent, and as unsatisfactory as possible. Besides, here I am, cooped up in a dirty balloon, with some one or two hundred of the *canaille*, all **2** bound on a *pleasure* excursion (what a funny idea some people have of pleasure!) and I have no prospect of touching *terra firma* for a month at least. Nobody to talk to. Nothing to do. When one has nothing to do, then is the time to correspond with one's friends. You perceive, then, why it is that I write you this letter—it is on account of my *ennui* and your sins.

Get ready your spectacles and make up your mind to be

1 The day is April Fool's Day, as it is in "Hans Pfaall." The name of the balloon is perhaps a nod to that optimistic atheist and visionary Percy Bysshe Shelley (1792–1822), author of *To a Skylark* (1821).

Poe may have also known the sailor's use of the word "skylark," meaning to mount the highest yards (called skyscrapers) and then slide down the ropes for amusement.

2 Rabble, scum, riffraff (from the Latin *canis*, dog)

3 The first engine-powered airship was built four years after Poe wrote his tale: a five-horsepower steam engine drove a ship with poor power-to-weight ratio, the invention of Henri Giffard. The gas engine was not built until 1860, and an airship using it (developed by German Paul Haenlein) was built in 1872; it managed a speed of nine miles per hour.

Are we forever to be doomed to the thousand inconveniences of the balloon? *Illustration by C. A. Stoddard*

In Poe's day, the balloon was the only type of aircraft that anyone would acknowledge as a realistic possibility—this was, after all, some sixty years before the Wright Brothers proved that a heavier-than-air machine could make it off the ground. During the heyday of the dirigible—the semirigid gigantic airship of the '20s and '30s—speeds of eighty mph were considered fast. The N-1, a 324-foot blimp built in 1951, had a top speed of ninety mph, and some proposed airships of the future were to have top speeds of 150 mph. The shape and mass of the lighter-than-air craft, however, preclude high-speed flying.

4 See "The Balloon-Hoax," note 26

5 Worthless

6 Much of the intended humor of the tale comes from the narrator's faulty knowledge.

The silkworm is the larva of various species of Asian (and African) moths that are now domesticated for silk production. The finest silk comes from the larva of *Bombyx mori*, whose eggs are so small that it takes thirty-five thousand of them to weigh an ounce. The silkworm eats the leaves of the mulberry tree, and, about thirty-two to thirty-eight days after hatching, spins its cocoon from a substance it produces called fibroin. The fibroin dries quickly in the air, hardening into a half-mile-long thread of silk that is gently unwound and used to make cloth.

Poe's mention of silkworms reflects the great interest in silkworm production at the time.

7 Mulberries of the family Moraceae are trees related to figs, that have a milky sap. Mulberry fruits, however, are the size and color of blackberries.

8 Papyrus is a sedge (*Cyperus papyrus*), a water-loving plant now almost extinct in its native Egypt but grown in many areas of the world as an ornamental. It was the basis for Egyptian writing material (also called papyrus), from which comes our word "paper."

annoyed. I mean to write at you every day during this odious voyage.

Heigho! when will any *Invention* visit the human pericranium? Are we forever to be doomed to the thousand inconveniences of the balloon? Will *nobody* contrive a more expeditious mode of progress? The jog-trot movement, to my thinking, is little less than positive torture. Upon my word we have not

3 made more than a hundred miles the hour since leaving home! The very birds beat us—at least some of them. I assure you that I do not exaggerate at all. Our motion, no doubt, seems slower than it actually is—this on account of our having no objects about us by which to estimate our velocity, and on account of our going *with* the wind. To be sure, whenever we meet a balloon we have a chance of perceiving our rate, and then, I admit, things do not appear so very bad. Accustomed as I am to this mode of travelling, I cannot get over a kind of giddiness whenever a balloon passes us in a current directly overhead. It always seems to me like an immense bird of prey about to pounce upon us and carry us off in its claws. One went over us this morning about sunrise, and so nearly

4 overhead that its drag-rope actually brushed the net-work suspending our car, and caused us very serious apprehension. Our captain said that if the material of the bag had been the

5 trumpery varnished "silk" of five hundred or a thousand years ago, we should inevitably have been damaged. This silk, as he explained it to me, was a fabric composed of the entrails

6 of a species of earthworm. The worm was carefully fed on

7 mulberries—a kind of fruit resembling a water-melon—and, when sufficiently fat, was crushed in a mill. The paste thus

8 arising was called *papyrus* in its primary state, and went through a variety of processes until it finally became "silk." Singular to relate, it was once much admired as an article of

female dress! Balloons were also very generally constructed
from it. A better kind of material, it appears, was subsequently
found in the down surrounding the seed-vessels of a plant
vulgarly called *euphorbium*, and at that time botanically
termed milkwee. This latter kind of silk was designated as **9**
silk-buckingham, on account of its superior durability, and was **10**
usually prepared for use by being varnished with a solution
of gum caoutchouc—a substance which in some respects must
have resembled the *gutta percha* now in common use. This **11**
caoutchouc was occasionally called Indian rubber or rubber **12**
of whist, and was no doubt one of the numerous *fungi*. Never **13**
tell me again that I am not at heart an antiquarian.

Talking of drag-ropes—our own, it seems, has this moment
knocked a man overboard from one of the small magnetic
propellers that swarm in ocean below us—a boat of about six
thousand tons, and, from all accounts, shamefully crowded.
These diminutive barques should be prohibited from carrying
more than a definite number of passengers. The man, of
course, was not permitted to get on board again and was soon
out of sight, he and his life-preserver. I rejoice, my dear
friend, that we live in an age so enlightened that no such a
thing as an individual is supposed to exist. It is the mass for
which the true Humanity cares. By the by, talking of Humanity, do you know that our immortal Wiggins is not so **14**
original in his views of the Social Condition and so forth, as
his contemporaries are inclined to suppose? Pundit assures
me that the same ideas were put nearly in the same way,
about a thousand years ago, by an Irish philosopher called
Furrier, on account of his keeping a retail shop for cat peltries **15**
and other furs. Pundit *knows*, you know; there can be no
mistake about it. How very wonderfully do we see verified
every day, the profound observation of the Hindoo Aries
Tottle (as quoted by Pundit)—"Thus must we say that, not
once or twice, or a few times, but with almost infinite
repetitions, the same opinions come round in a circle among
men." **16**

April 2.—Spoke to-day the magnetic cutter in charge of
the middle section of floating telegraph wires. I learn that **17**
when this species of telegraph was first put into operation by
Horse, it was considered quite impossible to convey the wires **18**
over sea but now we are at a loss to comprehend where the
difficulty lay! So wags the world. *Tempora mutantur*—excuse
me for quoting the Etruscan. What *would* we do without the **19**
Atalantic telegraph? (Pundit says Atlantic was the ancient
adjective.) We lay to a few minutes to ask the cutter some
questions, and learned, among other glorious news, that civil
war is raging in Africa, while the plague is doing its good work
beautifully both in Yurope and Ayesher. Is it not truly **20**
remarkable that, before the magnificent light shed upon
philosophy by Humanity, the world was accustomed to regard
War and Pestilence as calamities? Do you know that prayers
were actually offered up in the ancient temples to the end
that these *evils*(!) might not be visited upon mankind? Is it not
really difficult to comprehend upon what principle of interest

9 The common name for the Asclepiadaceae, perennial
herbs and shrubs characterized by milky sap, a tuft of
silky hairs attached to the seed, and often a climbing
habit of growth. Milkweeds have been used for food,
medicine, and fiber, as well as being a source of natural
rubber. When kapok was in short supply during World
War II, milkweed fiber was used as a substitute, and
recently, plans to grow the plant for rubber have surfaced
once again.

The Euphorbiaceae, a varied family of herbs, shrubs,
and trees, includes the spurges (which in turn include
the rubber tree, cassava, and castor-oil plant), poinsettia,
and cactuslike plants. They are not related to the above
group. Spurge was once touted as a wart cure.

10 J. Silk Buckingham, a British writer and traveler, is
mentioned in "Some Words with a Mummy," note 17.

11 A Malay word for latex obtained from certain ever-
green trees of the Far East. Gutta-percha is used in
adhesives, as well as in underground or underwater
cables.

12 Pure natural rubber. Unlike gutta-percha, it is elastic
and tough and does not deteriorate as rapidly.

13 Here our confused narrator mixes up several uses of
the word. "India rubber" is simply a general name for
rubber. A "rubber" of whist is a set of either three or
five games of cards, in order to ensure a clear winner.

Rubber got its name from its use as an eraser,
discovered by chemist Joseph Priestley about 1770.

14 From "pundit," the Hindu word for a Brahman who
is learned in Sanskrit, philosophy, law, and religion.

15 François Marie Charles Fourier (1772–1837), French
social philosopher who condemned existing institutions
and evolved a kind of utopian socialism. In the United
States, Horace Greeley touted Fourier's notion of "phal-
ansteries"—self-contained economic units of about sixteen hundred people (what we'd call "communes" today).
Brook Farm, of the transcendentalists, was Fourierist
for a while.

16 Aristotle, *Meteorologia* I, iii

17 Wireless telegraphy was still a long way off—1895,
to be exact—so here wires float on the ocean surface.
How they survive the stretching and stresses of high
seas is not explained. Even the Atlantic cable, laid safely
on the ocean floor, broke several times in the late-
nineteenth century.

18 Samuel Morse (1791–1872) first demonstrated the
telegraph in 1844, but so much of the foundation work
had already been laid by others that many question
Morse's claims to be the sole inventor of telegraphy.

19 *"Tempura mutantur, nos et mutamur in illis,"* means
"Times change and we change with them." The medieval
saying seems to be a misquote of a comment that
Matthias Bonbonius attributes to Lotharious I (c. A.D.
830): *"Omnia mutantur, nos et mutamur in illis,"* meaning "Everything changes . . ." (*Deliciae Poetarum Ger-
manorum*, Vol. I). At any rate, the quote is Latin, not
Etruscan.

20 Europe and Asia. Al Capp once referred to the
former as "Yurrp."

21 This elitist and cynical comment resembles Nietzche's opinion that war was an admirable remedy for a country that is growing weak, comfortable, and contemptible.

22 One wonders just how passengers manage to remain seated outdoors while the airship cruises along at 100–300 mph. Sounds just a bit breezy.

23 Charles Green (see "The Balloon-Hoax"). However, the first aeronauts were probably Joseph and Jacques Étienne Montgolfier, who in 1783 made the first balloon ascent, followed in that same year by Pilâtre de Rozier, who rose to a height of eighty-four feet.

24 "Savans" is an obsolete spelling of "savants."

25 Euclid (fl. c. 300 B.C.), the father of geometry, which is based on a series of axioms, and Immanuel Kant (see "Bon-Bon," note 3), *neither* of whom was a "disciple" of Aristotle

26 Sir Francis Bacon (1561–1626), whose contribution to philosphy was his application of the inductive method of modern science, as opposed to the *a priori* method of medieval scholasticism. He urged full investigation in all cases, avoiding theories based on insufficient data. Our narrator, however, has Bacon ("Hog") confused with poet James Hogg (1772–1835), who was born in the forest of Ettrick, in Selkirkshire and was a shepherd in his early life.

Interestingly, E. Cobham Brewer, in Dictionary of Fact and Fable (1894) states: "It may here be remarked that it is a great error to derive proper names of any antiquity from modern words of a similar sound or spelling. As a rule, very few ancient names are the names of trades; and to suppose that such words as Bacon, Hogg, and Pigg refer to swineherds . . . is a great mistake." (P 175) Not surprisingly, the first such derivation he corrects is "Brewer." "Bacon," he says, means "the fighter," while "Hogg" comes from the Anglo-Saxon word for scholar.

27 More etymological problems: "phenomenon" comes from the Greek *phainomenon* (*phainein*, to show). The narrator suggests that Aristotles's philosophy was based on naming things that might or might not be visible, while Bacon's was based on concrete things that could be shown.

our forefathers acted? Were they so blind as not to perceive that the destruction of a myriad of individuals is only so much

21 positive advantage to the mass!

April 3.—It is really a very fine amusement to ascend the rope-ladder leading to the summit of the balloon-bag, and thence survey the surrounding world. From the car below you know the prospect is not so comprehensive—you can see little vertically. But seated here (where I write this) in the luxuriously-cushioned open piazza of the summit, one can see

22 everything that is going on in all directions. Just now there is quite a crowd of balloons in sight, and they present a very animated appearance, while the air is resonant with the hum of so many millions of human voices. I have heard it asserted that when Yellow or (Pundit *will* have it) Violet, who is

23 supposed to have been the first æronaut, maintained the practicability of traversing the atmosphere in all directions, by merely ascending or descending until a favorable current was attained, he was scarcely hearkened to at all by his contemporaries, who looked upon him as merely an ingenious sort of madman, because the philosophers (?) of the day declared the thing impossible. Really now it does seem to me *quite* unaccountable how any thing so obviously feasible could

24 have escaped the sagacity of the ancient *savans*. But in all ages the great obstacles to advancement in Art have been opposed by the so-called men of science. To be sure, *our* men of science are not quite so bigoted as those of old:—oh, I have something *so* queer to tell you on this topic. Do you know that it is not more than a thousand years ago since the metaphysicians consented to relieve the people of the singular fancy that there existed but *two possible roads for the attainment of Truth!* Believe it if you can! It appears that long, long ago, in the night of Time, there lived a Turkish philosopher (or Hindoo possibly) called Aries Tottle. This person introduced, or at all events propagated what was termed the deductive or *à priori* mode of investigation. He started with what he maintained to be *axioms* or "self-evident truths," and thence proceeded "logically" to results. His

25 greatest disciples were one Neuclid, and one Cant. Well, Aries Tottle flourished supreme until advent of one Hog, surnamed the "Ettrick Shepherd," who preached an entirely

26 different system, which he called the *a posteriori* or *inductive*. His plan referred altogether to Sensation. He proceeded by observing, analyzing, and classifying facts—*instantiæ naturæ*, as they were affectedly called—into general laws. Aries Tottle's

27 mode, in a word, was based on *noumena;* Hog's on *phenomena*. Well, so great was the admiration excited by this latter system that, at its first introduction, Aries Tottle fell into disrepute; but finally he recovered ground and was permitted to divide the realm of Truth with his more modern rival. The *savants* now maintained that the Aristotelian and *Baconian* roads were the sole possible avenues to knowledge. "Baconian," you must know, was an adjective invented as equivalent to Hog-ian and more euphonious and dignified.

Now, my dear friend, I do assure you, most positively, that

I represent this matter fairly, on the soundest authority; and you can easily understand how a notion so absurd on its very face must have operated to retard the progress of all true knowledge—which makes its advances almost invariably by intuitive bounds. The ancient idea confined investigations to *crawling;* and for hundreds of years so great was the infatuation about Hog especially, that a virtual end was put to all thinking, properly so called. No man dared utter a truth for which he felt himself indebted to his *Soul* alone. It mattered not whether the truth was even *demonstrably* a truth, for the bullet-headed *savants* of the time regarded only *the road* by which he had attained it. They would not even *look* at the end. "Let us see the means," they cried, "the means!" If, upon investigation of the means, it was found to come under neither category Aries (that is to say Ram) nor under the category Hog, why then the *savants* went no farther, but pronounced the "theorist" a fool, and would have nothing to do with him or his truth.

Now, it cannot be maintained, even, that by the crawling system the greatest amount of truth would be attained in any long series of ages, for the repression of *imagination* was an evil not to be compensated for by any superior *certainty* in the ancient modes of investigation. The error of these Jurmains, these Vrinch, these Inglitch, and these Amriccans (the latter, **28** by the way, were our own immediate progenitors), was an error quite analogous with that of the wiseacre who fancies that he must necessarily see an object the better the more closely he holds it to his eyes. These people blinded themselves by details. When they proceeded Hoggishly, their "facts" were by no means always facts—a matter of little consequence had it not been for assuming that they *were* facts and must be facts because they appeared to be such. When they proceeded on the path of the Ram, their course was scarcely as straight as a ram's horn, for they *never had* an axiom which was an axiom at all. They must have been very blind not to see this, even in their own day; for even in their own day many of the long "established" axioms had been rejected. For example— "*Ex nihilo nihil fit*"; "a body cannot act where it is not"; "there **29** cannot exist antipodes"; "darkness cannot come out of light"— all these, and a dozen other similar propositions, formerly admitted without hesitation as axioms, were, even at the period of which I speak, seen to be untenable. How absurd in these people, then, to persist in putting faith in "axioms" as immutable bases of Truth! But even out of the mouths of their soundest reasoners it is easy to demonstrate the futility, the impalpability of their axioms in general. Who *was* the soundest of their logicians? Let me see! I will go and ask Pundit and be back in a minute. * * * Ah, here we have it! Here is a book written nearly a thousand years ago and lately translated from the Inglitch—which, by the way, appears to have been the rudiment of the Amriccan. Pundit says it is decidedly the cleverest ancient work on its topic, Logic. The author (who was much thought of in his day) was one Miller, or Mill; and we find it recorded of him, as a point of some

28 Germans, French, English, Americans

29 "Nothing comes from nothing," is an oft-repeated phrase, first used, as far as we know, by the Greek poet Alcaeus (d. c.580 B.C.). "Nothing will come of nothing" appears in *King Lear*, I, i, (and in the song "I Must Have Done Something Good," from the film version of *The Sound of Music*).

30 John Stuart Mill (1806–73) and Jeremy Bentham (1748–1832)

Mill, the English philosopher and economist, formulated the rules for the inductive process, and stressed the method of empiricism as the source of all knowledge. He also pointed to the possibility of a sentiment of unity that might develop a religious character under the right circumstances. An advocate of political and social reforms, he supported proportional representation, emancipation of women, and the develoment of labor organizations and farm cooperatives.

Bentham was the founder of utilitarianism, which held that the greatest happiness of the greatest number is the fundamental and self-evident prinicple of morality. He also disliked poetry. Neither of these attitudes was likely to please Poe, who pokes fun at Bentham every time he has the chance (see "Lionizing," note 17).

31 From Mill's *System of Logic*, Book II, "Of Reasoning," sections 5–7, although here confused with Joe Miller (1684–1738) of *Joke Book* fame. John Mottley compiled a book of jokes during the reign of James II, that he entitled *Joe Miller's Jests*, after the great comic actor of the day. A stale jest is sometimes called a "Joe Miller," implying that it is stolen from Mottley's compilation.

32 From Mill's *System of Logic*, although highly altered in tone

33 Again, from Mill, who actually says something quite different, namely that there is a difference between perception and belief

34 Johannes Kepler (1571–1630), the great German astronomer, stated three laws: 1) the orbit of each planet is an ellipse, of which the sun is one of the foci; 2) the radius vector of each planet moves over equal areas of the ellipse in equal times; 3) the square of the time the planet takes to orbit the sun is proportional to the cube of its mean distance from the sun.

Sir Isaac Newton (1642–1727) formulated the theory of gravitation, but Kepler's work was important in making its formulation possible.

35 In the nineteenth century, theorizing about scientific subjects began to take a back seat to empirical proof that something was so.

36 Jean François Champollion (1790–1832), the French Egyptologist who used the Rosetta stone to decipher the hieroglyphics that had confounded others for so long. It seems odd that our narrator, who so far has incorrectly spelled or named the most famous scientists and philosophers, should correctly name this less well-known scholar. Then again, if Poe tampered with the name, we probably wouldn't be able to figure out whom he meant.

As for "old moles," see *Hamlet*, I, v, 162–63: "Well said, old mole! canst work i' the earth so fast?/A worthy pioner!"

37 Many readers no doubt appreciate the thought.

30 importance, that he had a mill-horse called Bentham. But let us glance at the treatise!

Ah!—"Ability or inability to conceive," says Mr. Mill, very properly, "is in no case to be received as a criterion of **31** axiomatic truth." What *modern* in his senses would ever think of disputing this truism? The only wonder with us must be, how it happened that Mr. Mill conceived it necessary even to hint at anything so obvious. So far good—but let us turn over another paper. What have we here?—"Contradictories **32** cannot both be true—that is, cannot co-exist in nature." Here Mr. Mill means, for example, that a tree must be either a tree or not a tree—that it cannot be at the same time a tree and not a tree. Very well; but I ask him *why*. His reply is this— and never pretends to be anything else than this—"Because it is impossible to conceive that contradictories can both be **33** true." But this is no answer at all, by his own showing; for has he not just admitted as a truism that "ability or inability to conceive is *in no case* to be received as a criterion of axiomatic truth."

Now I do not complain of these ancients so much because their logic is, by their own showing, utterly baseless, worthless and fantastic altogether, as because of their pompous and imbecile proscription of all *other* roads of Truth, of all *other* means for its attainment than the two preposterous paths— the one of creeping and the one of crawling—to which they have dared to confine the Soul that loves nothing so well as to *soar*.

By the by, my dear friend, do you not think it would have puzzled these ancient dogmaticians to have determined by *which* of their two roads it was that the most important and most sublime of *all* their truths was, in effect, attained? I mean **34** the truth of Gravitation. Newton owed it to Kepler. Kepler admitted that his three laws were *guessed at*—these three laws of all laws which led the great Inglitch mathematician to his principle, the basis of all physical principle—to go behind which we must enter the Kingdom of Metaphysics: Kepler guessed—that is to say *imagined*. He was essentially a "theorist"—that word now of so much sanctity, formerly an epithet **35** of contempt. Would it not have puzzled these old moles too, to have explained by which of the two "roads" a cryptographist unriddles a cryptograph of more than usual secrecy, or by which of the two roads Champollion directed mankind to those enduring and almost innumerable truths which resulted **36** from his deciphering the Hieroglyphics.

37 One word more on this topic and I will be done boring you. It is not *passing* strange that, with their eternal prattling about *roads* to Truth, these bigoted people missed what we now so clearly perceive to be the great highway—that of Consistency? Does it not seem singular how they should have failed to deduce from the works of God the vital fact that a perfect consistency *must* be an absolute truth! How plain has been our progress since the late announcement of this proposition! Investigation has been taken out of the hands of the ground-moles and given, as a task, to the true and only true thinkers,

Could Poe have envisioned a vehicle such as the *Hindenburg* or even the Goodyear Blimp? *Illustration by R. Sayer*

the men of ardent imagination. These latter *theorize*. Can you not fancy the shout of scorn with which my words would be received by our progenitors were it possible for them to be now looking over my shoulder? These men, I say, *theorize*; and their theories are simply corrected, reduced, systematized—cleared, little by little, of their dross of inconsistency—until, finally, a perfect consistency stands apparent which even the most stolid admit, because it *is* a consistency, to be an absolute and an unquestionable *truth*.

April 4.—The new gas is doing wonders, in conjunction **38** with the new improvement with gutta-percha. How very safe, commodious, manageable, and in every respect convenient are our modern balloons! Here is an immense one approaching us at the rate of at least a hundred and fifty miles an hour. It seems to be crowded with people—perhaps there are three or four hundred passengers—and yet it soars to an elevation **39** of nearly a mile, looking down upon poor us with sovereign contempt. Still a hundred or even two hundred miles an hour is slow travelling after all. *Do* you remember our flight on the railroad across the Kanadaw continent?—fully three hundred **40** miles the hour—*that* was travelling. Nothing to be seen though—nothing to be done but flirt, feast and dance in the magnificent saloons. Do you remember what an odd sensation **41** was experienced when, by chance, we caught a glimpse of external objects while the cars were in full flight? Everything seemed unique—in one mass. For my part, I cannot say but **42** that I preferred the travelling by the slow train of a hundred miles the hour. Here we were permitted to have glass windows—even to have them open—and something like a distinct view of the country was attainable. * * * Pundit says that *the route* for the great Kanadaw railroad must have been in some measure marked out about nine hundred years ago!

38 The first balloons used hot air for lift, and no real progress was made in lighter-than-air craft until the second half of the eighteenth century, when experiments with other gases by Henry Cavendish, Joseph Priestley, and Antoine Lavoisier led to balloons filled with "inflammable air" (hydrogen).

Another problem was finding a material for the envelope that was both lightweight and strong, and impermeable enough to prevent hydrogen from leaking through. Jacques Charles and the brothers Robert used a solution of rubber to coat their silk envelope, capable of holding about nine-hundred cubic feet of hydrogen; this approach was standard for some time. Gutta-percha would be a poor choice as a coating for the envelope, since it is not elastic and deteriorates in air. However, Poe's narrator may mean it as a synonym for rubber.

Hot-air balloons are still in use today, but hydrogen long ago gave way to the much safer helium, discovered in 1868 by P. J. C. Janssen and isolated in 1895 but not produced in quantity until the 1930s. Could helium be this "new gas"?

39 The *Hindenburg* was designed to carry about seventy passengers and a crew of sixty; it was the largest passenger-carrying airship of the 1930s. The American *Akron* once made a ten-hour flight with 270 people aboard, at a top speed of 80 mph. While airships have gone as high as five-thousand feet, most cruised at a considerably lower altitude.

40 An old name for the Americas

41 The narrator is describing a sort of supertrain.

In 1844, New York businessman Asa Whitney tried to sell the idea of a transcontinental railway to Congress, and failed.

42 "Unique" in this sense is obsolete usage.

A train big enough to straddle tracks fifty feet wide ⟨bog⟩gles the imagination.

44 Building an interoceanic canal was suggested in early Spanish colonial times, and the United States showed interest as early as the late-eighteenth century. Active negotiations in 1846 led to a treaty in which the republic of New Granada (Panamá and Colombia) granted the Americans the transit rights across the Isthmus of Panamá. A Panamá railroad was built in 1848–55, but the canal itself had to wait until early in the next century.

45 Prairie dogs are known for their elaborate burrows, grouped in colonies or "towns." Poe may have read about them in Washington Irving's *A Tour on the Prairies* (1835).

46 " 'It's always best on these occasions to do what the mob do.' 'But suppose there are two mobs?' suggested Mr. Snodgrass. 'Shout with the largest,' replied Mr. Pickwick." (*Pickwick Papers*, Ch. 13).
 "The pitifulest thing out is a mob; that's what an army is— a mob; they don't fight with courage that's born in them, but with courage that's borrowed from their mass, and from their officers. But a mob without any *man* at the head of it, is *beneath* pitifulness." (Colonel Sherburn, in *The Adventures of Huckleberry Finn*, 1884; Ch. 22)

47 Nero. For Heliogabalus, see "Four Beasts in One," note 21.

In fact, he goes so far as to assert that actual traces of a road are still discernible—traces referable to a period quite as remote as that mentioned. The track, it appears, was *double* only; ours, you know, has twelve paths; and three or four new ones are in preparation. The ancient rails are very slight, and placed so close together as to be, according to modern notions, quite frivolous, if not dangerous in the extreme. The present width of track—fifty feet—is considered, indeed, scarcely

43 secure enough. For my part, I make no doubt that a track of some sort *must* have existed in very remote times, as Pundit asserts; for nothing can be clearer, to my mind, than that, at some period—not less than seven centuries ago, certainly— the Northern and Southern Kanadaw continents were *united*; the Kanawdians, then, would have been driven, by necessity,

44 to a great railroad across the continent.

 April 5.—I am almost devoured by *ennui*. Pundit is the only conversible person on board; and he, poor soul! can speak of nothing but antiquities. He has been occupied all the day in the attempt to convince me that the ancient Amriccans *governed themselves!*—did ever anybody hear of such an absurdity?—that they existed in an sort of every-man-for-himself confederacy, after the fashion of the "prairie dogs"

45 that we read of in fable. He says that they started with the queerest idea conceivable, viz: that all men are born free and equal—this in the very teeth of the laws of *gradation* so visibly impressed upon all things both in the moral and physical universe. Every man "voted," as they called it—that is to say meddled with public affairs—until, at length, it was discovered that what is everybody's business is nobody's, and that the "Republic" (so the absurd thing was called) was without a government at all. It is related, however, that the first circumstance which disturbed, very particularly, the self-complacency of the philosophers who constructed this "Republic," was the startling discovery that universal suffrage gave opportunity for fraudulent schemes, by means of which any desired number of votes might at any time be polled, without the possibility of prevention or even detection, by any party which should be merely villanous enough not to be ashamed of the fraud. A little reflection upon this discovery sufficed to render evident the consequences, which were that rascality *must* predominate—in a word, that a republican government *could* never be anything but a rascally one. While the philosophers, however, were busied in blushing at their stupidity in not having foreseen these inevitable evils, and intent upon the invention of new theories, the matter was put

46 to an abrupt issue by a fellow.of the name of *Mob*, who took everything into his own hands and set up a despotism, in

47 comparison with which those of the fabulous Zeroes and Hellofagabaluses were respectable and delectable. This Mob (a foreigner, by the by) is said to have been the most odious of all men that ever encumbered the earth. He was a giant in stature—insolent, rapacious, filthy; had the gall of a bullock with the heart of a hyena and the brains of a peacock. He died, at length, by dint of his own energies, which exhausted him. Nevertheless, he had his uses, as everything has, however vile, and taught mankind a lesson which to this day it is in no danger of forgetting—never to run directly contrary to the natural analogies. As for Republicanism, no analogy could be found for it upon the face of the earth—unless we except the case of the "prairie dogs," an exception which seems to demonstrate, if anything, that democracy is a very admirable form of government—for dogs.

April 6.—Last night had a fine view of Alpha Lyræ, whose **48** disk, through our captain's spyglass, subtends an angle of half a degree, looking very much as our sun does to the naked eye on a misty day. Alpha Lyræ, although so *very* much larger than our sun, by the by, resembles him closely as regards its spots, its atmosphere, and in many other particulars. It is only **49** within the last century, Pundit tells me, that the binary relation existing between these two orbs began even to be suspected. The evident motion of our system in the heavens was (strange to say!) referred to an orbit about a prodigious star in the centre of the galaxy. About this star, or at all events about a centre of gravity common to all the globes of the Milky Way and supposed to be near Alcyone in the Pleiades, every **50** one of these globes was declared to be revolving, our own performing the circuit in a period of 117,000,000 of years! *We,* with our present lights, our vast telescopic improvements, and so forth, of course find it difficult to comprehend *the ground* of an idea such as this. Its first propagator was one Mudler. **51** He was led, we must presume, to this wild hypothesis by mere analogy in the first instance; but, this being the case, he should at least adhered to analogy in its development. A great central orb *was*, in fact, suggested; so far Mudler was consistent. This central orb, however, dynamically, should have been greater than all its surrounding orbs taken together. The question might then have been asked—"Why do we not see it?"—*we,* especially, who occupy the mid region of the cluster—the very locality *near* which, at least, must be situated this inconceivable central sun. The astronomer, perhaps, at this point, took refuge in the suggestion of non-luminosity; and here analogy was suddenly let fall. But even admitting the central orb non-luminous, how did he manage to explain its failure to be rendered visible by the incalculable host of glorious suns glaring in all directions about it. No doubt what he finally maintained was merely a centre of gravity common to all the revolving orbs—but here again analogy must have been let fall. Our system revolves, it is true, about a common centre of gravity, but it does this in connection with and in consequence of a material sun whose mass more than counterbalances the rest of the system. The mathematical circle is a curve composed of an infinity of straight lines; but this idea of the circle—this idea of it which, in regard to all earthly geometry, we consider as merely the mathematical, in contradistinction from the practical, idea—is, in sober fact, the *practical* conception which alone we have any right to entertain in respect to those Titanic circles with which we have to deal, **52** at least in fancy, when we suppose our system, with its fellows,

48 i.e., Vega, a star with an apparent magnitude of 0.14, the brightest in the constellation Lyra.

In 1603 Johann Bayer introduced the reform of designating the stars in a given constellation by letters of the Greek alphabet, arranging the stars in their approximate order of brightness. Thus Vega (the traditional name) is the brightest (Alpha) star of the constellation Lyra.

Alpha Lyrae is mentioned also in "Ligeia."

49 In 1840–41, observers watched the longest-lasting sunspot ever recorded by astronomers, lasting eighteen months. Heinrich Schwabe in 1843 announced that sunspots appear in a cycle of 11.13 years on the average.

50 Alcyone is the central star of the Pleiades, in the constellation Taurus.

51 Johann Heinrich on Mädler (1794–1874) was the German astronomer who suggested that all solar systems within a galaxy revolve around a common center.

52 The Titans were the twelve primeval deities of Greek mythology, the children of Uranus and Gaea: Cronus, Iapetus, Hyperion, Oceanus, Coeus, Creus, Theia, Rhea, Mnemosyne, Phoebe, Tethys, and Themis. Led by Cronus, they deposed their father and ruled the universe until they were overthrown by the Olympians, led by Zeus. They were supposedly of great size.

revolving about a point in the centre of the galaxy. Let the most vigorous of human imaginations but attempt to take a single step toward the comprehension of a circuit so unutterable! It would scarcely be paradoxical to say that a flash of lightning itself, travelling *forever* upon the circumference of this inconceivable circle, would still *forever* be travelling in a straight line. That the path of our sun along such a circumference—that the direction of our system in such an orbit—would, to any human perception, deviate in the slightest degree from a straight line even in a million of years, is a proposition not to be entertained; and yet these ancient astronomers were absolutely cajoled, it appears, into believing that a decisive curvature had become apparent during the brief period of their astronomical history—during the mere point—during the utter nothingness of two or three thousand years! How incomprehensible, that considerations such as this did not at once indicate to them the true state of affairs—that of the binary revolution of our sun and Alpha Lyræ around a common centre of gravity!

April 7.—Continued last night our astronomical amusements. Had a fine view of the five Neptunian asteroids, and watched with much interest the putting up of a huge impost on a couple of lintels in the new temple of Daphnis in the moon. It was amusing to think that creatures so diminutive as the lunarians, and bearing so little resemblance to humanity, yet evinced a mechanical ingenuity so much superior to our own. One finds it difficult, too, to conceive the vast masses which these people handle so easily, to be as light as our own reason tells us they actually are.

April 8.—Eureka! Pundit is in his glory. A balloon from Kanadaw spoke us to-day and threw on board several late papers; they contain some exceedingly curious information relative to Kanawdian or rather Amriccan antiquities. You know, I presume, that laborers have for some months been employed in preparing the ground for a new fountain at Paradise, the Emperor's principal pleasure garden. Paradise, it appears, has been, *literally* speaking, an island time out of mind—that is to say, its northern boundary was always (as far back as any record extends) a rivulet, or rather a very narrow arm of the sea. This arm was gradually widened until it attained its present breadth—a mile. The whole length of the island is nine miles; the breadth varies materially. The entire area (so Pundit says) was, about eight hundred years ago, densely packed with houses, some of them twenty stories high; land (for some most unaccountable reason) being considered as especially precious just in this vicinity. The disastrous earthquake, however, of the year 2050, so totally uprooted and overwhelmed the town (for it was almost too large to be called a village) that the most indefatigable of our antiquarians have never yet been able to obtain from the site any sufficient data (in the shape of coins, medals or inscriptions) wherewith to build up even the ghost of a theory concerning the manners, customs, &c. &c. &c., of the aboriginal inhabitants. Nearly all that we have hitherto known of them is, that

---

53 Discovered (after being predicted some years before) in 1846, Neptune cannot be seen with the naked eye. A month after the detection of the planet, a satellite was discovered and named Triton, but the second satellite (Nereid) wasn't discovered until 1949.

54 Daphnis was a shepherd in love with a Naiad named Chloë, who comforted himself in his sorrow with sad songs on his pipe. His friends also lamented for him in song, and thus pastoral melody was born. His name means "laurel-like."

55 One recalls that the narrator of "Hans Pfaall" intended to describe the inhabitants of the moon in a future installment. Much of this description had already been furnished in "Discoveries in the Moon Lately Made at the Cape of Good Hope, by Sir John Herschel" (1835), known to us as "The Moon Hoax." (See "Hans Pfaall," introductory note.)

56 The description here echoes Coleridge's *Kubla Khan*, with its "stately pleasure-dome," its "gardens bright with sinuous rills,/Where blossomed many an incense-bearing tree," and its "mighty fountain," where one can drink "the milk of Paradise."

The Greeks used "paradise" as a name for the extensive parks and pleasure grounds of the Persian kings, and this usage was still common in Poe's time.

57 Manhattan Island, New York City. Although earthquakes are rare there, in Poe's day several other major disasters had occurred, including an outbreak of Asiatic cholera in 1832 and a disastrous fire in 1835 that destroyed thirteen acres and nearly seven-hundred buildings.

The fountain is Park Fountain, near City Hall. New York in 1820 had 123,706 people but was to grow to 1,164,673 by 1860.

they were a portion of the Knickerbocker tribe of savages **58**
infesting the continent at its first discovery by Recorder Riker, **59**
a knight of the Golden Fleece. They were by no means
uncivilized, however, but cultivated various arts and even
sciences after a fashion of their own. It is related of them that
they were acute in many respects, but were oddly afflicted
with monomania for building what, in the ancient Amriccan,
was dominated "churches"—a kind of pagoda instituted for
the worship of two idols that went by the names of Wealth
and Fashion. In the end, it is said, the island became, nine
tenths of it, church. The women, too, it appears, were oddly **60**
deformed by a natural protuberance of the region just below
the small of the back—although, most unaccountably, this
deformity was looked upon altogether in the light of a beauty. **61**
One or two pictures of these singular women have, in fact,
been miraculously preserved. They look very odd, *very*—like
something between a turkey-cock and a dromedary.

Well, these few details are nearly all that have descended
to us respecting the ancient Knickerbockers. It seems, however, that while digging in the centre of the Emperor's garden
(which, you know, covers the whole island), some of the
workmen unearthed a cubical and evidently chiseled block of
granite, weighing several hundred pounds. It was in good
preservation, having received, apparently, little injury from
the convulsion which entombed it. On one of its surfaces was
a marble slab with (only think of it!) *an inscription—a legible
inscription*. Pundit is in ecstasies. Upon detaching the slab,
a cavity appeared, containing a leaden box filled with various
coins, a long scroll of names, several documents which appear
to resemble newspapers, with other matters of intense interest
to the antiquarian! There can be no doubt that all these are
genuine Amriccan relics belonging to the tribe called Knickerbocker. The papers thrown on board our balloon are filled
with fac-similes of the coins, MSS., typography, &c. &c. I
copy for your amusement the Knickerbocker inscription on
the marble slab:—

This Corner Stone of a Monument to the
Memory of
GEORGE WASHINGTON,
was laid with appropriate ceremonies on the
19TH DAY OF OCTOBER, 1847,
the anniversary of the surrender of
Lord Cornwallis
to General Washington at Yorktown,
A. D. 1781,
under the auspices of the
Washington Monument Association of the
city of New York.   **62**

This, as I give it, is a verbatim translation done by Pundit
himself, so there *can* be no mistake about it. From the few
words thus preserved, we gleam several important items of
knowledge, not the least interesting of which is the fact that
a thousand years ago *actual* monuments had fallen into

---

58 "Knickerbocker" was a term used almost synony-
mously with "Dutch" in the early-nineteenth century,
particularly because of Washington Irving's *History of
New York by Diedrich Knickerbocker* (1809). There was
an actual Knickerbocker family, who came from Holland
about 1674 and settled in what is now Albany County.

59 Richard Riker (1773–1842) was a New York politician
who had been accused of graft but who also had dedicated
to him a poem, *To the Recorder*, by Fitz-Greene Halleck,
one of Poe's contemporaries.
 His fleecing the public leads to the wordplay on the
Golden Fleece sought by Jason and the Argonauts.

60 Poe and his fellow Southerners shared little of the
New England respect for profit and progress. In "Marginalia," XCVII, Poe writes: "The Romans worshipped
their standards; and the Roman standard happened to
be an eagle. Our standard is only one-tenth of an Eagle—
a Dollar—but we make all even by adoring it with
tenfold devotion." The reference is to the ten-dollar gold
piece, which had the American eagle on its face.
 "Churches" here refers to office buildings, the temples
of the business class, whom Poe assails in "The Man of
the Crowd."

61 See "Scheherazade," note 66.

62 Not the Washington Monument, in Washington,
D.C., but a proposed (but never built) memorial in New
York that was ballyhooed in 1843–47

63 From Laurence Sterne's *Sentimental Journey* (1768), Chapter 31, but also used by Senator Thomas Hart Benton (1782–1858), of Missouri, in a famous speech in 1837, when he tried to have President Jackson censured, but failed. Poe was no great admirer of Jackson either.

64 Charles Cornwallis (1738–1805), the English general whose troops were defeated by Americans in the decisive battle of Yorktown (1781), effectively putting an end to the fighting in the American Revolution. Cornwallis was not held responsible for the loss; he was later made governor-general of India, and then viceroy of Ireland—where he found himself in the midst of another rebellion (1798). True to form, when he was made governor-general of India again, he was forced to put down still another rebellion (1805) but died on his way to battle with his troops.

65 Compare this with the equally abrupt ending of "MS. Found in a Bottle."

66 "John Smith" is used for the commonness of the name. Zachary Taylor (1784–1850) was twelfth President of the United States, after winning several decisive victories in the Mexican War (1846–47).

67 Again, compare with "MS."

disuse—as was all very proper—the people contenting themselves, as we do now, with a mere indication of the design to erect a monument at some future time; a corner-stone being cautiously laid by itself "solitary and alone" (excuse me for **63** quoting the great Amriccan poet Benton!) as a guarantee of the magnanimous *intention*. We ascertain, too, very distinctly, from this admirable inscription, the how as well as the where and the what, of the great surrender in question. As to the *where*, it was Yorktown (wherever that was), and as to the **64** *what*, it was General Cornwallis (no doubt some wealthy dealer in corn). *He* was surrendered. The inscription commemorates the surrender of—what?—why, "of Lord Cornwallis." The only question is what could the savages wish him surrendered for. But when we remember that these savages were undoubtedly cannibals, we are led to the conclusion that they intended him for sausage. As to the *how* of the surrender, no language can be more explicit. Lord Cornwallis was surrendered (for sausage) "under the auspices of the Washington Monument Association"—no doubt a charitable institution for the depositing of corner-stones.——But, Heaven bless me! what is the matter? Ah, I see—the balloon has **65** collapsed, and we shall have a tumble into the sea. I have, therefore, only time enough to add that, from a hasty inspection of the fac-similes of newspapers, &c. &c., I find that *the* great men in those days among the Amriccans, were one John, a **66** smith, and one Zacchary, a tailor.

Good-bye, until I see you again. Whether you ever get this letter or not is point of little importance, as I write altogether for my own amusement. I shall cork the MS. up in a bottle, **67** however, and throw it into the sea.

Yours everlastingly,

PUNDITA

VON KEMPELEN AND HIS DISCOVERY

First published in *The Flag of Our Union*, April 14, 1849.

Poe was amused by the gold rush of 1848–49, and apparently saw this tale as a satirical commentary on man's lust for the precious metal.

"If you have looked over the Von Kempelen article which I left with your brother," Poe wrote publisher E. A. Duyckinck, "you will have perceived its drift. I meant it as a kind of 'exercise,' or experiment, in the plausible or verisimilar style. Of course, there is *not one* word of truth in it from beginning to end. I thought that such a style, applied to the gold-excitement, could not fail of effect. My sincere opinion is that nine persons out of ten (even among the best-informed) will *believe* the quiz (provided the design does not leak out before publication) and that thus, acting as a sudden, although of course a very temporary *check* to the gold-fever, it will create a *stir* to some purpose. . . ." (March 1849)

˙ Poe wanted the story published in the New York *Literary World*, and offered it to Duyckinck for ten dollars, or "whatever you think you can afford." He was turned down, and the story went to the less prestigious *Flag of Our Union* for fifteen dollars and did not get the wide exposure Poe had hoped for.

Poe's love of hoaxes seems in part based on elitest notions that show themselves from time to time in his tales. The common man will be taken in, but the educated, sophisticated reader will take notice of the many clues Poe has sprinkled about: Von Kempelen is "connected in some way with Maelzel," the trickster Poe had already uncovered in "Maelzel's Chess-Player"; the Bremen locales are fictional, and although the scientific men mentioned are all bona fide, none of their supposed reports on Von Kempelen ever existed. The references to the discredited "science" of alchemy are still another clue.

After the very minute and elaborate paper by Arago, to say [1] nothing of the summary in *Silliman's Journal*, with the detailed [2] statement just published by Lieutenant Maury, it will not be [3] supposed, of course, that in offering a few hurried remarks in reference to Von Kempelen's discovery, I have any design to [4] look at the subject from a *scientific* point of view. My object is simply, in the first place, to say a few words of Von Kempelen himself (with whom, some years ago, I had the honor of a slight personal acquaintance), since everything which concerns him must necessarily, at this moment, be of interest; and, in the second place, to look in a general way, and, speculatively, at the *results* of the discovery.

It may be as well, however, to premise the cursory observations which I have to offer, by denying, very decidedly, what seems to be a general impression (gleaned, as usual in a case of this kind, from the newspapers), viz.: that this discovery, astounding as it unquestionably is, is *unanticipated*.

By reference to the "Diary of Sir Humphrey Davy" (Cottle [5] and Munroe, London, pp. 150), it will be seen at pp. 53 and

1 François Arago (1786–1853) was director of the Paris Observatory and perpetual secretary of the French Academy of Sciences, and a well-known physicist and astronomer of Poe's time.

2 Benjamin Silliman (1779–1864) was professor of chemistry and natural history at Yale and founder-editor of *The American Journal of Science and Arts*, one of the most important scientific journals in the world at the time.

3 Matthew Fontaine Maury (1806–73) not only contributed to the *Southern Literary Messenger* (under the name of Harry Bluff) but was head of the Depot of Charts and Instruments in Washington, D.C., after 1842. Poe reviewed one of his navigation books in 1836. His *Wind and Current Chart of the North Atlantic* and other charts helped cut the sailing time from New York to San Francisco from 150 to 133 days.

4 The real Baron von Kempelen invented the automaton chess-player in 1769, although it was exhibited in the United States by Johan Nepomuk Maelzel, a Bavarian mechanic turned showman. The chess-player was constructed to make it appear that a mechanical man was

playing—and winning—chess games with human opponents, when in actuality it was operated by an assistant hidden inside (Poe wrote an essay exposing the fraud). The name of Von Kempelen is thus synonymous with hoax.

5 Sir Humphry Davy (1778–1829) was an English chemist and physicist who isolated potassium, sodium, calcium, barium, boron, magnesium, and strontium. He established the elemental nature of chlorine, and for good measure invented the miner's safety lamp.

At the end of an article on alchemy, Isaac D'Israeli records: "Sir Humphrey Davy told me that he did not consider this undiscovered art an impossible thing but which, should it ever be discovered, would certainly be useless" (*Curiosities of Literature*, 1823).

Although Poe never mentions it by name, the ancient art of alchemy is the basis of "Von Kempelen and His Discovery," specifically the alchemist's cherished dream of changing certain metals into gold. By the nineteenth century, metals were considered to be chemical elements, unalterable except through combination, and transmutation was therefore considered absurd.

In ancient times, however, alchemy was seriously practiced. Two metals were then said to be the same matter but specified by different *forms*. To change copper into gold, for example, one first removed the "form" of copper (a process referred to as the "death" or "corruption" of copper) and then introduced the new "form"—gold. The new form was drawn from a "spirit" that could be summoned to aid and direct generation and evoke new forms.

Alchemy originated in China in the fifth to third century B.C.; it was then brought to the West. Originally a species of metalwork, including the making of alloys, by its striving for perfection alchemy moved toward the transmutation of base metals into gold—the "most perfect" metal.

The philosopher's stone, also known as the elixir and the grand magistery, was a substance with which one could perform the transmutation of metals. It is interesting to note that current research suggests that at a very basic level transmutation *does* occur, for when a radioactive element disintegrates, one of a lower atomic weight results (when uranium 238 decays, for example, radioactive thorium is produced).

Transmutation of elements can also be achieved to some degree by the bombardment of elements with high-speed particles from accelerators.

Another kind of transmutation, this time on a truly cosmic level, takes place as a star burns out. Matter is compressed and burned, and elements are altered from the lighter hydrogen and helium to the heaviest metals, until a supernova scatters the matter throughout the universe.

We can see in alchemy the basis for modern chemistry, but alchemy always had a spiritual essence that is missing in contemporary science. An excellent book on the subject is Mircea Eliade's *The Forge and the Crucible* (Chicago, 1978), as is E. J. Holmyard's *Alchemy* (Penguin, 1957).

6 The Baltimore Athenaeum Library is still open today. While the bracketed statement is attributed to the editor of *The Flag of Our Union*, it is much more likely from Poe himself, an expedient way in which to get out of explaining something that does not exist.

7 The *Morning Courier and New York Enquirer*, whose editor, James Watson Webb, was a friend of Poe's and raised a fund for him after Virginia's death, in 1847

82, that this illustrious chemist had not only conceived the idea now in question, but had actually made *no inconsiderable progress, experimentally,* in the very *identical analysis* now so triumphantly brought to an issue by Von Kempelen, who, although he makes not the slightest allusion to it, is, *without doubt* (I say it unhesitatingly, and can prove it, if required), indebted to the "Diary" for at least the first hint of his own undertaking. Although a little technical, I cannot refrain from appending two passages from the "Diary," with one of Sir Humphrey's equations. [As we have not the algebraic signs necessary, and as the "Diary" is to be found at the Athenæum Library, we omit here a small portion of Mr. Poe's manu-
6 script.—ED.]

7 The paragraph from the *Courier and Enquirer*, which is now going the rounds of the press, and which purports to
8 claim the invention for a Mr. Kissam, of Brunswick, Maine, appears to me, I confess, a little apocryphal, for several reasons; although there is nothing either impossible or very improbable in the statement made. I need not go into details. My opinion of the paragraph is founded principally upon its *manner*. It does not *look* true. Persons who are narrating *facts*, are seldom so particular as Mr. Kissam seems to be, about day and date and precise location. Besides, if Mr.
9 Kissam actually *did* come upon the discovery he says he did, at the period designated—nearly eight years ago,—how happens it that he took no steps, *on the instant*, to reap the immense benefits which the merest bumpkin must have known would have resulted to him individually, if not to the world at large, from the discovery? It seems to me quite incredible that any man of common understanding could have discovered what Mr. Kissam says he did, and yet have subsequently acted so like a baby—so like an owl—as Mr. Kissam *admits* that he did. By-the-way, who *is* Mr. Kissam? and is not the whole paragraph in the *Courier and Enquirer* a fabrication got up to "make a talk"? It must be confessed
10 that it has an amazingly moon-hoax-y air. Very little dependence is to be placed upon it, in my humble opinion; and if I were not well aware, from experience, how very easily men of science are *mystified*, on points out of their usual range of inquiry, I should be profoundly astonished at finding so
11 eminent a chemist as Professor Draper, discussing Mr. Kis-
12 sam's (or is it Mr. Quizzem's?) pretensions to the discovery, in so serious a tone.

But to return to the "Diary" of Sir Humphrey Davy. This
13 pamphlet was *not* designed for the public eye, even upon the decease of the writer, as any person at all conversant with authorship may satisfy himself at once by the slightest inspection of the style. At page 13, for example, near the middle, we read, in reference to his researches about the protoxide of
14 azote: "In less than half a minute the respiration being continued, diminished gradually and *were* succeeded by analogous to gentle pressure on all the muscles." That the *respiration* was not "diminished," is not only clear by the subsequent context, but by the use of the plural, "were." The

sentence, no doubt, was thus intended: "In less than half a minute, the respiration being continued, [these feelings] diminished gradually, and were succeeded by [a sensation] analogous to gentle pressure on all the muscles." A hundred similar instances go to show that the MS. so inconsiderately published, was merely a *rough note-book*, meant only for the writer's own eye; but an inspection of the pamphlet will convince almost any thinking person of the truth of my suggestion. The fact is, Sir Humphrey Davy was about the last man in the world to *commit himself* on scientific topics. Not only had he a more than ordinary dislike to quackery, but he was morbidly afraid of *appearing* empirical; so that, however fully he might have been convinced that he was on the right track in the matter now in question, he would never have spoken *out*, until he had everything ready for the most practical demonstration. I verily believe that his last moments [15] would have been rendered wretched, could he have suspected that his wishes in regard to burning this "Diary" (full of crude speculations) would have been unattended to; as, it seems, they were. I say "his wishes," for that he meant to include this note-book among the miscellaneous papers directed "to be burnt," I think there can be no manner of doubt. Whether [16] it escaped the flames by good fortune or by bad, yet remains to be seen. That the passages quoted above, with the other similar ones referred to, gave Von Kempelen *the hint*, I do not in the slightest degree question; but I repeat, it yet remains to be seen whether this momentous discovery itself (*momentous* under any circumstances) will be of service or disservice to mankind at large. That Von Kempelen and his immediate friends will reap a rich harvest, it would be folly to doubt for a moment. They will scarcely be so weak as not to "*realize*," in time, by large purchases of houses and land, with other property of *intrinsic* value. [17]

In the brief account of Von Kempelen which appeared in the *Home Journal*, and has since been extensively copied, [18] several misapprehensions of the German original seem to have been made by the translator, who professes to have taken the passage from a late number of the Presburg *Schnellpost*. "*Viele*" has evidently been misconceived (as it often is), and what the translator renders by "sorrows," is probably "*lieden*," which, in its true version, "sufferings," would give a totally different complexion to the whole account; but, of course, much of this is merely guess, on my part.

Von Kempelen, however, is by no means "a misanthrope," in appearance, at least, whatever he may be in fact. My acquaintance with him was casual altogether; and I am scarcely warranted in saying that I know him at all; but to have seen and conversed with a man of so *prodigious* a notoriety as he has attained, or *will* attain in a few days, is not a small matter, as times go.

The Literary World speaks of him, confidently, as a *native* [19] of Presburg (misled, perhaps, by the account in *The Home Journal*) but I am pleased in being able to state *positively*, since I have it from his own lips, that he was born in Utica, [20]

8 "Kissam" is wordplay, obviously, and possibly used here as a friendly poke at George W Eveleth, who lived in Brunswick, Maine (see note 12).

9 Since we have no way of knowing what Mr. Kissam wrote, we can only assume that the fictional chemist didn't bring his discovery to public attention.

10 Referring to Richard Adams Locke's "Moon Hoax," which is discussed in "Hans Pfaall" and "The Balloon Hoax."

11 John William Draper, a professor at New York University, was a leading scientist of his day; he did much to improve the speed of early photographic plates. Poe apparently disliked him, as is evident from remarks made in a letter dated June 27, 1849.

12 Eveleth was a medical student at the Maine Medical School, in Brunswick, and had carried on a lengthy correspondence with Poe. But when Eveleth began publishing his own cosmological theories, Poe saw this as stealing thunder from his own *Eureka*. Eveleth had also consulted John William Draper while compiling his theories, which did not improve his case.

"Quiz" means a hoax or joke, so that the fictional name might just as well be "Hoaxum." Given this, "Kissam" could mean "kissing up" (currying favor), a definite slap at Eveleth's consulting Draper.

13 The diary is fictional; the source is actually Davy's *Collected Works*, III, "Researches Concerning Nitrous Oxide" (London, 1838):

"Having previously closed my nostrils and exhausted my lungs, I breathed four quarts of nitrous oxide from and into a silk bag. The first feelings were similar to those produced in the last experiment, but in less than half a minute, the respiration being continued, they diminished gradually and were succeeded by a sensation analogous to gentle pressure on all the muscles, attended by a highly pleasurable thrilling, particularly in the chest and the extremities." This is the first description of the effect of what was to be called "laughing gas."

Poe is manipulating phrases here that are not familiar to the average reader. His "corrections" are Davy's actual phrasing, but he gives the impression that he knows a great deal about the source in question. He also makes it clear from the laughing gas that the whole matter is laughable.

Davy's connection with alchemy is almost nonexistent, but Poe may have had in mind the scientist's discoveries in electrolysis; for example that the electrical condition of a substance can modify its chemical properties.

14 "Azote" was Lavoisier's term for oxygen. "Protoxide" is an early-nineteenth-century term for a compound of oxygen and another element, or radical, that contains the smallest proportion of oxygen. We use the term "oxide" today, and so "protoxide of azote" is nitrous oxide.

15 "Davy had learned caution since his early unfortunate hypothesis of oxygen as a compound containing light, and retreated to empirical definitions" (Cecil J. Schneer, *Mind and Matter*, Grove Press, 1969).

16 Although Davy was jealous of his protégé, Michael Faraday, and tried to block his election to the Royal Academy in 1824 (unsuccessfully), he was not so consumed with envy as to burn all his papers to prevent their falling into the younger scientist's hands. In fact, Davy did not burn his notebooks at all: they are in the

Royal Institution along with a large collection of manuscripts in his handwriting.

17 "Realize" is a pun on "real estate," while "intrinsic" seems to be a jab at the gold-hungry mobs, since gold does have its own intrinsic value. Poe suggests that the gold seekers want the gold only for what they can buy with it; for them the precious metal has little meaning in and of itself.

18 The New York *Home-Journal* had always been friendly toward Poe, but he had been upset by the paper's published appeal in 1847 to aid him while his wife was dying. He felt it was out of place and even insulting.

The mistranslation referred to here has nothing to do with the Von Kempelen story but everything to do with the appeal of 1847. *Viele Leiden* means "much suffering," a reference to Poe's anguish over his wife's death—and the *Home-Journal* had misinterpreted and publicized what he apparently felt was a strictly private matter. Poe's misspelling and noncapitalization of *Leiden* shows him less a master of German than French (although it could be a typographical error). He took the comment from Sarah Austin's translation of Prince Pückler-Muskau's *Tour* (1833): "*Leiden* does not mean *sorrows*, but *sufferings*" (p. 388).

The Pressburg *Schnellpost* was actually an American bi-weekly, the *Deutsche Schnellpost für Europäische Zustände, offentliches und sociales Leben Deutschlands*, which began publishing in 1843. Poe regularly saw copies while he worked at the *Broadway Journal*.

Pressburg was the German version of Bratislava, the former capital of Hungary and traditional home of instruction in magic (see "Morella").

19 The publication to which Poe originally tried to sell this story

20 A manufacturing city, certainly about as far away from the magic atmosphere of Pressburg as one can get. Poe uses the same device in "Bon-Bon."

21 Poe's "Maelzel's Chess-Player" (1836) is an essay debunking this notourious hoax of the period.

22 Again, the "editor" is probably Poe himself.

23 A cloven hoof?

24 Geniality, good nature. It should be spelled *bonhomie*.

25 In 1848 Poe spent some time at this hotel while courting Helen Whitman, the wealthy widow who could have pulled him out of debt once and for all. Unfortunately, at the insistence of her family, she divested herself of her property while engaged to Poe, and a drunken episode at the hotel bar later put a stop to the relationship.

26 The German North Sea port city.

in the State of New York, although both his parents, I believe, are of Presburg descent. The family is connected, in some **21** way, with Mäelzel, of automaton-chess-player memory. [If we are not mistaken, the name of the *inventor* of the chess-player was either Kempelen, Von Kempelen, or something like it.— **22** Ed.] In person, he is short and stout, with large, *fat*, blue eyes, sandy hair and whiskers, a wide but pleasing mouth, fine teeth, and I think a Roman nose. There is some defect **23** in one of his feet. His address is frank, and his whole manner **24** noticeable for *bonhommie*. Altogether, he looks, speaks, and acts as little like "a misanthrope" as any man I ever saw. We were fellow-sojourners for a week, about six years ago, at **25** Earl's Hotel, in Providence, Rhode Island; and I presume that I conversed with him, at various times, for some three or four hours altogether. His principal topics were those of the day; and nothing that fell from him led me to suspect his scientific attainments. He left the hotel before me, intending to go to **26** New York, and thence to Bremen; it was in the latter city that his great discovery was first made public; or, rather, it was there that he was first suspected of having made it. This is about all that I personally know of the now immortal Von Kempelen; but I have thought that even these few details would have interest for the public.

There can be little question that most of the marvellous rumors afloat about this affair are pure inventions, entitled to about as much credit as the story of Aladdin's lamp; and yet, in a case of this kind, as in the case of the discoveries in

. . . they traced him to a garret in an old house . . . and, coming upon him suddenly, found him, as they imagined, in the midst of his counterfeiting operations." *Illustration by F. S. Coburn, 1903*

California, it is clear that the truth *may be* stranger than [27] fiction. The following anecdote, at least, is so well authenti- [28] cated, that we may receive it implicitly.

Von Kempelen had never been even tolerably well off during his residence at Bremen; and often, it was well known, he had been put to extreme shifts in order to raise trifling [29] sums. When the great excitement occurred about the forgery on the house of Gutsmuth & Co., suspicion was directed toward Von Kempelen, on account of his having purchased a considerable property in Gasperitch Lane, and his refusing, [30] when questioned, to explain how he became possessed of the purchase money. He was at length arrested, but nothing decisive appearing against him, was in the end set at liberty. The police, however, kept a strict watch upon his movements, and thus discovered that he left home frequently, taking always the same road, and invariably giving his watchers the slip in the neighborhood of that labyrinth of narrow and crooked passages known by the flash name of the "Dondergat." [31,32] Finally, by dint of great perseverance, they traced him to a garret in an old house of seven stories, in an alley called Flatzplatz; and, coming upon him suddenly, found him, as [33] they imagined, in the midst of his counterfeiting operations. His agitation is represented as so excessive that the officers had not the slightest doubt of his guilt. After handcuffing him, they searched his room, or rather rooms, for it appears he occupied all the *mansarde*. [34]

Opening into the garret where they caught him was a closet, ten feet by eight, fitted up with some chemical apparatus, of which the object has not yet been ascertained. In one corner of the closet was a very small furnace, with a glowing fire in it, and on the fire a kind of duplicate crucible— two crucibles connected by a tube. One of these crucibles was nearly full of *lead* in a state of fusion, but not reaching up to the aperture of the tube, which was close to the brim. The other crucible had some liquid in it, which, as the officers entered, seemed to be furiously dissipating in vapor. They [35] relate that, on finding himself taken, Von Kempelen seized the crucibles with both hands (which were encased in gloves that afterward turned out to be asbestic), and threw the contents on the tiled floor. It was now that they handcuffed him; and before proceeding to ransack the premises, they searched his person, but nothing unusual was found about him, excepting a paper parcel, in his coat-pocket, containing what was afterward ascertained to be a mixture of antimony [36] and some *unknown substance,* in nearly, but not quite, equal [37] proportions. All attempts at analyzing the unknown substance have, so far, failed, but that it will ultimately be analyzed, is not to be doubted.

Passing out of the closet with their prisoner, the officers went through a sort of ante-chamber, in which nothing material was found, to the chemist's sleeping-room. They here rummaged some drawers and boxes, but discovered only a few papers, of no importance, and some good coin, silver and gold. At length, looking under the bed, they saw *a large, common*

27 Thousands of people from all over the world went to California, spurred on by tales of gold nuggets waiting to be picked up by the handful. Unfortunately, the easy pickings disappeared quickly, and the gold that was left, while plentiful, demanded time, effort, and a great deal of capital investment. Only a small number of prospectors found enough gold to make themselves rich, but the influx of people did make the development of the West an immediate and certain thing.

28 " 'Tis strange—but true; for truth is always strange; Stranger than fiction" (Byron, *Don Juan*, canto XIV, 101).

A particularly apt rendering of the old saying, and somehow very Poesque, is the anonymous "Truth is stranger than fiction, but not so popular."

29 Expedients made necessary by extreme circumstances

30 Johann Christoph F. Gutsmuths and Adam Christian Gaspari were the authors of well-known geopgraphy books of the day.

31 Ostentatious, showy. "Flash" also may be a reference to the language of thieves, also called by that name. See "The Man of the Crowd," note 10.

32 "Thunder god," i.e., Thor, the Norse god of thunder and lightning, and perhaps a wordplay on "flash." Thor is associated with iron, however, and not gold, but Poe may be suggesting the link between gold and the yellow of lightning.

33 The German names here are all fictitious.

34 The *mansarde* is the top story of a nineteenth-century Parisian house, directly beneath the roof. See "Rue Morgue," note 65.

35 This is the first clear reference to the alchemical process—no doubt the philosopher's stone itself.

36 The metallic element antimony was known to the ancients but not adequately described until the eighteenth century, long after alchemy had been relegated to pseudoscience. The element displays the properties of both a metal and a nonmetal, uniting with hydrogen to form a poisonous gas, stibine. It is used in making alloys, in the vulcanization of rubber, and in medicine.

37 The substance could be just about anything—in alchemy there were no-holds-barred rules in the search for the proper combination of chemicals that would induce the transmutation process. Here, for example, is a recipe from *The Experiments of Raymond Lully of Majorca* (1330; English edition, 1558):

"Take aqua fortis with his form, as I have taught you before, and in it dissolve 3 ounces of [silver]; then purify it 20 days, then take 3 oz. of [gold] and dissolve it in 18 oz. of the same aqua fortis with his form in which yet 4 oz. of the fixed salt of Urine ought to be first dissolved, as you have it in his Experiment. Then putrify these 2 bodies by themselves severally for 20 natural days. Then [remove the spirit of] them both severally by themselves, as well silver as gold, even to the rule delivered you before. . . ."

F. Sherwood Taylor, in *The Alchemists* (1974), translates this into modern chemical terminology as follows:

"Three ounces of silver is dissolved in nitric acid. Three ounces of gold is dissolved in 18 ounces of nitric acid in which was dissolved four ounces of a product chiefly consisting of common salt. Solutions (a) of silver nitrate and (b) of gold chloride are obtained. Both solutions are left for 20 days, then distilled to dryness. The distillates consisting (a) of fairly strong nitric acid and (b) of nitric acid containing some chlorine are preserved. The dry salts (earth) are heated till they give no more fumes. . . ."

The result, says Taylor, is "a very weak gold amalgam, and to such an anticlimax come all attempts to give a chemical interpretation to recipies for transmutation."

Taylor points to the belief among some scholars that the recipes were not chemical at all, but symbolic of some mystical operations, to which Carl Jung heartily concurs in his *Psychology and Alchemy*, 2nd ed. (Princeton, 1968). The material world was considered to be filled with "the projection of a psychic secret, which from then on appeared as the secret of matter and remained so until the decay of alchemy in the 18th century," he notes (p. 14). Alchemists searched for this secret spirit in the philosopher's stone, in order to transform imperfect metals into their perfect state. As with the Church, Jung notes, the object is redemption.

38 A hair trunk was a trunk covered with animal skin, with the fur or hair still attached.

39 If gold were transmuted from another metal, it would of course be absolutely pure, as opposed to that smelted from gold ore, which contains impurities.

40 The philosopher's stone was not necessarily a stone at all, but a substance of which even a small quantity would transmute a much larger quantity of base metal into gold or silver. It is first mentioned in Chinese texts. In a text dating back to the beginning of the Christian era, we find that "a gentleman of the Yellow Gate at the Han [imperial court], Cheng Wei, loved the art of the Yellow and White [alchemy]. Wei tried to "make gold in accordance with 'the great Treasure' in the pillow [of the King of Juai-nan, but] it would not come. His wife however came and watched Wei. Wei was then fanning the ashes to heat the bottle. In the bottle there was quicksilver. His wife said, 'I want to try and show you something.' She thereupon took a drug out of a bag and threw a very little into [the retort]. It had already become silver. Wei was greatly astonished, and said, 'The way of [alchemy] was near and was possessed by you. But why did you not tell me sooner?' His wife replied, 'In order to get it, it is necessary for one to have the [proper] fate." (Wu and Davis, "The Ts-an T'ung Ch'i of Wei Po-yang," *Isis*, Vol. XVIII, 2, no. 53, p. 258)

It was the Chinese (by the way of the Arabs) who contributed the notion of the philosopher's stone. Greek alchemists seemed to be more interested in the making of gold, rather than in a something that could transform other substances into the precious metal. There is, however, a certain amount of discussion in the *Pharmakon* of the "stone that is not a stone," but the reference seems to be to something other than what was later called "the stone."

41 Bismuth is another metal useful in alloys.

42 With a grain of salt. Poe is having some more fun at the reader's expense, again signaling the hoaxing nature of the tale—and at the same time playing with the fact that bismuth itself forms salts.

43 The quote lends an air of reality to the tale, but it is merely another Poe fiction.

38 *hair trunk, without hinges, hasp, or lock,* and with the top lying carelessly *across* the bottom portion. Upon attempting to draw this trunk out from under the bed, they found that, with their united strength (there were three of them, all powerful men), they "could not stir it one inch." Much astonished at this, one of them crawled under the bed, and looking into the trunk, said:

"No wonder we couldn't move it—why it's full to the brim of old bits of brass!"

Putting his feet, now, against the wall, so as to get a good purchase, and pushing with all his force, while his companions pulled with all theirs, the trunk, with much difficulty, was slid out from under the bed, and its contents examined. The supposed brass with which it was filled was all in small, smooth pieces, varying from the size of a pea to that of a dollar; but the pieces were irregular in shape, although more or less flat—looking, upon the whole, "very much as lead looks when thrown upon the ground in a molten state, and there suffered to grow cool." Now, not one of these officers for a moment suspected this metal to be anything *but* brass. The idea of its being *gold* never entered their brains, of course; how *could* such a wild fancy have entered it? And their astonishment may be well conceived, when next day it became known, all over Bremen, that the "lot of brass" which they had carted so contemptuously to the police office, without putting themselves to the trouble of pocketing the smallest scrap, was not only gold—real gold—but gold far finer than any employed in coinage—gold, in fact, absolutely pure, virgin, without the

39 slightest appreciable alloy!

I need not go over the details of Von Kempelen's confession (as far as it went) and release, for these are familiar to the public. That he has actually realized, in spirit and in effect, if not to the letter, the old chimera of the philosopher's stone,

40 no sane person is at liberty to doubt. The opinions of Arago are, of course, entitled to the greatest consideration; but he

41 is by no means infallible; and what he says of *bismuth*, in his

42 report to the Academy, must be taken *cum grano salis*. The simple truth is, that up to this period *all* analysis has failed; and until Von Kempelen chooses to let us have the key to his own published enigma, it is more than probable that the matter will remain, for years, *in statu quo*. All that as yet can fairly be said to be known is, that "*pure gold can be made at will, and very readily from lead in connection with certain other substances, in kind and in proportions,*

43 *other substances, in kind and in proportions, unknown.*"

Speculation, of course, is busy as to the immediate and ultimate results of this discovery—a discovery which few thinking persons will hesitate in referring to an increased interest in the matter of gold generally, by the late developments in California; and this reflection brings us inevitably to another—the exceeding *inopportuneness* of Von Kempelen's analysis. If many were prevented from adventuring to California, by the mere apprehension that gold would so materially diminish in value, on account of its plentifulness in the mines there, as to render the speculation of going so far in search of it a doubtful one—what impression will be wrought *now*, upon the minds of those about to emigrate, and especially upon the minds of those actually in the mineral region, by the announcement of this astounding discovery of Von Kempelen? a discovery which declares, in so many words, that beyond its intrinsic worth for manufacturing purposes (whatever that worth may be), gold now is, or at least soon will be (for it cannot be supposed that Von Kempelen can *long* retain his secret), of no greater *value* than lead, and of far inferior value to silver. It is, indeed, exceedingly difficult to speculate **44** prospectively upon the consequences of the discovery; but one thing may be positively maintained—that the announcement of the discovery six months ago would have had material influence in regard to the settlement of California.

In Europe, as yet, the most noticeable results have been a rise of two hundred per cent. in the price of lead, and nearly **45** twenty-five per cent. in that of silver.

44 Gold's value is dependent upon its scarcity, and Poe points out that if the precious metal were really as easy to make as the alchemists hoped, its value would plummet.

Poe may not have been aware that alchemists were also interested in the transmutation of metals into silver.

45 The ultimate joke: worthless lead now has value. Of course, if the secret of transmutation were known, soon both gold *and* lead would lose their value.

Some further reading in alchemy might include Johannes Fabricius' *Alchemy: The Medieval Alchemists and their Royal Art* (Copenhagen, 1976), which provides a fascinating coupling of both traditional and Jungian interpretations of the art.

LANDOR'S COTTAGE

A PENDANT TO "THE DOMAIN OF ARNHEIM"

First published in the Boston *Flag of Our Union*, June 9, 1849, this is a charming piece, although it is more a descriptive narrative than a short story. Poe here writes about an area he knows well, having first taken a tour of the Hudson River counties in the summer of 1848. He had originally hoped to write an account of his journeys, but it never came about. The house described here is Poe's own Fordham cottage, albeit with a much more idealized appearance than it actually possessed, obviously inspired by "The Landscape Garden."

A friend, Mary Gove Nichols, described Poe's "little cottage at the top of a hill" in these words: "There was an acre or two of greensward, fenced in about the house, as smooth as velvet and as clean as the best kept carpet. There were some grand old cherry-trees in the yard, that threw a massive shade around them. The house had three rooms—a kitchen, a sitting-room, and a bed-chamber over the sitting-room. There was a piazza in front of the house that was a lovely place to sit in summer. . . . There was no cultivation, no flowers—nothing but the smooth greensward and the majestic trees. . . . The floor of the kitchen was white as wheaten flour. A table, a chair, and a little stove that it contained seemed to furnish it completely. The sitting-room floor was laid with check matting; four chairs, a light stand, and a hanging book-shelf completed its furniture." ("Reminiscenes," London *Sixpenny Magazine*, February 1863)

In the last paragraph of the original manuscript, Poe mentioned the possibility of a sequel, but he never got around to it. This was the last story of Poe's printed in his lifetime. He would begin one more, "The Lighthouse," and leave it unfinished when he went to his mysterious death, in Baltimore.

1 Poe apparently walked from Fordham (then in Westchester County) through Putnam County to the north, and then into Duchess County (where, in Poughkeepsie, lived Andrew Jackson Davis, mentioned in "Von Kempelen and His Discovery" and "Tale of the Ragged Mountains)."

2 The village may be fictional, since it has not been identified.

3 The O.E.D. traces this to J. Hector St. John (Crèvecoeur, 1731–1813), who in 1778 described it as "a short interval of smoke and mildness" after the first frost. Mencken refers to the "balmy, smoky weather that usually prevails along the Atlantic Coast of the United States from the end of October until the onset of winter" (*American Language*, p. 117). See "A Tale of the Ragged Mountains," note 13.

During a pedestrian trip last summer, through one or two of **1** the river counties of New York, I found myself, as the day declined, somewhat embarrassed about the road I was pursuing. The land undulated very remarkably; and my path, for the last hour, had wound about and about so confusedly, in its effort to keep in the valleys, that I no longer knew in what **2** direction lay the sweet village of B——, where I had determined to stop for the night. The sun had scarcely *shone*—strictly speaking—during the day, which, nevertheless, had been unpleasantly warm. A smoky mist, resembling that of **3** the Indian summer, enveloped all things, and of course, added to my uncertainty. Not that I cared much about the matter. If I did not hit upon the village before sunset, or even before dark, it was more than possible that a little Dutch farmhouse, or something of that kind, would soon make its appearance—although, in fact, the neighborhood (perhaps on account of being more picturesque than fertile) was very sparsely inhabited. At all events, with my knapsack for a pillow, and my hound as a sentry, a bivouac in the open air was just the thing which would have amused me. I sauntered on, therefore, **4** quite at ease—Ponto taking charge of my gun—until at length, **5** just as I had begun to consider whether the numerous little glades that led hither and thither, were intended to be paths at all, I was conducted by one of them into an unquestionable carriage track. There could be no mistaking it. The traces of light wheels were evident; and although the tall shrubberies and overgrown undergrowth met overhead, there was no obstruction whatever below, even to the passage of a Virginian mountain wagon—the most aspiring vehicle, I take it, of its **6** kind. The road, however, except in being open through the wood—if wood be not too weighty a name for such an assemblage of light trees—and except in the particulars of evident wheel-tracks—bore no resemblance to any road I had before seen. The tracks of which I speak were but faintly perceptible—having been impressed upon the firm, yet pleasantly moist surface of—what looked more like green Genoese velvet than any thing else. It was grass, clearly—but grass **7** such as we seldom see out of England—so short, so thick, so even, and so vivid in color. Not a single impediment lay in the wheel-route—not even a chip or dead twig. The stones that once obstructed the way had been carefully *placed*—not thrown—along the sides of the lane, so as to define its boundaries at bottom with a kind of half-precise, half-negligent, and wholly picturesque definition. Clumps of wild flowers grew everywhere, luxuriantly, in the interspaces.

What to make of all this, of course I knew not. Here was *art* undoubtedly—*that* did not surprise me—all roads, in the ordinary sense, are works of art; nor can I say that there was **8** much to wonder at in the mere *excess* of art manifested; all that seemed to have been done, might have been done *here*—with such natural "capabilities" (as they have it in the books **9** on Landscape Gardening)—with very little labor and expense. No; it was not the amount but the *character* of the art which caused me to take a seat on one of the blossomy stones and gaze up and down this fairy-like avenue for half an hour or more in bewildered admiration. One thing became more and

Fordham cottage. *Illustration by C. A. Stoddard*

4 Compare this with a passage from Washington Irving's "Rip Van Winkle": "In a long ramble of this kind on a fine autumnal day, Rip had unconsciously scrambled to one of the highest parts of the Kaatskill mountains. . . . Panting and fatigued, he threw himself, late in the afternoon, on a green knoll, covered with mountain herbage, that crowned the brow of a precipice. From an opening between the trees he could overlook all the lower country for many a mile of rich woodland. He saw at a distance the lordly Hudson, far, far below him, moving on its silent but majestic course, with the reflection of a purple cloud, or the sail of a lagging bark, here and there sleeping on its glassy bosom, and at last lost itself in the blue highlands."

Like the narrator of "Landor's Cottage," Rip has set off on his walk through the river country of New York, accompanied by his dog, carrying a gun, and soon finds himself in fantastic surroundings. In Irving's tale, however, the magic is literal; here it is figurative.

5 Ponto, like Fido and Rover, was once a popular name for a dog. It is also the name of the narrator's dog in *Sheppard Lee*, the novel by R. M. Bird that Poe reviewed in 1836. The narrator has here left his gun behind, with the dog to watch over it.

6 Mountain wagons of the day were fairly high, with wheels forty-four to fifty-two inches in diameter, so that, fully loaded and with a driver, they could easily have been inconvenienced by low-hanging branches.

7 Velvetlike grass appears also in "The Domain of Arnheim" and "Bon-Bon." See also the description by Mrs. Nichols in the introductory notes.

8 Contrast William Blake: "Improvement makes straight roads; but the crooked roads without improvement are roads of genius" ("Proverbs of Hell," from *The Marriage of Heaven and Hell*, 1793).

9 Lancelot "Capability" Brown is mentioned in "The Landscape Garden" and "The Domain of Arnheim" (note 10) as the gardener who talked often of the capabilities or potential of an area.

He developed an artfully informal manner and devised many parks with wide expanses of lawns, clumps of trees, serpentine lakes, and other improvements that were a far cry from the very formalized gardens of the previous century. His object was to "tame" nature, and his idyllic parks were bounded by a thick planting of trees to protect the view from the "unimproved" landscape beyond. His probably apocryphal remark on his lake at Blenheim—"Thames, Thames, you will never forgive me"—pretty well sums up his attitude.

For more on this intriguing character, see *Capability Brown*, by Dorothy Stroud (Faber & Faber, 1975).

10 Meaning "in the style of a painter." In "The Land-scape Garden," Poe states: "No such combinations of scenery exist in nature as the painter of genius has the power to produce."

In *An Essay on the Picturesque as compared with the Sublime and the Beautiful; and, on the Use of studying Pictures for the Purpose of improving real Landscapes* (1794), Uvedale Price states: "Upon the whole, it appears to me, that as intricacy in the disposition, and variety in the forms, the tints, and the lights and shadows of objects, are the great characteristics of picturesque scenery; so monotony and baldness are the greatest defects of improved places" (p. 18). He also speaks of the relationship between painting and landscape design: "We may look upon pictures as a set of experiments of the different ways in which trees, buildings, water &c, may be disposed, grouped, and accompanied in the most beautiful and striking manner . . ." (p. 5).

Price defines "picturesque" as being "applied to every object, and every kind of scenery, which has been, or might be represented with good effect in painting, and that without any exclusion" (p. 34), but ultimately finds that too vague, and decides that "the two opposite qualities of roughness and of sudden variation, joined to that of irregularity, are the most efficient causes of the picturesque" (pp. 44–45).

11 "All the leading features, and a thousand circum-stances of detail, promote the natural intricacy of the ground; the turns are sudden and unprepared; the banks some times broken and abrupt; some times smooth, and gently but not uniformly sloping . . . ; no cut edges, no distinct lines of separation; all is mixed and blended together, and the border of the road itself, shaped by the mere tread of passengers and animals, is as uncon-strained as the footsteps that formed it" (Price, pp. 20–21).

12 A form of the magic-lantern show, in which pictures were projected on a curtain and then made to disappear, often to represent spirits.

13 A *chassé* is a gliding dance step.

14 Glance

15 "Monstrosity" seems out of place, for besides its meaning of enormity, there is the long-established idea of abnormal and contrary to nature. But see "Scheher-azade," note 33.

more evident the longer I gazed: an artist, and one with a most scrupulous eye for form, had superintended all these arrangements. The greatest care had been taken to preserve a due medium between the neat and graceful on the one hand, and the *pittoresque*, in the true sense of the Italian term, on the other. There were few straight, and no long uninterrupted lines. The same effect of curvature or of color appeared twice, usually, but not oftener, at any one point of view. Everywhere was variety in uniformity. It was a piece of "composition," in which the most fastidiously critical taste could scarcely have suggested an emendation.

I had turned to the right as I entered this road, and now, arising, I continued in the same direction. The path was so serpentine, that at no moment could I trace its course for more than two or three paces in advance. Its character did not undergo any material change.

Presently the murmur of water fell gently upon my ear— and in a few moments afterward, as I turned with the road somewhat more abruptly than hitherto, I became aware that a building of some kind lay at the foot of a gentle declivity just before me. I could see nothing distinctly on account of the mist which occupied all the little valley below. A gentle breeze, however, now arose, as the sun was about descending; and while I remained standing on the brow of the slope, the fog gradually became dissipated into wreaths, and so floated over the scene.

As it came fully into view—thus *gradually* as I describe it— piece by piece, here a tree, there a glimpse of water, and here again the summit of a chimney, I could scarcely help fancying that the whole was one of the ingenious illusions sometimes exhibited under the name of "vanishing pictures."

By the time, however, that the fog had thoroughly disap-peared, the sun had made its way down behind the gentle hills, and thence, as if with a slight *chassez* to the south, had come again fully into sight, glaring with a purplish lustre through a chasm that entered the valley for the west. Suddenly, therefore—and as if by the hand of magic—this whole valley and every thing in it became brilliantly visible.

The first *coup d'œil*, as the sun slid into the position described, impressed me very much as I have been impressed, when a boy, by the concluding scene of some well-arranged theatrical spectacle or melodrama. Not even the monstrosity of color was wanting; for the sunlight came out through the chasm, tinted all orange and purple; while the vivid green of the grass in the valley was reflected more or less upon all objects from the curtain of vapor that still hung overhead, as if loth to take its total departure from a scene so enchantingly beautiful.

The little vale into which I thus peered down from under the fog-canopy could not have been more than four hundred yards long; while in breadth it varied from fifty to one hundred and fifty or perhaps two hundred. It was most narrow at its northern extremity, opening out as it tended southwardly, but with no very precise regularity. The widest portion was within eighty yards of the southern extreme. The slopes which encompassed the vale could not fairly be called hills, unless at their northern face. Here a precipitous ledge of granite arose to a height of some ninety feet; and, as I have mentioned, the valley at this point was not more than fifty feet wide; but as the visitor proceeded southwardly from this cliff, he found on his right hand and on his left, declivities at once less high, less precipitous, and less rocky. All, in a word, sloped and softened to the south; and yet the whole vale was engirdled by eminences, more or less high, except at two points. One of these I have already spoken of. It lay considerably to the north of west, and was where the setting sun made its way, as I have before described, into the amphitheatre, through a cleanly cut natural cleft in the granite embankment; this fissure might have been ten yards wide at its widest point, so far as the eye could trace it. It seemed to lead up, up, like a natural causeway, into the recesses of unexplored mountains and forests. The other opening was directly at the southern end of the vale. Here, generally, the slopes were nothing more than gentle inclinations, extending from east to west about one hundred and fifty yards. In the middle of this extent was a depression, level with the ordinary floor of the valley. As regards vegetation, as well as in respect to every thing else, the scene *softened and sloped* to the south. To the north—on the craggy precipice—a few paces from the verge—up sprang the magnificent trunks of numerous hickories, black walnuts, and chestnuts, interspersed with occasional oak; and the strong lateral branches thrown out by the walnuts especially, spread far over the edge of the cliff. Proceeding southwardly, the explorer saw, at first, the same class of trees, but less and less lofty and Salvatorish in character; then he saw the gentler elm, succeeded by the sassafras and locust—these again by the softer linden, red-bud, catalpa, and maple—these yet again by still more graceful and more modest varieties. The whole face of the southern declivity was covered with wild shrubbery alone—an occasional silver willow or white poplar excepted. In the bottom of the valley itself—(for it must be borne in mind that the vegetation hitherto mentioned grew only on the cliffs or hillsides)—were to be seen three insulated trees. One was an elm of fine size and exquisite form: it stood guard over the southern gate of the vale. Another was a hickory, much larger than the elm, and altogether a much finer tree, although both were exceedingly beautiful: it seemed to have taken charge of the northwestern entrance, springing from a group of rocks in the very jaws of the ravine, and throwing its graceful body, at an angle of nearly forty-five degrees, far out into the sunshine of the amphitheatre. About thirty yards east of this tree stood, however, the pride of the valley, and beyond all question the most magnificent tree I have ever seen, unless, perhaps, among the cypresses of the Itchiatuckanee. It was a triple-stemmed tulip-tree—the *Liriodendron Tulipiferum*—one of the natural order of magnolias. Its three trunks separated from the parent at about three feet from the soil, and diverging

16

17

18
19

"Suddenly . . . and as if by the hand of magic—this whole valley and every thing in it became brilliantly visible." *Illustration by F. S. Coburn, 1902*

16 The setting sun is important in the concept of the picturesque. Uvedale Price says that "twilight does what an improver ought to do; it fills up staring, meagre vacancies; it destroys edginess, and by giving shadow as well as light to water, at once increases both its brilliancy and softness" (p. 126).

17 Salvatore Rosa (1615–73), painter, etcher, poet, actor, and musician, was the nineteenth-century's idea of the Romantic artist. He was even supposed to have been a bandit for a time, but this seems to have been a concoction of someone's imagination. He was a prolific painter of landscapes near his native Naples and is famed for his rather wild scenes in the Apennines.

18 Perhaps the Ichawaynochaway, a creek that flows into the Flint River, in Georgia. The cypress trees certainly indicate a southern locale.

19 See "The Gold-Bug," note 21.

very slightly and gradually, were not more than four feet apart at the point where the largest stem shot out into foliage: this was at an elevation of about eighty feet. The whole height of the principal division was one hundred and twenty feet. Nothing can surpass in beauty the form, or the glossy, vivid green of the leaves of the tulip-tree. In the present instance they were fully eight inches wide; but their glory was altogether eclipsed by the gorgeous splendor of the profuse blossoms. Conceive, closely congregated, a million of the largest and most resplendent tulips! Only thus can the reader get any idea of the picture I would convey. And then the stately grace of the clean, delicately-granulated columnar stems, the largest four feet in diameter, at twenty from the ground. The innumerable blossoms, mingling with those of other trees scarcely less beautiful, although infinitely less majestic, filled **20** the valley with more than Arabian perfumes.

The general floor of the amphitheatre was *grass* of the same character as that I had found in the road; if anything, more deliciously soft, thick, velvety, and miraculously green. It was hard to conceive how all this beauty had been attained.

I have spoken of two openings into the vale. From the one to the northwest issued a rivulet, which came, gently murmuring and slightly foaming, down the ravine, until it dashed against the group of rocks out of which sprang the insulated hickory. Here, after encircling the tree, it passed on a little to the north of east, leaving the tulip-tree some twenty feet to the south, and making no decided alteration in its course until it came near the midway between the eastern and western boundaries of the valley. At this point, after a series of sweeps, it turned off at right angles and pursued a generally southern direction—meandering as it went—until it became lost in a small lake of irregular figure (although roughly oval), that lay gleaming near the lower extremity of the vale. This lakelet was, perhaps, a hundred yards in diameter at its widest part. No crystal could be clearer than its waters. Its bottom, which could be distinctly seen, consisted altogether of pebbles brilliantly white. Its banks, of the emerald grass already described, *rounded*, rather than sloped, off into the clear heaven below; and *so* clear was this heaven, so perfectly, at times, did it reflect all objects above it, that where the true bank ended and where the mimic one commenced, it was a point of no little difficulty to determine. The trout, and some other varieties of fish, with which this pond seemed to be almost inconveniently crowded, had all the appearance of veritable flying-fish. It was almost impossible to believe that **21** they were not absolutely suspended in the air. A light birch canoe that lay placidly on the water, was reflected in its minutest fibres with a fidelity unsurpassed by the most exquisitely polished mirror. A small island, fairly laughing with flowers in full bloom, and affording little more space than just enough for a picturesque little building, seemingly a fowl-house—arose from the lake not far from its northern shore—to which it was connected by means of an inconceivably light-looking and yet very primitive bridge. It was formed of a

20 Arabia was not a center for perfume production, but a trade center for perfumes, spices, and incense during the Middle Ages, when the Crusaders brought these items back from the Holy Land.

21 "So blended bank and shadow there/That each seemed pendulous in air" is from Poe's "The Island of the Fay." See also Price's comments in note 11.

single, broad and thick plank of the tulip wood. This was forty feet long, and spanned the interval between shore and shore with a slight but very perceptible arch, preventing all oscillation. From the southern extreme of the lake issued a continuation of the rivulet, which, after meandering for, perhaps, thirty yards, finally passed through the "depression" (already described) in the middle of the southern declivity, and tumbling down a sheer precipice of a hundred feet, made its devious and unnoticed way to the Hudson.

The lake was deep—at some points thirty feet—but the rivulet seldom exceeded three, while its greatest width was about eight. Its bottom and banks were as those of the pond—if a defect could have been attributed, in point of picturesqueness, it was that of excessive *neatness*.

The expanse of the green turf was relieved, here and there, by an occasional showy shrub, such as the hydrangea, or the common snow-ball, or the aromatic seringa; or, more frequently, by a clump of geraniums blossoming gorgeously in great varieties. These latter grew in pots which were carefully buried in the soil, so as to give the plants the appearance of being indigenous. Besides all this, the lawn's velvet was exquisitely spotted with sheep—a considerable flock of which roamed about the vale, in company with three tamed deer, and a vast number of brilliantly-plumed ducks. A very large mastiff seemed to be in vigilant attendance upon these animals, each and all.

Along the eastern and western cliffs—where, toward the upper portion of the amphitheatre, the boundaries were more or less precipitous—grew ivy in great profusion—so that only here and there could even a glimpse of the naked rock be obtained. The northern precipice, in like manner, was almost entirely clothed by grape-vines of rare luxuriance; some springing from the soil at the base of the cliff, and others from ledges on its face.

The slight elevation which formed the lower boundary of this little domain, was crowned by a neat stone wall, of sufficient height to prevent the escape of the deer. Nothing of the fence kind was observable elsewhere; for nowhere else was an artificial enclosure needed:—any stray sheep, for example, which should attempt to make its way out of the vale by means of the ravine, would find its progress arrested, after a few yards' advance, by the precipitous ledge of rock over which tumbled the cascade that had arrested my attention as I first drew near the domain. In short, the only ingress or egress was through a gate occupying a rocky pass in the road, a few paces below the point at which I stopped to reconnoitre the scene.

I have described the brook as meandering very irregularly through the whole of its course. Its two *general* directions, as I have said, were first from west to east, and then from north to south. At the *turn*, the stream, sweeping backward, made an almost circular *loop*, so as to form a peninsula which was *very* nearly an island, and which included about the sixteenth of an acre. On this peninsula stood a dwelling-house—and

22 ". . . was of an architecture unknown in the annals of earth." The quote is from the original French version of the Gothic novel *Vathek* (1786), by William Beckford, a pastiche of the *Arabian Nights* and Voltaire's *Contes Philosophiques*.

The passage describes the capitals of watchtowers in a strange, mysterious land: "A death-like stillness reigned over the mountain and through the air; the moon dilated on a vast platform the shades of the lofty columns, which reached from the terrace almost to the clouds; the gloomy watch-towers, whose number could not be counted, were covered by no roof; and their capitals, of an architecture unknown in the records of the earth, served as an asylum for the birds of night, which, alarmed at the approach of such visitants, fled away croaking."

Mark Chadourne, in his biography of Beckford, *Eblis* (Paris, 1967), writes of the "infernal" climax of the tale: "The pen one had thought Voltairian is dipped into blacker and blacker ink; it is the pen of Edgar Poe, of Baudelaire. . . ."

23 The general effect of a person or object's appearance

when I say that this house, like the infernal terrace seen by Vathek, *"était d'une architecture inconnue dans les annales de la terre,"* I mean, merely, that its *tout ensemble* struck me with the keenest sense of combined novelty and propriety— in a word, of *poetry*—(for, than in the words just employed, I could scarcely give, of poetry in the abstract, a more rigorous definition)—and I do *not* mean that the merely *outré* was perceptible in any respect.

In fact nothing could well be more simple—more utterly unpretending than this cottage. Its marvellous *effect* lay altogether in its artistic arrangement *as a picture*. I could have fancied, while I looked at it, that some eminent landscape-painter had built it with his brush.

The point of view from which I first saw the valley, was not *altogether*, although it was nearly, the best point from which to survey the house. I will therefore describe it as I afterwards saw it—from a position on the stone wall at the southern extreme of the amphitheatre.

The main building was about twenty-four feet long and sixteen broad—certainly not more. Its total height, from the ground to the apex of the roof, could not have been exceeded eighteen feet. To the west end of this structure was attached one about a third smaller in all its proportions:—the line of its front standing back about two yards from that of the larger house and the line of its roof, of course, being considerably depressed below that of the roof adjoining. At right angles to these buildings, and from the rear of the main one—not exactly in the middle—extended a third compartment, very small—being, in general, one third less than the western wing. The roofs of the two larger were very steep—sweeping down from the ridge-beam with a long concave curve, and extending at least four feet beyond the walls in front, so as to form the roofs of two piazzas. These latter roofs, of course, needed no support; but as they had the *air* of needing it, slight and perfectly plain pillars were inserted at the corners alone. The roof of the northern wing was merely an extension of a portion of the main roof. Between the chief building and western wing arose a very tall and rather slender square chimney of hard Dutch bricks, alternately black and red:—a slight cornice of projecting bricks at the top. Over the gables the roofs also projected very much:—in the main building about four feet to the east and two to the west. The principal door was not exactly in the main division, being a little to the east—while the two windows were to the west. These latter did not extend to the floor, but were much longer and narrower than usual—they had single shutters like doors— the panes were of lozenge form, but quite large. The door itself had its upper half of glass, also in lozenge panes—a moveable shutter secured it at night. The door to the west wing was in its gable, and quite simple—a single window looked out to the south. There was no external door to the north wing, and it also had only one window to the east.

The blank wall of the eastern gable was relieved by stairs (with a balustrade) running diagonally across it—the ascent being from the south. Under cover of the widely projecting eave these steps gave access to a door leading into the garret, or rather loft—for it was lighted only by a single window to the north, and seemed to have been intended as a store room.

The piazzas of the main building and western wing had no floors, as is usual; but at the doors and at each window, large, flat, irregular slabs of granite lay imbedded in the delicious turf, affording comfortable footing in all weather. Excellent paths of the same material—not *nicely* adapted, but with the velvety sod filling frequent intervals between the stones, led hither and thither from the house, to a crystal spring about five paces off, to the road, or to one or two out-houses that lay to the north, beyond the brook, and were thoroughly concealed by a few locusts and catalpas.

Not more than six steps from the main door of the cottage stood the dead trunk of a fantastic pear-tree, so clothed from head to foot in the gorgeous bignonia blossoms that one required no little scrutiny to determine what manner of sweet thing it could be. From various arms of this tree hung cages of different kinds. In one, a large wicker cylinder with a ring at top, revealed a mocking bird; in another an oriole; in a third the impudent bobolink—while three or four more **24** delicate prisons were loudly vocal with canaries.

The pillars of the piazza were enwreathed in jasmine and sweet honeysuckle; while from the angle formed by the main structure and its west wing, in front, sprang a grape-vine of unexampled luxuriance. Scorning all restraint, it had clambered first to the lower roof—then to the higher; and along the ridge of this latter it continued to writhe on, throwing out tendrils to the right and left, until at length it fairly attained the east gable, and fell trailing over the stairs.

The whole house, with its wings, was constructed of the old-fashioned Dutch shingles—broad, and with unrounded corners. It is a peculiarity of this material to give houses built of it the appearance of being wider at bottom than at top—after the manner of Egyptian architecture; and in the present instance, this exceedingly picturesque effect was aided by numerous pots of gorgeous flowers that almost encompassed the base of the buildings.

The shingles were painted a dull gray; and the happiness with which this neutral tint melted into the vivid green of the tulip-tree leaves that partially overshadowed the cottage, can readily be conceived by an artist.

From the position near the stone wall, as described, the buildings were seen at great advantage—for the south-eastern angle was thrown forward—so that the eye took in at once the whole of the two fronts, with the picturesque eastern gable, and at the same time obtained just a sufficient glimpse of the northern wing, with parts of a pretty roof to the spring-house, and nearly half of a light bridge that spanned the brook in the near vicinity of the main buildings.

I did not remain very long on the brow of the hill, although long enough to make a thorough survey of the scene at my feet. It was clear that I had wandered from the road to the

24 Poe had a bobolink caged in his Fordham cottage, according to Mary Gove Nichols.

25 Poe is describing his ideal woman: slender, of medium height, a certain "modest indecision" in her walk, enthusiastic, romantically worldly and with haunting eyes.

26 "They were Americans, and they knew how to worship a woman," writes William Dean Howells in *The Lady of the Aroostock* (1879), commenting on the very worship of the feminine principle we find in many of Poe's tales. In *The Feminization of American Culture* (1977), Ann Douglas suggests that women, in league with the ministry, cultivated a realm of influence, becoming the cultural custodians, taking control of the schools, preaching a reverence for the very qualities that society imposed upon them: timidity, piety, childish naïveté, and a disdain for the competitive forces of the larger world.
The results, she points out, were "vapidity masquerading as sacred innocence," moral life seen as a perpetual childhood, an increasingly anti-intellectual church, and the middle-class woman idealized not as a doer but as a display case for the clothes and pretty objects a man could lay at her feet.

27 Poe's friend Mrs. Charles (Annie) Richmond, of Lowell and Westford, Massachusetts. Poe wrote a poem to her by that name.

28 The name comes from William Landor, the pseudonym for Horace Binney Wallace (1817–52), from whose novel *Stanley* (1838) Poe borrowed.

village, and I had thus good traveller's excuse to open the gate before me, and inquire my way, at all events; so, without more ado, I proceeded.

The road, after passing the gate, seemed to lie upon a natural ledge, sloping gradually down along the face of the north-eastern cliffs. It led me on to the foot of the northern precipice, and thence over the bridge, round by the eastern gable to the front door. In this progress, I took notice that no sight of the out-houses could be obtained.

As I turned the corner of the gable, the mastiff bounded towards me in stern silence, but with the eye and the whole air of a tiger. I held him out my hand, however, in token of amity—and I never yet knew the dog who was proof against such an appeal to his courtesy. He not only shut his mouth and wagged his tail, but absolutely offered me his paw—afterward extending his civilities to Ponto.

As no bell was discernible, I rapped with my stick against the door, which stood half open. Instantly a figure advanced to the threshold—that of a young woman about twenty-eight years of age—slender, or rather slight, and somewhat above the medium height. As she approached, with a certain *modest decision* of step altogether indescribable, I said to myself, "Surely here I have found the perfection of natural, in **25** contradistinction from artificial *grace*." The second impression which she made on me, but by far the more vivid of the two, was that of *enthusiasm*. So intense an expression of *romance*, perhaps I should call it, or of unworldliness, as that which gleamed from her deep-set eyes, had never so sunk into my heart of hearts before. I know not how it is, but this peculiar expression of the eye, wreathing itself occasionally into the lips, is the most powerful, if not absolutely the *sole* spell, which rivets my interest in woman. "*Romance*," provided my readers fully comprehend what I would here imply by the word—"romance" and "womanliness" seem to me convertible terms: and, after all, what man truly *loves* in woman, is simply, **26,27** her *womanhood*. The eyes of Annie (I heard some one from the interior call her "Annie, darling!") were "spiritual gray"; her hair, a light chestnut: this is all I had time to observe of her.

At her most courteous of invitations, I entered—passing first into a tolerably wide vestibule. Having come mainly to *observe*, I took notice that to my right as I stepped in, was a window, such as those in front of the house; to the left, a door leading into the principal room; while, opposite me, an *open* door enabled me to see a small apartment, just the size of the vestibule, arranged as a study, and having a large *bow* window looking out to the north.

28 Passing into the parlor, I found myself with *Mr. Landor*—for this, I afterwards found, was his name. He was civil, even cordial in his manner; but just then, I was more intent on observing the arrangements of the dwelling which had so much interested me, than the personal appearance of the tenant.

The north wing, I now saw, was a bed-chamber; its door

opened into the parlor. West of this door was a single window, looking toward the brook. At the west end of the parlor, were a fire-place, and a door leading into the west wing—probably a kitchen.

Nothing could be more rigorously simple than the furniture of the parlor. On the floor was an ingrain carpet, of excellent texture—a white ground, spotted with small circular green figures. At the windows were curtains of snowy white jaconet muslin: they were tolerably full, and hung *decisively,* perhaps rather formally, in sharp, parallel plaits to the floor—*just* to the floor. The walls were papered with a French paper of great delicacy, a silver ground, with a faint green cord running zig-zag throughout. Its expanse was relieved merely by three of Julien's exquisite lithographs *à trois crayons,* fastened to the wall without frames. One of these drawings was a scene **29** of Oriental luxury, or rather voluptuousness; another was a "carnival piece," spirited beyond compare; the third was a Greek female head—a face so divinely beautiful, and yet of an expression so provokingly indeterminate, never before arrested my attention.

The more substantial furniture consisted of a round table, a few chairs (including a large rocking-chair), and a sofa, or rather "settee": its material was plain maple painted a creamy **30** white, slightly interstriped with green—the seat of cane. The chairs and table were "to match"; but the *forms* of all had evidently been designed by the same brain which planned "the grounds": it is impossible to conceive anything more graceful.

On the table were a few books; a large, square, crystal bottle of some novel perfume; a plain, ground glass *astral* (not solar) lamp, with an Italian shade; and a large vase of resplendently- **31** blooming flowers. Flowers indeed of gorgeous colors and delicate odor formed the sole mere *decoration* of the apartment. The fire-place was nearly filled with a vase of brilliant geranium. On a triangular shelf in each angle of the room stood also a similar vase, varied only as to its lovely contents. One or two smaller *bouquets* adorned the mantel; and late violets clustered about the open windows.

It is not the purpose of this work to do more than give, in detail, a picture of Mr. Landor's residence—*as I found it.* **32**

29 The wallpaper is apparently that of a room in Sarah Whitman's home in Providence. Poe was engaged to her, but she called off the wedding when he became drunk while on a speaking tour.

Bernard-Romain Julian (1802–71) was a French painter and lithographer. "À trois crayons" refers to an engraving made from three separate plates to produce a three-color print that imitates the effects of chalk drawing.

30 A seat that holds two or more people, with a back and arms, and in America usually furnished with rockers. The O.E.D. suggests a fanciful origin in the word "settle."

31 An oil lamp that casts its light downward.

32 Poe's original manuscript continues: "How he made it what it was—and *why,* with some particulars of Mr. Landor himself—may possibly form the subject of another article."

Bibliography

ALLEN, MICHAEL. *Poe and the British Magazine Tradition*. New York: Oxford University Press, 1969. A particularly helpful look at Poe's relationship to the publications and reading public of the early-nineteenth century.

BONAPARTE, MARIE. *The Life and Works of Edgar Allan Poe: a Psycho-Analytical Interpretation*. London: Imago, 1949. Sometimes engrossing, sometimes baffling, sometimes maddening, this is still fascinating reading, even if you don't take Freudian psychology as gospel.

CARLSON, ERIC W., ed. *The Recognition of Edgar Allan Poe*. Ann Arbor: University of Michigan Press, 1966. A particularly useful compendium of critical commentary about Poe, ranging from contemporaries such as Lowell and Howells to recent evaluations and interpretations.

CIRLOT, J. E. A Dictionary of Symbols. London: Routledge & Kegan Paul, 1962. A Jungian approach to symbolism, which gives a different slant on some of Poe's writing from the works of Marie Bonaparte.

DOUGLAS, ANN. *The Feminization of American Culture*. New York: Knopf, 1977. Douglas gives one a good perspective of the worship at the shrine of woman that pervades not only Poe's writing but almost all mid-nineteenth-century American literature.

GUNN, JAMES. *Alternate Worlds*. Englewood Cliffs, N.J.: Prentice-Hall, 1975. This history of science fiction is important in tracing Poe's influence on later writers such as Verne and Wells.

HOFFMAN, DANIEL. *Poe Poe Poe Poe Poe Poe Poe*. Garden City, N.Y.: Doubleday, 1972. The best of the personal approaches to Poe's works, Hoffman's book is always enjoyable even if one doesn't accept entirely the writer's peculiar point of view.

HOWARTH, WILLIAM L., ed. *Twentieth Century Interpretations of Poe's Tales*. Englewood Cliffs, N.Y.: Prentice-Hall, 1971. Various critics' interpretations of some of Poe's more important stories.

JUNG, CARL G., et al. *Man and His Symbols*. New York: Dell/Laurel, 1968. The clearest and best general look at the chief interpretative ideas of Jungian psychology. Especially helpful in terms of Poe is the chapter "The Process of Individuation," by M.-L. von Franz.

KAYSER, WOLFGANG. *The Grotesque in Art and Literature*. New York: McGraw-Hill, 1966. A helpful guide to this most Poesque concept.

PENZOLDT, PETER. *The Supernatural in Fiction*. London: Peter Nevill, 1952. An invaluable historical and critical look at the various means writers have used to indicate supernatural themes and events in their writing. One can put Poe in perspective with the other writers of Gothic fiction.

POE, EDGAR ALLAN. *Collected Works*, Vols. II and III (Thomas Ollive Mabbott, ed.). Cambridge, Mass.: Belknap/Harvard Press, 1978. The most comprehensive examination of Poe's texts—almost bewilderingly so at times. This is not for casual reading, but if you want to check alternate versions of a particular tale, this is the only place to go.

QUINN, ARTHUR H. *Edgar Allan Poe: a Critical Biography*. New York: Appleton-Century, 1941. Although slightly dated, this is still an excellent overview of both Poe's life and his work.

REGAN, ROBERT, ed. *Poe: a Collection of Critical Essays*. Englewood Cliffs, N.J.: Prentice-Hall, 1967. Another fine grouping of varying points of view.

ROLT, L. T. C. *The Aeronauts: a History of Ballooning 1783–1903*. New York: Walter, 1966. For more background on Poe's three balloon pieces, this can't be beat for readability.

SYMONS, JULIAN. *The Tell-Tale Heart: The Life and Works of Edgar Allan Poe*. New York: Harper & Row, 1978. Symons tries hard to separate the writer from his work but doesn't always succeed. However, he does take a refreshingly no-nonsense approach to Poe which cuts through much of the murk surrounding his life.

WALKER, G. A. *Gatherings from Grave Yards*. London: Longman & Co., 1839. Reprinted New York: Arno Press, 1977. The title alone would make this a likely book to read in terms of Poe's sometimes morbid interest in tombs, vaults, and their often unwilling occupants. Fascinating!